P9-AQO-007

CHILD OF
THE PHOENIX

Barbara Erskine

VIKING

VIKING
Published by the Penguin Group
Penguin Books Canada Ltd, 10 Alcorn Avenue, Toronto, Ontario, Canada M4V 3B2
Penguin Books Ltd, 27 Wrights Lane, London W8 5TZ, England
Viking Penguin, a division of Penguin Books USA Inc., 375 Hudson Street,
New York, New York 10014, USA
Penguin Books Australia Ltd, Ringwood, Victoria, Australia
Penguin Books (NZ) Ltd, 182–190 Wairau Road, Auckland 10, New Zealand

Penguin Books Ltd, Registered Offices: Harmondsworth, Middlesex, England

First published 1992

1 3 5 7 9 10 8 6 4 2

Copyright © Barbara Erskine 1992

All rights reserved. Without limiting the rights under copyright reserved above, no part
of this publication may be reproduced, stored in or introduced into a retrieval system,
or transmitted, in any form or by any means (electronic, mechanical, photocopying,
recording or otherwise), without the prior written permission of both the copyright
owner and the above publisher of this book.

*Publisher's note: This book is a work of fiction. Names, characters, places and incidents either
are the product of the author's imagination or are used fictitiously, and any resemblance to actual
persons living or dead, events, or locales is entirely coincidental.*

Printed and bound in England on acid free paper

CANADIAN CATALOGUING IN PUBLICATION DATA

Erskine, Barbara
Child of the phoenix

ISBN 0-670-83834-9

I. Title.
PR6055.R7C5 1992   823'.914   C91-095817-3

For
C.N.P.R.M.M.B.J.M.G.
and P.

ACKNOWLEDGEMENTS

So many people helped me with their support and enthusiasm for this book, but I should like to thank especially the genealogists and archivists who contributed to the unravelling of the tale; I am very grateful for their patience and interest.

I should like to thank Janet Hanlon once more for her advice and also Jane, without whose organizational skills, help and humour present-day life would have disintegrated into a medieval miasma!

My heroine spent much of her life in four great residences. Of Fotheringhay virtually nothing remains. The site which once contained a great castle dreams on the banks of the River Nene, lost in memories of Mary, Queen of Scots, who died there and of Richard III who was born there. Of its far earlier occupants, the Earl and Countess of Huntingdon, nothing but faint echoes remain.

Kildrummy Castle too is a ruin, but an evocative and extensive ruin. I have been there several times since I was a child, but my last quick visit was one of the most enjoyable, entertained as we were with a lively account of the siege by young Scott Kelman, and the added information provided by his father, Tom.

At Falkland Palace we were made welcome by Elly Crichton Stuart and I should like to thank her for her hospitality and for showing us around the palace and for the help and advice which she and Thomas Puttfarken gave to me about the old castle.

Thanks also to Kathryn and Brian Gibson who made us so welcome at Pen-y-Bryn, the evocative and fascinating site of the Palace of Aber, of which tantalizing glimpses remain beneath and around their home.

And finally many thanks to Carole Blake and to Rachel Hore for their unfailing support and encouragement.

CONTENTS

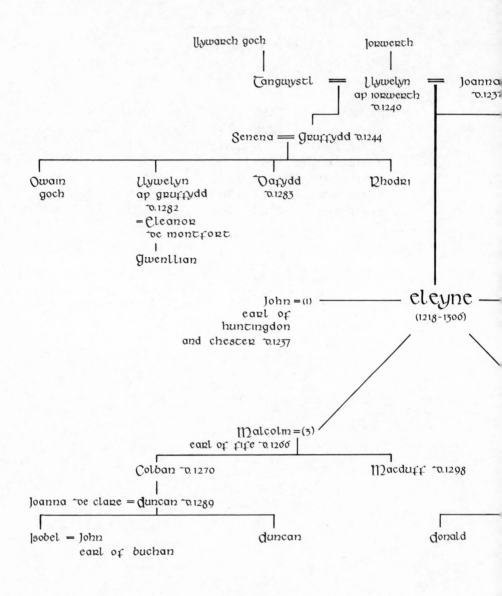

llywarch goch

Iorwerth

Tanguystl ═══ Llywelyn
ap iorwerth
ᴅ.1240

Joanna
ᴅ.123?

Senena ═══ gruffydd ᴅ.1244

Owain
goch

llywelyn
ap gruffydd
ᴅ.1282
═ eleanor
ᴅe montfort
|
gwenllian

ᴅafydd
ᴅ.1283

Rhodri

John ═ (1)
earl of
huntingdon
and chester ᴅ.1237

eleyne
(1218-1306)

Malcolm ═ (3)
earl of fife ᴅ.1266

Colban ᴅ.1270

Macduff ᴅ.1298

Joanna ᴅe clare ═ duncan ᴅ.1289

Isobel ═ John
earl of buchan

duncan

donald

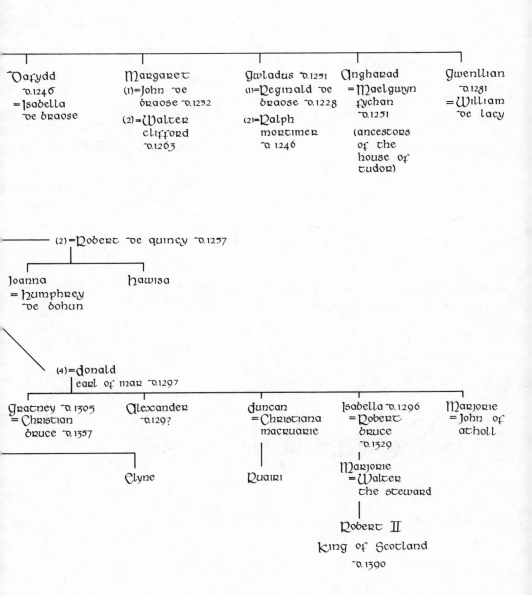

king John

Dafydd
ᴅ.1246
=Isabella
ᴅe braose

Margaret
(1)=John ᴅe
braose ᴅ.1232
(2)=Walter
clifford
ᴅ.1263

Gwladus ᴅ.1251
(1)=Reginald ᴅe
braose ᴅ.1228
(2)=Ralph
mortimer
ᴅ.1246

Angharad
=Maelgwyn
fychan
ᴅ.1251
(ancestors
of the
house of
tudor)

Gwenllian
ᴅ.1281
=William
ᴅe lacy

(2)=Robert ᴅe quincy ᴅ.1257

Joanna
=humphrey
ᴅe bohun

hawisa

(4)=donald
earl of mar ᴅ.1297

Gratney ᴅ.1305
=Christian
bruce ᴅ.1357

Alexander
ᴅ.129?

duncan
=Christiana
macruarie

Isabella ᴅ.1296
=Robert
bruce
ᴅ.1329

Marjorie
=John of
atholl

Clyne

Ruairi

Marjorie
=Walter
the steward

Robert II
king of Scotland
ᴅ.1390

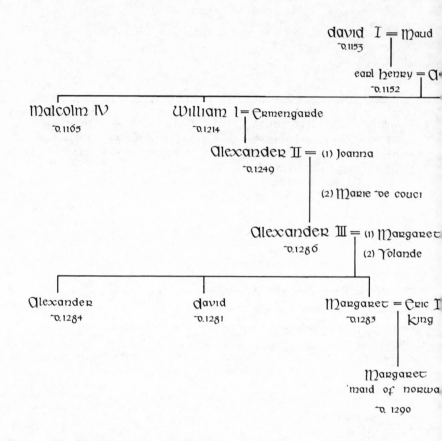

david I = maud
v.1153

earl henry = a
v.1152

malcolm IV
v.1165

william 1 = ermengarde
v.1214

alexander II = (1) Joanna
v.1249

(2) marie ve couci

alexander III = (1) margaret
v.1286   (2) yolande

alexander
v.1284

david
v.1281

margaret = eric
v.1283   king

margaret
maid of norwa
v. 1290

The Royal Line of Scotland

e waɾenne

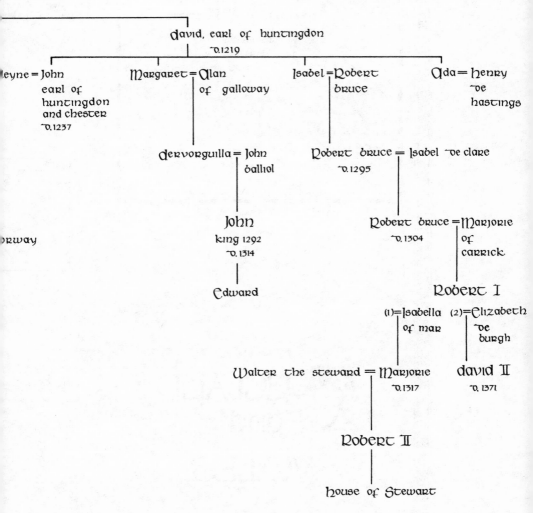

david, earl of huntingdon
ɒ.1219

eyne = John
earl of
huntingdon
and chester
ɒ.1237

Margaret = Alan
of galloway

Isabel = Robert
bruce

Ada = henry
ɒe
hastings

ɒɾway

dervorguilla = John
balliol

Robert bruce = Isabel ɒe claɾe
ɒ.1295

John
king 1292
ɒ.1314

Robert bruce = Marjorie
ɒ.1304   of
                 carrick

Edward

Robert I

(1)=Isabella   (2)=Elizabeth
of mar   ɒe
                 burgh

Walter the steward = Marjorie
ɒ.1317

david II
ɒ.1371

Robert II

house of Stewart

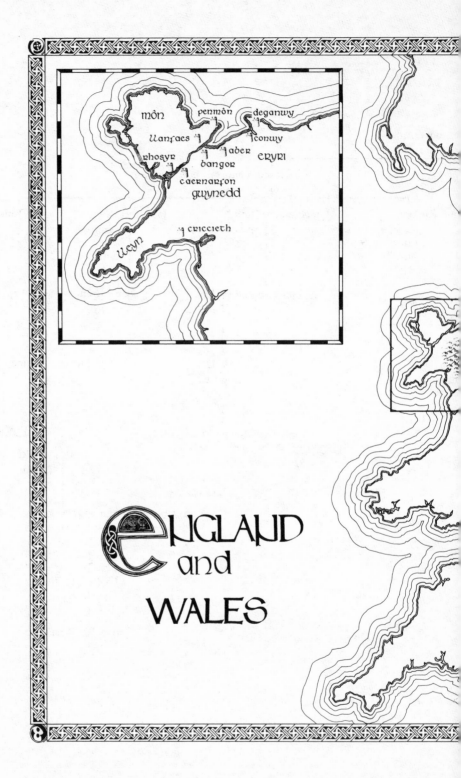

ENGLAND and WALES

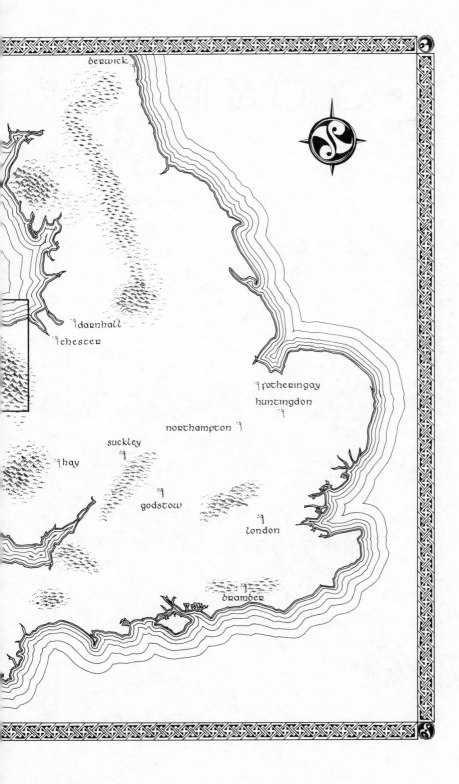

berwick

darnhall

chester

fotheringay

huntingdon

northampton

suckley

hay

godstow

london

bramber

PROLOGUE

LLANFAES, ANGLESEY ❖ 1218

The full moon sailed high and cold above the streaming clouds, aloof from the rising tide and the white-whipped waves. At the door of the hall a woman stared out across the water towards the glittering snows which mantled the peaks of Yr Wyddfa. Near her a man stood waiting in the shadows, silent, still, his hands clasped on his staff. Einion Gweledydd was tall, white-haired, austere in his patience. Soon the child would be born; the child whose destiny he had foretold; the child whose hands would hold three crowns; the child he would claim for the ancient gods of Albion. He smiled. The English wife had been in labour for three long days and soon she would die.

Behind the woman, in the hall, the fire had been banked up against the cold. A dozen anxious attendants crowded around the bed with its heaps of fur covers where their princess lay, too tired now even to cry out as the pains tore again and again at her frail body.

The men of the *Illys* had gone, sent out to allow women's work to be done.

Rhonwen turned from the door at last and went to stand before the fire. She watched it hiss and spit, contained in its pit in the centre of the hall, the smoke spiralling up towards the hole in the smoky roof beams which led it out and up towards the wind-blown clouds. Dawn was near.

Behind her Princess Joan screamed. Rhonwen stooped and picking up a handful of oak twigs she threw them into the flames where they flared blue and green, salted by the wind off the sea which tortured and twisted every tree on the island's edge. She watched them for a while, then she turned and went towards the bed.

Behind her a spark flew outward and lodged amongst the dampened rushes which carpeted the floor. It hissed a moment as if undecided whether to die or burn, then caught a frond of greenery and ran crackling along it to the next.

By the bed the women tended their exhausted princess and the tiny girl her body had spewed on to the sheets. In the hall already wreathed with smoke they did not smell the extra bitterness.

The fire ran on across the floor away from them and leaped towards the wooden walls with their embroidered hangings. The rustle of flame turned to a hiss and then a roar. When the women heard it and turned, it had already taken hold, devouring the wall, leaping towards the roof beams, racing back across the floor towards them.

One of them ran to ring a tocsin to summon the men, but they would be too late to save the hall. The others bundled the unconscious princess into her bedding and carried her as fast as they could towards the door. Outside Einion frowned: it seemed the princess would live; yet it was foretold that she would die.

Rhonwen was to be the child's nurse. She stood for a moment looking down at the baby crying on its sheepskin blanket. So little a mite, the last daughter of the Prince of Aberffraw; the grand-daughter of John Plantagenet, King of England.

A burning beam crashed across the floor near the bed. Rhonwen smiled. The fire was a sign. Bride, lady of the moon, was a goddess of fire. This child was thrice blessed and touched by destiny. She would inherit Bride's special care. Stooping, she gathered the baby into her arms, then she turned and ran amongst a shower of falling timbers for the door.

As the wind sucked the flames higher Einion Gweledydd raised his face to the east and his eyes widened in shock. The heavens too were aflame. The racing clouds flared orange and crimson and gold; where the wind had whipped the waves into towering castles they were purple and scarlet and gilded with sparks. The howl of the wind and water mingled with the greedy roar of the fire and the crash of thunder overhead. Before his awed gaze the clouds ran together and coalesced, their borders streaming flame as they reared up overhead. He saw the form of a great bird slowly spreading across the sky, its wings outstretched from the fire-tipped peaks of Eryri to the gold of the western sea.

The sun eagle. *Eryr euraid*. No! Not an eagle, a phoenix! His lips framed the word soundlessly. The bird of fire on its pyre as the sun was born in the east; as the last child of Llywelyn Fawr was carried from the burning hall; the child of Bride; the child of the fire; the child of the phoenix.

BOOK ONE

1228–1230

CHAPTER ONE

I

HAY-ON-WYE ✣ April 1228

'Don't look down!' Balanced precariously on the wooden walk-way at the top of the scaffolding which nestled against the high wall, the child turned and peered into the darkness. 'Tuck your skirts up in your girdle,' she called imperiously. 'No one's going to see your bottom in the dark!' Her giggle was lost in the wail of the wind. 'We're nearly there. Come on!'

Far below the dangerous perch the courtyard of Hay Castle lay in darkness. A fine mist of rain had driven in across the Black Mountains and slicked the wooden scaffold poles and the newly dressed stone. Beneath their leather slippers the planks grew slippery.

Isabella de Braose let out a whimper of fear. 'I want to go back.'

'No, look! Three more paces and we're there.' Eleyne, the youngest daughter of Llywelyn, Prince of Aberffraw, and his wife, the Princess Joan, was ten, a year her friend's junior. By a strange quirk of marriage and remarriage she was also Isabella's step-great-aunt, a fact which caused the girls renewed giggles whenever they thought about it.

Eleyne gripped Isabella firmly by the wrist and coaxed her forward step by step. They were aiming for the gaping window of the gutted tower to which the new wall abutted. In another week or so the masons would be starting work on renovating it so that it could once again become the focal point of the castle, but as yet it was a deserted, mysterious place, the doors at the bottom boarded up to stop anyone going in amongst the tumbled masonry and charred beams.

'Why do you want to see it?' Isabella wailed. She was clinging to the flimsy handrail, her fingers cold and slippery with rain.

'Because they don't want us to see what is in there,' Eleyne replied. 'Besides, I think there's a raven's nest inside the walls.' Letting go of the other girl's wrist, she ran along the last few feet of planking and reached the wall of the old tower. Exhilarated by the wind and by the sting of the cold rain on her face, she could hardly contain her excitement. She felt no fear of heights. It had not crossed her mind that she might fall.

'Come on, it's easy.' Peering over her shoulder she narrowed her eyes against the rain. Below, the roofs of Hay huddled around the castle, with here and there a wisp of rain-flattened blue smoke swirling in the darkness. She was very conscious suddenly of the brooding silence beyond the town where the great mass of black mountains stretched on either side of the broad Wye Valley into the heartland of Wales.

'I can't do it.'

'Of course you can. Here.' Forgetting the mountains, Eleyne ran back to her. 'I'll help you. Hold my hand. See. It's easy.'

When they were at last perched side by side in the broad stone window embrasure, both girls were silent for a moment, catching their breath. They peered into the black interior of the tower. The ground, four storeys below, was lost in the dark.

'It must have been an incredible fire,' Eleyne murmured, awed, her eyes picking out, cat-like, the blackened stumps of beam ends in the wall. 'Were you here when it happened?'

Isabella swallowed and shook her head. 'It was before I was born. Let's go back, Elly. I don't like it.'

'There was a fire when I was born,' Eleyne went on dreamily. 'Rhonwen told me. It destroyed the hall at Llanfaes. There was nothing but ash by morning when my father came.'

'This was burned by King John.' Isabella glanced down into the darkness, closed her eyes hastily and shuddered. 'There's no nest here, Elly. Please, let's go.'

Eleyne was silent. She frowned: King John. Her mother's father, descendant, so it was claimed, of Satan himself. In her mind she chalked up another black mark against her mother's hated family. Hastily she put the unpleasant thought aside and turned back to the problem in hand. 'The nest must be on a ledge somewhere on the walls inside. I've watched them flying in and out.' She stretched her hands out into the darkness as far as she dared. 'I'll have to come back in daylight. Rhonwen says the raven is a sacred bird and I want a feather for luck.'

'The masons will never let you in.'

'We could come at dawn, before they start work.'

'No.' Determinedly, Isabella started edging back on the sill, feeling with her foot for the wooden planks. 'I'm going back. If you don't want to come, you can stay here alone.'

'Please. Wait.' Eleyne was reluctant to move. She loved the cold rush of the wind, the darkness, the loneliness of their eyrie. And she was very wide awake. She had no desire to return to the room where they shared a bed, or to face the questions of Isabella's three sisters as to where they had been. They had left Eleanor, Matilda and Eva in the nursery – supposedly asleep but in reality agog to know where the

4

other two were going. 'If you stay, I'll tell you what it's like to be married.'

'You're not really married,' Isabella retorted scornfully. 'You've never even met your husband.' Nevertheless she settled back into her corner of the window arch, tucking her cold feet up under her wet skirt.

'I have.' Eleyne was indignant. 'He was at the wedding.' She laughed. 'Rhonwen told me. My father carried me, and he handed me to my husband and he went all pink and nearly dropped me!'

'Men don't like babies,' Isabella commented with dogmatic certainty.

Eleyne nodded gloomily. 'Of course, John was only a boy then. He was sixteen.' She paused. 'Shall you like being married to my brother, do you think?'

Isabella was to be married to Dafydd ap Llywelyn once all the formalities had been arranged between the two families.

Isabella shrugged. 'Is he like you?'

Eleyne thought for a moment, then shook her head. 'I don't think I'm like either of my brothers; and certainly I'm not like my sisters. Think of Gwladus!' Both girls giggled. Eleyne's eldest sister, fifteen years older than she, and married to Isabella's grandfather, Reginald, was a serious, devout young woman who had assumed assiduously a mantle of age to match her fifty-year-old husband. Her other sisters were also much older than Eleyne and they were all married; Margaret to another de Braose, Reginald's nephew, John, who lived far away in Sussex; Gwenllian to William de Lacy, and Angharad to Maelgwn Fychan, a prince of South Wales.

'Gwladus would be angry if she knew where we were,' Isabella commented anxiously. She resisted the urge to glance over her shoulder.

'But not half as furious as your mother.' Eleyne had good reason to regret the occasions she had aroused Eva de Braose's fury on this short visit. Unfortunately, it had happened with regrettable frequency. She paused, realising she had not given Isabella any reassurance about her brother. 'You'll like Dafydd. He's nice.'

Isabella laughed. 'You think everyone's nice.'

'Do I?' Eleyne pondered. 'Well, most people are.'

'They're not, you know.' Isabella sounded wise beyond her years. 'You wait till you want to do something they don't want you to do. Then you'll find out.'

Eleyne frowned. There was one person she didn't like. But that was her secret, and one that filled her with shame and guilt. 'Perhaps. Anyway at the moment all I want is for you to be my sister. We all want that, including our fathers. We'll have so much fun when you

5

come to Aber!' She linked her arm through Isabella's. 'How soon do you think they'll settle everything?'

Isabella shrugged. 'They always take ages to work it out because of all the dowries and lands and treaties about this and that. Come on, I'm cold.' Once again she began to edge off the window ledge on to the slippery scaffolding.

For a moment, lost in her dreams, Eleyne didn't move, then reluctantly she began to follow, feeling the wet stone cold beneath her bare buttocks as the wool of her gown caught on the rough window ledge.

It did not take them long to regain the ground. Once she was heading for safety, Isabella recovered her confidence and shinned down as agilely as her friend. At the bottom they looked at each other in the darkness and once more burst into smothered laughter.

'No one saw.' Eleyne was triumphant.

'You can't be sure.' Releasing her skirts so they swung down to warm her legs, Isabella shivered ostentatiously. 'I want to go to bed.'

'Not yet.' Eleyne kicked out at a pile of shaped stones, left at the foot of the wall. 'Let's go and see the horses.'

'No, Elly, I'm tired and cold. I want to go to bed.'

'Go then.' Suddenly Eleyne was impatient. 'But watch the Lady doesn't get you!' She issued her warning in a sing-song voice, dancing out from the shelter of the scaffolding into the teeming rain.

Isabella paled. For days Eleyne had been regaling the de Braose sisters with gruesome stories of the phantom lady she claimed to have seen on the walls of the castle.

'I don't believe in her. You only say that to frighten me.'

Nearby, a door opened and three laughing servants ran across the courtyard, diving through a door in the lean-to kitchens at the far side. They took no notice of the little girls standing near the ruined tower.

When Eleyne looked back for her friend she had gone. 'Bella?' she called. There was no answer.

Eleyne peered into the rain nervously. Suddenly she did not feel quite so brave. The night was cold and the large courtyard once again deserted. The guards were there, of course, on the curtain walls, staring out into the night; and the horses in their stables against the walls. And something else. Someone else. Always there. Watching. She glanced around.

'Are you there?' she whispered.

There was no answer but the howling of the wind.

II

Inside the solar the fire was blazing and a dozen candles were lit against the darkness.

'I think it's time I took Eleyne home to Gwynedd, my lady.'

Rhonwen had cornered Gwladus, Eleyne's eldest sister, second wife of Reginald de Braose, the Lord of Hay, in the newly finished west tower of the castle. 'She and Isabella are bad for each other.'

Rhonwen, unusually tall for a woman, with a beautiful, aquiline face and fair hair – visible only in the colouring of her eyebrows as her head was meticulously covered by a white veil – was at nearly thirty strikingly good-looking. But she was not attractive. Gwladus glanced at her surreptitiously. There was a coldness there, an aloofness, which antagonised people. Only with Eleyne, her special charge, did she ever show any warmth or human emotion.

Gwladus was a complete contrast to Rhonwen. She was a tall, tempestuous, handsome woman with black hair, a sallow complexion and dark flashing eyes beneath heavy eyebrows: colouring which had earned her the soubriquet of Gwladus Ddu. Looking haughtily at Rhonwen, she raised an eyebrow.

'If you mean Eleyne is bad for Isabella, I agree. However, it's too soon. I haven't completed my letters for father, and the emissaries who came with you are still talking with Reginald and William about the marriage agreement.'

She sat down on an elaborately carved chair near the fire and gestured Rhonwen to a stool nearby. 'You do know why you're here? It's not so the girls can be playmates. My father wants Isabella as a wife for my brother. Why?'

'Why, my lady?' Rhonwen shifted uncomfortably on the stool. 'Surely it would be a good match for Dafydd *bach*. Isabella is young and strong, and pretty as a picture.' She allowed herself a tight smile. 'And she's your husband's grand-daughter. The de Braose alliance is still very important to Prince Llywelyn.'

The de Braose family had been brought low by King John eighteen years before, but Reginald and his brother, Giles, Bishop of Hereford, co-heirs to the estates of their dead parents, had managed to reclaim them before the king's death in 1215, and the family was once again powerful in the Welsh borders.

'Exactly.' Gwladus pursed her lips. 'That was why he married me to Reginald, after Gracia died. What I want to know is, why does he need another marriage between the families?'

Rhonwen looked down at her hands. Did the woman want an honest answer? Could she not see that her husband was dying? She shrugged diplomatically. 'I am merely Eleyne's nurse and teacher, Lady Gwladus. Your father does not include me in his confidences.'

'No?' The dark eyes beneath the heavy black brows were piercing. 'How strange. I felt sure he would have.'

There was a long silence. Gwladus stood up restlessly and swept across to the window with a shiver. 'I hate this place! I keep begging Reginald to let us live somewhere else. She's still here, you know. His mother. She haunts the castle. She haunts the whole family!' She crossed herself and, closing her eyes, took a deep breath. 'If you are here merely as Eleyne's companion you'd better go and look after her. And stop her upsetting Isabella!'

III

The children were not in their bedchamber. Rhonwen set her lips grimly.

'Well?' She shook one of the nursemaids who had been sleeping just inside the door. 'Where are they?'

The frightened girl stared at the empty bed in the light of Rhonwen's streaming candle. 'I don't know. They were here when we went to sleep.'

Both servants were awake now, scrambling from their straw pallets to gaze round the room with frightened eyes. They were much in awe of the tall Welsh guardian of the little girl who was the wife of a prince of Scotland and the daughter of a prince of Wales. Secretly, they sympathised with her; the girl was a tomboy, uncontrollable according to the Lady Eva, Gwladus's daughter-in-law, constantly getting herself and her companion into scrapes.

Rhonwen strode across the room and glanced into the bedchamber beyond. The three small heads on the pillow showed that Isabella's sisters had not been included in tonight's escapade. She glanced at the shuttered window and sighed. Outside the wind and rain had increased threefold since darkness had set in. Whatever Eleyne had decided on, and she knew it was Eleyne, she hoped it was indoors.

IV

From her nest in the straw at the horse's feet Eleyne reached up and stroked the muzzle of the great stallion belonging to Isabella's father. It nuzzled her hair and blew at her companionably.

'I wish they'd let me ride you,' she murmured. 'We'd fly like the wind, you and I.'

She glanced up sharply as she saw the horse's ears prick. He raised his great head to stare into the darkness beyond her. A faint light appeared in the doorway and moments later a figure materialised out of the shadows. Thomas, the groom who had special care of his master's best warhorse, was carrying a lantern as he patrolled down the line of stalls. Small and wizened, his face was as brown as a hazelnut beneath his wild white hair.

'You again, my lady? I can't keep you away, can I?' He put the lantern down carefully, away from the straw, and leaned against the partition of the stall. Unsurprised by the appearance of the girl in the horse's bed, he pulled a wisp of hay from the net slung by the manger and began to chew it. The horse nudged his tunic hopefully, looking for titbits.

'You're not safe down there, child. He might step on you.'

'He wouldn't hurt me.' Eleyne hadn't moved.

'He wouldn't even know he'd done it. Look at the size of his feet!' Thomas ducked under the headrope and catching her arm swung her to her feet. 'Up, my little one. You should be in your bed.'

Eleyne pulled a face. 'Can't I stay here? Please. I'm not sleepy. And Isabella snores.' She flung her arms around the stallion's muscular neck. 'One day I'll ride him.'

'I don't doubt it,' said Thomas with a wry smile, 'but not without Sir William's permission, you won't. Now, away with you. I'm the one who'll get into trouble if you're caught here.'

Reluctantly she followed him out of the stable. 'I'll ask Sir William. I know he'll let me –' She stopped abruptly as a tall figure appeared out of the gloom in front of her.

'And what, little princess, will you ask me?' William de Braose, Isabella's father, shook the rain from his mantle as he ducked under the thatched roof. He did not seem surprised to see the child in his horse's stable so late at night.

Eleyne took a deep breath. 'I want to ride Invictus. Oh please, I know I could.' She caught his hand and looked up at him, her large green eyes pleading. He was the tallest man she had ever seen, his handsome features framed by wavy chestnut hair, darkened by the rain. His eyes, narrowed in the lantern light, were warm, alight with amusement.

He laughed. 'Why not? Tomorrow, princess, if the ground has dried a little, you shall take him for a gallop, if you dare. See to it, Thomas.'

'But, sir –' Thomas looked far from happy. 'The Lady Rhonwen would never let her –'

'Then we won't tell the Lady Rhonwen.' Sir William glared at him impatiently. 'This child has the heart of a boy, let her enjoy herself while she can. Would that I had a son with half as much courage!'

Thomas watched him thoughtfully as he strode away. 'Would that he had a son at all,' he said softly. 'Four girls, poor man. That bodes ill for the succession to the lordship. Still, there's time yet, God willing.'

'My brother will be his son if Bella marries him,' Eleyne said. She felt, inexplicably, that she had to provide some words of comfort.

'Aye, God help us all, for the Welsh alliance will only lead to trouble. It always does.' Thomas frowned, then he shook his head.

9

'Forget I said that, little one.' He began to walk slowly back towards his quarters at the end of the stable lines.

Eleyne followed him. 'When can I ride Invictus?'

'When you can escape the Lady Rhonwen. Don't you come to me with her in tow.' He gave an exaggerated shudder. Ducking inside he pulled off the sack he had draped over his shoulders against the rain and threw it into the corner. The other grooms and stable hands who shared the room were absent: probably playing knucklebones in the kitchens, he thought with a chuckle. Well and good, he'd have some peace for once. A small fire burned in one corner. Throwing on a branch, he held out his hands to the warmth with a groan of pleasure.

Eleyne had followed him in. She stood warily, staring at the flames. 'If I came early. At first light. Will that be all right?' She did not think that Rhonwen was going to be a problem.

'Whatever you want. Just so long as you come alone.' He studied her in the flickering light of the flames. She was a tall, thin child, with a fair complexion and deep red-gold hair – so unlike her sister it was hard to think they came from the same parents. He frowned. Lady de Braose – Gwladus Ddu – Black Gwladus – was the crow amongst the golden brood of Llywelyn ap Iorwerth of Gwynedd. He saw Eleyne shiver and he said, 'Here, come close to the fire and get yourself warm, then you must go.'

Eleyne stayed where she was, but held out her hands to the heat, staring at the fire. 'Do you ever see pictures in the flames, Thomas?'

'Of course. Everyone does.' He grinned. 'And if you listen to a fire, you'll hear the logs singing. Can you hear them? Listen.' He held up his hand. 'Trees memorise the song of every bird that sings in their branches,' he went on thoughtfully. 'When the wood is burned it remembers the songs and sings them in turn as it dies.' He rubbed his gnarled hands together.

Eleyne's eyes widened. 'That's beautiful. But so sad –' She drew a step nearer the flames. 'I can see a house. Look! With flames licking out of its windows and up its walls –' She was gazing unblinking into its depths.

Thomas gave a superstitious shiver. 'Enough of that, my girl. Of course there are flames. You're looking at a fire! Off you go now, and get some sleep. If you're tired you won't have the strength to hold that horse when you do ride him.'

Eleyne tore her eyes away from the fire with an effort. 'I shan't have to hold him,' she said after a moment's dreamy silence. 'I'll whisper to him and he'll do whatever I want!'

Thomas stood deep in thought for a long time after she had gone, a frown on his face. At last he shrugged. He kicked the door closed and settled down beside the fire with a sigh. With a bit of luck he'd get some sleep before the others came back with their winnings.

V

Horses had been part of Eleyne's life ever since she could remember, and Rhonwen, who in all other matters was strict and even over-protective, never interfered unduly with her when she was in the stables. Horses adored the child; they trusted her; the stout Welsh ponies at her father's court, the finer palfreys, the great warhorses, let her climb all over them.

'Let her be.' Einion Gweledydd had watched her from a distance and nodded his approval. 'She has the hand of Epona. The animals sense it. They will never hurt her.'

The old man, one of the most revered bards at Llywelyn's court, was one of those few survivors who, though he paid grudging lip service to the Christian church, in secret embraced the ancient beliefs which existed still in pockets in the mountains and forests of Britain. As a child Rhonwen had been taken to him by her fey, aristocratic mother and given to the great goddess. The rest of the family had disowned mother and child when they found out and later the heartbroken mother had died. Rhonwen was brought up by Llywelyn's beautiful lady, Tangwystl, his eldest son Gruffydd's mother. But Rhonwen had always remembered her destiny and remained faithful to her goddess – and obedient to Einion.

It was Einion who secretly supervised Eleyne's education, although he never went near her himself. Ostensibly it was Rhonwen who taught her everything she knew. How to read and write in Welsh and French and English; how to count; how to sew and weave and how to sing and play the harp; and it was Rhonwen who told her the stories of her father's principality, of the ancient kingdoms of Wales and the old gods and heroes who walked their mountains and forests. The child was bright and eager and learned quickly. Her father and Einion were both satisfied.

Princess Joan, Llywelyn's wife, who had in many eyes usurped the position of Tangwystl, and whose son Dafydd was destined to take Gruffydd's place as his father's heir, showed no interest in Eleyne, her youngest child. The rest of her brood were grown; her maternal feelings had been exhausted by them. It was left to Llywelyn to show Eleyne parental affection and this he did often. He adored her. The fact that he had married her as a two-year-old baby to the heir of his powerful neighbour, the Earl of Chester, a young man who was also heir pre-sumptive to the King of Scots, was almost forgotten. She would not go to her husband until she was fourteen. Until then she was his daughter and his delight.

Both the Prince of Aberffraw and Eleyne's distant husband were happy to leave the child in Rhonwen's care. She was competent and she was dedicated. Joan had been less happy with the choice of Rhonwen when she found out the young woman's background, but she was quiet and she was dutiful and Joan had better things to think about. After a while she put her objections to Rhonwen out of her mind, although she never bothered to hide her dislike. Had she known Rhonwen's feelings towards her and the nurse's passionate attachment to Tangwystl's son and the native Welsh cause, she would have been far more concerned. As both she and her husband would have been had they known that Rhonwen was still a follower of the ancient faith and that she and Einion Gweledydd had marked Eleyne for their own.

VI

Eleyne gave Rhonwen the slip the next morning, sensing, as old Thomas had, that she would not approve of the ride. Minutes later she was racing to the stables, praying Invictus was there and not out being exercised by one of the knights or a groom. Sir William was, she knew, in the great hall, seated with his father, Reginald, at one of the trestle tables. Reginald de Braose was better this morning. He appeared to have shaken off his fever and had come down to the hall to talk to his son. The two men were in deep discussion, a jug of wine on the table between them. With a quick evasive smile at them, Eleyne pulled her cloak around her and ducked out into the spring sunshine.

The heavy rain of the previous few days had stopped at last and the Wye Valley was brilliant in the clear air. Above her head she heard the hoarse call of a raven and she glanced up with narrowed eyes to watch it tumbling against the blue sky before it closed its wings and dived for the high ruined window of the tower. In daylight she could see the height of that window and she trembled at the thought that she and Isabella had been up there, so high above the ground. She turned away, the raven forgotten almost at once. Today she had a more important appointment.

Thomas saddled the charger, taller and rangier than the average battle horse, built for speed as much as weight, his dished head betraying the traces of Arabian blood amongst his ancestors, his huge dark eyes kind in the chestnut head. Thomas lifted her high on to the horse's broad back, then swung himself on to one of the palfreys. They had nearly reached the castle gates when Eleyne heard Rhonwen's cry.

'What do you think you're doing? Get that child off that horse!' Rhonwen had seen her from the doorway to the tower.

Eleyne glanced at Thomas, tempted to kick Invictus into a gallop, but Thomas had put a steadying hand on her rein.

'Sir William said I could,' she said defiantly as Rhonwen ran towards them.

'I don't believe you.' Rhonwen tightened her lips. 'No one would give permission for a child to ride that animal. That horse must be seventeen hands.'

Eleyne smiled. 'Yes, isn't he gorgeous? And he's as gentle as a lamb, really.'

'Get off!' Rhonwen's eyes were flashing dangerously. 'Get off him this minute. You are not going to ride him!'

'Why not, pray?' Behind her Sir William had appeared in the court-yard. As he strode towards them, they could see his father standing in the doorway in the distance watching them. Sir Reginald was leaning on a stick, his face grey with pain in the bright sunlight. 'I gave her permission to ride Invictus, Lady Rhonwen. She'll be safe with him.'

'I don't want her on that horse.' Rhonwen stood in front of Sir William, her fists clenched. 'Eleyne is my charge. If I forbid her to ride, she will not ride.' She loathed this man with his easy arrogant charm, his assumption that every female near him, child or adult, would succumb to his smile.

'Eleyne is my guest, madam.' William's eyes were suddenly hard. 'And this is my castle. She will do as she pleases here.'

Eleyne caught her breath, looking from one to the other. Without even realising it, she had wound her fingers deep into the stallion's mane. She was torn. She was passionately loyal to Rhonwen and she didn't want to see her bested, but this was a battle she wanted Sir William to win.

Rhonwen's eyes had narrowed. 'You would risk the life of this child? Are you aware, Sir William, that this girl is the Countess of Huntingdon. She is a princess of Scotland. The alliance and friendship of three nations rests in her!'

Rhonwen had never looked more beautiful. Watching from the back of the stallion Eleyne viewed her with a sudden dispassionate pride. She was wonderful – her head erect, her fine features tightened by her anger, her colour high, the gold braids coiled around her head gleaming beneath her veil. Eleyne straightened her own shoulders imperceptibly. Sir William too, she noticed intuitively, was very aware of Rhonwen's beauty. Nevertheless he frowned. 'Lady Huntingdon,' he emphasised her title mockingly, 'is my guest, madam, I shall let nothing harm her under my roof.'

'Lady Huntingdon,' Rhonwen retorted, 'is her sister's guest, under your father's roof.'

'And her sister is my father's wife.' William's voice was silky. 'And does as he commands. Shall I fetch her, Lady Rhonwen, and ask her to confirm that the de Braoses give their permission for this ride?' He held Rhonwen's gaze.

She looked away first. 'There is no need,' she said, defeated. 'If you're sure the horse is safe.' Her voice was heavy with resentment.

Eleyne found she had been holding her breath. She glanced at Thomas. He was waiting, his eyes on the ground, the perfect servant, seemingly not listening to the altercation, except that, she knew, it would be all round the castle within an hour of their return.

She looked at Rhonwen pleadingly, not wanting her to be hurt, but Rhonwen had turned away. Her head held high, she walked back across the courtyard and, passing Sir Reginald without even a nod of her head, disappeared into the west tower.

Sir William winked at Eleyne and smacked his horse lightly on its rump. 'Have a nice ride, princess,' he said cheerfully, 'and for pity's sake don't fall off, or we'll have three nations at each other's throats.'

He watched as Eleyne and Thomas rode off, followed at a discreet distance by an escort of men-at-arms. He frowned; he had made an enemy of Rhonwen and the thought made him uneasy.

VII

Rhonwen stood for a moment inside the door at the bottom of the new tower, trying to control her anger. Leaning back against the wall, she took a deep breath, then another, feeling the rough newly lime-washed stone of the masonry digging into the back of her scalp. Only when she was completely calm did she make her way slowly up the winding stair towards the bedchambers high above. At this time of day they were deserted. She stood for a moment looking down at the bed the children shared, then she walked across to the window embrasure and sat down on the stone seat. The forested hills beyond the Wye were crystal clear in the cold brightness of the sun, but there was no sign of any rider.

She wasn't afraid; Eleyne could ride any horse, however wild. She would cling along the animal's neck, whispering in its ear, and the horse would seem to understand. What worried Rhonwen was Eleyne's defiance, encouraged as it had been by de Braose.

She clenched her fists in her lap. She hated him as a man and she hated his family and all they stood for. To have to stay with them for however short a time, even though Gwladus, a daughter of the prince, lived here, was torture to her. They represented the loathed English who had insinuated themselves into the principalities over the last century and a half, and she could see no good coming of the prince's desire to be allied to them. Her knuckles whitened. William had publicly

14

challenged her; he had overruled her authority over Eleyne, an authority vested in her by the prince himself. For that, one day, she would make him pay. The de Braoses had fallen once from their power and influence in the March. Why should they not fall again?

VIII

It was many hours before Eleyne returned and when she did she was careful to avoid Rhonwen. Exhilarated, tired, her face streaked with mud thrown up by the thundering hooves, her hair tangled and her gown torn, she was happier than she had ever been. Leaving the stables with considerable reluctance, she looked around the courtyard. There was no sign of Isabella or her sisters. They had been there when Eleyne rode in so proudly at Thomas's side, and they had swarmed around as Eleyne dismounted. Then a maid had come to fetch them. The Lady Eva, their mother, wanted them indoors.

As the shadows lengthened across the cobblestones she stood for a moment watching the builders swarming over the castle walls. Wisps of hay danced and spun in the wind; a rowan tree, heavy with fruit, tossed its branches near the smithy.

She was seeing everything with a strange intensity: she noticed every detail of the stones the hod carriers lifted up the walls; the flakes and holes in the rough porous surfaces, the old dried lichen. She noticed the details of the men's faces, the different textures of their skins – some rough and weatherbeaten, one soft and downy as a child. She saw the clumps of primroses and cowslips, heartsease, the flowers intense purple and yellow, streaked with hair lines of black, and melissa with its glossy rumpled leaves, strays from the herb gardens, which had rooted at the foot of the walls.

Eleyne frowned. She was there again – the shadowy figure – watching the masons at their work. She was less distinct today, a wraith against the stone, fading, then gone.

Rhonwen was watching Eleyne from the shelter of the wall with its forest of scaffolding. She had watched the child ride in, and had forced herself not to run to the stable to meet her. She could see Eleyne's face, read fifty paces away the child's happiness, and she knew this was not the moment to go to her. This was a moment for Eleyne to treasure; a triumph she needed to savour alone, without the woman who had been her nurse. Time enough to speak to her later.

Rhonwen had thought about it often, dreading the moment when it would come, but this was what growing up would be from now on for this spirited and wayward girl. Steps to independence through defiance and even, sometimes, deceit. If she wanted to keep Eleyne's love and trust, she must know when to accept rebellion however hard

15

it proved to be. For she had come to realise over the years that keeping Eleyne's love was something she had to do. The child was her whole life; without her she would be nothing.

She frowned. Eleyne was listening again, her head cocked at an angle, her whole body alert, the recent ride momentarily forgotten. Watching her, Rhonwen felt the small hairs on her arms and at the back of her neck rise in warning. She pulled her cloak around her and stepped out into the cold evening sunlight.

Eleyne looked up at Rhonwen and smiled. The warmth and love in the smile soothed and cajoled, even if her words made Rhonwen frown.

'She's here again. Can't you feel her?'

'You're talking nonsense, my lady!' But Rhonwen glanced around in spite of herself. Oh yes, she was there, the strange presence who watched over Hay Castle. Rhonwen could sense her too, but she had no intention of encouraging the child: not yet. There had been too many nightmares – mostly Isabella's – already.

'Where is Isabella, child? I thought she would have found you by now?' Rhonwen straightened the girl's gown and rubbed at a pale streak of mortar dust on the red wool. The tear would have to wait until later.

'Their mother called them all inside.' Eleyne went to elaborate lengths to avoid Rhonwen's eye.

'Why?'

Shrugging, Eleyne drew a line in the dust with the point of her shoe.

'Had you been frightening them with ghost stories again?'

'They're not stories! All I said this morning was, *look, she's watching us*, and Isabella screamed.' Eleyne's chin set firmly. 'She was, Rhonwen. The Lady. She often watches us.'

'I see.' Rhonwen sat down on a piece of rough-hewn stone waiting its turn to be shaped and hauled up the scaffolding. Now was obviously not the time to talk about the ride. 'So, tell me, what does she look like, this lady of yours?'

'She's very tall, and her hair is a deep dark red, a bit like mine, and her eyes are grey-green and gold and alive like river water in the sun.'

'And do you know who she is, this lady?' Rhonwen asked cautiously. She remembered suddenly Gwladus's words, *She's still here, you know, Reginald's mother. She haunts the castle. . . .* Reginald's mother, Matilda de Braose, the Lady of Hay, who had built this castle, some said with her own hands.

Eleyne shrugged. 'I don't know, I expect she lived here. She is someone who loved this place. Sometimes I see her up on the walls

16

with the masons.' She giggled. 'If they could see her too, they'd fall off with fright!'

'But she doesn't frighten you?' Rhonwen stared up at the high new curtain wall.

'Oh, no. I think she likes me.'

'How do you know?' If it were Reginald's mother, this ghost of Hay, would she, who had been so brutally murdered by King John, really like this child, in whose veins ran that tainted royal blood? She shuddered.

'I just know,' Eleyne said. 'Otherwise she wouldn't let me see her, would she?' She stooped and pulled at Rhonwen's hand. 'Let's go in. I must change my gown before we eat, and I'm starving!'

As the innocent words echoed around the courtyard, Rhonwen paled. Secretly she made the sign against evil, as she glanced into the shadows. 'She doesn't know,' she whispered under her breath. 'Please forgive her, she doesn't know how you died.'

As they walked towards the door they stopped at the sound of shouting coming from near the blacksmith's shed. A man from Gwynedd had pulled a man from Hay by the nose, a knife had been drawn and within seconds a dozen men were fighting furiously on the muddy cobbles.

Rhonwen caught Eleyne's arm and pulled her back hurriedly. 'Inside,' she said. 'Quickly. There will be bloodshed if Sir William doesn't stop it.'

'Why do they hate each other so?' Eleyne hung back, wanting to watch the fighting.

'They come from different worlds, child, that's why.' Rhonwen compressed her lips. Her sympathies were with their own men. If she had been able, she would have been down there with them, tearing the eyes out of the hated English.

From the comparative safety of their position near the wall, they watched the fighting for a moment. Eleyne glanced up at her. 'You don't want Dafydd to marry Isabella, do you?'

'I don't care what Dafydd does.' Rhonwen's eyes narrowed. 'Just so long as he isn't made your father's heir. That position belongs to the eldest son by right, whether or not his mother was married to the prince under English laws. Gruffydd must have it. And Gruffydd is married to a Welsh wife.'

Eleyne sighed. 'I wish Gruffydd and Dafydd didn't quarrel all the time.'

'That is your father's fault. He should have stood up to your mother and made it clear that his eldest son would remain his heir.'

'If Dafydd becomes papa's heir instead of Gruffydd, Isabella will one day be the Princess of Aberffraw,' Eleyne went on thoughtfully. 'I hope she doesn't get big-headed.' She suppressed the treacherous thought quickly. 'But it will be nice to have her living at Aber so I can see her all the time.'

Rhonwen frowned. Eleyne had forgotten, as she was always forgetting, her own marriage to the Earl of Huntingdon, the Scots prince who would one day be Earl of Chester, the greatest earl in England. The reality of her position – that she would not be living at Aber forever – meant nothing to her yet, and it was something Rhonwen preferred not to think about. It would be four years at least before Eleyne would have to go to her husband. All the time in the world. Anything could happen in four years. She took Eleyne's hand. 'Look, they're fighting near the stables now. We must go in. If we go round by the herb gardens we won't be anywhere near them.' She dragged Eleyne away from the door and around the base of the tower towards the south side of the castle.

The sun was setting behind the distant peak of Cadair Arthur, Arthur's Seat, the greatest of the great beacons, sending long shadows from the walls across the ground. It was almost dark in the comparative peace of the little herb garden. Eleyne stooped and picked the heavy golden head of a dandelion and twirled it in her fingers. 'When will we go home, Rhonwen?'

'Soon, child. Don't you like it here?' In the small oasis of silence away from the fighting Rhonwen found herself glancing round suddenly and she shivered. Was she here too, that unseen presence whom Eleyne saw all too clearly, the woman who had laid out these herb gardens so many years before? She turned a speculative eye on Eleyne. The child was sensitive, but how much could she really see, and how much was due to an overactive imagination?

From the moment of Eleyne's birth she had watched and waited for the signs of Bride's hand on the child. Sometimes she thought it was there – the Sight – other times she wasn't sure.

'I love it here with Isabella,' Eleyne went on dreamily, 'but I miss the sea. And there is something here, something I don't like.' She frowned, holding the fluffy golden flower head against her cheek. 'I sometimes feel strange, as if I'm watching the world from outside, and I'm not really part of it.' She gave an embarrassed smile. 'Do you know what I mean?'

Rhonwen looked at her thoughtfully for a moment, but all she said was, 'It sounds to me as if you don't go to bed early enough, young lady.'

Eleyne laughed. She tossed away the flower. If she had been going to confide further in Rhonwen, she changed her mind. The strange feelings troubled her. They set her apart, made her feel distant sometimes, as if she were waiting for something to happen, something which never did. It made her restless and uneasy. She had mentioned them guardedly to Isabella, but her friend had laughed and Eleyne had never spoken about them again.

Eleyne moved into the shadow of the wall where it was already dark, and turned to look back through the archway towards the courtyard where sunlight still played across the cobbles. It was happening again now. She could hear the shouts of the men fighting in the distance; she could see Rhonwen standing near her, the blue of her gown vivid, very vivid, against the grey stone wall. Suddenly she could hear so clearly that the least sound hurt her ears. The birds' singing deafened her; the rush of feathers as a robin flew down near Rhonwen's feet; the crackle of dead leaves, the chiming of a raindrop as it fell to the ground from the lip of a gargoyle high on the old tower. She stared up to see where it had come from and felt her heart stop with fear. There were flames licking from the top window: the window where she and Isabella had sat in the darkness. For a moment she could not believe her eyes. Then she saw smoke pouring from the roofless walls.

'Rhonwen! Look! Fire!'

Terrified, she pointed. Figures were running in all directions. The flames were spreading as she watched. The old keep was already engulfed and beyond it the stables against the walls. She could hear the screams of the trapped horses.

'Sweet Christ!' She pressed her hands against her ears. 'Why don't they do something, Rhonwen? The horses! For Bride's sake, save the horses! Invictus! Where is Sir William?'

A flame ran along the top of the wall, where the wooden scaffolding had rested, and shot across the archway to the door of the main hall.

Eleyne was rooted to the spot, sobbing with shock. 'Rhonwen, do something! Where are Isabella and the others? *Rhonwen!*'

She felt Rhonwen put her arms around her, restraining her, and she pulled away violently. Her nose and mouth were full of smoke, her eyes streaming. 'Help them. We have to help them!'

'Eleyne, listen to me!'

She was aware that Rhonwen was shaking her by the shoulders.

'Eleyne! There is no fire!' Rhonwen slapped her face hard.

The shock pulled Eleyne up short. Trembling violently, she stared round. The fire had gone. The spring evening was as it had been; the robin still sat on a pile of earth near the bed of knitbone, and as she stared at the bird it began to sing its thin sweet trill into the clear air.

'What happened?' Eleyne swallowed hard. She was shaking uncontrollably as she stared round her. 'There was fire everywhere —'

'You had a nightmare.' Briskly Rhonwen pulled off her cloak and wrapped it around Eleyne's shoulders. 'You dozed off for a moment and you had some sort of a bad dream, that's all. It is all over now. There is nothing to be afraid of.'

'But I wasn't asleep –'

'You were asleep, *cariad*!' In her agitation Rhonwen spoke harshly. She put her arms around the child again. 'You were so tired you fell asleep where you stood. It is what I told you before. Too much running around the castle at night and not enough rest. You come now, to bed. Do you understand? Then I shall find you some broth in the kitchens and I'll put some valerian in it to make you sleep. You'll feel better in the morning and tomorrow I'll speak to the Lady Gwladus again about going home.'

She gave Eleyne no time to argue. Hustling her inside, she propelled her up the winding stair to the high bedchamber. There she pulled off the girl's shoes and pushed her, fully dressed, into the bed. Pulling the covers over her, she sat down for a moment beside her, chafing Eleyne's hands in her own. 'Don't think about your nightmare, child. Think about something nice. Think about the horse. He's well and safe and nothing will happen to him. Perhaps tomorrow you can ride him again.'

Eleyne looked up at her with frightened eyes. The concession alarmed her. 'You are sure the dream won't come back?'

'Quite sure!' Rhonwen spoke emphatically. At last it had happened, the thing she had dreaded for so many years. A cold breath of icy wind had reached out and touched the child she thought of as her daughter: the kiss of Bride's fingers. She closed her eyes, holding Eleyne's hand. When Einion found out she would lose her to him and what would she do then?

'Rhonwen?' Eleyne's voice was still hoarse from her screams. 'I'm cold.'

Rhonwen pulled another coverlet over her. 'Wait. I'll build up the fire, then I'll go down and get you something hot to drink.'

Reaching into the basket, she threw a couple of logs on to the fire, then with a glance over her shoulder towards the bed, let herself out of the room.

Eleyne lay still for a moment, then she sat up and, pulling the coverlet around her shoulders, she crept out of the bed. She stopped several feet from the fire and stood staring down at it. The damp bark threw off a thick aromatic smoke. She could smell the different woods – the sweetness of apple, the spiciness of oak, the sharp resin of pine; see the red and blue flames licking over the fissures in the bark, just as they had licked up the walls of the tower. She shivered violently. Whatever Rhonwen said, she had not had a dream. She had been awake and she knew what had happened. At last the strange other world, which before she had only glimpsed, had broken through the fragile barrier of her mind.

20

CHAPTER TWO

I

ABER, GWYNEDD ❖ September 1228

'You cannot prevent me from seeing my father!'
Gruffydd ap Llywelyn smashed his fist down on to the table.
'Where is he?'

'He is not here!' His half-brother Dafydd looked at him coldly. 'Here' was the *ty hir*, the long stone-built house which formed the royal family's private living quarters in the palace or *llys* at Aber on the northern edge of Gwynedd, nestling on its hillside on the edge of the mountains of Eryri, overlooking the sea and the Isle of Anglesey.

'You are lying!'

Gruffydd swung round to face his small sister who was standing miserably between them. 'Where is he, *cariad*?'

'He's not here – Dafydd's telling the truth.' Eleyne looked from one brother to the other unhappily. Their father had ridden towards Shrewsbury to meet his wife who had gone three weeks before to try to intervene in the quarrels between her husband and the King of England. In the continuing problems over the Welsh borders between Llywelyn and her half-brother, King Henry III, Princess Joan had proved herself an able and intelligent ambassador. That her efforts were all intended to ensure her son Dafydd's succession over Gruffydd's had not endeared her to the latter, nor to his followers.

'And in Shrewsbury she has tried yet again to interfere on Gwynedd's behalf with the English king, I suppose!' Gruffydd turned away in exasperation. 'Dear God in heaven! Can father not see what she is doing?'

'She is working for peace, Gruffydd,' Dafydd put in smoothly. 'By negotiating with her brother.'

'Her brother!' Gruffyd exploded into anger. 'King Henry recognises her as his sister now it suits him. Not so long ago she was just another of King John's bastards!'

'How dare you!' Dafydd had his hand on his dagger. 'My mother was declared legitimate by Pope Honorious III. And at least she's married to our father.' He laughed harshly. 'You are the bastard here, *brother*, and father can't wait to disown you, from all I see.'

21

Gruffydd let out an oath. 'That is not true!' he shouted. 'My father respects and honours me as he honoured my mother under Welsh law.'

'Does he?' Dafydd smiled. 'We shall see. If I were you, I should leave Aber now. Father knows what you have been up to – abusing his trust – working against him and against me, and he has sworn to clip your wings.'

Gruffydd's face was white with anger. Controlling himself with an effort, he turned his back on Dafydd and smiled grimly at Eleyne. 'When will father return? I need to see him.'

She shrugged. 'Soon.' She wanted to reach out and touch his hand, soothe his anger, just as much as she wanted to leap at Dafydd and scratch his eyes. She did neither. She was learning, slowly, not to become involved in her brothers' quarrels. As Dafydd had grown to manhood it became harder to pass their hatred off as jealousy and sibling rivalry. Llywelyn's determination to put his younger son first in everything had sown a deadly seed; instinctively Eleyne knew this was a quarrel which neither could win and where she should try not to take sides.

'Is it true Sir William de Braose has taken the field against father?' she asked, trying to change the subject. She bit her lip. Since his championship of her wish to ride his charger at Hay six months before, she had retained a secret fondness for Isabella's father.

'It is.' Gruffydd laughed harshly. 'The father of the bride! How embarrassing for you, Dafydd *bach*. How do you feel about your prospective wife now?'

Eleyne stared unhappily from one brother to the other. Gruffydd, older by some six years, was a short fiery-headed man with brilliant angry eyes. His broad shoulders and muscular build made him seem larger than Dafydd, though they were of roughly the same height. Dafydd, his pale gold hair cut long on his neck, his eyes green like his sister's, was the more handsome of the two. And the calmer. He had long ago perfected the art of goading his brother to fury and standing back to watch the results.

Now he was looking grim. 'There will be other ladies for me to marry. Isabella de Braose is no great loss.'

'But you must marry Isabella!' Eleyne cried. She saw her cherished plans vanishing before her eyes. 'It's not her fault that Sir William has to fight for King Henry. Once you are married, he won't fight any more.'

'Oh sweet naive sister!' Dafydd was exasperated. 'You don't understand anything. You're just a child!'

'I do understand!' She stamped her foot. 'He must still want Isabella to marry you. Gwladus won't be a de Braose any more now Sir Reginald is dead and he needs the marriage to keep the alliance. Besides, you are a prince.'

'But not the true heir,' Gruffydd put in quietly. 'No doubt he has noticed that fact. What a shame for de Braose that the true heir to Gwynedd is already married.' Gruffydd's wife, Senena, had recently given birth to their second son, who had promptly and tactfully been named Llywelyn after his grandfather.

'You are not, and never will be, his heir!' Dafydd put in, through gritted teeth. 'The eldest you may be, but bastards can't inherit!'

'I am the heir by Welsh law and custom!' Gruffydd hit the table with his fist.

Dafydd smiled. 'But I have been acknowledged heir by father; by King Henry, by the pope, and by the people. That doesn't leave much doubt, does it? Welsh custom has been dropped and feudal rules of tenure accepted. Now we all know where we stand! And you, brother, don't stand anywhere.' He picked up his cloak which had been lying across the table, and swinging it over his shoulders he walked out of the room.

Gruffydd closed his eyes in an effort to control his temper. 'He won't win, Eleyne. He can't take my inheritance from me! I have the support of the people, whatever he thinks.'

'And you and papa have been getting on better, haven't you?' Eleyne said cautiously. It was not altogether true, she knew. She hitched herself up on to the table, and put her arms around her knees. The atmosphere in the room had relaxed the moment Dafydd walked out. 'Papa will listen to you, I know he will.' She smiled hopefully.

Gruffydd leaned across and ruffled her hair affectionately. 'You have always been on my side, little sister, haven't you? Bless you for that.'

Eleyne bit her lip uncomfortably. 'You are the eldest. Rhonwen says you are the rightful heir.'

'And, by God, I'll win father's recognition of the fact, if I have to fight English-boy *David* for the rest of my life!' Princess Joan always called her son David.

Gruffydd smiled down at his little sister, winding her long, wildly curling hair gently into his hand. 'So, where is my champion, Rhonwen? It's not like her to leave you alone. Shouldn't you be at your lessons?'

Eleyne smiled. 'I've had my lessons today. Later we're going across to the island. We're to wait for my mother at Llanfaes.'

My mother, Gruffydd noticed, never *mama*.

'You don't want to greet her here, at Aber?' he said gently.

She shrugged. 'She'll have enough to talk about with papa and

23

Dafydd – and you of course,' she added hastily. 'She won't want to see me, or Rhonwen.'

Gruffydd's eyes narrowed. 'That's not true.' He hesitated. 'Your mother and Rhonwen are still enemies, then?'

'It isn't Rhonwen's fault –'

'I know, I know. If anything, it's mine. Rhonwen served my mother; Princess Joan could never forgive her that. I am sorry you should be so torn between them, little one.'

Eleyne tossed her head. 'I am not torn. Papa gave me to Rhonwen the day I was born. My mother had forgotten me! She would have left me to die in the fire if Rhonwen had not rescued me –' She did not try to hide the bitterness in her voice.

'Your mother was in no state to remember you, Eleyne. She was probably half dead; she was certainly unconscious –'

'She forgot me.' Eleyne closed her lips tightly. Rhonwen had told her the story many times. She turned away at the sound of the watchman's horn, glad of the excuse to avoid Gruffydd's scrutiny. She did not want anyone to know, ever, how much she hated her mother.

'Perhaps that is them, back already.' Gruffydd went to the first-floor window and looked down into the courtyard. His eyes narrowed at the sight of the armed men milling around the house. His father's standard flew jauntily above them, and nearby he saw that of his father's wife.

Llywelyn had already dismounted near the door to the great hall and had turned to help Joan from her saddle when Dafydd appeared at the head of the flight of steps. Running down two at a time, he bowed low to his father and kissed his mother.

Gruffydd frowned. 'Look how he runs to them. I knew it! He has told father I'm here. Already he is spreading poison.' Below them all three had turned to look up at the solar window. Eleyne, running to Gruffydd's side, saw Dafydd's face, politely inscrutable; saw her mother's smile vanishing, to be replaced by a frown, and her father's tired expression blackening to a scowl. She was suddenly afraid for the man at her side.

'Gruffydd, I think you should go.' She tugged at the sleeve of his tunic. 'Come back when papa has rested and is in a better mood.' She looked out of the window again. Her parents and her brother were already mounting the steps to the solar. She saw her father swing around with a curt word to his followers, who fell back and turned away. 'Please, don't wait for them.'

Hide, she wanted to shout. *Hide, run away.* She wasn't sure why. It was the strange feeling she got sometimes; the feeling that she knew absolutely what was going to happen. But what was the use? She knew he wouldn't listen.

They could hear clearly now the sound of spurs on the slate slabs

24

of the floor as Llywelyn and his son came through the storeroom below, and then their heavy tread as they mounted the wooden stair to the solar. Eleyne slid off the table and slipped across to the window seat, leaving her brother standing alone in the centre of the room. If her mother saw her, she would send her away.

Llywelyn stopped by the door and stared round. He looked very angry. 'So, Gruffydd, I do not remember giving you permission to come to Aber.' At fifty-five Llywelyn ap Iorwerth, Prince of Aberffraw, broad-shouldered and of powerful build, had the figure of a man in his prime. Though his hair and beard were grizzled, they showed still the signs of the red gold which had been his glory as a young man. He wore a corselet of steel over his gown and his sword was still at his waist.

'I wanted to see you, father.' Gruffydd went to him and knelt down on one knee. 'Alone.' He had seen his half-brother waiting in the shadows at the top of the stairs.

Eleyne pressed herself back into the window embrasure out of sight, but neither of them looked at her.

'There's nothing you can say to me which can't be said in front of Dafydd,' Llywelyn said stiffly. 'I hope there's to be no more nonsense about your claim, my son. All that is done with.'

His voice sounded very weary. Eleyne frowned, as always sensitive to her father's every mood. He was not well – she could see it at once – and Gruffydd was going to make him worse. Llywelyn might normally look far younger than his years but today, as he unbuckled his sword and laid it on the table, he was stooped as if in pain.

Behind him his wife had entered the room. She was petite and dark, a contrast in every way to her husband. 'So, Gruffydd, have you come to plague us again?' Stripping off her embroidered gloves, Joan sat down in the chair at the head of the table. As always Llywelyn's face softened as he looked at her. Even when he was at his angriest, Joan could soothe him.

Gruffydd managed a graceful bow in her direction. 'I haven't come to bother anyone, princess. May I ask how your negotiations fared with the king, your brother?'

Joan gave a tight smile. 'They went well. I brought back letters from Henry accepting your father's apology for interfering in England's affairs.'

'And you think that will stop a war?' Gruffydd could not keep the scorn from his voice. 'How could you bring yourself to grovel before Henry of England, father? Henry has ordered de Braose and the others to Montgomery to his standard. He has vowed to subdue you and all the Welsh with you. He is not going to withdraw, surely you can see that? If he invades Welsh territory again you will have to fight!'

25

'What do you want here, Gruffydd?' Llywelyn interrupted wearily. 'I am sure you have not come to tell me of the inevitability of war in Wales.'

'No.' Gruffydd glanced at Joan. 'I should like to talk to you alone.'

'Are you afraid of talking in front of me?' Joan's tone was mocking. 'Are you about to put some new hare-brained scheme to your father? He won't listen, you know. You have tried his patience too far!'

'Father!' Gruffydd exploded. 'Does this woman speak for you now?'

'Silence!' Llywelyn stood up stiffly. 'I will hear no word against your step-mother. Ever. Do you understand? I want you to leave Aber now. We can have nothing else to discuss.'

'We have to talk, father!' Gruffydd leaned forward threateningly. 'My God, if you don't listen to me here, I'll make you, later. You'll regret the day you turned me from your door!'

In the window embrasure Eleyne put her hands over her ears miserably. Why did it always have to be like this? Why couldn't Dafydd and Gruffydd be friends? It was *her* fault. Joan. Her mother. Eleyne's eyes went to her mother's face, noting the intent, hard expression, beautiful and youthful still in spite of Joan's forty-one years, the firm, uncompromising mouth, the steady blue eyes, so like, did Eleyne but know it, her mother's father, King John.

As if feeling Eleyne's gaze upon her, Joan's attention flicked briefly towards the window and mother and daughter exchanged hostile glances. To Eleyne's surprise, however, Joan, distracted, said nothing and her gaze returned thoughtfully to her husband.

'Enough, Gruffydd,' Llywelyn said slowly. 'If you threaten me, I shall have to take steps to contain you.'

Eleyne caught her breath, horrified by the threat implicit in the words.

'I do not threaten you, father –'

'You threaten the peace of this country.'

'No, it's Dafydd who does that. You have set him against me! You set the people against me! This is my land, father. This was my mother's land –' there was no mistaking the emphasis in the words as he glared across his father towards Joan '– and if it came to a choice between Dafydd and myself the people would choose me.'

'The people have already chosen, Gruffydd. Two years ago, the princes and lords of Wales recognised Dafydd as my heir –'

'No, not the people!' Gruffydd shouted. 'The people support me.'

'No, Gruffydd –'

'Do you want me to prove it to you?'

There was a long moment of silence. When Llywelyn spoke at last his voice was hard with anger. 'What you are suggesting is treason, my son.'

'Why do you let him talk to you like this, father?' Dafydd interrupted at last, abandoning his position by the door. 'This confirms everything I've told you. Gruffydd is a hotheaded fool. He's a danger to everything you and I believe in –'

He broke off as his brother hurled himself across the room and grabbed him, groping for his throat. As the two young men reeled across the floor, Llywelyn closed his eyes in bleak despair. When he opened them, his face was calm and resolved.

'Guards!' There was no trace now of fatigue in his voice. 'Guards –'

'No. Stop! Please –' Eleyne catapulted herself from the window seat and threw herself at her brothers. 'Gruffydd, don't! Please stop!'

But the guards were already there, leaping up the stairs two at a time, pulling the princes apart, as Llywelyn himself dragged Eleyne away from them. It took three of them to hold Gruffydd and as he struggled furiously to throw them off Dafydd retired to the far side of the room, mopping a cut lip on the sleeve of his tunic.

'Take him away and lock him up,' Llywelyn commanded.

'No, papa, you can't! Gruffydd is your son!' Eleyne clung to his arm. 'Please, he didn't mean it –'

'What is this child doing here?' Llywelyn shook her off.

'I gave orders she should be sent away before we got back,' Joan put in quietly. 'The Lady Rhonwen has seen fit to disobey me.'

'She has not!' Eleyne turned on her furiously. 'We all knew you had no time for me, so we were leaving this afternoon. You came back too soon.'

'That is enough, Eleyne! How dare you speak to your mother like that! She loves you, as she loves us all!' Angry, Llywelyn watched as his guards dragged Gruffydd from the room. They could hear the young man's curses echoing down the staircase until they were out of earshot. For a moment Llywelyn stood gazing at the empty doorway, then he turned his attention back to Eleyne, looking thoughtfully down at the child with her long untidy hair and her rumpled pale blue gown. His face softened. 'Go. Go and find Lady Rhonwen and tell her you are to leave at once. Where is she to go?' He turned to his wife, half regretfully. As a rule he enjoyed the company of his youngest daughter.

'They can go to Llanfaes. Eleyne needs to concentrate on her lessons. There is no room here at Aber and there are too many distractions.' Joan sounded irritable.

Llywelyn put his arm round Eleyne and, pulling her to him, dropped a kiss on her unruly curls. 'So, go to Rhonwen, little one, and tell her you must go now.'

'Yes, papa.' Eleyne shot a baleful look at her mother and then at her brother. 'You won't hurt Gruffydd –'

27

'Of course I won't hurt him. He must cool his heels for a while, that's all.' Llywelyn smiled gravely. 'Go now, Eleyne –'

II
LLANFAES, ANGLESEY

The prince's hall of Tindaethwy at Llanfaes had been rebuilt soon after the fire when Eleyne was born. Situated at the south-eastern corner of the island of Anglesey, it faced across the strait towards the great northern shoulder of the Welsh mainland. Rhonwen and Eleyne, with their attendants and guards, rode from Aber that afternoon across the meadows and marshland and over the sands to where the boats waited to take them to the small busy port at Llanfaes. It was a glorious September day, the sun gilding the water, the sands and the mountains as the horses cantered towards the sea.

Eleyne's cheeks glowed as they always did when she rode. She smiled across at her companion, Luned, who rode at her side. 'Race you to the boats!' Already she had kicked her pony into a gallop. Luned rode gamely after her, screwing up her eyes as the muddy sand, rough with worm casts, flew up in clots from the pony's hooves.

Rhonwen, following more slowly, sighed, thinking of the great war horse on which Eleyne had ridden at Hay. The Princess Joan had decreed that a rough-haired mountain pony was good enough for her youngest daughter. Eleyne, strangely, had accepted the dun pony and hugged it, and had not as far as she knew once gone to her father and asked for something larger or faster or with prettier markings. She had christened the animal Cadi and they had become more or less inseparable.

Now at the edge of the water Eleyne reined Cadi in, laughing, and slipped from the saddle. She looked up at Rhonwen who had followed more sedately. 'Are we going to spend long at Llanfaes?'

Rhonwen frowned. 'We must stay as long as your mother commands it.'

'Or my father. He may call me back.'

'I'm sure he will – if not at once, then certainly when the court moves to Rhosyr.' Rhonwen smiled.

Eleyne sighed. That sounded like a typical adult attempt to avoid the truth. She pulled the reins over Cadi's head and rubbed the pony's chin. 'What will happen to Gruffydd?'

Rhonwen frowned. She had made it her business to find that out before they had left Aber. 'He is being taken under escort to Degannwy. Your father has ordered that he be held in the castle there for a while.'

'Held there a prisoner?' Degannwy, a great castle built of stone in the Norman fashion like the newest parts of Aber, stood on the northern bank of the Conwy River on the eastern side of Llywelyn's lands. Beyond it, behind the mountains, lay the great earldom of Chester and beyond that the hinterland of England.

'That's what it sounds like.'

'So he'll be out of the way, while Dafydd is at father's side the whole time?'

Rhonwen nodded.

'That's not fair.'

'Life is never fair, *cariad*. But Gruffydd will find a way to make your father trust him again. You'll see.' Rhonwen smiled. 'Go on. Are you going to lead Cadi on to the boat? If she goes, the others will follow.'

The narrow strait was warm and flat calm. Sitting in the leading boat, Eleyne stared at the receding shore, her eyes following the foothills up towards the distant mountains, hazy in the light of the golden afternoon. Wisps of cloud hung around the invisible shoulders of Yr Wyddfa, drifting into the high *cwms* where already the shadows were gathering. Her father's land, the country of her birth – she trembled with suppressed excitement. Eleyne loved the mountains and she loved the sea and here she had both. She leaned over the side of the boat and stared into the glittering water, watching the whirling patterns made by the boatmen's oars, then she looked at Luned who was sitting beside her and she smiled. Her companion had, as usual, gone slightly green the moment the ferry pushed away from the sand.

Luned had been introduced into Eleyne's nursery by Rhonwen when the two girls were three years old. In a family where the nearest sister to her in age, Margaret, was ten years her senior, Eleyne would have had a lonely childhood without her. Now the two girls were friends. Later, Luned, an orphan from birth, would become Eleyne's maid. Both understood and accepted the situation happily. For both the future seemed very far away.

Eleyne turned back towards the far shore, trying to pick out the cluster of stone and wooden buildings low on the hillside which made up the great *llys* of Aber, but before she could make them out she was distracted by a flotilla of small ships which had appeared on the sea between them and the mainland. She watched, her eyes screwed up against the glare, seeing them wallow in the heavy swell which had developed near the shore.

'We're nearly there.' Luned's voice at her elbow startled her. 'I can see Cenydd with the others waiting on the quay!'

Cenydd was Rhonwen's cousin, the only one of her relatives to have kept in touch with her after the scandal of her mother's defection from Christianity and the lonely woman's death. He was seneschal at Llanfaes. Both little girls adored him.

Distracted from the boats, Eleyne studied the low shoreline ahead, where a group of figures stood waiting on one of the busy quays. A shadow had fallen across the glittering sea, and she shivered. The boats had vanished in the glare.

Impatiently Eleyne waited, listening to the laughing cry of the gulls and the shouts of the ferrymen as the horses were unloaded down the long ramps. As soon as Cadi was led on to the quay she ran to her. The horse whickered at her jauntily and within seconds Eleyne had jumped into the saddle.

Rhonwen and Luned watched in astonishment as pony and rider galloped up the track away from the port and along the shore towards the east. Rhonwen frowned and turned to Cenydd who had been waiting for them. 'You see?'

He smiled, accepting naturally the continuation, as if it had not been interrupted, of a conversation he and Rhonwen had commenced weeks before.

'She is wild still, certainly – and much loved for it. Shall I go after her?'

'She is a danger to herself, Cenydd. I am less and less able to control her. And now –' She broke off abruptly at the sight of Luned's eager face at her elbow.

'Now?' prompted Cenydd. He looked at her curiously. 'Is it as you feared?'

'Later.' Rhonwen glared at her kinsman, irritated at his lack of tact. 'You take the others up to the manor and settle them in. I shall go after her.' She mounted her own mare quickly and neatly and, kicking her into a hand canter, set off after Eleyne.

She was relaxed. There was no danger on this rich, gentle island, the heart of Llywelyn's principality, populated by loyal and true men and women, and yet it was wrong for Eleyne to ride off like that. It looked as if she had deliberately abandoned Luned and thumbed her nose at her escort and her companions. Rhonwen frowned. Almost certainly it hadn't been like that at all. She suspected that Eleyne had merely forgotten that the others existed. And that was where the problem lay. She should not have forgotten.

Cadi's hooves had cut deep holes in the sand, and already they were filling with water. At the shore's edge the oystercatchers and sanderlings, only momentarily disturbed, had returned to their patrolling. Inland from the low hill behind her came the whistling of a curlew.

Long gold streaks stained the tide race now. Ahead, in the distance, the huge hunched shadow of Pen y Gogarth lay, a sleeping giant in the sea. Somewhere on the shadowed lee of its shoulder lay Degannwy where tonight Gruffydd ap Llywelyn, the eldest son of the Prince of Aberffraw, would spend his first night as his father's prisoner.

Rhonwen scowled, reining in her horse to a walk. If Gruffydd were going to succeed his father as prince, he was going to have to learn to curb his temper.

She scanned the beach ahead. It was deserted. But still the hoof prints led on. Anxious suddenly, she kicked her horse on. A flight of gulls skimmed up the water beside her, easily overtaking the trotting horse, then she saw Cadi, riderless, her rein trailing. The pony was nibbling at the short salt-grass above the tide line.

Rhonwen felt a tremor of fear. 'Eleyne!' Her shout was lost in the empty air. 'Eleyne!'

She reined in and stared around. Then she saw her. Eleyne was standing at the sea's edge, her thin leather slippers in the water where the slowly rising tide had touched them. Her skirt, usually tucked up into her girdle, had fallen to its full length into the water and floated around her, a swirl of red. Eleyne was looking across the strait.

Rhonwen dismounted. Leaving her own horse to graze with Cadi, she walked towards the sea.

III

Eleyne had slowed her first wild gallop as soon as she was out of sight of the crowds and houses around the harbour. The strange need to be alone had come upon her quite suddenly, as it always did, and unthinking and unquestioning she had obeyed it.

She walked Cadi gently up the tide line, listening to the cries of the curlew – the messenger of death, the emissary of warning – and again she shivered. It was several minutes before she noticed the boats again. They had drawn nearer, out of the lee of the land, and were heading through the mist towards the island. She frowned. The mist had come suddenly, unnoticed, drifting over the water. The boats were crowded with men. She could see them clearly now – unnaturally clearly. They wore breast plates, gilded armour, helms. Spears glinted where the evening sun pierced the mist. There were more ships now – ten or fifteen abreast – and between the boats there were horsemen, hundreds of horsemen swimming their mounts towards the shore where she stood. Somewhere from across the water she could hear the beat of a drum, low and threatening in the echoing silence.

Suddenly afraid Eleyne turned, wishing that she hadn't ridden off alone. She gathered her reins more firmly as Cadi laid back her ears and side-stepped away from the sea. She must ride back. She looked over her shoulder, her mouth dry with fear, and to her relief she saw that she was no longer alone. Two women stood near her and beyond them a group of men. She frowned at their strange garb. Both men and women wore black robes, and all had long dishevelled hair. The woman nearest her wore a gold circlet around her arm, another around her throat. In her hand was a sword. Beyond her were crowds of others; the shore was thick with people now, all armed, all keening threateningly in their throats. They were staring beyond her towards the sea. The drumbeat filled Eleyne's ears. She felt the hairs on her arms rising in fear. She wasn't aware that she had dismounted, but then she was standing shoulder to shoulder with the women at the edge of the sea and all around them there were others, women, men, even children.

She looked for Rhonwen, for Cenydd, for some of the men of her escort, but she recognised no one. The crowd was growing and with it the noise. The sound of a hundred, perhaps a thousand voices raised in menace as, from the sea, she heard the soft shush of keels on sand as boat after boat beached and the armed men began to jump into the water.

She whirled around, wanting to run, trying to get away, but hundreds of people surrounded her, wielding weapons, and with a terrifying clash of metal they were fighting hand-to-hand. She felt the warm slipperiness of blood on the sand, heard their screams, smelt their fear and hatred. She couldn't breathe. They were being driven back, back from the shore. She found herself backing with them, stepping over the bleeding body of a woman. She spun round, panic-stricken, retreating with them towards the dark woods on the ridge behind them. The leaves of the oaks were russet and golden in the misty sunshine as the people broke and ran towards the trees and she knew, as they knew, that if they reached them they would be safe.

Then she saw the smoke.

The invaders from the sea were firing the trees, turning the ancient oaks into flaming torches and with them the people who were sheltering between them. She heard their screams, the crackle of flames as the air turned thick and opaque. Desperately she stretched out her hands, trying to reach a woman near her. If she could reach her, take her hand, she could guide her out of the smoke. Sobbing piteously, she reached forward but her hand passed through that of the woman as though it were a breath of air. Again she tried and at last she clutched it . . .

'Eleyne! Eleyne! Wake up! What's the matter with you!' She felt a stinging slap on both cheeks and a shower of cold sea water caught her full in the face.

Stunned, Eleyne opened her eyes and stared around her. She was on the lonely beach with Rhonwen. There was no one in sight. No ships; no soldiers; no men and women and children, dying in their blood on the shore. Fearfully she gazed up the beach to where the oak forest had stood. There was nothing there now but scrub and a few stunted thorn trees.

32

She found she was gripping Rhonwen's arm with every ounce of strength she possessed. She released it quietly. 'I'm sorry, I hurt you.' Her voice was shaky.

'Yes, you did.' Rhonwen sounded calm. She rubbed her arm. Beneath the cream wool of her sleeve, her flesh would later show ten livid bruises, the marks of Eleyne's fingers.

'Tell me what you saw.' She put her arm around Eleyne and hugged her close. 'Tell me what you saw, *cariad.*'

'An army attacking Môn; the men and women on the shore; then the fire, up there –' She waved her arm. 'Fire, everywhere.'

'You were thinking of the fire when you were born –'

'No!' Eleyne shook her head emphatically. 'No, this wasn't a hall. It was the trees. There on the ridge. A great grove of trees stood there, and they set fire to them with all the people sheltering there. The soldiers herded them there to burn – even women, even children, like me . . .'

'It was a dream, Eleyne.' Rhonwen was gazing over her head at the empty sea. She was completely cold. 'A dream, nothing more.'

'Am I going mad, Rhonwen?' Eleyne clung to her.

'No, no, of course not.' Rhonwen pulled her closer. 'I don't know why it happened. Too much excitement this morning perhaps. Come, let's catch the ponies and go back to the others. The wind is getting chill.'

Behind them a line of cats' paws ran down the channel and high on the misty peaks the dying sun brought darkness to the high gullies.

IV

'You are sure she has the Sight?' Cenydd leaned forward and refilled Rhonwen's wine goblet. He frowned down at the fire which burned between them. Behind them in the body of the hall men and women busied themselves at their various tasks. The children had retired to their sleeping chamber and Rhonwen had just returned from seeing that Eleyne was all right. She and Luned lay cuddled in each other's arms, dead to the world. Rhonwen had stared down at them for several minutes in the light of her candle before she turned away and returned to the hall.

'What else can it be? I don't know what to do, Cenydd.'

'Why must you do anything?'

'Because if she has this gift from the gods, she has to be trained. I have to tell Einion that she is ready.'

'No!' Cenydd slammed his goblet down on the table at his elbow. 'You are not to give her to those murdering meddlers in magic. Her father would never allow it.'

33

'Sssh!' Rhonwen said. 'Her father would never know. Listen, if it is her destiny, who are we to deny it? Do you think I haven't been praying this wouldn't happen again?'

'It's happened before?'

'When we were at Hay. She saw the destruction of the castle.'

'Does she realise –?'

'I told her it was a dream. The first time I think she believed me. This time, no. She knows in her heart it was no dream, at least no ordinary dream.'

'Did she see past or future?'

Rhonwen shrugged. 'I didn't like to question her too far. That's for the seer. He'll know what to do.'

She had struggled with her conscience for months, ever since the vision at Hay. If Eleyne had powers, they had to be trained, for the sake of her country and its cause under Gruffydd of freedom from England; she knew that. But once the seers and bards heard of Eleyne's gift Rhonwen would lose her to them and to her destiny.

'You're a fool if you tell him. He'll never let her go.' Cenydd reached for the flagon of wine. 'You wouldn't bring him here?'

'I must. I dare not defy the princess again. Anyway, there's too much unrest and unhappiness at Aber. Later – I don't know. It will be for him to speak to the prince if he thinks she has been chosen.'

'And her husband? What of the child's husband? He will surely not approve of his wife being dragged into paganism and heresy; I hear the Earl of Huntingdon is a devout follower of the church.'

'The marriage can be annulled.' Rhonwen dismissed the Earl of Huntingdon as she always dismissed him, with as little thought as possible. She groped surreptitiously for the amulet she wore around her neck beneath her gown. 'Everything can be arranged if it is the wish of the goddess, Cenydd.'

He frowned. He saw his cousin's passionate faith as alternately amusingly harmless and extremely dangerous. He did not like the idea of that pretty, vivacious child being turned into a black-draped, sinister servant of the moon. On the other hand, he shuddered superstitiously, if she had the Sight, then perhaps she was already chosen.

V

Eleyne was sitting at her embroidery lesson three days later when a servant brought the message that Rhonwen wanted to see her. She threw down her silks with alacrity. Although already a neat, accurate sempstress, with a flair for setting the colours on the pale linen, she soon grew bored with the lack of activity when she was sewing. Any variation of the routine was to be seized with enthusiasm.

Rhonwen sat at the table in the solar with an old man. There was no sign of Cenydd. Disappointed, Eleyne closed the door and went to stand near them.

'Eleyne, this is Einion Gweledydd. As you know, he is one of your father's bards,' Rhonwen said.

Eleyne dropped a small respectful curtsey but her curiosity already had the better of her. She loved the bards with their constant supply of stories and music, their recitations of history and the tales of her ancestors. She peered at him, not immediately recognising him. He was a tall, thin-faced, ascetic man, with brilliant intelligent eyes. His long hair was grizzled, as was his beard, and he wore a heavy, richly embroidered gown of the deepest blue.

He held out his hand to her, and hesitating she went to him.

'So, child. The Lady Rhonwen tells me you have had some strange dreams.' His hand was cold as marble. It grasped her hot fingers tightly. Frightened, she pulled away. 'Tell me about them,' he went on. He had not smiled and she felt a tremor of fear.

'They were nothing – just silly dreams.'

This time he did give an austere smile, visibly reminding himself that this was a child. 'Tell me all the same. I like dreams.'

She told him haltingly, her shyness slowly evaporating as she realised that he was listening with flattering concentration to every word she said. By the end of her story he was nodding.

'What you saw, child, was something which happened here more than a thousand years ago, when the Roman legions marched across our land. Their leader, Suetonius, gave orders that the Druids were to be killed. The Romans came here, to Anglesey, which was, as it still is, a sacred island. At first they were too afraid to cross the strait and attack, for they saw the Druids waiting on the shore. Do you know who the Druids were, child?' He waited a second, then seeing her nod, he went on. 'Even their women were there, ready to fight with their men, and the sight terrified the Romans. But at last they embarked across Traeth Lafan, just as you did when you first saw their ships, and they killed all the Druid people, burning the survivors of that battle in their sacred oak groves. They went on and destroyed every oak tree on the island.'

He was watching Eleyne closely. She had gone pale, her eyes fixed on his. It was several seconds before she whispered, enrapt, 'Was no one left at all?'

'Very few.'

'Why did the Romans do it?'

'Because they were afraid. The Druids were wise and fierce and brave and they did not want the Romans in Wales.'

Still she had not questioned the fact that she had seen these things.

Breaking eye contact with him with an effort, Eleyne walked across to the narrow window. She could see across the pasture to the shore where it had happened and from there across the strait. The mountains of Eryri were shrouded in cloud today; the tide high, the water the colour of black slate.

'Are you not curious, Eleyne, as to why you saw these things?' he asked gently.

Rhonwen sat watching them both, her fingers twisting nervously in her lap.

'It's because I walked in the place where it happened,' Eleyne answered simply.

'But why did you see it, and not the Lady Rhonwen?' he persisted.

She turned to face him and at last he saw a puzzled frown come to her face. 'Perhaps she wasn't looking.'

'And you were looking?'

'No. But sometimes I know things are there to see if I want to. I always thought it was the same for everyone, only no one talked about it, but now . . . now, I'm not sure.' She looked unhappy.

It had never happened to Isabella. When Eleyne had told her friend about her strange feelings at Hay, Isabella had laughed. She had never dared tell anyone else. Save Rhonwen.

'It's not the same for everyone, Eleyne. You have a precious gift.' He smiled again. 'I too can see into the past and into the future.'

'You can?' Her relief was obvious.

'It's a gift of our race. We are descended, you and I, from the survivors of those Druids you saw. Some of them escaped. Some of them lived to lead the opposition to Rome which finally chased out the legions. Your father descends from the ancient kings of Britain, and I from the Druid priests. And you, amongst all the children of your father, have been chosen for the gift of the Sight, for you are his seventh child.'

Eleyne's mouth had gone dry. Suddenly she wanted to run away. His seriousness oppressed her. The room was airless and hot. She glanced past Rhonwen to the driftwood fire which smouldered low in the hearth. The flames flickered up: red-blue fingers, beckoning, licking the wood they consumed. The smoke was acrid — salt from the old plank remnants of a boat thrown up by the gales.

'Can I go back to my embroidery now?' She directed the question urgently at Rhonwen. Her skin was icy with fear.

Rhonwen said nothing. She was staring helplessly at Einion.

It is my fault, she was repeating to herself, *I needn't have told him. Now he will never let her go.*

36

Once again he smiled. 'Of course you may return to your embroidery. But we shall see each other again soon. I am going to come here to Llanfaes to give you lessons myself.'

'What sort of lessons?' Eleyne asked suspiciously.

'Interesting lessons. You will enjoy them.' Again the smile. 'There is only one thing you must promise me. That you will keep our meetings a secret. Can you keep a secret, Eleyne?'

'Of course I can.'

'Good. No one must know I come here, save you and the Lady Rhonwen and I. Not even your little friend, Luned. Do you think you can keep a secret from her?'

'Easily.' She was scornful. 'I have lots of secrets from her.'

'Good.' He stood up. He was tall, lean, not stooped. Eleyne looked up at him in awe.

'I shall return in three days.' He turned to Rhonwen as he picked up his long wooden staff. 'By then I shall have chosen somewhere safe to meet. See that you have a story to cover her absence all day from the prince's hall. You did well, my daughter, to tell me about her.'

VI

'I don't want to go!' Two days later Eleyne was confronting Rhonwen with clenched fists. 'I didn't like him. What can he teach me? You teach me all I need to know.'

Rhonwen took a deep breath. 'You have to go –'

'I don't. My father doesn't know about it, does he? He would not approve. Nor my mother.' She pursed her lips primly. For two days she had pondered why Einion's lessons had to be secret. This seemed to be the only explanation.

Rhonwen took another deep breath. 'Eleyne, they are for your own good.'

'Why? What is he going to teach me?'

'I don't know exactly –'

'Then how do you know it will be good for me?'

'I just know. They are secret things, Eleyne. Even I may not know them. But you are special, as Einion told you. You are the descendant of the ancient kings. You have the Sight.'

'And he is going to teach me about what I saw? About the history of long ago?'

Rhonwen shrugged. 'I suppose that may be part of it.'

Eleyne paused. At last her curiosity was beginning to overcome her inexplicable feeling of dread. 'You will come with me, won't you?'

'I don't know.' Rhonwen looked away evasively.

'You must go with her.' Cenydd had appeared silently, pushing through the curtained doorway and pausing in the shadows, a frown on his face. 'You cannot let her go alone.'

Rhonwen went white. 'You don't know what we're talking about.'

'You are talking about Einion Gweledydd. I warned you, Rhonwen!' he sighed. 'I told you not to do it.'

Eleyne looked from one to the other, confused. 'Rhonwen?'

'Take no notice, *cariad*. Cenydd is jealous. He wanted to teach you himself.'

'And so I shall!' Cenydd smiled at her fondly. 'As soon as I return. I am summoned to Aber,' he added to Rhonwen in a low voice. 'There has been renewed fighting in the border march.'

'And Gruffydd?'

'He is still at Degannwy. Prince Llywelyn has sent Senena and the boys to join him there and he has kept Dafydd at his side.'

Rhonwen swore softly. 'So, Dafydd consolidates his position! We have to do something to help Gruffydd —'

'Dafydd has a new embarrassment on his hands which could help.' Cenydd smiled. 'It seems that the prince has captured de Braose.'

Eleyne's attention was caught by the name. 'Isabella's father?'

'Exactly.' Cenydd laughed out loud. 'It will be interesting to see how the negotiators handle that one. I suspect Llywelyn still hankers after the de Braose alliance. It neutralises Sir William, for all he rides with the king at the moment, and with the marriage formalised Prince Llywelyn will have an ally in mid-Wales.'

'What will happen to Gwladus now that Sir Reginald is dead?' Eleyne asked suddenly. 'Will she come home?'

'She will marry again, *cariad*,' Rhonwen said gently. 'Don't look to see her here. I doubt if she would want anyway to come back beneath her mother's roof.'

'And she'll want a younger man this time, I'll warrant!' Cenydd laughed quietly.

'Then I shall pray for her sake she gets one. But we will not discuss that now.' Rhonwen scowled at him.

'Will they bring Sir William to Aber?' Eleyne had missed the interchange. 'I would love it if he came with Invictus.'

'I don't know, child,' Rhonwen frowned again. 'I doubt if they'll bring him north. He will probably buy himself his freedom before we know it. We shall have to wait and see.'

VII

Einion had picked a deserted hermit's cell in the woods behind Penmon.

Rhonwen dismounted, staring at the closed door of the stone-built shack. A haze of smoke was escaping through the holes in the turf roof.

Eleyne remained in her saddle, her fingers firmly wound into Cadi's mane. 'You won't leave me.'

'I must if Einion orders it.' Rhonwen approached the door and after a slight hesitation she knocked. For several moments nothing happened, then slowly it opened. Einion was wearing a long black mantle over his embroidered tunic. In the shadowy doorway it made him look wraithlike, almost invisible.

'So, you are here. Where's the child?' He peered beyond Rhonwen into the trees where Eleyne waited. It was raining heavily, the raindrops drumming on the leaves, tearing them from the trees. The trunks glistened with moisture and the ground was a morass of mud beneath their horses' hooves.

Eleyne dismounted. She was wrapped in a heavy woollen cloak against the rain, and it dragged on the ground as she walked unhappily towards him.

'Good. You may come back for her at dusk.'

'No.' Eleyne turned and ran back to Rhonwen, clinging to her arm. 'No, I want her to stay!'

The old man studied her. 'Strange, I had not marked you for a coward, princess.'

'I am not a coward!' Stung, Eleyne straightened her shoulders.

'Good. Then you will do well. Come in.' He stood back, motioning her into the hut. As she stepped hesitantly into the darkness he glared over his shoulder at Rhonwen who hesitated in the rain. 'Dusk!' he said brusquely. 'And not a moment sooner.'

Eleyne peered around the dim interior, her heart thumping with fear as he shut the door. As her eyes grew accustomed to the light, she saw the cell was empty save for a table placed against the wall. On it a rush light burned with a feeble flame. In the middle of the floor a small circular fire had been lit in the centre of a ring of stones. It smoked fitfully, and her eyes burned with the acrid smoke.

She glanced fearfully at Einion. In the faint light his tall figure cast a huge shadow on the wall as he moved slowly to the table and shuffled various small boxes around on it.

'Sit down, child.' He spoke softly now, his voice more gentle. 'Don't be afraid.'

She looked for something to sit on and saw nothing in the semi-darkness save a folded blanket on the floor. After a moment's hesitation she sat down on it, putting the fire between herself and the man who stood with his back to her. Straining her ears in the silence, she heard him taking the lid off something and the rattle of some object inside a box.

'Listen.' He held up his hand. 'Tell me what you hear.'

Eleyne held her breath. The hut was full of sounds. The crackling and spitting of the fire as drops of water found their way through the roof, the rain outside on the trees, the heavy breathing of the man – but she could hear nothing else.

'I can't hear anything,' she whispered.

'Nothing?' He swung round to face her. 'Listen again.'

She swallowed. 'There is the rain,' she stammered, 'and the fire.'

'Good.'

'And our breathing.'

'Good. Listen now. And watch.'

He threw whatever he had in his hand into the fire. For a moment nothing happened, then there was a burst of clear bright flame and a hum from the burning wood.

Eleyne watched, enchanted. 'A man told me once the burning logs remember the songs of birds,' she whispered.

Einion smiled. 'So they do. And more. Much more. Look. Look close into the flames. Tell me what you see.'

Kneeling up, she peered into the heart of the flames. The heat burned her face and her eyes grew sore. 'Just the fire. The red centre of the fire.'

'And now.' He poured a scoop of some powdered herbs and another of juniper berries on to the logs. At once the fire died and threw off a bitter thick smoke. Eleyne shrank back, coughing, her eyes streaming. She was terrified.

'There is mugwort and wormwood and yarrow to help you to see. And sandalwood from the east and cedar. Look, look hard.' His voice was persistent. 'Tell me what you see.'

'I can't see anything –'

'Look, look harder.'

'It's all black.'

'Look.'

She stared as hard as she could, her eyes smarting. Now the heart of the fire was burning a deep clear red. She leaned forward, pushing her hair back from her hot face, then she reached out her hands.

'Look,' he whispered, 'look.'

'I can see –' She hesitated. 'I can see a sort of face . . .'

'Yes!' It was a hiss of triumph.

'A man's face, in the shadows.'

'Whose face?'

'I don't know. It's not clear.' Suddenly she was crying. The picture was fading. Desperately she tried to hold it, screwing up her eyes. Her head was aching and she felt sick.

'Enough.' Walking over to her, he put a cool hand on her forehead. 'Close your eyes. Let the pain go.' He left his hand on her head for a few moments. She felt the pain lessen. Slowly she relaxed. When she

40

opened her eyes, the pain had gone. He walked over to the door and threw it open, letting the cold woodland air into the hut.

Nervously she looked at the fire. It smoked gently on its bed of ash.

'Throw on some twigs. The pile is behind you, in the corner.' He was like a man trying to train a child not to be afraid of a wild beast. 'There, see how it takes the fuel from your hand. It's an ordinary fire again. There's nothing to fear. Now, for another lesson. Something less arduous.'

'That was a lesson?' Eleyne was still staring at the fire.

'Oh yes, child. You have to learn to command the visions. They must never rule you. That way leads to madness. You must learn to be their mistress. Now, how would you like to learn about the birds?'

'The birds?' She looked up hopefully.

'Legends about the birds; the omens of which they speak. The messages they bring us.'

'The curlews were there, crying of death when the Romans came in my dream.' She scrambled to her feet and went to the door. 'Where do all the birds go in the rain?'

'They find shelter when the weather is hard, but usually they go about their business. There's an oil on their feathers which casts off the rain.'

Now that he was speaking quietly, she found her fear had left her. She listened eagerly as the morning progressed. By midday the rain had stopped and a fitful sunshine slid between the branches of the trees. They walked for a long time in the woods, and he pointed out bird after bird which she had failed to see, telling her their names and the messages their appearance foretold. The sun slowly dropped in the sky. Her stomach growled with hunger but he talked on, pausing now and then to fire questions at her to check she was still attentive.

Twice she begged him to stop so they could eat or drink. He refused. 'You must learn to rule your body, princess. You do not run because it wants meat. You must tell it to wait.'

He knew exactly the moment when she began to grow light-headed and once more he took her to the hut and closed the door. He motioned her to sit again before the fire and once more he threw on a scoop of powder.

She put her hands over her eyes. 'No more, I'm tired.'

'Look.' He leaned over and tore her fingers away from her face. 'Look. Look into the fire.'

This time the picture was there, cold and clear. She stared at it in wonder. 'I see people standing about waiting for something to happen; crowds of people. The sky is blue and the sun is still low in the east behind the hills near Aber. It must be dawn. They are talking – now they are shouting. Someone is coming. A man. I see a man and they

41

are putting a noose around his neck. They are – no! No!' Suddenly she was sobbing. She scrambled to her feet and pushed past him to the door. Scrabbling frantically at the sneck she pulled it open as, behind her, the acrid smoke cleared, and ran outside.

It was nearly dark and it took a few moments before her stinging eyes could make out the figure of Rhonwen waiting beneath the trees. The two horses were tethered behind her.

'Take me home!' She ran to Rhonwen and clung to her. 'Take me home. Please.'

Rhonwen looked over her head at the darkened doorway. It was some time before Einion appeared. He seemed unmoved by the child's tears. 'She did well. Bring her to me again in three days.'

'Who was it?' Eleyne spun round. 'Who did I see?'

He shrugged. 'You did not hold the vision. That takes time to learn. Maybe when you come again we shall understand what you saw and read the warning, if there is one.'

'No. I don't want to see it again. It was horrible.' She pulled her cloak around her with a shudder. 'And I don't want to come again.'

Einion smiled coldly. He turned back to the hut. 'Bring her,' he called over his shoulder, 'in three days.'

VIII

'NO!' The next morning, having eaten and slept well, Eleyne's courage had returned. 'I will not go back, Rhonwen. I don't want to go to him. What he's doing is evil.'

'It's not evil!' Rhonwen was shocked into temper. 'Don't ever say such a thing. And you will go, if I have to carry you!'

'I won't. I refuse.' Eleyne's eyes were as defiant as her own.

'You will.'

'I shall run away.'

'Nonsense.' Rhonwen forced herself to speak calmly. 'Where can you go? I should find you anywhere on the island!'

'Then I shall leave the island and go to papa. If I tell him what you made me do, he'll put you in prison!' Her fists clenched, Eleyne was close to tears. The events in Einion's cell had frightened her badly. Under no circumstances was she going to return there, and instinctively she knew her father would be her ally in this. He had no idea, she was sure, that the stories and songs which Rhonwen had told her night after night since she was a baby were but a frame for a more sinister purpose. 'I don't want to learn from him, Rhonwen. I don't, and I won't. I'm going back to Aber. Now.' She turned and ran from the room.

'Eleyne!' Rhonwen shouted after her. 'Eleyne, stop! No boatman

42

will take you without my orders. You cannot go. Don't be so foolish!'

Eleyne raced across the great hall and out into the courtyard towards the stables.

'Eleyne!'

She heard Rhonwen close behind her, but she did not stop. Hurtling into Cadi's stall, she untied the pony's halter and backed her out. She had just managed to leap on to the pony's back when Rhonwen stormed into the stables. Nearly knocking her down, Eleyne kicked Cadi past her at a gallop, careering across the yard, scattering the manor servants as she fled out of the gates, down towards the shore.

There were no boats moored against the quayside in the harbour. Slowing Cadi, Eleyne bit her lip with frustration. Her pride would not permit her to go back. Rhonwen must not be allowed to win this quarrel.

She heard a shout behind her. Three riders were galloping after her, and glancing around she recognised Rhonwen's head-dress. There were two men with her.

Digging her knees into Cadi's sides, she put her at a gallop out of the small port and up the beach. There might be a fisherman mending his nets on the sands who would take her across the strait for a fee. She groped at her neck and was relieved to find her gold chain safely in place. That would no doubt buy her a trip to the ends of the earth if she should wish to go there.

There were no fishermen; as far as she could see round the ragged coastline the beaches were empty. The tide was midway, the water sparkling cheerfully in the light breeze.

The other, larger horses were gaining on her and she felt a surge of anger. Just because she was small they could force her to do what they wanted. It was unfair – unfair and wrong! She looked once more across the water towards the farther shore and the safety which was Aber. Almost without realising it, she began to steer Cadi with knees and halter towards the water. She had seen the Roman soldiers swim the strait. Why not Cadi? The tide was not too high, the water calm.

The pony's hooves splashed in the bright clear ripples. In two strides the water was up to her fetlocks. In two more to her knees. Eleyne heard the cries behind her grow more urgent.

Her own feet were in the water now. It was bitterly cold and she caught her breath. She felt Cadi hesitate. 'Come on, my darling. Courage. You can do it,' she whispered, urging the pony on. 'Come on. It's not so far.'

As if understanding what her young mistress wanted, the pony began to swim.

CHAPTER THREE

I

The water was icy. As it rose up her body, Eleyne began to tremble with cold. She leaned forward, throwing her arms around the pony's neck, feeling the sturdy pull of Cadi's legs as she struck out into the waves. She could hear nothing now of the shouts behind her; her ears were full of the rush of the sea. She clung desperately to Cadi, feeling the water pulling her away from the pony's back.

'Come on, my darling, come on, it's not far,' she whispered again, and the pony's ears flicked back at the sound of her voice.

On the shore Cenydd hurled himself from his horse. Tearing off his gown and mantle he ran for the sea, clad only in his drawers. Running through the waves, he dived into the deeper water and began swimming fast. The pony, hampered by the drag of her rider, swam slowly and doggedly. It was only a matter of moments before he was drawing near them. He did not waste his breath shouting; only when he was within easy earshot did he call out.

'Princess!' He saw the girl's head turn, saw her white, frightened face.

'Turn her head round, gently. Turn her now, or she'll drown.' With two more strokes, he was at the pony's side. He put his hand into the headband and began to pull the pony round, trying to avoid the flailing hooves.

'Hold on, princess, hold on.' He managed an encouraging smile. The pony was responding. He suspected that it too had reached the conclusion that the swim was too far and the tide too strong.

Slowly they made their way back, the man and the horse tired now, the child clinging between them. It seemed an eternity before the thrashing hooves found the sand and Eleyne threw herself into Rhonwen's arms, to be enveloped in the warmth of her cloak. It was Rhonwen who was sobbing as she hugged the shivering child to her.

II

'You should give her a damn good thrashing!' Cenydd was halfway down his second horn of wine.

'I have never beaten her!' Rhonwen retorted. She had put Eleyne

44

to bed with a hot stone wrapped in flannel at her feet, and a whispered promise that there would be no more visits to Einion in his cell in the woods.

'That's the trouble. She's never known any discipline! She could have drowned, woman!'

'I know.' Rhonwen sat down, pulling her cloak around her. 'It was my fault. I wouldn't listen. I said she had to go back.'

Cenydd laughed bitterly. 'I told you no good would come of that. You are a fool, cousin, and Einion will not let go. I've heard stories about him. He uses his powers to get his way, even with the prince.'

'No, he would not bewitch the prince!' She shook her head. 'He cares for Gwynedd above all else – for the whole of Wales. All he does is for the good of Wales.'

Cenydd raised a cynical eyebrow. 'By which I suppose you mean that he supports Gruffydd's claim as heir to the principality?'

Rhonwen looked nervously over her shoulder. 'For pity's sake, lower your voice! Of course he does. So does anyone of any sense. I had thought you were no supporter of the English party, Cenydd, or you would not be my friend.' She paused to take another drink of wine. 'I shall take her back to Aber. I can leave a message for Einion that the prince has sent for her. Even he cannot argue with that.'

'And when you get there? How will you confront the Princess Joan?'

Rhonwen shrugged. 'I shall tell her there was an accident. Tell her that Eleyne needed to be with her mother . . .'

Cenydd laughed. 'You imagine she would believe that?'

III

'So, Eleyne, you tried to swim the Menai Strait on a pony.' Llywelyn sat in his chair by the fire in the great hall at Aber. Near him Sir William de Braose lifted a goblet of wine. Both men were carefully concealing their admiration for the child. 'What made you think you could do such a thing?'

'The Romans did it, papa.'

'The Romans did it.' Llywelyn leaned back in his chair. 'But the Romans waited until low tide, Eleyne, as the drovers do, and they had a reason.'

'I had a reason.' She coloured indignantly.

'And what was that?'

How could she tell him that it was because here at her father's court she would be safe from Einion? Rhonwen had assured her that he would be told they had been summoned back to Aber, and that he would be content to wait. But wait for what? She was afraid. She had tried to wall off in some remote corner of her mind the strange vision she had seen in the depths of his fire, but it haunted her. It had not been a dream; it had come from outside. And she, under his instruction, had summoned it. But why? Why had she seen a man with a noose around his neck? A man being led to the gallows? Why, and who was he? Why had she not seen his face?

She met her father's eyes as calmly as she could. However much she disliked Einion and feared him, he had sworn her to secrecy and she would keep his secret. 'I was bored at Llanfaes,' she improvised bravely. 'I am too old for children's lessons. And I heard Sir William was here. I thought perhaps Isabella had come with him.'

Sir William smiled. 'I am not here voluntarily, little princess. Have you not heard? I was captured in battle. I am your father's prisoner.' He did not seem to be too upset by the situation, nor too uncomfortable, as he sat beside Llywelyn's fire, drinking his captor's wine. 'Isabella is not with me.'

'But she is still going to marry Dafydd?' Eleyne glanced from one man to the other anxiously, all her eager plans threatening to crumble before her eyes.

'That is one of the matters we are discussing, Eleyne.' Her father stood up. 'You may safely leave it to us. Now, what am I going to do with you?' He turned to look into the corner of the room where Sir William's guards stood to attention by the door. 'One of you, send to Princess Joan and ask her if she would grace us with her presence for a few minutes.'

'Did you bring Invictus?' Firmly ignoring the knot of unease in her stomach at the thought of her mother's presence, Eleyne sat down on a stool near Sir William.

He smiled. 'In a manner of speaking. He brought me.'

'Can I go and see him?' She found herself responding to his smile with a warm glow of happiness, and edged closer to him.

'That is for your father to say, little princess. Sadly, I am not allowed near him in case I escape.' His smile deepened.

'Then who is exercising him?' Eleyne's eyes were bright with excitement.

'Oh no, I'm not walking into that one.' Sir William laughed. 'You must ask your father.' The child was irresistible, with her beauty and her charm. Already she knew how to twist a man around her little finger.

'Could I, papa? Please, could I ride Invictus? He knows me. He likes me. I've ridden him before, at Hay. And,' she added ingenuously, 'Cadi is still so tired after her swim.'

'I take it that Invictus is that great chestnut brute you rode at Montgomery.' Llywelyn beckoned a page forward and jerked a thumb towards his empty goblet. 'No horse for a child, I should have said.'

'No ordinary child, no.' Sir William winked at Eleyne. 'Your daughter, your highness, is a witch with horses. Invictus would do anything for her. As I suspect any animal would.'

'Indeed?' Llywelyn looked at her thoughtfully. 'Why did you not tell me this before, Eleyne?'

'Because I forbade her to waste your time.' Princess Joan appeared at her husband's elbow. Both men rose. She was looking exquisitely beautiful in a gown of rose silk trimmed with silver thread and a mantle of deepest green velvet.

Eleyne saw Sir William's eyes light up with appreciation, and she felt a treacherous surge of jealousy as Joan greeted the two men calmly and took Sir William's proffered seat.

'What are we going to do with Eleyne, my dear?' Llywelyn put his arm around his daughter and pulled her against him fondly. Studying her mother, Eleyne was aware for the first time in her life of her own clothes. Her blue gown was too short at the wrists and showed her ankles. She had never before realised what an attractive woman her mother was.

'Why is she here?' Joan gave Eleyne a cursory glance and turned away.

'Because she grew bored at Llanfaes.'

'Bored!' Joan snapped. She did not hide her irritation. 'Has she completed her lessons then? Can she read and write and sew and sing and play the harp?'

'Yes, mother.'

'And she can ride like the wind,' Sir William put in softly.

Joan's eyes narrowed. 'Then perhaps we should teach her to ride like a lady.'

'She could not help but be that, your highness, being your daughter,' Sir William smiled. 'You must help me to persuade Prince Llywelyn to allow the little princess to ride Invictus for me. It's time he learned to carry a lady.'

Joan met his gaze, and gave a quick half-smile. Watching, Eleyne sensed a lightning spark of excitement flicker between them, but her father appeared to have noticed nothing. Suddenly she wanted to run away again. She did not want to stay in this claustrophobic palace with the adults; she wanted to be out under the sky, on a horse, with the wind in her hair and one of her father's great wolfhounds striding out at her side.

Her mother's smile had disappeared and was replaced by a scowl. 'No, it will not do. She must go back to Llanfaes,' Joan said crisply. 'I will not have my orders flouted in this way, and if the Lady Rhonwen cannot obey me she will be dismissed and someone who will obey me will take her place. This child is out of control. She must have discipline.'

'No.' Eleyne had gone white at her words, all her fear of Einion returning. 'No, I don't want to go back.'

Her father frowned. 'That's enough for now. We'll discuss this tomorrow.'

'Papa, please.' Eleyne flung herself at her father and put her arms around his neck. 'Don't send me back to Llanfaes. I don't like it there.'

He looked down at her thoughtfully. 'You're happy with the Lady Rhonwen?' His scrutiny of his daughter's face had uncovered something far deeper than boredom in her eyes.

'Yes, I love Rhonwen.'

'Then what is wrong?'

'Nothing.'

'There is something.'

'No, papa. Only I should like to stay here with you.'

He frowned. 'As to that, sweetheart, your mother and I will have to discuss it.' The smile he directed at his wife was warm. Then he turned back to Eleyne and scowled. 'I understand Cenydd saved your life when you tried to swim the strait.'

Eleyne looked down at her feet and nodded. 'He saved Cadi too.'

Llywelyn smiled. He pulled her on to his knee. 'I want you to promise me that you will take him with you wherever you go from now on. He is a brave man. I have already spoken to him and he's willing to be your personal escort and bodyguard. Later, when you are older, he shall be your steward. As a princess of Wales and Countess of Huntingdon you need more protection than I have hitherto given you. If there's anything frightening you, Eleyne, you must tell me, and you must tell him. He will be there to protect you. And,' he paused, 'your mother is right. You must try to behave a little more like a lady. A lady would not swim the Menai Strait.' He put his hand to his mouth to hide a smile of pride.

Eleyne looked down again. 'I'm sorry, papa.'

Gently he pushed her down from his knee. 'Good. Now go to your rooms. Your mother and I will discuss what to do with you later.'

IV

Einion stood patiently in the shadow of the wall, his arms folded, his eyes closed. He would know when she was near. He had long ago schooled himself in the absolute control of his emotions. Until he needed them, until he wanted to act he was relaxed, to an outsider indifferent, even asleep as the russet evening sun pierced the boughs of a mountain ash tree near the doorway to the great hall at Aber and warmed the rusty black of his mantle. In the silence he could hear the chuckling water in the river below as it tumbled over its rocky bed.

When Rhonwen walked around the corner, he opened his eyes and put out a hand to grasp her wrist.

'Where is she?'

Rhonwen caught her breath with fear. 'I left you a message. There was nothing I could do.'

'Where is she?'

'With her father.' The low sun was shining directly into her eyes.

'You must send her to me.'

'She won't come.'

'She must.' He tightened his grip. 'I have to see her again. I have to have her oath, child though she is.' His eyes were deep and expressionless like still lake water. 'I do not want to lose her; the gods, my gods, want her for their own. It must be soon or she will slip from me. And without me, without them, she will not know how to control her visions and will live in torment for the rest of her life.' He paused. 'You brought her here to avoid me.'

Faced with that cool all-seeing gaze, Rhonwen did not dare to deny it. 'She was so frightened,' she heard herself pleading. 'Besides, I could not stop her. She tried to swim . . . she's so young –'

'It's because she is young that she needs me so much.' He released her suddenly. 'She's too young to understand the powers she has been given. She needs strength and guidance.'

'She doesn't want to see you again. Please, Lord Einion. Wait a little; just until she is older.' Rhonwen despised herself for her weakness, but she could not help herself.

He took a deep breath. 'That is not possible, my lady. I have to see her again. Now, today. Bring her to me.'

'What if she won't come?'

'She will come. Tell her her father has commanded her to visit the hermit of the woods.' He smiled cynically. 'Tell her there is a horse for her to see. Tell her there are blackberries to pick. I am sure you can think of something. Bring her to me, Lady Rhonwen. You begged me to see to it that her marriage is annulled, but I will not do that until she has been initiated and blessed. Only after that shall I see that she belongs to no man. Bring her to me – now. I shall wait by the river beyond the village.'

Rhonwen stared after him. He had not waited for her agreement; he merely turned and walked away from the wall, beneath the gatehouse and down the hill towards the village with its mill and forge and church and the huddle of houses where the harp maker, the silversmith, the potter and the tradesmen and craftsmen lived, side by side with the twenty-four families who farmed the Aber land. He raised his hand in greeting and blessing to the men and women he passed.

Rhonwen swallowed hard. She did not dare to disobey him.

V

Eleyne was playing cats' cradles with Luned in the window embrasure, where the last of the sunlight lit their entwined hands. In another moment the sun would drop below the mountains and the *llys* would be in shadow.

'Is it nearly time for supper, Lady Rhonwen?' Luned asked.

'No, it's not that late.' Rhonwen was flustered as she came in. 'Please, Eleyne, come with me, your father has sent for you!'

'Me too?' Distracted, Luned let the string slip from her thumb and the intricate net of knots collapsed. Eleyne threw it down. Standing up, she gave Luned a gentle push. 'No, not you. You've got to untie the cradle.'

Luned's face fell, but she sat down obediently with the tangled string.

Rhonwen breathed a quiet prayer of thanks. Catching Eleyne's hand, she led her down the stairs and out of the *ty hir* into the courtyard. They hurried across it to the gatehouse. 'Down by the river.' She had to think of some reason for the walk, so that the meeting with Einion would seem an accident. If not, Eleyne would never trust her again. 'Your father wanted you to see some wild ponies on the hill beyond the village.'

Eleyne stopped. Her eyes were shining, but she looked puzzled. 'Why? Why especially tonight?'

Rhonwen shrugged. 'Perhaps he wants to catch one for you before they move away over the mountains now he knows how much you love horses. Perhaps he's noticed how you're growing. Soon you'll be too big for Cadi.' She hustled Eleyne down the track.

She did not want Einion to have Eleyne, but if the goddess had chosen the child who was she to fight her? Besides, it was better Eleyne stay here in the hills than go to a foreign husband – a man neither of them knew; a man fourteen years the child's senior. And it would happen. In four years' time John the Scot, the Earl of Huntingdon, would demand his bride. Rhonwen trembled at the thought of a man touching her child, her baby, mauling her, frightening her, hurting her, using her any way he wished. Almost as much she dreaded the thought that he might seduce her with sweet talk and gentleness, and steal away her loyalty and love. No, that must never happen. Better she be given to the goddess. That way she would remain a virgin; cold, chaste, pure as the silver moon. It was for Eleyne's good.

She had never lain with a man herself. Dimly in the far-off recesses

50

of her memory before she and her mother had come to the house of Tangwystl, there had been a man; a man who had pawed and hurt her mother and made her cry before he had turned his attention to the little girl. Rhonwen's mind had blocked out the rest of what had happened, but it had left her with a loathing and horror of men which she seldom bothered to hide.

Holding their skirts off the muddy path as they moved out of sight of the *llys* and through the village, they ducked beneath the tangled trees which grew down the deserted hillsides to where the river ran swiftly over the rocks. The sun had long gone from the deep valley and the air was cold and sharp. Old trees had fallen, rotting, across the river. The air was full of the rich scent of decay. They could feel the chill striking up from the wet boulders in the icy water. Everywhere carpets of moss and lichen clung to tree trunks, to the rocks, and even to the path beneath their feet.

Eleyne paused and looked round. 'Rhonwen, we shouldn't come here. It's too far from the hall –'

'I thought you loved the woods and the darkness,' Rhonwen retorted. 'I know you manage to slip out sometimes when you think I'm not looking. Besides, what danger could there be?' She was picking her way over the slippery stones, resisting the urge to take the girl's hand and pull her on.

'I don't know.' The skin at the back of Eleyne's neck was prickling. 'There's something wrong here. Please, Rhonwen, let's go back. We can come and look at the ponies tomorrow. It's getting too dark to see them anyway.'

'Only a little further.' Rhonwen walked on doggedly, praying that Eleyne would follow. The track was soft leafmould here, where the trees grew closer together by the water: alder and birch; hazel, ash and ancient oak, linking branches across the stream.

Einion was waiting by a bend in the river where the water hurtled over a small waterfall. Wrapped in his black mantle neither of them saw him until they were within a few feet of him. Rhonwen let out a small scream of fright, the sound all but drowned by the rush of water.

Eleyne stared at the tall man, paralysed with fear as he rose to his feet in front of her.

'Your next lesson, princess, will have to be here, as you are no longer at Llanfaes.' He held out his hand to her and she took it, unable to stop herself.

'Go.' He looked over her head at Rhonwen. 'I shall return her safely at dawn.'

'Dawn –' Rhonwen was scandalised.

'Dawn.' He nodded. 'Go.'

51

They seemed to have walked for hours. At first the woods were thick and the sound of water filled her ears, then they turned away from the river on to the open hillside and the noise of the water receded into the distance. Then they were near it again. Eleyne could see little in the darkness, but the man ahead of her must have had the eyes of a cat as he threaded his way onwards, sure-footed however steep and difficult the climb. When they stopped at last at the head of the valley, she was panting; he was calm, his breathing quiet and even. They had reached, she knew, the great waterfall which hurled itself down the cliffs below Bera Mawr.

'Here,' he called exultantly above the roar of the water. He released her hand. 'The spirits are come to greet you and make you theirs.'

Eleyne stepped back frightened. Her eyes strained into the darkness. In the starlight she saw the luminous flash of water as it hurtled from the falls high above them; felt the sudden cold striking at them from the cliffs.

'Take off your shoes.' She heard his voice dimly as he shouted against the noise of the water. She saw he was removing his own, so she followed suit, unable to defy him; still unable to run. He smiled. 'You're not afraid?'

Stoutly she shook her head, although she was, desperately afraid.

'Come.' He took her hand again and began to lead her nearer the foot of the falls. She could feel the spray; feel the ground shaking. 'Here, princess, drink this.' He produced a flask from beneath his cloak. 'It will warm you.'

She took the flask and, hesitating, sipped: it was mead. She drank eagerly, feeling the sweet warmth in her mouth and in her veins. Then she frowned. There was another taste in the mead beyond the sweetness of the honey. Malt and wine and bitter herbs. She spat some out, but it was too late. She had swallowed enough for the draught, whatever it was, to do its work.

'Is it poison?' she heard herself ask him. Her head was spinning. The roar of the water was all around her and inside her head and part of her.

He shook his head. 'Not poison. Nothing to harm you, princess. Herbs from the cauldron of Ceridwen and water from the everlasting snows. Come.' Again he took her hand. They seemed to be walking out into the deep pool at the foot of the falls. Stepping from stone to stone with bare cold feet, she felt their rounded smoothness, slippery with moss. He let go of her hand and as he moved away from her she saw him raise his arms. She heard him calling – calling the spirits and gods of the river and of the mountain, the incantation rising and falling with the roar of the water.

She stood still, her feet aching as the icy mountain water splashed over them, feeling her skirts grow wet, her hair soaked with spray. Her head was thick and woolly; she could not think or move and yet she could see. She could see as if it were daylight.

The moon was rising above the falls, its clear light falling through the spray, down the rock face on to the man and the child. She saw the moonlight touch his fingertips, his hands, his arms where the sleeves of his mantle had fallen back. It stroked silver into his hair and touched his face with cold lights. She felt the silver light touch her own skin and wonderingly she raised her hands to it and felt it warm.

As if in a dream she found herself wading deeper into the icy water. Her gown had gone. She was naked, but the water was warm. She felt it lap her body like milk. Then she was on the turf bank and amongst the trees, floating, her feet off the ground; flying up the waterfall, spinning like thistledown in the spray before she found herself again amongst the trees, her back against an old oak. She could feel its bark like soft velvet against her skin. She could not move; her limbs would not obey her. The tree was enfolding her, the moonlight in her eyes.

She saw the man in front of her, naked as she was. He carried water from the falls in a wooden bowl. He raised it to the moon and then dipped his hand in it and traced the secret sign upon her forehead and upon her chest where the small unawakened nipples stirred; then on her stomach and lightly, barely touching her, between her legs.

Then he was gone and she was alone. She tried to move, but the tree held her; the moonlight filled her eyes and she saw the gods of the forest dancing by the waterfall, their bodies half hidden in the spray.

VII

'Eleyne, for the love of the Holy Virgin, wake up!' Luned was shaking her shoulder. 'Come on, Rhonwen has been calling you for hours!'

Eleyne opened her eyes. She was in her own bed in the small chamber in the *ty hir* which she shared with Luned and Rhonwen. Luned was fully dressed and sunshine poured through the window and across the floor.

'Come on!' Luned pulled the covers from her. 'Have you forgotten you are going to ride Invictus today?'

Eleyne climbed slowly to her feet. She was still enfolded in her dream, still bemused by the roar of water and the numbing cold of her limbs.

There had been faces in her dream: men, women, children, people she had known through aeons of time. There had been love and death and fear and blood. Whirling pictures; laughter and tears; the crash of thunder and splinters of lightning in the black pall which had darkened the sky.

How had she come home? She remembered nothing of the journey back. She raised her arms above her head and lifted her tangled hair off her neck wearily. Her head ached and she felt far away.

She was standing naked in front of the window staring out at the hillside of Maes-y-Gaer, where the russet and gold of the bracken caught the morning sun, when Rhonwen appeared, a heap of green fabric over her arm.

'Eleyne, what are you doing? You'll catch your death!' she exclaimed, shocked at the blatant nakedness. 'Here. The sempstresses sat up all night to make you a new gown.' It had helped to pass the time while Eleyne was away; helped to quiet her conscience; and she too had noticed the previous day Eleyne's shabbiness as the child stood next to her mother.

Chivvying her impatiently, she dressed her charge in a new shift and slipped the gown over the girl's head.

'Say nothing to her,' Einion had said, the unconscious girl still in his arms. 'She will think it all a dream. The gods have marked her. She's theirs. In due time they will claim her for their own.'

'And you will make her father annul the marriage?'

Einion had nodded and smiled. 'Have no fear. I shall speak to him when she is of an age to choose a man. Then she will take whoever she wishes amongst the Druids. She will belong to no man and to any man as the goddess directs.'

'No!' Rhonwen pleaded. 'She must remain a virgin —'

'Virginity is for the daughters of Christ, Lady Rhonwen, for the nuns. The followers of the old gods worship as they have always worshipped, with their bodies.' He looked at her with piercing eyes and for a moment his gaze softened. 'If you have kept yourself a virgin, Lady Rhonwen, it was to assuage your own fears, not to please the Lady you serve. Do not wish the same fate on this child.'

Less than an hour of the night remained when Rhonwen tucked Eleyne, still deeply drugged, into her bed, her ice-cold body rigid next to Luned's warm relaxed form. Looking down at the two girls as Luned turned and put her arm over her friend, Rhonwen felt her tears begin to fall.

It was as Rhonwen was brushing her hair that Eleyne remembered. 'You knew he would be there, didn't you!' She jerked her head away from Rhonwen's hands and stood up. 'You knew, and you took me to him!' Behind her Luned, who had been sitting on the edge of the bed pulling on her stockings, looked astonished at the sudden vehemence. 'How could you! I thought you loved me, I thought you cared. You betrayed me!'

54

Eleyne had thought she was safe at Aber. She had thought he would not dare to follow her. She stood up, pushing Rhonwen aside: 'What did he do to me?'

'He gave you to the goddess.'

'Father Peter and the bishop would not like that.' Father Peter was one of the chaplains at Aber.

'You mustn't tell them. You mustn't tell anyone, ever.'

Rhonwen had realised that Luned was all ears. She turned towards her. 'Nor you, Luned. No one must ever know, no one.'

'What will happen to me now?' Eleyne still had her back to them. Her hands were gripping the stone sill of the window as she tried to clamp down on the horror and fear which had broken through the barriers and flooded through her. She was shaking.

'It means you can stay here in Gwynedd. When you are old enough Einion will tell your father what has happened.' Rhonwen's voice was calm and soothing.

'I won't have to go and live with Lord Huntingdon?'

'No.'

No, you will be given to the Druids; who will use your body for worship; for a temple; or for their plaything. Oh, great goddess, have I done right? Would she have been happier married to Huntingdon, living far away . . . ?

'I don't want to see the future, Rhonwen.' Eleyne was looking out at the russet hillside. There the old gods lived; the stones of their temple lay there still, tumbled on the hillside.

'You have no choice, child. You have the gift.'

'Einion would never have known if you hadn't told him.'

'I had to, Eleyne,' Rhonwen said guiltily. 'It would have destroyed you. Don't you see? He will tell you how to use your powers for good. To help your father, to help Gruffydd and perhaps Owain and little Llywelyn after him. For Wales. Besides, don't you see? I have saved you from marriage. I have saved you from going to a stranger like your sisters.'

There was a long silence. Then Eleyne turned back to her. 'I am not going to stay here. I never want to see him again.'

'Eleyne! You have no choice, *cariad*. You belong to him now.'

'No!'

'There is nothing to be afraid of –'

'No!' Eleyne was silent, then she turned back to the window. 'I will never belong to Einion. Never. You should not have allowed him to give me to the gods. My father is a devout follower of holy church, Rhonwen. I know he favours the canons of Ynys Lannog, who follow the way of the old anchorites, and he welcomes the friars and the Knights Hospitaller to Wales. Many feel he is too broad-minded, but he will not want me to turn back to the old faith.' She said it quietly and with absolute certainty.

Rhonwen felt a clutch of fear. The child had grown up overnight. Far from being more docile, there was a confidence in Eleyne's voice which brooked no argument. 'Nonsense,' she said uncertainly, 'he reveres the old ways in private.'

'No, Rhonwen. He respects them and he listens to the bards and the wizards of the mountains, but he had me baptised in the Cathedral of St Deiniol at Bangor. It was you who told me that.' Eleyne gave a tight little smile. 'And he will want my marriage to go on. The alliance with the Earl of Chester is vital. I heard him tell my mother. Lord Huntingdon will be Earl of Chester when his uncle dies. Father wants no more wars with Chester.'

'The days when Gwynedd and Chester were at war are over, Eleyne.'

'Exactly! And to seal that peace, father married me to Lord Huntingdon. He will not put that treaty at risk because Einion wants me for the old faith. Einion won't be allowed to take me.'

Rhonwen closed her eyes. 'It's too late, Eleyne. He already has you, *cariad*. You are his.'

Eleyne spun round. 'Never, I told you, never!' Suddenly she was a child again. She stamped her foot, then ran across the room and pulled the door open. 'And if you won't save me from him,' she sobbed, 'I must save myself!'

VIII

Rhonwen caught Eleyne in the stables as she was watching Sir William's groom throw the saddle up on to Invictus.

'Where are you going?'

'To Degannwy. I shall be safe there with Gruffydd.' The tears had gone. The girl's face was set and determined.

'You can't go without your father's permission.'

'Then you must get his permission, Rhonwen. Now. Quickly. I'm not going to stay here.' Eleyne's hands had started to shake and she clutched them together, waiting impatiently as the groom fitted the sharp bit between the stallion's teeth and settled the elaborate reins over his neck.

They both jumped as Cenydd appeared from the shadows. He was frowning as he saw the preparations for the ride. 'I gave your father my word that I would guard you, my lady. I must come with you if you are going out.'

Eleyne smiled uncertainly. 'Just as long as you don't try to stop me. My father gave me permission to ride Invictus.'

56

'I'll not try to stop you.' Cenydd threw a glance at Rhonwen. 'Is the Lady Rhonwen coming too?'

'No.' Eleyne scowled.

'Eleyne, please, *cariad*, wait,' Rhonwen cried. 'You can't go to Degannwy. You will only get Gruffydd into more trouble.'

Eleyne paused. 'Very well then, you go and ask papa if I can go. But I am going to ride on ahead. Now.' Any moment, she was sure, Einion would appear and manage to stop her.

Rhonwen had put her hand on Invictus's bridle. 'Lord Einion would want you to stay,' she whispered.

'No.' Eleyne shook her head.

Cenydd raised an eyebrow. 'I told you, Rhonwen. You were a fool to meddle. You had best make a clean breast of all this to his highness. Then at least the prince will thank you for saving his daughter for her husband.'

'But I am not. I don't want her to marry –'

'I am married, Rhonwen.' Eleyne stamped her foot again. 'Nothing can change that.'

'But it can, don't you see? The marriage is not consummated. It can be annulled. It must be annulled!'

'Don't be a fool, Rhonwen! The prince would never allow it.' Cenydd stepped forward, narrowing his eyes against the cold wind which whistled across the courtyard and into the stables. 'Accept the facts, woman.' He drew Rhonwen aside, his face angry. 'You didn't just do this to give her to your gods; or to save her from marriage. You did it to keep her for yourself, didn't you? But you won't keep her. The seer will get her unless you help her.'

Eleyne was staring at Rhonwen, her face white and pinched. 'Is that true?'

'No, of course it's not true.' Rhonwen held out her hands in anguish. 'I love you, Eleyne. I want only what is best for you.'

'Then you'll help me go to Degannwy.' At Degannwy she would be with Gruffydd and Senena whom she loved and the two little boys she adored. She signalled the groom to lift her on to the horse. 'I shall be safe with Gruffydd,' she said firmly, 'he won't let anything happen to me.'

Cenydd and Rhonwen looked at each other. Gruffydd was in no position to help her, but neither of them reminded her of the fact. Rhonwen reached up and touched her hand. 'Very well then, *cariad*. But wait. Wait for your father's permission. Otherwise you'll be in more trouble.'

Eleyne's face grew mutinous. 'I shall write to papa. He will understand.' She turned the horse, still terrified that Einion would be lying in wait for her in the shadows outside the gate.

The valley beyond the village lay in silence, sheltered from the wind and still bathed in mist as Invictus trotted on to the track which curved beside the river. Cenydd rode a few paces to the rear, his hand upon his sword; behind him were two of the prince's grooms, hastily beckoned from their work.

In the stable yard, Rhonwen, her heart in her mouth, turned to find the prince.

IX

Llywelyn frowned. 'You want to take her to Degannwy?'

Joan smiled. 'A good idea. Why not? She can stay with Gruffydd and Senena.' Her face betrayed the unfinished end to her sentence: three trouble-makers together, out of harm's way.

Rhonwen nodded, deciding to make the most of her unexpected ally. 'She can continue her studies there as Lord Gruffydd already has tutors for little Owain. They could help her.' Behind her a figure had entered the hall and was walking towards them. Her heart turned over with dread. She did not need to turn to know that it was Einion. She looked beseechingly at the prince, cold sweat suddenly filming her palms. 'May I go, your highness?' she whispered.

Llywelyn frowned. 'I see no reason why not. In fact, I shall give you a letter for Gruffydd. I don't want the boy to think I have forgotten him entirely.'

Joan's eyes narrowed. 'Surely that will merely encourage him to make more trouble.'

'He is my son.' Llywelyn silenced her firmly. He turned to Einion. 'Good morning, Sir Bard. You are welcome.'

Einion, leaning heavily on his staff, bowed before the prince but he was studying Rhonwen's face with narrowed black eyes. 'How is the princess, your charge, this morning?' he asked.

'Well,' Rhonwen murmured. Her mouth had gone dry.

'We have decided to let her go to Degannwy,' Joan put in, pulling her cloak more tightly against the cold of the hall. She eyed Einion with dislike.

Einion frowned. 'No, she must not leave Aber.'

Rhonwen felt her cheeks grow pale.

'Why not, pray?' Llywelyn frowned.

'Her place is with you, sir. At your side. It would be unwise to let her go to her brother at this stage.' Einion spoke with authority. He looked again at Rhonwen and it seemed to her that his eyes were sharp with suspicion.

'Why, my friend?' Llywelyn asked again.

Rhonwen held her breath. As the two men looked at each other Rhonwen felt the power of the older man's mind reaching out to his prince, trying to sway him. Llywelyn shook his head slightly as if feeling the pressure as a physical pain.

He doesn't know! Suddenly Rhonwen realised the truth – Einion was not all-seeing. He didn't know that Eleyne had already gone. She felt weak with relief.

Before Einion had a chance to reply Joan stood up abruptly. Her dislike of her husband's most senior bard was obvious. 'It is not your concern, Lord Einion, where our daughter goes, or why,' she said coldly, and with a sharp imperious nod to Rhonwen she turned away. The matter was closed.

X

The mountains on both sides of the road were shrouded in mist. The horses' hooves were muffled in mud. Looking behind her nervously for the tenth time, Rhonwen narrowed her eyes, searching the track for signs of pursuit. Surely Einion had seen her go? She had managed to arrange an escort and leave without the prince demanding to see Eleyne before she left, and she had been no more than two hours behind her charge when she turned east into the mountains. She rode fast, anxious to catch up, terrified even now that Einion would find a way to bring her back. In front of her, on the old Roman roadway, patches of mist drifted and swam, blocking out the view more than a hundred feet or so ahead. Trees vanished and reappeared, and in the silence she could hear, above the creak of the harness and the thud of the horses' hooves, the sound of the river. Then that too faded as the road turned away from its banks and across the hills.

It was early evening before Rhonwen came to the great river near the Abbey of Aberconwy which Eleyne's father had founded thirty years earlier, and caught up at last with Eleyne and Cenydd as they waited for a boat to take them across the water to Degannwy. To reach the castle they had to cross the river where it narrowed before the broad estuary opened out to the north, and then from the jetty on the far side make their way on foot up to the great castle, built around the twin scree-covered peaks of the Vardre.

There was no sign of pursuit. The road behind them was empty, shrouded in mist, and the water at their feet lapped dankly on the rocks with the rising tide. Rhonwen touched Eleyne's shoulder. 'The escort must take Invictus back to Aber. We'll be safe now.'

Eleyne hesitated. 'You're sure? You haven't told him where I am?' She gazed at Rhonwen: 'You have. You've told him!' Her voice rose in terror.

'Your mother told him, not me,' Rhonwen said. 'There was nothing I could do. But he cannot reach you here, *cariad*. You'll be safe here.'

DEGANNWY CASTLE ❖ October 1228

Gruffydd and Senena were waiting for them in the prince's solar. Eleyne hurled herself into her half-brother's arms and he swung her high off the floor.

'Oh, Gruffydd, I'm so pleased to be safe here with you.' She clung to him.

He frowned. 'What is it, little sister?' He had never seen her afraid. 'Sweetheart! you're trembling.' Setting her down, he glared at Rhonwen. 'What's happened? Why are you here?'

Eleyne collected herself. She drew herself up, walked away from her brother and stood in front of the fire, her hands to the flames, her back turned squarely towards him. 'Nothing has happened. I'm trembling because I'm cold.' She changed the subject hastily. 'Why do you keep making papa so angry, Gruffydd? You play right into Dafydd's hands every time you do it!'

'I know, sweetheart, I know.' Gruffydd grimaced ruefully. 'I curse myself and my stupid temper twenty times a day.'

'And I curse him another twenty!' Senena put in. She kissed Eleyne on the top of her head.

'So, little sister.' Gruffydd looked at her thoughtfully. 'What have you done to be sent to this prison? It seems a fearful sentence for one so young.'

'The Lady Eleyne is here to visit you, sir,' Rhonwen put in. 'She is not a prisoner.'

'No?' Gruffydd laughed bitterly. 'Are you sure? The children of Llywelyn are only sent here when they are in disgrace. Near enough to Aber for papa to keep an eye on us, but far enough away to forget us too!'

'Even so, sir, Eleyne is no prisoner,' Rhonwen insisted.

'No. I ran away,' Eleyne put in softly. 'I was afraid.' She was about to say more when she caught Rhonwen's eye and bit her lip.

'The Princess Joan was angry when we came back uninvited from Llanfaes,' Rhonwen explained. 'She would not forgive Eleyne for that.'

'Mother never likes me to be at Aber,' Eleyne went on. 'And Sir William de Braose likes me. That made her even angrier.' She said it wistfully. 'I think she likes him herself. So when I said I'd like to come here she agreed at once.'

Rhonwen and Gruffydd exchanged glances and Gruffydd let out a soft whistle. 'So, can the iron-willed Princess Joan be susceptible to mere human frailty after all? He is attractive to the ladies, is he, this Sir William?'

'Indeed he is!' Senena put in, teasing.

'And you like him too, do you, sweetheart?' Gruffydd chucked his sister under the chin.

Eleyne blushed. 'I like his horse.'

Gruffydd let out a roar of laughter. 'His horse, is it! Oh, sweet Eleyne! You've a little growing up to do, yet, I see.'

XII

Eleyne was playing with her little nephew, Owain, in the courtyard. He had set up a line of roughly carved wooden horses and was systematically knocking them down with his ball. Near them, taking advantage of the late autumn sunshine, the wetnurse was cradling the sleeping baby, Llywelyn, to her breast. Rhonwen was in the solar with Senena and her ladies, busy with her embroidery. Eleyne glanced up at the narrow window of the tower behind her and felt a stab of guilt. She should have been up there with them, but she was already feeling the restrictions of being incarcerated behind these high curtain walls. They made her feel safe from Einion, but she felt trapped, even though from the top of the tower she could see the mountains stretching away towards the east and south, to the west the estuary of the Conwy and beyond it the low misty hills of Anglesey.

She had no premonition of danger as she looked idly at a group of travellers who appeared through the gates. Then she grew cold. That tall spare figure in the centre of the group, even with the hood of his travelling cloak pulled up, would be unmistakable anywhere. For a moment she was paralysed with fear, then scrambling to her feet she looked around desperately for somewhere to hide – somewhere to escape those all-seeing eyes. She thrust Owain's ball into his hands and dived around the corner of the kitchens which were built up against the base of the western wall. Quickly she made her way down the path between the dairy and the back of the farrier's. Lost, there, in the constant coming and going of the castle servants, she could hide until Einion had gone in to see Gruffydd. But she was the one he wanted. Of that she had no doubt. And he would find her. Imprisoned in the castle, she had nowhere to run. Her heart hammering, she peered round the corner of the dairy.

'Eleyne!'

The small voice at her elbow made her jump nearly out of her skin. Looking down, she found Owain had followed her. The sturdy small child grinned up from a grubby face. 'Play hide and seek, Eleyne?'

She glared at him. 'Go back to your nurse!'

'No. Owain play hide and seek!' The shrill voice persisted. His hand crept into hers.

Eleyne peered around the corner once more. The party of visitors was moving towards the keep and the wooden staircase to the door of the great hall. Near them she could see the nurses. With Llywelyn clutched beneath the arm of one, they were hunting frantically for their lost charge.

'Go to your nurse, Owain, now.' Eleyne gave him a sharp push.

Owain let out a piercing wail and she saw Einion stop. Unerringly he looked towards her and she drew back into the shadows. 'Be quiet, Owain, please,' she murmured under her breath, but the child was now crying in earnest. Other heads were turning. The nurse was coming, clucking like an old hen. Einion had moved away.

With a little sob of relief, Eleyne saw him climb the stairs after his companions and disappear inside the shadowed door to the keep.

He was waiting for her as the household assembled that evening for supper.

'Come.' He held out his hand to her. 'I have messages from your father.'

'No.' She shook her head and backed away, her heart thumping with terror.

'You needn't fear me, Eleyne, I am your friend.' He rummaged in his leather scrip and brought out a sealed letter. 'I brought others for the Lord Gruffydd.'

She took her letter warily.

He smiled. 'You have had no more dreams and visions, child?'

She shook her head vehemently, feeling his eyes on her face.

'If you do, I want you to send for me. Don't try to bear them alone. I understand.' His voice was gentle, reassuring. 'You are greatly blessed, Eleyne. Don't fight your gift.'

That was all he said. He made no attempt to speak to her alone again.

XIII

DEGANNWY ❖ December 1229

Time had passed and weeks had turned to months, soothing Eleyne's fear; reassuring her; allowing her to feel secure. When the vision came back, it was unsought and unexpected. The first snows of winter had fallen and melted almost as soon as they had settled, and a light cold rain drifted in from the estuary, soaking the cold ground and turning the ice to mud. Most of the inhabitants of the castle were huddled around the huge fires in the great hall. In the nurseries Rhonwen and

Eleyne were helping the children's nurses stitch clothes for the swiftly growing boys. Tired, Eleyne put down her needle and stood up, chilled after hours of sitting still. She went to stand before the fire, looking down into the glowing embers as she felt its warmth begin to reach her aching bones.

The stones of the hearth were all at once so clearly defined that she could see the grain of the stone; she could hear the crack and hiss of the slivers of blackened bark as they peeled from the logs and shrivelled into ash. She put out her hand towards the fire, half intrigued, half repelled, but already she could see him, deep in the heart of the flame.

The man was standing, turned away from her. She could see his shoulders beneath a white shirt, the rope twisted around his wrists, and the other rope, the hempen noose, around his neck. She strained forward, trying to see his face, but already the picture was fading.

Rhonwen looked up. The child had let out a small despairing whimper. 'Eleyne?' she said sharply. 'What is it?'

Eleyne clenched her fists, fighting a wave of dizziness and nausea. 'Nothing. It was just the heat, that's all . . .' She turned and walked back to the others. She would not tell Rhonwen in case she told Einion. She would not tell anyone, ever again, when the pictures came.

XIV

When the snows had blanketed the countryside and the roads were closed, Eleyne grew less afraid that Einion would return.

Once she nearly confided in her brother. They were standing together on the walls one evening, watching the sun set in a bank of mist. Around them the encircling mountains and the distant hump of the Anglesey heartland were disappearing in the deep opal haze.

'Do you like Einion Gweledydd?' she asked. She did not take her eyes off the distant view.

'He's one of our father's most senior bards. He has been at court a long time.' Gruffydd blew into his cupped hands to warm his fingers.

'But do you like him?' she persisted.

Gruffydd considered for a moment. 'He's not the sort of man you can like,' he said with caution. 'He's too austere. There is a rumour that he holds to the old religion of the mountains and men are afraid of him for that reason. They believe he has magical powers.'

Eleyne's hand gripped the stone parapet. 'And do you believe it?'

Gruffydd laughed. 'I suppose everyone deep down believes in magic; but not in the old religion. Christ has vanquished that. Why do you ask, sweetheart? Has he been frightening you?' He gave her a searching look.

'No, of course not. I just wondered when he came here. He seemed so stern.' She bit her lip. 'What did papa say to you in the letter Einion brought?' she said, changing the subject. In all the long months since Einion's visit, Gruffydd had never mentioned the letter in her presence.

'Ah yes, the letter,' he said heavily. 'He said he loves me, but that he and Dafydd think it best I should stay here for a while longer. As if Dafydd would say anything else!'

Eleyne looked up at him miserably. 'I wish you and he could be friends, Gruffydd.'

He gave a grim smile. 'I am afraid that is not possible. Not as long as Dafydd usurps my place as father's successor.' His bitterness was savage.

She walked away from him and leaned on the stone battlements, gazing at the hazed glow in the mountains, all that was left of the setting sun. Aberconwy Abbey on the far side of the river, its tower surmounted by the cross of Christ, was a black blur in the deep lengthening shadows. She pulled her fur mantle around her tightly. 'How long can I stay here?'

Again, the grim smile. 'As long as father allows it, I suppose. I think he hopes that Senena can turn you into a lady.' He managed a wry grin.

Eleyne ignored it. 'It's strange that you want to leave and I want to stay.'

It was a world apart here: safe, cocooned. Far from Einion and from Aber; far from the thought of marriage. The only world she was not safe from was the world of her dreams. There had been one dream over the last few months which had come again and again. A dream she had had since childhood, but which had condensed and clarified until she could remember every detail. A dream of a man who was tall and red-haired with blue-green eyes and a warm smile. A man she knew and yet whom she could not name. A man as old as her father yet for whom she felt as no child should towards a parent. A dream which she welcomed guiltily and gloated over night after night in the privacy of the darkness, as she slept back to back with Luned in their tower bedchamber.

'It's terrible to have no freedom, Eleyne,' Gruffydd said. 'It's different for you. You are a woman. You will never have much freedom, sweetheart. Always a father or a husband to rule you. But for a man it's different. A man must be free.' He could not disguise the anguish in his voice.

Never to have freedom; always to be ruled by someone else. Put like that, starkly, life for a woman was indeed a frightening prospect. It was something Eleyne had never even considered, and now she pushed the thought aside. It belonged to that dark area of the distant future which she had walled off in a corner of her mind – that part of her future which concerned her husband, the Earl of Huntingdon.

'Sir William de Braose would know what I mean.' Gruffydd sighed, not noticing his sister's sudden silence. 'He knows he is a prisoner even if he is treated as father's guest.'

Eleyne seized on the change of subject gratefully. Every time she thought about Sir William she felt warm and special. She liked to say his name, and she sensed her brother's secret admiration for the man. Once or twice she had dreamed about him, adding his face gloatingly to that other face she dreamed about, the face about which she had told no one, not even Rhonwen, the face which she hoped belonged to the Earl of Huntingdon, but which in her heart of hearts she knew did not. The sixteen-year-old youth who had held her so awkwardly in his arms for a few brief moments after their wedding had fair hair and light blue eyes. If she remembered him at all, it was not as the man in her dream.

'Freedom is everything, Eleyne,' Gruffydd went on, his voice tight with frustration. 'To be held behind walls, however comfortable the surroundings, is a torment for someone who wants to leave. It is better than a dungeon, of course, but you are not your own master. I can't leave here until father agrees; Sir William can't leave Aber until he has paid his ransom and father gives him his freedom in exchange.'

'And when he has done that he can go home and then he will agree to Isabella marrying Dafydd.' Eleyne smiled with relief. 'I wonder if Dafydd is pleased.'

Gruffydd gave a rueful grin. When and if the wedding took place, Eleyne would be summoned back to Aber and he would lose his small companion. He glanced at her thoughtfully. She was pleased about the wedding, but would she be pleased to go back to Aber? She was afraid of something there. Mortally afraid. If only she would tell him what it was.

XV

DEGANNWY ❖ Easter 1230

'I don't want to go!' Tearfully Eleyne caught Gruffydd's hand. The letter she had dreaded had arrived at last.

'I know, sweetheart, but father has sent for you. There's nothing you can do. You have to obey him. You can't stay here forever.' Her hands were ice-cold in Gruffydd's and he could see the fear in her eyes. 'What is it, Eleyne? What are you afraid of?'

'Nothing.' She met his gaze, half defiant, half pleading, before she turned away. 'Nothing at all.'

65

After tearful goodbyes to Gruffydd and Senena and her small cousins who had to remain in their prison, Eleyne, Luned and Rhonwen, escorted by Cenydd and his hand-picked band of guards and by Llywelyn's messengers, embarked once more across the Conwy and set off west towards Aber. Tucked into Eleyne's baggage were several letters from Gruffydd to his father begging forgiveness; begging for leave to come to his side.

Eleyne rode upright, her face pinched with cold, her fear buried deep inside her. She could not tell Senena or Gruffydd, she would not tell Rhonwen, that she was still afraid. Instead she clung to the thought that Isabella would be at Aber waiting for her. Sir William had, it appeared, long ago paid his ransom and gone. The wedding arrangements had been made. It should be a lovely spring.

Above them in the mountains great swathes of snow still lay unmelted in the shadowy crevices and valleys, and over the peaks the crisp whiteness shone like caps of beaten egg-white. Wild daffodils, small tight spikes in the cold wind, only here and there showed a yellow trumpet. The wind cut like a sword. The mountain route west was impassable, so they took the road along the coast.

As Eleyne entered the crowded, noisy hall of the *llys*, still swathed in her furs after the ride, Einion was the first person she saw, standing behind her father's chair. She stopped in her tracks, shielded by the crowd of people around her. Behind her, Rhonwen too saw him and grew pale.

Einion spotted them at once, his eyes going unerringly to Rhonwen and then to the child at her side, and they saw him stoop and whisper into the prince's ear.

'No!' Eleyne turned away, trying to fight her way back through the crowd. Her heart was thumping with terror and she felt sick.

'You have to go on.' Rhonwen caught her arm. 'You have to greet your father. You have to give him Gruffydd's letters and plead for your brother's release.'

'No.'

'Yes,' Rhonwen insisted. Now she was near him, her own fear of Einion had returned and she was torn between her protective love for Eleyne and her duty and obedience to the seer. 'You are a princess, Eleyne! You are never afraid!' she whispered harshly. 'He's just an old man! He can't hurt you!' She crossed her fingers, afraid that he would know what she had said, then remembered, comforted, that he was not all-seeing. There were things he did not know.

Eleyne was rooted to the spot with fear, but somehow Rhonwen's words penetrated her terror. She clenched her fists, goaded by her nurse's tone. He was just a tired old man. He was nothing like the wild-eyed wizard of her nightmares. Besides, her father was there. She forced herself to walk on, her eyes avoiding those of the bard.

It was only when she drew near the dais where her father sat that Eleyne saw her mother. Joan was seated on the far side of the roaring fire, dressed in a gown of scarlet, stitched with gold thread. Over her shoulders was her mantle trimmed with fox furs. At her side, deep in conversation with her, sat Sir William de Braose. Eleyne felt her heart jump with happiness and surprise at the sight of him, and relief that beneath her heavy cloak she was wearing one of the new gowns Senena and Rhonwen had made her during the long winter days. It was a deep moss green, heavily stitched and embroidered, showing her colouring to perfection and every bit as beautiful, in her own eyes, as her mother's.

As she curtseyed to her father she glanced half defiantly at Einion. His expression was unreadable. He looked at her and then once more at the prince. 'Your daughter has been away too long, sir. Aber has missed her.'

'Indeed we have,' Llywelyn agreed heartily. 'Greet your mother, child, and take off your cloak. We are to have a recital.' He indicated the harp standing near them.

Eleyne curtseyed dutifully to her mother and then more animatedly to Sir William. There was no sign of Isabella.

Sir William smiled. 'So, do you want to ride Invictus again? I'll toss you for it tomorrow. My imprisonment is over, but it seems that I can't keep away!' His smile deepened. 'I have come back as a guest this time to make the final arrangements for Bella's wedding, so we can ride together. With your mother's permission.'

Eleyne's pleasure and excitement were strangely dampened by his glance at Joan. There was more warmth there than he had shown her; more intimacy. She felt a sudden sense of loss as if she had been excluded from something private and special.

'Eleyne, come here and sit by me.' The prince indicated a stool near his feet, but his eyes were on his wife's face and Eleyne, sympathetic, knew he felt the same as she. Instinctively she reached up and touched her father's hand. Llywelyn smiled and pressed her shoulder gently. At least he would never have cause to doubt his daughter's love and loyalty as he had begun, Christ forgive him, to doubt his wife's. He turned and nodded to the bard.

XVI
ABER

Rhonwen woke suddenly, every sense alert and straining, holding her breath as her eyes peered wildly around the silent chamber. The night was completely dark. Outside the narrow windows the valley was blanketed with mist; there were no stars; no moonlight pierced the gloom.

The tall figure was standing in the deeper darkness of the shadowed corner near her bed. Arms folded, he stared down at her.

'Where is the child?'

Rhonwen sat up slowly, holding the bedclothes tightly beneath her chin. 'What are you doing here? How did you get in?' She was terrified.

He ignored her question. 'Where is the child?'

Swallowing, Rhonwen could not stop herself looking across at the corner of the room where Eleyne's bed was invisible in the darkness. Without going near it, she could sense that only Luned lay there, fast asleep.

She shrugged. 'I don't know where she is. She often wanders around at night.'

'Find her. The lessons must continue.'

Rhonwen swallowed. 'She's afraid. Could you not leave it until she is older? Please . . .'

'It will be too late when she is older. Find her. I shall wait by the alders as before.'

Rhonwen closed her eyes. 'Please —' Her plea met with silence.

He had vanished. Climbing out of bed, she groped with shaking hands for the candle on the coffer near the door and thrust it into the fire. The light sent the shadows leaping and cavorting up the walls, running up the bed hangings and across the ceiling, racing across the floor and towards the door. The room was empty. She pulled open the door. The short spiral stair leading down into the darkness was deserted. The rush light in its holder at the first curved angle of the wall burned with a steady flame. No one's passing had caused it to flicker.

Closing the door, she went back to the bed and sat down, shivering. Had it been a dream or had Einion slipped through the walls, his body a wraith without substance as he sought the child? She glanced at Eleyne's bed again. Where was she and what was she doing?

XVII

Eleyne was in the stables. A small slim figure, wrapped in a thick dark cloak, she had slipped past the grooms unnoticed, ducking into Invictus's stall. He whickered a greeting, nuzzling her hands for titbits, and she gave him the crusts of wastel bread saved especially from the kitchens. She settled at his feet in the deep hay. Einion would not find her here.

She too had woken suddenly, aware of the questing mind of the bard seeking hers. She had sat up in the darkness, hearing the steady breathing of Luned and Rhonwen, feeling the warm solid weight of Luned's sleeping form in the bed with her. Hugging her knees miserably, she tried to blank off her mind, fighting him, shaking her head, pressing her hands against her ears, then she snatched her clothes, threw them on and tiptoed out of the room. In the stables, she knew instinctively, she would be safe.

'Well, well, what have we here!' The voice, loud, attractive, pulled her unwillingly out of sleep. 'Do you claim the ride because you were here first, little princess?' Sir William de Braose stepped into the stallion's stall and stood looking down at her, amused. The early morning sun blazed into the courtyard.

Eleyne stretched her cramped legs and yawned as the great horse lowered his head and nuzzled her hair, blowing companionably in her ear. She kissed his soft nose and then climbed sheepishly to her feet. 'I couldn't sleep last night. I often come to see the horses when I am –' She stopped. She had been about to say 'frightened' but that would never do. In daylight, with the palace bustling with activity, she would not admit even to herself her fear of Einion. 'When I can't sleep. I love it out here at night.' She smiled at him shyly. That at least was true. She never found the darkness frightening. The cool still magic time of night when everyone else was asleep and the halls and castles were silent, patrolled only by the night guard, was very special to her.

'So, are you ready for our ride?' As one of the grooms hefted in the heavy wooden saddle, Sir William stood back and put his arm around her shoulders companionably. He glanced down at the glowing, tangled red-gold hair and again found himself wishing he could have had a son with half her spirit.

Eleyne's eyes were shining. 'Are we going to toss for who rides Invictus?' She could not disguise the wistful longing in her voice.

He shook his head with a smile. 'No, there's a horse of your father's I'm keen to try.' He had decided the night before there must be no risk of disappointing her. 'You may take Invictus.'

It was as they mounted in the courtyard that the Princess Joan appeared, in a flurry of silks and furs, with two of her women attendants.

'I have decided to go with you, Sir William,' she called. She gestured at a groom to fetch her horse. 'I want to see this daughter of mine ride. I had no idea she was such a fine horsewoman!'

Eleyne looked at her in dismay. Her mother, beautiful, charming, her lovely eyes fixed on Sir William's face, had not once glanced at her. Already Eleyne knew the ride was spoiled, and she became conscious suddenly of her old, torn gown, snatched on anyhow in the dark, and stuck through with stems of hay from her night in the stable. Her mother's gown was new: a flattering gold, stitched with crimson silk.

Sir William leaped off his bay stallion and bowed to Joan. 'She's worth watching, your highness,' he said with a humorous glance across at the scowling child. 'And we shall both be honoured to have you with us.'

The two gazed at each other and Eleyne felt a shaft of jealousy knife through her. It was a reflex action to kick Invictus forward in a great bound and turn him for the gates. She did not look back. She knew the guards would follow her. So, in their own time, no doubt, would her mother and Sir William. Except that now Sir William would have no more eyes for her. He would, she knew, ride beside her mother.

'What's the matter, little princess?'

As they stopped to take breakfast after two hours' riding, Sir William walked across to Eleyne and sat beside her on the ground. Behind them the woods were pale green with new, reluctant leaves of birch and alder.

She stared down into the cup of ale which she had been given. 'Nothing's the matter.'

'Nothing?' He smiled. 'You didn't want your mother to come, did you?' He was watching her closely.

'She spoils everything.' Eleyne frowned. 'We have to go slowly because of her.'

'She loves you very much, you know.' Sir William was not aware that his expression softened as he glanced across at Joan, seated decorously on a fallen log between her ladies, a white napkin on her knees.

'She doesn't love me at all.' Eleyne was practical and unsentimental. 'And she's not interested in how I ride. She wanted an excuse to be with you.' She scowled.

Sir William did not deny it. 'I'll have a race with you, after you've drunk your ale,' he whispered. 'I bet you five silver pennies Invictus can't beat your father's new stallion.'

Eleyne looked up, her eyes sparkling. 'Of course he can.'

Sir William rose to his feet. 'We'll see.'

She won the race easily and, flushed and out of breath, claimed her prize. Then, contentedly, she agreed to lead the way back to Aber, steadying the prancing, excited horse with gentle hands – too preoccupied to think about Sir William and her mother riding side by side once more.

XVIII

The palace was silent. In the hearth the banked-up fire ticked and settled gently into the deep bed of ashes. Rhonwen leaned closer to her sewing and sighed. Her head ached and her eyes refused to focus on the tiny intricate stitches she was inserting into the green velvet gown she had promised to finish for Eleyne. She was well aware why Eleyne wanted the new gown so badly. The child wanted to impress de Braose. She smiled grimly. Well, let her try. At least it would take her mind off Einion.

Eleyne lay huddled beneath her blankets next to Luned, deeply and dreamlessly asleep. Excited by his race, Invictus had given her an exhausting, exhilarating ride and Sir William, when they had returned, gave her an affectionate hug and rumpled her hair, beneath the seemingly approving eyes of her mother, and promised her another ride tomorrow. Happy, excited and tired, she had not given Einion a thought. Nor Rhonwen. She had not noticed the cold stare Rhonwen threw at the hated de Braose, or the icy politeness with which she greeted Princess Joan.

Wearily Rhonwen put down her sewing, climbed to her feet and pulled her cloak around her. There had been no sign of Einion at Aber that evening, either in the great hall or in the outer courts and gardens. It would be safe to leave the sleeping children for a while. Folding the heavy velvet into her basket, she picked it up. She tiptoed down the stairs and beckoned one of the guards from the outer door. 'I have to go to Princess Joan's bower. Wait outside the Lady Eleyne's chamber until I return. Let no one in. No one, do you understand?'

She took a deep breath. Had Einion come to the chamber up the stairs and through the door, or had he floated, ghostlike, through the window? She shuddered.

Pulling her cloak around her she threaded her way towards Princess Joan's apartments in the tower at the west end of the *ty hir*. They were small, sumptuously appointed rooms hung with tapestries and furnished with richly carved and painted furniture. As she had suspected, there was no sign of Princess Joan. There were only two women in the ladies' bower, huddled over the fire, talking softly, and they greeted Rhonwen with a marked lack of enthusiasm.

'You shouldn't be here, Lady Rhonwen!' Marared, the daughter of Madoc, jumped to her feet, agitated. 'Princess Joan gave specific orders.'

Rhonwen frowned. 'Orders that I should not be admitted?' She found herself a joint stool and setting it in front of the fire sat down firmly and produced her basket. 'Be that as it may, I've promised little Eleyne this gown would be finished for the feast tomorrow and I need some more pairs of hands,' she said firmly. 'All I want is a little help. I'll not stay long.'

Marared glanced unhappily at her companion, Ethil, who had not moved from her own seat, her toes in the hearth.

Ethil shrugged. 'She just gave orders that she shouldn't be disturbed. And we can all guess why that is. Rhonwen can turn a blind eye as well as we can!' she commented tartly.

Marared knew of Rhonwen's antipathy towards Princess Joan, but she had already given in. 'I think we should all go through to the solar. The fire there is still hot and I can mull some wine,' she coaxed.

Ethil looked up, about to suggest that Marared bring the wine to her where she sat, but something in her companion's face changed her mind. She stood up. 'Good idea. Come, Lady Rhonwen, we'll be more private in the solar. I should hate our talking to disturb the princess. I don't want another tongue-lashing tonight!' They glanced at the door to the princess's chamber in the far wall – firmly closed. Rhonwen followed their gaze. 'I thought the princess would still be in the hall flirting with Sir William,' she said acidly. 'She didn't look to me as though she intended to go to bed early.'

There was a horrified silence. She looked from one to the other, then back at the door, and her eyes narrowed. For the first time she noticed the heavy cloak lying across a stool. 'So,' she whispered, 'she went to bed early after all. But not alone.'

Ethil seized her arm. 'For the love of the Sweet Blessed Virgin don't say anything! The prince would kill us all!' She dragged Rhonwen towards the small solar. 'Please, Lady Rhonwen, come through here. We'll do your sewing for you, and we'll have some wine. And you must forget whatever it is you are thinking!'

'How long has this been going on?' Rhonwen allowed herself to be pushed into the best seat and accepted some wine as Marared closed the door.

Ethil shrugged. 'It started when he was here before. When he was a prisoner. I don't think the prince ever suspected.' She closed her eyes miserably. 'When he went away I was so relieved, but then he came back . . .'

'So.' Rhonwen smiled. She bent to take the folded gown out of her basket and handed it to Ethil. 'Don't worry,' she said, 'your secret is safe with me.'

XIX

Eleyne sat up, staring into the darkness, her heart thumping with fear. Was he there again, his mind seeking hers, trying to lure her from her bed and down to the river? But no, the room was empty. She could hear the wind moaning in the roof timbers, swaying the trees in the valley below the palace. She shivered. Luned was fast asleep, burrowed like a small animal into the soft sheets. There was no sound from the other bed.

'Rhonwen?' she whispered.

She knew already that Rhonwen was not there and neither was the nearly finished gown which had been hung from a bracket near her bed so she could see it as she went to sleep.

Slipping silently from the bed, she pulled her fur-trimmed bed gown over her bare shoulders and padded over to the fire. The room was cold. She bent and pulled the turf off the banked coals and reached for a log. The fire hissed and a blue flame ran across the wood. She flinched, then, unable to look away, stared down into it.

She could see the gallows; see the crowds standing around its foot. The people were excited, rowdy, in the mood to be entertained; as she watched, unable to tear her eyes away, she saw them surge forward, shouting. He was there in their midst, surrounded by guards, his short tunic open at the neck, and already he wore the noose. She could see the rope against the softness of his skin, see the artery in his throat beating, throbbing with life. He half turned towards her and she strained forward, trying to see his face, but the crowds seethed round him cutting off her view.

'Wait! please wait!' she cried out loud. 'Oh, please . . .'

Behind her the door opened and the guard peered into the door.

'*Dew!*' He hurled himself across the floor as Eleyne sprawled forward into the fireplace, clawing at the burning logs. She was crying.

'Please, come back! I can't see you! *Please!*'

She let out a scream as the man grabbed her by the arm and pulled her to her feet. Behind them, Luned sat up in bed, frightened.

'What are you doing, princess?'

The man-at-arms half shook her, slapping in panic at her bed gown, which was covered in ash. '*Dew!* You nearly set yourself on fire! Did you drop something?'

Eleyne was trembling. Suddenly she began to cry. 'Rhonwen, where's Rhonwen?'

'She's gone to see the princess, your mother,' he said, and he found himself stepping back sharply as she pushed past him and ran out of the room.

Barefoot, she ran towards the ladies' bower and her mother's bed-room. She threw open the door into the solar and peered in. It was deserted. The fire had burned low and the candles were guttering. She stopped, panting. 'Rhonwen?' she whispered. Tears were streaming down her face. Then she heard the murmur of conversation from the bedchamber. Tiptoeing towards her mother's door, she lifted the latch and pushed it open.

The fire in the hearth leaped up at the sudden draught, sending

73

red-gold lights sliding up the walls and across the bed where the two naked bodies writhed together on the tumbled sheets. Eleyne stared. She saw her mother's face contorted with some strange emotion, her back arching towards the man who knelt between her legs, his broad shoulders shiny with perspiration in the leaping firelight. They laughed exultantly and he bent forward to smother her face with kisses, his powerful hands kneading the full white flesh of her breasts. Totally wrapped in their pleasure, the two did not hear the door open or see the small figure in the doorway.

Frozen to the spot, Eleyne stared at them for several seconds before she backed out of the room and pulled the door closed.

Blindly she turned. She did not seem surprised to see Rhonwen and her companions standing behind her. The three women had heard the outer door open and run into the solar in time to see Eleyne creep white-faced from her mother's room.

Eleyne stared from one to the other, wild-eyed. 'Did you see?' Her lips were stiff. She could barely speak.

Rhonwen nodded.

'It was Sir William.' Eleyne's voice was tight and shrill. She felt utterly betrayed. How could he? How could he do that with her mother? Her mother who had looked ugly and wild and like a sweating, rutting animal.

'Your father must be told,' Rhonwen said quietly at her elbow. She was suddenly, secretly, exultant. Sir William and Princess Joan. The two people she hated most in the world, trapped by their own lust. She bit back her triumph, anguished by the raw pain on the child's face. 'He has to know, Eleyne. What you saw was treason.'

Eleyne stared at her for a moment, her lips pressed tightly together. 'But he will kill them,' she whispered.

Then she nodded.

XX

Prince Llywelyn had fallen asleep in his great chair by the fire on the dais in the main hall. A half-finished cup of wine stood near him. Most of the men around him lay sprawled asleep across the tables.

Eleyne flew across the great hall and threw herself at him in a storm of tears.

It took Llywelyn a minute or two to understand what his distraught daughter was saying, then, white-faced, he stood up. Striding between his followers, all now awake and staring, he seized a burning torch from one of the sconces and made his way out of the hall, dragging Eleyne with him by the wrist.

'If you have made this up, I'll have you whipped,' he hissed at the terrified child. She had never seen her father like this. His eyes were huge and hooded, his mouth a thin line of pain. Frantically she cast around for Rhonwen, but there was no sign of her amongst the silent curious crowd pushing after them.

Llywelyn strode across the courtyard and into the *ty hir*. Climbing the stairs, he crossed the women's bower in long strides and flung open his wife's bedchamber door, holding the torch high.

Eleyne saw the two figures sit up in the bed, their faces rigid with shock; she saw Sir William snatch the bedcover and wrap it around his naked body as he leaped up, saw her mother's white skin gleaming with sweat, flaccid, exhausted, before Joan too grabbed at a sheet and pulled it over her. Then she found herself spinning across the room as her father, with an animal howl of grief and anger, pushed her away and threw himself on to Sir William, reaching for his throat. For a moment the two men grappled together by the bed, before the prince's men rushed forward and dragged Sir William aside. He had lost the sheet and for a moment he stood completely naked, his arms gripped by his captors, as he was dragged out of the room.

Llywelyn stood, panting, looking down at his wife. She stared back, rigid with fear, her beautiful hair matted with sweat.

'Whore!' Llywelyn shot the word at her with loathing. 'Slut! Harlot! You will die for this!'

Eleyne let out a little sob. Scrambling to her feet from the corner where she had fallen, she stood not daring to move, staring at her mother who was rocking backwards and forwards on the bed, moaning with a strange, high-pitched wail.

In the doorway Marared and Ethil hovered, not daring to approach her. It was Ethil who beckoned the frightened child and pulled her from the room. 'Go to your bed, princess, and don't say a word to anyone,' she whispered. 'Quickly now.'

Of Rhonwen there was no sign.

Eleyne fled to the stables. For a long time she stood staring at Invictus as he nuzzled her empty hands, then she put her arms around his neck and wept.

Rhonwen found her asleep in the hay between his great hooves several hours later. One of the grooms carried the still-sleeping child to her bed.

XXI

The world to which Eleyne awakened had changed forever. The palace was in shock. Sir William and his followers had been imprisoned, as had the Princess Joan. The prince's anger and grief had hardened into the need for revenge. Llywelyn's wife and her lover were to die. He refused to see Eleyne; he refused to see Dafydd; he refused repeatedly Joan's frenzied pleas for an audience. He closeted himself in an upstairs chamber of the new stone keep, admitting only Einion and his trusted friend and counsellor, Ednyfed Fychan.

Word of what had happened had spread like wildfire beyond Aber and across Wales. Already the crowds were gathering, baying for de Braose's blood.

Eleyne's mind refused to accept what had happened. She crept repeatedly back to the stables and at last Rhonwen, chilled by the expression on the child's face, let her stay there to find what comfort she could amongst the horses.

Where others had failed, Rhonwen managed to gain audience with the prince. His face appalled her. He had aged twenty years in as many hours.

'You must speak to Princess Eleyne,' she said urgently. 'The child is in torment.'

'I am in torment, lady!' the prince snapped back. 'Would to God she had not told me!'

'You would rather not have known your wife made a cuckold of you?' Rhonwen was deliberately harsh. 'When the whole court could see it? You had to find out.'

Llywelyn walked heavily across to the fire and threw himself into the chair that stood near it. 'Then the whole court will see how I repay treachery. Sir William accepted my hospitality at the sacred time of Easter and he abused every law of home and hearth. He will pay for it with his life like a common criminal, with no honour, on the Gallows Marsh.'

Rhonwen suppressed a triumphant smile. 'That's only just, sir, but I must take Eleyne away. You must see that. She's only a child.'

'Then it's time she grew up!' Llywelyn's face hardened. 'She can watch him hang.'

'No!' Rhonwen paled. This was not what she had intended. 'He befriended her –'

'Then she should learn to choose her friends with more care. It will be a valuable lesson.'

Rhonwen was silent for a moment. 'And her mother?' she whispered at last. 'Must she watch her mother hang too?'

Llywelyn put his face in his hands. He rubbed his cheeks wearily and she heard the rasp of his beard against his palms. He shook his head. 'I cannot hang her.' His voice broke. He gave a painful sigh. 'But she will spend the rest of her life in prison.'

There was a long silence broken only by the distant murmur of the crowds gathering outside the palace.

'Perhaps I could take Eleyne back to Degannwy?' Rhonwen persisted gently, 'afterwards.'

'Perhaps.' He stood up. 'Enough, woman. Leave me.'

Einion was waiting for her outside the door. He took Rhonwen's arm and pulled her into a quiet corner. 'I will take the little princess,' he said, 'she will be safe in my care.'

'No.' Rhonwen shook her head violently, her complacency turned to fear. 'No, she is too young and you have frightened her. She will not go with you now. If you had but left it; treated her more gently . . .'

'There was no time to treat her gently. She has grown into her full powers and she needs my guidance.' He drew himself up. 'This is a time of change for Gwynedd, lady, as you are well aware. The English princess and her compatriots are finished.' He smiled grimly. 'Under Prince Llywelyn's rule Wales can become a great and independent nation at last. It is vital that Eleyne takes her place at her father's side and, after him, at that of her brother, Gruffydd. She can help them. Guide them. We are agreed on that, I think.'

Rhonwen nodded unhappily. 'It is a pity that Dafydd's marriage to the little de Braose has not taken place yet. That would have spoiled his claim to be his father's heir,' she said with a sigh.

Einion gave a harsh smile. 'There are other ways of discrediting Dafydd *bach*. He is his mother's son, after all.'

'You are forgetting that Eleyne has the same blood,' Rhonwen reminded him, ruefully.

Einion smiled again. 'Her Plantagenet blood lies dormant. It is her Welsh blood which rules.' He put his hand heavily on Rhonwen's shoulder. 'Don't fear for Eleyne, lady. I shall take care of her. Once de Braose is hanged, I shall speak to her father and take her back to Môn.'

XXII
ABER ❖ 2 May 1230

Eleyne was sitting alone, huddled behind the stable block, watching the grooms strap the horses. She was still numb. This was the day chosen for Sir William to die. The crowds were increasing hourly – people riding in from all over North Wales to watch the scion of the hated de Braose family hang. No one spoke in his defence. Even had they wished to, how could they? To take another man's wife when you were a guest beneath his roof was a crime every man understood. Joan had already been sent away to her lonely prison.

Rhonwen found Eleyne at last in Invictus's stall. 'You have to come, Eleyne. It's your father's command.'

Eleyne's eyes darkened with horror. 'No.'

'You must, *cariad*. I'm sorry.'

Eleyne backed away. Why?' she whispered.

Rhonwen shrugged helplessly. 'I don't know.' She was full of guilt. Why had she not told Llywelyn herself? Why in her haste to destroy Joan and de Braose had she sent the child to find her father?

'You are a princess, Eleyne,' she said softly, 'you have to hold your head high and let no one see that you are crying inside.'

'I'm not crying!' Eleyne retorted unsteadily. 'He deserves to die!'

Slowly, head erect, her shoulders defiantly squared, Eleyne walked with Rhonwen out of the palace and down the river to Gwern y Grog, the Gallows Marsh. There she stood beside her brother Dafydd and her father as Sir William de Braose was brought to the gallows. They halted him before the prince and he bowed slightly.

'Your wife was innocent, your highness,' he said softly. 'I was the only one to blame.' He scanned the crowd anxiously as though afraid Joan had been brought to watch him die.

Beyond the royal party a crowd of several hundred people spread out across the marshy field, its earlier noisy excitement hushed as Sir William appeared. He wore nothing but a short tunic and breeches. They had tied his hands, but he stood proudly before Llywelyn, relaxing imperceptibly when he saw Joan was not there. Then his gaze fell on Eleyne and there was pain in his eyes as he bowed again.

'So, little princess, you come to watch my end. I should like you to have Invictus, sweetheart. My only bequest. With your father's permission, he is yours.' His eyes strayed to Rhonwen's face as she stood behind the child and suddenly he remembered that far-off day in his beloved Hay when he had made an enemy of Eleyne's nurse. With a wry inclination of his head he acknowledged her victory, then he turned and walked of his own accord towards the high gallows.

Eleyne closed her eyes, struggling to hold back her tears. She did not look as the hush from the crowd told her that they had put the noose around his neck, or when the deafening roar of cheers told her that it was done. She stared up at the brilliant blue sky and prayed she would not cry as she tried to control the panic which had swept over her. Her whole body had grown cold with horror for, now it was too late, she knew that she had seen this scene before. Sir William, the friend who had betrayed her as he had betrayed her father, was the man she had seen in her vision in the fire.

She could have saved him! She could have saved her mother and her father. And yet it was she who had told her father of Sir William's treachery; she who had set the chain of events in motion. She had been given the chance to alter the course of history and she had not understood.

'Eleyne, we can go now.' Rhonwen came between her and the gallows and put her arm gently around her shoulders.

Eleyne was clinging desperately to her self-control. She pushed aside Rhonwen's arm.

Why? Why had she not understood? She could have stopped it. She could have saved his life!

Trembling, she stood still, not seeing the crowds of people streaming past her, some with sympathetic glances for the child.

Rhonwen frowned unhappily. 'Come back to your room, *cariad*,' she whispered. 'There's nothing to stay for here.'

'I saw it and I didn't understand.' Eleyne's voice was husky. In the distance she could hear the whistling of the shore birds, feeding on the sands.

'Didn't understand what?' Rhonwen ached to take her in her arms. She saw Llywelyn, his face a mask of pain and anger, walking slowly by. He did not glance at his white-faced daughter.

'The hanging.' Eleyne's words were almost inaudible. 'I saw it in the fire . . .'

Rhonwen closed her eyes and murmured a prayer.

'I could have stopped it. If I had learned how to control the visions I could have saved him . . .'

'No, sweetheart, no.' Rhonwen hugged her now and this time Eleyne did not push her away.

'But don't you see? That's why I was allowed to see it. I could have warned him. I could have.' Suddenly the storm of tears broke. Sobbing, Eleyne clung to her. 'I could have stopped it, I should have. That was why I saw it in the fire. And yet it was me who betrayed him. Me . . .' Her voice broke and she choked on her sobs. 'Why couldn't I have saved him?'

Rhonwen frowned at the sky. 'Perhaps that was because it was his destiny,' she whispered.

XXIII
7 May 1230

Einion was with the prince when Llywelyn sent at last for his youngest daughter.

'You cannot stay at Aber.' Llywelyn looked down at the slight figure of the child with cold dislike.

'Sir, now would be a good time for me to take her to Llanfaes.' Einion stepped forward quickly. There had been no opportunity to speak to the child alone; he knew what she must be feeling; the fear, the uncertainty, the overwhelming guilt. He alone knew what she knew, had seen what she had seen in the fire. 'I have already spoken to you of the little princess's future at your side –'

'She has no future at my side,' Llywelyn snapped. He closed his eyes bitterly. Every time in the last few days that he set eyes on Eleyne it was the same: she reminded him of the night when his world had crashed about his ears. His tender fondness for her had been eclipsed by anger and heartache. Now he almost hated her.

'Then, sir, may I take her back to Degannwy, to Prince Gruffydd.' Rhonwen stepped forward.

Llywelyn shook his head. 'No.' He stood up slowly. 'My mind is made up. There is no longer a home for her in Wales. Eleyne, you will go to your husband; your place is at his side now.'

There was a stunned silence. Eleyne looked from her father's closed face to Rhonwen, who had gone white. She could not think clearly; her mind was numbed by her father's words.

Einion's eyes blazed with anger. 'Sir, this cannot be. She is too young, and her place is here, in Gwynedd.'

'She is not too young.' Llywelyn looked from one to the other, grimly. 'All is arranged. She leaves tomorrow. I do not wish to see my daughter again.'

BOOK TWO

1230–1241

CHAPTER FOUR

I

ABER ❖ May 1230

The prince's guards were at Eleyne's door; Princess Joan's ladies – those who had not been dismissed or followed their mistress into captivity – crowded the nursery quarters packing great coffers full of clothes and bedding and gifts. Although he refused even to bid Eleyne farewell, Llywelyn had made sure that she would leave Aber with a train suitable for a princess and a bride.

Eleyne sat silently amidst all the activity, frozen with unhappiness, unable to bring herself to believe what was happening to her. It had been so sudden. She could eat no supper and that night she lay awake fighting her tears. She could not go to the stable. The rooms were guarded. Beside her Luned slept heavily, worn out with excitement, for she too was to go to Chester.

Eleyne groped for her pillow and hugged it to her miserably, her brain whirling. Her husband was a man; he would want to take her to his bed; he would want to do the things that William de Braose had done to her mother – William whose body was still hanging out there in the darkness, carrion for the crows. She clung to the pillow, feeling sick panic clutch at her stomach. She could have saved him. She could have saved herself. She bit her lip, pressing her small, thin body harder into the feather bed, unconsciously clamping her thighs together in the darkness.

The line of wagons and carts and the escort of armed men stretched for over a mile as the party made its way north-east along the coast road, across the Conwy and, following the old Roman road to St Asaphs, over Afon Clwyd, turned south at last on to the flat lands of Dee. Riding behind Eleyne and Rhonwen came Cenydd and Luned, Luned mounted on Cadi. Somewhere behind them one of the knights led Invictus. Llywelyn had decreed that the horse might be a suitable gift for his son-in-law.

Eleyne's face was white and strained. There were dark rings beneath her eyes. 'What is he like, can you remember?' She rode closer to Rhonwen, her small hands steady on the gilded leather rein of her mother's favourite cream-coloured mare, an outcast as she was from the purge at Aber. She was very afraid.

'The Earl of Huntingdon?' Rhonwen too was numb with shock. 'He's nephew to the great Earl of Chester, and a prince of Scotland. That's all I know. And he is waiting at Chester Castle to meet us.' She tightened her lips. How could Einion have let this happen? Why, when Eleyne had been given to the goddess, had he been unable to prevent it? She closed her eyes wearily and eased herself in the saddle.

Eleyne edged her mare even closer to Rhonwen's, so that the two horses walked shoulder to shoulder. 'Will he . . . will he want to . . .' The question hovered on her lips. 'Will he want to make me his wife properly at once?' Miserably she blurted it out at last, and she saw Rhonwen's answering frown.

'It is his right, *cariad*, to consummate the marriage.' The older woman tried to keep her voice steady.

Eleyne closed her eyes. Yet again she saw the picture she could not keep out of her mind: the writhing bodies on the bed; the man between her mother's contorted thighs, thrusting at her; his great shout of triumph.

'Does it hurt very much?' she whispered. She wanted to reach across and hold Rhonwen's hand for comfort. Instead she wound her fingers into the horse's silky mane. She and Isabella had so often giggled and speculated about the consummation of their respective marriages, as had she and Luned. In the crowded uninhibited world in which they lived they knew what happened from an early age. Too often they had seen people in the shadows, beneath trees or against a wall, but always dressed, always shielded. Never frightening. Never before – never – had she seen a man and a woman coupling naked with such wild uninhibited lust. Never before had she seen a woman arch her back and thrust back at the man, seen the fingernails raking his back, heard a wild yell of triumph such as Sir William had given that fateful night. That act was now mixed inextricably in her mind with her vision of the man with the noose around his neck, the man whose body had jerked and grown limp and swung all day from the gallows tree on the marsh near Aber.

'Of course it doesn't hurt, *cariad*.' Rhonwen gave a wry grimace, trying to hide her own fear and anger and her despair: despair which the night before had led her for a moment to consider pressing the soft pillow over Eleyne's face so that she could die in her sleep rather than submit to this terrible fate. But she could not do it. Even to save Eleyne from marriage, she could not do it. She shook her head slowly. 'I've never lain with a man, but I don't think it can hurt or people wouldn't do it so much.'

'I think it's only the men who enjoy it,' Eleyne said quietly and again she thought of her mother's raking fingernails.

Already in the distance they could see the great red castle of Chester, rising in the sharp angle of the river, and behind it the city huddled around the Abbey of St Werburgh. In a few hours she would meet her husband for the first time since their wedding day, when she had been a babe-in-arms and he a boy of sixteen.

II

CHESTER CASTLE ❖ May 1230

John the Scot, Earl of Huntingdon, had been visiting his uncle, Ranulph, Earl of Chester, when the news came of the arrest of Sir William de Braose. The two men discussed the situation gravely but agreed, as men all over England were to agree, that Llywelyn's death sentence was justified and not a resumption of the war with England.

More surprising was the news which followed only days later that the Prince of Gwynedd intended to proceed with the match between his recognised heir, Dafydd, and Sir William's daughter, Isabella.

'A realist, our neighbour Llywelyn.' Ranulph reached for his goblet and sipped his wine. He was a small, stocky man in his late sixties, even now, dealing as he was with his correspondence, dressed for riding, his gloves and sword near him on the coffer. 'He wants to keep the alliance.'

'And no doubt the girl is now heir to at least a quarter of the de Braose estates,' John said lazily. In his mid-twenties he was a complete contrast to his uncle. He was tall and painfully thin, his handsome face pale and haggard from the illness which had plagued him all the preceding winter. Even now, warm and gentle though the weather was, he was huddled in a fur-lined mantle.

He picked up another of the letters brought by the messenger from Gwynedd and began to unfold it. 'That makes her a rich and influential young lady. It won't only be Builth she brings to Llywelyn now, though I doubt there will be much love lost between her and her new husband's family now they've hanged her father! No doubt she has the usual de Braose spirit – Holy Mother of God!' He stopped suddenly. He had begun reading the letter in his hand.

His uncle looked up. 'What is it?'

'It appears Llywelyn is sending me my wife!' John was silent for a moment, perusing the closely written parchment. 'He feels Aber is not the place for her at the moment. I should think not,' he interrupted himself, 'with her mother in prison and her mother's lover hanging on a gibbet – and he thinks it's time she came to me.'

Lord Chester frowned. 'With a large Welsh entourage, no doubt. So, Llywelyn feels this alliance needs strengthening too.'

John threw down the letter and, walking across to the window, stared out over the river towards the west. It was a glorious May day. From the keep he could see distant hedgerows covered in whitethorn blossom and the orchards beyond foaming with pink. The sun shone blindingly down on the broad river as it cut its way between low cliffs of sand towards the jetties where two galleys were unloading their cargoes.

'She's only a child still, uncle.' He counted on his fingers. 'She can't be more than eleven! What on earth will I do with her?'

'Send her followers packing for a start and take her off to show her your lands as far away as possible from here,' Lord Chester said succinctly. 'I want our friendship with that old fox kept firm, and I want the alliance kept watertight, but I would still rather keep him at arm's length. And you would do well to do the same. Train her up to be the wife you want. Show her who is master and she'll be an invaluable asset to you, my boy. When I'm gone, and you are Earl of Chester as well as Huntingdon, you will be one of the most powerful men in England. You will be allied to Wales, married to King Henry's niece and, if Alexander stays childless, you may well be king of Scotland as well. There will be few to oppose you in Christendom.' He grinned. 'You're a lucky man. I think Llywelyn is handing you a great prize.' He frowned as John turned away with a paroxysm of coughing. 'And you had better get a son or two on her as soon as she is capable, to safeguard your succession,' he added a trifle grimly.

John grinned ruefully, wiping his mouth. 'Perhaps she'll know some wild Welsh cures for the cough and turn me into a soldier for you, uncle,' he said quietly. He was well aware of the disappointment he was to his robust relative.

III

Eleyne was trembling by the time she rode beneath the huge archway into Chester Castle. She looked up at the standards flying above the tower and edged yet closer to Rhonwen. For a moment they sat without moving on their horses, then Eleyne saw a group of men appear in the doorway of the keep up a long imposing flight of wooden steps. Ranulph, Earl of Chester, was, she guessed, the shorter, distinguished-looking white-haired man with the ruddy complexion and piercing eyes, and next to him, was that her husband? She stared at the younger man. He was, as she had feared, nothing like the man of her dreams. Clean-shaven, slim, dressed in the robes of a rich cleric, his golden hair gleaming in the sunlight, he left his companion and ran down the steps towards her. She found she was holding her breath.

He made unerringly towards her. 'Lady Eleyne?' He took her hand in his and raised it to his lips. 'Welcome.'

Behind them the wagons and horsemen who had accompanied them were still moving into the courtyard and assembling around them. Eleyne did not notice: she was looking down into her husband's smiling blue eyes.

IV

'By all the saints, uncle! I can't bed that child!' John stared at the Earl of Chester in horror. 'She's a baby still.'

'There are girls on the estates here, a year younger than she is, get themselves with bastards,' Lord Chester retorted. 'She's old enough. And you'd be a fool not to make her your wife quickly. If you don't some other man will beat you to it and you'll find yourself raising a bastard as your heir!' His expression softened. He had not intended to draw attention yet again, even by implication, to his nephew's ill health. 'Do as I say, my boy. Send all her servants packing, take her to your bed and get a child on her as soon as possible. She'll soon develop some curves to titillate your fancy if you feed her up.'

'Thank you for your advice, uncle.' John was tight-lipped. 'But for now, I would rather she had apartments of her own. Aunt Clemence has allotted her and her servants two chambers in the west tower. Once she has grown used to me and the idea of living away from home, I shall consider your advice.' Turning away, he did not hear his uncle's exasperated sigh or see his sceptically shaken head.

V

'What do you think of it?' John appeared behind Eleyne without a sound as she stood at the high window staring down unhappily across the castle walls into the crowded streets of the city of Chester.

She jumped guiltily. 'It seems very big and noisy to me, my lord.' She glanced sideways at him. He had a kind face and gentle hands; he did not seem so frightening. And so far he had shown no inclination to drag her away from Rhonwen to his bed.

'Cities always are.' He smiled down at her, studying her thin, freckle-dusted face, her red-gold hair and big green eyes. Tall as she was for her age, she only came up to his elbow. 'You will have to get used to them. We shall visit many towns and cities each year.' He sighed. 'London, Chester, York, Edinburgh, Perth.'

'You mean we won't stay here?' She had known it of course. No one stayed in one place. Even her father toured his palaces and castles in Gwynedd regularly. But Aber was always home, always the favourite. And Aber was comparatively near Chester. She looked up at him, trying to hide her fear and misery. She could hear Rhonwen, bustling about in the next room with Luned. Their voices reassured her as she looked at this tall stranger. 'We will come back here?' she asked huskily. She was fighting her terror and despair, and trying to hide her feelings from his probing gaze.

He smiled and his blue eyes softened. 'We'll come back here often, I promise,' he said.

VI

It was two weeks later that the Earl of Huntingdon summoned Rhonwen to his presence. 'Lady Rhonwen, I understand that you have been my wife's nurse and companion since she was a baby?' He was seated by the fire in the solar. He studied her closely. The woman was beautiful in her way: her skin clear, her eyes a deep grey, her carriage erect and proud.

'I must thank you for taking such care of her all these years.' He rose stiffly from his chair and walked across to the table. 'She does you credit, madam, and I hope that this –' he picked up a purse from the table – 'will be a just reward for your efforts.' He put it into Rhonwen's hand.

She stared at it, feeling the heavy coins inside the soft leather. 'I don't understand.'

'It is our gift to you, Lady Rhonwen. My wife and I are anxious you should be rewarded.' He gave her a slight smile.

'Your wife . . .' Rhonwen lifted her eyes to his, her expression veiled to hide the hatred and jealousy of this man which had devoured her since their arrival at Chester.

'We should like you to return to Prince Llywelyn with the escort and the other servants when they go back,' he said gently. 'We leave soon for my lands in the south. It will not be practicable to take such a large contingent with us.'

'You are sending me away?' For a moment she couldn't grasp what he meant.

'I have all the servants and ladies my wife needs waiting for us at my castle of Fotheringhay, my lady.' Under the gentleness of his tone there was a hint of impatience.

'No, no!' Rhonwen threw down the bag of coins, her composure shattered. 'You can't send me away, you can't. Eleyne wouldn't allow it. She loves me –'

'She does as her husband commands, Lady Rhonwen.' John sat

down once more and reached for the goblet of wine on the table at his elbow. His hand was shaking slightly.

'No.' Rhonwen shook her head. 'You don't understand. We've never been separated. Not since the day she was born –'

'I know it is hard, my lady, and I'm sorry. But it's better this way.' There was a sharp edge to his voice. 'Now, please leave us. I have letters to write.' He raised his hand to beckon forward his clerk who was hovering near the window.

'No.' Rhonwen could feel the waves of panic rising. How she hated this man who now had absolute control over Eleyne's fate – and her own. 'You can't make me leave. You can't –'

The clerk came forward and bowed. 'Shall I call the guard to remove her, my lord?' he asked, bristling with disapproval.

'I am sure there is no need.' John stood up. He put his hand on Rhonwen's arm and she felt with a vindictive shock of pleasure the physical weakness of the man. 'Madam, please.'

With a sob, she turned and fled from the room.

VII

Eleyne was with the Countess of Chester, sitting nervously beside her new aunt, watching as the old woman checked some household accounts. They both looked up as Rhonwen burst in.

'Eleyne, you can't let him send me away. You can't! I have to stay with you. I have to.' Ignoring Lady Chester, etiquette long forgotten, Rhonwen sank to her knees next to Eleyne and, putting her arms around the child, began to sob.

Eleyne stood up, frightened. She had never seen Rhonwen cry before. 'What is it? Who is going to send you away?'

'Your husband.' She did not bother to hide the loathing in her voice. 'He is sending me, all of us, back to Gwynedd.' Rhonwen steadied herself with difficulty, suddenly aware of the Countess of Chester's eyes fixed on her face.

Lady Chester stood up stiffly. She was a small elegant woman in her mid-sixties like her husband, her blue eyes faded, but still shrewd as she looked at the sobbing woman in front of her. 'I am sure you are mistaken, Lady Rhonwen,' she said.

Rhonwen shook her head. 'He gave me a bag of gold and told me to go. I can't leave her. Please, my lady, I can't leave her among strangers like this –' She felt the waves of panic rising. Eleyne was her life; her child; her whole existence.

Eleyne's face was tense with fear. 'I am sure it is a mistake, Rhonwen. Lord Huntingdon seems so kind . . .' She hesitated, with a

89

nervous glance at her husband's aunt, uncertain what to do. 'Perhaps I should speak to him –'

Lady Chester shook her head. In the short time Eleyne had been with her she had grown extraordinarily fond of the girl. Childless herself, she felt endlessly guilty that she had not provided her husband with heirs to succeed him in his great inheritance. 'Later,' she said firmly. 'Never run to your husband to query anything he has ordered, Eleyne. That is one of the first lessons you must learn. If a wife wishes to get things her own way,' she tapped the side of her nose with a little smile, 'she must do it with subtlety. Let things remain as they are for a while. Then later, when you and he are alone and talking, and perhaps becoming closer acquainted –' she paused imperceptibly. Her husband had complained to her every evening for the last fortnight that his nephew was a weak-willed, soft-hearted, green-sick, womanly invalid who spent too long talking to the child and hadn't, as far as he could see, so much as kissed the girl's hand – 'then,' she went on, 'you can perhaps say to him how lonely you will feel if all your followers are sent away. Persuade him gradually. I know he doesn't want you to be unhappy.'

VIII

'Let's run away!' Eleyne pulled Rhonwen into the window embrasure; a heavy tapestry hid them from the body of the room where the Countess of Chester and her ladies were busy about their tasks. 'You and me and Luned. We could run away and no one would find us.' She was talking in a frantic whisper.

Rhonwen tried to suppress the quick surge of hope the child's words raised. 'But where would we go?'

'Home, of course.'

'Eleyne, *cariad*. We can't go home.' Rhonwen put her arms around the child and rested her lips against the veil which covered Eleyne's head. 'Don't you understand? Your father has forbidden you to return. Aber is no longer your home.'

'Then I shall go to Margaret at Bramber. Or to Gruffydd.'

'No, Eleyne, they will obey your father. They have to. They would only send you back to Lord Chester.' She closed her eyes to try to hold back her tears. She had written to Einion, smuggling the letter out of the castle the day after they had arrived at Chester, begging him to do something. He would think of something. He had to. Eleyne was sworn to the goddess.

'We could hide in the forest.' Eleyne looked up hopefully. Her eyes were feverishly bright. 'When Lord Huntingdon sends you all away, you go, as if you were doing as he commanded, and I shall hide in one

90

of the wagons. Once we are out of the castle you and I can slip away. Oh Rhonwen, it would work. I know it would work.'

Rhonwen bit her lip. '*Cariad* . . .'

'We can do it . . . I know we can.'

'And you would rather live as an outlaw in the woods than with Lord Huntingdon? Here you will be a very great lady.' It couldn't work. And yet she found herself seizing the idea, as if there were a chance they could escape.

'I hate it here.' Eleyne leaned against the wall, pressing her cheek against the cold stone. 'I don't want to be a great lady and I don't want to – I don't want to be anyone's wife. And I don't want to live in a city. Ever. I want to live with the mountains and the sea. And I want to stay with you, Rhonwen. I can't live without you.' Her eyes flooded with tears once more.

Rhonwen hesitated. So often in the past she had tried to curb Eleyne's impetuous ideas, but now every part of her wanted to fall in with this crazy plan and run away from the great castle with all its riches, this alien English stronghold, run by its arrogant English masters. But would it work? Could it work? The consequences if they failed did not bear thinking about.

She glanced into the shadowy room where the countess and her ladies talked quietly over their sewing and their spinning. Lady Chester was kind and understanding; Lord Huntingdon, whom she loathed and mistrusted, was a different matter. And it would be Eleyne who would suffer. Eleyne who would be punished. She pictured the handsome stern face of the earl with his fair skin and his intense intelligent blue eyes. What would he do to her if she were caught? Her child, her baby who had never been beaten in her life?

So little time . . . no time at all to plan. His mind made up, the earl had arranged for the baggage train and its escort to leave after mass, in three days' time.

Eleyne touched her hand. She smiled coaxingly at Rhonwen. 'I'll find a way,' she whispered. 'You'll see. I'll think of something.'

IX

That night Eleyne lay awake for hours, her stomach cramped again into tight knots of fear. Just before dawn she rose from her bed at last and crept down the stairs. It took her a long time, wandering through draughty corridors and cold stone passages, to find a way out into the courtyard where the stables were, and once there to creep between the horse lines to find her own particular friends. She found Cadi first and spent a long time with the gentle little mare, kissing her soft nose. Then she crept on, looking for Invictus. He was harder to find. He was already with the earl's horses, a groom constantly on hand should the animals become restless. Silent as a shadow, Eleyne slipped into the box and put her arms around the horse's huge head. She kissed his nose and his cheeks and felt her hot tears drip on to his coat. Walled up in the corner of her mind was the picture of the man who had loved this horse and of the noose around his neck. It was something she could not face.

The idea came with the dawn. As the castle came to life with the opening of the gates and the arrival of the first wagons loaded with produce from the city, Eleyne peered silently into the courtyard from the warm darkness of the stall. The stables were near the gatehouse. The guards were at ease, barely checking the incoming wagons, ignoring the men and women who bustled past them into the streets beyond the gates. The place was crowded, chaotic. No one paid any attention to anyone else. Silently she untied Invictus's halter. Scrambling on to the stall partition, she clambered on to his back and with the barest touch of her heels guided him down the line of stalls and out into the courtyard. A few people stared at the red-haired child astride the stallion, but no one recognised her and no one tried to stop her. Sitting very straight, her heart in her mouth, she smiled as confidently as she could at the guard as she turned the horse beneath the gatehouse arch. His hooves rang loud and hollow for a moment, then they were through and across the bridge. Holding her breath, she nudged Invictus into a trot, then a canter, turning east along the edge of the wharf rather than back into the city itself, following the road towards the city wall.

She was stopped almost at once by the Bridge Gate, which was still barred. As she turned uncertainly northwards into the city, she heard a shout behind her. In a panic she saw four horsemen galloping after her, weaving through the crowds. They wore the livery of the Earl of Chester over their mail. Desperately she looked round for a place to hide, but within seconds they were on her, two each side. Outraged, Invictus reared up and she grabbed at his mane to stop herself falling.

They took her straight to Lord Huntingdon. She was still barefoot, her hair loose, dressed only in her shift and bed gown – a dirty, unruly and stubborn child, her cheeks streaked by tears.

He looked at her for a long time after he had dismissed her escort. At last he spoke. 'Where were you going, Eleyne?' he asked gently.

She stared back at him defiantly. She had expected him to be angry, not gentle. 'To the forest.'

'The forest?' he repeated, astonished. 'Why?'

'I won't live here without Rhonwen. I can't. I'd rather be an outlaw or a beggar.' Tears began to trickle down her cheeks in spite of her efforts to stop them. 'I don't want to be a countess. I want Rhonwen.'

John walked across to his chair and sat down, perplexed. He didn't know what to do to comfort her, this ragged urchin who was his wife.

'Please, Eleyne, don't cry.' He knew he should be angry. Probably he should whip her. Certainly he should send her for a bath. The child smelt strongly of the stables.

'Please don't send Rhonwen away.' Her huge eyes, fixed on his face, were brimming with tears. 'Please, my lord –' She still didn't know how to address this tall stranger who was her husband. 'Please let Rhonwen stay.' Her sleepless night and the weight of her tears had reddened her eyes and underlined them with shadows.

He frowned. Certainly he regretted his summary dismissal of the entire Welsh entourage. Lord Chester was wrong. Such an action would antagonise the prince and needlessly make this child unhappier than she already was.

He rubbed his thumb against his chin. 'We are to travel across England to my lands in the Honour of Huntingdon, Eleyne. Would she wish to follow you there? She would find it very strange so far from Wales,' he said at last.

Eleyne stared at him, her eyes alight with hope. 'She would go with me anywhere, my lord.' She did not point out that she too would find it strange.

'Then perhaps I could change my mind and allow a few of your servants to remain with you. If it would make you happy and stop you running away again.'

'Luned and Marared and Ethil?' The girl's eyes were shining.

He nodded tolerantly. 'Very well. If it will convince you to stay with me you may keep half a dozen of your own ladies. But that is all –'

'And Cenydd. Cenydd saved my life when I swam the strait.'

'When you – what?' He blinked at her in astonishment.

Abashed she looked down. She should not have told him that. 'My father asked him to be my bodyguard,' she amended cautiously. 'He would die to protect me.'

'There are many here whose job will be to protect you with their lives,' he said gently. And he would want to know today exactly where they all were, to allow the Countess of Huntingdon to ride out of the castle as she had without an escort. 'But, yes, for now you may keep Cenydd too. But that is all.'

For a moment he thought she would fling her arms around his neck and kiss him but she remembered in time. Looking down, she gave a little curtsey. 'Thank you, my lord,' she said.

X

From the high window in the castle keep Eleyne and Rhonwen watched the huge train of wagons and carts move out of the courtyard. They were both numb with misery as this last link with home and Wales disappeared beneath the gatehouse arch with its massive portcullis, and headed west towards the ford which crossed the Dee.

Eleyne's head ached; her limbs felt like lead. If they could get away, lose themselves in the corridors and passages of the great castle, perhaps even now they could hide in the carts and be smuggled home.

The Earl of Huntingdon watched her for a long time from the doorway as she stood in the window embrasure with Rhonwen. Allowing Rhonwen and her companions to stay had helped Eleyne a little – his eyes went to the woman's protective arm around the child's narrow shoulders – but the frozen misery on the child's face, the lost bewilderment in her eyes, touched him deeply. She was his, this little girl, his to do with as he pleased. His countess, his child bride. Somehow he had to win her trust and if possible her affection.

'Eleyne?' Although he spoke her name gently, both women jumped at the sound of his voice. 'Lady Rhonwen can go to Lady Chester for now, my dear. I should like you to come down to the stables.'

One of his grooms had told him of the midnight visit; the tears, the anguished cuddling of the horses. With admiration, he had reported her fearless mounting of the great stallion, and Lord Huntingdon had seen a way of reaching her.

'The stables?'

He saw with satisfaction the sudden light in her eyes and he nodded. 'Your father gave me several horses as a gift and you have your own there too. I should like to look them over.' He held out his hand and, hesitating, she went to him.

Invictus whickered his usual welcome as she ducked into his box, her velvet skirts catching on the straw. Lord Huntingdon smiled. 'He obviously knows you well.'

Eleyne nodded. 'Sir William . . .' Her voice wavered and she bit her lip, unprepared for the wave of misery which the mention of his name brought. 'Sir William used to let me ride him. He . . . he gave him to me before . . .' her sobs tightened her throat, 'before they hanged him.'

Lord Huntingdon raised an eyebrow. 'So, this was de Braose's horse?'

Eleyne nodded numbly. 'My father wanted you to have him.' Her despair at losing her treasured inheritance after so short an ownership was obvious in her voice.

'He is not a lady's horse, Eleyne.' He smiled at her. Nor a slip of a child's were the words he left unsaid.

'No.' Her reply was barely audible.

'You must ride well if Sir William allowed you to ride him,' he persisted gently. Lord Chester's men-at-arms had told him as much.

She nodded. The germ of an idea had lodged in her mind. 'Could we go for a ride now?' She looked her husband in the eye for the first time. 'Please?'

He looked down at her, amused. 'I don't see why not.'

'And could I ride Invictus?'

'Ah, I see. You want to show me you are the mistress of my new stallion.'

She nodded shyly. 'I used to race against Sir William,' she said hopefully.

'Did you indeed?' He grimaced. 'I fear I don't have Sir William's prowess in the saddle, but we could certainly ride.

'Saddle him, and my horse too.' He turned to the groom who hovered behind them. 'Do you wish to change, my lady?' He smiled.

Eleyne glanced down at her velvet skirts and scowled. 'I never usually bother.' She did not want the moment to pass. She didn't want Rhonwen or Lady Chester or any of the strangers inside these high walls to cluck over her and try to dissuade Lord Huntingdon from letting her ride the great horse.

'I see.' He hid his amusement with difficulty. 'Then perhaps you had better not bother now.'

They were accompanied by half a dozen well-mounted knights who rode behind them as they turned south beyond the castle and out of the town walls into the forest. Eleyne glanced sideways at her husband, shocked to find him mounted on a staid gelding some two hands shorter than Invictus. He rode well, but stiffly, as if ill at ease in the saddle. Gently she eased Invictus's long stride back to match that of the smaller horse.

'I thought you would ride a destrier,' she said a little reproachfully after they had ridden in silence for some time, following the road out of the city and through the fields until they were beneath the new-green leaves of the oak forest.

He smiled. 'A warhorse, for a ride in the woods? In England we cherish our valuable horses, Eleyne.'

Her cheeks coloured at the implied rebuke. 'But it will be no race if we gallop,' she said sadly. 'No one here could keep up with Invictus.' She cast a professional eye at the mounts of the escort trotting two abreast behind them.

Lord Huntingdon hid a smile. 'I'm sorry we disappoint you. Come, why don't we gallop now?' Ahead of them the grassy ride broadened into an open track. He kicked his horse forward and with surprising speed it stretched its legs into a gallop.

Eleyne did not hesitate. The great stallion was like a coiled spring:

as she relaxed her gentle hands he leaped forward and thundered after his companion. In seconds they had overtaken him and, leaving the others behind, streaked away up the track.

She did not rein him in for a long time, enjoying the rush of wind in her hair, the feel of the horse's powerful muscles between her legs, the thunder of his hooves on the soft track. When at last she stopped, laughing, her hair was loose around her shoulders, her cap gone, her long skirts ridden high on her slim thighs and she was alone. The track behind her was empty.

She closed her eyes and lifted her face to the sun, exhilarated. For a moment she was tempted to ride on and on into the forest, to be lost forever away from her husband and his escort. Then slowly she walked the horse back the way they had come.

She thought he would be angry with her, but his frown was one only of concern. 'What if you had run into trouble? No one could have saved you.'

'I don't get into trouble. I've never fallen off in my life –' She was conscious of the admiring smiles, scarcely hidden, of the men around them, and she found herself sitting a little straighter.

'I am sure you haven't.' He was smiling too. 'But you might have met undesirable company. The march is a nest of robbers and thieves and outlaws. That is why the wife of an earl must always have an escort. Does Cenydd manage to keep up with you?' He threw her a quizzical glance.

She smiled at him unrepentantly. 'Only if I let him.'

'And you let him the day you swam the strait?' He hid a smile.

She blushed and nodded. 'He saved my life.'

'One day, Eleyne, I think you must tell me the story of the great swim, but in the meantime I think you must only ride Invictus if you promise to hold him in,' he said gently. 'Sir William bequeathed him to you and as far as I am concerned, he is your horse, but only if you ride him slowly. I want your promise.' His face was stern.

Her eyes were shining. 'I promise.' Then she frowned. 'Don't you want to ride him yourself?'

He shook his head. 'I've been ill, Eleyne. I can't ride fast yet. My bones are stiff and my body aches.' He laughed. 'But I improve daily and I shan't long be able to resist the challenge of having a wife who can outride me, I promise you. When I am recovered, I shall borrow him back and test his paces myself.'

XI

It took many days for the huge household to ride across England, and as they did so Rhonwen grew more and more depressed. The country was heavily forested, dull beneath lowering wet skies, even though around them hawthorn erupted in the hedges and the trees were full of birdsong as they crossed broad, shallow, slow-moving rivers and threaded their way across the flat central spine of England. From time to time they climbed hills and rode between small neat fields, the strips of crops showing green beneath the rain, but they had left the great mountains of Wales far behind and with them any hope of reprieve. No word had come from Einion, no ray of hope or explanation how his plans for Eleyne could have gone so far astray. She looked often at Eleyne, riding the cream mare some paces behind her husband, huddled in her cloak against the driving rain, and wondered what the child was thinking.

With every step their journey took them farther and farther from the land of their birth towards a new, strange life, but Eleyne was silent, her eyes only now and then flicking to left or right to note some aspect of the scenery they passed. The sense of desolation which had swiftly replaced her initial excitement when they had set out on their journey was overwhelming. The long days in the saddle, moving slowly but inexorably south and east, weighed on her, and it gave her time to think. There was no way now of avoiding the pictures which kept returning to her mind of the gallows; of her mother's bed and of Sir William's handsome face, and his rueful smile as he walked towards his death. Had he known? Had he known who it was who had betrayed him?

Again and again she tried to close her mind to the horror, tried to fight the guilt and remorse which threatened to overwhelm her. And again and again she failed. Hourly, or so it seemed to Rhonwen, her face grew more pinched and white and the shadows darker beneath her eyes.

XII
FOTHERINGHAY CASTLE ✧ July 1230

Lord Huntingdon called Eleyne to him three weeks after they arrived. 'I have had a letter from your father.'

He was still tired after the long journey, but the frailty and misery in the child's eyes dismayed him far more than his own failing health. Her face lit however at the mention of her father and she went to him eagerly. So, after all, he missed her as much as she missed him; he was calling her home; it must be that. Her eyes on her husband's face, she waited for him to hand it to her, but he held it curling loosely in his hand. There had been no message for Llywelyn's daughter in the long document, no piece of news of home which he could tell her, save one.

'Your father tells me your brother, Dafydd, is to be married soon to Isabella de Braose,' he said after a pause. 'It appears the wedding is to take place as though nothing has happened. She has arrived at Aber.'

'Isabella?' Eleyne looked stricken. 'But I wanted to be there.' Somewhere deep inside herself she had kept the hope that her father would relent, that he would allow her back for the wedding – the event she and Isabella had dreamed of and planned together for so long.

'I am sure you'll see her soon.' Instead of giving her the letter he dropped it into a coffer and locked it, then he turned back to her and smiled. 'So, how do you like this part of the country?'

'Well enough, my lord.' Crestfallen, she dragged her eyes away from the casket where the letter had disappeared, trying to hide her disappointment, and she forced a shy smile. She had seen little yet. The weather had been too wet for riding, but the rooms to which she and Rhonwen and her ladies had been shown were comfortable and richly appointed. Fotheringhay, one of the chief castles of the huge Honour of Huntingdon, was a large stone-built fortress set beside the River Nene in Northamptonshire amid a gentle landscape of flat meadows and fields, of fen and forest. The village outside its walls was small, augmented by a church and a nunnery of Cluniac sisters.

At Fotheringhay they kept considerable state, and the household had swiftly fallen into its routine. Lord Huntingdon was rich. He was important. His household was larger by far than even her father's, but to Eleyne it all seemed strange and alien. Her only comfort besides the presence of Rhonwen and her companions was that her husband had still shown no inclination to order her into his bed. Her suite of rooms was far away from his.

She explored the castle at his suggestion, sometimes with her ladies, sometimes just with Luned or alone, finding her way to the stables and to the walls from where she could stare out across the countryside, watching the thick mist of the early morning lie like foaming milk across the river meadows, where willow and alder rose disembodied from the whiteness. She explored the towers and the living quarters, smiling shyly at the men and women she met as she toured kitchens, bakehouses, brewhouses and storerooms, the great keep on its mound and the chapel. She sewed and read and played quiet absent-minded games with Luned and from time to time she rode. There was no further news from Aber. She might have been in a different world.

John gave her what he considered enough time to settle in and to grow used to the place, then he sent for her. 'In time you will oversee all my castles, but for now we'll let things stay as they are. I have competent chatelaines who will continue to run the establishments while they are teaching you how it should be done, and you can continue your lessons and your reading, and of course you may ride whenever you wish.' He walked across to the fire which smouldered sullenly in the hearth. He stared at it for a moment, trying to choose his next words with care. 'While we are alone, Eleyne, there is something I wish to speak to you about.' He frowned. 'I have been told that you have bad dreams. Is anything special worrying you?' He waited, hoping that she would trust him enough to reply.

She had gone pale. 'Who told you I had bad dreams?'

'One of your ladies mentioned it to my steward.' He turned and smiled gently. 'Secrets are hard to keep here, as I am sure they were at Aber.'

If he had hoped to comfort her, his words seemed to have the opposite effect. She stood as if paralysed, her eyes riveted on his face.

'If it is to do with —' He hesitated, at a loss how to put it. He had seen the way she shrank from his touch, sensed her physical fear of him as a man. 'If it is to do with becoming my wife, Eleyne, there is nothing to fear.' This was not the kind of thing a man discussed, but her helpless frailty touched him deeply. 'We shall wait to be man and wife properly until you are ready.' He smiled again, reassuringly.

She stared at him for a moment, her eyes on his, the relief at the implication of his words mixed with something else, something immediately veiled. 'Not until I am ready, my lord?' she repeated. 'But Rhonwen said I must give myself to you whenever you require it, when you are well again.' The view of the household, scarcely concealed, was that it was his uncertain health which kept their earl from his child bride's bed.

He shook his head. 'I am content to wait, Eleyne. We shall go to bed together when we both feel you are ready. Until then I shall not make that kind of demand on you.' He sat down stiffly. How could he even contemplate taking this child, this baby with her flat, boyish figure, her face still with the unformed features of a child? He was no baby-snatcher; the women he found attractive were mature, intelligent; he fell in love with their minds before he allowed himself to touch their bodies. That he was unusual, if not unique, in this, he knew to be true, but he could not help it. He was not attracted by the animal, by the scent of musk, the voluptuous curves and reddened mouths of the court ladies with whom he mixed, and he had not for a long time lusted after one of the farm girls or serving maids.

He was dragged back from his thoughts by the sight of the woebegone small face before him. He had so few opportunities to speak to the child alone, away from the ever attentive Lady Rhonwen who, however much she might have insisted to Eleyne that she must give herself to her husband when required, had nevertheless seen to it with malevolent care that they had no time together alone.

'Is there something else bothering you?' His voice was gentle, coaxing, as it would have been to a small animal. 'You can and should tell your husband everything, Eleyne. It is what he is there for.' He said it quietly with a wry inward smile at the quizzical eyebrow a more experienced wife would raise at the comment. 'Please. I should like to help you.'

She closed her eyes miserably, visibly struggling with herself.

'Come here.' He held out a hand to her and reluctantly she went to him. Resisting the urge to pull her on to his knee, he put his arm gently around her. 'Tell me. Once you have told someone your nightmares will stop.'

Suddenly she couldn't stop herself. Her voice punctuated by sobs, she told him everything: the visions, the dreams, the strange half-memories of the man with red hair, the meetings with Einion and that first harsh day of instruction in the smoke-filled hut where she had seen Sir William with the rope around his neck and not recognised him.

Christ and His Holy Mother! He could not bring himself to believe all he had heard. Eleyne had never tried to avoid attending mass with him every day in the castle chapel. She had never seemed, as far as he could tell, less than devout, and he had watched her carefully. Yet the child was a pagan, a witch, a sorceress and a seer! And still the words tumbled on. It was she who had caught Sir William in her mother's bed, and who had told her father.

'And why did you tell him, sweetheart? Why did you not keep it a secret?' At last he had a glimmering of the source of her terrible guilt.

'Because I hated him!' She stamped her foot, her voice anguished. 'He was my friend; he was Isabella's father. He had let me ride Invictus.' Huge wet tears were rolling down her cheeks and soaking into the soft gold velvet of her surcoat. 'And I hated my mother. She stole him from me.' She did not add that she had always hated her mother. That thought too brought anguish.

'You hated them so much you wanted them to die?' He was probing very gently.

'Yes! No! I don't know.' Her voice was so husky it was almost a whisper. She rested her head desolately against his shoulder in a movement so trusting and so intimate he found himself unbearably moved.

'Was anyone there with you when you saw them?' He had to try very hard to keep his own voice steady.

'Only Rhonwen.'

'Ah, Rhonwen,' he said drily. He paused. 'And what did she say?'

Again the almost inaudible whisper. 'She said it was treason.'

'Which it was. A wife must not ever betray her husband, Eleyne. Your mother not only defiled her marriage bed, but did so with a man who had been her husband's enemy and was subsequently his guest. She was guilty three times over.'

'But I shouldn't have told papa,' she persisted.

'If you hadn't, someone else would have done so. And rightly. He had to know.'

'Then why was he so angry with me?' she cried. 'Why did he send me away? Why did he blame me?'

The desolation in her voice was absolute. He tightened his arm around her, trying to comfort her, and noticed that she no longer shrank away from him. 'It was just a reaction, sweetheart. He was hurt and angry and some of it rubbed off on you. It will pass.'

'Will it?' She eyed him doubtfully.

'Of course it will. Prince Llywelyn is renowned for the love he bears his children.'

'And the dreams? Will they stop now?'

'I am sure they will.' He tried to sound confident. Dear God, surely a child her age should be occupying herself with dolls, not this nightmare tangle of love and hate and death!

'Have you had any strange dreams since?' He tried to make the question sound casual. 'Any more visions?'

'No. No more visions.'

'Your father's seer was wrong to teach you those things, Eleyne. You know that, don't you?' He was feeling his way carefully. 'They are absolutely contrary to the teachings of Holy Mother Church.'

She shrugged miserably. 'Einion does not go to mass.'

'No, I don't suppose he does. But I thought your father was a good Christian, Eleyne.'

'He is.' She coloured defensively.

'Then why does he allow this worship of ancient gods and spirits in his lands?'

'I don't think he knows.'

'Who told Einion that you could see the future, Eleyne?'

'Rhonwen.' It was scarcely more than a whisper.

XIII

'I should like you to return to Wales, madam.' John's lips were tight.

Rhonwen stared at him, her body growing cold. 'Why, my lord? Have I displeased you in some way?' Her eyes were challenging.

'I consider you to be an unwholesome influence, Lady Rhonwen, on my wife.' Humping his cloak higher on his shoulders, John paced up and down behind the long table. 'You have deliberately introduced her to practices contrary to our Christian faith.' He narrowed his eyes. 'Heretical practices which I will not condone under my roof.'

'No.' Rhonwen refused to meet his eye. 'That is not true.'

He swung to face her. 'Are you saying that my wife is a liar?'

'What did she say?' Rhonwen looked at him defiantly. She was pleating her fingers into the rich blue silk of her skirt. She could feel the perspiration cold between her shoulder blades.

'She said you encouraged her to go to this bard of her father's, Einion Gweledydd, who –' he stammered in his anger – 'who initiated her in some way –'

'He was helping her, did she tell you that?' Swiftly her courage returned. She leaned forward and put her hands flat on the table between them. 'Did she tell you about her dreams? Did she tell you about the visions which possess her? Did she tell you how they tear her apart?' She waited, her eyes on his.

'She told me she saw the death of Sir William de Braose long before it happened,' he said thoughtfully.

She narrowed her eyes. 'She told you that?'

'Yes, Lady Rhonwen.' Looking up quickly, he saw her expression. 'You look aghast. Did you not think she would confide in me, her husband? Perhaps you are not as indispensable to her as you hoped?' His voice was harsh now. 'She will have no more visions, Lady Rhonwen. I shall see to that. Please be ready to leave by the end of the week.'

'No!' The whispered denial was anguished.

He ignored it, and strode towards the door. 'By the end of the week, madam,' he repeated curtly.

She stood exactly where she was for several minutes after he had gone, staring round the empty room. From outside the deep embrasured windows she could hear the pure liquid trill of a blackbird. Behind it, in the distance, the call of the cuckoo echoed across the flat levels of the Nene. The room itself was silent. Her mouth had gone dry. She could feel a cold knot of fear in her stomach. This man had the power to tear her from Eleyne. He had the power to send her away.

Why had Eleyne betrayed her? Slowly, heavily, she went to the door.

Eleyne was nowhere to be found. With a snap of impatience Rhonwen made her way down the long winding stair which led from her solar into the great hall at the heart of the castle and then out into the courtyard.

Inevitably she was in the stables, watching a two-day-old colt staggering stiff-legged beside its dam as the pair were led out to the pasture.

Dressed in yet more new rich clothes, this time a kirtle of deep green over a saffron gown, the girl smiled at Rhonwen. Already she seemed older, more confident, more independent. Behind her Luned too was brilliantly dressed, and it was she who noticed the grim set of Rhonwen's features and faded hastily into the background.

'Why did you tell him?' Rhonwen caught Eleyne's arm. 'Why?'

Nearby two stable boys turned to stare.

'You broke your sacred oath!' Her voice though quiet was vibrating with anger.

Eleyne flushed guiltily. 'What do you mean?'

'I think you know.' Rhonwen almost shook her.

'I had to talk to someone . . .'

'You had to talk to someone!' Rhonwen echoed furiously. 'Why not me? Why did you not talk to me?'

The child's crimson cheeks drained of colour. 'I don't know why.'

'Not only did you tell him – Lord Huntingdon – about the hanging, you told him about Einion; about the most secret things . . .'

'I didn't tell him everything.' Eleyne turned to face her, wrenching her arm from Rhonwen's grasp. 'Anyway, I am supposed to tell him things. He is my husband!' There was defiance in her voice now. 'I am growing up, Rhonwen. I don't have to do everything you say.'

Rhonwen stared. What had happened to her? Could it be that he had already claimed her for his wife; seduced her away and she, Rhonwen, had not even guessed? 'I thought you loved me, Eleyne,' she whispered.

'I do –' The child stared at her stiffly then, relenting, threw herself towards Rhonwen and gave her a hug. 'I do love you. Of course I do.'

Rhonwen folded her arms around the girl's slight body, overwhelmed by her feelings of love and protectiveness. 'He is sending me away,' she murmured into the white coif which covered Eleyne's braided hair. As a married woman her hair was no longer permitted to tumble down her back. 'He is sending me away.'

Eleyne pulled out of her arms and looked up at her. 'I won't let him send you away, Rhonwen,' she said with astonishingly adult composure. 'I promise. I won't let John send you away.' It was the first time she had used his Christian name out loud.

He listened, half amused, half irritated by Eleyne's pleas, but he remained adamant. Rhonwen had to go. He had been shocked and outraged by Eleyne's confessions, and the full weight of his anger, horror and distrust was directed at her nurse.

'Please, my lord. Please!' In her anguish Rhonwen sought him out and threw herself on her knees at his feet the evening before she was due to leave. 'Let me stay! Eleyne can't live without me. We've never been separated, never, since the day she was born. Please. For the child's sake. You can't do this to her. You can't.'

'It is for the child's sake I am doing it, madam,' John said gravely. 'To bring her safely back to Christ. She has Luned and the others to keep her company and she has her husband. You will leave at dawn tomorrow, Lady Rhonwen, as arranged.'

XIV

Her eyes filled with tears, Eleyne turned from the gates and ran blindly across the courtyard, leaving her husband staring after her. After her anguished farewells, Rhonwen's horse had turned north on to the road outside and she was already lost to sight among the trees. Behind her the gates closed. John smiled. For the first time in many weeks he at last felt safe, and the realisation shocked him. Had the woman's influence been that malevolent? He was about to follow Eleyne when he stopped and shook his head. Give her some time alone, then he would speak to her.

Ignoring the men and women who stared after her Eleyne ran up the stairs and into the keep. Tears poured down her cheeks as she fled across the lower chamber and began to climb to the topmost storeys of the great tower. There were empty chambers there, places where nobody ever seemed to come, places where she could be alone and no one would see her grief.

Pushing open a door, she peered into a cold empty room. Ten years before it had been the bedchamber of Lord Albemarle who held the castle for a time while John, when he was a boy, still lived with his uncle at Chester. Now it was deserted, the bed frame dusty, the hangings long gone. John preferred to have his rooms above the newly built gatehouse. Hers were in the south tower behind the great hall, overlooking the river.

She walked into the silent room and crossed miserably to the window. It too faced south across the Nene. A ray of pale sunlight fell across the swept boards of the floor. In the opposite wall a low arched doorway led through to a small oratory in the thickness of the stone. The altar was still there; on it were half-burned candles and a carved alabaster crucifix. It was then that she smelt the incense. She frowned, puzzled. The smell was rich and exotic, pungent against the stale coldness of stone.

The woman was standing behind her in the shaft of sunlight, her black skirts rich and heavy, her veil silk, her pale, tired face strained as she stared towards the altar with an expression of resignation and sadness almost too great to bear. Eleyne stared back at her in shock, then a cloud crossed the sun. As the sunbeam faded the woman disappeared.

104

Terrified, Eleyne rubbed her eyes. She didn't dare move. Her husband had forbidden her to have visions. They were evil. It was because of her visions he had sent Rhonwen away. And this woman, whoever she was, had not been flesh and blood. She backed away from the spot where the woman had stood, her eyes fixed on the empty space. Who was she? Why had she come? And why had she shown herself now? Eleyne went back into the chapel and reached a hand out to the altar. But the rich scent of incense had gone. The great echoing bedchamber once more smelt of stone and dust and disuse. She was alone.

Trying to control her fear, Eleyne fled to the spiral staircase and began to run down it. All she wanted was to go back to her own bright rooms and find Luned, who would be as miserable as she was without Rhonwen. She put the thought of the lady in black, whoever she was, as far out of her mind as possible. John must never find out that she was still seeing things. Never.

Gasping for breath, she paused at the top of the steps outside the keep and stared down into the courtyard. While she had been in the upper chamber a line of wagons and horses had ridden into the castle. She moved back slightly, out of sight, wondering who they belonged to. Then she noticed that John was already out there ready to greet his guests; she could see his fair hair blowing in the sunlight. She frowned, the lady in black forgotten. She had never seen her husband look so happy, and even as she watched he stepped forward and helped a woman down from one of the horses. She saw him take her in his arms and kiss her on the mouth. Eleyne was stunned. A shock of something very like jealousy shot through her. She had never seen John take a woman in his arms before, never seen him kiss one or look so animated. She stood on the steps, staring down at her husband, feeling the wind cold on her face, and became aware that it was blotchy and swollen with crying. She looked like a stupid, ugly child while this tall elegant fair-haired woman was beautiful.

She realised they were looking up at her. Swallowing the lump in her throat, she began to walk down towards them, summoning as much dignity as she could: she was John's wife. Whoever this woman was, she did not have that distinction.

They were smiling.

'Eleyne, come here, my love,' John called. He had time only to whisper to his companion that she had arrived in the nick of time and to ask what in the name of all the saints had kept her. 'I want you to meet my most favourite person in the whole world,' he went on, oblivious of the desolation in Eleyne's face at his words — 'my sister, Isabel.'

Isabel, married to the irascible Scots nobleman, Robert Bruce, Lord of Annandale, had received her brother's letter at her manor of Writtle in Essex. It had begged her to come to Fotheringhay on her way back to Scotland and advise him on what to do about his wife. His brief summary of his problems had left her intrigued, amused and exasperated at the general helplessness of men when it came to matters of the emotions. Looking at Eleyne now, she saw a lonely and unhappy child. She had sensed as much as seen the moment of jealousy in the girl's eyes as she had watched John kissing her – so the child felt something for him then – and now she saw the wistful longing which replaced it, almost as if Eleyne had sent her an unconscious appeal.

Isabel removed her gloves, then she held out her arms. As she kissed Eleyne on both cheeks, she glanced over the girl's head towards her secret weapon, her son Robert. If Eleyne of Huntingdon were really a witch, a tomboy, a brilliant breakneck rider and an uncontrollable wanderer, twelve-year-old Robert could match her, fault for fault.

'You're crazy,' John exploded later as his sister unfolded her plan. 'I brought you here to try to inculcate some sense into her and to cheer her up, not bring her a playmate who will make her worse!'

Unabashed, Isabel reached for the glass of wine her brother had given her. For her he served nothing but the best in his richly enamelled, priceless Venetian glasses.

'You told me you wanted to get rid of that awful hunted look,' Isabel said firmly. 'And you want to hear her laugh. Rob will make her laugh. I guarantee it.'

XV

Three days later young Robert Bruce was lying in wait for Eleyne in the stables.

'I'm going riding with you,' he said as soon as he spotted her. 'Mama says you ride a great stallion.'

Eleyne felt her heart sink. She did not want this boy to ride Invictus. She did not even want him to see the horse. Dragging her feet, she walked towards Robert and gave him a determined brittle smile.

'He's cast a shoe,' she lied. 'If we ride we'll ride Sable and Silver.' The two mares were matched for height and speed, both well mannered and willing. She eyed her companion cautiously. She was two inches taller, but he was sturdier by far. They would probably be well matched in the saddle; but he would be heavier which would give her the advantage.

He caught her sizing him up and grinned. 'Do you know why we've come here?' he asked, his tone deceptively friendly.

Instinctively she knew she shouldn't rise to the question, but, as instinctively, she knew she would have to ask it.

'Why?'

He moved closer and lowered his voice confidentially. 'I saw the letter Uncle John sent mama. It said the most terrible things about you!'

'What things?' Stung, Eleyne felt her face growing hot.

'Dreadful things!' Robert crowed. He stepped back, ready to run if necessary.

'I don't believe you. Anyway your mother wouldn't have shown you John's letter.'

'She didn't! I sneaked it out of her writing box!'

'That's dishonest –' Eleyne's temper was beginning to flare. She stared at the boy in disbelief. Apart from Luned and Isabella, she had never had a friend her own age, and certainly not one who had taunted her like this. She didn't know what to do, and hesitated, torn between wanting to run away and wanting to know what the letter said.

'I don't suppose you can even read properly,' she said scornfully.

The barb went home. 'Of course I can,' he retorted at once. 'It said you were a strange, haunted child!' He stuck out his tongue at her. 'It said you saw ghosts in every shadow and that your nurse was a witch.' He danced away a few steps, tempting her to chase him. 'It said you were weird!'

'I'm not!' She was furious.

'You are. You see ghosts.'

'So what? Can't you?' She went on to the attack.

Her change of mood took him aback. He frowned, then reluctantly shook his head.

She sensed triumph: 'You would be scared out of your mind if you saw one.'

'I wouldn't.' It was his turn to be on the defensive.

'You would.'

'Wouldn't!'

'All right then. Prove it.' Caution was thrown to the winds. 'I'll take you to a room where I saw a ghost.'

Robert hesitated for a fraction of a second, then he nodded. 'Go on then.'

'What about riding?' Eleyne smiled, daring him to take the escape route. He shook his head firmly. 'Later,' he said.

Both had forgotten that she was Countess of Huntingdon and mistress of the castle. It was as two truant children that they dodged out of sight of the stables and raced across the courtyard towards the keep, sliding with the invisibility only children can manage across the lower chamber and up the dark stairs towards Lord Albemarle's bedroom. At the top of the stairs they stopped, panting.

'It was in here,' Eleyne whispered. The sun was on the far side of the keep this time and the room was in shadow.

Robert peered past her. 'What did it look like?' he hissed.

She smiled. 'Just a lady. A very beautiful lady in strange black clothes. She had lace here round her face,' she gestured with her hands, 'and a veil.'

'Did she say anything?'

Eleyne shook her head.

'She doesn't sound very frightening,' Robert scoffed.

Eleyne frowned. 'She wasn't frightening exactly,' she said. It was hard to describe the feelings she experienced when she saw these figures who slipped through the fine gauze curtain which was time and then slipped away again. She surveyed the room, then tiptoed through the rounded stone arch. 'Come on,' she said quietly. 'I was in the little chapel through here.' She gestured towards the doorway in the far wall. 'Then I looked back and saw her there, by the window.'

She crept into the oratory, Robert close at her heels. The tiny chapel was very dark. Both children held their breath as they stared round.

'Can you smell anything strange?' Eleyne whispered, her mouth very close to Robert's ear.

He swallowed nervously and gave a cautious sniff. 'I don't think so.'

'Incense,' she murmured. 'When she came there was a smell of incense.'

Robert felt the hairs standing up on the back of his neck; he wished they had gone riding instead. 'I can't smell anything.' His eyes swivelled round in his skull as he tried not to move his head. 'There's nothing here. Let's go.'

'No. Wait.' Eleyne could smell it. The rich exotic fragrance drifted imperceptibly in the still air of the oratory. 'She's here,' she breathed.

Robert stepped back and felt the rough stones of the wall cold through his tunic. His mouth had gone dry. Nervously, he turned his head so that he could see through the arch towards the window. There was nothing there. He frowned, staring harder, following her gaze, his hands wet with perspiration.

'Can you see her?' Eleyne asked softly. There was nothing there and the scent such as it was had gone. She glanced at him. He was shaking his head, his eyes screwed up with the effort of trying to see. His face was pasty.

'It's not the lady of Fotheringhay,' she said very quietly. 'Do you see? It's huge. And ugly. So ugly!'

Robert's face went whiter. He was pressing hard against the wall, wishing the stones would swallow him up.

'I can't see anything,' he gulped. 'I can't see anything at all.' He looked at her in mute appeal, then he stared. Her face had lit with suppressed laughter and she was giggling. 'If you could see your face, Nephew Robert,' she scolded.

'There's nothing there,' he said slowly. The fear and awe on his face vanished. 'There's nothing there at all! You've been teasing me! Why you –'

With a little shriek of laughter she dived past him. She raced across the empty bedchamber and pelted down the long spiral stairs, round and round and round, with Robert hot on her heels, bursting into the shadowy lower chamber just as John's steward appeared at an inner doorway. He stared at Eleyne as she stopped in her tracks, noticing with amused approval the flushed face and rumpled veil. 'Good day, my lady,' he said with a bow. 'His lordship was looking for you in the great hall.' His gaze strayed to the boy behind her and he hid a smile. 'It's good to see you again, Master Robert.'

Robert grinned impudently: 'And you, Master Steward.' He turned to Eleyne and bowed in turn. 'We mustn't keep Uncle John waiting, Aunt Eleyne,' he said severely. Then he winked. 'I'll race you!'

Eleyne hesitated for only a second, but already he was across the floor, scattering the scented woodruff which covered it, and out through the main door and out of sight.

XVI

The Earl and Countess of Huntingdon left the castle two months after Isabel and Robert had departed for Scotland. Eleyne had missed them enormously – after their ghost-hunting escapade they had become firm friends and he had kept the secret of her forbidden vision. Only the promise of another visit soon had consoled Eleyne as they rode away.

In her renewed loneliness she had turned to John more and more for company. She missed Rhonwen very much, but she also found it a relief not to have her constant supervision, and it was a pleasant surprise to find she no longer felt guilty enjoying her husband's company when they set off on a tour of his estates.

The lands which comprised the Honour of Huntingdon were for the most part flat. They stretched for miles, bisected by the black, slow-moving Nene, from the fens where they flew their hawks to the great forests of central England.

Eleyne was ill at ease in the flatness of the landscape and, try as she might to please John, she could not pretend to like the cities they visited. She did not like Cambridge or Huntingdon or Northampton, as they journeyed slowly from castle to castle; and most of all she did not like London, where he kept a town house. Instinctively she distrusted the slow-speaking, cold, suspicious easterners and she longed for the mountains and the wild seas; she longed for the quick-tongued, nimble-footed, warm-hearted people of Gwynedd where tempers might be quick to flare, but where vivacity and warmth and hospitality were second nature to the people. Twice John promised her that they would make the long ride to Chester and that from there she could, if her father agreed, visit Aber, but twice she was disappointed as John succumbed to the debilitating bouts of fever which returned again and again to plague him.

It was as the next long summer's heat settled over the flat lands of eastern England and they found themselves once more at Fotheringhay that he fell ill again and this time more seriously than before.

XVII
NORTHAMPTON ❖ May 1231

Rhonwen paused to move her basket of shopping from one arm to the other as she walked slowly back from the market to the house where she had found employment. Her new mistress was the wife of a wealthy wool merchant who had cheerfully given Rhonwen a place in the household as nurse to her brood of noisy children. Twice Rhonwen had despatched carefully worded messages to Luned to tell them where she was, but she had received no answer. She could not bring herself to return to Wales. She had to stay near Eleyne, and she had to find her way back.

Two men were leaning idly against the wall of the church on the corner of the street. One of them wore on his surcoat the arms of Huntingdon. Her mouth went dry. Had the earl found out where she was? Not that he had any jurisdiction over her here, she reminded herself sternly. She was a free citizen, honestly employed, within the city bounds.

She hesitated, then driven by her desperate need to have news of the earl's household she approached the men.

They stared at her with casual insolence. 'Well, my beauty. Can't resist us, eh?' The taller had noticed her watching them.

'Don't be impertinent!' Rhonwen drew herself up. 'You are one of Lord Huntingdon's men?'

The man nodded, then he winked. 'But not for long the way things are going.' He lounged back against the wall, picking one of his teeth with his forefinger. 'The earl is near death. I've come to Northampton to fetch a physician.'

'Near death?' Rhonwen echoed, her eyes fixed with such intensity on his face he shrank back. 'What's wrong with him?'

He shrugged. 'Fever,' he said non-committally. 'Who knows and who cares? It's his steward who pays me.' Reaching into his scrip he produced a silver penny and flicked it into the air. From the chink of coins between his fingers when he replaced it in the leather purse, there were plenty more.

'And where is he? Are they back at Fotheringhay?' Rhonwen asked.

He nodded. 'So. What about helping me spend some money while I'm waiting –' He stopped short. In a swirl of skirts, she had vanished into the crowds.

XVIII

FOTHERINGHAY

John's illness terrified Eleyne. It had begun without warning and she was devastated to see him so weak and helpless. Watching over him made her realise how fond she had grown of him, and she was very afraid that he would die. It had been her idea to send for the king's physician while he was at Northampton.

She was sitting at John's bedside, stroking his forehead, when Rhonwen found her. For a moment she stared incredulously at the woman, unable to move, then she hurled herself into Rhonwen's arms. But if Rhonwen had hoped to sit with Eleyne and watch John of Chester die, she was disappointed. It was obvious that Eleyne would do anything to save her husband's life; she wept and begged Rhonwen to help, and Rhonwen, unable to deny her beloved child, found herself setting aside her antagonism and resentment and, working harder than she had ever worked, she strove to keep him alive.

It was Rhonwen who made the decoctions of herbs which brought down John's fever; Rhonwen who spent hours in the stillroom making up soothing syrups for his cough. The physician was away, the messenger reported when at last he returned to Fotheringhay, but as soon as he returned to Northampton would be brought to Lord Huntingdon's bedside.

Eleyne was nervous John would find out Rhonwen was back. After that first visit to his sickroom when he was too delirious to recognise her, she was kept well away in the stillroom and in Eleyne's rooms in the tower on the far side of the courtyard. Eleyne brought the medicines in her own hands and watched with fearful eager hope as, slowly, he seemed to grow better.

When at last the king's physician arrived Rhonwen's medicines were swept scornfully away. The stout, white-haired man, with his huge bushy eyebrows and long black gown, bent over the earl and reached for his pulse, but the earl was already on the mend.

XIX
August 1231

The bedchamber was shady in the dusk. In the distance there was a rumble of thunder. Eleyne raised her hand and Luned stopped brushing her hair. There was no fire in the hearth and Eleyne had given orders for the lamps to be doused. Dearly though she loved her, it was a relief to be away fron Rhonwen, who followed her everywhere when she was not with John. Rhonwen was with Marared, sitting in the bower where a travelling minstrel from Aquitaine was entertaining the ladies with songs and roundelays redolent of the hot fragrant south. Pleading a headache, Eleyne had left with Luned, seeking the cooler silence of her rooms overlooking the river. For once, Rhonwen had not followed her.

On the far side of the courtyard, above the gatehouse, John was tossing in his bed, still tended by the physician. Eleyne had visited him before supper, putting her hand a little shyly in his and feeling the dry papery skin like fire against her own, then the doctor had peremptorily sent her away.

She frowned at the recollection: there had to be some other way of helping John. She was sure that under Rhonwen's care he had improved. For a long time that morning she had watched the physician carefully applying leeches to her husband's frail body, attaching the creatures with meticulous care to his chest and arms and waiting until they dropped, gorged with his blood, into the silver dish waiting for them. John had smiled at her calmly and asked her to read to him for a while. She had done it gladly, but every now and then her eyes left the crabbed black manuscript of the vellum pages and strayed to his face. He was too pale. He did not have enough red blood. Surely it must be wrong to drain even more. She found herself longing again for her father's court, with the wise men of the hills who attended it. Men like Einion, who might be a heretic and evil and wrong, as John so often told her, but it was he, so Rhonwen had said, who had taught her all she knew of healing, and that was much.

'That's enough,' she said sharply as Luned resumed her brushing. She stood up restlessly and walked over to the window, stepping into the embrasure so she could see out of the deep recess towards the west. Over there, beneath the moonlight, many miles away, lay the giant sleeping peaks of Yr Wyddfa.

'Go to bed, Luned.' Her mind was made up. 'Go to bed, I'm going down to the stables.'

It was months since she had done it; months since she had visited the horses in the dark. John had been adamant. The Countess of Huntingdon did not curl up in the straw like a stable boy – not now that she was a woman. She slept between silken sheets every night. The Countess of Huntingdon was not expected to seek out the shadows or explore the castle alone or gallop at the head of her men or disappear into the heaths when out hawking with her pretty merlin on her fist. She must be demure and ladylike and behave with propriety at all times.

'My lady.' The soft voice at her elbow stopped her as she reached the door into the courtyard.

'Cenydd?' She suspected he slept across her threshold once the castle was quiet at night.

'Shall I call for torches, my lady?' The big man was smiling down at her, his shoulders broad in his heavy leather jerkin. She became conscious of her hair, hanging loose down her back, free of the neat cap or head-dress she should be wearing.

'No, no torches.' She stepped out on to the wooden staircase which led down from the only door in the keep to the courtyard below.

'You should not go out alone, lady.' The gentle voice was persistent.

'I am not alone if you are there!' she retorted. Swishing her skirts in irritation, she ran down the staircase. At the bottom she stopped and turned. 'You may come with me if you wish. If not, you may return to the great hall and pretend you haven't seen me. I intend to ride Invictus.'

'In the dark, princess?'

'There is enough light. I do not want my husband to know about this, Cenydd. I do not wish to worry him. If you betray me I shall have you sent back to Gwynedd.' Her imperious tone left him in no doubt that she meant it.

'Very well, princess.'

She gave him a quick smile. 'Just this once, Cenydd, before I die of suffocation.' The charm had returned, and the small wheedling smile he could never resist – nor, he guessed, could any man. 'Please.'

If the grooms were surprised at being asked to bridle the great stallion for their small mistress, they hid the fact. He was led out and Cenydd lifted Eleyne on to the high back of the horse. He hastily mounted his own fast gelding, afraid she would gallop off into the dusk, but she walked the stallion demurely towards the gatehouse, beneath the portcullis, and reined in, waiting for the postern in the main doors to be opened, before urging the animal on to the track outside. The storm was drifting closer, imperceptibly, a deeper blackness in the sky to the south-west, sliced now and then by zigzags of lightning. Invictus sidled uneasily and snapped bad-temperedly at the horse beside him.

'If we take the road across the heath, we can gallop,' Eleyne said at last. The huge flat distances, mysterious in the moonlight, depressed

113

her, as did the vast unbroken canopy of the sky, this infinite eastern sky which rendered the land so insignificant and featureless.

'What of the storm?' Cenydd could smell the rain, sweet and cold, in the distance. Like the horses, he was ill at ease.

'I want to ride in the storm.'

'No, lady, think of your position. Think of your safety. Please come back.' He knew she should not be there. If anything happened to her, he would be blamed. He sighed, loosening his sword in its sheath for the umpteenth time. Her wilfulness was Rhonwen's fault. The child had never been disciplined and now she had a husband as weak-willed as the rest.

Invictus bared his teeth spitefully and Cenydd's gelding side-stepped.

'Come on. We can see well enough here.' She was gathering her reins and the stallion was on his toes.

'*Why*, princess?'

The forceful disapproval in his voice stopped her, fighting with the bit, holding the horse back on its haunches.

'What do you mean?' She raised her head defensively.

'Why must you ride like this? A countess, a princess, should behave like a lady . . .'

Even in the moonlight he could see the colour darken her cheeks. 'There are many kinds of lady, Cenydd. My husband has taught me that. I am the kind who rides like Rhiannon on her white horse, whom no man can catch.' She pronounced the soft Welsh name wistfully.

Cenydd stared across at her. 'Your husband told you this?'

She nodded emphatically.

She had been reading to him as he lay, his eyes closed, on the daybed they had arranged for him on the dais in the great hall. At first she had resented these hours at John's side, longing to be out in the sun, longing to be riding. Seeing this, he had kept her with him for short periods only, lengthening them infinitesimally until, one day, when the rain teemed down outside, sluicing off the roofs and pouring in waterfalls from the stone gutters jutting out from the parapets of the keep, he drew her down near him and with a smile handed her a packet wrapped in a piece of linen.

'A present.'

She looked at it with a sinking heart, knowing already from the feel that it was a book. Slowly she began to unfold the wrapping. To her delight the book was in Welsh, and as she turned the richly decorated pages she gasped in wonder.

'I asked your father if he could send a book of Welsh stories to cheer you up, Eleyne, and he had this made especially for you. The stories are as old as time. His bards and storytellers have been collecting them and writing them down for many years, I gather.' He waited, half amused, half anxious as she leafed through the pages spelling out the titles: The Dream of Maxen, the Countess of the Fountain, Peredur. She looked up at John, her eyes shining. 'I know these stories –'

'Of course you do.' He smiled. 'And I want to know them too. Will you read them to me?' He was watching her as he so often did, this strange child, the daughter of a Welsh prince, descendant perhaps of the ancient gods of the stories in the book she held. Maybe the stories would help him understand her better, and maybe they would help to relieve the homesickness which still robbed her cheeks of colour and filled him with such guilt whenever she came, trying so hard to hide her reluctance, to his side.

'Even so, princess,' Cenydd went on grudgingly, 'I am sure he did not mean you to ride without escort like this. These heaths and fens are full of robbers and thieves and outlaws.' He examined the still, moonlit landscape with its brooding shadows and the deeper pools of blackness beneath the trees, big enough to have hidden an army, and he shivered.

Eleyne laughed lightly. 'If there are any robbers here, we can out-ride them. And I have you and your sword to protect me.' Behind them a low rumble of thunder echoed around the horizon.

She waited for him in a patch of streaming moonlight, her hair wildly tangled on her shoulders, her blood singing with exhilaration, she and the horse tired at last. Then out of nowhere a bolt of lightning hissed out of the sky near them and exploded into the ground, making the stallion rear.

She had not seen the castle as she approached, but as she gentled the great horse she could see it clearly in the green eldritch light. The lightning vanished into blacker darkness leaving flames running along the walls, licking across the roofs, strung along the scaffolding poles like bright flags at a tourney. Dear God, the lightning must have struck the roof. Horrified, she watched, hearing the shouts and screams of the men and women trapped at high windows too narrow to let them push their way free. On the roof leads she saw a figure outlined by fire. As she watched, the man turned from the flames and climbing into the battlements hurled himself out into the smoke, his cry lost in the tumult below.

Dimly she was aware of Cenydd beside her now. 'Look. Oh, Holy Mother! Oh, the poor people! Can't we do something?' But there was nothing they could do; nothing anyone could do. They were sur-rounded by the roar of the flame and the rolling smoke, white and grey against the blackness of the night, sewn with a million sparks.

Another flash of lightning showed the broad band of the river between them and the castle and the line of armed men who stood unmoving between the castle and the water which could have saved it. She narrowed her eyes, trying to see the banner of the man at their head, but the smoke rolled down to the river once more and she could see nothing.

The rain came, as though a giant bucket had been overturned in the heavens, soaking the ground, the horses and the two riders within seconds, reducing the visibility to no more than a few feet. Eleyne narrowed her eyes, desperately trying to see ahead, but her eyes refused to focus now, seeing only the cold silver needles which stung her face and hands.

She realised that Cenydd had dismounted and was standing at Invictus's head, looking questioningly at her as he gripped the horse's sharp bit. She had not flinched from the rain. She sat upright, unmoving, her eyes on the distance.

'Are you all right, princess?'

She could barely make out his narrowed eyes, his hair plastered to his skin beneath his leather cap.

'I . . . I don't know.' She felt strangely disorientated. 'The castle . . . will they be all right? The rain will help put out the fire . . .'

Cenydd let go of the bridle long enough to cross himself fervently: 'You saw a fire?'

She stared at him. 'You must have seen it. There –'

Behind them the heath was invisible behind the curtain of rain. Another lightning flash zigzagged across the sky.

'There is no fire, my lady, and no castle,' he said gently. 'And there never has been. Not here.'

CHAPTER FIVE

I

BANGOR ❖ June 1231

The nuptial mass had been all Isabella had dreamed it would be. The cathedral at Bangor, with its sturdy pillars and its high arched roof, glowed with sunlight as, the marriage completed, Prince Dafydd ap Llywelyn, heir to Gwynedd and Aberffraw and all North Wales, led his young bride to the high altar and knelt beside her there on a faldstool embroidered with silver and gold. Behind him stood his father, alone. In spite of a stream of desperate, contrite letters from Joan, begging his forgiveness, she was still imprisoned. She had not been permitted to attend the wedding of her lover's daughter to her son.

Nearby, tight-lipped, stood Eva de Braose, her lovely face hidden by a black silk veil. Was she, she wondered, as she stared around the packed cathedral, the only person there to remember that her husband had been hanged by these people? She clenched her fists angrily as the voices of the choir soared aloft. Then a hand touched hers. Standing next to her, Gwladus, now married to Ralph Mortimer, remembered. She too had loved her dead husband's dashing son. In sorrow the two women bowed their heads and prayed.

Isabella was not thinking of her father. She ran her hands quickly over the front of her richly embroidered gown, then folded them meekly in prayer. On her thick curtain of black hair, brushed loose almost to her waist, sat a golden coronet studded with pearls.

She stole a look at her handsome husband. He was tall, his red-gold hair gleaming in the stray beams of sun which slanted across the hills behind the cathedral and in through the stained-glass windows. The air curled and moved with the smoke of incense.

Dafydd smiled at her. He found his curvaceous young bride much to his taste. Her dark eyes and hair showed off a naturally white skin; she was small – not yet fourteen – but the breasts beneath her bodice were well grown and her hips beneath the slender lines of the gown and kirtle were provocatively curved.

He had thought long and hard about the problem of her father and at last had cautiously brought up the subject with the prince.

117

'However right we were to hang him,' he said, with a wary eye on his father's face, 'the child is bound to feel resentment. It's only natural. Her mother does.' He grimaced; he did not like the stone-faced Eva.

'She must learn that the wages of sin are death,' Llywelyn replied, his face grim.

'I think she knows that,' Dafydd said slowly. 'But still it must be hard to bear. Can I . . .' he hesitated, 'can I tell her that it was Eleyne who discovered them together? It might be easier for her to come to terms with that idea, and if she can't,' he shrugged, 'no doubt it will take less time to get over it. And as Eleyne has left Gwynedd it hardly matters anyway.'

Llywelyn examined his son's face for a moment, surprised at the young man's cynicism. 'You mean you think Isabella needs a focus for her hate?'

'Of course she does.' Dafydd smiled. 'And Eleyne has gone. What better way of handling it?' He did not add that he had guessed that his father had done the same thing; only in his case he had shifted on to his daughter the blame of his wife. It was well known throughout the palace that Llywelyn had given orders for his wife's imprisonment to be made less harsh; that he missed her intolerably – and that he had sent no messages or gifts to the Countess of Huntingdon save one book, grudgingly, at her husband's request.

Isabella's reaction to his frank discussion was all Dafydd had hoped. Several days before the wedding he had drawn her aside into one of the window embrasures in the newly built stone keep at Caernarfon Castle, out of earshot of their chaperones.

'My dear, the shadow of your father is coming between us,' he said slowly, taking her hand gently in his. A master of the chivalric art of courtship, he had already plied his betrothed daily with poems and flowers and little gifts of love: scented kerchiefs and ribbons. 'I cannot bear that to be so.' He glanced at her solemnly and was touched to see her eyes had filled with tears. 'There is something you should know, Isabella.' He lowered his voice even more, so she had to bend close to hear him and he could feel the soft brush of her breath on his brow, see the fine bloom of youth on her rounded cheeks. He felt a sudden rush of desire and had to close his eyes to keep his feelings under control. 'I know she was your friend, but I have to tell you. It was Eleyne who betrayed your father. He trusted her; he loved her almost as a daughter, and yet she betrayed him.'

There was a long silence. 'No? Not Elly?' It was a plea.

'I am sorry, Isabella. But you would have found out in the end.'

She had cried a little, discreetly, so the chaperones would not see and interrupt their tête-à-tête, then slowly she began to realise what he had said. Eleyne, her friend, had killed her father! Anger replaced the tears, and then fire-spitting fury. 'How could she! I hate her! I'll never forgive her!' She had forgotten, as Dafydd had intended, that her father had not been alone in his sin. That Dafydd's — and Eleyne's — mother had been with him, and that they had both been in her bed.

The wedding feast dragged on for hours; course succeeded course, trenchers and plates were piled high with spiced food: sucking pig, swan, hare, pike, quail, partridge, stews, broths, mussels, trout, leek tarts, custards and honey cakes, and cask upon cask of Gascon wine, Welsh mead, ale and whisky were emptied, rolled away and replaced. Beside her husband Isabella was hot, tired and over-excited, and she had begun to feel sick. She stared around the hall uncomfortably, wondering if she should excuse herself again and run to the nearest range of chambers of ease, where she would have to brave a queue of jeering drunken men. It was that or the shame of being sick in the corner. She was still trying to make up her befuddled mind as she stared at the wheels of dripping candles when she found her husband beside her, helping her to her feet. 'Go, sweetheart. Make ready for me.' He pushed her gently towards a group of giggling ladies who seemed to be waiting for her. Swaying slightly, she stumbled towards them, only half conscious of the full-throated roar of approval from the prince's young friends and the chorus of lewd comments from the lower tables.

In the bridal chamber it was quiet and cool after the roar of noise and the heat of the great hall. To the accompaniment of much gentle teasing, Isabella's clothes were removed by her attendants, her face and body sponged with flower-water and anointed with sweet-smelling salves; her hair was brushed and then she was helped into the high bed, decorated all over with garlands and flowers.

Minutes later, as she caught the silk sheet to her breasts with a little shriek, the door flew open and Dafydd appeared, accompanied by a number of boisterous young men.

Hazily she watched as he tried half-heartedly to escape his friends; she saw him caught and watched, half amused, half afraid as they tore his clothes none too gently from his body. Then he too was naked. She gazed at him in awe. The lithe muscular body was the handsomest thing she had ever seen; and he sported a magnificent erection.

With a cheer the young men pushed him into bed beside her, during which manoeuvre she clutched tightly at the sheet, but they got a more-than-adequate view of the rounded charms of their new princess. Then reluctantly they fell to silence as the figure of the bishop appeared in the doorway, surveying the scene tolerantly. With a smile he walked into the room. '*Pax vobiscum*, my children.' He walked across to the bed.

Isabella closed her eyes as the holy water touched her face and breasts and realised with a sickening wave of nausea that the room was

119

spinning around her. She opened her eyes again, feeling her stomach lurch as, beside her in the bed, she felt with a shock the touch of her husband's thigh against her own. It seemed a long time before the bishop left the chamber, and with him her maidens and ladies and the prince's friends, but at last the door closed and they were alone.

With a swift, almost angry movement Dafydd brushed the flowers and ribbons from the bed and threw himself back on the pillows.

'Sweet Christ! I thought they would never go.'

Reaching out an arm, he caught her shoulder and pulled her towards him. 'My lovely Isabella –'

With a groan she pulled away. 'My lord,' she started to cry, 'I'm going to be sick!' She threw herself from the bed and ran naked to the garderobe.

It was a long time before she returned white-faced and shivering to the chamber. Dafydd was sitting in the bed drinking and gave her a sympathetic grin. 'Better?'

She nodded sheepishly, catching up a cloak and wrapping it around herself.

'Here.' He held out his silver goblet. 'Rinse your mouth with this. You'll feel better.'

She did as he bid, spitting ferociously into the ewer in the corner. Then she began to brush her hair.

'That'll teach you to mix your wine with mead!' His teasing voice was just behind her. She jumped. His hands were on her shoulders, peeling away the cloak. 'Come back to bed now and get warm.' He was naked too and she found she was trembling with excitement as they went back to the bed and scrambled in.

She liked his kisses. And she liked his hands upon her breasts. She lay passively, feeling strangely guilty that she should so enjoy the sensations of her body. Her mother had told her with a certain grim satisfaction that it would hurt, but this, this was ecstasy and her Dafydd gentle and kind. She opened her eyes sleepily and reached up her lips for another kiss.

They made love three times that night; the first time it did hurt and there was blood, but skilfully he kept her excitement at fever pitch and the second time was better. The third, when she was sated and sleepy, heavy with contentment, was as the first rays of the sun crept across the strewn rose petals on the floor and played across their sprawled bodies. Isabella, the wife of Dafydd ap Llywelyn, was very, very happy.

II

The fever had deepened. Eleyne lay tossing uneasily on her bed. In her delirium she was walking in a valley filled with flowers. With her there was a man with red-gold hair, who took her hand and kissed it and smiled at her with eyes so full of love she found she was crying, her tears warm and wet on her cheeks. Then she woke up, and Rhonwen was sponging her face with rose water and the man had gone and left her alone and she cried again. She barely recognised her husband when he rose from his own sickbed to visit hers.

The castle was hushed, the household concerned for their small countess, of whom most of them were very fond. The pinched face and huge unhappy eyes when she had first arrived had touched many a heart, as had her rare smiles, her concern for others, her careful attention to learning how to oversee them, her occasional irrepressible laughter and her wild uncontrollable rides from which she would return tired but with her spirit refreshed, just such a ride as had, this time, laid her so low.

Working silently in the stillroom, Rhonwen pounded the dried herbs in her mortar, searching her memory for a formula which would break the fever. She had to be so careful. The earl still did not know she had returned; he did not know it was she who had provided the physic which had made him so much better before the king's doctor had come. He did not know that Eleyne had thrown out the doctor's medicines, quietly replacing them with Rhonwen's; that Eleyne had smiled and nodded as the old man took the credit for the earl's improved health. Now it was happening again, but with Luned and Marared now carrying the potions to the countess's bedchamber. It was only at night when the castle slept that Rhonwen dared visit the child and smooth back her hair and bathe her wrists and temples with flower water.

She weighed the dried, powdered herbs carefully in her hand scale and poured boiling water over them. Their scent filled the small stillroom, already permeated with the smell of decades of dried herbs and flowers. As soon as the infusion was made she would take it to Eleyne herself. The bell for compline had rung from the nunnery beyond the walls a long time earlier. It would be safe to visit her charge.

Eleyne was asleep, her brow still damp with fever, her hair tangled on the pillow when Rhonwen tiptoed in. Beside her a single lamp burned. Ethil watched over her, dozing in the chair near her bed. She jumped to her feet as Rhonwen appeared. Rhonwen put her finger to her lips. Setting down the flask of liquid, she went to the bed and laid a cool hand on Eleyne's forehead.

'The fever is down, Lady Rhonwen,' Ethil smiled. 'The earl's physician says she is getting better at last.'

Rhonwen sniffed. 'If she is, it is none of his doing. See she gets this four times a day and give her nothing he prescribes. Nothing. Do you understand?' She stroked Eleyne's cheek gently. 'There, *cariad*. You'll soon be better –' She broke off as the door behind them opened.

The Earl of Huntingdon stared at Rhonwen for several seconds without speaking, his eyes hard. Then he stepped into the room. 'So my informant was right. You have sneaked back. What do you think you are doing here, madam?' He moved towards the bed and looked down at his wife as she murmured restlessly in her sleep.

'I am taking care of my child!' Rhonwen took a step back. Her heart was pounding with fear. 'Please, my lord, let me stay. You can't send me away, not now, not while she's ill.' She dodged back towards Eleyne and stood protectively over her. 'I'm the one who is curing her. Not your pompous old doctor. He knows nothing. *Nothing!*' She grabbed Eleyne's hand and clutched it to her. 'Who do you think made you better? Who do you think saved your life? It was me!'

John shook his head. His face was dark with anger. 'Enough! You disobeyed me, woman. I sent you away. I will not have you near my wife!'

'You can't make me go . . .' Rhonwen clutched Eleyne's hand more tightly.

'Oh, indeed I can.' John turned to Ethil. 'Call the guard.'

Ethil hesitated. 'Do as I say, woman!' His voice hardened. 'Call the guard. Now.'

Eleyne had awakened. She stared uncomprehendingly at the man and woman who stood over her arguing. Her eyes were unnaturally bright, her face flushed in the candlelight.

'John –' Her whisper was hoarse.

He looked at her and his face softened. 'Hush, my darling. Go back to sleep.' To Rhonwen he said, 'I mean it, madam. My physicians are perfectly able to take care of my wife. She does not need your care. You are the reason she is ill! If you had brought her up properly she would not have had this need to ride at all hours of the night! But for you she would have forgotten these nightmares and visions which torment her.' He swung around as two men-at-arms appeared in the doorway. 'Take this woman away. I want her off my lands by noon tomorrow.' He glanced at Rhonwen. 'Go back to Wales. You are not wanted here. If I see you near my wife again it will not go well for you.'

He watched, arms folded, as the two men advanced on Rhonwen. One of them took her arm and she spat at him, her eyes blazing. 'I shall

122

never forget this, John of Scotland,' she hissed as she was pulled away from the bedside. 'Never! One day you will die for this!'

III
August 1231

'So. Are you better at last?' The familiar gentle face of her husband swam into focus as Eleyne awoke. She moved painfully on the bed beneath the silk sheet as he put his hand on her forehead. 'The fever has finally broken.'

Beyond him the room was shadowy. The curtains of the bed were drawn back, the heavy bedcovers gone.

'Have I been ill a long time?' She stared round weakly.

'Indeed you have. You were caught in the storm, do you remember? Cenydd brought you back wet through and before we knew it, it was me visiting you, instead of the other way round.' After Rhonwen had gone the fever had worsened again and she had grown delirious. He himself had totally recovered. The long summer days and the prolonged rest ordered by the doctor had brought some colour to his cheeks. He was coughing less and, his appetite recovered, had put on weight. Each day he had been riding farther, determined, though he did not admit it even to himself, that when his wife recovered, he would no longer be put to shame in the saddle.

He eyed her slight frame, so painfully thin, with the newly appeared small breasts barely visible mounds beneath the sheet.

He had been frantic with worry as the fever had raged, watching in an agony of helplessness as Ethil and Marared nursed her, holding to her dry burning lips a succession of evil-tasting tinctures and decoctions of herbs which the physician had prescribed for her. And like them, he had listened to her delirious descriptions of the burning of the castle she had witnessed on her ride.

Cenydd, summoned to the earl, had reluctantly told him what had happened.

'She was sitting on the horse, staring, staring into the darkness, and her eyes were all over the place, watching, watching something I couldn't see. She was crying and complaining that the smoke was in her eyes and begging me to help. She said there were soldiers stopping the bucket men getting near the river . . .' His voice trailed away. 'But there was nothing there, nothing . . .'

John had rubbed his cheek thoughtfully. 'Have you seen her do this before?'

Cenydd shook his head. 'Luned knows about her visions, my lord,' he said slowly. For the child's sake it was better if it were all out in the open.

Luned was white-faced: 'It was a fantasy. The storm; the lightning. What she saw was the lightning strike a tree –'

'She saw a castle burning, child! You and I have heard her describe it again and again in her illness. She saw men and she saw a river. This was no ordinary dream.' He paced up and down the floor. 'She was warning us. Warning us of some attack. But where? Here?' He swung round and paced back towards the empty hearth. He was cursing himself roundly. He believed it! He, a man of education and sense, believed she was seeing the future and he was worried about it! He was as gullible as the lye-spattered women in the wash-houses beyond the walls. He turned back to Luned. 'I don't want anyone to hear about this,' he said repressively. 'No word, no word must get out, do you understand? If the servants heard her talk, it was her delirium speaking, that is all. And now, thank the Blessed Virgin, she is better and there will be no more talk of burning castles!'

Eleyne looked around the room. 'Where's Rhonwen?' she asked.

John sat down on the bed and took her hands in his. 'I've sent her back to Wales, my darling. I couldn't let her stay. She's all right. She's gone back to her own people.'

He saw her eyes fill with tears and he cursed silently. 'Luned and Marared and Ethil are still here to keep you company. And me.' He smiled. 'And Isabel is coming to stay and bringing young Robert. You have to get better soon so you can ride with him. You'll enjoy that.' He reached for the physic the doctor had left and helping her sit up held it to her lips. 'And your sister Margaret has sent you a gift from Sussex. She wants you to go and see her when you're better. She's sent you a beautiful necklace of pearls.'

Eleyne had grown while she was ill. He was astonished to find her now, thin as a reed, up to his shoulder. Her head still ached sometimes, so he would read to her in the evenings if there were no travelling minstrels or storytellers or guests. And he would talk to her of the future.

'Would you like to be a queen, little one?'

'In Scotland?'

He nodded. Great-grandson of King David I of Scotland, John, the only son of the elder John of Huntingdon and Maud, heiress to the Earl of Chester, was heir presumptive to the as yet childless King Alexander II.

Her eyes shone. 'What is Scotland like?'

'Beautiful. It has mountains bigger even than your great Snowdon, and lochs, great lochs as deep as the sea. One day soon we'll go there.

Your mother's sister, Joanna, is married to my cousin the king, so we are both near the throne.' He saw her frown. 'Your mother is well, Eleyne. Sad in her prison, but well. You must not go on blaming yourself for her imprisonment. It was she who sinned.' He looked at her. 'No more bad dreams, I hope?'

She shook her head. The man with the auburn hair was forgotten again, part of the whirling blackness of her fever.

'And no more burning castles.' He smiled. 'I keep wondering whether to stand to a bucket chain in case.' The violence of her descriptions was still in the forefront of his mind.

'It wasn't any of your castles,' she said, anxious to reassure him.

'Then where was it?' he asked softly.

'It was Sir William's castle. At Hay.'

There was a long silence.

'I understand Hubert de Burgh, the king's justiciar, has custody of Hay Castle,' he said at last. 'It must have been the past you saw, sweetheart. Your grandfather, King John, burned Hay after he destroyed Sir William's grandmother and grandfather twenty years ago.'

He saw her knuckles whiten.

'It's all over now. And best forgotten, Eleyne.'

'I know.' It was a whisper.

IV

The visitor did not realise the importance of the news he brought. He had been given fresh water to wash and food and wine in the great hall and then, as courtesy demanded, he repaid the hospitality with news of the country through which he had ridden. He had been in Hereford when he had heard of the sack of Hay Castle and the latest round of battles which raged in Wales.

'I hear they were still rebuilding the castle from the last time when the attack came. The women tried to hide in the church with their children, but that was burned too. The whole place has been razed to the ground, so I heard.'

John stared at him. Beside him Eleyne was as white as a sheet.

'Who has done such a thing?' John put out his hand and rested it over his wife's on the table.

'The Prince of Aberffraw. Your father, my lady. He burned Hay Castle.'

Letters came some time later from Llywelyn to John. He had done it, he said, to reduce the de Burgh influence in the march, and to remind the King of England not to encroach too far into Wales.

'That's not true,' Eleyne said huskily, the letter in her hand. 'He burned Hay for revenge. Because Sir William loved it there.' She took a deep unsteady breath, fighting back her tears. 'Poor Isabella. I wonder how she is enjoying life at Aber.'

She had written three times to her friend; there had been no reply.

'She'll be fine.' John tried to comfort her. 'Your brother Dafydd is a good man. He'll look after her.'

He did not mention the fire again and neither did she. She could not have saved Hay Castle from her father any more than she could have saved Sir William from the noose. She realised now, their destinies had been written in the stars. But how had she been allowed to see the future? And why?

V

The Earl and Countess of Huntingdon were summoned to Westminster within weeks of the burning of Hay Castle. John guessed that Llywelyn's motive must be of great importance to the king, and he warned Eleyne that the king would ask her about it.

'You won't tell him that I saw it all?' She looked at him anxiously.

'Of course not. Do you think I want the whole world knowing that my wife has visions of the future?'

She sat down at the great oak table where he had been writing, and picked up one of his quills. 'I do not do it on purpose.'

'I know.' Contrite, he squeezed her shoulder. 'But we cannot – must not – let it happen again. It's dangerous. And it makes you unhappy. The king will ask you about your father's motives. All you have to say is that you don't know. Tell him all your father's letters are addressed to me.' This was true.

King Henry III stood facing his niece, a quizzical smile on his face. 'Your father is thumbing his nose at me again, I think, my lady.'

Eleyne felt her face colouring. 'No, sire, that is not true.'

'My wife feels sure that the burning of Hay, at least, was a personal grudge, your grace.' John put a protective hand on her arm. 'A last gesture against the de Braoses.'

'Ah, the lustful Sir William who managed to win my half-sister's heart.' Henry smiled. 'The man must have been either a fool or so mad for love it made him so.' He looked around for approval for his joke.

At twenty-four Henry Plantagenet was an elegant, handsome young man with an artistic eye, amply demonstrated in his love of clothes and luxurious furnishings and in the extravagant plans he was drawing up for the rebuilding of Westminster Abbey. As yet unmarried, he was a pious, shrewd and sometimes obstinate man.

For a long moment he eyed Eleyne, then he turned away. She was still a child. Later, when she had more influence with her husband, would be the time to make use of her.

The Huntingdons were at home in their house in the Strand, a sprawling new suburb between London and Westminster, when news came that the Prince of Aberffraw had finally taken pity on his erring wife and forgiven her. After two years of imprisonment she had at last been allowed to return to her husband's side and was reinstated in his favour. Eleyne gave the messenger a silver penny, overjoyed with the news, and went to find her husband.

'I can go home! If papa has forgiven her, he will have forgiven me, won't he, my lord? Oh, please. Can I go home?' Not once in the last two years had they gone to the west.

John looked at her in astonishment and took the letter. It was the first she had ever received from Aber, and it came from Rhonwen.

'Home? To Gwynedd you mean?'

She nodded in excitement. 'Please?' Noticing his expression she stopped uncomfortably. 'I know I am your wife, I know I must come back to you when I am fourteen, but until then I could go home to Rhonwen. Back to Wales. Back to see Isabella —' Her voice died away. They stood looking at each other for a long moment, and slowly her face fell.

'I am sorry, sweetheart.' John shook his head. 'You must stay with me. Your home is with me now.'

'My home is in Gwynedd.' It was almost a sob.

'Not now, Eleyne. You are the Countess of Huntingdon. Wales is no longer your home. It never will be again.'

'But it must be!' Huge tears welled up in her eyes. 'It will always be my home. I love Wales. I hate it here!' The angry sweep of her arm encompassed not only the heavily oak-beamed room of the house with the endless rattle of carts and wagons outside and the hot, fetid smell of the crowded streets of London so close, but the whole of eastern England and her husband's domains.

'Then you must learn to like it, Eleyne.' His voice was unusually stern. He had not realised she still expected to go back to her father. He had thought she was happy with him. The wild ride of the night of the storm had not been repeated, and even before it she had appeared content to spend more and more time at his side, learning the intricate, sometimes tedious task of running the huge and complex administration. 'There is no question of going back.'

'Not ever?' The look she gave him was stricken.

He took a deep breath. 'No doubt a visit can be arranged at some point. When we go back to Chester we can consider it if your father wishes it. But at the moment he has made no mention of it. Neither, if you read your letter carefully,' he handed it back to her, 'does the Lady Rhonwen.'

*

Luned stared at Eleyne. 'We can't go back? Ever?'

Eleyne shook her head, biting back her tears. The brightly painted room with its terracotta walls and ornate gilded plasterwork between the beams was cool and shady compared with the street beyond the high gates. The small-paned windows let in a strange greenish light which cast ripples and shadows across the floor. The bitter smell of dry strewn herbs rose and tickled her throat as she moved.

'Then what?' Luned sat down heavily on the edge of a coffer.

'We go on as before. England is our home now.' Eleyne's voice was flat. 'Or Scotland, one day perhaps.' Scotland was a fairy tale; part of a dream of a queen with a golden crown. 'But we can visit Aber only if papa asks us. Luned,' she went and sat down next to her, taking her hand, 'I am going to write to Rhonwen. And to Isabella. I'll ask them to speak to papa. Bella would want me there. Aber won't be much fun on her own. There were so many things we were going to do together; so many adventures I had planned. She'll persuade them to let me come back, I know she will.'

The bleak reality of John's glimpse of the future was pushed aside. She could not, would not, believe it possible that she would never live in North Wales again.

VII

This time Isabella wrote back. Eleyne stared at the letter in disbelief, frozen with horror, oblivious of her husband's worried eyes on her. 'What is it, Eleyne?' The letter had been with his as usual courteous note from Llywelyn about march business.

Eleyne shook her head bleakly.

Leaning forward, John took the letter from her limp fingers and scanned the loose childish handwriting. Seconds later he had thrown it on the fire.

'Forget her.' His words were curt.

'But she is – was – my friend.' Eleyne was bewildered.

'I fear you have been made a scapegoat, sweetheart. Your brother has, it seems, blamed you for her father's death. You can see why they have done it. Life would be intolerable if she blamed your father. You are not there. It was the pragmatic answer.'

'But she was my friend,' Eleyne repeated. She could not believe such betrayal.

'Obviously not.' She had to learn the lesson now, hard though it was. 'A true friend would have believed in you.'

'I'll never go back home now . . .' The shock was wearing off and the full significance of the letter began to dawn. 'If she blames me, everyone else will be doing the same. My mother –'

John frowned. 'That may well be so, sweetheart.'

She stood up slowly and walked over to the low window. Through the dim glass she could see the altercation between two wagoners just outside the gates below. The wheels of their vehicles had become locked in the narrow street and, strain as they might, the oxen pulling in opposite directions could not extricate them. The fracas ended only when one of the wheels was wrenched off and the wagon tipped its load of heavy sacks into the filthy road.

VIII

The visit to London ended. John took Eleyne once again on the progress around the Huntingdon estates. Away from the city her spirits rose a little. She was happy to be riding again and, in spite of herself, she was becoming increasingly interested in the complexities of running the great earldom. John encouraged her, enjoying the blossoming confidence, the shrewd native intelligence, the occasional wry humour. He also enjoyed talking to her of deeper things: persuading her to tell him the stories of the old gods of the Welsh hills and in return showing her the gentle meekness of the Blessed Virgin Mary. Often he took her alone with him into the chapels and churches on his estates, to listen to the singing of the liturgy or to see the beauty of the gold and silver, the alabaster, the glass; above all, to feel the peace to be found at the feet of the Mother of God. Eleyne had more or less forgotten Einion and now she found that she could put Rhonwen too at the back of her mind. Her nurse was safe and happy at Aber, and her husband must now become the centre of her life. She would see Rhonwen soon, of that she was certain.

She fought the dreams consciously, never gazing into the fire, never allowing the veil which separated past, present and future to slip. As time passed it seemed to grow easier. She recognised the sensations which sometimes threatened her: the sharpening of perception, the intensity of feeling, the strange blankness which announced the closeness of another world. When that happened, she would clutch at the beautiful carved beads and crucifix John had given her and which now always hung at her waist. The more fixed she became in the present, the more she found herself becoming fond of John. At twenty-eight he was a good-looking man – serious, conscientious, gentle with his young wife.

He never mentioned the time when they would be more than friends. Her courses had started at last, a full eighteen months after Luned had blossomed as a woman. When it happened, she had held her breath and waited, sure that John would know, sure he would now insist she come to his bed. But he gave no sign of knowing that her thin, skinny body had become a woman's body. He treated her as he always had and never did anything to frighten her. As the months passed and she came more and more to rely on him and trust him, husband and wife grew more and more pleased with each other.

In March 1232 King Henry visited them at Fotheringhay and she helped to supervise the preparations for the vast number of men and women in his train. It was the first time she had really felt her role as countess and lady of the castle; the visit was a resounding success. It was all the more surprise therefore when, as the heat returned to the low-lying countryside, she fell ill again. When a summons came for John to attend Henry at Westminster, John was at his wits' end how to help her. He did not dare to suggest that she return with him to the Strand.

Eleyne's sister Margaret came to their rescue. 'Send her to me,' she said in her letter. 'As I suggested before, the air of the Downs will help her regain her strength.'

John showed her the letter and smiled at the sudden animation in her eyes when she looked up at him. 'Can I go?'

'Of course you can go. Spend the summer with your sister, and then we will come back to Fotheringhay together in the autumn.' He did not add out loud the thought which came into his head: And then, Eleyne mine, you must learn to be a real wife.

IX

BRAMBER CASTLE, SUSSEX ❖ July 1232

Bramber lay massive and prosperous in the summer sun as Eleyne rode across the bridges which protected it on its hill in the arm of the River Adur. The great castle, sixty miles from London, dominated the Sussex countryside around it, looking down on the busy quays at which were moored several ships which had come in on the high afternoon tide. In the distance the soft heights of the Downs were lost in the hazy sunshine.

Eleyne threw herself into Margaret's arms. After a hug of welcome, Margaret disentangled herself. Tall, flame-haired like Eleyne, and bubbling with infectious excitement, Margaret dragged Eleyne towards the keep. 'Come and meet my John.'

John de Braose, at twenty-five a year his wife's senior, was waiting at the head of the stairs. 'Lady Huntingdon.' Bowing, he kissed her hand formally, then he straightened and gave her a welcoming smile.

Eleyne's heart almost stopped beating: the eyes, the angle of the head. He was so like his dead cousin, William, she found herself speechless with shock.

'Eleyne?' Margaret took her hand. 'Are you all right? Come on. I want you to meet John's mother, Mattie – Lady de Braose.' She put Eleyne's hand into that of the woman standing behind John. 'Mother, this is my very important little sister!'

Matilda de Braose smiled. 'My dear. I am so pleased you have come to stay with us.' The face, framed by a snow-white wimple, was middle-aged, the eyes dark and vivid in the gentle face. Giving Eleyne a warm hug, she drew her arm through hers. 'Come in and have some refreshments. Then you may sit and gossip with your sister as much as you like!'

'She's nice, your mother-in-law,' Eleyne said shyly as Lady de Braose left them together. 'I thought perhaps she would hate me.'

'Hate you?' Margaret stared at her.

'Your husband's cousin, Isabella, blames me for Sir William's death.' Eleyne stood miserably in front of her sister, pulling off her soft kid riding gloves.

Margaret looked at her thoughtfully. 'Why?'

Eleyne stared in surprise. 'Because it was me who found them in bed together.' She raised her chin defiantly. 'It was me who told papa.'

'I see.' Margaret bit her lip thoughtfully. 'I cried when I heard papa had put mama in prison. She was always so just, so loyal to him. And so in love. It was hard to think of her as guilty of anything so terrible. It was William's fault of course; he must have bewitched her in some way.' She leaned forward and caught Eleyne's hand. 'William de Braose had few friends at Bramber, Eleyne, so you've nothing to worry about here. His father, Reginald, stole John's inheritance. John and his mother have been fighting for years to have it restored. When the family were reinstated after John's grandparents died, the king gave the de Braose lands back to John's uncle, Bishop Giles, because John was still a minor and under the guardianship of Mattie's father. But when the bishop died the king gave them to Reginald instead of John, who was the rightful heir. That was very wrong.' She grimaced. 'Anyway, enough of family talk for now. Come and meet my son, Will.' She gave Eleyne another hug. 'Oh, to think he's nearly nine years old! It makes me feel such an old lady to have a son so old, and my baby sister grown up at last!'

Was she grown up? Eleyne sat that night in the room she had been given with her ladies in the great gatehouse keep, and gazed thoughtfully into the polished metal mirror which Luned had taken out of her casket.

That afternoon, John de Braose had cornered her as she left the great hall after dinner had been cleared away. He had looked at her with a grave smile. 'I had no idea Margaret's little sister would be so beautiful,' he said softly. 'How can Lord Huntingdon bear to part with you?'

She blushed. 'My husband is waiting on the king at Westminster. He won't miss me.'

'No?' His eyes on hers were warmly quizzical. 'Then he is a fool. If you were my wife, I shouldn't let you out of my sight.' His arm around her shoulders was warm and strong. She swallowed nervously, unused to such blatant flirtation, half embarrassed, half excited by his attention.

Like his cousin, Sir William, he was a well-built man, strong, virile, exuding energy. Eleyne had a sudden vision of her mother's lover crouched over her mother's body and she closed her eyes, half dizzy with strange, conflicting emotions.

He felt her hesitate, felt the slight stagger as the memory hit her. 'Are you all right?' He removed his arm from her waist and took her elbow instead. She could feel the warmth and power of his fingers through the silk of her sleeve.

'I'm all right. Where's Margaret?' Her voice sounded strange – breathless.

He smiled. 'She's close behind us with mama. Why, are you afraid to be alone with me?' he teased and again she blushed.

'Of course not . . .'

'I can see I shall have to keep away from you, little sister.' His voice was low and amused. 'You have found your wings as a temptress and intend to practise on me.'

Her protest was cut off as he drew her arm through his and turned to wait for his wife and mother as they emerged from the hall.

Had he really thought her beautiful or had he been teasing her? She angled the mirror this way and that to get a better look at her face. It showed her a pair of large green eyes, fringed with dark lashes and broad upslanted eyebrows; a nose still upturned like a child's but showing already the strong lines to come; the cheekbones emerging from their round baby bloom. Her neck was long; her throat beneath her veil white and narrow; her mouth generous, quirky – quick to laugh and quick to scowl. She frowned and watched the light die from her eyes. Behind her the shadowed room was dark; the distorted reflection did not reach that far; but she saw a flicker of movement in the shadows. Dropping the mirror, she turned. Only Luned was in the chamber, bending low over a coffer, stowing away some of Eleyne's clothes. The corners of the room were empty.

That night as she lay in bed she thought about John de Braose, comparing him sleepily with her husband. This John was brash, confident, effortlessly attractive and flirtatious. He knew exactly how to charm, how to cajole. Her own John was so different. Quiet, serious, but kind. Sterner, but more gentle. And in his own way more handsome.

132

Hugging herself secretly beneath the bedclothes, she closed her eyes and tried to imagine what it would be like to be kissed – properly kissed – by John de Braose, but immediately her eyes flew open and she shuddered as the memory of William and her mother flooded through her. She tried to push it away, pulling herself up against the pillows. As her eyes closed, she vowed that never, never would she do *that* with anyone.

In her dreams someone came to her however. Someone who took her in his arms and kissed her; someone who was a part of her; someone without whom, did she but realise it, she was lonely. His face did not belong to John of Scotland or to John or William de Braose, and in the morning she had forgotten that he was ever there.

X

Eleyne shivered. The small bower at the end of the herb garden had grown cold in spite of the sun. She glanced at the sky, but there were no clouds in the intense blue. In the distance a heat haze danced over the Downs. She dropped her work on the bench beside her and looked around. Margaret and Mattie were busy in the wardrobe going through the monthly accounts with the castle steward and Will was with his tutor, so she had made her sewing the excuse to sit in the sun. There had been no sign of John. Over the past weeks she had grown used to looking for him, flirting with him, testing the strange new excitement which caught at her stomach when he was near, strangely like the emotions she had felt when she had been with Sir William – and yet different: more intense, more frightening. She felt the warmth rise in her cheeks even here, alone in the garden, and firmly she pushed the thought away. He was her sister's husband. She loved her sister and her sister's son, with whom she played frequently, and she adored Mattie de Braose, who was kind and gentle and motherly to the lonely girl. For she *was* lonely and to her surprise it was for the strength and friendship she had grown to rely on from her own husband.

Thoughtfully, she gazed down at the piece of work on her knee. At first she had imagined they were all so content at Bramber, but now, as her stay lengthened, she was beginning to feel the undertones and tensions around her. Mattie, frustrated and bitter for her son; Will, spoiled and indulged, and Margaret and John, outwardly so devoted and yet, inwardly, in some way estranged. Margaret had confided a little to her – their disappointment that there had been no other children after Will; John's dalliance with other women, a comment which had made Eleyne blush and hang her head. Seeing her, Margaret laughed and hugged her. 'Take it as a compliment, Elly. He only shows interest in the most beautiful women.' She paused and took her sister's hand. 'Are you happy with Lord Huntingdon? From what you tell me he seems a kind and sensitive man.' The way she said the words spoke volumes about her own husband. Eleyne wondered if she were wrong about John de Braose. He appeared so attractive, so amusing.

'But Margaret, you do love your John?' Eleyne stared at her sister anxiously.

Margaret laughed. 'Of course I love him,' she said lightly. 'And I'm lucky. Things could be so much worse. I have heard that Lord Huntingdon is often ill, Elly. Is that true?'

Eleyne nodded, unconscious of the wistfulness in her eyes as she thought of her husband. 'It was me who was ill last time, but he's ill a lot, though he was better when I left him.'

Margaret smiled. 'Then let us pray to the sweet Virgin to preserve his health as I pray daily for my husband.' She lowered her eyes. 'I have the king's assurance that, if anything happened to John, which the Blessed Virgin and all the saints forbid,' she shuddered, 'he will not force me to marry someone I don't like. You should do the same, Eleyne. If anything happened to your John you would not want Uncle Henry to choose you another husband against your wishes.'

Eleyne gasped. 'But that would be a terrible thing to do. It would look as if I expected John to die.'

Margaret shrugged. 'Men do die; if not of illness, then in battle, Eleyne, just as women die in childbed. It is God's will. It is best to be prepared.'

Listlessly Eleyne picked up her needle once more and screwed up her eyes against the glare as she began inserting the tiny regular stitches into the soft blue silk. She loved this quiet place; from the vantage point of the hill on which Bramber Castle stood she could see the Downs and though they were nothing like the great mountain of Yr Wyddfa they were better than the flat lands which made up the bulk of her husband's fief. And better still, to the south, beyond the busy quays and the broad tidal sweep of the Adur, lay the sea. She could smell the sharp saltiness of the mud now, as the low water narrowed the busy river to a trickle, leaving the ships and galleons at the wharf stranded until the next tide.

A shadow fell across her sewing. Again a cold breath had touched her skin, but the sky was still cloudless. For a moment she didn't move, then she tucked the needle into her work and set it down again. Her heart had begun to beat uncomfortably fast. There was someone here with her in the empty garden. She closed her eyes against the urgency of the emotions which were invading her: worry, anger, love and fear, yes, real fear.

'What is it? Where are you? Who are you?' She found she had spoken out loud. The answering silence quivered with tension.

Eleyne stared around. Near her the neatly clipped bushes of thyme and hyssop stirred slightly; the pale, fragrant leaves of costmary moved. 'What is it?' she whispered, frightened. 'Who are you?'

The silence was intense; even the shouts and bustle from the bailey beyond the hedge had died away.

'Please –' Eleyne moved away from the bench, her hands shaking. 'Please, what do you want from me?'

Again she was surrounded with silence.

'What is it, Eleyne, my dear? Who are you talking to?' With a rustle of rose-coloured skirts Matilda de Braose swept through the box hedge which sheltered the garden and stared round.

Eleyne looked at her white-faced. 'I'm sorry. I thought . . . I thought there was someone here . . .'

Below them a wagon rolled over the high cobbles and the sound of the heavy wheels reverberated above the shouts of the drivers. The presence in the small garden had gone.

Mattie drew the girl back to the bench and sat down with her. She picked up Eleyne's sewing and looked at it critically. 'You're a good little sempstress, Eleyne. This work is lovely.' Putting it down carefully she took Eleyne's hand. 'Who did you think was here?'

Eleyne shrugged. 'I don't know. It was just a feeling –' She glanced shyly at the older woman, overwhelmed by the need to confide. 'I get them sometimes.'

Mattie smiled, her gentle face framed by the crisp wimple. 'Tell me about them.'

'Sometimes pictures, like dreams . . .' Eleyne looked down at her hands. 'Like Sir William . . . I saw Sir William before . . .' Her voice trailed away.

'You have the Sight?' Mattie made it sound quite ordinary. 'I know many people in Wales have that gift. And you are your father's seventh child, are you not? Margaret told me. That is a special blessing.' She paused. 'And did you see something just now?'

Eleyne shook her head. 'No.'

'What then?' There was no impatience in the question. Mattie sensed Eleyne's loneliness and uncertainty, and impulsively she put her arms around her.

'I just felt there was someone here. Someone trying to speak to me.' Nestling into her shoulder, Eleyne sighed. 'And she is afraid –'

'She?'

'Yes.' Eleyne hesitated. 'Yes, it was a woman.'

Mattie smiled sadly. 'Perhaps you are right. I have sometimes thought . . . felt that there was someone in this garden. Another Matilda.' She stood up. 'My husband's mother. She never liked Bramber much, but this was her favourite place here. She built this garden. I think from time to time she comes to watch over John. He was always her favourite grandchild. She loved him so much.' Her eyes filled with tears as they often did when she thought about her adored mother-in-law, the woman whom her father, the Earl of Clare, had loved so devotedly for most of his life, the woman after whom she was named, the woman whom King John, this child's grandfather, had so viciously murdered.

Eleyne stared at her. 'Matilda? She is the lady . . . my lady who I saw at Hay Castle.'

'You saw her?' Mattie's eyes widened.

Eleyne nodded. 'I thought she liked me then. But not here, not now. She wants me to go.'

'No, of course she doesn't!' Mattie closed her eyes against the superstitious shiver which ran across her shoulders. 'Why should she want you to go? Silly goose, of course she doesn't want you to go.' She paused. 'What did she look like when you saw her at Hay, my dear?'

'She's very tall, with dark red hair and grey-green eyes –'

Mattie caught her breath.

'I used to see her shadow, sometimes strongly, sometimes just fading away.' She looked around the garden. 'But not here, I didn't see her here. I sort of felt her in my head. I don't even know that it was her . . .'

She broke off as young Will ran into the garden.

'I've been looking for you everywhere! I've finished my lessons. Now we can ride. We can, can't we, grandmama? Eleyne said she would ride with me.' He was tall for his eight years, with grey-green eyes and a shock of blond hair above a tanned face and a torn tunic. In only a few weeks, he had confided in Eleyne, he was to leave Bramber to serve as a page in the household of Sir Walter Clifford. He was reluctant to go; and Margaret was reluctant to let him. It was Mattie who had seen the danger; seen how he clung to his mother's skirts, and had persuaded her son to insist.

'Of course you can go, if Eleyne wants to.' Mattie smiled. She stood up and shook out her skirts.

'Oh yes I do!' Her face clearing, Eleyne said eagerly, 'Will has promised to take me to the sea.'

Watching them run together down the steps which led from the garden into the bailey Mattie frowned. The children were quite safe here. They would have an escort, and of course the devoted Cenydd would go with them, so why did she, too, feel a tremor of unease?

'May I ride Invictus one day?' The boy looked longingly at Eleyne on the great stallion as she arranged her skirts around her.

She shook her head. 'I've already told you, he's too big for you.'

'He's too big for you!' the boy retorted, and turned to his own pony, shorter by some half-dozen hands.

'I'm the only person who rides him now,' Eleyne said and bit her lip. It was true. Since Sir William had been hanged no one else, save the groom, had ridden the great horse. She leaned forward in the high saddle and fondled his mane. 'You're mine, aren't you, my love.'

They followed the curve of the broad river south, cut behind the port of Shoreham and rode west along the coast, from time to time riding down on to the beach where, with the tide still low, they could gallop on the firm sands. By the time they returned to Bramber they were exhausted, and the horses walked slowly through the warm evening sun.

In the inner bailey they dismounted. Will came round to Eleyne and patted Invictus's head. 'Please let me ride him, Eleyne. He's tired now. He won't mind.'

'No.' Eleyne stuck out her chin stubbornly. 'No one rides him but me.'

'Oh please,' the boy wheedled. 'Cenydd could lift me up. Just for a minute.'

'No!'

The air had grown cold as the shadow of the gatehouse cut out the westering sun. Somewhere in her head Eleyne could feel it again. The warning; the fear. 'No!' she repeated. 'No, you can't ride him. Not ever. No one rides him but me.'

'What's this?' Margaret and her husband had appeared from the great hall. The two figures stood watching the two children, amused at their bickering.

'She won't let me sit on her horse, papa!' Will whined, his voice heavy with grief. 'I only wanted to sit on him.'

'No one rides him but me.' Eleyne gritted her teeth.

John de Braose came down the steps and put his hand on the stallion's bridle. 'This, I take it, is William's horse?'

'He gave him to me,' Eleyne repeated stubbornly. 'Will is too small. He'd be thrown.'

'I wouldn't, papa. I'm a good rider.' Will, sensing parental support, was pleading, his eyes shining.

'You don't think him good enough?' John raised an eyebrow in Eleyne's direction. As always, his eyes were flattering, challenging, teasing.

'He's good.' She could feel her cheeks colouring. 'But no one rides Invictus but me.'

John looked amused. 'You have a very high opinion of yourself, young lady. You are beautiful and talented without a doubt,' his hand strayed to her cheek and she felt a small shiver of pleasure at his touch,

137

'but I think you will find others can ride him. Here, let me.' Firmly he took the horse's rein from her and beckoned one of his squires. 'Give me a leg up; I'll see how he goes. I can certainly ride any animal Cousin William could.' He smiled grimly. Invictus side-stepped as he reached for the high pommel of the saddle. The horse's ears went flat and he rolled his eyes.

'No, please,' Eleyne whispered, white-faced. 'You mustn't . . . you can't . . .' She could feel the fear all around her now. The air was full of anguish, bitterly cold and sharp; brittle, clear and yet shimmering as though reflected in water. As the squire humped John into the saddle, the horse let out a shriek of anger and bucked. 'Brute!' John's smile vanished and he dug his feet deep into the stirrup cups and jerked on the reins. Below the swirl of his long cloak Eleyne saw the huge rowels of his spurs. 'I'll tell you one thing: he's not safe for any child to ride –' He broke off as the horse, surprised and infuriated by the heavy hand on the savage bit, ran backwards for several steps and then reared up, pawing the air. John clung to the saddle, then with a cry he slipped sideways and crashed to the stone cobbles beneath the massive hooves.

No one moved. John lay absolutely still. Beneath his head a red stain spread slowly over the cobbles.

'John?' Margaret let out a small cry of disbelief, then flung herself towards her husband's still, crumpled body. 'John? *John!*'

Behind her the stallion stood trembling, his eyes wild as he pawed the ground. Eleyne ran to him. She soothed his neck gently, but her eyes were on her brother-in-law's inert body.

Margaret straightened. Still on her knees, her hands on her husband's cloak, her face was distorted with grief and shock.

'He's dead,' she whispered. 'He's DEAD!'

CHAPTER SIX

I

RHOSYR, ANGLESEY ❖ August 1232

Rhonwen had seen the messengers ride in from the east and had recognised with excited relief the insignia of the Earl of Huntingdon on the surcoats of the escort. Breathlessly she waited outside the hall of the palace, her eyes fixed on the doorway. There had to be a letter for her this time. Eleyne would not, could not have forgotten her.

From within she could hear a low murmur of voices and once a higher, louder shout of laughter, like a wave breaking on the shore.

Princess Joan was inside with her ladies. Two days before, Prince Llywelyn had taken the boat with Dafydd to Caernarfon. They had left the women behind.

Rhonwen hesitated. Princess Joan's displeasure and dislike were not things she relished; and the Princess of Aberffraw and Lady of Snowdon as she now liked to be called, following her husband's example, had made it clear that these were all she could expect. The day she had returned to Aber, Rhonwen had been summoned to the princess in the chamber where Rhonwen had last seen her, peering over Eleyne's head, three years before.

'So, you have been dismissed by Lord Huntingdon.' Joan's eyes were hard.

'No, highness.' Rhonwen managed to keep her voice meek. 'Lord Huntingdon has given me leave to return home for a visit.'

'A visit,' Joan repeated. 'No, you are mistaken if you think you are to go back. Lord Huntingdon's letter is quite clear. He does not wish you to attend his wife again. Ever.' She paused. 'When do you intend to visit your family, Lady Rhonwen?' Her voice was silky.

'As you know, highness, I have no family now.' Rhonwen's voice, though low, was steady. Cenydd was all the family she had who would acknowledge her and he was with Eleyne.

'So, if I send you away from here, you will have nowhere to go?'

'I shall write to Eleyne, highness. She will persuade Lord Huntingdon to take me back.' Rhonwen managed a note of defiance.

'I am sure she will.' The smile on Joan's face belied her words.

139

'But I'm sure there will be no need for that. You may serve me, Lady Rhonwen, as long as – ' her eyes narrowed – 'there is no suspicion of you ever, ever supporting my husband's bastard and his cause. Is that clear?'

'Quite clear, highness.' Rhonwen looked away from the hard eyes.

'She doesn't know!' It was Isabella who cornered her later. 'The princess doesn't know who betrayed her to her husband.'

Rhonwen stepped back in front of the small whirlwind who had entered the bower and slammed the door behind her. The two of them were alone.

'You were with Eleyne! You could have stopped her! You could have saved my father!'

'I could have done nothing!' Rhonwen's temper flared. 'If I hadn't found them, others would have. They were careless, flagrant; the whole court had seen them.'

'That is not true! She seduced my father . . .'

'No, lady, no.' Rhonwen felt sudden pity for this woman who was no more than a child, only a year older than her own Eleyne. 'Don't be under any illusion. They seduced each other. They could no more have stayed apart than could two moths from a candle. If Eleyne had said nothing, others would have spoken. There were too many whispers already. But why talk of it now? The past cannot be undone. Your father is dead, God rest his unhappy soul, and Llywelyn has forgiven his wife. Let it rest, lady.' She turned and picked up an armful of clean linen to return to the lavender-scented coffer.

'I'll never let it rest!' Isabella's eyes were blazing. 'I loved my father and one day I'll clear his name. I'll prove she seduced him. And I'll prove you and Eleyne trapped him deliberately – '

'Lady Isabella – '

'No, it's true. Perhaps the princess was part of it. Perhaps she did it just to ensnare and betray him. After all,' her voice dropped to a hiss, 'what happened to her? Two years in comfortable exile then she is back at Llywelyn's side as though nothing had happened. Dafydd says his father trusts her totally. He is using her as his adviser and negotiator as though nothing had happened. He has forced Ednyfed Fychen to accept her in her old role as ambassador. He is allowing her to negotiate with her brother the king as though nothing had happened. And my father is dead!' The last sentence came out as an anguished sob.

Rhonwen was silent. For a brief moment she had glimpsed the lonely and frightened child inside the brash young woman, and remembered the urchin who, bare-legged, had climbed the scaffolding at Hay with Eleyne. Then the child was gone. Isabella straightened her shoulders.

140

'Did Eleyne send you away?'

'No.' Rhonwen could not keep the pain from her voice.

'But her husband did. And Princess Joan doesn't want you. And neither do I.' She paused. 'I can have you dismissed if I want. I can have you sent into the mountains to starve.' She smiled brightly. 'Remember that, Lady Rhonwen, if I ever ask you to do anything for me.' Fumbling with the door handle, she left the room.

After that Rhonwen did her best to remain out of sight, choosing to eat and sleep with some of Princess Joan's less important ladies rather than run the risk of drawing attention to herself. And she had written. Several times she had written, enclosing her letter with those from Llywelyn to Lord Chester and Lord Huntingdon, and once she had paid for a messenger of her own from her meagre savings, directing him straight to Bramber and bidding him put the letter into Eleyne's own hands. None of the letters had received an answer.

Disconsolately she followed the court from Aber to Llanfaes, to Cemaes in the far north of Anglesey, then down to Caernarfon and back to Aber. And now they had come over the water again to Rhosyr on the edge of the drifting sands.

Twice she had seen Einion and both times he had asked after Eleyne. Her news had not pleased him. Shaking his head he had sighed. 'She needs me. Her gift will destroy her. This man, her husband, does he understand her?'

Rhonwen shrugged. 'He is kind to her,' she admitted reluctantly. 'He has not forced her. He is a good Christian.' She said the last under her breath.

'She is sworn to the goddess, Lady Rhonwen. Nothing and no one can change that. And nothing can change her destiny. When the time is right, she will return to us.'

Standing in the carved, ornate doorway to the hall, Rhonwen stared across the narrow strip of sea towards the wooded mainland. If there were a letter for her, would Joan tell her or would she throw it upon the fire as Lord Huntingdon presumably disposed of those she wrote to Eleyne?

'Are you waiting for someone or merely eavesdropping as usual, Lady Rhonwen?' Isabella's light voice made her jump guiltily. Beyond her a gull, flying low over the silver water, let out a long yelping cry.

Her slim body clothed in madder silks, her black hair covered in a net of silk sewn with pearls, Isabella looked a picture of elegance.

Rhonwen forced herself to smile. 'I was waiting to see if the messenger had brought me any letters —'

'Then why wait here? Why not come in and ask?' Isabella flounced past her and, pushing the door wide, hurried up the shadowed aisle of the hall to drop a pretty curtsey before her mother-in-law.

'The Lady Rhonwen is anxious to know if there is any news of Eleyne,' she announced.

Following her slowly, Rhonwen too curtseyed before the princess. Her heart was beating painfully.

Joan looked up and frowned. 'Indeed there is.' Her voice was thin and strained as she stood up with a rustle of silks and put her arm around Isabella's shoulder. 'My dear, I am afraid I have some terrible, terrible news.' Rhonwen went cold. Had something happened to Eleyne? Joan's hands, she noticed, were shaking. 'I have a letter from Bramber, from Lady Matilda de Braose. It is about your cousin, John. He has been killed. He was thrown by that wretched horse, the horse –' Her voice broke and the tears began to run down her cheeks. 'The horse your father gave to Eleyne!'

II

BRAMBER CASTLE

The chapel had been filled to overflowing for the requiem mass and the congregation had spilled out on to the hillside around the small square building with its squat Norman tower, built by the first William de Braose two hundred years before outside the walls of his castle.

Eleyne, swathed in black mourning veil like her sister and John's mother, had sobbed uncontrollably throughout the service.

It was my fault. She repeated the words again and again. *It was my fault. I could have stopped it. I could have seen what was going to happen.*

But she hadn't seen it and when the lady in the shadows had tried to warn her, she had not understood.

'Oh, my dear.' Mattie had taken her into her arms. 'You mustn't blame yourself, you mustn't. You did everything you could. You begged him not to ride the horse.'

It was Mattie who had countermanded Margaret's hysterical command that the stallion be destroyed. 'It could have happened at any time. John was a careless rider. He was too confident, too uncaring. He hurt the creature. Several people told me so.'

'She tried to warn me. She tried to tell me to go away.' Clinging to Mattie, Eleyne turned a tear-stained face to her. 'She knew!'

'So it seems.' Mattie held her close. 'My dear, we cannot change what is to be. We have to accept God's will. It is He who decides these things, not us. One thing at least is sure. John is with his beloved grandmama now. I have seen so much death, my dear, so much sorrow, so much suffering in my life. There has to be a reason for it. God must have a reason.' She steadied her voice with difficulty. 'At least John did not suffer. He died instantly.'

She did not speak out loud the cry in her heart. Why? Why when he was young and strong and healthy? Why could he not have outlived her? She, who had borne so many deaths, so many sorrows. Could not God have spared this one more? Why had he sent Eleyne, grandchild of King John, to take away her son, as the child's grandfather had taken away her husband?

Eleyne stood up restlessly and walked over to the window. For a long time she stood, staring into the courtyard below. 'Thank you for saving Invictus,' she said hesitantly.

'There was nothing to be served by slaughtering the animal.' Mattie swiftly regained control of herself.

'What will Margaret do now?' Her sister had refused to see Eleyne since the accident. Only Mattie and young Will, tearful and bewildered by the death of his father before his eyes, and not a little guilty that his noisy pleas to ride Invictus could have had such a dreadful outcome, had been allowed near the inconsolable widow.

'She will stay here with me and Will. She has the king's assurance that she will not be forced to remarry against her wishes.' Not for the first time, Mattie found herself wondering if Margaret too, in this family of the royal line of Wales, had a touch of the second sight. Why else would she have insisted on such an assurance from the king only months before the accident which had left her a widow?

III

FOTHERINGHAY CASTLE ❖ October 1232

Recovering from his latest bout of fever, John lay in his sickbed looking pale and wan. Beside him his physician was preparing to let more blood. Eleyne eyed the man's knives with a shudder. 'Are you feeling better, my lord?' Since their arrival at Fotheringhay after two months in London, her husband had lost his new-found robustness and sunk back into ill health. More and more, Eleyne found herself taking on the most onerous of his duties, and to her surprise found she was beginning to enjoy them. Young and inexperienced though she was, she found that the household, well trained and efficient, obeyed her and respected her decisions. That gave her a confidence which in turn inspired confidence.

'I've had a letter from my uncle.' John coughed slightly. 'He too is ill, it seems. He has not been well since his return from France. He wants to see us at Chester.'

Eleyne felt a sharp lift of her spirits. 'Can we go?'

'As soon as I am well enough we must.' He scowled as the physician laid a towel on the bed and sat down next to him. The opening of the vein was quick and easy, the gush of blood into the silver basin controlled. Eleyne, as always when she witnessed this sight, had to hide her horror. The doctors might insist that her husband's excess of blood caused the imbalance in the humours of his body and led to his frequent fevers and his chronic cough, but she could not believe that draining his blood until he was weak and pale would help him.

When it was done, and the wound sealed, she took the physician's place at his bedside. 'Perhaps we could visit Aber? Rhonwen could help you, I know she could,' she said cautiously.

John looked at her affectionately. Again she had grown while she had been away from him. She was turning into a beauty, this wife of his.

'She is a healer,' she went on reproachfully into the silence which followed her suggestion.

'I will think about it.' John frowned, easing his aching body on the bed. 'Isabel and Robert are coming in the next few days, on their way to Scotland from Essex.' He changed the subject adroitly. 'I had a letter from her this morning. If I am not well enough, you must entertain them for me. Will you tell the household to prepare?'

She nodded calmly, no longer thrown into a panic at the thought of having to supervise such a visit on her own with the extra work it entailed for everyone in the castle, but looking forward to seeing her sister-in-law and nephew again, and to the entertainment and music and laughter in the evenings and the hunting during the day, which she adored.

The night before the Bruces were due to arrive she toured the castle, checking that all was prepared. She was unaware of the admiration her husband's servants had for her as, quietly competent, she walked around the buildings, inspecting every detail, serenely assuming that things would run smoothly for John even if she weren't there. They knew better. They knew that without the firm hand of their young countess the household would grow lazy and slipshod and even the chatelaine would find it hard to keep everything running.

Candle in hand, she hesitated near the chapel. There was no need to go in, yet something compelled her to push open the door. The only light came from the lamp in the sanctuary. She walked towards the altar. She was there, the woman who haunted Fotheringhay: a darker shadow in the blackness, her unhappiness tangible. With a sudden flash of insight, Eleyne knew that she and this woman were linked by blood. She frowned, half holding out her hand, but the shadow had gone. The chapel was empty.

She completed her tour of the castle and returned to the lord's chamber where John, dressed in a loose tunic and swathed in a warm woollen mantle, lay propped on the bed. Outside the first autumnal gales were tearing the leaves from the trees, screaming in the castle chimneys, sending icy draughts through the building.

A servant was mulling some wine at the hearth, kneeling among the ashes.

'Is all prepared?' John looked up as Eleyne, wrapped in a warm cloak lined with squirrel furs, closed the door behind her and crossed the room to his bed.

She nodded, trying to shake off the sombre mood her experience in the chapel had induced. 'The cooks have been baking all day for the feast. I think Isabel will be well pleased with her welcome.' She kicked off her shoes and pulled herself up on to the bed, tucking her feet under her skirts. 'It's a wild night. I hope the weather improves before tomorrow or they won't come.'

'They'll come.' John leaned back and surveyed his wife fondly. Her face had lost its childish curves in the last few months; he could see the high cheekbones now, the soft breadth of her brow beneath the veil which covered her hair. His eye strayed from her slim white throat to the bodice of her gown where, in the flaring light of the branch of candles at the end of the bed, he saw the swell of her breasts all but hidden by the cloak. He felt a strange stirring inside him and, half shocked at his reaction, suppressed it sternly. She was still a child. But no. He counted surreptitiously on his fingers. She was fourteen years old. She was a woman.

'Would you like some wine?' She was leaning towards him, her hand lightly on his arm. He could smell the soft sweetness of her skin.

He opened his eyes and nodded and she beckoned the watching servant with the wine. 'If you are tired, I'll leave you to sleep.' Briskly and with adult composure, she dismissed his attendants and they sat alone, their hands cupped around the goblets of hot spiced wine.

'Not yet.' He leaned forward and put a finger to her cheek. 'Take off your veil, Eleyne. Let me see your hair.' He never saw her except when she was formally dressed, her hair hidden by the veils and caps she wore. No longer did she ride so wildly that her hair fell loose, or if she did he was not there to see it.

She smiled, and put the goblet down. Then she unpinned the silk veil and let it slip from her braids.

'Unfasten your hair.' He sat forward, conscious of a strange tension between them.

Her eyes on his, she slowly unpinned her hair and with lazy fingers began to unplait it, letting it ripple past her shoulders. Her hair loose, she sat watching him, unaware of the slight challenge in her eyes. He put out his hand and caught a handful of it, pulling it gently towards him. 'My lovely Eleyne,' he murmured. He broke off at the sound of a horn, eerily distant on the wind. Across the room a log slipped and fell

145

from the firedogs into the hearth, sending up a shower of sparks. Eleyne jerked away from him, the mood of the moment broken.

'Eleyne, come here.' There was a note of command in his voice she had never heard before, but she was distracted, slipping away from him, captured by the pull of the fire.

'In a moment, my lord. There is something I must do.' She slid out of his reach, and he watched helplessly as she ran to the fireplace and threw on another log. Her hair shone like copper in the light of the flames as it swung forward in a curtain hiding her face.

'Eleyne!'

'There is someone coming, my lord. You heard the watchman. There are messengers.' She was staring down unblinkingly into the flames.

'Messengers. How do you know?' A shiver ran down his back as the silence lengthened.

'It's your uncle . . .' she whispered.

He strained to hear her over the sound of the wind.

'Your uncle is dead!'

John sat bolt upright and swung his legs over the side of the bed. 'Are you sure?'

The violence of his words made her jump. 'I think so . . . I don't know . . .' Dragged from her reverie, she was confused and horrified that she had betrayed herself by telling him what she saw. But he did not reprimand her; he seemed to accept her premonition.

'We'll soon know.' He stood up, clutching his cloak around his shoulders, and walked to the chair by the fireplace. When the knock came, he was sitting upright gazing fixedly across the room. Eleyne sat opposite him, still demurely wrapped in her mantle.

Imperceptibly John relaxed his shoulders against the hard, carved wood as the messenger formally relayed the news. Ranulf de Blunde-vill, Earl of Chester, had died at the royal palace at Wallingford on the Thames on the twenty-sixth of October.

John's face was grey with exhaustion. 'So,' he said slowly, 'at last it has happened.'

Eleyne stared at him, astonished by the feverish triumph in his eyes. 'You're glad he is dead?'

He shook his head in irritation. 'Of course not! I shall order masses for the repose of his soul, but now – now I am Earl of Chester!'

Eleyne looked down at her hands. John had always been so passive; so gentle and accepting. The naked ambition flaring in his eyes frightened her. It excited her too.

She stole another look at him. It was his turn to stare into the fire, but his gaze was not dreamy. It was eager and full of determination.

IV
November 1232

In less than a month John was well enough to ride with Eleyne to the castle at Northampton. There, on the twenty-first of November, King Henry III confirmed him in his earldom.

Two days later a messenger found Eleyne as she was sitting on the dais in the crowded hall, watching the antics of some travelling acrobats who were putting on their show for the king. As they tumbled in the deep floor covering of sweet woodruff and hay, she turned to find a man bowing before her. She frowned, not immediately recognising the emblem on his shoulder.

'I have a letter for you, my lady, from Lady Clifford.' The man bowed.

Eleyne frowned. 'Lady Clifford?' She beckoned Luned forward to give the man a farthing. 'Do I know Lady Clifford?'

Hearing her comment, the king, who was sitting close to her, turned. 'A surprise for you, Lady Chester.' He gave her her new title with humorous formality. 'You know her well. Away, man.' He jerked his thumb at the messenger. 'It seems to be a family trait, changing your name suddenly.' He chuckled and turned back to the show.

With a puzzled glance at him, Eleyne broke the seal and began to read the letter, oblivious of the cheers around her as the entertainers reached the climax of their routine.

Dear Sister, I know you will be surprised to read this. Walter Clifford and I were married yesterday and today we leave for his lands in the march. We have known one another for many years; Walter's wife died two years ago, so when John was killed he asked me to be his. How strange that I shall return to live so near to Hay which John always wanted to reclaim as his own. Please understand that I am very happy.

Your loving sister,
Margaret

At the end of the letter Margaret had written a postscript: *Remember my advice. Ask Uncle Henry for his assurance that, should your husband die, you too can marry the man of your choice. M.*

Eleyne looked up. The king's eyes were on her face. 'So. The grieving widow has told you her news?'

Eleyne bit her lip. 'I didn't know, I never guessed.'

Henry smiled. 'She has been in love with Walter Clifford for three years at least, I hear. De Braose's death must have been a blessing to her –'

'No!' Eleyne couldn't believe it. 'She loved John. And what of Will? Who will take care of Will?'

147

'The boy?' The king sat back in his chair and stretched out his legs. 'I have yet to decide who has the wardship of him. But in the meantime his grandmother is to have his care at Bramber. His mother is too taken up with her new husband to want a child of the old . . .'

Eleyne had thought Margaret and John so in love; she had believed every bit of her sister's anguished mourning, and yet only four months later she was remarried. Now she understood Margaret's insistence that she be allowed to marry a man of her choice; the man had already been chosen!

John was waiting for her in their chamber, sitting in a chair by the fire, huddled in fur wraps. His hands were cupped around some pungent steaming brew. Eleyne stopped in the doorway and looked at him for a moment before she went into the room. He was pale again, and weakened by their ride through the cold November winds – too weak to stay up for supper and the entertainment in the great hall. Eleyne felt her heart sink. When she had seen that he and she were to share a chamber, sleeping together in the great curtained bed, she had felt a frisson of excitement. Those few moments at Fotheringhay when he had looked at her and touched her as if he were aware that the child was at last a woman had frightened her and yet exhilarated her. She was excited by a longing within her body, a longing which had not been assuaged. In the bustle of the next weeks he had not tried to see her alone again, but now that they were here, and his title confirmed, she had hoped that he would once more have time for her.

'How are you feeling, my lord?' She approached him and laid a timid hand on his arm.

He leaned back in the chair and smiled at her. 'Much rested, I'm glad to say. How did you leave the king?'

She smiled. 'In good humour. He hopes you will feel better tomorrow.'

'I'm better now.' He was watching her closely. 'Becoming Earl of Chester seems to have done me nothing but good.' There was no mistaking the message in his eyes as he pulled her towards him and put his arm around her waist. 'Here, fill up my goblet and have some yourself. The spiced wine is excellent.' With a gesture, he dismissed the attendants who hovered behind him. 'Now, come here.' He caught her hand and pulled her on to his knee. 'Do you have a kiss for your husband, Eleyne?'

His kiss was firm and light and tasted of cinnamon and mace and ginger. Closing her eyes, she returned it shyly, astonished at the excitement which paralysed her lungs and sent prickles of anticipation up and down her spine. Strangely comfortable perching on his knees, she relaxed into his arms and nuzzled his neck fondly as he began to unfasten her braids, letting her hair fall loose. Then he was opening the neck of her gown, his fingers straying inside, seeking her breasts. Eleyne caught her breath and, misunderstanding, he frowned. 'It is not too soon.' His words were lost in her hair. 'You are a woman now . . .'

'I know, I know.' Shyly she kissed his cheek then, unable to stop herself, his throat, and even his chest beneath the cool linen of his tunic, feeling her excitement rise with his. At last the moment had come; at last he was going to make her his. She gasped as his fingers tightened over her breast and eagerly she began to pull at the fastening on his tunic.

He paused as his wandering fingers dislodged the letter she had tucked into her bodice. 'What's this?' His voice was teasing. 'A love letter from one of your admirers?'

Eleyne smiled. 'Of course, my lord, what else?' she said coquettishly. 'My beauty has not gone unnoticed, you know.'

He laughed, holding the letter up between finger and thumb. 'What do I do if my wife receives love letters? Do I beat her? Do I challenge the writer to single combat? Or do I admire him for his good taste and condone his *billets doux* and poems?'

She was giggling now, her fingers gently playing with the curls of his hair. 'It's from my sister, Margaret,' she whispered.

'A likely tale.' Shifting her more comfortably into the crook of his arm, he began to unfold the letter.

'It is! She has remarried and goes back to live in the Welsh march.' Her eyes strayed to the looped flamboyant writing on her sister's letter, the shadows of the candelabra dancing on the crackling parchment. Suddenly, through the mists of contentment, Eleyne remembered her sister's postscript. She tensed. 'Please. May I have it?' She put out her hand. But he held it out of her reach, bringing it into the light of the candles. 'Surely you have no secrets from your husband.' He was reading, a scowl between his eyes. There was a long silence when he had finished.

Then: 'I'm sorry. I have a cramp.' He tipped her from his lap without ceremony and stood up. Dropping the letter on to the chair, he walked over to the fire, and stood looking down into the flames. 'So you expect me to die soon and leave you free to marry the man of your choice.'

'No!' She ran to him and put her hand on his arm. 'No, it's not like that. Margaret said —'

'Margaret!' He spun to face her, throwing off her hand. 'Margaret has some excellent advice for her little sister which you obviously discussed together — was it before John de Braose died or after? Perhaps it was a plan you both hatched to have him ride that accursed horse, to free your sister to marry her lover. Was that it?' His face was white with anger. 'Holy Virgin, but I've been mistaken in my estimation of you, my lady! Was I to ride it too? Was that the plan? It would be so

149

much easier, wouldn't it, for me to fall, sick and feeble as I am! Or perhaps you had decided not to bother with helping my demise along. After all, I'm likely to die soon anyway!' His face was hard and angry, his lips white as he glared at her.

'No.' Eleyne was beside herself with anguish. 'No, it wasn't like that. You must believe me, please.' He had pushed past her, making for the door. 'Please listen, let me explain –'

'No explanations are needed.' For a fraction of a second she saw the devastation in his eyes. 'Do you have a lover, Eleyne? Is that it? Or is there someone you want to marry? Someone you prefer to me?' He looked away. 'Suffice to say, my dear, that in future I shall be on my guard.'

She stared at the door for a long time after he had slammed it shut, then she turned miserably towards the bed she had hoped to be sharing with him and threw herself on to his pillow, kneading her fingers deep into the silk-covered down.

V

CEMAES, ANGLESEY ❖ November 1232

Isabella was walking in the gardens of the *llys*, ignoring the wet, straggling grasses which caught at the hem of her gown. She lifted her face to the unseasonably warm sun and closed her eyes, feeling gratefully the gentle heat on her skin. A gaggle of ladies followed, the garden noisy with their chatter and laughter, but she was paying them no attention. The pain had returned: a low, nagging ache in her back, coupled with a strange tiredness which frightened her. She stopped, conscious of how wet her shoes were. Behind her the ladies stopped too, their conversation unabated.

Princess Joan was resting indoors. She often rested now and, from time to time, her hand went unobtrusively to her stomach, as if she too had a pain. Isabella wasn't interested. All she cared about was her coming child. Was it all going to be this unpleasant? The nausea; the inability to keep any food down, save a warm milk pap and gentle syllabubs; the aching and the tiredness; the strange tenderness of her skin which made her hate it when Dafydd touched her, as he still did sometimes when he was there, laughing off her pleas that he leave her alone in her pregnancy. The women laughed too while they clucked around her; they cosseted her and gave her the food she asked for and held the basin when she vomited, but they still laughed and nodded their heads and said it was the same for everyone; it would pass; soon she would be better. She took a deep breath, trying to master the pain in her back, wishing she had not decided on this walk and had elected to retire to her bedchamber.

From her seat on the wall Rhonwen watched her sourly. Isabella was pasty-faced, bloated from the coming baby, though it was early yet for that; more likely it was her constant nibbling at sweetmeats. The girl looked unhealthy and discontented. Rhonwen hid a smile. For the first months of the marriage Dafydd had stayed close to his bride, petting her, chucking her under the chin, fondling her before the world, clearly delighted with her charms; but now, bored with her company perhaps or sated with bedding her, his duty done as her pregnancy had become obvious, he had left with his father for Caernarfon and Isabella had been left alone with the womenfolk. Rhonwen's eyes narrowed. She had not forgiven Isabella that letter to Eleyne. She saw Isabella stop and put her hand to her back, discomfort plain on her face. Her ladies, too preoccupied with their chatter to notice their mistress's distress, did not see as she leaned against the wall of the small windswept bower and tried to catch her breath.

Rhonwen stood up and approached her cautiously, half expecting to be dismissed, but Isabella did not seem to have noticed her.

'Are you unwell, highness?' Rhonwen saw the superstitious fear in Isabella's eyes as she noticed her. So she had heard it too, the story that Einion and Rhonwen served the old gods. The man who had spread the tale had died, his boat caught in a squall of wind off Pen y Gogarth, and Llywelyn, shocked, had firmly suppressed the rumour, but the gossip had stuck fast. Rhonwen and Einion had known it would and, each for their own reason, it had pleased them both.

'My back hurts.' Isabella's voice was peevish.

'The child is lying awkwardly,' Rhonwen said. 'If you wish I can give you a salve which can be rubbed on your back to ease the ache. Princess Joan used such a mixture when she carried her children and it helped her greatly.' She smiled at Isabella's ladies who had paused some feet away. 'One of your damsels can rub it in for you, or I will if you wish it.'

'You did it for Princess Joan?' Isabella pulled her cloak around her, emphasising her prominent stomach.

'I did indeed.' It wasn't a lie. Once, when Joan's handmaids had been busy elsewhere, Rhonwen had indeed stroked the scented ointment into the princess's taut, agonised back only days before Eleyne was born.

'Then you do it. They won't know how.' With a dismissive gesture to her ladies, Isabella turned towards the palace. 'Fetch it now. I ache so much I can't stand it another minute!'

'Spoilt little madam!' Rhonwen's muttered comment was lost on the retreating back as Isabella, followed by her attendants, swept out of sight.

She had a pot of salve in her coffer. For a moment as she rummaged

151

beneath her belongings, she debated whether to add some irritant to the mixture, pounding it into the soft sweet-smelling salve, but she thought better of it. If she was to help Eleyne, she had to win the trust of this plump spoiled princess who had once been Eleyne's friend.

Assisted by her attendants Isabella had removed her gown and kirtle and been wrapped in a silk and velvet bed robe. She was sitting on the great bed eating sugared violets and marchpane flowers rolled in cinnamon when Rhonwen arrived with her jar of precious ointment. When her plump white body was stretched out at last on the bedcovers, discreetly covered by rugs, Rhonwen exposed the girl's lower back and rounded bottom. She resisted the urge to give her patient a sharp slap on the backside and instead dug her hand deep into the jar of salve.

Isabella groaned with pleasure as Rhonwen's strong hands began to knead her cramped muscles.

'You're too tense, child,' Rhonwen murmured. 'Relax. Try to sleep while I work. Then the baby will lie more easily.'

'Why did Eleyne send you away?' Her head cradled on her arms, Isabella did not see the tightening of Rhonwen's face.

'She didn't send me. It was him – Lord Huntingdon. Now they'll be going to Chester, they'll summon me back.'

'Do you really believe that?' The muffled voice was just sufficiently short of incredulity not to be insolent.

'Yes, I believe it.' Rhonwen scooped more salve into her cupped fingers. Looking down at it, she felt the emptiness threatening to rise again and she fought it down. There had to be a way of going back, and if there wasn't then she had to see that Eleyne came back to her. And this spoiled girl was the key.

'No.' Isabella looked mutinously at the floor. 'I don't want her here. She killed my father!'

'No, princess. Your father killed himself.' Rhonwen kept her voice even. 'It is cruel to blame Eleyne, who loved you like a sister. Please, for her sake. Speak to your husband. Surely, now she is Countess of Chester, Prince Llywelyn would want to keep a dialogue between her husband and Gwynedd. And Dafydd *bach* can persuade him. He would do anything if you asked him to.'

Isabella was pouting. 'I haven't even seen Dafydd for two weeks.' It was a sore point; even when he had visited Rhosyr, on the other side of the island a few days before, he had sent no message; the ladies in the palace near the harbour at Cemaes were feeling ignored.

'It would give you an excuse to bring him to your side, princess.' Rhonwen's voice was low and confidential. 'And impress him with your grasp of the political scene. Tell him you have heard Lord and Lady Chester have taken up residence at Chester Castle and you think it would be a tactful moment for the Prince of Aberffraw to write to his son-in-law and invite him to Aber. Tell him that it will enhance his position with his father and with the King of England if he can repair this rift.'

ABER ❖ December 1232

The early winter was mild. The gales blew themselves out and late roses budded and came to bruised, torn flower. The roads remained in good condition, and so, at last, Eleyne came to Aber in the second week of December.

The last month had been bitterly unhappy. John had withdrawn from her completely. Since their quarrel over Margaret's letter he had remained angry and cold, refusing to believe her tearful insistence that she had not intended to ask the king about remarriage. Perversely, his health had improved. He had put on weight and he rode and hunted regularly now, a more robust colour animating his face, but he had made no further attempt to touch her. Their reading too had stopped. He was too busy, he said, with the administration of the additional huge earldom of Chester.

When the prince's letter had come, asking him and his wife to Aber for Yule, John had written back excusing himself, but Eleyne could go and welcome. She was ecstatic when he told her. She could go home; she could see Rhonwen; she could see her father. She closed off John's rejection in one corner of her mind and concentrated on preparing for the journey to the place she still thought of as home. She did not think about her mother or Einion at all. Nothing must be allowed to spoil her return.

John spoke to her once, on the eve of her departure, at her request.

'You are packed and ready?' He looked up from his desk without a smile.

She nodded. 'We leave at first light, my lord.'

'Good. Carry my greetings to your father and mother.'

'When shall I come back, my lord?' The excitement she felt at returning home could not fill the strange gap his withdrawal had left. She longed to run to him, to touch him, to feel him hold her protectively in his arms.

'I will summon you back when I want you, Eleyne. If I want you,' he said slowly. He laid down his pen. 'Do not return until you have heard from me. I'm not sure I still want you for a wife. I'm not sure at all. It is not too late to annul this marriage. It is not consummated in the eyes of God.' He turned back to his letters and did not look up

153

again. She turned slowly, fighting her tears, and walked from the room.

VII

Rhonwen was waiting for her in a guest chamber at Aber. Never again would the beloved nursery wing in the *ty hir* be hers. It was already being refurbished for Isabella's coming child.

'*Cariad!* but look at you! how you've grown.' For a moment neither of them moved, then Eleyne flew across the room and into the other woman's arms.

'Of course I've grown, Rhonwen. I'm grown up now!'

'You are indeed! A countess twice over, with a train of followers bigger than your father's!' Rhonwen held her away for a moment surveying her face. If he had taken Eleyne and made her his, she would know. She searched the girl's eyes. There was something there, but not what she sought. Of that there was no sign. 'You've been unhappy, *cariad*. I can see it in your eyes; see it in the thinness of you. What's wrong?'

'Nothing's wrong.' Eleyne turned from the sharp scrutiny. 'I'm tired, that's all. There is always so much to do at Chester, so many people to talk to.' The dowager had helped, staying on at the castle at Eleyne's frantic entreaty, but even so she had found herself busy at all hours, even when it was only the business of being entertained. Without John's support it had been a nightmare of strain and tension. 'My father, Rhonwen. When will I see him?'

'Soon, *cariad*.' Isabella had done her part; Dafydd had persuaded Llywelyn to issue the invitation, but that was as far as it had gone. 'I have no wish to see your sister,' he had said to his son firmly, and the day before Eleyne's arrival he had left Aber with a large contingent of followers to ride south.

Joan was there however, and only an hour after Eleyne's arrival she summoned her youngest daughter to her solar. Dry-mouthed, Eleyne stood before her, sharply conscious that she was now taller than her mother and far more richly dressed, for Joan was wearing a black gown and cloak – much to her husband's irritation, her habitual dress since her return from exile. But her eyes were the same, fiercely critical, as she looked her daughter up and down.

'So. You have become a beauty.'

Taken aback, Eleyne blushed. She still felt antagonistic towards her mother, but her fear had gone – and her respect. But for this woman and her betrayal of her husband, Aber would still be her home and she would still be sure of her father's love. Her disappointment at not finding him at Aber had been intense.

'Why have you come?' The directness of Joan's question shocked her.

'My father invited us,' Eleyne replied. She raised her head defiantly. 'And I wanted to come. I have missed you all.'

'Indeed?' Her mother's voice was dry. 'But your husband has not come with you.'

'He is too busy.' Eleyne answered too quickly.

'And you are not too busy,' her mother echoed quietly. 'You are not breeding yet, I see.' Her eye skimmed critically down Eleyne's slim figure. 'Your friend Isabella is six months gone.'

'Is she?' Eleyne turned away, but not quickly enough to hide her unhappiness from her mother's sharp eyes. Joan's expression softened slightly. 'You and your husband are content, Eleyne?'

'Yes, mama.'

'And he has made you his wife?' She paused. 'You do know what I mean?'

There was only the slightest hesitation, but it was enough. Joan frowned. Unexpectedly, and for the first time in the child's life, she felt a wave of tenderness for this wayward, fey daughter of hers. Her own unhappiness and loneliness over the last three years had made her more thoughtful, more understanding. Her attitude to other people had, she realised, changed.

She had been dreading seeing Eleyne again, well aware that it was Eleyne who had seen her that fearful, fateful night, but now, with her daughter sitting on the stool near her, gazing unhappily into the fire, she could feel her loneliness and misery as a tangible cloak around her. She responded to it with an unlooked-for wave of sympathy.

'Is it his illness?' she asked, her voice more gentle.

Eleyne shrugged. 'At first he said I was too young; then he was ill. Then, when I thought he wanted me at last . . . we quarrelled.' Her eyes were fixed on the soft swathes of smoke drifting across the fire as the flame licked at the damp logs. The air smelt sweet and spicy from the gnarled, lichen-covered apple.

'You must make up your quarrel.' Joan picked up her embroidery frame and selected a new length of silk for her needle. 'You have been lonely, I think.'

Eleyne nodded.

Joan squinted at the branch of candles, holding her needle up to the light. 'It was the same for me when I first came here. I was English and a stranger in your father's court. I was lonely and afraid.'

'You?' Eleyne turned to stare at her.

'Why not?' Her tone was defensive. 'I was young – oh not as young as you – and just as vulnerable and without the loving family behind me which you had.' She paused, unaware that her use of the past tense had brought tears to her daughter's eyes. 'I barely knew my father. He and my mother were together such a short time and yet here I was branded –' her voice grew heavy with bitterness – 'branded as the bastard daughter of King John. Not a princess, even though I had been declared legitimate, but the child of a woman of the night and a butcher!'

'Was he really so evil?' Eleyne's voice was quiet. Her grandfather had died four years before she was born, but she too had grown up in the shadow of the hate his name still roused.

'He did some bad things. He was a king,' Joan went on after a long pause. 'Kings and princes must sometimes be cruel if they are to rule effectively.' There was another silence.

Was she thinking of her own imprisonment, Eleyne wondered, and she realised with a shock that she had stopped thinking of her mother with hostility. This, the first real conversation they had ever had, had revealed a vulnerable, sensitive woman beneath the tough, unsentimental exterior, and Eleyne warmed to her.

Her needle threaded at last, Joan put the silver thimble on her finger and began inserting minute stitches into the linen in her frame. 'Why did he dismiss Rhonwen?'

The question dropped into the silence, then Eleyne shrugged. 'He doesn't like her.'

'Will you take her back with you?'

Again Eleyne shrugged. 'I love Rhonwen, but I don't want to make him angry.'

'Then leave her here. The woman plots and schemes like an alley cat. She will only complicate your life at Chester. You must learn one thing, Eleyne, and that is that there is no one you can rely on in this world but yourself. No one.'

VIII

Isabella could not hide her resentment and Eleyne felt it as soon as she walked into the room. The girl's look was hard and full of enmity in the streaming light of the torches; her dark eyes were calculating. 'So, you came back on your own.'

A gale had risen, screaming across the sea from the north-west, pounding the waves against the shore, rattling the window screens in the palace. Isabella clutched her wrap around her bulky body and sat in the chair nearest the hearth. Around her, her ladies, shivering too in the draughty hall, gathered as close as they could to the fire. Eleyne stood alone in the centre of the floor and felt the wave of hostility crest and topple towards her like one of the fat breakers on the beach below. Her heart sank. How could she have thought that she and Isabella could still be friends?

'My husband was too busy to leave Chester at the moment,' she said calmly.

'I heard he couldn't wait to get rid of you,' Isabella retorted pertly. 'Little princess icicle they call you, did you know? One of my ladies said the pages were betting long odds you would still be a virgin when you were twenty!'

Eleyne felt the colour mounting in her cheeks. Not all the sniggers from the listening women had been stifled; in fact, one or two had laughed out loud, their eyes brazen and mocking.

'I don't know what you mean!' She raised her chin.

'I mean, sister,' Isabella emphasised the word sarcastically, 'that if your husband had bedded you, you would have been with child long before this. Besides, it is well known you keep separate rooms!'

Eleyne thought she saw one or two of the women bow their heads, embarrassed by their mistress's waspishness, and she was comforted by it. Her initial hurt was passing and she felt her own temper rising. She clenched her fists.

'My private life is none of your business, Bella,' she retorted. 'But at least my husband and I live in the same town.' She closed her mind firmly to the fact that now they did nothing of the sort. 'My brother, I hear, has taken to putting the breadth of Gwynedd between you and him.' She turned on her heel, and walked, head high, across the chamber, conscious every step of the way of the staring eyes following her.

'*Murderer!*'

Eleyne stopped. For a moment she wondered if she had heard aright. Isabella's whisper carried as clearly as would a shout across the body of the large room. She turned, her face white, her eyes hard.

'What did you say?'

'I said "murderer",' Isabella repeated defiantly. She eyed Eleyne warily. 'Why not? It's what you are. You killed my father.'

The silence was total in the solar. Only the shifting of the fire stirred the breath-held tension. Eleyne was perfectly calm. Her temper ran cold as ice. 'Your father was a traitor. He seduced my mother and betrayed my father's friendship,' she said, her voice completely steady. 'He betrayed you and he betrayed me without a thought. I didn't sentence him to die, but it was the fate he deserved. My father,' she paused, 'had no choice but to send him to the death for which he had asked.' Conscious of the eyes fixed on her back, she walked slowly from the room, aware of a strange calm dignity, of the certainty that she was right.

Surprised at her coolness, she paused outside the door and examined her feelings with detachment. It was as if she had walked through an archway which led directly from childhood to adulthood. It was a step from which there was no turning back: yesterday she would have run from the room, shaking with anger, to throw herself upon her bed, pounding the pillows with frustration and fury; today, when she regained her bedchamber it was at a thoughtful walk.

Through the strange osmosis by which news and gossip spread through the palace, Rhonwen had already heard of the altercation. She laughed wryly. 'You touched a sensitive place there, *cariad*. The child was upset when Dafydd left her. She worships him you know, but now he's got a baby on her he's away.'

Eleyne sat down on the bed. 'Why is she so cruel?'

'You must try to understand how she feels.' Rhonwen noticed her calmness and was uneasy. 'She has to blame someone; and she's always been jealous of you.'

'I thought she was my friend.' Wearily Eleyne drew her legs up beneath her skirts.

'A fair-weather friend only,' Rhonwen said gently. 'And a dangerous enemy, *cariad*. You must watch your back when that young woman is around, indeed.'

It was hard to avoid anyone in the crowded palace over Christmas, confined as they were by the icy winds and the horizontal storms of sleet and soft snow which tore the last clinging dead leaves from the trees over the river, and brought the swirling brown waters down in spate. Eleyne kept as much as possible to her own rooms and to those of her mother, with whom she had several more quiet thoughtful talks.

Her father arrived late one night with an escort of ten men. Their torches spat and hissed in the wind; their fur cloaks were encrusted with frozen snow. Eleyne waited behind her mother, watching as Llywelyn tramped into the hall shouting greetings to his people. He did not see his youngest daughter until he was a few strides from her. For a moment father and daughter stared at each other in silence. Eleyne wanted to throw herself into his arms but she held back, her eyes on his face. He did not smile. A silence fell over the men and women around them. At last it was Joan who spoke. 'Welcome, my husband. Do you see who is here to spend Christmas with us?'

Eleyne stepped forward and curtseyed low. 'Papa,' she said.

Her father put out his hand and took hers. 'You are welcome here, daughter,' he said quietly. But he did not hug her and within seconds he had turned away.

It was a week later, after the supper tables had been cleared and the prince had retired to a private room with Ednyfed Fychan, the archdeacon of St Asaph's and several others among his closest companions and advisers, that the household, led by Princess Joan, settled themselves comfortably to hear a new harper from the land of Cornwall far to the south. Joan beckoned Eleyne to the seat next to her and Eleyne, with a look at Isabella who was scowling as usual, took the place with a smile, watching the grave young man before them lovingly tuning his instrument.

Her eyes wandered over the assembled company, men and women most of whom she had known all her life. There were some strangers, but they were seated in the body of the hall, their faces lost in the light and shadow of the wall sconces with their flaring smoky lights. All were quiet now, replete after their meal and eager to hear the new musician – all loving music, all appreciative, all critical of whatever offering was to come. Her gaze strayed back to the dais where the immediate family sat – all except her father – to Isabella, slumped in her chair, the bloated mound of her belly making it impossible for her to be comfortable. Even as Eleyne watched, she saw the young woman, who had ostentatiously turned her seat away from Eleyne, move awkwardly, obviously in some distress, her hand pressed against her side. Eleyne felt an overwhelming wave of sadness at the sight of her.

The first warm, enticing chords of the music drew her attention back to the performer and she was lost in the magic arpeggios of sound, her spine straight against the carved wooden chairback, her hands resting loosely on its arms, aware of the subtle change in the attention of the audience around her. The first notes had told them that this man was a master, equal to the best of their own harpers. Reassured, the audience sat back to enjoy the evening.

Isabella's scream cut the music short in mid-sweep, and there was total horrified silence in the hall. Then it was repeated, echoing eerily in the smoky rafters as Isabella half slipped, half threw herself from her chair, clutching her belly.

It took five agonised hours for her to lose the baby, during which time no corner of the palace seemed free of her screams. Rhonwen, her pot of healing salve in her hands, ran at once to help, but Isabella took one look at her and screamed again.

'Murderess! Sorceress! You did this. *You!* You did it for her. You hag! You witch!' Words failed her and once more she clutched in agony at the bed rail above her head. Rhonwen stood staring at the suffering girl, then slipped without a word from the room.

She put the pot of salve on the coffer near Eleyne and regarded it sadly. 'She is blaming me,' she said, her voice flat. 'She claims I did it for you.'

Eleyne grew cold. 'For me?' she echoed. They stared at each other in the shadowy room. The only sound was the moan of the wind. 'Did you?' Eleyne's whisper was barely audible.

IX

The snow started in earnest that night: soft, thick, silent snow, whirling in from the north, smothering mountains and valleys alike in deep feathery drifts which, as the grey dawn came, turned from shadow-white to grey and then to blue. The water of the river slowed to a sluggish crawl, held back by icicles and frost-hard tree roots, and in the stables the water in the horses' buckets was solid ice.

'I thought I'd find you here,' Rhonwen said quietly. Her breath was a cloud in the clean air. The horses too breathed dragon plumes in the silence. 'What happened to Invictus?'

Eleyne sighed. 'I left him at Chester. It would have been wrong to bring him back here. Lord Huntingdon will take care of him. He's a valuable horse.' The words sounded as though she had been trying to persuade herself. 'How is Isabella?' She hadn't turned from the door on which she was leaning, watched from a distance by her father's grooms.

'She'll live to bear more children, never fear.' Rhonwen pursed her lips. 'She's strong, that one.'

Eleyne shook her head: 'There will be no more children, not for Isabella.'

Rhonwen closed her eyes. 'So. Then that is the will of the gods. You saw that in the fire, *cariad*?'

Eleyne shrugged. 'No, there are some things I just know.'

'And what do you see for yourself, girl? Or is it just for others you have the Sight?'

Eleyne rested her chin on her folded arms. 'I have never seen anything for myself. Perhaps there is no future for me.'

'You mustn't talk like that.'

'I'm sorry. I am not very cheerful today.' Straightening, Eleyne looked at her directly and Rhonwen frowned, sensing yet again the new determination there, strengthened by the prince's lingering coldness. 'Where is Einion?'

'There was some scandal. The prince heard it and suggested Einion leave his court for a while. If you want to see him I'm sure I can find him –' Rhonwen looked doubtfully at the whirling whiteness in the courtyard.

'No!' Eleyne's voice was sharp. 'I don't want to see him!' She turned her back on the horses and pulled her cloak hood over her veil. 'Come. I want to speak to Isabella.'

X

'Keep away from me!' Isabella huddled beneath her covers, her eyes huge in her white face. 'You have bewitched me, all of us. You have

160

the evil eye! First papa, then Cousin John, and now me! Everyone you go near dies!' Her lip trembled and two huge tears welled up in her eyes.

'That is not true.' Eleyne had stopped near the doorway, conscious of the half-dozen pairs of eyes turned in her direction. At least two of Isabella's ladies crossed themselves and one, she saw, made the sign against the devil. 'I wish you no harm; I am your friend –'

'You are not my friend!' Isabella's voice was heavy with bitterness. 'You're jealous! Jealous of my marriage; jealous of my happiness; jealous of my baby –' She started sobbing loudly and was immediately surrounded by her women. One stayed behind and said: 'Please leave, Lady Chester. You see how upset the princess is.'

'It's not true.' Eleyne was still staring at Isabella. 'I'm not jealous. I wished her no harm –'

'Of course you didn't. Please go, my lady, please.' She ushered Eleyne to the door. 'Let my princess sleep now. I am sure she will be calmer later.'

The corridor was dark, lit by a single rush lamp at the corner of the passage, and for a few minutes Eleyne was alone.

The figure was barely a shadow, a darker place on the darkness of the wall. She looked at it and it was gone.

'Who's there?' she asked sharply. There was no reply. From Isabella's bedchamber behind her, there was no sound. There was nothing to hear but the wind.

She made her way down the passage to the staircase and peered down. The steps vanished into darkness. 'Who's there?' she called again, her voice steadier now. Almost without realising, she began to descend the stairs, her shoes silent on the wood, the only sound the soft swish of her skirts as they followed her, dragging a little down each steep step, catching now and then on a rough, splintered edge.

At the bottom she stopped again. The stairs ended in an inner hallway. To her right a curtained archway led into the great hall where the bulk of the household sat or sprawled, listening to a recitation by a poet from Powys. To her left a dark wooden passageway linked the hall with the other scattered buildings of the palace complex. Again without realising why, she turned down it. It was dark; from the far end she caught the unsteady flicker of light from the torch one of the watch had thrust into a sconce on the wall, perilously near the roof thatch. Beyond it a barred door led into the courtyard. There was no sign of the guard as she turned the corner. The whole of the building was silent, save for the wind which moaned in the roof timbers and howled in the doorways and passages before roaring on up the steep valley away from Aber.

She reached the door and looked around; there was still no sign of the watch. The passageway was empty. The kitchens beyond seemed deserted. The cooks, too, after scouring their pans and damping down the great cooking fires, had crept into the back of the hall to hear the poetry.

She turned to the door and, as if obeying some distant call, raised her hands to the bar which held it closed. It was heavy, cut from a plank of seasoned oak and slotted into two iron hoops, one on either side of the frame. She grasped the bar and pulled; it didn't move. She frowned, her head slightly to one side as if still listening to a voice in the wind, which moved her skirts around her ankles and made the torch behind her hiss and smoke. Was there someone there? Someone calling her? She listened again and the small hairs on the back of her neck stirred.

At her second fierce tug the door bar came away from one of its slots, rattling back and then, the end too heavy for her to hold, falling with a crash from her hands. With a determined effort she eased the other end free, and jumped back as the whole bar fell to the ground. Immediately the door swung inwards, opened by the pressure of the wind, and the torch behind her went out. Eleyne stood quite still, feeling the wind tearing at her clothes, listening to the roar as the trees on the hillside bent and streamed before it, then cautiously she stepped over the bar and slipped into the snow-covered courtyard.

There were two men on guard at the river gate, huddling for shelter beneath the wooden stockade which guarded the lower end of the palace.

'Open the gate!' Eleyne heard the words whipped from her lips and torn spinning into the distance. Her veil dragged at her hair, fighting to be free under the hood of her cloak.

'My lady?' One of the men held up his dark lantern. 'We have orders to allow no one in or out after dark.' His shadowed, angular face was highlighted by the faint glimmer of the burning candle behind the polished horn screens. There was a naked sword in his other hand.

Eleyne drew herself up. 'Those orders do not apply to me. Open the gate and close it behind me. I shall knock when I return.'

She saw the man glance uncertainly at his companion, saw the other nod, and saw the superstitious fear in the eyes of both. She didn't care; she didn't even know why she wanted to leave the palace so badly or where it was she was going in the deep, frozen snow. She waited as the gate was pulled back and walked through it, not glancing at the men as she passed. Then the gate was closed behind her and she was alone in the darkness.

She walked slowly, feeling the force of the wind trying to push her forward, her cloak flapping around her like a live thing. There was sleet in the wind out here – icy, hard in the blackness, stinging her cheeks, freezing her knuckles as she clutched her cloak, and somewhere in the distance she heard the howl of a wolf. She was on the slippery track, the road which bypassed the cluster of cottages around the church and mill, and had led up the river and across the mountains since before the Romans came; since the days of the old gods. She followed it easily in darkness made luminous by the snow.

Einion was waiting for her at the water's edge where the trees made it dark again. For some reason she was not afraid. She could see nothing, her eyes slitted against the sleet, but she knew he was there. His cloak was blacker than the blackness around him, his beard a white blur. Beneath her cloak her fingers touched her crucifix for reassurance – the crucifix John had given her.

Standing beside Einion on the bank of the river, she could not see the water, save for the occasional glint of foam as it roared down towards the sea, but the ground beneath her feet vibrated with the strength of it.

'You summoned me here?' She spoke at last, her voice loud against the wind. Beneath the sharp cold of the sleet, she could smell the scents of the earth: the bitter incense of the leafmould soaked with melted snow beneath her feet, the cold green smell of fern and moss, the tang of wet rock.

'It was you who wished to see me, princess.'

She could see his face now, his piercing eyes. Had she wished to see him? In those long days and nights when she had lain ill at Fotheringhay and the memory of her visions had spun in and out of her mind – had she wanted the reassurance of knowing how to control her dreams? When she walked so close to that other world – the world beyond the veil of the present – had she not wanted to know how to lift the veil and realised that Einion was her only key?

'I do need your help,' she said at last. 'I saw things, but I couldn't stop them happening . . .'

For a long time there was no reply, and she wondered if he had heard her over the roar of the trees and the water. At last he turned and held out his hands. She put her own into his without hesitation.

'Your path no longer runs through the mountains of Eryri, princess,' he said slowly. 'Your destiny lies far away. The day you left Aber to go to your husband you changed, as the hare changes to a cat or the doe to a horse. You no longer tread the path I hoped for you. But that is the will of the goddess and she has given you her blessing. She will allow you to see what you need to see and she will help you to understand if that is her intention. It is her path you follow now.'

'And where does my path lead? Can you see?' She stared into his face. His eyes were barely visible in the darkness; she could see nothing of his expression.

163

Again the silence. She felt the energy flowing through his hands into hers, felt his eyes looking deep into her skull.

'Your destiny lies in the far north,' he said at last. 'In the forests of Caledon, in the land of the Scots. It is there you will live the greater part of your life and there you will die.'

The ice-cold needles of sleet penetrated her cloak, soaking through her gown, making her shiver.

'And my husband will be king?' She whispered the question but he heard her.

'I see you at the king's side. I see you as the mother of a line of kings. You will be the life of a king and you will be the death of a king. The Sight will be yours and it will be denied you.' He stopped, his words snatched away into the darkness, and she felt the strength of his hands die away. He released her fingers and turned from her. 'Tomorrow I return to Môn. I have asked your father's leave to end my service with him. I wish to spend the last of my days alone, preparing myself for the next life.'

'Then who will I turn to for a guide?' She felt a wave of panic as she tried to grasp the things he had told her.

He smiled for the first time. 'That I cannot see. But it will not be me. I shall be dead before the snows have melted on Yr Wyddfa in the spring.'

'No!' Her cry was anguished.

'It is the will of the gods, child,' he replied gently. 'We cannot question their decisions. I have lived more than eighty summers in these hills. My business here is over. I waited only to speak to you and now that is done I shall rest in peace. Go now, back to your father's hall.'

'Will I see you again?'

'I think not in this life.' He smiled sadly. 'My blessings on you, princess, and on all you love. Now go.'

She raised her hand, but he had turned away. Huddled in his cloak, the hood pulled up over his hair, he was part of the shadows, part of the night. In a moment he had gone.

'Lord Einion?' Her voice was sharp and frightened. The wind howled around the spot where he had stood and the river hurled itself down between the boulders. She was alone.

CHAPTER SEVEN

I

ABER ✦ January 1233

The ashes were glowing beneath her feet as she walked in the fire; in front of her, in the distance, she could see mountains, blue beneath the haze. A figure was waiting for her, beckoning. She moved on, slowly, floating just above the ground. He was calling her name and she could see him drawing away from her, holding out his arms, his red-gold hair gleaming in the flickering light. 'Wait!' She tried to call, but no sound came from her throat. 'Wait . . .' But he was growing smaller, shimmering behind the heat of the fire. She began to run; she had to reach him, to see his face. The heat hid him, separating them. She had to get through the fire. 'Eleyne,' he was calling more loudly now, 'Eleyne.'

'Eleyne!'

Prince Llywelyn looked infinitely weary. Humping his fur-trimmed gown higher on his shoulders, he sighed. 'I cannot allow you to remain here, daughter. I am sorry.' He stood at the window of the solar, gazing out into the whirling snow. Eleyne sat alone, her eyes on the fire.

'You must see how difficult it is, with Isabella's illness. I'm told her megrims will pass and with them these tantrums, but meanwhile –' He shrugged helplessly. 'Dafydd will escort you to Chester. I am sure your husband will be pleased to have you back.'

She made no response, her eyes fixed unblinkingly on the smouldering logs.

'You and she will be friends again when she is with child once more,' he went on uncomfortably. 'This idea of hers, that it was your fault – no one believes it. It is no more than the raving of a mad woman, but then, women are like this sometimes, they tell me, when they have miscarried . . .' His voice trailed away to silence.

Again she gave no sign of having heard him. He moved closer. 'Eleyne, did you hear me?' He suppressed the wave of irritation which swept over him. He had come to Aber seeking peace; instead he had found himself surrounded by squabbling women. His daughter-in-law's

165

petulant voice and her uncontrolled sobbing rang day and night in his hall. Dafydd, in an effort to buy himself some quiet, nagged him constantly to get rid of Eleyne, whilst Joan could barely conceal her impatience with this girl her son had married, this daughter of the man who had been her lover. She kept begging Llywelyn to send Isabella and Dafydd to Dolbadarn or Dolwyddelan and allow Eleyne to stay at Aber. The servants and household gossiped about his youngest daughter endlessly; as for Rhonwen, if there were magic and evil in this palace, Rhonwen was the centre of it.

Still Eleyne had not looked up; she gave no sign that she knew he was there. He scowled. Her eyes, clear as the silver-green dawn light on the sea, stared unblinkingly at the embers. She seemed to be a thousand miles away in her dreams.

'Eleyne!' His voice was sharp. 'Eleyne, by the Holy Virgin, listen to me!' He stepped towards her and, putting his hand on her shoulder, pulled her to face him.

Her eyes were blank.

A superstitious shudder of horror swept over him. She had gone, his little daughter, his Eleyne, his seventh child, and the beautiful face looking up at him blankly was that of a stranger – a stranger who had stepped out of those glowing ashes to speak to him from another world. 'Eleyne, wake up!' His voice was sharp with fear.

Abruptly she was jerked to her feet. The picture in the fire vanished and she found herself staring into her father's furious green eyes.

'What's the matter? Can't you hear me?' The fear in his voice was raw.

'I'm sorry.' She tried to pull herself together, but her mind was far away, through the fire, seeking the man who had called her, the man to whom her soul clung.

'Are your wits addled, girl? Have I been talking to you all this time and you have heard not a word?' His moment of fear had made him doubly angry.

'I didn't hear you come in, papa. Forgive me –'

'Then listen now.' He didn't ask what she had been thinking about, where she had been. He thrust her away, ignoring his urge to take her into his arms as he used to do when she was little. 'I said you have to go. And go now. Today. You are not wanted beneath this roof. Your place is with your husband.'

'But, papa –'

This was the first time he had spoken to her alone since his return, and the first time he had really spoken to her at all. She felt a strange chill; once more she was the frightened child whom her father had sent away three years before.

'Why? Why must I go? What have I done? I don't understand.' She

166

tried to read the bleak, shuttered face. 'I can't go, papa. The weather . . .' She looked over to the narrow window behind him, the only one which was still unshuttered, where the snowflakes whirled crazily. Some had drifted on to the exposed sill and sat there unmelted in the cold. 'No one could ride in this; please let me stay at least until the storm clears.' She heard her voice rise unsteadily. 'Please, papa?'

He stared at her coldly. 'Dafydd will ride with you. There is no danger; the snow is not settling. You will leave as soon as you are packed. I am sorry, Eleyne. But you have to go. And take your woman with you.'

'My woman?' she echoed as the door crashed shut behind him. Rhonwen.

II

They sheltered that night in the guesthouse of the abbey at Conwy and rode on at first light, their faces muffled against the cold, their gloves rigid with caked ice on the reins of their horses. The snow whirled around them, settling in deep drifts in the sheltered gullies, torn and blown on the screaming west wind which as yet held no hard edge of ice. Dafydd had made no attempt to talk to her, to explain, but Rhonwen had known.

'It's the English bitch Dafydd took to wife,' she whispered as she threw Eleyne's clothes into her coffers. 'She spreads lies, like poison, round the *llys*; she screams and shouts and refuses to sleep until you've gone. She claims the child was lost because of you and that she won't conceive again while you're under the same roof.' She glanced sideways at Eleyne. 'Did you tell her what you told me? Did you tell her that there would be no other child, *cariad*?'

Eleyne frowned. 'Of course not! I have told her nothing. I haven't been near her. She wouldn't see me.'

'That's as well then. If you'd told her, she would have screamed sorcery and had you locked away for a thousand years.' Rhonwen closed the lid of the chest and began to fill the next. 'You're best back with your husband, *cariad*, and that's the truth.' She looked at Eleyne's bleak face, and knew without being told what Eleyne was thinking: *What if he won't have me back? What if he doesn't want me as his wife . . .?*

III

CHESTER CASTLE ❖ January 1233

The Earl of Chester's face was uncompromisingly stern. 'I did not send for you,' he said.

Eleyne raised her chin a fraction. 'I wanted to return.' She had forgotten how handsome he was, this husband of hers. She felt excitement beneath her apprehension.

Above her head the carved vaulted roof of the great hall of Chester Castle was lost in the shadows; after the comparatively small palace at Aber, it was a shock to remember the power of this great castle which was now her home.

She was intensely aware that the crowds of men and women, ostensibly busy about their affairs or gathered around one or other of the fires at either end of the hall, were watching and, if they were close enough, listening to the conversation between husband and wife.

Dafydd had exchanged only the briefest greetings with Lord Chester and then turned back into the storm, anxious to return to Wales before the snow closed the passes and locked the roads. He had offered no explanation for his sister's unheralded return. Rhonwen had slipped away into the depths of the castle without a word, terrified that the earl would send her back with Dafydd. Eleyne was left to greet her husband alone and unattended.

He looked stronger than she remembered him. Tall and good-looking, he was in the great hall surrounded by his friends and advisers when she was announced. They formed a laughing animated group which stood back in silence as she walked the length of the hall to the dais and stepped up to greet him. In the long weeks at Aber she had grown again; this time she was nearly as tall as he, and her eyes met his steadily for a moment before she dropped a deep curtsey before him, her heart thumping.

'What made you decide to return?' He dropped his voice so they could not be overheard.

'My place is at your side, my lord.'

'Did your lover reject you?'

Her steady gaze belied the tightening of her throat, the quickness of her breath. She clenched her fists. 'I told you before, my lord. I have no lover. You are the only husband I want.'

'Because, no doubt, you have now obtained the assurance from your uncle the king that you may marry whom you will when I die.' His eyes were watchful, his voice harsh.

'I have not seen the king; nor have I written to him, my lord.' It was becoming an effort to keep her eyes steady on his, but somehow she managed it, willing him to believe her.

He folded his arms thoughtfully. 'Your brother was in a great hurry to leave,' he said abruptly.

'The weather is bad, my lord. He didn't want to bring me to Chester, but I insisted. I wanted to return before it got so bad I was forced to stay at Aber until the spring.'

'I see.' There was a flash of humour in his eyes. 'And Aber was becoming untenable, was it? Or did your father send you packing?' He broke off as a flood of scarlet washed her cheeks. 'Aha! At last I have nailed the truth,' he said softly. 'You have been sent away a second time. What did you do on this occasion, wife?'

Eleyne tried to keep her voice under control. 'It was not my father, it was Isabella . . .' She was fighting her tears. Abruptly, she turned away from him and went to stand in front of the huge stone fireplace with its burning logs, holding out her hands to the blaze. Her gaze sought the depths of the glowing heat, but there was no message for her, and she stepped back as her eyes began to smart. There was a long silence in the hall, broken only by the spitting of the fires and the low murmur of voices from below the dais.

Then John was behind her, his hands on her shoulders. She felt herself grow tense.

'Eleyne, may I present a kinsman to you.' His voice was perceptibly more gentle. 'Come, turn round. This is a cousin of my grandmother's, Robert Fitzooth.'

Swallowing hard, she faced them and forced herself to smile. The young man was as tall as John and as good-looking, with an irrepressible twinkle in his eye. He swept a low bow.

'Lady Chester. I have heard so much about you and I had abandoned hope of seeing you before I left. Greetings, madam, and welcome home.'

She found she was smiling at him, responding instantly to his warmth and charm, so unaffected and uncomplicated after her husband's greeting. Almost without realising it, she allowed him to lift her heavy cloak from her shoulders and toss it over a bench, then he produced a cup of wine from a hovering page.

'You lucky man,' he called over his shoulder at the earl. 'You never told me how beautiful she is; that the storm would pass and the snow melt and the sun come up inside the hall when she came home.'

Eleyne laughed, and saw that John too was smiling, watching the two of them, arms folded with the tolerance an adult might show two children at play. 'She likes you, Robin,' he commented with a wry laugh. 'Lucky man. Make the most of it.'

After supper Robin organised games and dancing in the hall and led Eleyne into all the dances, leaving John in his chair by the fire. By bedtime Eleyne was exhausted.

Robin looked at her and laughed at his cousin. 'You will curse me for leaving your bride too tired for your private sport. Forgive me, my lord.'

John gave a forced smile. 'Eleyne has enjoyed herself. It's good to see her happy.' He stood up and, reaching across, took her hand. 'Nevertheless, as you say, it is late. Time for us to retire.'

They walked side by side from the hall, between ranks of bowing men and women, conscious that as soon as they had gone the dancing would start again.

Beyond the hall, the castle was bitterly cold; the wind had veered at last into the north and with it came the stranglehold of ice on the snow. Feeling the bite of it in her bones as they climbed the broad winding stair to the lord's bedchamber, Eleyne wondered briefly if Dafydd would reach home before the ice came. Dafydd and she had exchanged so few words on their ride to Chester; their mutual resentment was a physical barrier between them.

Above her, at the angle of the curving stair, John stopped and looked down at her. His smile had gone. 'You find my kinsman Robin attractive, I think.' His voice was flat.

She stopped too, raising her face to look up at him in the shadows, and her skin tingled with warning. 'He is indeed an attractive man.' She could hear the defiance in her voice.

'More so, no doubt, than your husband.'

Eleyne smiled sadly. 'No one should be more attractive than a husband to a wife, my lord,' she said softly. For a fleeting instant the image of William de Braose rose before her.

'No, they should not.' His mouth snapped shut on the words and he continued to climb.

Eleyne followed him, holding her heavy skirts clear of the stone steps. 'Are you at all pleased to see me, my lord?' Her voice, tentative above the howl of the wind, barely reached him.

'Of course.' He did not stop.

At the head of the stairs the gallery divided. To the east, it led to a small chapel and the lord's private apartments; to the north, it led around the great square of the keep to the apartments reserved for visitors of state. Eleyne paused, then taking a deep breath she turned after her husband.

At the door to his chamber he bowed to her courteously. 'You may make this room your own, Eleyne. I have given orders that your coffers and your servants be sent here. I myself will sleep elsewhere.' He looked at her, thoughtfully. 'Just until you are recovered from your journey.'

'And then, my lord?' She did not realise that her eyes were pleading.

'And then we shall see.' He reached out and touched her cheek. 'I trust you did not bring the Lady Rhonwen back with you from Wales, Eleyne.'

Eleyne froze, her eyes on his, unable to look away.

'You know how I mistrusted that woman,' he went on. 'She was

170

bad for you, keeping you a child, leading you into evil ways . . .' He paused, noticing her stricken expression. He said nothing, then slowly he sighed. He pushed open the chamber door and walked in.

Rhonwen was supervising the unpacking of Eleyne's boxes, standing in the middle of the floor as some half-dozen maids scurried around her, depositing armloads of linen in carved and painted coffers and chests around the walls. The lights flickered in the draught of the open door and Rhonwen looked around. For a long moment she and Lord Chester surveyed one another, then quietly, somehow hopelessly, he laughed: 'So that is the way of it.'

'You never said she couldn't return, my lord,' Eleyne cried. 'You never said she had to stay in Wales.'

'Did I not?' He looked at her coldly. 'I had thought you would have understood my intentions.'

That night Eleyne tossed and turned alone in the great bed, listening to the wind howling in the chimneys, and by morning she had reached a decision. After hearing mass in their private chapel at her husband's side, she waited until the household had broken their fast and then followed him to the side chamber where he was sitting at his desk. His face was pale, his hands stiff with cold as he reached for the first letter. His clerks hovered nearby waiting to begin work. One of them, his nose red and swollen, sneezed dismally into the crook of his arm and wiped his nose on his sleeve.

'I should like to talk to you alone, my lord,' she said boldly. Her back straight, her eyes steadily on his, she clasped her hands together to give her courage.

For a moment she thought he would refuse, then with a curt nod of his head he gestured the clerks towards the door. Bowing, they withdrew.

'If you are wondering where Robin was at breakfast, he has left the castle,' he commented curtly. 'He too was afraid of being caught in the snow. He asked me to pass his farewells to you.'

'I did not go downstairs to breakfast, my lord,' Eleyne retorted. 'Sir Robert's whereabouts are of no interest to me.' Her eyes were heavy from lack of sleep and her head ached. She must not lose her temper; she must keep up her courage; she must remember what she had vowed to do. 'I came to talk to you about Rhonwen. If it is your wish, I shall send her back to Wales. All I ask is that we give her a dowry to enable her to marry well. I love her as a mother. I should not like her thrown destitute upon the world.'

John looked at her closely. 'Have you told her that this is what you intend?' he asked shrewdly.

Eleyne hung her head, then once more straightened her shoulders.

171

'Not yet, my lord,' she said honestly. She smiled wearily. 'I didn't have the courage. But I shall do so at once if it is your wish.' The pain in her eyes was obvious, in spite of the resolution in her voice.

He frowned. 'You really love that woman, don't you? Even knowing she is not a Christian.'

'She will attend mass if I ask it of her, my lord,' Eleyne said firmly. She took a deep breath. 'I was a child when I came to you. I did not realise that the things I had been told by Einion were bad. He had offered to help me understand my dreams. For that I was grateful. But I know what I did was wrong. I am no priestess of the Welsh gods of ancient times. I am your wife and I am no longer a child. I have put Einion's teachings behind me, and Rhonwen understands that. I saw Einion . . .' She hesitated. To tell him was a risk; it was also perhaps the key to the future. 'I saw him before I came back to Chester and he confirmed what I already knew in my heart. That my place is at your side. And that our future lies in Scotland.'

She saw the excitement flare in his eyes, and she felt an answering excitement inside herself.

'In Scotland?' he repeated. 'He said that?'

'Yes, my lord. He said that my place was with the King of Scotland and that I would live – and die – in that country.'

John stood up. He threw the letter which had been clutched in his hand on to the table and watched as it slowly refolded itself. 'So. It is to happen. When?' He rounded on her, his face alight with suppressed fire.

She shook her head. 'He showed me no calendar, my lord.' She smiled, her heart thumping with excitement.

'And the future? Did he see children?' The eagerness and fear in his voice made her blush as she replied: 'He said I should be the mother of a line of kings.'

'So!' He smacked his hands together triumphantly. 'I knew it! I felt it in my bones! And you –' He reached out and took her hand. 'You are to be the mother of my heir.'

She smiled. 'So it would seem, my lord.' She looked up at him as he pulled her closer and she could feel her breath coming in small gasps. It was working; working more surely than ever she would have dreamed possible. Let it be now, she thought incoherently as she reached up, seeking his lips with her own, now while he is excited and optimistic and strong. Let it be now.

As if reading her thoughts he murmured through his kisses, 'Why don't we retire to the bedchamber, my Eleyne? Dear God, you've been away too long and I have missed you.' He held her away from him as if trying to reassure himself that she was indeed a grown woman now, eager in his arms. 'You're not afraid?'

Her heart was hammering wildly beneath her ribs. 'Oh no, my lord, I am not afraid.' She reached up again to kiss him, her lips tracing the angle of his jaw, finding the soft skin of his cheek beneath the rough neatness of his beard as he caught her hand and pulled her towards the door.

Outside the three clerks were waiting dutifully to be summoned back to their master's office. They looked up as the door opened, but neither the earl nor the countess noticed them, even when one sneezed yet again as they walked past. Holding Eleyne by the wrist, John walked swiftly across the stone flags towards the staircase. Almost running to keep up with him, Eleyne was oblivious of the interested faces watching from the shadows as she followed him upwards, concentrating, as he was, only on what was to happen once they reached the privacy of the bedchamber. He flung back the door and stood still.

Rhonwen sat by the fire with two other women. They were gossiping softly in the intimate warmth of the hearth. The three faces turned in surprise as the door crashed against the wall.

'Out!' John jerked his thumb towards the door. The women rose and, dropping their spindles, scuttled past him. Rhonwen hesitated for a second as though she were about to speak. One glance at John's face made her change her mind and she followed the others, closing the door behind her.

'At last.' John turned the key in the lock. Unclasping his mantle, he let it drop to the floor. 'Wife —' He pulled her to him and kissed her. She could feel the strength and power centred within him, so different from his habitual gentle reserve. Lifting her mouth to his, she felt herself grow dizzy with longing. He felt her excitement and smiled. 'So, you are eager for your husband at last.'

'You know I am,' she whispered. She longed to tear off her clothes, to feel his hands crushing her breasts, to feel his skin against hers; to throw herself to the ground and roll on the floor naked before the fire. Her whole body sang with life. But then, dimly, in some recess of her mind, she heard a small voice of caution. She must not shock him with her eagerness; she must not let him think her wanton; she must let him lead.

Closing her eyes she pressed against him, feeling his arms tighten immediately around her. 'Sweet Eleyne,' he murmured, his lips against her ear, and now he was slowly, gently, feeling for the lacings of her gown. She stood still, trembling with anticipation as he undressed her, removing each garment slowly and carefully until even her shift had gone. For a long time he did nothing. He stood looking at her with an expression of wonder on his face. 'I hadn't dreamed you were so beautiful.' His voice was hoarse. Not touching her body, he reached up to the braids wound around her head beneath her veil. Unpinning the fine fabric, he began carefully to unplait her hair until it hung in a rippled curtain around her breasts. 'You are sure you're not afraid?' He had felt her trembling.

She shook her head, her eyes lowered, shy suddenly before the intensity of his gaze. 'No, I'm not afraid.'

'My love.' His hand on her shoulder was featherlight. She scarcely felt it as it traced along her collar-bone and down towards her breast. But his gentle touch on her nipple sent a bolt of lightning knifing through her body. She gasped and he looked up, frowning. 'I didn't hurt you?'

'No. No, my lord, you didn't hurt me.' Her words came in a rush.

'I wouldn't hurt you for the world, Eleyne –'

'You won't, my lord.' Her voice dropped, instinctively low and seductive as she caught his face in her hands and brought it towards hers. 'You won't.'

He kissed her long and hard, then he drew her towards the bed. She followed him, her breathing quick and shallow, her pale skin flushed in the light of the fire.

His body was painfully thin, his skin as soft and white as a girl's. To Eleyne it was the most beautiful thing she had ever seen. Mesmerised by the intensity of his gaze and the light touch of his hands on her belly and flanks, she lay back on the bed, her hair spread loose on the silk sheets and pillows, unaware that as her arms drew him down towards her, her legs had parted as naturally and wantonly as any village girl's with her man in the hay.

With a groan, he buried his face in her hair and she felt with a quick exultation his weight come down on her slim body.

There was very little pain. For the few short moments he was inside her, she felt her exhilaration rise as his sweat turned the skin of his shoulders slippery beneath her clinging fingers and she felt the thundering of his heart against hers. Then it was all over. Triumphantly he rolled away from her. He lay still, breathing heavily as he gazed up at the shadowy tester above their heads. The flickering lights from the fire slid back and forth across the damask till it glowed like a sea of living gems. He heaved himself up on one elbow and looked at her with a smile. 'Are you happy, my love?' On the damp sheet below her hips he had seen the small smears of blood. The servants would find them later, and draw their own conclusions. He smiled triumphantly and Eleyne smiled back at him. 'I'm very happy.'

'And now you are truly my wife.' He pushed the hair back gently from her face and reached down to pull the covers over her. Tenderly he kissed her on the forehead, then he slipped from the bed. She watched as he pulled on his clothes. The long dark green tunic clasped at the waist with a leather belt, engraved with gold, then the heavy mantle, green too, though a lighter shade, dyed with mountain lichens, the embroidered border gleaming with gold and vermilion threads. His light gold hair, darkened with sweat, framed his face as he pushed his feet into his shoes.

He came back to the bed and sat down beside her, resting his hand for a moment on her breast. 'Sweet Eleyne. Sleep now, my darling. We'll talk later.' He strode from the room.

Obscurely she felt a little disappointed. Her body still yearned for his; it felt alive, her skin so sensitive that the slight draught straying over the floor from the doorway touched her like the caress of a man. Never had she felt more alert. But he had gone.

IV

DUNFERMLINE CASTLE, SCOTLAND ❖ March 1233

In their bedchamber at Dunfermline Castle the King and Queen of Scots were alone at last. Alexander II, a handsome, broad-shouldered man of thirty-six, stood gazing out of the narrow window towards the gleaming blue ribbon which was the River Forth. His flaming hair and beard, already streaked with grey, were glinting in a stray ray of sunlight which slipped through the window and glanced off the deep embrasure wall.

He closed his eyes and took a deep breath, willing himself to composure. 'Are you sure, this time, my love?' His voice was gentle, but Joanna could hear the uncertainty, the disbelief, above all, the hope.

'I'm sure,' she whispered. 'I'm into the third month and all is well.'

'So!' He smiled exultantly. 'At last there will be an heir for Scotland!' He caught her to him. 'Make sure it's a boy, sweetheart. A boy to lead Scotland forward to greatness.'

'Scotland is already great with you as her king.' Joanna reached on tiptoe to kiss her husband's cheek. She sighed and, wrapping her arms around herself, she danced an excited pirouette. The eldest daughter of King John of England, and the sister of England's present king, half-sister to Eleyne's mother, Joan of Gwynedd, Joanna had been married to Alexander since she was eleven years old and she worshipped her handsome husband. She would have done anything in the world for him; she would have died for him. The only thing she had seemed unable to do in their thirteen years of marriage was to produce a child. Month after month, year after year she had offered prayers to the Blessed Margaret, to St Bride, to the Blessed Virgin herself, but month after month her prayers had proved fruitless and she remained barren. Until now.

175

'When shall we tell everyone?' She ran to him again and caught his hand. 'I should so like everyone to know.'

'And I, sweetheart, and I.' Seeing the joy and excitement in her face, his doubt vanished and he laughed out loud, suddenly aware of the enormous relief which had succeeded his initial caution. A son! An heir! At last Scotland would have the stability she needed, the stability which the succession of his first cousin, the Earl of Chester – English-born and so often ill – would so badly have compromised. He looked again at his wife's slim body – no trace yet of a thickening at her waist – and at her radiant smile, and again he laughed out loud. Picking her up, he whirled her in the air until she shrieked with laughter, then he took her in his arms and kissed her.

V

ANGLESEY ✧ March 1233

As the ice melted and the first small field daffodils turned the sunlit corners of the meadows to palest yellow, Einion, his proud bones weary and aching, walked less and less often to the headland to gaze across the narrow strait towards Eryri and the distant invisible summit of Yr Wyddfa. The snow in the high passes lay thick and undisturbed, blue in the crevices and in the early shadow of the night. The air around him was scented with burning oak and apple from the small settlement of monks at Penmon and, to the west, from the clustered roofs of Llanfaes, but behind and over the smoke and salt of the sea he could smell the clean sweet air of the mountain and its snow.

He saw her less now: the child, the young woman, for whom he had spent the winter in prayer and supplication; the pictures were fading, the future misty and indistinct, but through the darkness had come one message, the message from the fire, the message which held her destiny. When he understood at last what it meant, he had wept. If she should fail to understand, if she should quail before the wishes of the gods . . . Once more he had to meet her, to warn her of what was to come. Then she must go forward alone.

His fingers an agony of rheumatic pain, he managed to clasp the quill and pen the letter to her, commanding her presence without delay in the name of the powers she acknowledged and worshipped as he did, at his retreat on the headland at Penmon. He addressed it formally to the Countess of Chester and entrusted it to a messenger summoned from the prince's *llys* at Llanfaes.

Then he turned his pale, filmy eyes south towards the mountains once more and prayed the gods would grant him a reprieve, a few more weeks of life, to tell her what she had to know.

CHESTER ❖ April 1233

'We must travel!' John's eyes were burning with zeal. 'Now I'm well again we shall visit all my northern estates. Then, all being well, we'll go on to Scotland and I shall present you to the king and your aunt.' He smiled. 'It is time you became acquainted with our future kingdom.'

She nodded, pleased as always to see him active and busy with plans for the future. But part of her, a small, cautious part, watched in concern, noting the speed with which he rushed at things, as though afraid there would be no time to accomplish them all, noting the high colour of his skin and the brightness of his eyes. At night sometimes, as she lay beside him, listening to his deep breathing, she would put her hand gently for reassurance on the place where, beneath his ribs, she could feel the steady beating of his heart, as if to comfort herself that all was well with him.

It was the end of April when they set out from Chester for the east, riding at the head of a long line of attendants, knights, and men-at-arms, servants, wagons and carts. Seated on Invictus, his gilded harness newly sewn and accoutred, her saddle spread with a silken caparison, Eleyne glanced sideways at her husband with enormous pride. He rode upright and calmly beside her, astride a great black destrier which matched Invictus stride for stride. It was an old horse and steady, but it stepped out with style.

Their first stop was in South Yorkshire at an old manor house which lay in a soft fold of the moors beneath the peaks. It was a small place, barely housing a quarter of the big household, which had to find places to camp around the manor walls.

Tired after the long ride, Eleyne retired early to the solar. Their own bed had been set up, the hangings, embroidered with the Chester coat of arms, hung in place and their coffers were unpacked. Rhonwen had stayed at Chester. Never again, after that first night back from Aber, had John mentioned Rhonwen's name, and Eleyne had steadfastly refused to contemplate sending her away. All she had done that first devastating day was to hug her and beg her to stay out of her husband's sight. Then John had taken her to his bed and Rhonwen had been forgotten. She was fed and clothed and, as a senior lady-in-waiting and Eleyne's nurse, had status and regular annual payment of clothes and candles. What more could she want?

Now, as Eleyne sat on a low stool before her mirror allowing Luned to brush out her hair, she caught her eye suddenly in the reflection. 'I wish Rhonwen were here,' she said slowly.

'It's as well she isn't.' The young woman dragged energetically at the thick hair with her comb. 'She knows Lord Chester doesn't want her near him. She preferred to stay behind. She said you did not need her now.'

Eleyne frowned. 'But that's not true. Of course I need her.'

Luned shook her head. 'Not while you sleep in Lord Chester's bed. That's what Rhonwen said.'

Eleyne felt her face colouring. 'My place is in his bed,' she said sharply.

'Of course.' Luned smiled enigmatically. She, at sixteen, had grown into a comely young woman, possessed of a neat waist and high, firm breasts. Her glory was in her eyes. They were a deep seductive grey, fringed by the longest of black lashes, and every young man who saw them fell instantly in love with her. She was being courted by two squires and twice as many pages, and hardly a day went by without her finding small gifts and poems hidden beside her place at dinner or pushed shyly into her hand as she waited on Eleyne in the great hall.

'Rhonwen says she will be there when you need her; when my lord falls ill, or when you are with child. Then you will remember her and ask for her. That is what she said.' She moved behind Eleyne again and set to once more with the comb.

'When I am with child?' Caught by the words, Eleyne heard the echo of Rhonwen's bitterness in them. 'But I'm not, not yet.' She caught a ringlet of her hair and twisted it round her finger.

'Plenty of time for that,' Luned commented tartly, 'when my lord is stronger.' So others too had noted the passing weeks and counted. 'Rhonwen told me she can give you powders to put in his wine that will give him the strength to father children –' She broke off as she caught sight of Eleyne's face in the mirror.

Eleyne jumped to her feet. 'How dare you! How dare she! What do you mean? There is nothing wrong with my husband! Nothing! He is strong and well. He is completely recovered.'

'I'm sorry, my lady.' Luned looked frightened by the unexpected burst of temper. 'I didn't mean to make you cross. And nor did Rhonwen. She only wanted to please you.'

'Well, she hasn't.' Eleyne walked over to the fire and stared down at the smouldering log. The room was cold and damp. 'And I wanted her here. I wanted to talk to her. I need her.' For a moment she was a lonely child again.

It was dark outside and the wind was howling across the moors when John came at last to bed after spending some hours closeted with his chamberlain and the steward of the manor, arguing over the accounts of the previous year's harvest. Climbing into bed beside Eleyne he reached out, as he so often did, to stroke her hair and touch her shoulder as though to reassure himself that she was really there. Then, as he so often did, he turned wearily away and fell into an exhausted sleep, leaving her staring into the darkness.

VII
CHESTER CASTLE ❖ April 1233

The Welshman pulled his rough sheepskin cloak around him and peered furtively over his shoulder. It was some time since he had passed the coin to the servant and asked for the Lady Rhonwen. Behind him the sun had set into a bank of crimson cloud and the cold wind was rising, blowing steadily from the north. With the earl and countess away, the castle was strangely empty. The garrison remained; the administrative officers were still there, but the rest of the great household had moved on to progress around Lord Chester's vast estates.

It was nearly dark before she came, muffled as he was against the cold. They stood in the shelter of the stable block and talked for a few minutes in hurried Welsh. A letter passed between them, then some coins, and the Welshman faded back into the night. At first light, when the gates opened, he would be gone on the journey back to Degannwy.

Rhonwen tucked the letter into her bodice and retraced her steps back to the women's bower. There were fewer ladies there now; those who served the aged dowager and the chatelaine and two young women near to giving birth, that was all. It was comparatively easy to find a secluded corner and settle with her flickering candle to read the letter which Gruffydd had written to Eleyne.

Cautiously worded though it was, it was clear in its message. Gruffydd had had meetings with his father and at long last Llywelyn was talking of allowing his eldest son his freedom once again. There had even been a vague promise that Gruffydd would be given the Lleyn Peninsula and that he would be allowed to work again with Dafydd if he would recognise Dafydd as his father's heir.

Rhonwen dropped the letter on to her lap and gazed unseeing at the heavy wooden shutter which had been pulled across the window. If only he had the sense to agree; to bide his time. She sighed and pulled from her gown her other letter. There had been two that day, both addressed to Eleyne. This one had been carried by a messenger in the livery of the Prince of Aberffraw. He had been reluctant to give it up to her; he had been paid and well paid to put his letter into the hands of the Countess of Chester and no other, but in the end he had relented. Did not everyone know that the Lady Rhonwen was the countess's nurse, her friend, her confidante? She could be trusted to pass on the letter the quickest way possible.

Reading it again now, Rhonwen frowned. Einion's hand had grown feeble; his writing shook and strayed across the roughly scraped parchment, but the urgency was clear. He wanted Eleyne to return to Môn.

Rhonwen frowned again. Eleyne had summoned her to her chamber once when the earl had ridden out for the day. They had hugged one another as they had when Eleyne was a child.

'I am his wife now, Rhonwen,' Eleyne had whispered, her eyes shining, 'really his wife.' She caught Rhonwen's hands. 'Oh Rhonwen, I love him so much. Give me time. Please. He will grow to like you. I know he will.' Rhonwen had suppressed the agonising pang of jealousy which Eleyne's words had caused her, melting before the excited pleading eyes, and she had not, as she had never, been able to deny Eleyne what she wanted.

'I'll wait, *cariad*,' she had said, hiding her sadness. 'I'll keep out of his way, and wait.' Nevertheless she had been hurt by Eleyne's attitude in those last few weeks before they left on their progress around the country. It was as if Eleyne had forgotten her existence. But Rhonwen had watched and waited and kept out of the earl's way as she had promised. And when the time came for the household to leave Chester she had shaken her head and pleaded exhaustion and told Luned to wait on Eleyne with extra care.

She looked down at Einion's letter again: it must be important. Einion would never summon Eleyne back unless he felt it was vital; Einion, to whom she had entrusted Eleyne as she would have trusted herself; a man she respected and honoured more even than she honoured the prince. To disobey him would be to disobey the wishes of the gods; to obey him would be to reclaim Eleyne from her husband; to travel with her once more to Gwynedd; to go home.

She walked slowly across the room, her skirts catching in the dried, dusty herbs strewn upon the ground, her eyes shining. These two letters gave her the power to summon Eleyne back, to bring her home. She stood for a long time before the fire, unaware of the eyes of the other women looking up from their spinning and sewing and watching her warily. Her temper had grown uncertain in the weeks since her return from Gwynedd, her arrogance more defensive. Her beautiful face was drawn now and thin, her eyes haunted, and she seemed unaware of the women around her.

What would Eleyne want her to do? Would she want to go back to Gwynedd and the convoluted politics of her brothers' quarrels, and to Einion, or would she want to remain with her husband, a countess touring her estates? She pictured Eleyne's face yet again: the shining eyes, the knowledge of something which Rhonwen would never know, and she heard again her voice: *Oh Rhonwen, I love him so much*, and she knew what she must do.

Slowly and deliberately she dropped the two letters on to the fire and watched them shrivel and blacken in the heart of the flames.

VIII
PENMON, ANGLESEY ❖ April

In his lonely hermit's cell Einion sat staring deep into the flames, feeling the ice-cold draughts playing across his shoulders and down his spine. The pain in his bones distracted him from his meditation and he could think of nothing now but the cold wind which howled across the island and whipped the strait into white-topped breakers.

Leaning forward he reached for a log to throw on to the fire. He had seen the messenger in the flames that morning; seen him hand the letter to Rhonwen and he had smiled, reassured. Rhonwen would understand the urgency. She would see that Eleyne came back. Only a few more days and she would come; only a few more days . . .

He frowned. Suddenly, it hurt to breathe. The hut was full of smoke. The sound of the wind had risen to a scream. He stared at the fire, his hand pressed against his chest, trying to see. He was struggling to rise to his feet when the pain hit him: a grip like an iron bar across his heart, crushing him, blinding him with agony. He heard himself cry out loud, expelling his last breath as his lungs ceased to function; the deep blackness was enfolding him, numbing his mind as one last certainty flashed through it. Eleyne was not going to come after all. He would not, as he had always known in his heart he would not, see her again. Rhonwen had betrayed her gods. She had thrown the letter on the fire – he saw her do it in one flash of blinding clarity – and because of her Eleyne must face the future without his warnings.

As the blackness became total and the howl of the wind filled his ears, he staggered a few steps into the darkness and pitched full-length across the fire.

181

CHAPTER EIGHT

I

YORKSHIRE ❖ April 1233

'The Queen of Scots is with child!'

The messenger took a certain malicious joy in relaying the message to the stunned household of the Earl of Chester. 'It is his grace's command that all his subjects share in his joy and give thanks that his prayers have been answered at last. Your aunt, my lady,' he went on, turning to Eleyne whose face had drained of colour, 'sends you her especial greetings and hopes that you and your husband will travel north soon to visit her and the king.'

'You told me I should be king one day!' John rounded on Eleyne as soon as they were alone. 'Holy Virgin, and I believed you! How could you tell me such lies?'

'They weren't lies,' Eleyne cried, 'I told you what was told to me.' He was standing in the centre of the room, his hands clasped tightly, his knuckles white, visibly trying to control himself. 'This means nothing.' She ran to him and put her hands over his. 'A baby not yet born –? So much could happen. Your succession might not be for many years – King Alexander is not an old man –'

She had meant it as a reassurance, but his face darkened. 'He is only eight years older than I. Eight years, Eleyne!' John smiled at her sadly. 'And he is a robust man, whereas I . . .' He left the sentence unfinished.

'You are well now and stronger than you have ever been,' she said firmly. 'Besides, he is far more likely to die in battle before you, being a king! He has often led his men against the rebels in his kingdom, you told me so yourself.'

'And I? If I should lead my men to battle, how do you think I'd fare, sweetheart?' The humour returned to his eyes.

'Your men would follow you to the ends of the earth.' She was trying to keep the impatience out of her voice. 'And you know it. Though I pray to the Blessed Virgin that your cousin leaves you a peaceful inheritance when the time comes. And now, you must send a letter congratulating him on his news and telling him that we shall visit him as soon as it is possible. I want to see this country where I shall be spending so much of my life with its king.' Reaching up, she kissed him on the lips, and his face showed that the despair had left his eyes. Seconds later his arms were around her and his mouth came down hungrily on hers.

'You have seen it again? Seen it in the fire?' he asked. 'You know what will happen, don't you?' He had forgotten that he had forbidden her to look into the fire; told her to close her eyes and pray if she feared the visions were close. The touch of her lips had awakened him. She could see the excitement in his eyes. Reaching up, he began to unfasten her mantle. 'Tell me, Eleyne. Tell me what you saw.' In his hurry he had torn the neck of her gown. Bending, he kissed her breasts. Her excitement rose with his, and she wanted to reassure him, to tell him what he so badly needed to hear, but she couldn't. About the Sight she couldn't lie.

'I've seen nothing, my love, nothing,' she breathed. 'We must wait.' She was naked now, her gown and kirtle around her knees, cradling his head to her breast as he caught hungrily at the nipple with his teeth. The pain sent the excitement knifing through her belly, and she found she was pulling at his hair, willing him to throw her down and mount her, there on the floor. But already his ardour was cooling; he glanced ruefully at the beauty of her pale body and reached for her gown. 'Someone might come in –'

'Then bar the door, my lord.' She smiled at him, her hunger in her eyes. 'Quickly –'

She pulled the cover from the bed and throwing it down on the floor before the fire, she knelt on it and began with shaking hands to unbraid her hair.

'Eleyne –' His voice was husky.

'Bar the door, my lord.' She heard the imperious tone in her voice with faint surprise and expected him to frown, but he obeyed her at once. Her fingers still busy with her hair, she knelt upright on the rug, conscious that her breasts beckoned him, conscious as he fumbled with the buckle of his girdle that this time he could not resist her.

When he had finished she lay a long time on her back, gazing at the vaulted stone arch of the ceiling. The sunlight slanted through the mullioned windows, striking the warm colours of the embroidered hangings on the wall, animating them into strange and wonderful life. She felt the chill of sweat drying on her skin. His, not hers: as always, her excitement had died and she was left cradling his head in her arms, her body tight with longing, unslaked and lonely.

Below them the manor house was quiet. Everyone was out about their chores, even the women taking advantage of the cold spring sunshine to gain a respite from the badly ventilated hall. In the lord's solar the only sound was the sighing of the ashes as they cooled.

183

'Sire, you must speak to the queen.' The distraught official was hovering behind Alexander as he paced the great hall. 'She is pleading for you, sire.'

'No!' Through clenched teeth Alexander repeated the word for the tenth time. 'No! No! No! I do not wish to see her.'

'But she blames herself, sire —'

'With good reason!' The king swung to face him. 'She was warned to rest. All the signs told her to rest. It was written in the stars themselves!' He flung his hand towards the distant roof of the hall. 'But she took no notice! She knew best! She had to ride with her hawk and now she's lost the bairn. Oh yes, I blame her. And I do not wish to see her. Now get out of my sight!'

The man bowed unhappily and scurried towards the door at the west end of the hall, his face a picture of disapproval. Outside a cluster of women waited in agitation. One look was enough to tell them the king's response and dejectedly they hurried away.

The queen's rooms were full of the sound of her sobbing. It was three days since her miscarriage, but still she could not stop crying. She had not eaten or slept and cried constantly for her husband.

'Hush, madam, please.' The distraught lady at the bedside dabbed at her face with a cloth wrung out in rose water. 'You'll harm yourself. There will be other babies, you'll see.'

Joanna spotted the women clustered by the door. She pulled herself up on the pillows, her face swollen and blotchy with tears. 'Where is he? Is he coming?'

The Princess Margaret, the king's youngest sister, came forward. She shrugged and shook her head. 'Soon, my dear, soon. Alexander doesn't wish to tire you . . .'

'That's because he blames me. He does, doesn't he? It's my fault! He knows it's my fault!' Her voice rose in a wail. 'If I hadn't gone riding; if I had stayed at home and rested . . .'

'Hush, hush.' Margaret took her hand and stroked it unhappily. 'Don't upset yourself so much. Rest now.'

'No! I must see him, I must!' Joanna's voice rose in a hysterical scream. Pushing back the sheets, she threw her thin legs over the edge of the bed and staggered to her feet.

'Your grace, please! Please, come back to bed —' Her ladies clustered around her, frantically trying to push her back.

'Where is he? Where is the king?' Tears were streaming down her face.

'Joanna, I don't know where he is — please, please calm yourself —'

Margaret caught her arm. 'You'll do no good by trying to find him. He'll come to you when he's ready.'

'But he won't, he won't.' She pushed at the other woman so violently that Margaret staggered backwards as Joanna ran for the door, her long bed gown trailing behind her, her feet bare.

No one else tried to stop her but her ladies followed her down the long winding staircase as fast as they could. Instinctively, she knew where to find him. In the royal stables, waiting impatiently whilst his grooms threw saddle and bridle on his great stallion. There was a goblet of wine in his hand. He had been drinking heavily all morning, but he was far from drunk when he saw his wife running barefoot towards him across the high cobbles, her hair flying, her face streaked with tears.

The sight of her sliced through his anger and disappointment with ice-cold shock; for the first time he thought of her misery and pain.

He threw down the goblet, splashing the cobbles with the blood-red wine, and strode towards her. 'Joanna! Joanna, lass.' He scooped her up in his arms and buried his face in her hair. 'It doesn't matter, lass. There will be others. You'll see, there will be others.'

Sobbing, she clung to him. 'I'm sorry, I'm so sorry. It was all my fault . . .'

'No, no, it was God's will.' He was carrying her back towards the door, neither of them seeing the men and women around them. He carried her inside and up the stairs, soothing her as if she were a small child who had had a nightmare, and gently he put her down on the bed. Then he sat beside her and took her hand. 'All I want now is for you to get better quickly. Then,' he smiled, 'we'll try again. Now, you must rest. I'll call the physician to give you something to help you sleep.' He pulled the covers over her tenderly and leaned forward to kiss her forehead. As he walked from the room his face was bleak.

Impassively his clerk took down the letter to the Earl of Chester informing him of the Queen of Scots's miscarriage and commanding him to come to Scotland. It was time the heir presumptive to the throne became better acquainted with his future kingdom.

III
CHESTER CASTLE ❖ May 1233

Rhonwen woke with a start and peered around in terror. The chamber outside the bed curtains was completely dark. The fire had died. She could hear nothing at all, but she was shaking and could feel the perspiration cold on her body. The covers of her bed were tangled. She lay still, rigid with fear. A gentle snore came from the fireside where two of the serving girls lay, curled up on pallets, huddled into tight cold humps beneath their rugs. Across the room her companions were invisible behind the curtains of their bed. The room was full of people, and yet it was totally silent. She thought about the rush lights in their box near the pricket and the flint and tinder near it, but she couldn't move.

'Einion?' She breathed the name into the silence.

He knew. He knew she had burned his letter and he was displeased. More than displeased: she could feel his anger whipping around her in the dark. She clutched a pillow in front of her, her eyes wide, huddling back into the wall, feeling the stone against her shoulder blades beneath the heavy embroidered hangings.

'I did it for her.' Even as she mouthed the words, she knew it was no excuse. He had commanded Eleyne to return and she, Rhonwen, had intercepted that command. With a little sob, she clutched the amulet she wore at her throat, but what could an amulet do to protect her when the gods themselves were angry?

With a groan, one of the girls by the fire sat up, shaking with cold. She looked around in the darkness and then, feeling in front of her, found the cold cinders at the edge of the fire. It was her job to keep the fire in. She groped through the litter in the hearth, her fingers floury with ashes, feeling for warmth, feeling for the tiny spark which could ignite new kindling. She found it, burning her hand suddenly on a hidden ember, and scrabbling the rubbish of twigs and leaves from the hearth's edge to it she blew gently on the fragment of bark, watching as it glowed, seeing the reassuring wisp of smoke as the tinder ignited. In minutes the fire leaped to life once more.

Through the crack in her curtain Rhonwen saw the flame. She stared into the shadows and took a deep breath: he had gone and with him the anger and despair. She rested her damp forehead on her knees, feeling her hair fall forward around her shoulders. Perhaps it had been no more than a warning; perhaps she could still send a message to Eleyne to return to Wales. She closed her burning eyes, cutting out the shadows where the servant girl, the fire made up and banked to her satisfaction, had once more settled to sleep.

The next morning Chester Castle was buzzing with the news. The Queen of Scots had miscarried her child and the earl and countess were leaving for Scotland immediately without returning to Chester. They would be gone until the autumn.

Rhonwen listened tight-lipped. She had lain late, missing mass as was her custom, and taking no food. She had drunk only a cup of watered wine brought by one of the servants. So, Eleyne was moving north with no message to her; no summons for her to join the household. Her head throbbed. She gathered up some embroidery, used always to having her hands employed, and wearily made her way to the women's bower. Outside the spring sunshine was warm after the chill of the night. From the city beyond the castle walls she could hear the noise of the new day: shouts, yells, laughter, music, the rumble of iron-bound wheels on cobbles, the bellowing of cattle penned out beyond St John's waiting to be brought to the market. The other women had taken their work outside; she was alone. She sat in the embrasure and allowed the thin sunlight to fall on the fabric on her knee; reaching for her needle, she began to thread a length of madder silk.

Take her the message. The words were so loud in her head she thought someone had spoken. *Tell her . . .* Slowly she put down her sewing. She could feel her heart thumping unsteadily beneath her ribs.

'Who's there?' Her voice sounded thin and reedy in the silence.

There was no reply.

She thought of Eleyne, perhaps already on the long ride north. She would not return now; no summons however urgent would call her back to Gwynedd. She shivered. Einion's message had boded ill: did he have a warning for Eleyne? A message from the gods? She closed her eyes.

Tell her . . . The words were fading now, indistinct inside her head. Perhaps they had not been there at all.

'She won't come back! She can't come back!' she cried out loud into the shadows. 'Don't you see? She has to go with him. She doesn't belong to us any more.'

IV

DUNFERMLINE CASTLE ❖ June 1233

The ferries and boats had carried them at last across the broad glittering waters of the River Forth, and in the distance they could see old King Malcolm's castle of Dunfermline, with the abbey church silhouetted against the skyline.

Eleyne looked at John. His face was white with exhaustion, but his eyes were bright and excited, his fists hard on the ornate reins of his horse's bridle as he gazed up at the huge floating banner above the castle keep: the ramping lion of Scotland on its field of gold.

They had ridden the eastern route, from York to Northallerton and Darlington, on to Durham and Newcastle and thence across the bridge over the Tweed at Berwick and into Scotland at last, growing more excited with every mile. Now the gates in the castle wall stood wide in welcome and as they rode towards them they could hear the heralds trumpeting their approach.

Eleyne was breathless with anticipation as they dismounted in the courtyard and made their way into the great hall where the King and Queen of Scots stood together, waiting to greet them. Eleyne's eyes went sympathetically to her aunt, trying to see a likeness to her mother in the slim, delicate woman who stood, a little apart from her husband, dressed in a gown of black. Joanna's face was drawn and pale, her figure painfully thin beneath her mantle. There was no likeness to her half-sister, Joan, save in the eyes, the brilliant Plantagenet eyes, startling in the gentle face – eyes which were fixed on her and which, Eleyne realised with a shock, were far from friendly.

She looked away hastily, her gaze going to the king, and she caught her breath in stunned shock. She knew him! His was the face she had seen a thousand times in her dreams. He was tall, as tall as John, with flaming gold hair and beard to match, and broad-shouldered beneath his mantle. John bowed to him and he stepped down off the dais and clapped his cousin on the shoulder.

'So, you have brought your wife to meet us at last.' Already he was holding out his hands to her. She took them hesitantly, knowing her own were trembling badly. Still overcome with shock and strangely breathless, she curtseyed low, her eyes on his face, dazzled by the golden splendour of the man. It was true. He was the man in her dreams, and he was the most attractive man she had ever seen.

'Well, niece, how do you like Scotland?' His voice was mellow as he raised her and kissed her cheek. 'I hope you are going to cheer your aunt with your company. She's been sad, these last weeks.' He stared at her, open appreciation in his eyes, and she felt herself grow warm. Then his expression changed: 'I know you.' His voice was husky. 'Sweet Virgin, but I know you from somewhere.' Then he shook his head; the moment was gone.

'Cousin,' he called over his shoulder, 'you didn't tell me your countess was so beautiful. There won't be a red-blooded man in the whole of Scotland who doesn't fall in love with her!' For a moment longer he gazed at her, a slight frown between his eyes, then he mounted the dais again, waving them to chairs and beckoning for wine to refresh them.

Eleyne sat down; she was still shaking. So, he had felt it too, but how was that possible?

The emotion was immediately followed by guilt. How could she be so disloyal to John? She glanced at her husband and saw that he had relaxed, melting, as she had under the king's charm. Next to her the queen was silent, locked in her own misery, conscious that every man and woman in the great hall knew that the Earl of Chester was here as heir presumptive to the throne; that her failure to produce a child meant that, whatever reassurance she had been given that she would conceive again, they believed there would be no son now for Scotland's king.

She looked at Eleyne, so young and fresh and eager, her eyes glowing, her cheeks slightly flushed as she gazed at Alexander. She, now, was Scotland's hope, and Joanna could feel her resentment welling up like poison inside her. Feeling Joanna's eyes upon her, Eleyne looked at her aunt. For a moment they stared at one another, then Eleyne smiled. Impulsively she jumped to her feet and knelt beside the queen's chair, catching her hands in her own. 'I was so sorry . . .'

The sympathy in Eleyne's voice brought tears of self-pity to Joanna's eyes. 'You! Sorry?' She rounded on the girl in her misery. 'You should be pleased. You'll be the one now to give Scotland an heir!' Through her sobs her voice rang out loudly in the hall and there was a sudden silence around them.

The king frowned. 'Joanna, lass –'

'It's true! So why pretend?' Forgetting where they were, forgetting the protocol due on such a public occasion, Joanna jumped to her feet. She pushed past Eleyne and nearly knocked her over in her haste as she ran across the dais. She did not pause even to curtsey before her husband as she fled from the shocked eyes around her.

Eleyne scrambled to her feet. 'Oh please, wait . . .' she called. She looked helplessly from John to the king. 'Please, may I go after her? I didn't mean to upset her.' She was scarlet with embarrassment.

Alexander smiled. For an instant his eyes seemed to caress her. 'Aye, go after her if you wish. See if you can comfort her. I surely can't.' He sighed and turned back to John.

A servant led her up to the queen's bedchamber. Behind her Luned and three of her ladies ran to keep up as she hurried after the queen.

Joanna was lying sobbing on the high bed, surrounded by her attendants as Eleyne came in.

'Please, your grace – please, Aunt Joanna, don't be upset.' Ignoring the other women, Eleyne ran to the bed and caught the queen's hands. 'You'll have other babies. I'm sure you will. You mustn't mind us coming here. For the country's sake it must be known that there is a man at hand to take over should anything happen to the king, which God and the Blessed Virgin forbid.' She crossed herself hastily. 'But that is for show. King Alexander will live for many many years and you will have many children, I'm sure of it.'

The conviction in her voice reached through the queen's misery and slowly her sobs died away: 'Do you really believe that?'

Eleyne did not allow herself to hesitate: 'I do believe it,' she whispered.

Joanna forced a smile. She was still gripping Eleyne's hand. 'You're such a child. How can you know?'

'I know.' Eleyne met the other woman's eyes. It wasn't true, there would be no more children, not if John were to be king. She hated to lie, but how could she tell the truth? She was torn with pity. This woman's misery was nothing like Isabella's; she could feel the raw edges of it cutting deep inside Joanna's soul.

A rustle of movement from the women around the bed distracted her and Eleyne looked up. The king was standing beside her, his eyes on his wife's. Staring unobserved into his face, Eleyne felt a pang of loneliness. The love and compassion in his gaze were total, the strength and power of his personality directed at his wife alone; it excluded her and she felt lost.

Joanna's grip on her hand relaxed and she lay back on the silk pillows with an attempt at a smile: 'My lord, I should not have run away just now.'

'Indeed you shouldn't.' His face was stern again as he turned his gaze thoughtfully towards Eleyne. The girl's vivacity and warmth had died visibly as he came in, but not because of him; she hadn't known he was there. It was because of something she had said or thought, of that he was sure. She was staring down at her hands as they gripped those of his wife on the embroidered silk bedcovers, and he could feel the intense unhappiness which had swept over the girl, an unhappiness which equalled that of the woman at her side.

He had been about to give her a quick smile of reassurance and a command that she rejoin her husband, who had already been escorted with due ceremony over to the guesthouse of the abbey where he and Eleyne were to be lodged in a style and spaciousness which the crowded keep could not afford them. But now he hesitated, trying to see her face. She kept it turned from him, as if she knew he was trying to look at her.

'Lady Eleyne —' His voice was sharper than he intended, but it had the desired effect. She raised her eyes. What he saw there surprised him: the face was beautiful, the eyes large and clear and steady, but they were full of guilt.

He was suddenly doubly curious about his wife's niece.

'Come, we'll leave your aunt to rest.' He smiled and held out his arm, and after a moment she took it. In the broad passageway outside the chamber the king drew her towards one of the windows. Below them a deep glen dived, in a natural moat, into the woods beyond. Over the trees she could see, far away, the glittering water of the Forth.

'You must forgive your aunt, Eleyne. Losing her baby has changed her; turned her mind.' His deep voice was quiet. He was looking at her

190

closely. 'I am sure she will be herself again soon. Don't let her upset you.'

Eleyne raised her eyes to his. 'I wanted to be her friend –'

There was a tense silence between them.

'And so you will, you'll see. Give her time, and in the meanwhile I want you to enjoy yourself. You will like Scotland.' He paused. 'Forgive me, my dear, but I feel I know you so well.'

Eleyne shook her head. 'I've never been to Scotland before, sire. You must be thinking of someone else.' But he wasn't: somehow, somewhere, they had known each other before. She felt her face growing hot, and she tore her eyes away, looking beyond him to the crowd of courtiers and attendants who waited for them. Luned was there, giggling at the attentions of one of the handsome Scots squires.

'Do you like to ride, my lady?' The king had taken her arm again, and they walked towards the narrow staircase.

'I do, your grace, very much.' Eleyne seized with relief on the change of subject.

'Good. Then we'll hunt together, I think. And I have a court full of young gallants who will vie with their king for a chance to ride beside you. Robert Bruce, the Lord of Annandale, is here at court. His son, your nephew, is a friend of yours, I hear,' and he smiled, his hand firm beneath her elbow.

The lofty guest chambers of the abbey guesthouse, rich in warm hangings of embroidered wools, were crowded with their own servants as Eleyne joined her husband to inspect their bedchamber. Her head was whirling with impressions. The castle on its crag swarmed with people: the king with his charm and gallantry; the queen, taut and resentful; the courtiers and a crowd of gossiping, whispering faces, some already, did she but know it, aligning themselves with John, planning to curry favour with the man who might one day be their king.

'Did you comfort the queen?' John moved to her side and took her hand. His face was pale and drawn.

Eleyne shrugged. 'I wanted to comfort her, but . . .'

'But you know she will have no more children . . .' His voice had dropped to a whisper, but his eyes glittered. 'Tell no one of your gifts, Eleyne, nor of Einion's prophecy, no one at all. It is dangerous to know the future, especially in the courts of kings.' He raised his hands to her veil.

Eleyne frowned. 'We do not know that she won't have children, my lord,' she whispered unhappily, 'only that they will not succeed to the throne. Maybe she will have babes to comfort her . . .' She stopped, wondering whether it were better to lose a child one had never known or to lose a living baby once one had grown to know and love it, perhaps when it was a boy or a young man.

John shook his head, untroubled by such thoughts. 'There will be no more children. We both know it, Eleyne. It is written.' Hungrily, his mouth sought hers. The servants busied themselves around the room, and someone stirred the fire, releasing the sharp salt tang of burning driftwood.

'Out.' John did not take his eyes from hers as he gestured with his hand. The door opened and the servants melted through it. They were alone. This time he did not undress her. Pushing her skirts up to her waist, he almost threw her on to the bed and thrust into her repeatedly, his face set, his eyes remote. Eleyne felt a tremor of fear. It was as though he didn't know she was there.

In seconds it was over and he had rolled away, panting. Between her thighs she could feel the warm seed trickling uselessly from her body on to the bedcovers, where it grew cold and died. She wanted to cry.

V

July 1233

The Earl of Fife was beside her again, dark, handsome, his gelding matching Invictus stride for stride, the bright gilded leather of his horse's trapping fluttering as they raced after the king. Somewhere to their left, far ahead, they could hear the huntsman's horn and the baying of the deerhounds. The forest was brilliant with new green.

Malcolm Fife laughed exultantly. 'They scent blood, lady. Come!' He wheeled his horse and plunged into the wood. Without hesitation Eleyne followed, her long skirts, trailing from the saddle, catching in bushes and trees as the horses thundered on. Excitedly she kicked Invictus on, only half aware that the riders behind them, including Isabel Bruce and Lord Annandale and Robert, had not followed them but galloped straight up the main ride.

'We'll be up with the king in seconds!' Malcolm called over his shoulder. He reined his horse over hard, plunging up an even narrower overgrown track. 'Does your husband never hunt, my lady?' he shouted.

'Never!' she called back. It wasn't true, but Lord Fife's mood had affected her; his high spirits, his daring. She didn't want to think about John, sitting with his books in the dark rooms of the abbey guesthouse as he nursed a heavy summer cold. To do so made her feel guilty. She should be with him, not hunting with the king.

Gritting her teeth, she urged Invictus on, stung by the earl's arrogant assumption that his horse would lead. On three occasions now he had challenged her: twice she had won and once his horse had been in at the kill at the king's side as the huntsmen crowded round to cut the throat of the stag the dogs had brought down. Today, she had vowed she would be at Alexander's side, she and she alone, above all his followers. With a shout to Invictus, she brought the loop of the rein down on his sweat-streaked rump and felt the surge of power as the stallion shot forward.

The ravine had opened before either of them saw it. Both horses stopped in their tracks, rearing, their hooves slipping in the crumbling earth.

'God's bones!' Malcolm's face had gone white as he clung to his plunging horse. 'Are you all right?'

Eleyne nodded, aware that her legs were shaking violently as she peered down through the trees which clung to a deep cleft in the rocks, disappearing almost vertically below them. Somewhere in the distance they could hear the rush of water from the burn which coursed through the glen at the bottom.

Not giving herself time to think, Eleyne wheeled Invictus around. 'This way! I can still hear the horn!' But the other horse barred her way. There was no room to pass and the earl was dismounting. He was a stocky young man, fresh-faced and good-looking with a shock of dark unruly hair. 'I think he's lame. Hold a moment, my lady.' Ducking beneath his mount's head, he ran a hand down the horse's foreleg.

Eleyne trembled with impatience: 'We'll lose the king —'

'Do we need the king?' Before she knew what he was doing, he had straightened. His hands were on her waist and he had pulled her from her saddle. She did not react, too surprised to resist, then his hands were on her breasts.

Eleyne froze. 'My lord —'

Pulling her to him, he crushed her lips with his own, bending her backwards over his arm as he devoured her mouth, one hand greedily groping inside her gown. She struggled furiously, but his strength was enormous. She could feel herself losing her balance, feel the soft earth at the edge of the ravine crumble beneath her feet. Clawing at his face, she heard him swear as her gloved finger caught his eye. His grip slackened and she broke away from him, staggering towards Invictus, feeling the tightly braided coils of her hair slipping from beneath her head-dress. Pulling herself into the high saddle, she wheeled the horse and pushed him into a gallop back up the track the way they had come.

The king was standing among his followers staring down at a magnificent stag. He looked at her quizzically as she rode up: 'I thought

193

you vowed to be at the kill, my lady,' he called, teasing. She saw him eyeing her torn gown and dishevelled hair.

'It looks to me as though a little hunting has been done away from the main chase.' His smile was forced. Beside him Lord Annandale frowned.

Eleyne felt her face going crimson. 'One of your lords, your grace, seems to know little of the code of chivalry,' she retorted. 'He tried to dishonour me – and my husband . . .'

'Oh come.' The king walked across to her. 'Hardly that, I'm sure. Most ladies take it as a compliment if a man shows them his admiration.' He reached up and put his hand over hers. If he could feel them shaking he made no sign. His eyes became serious, holding hers. 'Lord Fife is a hothead, lass, and he's made no secret of his admiration for you,' he said with quiet urgency. 'It was he, I take it?' He searched for the missing earl among the crowded courtiers. 'The two have made him a little over-eager for a kiss, that's all. Least said, the better, don't you think?' He was smiling, but she could hear the command in his voice.

'But your grace –'

'Enough, Eleyne.' His fingers tightened. He was holding both her hands over the pommel of the saddle, crushing them in his grip. 'I'll have a word with Lord Fife.' His words could be heard by her alone. 'I'll tell him to flirt less and remind him you're a married lady, for all you're so fresh and young and enticing.'

Oh, he was the handsomest man she had ever seen, this King of the Scots, with his golden hair and beard and his fierce commanding eyes, but he frightened her! She felt the strength in the hand which so easily held hers imprisoned, sensed the power of his will as he looked up at her. Suddenly shy, she looked away, and at once he released her hands. 'Enough,' he said softly, 'I don't think any more need be said.'

She watched as he strode away, once more absorbed in the crowd of huntsmen and courtiers, noblemen and servants who surrounded him, heard the talk and laughter, saw the carcass of the stag being trussed and slung between poles, and she felt terribly alone.

VI

'Did you enjoy the hunt?' John asked wearily. His eyes were sore from reading and his head ached.

'Not very much.' Eleyne tossed her head. 'I don't think I like it here, my lord.' Her pride was still stung by the king's rebuke and her temper dangerously high.

John frowned. 'You have not annoyed the king or his henchmen, Eleyne? You know how important it is for them to like me.'

194

'Do you not think to ask if they might have annoyed me?' she flung back at him.

John stood up, and threw down his pen. 'What happened?'

'The Earl of Fife forced me to kiss him; he tried to touch me, to force me –'

'Oh, surely not. The Earl of Fife is one of the most influential men in the kingdom –'

'And he tried to force your wife!' she repeated. 'When my father found another man in bed with my mother, he hanged him like a common thief!'

'De Braose was your father's enemy, when all is said and done, Eleyne. The cases are not the same. And Lord Fife was not in bed with you. He snatched a kiss, that's all.'

'And you don't mind?'

'Yes, I mind.' He folded his arms beneath his cloak. 'But I am not going to be foolish about it. No harm was done. He paid you a compliment. Just make sure you are not alone with him in future.'

'And that is all you are going to say?' She was almost speechless with indignation. Her cool, stern husband was not even ruffled by her news. 'You are like the king. You think it a joke! The great Earl of Fife tried to kiss Lady Chester in the woods. Oh, she's not dishonoured, she's not even supposed to be angry! She is supposed to laugh it off and consider herself flattered!'

'You told the king?' John frowned. 'Eleyne, I don't want him to think you are going to cause trouble among his followers.'

'Cause trouble!' Eleyne was incensed. 'Perhaps, my lord and husband, if you had been there, hunting with everyone else, it would not have happened! Perhaps if you were in the great hall more often after supper it would not happen –'

'That is enough!' he exclaimed angrily. 'May I remind you that neither would it have happened if you had remained here with me! In future you will stay here, at my side, and behave like a dutiful wife. Then men will remember that is what you are.'

That night he slept with his back to her, a bed cloak wrapped around his thin shoulders against the damp and cold of the rain which had swept north across the Forth in the darkness and which seeped in through the very stones of the building. At dawn he began to cough again.

VII

The great castle of Edinburgh was black on its rain-soaked rock. Staring up at it, Rhonwen felt her heart clench with fear. Was this where Eleyne would spend the rest of her days? Her carefree, bright child a prisoner in this cold northern land. She huddled into her cloak and looked around intently. Her servants and horses were as tired as she was after the long ride north, and now they were disappointed. The court, they had been told, had been in Dunfermline across the broad River Forth for many weeks. They had farther yet to go.

It was already growing late. They had to find somewhere to sleep in Edinburgh and in the morning go on to find the Queen's Ferry which, they had been told, would take them on their journey. They were fighting their way down the busy high street with its market crowds, and Rhonwen was mentally counting out the last of her precious hoard of silver coins. Were there enough left to buy bread and meat and sleep tonight in a clean bed with a minimum of others to share it? And then to pay for a guide and the ferry in the morning?

She watched wearily as one of her servants stopped a tall, thin-faced man with high cheekbones and dark hooded eyes, asking him for somewhere to stay. She saw the puzzled looks on both their faces as they struggled to understand one another's tongues, then the Welshman turned, nodding. He waved ahead down the street. 'We are to go out of the town by the Nether Bow Port and on through the canon's burgh, then we'll find a guesthouse at the Abbey of the Holy Rood on the edge of the forest,' he called. 'It's not far to the ferry in the morning.'

Rhonwen kicked her horse on down the steep road through the thronging market crowds. Now that she was so close to Eleyne, she was beginning to feel nervous; what would Eleyne say when she saw her and when she heard, as she must, that Rhonwen had burned Einion's letter with all its urgency, and – the fact which had terrified Rhonwen into starting her frantic journey north – that the old man was dead and with him the message which had been so important it needed Eleyne's immediate return to Môn?

VIII

DUNFERMLINE

That night Eleyne dreamed again about the king. She awoke, her husband's implacable back turned towards her in the darkness, aware that her body was alive with longing, that her skin was warm and eager beneath the sheets, her nipples hard, her thighs flaccid and welcoming. It was the third time she had dreamed of Alexander in as many nights, and each time she had buried her face, hot with shame, in the pillows. What kind of wanton was she that she dreamed of her husband's cousin – her aunt's husband – in such brazen detail? She stroked her hand surreptitiously across her flat belly and up to her breasts, feeling them tense beneath her fingers. Outside she could hear the heavy summer

196

rain pouring endlessly on to the lead roofs of the guesthouse and gurgling from the gutters. The rich smell of the earth, newly drenched, rose through the open windows and filled the room. Beyond the bed curtains she heard a movement from one of the truckle beds which lined the room, then a whisper and the creak of wood followed by a stifled giggle.

She turned over, staring towards the heavy tester over the bed. Beside her was John's deep regular breathing. Cautiously she reached out and touched his back, running her fingers down the length of his spine. He moved slightly and groaned, then he slept again. Beyond the curtains the room had grown silent.

IX

'Lady Chester!'

Sometimes the king addressed her formally; sometimes he called her Eleyne and sometimes he addressed her, as he addressed his wife, as 'lass'. She never knew which was coming or, when she looked into his face, if he were serious or teasing.

'We have a visitor who will interest you.'

Beside him on the dais Joanna was sitting near the smouldering fire, attended by Robert Bruce, Eleyne's nephew, newly raised from page to squire in the queen's household and celebrating the fact by sticking his tongue out at Eleyne when he thought no one else was looking. The queen's face was pale and she had grown even thinner over the last few weeks, but her eyes were calm now, and no longer red with weeping. Robert alone was sometimes able to make her smile.

The visitor, as Eleyne made her way across the hall beside her husband, was a tall man, dressed in a black gown and mantle, his white hair and beard moving silver in the light of the flickering candles. He's a bard, she thought, like Einion. Perhaps he's a seer – and she was afraid.

She walked towards the dais at John's side, aware that many eyes had followed her from the moment she entered the hall, aware that she was being gossiped about, her name linked with the Earl of Fife even though she had never been alone with him again or hunted since that fateful day. And even though she slept every night with her husband and seldom left his side at all, by his decree.

She raised her eyes and met those of the queen, who smiled at her. The two had become friends after a fashion during the long weeks of their stay, Joanna's resentment tempered by Eleyne's warmth and open friendliness, so different from the bitchy, manoeuvring ladies of the court. Reaching the dais, Eleyne curtseyed to the king and queen. Near them the tall man rose. He bowed. His eyes were clear quicksilver in his face; depthless, swift-moving, all-seeing.

'This is Michael.' The king too rose. 'The greatest seer in all Scotland if not all Europe.' He smiled gravely. 'He comes to tell my fortune, is that not so, Sir Wizard?'

Joanna had sent for the man, desperate to know the future, but he had talked to her of the waning moon and the obscuration of the firmament and the alignment of the planets and told her nothing.

Eleyne could feel his power. Like Einion's it came from him in waves, probing, all-seeing, frightening. She stood still, feeling it encircling her like a tangible web, testing her, questing into the corners of her mind. Her fear passed as quickly as it had come, and she met his eyes with something like relief. That he would find a way of talking to her, she was certain. Not now before the king and his court and her husband, but later, alone.

X

'What did you see for the queen?' She hardly dared meet his gaze. In the darkness of the deep glen the water flashed white against the stones. He had arranged their meeting as she had known he would, his servant guiding her to this remote corner within the span of the outer castle walls, whisking her past servants and guards as though he had thrown a cloak of invisibility about her shoulders.

'What I see for the queen is between the gods and her, my daughter.' The man was as slim as a reed in his cloak of black, upright, though he leaned on a staff.

'She will have no more children.' Eleyne hardly dared breathe the words out loud.

'Yet there will be a son for Scotland.' Michael smiled coldly. 'You have power, madam, but it is untrained. That is dangerous.' Eleyne looked away from him. Her heart was thumping with excitement, hearing only the first part of his statement. A son for Scotland – her son.

'You must learn to guard the truth and ponder it, for it may not be the truth you seek. The gods are pleased to speak in riddles,' he went on sententiously. 'There is danger here in Scotland for you. Did your visions tell you that? Your eyes are full of golden diadems, but first comes death.'

Eleyne felt a cold shiver cross her flesh.

'Death must always come before the throne passes from one man to another,' she whispered. She had closed her mind to the fact that the death must be Alexander's.

He smiled: 'That much is true. I should like to teach you, lady; it is a long while since I had an apprentice.'

198

She laughed, relieved at the sudden lightening of the atmosphere, and for a moment she was almost tempted. To have the power – the Sight – to command, and the knowledge it would bring, would be wonderful. But it would also be terrifying, and regretfully she knew her initial reaction had been right. This was something she must turn her back on. 'I'm afraid that road is not for me,' she said sadly. 'My place is with my husband. What pictures I see I must try to understand alone. If only they were clearer, if only they showed me more.'

'The interpretation of dreams and visions takes study and prayer and fasting, too great a task for a glittering countess.' His smile was malicious.

She was silent, indignation fighting with temptation as she recognised his challenge. She straightened her shoulders. 'Then I must remain in ignorance and wait for the will of the gods to be made clear.' She paused. 'Will you answer one question for me?'

He raised an eyebrow. 'Only one?'

She gave a nervous smile. 'It's about the king.' Her voice dropped to a whisper. 'It's as if I've known him all my life. Yet that's not possible.' She raised her eyes to his fathomless silver gaze. 'Is it?'

He leaned thoughtfully on his staff, looking away from her. 'It is possible,' he said, 'that you have known one another through all eternity.'

A strange shudder touched her spine. *And did I love him?* she wanted to ask. *Did I love him through all eternity?* But she didn't dare. She too looked away, ashamed and frightened by her thoughts. 'Why do we have dreams and visions,' she burst out, 'if we cannot change our destinies whatever we may see?'

He smiled: 'That, my lady, is where you are wrong.' He stared down at the burn which ran at their feet, listening to the gentle chatter of the water in the dark. 'The gods send us warnings that we may heed them, if we poor mortals can but understand them.'

She swallowed. 'William? I could have saved William?'

He shrugged. 'I know nothing of a William. But destiny hangs heavy over you; I see it in the air around you; I hear it in the clash of swords; I see it in the stain of blood. I see it in time past and time to come.' He looked at her again, but his eyes were unfocused, as if they did not see her. 'I see you as the mother of a line of kings.' It was what Einion had said.

'And will I be a queen?' Her question was breathless, almost inaudible against the sound of rushing water.

Michael was still for a long time. Then his eyes focused once more. Nearby an owl floated through the trees, a white ghost in the darkness. As it crossed the burn, it screeched once, a harsh defiance of the silence. Michael shook his head: 'I see no more,' he said at last.

Above them the trees were thick canopies in front of the stars.

XI

The hall was crowded with people. It stank of wine and roasted ox and sweat and floral toilet waters and perfume. As she threaded her way through the crowds, still wrapped in her cloak and deafened by the roar of music and laughter and shouting, Eleyne's eyes were on the two men who sat side by side at the centre of the high table. The king and the earl were deep in conversation, seemingly oblivious of the noise around them. As she walked, a slim lone figure swathed in silk of rich scarlet, she saw Alexander lift his head. Their eyes met and she felt the strange shock of recognition shake her as it always did when they looked at one another. Beside him, John, her pale handsome husband, was suddenly like a stranger to her.

XII

Rhonwen stood very straight before the Earl and Countess of Chester, her hands clutched in the soft wet wool of her cloak, her hood, soaked with rain, pushed back on her shoulders. Some frowns, some smiles had greeted her as she threaded her way across the room. She saw them without registering that she had done so, and noted in some secret part of her mind who was still a friend, who an enemy.

Neither the earl nor the countess had smiled as Rhonwen curtseyed before them.

'I have brought messages from Gwynedd, my lady.'

Eleyne stepped forward and taking Rhonwen's hands kissed her on the cheek. 'I'm glad to see you.' There was a note of defiance in her voice.

'Are you, *cariad*?' Rhonwen scanned her face. The child looked well; and yet there were shadows in her eyes. All was not as it should be with the Chesters. She looked over Eleyne's shoulder at John of Chester. He had a half-smile on his face and, catching her eye, he raised an eyebrow.

'As you see, Lady Rhonwen, my wife is glad to see you. I'm sure she will welcome your company.'

Rhonwen stiffened. Although his voice lacked warmth, there was no particular hostility in the man's demeanour. It was as if he were distracted – his mind elsewhere.

She hugged Eleyne. One of her worries at least had been allayed, and at last she felt the child relax.

'My father and mother, Rhonwen, how are they?' Eleyne pulled her into a private corner.

'They are both well, *cariad*.' Rhonwen made sure she was not over-heard. 'As are Gruffydd and Senena. They are free, free at long last! And your father has given Gruffydd part of the lands of Lleyn and he and Dafydd are friends, for now.' She lowered her eyes and Eleyne smiled.

'So, Gruffydd still plans to win back his inheritance one day?'

'He will, soon. He will.' Rhonwen had ridden to Degannwy from Chester and spoken to Gruffydd before her ride north. After that she had journeyed to Aber and spent an hour in private conversation with Llywelyn. The results of the conversation had surpassed her wildest dreams and put the death of Einion temporarily out of her mind. The prince did not speak of restoring to Gruffydd his birthright of North Wales, but he spoke of a far greater scheme and he had entrusted her with verbal messages for Eleyne and through her to Lord Chester and the King of the Scots. Nothing was to be written; nothing risked. Correctly judging that in this matter at least Rhonwen would be inestimably useful, Llywelyn had trusted her with the secrets of three nations.

'We must talk alone, *cariad*,' Rhonwen said softly. 'Soon. I have messages from your father.'

Eleyne scanned the other woman's face and nodded. 'We join the king and queen for supper in the castle hall. After that we'll talk.'

The candles had burned low, the soft beeswax clotting in sweet yellow lumps on the table. They had talked for a long time of Llywelyn's plan for an alliance between himself and Alexander and the leaders of the growing baronial opposition in England to King Henry. Later, when he returned from the king's hall they would talk, in secret, to John, but for now the topic was closed. Rhonwen, whose eyes had burned with cold fanaticism as she described the plan, sat back exhausted, too tired even to reach for the mead the servants had poured before they left the two women alone in the small guest chamber. But still Rhonwen was holding something back. Eleyne leaned forward, her elbows on the table, and looked through the flame of the candle at the other woman's face with its shifting mask of shadow. The room was intensely quiet after the noise of the great hall.

'What is it, Rhonwen? What have you not told me?' Her voice was gentle, persuasive, but Rhonwen noticed there was an undertone of command there, an echo of her father.

She sighed. 'When the snows were still thick on the ground, you had a letter from Lord Einion.' There was a long silence. Eleyne's eyes did not leave her face. 'He commanded you to go to him on Môn.'

'And what happened to the letter?' Eleyne asked.

'I burned it.' Rhonwen could feel the cold draught at the back of her neck. Her mouth had gone dry. 'I wanted you to be happy with your husband. I knew you did not want to come back so soon to Gwynedd.'

'And did you tell Einion that?'

'He knows.' Rhonwen shivered and Eleyne saw her hand go surreptitiously to her throat where the amulet lay hidden beneath her gown. 'And he was angry with me.'

'What did he want to tell me, do you know?' Eleyne asked.

Rhonwen put her hands over her eyes. Silently she shook her head.

'Then I shall go to see him when we return south. We are going home soon.'

'No, no, *cariad*, don't you understand? He's dead!' Rhonwen cried. 'He died after he wrote the letter. Even if I had sent it to you it would have been too late!'

It was no less than the truth, but she didn't believe it herself. If Eleyne had been coming, he would have waited for her – he would have found a way to stay alive until she came.

'I wonder what he wanted to say to me,' Eleyne said after another silence. There was no reproach in her voice, no anger, only curiosity.

Rhonwen swallowed. 'He's tried to tell me,' she whispered, 'three times he's tried to tell me . . .'

Eleyne felt the hairs on the back of her neck lift and stir. Einion and Michael had both seen her destiny. What else could Einion have seen that he would have held death itself at bay to tell her?

CHAPTER NINE

I

ROXBURGH CASTLE ✧ July 1235

'Don't go! Please, don't go!' Joanna threw herself at her husband's feet, sobbing.

'Joanna, lass . . .' The king's patience was wearing thin.

'Please. You'll be killed! You mustn't go.'

'I have to go.' Pulling her to her feet, he set her aside as if she had been a rag doll in his path and beckoned forward once more the men who had been trying to arm him. 'I have had enough of these rebels in Galloway. I mean to bring those people under my rule once and for all. They have disobeyed me and tried to set up a bastard lord as their leader. I mean to make them accept Alan of Galloway's daughters as his heirs, with my sheriffs to uphold my authority. Now please, my sweet lady, leave me.'

'Lord Chester isn't going with you, and Alan's widow Margaret is one of his sisters!' she flung at him. 'He cares about what happens to Margaret and his nieces, but he has more sense than to ride into a nest of thieves and rebels!' Her voice had risen again to a panic-stricken shriek. 'Perhaps he means to stay here and keep himself safe to inherit your throne when you are killed – '

After two years of travelling around the Chester and Huntingdon estates, and three more visits to London, Eleyne and John had once more been invited north to Scotland.

Alexander frowned. 'That is not true. Lord Chester is not well enough to ride and you know it.' He raised his arms as the mail hauberk was settled on his shoulders over his heavy, padded gambeson. The armourer buckled the cuirass over it, and finally came the surcoat. 'I'll be back for Margaret's wedding, lass, you'll see.' He spoke heartily, trying to cheer her. 'You help her with all her finery. That'll keep you busy and I'll be back before you know it.'

Joanna gave a weak smile, trying to pull herself together. She was ashamed of her tears. She had seen her husband off to war so many times, always fearful but always courageous – until now. It had been as much a shock to her as it was to him to find that she was shaking, wanting to cling to him, wanting to keep him with her. They both knew why. Unspoken between them was the tally of months since the miscarriage with still no sign of another pregnancy, and the presence of the Earl of Chester, summoned back to Scotland ostensibly for the wedding of the king's sister to Gilbert, the Earl Marshal of England, but in reality so that the heir presumptive would be on hand should anything happen to the king.

Alexander waved his men aside and, shrugging his shoulders beneath the heavy weight of his armour, strode towards the door. 'I shall bid you farewell outside before the court, Joanna. See to it you send me to war with a smile and your favour in my helm.' She was the queen; she must find it within her to be strong.

The army which had been gathering for days beyond the castle walls had broken camp at last. The ranks of armed men were ready to march, waiting only for their king to lead them. In the courtyard before the tower Alexander turned and kissed his wife's hand. Joanna's eyes were red and swollen, but she managed to restrain her weeping. Beside her stood Eleyne, her face white. As Alexander took her hand, she curtseyed low, not looking at his face. 'Sweet Christ go with you, your grace.' Her voice was a whisper. He tightened his grip on her fingers briefly, then moved on to his sister Margaret, pretty gentle Margaret, soon to be the wife of the Earl Marshal of England. He smiled at her, and received a reassuring smile in return. His farewells made, he raised his hand to the assembled courtiers and turned towards his horse.

II

Eleyne stood looking out of the deeply embrasured window, clutching her mantle around her as if she were cold, her embroidery – a panel of Margaret's wedding dress – discarded on the stone seat near her. The day was hot and airless. Behind her in the body of the room the queen and her ladies chatted listlessly over their work. There had been no word from Galloway.

Torn with guilt about his sister's safety and his nieces' inheritance, and knowing he should be there with the king and his brother-in-law, Lord Annandale, John had closeted himself in the guesthouse with the officials who travelled regularly from Chester and the lands of Huntingdon, immersing himself in day-to-day administration. He was there now, gaping up at the stone vaulting above his head. What if the king should die? What if a messenger should come that very morning with the news that Alexander had been mortally injured? He closed his eyes and brought his mind back to the business in hand.

Eleyne could not focus on the fine stitches of her embroidery. Her head ached. Even in the cool stone of the old keep the air was unpleasantly humid, and she had given up trying to listen to the conversation around her. It faded into the distance and for a moment she felt her eyes close.

At seventeen she had blossomed into a composed, beautiful young woman, outwardly confident, popular with her servants and her companions. She was eccentric still in her love of her own company, her passion for her horses and her strange abstracted moods, but she was kind and thoughtful and she was a princess and they were prepared to forgive her much. But she was still childless. That preyed on many minds, not least her own.

The sound of the watchman's horn from the high gatehouse brought all talk to a halt. The embrasure was suddenly crowded as Margaret and three of the other ladies craned past her to try to see out of the window. Behind them the queen sat unmoving; Eleyne saw that her knuckles were white.

The messenger was weary and covered in dust, and still out of breath from his long ride as he knelt before Joanna.

'The king was attacked, madam, after he entered Galloway. The rebels fell on our men as they were making camp.' He gulped for breath. 'But the rebels have been defeated. By God's mercy the Earl of Ross was delayed in joining the main body of the army with his men. He was able to attack them from the other side and take them by surprise. Their defeat is total.'

'And the king?' Joanna's voice was flat and hard. 'Is the king all right?'

'He is safe, your grace. He has ordered Walter Comyn to remain and complete the rebels' defeat. He bid me return to tell you that he and his lords are on their way back for Princess Margaret's wedding.'

Joanna closed her eyes as relief swept over her: 'The Blessed Virgin be thanked.'

Eleyne silently echoed her prayer; she hadn't realised that she had been holding her breath.

Rhonwen was standing by the table where she had been sorting silks. Eleyne saw that she was watching her closely, a thoughtful expression on her face, and suddenly she was afraid: it was almost as though the other woman had guessed her secret. But how could she? It was a secret so terrible that Eleyne barely acknowledged it to herself. A secret which bit deep into her soul: that she had fallen in love with the man who was her aunt's husband and so her own uncle – Alexander of Scotland.

Later, before the shrine of Queen Margaret in Dunfermline Abbey, the court lit candles and gave thanks. At Joanna's side Eleyne raised her eyes to the great carved crucifix upon the altar. Had her husband secretly prayed for Alexander's death? If so, she had not known about it. In her heart she was giving thanks over and over again that the man of whom she dreamed so often was alive.

III
BERWICK-UPON-TWEED ❖ 28 July 1235

King Alexander had held a meeting of his council at Berwick. He needed money to pay for the campaign in Galloway and money for the wedding which – the better to defy King Henry who had not yet given it his blessing – was to be a splendid and royal affair.

He and John had talked long and privately once more about Llywelyn's proposals. The possibility of an informal Celtic alliance against England's predatory king was becoming more and more viable, and both had known that they had the perfect go-between. Intelligent, energetic and impetuous enough to escape suspicion should she take it into her head to ride about the country, Eleyne would make the ideal messenger between the parties involved. 'If she returns from Chester to see her father it would not be remarkable,' Alexander said slowly, leaning back in his chair.

'She'll be glad of the excuse, I'll warrant,' John smiled. 'Each time she goes home my hothead wife gets chased away for yet another misdemeanour. She has enemies in the English faction in Gwynedd.'

Alexander raised an eyebrow: 'Her mother?' His own wife had never meddled in politics the way her half-sister did, and for that he was profoundly glad.

John shook his head. 'I have a feeling things are better with her mother. It is the little de Braose. Friendship gone sour is always the worst kind of enmity.'

Alexander laughed. 'Nevertheless, your wife will find a way to her father's ear, I'm sure. She has a winning way with her.'

'Perhaps it would be better if it were less winning.' John scowled. 'There are those among your lords who still fawn on her too much.'

'But you guard her well.' The king spoke lightly. 'Almost as though you did not trust her.'

John pushed his chair back abruptly as if he were about to rise. Then, remembering he was in the presence of the king, he subsided once more on to the embroidered cushion. 'I trust her with all my heart,' he said coldly, 'she would never dishonour me. Not with any man.'

There was a moment's silence.

'I am glad to hear it, cousin,' the king replied. 'Then you have no need to worry when she comes to Scotland without you.'

206

August the first was the date fixed for the wedding of the king's youngest sister to the Earl Marshal of England, an act of defiance against King
Henry worthy of Llywelyn himself, and an occasion to which the court
had been looking forward with much excitement.

The rumour was that King Henry had fallen in love with Margaret
four years earlier and had wanted her for his queen. She too had been
much smitten by the handsome young King of England, but her elder
sister was married to Henry's justiciar, Hubert de Burgh, a man now
rapidly falling out of favour in England, and Henry's advisers persuaded
him that it would not be suitable for the king to marry de Burgh's
wife's younger sister. Margaret was heartbroken, but with the passing
of time it seemed her heart was willing to be mended.

The first part of the wedding feast over, the guests were wandering
across the meadow which lay at the foot of the castle walls. Beyond it
flowed the Tweed, silver in the afternoon heat, and beyond it the border
with England. Nearby a group of minstrels played a selection of the
latest popular dances as they side-stepped and dipped across the turf,
a group of people dancing and clapping to the noisy refrains.

Rhonwen had stopped to supervise a servant who was pinning up
Eleyne's hem, caught beneath the enthusiastic foot of the lady next to
her in the ring dance. The repair completed to her satisfaction, she
waved the girl away.

'What is wrong between you and Lord Chester, *cariad*?' Making
sure that they would not be overheard Rhonwen caught her arm.
'When I saw you together in Chester Castle you were like lovesick
doves, the pair of you, but in Scotland he watches you as wistful as a
dog outside the kitchen, and you jump with guilt every time you see
him.'

Eleyne pulled her arm away. 'Nothing is wrong. What could be?'

'The handsome Lord Fife for one?' Rhonwen narrowed her eyes.
'I've seen him watching you.'

'Oh, him.' Eleyne dismissed him with a shrug. 'The king my uncle
has told him to stay away from me.' She felt the colour rise in her
cheeks and turned away to look at the river. The tide was low and the
sun reflected on the mud, turning it to rich silk stained with gold.

'The king your uncle, is it now?' The soft voice at her elbow was
gently probing. 'And the queen your aunt, what does she say in the
matter?'

'She thinks it amusing,' Eleyne replied dry-lipped. 'She teases me
about my followers.'

There was a burst of laughter near them and a group of girls scam-
pered past, giggling, pursued by two young men. The wind was rising.
The ornate tents set up around the castle walls began to flutter and

thrum, a background accompaniment to the steady beat of whistle, viol and cymbals, timbrel and cittern.

Rhonwen smiled. There was more. Oh, yes, there was more there. She could always tell when Eleyne had secrets, and she could always worm them out of her. In the end.

The Chesters were being accommodated in a large tent, the gaudy canvas surmounted by pennants, the tall conical roof surrounded by scalloped bunting.

Chairs had been placed outside the tent near the fire which had been lit as soon as dusk fell. The revelry continued all around them, the noise as loud as ever. Glancing up at the high stone walls of Berwick Castle above them, Eleyne shivered.

The banquet over at last, the bride and groom had departed to their chamber in the great keep. At last she and John had been able to leave the hall with its reek of cooking and wine and hot excited humanity, and pick their way through the dozens of fires to their own. Their servants were mulling wine, and inside the tent she could see in the warm lamplight the piles of rugs and furs unnecessary on such a hot night, but nevertheless a soft bed awaiting them.

John sprawled in one of the chairs and let out a great sigh of exhaustion. 'Perhaps we can rest a few days here before we ride south.'

'The burgesses of Berwick won't thank us; they are already complaining at the number of people camped in the town,' Eleyne said drowsily. 'They hope to see us all on our way as soon as possible.'

John snorted. 'We'll be gone soon enough. They should be glad their town has been honoured with a royal wedding. Burgesses were ever tight-fisted. You –' He beckoned a young minstrel who had paused near them, his instrument across his back. 'Can you play us a lullaby to ready us for bed?'

The boy gave a slow rich chuckle. 'Aye, my lord.' He pulled the viol from his shoulders and squatting near the fire tweaked the instrument into tune. Then he began to play.

Eleyne closed her eyes. She had eaten and drunk and danced since dawn, or so it seemed, and she was tired. And she wanted to leave Scotland. She still dreamed of the king; she found herself watching him; her fingers longed to touch his springy golden hair. She spent hours on her knees in prayer begging forgiveness – of whom she was not quite sure – the Holy Virgin who was so pure in thought and body? Would she understand and help a mortal woman fight the sins in her heart? Or St Bride, who was her own goddess, the patron of her birthday, surely she would help? And the Blessed Queen Margaret, whom all Scotland revered as a saint and whose miracles were manifest. She too might intercede.

She must not let herself think about him, must control her dreams. She must leave Scotland; never see him again. She was doubly guilty because she loved her aunt, and Joanna had at last, she thought, come to love her. In spite of herself, she looked once more at the castle walls, their battlements lost in the dark. Desolation and loneliness hung over this place. However loud the music, however joyful the crowds, she could feel the sadness: sadness past and sadness to come. Beyond the encampment, beyond the ditches and palisades which surrounded the town, the black rolling hills stretched out into the dark.

The boy was playing more softly now – the music compelling and clear against the background noise which swelled around them. She leaned forward to hear better and, opening her eyes, found that she was staring into the fire.

IV

DOLBADARN CASTLE, GWYNEDD, ❖ Late August 1235

'Why? Why must I stay here?' Isabella glared at the slate-black skies and dark mountains all around her. Standing on its rock on the route from Caernarfon to the upper Conwy valley, Dolbadarn Castle, with its enormous stone keep and majestic hall, lay below high gorse and scree-covered ridges in the heart of the great mountains. It was a desolate place.

'I want to be with your father's court. There at least I have some fun.' Sulkily she turned her back on the window. 'Is it because Senena is there? Does she object to my Englishness?' Her voice was heavy with sarcasm.

Dafydd sighed. 'Gruffydd is in the Lleyn and Senena is with him. We are here at my father's orders, Bella, you know that as well as I. There are matters here that need sorting out.'

'I think we are here to keep us out of the way.' She flounced across the room towards him. 'And if you are too stupid to see it, I'm not! Your father has something up his sleeve, Dafydd, don't you see? He's up to something. And he doesn't want you there. So it must be something to do with Gruffydd. How can he be so foolish as to trust him!' In an anguish of frustration, she turned with a swirl of skirts and paced back to the window.

Dafydd smiled ruefully at her back. She was shrewd, his little wife, and as so often right in her assessment of the situation. Save in one respect. The plot Llywelyn and Gruffydd were hatching included him. It was Isabella and Isabella alone they wanted to exclude from Aber.

'Sweetheart.' He followed her to the window and put his hands on her shoulders. If it took a lie to allay her suspicions, then lie he must.

'I can see I must let you in on a secret. It is Gruffydd and I who plan a meeting. I ride to Criccieth to see him tomorrow. I'll be gone only two days. I want you to remain here so that it seems that I am still here. I'll be back before you know it, then you and I shall ride together for Caernarfon to join the princess my mother.' He dropped a kiss on the top of her head. He had no intention of going to Criccieth. The family meeting with Eleyne was at Aber.

It never occurred to him that she would disobey him.

V

GWYNEDD ❖ August 1235

It was Eleyne's first visit to Aber since Isabella's miscarriage and her own ignominious return to Chester. Then it had been mid-winter. Now the countryside was heavy with summer. The clouds hung low over the mountains and thunder rumbled around the hidden peaks of Eryri. Her party was small: this was a private visit by the Countess of Chester to her mother. Attended by Rhonwen and Luned and two ladies, only a dozen men-at-arms escorted them over the high, rough road from Conwy to Aber through the clinging mist and down towards the river.

Eleyne was silent as she rode, her head whirling with thoughts as she guided her mare over the rough track, all that was left of the broad Roman road which swung high here across the shoulder of the mountains. She had messages from King Alexander and John for her father; she had messages of goodwill, albeit stilted, from Joanna to her half-sister; and she was still thinking about the wedding with all its pageantry and state. Now that she was away from John – he was waiting for her at Chester – she found to her shame that she was thinking even more about Alexander, and guiltily again and again she tried to push all thoughts of him from her head.

'We'll be there before dusk.' Rhonwen rode up beside her. She saw Eleyne's troubled face. 'What is it, *cariad*? Don't you want to go home?'

Eleyne dragged her attention back to the present. 'Of course I want to go home. I've missed Wales.' Her voice trailed away. Lightning flickered on the horizon and there was an ominous rumble of thunder far away in the west.

'Will you speak to Einion?' Rhonwen's voice was very quiet.

Eleyne frowned. 'What do you mean?' she said sharply. 'Einion is dead!'

'You can still speak to him, *cariad*. Here in Gwynedd.' Rhonwen's tone became urgent. 'I can feel it. He wants you to contact him, to listen! Here, where his spirit is still strong.'

210

Eleyne's eyes opened wide, and she shivered in spite of the oppressive heat. Out of habit, her hand went to her crucifix. Rhonwen saw the movement and scowled. 'You cannot turn your back on the old gods, you belong to them,' she said caustically. 'They won't let you go.'

'Of course they will,' Eleyne retorted. 'I want nothing to do with Einion. Nothing! I don't want to know what he wanted to tell me. Do you understand? I don't want to know!'

VI

ABER

Llywelyn greeted his youngest daughter with a hug. 'So, Eleyne, you are well, I see.' Her sparkling eyes and radiant smile told him that much. He held her briefly, looking at her as though hoping for more, then he released her and she found herself hugging Gruffydd and, more restrainedly, Dafydd.

'And my mother, is she not here?'

Gruffydd looked at his father and shrugged. 'Your mother does not wish to be here if I am here, it seems. She prefers to wait at Caernarfon, and that is fine by me. What we talk of here does not need the presence of King Henry's spies.'

'That is enough, Gruffydd!' Llywelyn said impatiently. 'Your stepmother is true and loyal to us all. I'll hear no word against her.'

There was a moment's tense silence.

'And Isabella?' Eleyne asked at last. 'Where is she?'

'At Dolbadarn.' Dafydd did not volunteer any more information and Eleyne did not ask for any. It was a relief to know Isabella would not be there.

It pleased Eleyne enormously to sit at the long polished oak table between her father and her elder brother, facing her younger brother and taking part in their discussions as an equal. She had been to Scotland and spoken to the king; she knew his views; she was spokeswoman too for her husband. The three Welshmen found her shrewd and well informed. She was no longer the baby of the family, the scapegoat and the trouble-maker. She was proving herself a skilled negotiator like her mother. Their talks went on for two days and Eleyne made careful mental notes of what she was to say to her husband and of the messages she had to take back to the King of Scots.

She had not realised she would have to see him again at once. She almost betrayed herself as the colour rose in her cheeks, but she calmed herself sternly and kept her eyes on the candles which burned in the centre of the table. Outside, the hot August night grew dark and the bats wheeled and swooped beneath the stars, their high-pitched cries reaching her ears in the long measured silences as Gruffydd and her father felt their way towards agreement.

She would have to ride north without John. For the Earl of Chester to meet the King of Scots again so soon would cause comment and speculation, but for his wife to visit her aunt, with whom she had become firm friends, would be regarded as natural.

Her heart began to beat fast again; she felt a frisson of panic. She did not want to see him; she could not cope with the guilt and fear her feelings aroused, but she knew she could not resist; indeed she could not refuse her father's instructions that she should see Alexander.

Somewhere out beyond the walls she heard an owl hoot. *Tylluan*. The bringer of ill luck. She shivered.

VII

Isabella arrived when the midday sun was at its hottest. Dressed all in white, her raven hair covered by a jewel-studded net framed by a linen fillet with a golden coronet and a barbette beneath the chin, she slid from her horse in the courtyard of the palace and swept unannounced into the presence of her father-in-law. There was a long silence as she stared around the upper chamber, her eyes going immediately to Eleyne. Her face darkened. 'So. I decide to return to Aber and I find this is where you are! I might have guessed you would be behind all this deceit. Dafydd has never lied to me before.' She flicked her husband a look of contempt. Approaching the prince she curtseyed low, then she took a seat at the end of the table as far from the others as possible. 'I am excluded from this conclave, am I?'

Llywelyn smiled at her, the intense irritation which the sight of her always provoked in him carefully concealed. 'You are welcome, daughter-in-law, as always.' He rose stiffly from his chair. 'Our discussions were in any event over for the day. Your presence will serve to lighten what had become too serious an afternoon. Come.'

He put his hand out to Eleyne and, rising, she took it. Her immediate unease at seeing Isabella had lessened as she heard her father's tone, although the thinly veiled irony had been totally lost on Isabella.

The prince led her towards the door. 'I have a horse on which I should like your opinion, daughter.'

Gruffydd caught up with them at the foot of the stairs. He bowed to his father with a rueful grin. 'I have left Dafydd coping with his wife.' He raised his eyes heavenwards. 'The gods help him, he is taking a tongue-lashing as meekly as a whipped pup!'

Llywelyn laughed. 'I fear that lady is not the obedient wife he might have wished, for all her tender years. No more than you, I suspect,

212

Eleyne.' He smiled fondly at his daughter. 'Heaven preserve us men from all your sex!'

Isabella found Eleyne later in the solar. The two young women looked at each other in silence. Eleyne had been about to dictate a letter to her sister Margaret to one of Llywelyn's clerks. Waving the man away she stood up, unaccountably reassured to find she was taller by a head than Isabella.

'I am pleased to see you, sister,' she said cautiously.

'Are you?' Isabella put her hands on her hips. 'I am surprised. No one else is. So, you are part of their secrets, are you? Important, beautiful, clever Eleyne. But where is your husband?' Her voice had taken on the sing-song lilt of the mountains. 'Can it be that he is ill again? Or don't you bring him with you on these trips? You leave him at home with your horse. My father's horse,' she finished with a sneer.

Eleyne tried to interrupt her, but Isabella swept on. 'They all hate you, you know. Whatever you are here for, it is only because you are useful. When you are away they forget about you completely. And they all say what a liar and a sneak you are.'

Eleyne took a deep breath. Her first reaction had been to throw herself at Isabella, pull off her fine head-dress and then pull out her hair for good measure, but that would be playing the girl at her own game; that would be childish and stupid. She forced herself to smile, knowing that by remaining calm she would infuriate Isabella more. 'My, you sound just like the Isabella I played with at Hay. The Isabella who was ten years old. Does Dafydd mind that you never grew up?' It was true, she realised. Isabella was still the spoiled little girl who had been her father's favourite child; Dafydd spoiled her now, no doubt to keep the peace, and Isabella had never changed. The disappointment she felt at still being childless had embittered and frustrated her; it had not matured her.

'Oh, I've grown up.' Isabella's eyes flashed. 'I am not the one who is playing games, pretending to be a spy. Tell me, do you still climb trees and ride like a hoyden on men's horses, or has your husband beaten it out of you?'

'My husband has never beaten me.' Eleyne raised an eyebrow, suddenly thoughtful. Was that it? Had Dafydd beaten the girl in an attempt to gain mastery over her? If so, it had not worked. She felt almost sorry for Isabella. 'Yes, I still ride like a hoyden, and I'd climb trees if I needed to. Why not? One thing I have learned, Isabella, is that if you are one of the highest in the land, you set the fashion as to how a lady behaves, you don't follow it. That is something you might remember if you wish to succeed as a princess of Gywnedd.' She walked slowly to the door and pulled it open. It was the perfect exit.

Rhonwen had been listening in the passage outside. 'You've made an enemy for life there, *cariad*,' she said, shaking her head as they walked together towards the stairs. 'If you were hoping to patch things up between you, I'd say you've put an end to that chance forever.'

'There never was any chance, Rhonwen. We both know that.' Eleyne sat on the bottom step of the staircase and buried her face in her hands wearily. She felt very sad. The scurrying servants stared in astonishment at the Countess of Chester sitting on the stairs, then skirted around her with carefully bland faces as Rhonwen stood looking down at the pale silk of the girl's veil.

'You should at least try to keep on speaking terms, Eleyne. Think of the mission you are engaged in. You may one day have to act between Dafydd *bach* and the king. What would happen if madam put her oar in and forbade you the *llys*?'

'Dafydd would not let her.'

'He's well under her thumb, that one.'

Eleyne shook her head. 'He may let her think so, but he'll never let her make a fool of him again. He knows the whole world has watched her disobey him. If his wife does not obey his authority, why should the people of Wales?' She smiled ruefully. 'Dafydd's ambition will see to it that he keeps Isabella in order, you'll see.'

'And if he can't, there are other ways of putting an end to her nonsense.' Rhonwen narrowed her eyes. 'I'll not let her cross you; and I'll not let her endanger the chances of Gruffydd inheriting from his father.' She smiled enigmatically. 'It's Gruffydd who favours the Scots alliance, you know. Henry has recognised Dafydd as his father's heir, so Dafydd keeps his options with the king of the English open. The prince is a fool to trust Dafydd with his secrets.'

'That's not true, Rhonwen,' Eleyne frowned. 'Dafydd fights for Wales too.'

Rhonwen made a gesture of disgust. 'Dafydd fights for himself. It is Gruffydd who fights for the truth. And Einion – still. You'd best remember that. Don't forget which gods you serve for all your jewelled rosaries, and don't forget whose side you are on with all your importance as a king's messenger.'

Eleyne's eyes flashed. 'That is impudent, Rhonwen.'

'Yes – and it is your nurse's business to be impudent if you get above yourself and ignore your duty!' Rhonwen's colour had risen. 'Never forget that, madam, however close to a throne you may be!' She stormed across the hallway and slammed the door into the courtyard behind her.

Eleyne stood up thoughtfully. Rhonwen was presuming too much. Llywelyn's decision to use her to carry the first message had given her an exaggerated idea of her own importance. Eleyne mentioned this to her father later, cautiously, not wanting him to be angry with

214

Rhonwen, but worried. To her astonishment, Llywelyn threw back his head and laughed. 'I used the Lady Rhonwen because I knew her passionate support of Gruffydd would bind her to our cause,' he said, 'but also because she is expendable.'

'Expendable?' Eleyne echoed the word softly. She had gone cold.

'Of course. Had she betrayed us we could have denied all knowledge of whatever she claimed. No one would believe the ravings of a servant already suspected of heresy and of having procured the death of an unborn child. She could easily have been disposed of.'

'You would have killed her?' Eleyne was appalled. 'You would have killed Rhonwen?'

'I will kill anyone who betrays our cause, Eleyne, if it is necessary,' he said sternly. 'And you must remember your priorities in this. The woman was your nurse and you love her, but the affairs of princes and kings and of nations take precedence over all personal sentiment, particularly as she is a heretic. I thank Our Lady daily that you have not been contaminated by her heresy.' He paused. 'I was afraid once that she and Einion Gweledydd might try to suborn you for their unchristian ceremonies, but your mother persauded me there was no danger. Now Einion is dead, that little pocket of belief in the old ways is dead with him, Christ be praised.'

He surveyed her shocked white face, then he smiled. 'Now while I prepare letters for the King of Scots, which you will give him, and upon which you will be able to elaborate personally, I suggest you ride to Caernarfon to see your mother. She would enjoy a visit from you, if only for a day. Her health has not been good.' He allowed himself a small scowl, and Eleyne saw a worry which he had so far concealed.

'What is the matter?' Her indignation over his cavalier and cynical dismissal of Rhonwen was eclipsed by a sudden new fear.

'She is tired; she is no longer strong.' There was a moment's silence; both were thinking of her years of imprisonment and exile in the austere, cold convent. 'She was happy last time you came when you and she became friends. It would be a kindness to visit her.'

'She should be at Aber, papa, or Llanfaes. She loves it there, and Caernarfon is a cold bleak place to be if she is ill.'

'She would not come here. Not while Gruffydd and Senena were here.'

'But she could come now. Gruffydd goes back to the Lleyn tomorrow.' Eleyne looked hard at her father. 'You and she have not quarrelled, papa?'

He shook his head.

'But she is angry that you and Gruffydd are close again?'

'She is afraid I shall grow soft and change my mind about Dafydd's succession. I have told her that there is no need to fear. I have made

215

my decision: Dafydd is my heir. Gruffydd is not the son of my true wife, and even if he were entitled by Welsh law to share in the inheritance, he is too much of a hothead; he does not have the support of the country.'

'Of course he doesn't, because you have repeatedly forced your followers to swear allegiance to Dafydd. You have weaned all support from Gruffydd.' Eleyne kept her voice carefully neutral.

'And so it will remain.' Llywelyn was growing irritable. 'Enough! Go and tell your nurse to pack. Stay two nights with your mother and when you get back I shall have the letters ready. Then you can return to Chester before you ride north. Your husband is well?' He had asked before, as a formality, but as he peered at her from beneath his bushy eyebrows she sensed a more genuine interest – and worry.

'He is well, papa. The journey back from Scotland made him cough again, but he has recovered. I left him in the best of spirits.'

'But still there is no babe?'

Eleyne looked away from her father's probing eyes and shrugged. 'God has not seen fit to send us a child yet.'

'But you are his true wife? The marriage is consummated?'

She could feel the colour rising in her cheeks. She looked defiantly up at him: 'Yes, papa, the marriage is consummated.'

VIII

CAERNARFON

Joan was in bed when Eleyne was shown into the bedchamber in the new-built stone keep at Caernarfon. She held out her hands to Eleyne with a smile. Her face was pale and drawn, but her eyes were alert and she sat forward on her pillows and drew Eleyne to sit on the bed beside her.

Eleyne felt a sudden rush of sympathy for this woman who was her mother and whom she still barely knew. 'What is wrong, mama? Are you ill?'

Joan's ladies had withdrawn to the other side of the room.

Joan shrugged. 'I get a pain sometimes. It seems to drain my strength. But it is nearly gone. I shall be well enough to get up soon.' She smiled. 'Tell me your news. And tell me what your father and those sons of his have been plotting while I have been safely out of the way.'

Eleyne smiled. She kissed her mother's cheek. 'Would you not rather hear about Joanna and her life in Scotland and the wedding of Princess Margaret?'

Joan frowned. 'Joanna and I are not close. You know that. We are

216

only half-sisters. She is unlikely to forget that I was not the child of her father's queen.' She sounded bitter.

'But Uncle Henry declared you legitimate,' Eleyne reminded her gently. 'And Joanna speaks of you with much affection. She sends you her fondest greetings.'

'I'm surprised she can remember me.' Joan caught her breath as a spasm of pain wrenched at her stomach.

Eleyne jumped to her feet in distress. 'Can I get you something to drink? Have you medicines? What do the physicians say, mama?'

Joan shook her head. 'Nothing, nothing. It will pass. Don't fret! Yes, tell me about the wedding.' She lay back on the pillows and closed her eyes. Her face was grey.

When she slept at last Eleyne slipped from the chamber and slowly descended the stairs to the great hall, but they spoke again that evening. Joan, her hair brushed and her face sponged by one of her waiting women, looked stronger. She smiled at Eleyne. 'I wish you and I had been friends sooner,' she whispered. 'Eleyne, I should like to see Margaret and Gwladus and Gwenllian and Angharad. Write to your sisters, child. Tell them to come.'

'Mama,' Eleyne was afraid, 'you're not going to die?'

Joan smiled and shook her head. 'No, of course not. I am just feeling silly and weak and sentimental. What better reason to ask one's children to come and see one?' She reached for Eleyne's hand. 'I wish I had not given you to Rhonwen. I stayed much closer to the other girls. She made us enemies, you know.'

'Rhonwen would not do that.' Eleyne was on her guard at once.

Joan nodded. 'Oh yes, she was jealous because she had never given birth. She wanted you for her own. You were so much younger than the others, Eleyne.' She paused. 'Rhonwen wanted us to call you Bridget, you know, for the day you were born in the fire, but we named you after St Helena. She was a great ancestress of yours; a daughter of King Coel . . .' She seemed to drift away for a few moments, then she opened her eyes again. 'Someone told me that Ellen too was a goddess; a goddess of light.' She was silent again. 'Your father was afraid once that Rhonwen would contaminate you with her heathen ways. I told him she wouldn't dare.' She lay staring at the opposite wall. It was freshly plastered and painted with bright roses. 'One of your father's bards believed in the old ways. These mountains. They are full of such people . . . enemies of Christ. Your half-brother, Gruffydd, I sometimes think he is one of them.' Her voice was growing weak.

Eleyne said nothing, her eyes fixed on her mother's. Her fingers strayed once more to the beads at her girdle.

'Eleyne!' Her mother's voice was suddenly sharp. 'Are you paying

217

attention? Remember, Rhonwen is evil. I am so glad she is no longer with you . . .'

Rhonwen was downstairs in the great hall listening with most of the household to a travelling harper who had ridden into the city the night before. 'Rhonwen is not evil, mama. She loves me. She would do nothing to harm me,' she said gently.

'No? Perhaps not. But she would not hesitate to harm anyone else who crossed her path. Or yours.' She gave a little half-smile. 'It was she who told you to betray William and me to your father, wasn't it?' It was the first time she had ever made any reference to that night.

Eleyne bit her lip. 'Mama, it was so long ago. It's all forgotten now.'

'Forgotten!' Joan's eyes blazed. 'No, it's not forgotten! I loved him, you know, though not the way I love your father.' She subsided back on to the pillows and took Eleyne's hand almost pleadingly. 'It was something strange and new and forbidden. It was an excitement in a world where I had come to accept the fact that I was growing old. I was used to the flattery of courtiers, but William was different. He made me feel alive.' She closed her eyes and Eleyne felt her fingers growing slack. 'You were jealous, weren't you, child? You didn't want your old mother taking his attention from you and that monstrous horse. You didn't understand. I wouldn't have betrayed your father for the world. I loved him so much, but . . .' Her words trailed to a stop.

In spite of herself, Eleyne saw again the picture of her mother and William naked on the bed. She trembled. But at the same time she had begun to understand. She groped for the right words. 'You loved father, but he never gave you pleasure,' she murmured.

Joan's eyes flew open, and she studied Eleyne's face. 'You do understand,' she said at last.

Eleyne nodded. 'I think so.' She smiled sadly.

'So.' Joan caught her hand again and squeezed it. 'Is it the same for you? But your husband is kind? Llywelyn was always kind. And it is not as though you have ever loved anyone else.'

Eleyne shook her head violently. 'I would never, never betray my husband.' It sounded sanctimonious and she was immediately sorry she had said it. She had not meant it that way; she had been thinking about herself.

Joan gave a bitter laugh. 'That is so easy to say. Perhaps you have not had the opportunity. Try to put yourself in my place. What would you have done if your lover had beckoned you one night and kissed you in the shadows beneath the moon? What if he beguiled you away from everyone else on a ride and you found yourself alone with him on a mossy bank covered in dog roses and violets?' She began to sob.

'Mama!' Eleyne leaned forward and kissed her forehead. 'Mama, don't cry.'

218

IX

September 1235

She had not wanted to return to Scotland so soon. She had not wanted to return to Chester. Her mother's illness and her father's worry frightened her. She wanted to wait until her sisters were there. She wanted them all to be together, but Llywelyn was adamant.

'It is your duty, child, you must convey our messages. Your mother will have the other children. It is not as though she is going to die.'

Eleyne scanned his face, trying to see the truth. What she saw was his blind determination that what he said was the truth. And with that she had to be content.

She rode fast to Chester and spent three days with John, then she was on the road again, riding north with a small escort of chosen knights and just two ladies, Rhonwen and Luned. Ostensibly she was answering an urgent summons from her Aunt Joanna to come to her sickbed at Kinghorn. In reality she carried two letters sewn inside the bodice of her gown, one from her husband and one from her father.

Free of the burdensome escort of the huge household which had accompanied them on their last trip, Eleyne set a fast pace, feeling the power of the great stallion beneath her as they rode the long road north. The nearer they got to Scotland the more nervous she became. The thought of seeing Alexander obsessed her. She wanted to be near him; she longed to see his face, to hear his voice, but at the same time she was bitterly ashamed of the longing and consumed with guilt. Why did she feel this way? She loved her husband. John was kind and understanding and handsome; what more could she want? It was so much more than many women had. The king had never really noticed her in any special way; he teased her, he was off-handedly affectionate – she was after all his niece and the wife of his heir. Each time her thoughts reached this point she would try to blank them off. Every thought was mortal sin. Her soul was damned and yet she could not stop her dreams.

As they forded the glittering silver sands of the Solway and struck north through the forest of Ettrick and Teviotdale the weather worsened markedly. The wind rose, the clouds settled on the hills and the rain drove across the tracks soaking horses and riders alike. Huddled in her cloak on the wet, cold saddle, Eleyne shivered, her teeth chattering.

The Forth was rough, the wind whipping the water into sharp, white-topped waves as they embarked on the ferry at Dalmeny and set out from the shelter of the land, leaving the horses behind. The far shore was invisible in the murk. Chilled and uncomfortable in her wet clothes, Eleyne refused the shelter of the rough, open cabin and settled in the lee of its walls, staring out into the gloom. The sailors had raised an old patched sail to aid the oarsmen and the boat lurched forward alarmingly, creaming through the water, its rigging creaking and flapping as the steersman, his eyes narrowed, tried to edge downstream before the wind.

'I'll be glad when we're there.' Rhonwen, her eyes streaming from the cold, sat down beside her and pulled her hood forward over her face. 'It's only a short ride to the king's manor at Kinghorn, the ferryman assured me.' She shuddered as the vessel shipped a shower of cold spray.

Eleyne rested her head in her arms, thinking yet again about the king. Her stomach was taut with anticipation.

'What is it, *cariad*, are you sick?' The solicitous voice would not allow her even that much privacy. Irritated, Eleyne shook her head. 'I'm tired, Rhonwen, that's all. Please, let me rest.' She gasped as another douche of cold water cascaded over them. The bottom boards of the boat were running with water; her gown was soaked, her feet like blocks of ice.

Horses were waiting on the shore to take them along the well-beaten track which followed the coast to the east. After a while it plunged into the woods, sometimes staying down near the shore, sometimes climbing to the top of the low cliffs, but always following the curve of the coast, every now and then affording a view of the wind-lashed waters of the Forth.

The king's royal manor lay near the port of Kinghorn at the foot of the low red cliffs, and Joanna was waiting for her visitor in the queen's bower attended by her senior lady-in-waiting, Auda de Boellis and her valet, Hugh de Gurley. She greeted Eleyne with open arms: 'See how ill I look! We must let the rumours fly around the kingdom that you visit me out of compassion and are summoned to my deathbed. Isn't that the story we have concocted?'

Eleyne laughed, unable to resist the queen's infectious good humour. The king was not there. The whole atmosphere at the manor told her that; the stables were half empty and it was the queen's standard, not the king's, which flew from the watchtower at the gate. Half disappointed, half relieved, she hugged her aunt in return. 'You look so much better than when I last saw you, aunt.'

'I am.' Joanna caught her arm and pulled her towards the fire as her attendants withdrew. 'I have my own news! I think I am with child again!' Her excitement was vivid.

Eleyne stared at her in amazement, the king forgotten, John's face suddenly before her. 'Are you sure?'

'Not sure, not yet. But more than a month has passed and I haven't bled. Oh, Eleyne, dear Eleyne! I am sure my prayers are answered!'

'The king must be pleased.' Eleyne clenched her fists. Where was he?

'I haven't told him yet.' Joanna's face lost a little of its animation. 'I haven't dared. I have to be sure.' She sank heavily into a chair. 'If I am wrong he would be so disappointed.'

'Where is he?' Eleyne could not stop herself from asking.

Joanna smiled. 'Of course. You are anxious to deliver your messages. He will join us tomorrow or the next day. We didn't know how long it would take you to ride north –' She smiled. 'You have made as good speed as the royal messengers. Alexander thought you might ride more slowly. He did not wish to be here when you arrived. It was me you were coming to see in the world's eyes. But we will send messages at once for him to come. He is only at Cupar.'

X

KINGHORN

The king was in the small room off the great hall which he used for his private office when he summoned Eleyne the next afternoon. Closeted with her aunt, she had not even known he had arrived.

The chamberlain who had shown her into the room left them, pulling the heavy oak door shut behind him. They were alone, save for the great hound which lay in front of the fire. She dropped a low curtsey.

The king had been standing by the window reading a letter in the dull, stormy light. He turned to her with a smile and threw the letter down on the table. The cluster of candles in the huge silver candelabra smoked in the draught. 'So, Lady Chester.' For a moment he did not move; he stared at her with a frown.

His silence unnerved her completely. 'I have letters, your grace.' Nervously she held the two letters out to him. The evening before she had unpicked them herself from her bodice, in the flickering candlelight before she went to bed. They had spent the night beneath her pillow.

'How are you, Eleyne?' He did not make a move to take the letters and she was left holding them out in front of her. Her hand dropped slowly back to her side.

'I am well, uncle, thank you.'

'And your husband?'

She looked down at the floor, praying he could not see how agitated she was. 'He is well too. He sends his loyal greetings.'

Her hands were growing clammy. She swallowed and tried to smile.

'Are you enjoying the role of royal messenger?' He seated himself on the edge of the table, lounging now, his hands clasped around his

221

knee. She could see that the heavy gold thread of the embroidery on the hem of his mantle was snagged and torn. The garment was damp and muddy from his ride.

'Very much, sire.'

'I suspected you would enjoy being a spy.' He smiled. 'Are you ready to go and worm secrets out of your Uncle Henry at the English court?' His tone was humorous, but there was an underlying note of seriousness in the words. 'I would appreciate a woman's view of the world. I suspect your sex sees with a clearer eye sometimes than we poor men. We huff and we argue and we pick at the minutiae of our quarrels and we don't always stand back and see the greater picture. Your mother was ever a great help to your father. She has always had her brother's ear. Do you have it too?'

Eleyne hesitated. 'I hardly know my uncle, your grace. We have met often since I was married, of course, but never spoken much. I think he likes me, but –' she shrugged – 'I have been just a lady of the court, or once or twice his hostess, no more.'

'But he speaks freely in front of you?'

'Only in so far as he speaks freely before anyone at his table or at his side. I have never been admitted to his discussions with his advisers.'

'Nor with your husband?'

She shook her head.

Alexander frowned. 'Then you must practise using a little more of your charm on him. Wheedle a little, I am sure you are good at wheedling.' He smiled again, his eyes narrowing mischievously.

She could feel herself blushing. Without realising it she had begun to twist the letters in her hands.

He folded his arms. 'You get on well with Joanna. I'm glad. She's had a sad time.'

Eleyne searched his face for any sign that he had guessed Joanna's news. 'She seems much more cheerful,' she said guardedly, 'I am glad she is in such good health.'

'Did she tell you she was breeding again?'

He went to stand before the fire, rubbing his hands together slowly. The dog thumped its tail a couple of times and lay still. 'Aye, I can tell she did. It's all in her head. The physicians have told me. She's not with child and not likely to be.' He slammed his fist into the palm of his hand. 'So, lassie, unless things change radically, if anything happens to me, you will be the next Queen of Scots.'

He turned his back on the fire and studied her again, noting her troubled face. 'What's the matter? Does the idea not please you?'

Eleyne shook her head. 'I should hate anything to happen to you . . .'

He roared with laughter. 'So should I, believe me! Here, give me

222

those letters before you knead them to pulp.' He reached out and took them from her hand. For a moment their fingers touched, then he turned away to the table.

She stood by the fire gazing down into the flames while he read. The wood burned with the green salt flame of beached timber collected on the strand. As it dried and split and turned to ash-drawn squares, she watched the flames lick and devour and race one another into the smoke. Outside, the rain lashed the walls and splattered through the open window on to the floor. The shutter lay against the wall where the king had put it when he removed it to see better in the gloom. Near it a puddle began to form on the stone flags. The dog sighed and smacked its lips in its sleep.

She could see a horseman in the flames, riding low over the animal's neck, lashing it with the reins, his cloak flying out behind him. Around him she could see the trees, their branches streaming before the gale; she could see the lightning; hear the thunder roll in the low crackle of the flames. Without realising it, she went closer to the fire and knelt on one knee, trying to see more clearly.

The king lowered his letter and watched her with a frown.

She could see now: the horse's hooves pounding down the sandy track, the puddles reflecting the fire. She could hear the reverberation of the wind, see the dancing, flailing shadows which hid the path, feel the shock of the lightning as it blinded horse and rider – hear the scream of the horse as it fell . . .

'Eleyne!' The king's voice was sharp. As she had crouched nearer the fire, her veil trailed near the sparks. Her hands were reaching almost into the flames.

'Eleyne!' Dropping the letters, he was across the room in two strides. Seizing her arm he swung her to her feet. 'You'll set fire to yourself, lass! What's the matter with you?'

For a moment they stood, staring at each other. He was still holding her arm and she could feel his fingers biting into her flesh. Their eyes were locked. Then at last she spoke. 'I'm sorry, I . . .' She hesitated, feeling his fingers red-hot through the silk of her sleeve. 'I felt dizzy for a moment. I . . .'

'You are expecting a bairn?' He was still holding her, his face close to hers.

She shook her head. 'No, no, I'm not. Please.' She tried to twist her arm free of his grip, frightened by his strength.

Abruptly he let her go. 'Then what?'

'I leaned too close to the fire, that's all. I lost my balance, the heat was too great. I'm sorry.' Her heart was hammering in her chest and she felt sick.

He looked angry as he turned back to the table and picked up the letter again. 'Lean out of the window and take a breath of air to clear your head,' he commanded curtly, 'then you can talk to me about this,' and he shook the letter at her.

The wind was icy on her burning cheeks, and the rain, driving full into her face, stung her eyelids and ran down her neck, soaking the front of her gown in seconds. She stood there for a moment trying to compose herself, then she turned back into the room.

He raised his eyebrows. 'First she tries to burn herself to death. Now she attempts to drown. It seems she will go to any lengths to avoid serving her king. Come here.'

She went to him. She was no longer trembling as she stood before him, her eyes on his. His expression was preoccupied, as if distracted by some conflict deep within himself. Then at last he spoke: 'I do know you. The Blessed Virgin knows where from, but I feel I've known you all my life.' He drew a deep unsteady breath. 'Sweet Virgin, lass, but you're beautiful!' He said it almost wonderingly as he reached for the corner of her veil and raised it to dab gently at her face, drying the rain which lay like tears on her cheeks. He touched the end of her nose gently with the tip of his finger and turned away. 'Now, to the business in hand.' His voice was carefully neutral.

'I shall want you to visit my sisters in England, and then I shall want you to talk to their husbands.' He frowned suddenly. 'This could be dangerous for you, as a subject of King Henry. Like all who hold lands in both England and Scotland, your allegiance is finely balanced. Our countries are at peace at the moment and pray God it will continue so, but Henry tries the patience of a saint sometimes, as all his subjects will tell you. Hence a ring of allies who can resist him if necessary.' He gave her one of his most knowing smiles.

She smiled in return – calmer now, her vision all but forgotten, the touch of his hand receding. She was once more in command of herself.

Neither of them heard the footsteps outside. When the door swung open, they turned as one. Joanna stood there, her hair loose, her face working. There was blood on her hands and on the skirt of her gown. She stood unmoving, looking from one to the other of them, then she burst into tears.

'There is no baby,' she screamed. 'Again, there is no baby!'

XI

'She is resting, sire.' Eleyne stood before the king as he sat pale and exhausted in the great chair before the fire. The household was subdued, even the hound, sensing his master's depression, lay with his head on his paws, his eyes watchful. 'My lady, Rhonwen, has given her a sleeping draught and the Lady Auda is watching over her.'

'Sit down, Eleyne.' The king's voice was husky. 'I am glad you were here when it happened. Her ladies cannot calm her.'

'You mean it has happened before?' Eleyne was appalled.

'Once, yes. But not . . . not like this.' He was silent for a moment. 'She spends more and more time here at Kinghorn. The life of the court makes her unhappy; the sight of another woman's belly beginning to swell makes her cry. I have told her again and again that it does not matter — but of course, it does matter. It matters a great deal. I thought at first the sight of you would send her mad. You are young and happy and can have a dozen bairns. I thought she would be jealous, but you won her round. Perhaps she sees that if you and John are there, all will be well with Scotland if anything should happen to me.' He rubbed his chin wearily. 'I don't know what she will do when you do produce a baby.' He said it thoughtfully, quietly, but there was a slight inflection at the end of the sentence which turned it to a question.

Eleyne stared into the fire: the flames were empty, there were no pictures now. 'There has been no baby yet,' she said at last.

The king said nothing. She could read his mind. Was she another barren wife; was Scotland's line to die with her? She wanted urgently to tell him, tell him that she knew the future, but she remembered John's warning and remained silent. It did not do to speak of such things, especially to a king.

The following evening Alexander summoned her again to his private room. He was seated at the broad oak table when she curtseyed in the doorway. Once more he was alone. Without a word he walked to the door and pushed it closed behind her. 'You've seen the queen today?'

Eleyne nodded. 'She is better.' Joanna had been lying in the darkened room, staring at the ceiling. She had said nothing at all when Eleyne went to see her.

The king sighed. 'By the Virgin, I wish she was! So, Lady Chester. What do I do?' His eyes on hers were half sad, half quizzical.

She returned his gaze, trying to read his expression. 'You must be gentle with her, sire. She is very unhappy.'

'So am I, unhappy.' He looked at her thoughtfully. 'And you, Eleyne. Are you unhappy too?' His voice was very quiet.

She shook her head, not daring to breathe. Her fists, hidden in the folds of her mantle, were clenched so tightly her nails cut into the palms of her hands.

'Do you have the letters I am to take to my father, sire?' Her reply came out as a whisper.

Slowly he stood up and walked across to her. He was frowning as his hand came up and he touched her cheek almost absent-mindedly.

225

'No.' Shaking her head, she backed away from him and he let his hand fall. 'I'll have the letters for you tomorrow,' he said quietly. 'Leave me now.'

XII

She spent five days at Kinghorn. On the fifth day a messenger arrived with a letter from Eleyne's sister Margaret. She read it with dismay. Their mother had returned to Aber, and as soon as she had arrived there she had had a relapse which had left her so weak that her life was feared for. Their sisters, Gwenllian and Angharad, were there with her, but Joan kept asking for Eleyne.

'Don't you see, I must go at once!' Eleyne had found Joanna lying on her bed, still too listless to get up. The king had returned to Cupar two days before. He had gone without warning or explanation and until he went Eleyne had avoided him, remaining in her room or her aunt's, suddenly acutely aware of Rhonwen's watchful, puzzled gaze which followed her everywhere. She had not seen him again before he left.

'No, don't go. You must stay!' Joanna sat up in agitation. Her hair was uncombed and her face pale and drawn.

'I must, aunt. Mama is ill; she might be dying.' Eleyne's voice rose unsteadily. 'Please, give me your good wishes for her and let me go.'

'You can't go, not without Alexander's permission.' Joanna lay back triumphantly. 'The reason you are here was to see him, after all. You can't just leave. He has letters and messages for you to carry.' It was true.

Eleyne took a deep breath. 'Then I must find him and ask him for them.'

Margaret's messenger, riding hard, had taken several days to reach Kinghorn from Aber through the mud and heavy rain. Already it might be too late. Eleyne gave orders for her companions to pack. Despite Joanna's pleas she had resolved to leave Kinghorn at once, find the king and ride south. Her need to see the king was solely to collect the letters for John and her father; she refused to countenance the idea that it was because she longed to see him before she left. That was unthinkable.

The roads were like quagmires, muddy and full of potholes, and the horses made slow progress. It was well past noon when they cantered into the burgh of Cupar and rode up the high street towards the castle.

The king was surrounded by petitioners as he sat on the dais in the great hall. For a moment Eleyne hovered on the outskirts of the crowd watching him, staring at his handsome face as, preoccupied, he spoke to the man who stood before him. With a sinking heart, she realised that he was talking to Lord Fife.

Cenydd had cleared a way for her to approach the king, and after a moment's hesitation she walked forward. After all, Lord Fife could hardly accost her here, in front of his sovereign and hundreds of people.

When the king saw her, he broke off his conversation; he did not look pleased to see her. 'Lady Chester?'

Her throat was constricted as she curtseyed before him. 'Forgive me, sire, but I have to return to Wales. My mother is ill.' Her voice faltered. 'She is dying. I must cut short my visit.'

She saw a frown of irritation cross his face and she looked down miserably. Her visit was supposed to have been a private one to her aunt. Would people wonder why she had ridden miles in the wrong direction to say farewell to him? But it was too late now to worry about that. All she could think of, all she must think of was a speedy start towards the south.

The king had collected himself if she had not. 'Forgive me, my lords. I would speak with Lady Chester before she leaves.'

She thought she was going to see him alone, and her heart began to beat wildly but, bowing, the men withdrew to the far end of the hall and waited. Alexander sat down again and held out his hand so that she had to move nearer to him. Their privacy was to be notional. No one could overhear their conversation, but they would not be alone. She was half disappointed, half relieved.

'I have had no time to write letters,' he said quietly. 'You are going to have to remember what I tell you. Say to your father that I am going to wait. There is still a chance of a treaty with Henry and I have no wish to jeopardise that or the chance of a meeting with him next year. Visit us again in the spring, when I shall have revised my plans and decided what action needs to be taken. You can say the same to the earl marshal when you visit Margaret.' He smiled. 'I am sorry to hear of your mother's illness. I shall pray for her.'

That was all. She waited a moment, searching his face, wondering if he were going to say something else, but already he had beckoned Lord Fife back to his side.

The earl smiled at her, his gaze running hungrily over her body as he bowed. 'Lady Chester, I am sorry to hear you are leaving so soon. I had not realised you were in Scotland or I should have paid my respects much sooner.'

Eleyne stepped away from him. 'I was on a private visit to my aunt, my lord. I did not intend to see anyone but her, and the king my uncle. Forgive me, but I am leaving now.'

'Then let me ride with you.' Lord Fife turned to the king and bowed.

'Sire, may I escort your beautiful niece as far as the border? My business here is done and I should deem it an honour to go with her.'

Eleyne's eyes flew to the king's face, pleading. 'Please, my lord, there is no need. I am going to be riding very fast . . .'

Alexander grinned: 'You are sure you would not like an escort, Lady Chester? Lord Fife can move very fast when he wants to –'

'No. Thank you, your grace, but no.' With a flash of impatient anger she realised he was laughing at her.

Alexander frowned. When she was with him the girl guarded her feelings most of the time, masking them with a cold, almost austere formality, but he had seen fury and disappointment in her eyes just then and, when she looked at Malcolm of Fife, cold hatred. Her volatility was captivating, as was the hint of longing he had caught in her eyes when she looked at him. She intrigued him, this beautiful niece of his wife's; this woman he felt he had known for a thousand years. He found her more attractive than any woman he had met for a long time, and that was why he had left Kinghorn so abruptly. She was dangerous, she was forbidden fruit. Wife to his heir, daughter to his ally, niece to his enemy, and so close to him by marriage that even to think of her too much was incest.

He turned back to the earl, and looked at him coldly. The man was almost visibly panting. 'Then I shall feel no guilt in asking Lord Fife to remain here. I have need of his services, and clearly you do not.' He bowed with stiff formality. 'Farewell, niece, and God go with you.'

XIII

ABER ❖ February 1237

In the bed which she had not left for many months, Joan grew weaker.

She had been lying there when Eleyne had arrived, exhausted and covered in mud from the long wet ride south from Scotland sixteen months before. The last few miles had been ridden by the light of flaring torches, hissing and spitting as the rain sizzled on the slow-burning resin, and Eleyne's fear that her mother would be dead before they got there had grown with every mile as Aber drew closer.

In the event, Joan had been well enough to welcome her youngest daughter, and she had seemed stronger than they had dared hope.

They stayed only a few weeks, returning to Chester after Martinmas, and in the spring Eleyne was able to convey her messages to Alexander's sisters at last. As she and John rode around England, they found themselves several times in King Henry's presence, as the court moved from Westminster to Windsor, to Winchester and Northampton. It was at Nottingham that letters caught up with them, informing them that Joan had had a relapse, and they had ridden west once more. There had been two more visits as her health began to decline faster and now they had made the journey through hard-packed snow and icy winds to the princess's bedside for the last time.

They were all there, Joan's six children: Dafydd, with Isabella, Margaret, Gwenllian, Gwladus, Angharad and Eleyne, and the end was very near.

Rhonwen sat at the table, her nimble fingers sorting through the candles, counting under her breath. There were some missing. There had been a hundred in the candle box, enough for two days more at this, the darkest time of the year, and she had been about to order another gross to be sent up from the storeroom beneath the *ty hir*. Now there were enough for only one more day. She watched the boy walking round the room lifting the candle stumps from the prickets with his knife and tossing them into his leather bucket, and she frowned. The wax candle ends were a valuable perquisite of the household officials; stolen candles were another matter. The thief had to be found. Pursing her lips, she closed the lid of the box and stood up. There was no supervision in the *llys*; no order. Senena was at Criccieth with Gruffydd, and as for Isabella – she shook her head as she searched for the missing key to the candle box – Isabella was still a child, alternately spoiled and berated by her husband, disliked by the servants, as poisonous as a snake and as little use.

She found the key where it had obviously lain for many months, in the stale rushes beneath the coffer. Eleyne would have to give some orders to the servants or somehow shame Isabella into supervising the royal household.

It was strange, but Eleyne, the youngest by far of all the daughters, was the most composed now that Joan's death was near. And that, Rhonwen had decided, was because her mind was elsewhere. It was still, as it had been for the last sixteen months, in Scotland.

The visit to Kinghorn had told her all she wanted to know. Listening and watching in the shadows, Rhonwen had seen it all. She loved him! Her child, her Eleyne, loved the King of Scots! It had been so obvious: the blushes, the stammering, the defiance, the interviews alone and unchaperoned, the stolen glances, the sleepless nights when Rhonwen in the truckle bed had heard her sigh and toss and turn. She had got it all wrong. It was not the Earl of Chester the girl loved at all. She had saved his life to no purpose. Rhonwen had spent a great deal of time thinking over the implications of her realisation, then slowly, over the long months, she began to plan.

ABER ❖ February 1237

Joan died at last on Candlemas Day. Her husband and all her children were at her bedside. Llywelyn, the tears running down his face, was holding his wife's hand. She smiled as, one by one, they came to the bedside and kissed her. She was too weak to speak or move her head, but they could read the message of blessing and farewell in her eyes. One by one, the men and women in the room sank to their knees in prayer. When the end came, it was so gentle that it was several moments before Llywelyn realised that the hand in his had fallen limp and that she had left them.

The funeral was lavish. The sons-in-law arrived and joined Llywelyn in following Joan's body as it was carried in state over the Lafan sands and ferried across the strait to Llanfaes. It lay there one more night in the prince's hall before it was interred in a ceremony conducted by Bishop Hugh of St Asaphs in the new burying ground especially prepared to receive it nearby.

Rhonwen did not go to the requiem mass or to the interment. In the solar she waited alone for the mourners to return. The room was dark; it was early yet so she had ordered no candles, but the lowering sky was heavy with more wet snow and the sea was like black slate. She shivered: Einion was here again; the air was heavy with anger and reproach.

Each time she had come with Eleyne to Gwynedd she had felt him. And so had Eleyne, she was sure of it; but the girl refused to acknowledge him, refused to allow him in, clutching at her crucifix and backing away from the shadows, never letting him come near her, never letting him give her his message. And each time his frustration and despair had grown. And so had Rhonwen's; she was racked with guilt.

The moment they had set foot on the island of Môn, as part of the funeral cortège, the plan had come to her. The mourners would be back soon from the burial ground and the feast would start; the place would be full of people. She would force Eleyne to come with her, now while she was here on the island, his home and his body's resting place. Rhonwen smiled grimly. With the Englishwoman dead at last, and Eleyne too exhausted by grief and the cumulative strain of the long months of her mother's illness to know what she was doing or to argue, it would be easy to take her to Einion and do what must be done. Then and only then would her conscience be clear.

She pounced on Eleyne as the girl appeared in the doorway, her eyes red with tears. 'Quickly, now, before you take off your cloak!' Rhonwen was almost hysterically insistent. 'There is something we have to do. It won't take long! I have horses waiting. No one will know we've gone. You will be back before they've missed you. All you have to do is come to where Einion is buried. You owe him that much! The rest of the night, the rest of your life you can grieve for your mother! But tomorrow you will leave the island. You may never come back. You have to come with me now. You have to.'

Eleyne was too tired and depressed to do more than shake her head. Slowly and heavily she sat down on the bed and began to pull off her embroidered gloves. 'Don't be foolish, Rhonwen. My place is here. I've told you a dozen times, I don't want to see Einion's grave!'

Rhonwen stood over her. 'Have you never wondered, *cariad*, what he wanted to tell you so badly?' she hissed. 'Your destiny lies in Scotland, yet you bear Lord Chester no children. Why?' She leaned so near, Eleyne could feel her breath on her cheek. 'Supposing Einion can tell you? Supposing he was going to tell you about the King of Scots!' Her eyes glittered with triumph as she saw the start of guilt and the rush of colour to the girl's cheeks.

'What do you mean?'

'You know what I mean. You think I don't see you count on your fingers every month in the hope that you have conceived. But nothing happens. Your milksop earl can't father a child. He's impotent! And Queen Joanna is barren!' Rhonwen leaned even closer. 'Ask Einion! Ask him what is to be. Now! With me!' Her hand closed over Eleyne's wrist.

Slowly, only half knowing what she was doing, Eleyne allowed Rhonwen to pull her to her feet. Still wearing her heavy furs, her hair and face swathed in a black veil, she followed Rhonwen to the side door in the wall. Behind them in the great timber hall the funeral feast was already in full swing. She had not been missed. People assumed she was prostrate with grief like her sisters Angharad and Margaret.

The doors to the hall had been pushed open to clear the smoky fetid air and the noise of the feast, subdued at first as always at funerals, had risen almost to the usual level, although there were no musicians. The only music the whole day had been the chanting of the monks and the slow dirge of the bards in the rain.

XV

Rhonwen had found the exact spot. Deep in the woods Einion lay in a grave marked by a slim upright stone. There was no carving on it, no name, no sigil – only a shadow of lichen which had been there long before the stone was raised. Who had found his body, sprawled across the dead ashes in his lonely cell, she did not know; nor who had buried him here, far from consecrated ground, blessed only by the rites of his own faith. All she knew was that he wanted Eleyne to come. Rhonwen dismounted before the grassy mound with its streaks of melting snow. The trees which interlaced their boughs above were stark against the cloud wrack. Behind the storm there was a full moon.

Eleyne did not move: her head was a whirling confusion of sorrow and exhaustion. Like her sisters, she had sat up for the last few nights at her mother's bedside, and like them she had slept little since her mother's death. The ride through the cold night had been numbing. It was farther than she had expected and as they rode deeper into the woods she grew more and more tense. Rhonwen was right. He was here beside them. He was in the trees, in the scattered, fleeting moonlight, in the howl of the wind.

And he wanted to speak of her destiny.

'Get down, I'll tether the horses.' Rhonwen was at her stirrup, her hood blown back, her hair whipping around her face where it had been torn from her braids.

Eleyne did as she was bid. She stared at the grass mound and her mouth was dry with fear.

Rhonwen lit a fire in the small brazier which she had carried at her saddle bow and set it gently on the grave. She had a leather pouch at her girdle. In it, gathered the summer before for this specific purpose, were dried hemlock and poppy seed, dittander, mugwort, rowan and sallow bark. She handed it to Eleyne. 'Scatter some on the flames,' she instructed in a whisper. Eleyne put her hand into the pouch, feeling the crumbly brittle petals, smelling the bitter spicy aroma of the herbs. Taking a handful, she let them fall into the brazier. He was very close.

Rhonwen began a low keening chant, her voice so quiet it was almost lost in the moan of the wind in the branches above their heads. Mesmerised by the sound, Eleyne dug her cold fingers once more into the pouch and scattered a new handful of herbs. The wind caught them and whirled them away into the shadows.

Rhonwen's eyes were fixed on the snow at their feet, almost invisible as the moon disappeared behind the clouds. Imperceptibly her keening grew louder and throwing back her head she raised her arms, staring at the sky behind the trees.

'Come!' she screamed. 'From beyond the grave, I command thee, come. My lady awaits you! *Come!*'

XVI

John was seated beside Margaret, toying half-heartedly with the food on his platter. Several times he had left the table to search for Eleyne, but had failed to find her. Then Cenydd was at his elbow. 'May I speak to you, my lord?' The man's face was creased with worry.

John threw down his napkin, rose and followed Cenydd out of the hall.

'It's my fault, my lord.' Cenydd was furious with himself. 'They gave me the slip. Rhonwen must have planned it. But I know where they've gone. I think we should follow them.' He half guessed what his cousin planned to do and his skin crawled at the thought.

John scanned his face thoughtfully, then nodded curtly. 'Bring four men, as quick as you can.'

They left the men with their horses on the edge of the woods, cautiously following the hoofprints of Rhonwen's and Eleyne's mounts in the moonlight. At the edge of the clearing they stopped, hidden by the tangled undergrowth and the near darkness. The clear low notes of Rhonwen's chant carried easily in the cold air.

'What are they doing?' John breathed. He could see the two women and between them the smoking vessel on the low mound of the grave.

'It's the burial place of the seer, Einion,' Cenydd whispered back.

'Sweet Christ!' John crossed himself. He felt the hackles on his neck prickling with fear. His wife, her face almost lost in the shadows of her black hood, looked preoccupied, dazed, as she gazed at the red glow of the smoking brazier. Around it, the melting snow was full of crimson reflections.

The two men looked at each other and, abruptly, Cenydd drew his sword, the rasp of metal ugly against the moan of the wind. 'We have to stop them,' he said.

'Eleyne!' John pushed his way out of the undergrowth. 'Don't you see what that woman is doing?' His voice was harsh with anger. 'Stop her!'

Eleyne did not appear to hear him. John grabbed the sword from Cenydd's hands and reversed it, holding it up to form a cross. 'Be silent, woman!' he thundered. His nerves were raw. 'I forbid this. Eleyne — go. Go now. While you can! Run!' Holding the sword before him, he stepped forward and stopped. The air around her was like ice: a tangible barrier between him and his wife.

'*Eleyne!*'

She did not seem to hear him. She was standing completely still, gazing down.

John swore at Cenydd, who was standing as if paralysed behind him. 'Grab Rhonwen, you fool. Grab her! Stop her mouth! Don't you see what she is doing? She is summoning the dead!'

Cenydd stepped backwards, his eyes rolling. 'Don't touch her, my lord. Don't go near her!'

Rhonwen whirled to face them, as though conscious of their presence for the first time, and they saw the glint of a knife in her hand. 'He is here!' she hissed. 'Listen, Eleyne, listen! He is here. Listen to his message!' She raised her hands again and there was a roar from the wind. It whirled into the treetops and rose to a scream, tearing the branches, shredding the clouds to reveal the cold distant moon.

Eleyne raised her head: 'Einion . . . ?'

In the shadows one of the guards had followed John and Cenydd. He peered petrified from his hiding place in the trees.

'*No!*' With a roar of anguish John launched himself at her. He tore the pouch from her hands and hurled it to the ground. 'Einion is dead! He is *dead*, Eleyne! He has no message for you!' He couldn't make himself heard above the scream of the wind. 'This woman's mad, don't you see? She is mad!' He seized Eleyne's wrist and dragged her away from the grave. 'Cenydd, call the men!'

'Let go of her!' Rhonwen turned, light-footed as a cat, and positioned herself in his path, the knife still in her hand. 'She is ours! Look!' She was triumphant. 'Look, John of Scotland. Look!'

In spite of himself, John followed her pointing finger. In the streaming moonlight he could see a tall wavering figure with long white hair and a dark robe, a staff in its hand, hovering in the shadows behind the grave.

Rigid with fear, he dropped Eleyne's wrist and the sword wavered. In his hiding place amongst the trees the guard fell to his knees and covered his face with his hands.

'Speak, Lord Einion!' Rhonwen screamed. 'See, I have brought her to you. Speak. Give her your message!'

'No, you scheming hellcat, no!' Cenydd recovered first and threw himself at Rhonwen. 'You evil witch! You −!' His hands grappled for the knife and they swayed back and forth together in the shadows.

John threw his arms around Eleyne. 'Come away. For sweet Christ's sake, come away!'

'He's gone.' She was staring white-faced at the place where the spectre had been. As suddenly as it had come, the whirling wind had died and the night was silent save for the heavy breathing of the man and the woman as they grappled in the snow.

'He was never there! It was a trick of the moonlight. He was never there, Eleyne!' John dragged her towards the trees. 'Come away, quickly, before −'

He stopped and swung around as a bubbling scream rang out behind them. Slowly, Cenydd sank to his knees in the snow, his hands clasped to his stomach. The blood welling from between his fingers and from his mouth was black in the moonlight.

'Guards!' John's voice rang out in the silence. 'Guards!' He pushed Eleyne aside and flung himself towards Cenydd.

Rhonwen's eyes were wild. Her teeth bared in a grimace of hatred, she leapt at John, the knife still in her hand. For a moment they wrestled as he tried to dislodge the weapon from her grasp, but it was slippery with blood and his fingers lost their grip.

Behind them the guard had finally recovered his wits enough to scramble to his feet and run to John's aid as his colleagues burst out of the darkness. As they threw themselves at Rhonwen she thrust the knife with all her remaining strength at John's heart. The thick folds of his cloak deflected the blade and he felt it graze his arm, but it was over. As the men seized Rhonwen's arms and pulled her back the knife flew harmlessly to the ground.

Panting, John knelt beside Cenydd's body and felt below the ear for a pulse. He looked up. 'He's dead,' he said.

Rhonwen ceased struggling. She stood still between her captors, looking down at the earl as he knelt in the snow, and her face contorted with rage. 'I curse you, John of Scotland!' she screamed. 'I curse you in the name of all the gods. May you roast in eternal hell for interfering here tonight!'

CHAPTER TEN

I

LLANFAES

The cell had only one window, high under the roof. Through it Rhonwen could see the moon, high and lonely far beyond the cloud wrack which raced across it. They had put chains on her wrists and ankles and given her straw to lie in, like an animal. She could remember screaming – a long high-pitched scream, which went on and on, echoing inside her skull. Cenydd's blood had dried on her gown. She could feel it, crusted and stiff in the darkness. Dimly she remembered the dagger in her hand. The blade had glinted, and in its reflection she had see Einion's anger and frustration, his desperation to speak.

Eleyne had screamed too. Why had she screamed? Was it when Lord Chester flung himself across the grave and tried to snatch the dagger? Had she tried to stab him too? She couldn't remember. But she could remember the fury in Einion's eyes before the guards had closed in on her and dragged her away.

Where was Eleyne? Why didn't she come? And Cenydd. Where was Cenydd? She had always been fond of Cenydd.

She tried to settle herself more comfortably against the wall, linking her manacled wrists over her knees and hugging them for warmth. The cell was quite clean; it had been used as a storeroom over the winter, but the damp and chill of the earth floor struck through the straw and she felt a dull ache beginning to seep into her bones. Quietly, she began to cry.

II

'Papa! Please let me see her!' Eleyne was distraught. 'Please. She did it for me!'

'She killed your bodyguard, her own cousin, for you?' Llywelyn stared at her. His anger and horror vibrated in the air around him. Lord Chester had told him what had happened. Sorcery. Necromancy. Murder. Sweet Jesus, *Dew!* His daughter was a necromancer!

Eleyne took a deep breath. 'Lord Einion wrote to me before he

236

died. He wanted to see me urgently, but Rhonwen burned the letter. When he died it preyed upon her conscience that I would never know his message.' She caught his hand as she used to when she was a little girl. 'Please, papa, I have lost my mother. Don't take away my nurse. I love her.' There were tears in her eyes.

'The woman has committed murder, Eleyne. She must pay the price.' Somehow he kept his voice steady. Eleyne must be kept out of this, and her involvement concealed.

Eleyne clung to him. 'No, please, you can't kill Rhonwen! You mustn't.' She was sobbing now. 'She did it for me!'

'She has killed a man, Eleyne, and by the laws of Wales she must pay the price,' Llywelyn said heavily. By Our Lady, didn't she realise the penalty for necromancy was death? Death for both of them! He had aged ten years in the few short days since his wife had died. His strong, lined face had grown puffy, his eyes were swollen from lack of sleep. Across the courtyard in the great wooden hall the funeral feast was still going on. When the prince had been called away, he had given no signal that it should cease.

'Cenydd was my servant. She must pay the price to me,' Eleyne said desperately. 'I will see that she is punished, papa.'

'Cenydd's family will require more than that, Eleyne.'

'Cenydd's family is her family. They won't want her life!' She rushed on. 'She didn't mean to kill him. She loved Cenydd, he was her cousin. She trusted him.'

'Your nurse, Eleyne, is a heretic,' Llywelyn said. 'She is in a state of the most mortal sin. As you are.' He added the last words with terrible emphasis.

Eleyne froze. She looked at her father, then at her husband who was sitting in a chair near the fire. There was blood on his mantle.

'Papa.' Eleyne's words were anguished. 'You can't punish us for summoning Einion –'

'It was the Lady Rhonwen who summoned him,' Llywelyn said slowly. 'Your husband and I have discussed your part in the ceremony, such as it was, and we have decided that you were there in complete ignorance of what she intended. She, as its instigator, must pay the full price. Your husband will deal with you as he sees fit.' He folded his arms in his mantle. 'She has caused nothing but trouble as long as I have known her,' he said grimly. 'And now she must be punished for her crimes. Your husband agrees.'

Eleyne looked from one man to the other; she was sick with horror. 'John dislikes her because she loves me, don't you understand?'

'The woman has proved herself a common murderer.' John's voice was weary. 'The penalty for that is death.'

'No!' She began to sob again, softly. 'No, you can't! You can't put her to death. I won't let you –' She flung herself on her knees and clung to the skirt of her father's gown.

Llywelyn put his hand gently on her head. He sighed. 'We shall leave it for God to decide, Eleyne. Tomorrow she will stand trial before Him. If He deems her innocent she will go free. I can do no more for her.'

Eleyne's eyes were round with horror as her hands fell from his gown. 'What do you mean?'

'A trial before God. I have given orders that she must face the ordeal of the hot iron . . .'

'*No*, papa, no!' Eleyne was as white as a sheet. 'Dear sweet Christ –'

'Sir,' John put in quietly, 'it is some twenty years since the Lateran Council forbade such trials to be conducted by the clergy in Christendom. You cannot mean to . . .'

Llywelyn swung round. 'Don't presume to question my decision, my lord! That woman has defiled my wife's memory and led my daughter into mortal sin. Only God can judge her fairly for, as Blessed Christ is my witness, I can't! She will face the ordeal tomorrow. If she is guilty, she will die!'

III

The Chesters had been given a small private room in one of the buildings which surrounded the courtyard. Rugs and furs were spread on the rough bed. Their light came from a tall candlestick which stood in the corner.

It was Luned alone who undressed Eleyne and wrapped her once more in her warm cloak against the cold.

'Where is she?' Eleyne whispered. John had gone out into the darkness.

'They have chained her in a cell.' Luned bit her lip, her huge eyes brimming with tears. 'Is it true she must undergo trial by ordeal?'

Eleyne nodded, still numb with horror.

'And did she . . . is it true she summoned Lord Einion from the dead?' Luned crossed herself fervently.

Eleyne stared at her dully. 'Who told you?'

'One of the guards followed you into the forest and spied on you. It is being whispered in the hall.' Luned shivered. 'He says Einion rose up out of the grave, as tall as a tree, with flames coming from his hands –' She broke off with a cry of fear as the door opened.

John ducked inside, stamping snow from his boots; the candles dipped and smoked as he pushed the door closed. 'The wind is rising again.' He unlaced his cloak at the throat and threw it down. 'Go, girl. Return to your mistress at daybreak, she will need you then.' He waited until Luned had slipped into the dark. 'The trial will be held after terce.'

Eleyne bit her lip miserably. 'Poor Rhonwen.'

'She is guilty. She must pay the price.' John put his arm around her. 'You must resign yourself to that, sweetheart. You cannot save her. Only God can do that now.'

Her eyes filled with tears again. 'She did it for me.'

'Then she was very foolish. You have no need of magic or murder. Christ and Our Lady are all anyone needs for protection.' He held her at arm's length, his eyes full of compassion. 'I know you love her, sweetheart. I have given in to you often enough on the subject of the Lady Rhonwen, but not this time.' He pulled her to him again.

She gasped; the movement had pushed up the sleeve of his gown revealing an ugly, puckered wound across his forearm, the blood clotted into uneven scabs. 'Did she do that?'

He nodded grimly. 'You must forget her, Eleyne. She is evil.' He paused. 'You let her do it, Eleyne. You must take some blame. You helped her in her evil arts. You would not listen when I shouted to you to stop. Only Our Lady can guess the penance the priest will give you for your sins.'

Eleyne paled, her fear for Rhonwen eclipsed by fear for herself. She had never seen John so cold.

'No.' She backed away from him. 'I can't confess!'

'You must, Eleyne, for the sake of your soul.' His face very grave, he pushed her cloak back so that he could see her body and he touched her breast, running a finger from it up to her throat. Their breath was misty in the cold candlelight. 'Tomorrow, before mass. And tonight I must chastise you.'

He took no pleasure in beating her. She had defied him and gone off to the forest alone, to practise sorcery and necromancy. She had risked her life, and indirectly risked his, for Rhonwen had nearly killed him. For her own sake, she had to be punished and punished severely.

IV

Rhonwen stared at the door in terror. They had told her what was to happen. The door ward and the priest, with his crucifix held before him, had been explicit in giving her the details of the ordeal before her. And they had told her that Eleyne could not save her.

Rhonwen looked at the door again, holding her breath. The moonlight had long gone from the window, but the sky was still dark. It could not yet be morning.

'Who's there?' she whispered. She knelt up, restricted by the unwieldy chains, her eyes straining in the darkness.

It was probably rats or perhaps a yard dog, sniffing at the bolts and

239

pausing to cock a leg outside the cell. There it was again – a soft scraping as the bolt was inched back a little further. Her heart began to beat very fast; she pressed back against the wall, her hands clasped before her, feeling the weight of the iron dragging on her wrists. Were they coming for her early? Were they going to strangle her here alone, and throw her body, unblessed by the gods, into the sea? The sweat poured down her back, in spite of the biting cold. Her skin was clammy, her whole body shaking with fear. She could hear the heavy wooden bar moving now, the soft animal squeak of the wood as the hasp was moved, the slight groan of the hinges as the pressure of the locks was eased.

Blessed Bride, be with me. Spittle ran down her chin as she began to gabble incoherently.

The door was opening. Still she could see nothing, for the darkness was as intense outside. The torch on the side of the building had gone out. Sobbing with fear, she scrambled to her feet, hampered by the chains around her ankles; she pressed harder against the wall, trying to back away from whatever was coming. She could see a little now: a torch on the far side of the courtyard still flared. It backlit the whirling sleet and outlined a figure standing in the doorway. There was no sound but the hiss of the wet snow against the wooden wall of the cell and the cry of the wind.

'No, please.' She had dug her nails into the palms of her hands and felt her fists slippery with her own blood. 'No, please, please . . .'

She fought the chains frantically as the figure stepped inside. For a moment the silhouette blocked the doorway, then it came towards her. She was conscious of a strange thundering in her ears, then everything went black and she slumped to the floor.

V

The Countess of Chester had screamed only once when her husband had beaten her, then her cries were muffled in the furs on their bed. But they had known, the gossips, the spies, the listeners at keyholes. In the guest room across the courtyard, Isabella had heard the whispers of her maid and, still dry-eyed after the funeral, she laughed as she climbed into her husband's bed.

Thin cracks of daylight showed around the shutters of the small window. Eleyne lay for several minutes, trying to make out the shadowy corners of the room. Her body was stiff and aching. Beside her, John lay asleep, his back towards her. She moved away from him and, teeth chattering, pulled a fur rug over her chilled shoulders. She lay still, feeling the warmth slowly coming back to her, then, rolling on to her stomach, she buried her face in her arms and began to sob.

John was awakened by the sound. Turning to her he pulled her to him. 'My darling, never make me do that to you again.' He held her gently, cradled on his chest, and kissed her wet eyelashes. 'You had to be punished, for your own good.' He shook his head. 'Supposing we had not been there. You could be facing trial with her today. Sweet Jesus, Eleyne, I couldn't bear it if anything happened to you.'

Eleyne closed her eyes, her face buried in his shoulder. 'Can't we do something to save her?' she whispered. Her voice was husky.

'It's out of our hands, Eleyne. She must stand judged by God.'

Eleyne pulled away from him and knelt up, suddenly rebellious. Her hair fell forward over her breasts: 'Do you really believe it? That God will judge her by this ordeal?'

He was distracted by her nakedness in the dim light filtering around the room. 'We must believe it.'

'I asked if you believe it.'

He saw a red welt, a mark from his belt, curving up her thigh and across her buttock. The skin on either side was bruised.

'Of course I believe it. I believe – we must all believe – what the church tells us.'

He reached forward and caught a handful of her hair, pulling it so that she overbalanced towards him. 'Enough, Eleyne, forget her,' he commanded. He pushed her back on to the bed and began to kiss her breasts, unaware of the misery and anger on her face.

It was several minutes before either of them noticed the shouting in the courtyard outside. John raised his head and listened, then with a groan he climbed to his feet and reached for his clothes.

'What is it? Is it time?' Eleyne sat up, trembling.

'No. It is not time,' John said grimly. He strode to the door. Unbarring it he pulled it open. Brilliant cold light flooded into the room. It had snowed hard in the night and the courtyard was clean and crisp, the surrounding roofs hung with icicles.

Eleyne gasped as the cold air hit her and pulling the rug over herself, she scrambled from the bed and ran to find her clothes, where Luned had left them, hanging cold and damp with condensation from a bracket on the wall.

VI

The door was still barred from the outside when the guards had opened the cell, and they had not left their posts all night, or so they claimed, but the cell was empty. Of Rhonwen and her chains, there was no sign. The straw lay flat and undisturbed, the bowl of water left for her to drink had frozen through. Not a drop had been spilled. There were no footprints in the heavy white carpet of snow leading to or from the cell.

The view of the men and women who peered nervously through the open door was that the devil had claimed his own. The men who had been heating their irons laid them aside to cool, half relieved, half disappointed, and the priest of St Mary's was called in to sprinkle the cell with holy water.

'Do you think she escaped?' Eleyne had given thanks to Our Lady and then, to be on the safe side, to the ancient gods as well.

John shook his head. He was watching Luned plait his wife's hair. 'It's my bet your father had her quietly strangled. That's what I would have done in his shoes. Now, finish getting ready, it's time for your confession. I want to leave for Chester after mass.'

VII
ABER ❖ March 1237

Isabella grimaced. She hated Lent. The diet of salt fish and bread left her feeling lethargic and turned her complexion pasty. Dafydd had not come near her for weeks, and she had amused herself by reorganising her father-in-law's household at Aber. Now that she had put her mind to it, she found she rather enjoyed it. She especially enjoyed pensioning off Princess Joan's ladies and despatching them to various local nunneries. She let it be known that she would welcome the services of some young, lively maidens from the families of Dafydd's supporters, and she made it clear that Senena, her three sons and the new baby, were no longer welcome at the prince's court. About Gruffydd she could do nothing. She smiled grimly: Dafydd would see to his brother in good time, if Gruffydd did not disgrace himself first with his father yet again. The man seemed incapable of holding his temper or his thoughts in check.

'So, daughter-in-law, you run my home with great efficiency.' Llywelyn smiled indulgently; he had begun to think he was mistaken in his assessment of the girl. She had steadied and grown into her responsibilities, and she had slimmed down, her face thinner and more becoming. She had always been pretty but now, as the poets of his court had not failed to notice, she was becoming beautiful. He was pleased. He missed his own daughters who had all returned to their homes and husbands, and as Dafydd took over more and more the running of affairs in the principality he enjoyed sitting by the fire and being waited on by the pretty, lively ladies of his daughter-in-law's household.

He missed Joan. Oh, how he missed Joan. More and more now he

242

thought about death. His own robust frame had shrunk; his will for life had gone. With Dafydd there to take his place, it was time to turn his thoughts to God.

He sighed as he sat by the fire in the solar he had appropriated as his private office. How he longed for the spring; winter had been too long. It had left him trapped between his sons. They were quarrelling again – Dafydd the reasonable, the systematic, his choice for heir, and Gruffydd the romantic hothead, fighting with his neighbours, fighting with his brother and his brothers-in-law. Gruffydd drove him to despair, but he loved his eldest son. He could see a lot of his younger ambitious self in Gruffydd, and he adored his four grandsons. Owain, serious, quiet, much like his mother; Llywelyn, the boisterous, clever, outgoing one; Rhodri, already a dreamy, musical child; and now the baby, Dafydd, named, Llywelyn suspected, as a half-hearted gesture of appeasement to his brother. It was time he saw them again; perhaps in a day or two he would feel well enough to ride.

He rose and walked stiffly to the desk where a pile of letters awaited him. One, he could see at once, bore the great seal of Chester. He frowned. Yet again Eleyne had disrupted his life; she had disrupted the court and Joan's funeral and tainted the memory of that sacred occasion.

He had decided to found a Franciscan friary over Joan's grave. The brothers would pray in perpetuity for her soul, sanctify and wipe away the desecration of that night. Even the thought of it made him angry. How could she? How could Eleyne have contemplated visiting another grave; how could she have allowed that woman to perform who knew what ceremonies over it to raise the dead? Agitated, he drummed his fingers on the table. Eleyne had not known what was going on, of course.

Did he really believe that? Lord Chester had assured him that his daughter was innocent of any complicity, and yet . . .

Now they would never know. Rhonwen had disappeared unpunished, claimed, so his courtiers whispered, by the devil she worshipped. He could feel the frustrated anger rising in him yet again, the throbbing inside his head. He turned sharply to the page who was waiting in the corner of the room: 'Bring me a drink, boy, *chwisgi*! Then call a clerk.' He put his hand to his eyes and leaned on the table. He must not let himself get so angry, it always gave him an infernal headache. He must stay calm and get on with the letters. He reached out towards the first. His hand wavered slightly, finding difficulty in locating its target, and his sleeve caught the inkwell. Perplexed, he watched the stream of black ink run, slow and viscous, across the table. The room was spinning now, the pain in his head unbearable. With a sharp cry, he put his hand to his temple, then he collapsed across the table, his hands clawing at the inky wood. The page found him lying on the floor, the ink dripping slowly on to his face.

VIII
FOTHERINGHAY ❖ March 1237

The flames were burning more clearly now, licking the back of the chimney, embracing the logs, devouring the dry twigs as Eleyne fed them slowly into the blaze. A log cracked loudly and she glanced over her shoulder, nervous that someone might have heard. The door was closed and she had turned the key in the lock. She was alone. The candles had long since burned down and the room was dark. She threw on the last stick and knelt for a while, holding her bed gown tightly around her shoulders, listening to the sound of the rain pouring outside. John had ridden with most of the officers of his household to Northampton to see the king. It had been her choice to remain at Fotheringhay, her wish that now, at last, she should be alone, and he had left her, believing that she was unwell, hoping that she might at last be pregnant.

She had collected the herbs from the stillroom over the past few weeks, hiding them in a small coffer, to which she alone had the key. Luned thought it contained letters. It was the night of the full moon — the most propitious time for what she had in mind. No moon would pierce the clouds tonight, but she could feel the power of it, up there, above the rain; feel its magic, its pull.

It had taken a while to pluck up the courage to do it, but her guilt at Rhonwen's death (if indeed she was dead at all) and her increasing anger with John had festered. She missed Cenydd's quiet presence and she was very sad about his death, but it had after all been John's fault! If he and Cenydd hadn't spied on them, none of it would have happened.

Something had changed between her and John. Perhaps it had changed before, when she was riding to and fro between Scotland and Wales, but she was no longer a child in any sense. She felt herself his equal now, and her independence had begun to assert itself. The night he had beaten her, he had awakened a sense of rebellion, and with her rebellion had returned her longing to ride alone. Now there was no faithful Cenydd to follow her.

She rose to her feet and let the bed gown slip to the floor. Away from the fire the room was cold and she felt the gooseflesh stir on her skin as she unlocked the coffer and took out a small silver dish and spoon and the packages of herbs. She mixed them carefully in the dish, then took it to the window, where earlier she had opened the shutters.

Standing by the sill, she offered the mixture to the sky, feeling spots of icy rain on her cold skin, then, not giving herself time to think, she threw the mixture on the fire. Thick pungent smoke filled the hearth and spilled into the room, and she found herself spluttering and coughing as she knelt waiting for it to clear. At last she could look deep into the flame and with her voice low but determined, she called Einion to come to her.

The flames shrank and hissed and she heard the wind moan in the stairwell outside her door. The draught rattled the hinges and lifted the tapestries from the wall and she realised that there was a picture in the fire. She leaned forward, straining her eyes, feeling the heat searing her eyelids: there was a figure lying on a bed, and around it other figures, indistinct, fading. Who was it? Einion had died alone. Surely it was not John? Dear God, it could not be John.

'Einion,' she called, her voice sharp with fear, 'Einion, come to me.' But the picture was dissolving; it had gone. She slumped on her heels with a scowl of frustration. In spite of all her careful preparations, she had failed. Her questions were still unanswered.

The fire settled and her eyes flew open again. 'Please,' she knelt up, and held out her hands in supplication, 'please come.' There was another picture; she saw a horse, cantering proudly, its eyes huge and staring in the thunder, its saddle slippery with rain, its hooves sliding in the mud. The rider leaned forward, urging it on, the thunder of hoofbeats filled her ears, then the horse was screaming, its feet scrabbling for a foothold, and she saw the rider flying through the air. As fast as it had come, the picture was gone.

She sat back on her heels again, trembling. Who was it? Who did she keep seeing, riding to what death? Not John, of that she was certain. The seat in the saddle was too sure, the shoulders too broad, but always the billowing cloak hid the face from her.

'Oh please, show me his face,' she whispered. 'And show me Rhonwen. Tell me if she is truly dead, or if she is my father's prisoner. Show me what has happened to her.' She knelt forward for a third time, her head swimming from the fumes, straining her eyes into the heart of the flame. She saw the bed again. It was at Aber, and she could see the bedchamber clearly. 'Papa!' she whispered, 'it's papa.' She rubbed her eyes, her heart pounding with fright. But there was nothing there. The pictures had gone.

Dragging on her gown, Eleyne went back to the window and leaned out as far as the grilles would allow, letting the cold rain pour in on her face, battering her eyelids, soaking her hair. She was shivering violently. 'Papa,' she whispered to the night. 'Papa.' Behind her the fire burned low, but the pungent smell of herbs remained.

High above, the cloud grew thin for a moment and shone with a pearlised glow where it veiled the cold spring moon. Then it thickened and the night was once again dark.

John looked down at the letter in his hand. It was from his brother-in-law, Dafydd. The old prince had had a seizure and lay unconscious at Aber. He begged the Earl of Chester to inform King Henry and reaffirm his own loyalty to the king, and he also begged John not to tell Eleyne: *Sadly, she will not be welcome here, unless, of course, father should die, in which case you would both be expected at his funeral.*

The words, formal and penned by a scribe, were cold and unfilial. He wondered how Gruffydd was feeling about the situation.

King Henry was listening to a seemingly endless list of petitions when John approached him. The king signalled for the clerks to wave the patient crowds back.

'So, my Lord Chester, have you come to rescue me from my duties?' Henry gave a cold half-smile. As always he was richly dressed, today in a parti-coloured gown, stitched with gold, and a scarlet cloak with a border sewn with gems. Eleanor, his young wife of a year, was beside him on the dais. Only fourteen years old, her face was set with boredom.

'Sad news, sire.' John bowed. 'I have a letter from Dafydd ap Llywelyn. He bids me tell you that his father is ill and may be dying.'

Henry frowned. 'That is black news indeed. North Wales has been well ruled by Llywelyn.' He stood up with a sigh and threw the silken sweep of his mantle over his left shoulder. 'I can't say I am surprised though. I had been told that he lost the will to live when my half-sister died. May I see the letter?' His sharp eyes had spotted the folded parchment still clutched in John's hand.

John handed it over reluctantly and watched as the king read it. Henry looked up at last. There was quizzical amusement in his eyes. 'Your wife has been a thorn in Llywelyn's flesh on more than one occasion if I remember right. Where is she? We have missed her here at Northampton.'

'She is at Fotheringhay, sire.'

'And will you be able to keep her there, do you think?' Henry's smile was almost mocking. The rumours of Eleyne's wild rides had reached court.

John felt a rush of heat to his face. 'Oh, I shall keep her there, make no mistake, sire. Although it will break her heart that her father does not want her.'

246

'It sounds as if Llywelyn is past knowing what he wants,' Henry retorted. 'We can both guess who is behind that remark by Dafydd ap Llywelyn. And it bodes ill for Llywelyn's inheritance if the heir, good man though he is, is led by the nose by that she-cat he married. The de Braose family have always been trouble.' He sighed and was about to beckon back his clerks. Then he paused. 'Eleyne visited her aunt in Scotland again several times last year, I hear?'

John tensed. 'Your sister, the Queen of Scots, was unwell, sire. She seems to have taken a great liking to her niece.'

'As you have to the idea of a kingdom of your own, no doubt.' Henry smiled coldly. 'Just so long as you remember where your first loyalty lies, as Earl of Chester and, even if the time should come, as King of Scots.'

John bowed slightly; the gesture allowed him to avoid the king's eye. He murmured something which could have been taken for agreement and was much relieved to see that it had been taken for one of farewell by the men waiting to catch the king's attention. With another bow John turned away. He did not like the turn the conversation had taken. It was time to return to Fotheringhay to break the news of her father's illness to Eleyne.

X

CRICCIETH CASTLE ❖ April 1237

'I will not have that woman under this roof!' Senena faced her husband, her eyes blazing.

Gruffydd glared at her. 'God's bones, woman! I won't be spoken to like that. If I say she stays, she stays!'

Beyond the narrow windows of the keep of Criccieth Castle the sea crashed against the cliffs, the rollers creaming in from the south-west, piling into the bay and hiding the sands in clouds of spume. Rain streamed before the wind and the red lion flag high above the newly built keep stood out stiffly, pointing towards Eryri and the grey mass of cloud which hid the mountains.

'Oh no!' Senena shook her head. 'I obey you in most things, my lord and husband, but in this never!' She swept away from him, her woollen gown bulky around a figure still thickened from bearing her last baby. She was a tall woman, as tall as her husband, and when roused, as now, her temper was as formidable as his. 'You get her out of here! Get her right out of Gwynedd; out of Wales, you hear me?'

Gruffydd sat down and put his elbows on his knees. He glared at her, supporting his chin on linked fingers. 'And what do you suggest I do with her?'

'Send her away! Send her back to your sister. That's where she wants to be.'

Gruffydd frowned. 'She can't go to Eleyne. Lord Chester would arrest her. She can't go to her family; they have never recognised her anyway, and they have sworn the bloody vengeance of the *galanas* on her for killing Cenydd.'

Senena shuddered. 'An eye for an eye; a life for a life. It is just. Why did you have her brought here?'

'For Einion's sake; she served him faithfully.'

Senena shook her head. 'That is where you are wrong. It is Eleyne she serves. Whatever she did that night, she did it in her own twisted mind for Eleyne, and Eleyne alone.'

Gruffydd raised an eyebrow. 'I should have thought such loyalty was to be commended.'

'Maybe,' Senena said, 'but not when she is living beneath our roof and Eleyne is hundreds of miles away. Her loyalty is too violent and too partisan! I want her out!'

Gruffydd rubbed his face in his hands. 'And who is to tell her this, pray?'

'You.' Senena snapped her mouth shut on the word like a trap.

'And what if she curses us as she cursed John of Chester?'

Senena was silent. She could feel the throb of the wind against the stone walls, for all their thickness. Far away, above the howl of it, she heard the yelping cry of a gull. She shivered. There was an omen there, she was sure. She straightened her shoulders. 'Then we will spit on her curse and throw her into the sea.'

Gruffydd paled: 'Blessed Bride! Are you mad, woman?' He stood up. 'I forbid you to say a word to her. I shall tell her myself.' He swung around as the door behind him opened. 'Did I send for anyone?' He stopped in mid-sentence. Rhonwen stood in the doorway, wrapped in a thick plaid cloak, her hair covered by a heavy white veil in the manner of the Welsh mountain women. Her face was pale and drawn.

Senena found her mouth had gone dry. How much had she heard? Against the noise of the storm and the crashing of the waves on the rocks below, surely she would not have heard anything. But then, who could tell what powers this woman had? Senena smiled nervously, ashamed of her own twofacedness: 'Lady Rhonwen, you are welcome.'

'Don't lie to me, princess. I am as welcome as the raven at a wedding feast! A woman with blood on her hands is not going to be a favoured guest anywhere; I am well aware of that. But you have nothing to fear. Your husband saved my life and I have always been his friend.'

Rhonwen walked painfully across towards the fire, which smouldered fitfully as the wind blew down the chimney and threw sparks out across the floor. When Gruffydd's henchman had cut the chains from her ankles his chisel had slipped from his frozen fingers and cut deep into her leg. The wound had festered and in spite of her ministrations had refused to heal.

She seated herself in Senena's chair without invitation and leaned back, her eyes closed for a moment against another wave of throbbing heat which spread outward from the wound and mounted towards her knee. Gritting her teeth, she noted with grim amusement that Gruffydd's fingers were crossed. 'So. You want me out of here, no doubt.'

Gruffydd looked at the floor. 'My father's men will come soon. It is only a matter of time.'

'But you would not betray me to them?' She regarded him steadily.

'Of course not. But you will never be safe as long as you stay in Wales. The *galanas* is powerful, its reach is long, you know that as well as I.'

'And you don't think my magic powers will protect me?' She laughed grimly. 'And you are right. For all the stories that I flew out of that cell disguised as an owl you know the truth. I have no magic powers. I have the temper of a wounded cat, that's all.' She paused reflectively.

'But you summoned Einion from the dead,' Senena put in. 'The whole of Gwynedd talks of it.'

Rhonwen shook her head. 'Einion came because he wanted to. Oh, there was magic there that night, and power. But the power did not come from me.'

'Then where —?' Senena whispered.

'From Eleyne, of course.' Rhonwen looked at her triumphantly. 'Didn't you realise? All the power comes from Eleyne!'

There was a long moment of silence. 'I had heard that she has the Sight,' Gruffydd said cautiously. 'Is that what you mean?'

Rhonwen gave a mocking smile. 'Oh she has more than the Sight, much more. And her destiny is written in the stars!' She hugged herself as another spasm of pain shot up her leg. 'She will show them! the Lord Llywelyn; Dafydd; that English minx, his wife. She will show them all. Where is she?'

Senena looked across at her husband. 'Eleyne has returned to England. I believe they are at Fotheringhay.'

'And she hasn't sent for me, because Lord Chester hates me. I nearly killed him too, you know.'

'I know,' Gruffydd replied grimly. 'You were a fool, my lady, if you will forgive me for saying so. You have made powerful enemies. But as to why Eleyne has sent you no message, it is because all the world thinks you are dead. The rumour at Aber was that the prince had you secretly killed, and I saw no reason to deny it. Only he knows that is not true, and he is too ill to tell anyone.'

249

'She will know. Eleyne will know I am alive. She will have seen it in the fire.' Rhonwen gazed at the fire as though seeking confirmation in the hissing coals.

Senena stepped forward and put a hesitant hand on Rhonwen's shoulder. 'What are you going to do? Where will you go?'

'To Eleyne, of course. She needs me. As soon as my leg is better and the weather has cleared a little I shall beg a horse from you and go to her. You need not fear that I shall stay here a moment longer than necessary.'

'But what of Lord Chester?' Gruffydd enquired soberly. 'He is not going to welcome you, my lady.'

'He has never welcomed me.' Painfully Rhonwen pulled herself to her feet. 'I am no longer sure that Lord Chester is part of Eleyne's destiny. I don't think I need worry myself about him. I shall see to it that he does not get in our way. I cursed him at Einion's grave and I curse him every night!' She laughed out loud suddenly. 'Oh no, Lord Chester will not bother me.'

XI

FOTHERINGHAY ❖ April 1237

Carpets of snowdrops grew on the banks of the Nene beyond the walls of the castle at Fotheringhay. Slipping from her saddle, Eleyne began to pick some, keeping her back to her husband so he could not see her tears. He had waited until the end of the day's hunting to tell her. They had been tired and content, nearly home, the horses walking steadily across the flat marshlands towards the castle when he had called her aside and dismounted on the river bank.

'If it were up to him, Eleyne, of course he would want to see you,' he said slowly. 'He is not dead. It is some kind of seizure. He may well recover.'

'He cannot move his hands; his speech is affected,' she said.

She had not seen the angry look he had given her when she confessed that she knew her father was ill. Every further detail of knowledge she betrayed made him more horrified.

'He may get better. There is no point in rushing off to Aber until we know how he is.'

'He would want me with him. That is why I was shown his illness . . .' She began to tremble violently beneath her cloak of warm furs.

'No, my darling, he would not want you there.' He sighed. That at least she hadn't seen: her brother's prohibition. 'And neither would Dafydd. I'm sorry.'

250

'You mean I am forbidden to go to him?' She looked at him, stricken, the flowers clutched in her gloved hand. He could see the tears swimming in her eyes, clinging for a moment to her eyelashes, then she turned away. She walked slowly towards the river and stood for a moment on the muddy bank, then bringing the flowers up to her lips she tossed them high in the air and watched as they scattered across the dark slow-moving water.

John followed her and put his hands on her shoulders. 'He will always love you, Eleyne. It's just that your mother's death is still very much on his mind. Give him time.'

'And what if there is no time?' She swung and faced him. 'What if he is dying? What if he is already dead?'

'Then that is God's will.' The cold air caught his throat and he began to cough. Stepping back as he gasped for breath, he pressed his hand to his chest.

She stared as she saw the colour drain from his face except for two hectic patches which had appeared on his cheeks. 'You should not have come out today,' she said almost absently, 'I didn't know you were ill again.'

'I'm not ill.' He controlled the cough with a monumental effort. 'It's just the cold wind. Come on, let's ride back now, it's growing dark.'

Patches of mist were drifting up from the river across the marshes and into the meadows and woods as the light faded. They could see the castle in the gloom, a black silhouette against the lowering sky.

'Here. Let me help you mount.' For a moment he stood looking into her eyes. 'You know that I love you, don't you?' He looked down, as abashed as a boy.

She stared at him for a moment, then she began to cry.

'Eleyne.' His arms were round her. 'Eleyne, my darling.' He could not feel her figure through the thick cloak, or touch her hair. Her cheeks were like ice, but her tears were hot as they ran into the collar of his cloak. He held her tightly, oblivious of the assembled attendants watching as their horses stamped impatiently in the cold. His lips sought hers as he pulled her into the shelter of his cloak.

They did not stay long in the hall that night. As soon as supper was finished they withdrew to their bedchamber and John called for the candles to be lit. Sitting at the fireside Eleyne watched the servant move from candle to candle, his taper wavering as he held the flame to each new wick, the shadows in the room drawing back into the corners. Beyond the shutters the night was still; a heavy white mist hung over the river, wrapping the castle in soft dripping silence. There was no sound from the great hall below. A travelling minstrel was entertaining the household with a succession of soft dreamy ballads and, the supper dishes cleared away and the cooking fires doused for the night, the

251

whole castle had settled early into quietness. Lighting the last candle, the servant bowed and withdrew. John threw himself into his chair and thrust his feet out towards the fire. 'Will you sing to me?' He smiled at Eleyne and held out his hand.

She went to him and sat at his feet, her head resting against his knees. The loss of Rhonwen and her mother had been devastating, but through everything John had been with her. Even when she was angry with him he had given her strength, as he was giving her strength now, just by being there and by loving her. 'I would rather hear one of your stories.'

Her tears were long dried. It had happened too often before: the rejection from Aber, the hurt, the sorrow. If her father were dead, she would have known. Probably every passing day without news meant that he was growing stronger. She reached for John's hand and felt his grip at once, strong and reassuring. 'You really want to hear one?'

He smiled down at her, and he nodded.

He made love to her with great tenderness that night and she fell asleep at last, secure in the circle of his arms. Outside the mist thickened. It swirled and licked against the heavy shutters and glistened on the castle walls. The men of the night watch strained their eyes from the gatehouse tower and the wall walks and, seeing nothing, turned gratefully back to their braziers.

John lay awake, staring at the hangings of the bed, seeing the glow of the banked-up fire reflected on the heavy beams of the ceiling. He had begun to sweat heavily and could feel his limbs beginning to shake. He eased his arm from beneath Eleyne's shoulders and sat up, staring down at her. He could not see her face, but she gave a little moan as he moved, and snuggled closer against him. He smiled, his hand gently stroking her hair, and after a moment her breathing steadied again. John pushed his legs over the side of the bed and stood up; immediately the heat left his body and he began to shiver. He pulled his bed gown around his shoulders, went over to the fire and kicked at the turves which covered the logs. It burst into life at once. He could feel the sweat, ice-cold on his forehead; he could smell it, rank upon his body. Sitting down, he hugged his gown around him and rocked back and forth as the nausea began to build. He could hear the silence outside, a tangible wall, like the mist which drifted up from the River Nene. He shivered again and not for the first time he remembered Rhonwen's curse.

ERYRI ❖ April 1237

The horse was lame. In the distance she heard again the liquid trill of a curlew. Her sodden cloak dragged at her shoulders as Rhonwen bent and felt the horse's leg with stiff cold fingers. The mountains were swathed in mist, the ground a quagmire of mud and slush. Twice she had lost the packhorse trail and spent precious time hunting back and forth among the heather and bilberries until she found it again; now it was growing dark and she could see the pale flicker of corpse lights, the strange fairy lights which showed above the bog cotton in the twilight and made her mouth go dry with fear.

Senena had given her the horse and the money and the spare gown and shoes which were all wrapped in the bundle which hung from her saddle. She had wanted to stay, to remain in the shelter of the castle at Criccieth until her leg was better, until the weather had cleared; until the hunt for her had been called off, for Senena had warned her that Dafydd did not believe the devil had taken her. He believed she had escaped and the alarm had been raised across Gwynedd and beyond. But they wanted her gone, and she was afraid. If Dafydd's men came to Criccieth, would Gruffydd hide her then? If she could reach Eleyne, she would be safe. Eleyne would help her and in return she could help Eleyne to her destiny.

Rhonwen straightened her back and surveyed the wet fog which surrounded her. The horse could go no further tonight, and she had to find shelter. She strained her eyes, trying to make out the shapes of trees and rocks in the gloom, trying to listen for the sound of a stream nearby, but the mist blanketed everything.

The old man's dog found her. She heard the bark and stared round, her heart thumping, trying to place the sound. Then she heard the slithering footstep on the loose scree. Nimble in his flat-soled, soft skin shoes, a sheepskin around his shoulders, he was within a few feet of her before she saw him. 'Greetings, mistress, have you lost the road?' He was small and wizened, and his eyes darted inquisitively over her horse, lingering on the bundle, then returning to her.

'My horse is lame.' She forced her voice to be strong. 'Is there somewhere near here where I can stay?'

He laughed – a croaky, wheezy sound which was not entirely pleasant. 'You are welcome to my house, mistress, if you wish. It is but a short way from here. I can see to your horse, my wife will give you food and you are welcome to share our bed.' He put his hand on the horse's bridle. 'You have come a good way up from the track. It's a good thing I found you, the mountain is treacherous to those who don't know it.'

She limped after him as he led her horse back down the steep hillside. It seemed a long time before they stopped, but at last she saw a small dwelling materialise out of the fog. At the old man's shout a square of light appeared as someone pushed back the covering which hung across the doorway. He gestured her inside. 'Go, warm yourself. I shall see to your horse.'

Unhooking the bundle from her saddle, Rhonwen turned with relief towards the light and ducked inside the small cottage. It was blessedly warm, with a bright fire burning in the centre of the single room. Beyond the low partition which formed the wall at the left-hand end a cow and several sheep huddled together in the darkness. The old man's wife, Rhonwen saw as she shyly motioned Rhonwen to the piled bracken which served as bed, seat and table, was scarcely more than a child. As the girl dipped water from her cauldron for her guest to wash her hands and face, Rhonwen caught a glimpse of the pale hair beneath the coarse white veil.

'You are injured, mistress?' The child's sharp eyes had spotted the limp. Rhonwen sat down, pushing her bundle behind her as a back support, and with a groan kicked off her sodden shoes. The girl knelt before her. With gentle fingers she folded back Rhonwen's wet, muddy skirt and stared at the linen which covered the wound. Fresh blood and pus mingled with the dirt on the bandage.

The heat was beginning to make Rhonwen feel drowsy. She watched as the girl fetched a bowl of fresh water and clean rags, and saw her put a thick green ointment on the wound before she rebandaged it. Gratefully she accepted a bowl of mead to drink. When the man returned, she was nearly asleep.

'I have seen to your horse,' he said. 'It's next door with the other animals. I've moved the stone in its hoof, and the bruising will be better by tomorrow.' He sat down beside her and accepted a bowl of mead from his wife. In the cooking pot over the fire something bubbled gently with an appetising smell, and he sniffed hungrily.

'Where are you bound?' He eyed Rhonwen curiously and she stiffened at his uncouth manners. No host should ask where his guest was going, or how long they wished to stay. She forced herself to smile: 'I ride to Chester.'

'Chester?' He stared at her blankly. 'That's a long way.' His eyes had strayed from Rhonwen's face to the bundle against which she was lying. 'Especially for a lady such as yourself, alone.'

Rhonwen's attention sharpened. 'I became separated from my companions,' she said quietly. 'They cannot be far away. Once this accursed mist lifts they will find me.'

'Indeed. I am glad to hear it. It's dangerous to ride these roads alone. There are all manners of thieves and outlaws in the mountains.

It is no place for an unescorted lady.' He watched as his wife ladled the contents of the cooking pot into three wooden bowls. She reached into the crock for some coarse bread and, breaking it into pieces, gave Rhonwen her share.

'My name is Annest,' she said shyly. 'And my man is Madoc.'

'I am Rhonwen.' The words were out before she could stop them, but her host gave no sign that the name meant anything to him. He was too busy pushing the stew from his bowl into his mouth. Rhonwen tasted hers. There was a heavy flavour of leek, and some kind of game bird – the grease floated on the thin stock in great shining gobbets – and it was very hot. After a moment's hesitation, she began to eat it eagerly, feeling the warmth run through her veins.

They ate in silence, the small room lit only by the fire. Beyond the wall, she heard the animals moving about; caught the heavy smell of dung. Twice Madoc leaned forward to refill her bowl of mead and twice she found she had drained it. She put down her bowl and, the last of her bread eaten, lay back against her bundle.

The fire had died when she awoke, and the room had become very cold. Her head was aching violently. Her eyes still half shut, she groped for her cloak. It had dried by the fire and she pulled it over her, thankful for its heavy folds. She was almost asleep again when she heard someone whispering. She tensed, straining her ears, aware that her hosts were no longer by the fire with her. In the darkness she had not noticed that they were gone, but now she missed the staccato snoring of the drunken Madoc and the snuffling whimpers of his wife. They were outside, and she realised that the cold draught which had awakened her had come from the loosely flapping sacking across the doorway. They appeared to be arguing about something in hushed tight whispers. Again she strained her ears, but she could not make out what they were saying. Fully awake and every nerve tense, she edged herself into a sitting position, feeling for her precious bundle and pushing it behind her. Something was wrong. She had mistrusted Madoc from the first moment she set eyes on him; she should have obeyed her instincts. If only she had a knife. She had asked Senena for a weapon and the stupid woman had laughed: 'Haven't you done enough damage?' she had said. She had given Rhonwen money, clothes and shoes, but no weapon.

There was a sound in the doorway and she held her breath. She heard the slither and drag of the bracken as the two figures crept back inside. It was pitch black, then a small flicker of light showed as Madoc squatted before the fire and pushed aside the turf covering. He paused, silhouetted against the faint glow, then turned towards her. She had half expected him to be holding a knife, but in his hand was a coil of rope.

Her heart thudding with fear, she had almost sat upright when her

255

face was enveloped in a suffocating blackness. Annest, creeping around behind her, had dropped a length of sacking over her head. In seconds she felt the rope looped around her flailing hands, and moments later her ankles were bound as well. Only then was the sack removed. She had been left lying on her side, her ankles pulled up to her wrists so that she was trussed like a fowl ready for the spit.

Madoc kicked at the fire with a chuckle and sat down opposite her, his face illuminated by the flames. 'So, my fine lady. When I spoke of outlaws in the mountains, little did I realise that I was entertaining one of them under my roof.' He rubbed his hands together. 'See what she has in that bag she's been guarding so carefully, *cariad*!' he instructed his wife, who knelt trembling near the door. Annest glanced at Rhonwen in terror and shook her head.

'Go on, woman, she can't hurt you!' Madoc reached for his jug of mead and poured out the last measure. Shaking the jug regretfully upside down, he tossed it over his shoulder into the shadows. 'She's going to make us rich, this lady. The prince has offered a reward for her capture, and the family of Cenydd ap Maredudd want her dead or alive.' He narrowed his eyes. 'Maybe they will pay even more than the prince, who knows?'

In spite of herself, Rhonwen groaned. Her wrists and ankles hurt savagely and the wound in her leg was sending a knifing pain up to her knee. 'Please. Let me at least sit up.' She despised herself for the whimper in her voice.

Madoc ignored her. His eyes were on the bundle which Annest had pulled into the firelight.

'Go on. Open it.'

She did so and dragged out the spare gown — a soft rich red wool — a fine linen chemise, the pair of leather shoes and the small bag of coins. Taking the purse into her hand, Annest tossed it up and down on her palm. Madoc's eyes glinted at the sound of the coins.

'Empty it!' he hissed. She fumbled with the thongs which bound the mouth of the bag and with an exclamation of impatience he reached into his belt and tossed her his dagger. 'Cut it, you stupid bitch! Cut it.'

The girl's hands were shaking as she inserted the blade beneath the leather thong and snicked it. A small pile of shining coins spilled on to the bakestone. Welsh silver pennies with the cross of the Rhuddlan mint lay gleaming in the light of the fire. Madoc licked his lips. 'So. You carry a fortune with you, Lady Rhonwen. To buy your way across Wales, no doubt.' He hiccuped morosely. 'Did you not realise that your name has been cried from every market, from every pulpit, from every mouth, from every passing eagle?' He snatched a new flagon of mead from his wife, who had produced it from the back of the room without being asked. Drawing the stopper with his teeth, he tipped the bottle and drank deeply, wiping the sticky residue from his lips with the back of his hand before he lay back on his elbow and stared reflectively at the coins. 'Beautiful,' he said dreamily, 'beautiful.'

'What are you going to do with me?' Rhonwen asked at last. She was still trying to ease her position.

Madoc stared at her, bleary-eyed. 'I haven't decided. Maybe I'll let them haggle over you like a mare at the horse sales!' He gave a contented smile and belched. 'Perhaps we should fatten you up a bit, eh? Get a better price for you that way. In foal!' He let his eye run insolently over her body.

Rhonwen felt herself shudder with loathing. The hatred she felt for this man was greater than anything she had felt in her life. She could feel it burning through her like fire; like vitriol, corroding her veins. She was almost surprised not to see the ropes which bound her falling away from her limbs, smoking. Her dazedness had gone, and her brain was working as clearly and keenly as a honed knife. He was not going to kill her, that much was clear. She had time to work out how to escape. She eased herself again, feeling a new ache in her back from the awkward curled position in which she lay. She tried to ease her wrists apart, but he had tied the ropes cruelly tight. She heard a quiet chuckle from across the fire, and saw that he was watching her. 'Trussed like a fowl, you are, my beauty, you'll not escape,' he said smugly. He lifted the flagon again, and she watched his Adam's apple jumping up and down as he swallowed, the shadows from the fire playing across his weathered skin. Behind her Annest sat down quietly and pulled her cloak around her, shivering. She had not touched a drop of the drink.

The fire had burned low again before the jug was at last empty and Madoc lay snoring on the bracken, his mouth open. Rhonwen saw the dagger back in his belt. The bag of coins, carefully gathered again, lay beneath his hand.

'Annest!' She could not see the girl from where she lay. 'Annest, are you there?'

She heard a rustle in the bracken, but there was no answer. 'Annest, please, my leg hurts so much. Could you not loosen the ropes a little?' Again there was no answer, but she could hear the silence of the girl holding her breath. 'Please. You helped me; you bathed my feet and gave me hospitality; you tended my wound. All I am asking is that you loosen the rope around my ankles. He would never know.' The pain in her voice was real.

Annest sat up and pushed the hair out of her eyes. She said nothing.

'Please, Annest.'

'I don't dare,' the girl whispered.

Rhonwen gave a small smile – Annest had answered; her will was weakening.

'Please help me, Annest, I am in such pain.'

There was another slight rustle as Annest crawled towards her. In the dying firelight it was almost dark, but Rhonwen could see the girl's long flaxen hair hanging forward over the shoulders of her gown.

'If I loosen the ropes, you won't do anything?'

'No, of course I won't do anything.' Rhonwen bit her lip as another wave of agony swept up her leg.

Annest touched Rhonwen's ankles. The rope was very tight, strapping her wrists to her feet, pulling her head almost down to her knees. Her flesh was so bruised and numb she could barely feel Annest's cold fingers groping their way around the knots.

'I can't undo them, they're too tight.'

'Then cut them. Please, Annest, in the name of pity.' Suddenly she was sobbing.

'Oh please, don't cry. You'll wake Madoc,' Annest said unhappily. 'I don't know what to do.'

'Cut the ropes around my ankles. I can't escape if my hands are still tied; and anyway I can't walk with my injured leg, you know that.' Madoc snorted and shifted his position on the far side of the bakestone. They held their breath. Almost at once his snores began again, softer now, muffled by his arm.

'He'll see. In the morning, he'll see I've helped you. He'll beat me.'

'He won't see if we burn the cut ropes, and he won't remember what he did after all that drink anyway. Oh, please.' Rhonwen closed her eyes as another wave of pain hit her. 'Have you got a knife?'

Annest nodded, reached into her girdle and pulled out a small knife. With a glance across the embers at her sleeping husband, she began to saw at Rhonwen's bonds. It took what seemed like an age to cut through the bands around her ankles. The knife was blunt and the rope had tightened deep into her flesh, but at last it gave and with a groan Rhonwen was able to straighten a little. 'Here, again, cut this one too.' Her lower lip bled with the effort not to cry out in pain.

'I don't know if I should . . .'

'Of course you should. Go on, otherwise he will see. The rope is not yet free.' She felt the blood flowing back into her wrists as the knots loosened.

'You won't do anything —'

'I have already told you that.'

In another moment she would be free. She eased her cramped body, feeling the brush of the girl's long hair on her arms, smelling her unwashed skin.

'Eh! What's going on!' Madoc's shout was loud in the hut. With a terrified cry, Annest dropped the knife and jumped backwards almost into the fire.

'You stupid bitch!' Madoc staggered to his feet cursing. 'What are you doing? Leave her alone! Do you want her to escape?'

As he lurched towards her Rhonwen grabbed with her bound hands for the knife Annest had dropped. She jerked herself up on to her knees as Madoc reached her and brought the knife up in one swift movement through his jerkin and under his ribs. He let out a howl of rage; his arms flailed and he staggered back as Annest cowered sobbing in the darkness.

'Don't come near me, you bastard son of a pig!' Rhonwen breathed. She still had the knife, and the warm blood running down the blade told her it had found its target. 'Don't you ever come near me again.' She held it, point out, towards him, marking him as he stumbled into the red-hot embers and fell on one knee near her. His hands were clutched to his middle and he had begun to breathe with harsh rasping sounds.

'Bitch, bitch, bitch! Annest! *Annest, help me!*' He had fallen to both knees now. Rhonwen sawed frantically through the last of the rope that held her feet, and somehow got the blade of the knife under the rope around her wrists. It was too blunt; without sawing it would do nothing. She was shaking so much she could hardly hold it. 'Don't drop it,' she muttered between her teeth, 'don't drop it!' Across the fire she could see faintly the huddled silhouette of the man. His curses were barely audible. Annest had not moved; sobbing hysterically, she was pressed against the wall on the far side of the cottage, clutching her cloak around her.

Gritting her teeth, Rhonwen sawed on as best she could, feeling first one then another strand of the rope loosen and snap. With one final frantic effort, it was done. The rope fell away and she was free. Grimly she forced her limbs to move, crouching, knife in hand, as she waited to see what Madoc was going to do.

His breath rasped in his throat as he hauled himself to his feet, feeling for the dagger at his belt. She saw its blade catch the light of a stray flame as he held it before him. 'I'm going to get you, bitch! I'm going to deliver you to your family flayed and gutted!'

There was a wail of anguish from Annest. Neither gave her so much as a glance. Their eyes locked, they faced one another, knives before them. On the front of Madoc's jerkin a slow stain, black in the dim firelight, was spreading downwards. He clutched his stomach and when he took his hand away it was wet with blood. 'Bitch!' he shouted again. 'Bitch! I'm going to kill you for this!' He coughed painfully.

Rhonwen was totally calm now, the knife handle alive in her hand. She caressed it, waiting. Everything depended on the next few moments. If she was ever to see Eleyne again, she had to win. Straightening a little, she took a step forward and saw the surprise in his eyes. She smiled as she saw that he was afraid. 'The gods are with me, old man,' she whispered, 'you can't kill me, you are already dead. See your lifeblood is leaking to the floor like so much rat's piss.'

259

'Annest!' His voice was weaker now, piteous. 'Annest, help me. Kill her –'

Rhonwen side-stepped, her back against the wall. She could see Annest now. The girl had not moved.

'She won't help you, old man, she hates you. You have beaten her once too often,' she said. 'Look at the blood. Can't you feel your life running away between your fingers? You leak like a sieve!' She laughed softly.

He looked down and she heard him give a yelp of pain and fear. As if realising for the first time how badly he was hurt, he staggered and fell to his knees. 'Die, old man, die!' she said. There was something like elation in her voice. 'See what happens to those who meddle with the will of the gods!'

'No!' Annest let out a scream. 'No, you evil woman! He's not going to die. He's not.' She hurled herself at Rhonwen, her fingers clawed. 'Leave him alone, you witch!'

The two women grappled back and forth on the floor, then Annest fell back. With a little sigh, she collapsed at Rhonwen's feet, the dagger in her heart.

Rhonwen narrowed her eyes. 'Stupid child,' she said quietly, 'there was no need for you to die.' She pulled the knife from the girl's body with an effort and turned back to Madoc. 'But there's every need for your death, old man,' she murmured, 'you broke the rules of hospitality. And you defied the gods.' She stepped towards him.

Madoc cringed, his strength almost gone, his hand still clutched to his belly, the other holding his dagger before him. He snarled like a cornered animal, lunging towards her with the weapon. She dodged back, almost losing her footing as a shaft of pain ran up her leg. Then she went at him again, slowly, holding his gaze, part of her uninvolved, astonished by her own lack of fear.

It was over in a moment. Her movement was too quick for him. He never saw the blade flash. He felt only for a moment the searing pain in his throat, then all went black.

For a long time Rhonwen stood without moving, then at last she dropped the dagger and walked to the doorway of the house. The mist had cleared, and in the east, over the rim of the mountains, the sky had lightened a little. The air was fresh and cold and blessedly clean. Somewhere nearby she could hear running water where she would be able to wash away the blood. She must purify herself with water, and the house with fire. Then she would go to Eleyne.

CHAPTER ELEVEN

I

FOTHERINGHAY CASTLE ❖ April 1237

'Your father is well again!' John, followed by his hurrying train of attendants, carried the letter through to the stillroom where Eleyne was supervising two of her women as they checked her supplies of herbs and medicines.

He thrust the letter into her hand with a smile. His face had grown thinner again and he looked very weary. He began to cough and she saw his hand pressed against his chest.

The letter was from her father's steward. 'The prince is much restored, the Lord be thanked. He can speak again and has regained the use of all his limbs. We give thanks every hour that he has been spared and is once again in full control in Gwynedd. He has given part of western Gwynedd to his son, Gruffydd, together with a part of Powys, and trusts his elder son more each day.'

'Happy now?' He was amused at the radiance which had illuminated her face.

'Very happy.' She ran to him and threw her arms impulsively around his neck. 'Oh, I am so pleased!'

'And now we can move on without you constantly worrying about him?'

'We can go tomorrow if you wish.' She twirled around ecstatically, much to the enjoyment of their attendants.

The long round was due to begin again: the circuit of their estates, the attendances at court, a visit within a couple of months to Scotland. It would be a busy year.

At their manor house at Suckley John was taken ill again. As the soft greenness of spring settled over the border countryside and daffodils clouded the riverside fields, he retired to bed, coughing and racked with fever. Eleyne summoned the physician and sent Luned to search the coffers for the tinctures and elixirs they had brought from Fotheringhay. Then she sat beside him, holding his hand. 'You must get better soon, there is so much for us to do.'

He nodded. His breath was shallow and harsh, his skin flushed and damp.

261

She drew her legs up beneath her skirts and snuggled close to him. 'There is something I want to tell you.'

It was too soon to know, too soon even to hope, but for the first time her courses were late and that morning she had awakened feeling sick and heavy. As Luned bathed her forehead they had looked at one another and smiled with hidden excitement. Looking at John, she had felt a sudden panicky terror that he might not get well, that he looked too weary, too grey, and she had known that she must not keep her secret excitement from him. She had to give him hope; to give him the will to live.

'I think I may be going to have a child.' She saw the sudden leap of joy in his eyes.

'Are you sure?'

She shook her head. 'It's too soon to be sure, but I have a feeling I'm right.'

'Oh, Eleyne, my darling.' He raised himself on his elbow and drew her to him. 'I can't tell you how happy that makes me. It's been so long. I wondered . . .'

'You wondered if, like poor Aunt Joanna, I couldn't have a baby.' She felt a stab of pain as the thought of Alexander rose unbidden in her mind and as always she pushed it away. 'Rhonwen said it was because I was too young. All I had to do was wait.' Her voice faded at the mention of Rhonwen's name; she still missed her, still thought about her, even though a small guilty part of her was relieved to be rid of her prying and her hostility to John. But, however much she disliked him, Rhonwen would have given Eleyne medicines for John at the first sign of his illness if she had begged her to do so, and her medicines, unlike those of the doctors who followed him everywhere he went, had always worked. She glanced up at him, and was pleased to see how bright and animated his eyes had become. The physician entered and bowed. As Eleyne kissed John and wriggled reluctantly away from him off the bed she saw the doctor reach for her husband's pulse. She did not notice the man's worried look when he saw the Earl of Chester's glowing skin and fevered eyes.

II

CHESTER CASTLE ✣ May

Her head wrapped in a white shawl, Rhonwen stayed long enough in the precincts of the castle to find out what she needed to know. The earl and countess were still at Fotheringhay. She had two animals now, her own and a packmule which she had found with the beasts in the byre end of Madoc's house. She had methodically ransacked the *hafod*, taken what few possessions they had which were of value – a cooking pot, Annest's Sunday shoes, their few pennies buried beneath the bakestone, and an extra woollen shawl. Then she had turned the animals loose and set fire to the cottage. There was little that would burn; the turf roof was wet, the walls were stone, but she needed to burn it to cleanse it and to be rid of the bodies. By the time full light had come she had been on the road long enough to put a distance between her and whoever might come to the lonely dwelling on the hill. It had taken four more agonising days to reach Chester, and now she faced another long ride across the middle of England, but her days of skulking in the mountains were over. No one would be looking for her once she was clear of the border march. She had two animals and before she left the city she would have found herself a servant and escort. No one would see her as a woman travelling alone again. And this time she was armed.

III
SUCKLEY

'For the love of the Blessed Virgin, Eleyne, you must not ride!'

John was out of bed within three days. Beyond the walls of the manor house a soft sun coaxed the full leaves to unfurl on the hedges. The buds on the blackthorn were like clusters of tiny seed pearls, catkins hung gold on the hedgerows and the first feathered leaves burst out on the willow trees by the brook. Her hand on Invictus's bridle she turned to him, astonished. 'Why? I'm perfectly well.' It was he who looked unwell, leaning on his servant's arm, his face ashen.

'Please, Eleyne, don't do it.' Pushing the man away, he stood upright with an effort. 'I forbid it.'

She felt the familiar rebellion surging through her body, almost choking her with humiliation and rage. It had been a long time since she had felt like this; for weeks they had been friends, lovers. She trusted and respected him. She worried and fretted ceaselessly when he was ill. But when he was ill she was in charge, she ran the household, she did as she pleased and rode when she liked. Her hand tightened on the stallion's bridle. The groom was watching her, and she saw the shadow of mocking amusement in his eyes. He admired her, she knew, but he enjoyed seeing her discomfited. She bit her lips in fury and reluctantly released the bridle. 'You take him, Hal. Give him a gallop and then bring him back. I may use him to fly my bird later.'

Head high she took John's arm. 'Leave us,' she commanded as the servant fell in step behind them, 'we'll walk in the garden.'

There was a lovely garden at the west end of the manor house,

263

near the moat. Bulbs were already pushing up through the grass and the walls were hung with newly budding sweet-briar and ivy.

As soon as they were alone she dropped his arm and turned to him, her eyes flashing. 'Why? Why do you humiliate me in front of the servants? Why shouldn't I ride?'

'Surely I don't have to tell you that, after what happened to the Queen of Scots.'

'The Queen of Scots's physicians had warned her not to ride. She had threatened to miscarry. It's not the same for me. I don't even know for sure that I am with child!'

'Of course you are.' He reached across and took her hand. 'Don't be angry, sweetheart, I'm concerned for you.'

'Then please don't stop me riding. If I'm worried about my health I will take care, I promise you.' She gave him a winning smile. 'It's you we must take care of, my husband. You look so tired. Did the physician say you could get up?'

He hunched his cloak on to his shoulders. 'The man is a fool. He bleeds me constantly and leaves me weak as a woman. I do better to get up and walk about. And your medicines have always been better than his.' He gave a sheepish grin. 'Perhaps that's why I want you with me. Pure selfishness.'

Her temper was receding. 'Those medicines were Rhonwen's. I do wish she were here, she knew so much of remedies and charms to make people well.' She paused. 'John? What is it? Why do you look like that?'

He had dropped her hand and turned away. 'Rhonwen had no love for me, Eleyne. Sometimes, I think . . .' His voice tailed away and he bent over a rosebush, examining the soft red buds of the leaves.

'You think what?'

'She cursed me, that night, over Einion's grave. She cursed me.'

'And you think her curse has made you ill again?'

'I did wonder.'

'But she loved me, and she would never harm anyone I loved.' She caught his arm and hugged him close to her. 'You must not believe that she would or could hurt you. She was beside herself that night; she didn't know what she was doing.'

'Oh, she knew.' He was silent for a moment, then he began to cough.

'No. Please don't say that.' Eleyne walked away from him across the long damp grass, with its drift of golden buttercups. 'Do you think she is dead?'

'Yes.' His reply was terse.

'You think my father had her killed.'

'I think someone did.'

'One of my mother's ladies wrote to me. She said Dafydd has had her declared an outlaw and offered a reward for her capture.'

'That had to be done, otherwise they would have been admitting that she was dead. Forget her, Eleyne. She has gone. We'll never see her again.'

She frowned. 'But she hasn't gone, she haunts you. You told Father Peter at Fotheringhay, didn't you? What did he say?'

'He sprinkled holy water and swung the incense and muttered prayers. Then when he thought I wasn't looking he made the sign against the evil eye and touched an amulet around his neck beneath his crucifix. The man is a superstitious fool.' He grinned. 'But I am no better. I'm afraid of her.'

A week later he was stronger and, the rents at Suckley collected, the household set off again. Eleyne rode a gentle old mare next to her husband, Luned on her other side, a huge heavily cushioned wagon close behind in case she should need to rest. She didn't. That morning the blood had come, flooding between her legs, washing away all her hopes, and she had cried. She had not yet dared to tell John. He looked so much better, so much stronger, so proud as he rode beside her. She straightened her back to ease the nagging pain which dragged between her hips. She wanted Invictus, she wanted to gallop and gallop and gallop until the cold wind and the sunlight had washed her mind clean and empty as her womb, but the horse was at the back of the train somewhere, led by his groom.

John would understand. He would be disappointed, but not angry. She glanced across at him, wanting to speak, wanting to tell him, but her courage failed. It had to be when they were alone, in case she cried again.

IV
FOTHERINGHAY ❖ May

Rhonwen reached Fotheringhay two days after the Feast of the Annunciation. They received her there with honour, if with a few sideways looks and much crossing of fingers, and it was with fresh horses and the addition to her small train of a lady's maid from the village that she set out once more after the Chesters, retracing her steps towards the Welsh borders.

John took Eleyne in his arms and kissed her. Outside the window a blackbird was carolling from the branch of an ash tree, and the joyous song poured on and on, liquid and golden in the twilight.

'It doesn't matter, little love,' he murmured. 'I don't mind, there will be other times, many other times. We will have a dozen children at least! That is your fortune, remember? Your future. You told me: it's written in the stars.'

She snuggled up to him, comforted at last. He was quite better now, and they had ridden out that morning after the hounds in pursuit of hare. The day had been glorious and they had returned exhausted. They had eaten well and retired to bed, where they made love until they had fallen at last into a deep sleep. It had been still dark when John had awoken her, his hand questing beneath the sheets for her body, greedily seeking every part of her. When they had made love again, they lay and talked until the first tentative notes of the dawn chorus made its way between the heavy curtains of the bed.

VI

DARNHALL, FOREST OF DELAMERE
The Feast of Helen of Caernarfon

Rhonwen caught up with them when they were almost back at Chester, on Eleyne's name day. She halted her horses at the smithy in the village and wearily asked the way to the manor house.

'Is the countess there?' she asked the smith as he came out into the sunlight, blinking after the darkness of the forge.

'Oh, aye, she's there, God bless her.' The smith grinned and rubbed his hands down the front of his leather apron. 'I went up there nobbut three days ago to shoe that great stallion of hers.'

Rhonwen closed her eyes with relief. 'And the earl? He is here too?'

'Oh, aye. He's here. They're staying here awhile, so I heard.' The man ran a professional eye over her mounts. 'You'll have come a long way.'

Rhonwen gave a grim smile. 'Indeed I have. Here.' She reached into her scrip and found the last halfpenny of her hoard. She tossed it to him. 'Take this for your trouble, my friend.' She hauled on her horse's reins and set off in the direction he had pointed, her servants trailing in her wake. The smith watched until she was out of sight, then he stared down at the half coin. He bit it tentatively: it was good. The woman must have been mad.

She rode into an orchard, pink with apple blossom, and dismounted beneath the trees. 'Go and find Luned, Lady Chester's maiden. Tell her to come to me here. Speak to no one else, do you hear,' she directed the serving girl who had dismounted beside her. 'Hurry.' Now that she was so close she could not wait to see Eleyne again, but she had to be careful. What if Lord Chester arrested her? What if he sent her back to Gwynedd to face trial? For her sake, as well as Eleyne's, Lord Chester would have to be dealt with. Leaving the horses to the manservant, she walked slowly across the orchard and leaned on the lichen-covered gate. At last she had found her child.

The sun had travelled across the orchard and settled into the mist behind the wood before anyone came. It was Luned. She ran across the dew-wet grass and threw herself into Rhonwen's arms. 'We never thought we'd see you again. They told us you were dead!' They clung together for a long time, then Rhonwen pushed her away.

'How is Eleyne? I long to see her.'

'She's well.' Luned clutched her hand. 'She's very well, she and the earl are happy.'

'She is happy, thinking I am dead?' Rhonwen could not keep the shock from her voice.

'No, no, of course not. She misses you terribly. We all did. But she had no way of finding out what had happened.'

'She had a way.' Rhonwen's voice was tight.

Luned let go of Rhonwen's hand and leaned on the gate beside her. 'She stares into the fire sometimes and I can see in her face that she is seeing things. But the earl doesn't like it. He beat her, you know, after what happened. And he has forbidden her to look into the flames. The servants had begun to whisper. The priest of Fotheringhay spoke very strongly to the earl about her and my lady had to do penance.'

Rhonwen stared at her, cold with horror. So, he had beaten her and he had tried to forbid her the Sight – for that he would pay. She forced herself to speak calmly. 'She will not have stopped looking into the flames. She can never stop doing that. She can pretend . . . to him. But she won't stop, she can't. She did not do the penance?'

'She did and she goes to mass every day with the earl. She is very devout.' Luned frowned. Could she so soon have forgotten Rhonwen's intransigence; her intolerance.

'And where is she now? I expected her to come.' Rhonwen's voice was hard.

'I couldn't tell her; she was with him. You can't come up to the manor house, Rhonwen. The earl would have you taken by his men. I have heard him talk about you. He never liked you, and now I think he is afraid of you too.'

'Afraid?' Rhonwen raised an eyebrow.

'You cursed him. He blamed you when his cough came back and he was ill.'

Rhonwen leaned her back against the gate, staring at the shadowy branches of the apple trees. It was growing dark. She gave a bitter laugh. 'He has reason to be afraid.'

'What will you do?' Luned peered at her cautiously.

'I don't know. I have nowhere to go. No money.'

'I can give you money.' Luned slipped her hand through the slit in her gown and groped for the purse she carried at her waist. 'Here, and I can get you more. But you musn't stay near here, it's not safe.' She paused. 'I suppose you could go to the abbey at Vale Royale. No one would dream that you would go there. Stay in the guesthouse and keep your face covered. I will contact you as soon as I can, but don't let anyone know who you are. You would never be safe if the earl found out you were alive. I'll tell Eleyne you are here as soon as I can, tonight if I get the chance.'

'If you get the chance? Don't you see her every night?'

Luned smiled. 'Sometimes they send the attendants away. The earl undresses her himself. They are very much in love.'

Rhonwen flinched as though she had been struck. 'That's not true! She loves someone else. Oh, she's a clever one, my little Eleyne. She would never betray herself, but I know it. The earl has her under some kind of spell.' She smiled coldly. 'But I can always break it. Sweet goddess, how she must have longed for me to help her!'

Luned looked at her doubtfully. 'Are you sure? She seems so happy to me.'

'I'm sure.' Rhonwen straightened wearily. 'So, tell me where this abbey is. I will wait there for a message from you. I hope it's not too far, I'm aching all over after riding three times around England looking for you!'

'It isn't far. You'll get there before dark, and they will treat you with great hospitality as long as —' She hesitated. 'Don't offend them, Rhonwen. Don't let them see you don't believe as they do. Word will get round so fast.'

'Do you take me for a fool!' Rhonwen snapped. 'Of course I won't offend them. They won't get me to their masses and their prayers, but I shall be polite and pay my dues. What more can they possibly expect?'

VII

DARNHALL MANOR HOUSE

'Robin!' Eleyne recognised the tall visitor in spite of the all-enveloping cloak in which he was muffled. 'So, you have come to see us after all.'

'My lady.' Robert Fitzooth stooped to kiss her. 'How could I not come to welcome you back to Chester? How are you? And how is my cousin?'

Eleyne took his hand and led him to the chairs on the dais. 'He is well. He is with our steward at the moment, but he will join us soon. I will send a messenger telling him you've come. He'll be pleased to see you. Luned, ask the servants to bring us some wine.'

Luned beckoned a page forward. It was nearly midday and still she hadn't found a moment alone with Eleyne to tell her about Rhonwen, and, she realised as she supervised the jug of wine and the goblets on the tray carried by a nervous new maid from the village, she was reluctant to do so. She loved Rhonwen as Eleyne did; they had been brought up by her together after all, but Rhonwen had changed. She had grown bitter and possessive, and her presence had became a threat.

'Luned? Luned, the wine!' Eleyne's voice jolted her out of her thoughts. Eleyne left her guest and crossed to the table where Luned was standing. 'What is it? Is anything the matter?' She smiled fondly at her, troubled by the girl's unhappy expression.

Luned glanced across at Sir Robert, who was talking to one of his companions. 'I have been trying to speak to you, my lady,' she whispered urgently, 'but there is always someone there.'

'What do you mean? You only had to say . . .'

'It had to be alone, in private.' Luned's voice was anguished.

Eleyne looked at her hard, then she turned. 'Robin, will you forgive me? A crisis is at hand. Drink some wine and warm yourself by the fire and I shall return at once.'

Gathering her skirts, she swept out of the hall in front of Luned and into the bright sunshine. 'Here, in the arbour. We won't be overheard. What is it?'

'Rhonwen is here.'

Eleyne stared at her. 'Rhonwen! She's alive? Where? Where is she?'

'I sent her to Vale Royale. It wasn't safe for her to stay nearer. I didn't think you'd want her here.'

Eleyne closed her eyes, stunned by the news. 'You're right. Dear God, I never thought to see her alive again! Is she all right? Is she well? What happened to her? Where has she been?'

Luned laughed. 'I'm sure she'll tell you herself.'

'I must go to her.' Surprised at the reluctance which vied with her relief that Rhonwen was alive, Eleyne went on, 'Go now, and order them to saddle my new mare. We'll say I couldn't wait to try her out. Come with me and bring two men as escort. I'll explain to Robin.'

In a whirl of skirts, she ran back to the house. Shaking her head, Luned turned towards the stables.

VIII
VALE ROYALE ABBEY

The abbot was waiting for her in his lodging, a stone building set apart from the other monastic buildings. It was cold in the room, but Eleyne found herself waved towards one of two comfortable chairs standing on either side of a spacious but empty hearth. 'May I give you some wine?' The abbot was preparing to serve it himself.

She nodded, gratefully. 'My lord abbot, I came to seek a friend who I hoped had lodged in your guesthouse last night.'

He frowned. 'I thought perhaps that was it.' He handed her a brimming goblet with a bow. 'I am afraid I had to ask your friend to leave.'

Eleyne froze. The abbot, a small, thin man with a kind, careworn face, his fringe of hair silver above watery grey eyes, seated himself opposite her. He had taken no wine himself.

'I am sorry, my lady, if this causes you grief, but the woman who came here last night was an outlaw, wanted by the king's men. She is a heretic and a murderess. I could not allow her to spend a night beneath my roof. I should have told my guest master to arrest her, but –' He sighed and shook his head. 'Perhaps I did wrong, but I felt compelled merely to send her on her way. She had sought Christian hospitality, and was given food and water to wash in. I could not send her to the gallows after that.'

Eleyne licked her lips, which had gone dry. 'What made you think she was an outlaw, my lord abbot?'

The abbot sighed. 'I was at Chester when word went round of what she did. I am sorry, Lady Chester, but everyone knew your lady, Rhonwen. She was too vivid, too striking for men not to remember her. When my guest master came to me and said he was worried because a guest under our roof had said she would not hear mass, I came to speak to her, thinking I could offer her some advice or reassurance. Then I recognised her and sent her on her way. I kept her servants here, and gave them absolution this morning, then I dismissed them with a small payment which will enable them to move on until they find new employment.'

'And Rhonwen. Where did she go?' Eleyne asked at last. The wine was untouched in the goblet in her hand.

'She went into the forest. What else could she do?'

'And you think that a Christian action? To send an unprotected, gently born woman into the forest to live amongst outlaws and thieves and murderers?' Eleyne stood up. A little of the wine slopped on to her skirt but she didn't notice. 'My lord abbot, I think you have done her a great wrong.'

'You think she was innocent?' The abbot had risen as well.

'She killed a man, but it was in self-defence. She had no option.'

The abbot raised an eyebrow. 'Forgive me, my lady, but that is not the way I heard the story. However, it is not for me to judge. I sent her on her way and she has gone with her horse and her life. No doubt the earl can find her; he has but to put the word around and offer a reward and every cutpurse in the country will search for her.' He paused, his face full of compassion. 'I understand she was your nurse, my lady, and I realise you must have loved her, but don't be misled by her. That lady is a danger to everyone around her. She is evil. I recognised it in every part of my body and soul.'

Eleyne put the goblet down untouched and turned towards the door. 'As you said, my lord abbot, she was my nurse and she loves me, she said. 'And I love her.'

IX

John was sitting playing chess with Robin when Eleyne walked at last into the great hall. Both men rose.

'Where have you been?' John asked. 'It's late. You missed both dinner and supper.'

She pulled off her gloves and threw them down next to the chessboard. 'I am well aware of that,' she said sharply. She was hungry and tired and disappointed. 'I rode to the abbey. The abbot delayed me there and then on the way back through the forest we took the wrong track.'

'Then what you need is some wine and some delicious titbits to tempt your appetite, my lady.' Robin pulled forward his own heavy chair. 'Here, sit by the fire. Don't bully her, John. Your lady is not to be upset!' He grinned at his cousin impudently. 'She can tell us about her adventures when she is rested and not before.' He lifted Eleyne's cloak from her shoulders and guided her to the chair.

Eleyne saw that John was watching her closely, but his worry was only for her safety, she was sure of that. He had not guessed about Rhonwen. How could he? Unless Rhonwen came to the house he would never know that she was nearby. But would she come to the house? Eleyne remembered Luned and looked for her, but there was no sign of her in the crowded hall; Luned, who had comforted her on the return ride with the words: 'She knows where you are. She'll find you . . . somehow.'

In spite of herself, Eleyne began to enjoy the evening. Robin had brought her wine, serving her on one knee with a clean napkin over his arm. Then he had brought her a silver platter, full of dainty pieces of food, somehow reheated, although, she was sure, the great oven fires must long ago have been damped and the kitchens swept clean.

Secure in her love, John no longer found himself racked with jealousy as his cousin flirted and laughed with Eleyne. He was glad that the pain which had shown around her eyes when she walked in had gone. Whatever had been worrying her had been forgotten. He relaxed and found himself laughing, responding to the young man's charm and humour, wishing, not for the first time, that he had a son like Robin. Eleyne laughed and opened her mouth as Robin poked a piece of pastry at her. John sighed and pushed the thought away, beckoning the musicians who had been waiting hopefully at the foot of the dais.

The noise lessened as men and women found themselves seats on the forms ranged around the edge of the hall, or on their spread cloaks on the rush-strewn floor. The dogs settled before the fire and with an expectant hush the eyes of everyone present turned to the musicians as they began to tune up. The leader of the troop bowed to Eleyne.

'My Lady Chester. What would you like us to play? A love song perhaps?' He raised his eyebrow suggestively.

'Yes.' Eleyne smiled. 'A love song, please.' She held out her hand to John. He came and stood behind her, taking her fingers and pressing them to his lips. Robin watched them for a moment, then with a little shrug he stood back and, offering John his chair, he went and squatted on his haunches by the fire.

They sat a long time that evening, contentedly listening to the music. Eleyne was too tired to move from her chair. She leaned sideways until her head was on John's shoulder, feeling his warmth through his mantle. Robin sat by the fire, his arms wrapped around his legs, his chin sunk thoughtfully on his knees, his eyes shut. The great hall was silent save for the occasional snore, quickly hushed, from a man-at-arms asleep in the corner. The night was cold and clear; the stars seemed very far away.

X

Near the door a kitchen maid was lying beside one of the pantrymen. He had spread his cloak over them both and his hands were busy under her skirt. She lay still, trying not to giggle, feeling the excitement mounting, knowing that soon they would creep away into the stables. Opening her eyes sleepily, she saw that the door was close by. No one would notice if they crept outside. She turned to the man at her side and firmly removed his hand from between her legs. He scowled, then understood. He stood up and, picking up the cloak, took her hand. They tiptoed along the edge of the hall, stepping over other somnolent bodies, and made their way towards the door.

The courtyard was very cold. Their breath showed in clouds of white as, unable to wait, he pulled her to him and thrust his hands inside her gown, fumbling at her breasts.

'Not here. The countess would send me off if she found out. In the stables – it's warmer,' she breathed. Capturing his hand, she began to lead him across the courtyard, but almost at once she stopped.

'What is it?' It was his turn to pull her.

'I don't know, look.' She found she was holding her breath.

'Where?' There had been fear in her voice, and he found he was no longer feeling quite so lusty.

The white figure was standing in the shadows near the angle of the wall and the western range of buildings. It was indistinct, a wraith in the mist which seemed to surround it. It began to move, gliding towards the door of the great hall.

'Blessed Virgin!' the man gasped. He stood paralysed, unable to turn or run. Beside him the girl seemed to have stopped breathing.

They watched the figure as it moved away from them towards the corner of the hall. There it stopped, seemingly unable to decide whether or not to go in, then it turned and glided away again. Seconds later it had disappeared into the darkness.

XI
DARNHALL ❖ St Columba's Day

Luned pulled the pins one by one from Eleyne's hair and reached for the comb. 'Is he no better, my lady?' she asked sympathetically as Eleyne closed her eyes wearily.

'Perhaps a little, I don't know. The physician says so, but he was still feverish.'

She had just returned from the small side chamber where John lay tossing and turning on the narrow bed erected there for him. He was coughing violently, his body convulsed with the force of the spasms which swept over him.

She looked at Luned, her eyes clear in the candlelight. 'He told me he had seen Rhonwen's ghost.'

Luned bit her lip. 'The whole manor is in turmoil about it. Four people have seen her now. What shall we do?'

'Why doesn't she stay away!' Pushing aside the comb, Eleyne walked over to the fire and stared down into it. 'We go into the forest and she is nowhere to be found; then she comes here and haunts us!'

'You don't think –' Luned hesitated. 'You don't think it really is a ghost? If something had happened to her in the forest, something awful, wouldn't she come to try and find you?' The girl had gone pale.

'Nonsense, she is as alive as you or I.'

273

'Then why does she wear white? Why does she move so quietly? Why can no one get near her?'

'Because they are scared of her.' Eleyne came back to the stool and sat down again. 'And please God no one does get near her.'

'You haven't told the earl or Sir Robin that she's alive?'

Eleyne shook her head. She picked up the comb and began to pull it through her hair.

'Are you going to?'

'No. I want to see Rhonwen, I want to speak to her and give her money. Then I want her to go away.'

Luned nodded. There was something she had to say, something she could put off no longer. It had been gnawing at her day and night.

'My lady, when I spoke to her she told me . . . she told me that she thought you loved someone other than the earl.'

There was a moment's total silence. Throwing the comb down Eleyne stood up. 'That is a lie! How dare she! It's not true. I have never loved anyone but John, never. And I am faithful to him. I always have been. How could you –' she glared at Luned – 'how could you, of all people, even repeat such a scandalous suggestion?'

'Because I heard it being whispered in the hall tonight,' Luned replied softly. 'That is why. And I wondered where the rumour could have come from.'

There was another long silence. Eleyne closed her eyes. 'It's not true,' she whispered at last, 'you must stop it.'

'I'll do my best.'

'It would hurt John so much and it's unfounded. Totally unfounded.'

She brought food to John herself, sitting by his bed and holding the bowls of fragrant stews and possets and his favourite *doucettes*, sweet pastry tarts filled with cream and eggs and sugar, but his appetite was small and he was losing weight before her eyes. The Feast of the Trinity came and went. The weather turned unseasonably wet and cold and they listened to the wind wuthering up the valley from the south-west, tearing the leaves from the trees. Robin ran the earldom with Eleyne's help, dealing with the important matters as they came in, sorting out a few problems each day to take to John's bedside. Of Rhonwen there had been no word or sign for two weeks and Eleyne had stopped riding into the forest, her mind too preoccupied with what was happening at the manor.

Then at last John began to improve. His fever left him and he lay back on the pillows, his eyes clear. Eleyne, white with exhaustion, went to sit with him and he took her hand. 'My darling, you look so tired. I'm sorry, each time it's more of a burden on you.'

She kissed his forehead gently. 'As long as you are well now.'

'I am well. I thought that woman's curse had killed me for sure this time.' He gave a wry grimace. 'In the sun, with the candles gone and the birds singing outside, I find it hard to believe in her malice, but at night, when the fever had me in its grip I thought I saw her every time I closed my eyes.'

'What woman?' Her mouth was dry.

'Your beloved Rhonwen. Did you not hear that her ghost was seen?'

Eleyne looked down at her hands. 'Yes, I had heard.'

'And you didn't want to think that she was dead.' His voice was gentle. 'I do know how much you loved her, Eleyne. You were too young to realise that she was evil, my darling. It was not your fault that you loved her. I am only thankful that she has gone.' He heaved himself up higher on the pillows. 'Where is Robin?'

'He is closeted with your clerks, wrestling with affairs of state.' She smiled. 'Poor Robin. He has grown quite thin and pale these last few days. We are lucky he was here while you were so ill. He acts . . . he acts as though his interests were the same as yours.'

'You mean as if he were my heir?' John scowled. 'Would that he were. It would take a load from my mind. As it is my nieces and my sisters are heirs to the estates should anything happen to me. As to the titles, I don't know. Perhaps Robin has as good a claim as any, at least to Huntingdon.' Preoccupied with his own bitterness, he did not notice her face. Then he looked up and saw the tears in her eyes. 'Sweetheart, forgive me, that was cruel. It is not your fault that we have no children yet. There is still time, plenty of time.' He pulled her to him. 'You will give me six fine sons and six beautiful daughters and between them they will rule the world.' He ruffled her hair gently. 'You'll see.'

XII

'She will be in the old charcoal burner's hut near the Chester road,' the messenger had said. 'Come at midday and come alone.'

'You can't go alone,' Luned said firmly. 'I will go with you and wait near at hand with a couple of men-at-arms.'

Eleyne was torn between longing and irritation that after causing so much rumour and anguish Rhonwen should openly and arrogantly send this message now, as John was getting better. She had hoped that Rhonwen had gone away.

The forest was sweet with summer, the leaves heavy on the trees, the rides carpeted with late bluebells. As she rode towards the charcoal burner's hut and dismounted near the remains of one of his fires, she peered warily around. There was no sign of anyone in the clearing; the hut was ruined and deserted. Tying the horse to the branch of a tree

275

she walked across and peered in. Rhonwen was waiting inside. She was thin and pale and her clothes were torn and ragged. Her shoes had fallen almost to pieces, and she was wearing a heavy white woollen cloak.

At the sight of her, Eleyne's irritation fell away. They clung together for a long time, then sat side by side on a fallen log in the clearing while Rhonwen told her story.

'So it was Gruffydd who helped you,' Eleyne said at last. 'I'm glad, I should have guessed. But now. Where will you go?' She looked at Rhonwen steadily. 'You cannot return to my service and you cannot go back to Wales.'

'I can.' Rhonwen's eyes were feverish with triumph. 'I can go anywhere with a king's pardon. You can get it for me. The King of England is your uncle, and he will give you anything you ask for.' Rhonwen caught her hands; her grip was very strong. 'Surely I do not have to beg this from you? With the king's pardon even the Prince of North Wales can do nothing against me. I will be safe.'

For a moment Eleyne had almost caught her optimism, but then she shook her head. 'John would never let me go to the king for that. You made him very angry, Rhonwen.' She did not add that he was afraid.

'Pah!' Rhonwen spat on the ground. 'I don't give that for your English earl! Besides, I heard he was dying.' Her eyes grew still on Eleyne's face. 'You love a king, *cariad*, remember that. Your future is in Scotland with him, not with your milksop earl.'

Eleyne was too shocked to speak immediately: 'So, it was you who started these evil rumours!' Her eyes flashed with anger. 'How dare you! And you are wrong. What you are saying is wicked, evil! It is John I love. John!' The forest was silent as the two women faced each other, save for the distant ringing call of a blackbird hidden in the thicket.

'So.' Rhonwen raised an eyebrow. 'You really believe that? Oh, how he's got you tamed! I can see the jesses around your ankles.' She stood up restlessly. 'He's not man enough to have got you with child yet, I see.'

Eleyne coloured violently. 'That's a vicious thing to say . . . and not true. I was pregnant, I think. Only I lost it before it was real, and that was my fault. I love John. He is kind and good and caring, and he is my man. I want no other.' She too stood up. 'I want no more of this gossip. I understand why you are bitter and unhappy but it's all your fault. How could you kill Cenydd? He was a good man. I thought you loved him.'

'I did love him, after a fashion.' Rhonwen was defiant. 'I did not mean to kill him. He was useful.' She grimaced. 'I had never killed a man before. Now I have killed three people.'

Eleyne closed her eyes. The unease she had felt from the first moment Rhonwen had begun to speak deepened into horror. She looked at Rhonwen for some sign of sorrow or remorse. She saw neither.

'You are in a state of mortal sin,' she whispered.

'Sin?' Rhonwen gave a bitter laugh. 'Maybe. For Cenydd I shall have to pay, one day. For the other two, no. They were robbers, nobodies. Cutting Madoc's throat was no harder than wringing the neck of a chicken. I'll not burn in your Christian priests' hell for them.'

'Oh, Rhonwen.' Eleyne was despairing.

'You're shocked. Now our roles are reversed, *cariad*. Suddenly you're the dutiful lady and I'm the rebel, in my stolen monk's cloak and my threadbare shoes.' She stood very close to Eleyne. 'I was like a mother to you, you will not forsake me now. You will find a way to go to the king and obtain my pardon. Your English earl does not have to know.'

'Of course he has to know. I won't deceive him.'

Rhonwen narrowed her eyes. 'Are you saying you won't help me?'

'Of course not! I will help you in every way I can.'

'As long as you don't have to go to the king.'

'I will try to persuade John –'

'No, *cariad*, your earl will not lift a finger for me. He would have me arrested, so I would have to disappear into the forest forever. You would never see me again.'

Eleyne frowned, but not with the fear Rhonwen had hoped to see. She had changed, had learned to live without her. 'You'll never find me,' she repeated, 'never.'

'Then how will I reach you?'

'You won't. When you have the pardon I will reach you. The people of the greenwood have their methods.' The mocking smile deepened. 'But don't leave it too long, *cariad*. I need that pardon.'

XIII

Robin threw back his head and laughed. 'So, your nurse is a forest outlaw, with a string of murders behind her! Does this explain why my lady countess is such a spirited rebel?'

'It's not funny, Robin. I have to find a way to help her.' Eleyne had reined in her horse beside him, a pretty merlin on her wrist.

'You have offered her money?'

'Of course.'

His eyes were shrewd in the bright spring sunlight. Their attendants had drawn back and they could talk alone. 'Am I right in thinking you don't necessarily want her back?'

'She frightened me.' Eleyne sighed. 'But I want what is best for her. And I want what is best for my husband.'

'He loathes her of course. He has spoken to me about her. You know he thinks she is dead. It might be best if he went on thinking that.' He wrinkled his brow thoughtfully. 'Of course, you could always do both. Promise her you will speak to the king when you see him, on condition that she goes as far away as possible, and in the meantime give her enough money to live comfortably in London or Winchester or somewhere far away, under an assumed name.'

Eleyne stroked the soft russet breast feathers of the bird on her wrist as it settled trustingly against her. 'It might work.'

'It will work, if you are firm enough. Then you can forget her. John wants to go back to Chester. She won't dare follow you there.' He gazed up at the trees, their leaves dappled by the sunlight against a sky of purest sapphire. 'You know,' he went on, 'I almost envy her her life in the forest. At this time of year it must be glorious to acknowledge no master, to lie where you please, to eat the king's deer till you are too fat to move.'

'I don't think so. She is afraid, and the nights must be cold and wet and lonely.'

'Don't you believe it. She will have found herself a man by now.' He gathered up his reins. 'Come on, we have a long way to go.'

XIV

'So you are going to send me away.' Rhonwen clutched the bag of coins Eleyne had pressed into her hand.

'Only until I can see the king and speak to him about you. You can't come back with me, you must see that.'

'Oh yes, I see that.' Rhonwen's voice was bitter. 'You dare not upset your husband. You dare not ask him a favour or beg for your old nurse.'

'It's not that I don't dare, Rhonwen.' Eleyne tried to keep the impatience out of her voice. 'It's that there is no point. He will not relent, and I do not wish to have him upset. He has not been well.'

'Again.' Rhonwen threw the money on the ground beside her. 'So you will not be leaving after all?'

'We are, we leave at first light. That is why I wanted to see you, to say goodbye and to promise that I will do my best. There is enough money here to last you a long time. It will buy you a roof and food and a servant wherever you want to go. When you have found somewhere to live, write to me with your address. You must choose another name, a name only you and I will know.'

Rhonwen looked down at the heavy bundle of coins near her feet. 'What name shall I choose, *cariad*?' she asked with an enigmatic smile.

Eleyne breathed a sigh of relief. 'We shall call you Susanna. And you shall be a poet and a scholar, writing to me of matters of deep philosophy and wit. From time to time, when we are at the court in Westminster or Winchester or wherever it is that you are living, I shall call on you privately and buy your books for enormous sums of gold.'

'So you don't envisage the king giving me a pardon very soon,' Rhonwen said drily.

'I will try.' Eleyne kissed her. 'I promise.'

'But still the earl stands between me and my freedom.' Rhonwen hesitated, then almost sadly she put her hand into her scrip and pulled out a small linen pouch. 'To show I am more forgiving than he, I have gathered some herbs in the forest for him, to stop his weakness returning. Infuse these and make him drink them.'

Eleyne took the pouch and clutched Rhonwen's hand with a sudden rush of gratitude. 'I have missed you so much while he has been ill. It was always your medicines which helped him. Thank you.'

Rhonwen raised an eyebrow.

'So, you have missed me? I was beginning to wonder whether I should do better to forget you. No, don't swear your undying love. I know you love me, but you have grown up now. You have changed, moved on. You don't want your nurse with you any more. You are mistress of vast estates. Your husband is a great nobleman. Why should you want your nurse?' She stooped and scooped up the bundle of money. 'I shall write to you, *cariad*, and I shall be there when you need me, have no fear of that.'

XV

Eleyne put the bundle of herbs in a small coffer beside her bed. The household was packed and ready to leave. At first light the long train of horses and wagons would wind its way the last dozen or so miles to Chester.

She smiled at John, already undressed and wrapped in a heavy bed gown, who was sprawled in a chair near the fire. His face was pale and strained, his cough still bad, but he insisted that he was well enough to travel. He longed for the space and comforts of Chester Castle. This small manor house, at first so beautiful and quiet, had become cramped, and it lacked privacy, save in this small bedchamber above the hall. He watched as Eleyne's maids undressed her and brushed her hair, then he gestured them away. 'Come and sit by me.'

She knelt beside him, her head on his knee, and felt his hand gentle on her hair. It was a long time since they had made love.

'Are you happy to be moving on? It has been a hard few weeks for you, here.'

279

She smiled up at him. 'Robin has helped me; I was sad when he left today.'

John nodded. 'I trust you've not grown too fond of him.'

Eleyne smiled again. 'No, I've not grown too fond.' She thought suddenly of the rumours Luned had said were still rife in the hall: that she was unfaithful to the earl. Some of those rumours linked her name with Robin's for want of another. She reached for his hand. 'Shall we go to bed, my love? We have a tiring day tomorrow.'

'So eager for your husband? Why not? Call the boy to make up the fire.'

They made love tenderly, gently, as if each were afraid that the other might break, then John lay back exhausted on the pillows. Suddenly he began to cough. For a few minutes she lay listening to him, then she slipped from the bed and, lighting a taper from the fire, she brought a candle to the bedside. 'John, are you all right?' He was coughing convulsively, his whole body racked with the force of the spasms, and a trickle of blood had appeared on his chin. 'Shall I fetch the physician?'

He shook his head violently. 'A drink,' he gasped, 'just get me a drink.'

She ran to the coffer on the far side of the room where a jug of wine had been left with two goblets. With shaking hands she poured a cupful. She managed to raise him and hold the drink to his lips while he swallowed a little, then he lay back. He was pouring with sweat. 'Stupid,' he whispered, 'must have got some dust in my throat.'

She smiled, setting down the wine. 'Rest now, I'll bring you some medicine to soothe your cough.'

Luned came at once when she called, stoked up the fire and fetched a small cooking pan while Eleyne sorted the herbs from Rhonwen's pouch. There was wild thyme there, from the sunny hilltops beyond the forest, and cowslips and valerian root, leaves of agrimony and flowers of hawthorn and wormwood and powdered bark of alder. She smelt them, running them through her fingers. There were other things there too, bitter, dark leaves she did not recognise, leaves from the thick forest which Rhonwen now called home. She tipped the whole mixture into the boiling water and drew it off the fire to infuse, sniffing the thick earthy smell which came from the brew. John was dozing now, his breathing laboured, the sweat standing on his forehead.

Luned came over to the bed. 'Shall I fetch the doctor?' she whispered.

Eleyne shook her head. 'Let him sleep. When he wakes I'll give him Rhonwen's medicine. It always soothes him.'

She lay down beside him, listening to his laboured breathing. Once or twice she slept, jerking awake at his slightest movement as he shifted uneasily on the pillows.

Dawn came and with it the earl's chamberlain. He looked at the sleeping man and shook his head. 'Shall I tell the household we won't leave today?' he asked. Eleyne nodded. Servants came and went, tiptoeing about the room as they built the fire and replaced the candles, and at last the physician came with his knives.

Eleyne stood between him and his patient. 'You are not going to let his blood, he is too weak.'

'My lady.' The man clicked his tongue with irritation. 'It is the only thing which will save him; I have to do it.'

'No. Let him sleep. He will be stronger when he is rested.'

'My lady —'

'No! Leave us. I won't have him bled.'

The man scowled. 'Then be it on your own head, lady, if he dies.' He turned and swept out of the room.

Behind her John stirred. 'Well done, my love,' he whispered, 'a victory indeed.'

She sat down beside him and took his hand. 'How are you?'

'Tired.' He tried to smile. 'So very tired. Fetch me some wine, and I should like to see the priest.'

She leaned across to the coffer where the herbal brew, cool now and strained through a piece of muslin, waited in a glazed bowl. The liquid was green as a cat's eye. She raised John's head gently and held the bowl to his lips. 'Not wine, my love, medicine, that is what you need.'

He scowled. 'And as foul tasting as any of your concoctions, no doubt.'

'No doubt, but they do you good. Drink it.'

He swallowed it with difficulty and then lay back, his eyes closed. 'The priest, Eleyne. Please call him.'

She sent Luned and the priest came, shuffling into the room, the viaticum in his hands. He had done this so often before for the earl, he scarcely took notice as he listened to the confession and gave him absolution. His prayers said, the priest gave his blessing and withdrew to the hearth, where he sat down while Eleyne resumed her place at John's side.

For a long time there was silence and she thought he was asleep, then he opened his eyes. 'Eleyne, did you ever get your letter from the king?' He paused, trying to catch his breath. 'Like your sister, Margaret. Saying you could choose your next husband.'

'No!' She caught his hand. 'You know I didn't. I never want another husband.'

He grimaced. 'I think you may find you have to, my love. No,

281

listen.' He held up his hand and rested his finger against her lips. 'If
. . . if anything happens to me, I want you to promise me something.
I want you to go to Alexander.' He coughed and she saw him wince
with pain. 'He will take care of you and see you have your rights.
Promise me.'

Alexander.

Eleyne shook her head miserably. 'Nothing is going to happen to
you. You are going to get better and tomorrow or the next day we are
going to ride to Chester.'

'I don't think so.' His whisper was so faint she could hardly hear it.
'Promise me, Eleyne. Don't go to King Henry. I know him, I know
what he –' He coughed again, clutching at her hand with surprising
strength as the paroxysms grew stronger.

He never finished the sentence. The blood was brilliant arterial
blood, spewing out over the bedcovers, soaking her gown as he began
to choke.

It was all over very quickly, but still she sat cradling his head in her
arms. Behind her the room filled with people. Luned tried to lead her
away, but she would not move. Afternoon came: the sun shone directly
into the room through the narrow windows which looked out over the
trees. A strange silence hung over the manor house, and the village
beyond it, where the news had quickly spread. Messengers had set
off to Chester, to Scotland and to the king, despatched by the earl's
chamberlain.

In the bedchamber the silence was broken by the physician. He
pushed his way in and stood looking down at the bed. 'This is your
fault, my lady. You killed him,' he said grimly. 'You sent me away and
gave him potions of which I knew nothing. For all I know they were
poisoned –'

Eleyne stared at him. She was numb; as cold as the body she still
held in her arms. 'No, I loved him.'

The man scowled. He seized the cup on the coffer beside the bed
and sniffed at what remained of the medicine. 'Atropine! There is dwale
in this and henbane. The earl has been poisoned!'

Eleyne shook her head.

'My lady, do you dare to question my knowledge? But of course
you do. You have questioned it often. And now we know why.' He
turned to the crowd in the room, who were listening in horror. 'This
potion is poisoned. Your countess is a murderess!'

CHAPTER TWELVE

I

DARNHALL ❖ Midsummer Day 1237

The halfpenny Rhonwen gave to the boy from the village had come from Eleyne's purse. He had run on bare, silent feet up the forest ride as the bells at the abbey had begun to toll.

'So,' she breathed, 'she is free.' She watched as the boy disappeared once more into the forest, then stooped and gathered up her belongings, slinging them on the saddle of her horse. It wasn't a long ride to the manor and this time she would have nothing to fear, with her enemy gone and Eleyne in charge.

The manor was in turmoil. Carts and wagons which had been packed ready for the early start had been abandoned; mules and horses were standing in rows while servants and men-at-arms milled round aimlessly, spilling in and out of the great hall in a constantly moving tide of humanity.

Sir Robin, overtaken by a fast-riding horseman, had arrived back just before her, and run at once to the bedchamber where Eleyne still watched over the body. The room was almost empty now. The body of the earl had been laid on the bed, washed and dressed in a velvet mantle, a crucifix between his folded fingers. Candles burned at his head and feet, and Eleyne, her bloodstained bed gown gone, a black velvet wrap around her thin body, knelt at his side. The priest still stood near the bed, murmuring prayers, whilst the chamberlain faced Robin near the door, talking to him in an agitated undertone.

Rhonwen stood in the doorway, looking around as the servant bowed and left her, then she stepped inside and called Eleyne's name.

Eleyne rose to her feet. 'You! It was you. You gave me the herbs! You killed him!'

Rhonwen met her gaze steadily. 'How can you think such a thing, *cariad*?'

'They have accused me of murder!' Eleyne's voice was shaking. 'The doctor says there were poisons in the plants you gave me for him –'

'If I had put poison in the mixture, would I have come here?' Rhonwen replied slowly. She narrowed her eyes. 'Would I have come to your side? Who accuses you of this? The doctor, you say? The same man who has nearly killed the earl a hundred times with his leeches and his knives?'

The chamberlain cleared his throat. 'I have already made it clear there is no question of murder,' he mumbled. 'It is an outrageous suggestion! The earl has been ill for many years. We all knew that it was merely a matter of time. He has weakened with each attack. It has been the countess who has kept him alive so long with her love and her care.'

'And with my medicines!' Rhonwen flashed. 'If the physician was so sure of poison, why did he not give the earl mithridate to counteract it? I suggest it is the physician who should be accused of hastening the earl's death by treating him with sulphur and vitriol and saltpetre!'

'Rhonwen.' Eleyne, her face grey with exhaustion, took a step towards her. 'Rhonwen, please . . .'

'It's all right, *cariad*.' Rhonwen took her hands. 'You are distraught. That's why I came as soon as I heard what had happened. I knew I had to be with you, regardless of the danger.'

The chamberlain frowned. 'I am sure that under the circum-stances –'

'Under the circumstances Rhonwen is staying with me. I need her.' Eleyne still hadn't cried. Her whole being was numb with shock. When they had finally prised her away from John and laid him back on the pillow, she had looked at him for the first time since he had died. He wasn't there; he had gone; it was as though she were looking at a stranger.

Luned had washed her hands and face and helped her to change out of the bloodstained gown, then she had led Eleyne back to John's side where she knelt beside him, her mind a blank. She had not whis-pered any prayers for his soul. She had not whispered to him of love or sadness or even anger that he had gone so suddenly from her. He had gone – there was no sense in speaking to an empty shell. She was oblivious of the coming and goings in the room behind her; she had not noticed Robin or his urgent conversation with the chamberlain. She had noticed nothing until Rhonwen came.

The funeral was to be at Chester. The long cortège wound its way slowly to St Werburgh's Abbey and there John of Scotland, Earl of Chester and Huntingdon, was laid to rest near the high altar.

Gruffydd came to the funeral and announced afterwards that he was taking Eleyne back to Aber.

'No!' Rhonwen had cornered her in her bedchamber in Chester Castle, her eyes narrowed with anger. 'No! Don't you see? You have to go to Scotland. You told me yourself that the earl said you were to go to King Alexander.'

'I can't.' Eleyne rounded on her. 'I can't. It would be wrong.' She wouldn't, couldn't think about Alexander now.

'It would be wrong?'

'I owe it to John's memory. I can't go to Alexander! It would look as if —'

'It would look as if you were obeying your late husband's last wish,' Rhonwen said tartly.

'Rhonwen, don't be angry.' Eleyne sat down, her pale face framed by the severe white of the wimple she wore. 'I know you can't go with me; I know I need you, but I need to see my father more. Gruffydd says he is still not well and he spends more and more time with the monks in prayer as though he knows he hasn't much time left. He wants to see me; I have to see him, and I want to go to Aber. Later I will go to Scotland, but not yet.'

II

ABER ❖ July 1237

Isabella was seated on the dais, attended by a bevy of pretty girls. She had grown very plump once again in the months since Joan's death.

'Of course, you know why papa wanted you back at Aber.'

'Papa?' Eleyne stared at her, raising her eyebrow at her sister-in-law's proprietary use of the word.

Isabella smiled. 'He asked me to call him that, as he has no daughters left at home. He wants you here so he can marry you off to someone else. Gwynedd needs allies, but I doubt if he will find you such a good match as the Earl of Chester. I wonder how you will cope with being the wife of a mere lordling!'

Eleyne flinched as if she had been struck as the pain of her loss hit her yet again, but determinedly she closed her eyes and took a deep breath. 'I don't think papa means to find me a husband. Besides,' she was aware of the listening women around them, but unable to keep her hope to herself any longer, 'I think I might be expecting a child. John's heir. My duty would be to bring him up and help him until he was old enough to inherit the earldom.' Six weeks had passed now, since she had last bled. Surely that could mean only one thing?

Isabella laughed. 'You don't look pregnant,' she said unkindly. 'Well, well. Lucky you!' This time the tone was openly caustic. 'But it won't save you from the marriage market.'

'Oh, indeed it will,' Eleyne said firmly. 'Believe me, papa will not marry me to anyone against my wishes, and nor will King Henry. I am quite sure about that. I never want to marry again!'

Isabella let out a peal of laughter. 'Eleyne! I'm twenty! And you're a year younger than me! You'll have to marry. Won't she, papa?'

Unnoticed by Eleyne, the prince had entered the hall and walked slowly towards the dais. He leaned heavily on a stick, but apart from that he seemed to have regained his former vigour.

'Won't she what?' With a groan Llywelyn lowered himself into his chair. 'How are you, sweetheart?' He held out his hand to Eleyne.

'Marry, she'll have to remarry.'

He frowned. 'In due course, perhaps. There is no hurry to decide. I am sure the king will allow Eleyne to do as she wishes. She is a rich and powerful young woman now. Her dower lands will be immense.' He smiled at her fondly. 'But before all else we must get some colour back into her cheeks and comfort her sorrow. I know what it is like to be lonely and there is no healer but time.' He squeezed her hand again.

'Or another man,' Isabella murmured, not quite inaudibly.

Llywelyn smiled into his beard as Eleyne gritted her teeth. 'Take no notice, child,' he said softly. 'Madame is as sharp-tongued as ever, as my son knows to his cost. And if you're with child,' he peered at her thoughtfully, 'she'll never forgive you.'

'I think I am.' She smiled, unable to restrain the temptation to place her hands protectively, just for a second, on her still-flat belly. A baby for John – an heir. How much he had longed for it and now he would never see it. Her eyes filled with tears, in spite of her vow never to give way to them in public, and she turned her back to Isabella. 'I think I might go and rest, papa, if you will excuse me. I am so tired.'

'Of course.' Llywelyn rose to his feet stiffly. 'Rest as much as you can, child.' He put his hand on her shoulder and gently drew her into the crook of his arm. 'I am glad you've come home.' He led her away from the others towards the door at the far end of the hall. 'Your nurse, the Lady Rhonwen,' he said awkwardly, 'she came between us so often. I must tell you that it is almost certain that she is dead, and I am glad of it.' As he felt her stiffen, he pulled her closer: 'I don't know what happened to her, but had she remained in custody she would surely have paid the severest of penalties for what she did on the night of your mother's funeral.' He paused as they reached the door, staring out across the courtyard. 'She was evil, Eleyne, a servant of the devil. I like to think that I am growing more devout in my old age, and I pray more than I used to. Perhaps that has made me see what I should have seen from the start. She was a bad influence on you. She came between you and your mother. She is better dead.' He had not looked at her.

Eleyne had closed her eyes. Rhonwen had stayed at Chester with the dowager and her ladies. Her fists clenched in the folds of her black skirts, she said nothing. What was there to say?

III

Over the next two weeks Eleyne had little time for grieving. Day after day a string of messengers came to see her with condolences from the kings of England and Scotland and all the nobles of the land. Bailiffs and clerks came endlessly too as the vast inheritance of Chester and Huntingdon was surveyed, ready to be split amongst its heirs, and as Eleyne's dower lands were apportioned.

One of them, the king's clerk, Peter de Mungumery, stayed at Aber before setting off to Fotheringhay. There he was to list and value all the vast possessions of the Honour of Huntingdon in Northampton, Rutland, Bedford, Huntingdonshire and Middlesex, for if there were no direct heir, the earl's three surviving sisters, Maud, who had never married, Isabel Bruce, the Lady of Annandale, and Ada, Lady de Hastings, together with Christian and Dervorguilla, the two daughters of John's eldest sister, Margaret, Lady of Galloway, who had died the preceding year in Scotland, would inherit these vast estates. Already a legal battle had begun as Alexander of Scotland claimed seisin over the lands of the earldom of Huntingdon and Robert Fitzooth claimed the title.

If there was no direct heir . . . Peter was waiting to find out if there was a child. As each day passed, Eleyne prayed, her only comfort that maybe she would bear John's child.

It was not to be. The symptoms her body had shown and over which she had watched so hopefully were not those of pregnancy. As the long July days slid by and her body rested, recovering from the shock of John's death, her courses resumed naturally and she was forced to acknowledge that there would be no direct heir to the earldom of Chester. To have to make such a private moment so public, knowing that so many, from the king to the least servant of the earldom, were waiting and watching to see what happened, was humiliating enough, but the moment was made more devastating by Isabella's obvious pleasure at her distress.

King Henry's messenger had spent a long time closeted with Llywelyn, and Eleyne, used by now to such visitors, waited in the arbour at Aber for a summons to their presence, expecting more interminable, impersonal discussions of rents and tenancies and dower lands.

She was sitting on the turf bank, idly picking daisies as she watched her ladies playing with the baby of one of Isabella's women, when she saw her father and his visitor walking towards her beneath the trees.

She could see at once that something was wrong: Llywelyn's face was grey with fatigue and his mouth was tight.

She rose to her feet, her throat constricting with fear, dimly aware that the ladies around her had scooped up the baby and withdrawn to the far side of the garden. Llywelyn stopped in front of her. 'King Henry has commanded you to return to Chester,' he said without preamble. 'This gentleman is here to escort you.'

'But why?' Eleyne stared from her father to the stranger and back. The visitor bowed. He was a tall thin man, dressed as she was in black, a colour which drained any semblance of animation from his face and left it looking cadaverous.

'Permit me to introduce myself, my lady. I am Stephen of Seagrave, former Justiciar of England, one of his grace's officers. King Henry has ordered that I take charge of you and escort you back to Chester and that you be kept in honourable and fitting state there until certain enquiries have been completed concerning accusations made against you, that you procured your husband's death by use of foul poisons.'

'Those were lies!' Eleyne exploded. 'Terrible, cruel lies!'

Stephen gave a shrug. 'I am sure that will be quickly established. Whatever the case the king wishes you to be held there until he decides what is best to do with you.'

'To do with me?' Eleyne echoed.

Stephen bowed. 'Those were his grace's words.'

'He means to give you in marriage to one of his supporters,' Llywelyn put in heavily.

'No!' Eleyne stared at him. 'No, he can't! I don't want to remarry –'

'I am sorry, my lady, it is the king's command,' Stephen said crisply. She saw the glint of metal beneath his mantle and realised that he wore full mail under his robe. 'His grace waited in case you were *enceinte* with the earl's heir, but it has proved not to be so and it is his grace's wish to make provision for you. You are young, and if I may say so very beautiful. It would be a crime if you were not to remarry.'

'And you are very rich and the king wants to secure the support of someone or other at his court, no doubt,' Llywelyn added, his voice weary. 'Would that I could spare you this, Eleyne, but there are reasons why I must agree to the king's wishes.'

Eleyne tightened her lips. She was angry as she had never been angry in her life before. 'You mean it is convenient for you – or perhaps for Dafydd! That's it, isn't it? It would be good for Dafydd if you were seen to be supporting King Henry at the moment. And no doubt Isabella has had her say!'

'No, my darling, Isabella doesn't even know . . .'

'But Dafydd does.'

'Yes.'

288

'And Dafydd advised you to agree without argument . . .'

'Yes, he did, but –' Llywelyn's temper was rising too.

'And Gruffydd, does he know what's going on? Does he know what's planned for me?'

'No.'

'Why not?'

Llywelyn frowned, anger beginning to colour his face. 'Gruffydd is, as you know, in Powys. Eleyne, please allow your brother and me to know what is best for you.'

'Best? I have just lost the best husband in the world, a man I loved and respected, a man I wanted to spend the rest of my life with. I do not wish to remarry.'

'Your marriage to Lord Chester was arranged, Eleyne. May I remind you that you were married to him when you were but a small child. Your next marriage has every chance of being as happy. Lord Chester would have been the first to understand. He would not have expected you to remain alone.'

No, he told me to go to Scotland. She did not say it out loud, but his words returned to her. *Don't go to King Henry.* The last words he had uttered on this earth. He had foreseen this and had tried to save her from it. She closed her eyes, trying to steady the mounting anger which was surging through her. 'What of King Alexander in all this? Does he not have a say in the remarriage of his heir's widow?'

Llywelyn frowned. 'King Alexander has already proclaimed your husband's nephew, young Robert Bruce, the eldest male descendant of King David of Scotland after himself, as heir presumptive until he has a son of his own. And the King of England is negotiating to buy the lands of Huntingdon back from Lord Chester's sisters so that the Scottish connection with the earldom of Huntingdon will finally be brought to an end,' he added. 'I understand Sir Robin Fitzooth has put in a claim for the earldom for want of a closer heir. King Alexander will have no interest in what happens to you, my darling. He will agree that King Henry's decision is the best.'

Eleyne stared at him. 'He will agree?' she echoed. 'He is to be consulted, then?' A surge of hope flowed through her.

'He will be informed as a matter of courtesy,' Stephen put in. 'King Alexander has been in negotiations with King Henry for some time over peace talks beween the two countries. I doubt if he would wish to jeopardise the progress that has been made by interfering in any decisions King Henry may make about you.' His hard green eyes glittered with satisfaction. He had seen this wayward girl at court and he had heard of her reputation. It gave him much satisfaction to be part of the process that was going to trim her wings. He even had a rough idea of who the king would give her to. His hooded eyelids veiled his expression as he smiled at her.

'We can leave for Chester whenever you are ready, my lady,' he said with unctuous humility. 'His grace has ordered that the Chester estates be administered by three royal servants for the time being: Henry of Audley, Hugh Despenser and myself. I am now appointed Justice of the County of Chester. I have to return at once to my duties, but I realise you will have farewells to make and that your servants will need to make ready for the journey. Would two days hence be satisfactory?'

'Two days?' Eleyne was aghast.

'Three, if you prefer. I am at your service, as is his grace's escort.' Stephen smiled again. The king himself had warned him of Eleyne's propensity for taking off on horseback and riding wildly around the countryside. That was something she would not do once she was in his care. He eyed her tall slim figure critically. She was undoubtedly the most dangerous type of woman: a temptress, designed to lead men astray and put their souls in jeopardy. He shuddered elegantly beneath his black gown and turned away from her.

IV

'No!' Eleyne lay on the bed, face down, pounding the pillow with her fists. 'I won't go with him, papa can't make me!' Her fury had jolted her out of her deep depression.

'Ssssh!' Luned glanced over her shoulder into the quiet darkness of the room. 'What can you do?' She was upset too.

Eleyne sat up. 'Suppose they found me guilty of trying to murder John?' She closed her eyes and shook her head. 'It's not possible, no one would believe that, no one.'

Luned scowled. 'You don't think . . . what I mean is . . . Rhonwen had no reason to love Lord Chester,' she finished in a whisper.

'No, she wouldn't.' Eleyne put her knuckles to her eyes. 'She couldn't. I won't believe it. There was no poison. It was that stupid, jealous doctor and his fear his incompetence would be exposed. I must see Uncle Henry myself. If I speak to him, I can make him understand. I can make him see how foolish this is. He can't do this to me, he can't. He allowed Margaret to choose her own husband. He must allow me to do the same. If I must remarry, at least I can get his promise that I can choose who it is.'

'And you think that black crow will allow you near the king?' Luned asked quietly. She had seen the expression on Stephen's face as he watched Eleyne.

'Of course he will if I order him to.'

'I don't think so.' Luned shook her head. 'He has his orders, and he is the type who can see neither to left nor right of the path he has been shown. And he hates women.'

Eleyne frowned. 'Yes, he does. And he's afraid of them. So, if I go, I must go without his permission.' She drew her legs up beneath her gown and hugged her knees, her face thoughtful.

Luned suppressed a smile. She recognised that expression. 'I'll come with you,' she said softly.

Eleyne smiled. 'I wish I had Invictus here.'

'I'm glad you haven't, I'd never be able to keep up with you, but there are plenty of fast horses in your father's stables. When shall we go?'

'I suppose it ought to be as soon as possible.'

'Tonight, you mean?' Luned looked towards the door.

'Tonight.' For the first time in many days Eleyne's face lightened. 'Now! That will be a shock for the black crow. Can you pack us each a bundle while I find us some money?' She scrambled off the bed and ran to a small coffer on the table. In it was a pile of silver which she had brought with her from Chester to distribute as rewards and pensions to those amongst her father's servants and her own who had served John. Gathering the pennies into a leather pouch, she tucked it securely into her bundle and reached for her cloak. The candles had burned down less than half an inch since the idea of flight had come to her.

Extinguishing all the candles but one, Luned picked up her belongings and pulled open the door. The hallway was empty. At the far end the staircase led downwards out of sight. They could see the faint shadow where a torch in the main entrance to the building flickered in the draught.

Her finger to her lips, Eleyne led the way on tiptoe, her bundle under her arm beneath her cloak. Cautiously she began to descend, holding her breath as the steps creaked, her ears straining in the silence. The *llys* had long since gone to bed, the fires damped, most of the lights extinguished. At the last turn of the stair she peered around. The guard at the doorway was asleep. Even as she watched, she saw him shift his position, smack his lips and settle back, his neck bent down on his shoulder as he sank against the wall as though it were a soft pillow.

She smiled at Luned. They both knew him, he was one of her father's oldest men-at-arms, retired to this, one of the least onerous posts within the palace.

They were past him in seconds, the warm summer air flowing in through the opened door stirring his hair a little but not disturbing his sleep. Then they were running across the courtyard. There was no chance of taking a horse from the stable; too many boys slept there in the straw, to say nothing of the couples who found privacy in the fragrant darkness. Instead they made their way to the gatehouse. The guards there were alert, but they had had no orders to forbid the prince's daughter to go out into the night and they let them pass. Eleyne had after all done this before.

She frowned as she thought again of Einion and his mysterious summons to her from the darkness; it seemed so long ago. And what had he told her? Her skin prickled with fear and excitement and she stopped so suddenly that Luned nearly bumped into her. Einion had said that she would become the ancestress of kings. That her future lay in Scotland. Of course! She would be a fool to ride to Henry, she would go north and seek out Alexander as John had told her.

The horses were grazing at the far side of the meadow, where the river broadened and flowed more slowly over the flat lands towards the sea. They were ghostly shapes beneath the stars, fetlock deep in soft white mist.

'How will we catch them?' Luned breathed, awed by their ethereal beauty.

'I'll do it.' Eleyne slid her bundle to the ground. She reached for the two plaited girdles she had brought to act as halters, realising that the harness rooms would be too securely locked to reach without waking someone; these would have to do. Gathering her skirts, she climbed lightly over the gate and began to walk across the dew-soaked grass. Luned watched her, a slight figure, no more than a shadow in the starlight, moving silently through the mist.

One horse spotted her and then the others. They raised their heads, ears pricked, and watched as she drew near. Luned heard a whicker in the darkness and she smiled; they would not be able to resist her. What horse ever could? Sure enough, in seconds they were gathering around her, nuzzling her hands as she selected two and slipped the girdles around their necks. Like a virgin capturing unicorns, Luned thought. They were coming now, a horse on each side of her, the others behind, inquisitive, light-footed, manes and tails flowing.

Swiftly Luned strung their two bundles together to go across her horse's withers. She pulled open the gate as Eleyne led their mounts through, and shut it to stop the rest of the animals following.

Her slim wrists moving deftly in the darkness, Eleyne knotted head-collars for the horses and helped Luned to mount from the gate, then she jumped astride her own, a light-footed silver mare, part of the starlight itself.

'We'll take the mountain road,' she called, 'and then we'll make for Scotland.'

Suddenly she laughed out loud.

Rhonwen stared out across the rooftops of Chester and sighed. The embroidery on which she had been working lay on the table behind her, the silks and needles and shears all jumbled in a heap. Her head was splitting.

The old Countess of Chester looked up. 'They will find her, my dear. She cannot have got far, you know.' She glanced almost reproachfully at the door of the solar and frowned; behind it stood one of the king's guards.

Returning to Chester without Eleyne, Stephen had put the whole castle on alert and more or less imprisoned those of the earl's and countess's personal household who remained. The castle flew the king's standard now, and the day-to-day administration was in the hands of Stephen and his two colleagues. John de Lacy, Earl of Lincoln, had been made constable of the castle.

It had not taken them long to find that Rhonwen was Eleyne's particular confidante, and even less time to assimilate the interesting information that she was a wanted murderess and a heretic. But they were biding their time. She could not go anywhere. All the women were imprisoned, and she might in some way hold a clue to Eleyne's destination.

Stephen had sent riders in every direction when Eleyne's flight had been discovered and had guards patrolling all the roads south. He knew the way her mind was working. She would try to reach her uncle and beg him to change his mind. He had expected to catch up with her within hours, but to his fury she and her companion had completely disappeared, and with her two of the prince's best horses.

'Sit down, my dear.' Countess Clemence's voice was surprisingly firm. 'Don't let that boorish man see that you are upset. He will be here in a minute.' She pushed Rhonwen's embroidery towards her. 'You do know where she's gone, don't you?' she asked quietly.

Rhonwen shrugged. 'I can guess.'

'Is it Scotland?' The dowager smiled. 'I know dear John was always so in love with the place. I cannot believe he didn't infect her with his own longing. And Alexander would shield her against Henry's ridiculous schemes.'

Rhonwen glanced warily around the table. The other women were listening, and any one of them might betray Eleyne.

'I don't know, my lady, I really don't. There are so many people who would take her in. People right here in Chester. He will never find her once she is among friends.'

'She is indeed much loved.' Clemence nodded. 'Poor child, she must have been so disappointed to find she was not going to have John's child. That was a cruel trick of fate.'

'Indeed.' Rhonwen nodded meekly. 'I was very sad when I heard the news.' Eleyne would reach Scotland – and then she would send for her friends.

VI

THE ROAD NORTH ❖ August 1237

It was only when daylight came that they realised the magnitude of their task. They had to ride to Scotland, a journey which would take them many days, avoiding the main roads, avoiding towns and villages. They had no saddles or bridles for the horses, no escort, no food. They did have money, but when they stopped to use it they might be recognised. Eleyne was under no illusions. Stephen would not take her disappearance lightly. They would have had only a few hours' start, if that, and already the king's escort, which was to take her back to Chester, would be scouring the country for her. It was Luned, wrapped in her dark cloak, who went to lonely homestead doors and bought bread and cheese; it was Luned who, pretending she had lost her own, brought extra cloaks for them at different places along the way to protect them against the cold hard ground at night. But it was a long time before they dared to try and obtain bridles for the horses.

'We have to try and we must hire a man to escort us,' Eleyne commented as they rode off the path yet again and waited in the shelter of some trees as a wagon rumbled past. 'Like this, we attract too much attention.'

'You should have picked a less showy horse,' Luned commented wryly. The delicate mare with her silver mane and tail had attracted many covetous stares over the past three days, as had the sight of two unescorted women riding bareback.

'The next town we reach, you will go and buy us bridles,' Eleyne said firmly.

'And that will not attract attention? Me, alone, going to the harness-maker and buying two bridles?' Luned's voice was tart. 'I thought we had decided that we couldn't risk it.'

'Not if you say they are a gift for your sweetheart,' Eleyne said. 'Of course, you will have to buy rather fancy ones if they are a gift, but it will be worth it, and I have the money. It must be safe to stop now. We have been riding for days and we can't be far from the Scottish border. The last man you spoke to said we would reach Kendal soon. Let's stop there and buy some food and two bridles.'

The route so far had been relatively easy and flat, following the road due north almost the whole way from Chester, which they had bypassed at a safe distance, but now they could see mountains to the east and north and the tracks had begun to climb. It was still early morning when Eleyne led the way off the road once more, and already it was blisteringly hot. The sun, high overhead, shone from a cloudless sky, and with relief they rode into the shade of a copse and dismounted.

'Rest a little, then we'll go on.' Eleyne sat down wearily on a fallen tree, the mare's plaited rein slack in her hand. The horse lowered her head and began to graze on the thick rich grass.

Luned glanced at her with a wave of sympathy as she tethered her own mount to a birch tree nearby. 'You're exhausted. Let me go into Kendal alone. It would be safer in the long run anyway. We can't risk you being recognised now we've come so far.' She saw Eleyne hesitate and, sensing victory, she went on quickly, 'I'll rest, then I'll beg a ride on one of the wagons we've seen on the road. I can't ride into the town without a bridle anyway – they'll think I've stolen the horse. I'll be safe on my own; no one is looking for me.'

Eleyne had to acknowledge that. She could not take the risk of being found this side of the Scottish border. If King Henry's men were following them, they would stop at every guesthouse, monastery and inn; at every castle – at every place the two might have stopped. Luned pulled their bundles from her horse and threw them on the ground. Eleyne was determined and more courageous than anyone she had ever known, but the strain of the past few weeks was beginning to tell. Luned had seen the exhaustion on her face. She cried softly in the night; Luned had heard her and now, in the daylight, though her eyes were bright and there was excitement in them, she was almost too tired to stand.

Eleyne nodded and sighed. 'You're right, it would be safer. Take some money and buy bridles from two different saddlers, so they do not grow suspicious. Then we can buy saddles one at a time later.'

'You won't have enough money for saddles, my lady.' Luned had looked into the money bag. 'They are expensive and we should keep as much money as we can – we may need it.'

'It's not that far to Scotland,' Eleyne countered. All her life she had been wealthy and it had never crossed her mind that she might one day find herself without money – that without the small, steadily dwindling pile of coins they would find themselves destitute.

'It will be five or six days' ride to Edinburgh at least, and each night we have to find somewhere to stay, unless you intend to continue sleeping in the forest like an outlaw,' Luned said firmly. 'We don't need saddles.'

Eleyne sighed. 'I don't know that we dare show ourselves even in

Scotland until we reach Alexander,' she said. She kicked off her shoes and pushed her feet into the grass.

'But once we get to him, we'll be safe.'

'Of course.' Eleyne smiled. She was staring into the distance, where the green shade of the trees hazed into a blur. Crossly, she rubbed her eyes and turned to Luned. 'Go on, if you've rested enough. It looks as though it must be market day. There are a lot of people on the road.'

She watched Luned thread her way back through the trees and descend the rocky slope, where she disappeared from view. Within minutes she had found herself a ride with a plump woman who was driving a wagon. A few minutes later she wished that she hadn't: the wagon, attended by clouds of bluebottles, was laden with stinking half-cured hides.

Eleyne led both horses deeper into the shade and tethered them securely, then she stowed their bundles beneath a clump of elder, before wandering into the copse. Behind it a meadow, spangled with wild flowers and bisected by a narrow, tumbling beck, separated the copse from a larger, more dense area of forest which filled the valley and rose up the side of the hill before the mountains shook themselves clear of the trees and rose high in the sunlight. She walked down towards the water and sat on the grass to wash the dust of the road from her hands and feet. The water was ice-cold and refreshing and she drank long and gratefully from it. She was hungry, but they had eaten the last of their provisions that morning, and she would have to wait to eat until Luned returned, which might not be until dusk. Still barefoot, she wandered along the bank to where the trees came down to the water's edge. There, in the dappled sunlight, she found some wild strawberries. Lying back in the long grass and staring up through the leaves of a graceful birch tree, she began to eat them.

She must have dozed, for when she next looked up the sun had moved several degrees towards the west and the shadows had lengthened. She wondered what had wakened her, then she saw a squirrel sitting above her washing its face with its paws. It tensed, chittering at her in fury, then disappeared.

She sat up. With the squirrel gone, the woods were unnaturally silent. She frowned, every sense alert – she was not alone, she was being watched. She scanned the hazel break on the far side of the beck, then as casually as she could, she looked behind her. The wood was darker than she remembered, the trees closer together. The afternoon was very still and even the cheerful ripple of the water at her feet seemed quieter, more distant. She cursed herself for wandering away from their horses and their bundles, where her only weapon – a small knife – was hidden. The feeling of being watched became stronger and she felt the hairs on her neck prickling. The shadow of the trees had crept nearer. Now it had reached the grass where the skirt of her black gown lay spread around her. The fabric dulled, like a dark flame extinguished.

Had they been followed after all? Were Stephen's men in the wood even now, watching her? She rose to her knees, keeping her movements as natural as possible, then she dusted the dried grasses from her skirt and stood up. The feeling was overpowering now; she wanted to turn and run, but she forced herself to retrace her steps casually, feeling eyes on her from somewhere in the dark trees across the stream, expecting every moment to feel an arrow in her back.

Nothing happened; the silence pressed around her. The world was holding its breath with her.

At last she regained the trees and slid into the shadows, thankful, not for the first time, for her black gown. She stopped by an ancient oak, its trunk swollen and gnarled, broad enough to hide a dozen men. Slipping behind it, she peered back the way she had come, her hands on the rough bark, taking comfort from it. She could hear her heart beating in her ears. The woodland seemed deserted. Nothing moved, but she could feel it again: a presence in the hazy green distance. A presence that was not human.

'Einion?' she breathed. She felt the perspiration icy between her shoulder blades. She strained her eyes into the dappled shadows. This new unseen threat was even more frightening than the thought of King Henry's men hidden in the trees.

How could Einion be here, so far from Wales? Why had he followed her? She could feel him around her, his frustration beating against the barriers of silence which separated him from her; she could sense his raw emotion, tearing at her, crying to be heard.

'What is it?' she cried, her voice husky with fear. 'What is it? Tell me.' But only the silence of the hot afternoon answered her. She rested her forehead against the tree; it was warm, reassuring, solid.

The fire, look in the fire.

Were the words in her head, or had she heard them? She swallowed, trying to calm herself.

The fire, look in the fire.

It was a long time since she had tried to see pictures in the fire; the last time she had seen her father's sickbed. The fire had not told her that he would recover or that John would die. There had been no clue that she would have so short a time with her husband; no clue that he would leave no heir. Everything Einion had told her had been wrong. She would never be the mother of kings. Was that what he wanted to tell her – that he had made a mistake?

'I know you were wrong!' she called. 'You were wrong about

297

Scotland. John is dead!' Her eyes filled with tears. 'He's dead! He will never be Scotland's king –'

Look in the fire . . .

'I can't see anything in the fire. I don't understand.'

Look in the fire . . .

She stared around in despair, her hands shaking. Her breath was coming in painful snatches, deep within her chest, knowing she would have to do it. She could not argue with this strange voice which filled the silence of the woods, because she wanted to know what it was he so desperately wanted to tell her.

Almost sleep-walking, she made her way back to the clearing where she had left the horses. They were dozing, hip-slack in the heat, their heads low, their eyes closed, not bothering to look up as she crossed the grass towards them. Kneeling, she pulled the bundles from the bush, and inside Luned's she found the flint and steel. She took them to the far side of the clearing and scraped a hollow in a patch of dusty soil. She collected flakes of birch bark and dry leaves and some brittle summer-dried moss and lichen. Piling them up, she began to strike the flint. It was several minutes before she managed a spark. Her hands were shaking and her fingers were all thumbs, but at last she had a wisp of smoke and minutes later a small flame. Throwing down the flint, she cupped her hands and blew gently.

It took some time to get the fire she wanted, a small steady glow, fed by lumps of rotten timber and made smoky with fragrant leaves. I'm mad, she thought, quite mad. What am I doing? Lighting a fire on the orders of a ghost! She prayed that the wisp of smoke would not be seen from the road, and it was a long time before she saw any pictures in the glowing embers. Her eyes were sore from the smoke, her head was heavy, and she was too conscious of the brooding presence waiting. Then slowly they came, flickering, indistinct: horses, galloping through the smoke. She could see a sword glinting in a rider's hand, a banner flogging in the wind, its device indistinct. Frowning, she leaned forward. 'Show me,' she whispered, 'show me! I am watching . . .' She reached forward with her hand into the fire as if trying to part the smoke, watching, strangely detached, as the small blue flames licked at her fingers. She felt no pain. The flames nudged at her hand, companionable, friendly, and at last, through them, she saw his face: the thin, ravaged flesh, the white hair, wild as smoke, the skeletal hand raised towards her as he began to speak. She strained to hear, her mind reaching across the smoke, groping for understanding.

Behind her Luned had walked into the clearing, a heavy sack in her hand. Eleyne was kneeling beside a small fire, her hands in the embers, her eyes open, unseeing, fixed on some object Luned could not see. Luned threw herself forward. 'Stop it!' she screamed, and

298

dragged Eleyne back from the fire. 'What are you doing? Are you mad? Sweet Virgin! Look, look at your hand! You are burning!'

Eleyne's face was blank – she didn't know where she was and she didn't recognise the woman pulling at her arm. Then the mist cleared from her eyes and she became aware of the agonising pain. Stunned, she looked at her fingers; the flesh of one hand was red and shiny, stained with soot.

'Put it in the stream. Quickly, it will cool it. Come *on*!' Luned pulled at her angrily. 'What were you thinking of, putting your hand in the fire?' Scolding and cajoling, she pulled Eleyne across the meadow and forced her to kneel at the water's edge, plunging the burned hand into the ice-cold water. Eleyne cried out with pain and struggled to pull free, but Luned, with gritted teeth, held her wrist firmly, pushing the blistered fingers deeper into the beck. 'Keep it there. You have to take the fire out of the flesh. Rhonwen showed me when I was little and fell into the embers in the nursery in the *ty hir* at Aber.'

Eleyne's teeth had begun to chatter, as much with shock as with the sharpness of the mountain water. 'For pity's sake, that's enough.'

'No, not until the heat has gone.' Luned touched one of the burns cautiously with her fingertip. 'I can still feel the fire. Leave it until it's cold. What were you doing?' Kneeling at Eleyne's side, Luned looked at her curiously: 'You didn't light the fire for heat, and there was nothing to cook.'

'No.'

'Then what?'

Eleyne watched her fingers trailing in the water amongst the green soft fronds of the river weed as Luned released her wrist and sat back on the bank.

'You were looking in the fire for your future?'

'Perhaps.' She could not tell Luned of the wraith amongst the trees, the agony of a man who had died with a message unspoken, of the future which swirled and battered against her brain in a series of untold riddles.

'And did you see anything?'

Eleyne shook her head. 'The pictures were starting to come as you pulled me from the fire.'

'Just as well I did. You would have thrown yourself on the flames if I had been any later.'

Eleyne sat back at last, holding her hand before her. 'The redness is quite gone.' She looked at Luned, 'You came back sooner than I had thought.'

'I have the bridles and I have some food. And I have news.' Grimly, Luned turned back her skirt and tore a strip off the bottom of her shift to bind Eleyne's hand. 'The king's messengers have been in Kendal.

They have guessed you are trying to reach Scotland and they are asking for you by name everywhere. They have our descriptions and those of the horses we ride. I wasn't recognised on my own and without a horse, but we are going to find it very difficult from now on.'

Eleyne bit her lip and looked across the meadow towards the wood. The trees were empty now, Einion had gone. The shadows where the westering sun had sunk behind the hill at the end of the valley threw long black lines on the ground, but they were empty of menace. Shivering, she sat on the bank, looking glumly at her bandaged hand. 'We'll have to ride at night then.'

'And keep away from towns and villages. It shouldn't be too difficult.' Luned smiled. 'Shall we eat, then we can set off. At least the horses are rested. We can ride as long as the moon is high and sleep at moonset.'

They could not ride so fast in the darkness; the horses picked their way cautiously up the steep tracks and both young women were acutely aware of the cavernous black shadows behind trees and rocks as the path grew wilder and more steep. The night was cold and crystal clear. Every sound from the horses' hooves, every jingle of the new bridles was magnified a thousand times and seemed to echo from the rocks behind them.

The moon dropped away into the west. For a while they continued in the starlight, then as dawn began to break they saw a huddled village in the valley below them. 'We daren't go down,' Eleyne whispered, reining in her mare with her good hand. 'We have followed the most direct road. They will look for us there.' She peered into the shadows, looking for shelter, but high on the pass there were few trees. In the east behind the mountains the sky was paling to green. 'We'll have to ride well away from the track.' She led the way up a small glen and into the shadow of a group of tall pine trees, where she dismounted. 'There is grazing here, and water. I don't think we'll be seen from the main road —' She broke off. 'What is it?'

Luned had cocked her head, listening, her hand over her horse's nose to stop him calling. 'Horses, behind us,' she whispered.

They held their breath, pressing back into the darkness as the sound of hooves grew louder — there seemed to be a considerable number of horses riding purposefully up the road beneath them. Then they heard a sharp command ringing up the valley and the horses drew to a halt.

'We've been followed,' Eleyne breathed, her heart thudding with fear.

'But how? I wasn't recognised.'

'You must have been. Come on.' Eleyne began to lead her mare further up the defile, picking her way over the rocky ground, praying

300

there was a way out at the top of the small valley. If there wasn't, they were trapped.

Behind them the horses hadn't moved, but a new sound reached their ears: the excited yelp of a hound.

Eleyne bit her lip. 'They have dogs. We'll never get away now.' She looked at the rocky cliff above them. 'Unless –' she put her hand on the rock. It was icy, black in the pre-dawn twilight. 'Leave the horses,' she whispered, 'leave everything. Climb.'

Luned stared at her. 'I can't.'

'You'll have to, there is nothing else for it. The dogs are following the horses. They will not know where we have gone.'

She gave the grey mare a regretful kiss on her silky nose and turned soundlessly to the cliff.

Her hand hurt intolerably. It had ached and burned all night, and as she used her fingers to hitch her skirts into her girdle the pain became worse. Gritting her teeth, she set her foot on a small ledge and pulled herself clear of the track. Luned followed her. The rock was slippery with dew and very cold. Clinging to it, Eleyne looked down and saw them. Three men on foot, following two dogs. They were almost below them.

She forced herself to look up and saw an overhang above her – there was no way up, nothing to be done but to cling to the rock face and pray that the men would not see them. She held her breath, waiting, aware of Luned hanging motionless beside her.

In the clear dawn air they could hear every word of the men below as they drew closer.

'I'll be glad when I'm back in a warm bed,' one called, 'with a hot-blooded wench to heat my feet.' The retort of a second was lost in a shout of laughter.

The men were casual, unarmed as far as Eleyne could see, confident as they came upon the two horses.

'Here they are.' The words were clear and ringing. 'The dogs will soon find the women. There's no way out of this valley. Then we can get back to our beds.'

For a brief moment men and dogs were lost to view in the brush at the foot of the cliff, then Eleyne saw them emerge immediately below them. The dogs were barking wildly; all three men looked up.

'So, our flyaway birds have roosted on the cliff!' With a shout of laughter the leading man stood, hands on hips, and stared at them. 'Come down.'

Eleyne clung to the rock more tightly and closed her eyes, paralysed with fear. Seconds later, there was a sharp ping as an arrow hit the rock a few feet to her left.

'Come down, Lady Chester, or the next will be through your maid's back.' The banter had left the man's voice.

'All right.' Eleyne's voice was hoarse. 'All right, we'll come down.'

By the time she reached the bottom of the cliff, she was shaking like a leaf and her burned fingers were bleeding through the bandage. Unable to stand, she sank to the ground helplessly as Luned jumped the last few feet and landed beside her.

The man looked concerned. 'Bring the horses up here; I don't think her ladyship can walk.' He stepped over to her.

'Leave her.' Luned pushed him away. 'Let me see her hand.'

He stood back as Luned unwrapped the dirty bandage and pulled it gently away from Eleyne's blistered and bleeding fingers. 'I'll have to bandage it again,' she said softly, 'does it hurt very much?'

'I'll manage.'

'We'll ride back to Kendal immediately,' the man said, 'and find a physician to dress it for you before we go back.'

'Go back?' Eleyne looked at him wearily.

'To Chester. The king has ordered that you be taken back there the moment we find you.' He gave a half bow. 'I understand his grace does not think it an appropriate time for you to be visiting Scotland.'

The two horses were led up to them.

'Allow me, my lady, I'll help you into the saddle, then we'll rejoin the escort on the track below.'

VII

CHESTER CASTLE ❖ August 1237

Eleyne slept in the earl's bedchamber and was given all the state of the Countess of Chester. But she was a prisoner. John de Lacy, Earl of Lincoln, had made that quite clear. She was not to ride or to visit the town; she couldn't receive envoys or messengers unless he was present, and she could not write to her father or to her aunt or uncle in Scotland. Her vision faded and she did not have the heart to summon it again. Whatever destiny had in store for her, it would come without her aid.

Rhonwen anointed her hand with salves which softened and healed the burned skin, and scolded her alternately for running away and for getting caught. 'That has put you in the wrong, *cariad*. Now they are on their guard. They expect you to try again.' She tied the cool buttered silk bandage tighter and settled Eleyne's arm into the scarf knotted around her neck as a sling. 'You should have bided your time. You should have waited for King Alexander to ask for you to be sent to him.'

'He hasn't asked –'

'He has. Countess Clemence told me. He has written to King Henry in the strongest possible terms and demanded that, as the widow of the heir to Scotland, you be allowed to return there. King Henry has refused.'

'Of course.' Eleyne walked sadly to the window of the solar and looked down across the walls into the busy street. 'He has already selected my husband, it seems, but he does not deign to tell me his name.'

She turned with a flash of impatience. 'Dear sweet Christ! for two pins I would throw a rope of sheets across the battlements and slide down! How dare he do this to me! I am one of the highest-born ladies in the land, I am a princess of Wales and of Scotland, and he treats me like a brood bitch to be mated at his command!'

'It was ever so, *cariad*.' Rhonwen wrinkled her nose fastidiously at the metaphor.

'I won't do it!' Eleyne swept back to the table where Rhonwen was sitting and stood glaring down at her. 'I'd rather die!'

'You don't mean that, it's not you that should die; it's the man who lets himself be mated with you when he knows you're unwilling.' Rhonwen paused, her eyes hard, then she shook her head. 'He must be a great man, to be married to the Countess of Chester – a prince at least.'

'There are no princes who are not related within the prohibited degree.' Eleyne paced the floor again. 'How could he do this to me? Why does he keep it a secret? Surely I should be told whom he has chosen, or is he too afraid to tell me? Is he afraid what I will do when I find out whom he has selected?'

Outside the castle walls the town was busy; the noises of the street drifted up to the windows of the keep, and with them the stench of refuse. The long August days were unremittingly hot; there was disease in the merchants' quarter and night after night the sound of fighting drifted up from the town as men's tempers grew short.

Eleyne's hand had healed, leaving only two small red scars across the knuckles of two fingers. Her grief for John was contained now, sealed deep within herself, buried beneath the worry and frustration which grew daily. Day after day she paced the floor of the solar or walked in the small garden within the inner walls – ten paces towards the setting sun, four paces back and forth north and south, the flower-strewn grass bank which bordered it long turned to grey barren dust. Beyond the castle walls the river ran low between its banks, the mud shining briefly as the tide receded, then cracking open like a desert.

The trees outside the walls began to look jaded and the leaves yellowed. Peter de Mungumery returned from his survey of the estates of Huntingdon and closeted himself with Lord Lincoln and his justice and chamberlain, Richard de Draycott and Richard de Gatesden, and her old antagonist, Stephen Seagrave, for hours in the castle scriptorium. Eleyne was neither consulted nor told the outcome of their deliberations. Her haughty enquiries were treated with tolerant scorn and tight-lipped silence. September came, then October. The drought broke at last and torrential rain turned the dusty roads and fields to quagmires within hours. At last, with the first gales from the west, came news of Eleyne's husband-to-be.

John de Lacy never summoned her to the great hall. Instead he would beg for her presence there, sending messengers who would let it be known that they would wait until she came. He and Stephen Seagrave sat in the two great chairs on the dais, near the fire; Peter de Mungumery stood near. As Eleyne walked towards them, followed by two of her ladies, they both rose. She walked calmly to the earl's chair, vacated by John de Lacy, and sat down, eyeing them with distaste.

'You wished to see me, gentlemen?'

The castle shook with the strength of the wind, shutters rattling, doors banging back and forth on the latch, the floor coverings stirring and whispering, wall hangings billowing uneasily. Everywhere, the fires smoked unpleasantly.

De Lacy bowed. 'The king has sent news at last, my lady. The accusations of murder against you have been dropped.' He paused. 'The king has found someone, it seems, who is prepared to take you, even with the suspicion unresolved. Your marriage is to be celebrated here, next month, on Martinmas Eve.'

Eleyne felt her stomach tighten but she kept her face impassive. 'Indeed. And I am to be told the name of my husband-to-be?'

'Of course, madam.' De Lacy could not keep the triumph out of his eyes. 'It is someone I know well. The king's letter informs me that this – gentleman,' he paused, 'is to be knighted next week by the king himself. It is none other than my late father-in-law's brother, Robert de Quincy.'

'His youngest brother,' Stephen Seagrave put in softly. 'A young man of about your own age, I believe, madam.'

Eleyne stared incredulously from one man to the other: 'I am to be married to the youngest son of an earl, a man with no title?'

'You will, of course, under the circumstances, keep your late husband's title, madam . . .'

'A man not yet knighted –' she swept on without heeding him.

'He will have his knighthood before the wedding,' Stephen added reassuringly. He was enjoying this. 'His grace has asked me to give you a loan, madam, of fifty marks to buy finery for the wedding. Just until the sum of your dower has been agreed. I understand Robert has little or no wealth of his own.'

Eleyne looked at him coldly. 'I don't even know this Robert de Quincy —'

'No, madam, though he is of course a brother-in-law to your late husband's Aunt Hawise. I believe he serves his elder brother, the present Earl of Winchester. They have been much in Scotland in the service of King Alexander. As you know, Lord Winchester's wife, Elena, brought with her the office of Constable of Scotland. I am sure the King of the Scots will heartily approve the match.'

'No.' Eleyne shook her head slowly. 'No, he will not approve it. I will be disparaged by this marriage, sir. I am a princess of Wales. It is unthinkable that I should marry a man with no title.' She rose to her feet.

The men rose too, and Stephen did not attempt to hide his smirk of triumph. 'The king, your uncle, feels the match is a good one, madam,' he said smoothly. 'It will please the Earl of Winchester greatly.'

'So that's it.' Eleyne's eyes blazed. 'I am to be given to this . . . this nobody, to win the Earl of Winchester's support for my uncle!'

'So it would seem,' Stephen nodded, smiling openly at the Earl of Lincoln. 'And of course, it will remind the Prince of Gwynedd that he is no more than a vassal of the King of England. Prince David also needs to be reminded of that fact occasionally, I gather.'

Eleyne stared at the earl, speechless with indignation. 'Have you thought what my father and my brothers will do when they hear this news?'

John de Lacy shrugged, 'They will do nothing, madam. I guarantee it.'

VIII

CHESTER ❖ November 1237

'He's arrived.' Nesta had stationed herself in the window embrasure at first light. A large, ungainly woman, her wild brown hair barely restrained by her coif, Nesta had been born and bred in Chester and in service in the city since she was twelve. To serve the Countess of Chester was honour indeed. 'Are you going down to the great hall to greet him?'

'I am not.' Eleyne's fists were clenched so tightly her knuckles were white.

'You'll have to go when they summon you.'

'Not unless they carry me.' Eleyne sat back in her chair, staring at the small fire in the hearth. It was three weeks since she had been told the date of her marriage; three weeks since she had seen Luned or Rhonwen or any of her own servants. When she returned from her interview with John de Lacy and his colleagues, she had found she was a prisoner indeed, not allowed beyond the walls of her solar and the bedchamber. Worse, she was to be waited on by strangers, employed for the purpose. There had been no chance to send letters to her father, whose impotent fury at hearing the name of her proposed husband had nearly caused a second seizure, or to Scotland. There was no possibility of escape, no way of finding out what had happened to her companions. There was nothing she could do; she was helpless.

'If that's him, on the horse in the front, he's ever so handsome,' Nesta went on from her viewpoint in the embrasure. 'There, he's dismounted now. Tall, he is taller than the groom. He's very dark, swarthy, I'd say . . .'

'Come away from the window!' Eleyne commanded sharply, 'and get on with your sewing. We are not peasants to run and stare.' Her mouth was dry with fear; her throat constricted.

Nesta ignored her. 'He hasn't got many attendants. There are only four menservants and one wagon. I expect that's your wedding gifts. He's coming towards the keep now, and he's, yes, he's looking up.' She giggled shrilly. 'I think he saw me.'

'I'm sure he did.' Eleyne's voice was icy. 'Close the shutter at once and come away from the window.'

When the invitation to the great hall for supper came Eleyne declined. Minutes later Stephen Seagrave arrived, panting slightly, pushing past the servant at the door.

'I am sorry to hear you have a headache, madam; however on this occasion I think you must ignore it. Your betrothed has arrived and he would like to meet you.'

'I am sure he would,' Eleyne replied quietly, 'but I feel I must disappoint him.'

'You mean, you refuse?'

'I mean, I refuse.'

'You will have to meet him tomorrow at the wedding ceremony.'

'I don't think so.' Eleyne had not looked at him. 'I have already told you, I will not marry Robert de Quincy.'

'Indeed you will, madam,' Stephen spoke through clenched teeth, 'it is the king's command.'

She smiled faintly. 'I think not. If his grace wishes me to marry, he must tell me so himself. I will not take his messages from a lackey.'

She had still not looked at him and missed the glitter of hatred in his eye.

'Oh, I think you will find lackeys . . .' he paused as if to contain his anger, 'have methods of making you obey them, my lady. Lord Lincoln has given me authority to use any method I choose to persuade you, so that he is not embarrassed before his wife's uncle.' He said it so quietly she could barely hear his words. 'Make no mistake about it, you will be in the chapel tomorrow for the nuptial mass after you have made your vows.'

'You've made him very angry,' Nesta whispered as he closed the door behind him.

'I don't care.' Eleyne closed her eyes and leaned back in the chair. 'The man is a fool.'

'I don't think so, my lady.' Nesta had grown fond of Eleyne in the three weeks she had served her, and she had not liked the look on Stephen's face.

IX

Robert de Quincy had found the ride to Chester painfully slow because of the wagon, and he was tired and bored. But it had been worth it. Unconsciously, he licked his lips. His bride-to-be was beautiful, young, rich and of the highest rank, so the king had informed him, in person. A forty-pound gift from the royal wardrobe had allowed him to order new clothes, a fine brooch for his mantle, two pairs of soft leather boots – and his hair and beard had been freshly barbered only this morning. Any future clothes he wanted, the king had assured him, would be paid for by Lady Chester.

That the marriage had been arranged by the king with cold impersonal calculation mattered to him not a bit. He put that firmly to the back of his mind. What mattered now was that Eleyne of Chester, and her dower, would soon be his.

He had looked up at the steps of the keep, expecting to see her waiting for him, but two soberly gowned men stood in the doorway. He could see no women at all save the servants who scurried around the courtyard. He scanned the windows in the high wall. She was probably there, peeping, dying to see what her new husband was like. Smiling to himself, he swaggered slightly as he began to climb the stairs.

Stephen Seagrave bowed as the young man came level with him. 'Sir Robert, you are welcome to Chester. I have sent a messenger to inform the countess of your arrival.' He had summed the young man up at a glance: shallow, vain, and probably with an overdeveloped sense of his own worth as a result of his impending marriage. Stephen smiled grimly to himself; the introduction of the bride and groom would be a shock to both.

Robert grinned at him amiably. He accepted a cup of wine and walked into the great chamber, staring around. The king had never said as much, but it was possible, very possible, that when he realised what a worthy young man Robert was, he would elevate him as Earl of Chester and make him lord of all this. Another servant was whispering in Seagrave's ear, and the man's face darkened with anger. Without a word to Robert, he strode out of the hall.

Robert drank his wine and put down the pewter goblet. He walked back and forth a couple of times. Where was Seagrave? And more to the point, where was his bride? He felt his temper rising, he had expected a better welcome than this.

'Sir Robert!' When Seagrave at last returned, he looked angry. 'I'm sorry. It appears that Lady Chester has a headache and doesn't feel able to come down this evening.' He smiled unpleasantly. 'Her ladyship is an arrogant young woman, Sir Robert, used to getting her own way. She is not pleased, it seems, with his grace's choice of husband for her.' His eyes gleamed maliciously and his words were audible throughout the hall.

Robert's mouth dropped open – he was too astonished to speak. Then his face suffused with anger.

'Are you telling me she refuses to meet me?' His voice was very quiet. He was conscious of the men and women around them. In the crowd someone sniggered.

Stephen Seagrave eyed him coldly and Robert received the clear impression that he was enjoying the young man's discomfort.

'As I said, she is an arrogant young woman, with an exaggerated view of her own importance. I feel sure she will benefit enormously from the security and mastery that a strong husband will provide.' He eyed Robert, then looked away with a dismissive shrug. 'She will be at the wedding, Sir Robert, I promise you.'

'I am very glad to hear it.' The suppressed fury in Robert's voice was almost tangible. 'And once we are married, I shall have to teach my wife some manners, which is not what I expected to have to do to so great a lady.' He seized his goblet from the table. 'Wine!' he shouted at the staring servants, 'wine and then supper and tomorrow we have a wedding!'

X

Eleyne was woken next morning at first light and, still in her bed gown, was summoned from the bedchamber into the solar where the fire had just been lit. It flared brightly, without warmth. Stephen was sitting in her chair in front of it and with him were two men-at-arms. Between them stood Rhonwen. There were chains on her wrists.

Stephen squinted up at Eleyne, taking in her long flowing hair, her bare throat and the cleavage of white bosom where she clutched the gown around her.

'Good morning, my lady.' He smiled. 'I have come to wait for you. When you are dressed in your wedding finery, we shall go down together to the chapel where Sir Robert is expecting you.'

Eleyne had gasped at the sight of Rhonwen. 'What is Lady Rhonwen doing here? Why is she in chains?'

Stephen inclined his head. 'Oh come, my lady, you are an intelligent woman. Surely I do not have to spell it out for you? Lady Rhonwen is wanted by the authorities on charges of murder, necromancy and poisoning. She is implicated too, I understand, in the charges against you. I would be doing everyone a service if I hanged her without further delay . . .'

Rhonwen caught her breath in terror and Stephen smiled more broadly. 'Exactly. I *could* be persuaded to spare her life, but only after you have been through the marriage ceremony.'

Eleyne glared at him. 'This is unspeakable —'

'It is your doing, my lady. Had you agreed to obey your king, I should have had no need to use such a lever. Make ready.' He turned to one of the men-at-arms who produced a coil of rope. He proceeded to throw one end over one of the ceiling beams and the other he knotted into a noose. Deftly he slipped it over Rhonwen's head.

Eleyne ran towards him, but the man pushed her back.

'No! You can't do this!'

'I can, my lady.' Stephen narrowed his eyes. 'But I won't, if you obey me. Go now and put on your wedding gown.' His voice had lost its customary quietness and was harsh.

Rhonwen's face was grey; she had not said a word.

Eleyne stared at her in despair, then slowly turned towards the bedchamber. 'I shall expect to see that rope gone and the chains removed before I come back into this room.'

Stephen laughed mockingly. 'I am afraid you expect in vain, madam. The rope will be removed after your vows are made and not before.'

The gown was cloth of silver. She had refused to allow it to be fitted so it hung loosely around her waist, but the effect was one of ethereal beauty as Eleyne walked across the inner court to the door of the chapel where the bishop was waiting to celebrate the marriage.

Her husband-to-be was also dressed in silver, with a scarlet-lined cloak over his mantle. He was indeed tall, taller than Eleyne, and very slim, his dark face austerely handsome beneath a heavy black beard, his eyes a clear nut-brown. He gazed at her for a long minute, his face cold.

'Madam.' He held out his hand. Eleyne inclined her head. Her hand, when she gave it to him, was ice-cold.

The vows took only a few minutes, then they processed into the chapel and stood side by side before the altar. Eleyne was numb. She had looked only once at her husband: his eyes had been alight with greed.

After the mass Eleyne stopped on the steps of the chapel. The procession which had formed behind them stopped too. She withdrew her hand from her husband's arm and turned to Stephen Seagrave, who stood immediately behind the Earl and Countess of Lincoln.

'Send Rhonwen to me. Now.'

Stephen bowed. 'All in good time, my lady . . .'

'Now,' she repeated, her voice icy. 'I do not move from here until she comes to me.'

Robert turned a speculative look on his new wife, but said nothing.

Stephen hesitated. He glanced at Lord Lincoln and raised an eyebrow. Receiving an imperceptible nod, he turned back to Eleyne. 'Very well. It serves no purpose to detain her any longer. Fetch her.' He snapped the order at one of the clerks standing near him.

The procession remained where it was in the freezing November wind. Eleyne was so cold she could barely feel her hands or feet, but still she did not move. Her head held high she stood without looking at her husband. Behind her, the chapel congregation waited, whispering among themselves.

When Rhonwen appeared, the chains had been removed. She was pale but smiling.

'Now. Perhaps we can go in to the wedding feast?' John de Lacy said, his voice pained.

Eleyne stepped away from her husband and kissed Rhonwen's pale cheek. 'Are you all right?'

Rhonwen nodded. 'You saved my life, *cariad*.'

'Yes.' For a moment Eleyne looked at Rhonwen, her face bleak. Then she turned to her husband's side.

The nuptial bed had been set up in the castle's great guest chamber, and there at last Eleyne found herself alone with Robert de Quincy. He had drunk a great deal at the feast and his handsome face was flushed. He had insisted on watching as his wife's gown was removed by Luned and Nesta, and as Rhonwen, tight-lipped, had brushed out her hair. Eleyne had kept on her shift and had pulled over it the velvet bed gown. Now she turned to him; he was still fully dressed.

'Do you wish me to call your servants, sir?'

He smiled. 'There is no need, you can undress me.'

She stared at him. 'Me?'

'Yes, you, wife. You can be my servant.' His voice was insolent. Stephen Seagrave's advice had been clear enough: his arrogant young wife had to be mastered. And if in mastering her he indulged some of

310

his favoured pleasures, so much the better. He would begin at once. He stuck his feet out in front of him as he lounged in the heavy carved chair. 'Remove my shoes first.'

Eleyne hesitated and his face darkened. 'You have just promised before God to obey me, woman. Remove my shoes.'

'I am not your servant,' she retorted hotly, her eyes flashing with indignation. She walked across to the door and pulled it open. 'Call Sir Robert's manservant,' she said to the guard outside. Closing the door, she turned to him. 'Do you know who I am?'

He threw back his head and laughed. 'Yes, you are my wife.'

'I am the Countess of Chester, sir, a title I shall keep until the day I die as you have none to give me.'

The door opened and a man peered around it. 'You sent for me, Sir Robert?'

'No,' Robert leaned back in his chair, 'I did not. My lady wife will wait on me. You may go, Edward, I shall not need you again tonight.' He waited until the door closed, then he stood up. He walked across to Eleyne and stood in front of her, smiling.

She did not see the blow coming. His hand moved so fast she had no time to dodge and his open palm caught her full across the face. He smiled again. 'It seems a pity that the whole castle will see from your bruises that I have had to chastise my wife so soon.' He folded his arms as she regained her balance. 'I understand that woman you summoned after the wedding service is a common murderer,' he went on, his voice very quiet. 'Master Seagrave tells me that if I have difficulty in ensuring your obedience I should give the woman up to the hangman.'

Eleyne gasped and a look of triumph crossed his face. 'My shoes, madam,' he commanded again. He did not sit down and, almost blind with rage, she was forced to go down on her knees to remove his shoes and then his hose. She lifted the heavy mantle from his shoulders and hung it, at his instructions, on the peg on the wall, then she unfastened his gown, hanging the heavy girdle beside the mantle. His chest was covered in black hair and his shoulders were very broad. She felt a catch of panic as he stood before her dressed only in his linen drawers, then – deliberately and slowly – he raised his hand and unfastened the ties that held them up, allowing them to fall.

'Now you, wife,' he said. 'Take off that hideous shift. Let us see what I have got for my side of the bargain.'

Fists clenched, she tried not to look at him as he stood so blatantly before her. There was complete silence in the room, then he laughed. 'Perhaps I should call my manservant to undress you, Lady Chester,' he said quietly.

She closed her eyes and swallowed hard. Somehow she steadied her hands so she could untie the ribbon which fastened her bed gown and let it fall to the ground, then, almost defiantly, she pulled open the neck of her shift and allowed it too to slide from her shoulders. She did not look at him. She felt his hands running over her body; she was completely cold. She allowed him to lead her to the bed and she lay down when he commanded it, and allowed him to force her legs apart without protest. It was as if a screen separated her from her body.

It hurt; it hurt very badly and she bit back her tears, turning her head away on the pillow so that he would not see her face, but it was soon over and he withdrew, leaving her feeling strangely inviolate. He might do what he wished with her body, but he could not reach her.

When he lay at last, snoring loudly, sprawled across the bed, she crawled away and pulled on her bed gown. Then she went to the fire. She was completely numb.

The fire had died almost to nothing – the ashes were white and the log which still burned was sour and smoky with its last heat. Stooping wearily to the pile of wood in the basket, she threw some on. For a moment nothing happened, then the flames began to flicker into life.

A horseman was galloping fast towards her, one hand on the reins, one held out towards her. She heard him call her name.

'Who are you?'

She breathed the words out loud, leaning closer to the fire. Her hair fell across her shoulders.

He was coming closer now and she could almost see his face. He was smiling. 'Wait for me,' he called. 'Wait for me, my love.' She could hear the thunder of his horse's hooves, see the swirl of its caparison, and suddenly she recognised him.

'What in the name of the Blessed Virgin do you think you are doing?' The hand on her shoulder was so heavy she lost her balance and sprawled forward in the hearth. Her husband stood over her, naked, his face white with fury in the firelight. 'Who were you talking to? Who?' She tried to dodge his kick but it struck her thigh and she winced. 'What were you doing?'

She looked up at him through the dishevelled curtain of her hair and saw fear in his eyes behind the anger.

She laughed. 'What do you think I was doing?' she whispered. 'I was looking into the flames to see the future. Scrying. Seeing the outcome of my marriage.'

He licked his lips nervously. 'And what did you see?' In spite of himself, he had to ask.

'I saw death,' she answered slowly and she saw him blanch.

It was untrue. She had seen Alexander of Scotland.

CHAPTER THIRTEEN

I

At dawn Eleyne crept from the bed and went to the stables. The grooms stared at the bruises on her face and were embarrassed as they brought out one of the palfreys for her to ride. She gave Invictus titbits, kissed his nose and left him behind. She knew already she could never let Robert know how much she loved the horse.

She did not see her husband again until supper, when she sat beside him at the high table, sharing his dish as she had shared John's. He appeared to be in high good humour.

'So you rode out without me?' He dabbled his fingers in the silver basin of rose water the page held for him and reached for the napkin. 'Why was that?' His voice was innocently quiet, his face bland, pleasantly interested.

'You were asleep,' she replied. 'I didn't want to wake you.' She waved the page away and signalled for the meal to begin.

He smiled, holding out his goblet for wine. 'In future you will remain in bed until I give you permission to rise. Then we will ride together.'

'If you wish.' She felt her temper flare, but she forced herself to smile back at him. She was not going to defy him before the whole household and give him the chance to rebuke her publicly.

She ate little and drank less, watching silently as he called again and again for wine. The other men at the high table were watching, their expressions inscrutable as they saw Robert's hand waver on the stem of the goblet and tip a few drops of wine on to the table.

'We have musicians with us from Provence,' John de Lacy said at last. 'Shall I ask them to play?'

Robert rose unsteadily to his feet, stared around and then smiled. 'My wife and I are going to bed,' he announced, shaping his words with care. 'You may ask the devil to play for you, if you wish!' He caught Eleyne's wrist and pulled her to her feet. 'Madam.'

Eleyne was calm, conscious that every eye in the crowded great hall was on her. As they walked between the tables to the door at the far end of the hall, a total silence descended on the assembled household.

The bedchamber was dark, the fire banked and warm. Robert

released her wrist and walked to the centre of the room. 'Why is there only one candle?' He sounded peevish.

'They did not expect us so soon from supper.' Eleyne went to the table and touched the candle to the others in the candelabra. As each flame caught and flared, the room grew brighter, though the vaulted ceiling stayed dark. Outside it was bitterly cold; the wind was sighing in the battlements.

'Boy!' Robert bellowed for the servant who had followed them from the hall. 'More lights. I want to see what I am doing!' He threw himself down on the chair by the fire and watched as the boy moved round the room, lighting branch after branch of candles. On the far side of the chamber, the bed loomed dark beneath its hangings.

'Enough. Now fetch a bucket of water.' Robert sounded completely sober.

'Water?' Eleyne echoed.

'Water,' he repeated, and he laughed.

'Why do you want water?' A small unacknowledged knot of fear tightened in her stomach.

'You will see.' He folded his arms.

It was a long time before the boy reappeared, panting, with a large bucket of water. He put it on the floor with relief, slopping some over his shoes. From the door and down the stairs a wet trail showed the way he had come with his burden from the well.

Robert smiled; he did not seem to have grown impatient with the long wait. 'Throw it on the fire.'

'Sir Robert?' The boy stared at him.

'You heard me. Throw it on the fire.' Robert stood up and the boy hastily picked up the heavy pail. Staggering slightly, he carried it to the hearth and tipped the water over the fire, which hissed and died in clouds of steam. Immediately the room began to grow chill.

Robert nodded grim approval. 'Now leave us.'

The boy ran for the door, the pail banging against his knees.

'Why did you put out the fire?' Eleyne kept her voice steady with difficulty. She could feel her anger and fear mounting.

He folded his arms. 'I've done it for your sake, wife. We don't want you staring into the future too often, do we? Particularly if what you see frightens you.'

He began to unfasten his cloak. 'Now, you may remove my shoes, if you please.'

She moved away from him. 'No, I am not your servant.'

'Oh, but you are, if I say so.' He let his cloak fall to the floor. 'Think of the Lady Rhonwen, my dear, with the rope around her neck.' He moved so swiftly she did not have time to dodge. 'I think you have to

314

learn a little about obedience. I think your grand titles have gone to your head! Now, undress me.'

She side-stepped. 'No. You are a knight, sir. You should be undressed by a man, by your squire. Surely it demeans you to be undressed by a woman.' She could not keep the scorn out of her voice.

'Not if that woman is a princess,' he sneered. 'Are you going to do as I say?'

'No.' Even the danger to Rhonwen was forgotten. 'I shall go to my uncle the king. I shall show him what you have done to me.' She fingered her cheek. 'He will protect me.'

Just for a moment he hesitated, then he shook his head. 'You will have to reach him first, my dear. Oh, I want you to see the king; I want you to see that I am given office at court, but first we are going to have to ensure that you have learned to be a good wife.' His voice dropped menacingly. 'Perhaps in future we should see that your bruises are not quite so obvious.' As he lunged, she ducked away, dodging him, hearing his breath rasping in his throat as he spun around to follow her. She threw herself at the heavy door, her fingers scrabbling for the latch. She found it and pulled it half open but he was right behind her and, slamming it shut with his fist, he shot the bolt across. As he gripped her arm and swung her to face him, she caught the full blast of his wine-sodden breath and realised just how drunk he was.

She kicked at him but he ignored her, cursing as he dragged her across the room towards the bed. She fought him but he was too strong for her. He had no difficulty holding her with one hand as he ripped down the ornate woven cord which held back the bed hangings, letting the heavy curtains fall around the end of the bed. He pulled the cord tightly around her flailing wrists and pushed her face down on to the bed, binding the rope again and again around the oak bedpost, pinioning her securely.

He was panting as he stood back to survey his handiwork. Her veil had been torn off in the struggle, and her hair had fallen loose around her shoulders. Looking at her as she lay helpless before him, he smiled again then carefully he drew his dagger. His smile deepened as he heard her frightened intake of breath at the sight of the gleaming blade. He tested it with his thumb, enjoying her fear, then methodically, with exaggerated care, he began to cut off her clothes, reducing gown and mantle and shift to a tangle of brilliant rags.

Satisfied that she was naked, he left her and went to the coffer by the wall. He had obviously put the slender birch whip there during the day in anticipation of this moment. He took it out and flexed it, the smile still frozen on his face. 'Your bruises will be where even the king will not see them, princess mine,' he said softly.

She was helpless. All she could do was bite her lips, so as not to give him the satisfaction of hearing her cry out as he hit her again and again. When at last he stopped, she lay slumped across the mattress only half conscious that he was untying her.

'Are you still going to tell the king?' His mouth was close to her ear; she felt his hot stinking breath on her face. 'If you do, I shall give you Rhonwen's head to take to him as a present.'

Pushing himself away from the bed, he began to remove his own clothes. She raised her face, her hair in her eyes, her face burning in spite of the bitter cold of the room. Her whole body ached, the welts across her thighs and buttocks stung, and she felt the stickiness of the blood from the worst of the wounds, but she was not going to give him the satisfaction of thinking he had defeated her. She dragged herself to her feet as he removed the last of his garments.

'Where do you think you are going?' He was smiling again, naked now as she was, his hands on his hips, his member massively erect. 'Get back on that bed.'

She found the courage to shake her head. 'No.' Her mouth was so dry she could hardly speak. 'No, I will not sleep with you. Get out.' It was not a plea; it was a command.

His face darkened and he stepped forward, meaning to catch her wrist, but she was too quick for him. Her fingers clawed, she dragged them down his face, seeing with satisfaction three ribs of black oozing blood open down his cheek. He let out an explosive curse and grabbed her, throwing her to the floor, then he reached with both hands for her hair. She screamed with pain as he pulled her on to her knees and held her for a moment, her head forced back, before he made her take his red, engorged penis in her mouth. Retching, she clawed at him, blind with fury and disgust, but she could not free herself until, satisfied at last, he pushed her away.

As he threw himself on to the bed, laughing, she crawled to the garderobe and vomited again and again down the latrine hole into the darkness, her naked body ice-cold and sheened with sweat. She knelt there for a long time, her forehead resting on the rim of the cold wooden seat before she found the strength to stand. Her hands still numb from the ropes, she pulled off the wedding ring her husband had given her the day before. She cupped it in her palm, feeling the weight of it for a moment, then let it fall four storeys into the fetid ditch below.

She was shaking uncontrollably as she walked back into the bedchamber. Robert was snoring. She pulled the torn curtain from its hook and wrapped it around her shoulders, then she turned away, fighting back a new wave of nausea. She had time to take only a few steps towards the bolted door before she collapsed on to the stone floor.

316

II

When she awoke, she was so bruised and stiff she could hardly move. The bed was empty; the fire had been made up, and Luned was bending over her.

'Where is he?' As Eleyne sat up a wave of dizziness swept over her.

Luned was tight-lipped. 'I've sent for hot water and salves.'

The smears of blood on the curtain were evidence enough of what had happened. Silently Luned helped Eleyne to wash and anoint her bruises and cuts, then she dressed her in a shift of softest silk before putting on her gown.

'I put the whip on the fire,' she said as she brushed Eleyne's hair.

'Good.' Their eyes met. 'Did you see him this morning?'

For the first time Luned smiled. 'Everyone saw him. He will carry those scars on his face for a very long time.'

III

'You have to go, don't you see?' Eleyne shook Rhonwen's arm. 'As long as you are here he has a hold over me. He can make me do anything he wants. I can't fight him while you are here.'

'The man is an animal!' Rhonwen spat at her. 'He can't be allowed to live! I can get rid of him for you. I can see to it that he dies – '

Eleyne turned away. 'No, that is not the answer.' She pushed away the thought of John dying in her arms; of the empty goblet of dark green, earth-smelling infusion which he had drunk. She could never again allow that suspicion to rise to the surface of her mind.

'Then what shall I do? I have to help you . . .' Rhonwen's eyes were narrow with hate.

'You have to go while I work out how to deal with the situation.' It was too painful to sit down. She leaned against the table, conscious that her sleeves, long as they were, failed to hide the rope marks on one of her hands.

Rhonwen frowned. 'How can you deal with him? He can always resort to violence. That is the only language men understand, and before it we are powerless.'

'I will think of something,' Eleyne said grimly. 'But you must go, don't you see?'

Rhonwen sighed. 'Where?'

'As we planned before. I can give you money – ' Eleyne paused, realising that even that was no longer certain. 'You must go where no one knows you and you can live under an assumed name. I know it will be hard, but you will be safe. I shall obtain a pardon for you somehow, I promise. One thing I know already: my husband longs to have a position in court. Secretly I think he delights in being married

317

to the king's niece, but he will have to take me to the king if he wants preferment.'

Countess Clemence helped her. She had swiftly formed a shrewd opinion of the young man who stood now at Eleyne's side. He was obviously shallow, greedy and vicious and nothing Eleyne told her disabused her of this view. She nodded at once at Eleyne's whispered, heavily censored tale, and said, 'I shall give Rhonwen and Luned money. They can go to London, where I have houses. It is unthinkable that you should be threatened like this.' She frowned, 'Be careful, child. He is a spiteful young man.'

'I'll be careful.' Eleyne took Clemence's hands in hers. 'You have been like a mother to me. I shall miss you so much when we leave Chester.'

Clemence smiled sadly. 'And you have been the daughter I never had. You will always be in my prayers. I don't know what will happen to the earldom of Chester now. I know your husband hopes he will get it through his marriage to you.' She snorted derisively. 'John de Lacy thinks he will be given it too, but I think the king will make the lack of a direct heir the excuse to take the earldom into his own hands. I shall have to move on of course. I'll not stay under this roof with the king's men in charge. I shall go to my own dower lands, and offer a home there to Lady Rhonwen and to your little Luned if they wish it. But in the meantime they will be safe in London.'

IV

The night after Rhonwen had left Eleyne countermanded her husband's order about the fire.

'Leave it,' she ordered as the servant staggered in with the water to douse the flames. 'We will keep a fire tonight.'

Robert frowned. 'I said it should be put out.'

'Not tonight.' She spoke so forcefully that he hesitated and she seized the advantage. 'You may go, take the bucket away. Sir Robert has changed his mind about sleeping in a cold room.' She smiled at the boy, waiting to hear Robert's shout of fury, but it didn't come. He waited until the door had closed.

'You will be sorry you did that,' he said softly. 'I do not expect my wife to defy me.' Three parallel scratches flared angrily on his cheek.

Eleyne had been waiting for this moment, her fear eclipsed by her fury. 'If you wish to sleep in the cold, sir, I suggest you go out to the stable. If you wish to sleep with me, you will behave as a knight and a gentleman. If not, the king shall hear of it. I have already written to him telling him that I am coming to see him. And do not think, sir, that I would be afraid to show the king my backside as evidence of your treatment to me. I will show him every inch of my body if I have to.' The words echoed in the silence.

Robert looked uncertain. 'Are you challenging me?'

'I am telling you how this marriage will be conducted in future.'

'A future without your nurse presumably.' His eyes glittered.

She nodded. 'A future free of your threats. Rhonwen has gone, so has Luned. There is no one here now that I care that much for –' She snapped her fingers beneath his nose. 'If you wish to be a husband to me, sir, it will be on my terms if you hope for a career in the king's service.'

He could of course lock her up and keep her from the king; he could, by law and custom, do anything he liked with her, except actually kill her, but she was fairly sure he wouldn't. He wanted the king's favour, and she was his only route to it.

V

December 1237

When the time came to leave Chester the baggage train was shorter than anything Eleyne was used to. It included her horses, her belongings, her dower plate and bedding, the wedding gifts she had received including two silver basins and a jewelled chaplet from the Queen of Scotland and a tapestry from Arras from her uncle the king. There were only a few servants: Robert announced on the last day that he could afford no more. It was hardly an escort fit for the Countess of Chester.

At least to begin with they were to live at Fotheringhay. Eleyne took comfort from the familiar surroundings, which had seen so much of her marriage to John, but it was small compensation for the misery of her new life. She was trapped. Her dreams had come to nothing. Einion's predictions were so much dust, blown and vanished on the wind. To keep herself sane, she allowed a tenuous thread of hope to remain deep inside her, that Alexander would hear of her plight and find the means to rescue her and declare her marriage invalid – but reality was too pressing and too unhappy to allow her time for dreams.

Robert had not mentioned the missing wedding ring. He had taken note of her threats and ceased his overt tormenting of her, often drinking himself insensible in the hall and sleeping there amongst his companions. But when he was sober enough to come to her room, he took every opportunity to assert his will, and in bed, where she had no choice but to obey him, he hurt her viciously and frequently, never enough to leave a mark, but enough to make her dread each day's end. There was little to distract him save hunting: there was no earldom

319

now, no great estates to administer. Eleyne's dower lands were still the subject of royal enquiry; even the manor and castle of Fotheringhay might be taken from her, though now she had letters confirming that she could for the time being consider Fotheringhay, Nassington and Baddow as part of her inheritance to give her and Robert an income to live. Robert instructed bailiffs in her name to visit them and raise money.

When the chance came at last to ride to London, they both – for their own reasons – seized it with alacrity. The court was at Westminster and Robert's brother, Lord Winchester, had suggested that they join him in the south as the February ice began to give way to the long-hoped-for thaw.

They were guests in a stone-built house in one of the new fashionable suburbs of London south of the River Thames at Southwark and there a letter came for Eleyne. She took it with a glance at her husband, hoping he had not seen it, but he had spotted it at once. The seal was blurred. She could not immediately recognise it.

'A letter, madam,' he said with the smooth smile which she had come to loathe. 'Please, allow me to see it.'

'It is addressed to me, sir,' Eleyne retorted, her voice tight with anger. She saw the raised eyebrows of her husband's family around them and forced herself to smile. 'Come, you cannot ask to see my billets-doux. What would my lovers think!'

The message was from Rhonwen, she was sure of it. Dear God, how could the woman have been so foolish as to send it openly here? It was three months since Rhonwen and Luned had ridden out of Chester Castle into the icy winter's night. They had not been heard of since.

Robert laughed heavily. 'If that is a billet-doux, sweetheart, all the more reason for your husband to see it. I wish to know who your secret admirers are.' Stepping forward he snatched the letter from her hand. She saw his brother's frown of disapproval. The Earl of Winchester seemed to have little time, normally, for his youngest brother and she suspected that their invitation now was due solely to his curiosity about his new sister-in-law.

She glanced at Robert as he broke open the seal on the letter and watched his face nervously as he read the contents. It was several moments before he looked up. Far from registering fury he looked pleased.

'This is from your aunt, the Queen of Scots. She has arrived in London and wishes you to call upon her.'

'Aunt Joanna?' Eleyne was quite unprepared for the jolt of shock and excitement which swept through her. 'And the King of Scots? He is not in London?' She realised it was impossible even as she said it.

320

Her heart had started beating very fast. Terrified he might see the longing in her eyes she looked down at the floor.

'Of course not.' He tossed the letter on to the table. 'The queen has been visiting the shrine of St Thomas at Canterbury, it seems. She is on her way back to Scotland.'

'Then I shall go to her.' Eleyne could not hide the happiness in her eyes. 'It is a long time since I saw Aunt Joanna, and she was so ill then. I shall go today.'

'You will go when I can spare you,' Robert said heavily. 'And then I shall go with you.'

Eleyne stared at him, her heart sinking. 'But, has she asked to see you too?'

'You do not go alone.' Robert scooped the letter off the table and walked deliberately across the small room to drop it on the fire. Eleyne had not had the chance to see it at all.

Lord Winchester frowned. 'You cannot go to see her grace of Scotland, Robert, if she has invited Eleyne for a private family visit. I have heard that the queen's health is still not good. She will not wish to receive you.'

'Then Eleyne must wait until she does.' Robert scowled. 'She will in any case be busy with me at court. We are to call upon her uncle tomorrow.' He had ordered himself a complete set of new clothes at Eleyne's expense: an embroidered, long-sleeved tunic over which would go a rich tabard. With these would go new stockings, cross-gartered in scarlet, and soft shoes buckled in silver. Over the whole outfit he planned to throw a new mantle, lined with miniver. His wife, he had decided without consulting her, would wear her silver gown, something she had not worn since their wedding day, and with it the ornate head-dress that the Queen of Scots had sent her as a wedding gift.

He himself had given her a cloak lined with sables paid for by her rents. It pleased him that it would contrast nicely with his own.

Eleyne did not argue. It did not matter to her what she wore; what mattered was that she should manage to catch the king's ear alone and she was afraid this was almost certain to be impossible. She wanted the king to know what he had done in marrying her to Robert de Quincy and she had to try to obtain the pardon for Rhonwen.

There had been no word from the latter, no clue as to where she and Luned might be staying, and there was nowhere she could send to find out. She did not trust any of the servants now, nor seek to make special friends of them. They all liked her, of that she was fairly certain, but it would not be fair to expose any of them to her husband's vindictive wrath. She had seen him flog a page boy for dropping a basin of water which splashed across his master's shoes. The child had nearly died. If anyone defied Robert de Quincy it could only be his wife, and she defied him, she knew, at her peril.

The Norman Abbey of Westminster with at its east end the new Lady Chapel which housed the shrine of St Edward the Confessor lay bathed in sunshine next morning as the Countess of Chester and her husband made their way to the Palace of Westminster and into the presence of the king. With him was his young queen, Eleanor, and beside her sat the Queen of Scots and Margaret, Countess of Pembroke.

'So, niece, how do you like your new husband?' Henry called out jovially as she appeared. He reached across for the queen's hand. Eleyne, curtseying before him, did not answer. Her face was bleak. 'It is good to see you again, my uncle.'

He frowned with a glance over her shoulder at Robert who had bowed before him with an elaborate flourish. Then he went on. 'As you see, your Aunt Joanna is here. And the Princess Margaret. They especially asked to be here when I told them you were coming this morning.' He smiled across at his sister and then at the woman with whom he had once been so in love.

Joanna looked very pale and tired. Her eyes were full of unhappiness as she smiled at Eleyne. 'I hope you will come and visit me at my lodgings in the Tower, Eleyne. I return to Scotland soon and I would like to talk.'

'I should like that too, your grace,' Eleyned smiled. 'If I can persuade my husband to allow me out of his sight.' She softened the words with a smile but there was no mistaking the harsh note in her voice.

Henry raised an eyebrow. 'I am sure he will allow you to visit whoever you wish, Eleyne.' Not for the first time he felt a twinge of conscience about the way he had hustled his niece into this marriage. He had comforted himself that Robert was a handsome young blade and must be a damn sight better husband than the constantly sick Earl of Chester had ever been, but seeing them together he knew in his heart that was not the case. Robert's obsequious smile did not extend to his eyes, and however smart he looked – the king took a minute to examine the cut of his clothes with a professional eye – he could not hide the unpleasant arrogance of his demeanour, nor the possessive way he now took his wife's arm. Henry's gaze lingered on the place where Robert's fingers crushed the silk of her sleeve.

'I shall require you to wait on me here, Sir Robert,' he said firmly. 'And you will allow Eleyne time to visit her aunt whenever she wishes.'

The gratitude in her eyes did not make him feel any more comfortable.

'Why did you marry him?' Joanna was reclining in her bed, her ladies banished to the far side of the room so she and Eleyne could talk privately.

'I had no choice.' Eleyne outlined what had happened, as her aunt's eyes rounded in horror.

'Alexander knew nothing of this, I am sure of it. When he met Henry at York, they spoke of you, he told me so. He told me Henry said you had agreed to the marriage and were pleased with it.' Joanna lay back and closed her eyes. 'It made him angry that you should be married to someone without title. He said you must have fallen desperately in love with the young man and the king was granting your whim.'

Eleyne stared at her in horror. 'How could anyone think that I would choose to marry Robert?' she cried. 'I hate him!'

Joanna bit her lip. 'I can see you do. Poor, sweet Eleyne. My brother is a fool. Had it been a dynastic marriage no one could have queried what he ordered. But to marry you to a nobody –' She shuddered.

'It was to insult my father.' Eleyne wrapped her arms around herself, cold in spite of the huge fire which burned in the grate. 'I can think of no other reason for him to act so quickly and so cruelly. It made papa so angry.' She shook her head. 'And yet the king allowed my sister, Margaret, to marry the man she loved.'

'I remember,' Joanna said, 'but she obtained a release from him in writing. You told me.' She glanced at Eleyne thoughtfully. 'Do you love someone then, someone you could have married?'

Eleyne could feel the heat in her cheeks. 'No, there is no one I could have married.'

'I see.' It was several seconds before Joanna went on. 'That must make it a little less hard to bear.'

'No, it doesn't. I have to spend the rest of my life with that man; I have to obey him. I have to carry his children!'

It was a thoughtless remark. She knew it as soon as she had said it. 'I'm sorry, I forgot.'

Joanna said, 'I went to the shrine of St Thomas at Canterbury and I have visited the shrine of St Edward at Westminster. I have prayed that they will intercede, as I have prayed to our own Blessed Margaret and to St Bride. I have lit enough candles to bring daylight into the great hall at Westminster Palace!' She smiled wanly. 'One of them will hear me.'

'Of course they will.' Eleyne took her hands and squeezed them gently. 'You are but young still, so much younger than mama when she had me.'

'I am twenty-eight. By the time she was my age your mother already had four children.' Joanna lay back listlessly.

Eleyne smiled ruefully. 'I understand a little. I prayed so hard that I would have John's baby, but it was not to be.'

They sat in silence and, taking a cue from their obvious sadness, Joanna's lady-in-waiting, Auda, moved towards them with her lute and began softly to play.

VII

LORD WINCHESTER'S HOUSE, SOUTHWARK

'So, did you remember your obedience to me?' Robert was standing with his back to the fire, his arms folded across his chest. The servants had left them for the night.

Eleyne was combing out her hair, making the task last as long as she could. 'I tried not to remember you at all,' she said tartly. 'The Queen of Scots and I talked of family matters.'

'And you did not complain to her that I abuse you?'

'What would be the use of complaining?' Eleyne swung round to face him. 'The queen could do nothing. It is her brother, the King of England, who will act if I ask him.'

'But you won't ask him.' Robert's voice dropped to a whisper. 'Will you?'

She held his gaze. 'He is responsible for marrying me to you,' she said softly, almost unaware of the thread of menace in her voice. 'And he is sorry for it.'

He raised an eyebrow, stung. 'What do you mean, sorry?'

'He regrets it already. He has wasted a valuable asset.' She smiled humourlessly. 'But a woman is a reusable commodity. Widowed once, she can be widowed again.'

He went white. 'What are you saying?'

She stared into her mirror, 'I am saying nothing, my husband,' she said slowly, 'except that I could wish for greater happiness in my marriage.'

A petulant frown appeared on his face. 'How can we be happy? You are always fighting me!'

'Because you force me to do things I do not wish to do.'

He glowered at her. 'That is a husband's right.'

'I don't want a husband who enforces his rights. I want a husband who earns them. I want a husband who is considerate. I want a husband who is gentle. I want a husband who is a perfect knight!'

She looked into the mirror to gauge his reaction. Such a speech could earn her a beating or worse, but she saw that he was thoughtful. Her oblique threat had struck home, as had the intriguing idea that he might be the perfect knight! Then his expression closed and she knew the moment had passed. There would be no change in Robert.

VIII

THE TOWER

The Queen of Scots's maid had been gone a long time. When she returned to Rhonwen, she was breathless and her flushed cheeks betrayed that she had wasted several minutes in the narrow stone passage, kissing a handsome squire.

'Her grace will see you now, my lady,' she gasped, straightening her cap. She was enjoying her stay in the royal apartments of the great Tower of London.

Rhonwen gravely followed the girl back up the long staircase and from there she was escorted by Hugh de Gurley, the queen's valet, into the east-facing bedchamber where Joanna lay propped on a heap of soft pillows.

Joanna acknowledged her curtsey with a wave of her hand. 'Have you brought a message from Lady Eleyne?'

'I have not seen Lady Eleyne for many months, your grace.' Rhonwen was holding a box containing gifts: honey and sweetmeats and pastries to tempt the ailing queen's appetite. 'Her husband threatened my life. He used his threats as a lever to force her to obey him. It was a situation which could not continue. I have been living in London in a dower house belonging to the old Countess of Chester.' Rhonwen was studying her carefully, noting with professional interest the pale skin, the dark rings beneath the queen's eyes, her languid movements. 'It is only until Eleyne can reach the king and obtain a free pardon for me.'

'Oh yes, the death of the Prince of Gwynedd's bard.' Joanna lay back. 'We heard about that. I expect Eleyne will petition my brother while she is here.'

'She is here then?' Rhonwen smiled. 'I had heard rumours but I wasn't sure. That was why I begged an audience, knowing she would come to see you if she were in London.'

The queen smiled. 'She and Sir Robert are in Southwark, across the river, staying with the Earl of Winchester. He is our constable of Scotland and will be escorting me home soon.'

Rhonwen shook her head. 'I sent messages to Fotheringhay to tell her where I was, but I doubt they ever reached her.'

325

Joanna nodded. 'She told me something of the marriage. It is not a happy one.' She sat forward suddenly, her eyes alight at the thought of intrigue. 'My lady, if you wish to meet Eleyne safely, then you must come here. The king has told Sir Robert to allow her to visit me alone – Sir Robert seems afraid to allow her anywhere without him in constant attendance. Poor Eleyne, she can't even ride that fearsome great horse of hers. But here at the Tower she can be away from him for a few hours at least.'

Rhonwen smiled. 'That is a kind offer, your grace, and one I accept most gratefully. I've missed Eleyne so much.'

The thought of outwitting Robert de Quincy pleased Joanna enormously and distracted her a little from her lassitude and unhappiness. She reached for the box which Rhonwen had put on the bed, pulling at the pale green ribbons which fastened it.

Rhonwen watched, amused. The woman was a fool, but for the time being she was useful. So for just a while longer her existence could be tolerated.

IX

THE TOWER

Their reunion was a happy one. They clung together for a long time before Joanna's amused gaze, then at the same moment they held each other at arm's length. It was scarcely three months since they had been parted, but it had seemed like forever.

Rhonwen was smartly dressed in a new gown with fine linen gloves which she had tossed on to the table. Countess Clemence had employed her officially as housekeeper to one of her houses in the city and, after the initial shock of settling into the cut and thrust of city life, Rhonwen had begun to enjoy herself running the rambling old building in Chester Court off Gracechurch Street. Away from the protocol of life in the prince's household in Wales, or that of the countess at Chester, she was undisputed head of the house, with freedom to run it as she wished. She did it well and with energy; the only thing which had spoiled her enjoyment was the thought of what might be happening to Eleyne.

'And Luned? How is she?' Eleyne was sitting opposite her, near the fire, beside the queen.

Rhonwen frowned. 'Married.'

'Married? To whom? When? Where is she?'

'To a London silk merchant; last month; she is living in Milk Street. I told her she should seek your permission, but she would have none of it. She told me she would like mine, but if I didn't give it she would go ahead anyway. She was determined to be married before Shrovetide.

She wouldn't wait. They were married on Valentine's Eve. He is a wealthy young man, good-looking in his way, I suppose, and besotted with her. What could I say?'

Eleyne smiled. 'Is she happy?'

Rhonwen nodded. 'Oh yes.'

'Then I'm pleased for her. Tell her she has my blessing. I'd like to see her.'

'Tell her to come to us here,' Joanna put in. 'If she is married to a silk merchant, perhaps we can buy some of her husband's wares.'

X

They met three more times, the last with Luned there, dressed now in clothes finer than those Eleyne wore. Robert, handling the money due to her from her dower, used much of it for his own wardrobe. His wife, he announced, had enough clothes already and, seething with anger, Eleyne had to abide by his decision. She saved her finer gowns for audiences with the king and the Queen of Scots. The rest of the time she had to wear gowns and mantles which were darned.

This last meeting did not go well. Joanna, attended as usual by Auda and the faithful Hugh de Gurley, was sick and fretful and had decided to move on.

'I am going home,' she said, dipping into the new box of sweetmeats Rhonwen had brought her. 'Back to Alexander.' Her eyes strayed to Luned who, as she directed the boys who had accompanied her, laden with rolls of silk, showed as yet no sign of the pregnancy she had excitedly and confidently announced to them all. 'Some of this silk can make me new gowns to please him at the Easter celebrations at Dunfermline.'

'These are the latest designs, your grace.' Luned smiled with professional pride. 'Straight from the looms of some of our best weavers, and you will find none better. Even the Queen of England has not seen them yet.'

Eleyne touched the silk gently and found herself smiling at the irony which had just dawned on her. She would not be able to afford Luned's wares.

The queen bought four dozen ells of silk and at once she presented two dress lengths to Eleyne. 'A gift from your uncle and me,' she said.

Eleyne examined the stuff in delight, fingering its featherlight texture. Joanna had given her one of green, spun with madder thread, and one of scarlet samite.

Rhonwen joined her to admire them. 'I'll take them and turn them into gowns for you, *cariad*,' she said softly. 'If you take them home,

327

your husband will probably insist on having them made into tunics for himself.'

Eleyne hid a smile; the same thought had occurred to her. 'Would you, Rhonwen? No one makes gowns like you.'

Rhonwen nodded, pleased. 'I have two first-rate dressmakers in Milk Street. They will sew to my direction, and they embroider as well as I do. Come to me in three days and you can have a fitting.'

'I'll find a way of getting there,' Eleyne agreed. 'In this case the truth will do: I am to visit a dressmaker. Once the gowns are made he cannot unstitch them!' She hugged Joanna. 'You are so kind. When will I see you again?'

Joanna thought for a moment. 'Come to us in Scotland. Your husband was often at Alexander's court with his brother; persuade him to come again. Lord Winchester holds many lands in Scotland, and I am sure there are reasons why you could come north.' She smiled wistfully. 'I know Alexander would love to see you.'

There was a short silence. Eleyne could feel her cheeks colouring and quickly she turned away to watch the silk boys refolding the lengths of fabric and wrapping them. 'Then I shall come,' she said at last, her mouth dry, 'of course I shall.'

XI
THE PALACE OF WESTMINSTER

'So, you want a pardon for this murderess.' Henry sat back on his chair of state and belched reflectively. 'She must mean a great deal to you.'

The Earl of Winchester and his brother had left the hall to view some new horses of the king's. She had hung back and begged her uncle to listen to her plea.

'She was put in charge of me by my mother, sire. She has looked after me since I was born. She killed poor Cenydd in self-defence – in my defence.'

Henry frowned. 'I am not sure that is the story I heard.'

'Then you were not told the truth, sire. Had you been fully informed, you would already have pardoned her,' Eleyne pleaded. 'I need her, your grace. I do not have many friends or servants in Robert de Quincy's household.'

She held his gaze and saw him shift uncomfortably in his chair. He had ordered the marriage of several lords at court to foreigners from his wife's entourage, and that action too had earned him nothing but hatred and anger. He set his mouth in a stubborn line. 'You are not complaining of my choice of a husband for you, I hope.'

'Of course not, sire.' Her face was as stubborn as his. 'But I am sure that you will allow me the company of the Lady Rhonwen in the life you have chosen for me.'

'I suppose it would be all right, if it will make you happy. Very well. I can't believe the woman is a danger to anyone else. Come next week and I shall have a pardon drawn up.'

'Could you not do it now, my uncle?'

He shook his head testily. 'No, I could not. Now go, go with your husband before I change my mind!'

XII

Robert made no difficulty three days later when she announced that she was going out. He had been summoned to the court with Lord Winchester to attend the king and was anxious to leave at once.

The house in Chester Court was just off Gracechurch Street. It stood end on to the narrow, dark alley, but behind the high gates it was large and rambling. Fully occupied only once or twice a year in the past when Countess Clemence had visited London, it had remained empty for several years now as her increasing age prevented her from travelling. Rhonwen ran it with a well-trained, obedient staff and lived in more state than Eleyne had enjoyed on her last visit to Fotheringhay.

The gowns were hanging in a large airy bedchamber which looked out on a small central garden with gravelled walks and formal rose beds. The two dressmakers were waiting, and Rhonwen was smiling. Eleyne had told her the news of the pardon and she could not contain the elation which had swept through her.

The fittings took only a short time. Rhonwen had remembered Eleyne's measurements with complete accuracy, but she scowled at the amount of weight Eleyne had lost. 'You are like a starving waif, *cariad*.' She took Eleyne's hand gently. 'You are not ill?'

'No, of course not. I'm never ill, you know that.'

'Then you are still unhappy?'

'Of course I am unhappy! What do you expect? Oh, he doesn't beat me any more; he doesn't force me to do anything I don't want.' She gave Rhonwen a rueful grimace. 'But that is because he has no lever to use against me now; and besides, he wants me to help advance him with the king. He would do anything for that.'

'But you would rather be in Scotland.' Rhonwen said the words so quietly that the dressmakers could not hear them.

'Rhonwen, I have told you –'

'Tschk! I know what you told me, but you are no longer married to that milksop earl! He is gone. Your heart is free to go where it wishes.'

'It does not wish to go anywhere, Rhonwen.'

'I think it does, *cariad*. And I think you will soon have your heart's desire.'

XIII

Thursday 4 March 1238

Four days later Eleyne presented herself before the king wearing one of her new gowns. When Robert had seen it, he had gone white with anger.

'Where did you get the money for that? Sweet Christ's bones, do you think you still live in the style of your former life? You will bankrupt me, madam.'

Eleyne refrained from mentioning that her husband's mantle was also new, the third she had seen since they had arrived in London, and that the money for it came from her coffers.

'It was a gift, sir,' she said with a cold smile, 'from the Queen of Scots.'

'Indeed. In that case I suppose we must be thankful for her generosity.' He scowled with bad grace and was still scowling when they arrived at the Palace of Westminster.

This time he could not speak to the king alone, and she was acutely conscious of Robert at her shoulder when she asked her question. 'The matter we spoke of last week, your grace. Do you have it for me?'

Henry looked at her, his expression puzzled. 'What matter, niece?'

'The pardon, sire.'

'The pardon?' He rubbed his cheek with the back of his hand. 'Ah, yes, the pardon. I have had no chance to think about it, ask me again next week.'

'But your grace —'

'Next week!' He squinted up at her. 'I have not decided yet whether I am going to grant the woman a pardon at all. I have to make enquiries . . .'

Eleyne was speechless for a few seconds. 'But you promised —'

'I did not promise anything, Lady Chester.' He emphasised the formal address. 'I shall think about it. Next week.'

Out of the corner of her eye Eleyne saw that Robert was frowning, his mouth tight with anger. 'But, my lord king, uncle, please listen —'

'Leave us!' Henry snapped so loudly that men and women below the dais fell silent and stared up at the group of figures around the king's high seat. He turned to a messenger who had just come in. 'Well, what is it, man?'

Eleyne was dismissed. She drew breath, stunned by his betrayal, but the gasped message of the man who had dropped to his knees in front of the king stopped her short as she turned away.

'It is the Queen of Scots, sire. She is dying!'

Henry rose. 'What did you say?'

'Your sister is dying, sire! She was to have left for Scotland today, but she was taken ill in the night. This morning she went into a convulsion and now she lies near to death.'

'No.' Eleyne's whispered protest went unheard.

The king looked at the messenger as if he could not understand what the man was saying. 'My sister?' he repeated under his breath, 'Near to death? But how? She was well. She came to bid me farewell only two days ago. She was to take messages from me to the King of Scots. I gave her gifts −' He shook his head, trying to absorb what the man had said. 'Are there physicians with her?'

'Yes, sire.'

'And don't they know what is wrong? Can't they help her, for Sweet Christ's sake!'

'They say she is beyond help, your grace. Only divine intervention can save her now.' The messenger crossed himself, and the king and those around him followed suit.

'I must go to her.' Eleyne was one of the first to recover from the shock. 'Please, uncle, let me go to her now.'

He nodded vaguely. 'And I. The queen and I shall go to her bedside. Poor Joanna −'

At a run Eleyne threaded her way down through the crowded hall to the door, leaving Robert standing at the king's side.

The huge courtyard was milling with people and there was no sign of the de Quincy horses. She saw two knights riding in through the main gateway, both mounted on high-stepping horses, fresh from their stables. Gathering her new scarlet skirts above the mud, she ran towards them.

'Please, sirs, will one of you lend me your horse and the other ride with me to the Tower? It is a matter of life and death.' Her hand was already on the bridle of the horse nearest to her.

The man gaped at her, then his face broke into a grin. He didn't know this vision in scarlet, but the huge green eyes and beautiful face were enough. 'Of course, my lady. For you, anything!' He slid from the horse and handed her up into the high saddle. 'Escort the lady wherever she wants to go, Edmund,' he called to his companion. 'If she wants to ride to furthest Cathay itself, take her there with my blessing!' He swept a low bow.

Eleyne touched her hand to her lips, automatically reacting to his handsome good humour, but already she was kicking the horse out past the king's guard towards the bridge over the Tyburn away from

331

Westminster, towards the City of London. Edmund cantered at her side. 'Sir Edmund de Merton, at your service, my lady,' he called. 'May I ask what quest we ride on so frantically?'

'The Queen of Scots is dying,' Eleyne cried. 'She is my aunt and I love her.'

Sir Edmund kicked his horse to keep up with her, but she had drawn away from him, urging her mount through the traffic of wagons and carts which thronged the road. He found it hard to keep up, but when at last they reached the Tower he was still at her side. Eleyne threw herself from the horse. 'Thank you.' The smile she turned on Edmund as she flung the reins of the borrowed animal at him was so full of sadness that he stood still, stunned. Then she was gone.

Joanna lay in the darkened room, surrounded by her servants. She was completely still, seeming barely to breathe beneath the velvet bedcoverings. The men and women around her stood back as Eleyne approached the bed on tiptoe and took Joanna's hand. It was cold.

'She cannot hear you, my lady,' Auda whispered through her tears as Eleyne breathed Joanna's name. 'She is sinking fast.'

'But how? Why? How can she be dying?'

An old man in the black robe and carrying the staff of a physician stepped forward.

'The queen has been ill often, my lady. She has a fever in her womb. It was that condition that deprived her of children and it was to cure it that she made her pilgrimage to Canterbury. It seems,' he crossed himself, 'that it was too late even for St Thomas's intervention.'

'But she was better, she told me she was better.'

'She told you what she hoped, my lady. She could not accept the truth.'

Joanna died as the early dusk fell across the city beyond the high walls of the great castle. The king, her brother, Queen Eleanor and Eleyne were at her bedside, with her entire household ranged behind them. Most were crying softly, but Joanna knew nothing of it. Her life slipped away so gently that for a while no one realised she had gone.

On the table beside the bed stood a small empty box. The length of green silk which had tied it lay beside it, in a dust of sugared crumbs.

XIV

SOUTHWARK

'You deceived me!' Robert lifted his hand again and struck her across the face. He had come to her room soon after their return from Joanna's deathbed. 'Running to the king and begging for a pardon for that woman! How dare you defy me! Do you wish to make me a laughing stock?' He raised his hand again.

Eleyne faced him, her eyes blazing. 'Rhonwen is my servant. My nurse. If I chose to speak to the king about her it is none of your business.'

She broke off as with a sharp slap his hand connected once again with her cheekbone. 'I will not have her in my house,' he said through gritted teeth.

'May I remind you that the houses we live in are none of them yours, sir.' She moved out of range, her back ramrod stiff. If he hit her again, she knew she would hit back. 'This house is your brother's. Fotheringhay is part of my dower. You married me with nothing but a wagonload of goods and four servants. The church, even the king, may give you nominal rule over me, husband, but God sees what you do. He judges!' She put the length of the oak table between them. 'You abuse your power over me, you squander my dower and now you dare to question my dealings with my uncle, the king. The king you hope to serve!' She leaned forward, her fists on the table. 'I have only to say to the king that you are unfit for royal service and he will send you to the farthest ends of his kingdom.'

Robert paled, but he managed a thin smile. 'If he does, you will come with me, wife.'

'Nothing would give me greater pleasure. I love the wild places, remember? The forests and the mountains are my home. The gods of those places protect me.' To her great satisfaction, his face grew whiter still. 'If we are tied together for eternity in hell, husband, it is I who will thrive,' she went on relentlessly. 'I love the fire and I love the ice! Wherever hell is it will be my home and your downfall!'

Outside the door Nesta and two serving boys stood, their ears to the thick oak panelling. Nesta held her breath, waiting for his retort. None came. Robert tried to shrug nonchalantly as he threw himself down in a carved chair.

'I wonder if the king knows he married me to a she-devil,' he commented at last.

'Oh, he knows.' Eleyne pressed her advantage home. Her hands were shaking and she kept them on the table to steady them. Her eyes were emerald green in the candlelight. 'And he hears every time you strike me, every time you squander my inheritance, every time you abuse my servants, and he waits.'

'He won't dare to harm me. He needs my brother –'

'And he is afraid that your brother's allegiance may go to Alexander of Scotland.' Eleyne hid the wave of grief which threatened to make her voice waver. 'Which it may. Do you think marrying you to me has had any effect on Roger's allegiance either way? Give your brother more credit than that.'

'Ssh!' Robert looked helplessly towards the door.

'I won't ssh! Not now, and not when I next see the king. Not if you persist in your foul treatment.' Eleyne left the table and walked towards him. In her scarlet gown, over which she had thrown a black mantle as a symbol of mourning for her aunt, she looked very determined and very beautiful. She stopped near him. 'And don't think you can stop me seeing the king. He will ask for me if I do not go to the palace.'

'I wasn't going to.'

'If you want to succeed at court, husband,' she went on without pausing, 'you have to keep me content, or I swear I will bring you down.'

'And if I keep you content?' His eyes narrowed, and there was a sarcastic edge to his voice.

'Then maybe you will find your fortune at King Henry's court.'

XV

The body of the Queen of Scotland was taken to the abbey at Tarrant, to which she had bequeathed it in her will, and there laid to rest with great ceremony beneath a marble tomb made in haste by Master Elias of Derham at Salisbury. Two days after her death two prisoners were released for the sake of her soul, by her brother, King Henry. On 13 March sixteen silk cloths of Arras were delivered to offer with the body of the king's beloved sister, together with silk and gold clothes worth thirty-five shillings each. Wax candles were to burn before her tomb forever. Her husband, the King of Scotland, did not come south for the funeral.

XVI

Lady Day 1238

'The king still has not given me the pardon!' Eleyne, swathed in her sable mantle, had fought her way out of the gale and was standing in the hall of Rhonwen's house. 'I have asked him a dozen times, but he claims he is too grief-stricken by Joanna's death to conduct any but the most urgent business!' She threw down her cloak and walked over to the fire. 'It makes me so angry. He has but to tell a clerk to write it and affix his seal. It would take him no more time than it takes to draw breath.'

Rhonwen stood near the hearth, her hands pushed into the sleeves of her mantle.

'And you, *cariad*? Are you too grief-stricken by Joanna's death to do anything?'

'I am upset, of course I am. You know how fond I was of her . . .'

'But not so fond as you are of her husband. Why deny it? Your aunt is dead. He is no longer your uncle. There are no blood ties now to make your love a sin.'

Eleyne was shocked. 'You shouldn't say such things. Suppose someone heard you?'

'There is no one to hear, nothing but the wind rattling in the hangings. Your destiny lies in Scotland. Remember Einion's words. Your future does not lie with that spoiled brat who is your husband; it lies with kings.'

Eleyne stared down at the fire. There was no denying the tight knot of excitement in her stomach. 'If I could go to him . . .'

Rhonwen asked, 'Who better to take the king's condolences to his brother-in-law?'

'But Robert would come with me.'

'You would need him there, *cariad*, to avoid a scandal. Once there he can be distracted – or disposed of.'

Unbidden the image of a trailing length of green ribbon came to Eleyne's mind, the ribbon at the bedside of the dying queen. After it flashed the image of the earth-green medicine which had stood beside John's bed as he too died. Her eyes on Rhonwen's, she tried to read the woman's mind. Was she capable of such cold-blooded murder? She was deeply afraid as she stared at her nurse's face. Rhonwen met her gaze and held it steadily. Her expression was impenetrable but there was a pitilessness there which repelled Eleyne. But it wasn't true, Rhonwen would never do such a thing; she couldn't. A picture of Cenydd floated into her mind; quickly, she suppressed it. That had been a terrible accident; they had struggled in the heat of the moment. It was not calculated, it could never have been calculated. Even to think it was a vicious calumny and a projection of her own secret wish for Robert's death.

She watched as Rhonwen took the chair opposite her, arranging her skirts with meticulous care. The moment had passed.

'I won't be able to come with you, *cariad*. If asking for a pardon causes trouble between you and the king, it is better forgotten for now. I am content now I know how you are. Leave me here. Seek the king's permission to ride north. Go to Alexander. I will come if you need me.'

XVII

It was so easy in the end. The king agreed that Eleyne should be the official carrier of his condolences; and Robert was to go with her. They set off into the teeth of a violent March gale, a party of some two dozen riders and ten sumpter horses, splashing through the mud, forcing their way against rain and sleet on the long ride north.

Alexander was in Edinburgh. He received Robert and Eleyne on a grey afternoon when snow still whipped through the air, clinging to their eyelashes and freezing their gloves to the reins of their horses. Edinburgh Castle, high on its rock, was cold and draughty, the huge blazing fire in the great hall roaring towards the darkness of the sky far above. The king, a black cloak over his embroidered tunic, rose from the table where he had been poring over a pile of letters with a group of his advisers.

Eleyne stopped so suddenly that the servant behind nearly bumped into her, and she realised that her heart was thumping fast as she watched him walk to the edge of the dais.

'Lady Chester, Sir Robert, greetings.' His tone was formal.

Beside her, Robert had stopped too, taking his lead from her. She forced herself to walk on towards Alexander, her head high, her eyes on his. At the edge of the dais she curtseyed low. 'We bring you the King of England's greetings and condolences, sire. He was – we were with your queen when she died . . .' Her voice trailed away and there were tears in her eyes.

Alexander stepped from the dais, took her hand and raised her to her feet. 'I'm glad you were there. She always loved you, lass. It was good of you to make the long ride north.' He smiled at Robert and bowed. 'And you, Sir Robert.' He looked at him, perhaps a moment longer than was necessary, then he turned his attention back to Eleyne. 'Come, sit by the fire and take some refreshment. Tomorrow we ride to Dunfermline to prepare for the Easter celebrations, and there I can make you welcome in more style.'

XVIII

DUNFERMLINE CASTLE

It was two days after Easter before she saw the king alone, five days and nights of tormented, sleepless anguish as she tried to hide her hopes and fears from her husband and even from herself. Alexander was in his office at Dunfermline with three of his clerks when he sent for her. As she curtseyed to him, her heart thudded with fear and excitement. She took the proffered chair and he ordered the three men from the room.

On his desk a small coffer lay open, and she could see that it contained jewellery. He leaned against the desk, his arms folded.

'Joanna made her will twelve days before she died. She wanted you to have something to remember her by. I have chosen some rings and chains which I thought you might like.'

She had dreamed so often of being alone with him, but now she could think of nothing to say. She was drowning in his presence, aching for his touch, yet this small casket of jewels stood between them like a stone wall. They represented Joanna and guilt.

She bit her lip. 'Thank you, sire, that would please me very much.'

'Come here and look at them.' He had not moved from the desk.

She moved numbly towards him. The coffer was in the middle of the desk; to reach it she had to lean past him.

'Do you wish me to choose something, sire?'

'They are all yours. Here, let me try some of them on.' He pulled out a ring of garnets and sea pearls and held it out. She gave him her hand, holding her breath as he placed it on her finger. His touch burned her skin like fire.

'Are you happy with your new husband?' he asked quietly, his concentration entirely on her hand.

'No.' She did not elaborate.

'You married him against your will?'

'Yes.'

'I cannot believe the fiery Lady Chester allowed such a thing to happen.' His lips twitched into a quizzical smile.

'I had no choice, I was forced. By the King of England's order.' She looked into his face, unaware of the transparency of her expression. It was all there for him to read – hope, fear, love, longing, frustration and the blind resolution that he should see none of them. 'They told me that you agreed.'

'I was not consulted. Henry told me he had arranged a suitable match for you and that you were pleased with it. We were at York –'

'And you did not wish to jeopardise the treaty with England.' Her voice heavy, she pulled her hand from his. 'And women's lives are of so little importance.'

'That is not true, Eleyne. You had enormous wealth, it was important that you marry –'

'Why? To give my wealth away? To allow a thriftless callow nobody to run through it, spending a fortune on tabards and herygouds and embroidered garnaches to decorate his person while his wife wears darned gowns, cuts the number of courses at meals by half and can find no money to pay her servants!' The colour had risen in her cheeks. 'I shall have to ask you to tell my husband, sire, that you have given me these jewels or he will take them from me to pawn or sell. He would have taken the material Aunt Joanna gave me for new gowns had I not sneaked it away to be made up before he could lay his hands on it.'

337

Alexander stared at her. 'I am sorry, his brother is made of finer stuff.' He walked across to the window; unglazed and unshuttered in spite of the cold, it looked south across the Forth, which gleamed brilliant blue in the icy sunshine. In the far distance was the grey of the Pentland hills, and towards the east the humped shoulder of Arthur's Seat, brooding next to the black silhouette which was his great rockbound castle at Edinburgh. When he turned, he had control of his anger.

'Come, see what else I have for you. Joanna would want you to look at them.' He cursed himself for speaking her name, but knowing he had to. 'I shall speak to your husband. He will not take anything from you again.' There was an underlying note in his voice which made her look up, startled. What she saw in his face brought the colour flooding to her cheeks.

'Your grace –' Her voice was breathless. Without realising it, she had taken a step towards him.

For a long time he looked at her in silence without moving, then at last he reached towards her and pulled her into his arms. His mouth was hungry as it found hers, his grip fierce, imprisoning her so tightly she couldn't breathe. She didn't want to breathe; she wanted to cease to exist and find herself in eternity. She wanted to melt into him as the cold winter snow melts in the blazing heat of a summer sun. She could feel her body quivering with longing, her hips pressing shamefully against his, her breasts aching for the touch of his hands. She did not think of John or of Joanna. She did not think of Robert. This man was her whole world, her whole existence, her destiny.

Still he had not spoken, nor did she want him to. She did not want words to come between them.

Almost without realising it she was pulling at the fastenings of her gown, offering him her throat, her breasts, gasping as he reached greedily for her nipples. Then he was wrenching her garments from her shoulders, stripping them down, so that she was naked as he bore her to the floor, dragging at his own gown so that flesh met flesh without impediment.

She clung to him, pulling him on top of her, wrapping her legs around his hips, feeling him thrusting inside her with a force which was as agonising as it was exquisite.

When her pent-up excitement was released in a long animal howl of triumph, the king put his hand across her mouth. He smiled down at her, his eyes silver slits. 'You'll bring every guard in the castle to us if you scream,' he said softly, his voice husky with passion. He dropped his mouth to her breast and she felt her breathing quicken again.

'What if someone comes in?' she gasped. She could not have pushed him away if she had wanted to. Her whole being had fused with his, cleaving to him as though it had found a part of itself.

'No one will come in,' he said softly. Easing his weight slightly, he rested on his elbows, staring down into her face. Then he knelt up, sitting astride her, keeping her imprisoned between his thighs, his gown rumpled around his hips. He groped above his head on the table and brought his hand down laden with jewels from Joanna's casket. As Eleyne gasped at their coldness, he festooned her naked body with golden chains and precious stones, nestling a circlet of pale river pearls in the silken hair which covered her most secret place.

'Sweet Virgin, lass, but I have wanted you for so long,' he murmured at last. He stroked her face. 'Since I first laid eyes on you.'

'And I you.' She gave a languid smile. Her body seemed to be cushioned on air; she was floating on contentment. 'Have we done wrong?' She felt no hint of conscience or shame.

'How could it be wrong?' He narrowed his eyes. 'My wife is dead, and so is the husband you loved.' He paused. 'Your present husband –'

'Means nothing.' For the first time her voice was sharp. 'I was meant to be yours. Even John . . .' she hesitated, then went on, 'even John told me to come to you.'

'Had you been free now, I could have made you my queen.' He stroked her belly almost absent-mindedly, resting his finger thoughtfully on the trinket he had pushed into her navel. 'Queen Eleyne. You would give me sons, lass, wouldn't you? Bonny, strong, healthy sons.' He leaned down and kissed her lips fiercely.

'I would give you anything.' She smiled up from beneath her lids. Everything was what she meant, everything.

Neither of them reacted immediately to the knock on the door, then abruptly the king rose. 'Wait,' he shouted as he adjusted his gown, pulling the heavy folds straight. Eleyne lay still at his feet, half smiling as the firelight played across her body. The king laughed. 'Up you get, lass, or I'll be asking my clerks to step across you to write my letters.'

She narrowed her eyes. 'Would they enjoy that, do you think?'

'No doubt, but I would not.' He stooped, picked up her gown and tossed it over her. 'Hurry, there is much to be done and you are distracting me shamefully.' His voice was stern but his eyes, she checked quickly, were still laughing. She scrambled to her feet and pulled her clothes on, dropping the jewels one by one back into the casket. Her body was languid; contented. For the first time in her life she felt complete.

XIX
DUNFERMLINE CASTLE

Robert found the casket of jewels that same afternoon, concealed in one of her coffers. He picked it up and opened it, pawing over the gems. Then he turned to her. 'Where did you get these?' His face was sharp with suspicion.

'They were bequeathed to me by my aunt.' She took the box from his hand and put it down on the table next to her mirror.

'So many?'

'She loved me and she had no children of her own.' She was hugging the memory of the king's lovemaking to her, conscious of the feel and smell of him still on her body.

Robert, suspicious, sensed the change in her. 'Where did you get them?'

'From the king.' She met his gaze with wide-open challenging eyes. 'And in case you are thinking of selling any of them they are all listed and recorded.'

'Part of the Scottish inheritance, no doubt,' he said softly. His gaze sharpened. 'Your gown is torn.'

'Is it?' Without thinking she put her hand to her throat.

He smiled. 'Your lover perhaps? Too eager, was he?' He was not serious. He was taunting her as usual; even so she felt her colour rise.

'You talk nonsense.' She turned from him, but he caught her arm.

'I may talk nonsense, wife, but you will take heed of what I say,' he said quietly. 'I think you should change your gown before supper, then perhaps you can wear some of your newly won finery.'

'I will change when Nesta comes up.' She stepped away warily.

'You will change now.' Without fully realising it, he could smell the sex on her; it excited him and he felt himself growing hard. She was beautiful and proud, not bothering to hide the disdain she felt, so her subjugation would be all the more enjoyable. He wanted her on her knees, taking him in her mouth, her fury and humiliation burning in her eyes. And here he could force her to do it – she was far away from King Henry; her threats to tell him would mean nothing. She was in his power and he could do what he liked with her.

He turned the heavy iron key in the lock.

CHAPTER FOURTEEN

I

DUNFERMLINE CASTLE ❖ June 1238

'We are going to Falkland.' Robert stood in front of his wife, hands on hips. 'As the guests of the Earl of Fife.'

'No.' Eleyne shook her head. 'That's not possible; the king would not allow it.'

'Because he is so fond of your company?' His voice dropped, heavy with sarcasm. 'Do you think I don't know what is going on? Do you think anyone in the castle doesn't know? You behave like a strumpet, you flaunt yourself when you're near him –'

'That's not true!' Her moment of panic had vanished. In its place came the cloak of frozen dislike which cocooned her whenever her husband came near her. 'How can you say such a thing when my aunt is scarcely cold in her grave?'

'Exactly, your aunt. I am sure the king, your uncle,' he emphasised the word carefully, 'will give us leave to go to Falkland.'

'I think you must go.' Alexander put his hand gently to her face. 'He is right, people are noticing. How could they not when I follow you around like an adoring puppy, fawning in your lap?' The firelight played softly over their skin, softening and blurring the shadows over the curves and angles of their bodies as they lay in one another's arms on a pile of furs before the fire. 'Besides, I neglect my kingdom shamefully.'

'But I can't leave you . . .'

'You must, just for a while.' He raised himself on his elbow and pulled her face towards his, kissing her fiercely. 'Do you think I want you to leave me? Do you think I can bear the thought of you in your husband's bed when you should be in mine?'

He ran his hands down her body, tasting, devouring her flesh as she lay quivering beneath him, her thighs parting slackly at the command of his questing fingers. It was several minutes before she could speak again.

'You could send him back to England –'

'Aye,' he smiled. 'Maybe I'll do that. Send him on his way and volunteer to take care of you myself.'

'Then I needn't go to Falkland?' She arched her back, throwing back her head so her hair trailed across the furs in a gesture of abandoned sensuality. 'I needn't see Lord Fife again?'

The king raised his head, his eyes narrowed. 'You are not still afraid of Lord Fife?'

She could not explain the strange dread she felt whenever the man came near her. 'Not as long as I have your protection.'

'Sweet Eleyne, you have my protection – and he knows it. And,' his voice became stern, 'while you are at Falkland you will have your husband's as well.'

II
FALKLAND CASTLE ❖ June 1238

Falkland Castle stood on the central plain of Fife in the shadow of the Lomond Hills. The great fortress of the Earls of Fife boasted a vast circular tower, a hall, a chapel and numerous other buildings within its high curtain wall.

It was three days before the Earl of Fife managed to find Eleyne alone on her way back from the stables, where she had been looking at his horses.

'So, my lady, I think you have been avoiding me.'

'Lord Fife.' Eleyne looked round swiftly. Her ladies had moved on out of earshot, chattering amongst themselves.

'I have not congratulated you on your new husband.' He raised an eyebrow. 'Or should I perhaps commiserate?'

She straightened her shoulders haughtily: 'I don't understand you, sir.'

'Don't you? Well, remember, if you need a man, a young man –' he paused for a fraction of a second, allowing the weight of innuendo to fall on the penultimate word – 'to champion you in any way, I am at your service.'

Her eyes sparkled with anger. 'If I need a champion, Lord Fife, I already have one to serve me.' She tried to keep her dislike of him from her voice.

He bowed. 'Then I shall bide my time. You may yet call upon me one of these days. Meanwhile, you will be pleased to know that the king will be my guest for the first hunt of the season on Midsummer's Day. We have some fine harts here in the forest of Falkland.'

He had not come near her but she felt his eyes moving over her body, devouring her greedily, touching her with all the intimacy and

342

hunger of a lover. Neither of them moved then, with a bow, he left her staring after him, her heart heavy with foreboding.

For the hunt on Midsummer's Day, Eleyne wore her gown of silver samite and a mantle of dark green silk, her hair bound beneath a veil of finest gauze. She was to ride a milk-white palfrey, caparisoned in blue and silver, a present from Lord Fife. She had not wanted to accept it, much as she loved the horse on sight; but Robert had insisted. Ever greedy, he had calculated the horse's value – at least forty pounds, he reckoned – and he had accepted for her.

As she curtseyed before the king, she was conscious of a hundred pairs of eyes watching her from the crowds who mingled around them at the start of the day. Alexander touched her hand and smiled gravely. They had gathered to breakfast beneath the trees at the edge of the forest. As soon as the huntsmen had located the first stag they would be off, the king with his nobles at the head of the field. Eleyne intended to be at the front with them. As the king moved off, young Robert Bruce approached Eleyne, his grey eyes full of mischief. He bowed low. 'Mama sends you greetings and best wishes from Lochmaben, Aunt Eleyne.' He emphasised the title gravely. 'She misses her visits to you at Fotheringhay.'

Eleyne had torn her eyes from the king with difficulty, but Robert's charm was irresistible. 'You must stop calling me Aunt Eleyne,' she scolded, 'I'm younger than you, Rob!'

'Rubbish! You're a hundred years older!' Robert bowed again, his eyes teasing. 'Unless of course you can prove you're not by being in at the kill.'

John's handsome nephew had been named by King Alexander as heir presumptive now John was dead, and was frequently to be found at court near the king. The realisation that Robert and his sons might be the future of Scotland had given Eleyne a pang of misery when she first realised the significance of Robert's new status, but that had not changed her liking for him.

She laughed. 'I'll be there, nephew,' she said, 'have no fear on that score!'

A fine linen tablecloth had been spread on the ground for breakfast and, as they all followed the king's example and sat down around it, Eleyne was conscious of her husband at her side. He was sitting so close that he was crushing her gown. She pulled at it, irritated, and heard the fabric rip slightly in her hand. The king was talking to his neighbour on the other side and didn't notice; nor did Lord Fife who was standing on the far side of the cloth, frowning slightly as he checked the preparations for the hunt.

Seeing her restlessness, Robert moved closer to Eleyne. 'We ride together,' he said quietly. 'At the back of the field.'

She was furious. 'Why?'

'Because I say so. I have no desire to ride with the king.'

'Well, I have. I am never at the back of the field, never.' Again she tried to rise, but he was pinning her down. 'You can't make me ride at the back. Everyone would think there was something wrong with me.'

'Something wrong, because you choose to stay with your husband?' he mocked. 'I think you will find that the ladies of the court,' he paused significantly, 'will be rather pleased to see you playing the obedient wife, for once.' He reached forward for some wine.

Eleyne waited, impotent, as one by one the members of the party rose and went to find their horses. She gazed longingly at the white palfrey which was standing with Robert's beneath the trees at the edge of the clearing.

When at last the king rose, he turned to her and smiled. 'Are you accepting any wagers this time, my lady? On who will be first at the gralloch?'

'My wife is going to follow at the rear of the hunt today, sire.' Robert stood up and pulled Eleyne to her feet. He kept a firm hold on her arm.

The king was concerned. 'You are not ill . . .'

'No, she is not ill, merely content to ride with me.' Robert met the king's eye, then he looked down. Alexander raised an eyebrow but said nothing. She stared after him in disbelief. Surely he wouldn't leave her without another word?

It was Lord Fife who intervened. He stepped across the cloth, pulling on his gloves; it was obvious that he had heard the exchange. He gave her a conspiratorial wink. 'I trust you like your horse, Lady Chester?' he said loudly. 'He is one of the best in my stable, and I beg leave to ride with you as you test his paces. I am sure Sir Robert won't object – a host's privilege.'

Eleyne pulled her arm from her husband. 'Thank you, my lord, I accept your offer gladly.' She shot a venomous look at Robert and stepped away from him. Any escort was better than her husband, and Lord Fife would, at least, keep up with the best.

'You like him?' As they trotted side by side up the grassy ride, Malcolm of Fife looked across at her horse. The gelding was a high-stepping, showy horse, with flowing mane and tail. He carried his head proudly, as if aware of the beauty of the woman on his back, aware too that she would be more than a match for him if he chose to show his paces. 'I called him Tam Lin.'

She was intrigued in spite of her antipathy to the man. 'That's a strange name.'

Fife's handsome face lit out of its usual sulky expression. 'After the elfin knight, who rode a milk-white steed. But you must call him whatever you wish.'

Eleyne shook her head. 'Tam Lin it shall be.' The huntsman's horn rang through the trees. 'They've found the stag. Now we shall see how this horse can run.'

They had killed four times by evening and riders and horses were tired as they rode back into the courtyard of Falkland Castle. Eleyne was riding between the king and the earl, ecstatically happy; it had been a wonderful day. Lord Fife had remained at her side, but they had been close to the king for much of the time and both men had flirted with her – complimenting her, teasing her, giving her all their attention. She had not seen her husband for several hours. Dismounting, she gave Tam Lin a hug, then she turned to the king who was watching her, amused.

'Do you always kiss your horses with such passion, lass?' he asked humorously.

'If I like them.' Throwing her veil back, she stretched her arms above her head to ease her stiffness, a gesture of sensual abandonment which occasioned a few raised eyebrows among the court ladies dismounting near them. They had missed no detail of Lady Chester's day; seen every look and smile the king and the earl had thrown her. 'I love my beautiful Tam Lin,' she went on. 'Lord Fife gave him to me. Aren't you jealous that I should get such lovely gifts?'

'Indeed I am, I shall have to watch my Lord Fife, I can see.' The earl was talking to the huntsmen and for a moment the king's voice grew serious. 'Can it be that you have got over your dislike of the man? Perhaps I should ask him to visit some far outpost of my kingdom while you are in Scotland.'

'He could take my husband with him,' Eleyne agreed.

People were crowding around them; someone slapped the king on the back. The huntsmen were carrying in the carcasses; Eleyne was separated from Alexander and turned happily towards the castle. There would be feasting in the hall that night, but first she wanted to change her gown. There were tears where Robert had sat on it, and others where she had galloped through the trees, veil and skirts flying, in pursuit of the king. She had been beside him at the first kill.

Nesta was waiting for her in the bedchamber, a jug of hot, scented water standing on a trivet over the fire ready for her to wash. To her relief, there was no sign of Robert. She stepped out of the ruined gown as Nesta poured the water into a bowl.

'Will you be able to mend it?' As she bathed her face and neck, she saw the maid gather up the gown and fold it over her arm.

'I expect so, my lady, I've never failed you yet. Your scarlet is waiting for you –' Nesta broke off as the door opened and Robert

345

walked in. He surveyed the scene as Eleyne straightened, the warm water running down her throat and arms, soaking into the low-necked shift, which was all she wore.

'Out.' He gestured at Nesta with a jerk of his head. Nesta curtseyed and scuttled past him, leaving them alone.

'You disobeyed me and made me look a fool before the whole court,' he said slowly.

Eleyne eyed him defiantly, still standing over the basin, her damp hair curling over her shoulders. 'If you looked a fool, it was because you could not keep up,' she said coldly. 'If you had been at the front, you would have been at my side.'

He smiled. 'Next time I shall ride the grey, then perhaps I shall be well enough mounted. And if I don't like the animal, I shall have it knocked on the head.' Her face went white. 'Oh, I heard how you flung your arms around the horse's neck. The whole court makes sport of your love of the creature.' He sat down astride the chair which stood by the table, his arms folded over the high back.

'Why do you wash in your shift?' He changed the subject abruptly. 'Such modesty seems odd in such a forward woman. Take it off.'

'We are expected at the high table –'

'And we will be there. We don't want to disappoint our host or his king, do we?'

She looked at him warily. 'Then I should dress . . .'

'Soon. First, take off your shift. Think of the horse, Eleyne, it would be sad, wouldn't it, to kill such a beautiful animal?'

She knew what he would do. He would humiliate and degrade her, then he would beat her. Then with exaggerated politeness, he would help her to dress. It had happened too often. She knew it excited him to think he was her master, but not this time. She stepped back from the basin of cooling water and reached for the towel which Nesta had dropped on the bed.

'If you touch that horse, I shall tell the king what you do to me,' she said desperately, 'and he will have you killed. Don't think he hasn't thought of it already –' She saw his face blanch. 'You are in his way. It's only my pleading which has spared you so far.' Her fear for the horse had given her strength. She stepped towards him and was pleased to see him flinch. 'If anything happens to Tam Lin, anything at all, if he so much as gets a stone in his hoof, I shall know who to blame.'

'The king wouldn't dare to harm me, an envoy from England –'

'An envoy? I was Uncle Henry's messenger, not you! You are no envoy.'

His eyes narrowed triumphantly. 'That is where you are wrong: I carried the letters from King Henry, I have the official safe conducts to travel north, and I serve as one of Henry's officials.' He smiled at the expression on her face. 'You didn't know that, did you? And if I am killed by the King of Scots, or anyone else in Scotland, Henry will want to know why. And your Alexander's precious peace will not be worth a farthing bannock! No, King Alexander can't touch me, Eleyne. If he could he would have done it already.' He folded his arms. 'And you know it, sweetheart, or you would have crawled to him before now with your list of complaints. Do you want to be responsible for a war between England and Scotland? Do you want the whole world to know that the King of Scots commits incest with his niece? Do you know the penalty for incest, wife, if the church finds out?'

Eleyne's mouth was dry, her defiance had crumbled into ashes. 'I suggest that we get ready for the feast,' she said tight-lipped, 'this conversation gets us nowhere.'

'It gets *you* nowhere.' He pushed himself from the chair and before she could turn around his hands grasped her wrists. She fought frantically, but as always he was much the stronger. He bound her hands behind her back with her own girdle and forced her to her knees. Then he undressed. As always, her mute fury and the fear in her eyes excited him. By the time he was ready for her he was enormous.

Her bruises, as he had promised, were all hidden as she walked at his side into the great hall and took her place at the king's side. Her face was pale, but she managed a smile. On her right, Robert was wearing a gown of stiffly embroidered black silk. He was looking immensely pleased with himself as he raised his first goblet of wine. Before the meal was half over he lay sprawled across the table, his head amongst the dishes.

The king glanced past her and raised an eyebrow. 'Your husband seems to have caroused too much. Shall I have him taken to your chamber?'

'I think fresh air would do him more good,' Eleyne retorted tartly. She had hardly spoken all evening.

Alexander beckoned attendants from the corner of the dais. 'Take Sir Robert to the courtyard and leave him to sleep it off under the stars,' he directed. When they had gone he turned back to her. 'Did you not enjoy the hunt?'

'I enjoyed it enormously.' She wanted to throw herself into his arms; to cry, to beg him to help her, to show him her bruises and wait while he stormed outside to kill Robert with his own hands. But she had to be calm. She could not risk two countries going to war because her husband beat her, nor could she risk, ever, the chance of Alexander's being excommunicated – or worse.

Alexander put his hand over hers. 'I must talk to you later, alone. Your husband is too drunk to know or care what we do –'

'No!' her cry was almost frightened, and she saw him frown. 'No,'

347

she repeated more softly, 'not here. Falkland is too public, there are too many eyes. Everyone will know –'

'I suspect everyone knows already, sweetheart,' Alexander smiled, 'but they indulge their old king by turning a blind eye.'

III

The castle was asleep when the king's servant knocked softly on the stout door. He whispered to Nesta, and Nesta tiptoed to Eleyne's bed. Eleyne was lying awake, trying to ease her painful body on the mattress. Outside the night was luminous, barely dark, though it was long after midnight and she had left the bed curtains undrawn.

'The king wants you,' Nesta whispered importantly. She put her candle down beside the bed, picked up Eleyne's velvet bed gown and held it up. At last the king would see the poor lady's bruises: he could hardly miss them this time. He had tipped her and tipped her well to act as a messenger between her mistress and himself since the beginning of their stay in Scotland, and she was happy to do her best to help Eleyne. Like all the Chester servants, she had a low opinion of Sir Robert.

Eleyne was tempted to send a message to say she wasn't well, but her longing for him was too great. Wrapped in her gown, a candle in her hand, she followed the king's servant on tiptoe to the state bedchamber, which was almost next to their own. A fire had been lit there, in spite of the warmth of the night, to take the chill off the stone of the room, and the king sat beside it in the light of a single candle. As the servant pulled the door shut, he rose and held out his hands. They did not speak. She clung to him, her face buried in his chest, and it was several minutes before he realised that she was crying.

'Eleyne?' He held her away from him and looked down at her face. In the shadowed candlelight he could hardly make out her features, but he felt the hot tears as he touched her cheek with his forefinger. 'What is it, lass?'

She did not trust herself to speak, just wanting to feel his arms around her again, but he held her away firmly. 'Tell me!' His voice was sharper, full of anxiety.

'I can't, it doesn't matter. As long as I'm with you.'

'It does matter, Eleyne. I've never seen you cry.' Abruptly he released her. He turned to the table and taking the candle he used it to light half a dozen more so that the shadows drew back and he could see her face more clearly. He swore softly and took her in his arms again. 'Has that bastard de Quincy hurt you?'

She nodded. 'It doesn't matter, I'm used to it –'

348

'Used to it?' His whisper became a roar. 'By Christ I'll make him sorry he was ever born! I'll have his head on a spike on –'

'No, no! Please, you mustn't! You can't.' She was sobbing openly now. 'Don't you see? He has threatened to tell King Henry of our affair; he has threatened to tell the church that we commit incest.' Her voice broke and she flung herself down on her knees on the cushions he had thrown ready for their lovemaking in front of the hearth. 'He says it would lead to war,' she went on, 'Uncle Henry would make it the excuse to invade Scotland. Oh my dear, don't you see he's right, we can do nothing.' Knuckling her eyes, she rocked back and forth on her knees.

'He overestimates his importance,' the king said succinctly.

'I know, but at the same time he's right. Henry could make it an excuse to cause all kinds of unpleasantness. Oh, please, don't you see . . .'

Alexander stared down at her, his fury tightly in check. All his instincts told him Robert de Quincy had to die, but she was right. Above all, the king was a statesman and Scotland must come first, even before this beautiful wild creature whom he loved, as he had at last acknowledged to himself, almost to distraction.

He knelt beside her and pulled her against him, gentling her sobs, then slowly he kissed her on the lips. She responded, unable to resist the longing which his kisses kindled, allowing him to pull off her bed gown. She heard him catch his breath as he saw the bruises on her buttocks and she felt his fingers tighten on her shoulders until she cried out with pain.

'It doesn't matter, love,' she whispered. 'Nothing matters as long as I still have you.' She put her arms around his neck, pulling him down towards her. 'If harm came to Scotland because of me, you would grow to hate me. I could not bear that to happen. Leave it, my love.' Her tongue was in his ear, fluttering down his jaw line, dipping, seeking the small erect nipples hidden in the golden chest hair where she was pressing her face as his gown fell open.

The firelight made a golden halo of his hair. Smiling up at him, she lay back on the cushions, pulling him with her, holding his head in her hands, bringing it down to her breasts, wanting to lose her pain and fear and humiliation in the golden, worshipping body of the king. She gasped as his lips caught at her nipple, teasing it, sucking, and her body arched towards his from the soft pile of cushions.

She flung her head sideways, staring at the fire, unseeing, turning inwards, feeling only the growing rush of pleasure as it built towards its crescendo and final explosion.

The horseman in the flames was riding fast, his cloak streaming in the wind, the lightning flashing in the flaming logs which framed the picture, the banner above his head a roaring, ramping lion. He was riding too fast, not able to see the rough track beneath the horse's feet, unable to steady the animal, not caring, urging it faster, faster still, laughing exultantly into the rain . . .

'Eleyne, what's the matter?' The king's voice was sharp. Just as her body seemed ready to crest into a climax, she had become still, withdrawn, almost as though she no longer knew he was there. He felt the heat leaving her skin beneath his hands. Around them the room had grown cold. 'Eleyne!' He knelt up, cupping her face in his hands. 'What is it? Where are you?' Fear knifed through him.

She stared at him blankly as he knelt over her, her mind still with the galloping horseman, then she glanced back at the fire. But he had gone. The flames had died, leaving a red, glowing bed of ash as the logs collapsed into cinders.

Alexander followed her gaze, the hairs stirring on the back of his neck. 'You saw something in the fire?' he asked sharply.

She nodded, shaking violently. 'Don't be angry.'

'Why should I be angry?' He sat up and pulled one of the rugs around her shoulders before reaching for his own gown.

'What did you see?'

'A man. Riding.'

'Who?'

She shrugged. 'I never see his face.'

'You've seen him before?' He felt her fear.

She nodded miserably. 'Several times. And I've seen other things.' Suddenly she didn't want to have any secrets from him. 'I saw Hay Castle when it burned; I saw my father's illness. Once when I was a child I saw the massacre of the Druids on Môn.' She stopped abruptly. There was someone in the room with them. The temperature had dropped so sharply she could see Alexander's breath as a cloud in the air between them. Two of the candle flames paled and smoked and went out, leaving a trail of acrid blue smoke.

She saw the king look round as he felt it too. His face was white. Silently he rose and reached for his mantle. From its folds he produced a dagger and pulled it from its sheath. But the shadowy bedchamber was empty.

'Einion –' She had whispered without realising it, searching the shadows, her fingers clamped into the rug she was holding around her shoulders. Her part in Scotland's future, if she still had a part in Scotland's future, had been Einion's secret and Einion's vision. He had seen her at a king's side; he had seen her as the mother of a line of kings. Unconsciously she put her hand to her stomach beneath the thick folds of the rug.

'What is it?' Alexander's whisper was harsh. He had backed towards

350

the wall, lightly hefting the dagger from hand to hand, his eyes everywhere, his whole body poised for attack.

Eleyne shook her head. 'It's nothing, it will pass . . .'

'Nothing! There was someone here –'

'Yes, my lord, and he has gone.' Eleyne smiled wanly. She was still trembling.

'You spoke a name.'

'Einion. He was my father's bard. It was he who taught me to look in the fire.'

'Sweet Christ!' Alexander peered around the room again. The remaining candles had steadied, and the strange unnatural cold, the cold of the grave, had lifted. Still holding the dagger in his right hand, he pulled his mantle over his shoulders, then he bent and threw a couple of pine logs on the fire.

'So. My Eleyne is a seer.' His voice was carefully neutral. 'And protected by the spirits of the dead.' Behind him the logs spat blue sparks up the chimney.

'No, it's not like that. He wants to tell me something –'

'He wants to tell you something!' Alexander sheathed the dagger in his belt and threw it back on the stool. He folded his arms across his chest. 'He doesn't choose his moment with any tact, this bard of yours, does he?'

Eleyne gave a wry smile. 'I'm sorry.' She leaned past him towards the rugs and pulled another around her shoulders. 'Do you hate me now?'

'Why should I hate you?' He was recovering rapidly. 'There are seers in Scotland, it's a gift of our people as it is of yours. You met Michael.' He put his arm around her shoulder. 'But you're afraid.'

'I can't control the visions and I can't understand them. This one,' she flung her arm in the direction of the fire, 'it's a warning, I know it's a warning. But of what? Who is he? Who is it I keep seeing? That's why Einion came. He wants to help me understand.' There were tears in her voice.

He pulled her against him. 'Perhaps it was me you saw?'

The lion flag; the billowing streaming standard. Was it the standard of the king? Perhaps. But the shoulders of the man in the cloak, the angle of his head – she did not recognise him. 'I would know if it were you, my love,' she whispered. 'I am sure I would know if it were you.'

IV

It was still early when the king summoned Robert de Quincy to his bedchamber the next morning. The ashes of the fire had grown cold many hours before, and the candles had burned down into pools of wax. There was no trace of the strange coldness which had permeated the room. The two narrow windows let in broad slashes of early sunlight which spilled across the floor and lit the far walls.

Robert's head was pounding and his tongue felt like old leather as he stood before the king. He had drunk so much the night before, his mind was a blank. He looked at the king warily, wondering why he had been summoned, but Alexander's face gave nothing away as he stood with his back to the empty hearth. He had seen to it that they were alone. The young man's face was the colour of cold lard, but his eyes, small, brown and intense, were confidently insolent.

Alexander flexed the joints of his hands together, then he smiled. And for the first time Robert felt a quiver of uncertainty.

'You are a messenger of the King of England,' Alexander said at last.

Robert nodded, watching the king's face cautiously, but Alexander's expression remained unreadable.

'I have messages for my brother-in-law of England,' the king went on, 'which I should like you to deliver without delay. You will ride south this morning.'

'But, sire –'

'You will leave your household here, Sir Robert, to allow you to make best speed, and you will – you must – reach Westminster by the feast of Peter and Paul. I know I can rely on you.' He had given him four days to reach London.

Robert narrowed his eyes, wishing his brain was thinking more clearly. His wife . . . she was behind this. She and her kingly lover wanted him out of the way.

'Eleyne must go with me, sire –'

'No, Sir Robert.' The king folded his arms. 'Your wife would be safer here. No harm will come to her while you are away.' Something in the way he said those words made Robert's hair stir uneasily on his scalp. So. The bitch had told him, and no doubt shown him her bruises. He shook his head, trying to clear it. Last night, before he had drunk all those jars of Gascon wine, what had he done to her? He shuffled his feet. No more than usual, no doubt.

'You need me here, your grace,' he said slowly, allowing a slight undertone of menace to enter his voice. 'Eleyne cannot stay here alone.'

'She'll be safe here,' the king repeated.

'She won't be safe from scandal. And the condemnation of the church.' Robert forced his lips into a leer. 'You, as a king and a widower, may be beyond the reach of either, but she isn't.'

Alexander clenched his fists. 'There will be no scandal, Sir Robert.' He paused. 'There would be even less chance, of course, if your wife were a widow, but I am sure it will never come to that.' He held Robert's eye and saw the young man flinch. 'And do not be misled into believing that your death would cause an incident of any importance,' he went on relentlessly. 'The King of England needs peace with Scotland as much as Scotland needs peace with him. The death of an unimportant messenger on some lonely moor at the hands of a few footpads would not even occasion an exchange of letters.' The king took a step forward. 'I shall not expect replies to my letters from King Henry. Do I make myself clear?'

V

Lord Fife was waiting for him as he walked towards the great hall, the king's pouch of letters dangling from his hand.

Fear and anger were still vying for priority when he found himself confronted by his host and drawn into a private corner. 'Is he sending you away?' Lord Fife wasted no time on formalities.

Robert raised his chin slightly. 'He has an urgent message for the King of England. I am the only one who can be trusted with it –'

Fife laughed. 'And he has got his way. You will be in England and Eleyne will be in Scotland – alone.'

Robert glowered. 'What is that to you?'

Lord Fife shrugged. 'Nothing, but I dislike seeing our sovereign make a fool of himself. He must be detached from her somehow. Why not order her to remain here at Falkland? I'll look after her if you give the word.'

'Against the king's wish?' Robert could not keep the scorn out of his voice. 'You think he would quietly ride off and leave her, even if you dared to defy him?'

'Oh, I would dare.' The expression in the earl's eyes was formidable and Robert felt a moment of unease. He scrutinised the other man's face, trying to read his meaning.

'You are going to do it anyway,' he said at last, astonished at the ease with which he could read the man's mind. 'You are going to keep Eleyne here, and tell the king she's gone with me. That's it, isn't it? You want her for yourself!'

The earl smiled grimly. 'I wouldn't do anything to anger my king, Sir Robert. Believe me, I would do nothing to anger my king.'

Lord Fife was waiting in the stables when Eleyne went to Tam Lin. She did not see him until it was too late. As she entered the stall and began to make a fuss of the horse, the shadow of his stocky figure fell across her.

'So, my lady, my gift still pleases you.' The earl smiled. He was very

353

close to her and she could not back away because of the wooden partition in the stall.

'He pleases me enormously, my lord.' She turned to face him, her hand still caressing the horse's soft muzzle. The wonderful feeling of release she had experienced as Robert rode away with his escort of two companions was still with her, but she eyed Malcolm uneasily. 'I'm very grateful.'

'How grateful?' He lowered his voice. 'Your affair with the king can't go on, my lady,' he said gruffly. 'You must know that. Already it is being talked about. The king has to marry again. He has to get an heir . . .'

Eleyne had gone cold. 'I don't know what you're talking about,' she retorted. 'What I do is none of your business. Nor is anything the king may choose to do!'

'Oh but it is.' Malcolm's voice was silky. 'I am the most senior earl of the kingdom, and the king listens to my advice. It will be my honour and my duty one day perhaps to crown Alexander's son. Don't demean yourself, Eleyne, you are worth too much. Come away with me –'

She stared at him in fury. 'How can you suggest such a thing? Never!' She ducked under Tam Lin's head so that the horse was between them.

'Aunt Eleyne?' The voice from the end of the stalls made Malcolm swing round with an exclamation of anger. Young Robert Bruce was standing there, hands on hips, a quizzical smile on his face.

'Rob!' In relief Eleyne moved towards him. 'Lord Fife was just looking at Tam Lin again.' Flustered, she clutched her nephew's arm.

He grinned. 'His grace the king is asking for you, Aunt Eleyne. I think he plans to ride out with his hawks.' He bowed gravely to the earl.

Malcolm glared at the young man, then he smiled. If there were no royal son, young Robert Bruce might one day be his king. Better keep him sweet. He could wait for Eleyne of Chester.

VI

Robert de Quincy slowed his horse and looked across at his companions. They had been riding hard at his insistence and the horses were blown. As the road climbed high over the Pentlands and dived down into the Ettrick Forest, they drew rein.

Robert reached for the wineskin at his saddle bow and raised it to his lips. 'We'll be at the border by nightfall.' He passed the wine to James Comyn. 'Then we'll stop and think this through.'

'Think what through, my friend?' James asked 'You have to get the king's letters to Westminster fast. There's nothing to think about there.'

'No?' Robert reached for the sealed letter pouch and felt it thoughtfully. 'Alexander wants me out of Scotland, and these are his excuse. I doubt if they are important. I'm tempted to turn back.'

'Then you're a fool, man.' James handed back the wineskin and gathered up his reins. 'And I for one don't intend to be there if you do!'

The road dipped from the moorland into thick woods and the air grew oppressively still. Robert reached for the wine again, allowing his horse to pick its way after its companions, the reins lying loose on its neck.

The men were waiting for them in the shadows of a thorn thicket, their drawn swords gleaming in the stray rays of sunlight. James Comyn did not stand a chance – before he could draw his weapon the sword had entered his stomach beneath the ribcage and he had slumped to the forest floor. John Gilchrist fared little better. He drew his sword and had time to flail it wildly around his head with a cry of 'footpads' before he too fell from the saddle. The two riderless horses thundered away up the grassy ride.

Robert, terrified, hurled the wineskin in the direction of the robbers and lashed his horse's sides. The animal bolted back the way it had come and within minutes he was lost in the forest.

It was a long time before he brought the fear-crazed horse to a halt. He listened intently: the silence of the broad forest rides and the narrow deer trods was total. There was no sound of pursuit. Whoever had lain in wait had been content with his two companions, at least for now. Sober and scared, Robert looked up for the sun and turned his weary animal once more towards the south.

VII

STIRLING CASTLE

The news that the bodies of James Comyn and John Gilchrist had been found, robbed and mutilated, in the Forest of Ettrick hit the country with a wave of shock. As did the news that there was no sign of Robert de Quincy, who had been with them. The king received the news in silence, then gave orders that the robbers be found and dealt with. Holding up a king's messenger was a serious offence. But the robbers were not found and there was no news of Robert.

They spied on her the whole time: the women of the court, the servants, the king's advisers, even his friends. Each time she went to his chamber she felt their eyes upon her from every doorway and window squint; each time he summoned her to his private rooms she

355

sensed ears at the keyhole, and heard the chain of gossip as it flew around the castles of the king.

She walked proudly, ignoring it, her eyes deliberately ahead, but she was deeply troubled. She wanted Robert dead – in the depths of her soul she wanted him dead. But to wish him dead was a sin. How could her happiness with Alexander be based on that? She did not let herself wonder whether Alexander had arranged the murder. If he had it was as great a sin for him. She prayed, but her prayers always ended with one petition. 'Please, sweet Blessed Virgin, Blessed Bride, let Robert de Quincy be dead.' If Robert were dead, she would be free to marry again and her husband would be a king. The matter was now urgent, for she had begun to suspect as the weeks passed that she was pregnant.

She was never completely alone; her servants were always with her. They slept in her chamber at night, they followed her by day; when she was summoned to the king, it was by one of his attendants. And now more than ever she needed to be alone. She wanted the chance to see into her future. She could not bear the suspense; could no longer tolerate her position. She had to know. Was the destiny Einion had predicted hers at last? Was she to be the next Queen of Scots, in spite of the opposition to her? For there was opposition. It wasn't only the Earl of Fife who did not want her to be queen. The Earl of Mar, the Earl of Buchan, the Earl of Dunbar, and of course the Constable of Scotland, Robert's brother, Roger de Quincy, were all adamant that when the king remarried – and for Scotland's sake that had to be soon – it could not be to the Countess of Chester. Too much doubt and jealousy and scandal clung to her now, and how could the king marry a woman whose husband might still be alive?

Her nights in Alexander's arms were a haven, but never once did she dare to ask him what was to happen, and never once did he give her any sign. Together, in silence, they waited for news of her husband. Until it came, they could do nothing. And still she had not told him her secret.

VIII

John the Baptist's Day, 29 August 1238

They were at Scone again. The hot muggy August days stretched out and thunder was never far away. The beautiful old palace of Scone lay in a heat haze. It was very silent in the king's rooms where Eleyne lay in Alexander's arms. They were both naked.

The knocking on the door was quick and urgent. Alexander sat up and frowned. His servants had orders that he was never to be disturbed when he was alone with Lady Chester.

The knocking was repeated, light, so as not to be heard far away, but insistent.

Pulling on his gown, he went to the door and unbolted it. A shadowy figure waited outside in the dark corridor. The king heard the whispered message and scowled.

'I have to go, my love.' He was dressing swiftly. 'But wait here, I'll be back soon.' He knelt and put his hand on her breast as she lay sleepily where he had left her. 'Lock the door behind me.'

She needed no second bidding. Her hands were shaking as she struck flint to steel and coaxed a spark into the fire laid in the hearth. It had not been lit for days and the kindling was dry as dust. She had no herbs to conjure up the scented smoke. This time she had to do it alone.

Kneeling before the flames, still naked, she waited impatiently for them to heat and steady, emptying her mind, seeking the pictures she knew would be there.

Outside footsteps approached up the stone-flagged passage. She held her breath; they came nearer – she heard the double beat of the heavy boot, heel and toe, and then the jarring metallic ring of the long spurs. They reached the door and paused, then they moved on. She closed her eyes with relief.

The future, her future, her destiny. Would she marry the king? Was the child she was now certain she was carrying going to be the heir to the throne of Scotland? She had to know.

Show me, show me the future. She knelt closer to the fire, her hands outstretched. *I must know.* Her eyes were reddening; sore and dry from the heat. The sweat was pouring down between her breasts, and her fingertips tingled warningly. 'Please show me,' she begged out loud.

Were the flames condensing into a picture? She leaned closer, her hair falling forward over her shoulders, her bare knees on the sprinkling of broken twig and bark which lay in the hearth.

There, against the grey stones of the chimney, still cold and impervious to the new heat, was that a picture? 'Einion, help me! Tell me what is to happen!' She shook her head to clear her eyes. 'Tell me my future.'

The flames crackled up merrily, devouring the dry sticks, licking at the log which lay ready to heat the room on the first cold night. Outside, the sunlight had turned coppery; thunder rolled around the Perthshire hills.

She did not hear Alexander's soft leather-soled shoes. His knock was imperious. 'Eleyne, open this door!' For one long moment she remained where she was, kneeling before the empty flames, then she rose to her feet.

357

Alexander stared at her and slammed the door behind him. 'Never, *never* open the door with no clothes on again. Supposing someone had seen . . . Eleyne, what is the matter? Why in the name of all that is holy have you lit a fire?' He strode over and kicked at the logs, scattering them. Then he turned. 'You were looking into the future?'

She was still standing by the door, her long hair curling down over her breasts, her hands and arms streaked with wood ash and soot. Her eyes were red.

'Or were you summoning the dead?' His face darkened angrily. 'Is that it?'

She was frightened. 'No, I was trying to see . . . to see the future . . . I needed to know,' she finished in a whisper.

'You needed to know. What pray did you need to know?'

'What will happen.' She looked at him in anguish. 'It was prophesied by Einion Gweledydd that I should be the mother of a line of kings. I had to know,' she rushed on. 'I had to know when. We always thought he was speaking of my marriage to John.' She took a deep agonised breath. 'But that wasn't to be. And now . . .' Her voice faltered to a halt.

'And now,' he echoed.

She saw the vivid blaze of his eyes and suddenly she was reminded of John. How he had looked when she had told him the same thing. She put out her hand timidly and touched his arm. 'Is Robert dead?' she whispered.

He nodded.

'You gave the order?' she forced herself to ask.

'I gave the order.' He spoke heavily, staring down at the remains of the smouldering ashes. 'God forgive me, I gave the order. I had to have you. Sweet Blessed Christ, I had to have you for my wife!'

Eleyne clenched her fists. Her breath was coming in tight, painful gasps. 'I'm carrying your child, my lord.' She hadn't meant to say it like that – straight out.

'Are you sure?' Words he had spoken before, to his wife, but this time he already knew the answer. The curves of her belly, the full breasts, the slight broadening of her hips: the signs which he had subconsciously noticed and enjoyed without realising their significance.

'I'm sure.' She spoke in a whisper.

'Sweet Jesus! how long I've waited for this moment!' He took her in his arms, her soft white body crushed against his robe. He threaded his fingers through her hair and gently pulled back her head, raising her lips to his.

'You will marry me? You will have to marry me now.' She arched her throat to his kisses, feeling herself growing weak, as always at his touch.

'Yes,' he breathed, 'I'll have to marry you now.'

'And Robert?'

'Robert is dead, I told you.'

He was pulling at his clothes, pushing her down, his mouth on hers. She shut out the shiver of unease his tone had brought. She had always known that Robert would have to die to set her free.

She lay back beneath him, her lips against his, her mind spinning out of thought into animal sensation. If this was the will of the gods, if this was her destiny, who was she to feel guilt at the death of one man?

IX

LONDON ❖ September 1238

The River Thames lapped greedily against the wall, small wavelets slapping at the stone, teasing the weed and rubbish which floated there. It was full high tide. The messenger drew Robert de Quincy into a dark corner in the angle of the Water Gate Tower and the wall and glanced over his shoulder before he put his mouth to Robert's ear.

'Your wife is with child by the King of Scots.'

Robert's eyes widened. 'Who told you?'

The stranger shrugged. 'I was told to tell you. It was the king who tried to have you killed. They think you're dead and that she is free to marry him.'

Robert put his hand to the throat of his new gown and shivered. 'How do they know it's the king's child?' he blustered. 'It might be mine.'

'Then you must claim it.' The man eyed him insolently. 'If you dare.'

Robert's mouth was dry with fear, but a slow steady anger churned in his stomach. How dare she? They had made a cuckold of him before the world and now they wanted to dispose of him like so much rubbish. Well, she was not going to find it that easy. Not once he had told King Henry what was going on.

X

DUNFERMLINE CASTLE ❖ October 1238

'It won't be for long, lass.' Alexander's hands were on her shoulders. 'What is it?'

It was unlike her to cry, but the tears slipped down her face in spite of her efforts to check them. 'I don't want you to go.' He was riding to the far west of his kingdom.

'Neither do I, Eleyne,' he said, growing impatient. 'But it has to be; you know that as well as I do.'

Her belly was showing now. If she were careful, always draped in a full mantle, no one could see it, but her servants knew; Nesta knew, for she had had to let out the seams of Eleyne's gowns. And she was sure some of the men and women of the court had guessed. But still Alexander had not acted. It was only three or four months before her baby was due; they had to be married soon.

She had stopped riding, terrified of harming the baby, her whole being tied up with the scrap of life who would one day wear a crown. She did not know that messengers had arrived from the court of King Henry, and that one of the messages they carried was that Robert de Quincy was alive.

XI

STRATA FLORIDA, WALES ❖ 19 October 1238

All the lords and princes of Wales were gathered at the command of Prince Llywelyn. Once more he wanted their assurances and their oaths of loyalty: for Dafydd.

Isabella sat watching as her husband's attendants put the finishing touches to his clothes, tweaking, brushing, pulling at the folds of his cloak. She was shivering in spite of the lighted brazier which threw out a shimmering wall of heat from its glowing coals.

'Is your father well enough to attend the meeting?' She was growing agitated now that the day had finally arrived.

Dafydd nodded. He waved away his servants and turned to face her. 'So, how do I look?' He was wearing the *talaith*, the coronet which was the symbol of his rank.

'Handsome.' She smiled with some of her old coquettishness. 'Every inch the greatest prince Wales has ever seen.'

'No prince will ever be greater than my father, Isabella.'

'You will.' She stood up and moving towards him with a rustle of silks she stood on tiptoe to kiss his mouth. 'You'll see, Dafydd *bach*, after today you will rule all Wales.'

Outside the guesthouse the wind had risen, roaring through the trees in the valley beyond the abbey. The lonely hills were dark under the speeding clouds.

'Not as long as Gruffydd holds so much of Gwynedd and Powys. Father means him to succeed Gwenwynwyn as leader in central Wales. If he does he'll be a thorn in my flesh for the rest of my days.'

'Then he mustn't succeed.' Isabella's eyes narrowed. 'Once the princes have sworn allegiance to you, my husband, he will have no friends. And your father will go back happily to his prayers at Aberconwy. The field will be yours.'

'My thoughts exactly! Though I must move carefully. Remove his lands little by little, isolate him. With my allies and my sisters' husbands with their lands ... Angharad and Maelgwyn Fychan, Gwladus and Ralph Mortimer, Gwenllian and William de Lacy, Margaret and Walter Clifford. It's a formidable list.' He paused. 'It's a pity that Chester is now so irrevocably in Henry's hands. With the earl as our ally we were far more secure.'

Isabella frowned. 'Where is the Countess of Chester now, do we know?'

Dafydd smiled. The minx was showing her claws again. He could tell by the tone of her voice. She knew very well where Eleyne was. He shook his head at her gravely. 'She is, I hope, working on strengthening the prospects of a Welsh alliance with Scotland.'

Isabella laughed shrilly. 'Is that what it's called? That is not what Robert de Quincy called it when he came to see papa.'

If Robert de Quincy had hoped for sympathy from Eleyne's father when he came to Aber the month before, he had been sadly disappointed. Llywelyn, on his way back to Aberconwy, where he spent more and more of his time in prayer, had been curt to the point of rudeness to his unwanted and unloved son-in-law, pointing out that a wife was a man's own business and if he could not control Eleyne he should perhaps look to his own character for the reason.

The news of Eleyne's attachment to the King of Scots had pleased Dafydd enormously; her marriage to him would be the best and biggest insult to Henry anyone at Aber could conceive. He had said as much to his father.

'If that young man should meet with an accident on his way out of Wales, we would be doing the whole world a favour!' he had said succinctly as Robert de Quincy left Aber.

Llywelyn had frowned, groping with shaking hand for the crucifix he wore around his neck. 'Murder is not the answer, my son, though I'm tempted, sorely tempted. The alliance with the royal house of Scotland would be good for Wales, very good.' He smiled with a glint in his eye, quite like his old self. Then he sighed. 'But I don't wish to die with that wretched young man's death on my conscience. Or on yours –' he added hastily.

Both men had thought for a moment with regret about Gruffydd. He would not have hesitated. But Gruffydd wasn't there.

XII

DUMBARTON CASTLE

William, Earl of Mar, was sitting near King Alexander. He glanced at his companions with a scowl. They had wished this on him after long discreet discussions by the fireside, and now they had turned to talk among themselves, leaving him alone with his king.

Alexander lay back in his chair and sighed. 'So, William, another two days and we can ride back to Roxburgh.'

'I hope so, sir.' What kind of fool was he to try this? How could he even begin?

Someone cleared their throat in the room behind him. William took the hint.

'I hear Sir Robert de Quincy is bragging at Henry's court that he is to be a father, sire.' He kept his eyes on his hands, watching the fire glint on the stone in his ring. 'He claims his wife was cohabiting with him when the child was conceived and claims to know when it will be born.'

He risked a glance at the king's face, and wished he hadn't. The pain was raw.

'Sir Robert is also claiming that you tried to have him killed, sire,' he said softly. 'Even if he released her –' he paused – 'or if he died, there would always be doubt. Even with a papal dispensation, as the widower of her aunt,' he ploughed on manfully, 'you cannot marry her. Scotland would be torn apart.'

'I know.'

For a moment William did not believe what he had heard. The king's strangled whisper had been so soft.

The other three men watching covertly from the shadows saw their king put his face in his hands. 'How will I tell her, William?'

Lord Mar bit his lip. 'I am sure she will understand,' he said hopefully. Privately, he doubted it. The beautiful Lady Chester had a fiery spirit which did not, as far as he could see, tolerate any contradiction of her wishes.

The king's wry smile seemed to imply that he felt the same.

'You could just stay away,' William said, 'until she is brought to bed.'

Alexander shook his head. 'That would be cruel, and it would be cowardly.' He straightened. 'So, William, tell me: whom do my lords think I should marry? Do you have a list of your daughters ready? Or must I marry a foreign princess?' He stood up abruptly. 'I love her, William.' It was a cry of anguish.

'She is a very beautiful woman, sire.' William stood too. 'I am sure she will continue to –' Embarrassed, he groped for words.

'To be my paramour?' Alexander laughed bitterly. 'But she deserves better than that, William. Far better.'

XIII
PERTH CASTLE ❖ February 1239

Eleyne was sewing with her ladies in the solar above the hall. The gales had grown worse, uprooting trees, tearing roofs from buildings, screaming banshee-like in the chimneys, hurling the rain against the narrow windows. It was hard to sew by the flickering candlelight and the women were talking idly around the table, only now and then inserting stitches into their work. Eleyne had had a letter from Alexander that morning; he was still delayed in the far west. It would be another week at least before he could come to her.

She knew of the rumour that Robert was alive, but she had no way of finding out the truth. As the weeks passed, she had grown more miserable and uncertain. She did not eat; she did not sleep. On the one hand, his survival meant that Alexander had not after all been guilty of murder. On the other, it meant she was not free. Had Alexander petitioned the pope for an annulment of her marriage? Was he even now awaiting word from Rome?

She sighed, moving uncomfortably in her chair as the baby kicked beneath her ribs. Why was the king taking so long? Couldn't he see that time was running out? They had to be married before the baby was born; surely that was more important than yet another squabble among his quarrelsome subjects. He had people to do that for him, he did not have to be there in person. The needle slipped in her hands and she gave an exclamation of pain and annoyance as a spot of blood appeared on her finger.

The noise of the wind disguised the sound of feet. When the door burst open, the women looked up in amazement. Robert de Quincy had a drawn sword in his hand. Behind him were several armed men who wore the insignia of the Earl of Fife.

'So this is where you are, sweetheart.' He peered around the room as the shadows leapt from the wildly flickering candles. One of the ladies gave a scream; the rest stared at him, too afraid to move.

'Come, we are leaving, King Henry wants us in London.'

Eleyne rose to her feet. Her face was white and strained, her heart thudded sickly in her throat. 'I am not going with you. Our marriage is over.'

'Our marriage isn't over.' He laughed humourlessly. 'My dear, it has hardly begun. Fetch her cloak.' His eyes had flicked over the cowering women and settled on Nesta. 'We ride south tonight.'

Nesta licked her lips nervously. 'My lady is in no condition to ride, Sir Robert,' she said cautiously, amazed at her own courage.

'No condition?' Robert raised an eyebrow. 'Nothing stops my wife from riding, surely.' He had to raise his voice against the sound of the wind. 'Not even the fact that she is carrying my child.'

'This is not your child.' Eleyne's hand went protectively to her stomach. 'And you know it. I am carrying the king's son.'

'You are carrying my son, madam,' Robert's voice was harsh, 'and he will be born under my roof. We ride south tonight.'

'No.' She backed away from him. 'The king –'

'The king is a hundred miles away. You and I will be in England before he even hears that you have gone. You are my wife, any child you bear is my child, and I insist it is born in England. Fetch her cloak.' The last words were shouted at Nesta as Robert strode towards Eleyne and grabbed her wrist. He was wearing armour beneath his mantle and cloak, his sword still in his right hand.

'Guards!' Eleyne screamed, 'where are the guards?' She tried to pull away from him.

'The guards are elsewhere, and they have no orders to keep me from my wife.' He had his arm around her shoulders now. 'I advise you to come with me without any fuss, sweetheart, if you don't want to hurt yourself and my son.'

Nesta, white-faced, scuttled away to fetch Eleyne's thick cloak. 'I'll come too.' She put it gently around Eleyne's shoulders, but Robert pushed her away. 'She needs no servants. Out of my way, woman.' He was sweating as he turned for the door, dragging Eleyne with him.

She kicked out at him and tried desperately to pull free, but she knew he was too strong for her.

'Call for help,' she screamed over her shoulder. 'Tell the king, for sweet pity's sake, tell the king –'

With a curt nod, Robert pushed Eleyne towards one of his men and the man swept her off her feet. In seconds she was being carried towards the door.

Robert turned back into the room, where the women cowered. 'No one is to call for help,' he said softly, 'no one at all.' He raised the sword and very gently put the tip against Nesta's throat. She moaned with fear, her eyes rolling towards the ceiling. 'If they do, I shall pull the necks of every woman in this room, for the squawking hens you are.' He gave a small flick of the sword and a speck of blood appeared on the white fabric of Nesta's wimple. She moaned again, half fainting with terror, and he gave a humourless bark of laughter as he withdrew the sword. Following the other men outside, he pulled the door closed and locked it, and on the way across the lower floor of the keep he tossed the key into the well.

He took Eleyne on his horse in front of him and kicked it forward through the gates. On either side his men carried flaring torches to light the road as they turned south at a gallop.

The wind was mercifully behind them, but within seconds the riders were soaked through. Eleyne was shaking with cold and fright and anger, but her only thought was for the baby as the horses thundered along the track. Robert's mailclad arm was viciously tight. She could scarcely breathe. At one point the horses plunged across a broad river and she felt the icy water dragging at her skirts, her cloak drenched afresh by the spray from the horse's hooves, then they were on the road again.

It was growing light before they reached their destination. The horses walked in single file through a gate in a high curtain wall and halted in a courtyard before a small tower. Robert dismounted and lifted her down. 'We'll rest here for a few hours.' He took her arm and turned towards the door, where an old man was standing, waiting for them.

'Where is this place?' Eleyne could hear the sound of distant waves crashing against the rocks, and she could smell the sharp green smell of the sea. She took a step forward and winced with pain. Her feet were numb and she was stiff and aching in every muscle.

'A friendly castle.' Robert grinned. 'One where your lover will not find you.' Taking her arm he pulled her towards the door.

The man who was waiting there was a complete stranger to her. He bowed before them. 'My wife and her servant have prepared a room for your lady, sir. She will be comfortable there.'

'Thank you.' Still holding her arm, Robert followed the man indoors. A turnpike stair twisted up in the thickness of the wall on the eastern side of the chamber and in single file they followed him up it.

The bedchamber was at the top of the tower. A fire had been lit and a bed prepared. Too tired to think of anything but sleep, Eleyne scarcely allowed the woman to remove her wet clothes before she collapsed into the bed and felt the bedcovers being heaped over her. The chatelaine chuckled quietly to herself as she wrapped hot stones in cloths and packed them around Eleyne's feet. Within minutes Eleyne was asleep, her arms crossed protectively across her belly.

It was late morning when she awoke but the room was still dark. It was full of the sound of the sea. Robert was standing by the bed. 'We have to ride on. Mistress Gillespie has dry clothes for you and food.'

Now that she was rested, Eleyne's resolve had returned. 'I am riding nowhere. Do you want me to lose this child?'

Robert's eyes narrowed in the light of the candle he held. 'My child?' he said quietly. 'No, I don't want you to lose it. I want it to be born at home. At Fotheringhay. We'll ride slowly once we are out of

Scotland, I shall get some kind of conveyance for you if it is easier. We should be at Berwick tomorrow.'

'I am not going.' She could feel waves of panic rising inside her and desperately she fought them down. 'You can't do this. The king will kill you —'

Robert smiled humourlessly. 'I don't think so. Don't you think he would have married you by now if he were going to? Sweet Eleyne, the king is not going to marry you. And I'll tell you why. He knows this child isn't his.'

'It is.' Her cry was full of anguish.

Robert put down the candle and sat on the bed beside her. 'Poor Eleyne. So ambitious. Not content with being Countess of Chester, she wants to be Queen of the Scots. Well, sweetheart, it isn't going to happen, you are my wife and my wife you are going to stay. And all your children . . .' he put his hand heavily on her stomach, 'are going to be mine. Is that clear?' He sat looking at her for a long moment, then he stood up. When he left the chamber she heard the bolt shoot home on the door behind him.

Dragging herself out of bed she went to the window and pulled the shutter open. The wind had dropped, but it was still ice-cold in her face as she leaned out across the broad wet sill and peered through the narrow lancets. The tower was built high in the woods above the sea. She could see the waves crashing on to the shore in the distance, sending up clouds of spray. On the horizon a multitude of small islands stood out of the mist. There was no escape that way. Turning from the window she surveyed the round room. It was sparsely furnished. Two coffers and a bed were all the comforts it afforded. The two archways with curtains across them revealed the garderobe and a small oratory in the thickness of the massive wall. She stood for a moment before the crucifix which stood on the altar. The narrow windows above it had small yellowish panes of glass set in a leaded frame. It was very dark.

The prayers she had thought to make would not come. Instead, she found herself concentrating on the dull ache in her spine. With a groan she braced her hands against the small of her back in the time-honoured gesture of the heavily pregnant woman and went to sit on the bed.

She ate the food she was brought and put on the clothes. She knew enough about Robert to be certain that he would have no compunction about forcing her if he had to and that he would enjoy doing it. She refused to give him that satisfaction. Her only chance of escape was to use her head. Mistress Gillespie had refused to speak to her, shaking her head sternly when questioned as to where they were, but Eleyne guessed they were somewhere in Fife. The men who had ridden with Robert wore the Earl of Fife's blazon on their surcoats. But why should

Malcolm of Fife help Robert? He wouldn't want to make an enemy of his king, and besides, he still seemed to want her himself.

She was no wiser when Robert came upstairs to collect her. He eyed her clothes, smoky but dry from the fire, and nodded. 'I'm glad you've decided to be sensible. The horses are ready.'

Even now she could probably outride him, given a decent horse. It was the only chance of escape. Gritting her teeth against the nagging ache in her back, she followed him down the narrow spiral stair.

'I'll ride my own horse!' She saw with alarm that he intended her to sit behind him.

'I think not. It's safer for the baby if you are with me. Besides, we are not going far.'

It was barely half a mile down to the small harbour where a boat was waiting, jerking at its mooring rope on the choppy water.

Eleyne stared at it in horror. 'I'm not going in that.'

She saw her hopes of escape receding fast and she could feel her panic growing.

'Indeed you are, sweetheart. The ferryman is going to take us across the Forth. I have fresh horses waiting on the far side.' Throwing his leg over the pommel of the saddle, he slid to the ground and pulled her after him. Two of Lord Fife's men were going with them and she was lifted into the bucking boat. 'No!' Desperately she tried to rise, but already Robert was beside her. 'Sit quietly or you'll fall overboard,' he shouted against the wind and she found herself sitting helplessly in the shelter of his arm as the sail was raised and the boat drew away from the jetty, hurtling before the sharp north-easterly wind towards the south.

They made landfall on a deserted sandy coast where two horsemen were waiting with spare mounts in the shelter of a pine wood. The ferryman ran the boat up on to the sand and Eleyne was lifted out. She was wet through from the spray and chilled to the bone, and her back ached worse than ever. She had never been seasick in her life, but Robert had spent most of the journey leaning over the side and he was still green as he staggered up the beach.

Eleyne paused to catch her breath, feeling her shoes sink into the soft sand. 'I can't go any further.'

Robert stopped. He felt like death and his legs would hardly support him. However much he knew they must ride south quickly and put as much distance between themselves and the King of Scots as possible, all he wanted at this particular moment was to lie down and die. 'I'll ask the men with the horses if there is somewhere we can rest,' he said. It was obvious to Eleyne that he could not face going any further himself, but he still sounded grudging.

They were taken to a small cottage on the edge of a fishing village nearby. The horses were led away and Robert shown to a shed full of hay where he could sleep, while a cheerful young woman, barefoot, her skirts kilted up to her knees, shyly led Eleyne inside. The whole place smelt strongly of fish, but the bed was a pile of dried heather and bracken, spread with sheepskins, and to Eleyne it was the most comfortable place on earth. She sank into it, too tired even to feel the young woman removing her shoes and pulling her wet cloak from her shoulders.

She woke much later with terrifying suddenness as a vicious pain knifed across her back and cramped her womb. Night must have fallen while she was asleep. The fire was damped and she could see in its faint glow the figure of her hostess dozing on the far side of the hearth. The pain came again and she heard herself cry out.

The young woman awoke with a start and scrambled to her feet. 'My lady? Are you all right?'

Eleyne lay still, shaking. She could feel the chill of perspiration drying on her face. 'My baby,' she gasped, 'I think it's coming.'

The woman deftly pulled aside the turves which were heaped over the fire. She found some twigs from the pile of driftwood in the corner and fed them to it. By the time it was blazing, she had lit one of her precious tallow candles and set it on the iron pricket on the chest in the corner. Then she turned to Eleyne and laid a comforting hand on her head.

Eleyne groaned again. She knelt up on the bed, rocking back and forth, her arms wrapped tightly around herself.

'What are we going to do?' she cried. 'You must get help.' Alexander, where was Alexander?

The woman's frightened shout brought Robert into the cottage, then, a shawl thrown over her head, she ran into the night to fetch her neighbour.

Robert stared at Eleyne, his face white and drawn in the smoky light; he did not dare to go right into the room. There was a strange smile on his face. At the sight of him standing in the doorway something snapped inside Eleyne.

'This is your fault,' she screamed. 'If I lose this baby it is your fault! And I shall kill you myself, if Alexander doesn't do it first, so help me, I will!' The tears were streaming down her face. She was aware suddenly of water, warm and salty, pouring between her legs, soaking into the sheepskin on which she was kneeling.

Robert didn't move. He took in with dispassionate disgust every detail of the dishevelled woman kneeling on the bed in her stained gown, with her huge belly and her wild eyes and her hair deep red in the smoking tallow light.

The fisherman's wife reappeared almost at once with an older woman behind her and in seconds Robert had been banished from the cottage. He stood outside, wrapped in his cloak, looking across the shore to the black waters beyond. Somewhere out there, this woman's husband and his colleagues were in their little boats, fishing the dark, storm-bound waters, or even now fighting their way back towards the land. His mind worked furiously as the wind pushed his hair back from his cold forehead, his fear of pursuit eclipsed by his anger that once again she had outwitted him. The child was going to be born in Scotland after all.

Eleyne screamed once, just as the sun was rising in a blaze of stormy crimson out of the eastern clouds. Then the eerie silence descended once more on the cottage. It was a long time before the fisherman's wife appeared at Robert's side. When he didn't turn she touched his elbow timidly.

'The babe is born, my lord,' she whispered. 'It's too small to live. I'm sorry. Do you want to see it?'

'What is it?' His voice was expressionless.

'A boy.'

'A boy.' He repeated the words slowly, then he shook his head. 'No, I don't want to see it.' He walked away from the cottage towards the water.

Eleyne was propped against a pile of sacks – there were no pillows in the house – the child wrapped in a bloody piece of torn shift in her arms. He was so tiny, this little mite, her dream of Scotland's future, his features perfect, too early for pudgy baby fat, his hair a glorious red-gold, his minute fingers curled on themselves like sculptured wax. His eyes fluttered slightly behind transparent lids and his mouth parted a little for the breast he would never have the strength to take.

Tears pouring down her face Eleyne kissed his little face and held him to her as he died.

The old woman who had delivered him had baptised him Alexander at her request.

CHAPTER FIFTEEN

I

ABERDOUR CASTLE ❖ March 1239

As soon as she was well enough to travel, Robert took her back across the water to Aberdour. He carried her upstairs to the chamber in the tower and left her there, in the care of Mistress Gillespie. Then he sent for Nesta and her ladies.

Eleyne had not spoken since the baby died. There had been no anger, no rage, just a terrible silent grief. It had been many hours before they had been able to take the baby from her. She rocked the little body in her arms, her lips against his soft hair, and she wept as though her heart would break. When at last the two women had managed to take him and wrap him in a piece of clean woollen cloth – the only shroud that could be found for the son of the king – she had lost so much blood that she was too weak to stand. Neither she nor Robert was present at the burial in the churchyard on the shore.

Easter came and went and Robert returned to England alone. He simply rode away one day and left her at Aberdour. He felt no desire to take her with him, he felt no desire for her at all. He felt only increasing fear at what Alexander would do when he found out what had happened. It was several days before she wondered if he were coming back; two more before she realised she was no longer a prisoner. It was six days before Alexander came.

He sat down on the bed and took her hands. For a long time neither of them spoke, then at last she looked at him. His face was grey with pain.

'How did you know I was here?'

'Malcolm of Fife told me.'

'It was his men who helped Robert kidnap me.'

The king frowned. 'He says he told Robert he could use this place. He didn't know you were here.'

'Didn't you look for me?'

'Of course I looked for you!' For the first time his voice betrayed emotion. 'Holy Virgin! I nearly died when I found you had gone. I scoured the kingdom, but no one even knew in which direction he had taken you!'

'Why did you leave it so long before you came back to me?' She was leaning against the pillows, wrapped in a linen shift with a woollen cloak around her shoulders. She had grown very thin. 'We could have been married. You could have had a son.' Her voice broke, but there were no tears. There were no tears left.

'You will have other children, Eleyne. You are very young.'

You. Not we.

'You aren't going to marry me. You never intended to marry me.' It was a whisper.

'You are already married, Eleyne. If you hadn't had a husband . . . if you had been mine from the start.' He paused. 'We don't even know for sure that the child was mine.' His voice was gentle but firm.

She closed her eyes. Outside the wind was moaning again, stirring the waves as they whispered on the rocks below. There was a smell of snow in the air. 'He was yours. He looked like you. He had your colour hair.' Her voice wavered and she clenched her fists.

At last he spoke. 'Eleyne, we cannot go on seeing each other. You know that, don't you? There must be no more scandal. The wellbeing of Scotland must come before all else, even before our happiness. If I had been anyone but a king, anyone at all, no one would have kept you from me. No one.'

'You are going to send me back to Robert?' Her voice was toneless, and she did not look at him. There was going to be no punishment for her husband; no retribution for the murder of her baby.

'You never left him,' Alexander said gently. 'You are his. That is God's will.'

'God's will,' she echoed. 'No, that is not God's will.' Her voice rose. 'It was God's will that I bear you a child, that I be the mother of a line of kings! That was written in the stars. If you don't marry me, you are defying God's will!'

He shook his head. 'No, lass, I'm sorry.'

'You are not sending me away?' It was as though she had only just realised what he was saying. 'I can't live without you. For pity's sake!' She threw herself from the bed and into his arms, sobbing wildly.

He closed his arms around her and held her for a long time in silence, listening to the gentle sigh of the sea in the distance. 'I shall always love you, lass, always,' was all he said at last. Reluctantly he pushed her away from him and turned towards the door.

She did not move. Ten minutes later, when Nesta put her head into the room, she was still sitting on the edge of the bed, staring blankly at the wall.

II
April 1239

The king was once more at Dunfermline. She rode Tam Lin slowly into the great courtyard below Malcolm's Tower, well again physically, although she was still pale and very thin. She dismounted, unaware that her brilliant hair was the only touch of colour about her; her cloak of white furs, her white face, her milky horse, they all seemed fairylike against the light scattering of April snow; more than one man crossed himself as he saw her.

She was not expected and had no escort save for the faithful Nesta and Master Gillespie who had ridden with her, and no one sprang to welcome the Countess of Chester and escort her with ceremony into the king's presence. She looked around ruefully and smiled at Nesta. 'Is this how those who fall from favour are welcomed?'

Nesta bit her lip. She was afraid.

Eleyne walked towards the door. The guards stood to attention, their eyes carefully impersonal, and let her pass, as did the chamberlain who had been summoned to the hall. The king was with Lord Fife and Lord Mar in his private room, and they were attended by two of the king's clerks.

He looked around as she appeared and she saw the sudden frown between his eyes. There was no message of hope there, no chance then that he would change his mind.

She walked towards him, very straight in her white cloak, and curtseyed deeply.

'Sire.'

He took her hand and raised her to her feet. 'Lady Chester.'

He waited courteously for her to speak and she was conscious of Malcolm of Fife's eyes on her face. His expression was unreadable.

The king was not going to make it easy for her.

'I have come to take my leave, sire.' Her voice sounded loud in the silence of the room. Five pairs of eyes watched her covertly as she stood before him. She felt as if she were naked.

'You are returning to Fotheringhay?' His voice was husky.

'No, I won't go back there.'

'Then where?' He hated her quiet pride more than he had hated her pleading. It reminded him that she was of royal blood, a princess, and because of that he could not treat her as a common whore and drag her to his bed to assuage his lust and his terrible guilt. Suddenly he could stand it no longer. He snapped his fingers at his companions. 'Leave us, I will speak to Lady Chester alone.'

She did not let herself hope. She had not seen any change of heart in his eyes.

'You should not have come here,' he said as soon as the door closed behind the last servant. 'You are not making it easy for either of us.'

'I did not come here to make it easy.' She clenched her fists, fighting her need to run to him, forcing herself to remain where she was. 'Have you decided whom you're going to marry?' Her voice was hard.

He sighed. 'Don't torment yourself, lass.'

'Have you?' Her eyes flashed dangerously. 'Tell me. You owe me that much. Or do I have to wait to hear it from the gossips?'

He shook his head impatiently. 'I am to marry a lady from France. Marie, the daughter of Baron de Couci. We will marry later in the spring.'

'I see.' It was the ghost of a whisper. 'And then you will forget me.'

'I shall never forget you, Eleyne.' The agony in his voice was intense. 'Sweet Jesus, I shall never forget you. How could I? You are a part of me!' There was a long silence, then he was suddenly brisk. 'You have the gifts I gave you? I want you to keep them. They will give you . . .' he groped for the word, 'security.'

Her lips tightened. She wanted to throw his gifts at his feet, but she couldn't. He was right. They were all that stood between her and poverty unless she went back to Robert.

The king was finding it very difficult not to touch her. He wanted her so badly his loins ached. His heart ached. He had only to smile; to hold out his arms. But he owed her more than that, his beautiful Welsh princess. If she could not be his queen, he would not insult her by asking her to be his mistress. There was only one thing he could do for her now.

'I shall give you letters for your father, Eleyne. If you would, deliver them for me, to Wales. As a royal messenger you will have an escort and my safe conduct to protect you, and it will give you a reason to go home.'

She gave a wistful smile. So she was to hide her hurt pride and her broken heart in Gwynedd. But at least Robert would not come to find her there, even if he heard where she had gone.

Alexander stepped forward and kissed her once, on the forehead, then he left her.

In the morning he had two letters for her, one for Llywelyn and one for Dafydd. Under his arm there was a small squirming wolfhound pup, which he put in her hands. 'I know it won't fill the gap in your heart, lass,' he said softly, 'nothing can do that, but he'll serve you with his life. He's the same line as old Gelert; Joanna's father gave one pup to your father, one to us.'

Her arms closed around the dog; she felt its tongue, rough and eager, on her nose. Then she turned away, so he could not see her tears.

III

LLANFAES, ANGLESEY ✥ May 1239

Llywelyn settled her in the manor at Llanfaes, where she did not need to see Isabella too often, but nevertheless Isabella came. She was smiling. Her pretty face had lost its puffiness again, her hair was wreathed in a coronet of twisted gold.

As she was shown into the hall, Eleyne felt her stomach clench warningly, but she rose and stretched out her hand with a smile. Isabella dimpled and sat down next to her with a rustle of silks. It was unseasonably hot outside, but it was cool in the hall.

'Did you know that Dafydd has had to send Gruffydd and Owain back to Criccieth?' Isabella asked at once.

Eleyne nodded. Llywelyn, tired and ill, had retired permanently at last to the Abbey of Aberconwy and donned the cowl of the monks to spend his last days in prayer, leaving Dafydd in full control of all his lands. She had been told of the trick by which Dafydd had immediately captured his brother, luring him into a trap with his eldest son and making them both prisoners. He did not mean to brook any opposition in his final bid to become Llywelyn's only heir. Already Eleyne was planning a visit to her father on Gruffydd's behalf.

Isabella smiled. Obviously this was not the purpose of her visit. Her next words revealed what it was. 'Dafydd has had letters from Scotland.' Her voice rose a little as she faced her sister-in-law under the curious gaze of their attendants. 'I thought I should be the one to tell you.'

Eleyne already knew what Isabella was going to say; it had come to her in her dreams. Alexander was married. Another woman was his queen. She clenched her fists, tired of always having to show a brave face, tired of the pain, tired of the pleasure others seemed to take in her unhappiness, yet unable to fend off this new wave of grief.

'You know, don't you?'

She realised that she had risen from her chair and that Isabella was standing behind her. 'Your lover has married – a baron's daughter, from France.'

'I know.' Eleyne managed to keep her voice steady.

'What will you do?' The spite in Isabella's tone had softened; in its place there was genuine curiosity.

'I don't know.'

'What about your husband?'

'I don't know that either.'

'You have to go back to him.'

'No, I'll never go back to him, never.'

It was easy to be alone at Llanfaes. Dafydd and Isabella had spared her few servants, but she had not wanted more. Her body needed rest to heal. Her soul needed silence. She often walked alone and the servants respected her orders not to be disturbed. It was easy to extend that order to the long rides through the soft Anglesey countryside, with its rich corn fields and its woods, accompanied only by the pup. Alexander's gift had become inseparable from her. She had called him Donnet. It meant 'given'.

There was something that she had to do: she had to summon Einion.

It was hard to find where he was buried. Rhonwen had led her there in the dark and so much had happened since that terrible night; a lifetime of happenings which had left them, for the time being at least, far apart. Rhonwen was still safe in London.

She began at the hermit's cell which Einion had made his own. The roof had fallen in and weeds had grown through the floor. Tethering Tam Lin in the clearing and telling Donnet to stay with him, she walked slowly towards the collapsing stone walls and stared around.

In the distance a curlew called, a lonely cry which echoed in her ears. Her skin prickled with fear, but she forced herself to move on, stepping across the threshold and pushing her way through a tangle of nettles and willow herb to the centre of the hut.

His few possessions were still there on the rudimentary shelf. So great was the respect in which he had been held that no one had touched them. The little boxes of herbs and spices lay tumbled in a heap, the boxes swollen with damp and mildewed. Some of them had fallen to pieces and their contents had long disintegrated or rotted away. His books, his knives, the little cauldron he had used to infuse his herbs – they had been buried with him.

She looked around warily, but there was no feel of him. She was alone. Picking up one of the rotting boxes she sniffed it curiously. It smelt of the damp forest floor in autumn. There was no clue to what it had held, no clue to what Rhonwen had used to summon his spirit.

The sun beat down on the top of her head beneath her veil and she could feel her temples starting to throb. She stood for a while in the clearing. Beneath the trees she felt better. Taking the horse's rein, she began to walk slowly into the trees with Donnet at her heels. The track was indistinct now, overgrown, but she remembered it from that single afternoon so many years before when Einion had led her into the forest and taught her about the birds.

His grave lay beneath an oak tree some yards off the track. She recognised it by the stone. She dismounted and tied Tam to a tree, then she called Donnet and put her hand on his head. 'Stay close,' she whispered, and the dog whined.

She had no herbs, no flint to light a fire. If he wanted to speak, he must come on her terms. He was the one who had lied.

'Why?' she called out loud. 'Why did you tell me I should be a queen?'

Nearby she heard a wren singing in the undergrowth. The wind stirred the trees and Donnet growled quietly in his throat.

'That was what you wanted me to know, wasn't it? That you were wrong? That I had no destiny in Scotland?' Her voice rang amongst the trees and further up the ride a hare stood up on its back legs before it bolted into the shadows. 'Well, now I know! Your gods were wrong, Lord Einion. They had no great plan for me! How they must have laughed when they saw me with my dreams!'

But, as her voice echoed in the silence, she knew there was no one there to hear.

V

Eleyne went to see her father three days later.

She did not speak of Alexander, what was the point?

'You cannot let Dafydd lock up his brother like this!' She sat close beside him, knowing his eyes had grown weak. 'Please, papa, you are still the prince!' Her hand strayed to the head of the puppy at her side.

He shook his head. 'You must speak to Dafydd, Eleyne. He rules Gwynedd now.'

'And unjustly,' she said heatedly.

He smiled. 'Are you still as hotheaded as ever, child? No, he does not rule unjustly. He was the right choice.'

She went to Dafydd, risking Isabella's acid tongue, and she went to Criccieth to see Gruffydd and Senena, but she could do nothing. Dafydd was adamant.

Gruffydd was a close prisoner in his castle on the Lleyn Peninsula. She could come and go by Dafydd's order, with her white horse and her growing, adolescent hound, but her favourite elder brother could not go with her, and when the old prince died the following year Gruffydd was not allowed to leave the castle to attend his father's funeral at Aberconwy.

Eleyne went with Dafydd and Isabella and her sisters and their husbands, and it seemed as though the whole of Wales was weeping. She had loved him and he was gone. She went back to Llanfaes, but she knew it would not be for long. She had seen Isabella's face as they stood for the requiem mass.

VI
August 1240

'The scheming bitch has persuaded King Henry to attack us!' Isabella shouted. 'She has begged him to free Gruffydd! So much for her claims to be a patriot!' Her anger hid real fear, and her quarrel with Eleyne was for the moment forgotten. The news brought by the exhausted, dust-covered messenger had reduced her to panic.

Senena, it appeared, had left Criccieth secretly and ridden to Shrewsbury to meet the king.

The old prince had hardly grown cold in his grave before Wales had erupted into dispute. Quarrels, dissatisfaction and jealousies which no one had dared to voice whilst Llywelyn was alive had been whipped into life. Dafydd's peaceful succession had disintegrated into chaos, and Henry as his overlord had summoned him to Shrewsbury to explain the situation. Furious, Dafydd had no choice but to agree to abide by the King of England's arbitration; but when the appointed date arrived he did not go. Instead he had assembled his armies.

Far to the east, beyond the mountains, Henry, leaving his wife and year-old son Edward behind in the castle, left Shrewsbury for Rhuddlan, encouraged by Senena's message, marching purposefully towards the heartland of North Wales. In front of him Dafydd, without allies and without friends, moved steadily back. At Degannwy he delayed to pull down the castle, so that Henry could not use it as a base, then he retreated into the heat haze which hung over the mountains.

'Sweet Christ! I cannot fight him!' He ran his fingers through his hair, looking from his wife to his sister and back. He had invited Eleyne to join them at Aber for safety, not really believing that Henry would invade Wales. 'Even the weather is against me. He marched his army across the marshes as though they were hard ground! Nothing seems to delay him! He'll be at the Conwy any moment.'

'Go and negotiate,' Isabella pleaded. 'What else can you do? Do a deal with him. He doesn't want to fight you. He's making a point, that's all. He wants you to recognise him as your overlord and submit, then he'll help you put down the revolts against you. He'll help you deal with Gruffydd and Senena. For God's sake, Dafydd, you have to do it. Do you want him here at Aber?'

'She's right, Dafydd.' Eleyne felt sorry for her brother. His allies had deserted out of jealousy, because Llywelyn had left him too strong and they were afraid. 'Negotiate now before it's too late.'

'What you mean is surrender,' Dafydd said.

There was an uncomfortable silence.

'It's that or lose Gwynedd,' Eleyne murmured at last.

It was the advice Ednyfed Fychan, his father's chief adviser, who was now his own, had given him too.

The night before Dafydd left Aber he called Eleyne to him in the small room which had been his father's study. 'There is something you should know. Isabella has written to your husband and told him you are here.'

'I don't believe you!' It was as though every part of Eleyne had turned to ice.

'I'm afraid it's true, and I'm sorry. I'm only surprised she left it so long.' He smiled apologetically. 'She's very loyal to me, Elly. I think, all things considered, it might be better if you left Gwynedd.'

Eleyne closed her eyes. Would Isabella never allow her any peace?

Dafydd gave her an escort of four men and two women to accompany her and Nesta away from Wales. He did not ask her where she was going and she did not volunteer the information. He kissed her gravely under Isabella's watchful eye and gave her a little money. 'Yours, under papa's will,' he said quietly. She blessed that money. It would give her something to live on for the immediate future without having to sell any more of Joanna's jewels.

VII

LONDON ❖ October 1240

Her men wore no insignia and, as she drew near the old Countess of Chester's town house in Gracechurch Street with Donnet at her horse's heels, she pulled her veil across her face. She wanted no one to recognise her.

The house was quiet, but there were servants to open the heavy gates and lead away the horses. Eleyne followed the old woman who had greeted her and found herself in a shadowy parlour on the first floor of the house, where she was left alone.

It was a long time before Rhonwen came. She stood in the doorway without a word, then ran to Eleyne and folded her in her arms, tears pouring down her face. 'I've missed you so much, *cariad*, and I've been so afraid for you. Where have you been?'

Eleyne was crying too. 'I've been at Llanfaes. I was with papa when he died, and Dafydd let me stay on. I couldn't send for you, not to Gwynedd, you know that.'

'I had thought you were still in Scotland.' Rhonwen shook her head. 'Have you seen your husband?'

'Isabella told him that I had left Scotland, and he now knows that I no longer have Alexander's protection.' Eleyne found she could say it calmly, as if she did not care. 'Isabella told him I was in Wales. That's why I had to leave. That's why I came here. I had nowhere else to go.'

Rhonwen sighed. 'Your husband does not care for war, so the king left him here in London! He has been to this house a dozen times, swearing that he'll hang me if he finds me.'

'Then why are you still here?' Eleyne was shocked.

'I like it here. I've become a city dweller.' Rhonwen smiled. 'I like being my own mistress; old Lady Chester is a fine employer. She leaves me to run her house as I see fit. Robert de Quincy isn't going to chase me away from here.' She folded her arms. 'Perhaps he's ridden to Wales to find you. If he has, you'll be safe here for now; I shall look after you. Don't worry, *cariad*, we'll think of something. That bastard is not going to find you, I swear it!'

VIII

As the months passed Eleyne hated London more and more. Rhonwen's anger and sympathy when she found out at last about Eleyne's dead child from Nesta strained her patience to the limit. And as time went on and there was still no sign of Robert, her fear of him was beginning to give way to anger and impatience.

'Fotheringhay is my home, it's part of my dower, and I should be allowed to live there. I'll go and see the king now he is back at Westminster and ask him to forbid Robert to come near me.'

Rhonwen raised an eyebrow. 'And you think he will agree?'

Eleyne sighed, pacing the floor like a caged animal. 'I don't know, but I can't stay in hiding for the rest of my life, it would drive me insane! Besides, Robert will find me in the end.'

They both knew that if he found her he would take her back by force.

IX

WESTMINSTER ❖ August 1241

King Henry granted her an audience almost at once. He was in jovial mood.

'So, niece, how are you? I'm glad your brother decided to come to heel and that ridiculous business in Wales is over. You know he is coming here to London?'

Eleyne hid her surprise. She gazed at her uncle in some dislike. 'I didn't know, no.' A survey of the great hall at Westminster had reassured her that neither of the de Quincy brothers was in attendance on the king.

He smiled. 'Indeed he is, and I have brought Gruffydd and the Lady Senena to London as my guests at the Tower.'

Eleyne was almost speechless with horror. She had known nothing of this. 'Your prisoners?'

'My guests.' He gave her a hard look. 'I am glad to see you here at last. You've been too long in mourning for your father. We have missed you at court.' There was a pause. 'Your husband has been lost without you. He will be very glad to hear of your return.'

'Your grace –' She tried to interrupt, but he held up his hand. 'He has told me how much he has missed you, and how much he looked forward to having you once again at his side. Wales is too far from Westminster, Eleyne, and so . . .' his eyes were gimlets, boring into her skull, 'is Scotland. Your place is at your husband's side. Here, at court.'

The conversation was not going as she had planned. In panic she tried to speak, but he went on ruthlessly.

'I remember . . .' he smiled without warmth, 'that you asked me to draw up a pardon for a woman of your household. The Lady Rhonwen, was it not?' She stiffened with suspicion 'Your husband has spoken to me about the case and pleaded her cause. I think, Eleyne, it will be possible to give her that pardon.' He smiled again. 'Once you are back in Sir Robert's bed, where you belong.'

It was all so neat. Robert had baited his trap and waited, and she had walked straight into it. She dropped her head in bleak despair as she left the king's presence chamber. Robert had grown clever, she had to give him that. Clever and devious and patient. All he had had to do was wait and she had come as meekly as a lamb to the slaughter. She could not disobey the king's direct command.

X

August 1241

'I will return to your hall, and to your fireside.' She confronted her husband in the panelled solar in the Earl of Winchester's house. They were alone for the first time since he had left her at Aberdour more than two years before. 'But I will not sleep in your bed.'

'Then you can sleep on the floor.' His tone was mild, though his face was hard.

'Willingly.' The silence which followed her retort was broken by the rattle of wheels on the cobbles outside the window.

'Hardly the spirit to earn a pardon for your viperous nurse.' Robert curled his lip.

'Before the world I shall be your wife again. Is that not enough to appease your vanity?' She took a step towards him and involuntarily he shrank back. She had grown very thin, her face almost austere in its gravity, and there was a coldness about her which repelled him. He had been looking forward to taking her back, looking forward to the excitement her anger and disdain always raised in him; above all, he had been looking forward to dominating her, but now, looking into those chilling eyes, he felt his confidence waver.

'Do you want your pardon or not?' he asked sulkily. His voice was still arrogant, but he had turned away from her. Pulling his dagger from the ornate sheath at his belt, he began to pare his nails with exaggerated casualness.

'Yes, I want the pardon.'

He wasn't sure if it was resignation which flattened her voice or hatred. Either way it gave him no pleasure.

'Then I shall go to the king and get it for you.' He sheathed his dagger and stood up. 'I shall stay with you in Gracechurch Street as long as the court sits at Westminster. I am sure Countess Clemence will not object. Then we can ride to Fotheringhay.'

XI
FOTHERINGHAY CASTLE ❖ September 1241

The summer had been one of soaring temperatures and devastating drought. The corn shrivelled in the fields and throughout the land men and women searched the skies for some sign of rain. Autumn brought no relief.

Eleyne watched anxiously over her horses, to which she gave more and more of her time, seeing the grazing disappearing and knowing there was little hay for the winter. When Robert wasn't pursuing the succession of obsessive legal battles he had undertaken to consolidate Eleyne's claim to her dower lands, he had taken to drinking outside, carrying his wine to the shade of the woods where two local girls amused him in the time-honoured way. He did not sleep in Eleyne's bed.

They had left Rhonwen in London with her pardon. Tacitly the two women had agreed that for the present this was best. If Eleyne needed her, Rhonwen would come, and Eleyne found that she had parted from Rhonwen with something like relief. Fond though she was of her nurse, there was something about Rhonwen which made her more and more uneasy; a cold core to the woman's soul even when she smiled.

Her sleeves rolled up, her head shaded by a broad-brimmed straw hat, Eleyne was with the farrier examining a wound on the hock of one of her mares when Robert found her. Donnet, as always, was nearby, asleep in the shade. Robert stood watching her, displeased by the sight of her tanned arms and roughened hands, then he remembered why he was there. He felt in his pouch for the letter.

She watched him cautiously as he approached. He had been drinking heavily already, although it was not yet noon, but his hand was perfectly steady as he unfolded the crackling parchment.

'A letter, sweetheart, from my brother in Scotland.'

She took off her hat and rubbed her arm across her forehead. It left a small dusty streak which for some reason pleased him greatly. 'He thought we would like to know: the Queen of Scots is safely delivered of a son at Roxburgh.'

She was completely unprepared. He saw the pain and shock in her eyes as though he had dealt her a physical blow. At last he had penetrated her defences. He refolded the letter. It would be so easy to turn the knife in the wound, to watch her wriggle and suffer like a lizard skewered on a dagger. 'I think we should go north, don't you? To pay our respects to the little prince,' he went on. 'Roger says the king has commanded your attendance on him. I expect he wants to show off his son to you.'

XII

ROXBURGH CASTLE ❖ September 1241

She could no more keep away than she could stop breathing. However much pain she knew it would cause her, she had to go to Alexander if he had summoned her. To be near him, to be in the same room, even with his wife and her child, was something she could not resist. She knew Robert believed it would be a punishment for her; she knew he would watch and enjoy every moment of her suffering but still she had to go.

The drought still held, but in the cooler north there was more grass in the meadows, and the trees, already turning golden and russet in the sun, were not so jaded. They found lodgings in Roxburgh, near the castle wall. Rhonwen, summoned by urgent messenger to Eleyne's side, was with them and it was she who helped Eleyne change into her most beautiful gown. It was of deep blue silk, trimmed with silver, held in at her too-thin waist by a heavy girdle stitched with chased silver ornaments.

They presented themselves at the castle at noon on the day after their arrival, and Robert gave their names to the official who was overseeing the crowds of petitioners waiting in the courtyard. They were ushered in at once. The king and queen were seated on a dais at the far end of the hall. Eleyne forced herself to walk beside Robert, her head high, her step firm, conscious of the whispers as she drew near the king and curtseyed. He had risen as they appeared and for a moment her eyes met his. He did not, after all, look pleased to see her.

'You haven't met Lady Chester, the widow of my cousin John,' he said at last to his wife. 'And Sir Robert de Quincy, her husband.'

Queen Marie was sitting back in her carved chair, her wrists hanging loosely on the armrests, her dark eyes watchful. Her face was heavy and olive-skinned, her hair black, looped around her ears in an elaborate style which emphasised the breadth of her chin. Eleyne realised at once that the queen knew exactly who she was.

Robert smiled at the queen. 'Madam, we have come to offer our congratulations on the birth of your son. This is a wonderful event for Scotland.'

'Indeed it is.' The queen's voice was heavy and without humour. 'Something for which Scotland has waited a long time. It was kind of you both to come and convey your good wishes. I understand you are on your way to stay with your brother, Sir Robert?'

'Indeed, madam.' Robert bowed.

Eleyne glanced up at Alexander; his eyes were on her face.

'Then we shall not detain you.' The queen had not looked at Eleyne. She held out her hand to Robert and he kissed it.

Alexander narrowed his eyes. She looked ill; unhappy; her face was thin to the point of gauntness, but she was still the most beautiful woman he had ever seen. And his wife was publicly snubbing her.

'It would be churlish to allow you to move on so soon after your arrival, Lady Chester,' he said, forcing the words from a throat tight with emotion. 'I should like you and your husband to stay at the castle. The Constable of Scotland is commanded to wait on me here. You do not need to travel further to see him.'

A small sigh passed around the spectators in the body of the hall and the queen's colour heightened.

So did Eleyne's. She met Alexander's gaze and gave a hesitant smile. It was a small enough triumph, but it was better than nothing.

As Countess of Chester, she sat next to the king at the high table. It was a long time before the level of conversation had reached such a volume that he could turn to her and speak without their being overheard. On her other side, Robert had already drunk more than enough to lull him into a stupor over the heavy spiced food.

'Why did you come?' he asked.

'You sent for us.' She kept her voice steady.

'No, lass, I wouldn't have done that to you.'

She sighed. 'I should have guessed.'

'Are you content with him now?' Alexander's hand, his fingers clenched around his knife, lay near hers on the table.

'How could I be content!' Her eyes were fixed on the dish of stewed

383

capons in front of her. There was no bitterness in her voice. 'I know it was the only way, and I'm glad for you. You have your son at last.'

'Aye.' He smiled broadly. 'Alexander. He's a beautiful bairn. You shall see him presently.' He did not notice the pain in her eyes as she thought of that other little Alexander buried in an unmarked grave on the cold windy shore of the Firth of Forth.

She and Robert shared a bed that night in the gatehouse tower of the castle, overlooking the River Tweed. He did not touch her. He was drunkenly asleep as soon as his head touched the pillow. Silently she cried herself to sleep, aware of Rhonwen and Nesta in their beds beyond the curtains and Donnet on the floor at the foot of the bed.

The baby was plump and healthy and screamed lustily as the wet-nurse picked him up and put him in Eleyne's arms. He was warm and heavy, his eyes a deep blue as he gazed up at her, his small mouth puckered into a brief toothless smile as his cries stopped. Her heart lurched with pain as her arms tightened around the child – Alexander's child, the child who should have been hers – and her eyes filled with hot tears.

'I want you to be his godmother,' Alexander said in the short silence as his son and heir paused to refill his lungs.

It was his way of saying he understood.

She sniffed, burying her face in the tightly swaddled shawl. When she looked up, she had recovered enough to give him a small smile. 'And the queen? Does she want that too?' She hugged the baby more tightly.

'Indeed she does.' He caught her eye and winked. 'It's Marie's greatest wish.'

She looked away, unable to bear him so close to her, wanting to reach out to him, wanting him to reach out to her, but the nurses were impatient. The king's servant was hovering, trying to catch his attention; across the room some ladies were waiting for the queen. A dozen pairs of eyes were on her and she had the feeling that each one of them could read her mind.

'Eleyne.' His anguished whisper was so quiet, she wondered if she had imagined it.

Ducking her head to kiss the baby's small nose she allowed herself to glance up. What she read in his eyes made her catch her breath.

It was as if they were alone in the world, she and the king and the small child in her arms. Then it was over. The baby began to cry again. Clucking, the wetnurse hurried forward to take him, the voices of others in the room intruded again and the king was surrounded by his attendants.

She didn't mind. He would find a way – somehow.

It was three days before he did. Rhonwen had arranged it.

Swathed in heavy cloaks, the two women slipped from the postern gate and into the teaming burgh outside the walls. Rhonwen led her down a narrow wynd and into a small court. An outside staircase led up above the baker's shop and Eleyne followed her into a small room, full of the scent of new bread. Outside the high narrow window the River Tweed ran low and slow down the centre of its stony bed. It was full of rubbish, tossed from the town.

'Lock the door after me,' Rhonwen whispered. 'Open to no one unless they knock six times like this.' She rapped with her knuckle on the frame of the window. 'There's wine and pasties here in the basket, if loving makes you both hungry.' She winked. 'The bed's not over-clean, but if it's fit for a king it's good enough for you!' Chuckling, she punched the coverlet and they wrinkled their noses as a cloud of dust flew up. Rhonwen stared round the room once more and then she let herself silently out of the door.

Eleyne walked to the window: a thick unpleasant smell of mud and rubbish wafted from the river, and the room was airless and very hot. She longed to throw off her clothes but she did not dare. Not yet, not until she knew what he wanted from her. Rhonwen had been so sure, but was it possible after all that had come between them that he still loved her?

She paced up and down. In the distance the bells from Kelso Abbey called the monks to nones. Her skirts stirred small eddies of dust from the bare boards and she heard voices from the shop downstairs as the women of the town brought their dough to the baker's great oven. A dog barked endlessly, tied to the door across the narrow street; wheels rattled on the cobbles of the main road towards the castle.

Shouts and the sound of splashing took her back to the rear window, and she stood watching as three small boys stripped and leaped laughing in the river, drenching one another with the near-stagnant water. She stood for a long time watching them, then she went and sat on the bed, lying back, her arm across her eyes. She must have dozed, for when she went back to the window some time later the sun had moved behind the houses and the boys had long since disappeared. Downstairs the shop was silent now, and even the street noises had died away.

He's not coming.

Her mouth was dry, her stomach was no longer tense with anticipation. A heavy resignation began to swamp her. She lifted the cloth from Rhonwen's basket and peered inside. The wine would be welcome and at the sight of the food her stomach gave a growl of hunger.

She was sitting cross-legged on the bed with a cup of wine in one hand and a pasty in the other when she heard footsteps in the wynd outside. They stopped. She held her breath, listening. She heard some-one on the wooden staircase, mounting two at a time. Her knuckles whitened on the cup as she saw the doorlatch jiggle up and down. Outside someone swore under their breath. There was a pause, then a quick rapping on the doorframe.

One two three four five six.

Alexander had come at last. Setting down her cup so quickly she spilled some of the wine, she scrambled to her feet and brushing crumbs of pastry from her gown she ran to the door and fumbled with shaking hands for the bolt.

He was wrapped, as she had been, in a heavy homespun cloak, a hood over his red-gold hair. He slammed the door shut behind him with his foot in the same movement as he pulled her into his arms.

'Eleyne, sweet Eleyne, did you think I'd never come? Dear God, lass, but I've missed you!' He pulled her to him so hard she gasped for breath. 'My Eleyne, what have I done? You should have been Alex's mother! You should have been my queen! Sweet Christ, how could I have been so stupid? When you are away from me, it's as though a piece of me is missing!' His face was in her hair. 'I don't think I can ever let you go again.' He held her at arm's length, his eyes on hers. 'How can our destinies keep us apart like this?' It was a cry of anguish.

She clung to him. 'You are a king. Your destiny is not yours to direct,' she said bleakly. She looked up, her eyes on his, shaken by the passion and anger in his words. Why, if he felt like this, had he turned his back on her? Why had he married Marie?

Reading her thoughts with ease he groaned. 'You are right. My destiny must be ordered by my duty, by my country. If I had married you it would have brought disaster, and yet I know now that I can't live without you!' He was rocking her back and forth in his arms. 'Oh, what are we to do, lass?'

'Make love,' she whispered gently. 'If our love was made by the gods, it doesn't need the blessing of church or man.'

For a single breathless moment they were drowning in each other's eyes, then his lips were on hers, then on her hair, her eyes, her cheeks, and his hands were already busy with the laces at the back of her gown. He continued to kiss her as he undressed her until he was holding her naked in his arms.

'Aren't you going to undress?' She freed her hands from his embrace long enough to unfasten the golden brooch at his shoulder.

'In a minute. I want to see you first.' He stood back, his eyes caressing her body with such love she could feel the touch of his gaze on her skin, stroking, inflaming her, and she found herself breathing heavily and deeply as if he were already inside her.

'Unbraid your hair, lass.' His voice was husky. At last he was pulling off his tunic. She undid it with shaking hands and shook her head so the tangled curls flew in a cloud around her face.

He smiled. 'You're too thin. Why don't you finish your pasty?' He had noticed the remnants of her meal lying on the napkin on the bed.

'I couldn't eat anything now.'

'Later then.' He stepped towards her.

It was much later. It was dark when they sat up and ate and drank together in the bright starlight which filtered through the open window.

Eleyne giggled, leaning against his shoulder. 'I'm covered in crumbs.'

'I'll lick up every one. Here, my love, have some more wine.' The jug clicked against her cup and she felt the velvety wetness splash on her breast.

'Do we have to go?'

'You know we do. And separately.' He sighed. 'We'll both have been missed. I hope the Lady Rhonwen has a story to tell your husband as to where you are.'

'She will.' Eleyne didn't want to know what Rhonwen told Robert; she didn't care as long as she was in Alexander's arms. 'Can we come here again?' she whispered.

'I'm sure we can.' His voice was grim. 'Somehow.'

It was nearly dawn when he dressed at last and let himself quietly from the room. 'Don't come to the castle until the main gate is open,' he commanded, 'then come in with the first townspeople. You won't be noticed in the crowds.' And he was gone.

XIV

They met three more times in the room above the bakehouse before Alexander and his court prepared to ride north to Stirling. No one appeared to have noticed their rendezvous and, that first night, the only occasion when Eleyne was absent all night, Robert had been drunk and insensible in the great hall of the castle. Each day she dreaded the row there would be when Robert said they had to go back, but he seemed content to wait for his brother.

There was no sign of Roger.

XV

STIRLING CASTLE ❖ October

Two weeks after their arrival at Stirling Rhonwen hustled Eleyne once more into her heavy cloak.

'Hurry. It's not so easy to get out unobserved here. I have a note from the king that you are to meet him at the house of the knifegrinder at the foot of Castle Hill. Sir Robert has ridden out with his brother, I saw them leave myself and the queen is, as always, with the child. There should be no trouble.' She tweaked Eleyne's cloak into place. 'You are happy, *cariad*?'

Eleyne nodded. 'I love him so much, I can't live without him.'

'Even though you can never be his queen?'

'Even though.' Eleyne smiled. 'Einion was wrong. We must accept that; or the gods have changed their minds.'

'You haven't seen the future again?'

'No.' Eleyne gave a crestfallen Donnet the order that he must once again stay behind. 'I don't want to see the future, Rhonwen. I want the present, that's all, with Robert out of my bed and the king in it. Is that so very terrible?'

For a moment neither woman spoke, then slowly Rhonwen shook her head. 'All that is important for me, *cariad*, is that you are happy.'

The narrow street was deserted as they made their way over the rough cobbles, searching the housefronts for the sign of the knifegrinder. They found it, set back in the shadows of the castle wall itself. A covered wagon pulled by two oxen was drawn up outside. The beasts, their heads buried in nosebags, dozed in the heat. The shopfront was closed and shuttered, and there was total silence in the house behind it. Rhonwen led the way down the side of the building. The evil-smelling close was dark, but Eleyne didn't notice. She was too tied up with her own inner excitement. Her skin was tingling with anticipation, her stomach a fluttering hollow of longing. At the back of the close a small door stood half open.

'This way,' Rhonwen whispered. 'Keep your head covered in case we meet someone.' She pushed the door cautiously and led the way inside. A narrow inner stair led to an upper room where the closed shutters allowed only a dim light to filter through. It was enough to reveal four figures, swathed in black cloaks, waiting in the shadows.

Rhonwen whirled. 'Run!' she screamed, but it was too late. Another man had appeared at the bottom of the stairs behind Eleyne. There was a dirk in his hand.

'Good afternoon, sweetheart.' Stepping forward as he threw off his cloak, Robert bowed. 'I'm sorry to disappoint you, but this is one tender meeting his grace the king is not going to attend.' He smiled. 'But so that you don't feel slighted, the queen has honoured us with her presence instead.' He bowed at the figure standing to his left and she took a step forward, pushing back her hood.

'Lady Chester,' Marie smiled with a gracious nod. 'I wanted to come myself, to be sure.'

'To be sure?' Eleyne echoed.

'To be sure the rumour was true: that you would stoop to being my husband's whore.' She smiled again. 'It was I who wrote the note and sealed it with his seal. Take your wife away, Sir Robert. We do not wish to see her at court again.' The queen stood back, holding her skirts fastidiously off the dusty floor.

'No.' Eleyne took a step backwards down the stairs, but the man behind her had his foot on the bottom step, the dirk upright in his hand.

'No,' Eleyne repeated as Robert came towards her. She took another step away from him, straight into the arms of the man with the knife. He grabbed her from behind and as she screamed she felt his hand, rough and stinking of the oxen he had been tending, clamp over her mouth. It took only moments for them to tie her in her cloak, to push a gag of rags into her mouth and pull the hood down over her face, then she was carried unceremoniously down the stairs, through the front shop and thrown heavily into the wagon. A whip whistled, the wagon lurched into motion and, with much creaking and groaning, began to swing slowly down the steep hill towards the centre of the town.

Faint with fear and anger and half stifled by the gag and the hood of her cloak which they had pulled right down over her face, Eleyne found herself rolling helplessly from side to side in the bottom of the wagon. Her arms, pinioned to her sides, could not steady her and her ankles were strapped with a thong of hide. Her elbow struck something hard and she almost blacked out with pain. After that she was too dazed to know what was happening. She did not know if Rhonwen was with her. The only sounds were the creak and groan of the swaying vehicle and the occasional crack of the carter's whip.

She lost all track of time. She didn't know if it was minutes or hours before the sound of galloping horses blotted out the plodding gait of the oxen and they lurched to a stop. Robert leaped into the wagon and pulling her into a sitting position against the side, pushed back her hood and removed her gag. She noticed, dazedly, that he was for once completely sober. Rhonwen lay beside her, her trussed body inert.

'Rhonwen?' Eleyne forced her dry mouth to form the words. 'Is she all right?' She felt sick and dizzy and afraid, but above all she was angry. Furious with herself for being so easily tricked and furious with Robert.

Robert prodded Rhonwen viciously with his toe.

'Move her gag, she can't breathe.'

'Good.' Making no attempt to help Rhonwen, Robert perched on the backboard of the wagon, glaring at his wife. 'Comfortable, sweetheart?'

'You can see I'm not.' She kept the anger out of her voice as she tried to shift into an easier position. Her arms were numb and her ankles had swollen painfully. She was desperately hot inside the heavy cloak. Her eyes kept returning to the still body on the straw-covered floor near her. 'Where are you taking us?'

'To stay with a friend. Somewhere the king will never find you.'

'Aren't you going to kill me?'

The defiance and scorn in her voice made him scowl, but he laughed harshly. 'You are no use to me dead, wife. I would lose your income, wouldn't I? But I don't intend to be the laughing stock of Scotland, be sure of that. From now on you will be an obedient and faithful wife and you will never see your beloved Alexander again.'

CHAPTER SIXTEEN

I

CAERNARFON ❖ September 1241

'You are going to London?' Isabella asked Dafydd, her eyes round with astonishment. 'But why?'

'It is the king's command.' Dafydd kicked angrily at a stool near him and it rocked sideways and fell to the floor. 'He wants to consolidate the agreement we reached at Rhuddlan last August.'

'Where you let him take Gruffydd as a prisoner to London.' Isabella raised her eyebrow tartly. 'Are you now going to beg for his release?'

'I am not. Nevertheless, I don't like Gruffydd being there. It isn't right. Our quarrel is our own, it's not Henry of England's business.'

'Then you should not have surrendered to him, should you?' She could not resist the dig even though she saw the angry colour flood into her husband's face.

'I had no choice. You yourself urged it, if you remember, and my friends had deserted me.'

'You had been too soft with them. It would not have happened to your father.' She flounced over to the window. 'I shall come to London with you. It will be wonderful to visit the big city.'

II

LONDON ❖ Michaelmas

The court was all she had dreamed: noisy, rich, crowded, colourful, constantly exciting and full of gossip. And one of the first pieces of gossip she heard was about the strange disappearance of the Countess of Chester.

She heard it from Isabel Bruce, Eleyne's sister-in-law, and Lady Winchester, both of whom had recently ridden south from Stirling.

Lady Winchester swept Isabella into her circle with a generous charm only partially motivated by curiosity as to what the little de Braose was like. She had always liked Eleyne and she detested her brother-in-law, Robert de Quincy.

Her real concern for Eleyne was mixed with lively speculation. 'You know they say she is Alexander's mistress!'

'That was when she hoped to marry him.' Isabella had quickly realised that she had acquired a certain notoriety as the missing countess's sister-in-law.

Lady Winchester smiled. 'But they resumed their affair after Eleyne returned to Scotland. Didn't you know? Isabel Bruce told me she and the king could not keep their eyes off one another!'

'Then perhaps he has spirited her away to a love nest in the distant mountains.' Isabella's crisp sarcasm could not quite hide a wistful note.

'I don't think so.' Lady Winchester was thoughtful. 'I hear the king is seriously worried about her, though he tries to hide it. My brother-in-law, Robert, told him she was safe at Fotheringhay, but she isn't there! And if she had intended to go there, why did she not take her dog? She adores that creature. Nothing would induce her to be separated from it.'

The three women looked at one another in silence.

'Do you think something terrible has happened to her?' Lady Winchester whispered at last.

III

STIRLING ❖ October 1241

Alexander threw the letter down on the table in front of him with an exclamation of impatience. 'Does the man really think I'd believe this!'

At his feet Donnet stirred and pricked his ears, his eyes reproachfully on the king's face. He had accepted grudgingly that this man was for some strange reason his new master, but he still pined every second of the day for Eleyne.

Queen Marie glanced at the letter, eyebrow raised. 'Sir Robert has written again?'

'From Fotheringhay. He tells me his wife is well. He tells me she no longer wants the dog.' He thumped the table with both fists. 'Sweet Christ, does he think I'm a fool?' He swung round on his wife. 'You know more about this than you'd care to admit, madam. Do you think I don't know?' His eyes blazed. 'If anything has happened to her —'

'I'm sure it hasn't.' Marie's voice was irritatingly patronising. 'Husband, can you not accept that the woman grew bored with you? She's a whore. She likes a frequent change of lover. It adds piquancy, no doubt, to her jaded appetites.' She smiled, as aware of the furious clenching of her husband's knuckles and of her own immunity from his fury as she was of the search parties he had sent to quarter the length and breadth of his kingdom. She stood up.

392

'Please. Throw that dog out into the yard where it belongs. It smells.' She gathered her embroidered mantle around her and swept haughtily from the room.

IV
THE TOWER OF LONDON ❖ October 1241

King Henry had been at prayer in his private chapel when Dafydd and Isabella arrived for their final audience at the king's apartments in the Tower.

'You have visited your brother?' Henry threw himself into his high-backed chair and gestured them to smaller seats near him.

'We have indeed, your grace,' Dafydd replied. He was glum. Gruffydd had been bitter and scornful and Senena's tongue had been at its most vitriolic when he and Isabella had been ushered into the spacious chamber, one of the three Gruffydd and his wife had been allocated in their honourable, not to say comfortable, imprisonment.

'The Lady Senena constantly reproaches me for not honouring some agreement she thinks I made to place Gruffydd in your shoes.' Henry leaned back, his eyes half lidded. 'I should imagine it is to your advantage to have Gruffydd out of your way.'

Dafydd gave a slight bow. 'I do not like to see any Welshman in an English prison, sire,' he said firmly.

'Quite.' Henry beamed at him. 'And Welsh women? I should be more than happy for you to take the Lady Senena with you when you leave London.'

Dafydd hid a smile. 'That is for the lady herself to decide, sire. At the moment she is resolved to stay with her husband. I think she feels she is of more use here, where she hopes to be able to persuade you to release him.'

'I see.' Henry's face was impassive as he rose to his feet and, walking across to the window, stood looking down into the courtyard below. Two ravens were squabbling over a pile of rubbish in the corner, tearing at the carcass of some dead animal. 'She is content not to see her youngest children for so long?'

'They are well looked after at Criccieth, sir.'

Henry scratched at part of the glass's leaded frame with his fingernail. 'I have been thinking about the question of the succession,' he went on after a short pause during which Dafydd and Isabella watched him in silence. 'Your succession.' He looked first at Dafydd and then at Isabella. 'You are still childless, I understand.' His tone was impersonal.

Colour flooded Isabella's face. 'We hope all the time for a baby, sire –'

'I am sure you do.' Henry brushed aside her anguished interruption smoothly. 'And I am sure you will soon be blessed, but until then I am not happy, as I am sure you are not happy, with the idea of your half-brother or his children succeeding to any of the principalities of North Wales.'

When Dafydd spoke at last, his voice was heavy with suspicion. 'What are you saying, sire?'

'I have drawn up an agreement.' The king gestured to the table where a document lay next to the inkwell and pens. 'I think it would be advisable as an interim measure for you to appoint me as your heir.'

'No!' Dafydd smashed his fist on the table, making the quills jump.

'No?' Henry repeated mildly. 'I think you will find, if you think about it,' he paused, 'that it is an excellent suggestion.'

V

'Now see what you have done!' Dafydd had scarcely waited until the door of their room was shut before he turned on Isabella. 'If we had children . . .'

'It's not my fault that we have no children.' Isabella's voice rose hysterically. 'You know I can have children. Did I not prove it to you? Did you not see the baby I gave you –'

'That was not a baby, Isabella! Whatever it was,' he shuddered, 'it was dead.' He crossed himself. 'And you have not quickened since.'

'And you know why!' She leaned forward, her eyes glittering. 'Because your sister cursed me.'

'No, Isabella –' It was a long time since she had brought up that particular grievance.

'Yes! She cursed me. She made me barren, she and that servant of the devil who was her nurse.' Little flecks of spittle appeared at the corner of her lips and Dafydd regarded them with fascinated distaste. 'If you want an heir, Dafydd ap Llywelyn,' she rushed on not giving him time to speak, 'you find your sister and make her lift her curse! Until you do that, I will never have a baby, and when you die, Gwynedd will be handed on a plate to your Uncle Henry or little Prince Edward, with your signature to speed its going! And God help you, husband, when the people of Wales find out what you have done.'

She walked past him to a stool and sat down, then she burst into tears.

Dafydd frowned uncomfortably. 'If I make Eleyne lift this curse, if it exists –'

'Are you calling me a liar?' She lifted her head, her eyes glittering with tears.

'No, no, of course not.' He frowned with irritation. 'For the love of the Virgin, Isabella, why didn't you say all this when Eleyne was at Llanfaes? If you really believe it, why wait until now when she is in Scotland?'

'Because now it is urgent. And she isn't in Scotland. Robert de Quincy says she's at Fotheringhay.'

'Then we'll go back that way.' Dafydd gave an inward sigh of relief.

'And if she isn't there?' Isabella dabbed her eyes. She had not passed on to Dafydd the gossip that his sister was missing.

'If she isn't there,' Dafydd replied in exasperation, 'I shall find her.'

VI

LOCH LEVEN CASTLE ❖ February 1242

Days of heavy ceaseless rain and cold gusty winds had turned the small bedchamber into a damp, dismal prison.

Huddled over the fire, Rhonwen turned to the window, where Eleyne was staring out across the black waters of the loch. 'For pity's sake, put up the shutters, *cariad*. What is there to see out there, anyway? Let's at least keep out the cold.'

The side of her face was still swollen from the massive bruise she had sustained when one of Robert's henchmen had hit her with a wooden club three months before. It had been a full day before she had regained consciousness when they had reached their destination.

The two women had been transferred from the oxcart to a light, horse-drawn wagon and for the last few miles they had been thrown across two sumpter horses like so much baggage. When the horses came to a halt at the edge of this great wild loch, they had been thrown into the bottom of a boat and rowed across the water to the lonely castle on its island.

Stiff, bruised and frightened, still thinking that Rhonwen was dead, Eleyne was dragged to the castle's bedchamber and Robert allowed his frustrated anger its full rein. When he left the castle at last in the stern of the rowing boat which had brought them, his wife lay insensible across the bed.

The castle had a garrison of three and as many servants. Eleyne and Rhonwen were allowed wherever they liked on the small island. Where was there for them to go? There were no boats. Supplies came every few weeks from the shore; the rest of the time they were cut off from the world. Slowly Eleyne nursed Rhonwen back to health, and slowly she too recovered from her bruises, learning from Rhonwen how to find healing herbs on the tiny island and how to make them into potions and medicines she had never dreamed existed.

In her loneliness Eleyne found an unexpected companion on the silent island. A woman in a black gown and stiff lace ruff was often there, standing in the shadows. Eleyne caught sight of her as she walked alone through the twilight by the high barmkin wall and she stopped, staring. 'You?' She rubbed her eyes. It was the woman she had seen at Fotheringhay: the black, shadowy apparition who haunted the upper floors of the keep in faraway Northamptonshire. Yet how could that be? The two women looked at each other, silent, both locked in their own misery. Eleyne saw recognition in the other's eyes, then darkness fell, the shadows grew black and the woman disappeared. Eleyne could feel her heart thudding uncertainly beneath her ribs. She stepped forward, peering into the darkness. 'Where are you?' she called softly. 'Who are you? Why do you come to haunt me?' She knew already there would be no answer. The woman was from another world.

It was a long time before Eleyne realised she was pregnant.

'It's the king's child?' Rhonwen kissed her gently and took her hand.

'Of course it's the king's child. Robert hasn't – hadn't –' she changed the word with a shudder – 'been near me in months.' She was standing looking across the black waters towards the low hills which divided her from Alexander.

'Then perhaps the prophecy was true after all,' Rhonwen whispered under her breath. 'Perhaps that child, in your belly, will one day be a king.'

When Robert came back, her pregnancy was already showing. Outside, the winter gales roared across the loch, churning the shallow water to waves, hurling spume against the walls of the keep. He threw off his cloak in the tower room below her bedchamber and turned to look at her, his dark hair sleek with rain. The expression on his face turned first to thoughtful calculation and then to cold anger as his eye travelled slowly down her figure.

'Your lover's child, I take it – not mine, certainly.'

Eleyne pulled her cloak around her defensively. The chamber was cold in spite of the fire which burned in the hearth.

'The king's child.' She raised her chin. 'And this time you will not dare to lay a hand on me.'

'No?' He spoke with deceptive mildness.

She swallowed. The baby kicked her sharply and she brought her arms involuntarily around herself to protect it. 'He knows,' she said desperately. 'He knows about the baby. If anything happens –'

'He doesn't know,' Robert smiled. 'He believes you to be safely at Fotheringhay, whence you were summoned by your uncle. Your other uncle.' He looked around the room. Rhonwen was seated unobtrusively in the shadows, and the other two women squatted near the fire, their

396

eyes on the couple in the centre of the shadowy room. Of the lady who haunted the shadows there was no sign. There were no candles alight, though indoors it was nearly dark. Outside the February afternoon was as colourless as the leaden water of the loch.

'What a merry household!' Robert shouted suddenly. 'I come back to see my wife and all I see is gloom. Wine! Fetch me some wine! And lights and food. God's bones, what kind of welcome is this?'

No one moved. Robert scowled. In three paces he was beside Rhonwen. He grabbed her arm and, swinging her to her feet, flung her towards the door. 'You heard me, woman! Wine!'

'There is very little wine, Robert, and candles are short. So is the firewood.' Eleyne's voice was weary. 'The storms have been so bad the boat has not been able to get here.'

'I got here!' His eyes blazed angrily.

'Then you should have brought supplies with you.' Eleyne moved away from him to Rhonwen's chair and sat down. 'You are not welcome here, Robert.'

'So I gather,' he said. 'And you will be glad to hear that I don't intend to stay long. Not long at all.'

He stayed barely two days and during that time he did not touch her; instead he finished the last cask of wine in the cellar. He was very drunk when he summoned Eleyne from her bedchamber.

'I'm going back to England.' His words were slurred, his eyes bleary. 'I am going back to England,' he repeated carefully, 'and I am leaving you here to rot. You and your bastard.' He slumped against the wall, his legs braced in front of him. 'It's a very easy place to forget, Loch Leven Castle.' He pronounced the words with enormous care. 'Very easy.' He gave a sudden high-pitched giggle. 'I shouldn't be surprised if I forgot you forever.'

'I hope you do.' Eleyne's voice was cold.

'You want to be forgotten?'

'By you, yes.'

Robert giggled again. 'And by the king, oh yes, by the king. I went to see him at Roxburgh on my way here. I sent him your greetings and told him you were well and happy. You are well and happy, aren't you, sweetheart?' He pushed himself away from the wall and gave a small hiccup. 'Though I can't imagine how you can stand being cooped up here with that woman.' He made an obscene gesture at Rhonwen. 'In fact, I think I shall do you one last kindness. I shall relieve you of her company.'

'That is not necessary, Robert.' Eleyne's voice was steady, though her stomach had turned over with fear. Sensing it, the baby kicked feebly beneath her ribs and she flinched.

'Oh, but it is.' He lunged towards Rhonwen and caught her wrist.

'Peter!' he shouted. 'Peter! Some rubbish to dispose of on the way to the shore.'

'No!' Eleyne screamed. 'No, you can't.' She clawed at his arm desperately, but he pushed her away.

'Yes, sweet wife. Take her.' He pushed Rhonwen towards his manservant, who had appeared at the top of the stairs. 'Put her in a sack and take her to the boat.'

'No!' Both women were screaming now. Rhonwen was kicking frantically as the tall young man dragged her from the room. Sobbing, Eleyne ran towards the stairs after him, but Robert caught her. He slapped her face. 'Do you want to risk your precious royal bastard?' he shouted. 'Leave her!'

'Why? Why are you doing this? For pity's sake, Robert.'

'For pity's sake,' he echoed, high-pitched. 'Think about it, my dear, just think what you have done to me and think well. Perhaps this is your real punishment.' He ran down the stairs and out of sight.

Eleyne followed him, but at the narrow door in the undercroft she was stopped by the old castellan. 'Please, Andrew –'

'I'm sorry, my lady, there's nothing you can do. There's nothing any of us can do.' He braced his arm across the doorway. Behind him the small courtyard was already empty, and she could hear nothing but the plaintive murmuring cry of overwintering geese echoing from the bleak shores beyond the loch.

That night she called for a fire in her room. Andrew piled the kindling high, though there was little left on the island, and lit it with a sidelong look at the countess. She was rocking herself back and forth, her arms around her belly, her tears long dry, but her face so drawn in misery that even his unsentimental old heart was touched. He had liked the Lady Rhonwen – for all her tart tongue, she had been fair with him.

'Shall I ask my wife to come and sit with you, my lady?' he ventured when the fire was drawing to his satisfaction. His Janet was a kind soul whose views on Sir Robert had been so outspoken he'd had to slap her face for fear she would be overheard by de Quincy or one of his men. It was Sir Robert, after all, who was paying them to look after the countess and keep her on the island, and paying him more than he had ever dreamed of.

Eleyne shook her head dumbly.

'I'll leave you then, my lady.' He didn't like the look of her at all, but what could he do? He was now the senior member left in the household. Household! He snorted to himself as with a bow he shuffled towards the door. There was him and Janet, Annie, the cook, and three men to mind the walls.

Eleyne sat a long time without moving after he had gone, then slowly she stood up. The fire had settled to a friendly blaze, smoking from the damp in the wood. The night beyond the narrow window was starless, the waters of the loch black and forbidding, as she stood staring out. She felt empty and afraid and lonely as the slow tears began once more to slip from beneath her lids. Of her ghostly companion in imprisonment there was no sign.

For a long time she stayed there, feeling that just by looking at the water she still had some link left with the woman she had loved. At last, frozen and stiff, she turned from the window and went to the fire. She bent awkwardly to throw on another log and caught her breath. There was a picture in the flame. Falling to her knees in the dusty ashes at the edge of the small hearth, her heart thumping with fear, she stared into the heart of the fire.

He was there, the horseman, filling her head, filling the scene in the fire, riding away from her to who knew what fate. But who was he and what had he to do with her? Still she did not know.

Alexander, where are you? Come to me, please.

The position she was kneeling in was uncomfortable. Her back ached and the baby kicked resentfully beneath her ribs. Please. She was talking to the fire as though it were alive and slowly she reached out towards the flames. This time, as they began to lick playfully towards her fingertips, there was no one to pull her back.

VII

De Quincy's men had bound Rhonwen with a single rope around her body, pinioning her arms before pulling the big flour sack over her head and tying its neck around her ankles. Half fainting with fear, and choking from the flour dust still clinging to the hessian, Rhonwen felt herself lifted by the two men and hauled roughly over the ground. Twice she was knocked against something, then at last she was dropped, doubled up, on the bottom boards of the boat.

Frantically she struggled inside the sack as the men walked back up to the castle from the small landing stage, their voices growing fainter, then from the silence she guessed that she was for the time being alone. All she could hear was the gentle lapping of the water and the beating of her own heart. The rope around her body had been carelessly tied; almost at once she felt it loosen as she fought against the stifling folds of sacking, but the rope around her ankles was tight, knotting the neck of the sack. She flailed out with her arms and, humping over, tried to reach her feet, tearing her fingers on the rough material. She was concentrating so hard that she didn't hear the men returning. The sudden dip and buck of the boat as one by one they jumped aboard, and a sharp agonising blow in the breast as someone kicked out at the sack, was the first she knew of their return.

'Sweet Bride, preserve me,' she whispered desperately as she heard the unmistakable sound of Robert's drunken laughter close to her head. 'Sweet lady, help me.'

She could not hear what they were saying. The boat had steadied now and she could feel it travelling through the water, the cold black water which she could sense close beneath her body, on the other side of the thin planking. Panic gripped her and she began to shake all over. Any moment they would stop rowing.

'Sweet lady, save me, please.' She was tearing at the inside of the sack now, not caring if they saw her; moments later another vicious kick told her that they had. It was a while before she realised the boat had lost its swinging momentum through the water. There was another low laugh and she felt hands groping for the corners of the sack.

She screamed again and again as they struggled to move her towards the edge of the boat, rocking it wildly on the black water, then she felt the sharp gunwale beneath her ribs; she hung across it for a long moment before her captors, with a shout of triumph, lifted her feet in the air and tipped her head first over the side.

The sack floated around her, filled as it was with air, then it began to sink and Rhonwen felt the ice-cold blackness closing over her head.

VIII

As Eleyne's screams echoed down the staircase, Andrew dropped the flagon of small beer he had been carrying to the table and raced towards the sound, panting heavily as he climbed the spiral stair in the thickness of the wall.

When he reached the room, he was so appalled he could not move. She had sprawled forward into the ashes and flames were running around her head.

'Blessed Jesu!' He hurled himself across the room and tearing a rug from the bed threw it over her, pummelling out the flames.

'Janet!' He pulled Eleyne back on to the floor and shouted as loudly as he could. 'Janet! For Blessed Christ's sake, woman, get yourself up here quickly!'

He could hear his wife panting as she hurried up the stairs, hampered by her heavy bulk.

'What is it? Is it the bairn?' She arrived, gasping for breath, her face glazed with perspiration.

'My lady's had a fall. Help me, woman, she's too heavy for me.' He was pulling ineffectually at Eleyne's arms. 'Let's get her on the bed.'

'Is she dead?' Janet hadn't moved from the doorway.

'Of course she isn't dead! Stop havering and help me, or she soon will be!'

Between them they pulled Eleyne on to the bed and Andrew cautiously peeled back the blanket he had thrown over her.

'Oh sweet Virgin, look at those burns!' His wife stared down in anguish. 'Oh poor lady!'

'Get something to put on them – quickly.'

'Buttermilk, I'll get some buttermilk.' The woman scurried back towards the stairs as, gently, her husband began to pull away the burned remnants of Eleyne's veil and hair. They still had not seen her hands.

IX

As Rhonwen fought the enveloping wet sackcloth, her fingers became entangled in the loosened seam at the side of the sack. Her lungs were bursting; red stars shot through her head and exploded in her brain. Her struggles were growing weaker. Any second she was going to have to take a breath, to inhale the soft black water which would fill her lungs and seep into her arteries and draw her to itself forever. With one last desperate effort she tore at the seam and felt it part. She pushed her arm through the gaping hole in the clinging wet hessian and then her head. The water was thick with reeds. Her fingers grasped them but they slid away, slippery and tough as wet leather. Then, as her bursting lungs drew in that final lethal breath of water, her fingers broke the surface and clawing towards the stars locked on to a half-submerged tree stump.

X

'Her lovely hair; oh Andrew, her lovely hair.' Janet was soothing the buttermilk over Eleyne's face and head with a pad of soft lambswool.

'Aye.' His face was grim; the woman would be terribly scarred. 'Is the bairn all right?'

Janet shrugged. Wiping her fingers on her apron she put her hand on Eleyne's stomach. 'I can feel it moving, but who knows . . . I wish Lady Rhonwen were here.' Her eyes were round with fear. 'I don't know what to do.' Her soft plump face, reddened and weathered by the winter winds, was crumpled with misery and she started crying.

'You're doing fine, woman, just fine.' He sounded more confident than he felt. Slowly, wearily, he picked up the remnants of Eleyne's burned head-dress and the charred scraps of her hair. After wondering what to do with them, he dropped them with a shrug on to the fire, which hissed and shrivelled them into ash.

Janet worked slowly over the woman lying unconscious on the bed – her face, parts of her scalp, her hands and forearms and shoulder. Painstakingly, she smeared on the cooling buttermilk, tearing away the burned fabric of Eleyne's clothes, binding her hands with strips of cloth she had torn from her own shift. 'It's not all her hair, the Lord be praised,' she murmured to her husband as she worked. 'It's just the one side here, but her face – oh, the poor, poor lass.' She blinked away her tears.

'Just pray she doesn't wake up yet awhile.' He turned away to hide his own emotion. 'It's maybe she won't want to go on living after this.'

XI

Her hands were like claws, clamped on to the wet trunk, her body humped over the body of the tree, her face hanging inches from the water. Her last convulsive heave before she lost consciousness had half dragged her into a position where her head hung down, her mouth open. The loch water drained out of her, leaving her suspended like a bag of old rags. It was raining hard. She could feel the cold sweeping down her neck. Perhaps it was that new, colder cold which had awakened her.

It was just growing light. With a tremendous effort, Rhonwen raised her head and looked around. As far as she could see, water surrounded her. She could see the luminous glow of it in the receding darkness, smell its cold dankness, see the bright trails in the distance where the sunrise was beginning to send pale gold across the Lomond Hills. Cautiously she heaved herself up higher on the log and felt it roll slightly under her weight. She lay still, her eyes closed, her heart banging with fear. She could not feel her feet; the rope still bound them and the hideous wet sacking clung around her waist, turning her into a travesty of a mermaid.

Too tired to move, she lay there a long time, watching it grow light, too cold now to feel cold, letting herself drift into unconsciousness as the first crimson sun path across the water rippled towards her trailing feet.

XII

Eleyne lay staring at the ceiling as the girl rebound the bandages around her hands. She was a small thin young woman, scarcely more than a child, her clothes ragged, her unkempt hair loose around her thin intense face.

'Who are you?' Eleyne could barely whisper; her blistered lips were very sore.

402

'Annie, my lady, I am the cook here.' She seemed well aware of the ironic grandeur of the title she claimed and amused at her self-mockery.

'And where, Annie, did you learn to care for people with such kindness?'

Annie shrugged. 'I used to go with the boat sometimes to St Serf's Island and watch the infirmarian at the priory there. He taught me which herbs to use. When the prior found out, I was forbidden to go there again. But I remembered what he showed me.'

'That's lucky for me.' Eleyne paused. 'Is my face very bad?' There were no mirrors in the castle and she was too ill to bend over a bowl of water looking for her reflection.

'Aye, it is now, but it will get better.' Finishing at last, Annie straightened and tucked the sheet back around her patient. 'I've bathed all the burns with lavender and put on flaxseed poultices; most of them will heal cleanly without a mark. Luckily your scalp wasn't burned. The ash on your face saved you.' She frowned. 'But you have to eat to get better, my lady, and for the baby. Shall I bring you something now, before you sleep?'

Eleyne shook her head. She lifted her hand towards the girl as if to detain her, and then let it fall, flinching at the pain.

'Rhonwen –' she whispered.

Annie looked at the floor and shook her head. 'I'm sorry, my lady –'

'Robert took her?'

Annie nodded. Everyone in the castle had watched the struggling, heaving sack being carried down to the boat, knowing they could do nothing to help against de Quincy's thugs.

'She's dead then.' Eleyne's voice was despairing.

'We don't know for sure.'

'We do. He wanted her dead for so long.' Eleyne turned her face away as the tears began to ooze from beneath her swollen eyelids.

XIII

When Rhonwen next awoke it was full daylight. She lifted her head and looked around. In front of her the water was green with reeds and water plants and about fifty yards away she could see the shoreline rising towards some trees. Cautiously she pulled herself higher on the log. It twisted beneath her but she could see now that it was firmly held by a tangle of branches. If she could just free her feet . . .

It took a long time. The rope was sodden and matted into the sacking and her feet had swollen at the ankles but in the end she managed to unknot it and kicked away the sack. She lay for a long time after that trying to regain her strength and pluck up the courage to relinquish her hold on the tree stump which had saved her life. Finally, she forced herself to let go by sheer will-power. She flopped into the icy water and floundered her way across the reed bed with its clinging mud bottom towards the shore. It seemed to take forever and she could feel her last reserves of strength draining away as she fought her way forward, but at last the ground was firmer under her feet and the water began to shallow and finally she was crawling up the beach into the shelter of some low bushes, where she collapsed into unconsciousness once more.

The rain woke her. The sun had vanished and the sky was heavy. A cold wind was blowing from the north. She could see Loch Leven Castle, low on its island in the distance. Eleyne was there, and for the time being she was safe, but for how long? Wearily Rhonwen pulled herself into a sitting position and began to rub her feet. She had to reach the king.

When the Earl of Fife's steward found her she was wandering in wider and wider circles, staggering slightly as though she were drunk. At first he was going to ride past her, but something made him slow his horse and turn it off the road. It was several seconds before he recognised, in the mud-stained woman with her trailing hair and bare bleeding feet, the nurse of the Countess of Chester. He reined in and slid from the saddle.

He lifted her behind him on the sturdy palfrey and turned towards Falkland Castle. Three times she swayed and nearly fell; after that he tied her to his waist with his leather girdle and made better speed, feeling her head flopping weakly against his shoulder blades. At Falkland she was put to bed and fed a bread-and-milk pap and at last she was allowed to sleep. She could not remember now who she was or what had happened.

The fever burned for four days then at last she awoke clear-headed. Minutes later the earl himself had been summoned to her bedside.

He listened to her story, incredulity and anger vying for predominance in his face, and when at last she had finished he frowned. 'You are welcome to stay at Falkland as long as you wish, Lady Rhonwen. In fact you can make it your home if you can no longer serve Lady Chester for fear of her husband, but I don't know what I can do for her. If her husband wishes to keep her at Loch Leven —'

'It's your castle —'

'But not in use at the moment. He asked me some time ago if he could use it as a hunting lodge.'

'Did he tell you what he would be hunting?' Rhonwen's eyes blazed with something of their old spirit. 'How can you let such a man live, never mind abuse his wife as he does?' She was trembling with rage.

404

'I thought you felt something for her yourself, my lord. The horse you gave her was a lover's gift, surely!'

His face flooded with angry colour. 'She wants none of me, Lady Rhonwen. She is besotted with the king.'

'Then you must love her from afar.' Rhonwen forced herself to smile, aware that she had to use her wits to overcome his hurt pride. 'And you must show her your devotion in your actions. To tell the king of her plight would gain you great favour with him and my lady would see how much you love her.'

She watched his face carefully. Malcolm was a bluff soldier, a good-looking man of few words; tough, fair, no courtier, but she could see that this idea of himself as a chivalric lover pleased him. She prayed under her breath. If he would not help her, she had to find the king without delay and she doubted if she had the strength to stand, let alone ride across Scotland. She waited several seconds more, then: 'If you love her, my lord, you cannot stand by and watch her suffer like this. That place is a vile prison.'

He nodded soberly. 'Very well. I shall ride to the king today and tell him where she is.'

XIV

It was several days before Eleyne was able to rise. She was still in great pain, but each day she was stronger and calmer. The supply boat had still not appeared, and supplies in the castle were very low indeed, but they could manage with what they had. There was no wine, but the well water was fresh and the cow in milk; they had hens and there were plenty of squabs in the dovecote. Annie had concocted healing broths from plants she had found in the small wood outside the castle walls and with calm amusement she had seen her reputation as a healer spread. She was now allowed to treat Andrew for his gout and his wife for her headaches and her troublesome teeth.

It was Annie who first saw the boats.

'They're coming!' She ran inside the castle, waving her basket around her head, scattering snowdrops and coltsfoot, dog's mercury and celandine. 'There's two boats coming over from Kinross, my lady. It will be the food and wine at last!'

'Please God it is not my husband.' Eleyne's face was grim as she climbed painfully to the walls with the others and watched the slow progress of the boats across the sunlit water. Her burns were still raw, but her strength had returned and the baby seemed, miraculously, unharmed.

There were a dozen men in each boat besides the barrels and boxes

405

which proclaimed themselves as supplies. She felt a new flutter of fear. 'Those are not the usual boats.'

'No, my lady.' Andrew was shading his eyes against the glare off the water. For a long time he didn't speak. When he did his voice was heavy with disbelief. 'It is the king.'

Eleyne gasped. The shock of relief and joy shook her whole body. 'Are you sure?'

'Aye, madam, I'm sure. See for yourself. In the second boat. You can see his standard clearly now.'

She frowned into the sun, trying to focus her eyes, then she let out a low cry of dismay. 'No, I don't want to see him. I don't want him to see me.' She pulled the thick veil which was draped over her ruined hair half across her face. 'I can't –'

Janet and Andrew watched as she ran towards the stairs.

'She won't see you, your grace.' The old man greeted the king on his knees. His hands were shaking.

'What do you mean, she won't see me?' The king glared at him. Donnet was at his side. 'Of course she will see me.' His mouth was dry with anticipation, his hands trembling.

Andrew glanced at his wife and shrugged. 'A lot of things have happened here, sire –'

'I know. The Lady Rhonwen told Lord Fife.'

'Lady Rhonwen is alive?' The old man's face broke into a great beam of pleasure.

'She's alive.' The king pursed his lips. 'I doubt if de Quincy will show his face in Scotland again, but if he does he will pay with his life for what he has done here. Lady Rhonwen is at Falkland. She is still very unwell I understand. Now, I wish to see Lady Chester.'

'Sire.' Janet pushed her husband aside. 'You don't understand. There was an accident. The night Lady Rhonwen was taken.' She grimaced at her husband, who was plucking at her sleeve. 'No, I won't hush! He has to know. She was burned. Badly burned.'

'Sweet Jesus! How, in God's name?'

'I don't know, sire, she was alone. She must have fallen.'

'It's her damned obsession with fire!' Alexander shook his head. Suddenly he was terribly afraid for her. 'I should have guessed something like this would happen one day. Where is she?'

He sat on the bed and put his hand gently on her shoulder. Donnet had found her first, streaking up the stairs ahead of him, and was sitting ecstatically by the bed, his great head resting on her feet. 'Speak to me, sweetheart, please.'

She shook her head mutely. 'Go away.' She was facing the wall, the heavy veil pulled down over her face. 'Please.' Her voice was muffled with tears.

'No, I won't go away.' He took her shoulders and pulled her towards him. He could see nothing through the black swathes across her face but there was a long silence as he noticed her swollen figure.

'You are carrying my child?' Her veiled face was forgotten as he rested a hand on her stomach. 'Oh, my darling, I didn't know.'

She groped for his hand with her still-bandaged fingers.

He smiled. 'He is kicking.'

'He kicks a lot.'

He moved his hands up towards her face. Taking the edge of her veil, he lifted it and folded it back. She waited, frozen, to see revulsion in his face as his eyes travelled slowly over her features, but there was none. He brought a finger gently to her temple. 'Poor darling, your lovely hair is gone, but it will grow again. See, already I can see down, here.' His finger traced a line across her brow. 'It was only the ends that were burned. It's not so bad.'

'And the scars?' Her voice was husky.

'The scars will heal.'

'I can't see them, I have no mirror.' She looked at him pleadingly.

'Then I shall be your mirror.' He smiled. 'See, they don't upset me at all, except that they hurt you.' He put his hand over hers and saw her flinch. 'Was it the pictures again? Our baby's future in the flames?'

She shrugged. 'It was the man on the horse. Not you. Someone else. I wanted to touch him, to make him turn so I could see his face.' She pulled the veil back over her head. 'I wanted to see if it was my son.' The tears began to trickle down her cheeks again.

He stood up and walked to the window. 'Does de Quincy know it isn't his?'

'Yes.'

There was a long silence. 'How long did he intend to leave you here?'

'I don't know. Perhaps forever.'

The king stayed four days and they were happy days. They walked around the island, they lay together on the bed and he kissed her belly and her breasts and, again, her poor sore face and hands. But when it was time to go he left her there. 'The castle is in my custody now. You shall have food and wine and servants and guards to keep you safe from de Quincy and his men.' He paused. 'It is safer for you here, Eleyne.'

An image of the queen arose unacknowledged between them and she nodded. 'I don't want to leave, not now. Not until the baby is born and my face is better.'

To allay her fears, he had sent for a Venetian glass mirror and she spent hours staring at her face, tiptoeing with her fingers around the scars. She wept and Annie had scolded her. 'They'll go, I promise. See the ointment I've made? It softens the skin and soothes it. It will get better.'

XV

Lord Fife brought Rhonwen back three days after the king left. He brought Eleyne gifts too: lengths of rich silk; ivory combs for her hair as it grew back and a small book of hours. He kissed her hands and left.

Eight weeks later her baby was born. Rhonwen, Janet and Annie attended her and her labour was quick and easy. A priest, brought over from Kinross, baptised the baby John.

He lived only seven hours.

BOOK THREE

1244–1250

CHAPTER SEVENTEEN

I

LONDON ❖ 1244

The house in Gracechurch Street was very dark. Outside, the sky was black; thunder echoed across the narrow court and the rain poured down, splashing into the puddles and racing down the central gutter carrying a tide of rubbish with it. Though it was noon, the house was lit by candles.

Robert de Quincy was standing by the table. In his hand was a document which bore the seal of the King of England.

Eleyne, standing by the fireplace, was staring at it, but she had made no move to take it.

Robert laid it on the table. 'There you are. As I promised. The king's permission to visit your brother Gruffydd in the Tower.'

'Thank you.'

Her hair had grown back with silver streaks amongst the red-gold, even though she was only twenty-six years old, but her curls were as rampant as ever. Her face was still beautiful; there were scars on her forehead partially concealed by her head-dress, another at the corner of her mouth; one hand was badly marked with tight shiny red scars across the back of her knuckles.

This was only the second time he had seen her in three years. King Henry had made it clear Robert was not to go to Fotheringhay; he had not asked what Henry knew or where the pressure came from to leave Eleyne alone. For a long time he had gone in terror of his life, then, slowly, the fear had receded and he had stopped gazing over his shoulder, expecting a dirk in his back. He had come now to the dowager Countess of Chester's town house by invitation, to deliver the king's letter, and at least until he had actually confronted Eleyne at last he had regained something of his old swagger. Now, looking at her cold face, he was not quite so confident.

'Are you well?' He smiled tentatively.

'Yes.'

'I'd better leave.' He had come as a messenger, to test the water, thinking to win her favour by arranging for her to see Gruffydd. Her face was not encouraging, as she walked over to the table and picked up the document.

'Eleyne – '

'Please go now.' Her voice was colourless. She folded her arms, holding the letter across her chest tightly, like a shield.

He shrugged and walking towards the door he opened it, then he hesitated. He turned. 'Greet your brother from me.'

She made no response. For a long time after he had gone she did not move.

II

THE TOWER OF LONDON ❖ March 1244

Either by accident or design the date of the visit to the Tower had been arranged for St David's Day. Eleyne and Rhonwen found Gruffydd housed in some comfort in one of the private apartments in the White Tower. He waited until the guard had withdrawn before he spoke.

'Eleyne. At last. How are you, little sister?'

Eleyne stared. Her handsome, red-haired brother was a travesty of his former self: he had grown very fat and he was balding.

'For pity's sake, Gruffydd, what have they done to you?' She threw herself into his arms.

'The old stomach, you mean? That'll soon go, girl, when I'm free. You'll see. Senena called me fifty different names last time she came to see me.' His face saddened. 'God, how I miss them! But I'm glad they've gone. It was no life for them here. Have you seen her and the boys?'

Owain was still with him in captivity; the others were with Senena at Criccieth.

'It's no place for anyone here!' Eleyne retorted. 'No, I haven't seen them. I haven't been back to Gwynedd since papa died.'

'So you haven't seen our beloved brother then?' Gruffydd's voice was harsh.

'No, I've not seen anyone.'

Rhonwen had retreated to sit on the window seat which was furnished with cushions; there were hangings on the walls, a table, benches and stools and a chair near the fire. On the table amongst the candlesticks she could see all the paraphernalia for passing the time: a game of chess, abandoned halfway through; parchment and pens, books, a little leather box of dice and several empty wine goblets.

'Gruffydd, how could you stay here? What has happened to you? How can you live without riding and laughing and fighting?'

'I have no choice.' He put his arm around her. 'I live here because

412

I'm a prisoner, little sister. You know that as well as I do, and you know why. Because of the treachery of our brother!' His voice was full of bitterness. 'But we don't want to talk about me. Tell me about yourself. Why aren't you in Scotland?'

'Alexander doesn't want me any more. I bore him two sons, Gruffydd, and they both died. What use am I to him?' Her voice was husky and she turned away.

He frowned. 'I thought he loved you, *cariad*.' He put his hands on her shoulders and turned her back to face him. 'He has a wife to breed for him. He wanted you for love, did he not?' He was looking into her face with enormous compassion. 'Have you not seen him at all?'

She shook her head wordlessly.

He had sent messages and gifts, but she had been too sunk in misery to acknowledge them when he did not come himself. She wanted him, not gifts. Two weeks after little John's burial she had left Loch Leven Castle and begun the long ride south. He had sent no one to stop her.

She had ridden back to England in a daze, unaware of the countryside around her, her face swathed in a black veil. When she reached Fotheringhay she had gone to her bedchamber and begun her mourning for her children and for her love.

It had never occurred to her that Robert might appear at Fotheringhay, and he had not done so, for which she thanked the gods nightly. She did not wonder where he was or who kept him away, it was enough that he did not come. Comforted by her dog and her horses and by the quiet beauty of the countryside, she had recovered. She rode and walked and once more took up the reins of running what estates were left to her as dower lands.

Alexander sent her more gifts and letters there, but she had never replied. He had not come himself, he had left her to mourn alone. Her pride would not allow her to beg him to come, and now it was too late. However much she longed to throw herself into his arms, she couldn't rid herself of the lump of ice which seemed to fill her heart; the thought of her tiny John, lying so still and white in his royal cradle, devastated her every time she let herself think about Scotland and Scotland's king.

There had been no word of Robert until that night when she had been on a visit to London to see Luned and her brood of noisy, happy children when she had received the letter from him saying that he had interceded for her with King Henry so that she could visit Gruffydd, something Henry had steadfastly refused to allow before.

'Have you written to Alexander? Or sent him a message?' Gruffydd persisted gently.

'If he wants me he knows where to find me.'

'Perhaps he is waiting to see if you want him?'

She considered the idea, then she smiled. 'I don't think so. He has a wife now to keep him amused.' She broke away from Gruffydd and walked across to the table. She studied the chessboard, then she picked up one of the carved ivory pieces and moved it thoughtfully. 'We are a pair of miserable fools, aren't we?' she said slowly.

'Looks like it.' He grinned.

'I, at least, have an excuse,' she went on. 'You do not. Look at the state you are in, Gruffydd. How could you allow yourself to become such a passive victim? How can you stand by and watch Henry inherit Gwynedd if Isabella never gives Dafydd a son? Don't you care about your inheritance any more? Doesn't Owain? Don't you owe it to him? And to Llywelyn and Rhodri and Dafydd to get out of here?' Her eyes flashed with anger. 'Don't do that to them, Gruffydd. You seem to have few guards. If I had been you, I would have long since escaped. Or do you really like this fat living?' She tapped his stomach so sharply he winced. 'I'm surprised at you, brother, I thought you were made of sterner stuff. Wales needs you there, not mouldering away in London!'

He flushed angrily. 'What am I supposed to do? They keep the doors locked and bolted and didn't you notice that there are guards? This is the king's fortress, Eleyne! I'm not here for my health. I'm a prisoner of state!'

'There are no bars on the window. Go that way!' she retorted. 'Think of something! Other people have escaped from the Tower. The boys won't even remember their father at this rate.' She sat down crossly on one of the carved stools.

He smiled. 'Same old Eleyne. Still a firebrand.'

'No, not any more. I just live in the country with my horses and my dogs like a sturdy yeoman.'

Gruffydd laughed out loud. 'My yeoman sister! And she dares to criticise me for growing fat!'

'I am criticising you for giving up.'

'And what have you done, Eleyne?' He was goaded into retaliation. 'You have resigned yourself to living alone, leaving your lover to his shrewish wife! You take no part in politics. You have not even been sufficiently interested in what Dafydd is doing to visit him since he inherited my lands.' He had grown red with anger.

Through the window they could hear the ravens croaking far below in the courtyard, as they fluttered over the carcass of a dead dog. In their cages nearby two leopards prowled restlessly as they smelled the blood. Rhonwen was studying her fingernails as brother and sister faced each other with sudden hostility.

'I have no lover,' she whispered at last.

'Did he say that?'

'No, but –'

'Eleyne, go to him.' He sat down and leaned forward, his elbows

414

on his knees. 'I'll make a pact with you – I'll try if you'll try. I'll wager a hundred pounds that I can be eating my dinner at Criccieth with Senena before you sit on your lover's knee at Roxburgh.'

She smiled. 'I don't have a hundred pounds, Gruffydd.'

'Nor do I. Sixpence, then, sixpence and a kiss.'

He waited, watching her face, trying to read her thoughts as she stared into the fire.

It had been so long since she had allowed herself any hope; so long since she had allowed herself to think about Alexander at all without the tiny pale figures of her babies coming between them, but now, as she sat in Gruffydd's chamber in the Tower, she felt a glimmer of optimism.

Gruffydd saw it and smiled. 'We're fighters, you and I, and we've both forgotten it,' he said softly.

In the window embrasure Rhonwen listened intently. Gruffydd was succeeding where she had failed. She held her breath, not daring to move lest she break their mood.

'I suppose it would do no harm to ride north and see.' Eleyne's heart had begun to beat rapidly.

'No harm at all.' He nodded vigorously. 'And we must both set off on our journeys within the week. That is part of the wager. By God, Eleyne, you're good for me. You're right, I have accepted captivity like a capon waiting for the cook. I'll go! I'll go back to Wales and fight for what is mine.' He took her hand and pulled her to her feet, then he hugged her so tightly she gasped for breath. 'We won't meet again here in London.' He held her at arm's length, suddenly serious. 'God bless you, little sister, and keep you safe and happy.'

'And you, brother.' Eleyne kissed him on the cheek. 'I'll come again to Wales and bring you the King of Scotland's greetings.'

'Done!' Gruffydd spat on his palm and smacked it against hers.

III

GRACECHURCH STREET, LONDON

Now that she had allowed herself to think about Alexander, Eleyne could think of nothing else. Her whole being ached with longing. Some part of her which had been walled off in misery had come alive again.

'So, at last you have come to your senses,' Rhonwen remarked. 'How I bless the Lord Gruffydd for talking some sense into you.'

'Do you think Alexander will still want me?' Eleyne wavered and her hand went unconsciously to her temple, where the worst of her scars still showed beneath the soft loops of her hair. Was that her real reason for not facing him again? Her terror of what he would say when he saw her scars?

'Of course he will want you,' Rhonwen said. 'I guarantee it. The love he has for you is something very special. I have never seen a man so in love.'

'Then why didn't he come after me?' Eleyne moved to the mirror, studying her face, something she very rarely did. She touched her forehead with her fingertips. The scars had faded: in the evening, in the candlelight they hardly showed at all. Did they make her look ugly? She tried to view them dispassionately, as a man would, assessing them in a way she had not brought herself to do before . . . but she could not judge. The scars which hurt were inside her.

Would he still want her? She stared into her own eyes seeking an answer, and found none. Instinctively she glanced across at the fire. But there was no answer there either.

'He didn't follow you because he respects you too much. He wanted what you wanted, even if it destroyed him to wait,' Rhonwen said softly. 'But he has waited, and he has never given up hope.'

'How do you know?' Eleyne turned from the mirror and looked at her.

'I just know.' Rhonwen smiled enigmatically, her eyes still with that strange feral blankness which had lurked in them since her experience in the loch. 'Alexander of Scotland is one of the few men I have ever admired unreservedly; the only man I have ever met who deserves my Eleyne. Unlike that filth who is your husband.'

Eleyne smiled. 'I wonder if you like Alexander because he is a king.'

Rhonwen grinned. For a moment she focused totally on Eleyne's face and Eleyne felt something of her old warmth. 'It helps,' she said candidly. 'But above all he is a man of honour. He will be waiting for you if you have the courage to go to him – and you have the courage.'

'Yes, I think I do at last.'

'And to win your brother's bet we must go soon.'

'I think I can afford to lose sixpence . . .'

But Rhonwen was shaking her head. 'No, no, we must go at once. Don't you see, he might try to stop you!'

'Gruffydd?'

'No, not Gruffydd, de Quincy!' Rhonwen's voice hardened. 'He has seen you again. You have spoken to him. He has remembered you and he has the king's ear. Don't trust him, *cariad*, he will try to get you back. I'm sure of it!' Her eyes burned with fury. She had not seen Robert when he came to see Eleyne but she had sensed him there, his presence like a loathsome wart in the house she still thought of as hers. 'Let me start packing. Let's go soon. What is there to wait for?'

For a moment Eleyne was silent, then she nodded. What was there to wait for? She wanted Alexander, she wanted him so badly she could not imagine how she had lived without him all this time.

IV
THE TOWER

Gruffydd peered at the courtyard three storeys below. In the soft moonlight the cobbles looked like beaten earth, the shadows black holes in the wall. It was at night that the animals in the king's menagerie grew restless; in the silence he could hear the snarling of a leopard. It was at night too that the fetid air from the moat and the cold mud smell of the river merged with the cooler winds and sometimes, through the high window, he imagined he could smell the cold clean winds of Yr Wyddfa.

He turned to look at his companions as they sat before the fire, the chessboard between them: two Welsh men, Ion and Emrys, who had loyally volunteered with so many others to share his exile and his imprisonment and with them his eldest son, Owain.

Eleyne's visit had made him restless. When she had gone he had stood a long time looking down out of this same window, to see if he could catch a glimpse of her as she left the Tower. Had he ever intended to try to keep his part of the wager, or had he done it to goad her into going after some happiness in a bleak world? He wasn't sure. He had hated to see her so unhappy, and he had guessed that one of the real reasons for her reluctance to go back to Scotland was her fear of Alexander seeing her scars. But they were nothing. Court beauties he had seen in Henry's apartments had worse disfigurements by far than the marks he had seen on her face. They added, if anything, to the quirky nature of his spirited sister's beauty. He did not know if Alexander still loved her, but she had to find out and, if she wanted him, fight for him!

He sighed. He used to be a fighter, but the mood had gone. There was so much against him: his father's wishes, Dafydd's success, and now the combination of Dafydd and Henry of England. His fate seemed inescapable.

He sighed and leaned forward, his elbows on the broad sill. He had never really thought about escape. Everyone knew it was impossible to escape from the Tower unless one had friends and money, and even then it wasn't easy. Yet now, looking down into the inner ward far below, a plan began slowly to form. Once down there it would not be hard to hide in those dense black shadows until daylight came; then, when the heavy gates opened to admit the supply carts from the city, he only had to find an empty one ready to leave, climb in, lost in the milling crowds, and crouch under some empty sacks. He doubted if the security was tight. What had Londoners to fear? Certainly not one fat, middle-aged Welshman who had lodged in the Tower for two and a half years without making the slightest attempt to escape. Eleyne was right. Why hadn't he done it years ago?

He leaned further into the window. The problem was reaching the ground. The doors were locked and there were guards at every cross landing on the main stairs in the great keep. He had seen them when he had been summoned to King Henry's apartments on the floor below his. He had not considered the window until Eleyne's remark about there being no bars; her challenge. He inched forward and peered down. It was a long way down from the great double stone lancets, but as a youth he would have thought nothing of shinning down a rope from a window higher than this!

Perhaps, after all, all bets were on. He smiled to himself. Why delay? St David's Day was perfect. What better day to set off on his journey home?

'Ion. Emrys. Owain. A word.' He turned towards the chess players.

There were plenty of sheets to knot together. The three men leaned out in turn and made the calculation, then they compared notes. They were within two sheets of one another in their guesses. They would wait until the darkest hour of the night, just before the guard changed, when the sentries were cold and tired and huddled around their braziers. Then they would go.

Ion cast a wary eye up at the brightness of the moon. 'By then it will be around the side of the keep and this window will be in deep shadow.' He grinned. They were all excited now, Gruffydd's mood deeply infectious.

They piled pillows in the prince's bed and covered them with blankets, then did the same for the other beds. The guards seldom checked on their prisoners, and breakfast was always brought late in the knowledge that a long night's drinking was not conducive to early rising. But they could afford to take no chances. The longer start they had on their pursuers the better.

'I'll go first.' Ion slapped the prince on the shoulder. 'It's time.' They had enlisted the help of one of their most loyal servants. He would release the sheets after the last man and go back to a sodden boozy sleep. The jug of wine on the table was still full, and he had been promised it all.

The shadow had come round to the window. Ion climbed on to the inner sill and looked down. It took some manoeuvring, but at last he managed to kneel backwards on the sill and shuffled back, his hands firmly gripped on the sheets knotted around the stone mullion. He vanished from view, letting himself down hand over hand, his legs braced against the wall. In two agonising, endless minutes he reached the ground. He grinned up from the darkness and Gruffydd saw the pale blur of the man's upturned face. Then Ion ran for the deeper shadows.

'Me next.' Gruffydd's heart was pounding very fast.

'Good luck, my friend. God speed.' Emrys clapped him on the shoulder.

'Good luck, father.' Owain grinned at him and shook his hand, then he gave him a hug. 'See you down there.'

They watched in breathless silence as Gruffydd hauled himself into the deep embrasure and edged his way towards the window, feet first. The gap was narrow and he felt it catch his hips. He wriggled hard, sweat breaking out all over him. Why had he let himself get so fat? He pushed again. Sweet Christ! He couldn't do it. He would not fit. 'Push!' he gasped. 'Push me.'

Emrys braced his hands against his prince's shoulders and pushed hard, but Gruffydd did not budge. Desperately he wriggled back inside, his face covered in sweat, heavy with disappointment. Then Owain grabbed his arm. 'Upstairs, on to the roof! The door isn't locked, I've been up there! We can put the rope around the battlements.' Already he was scrabbling with the knots which had pulled tight under Ion's weight.

Gruffydd's mouth was dry with fear and anger. He watched as Emrys pulled up the long rope of sheets, wondering what Ion was thinking as he stared up at the window. 'Come on, man,' Emrys urged, 'we'll have you down there in no time!'

'Wait! Another sheet,' Owain cried. 'The rope won't be long enough from the battlements.'

Gruffydd took a deep breath. 'Lucky you remembered that, boy,' he said with false joviality, slapping his son on the back.

The rooftop was silent, the leads ice-cold. Above London the night was frosted with a myriad stars. All three gazed upwards, then Emrys took the rope and began to knot it around one of the great stone merlons. He worked fast, his fingers tying the sheet again and again until he was sure the rope was secure. Then he leaned out through the embrasure. Christ, but it was high! He studied the shadows of the inner ward, listening intently, then at last he let the coils of the makeshift rope fall into the darkness. He made a thumbs-up sign to Gruffydd.

From somewhere in the dark Gruffydd heard the deep barking roar of a lion from the menagerie. It was a lonely, primeval sound and he shuddered. He climbed on to the embrasure and peered over, then he turned his back to the void and began to edge backwards on his knees, his hands gripping the knotted sheets. He could see nothing behind him, and he had no way of knowing if any of the guards were standing in the courtyard waiting for him. He had to trust to luck. He wriggled a little further, feeling his legs dangling disconcertingly into space, and he tried not to think of the drop as he pushed grimly on. The stones at the sides of the embrasure caught at him, grazing his hips. He wriggled harder.

And then he was through. His centre of gravity moved sharply outwards and for a moment he was hanging by his elbows. He closed his grip more firmly on the sheets and pushed himself over the edge. There was a sharp tearing sound and his heart stopped beating, but the sheets held and slowly hand over hand he began to edge his way down. The tendons in his shoulders cracked and the joints in his hands ached. Sharp sweat dripped into his eyes. There was another slight give in the makeshift rope and again his heart jumped frantically! Sweet Christ, he had nearly let go in fright.

Above him in the darkness the reef knot joining the second and third sheet strained and looped, and the ends began to pull free.

Not far, now, not far. Doggedly he let himself down, hand over hand. He saw the great bulk of the keep above him against the stars, the black spaces which were the windows like gaping mouths in the white-washed stone. He could not see the rope, but he felt it slip again and the sweat on his shoulders sheened over with ice.

Sweet Jesus, hold on. Please let it hold on. He was trying to hurry now, fumbling with his legs, but his muscles were weak and his whole body was screaming with protest at his weight.

When the sheets parted, he was still thirty feet from the ground.

V

GRACECHURCH STREET

Eleyne watched with increasing impatience as the grooms and servants loaded the last boxes into the wagons. It had taken all night to make the preparations, to pack, to load the wagons and saddle the horses. She had stifled the urge to jump on a horse and gallop northwards alone, to feel the wind sweeping her hair back from her face, the pull and thrust of the horse's powerful leg muscles beneath her, carrying her on, but she waited. She stood as Rhonwen pinned her cloak around her shoulders and watched as Tam Lin was led towards her, his neck proudly arched, his caparison fluttering in the cold March wind. Now that they were setting off, she was afraid.

Hal Longshaft, her steward, stepped forward. 'We're ready, my lady.' He was smiling. The whole household had caught her excitement.

'Thank you, Hal.' She took the horse's rein.

She was already mounted when the troop of royal horsemen swept around the corner and down the narrow street, their hooves loud above the low rumble of early morning traffic.

The riders wheeled into the gates which had been opened wide for the departure of Eleyne's household. The officer in charge dragged his horse to a rearing halt before her and saluted with a drawn sword.

'Lady Chester. I have a warrant for your arrest!'

Eleyne stared at him in horror. 'By whose order?' she demanded numbly. She had gone cold all over. She was very conscious of Hal Longshaft and Rhonwen standing protectively near her. Tam Lin scraped impatiently at the ground with a foreleg and shook his head. Hal put his hand on the horse's bridle and gentled him.

'By order of the king.'

'And what am I charged with?'

'With aiding and abetting the attempted escape of a prisoner from his grace's fortress of the Tower.' The man stepped forward.

'Gruffydd?' She whispered his name under her breath.

If he heard the name he gave no sign. 'You are to accompany me now to the Tower, my lady. Command your servants to return to the house. You will not be leaving London today.'

Stunned, she turned to her steward. 'You must see to it, Hal,' she said quietly.

'Yes, my lady.'

'My ladies will accompany me,' she said to the officer, keeping her voice as firm as she could. She gestured to Rhonwen and Nesta to mount and then she kicked Tam Lin forward. To keep up with her, the man had to leap for his horse.

As they rode through the walls into the inner ward of the Tower there were knots of people everywhere, whispering: soldiers, servants and townspeople. Eleyne felt their eyes watching her, sensed they were whispering about her and suddenly she was filled with dread.

King Henry was waiting in the royal apartments in the White Tower.

'So!' He swung to face her as soon as she appeared. 'Are you satisfied now? You always were a trouble-maker! I should have known you wouldn't change! I should have remembered your capacity for creating mayhem.' He swung round the table towards her in a swirl of scarlet and gold, and his attendants cringed back against the walls. 'Well, madam, you have meddled for the last time!' He thrust his head forward in a characteristic gesture of fury. 'I listened to Alexander of Scotland when he begged me to allow you to live alone; I kept your husband by me at his request and kept him out of your way as he asked. But no more!'

Eleyne stared at him, trying to come to terms with what he was saying, but Henry swept on. 'That is over! I am going to send you back to de Quincy and he can have the governance of you from now on. You will learn in future to live in obedience to him as the church and the law require. I wash my hands of you. I do Alexander no more favours! I should imprison you for what you have done!'

Eleyne could feel her hands shaking. Her mind was spinning in confusion.

'I don't understand. Where is Gruffydd? I want to see him. Whatever he did it was not of my doing. How could I have helped him? What have I done?'

'What have you done?' he spluttered.

'Your grace.' A priest who had been seated on a bench at the back of the room stood up and stepped forward. 'Lady Chester has obviously not heard what has happened.'

For a moment Henry was taken aback, but his fury was unchecked. 'Then I shall have to tell her! Your brother, niece, is dead!'

'Dead! My brother?' Eleyne stared at him, her face white.

'Your brother, Gruffydd, my lady. The prince was killed last night.'

'Killed?' She was ashen.

'Killed,' Henry repeated. 'You talked him into trying to escape when you visited him yesterday, didn't you? For three years he has been content to live as our guest here in the Tower. You visit him and that same night he tries to climb from the roof and, Sweet Lady! I lose my hostage and now your other brother will no doubt stir up the whole of Wales again!' He thumped the table with both hands.

Eleyne was trying to hold back her tears. 'Where is he?' The king was right. It was her fault. Gruffydd's death was all her fault.

'He lies in St John's Chapel, my lady.' The priest looked at her stricken face with some sympathy. 'I am sure his grace will allow you to see him to say goodbye.'

Henry nodded grimly. 'Say your farewells to him, then you will return to Fotheringhay with your husband. I have told him to keep you there. It will not be possible for you to go to Scotland again, nor will you ride to Wales.' He folded his arms, his malice a clear expression of his fury. 'And I do not wish to see you or your husband at court again.'

VI

FOTHERINGHAY ❖ March 1244

'It's all your own fault!' Robert de Quincy was seething with anger. 'It suited us both, the way things were, and now we are both exiled.'

He was watching the long baggage train ride into the courtyard at Fotheringhay from the steps to the door in the keep. 'And I am appointed your jailer! By the king this time.' He gave a grim smile. 'What irony. You must appreciate the humour of the situation. To have brought all this on yourself was quite some feat, was it not?' His mood changed. 'It will be pleasant, sweetheart, will it not, to play house again together at last?'

'I hardly think so, for either of us,' she retorted. She would not wait even a day. Tam Lin was still fresh; they had ridden barely ten miles on the last leg of the journey. As soon as Robert was nodding over the last of their midday meal, drugged with wine, she would ride north alone.

Rhonwen had stayed in London at her insistence, as had Hal. There was no one here to whom she could reveal her plan. She would ride alone and fast and pray that Alexander would welcome her. Ducking into the keep out of the wind, she stood in the cold, dark chamber on the first floor. Someone had lit a fire but it still smouldered sullenly, smoke curling from the damp logs and being sucked sideways across the floor. The floor coverings were stale and no furniture had yet been set up. It was not a welcoming place.

She shivered, then glanced around. One friend at least was still here, in the shadows: the lady who had haunted Loch Leven Castle – the lady with whom, by some strange alchemy, she shared her blood.

'Grim, isn't it?' Robert was at her shoulder. 'We shall be hard put to keep ourselves amused.' He took her arm and she felt the familiar cruel grip of his fingers with a shudder. 'You are to be guarded, sweetheart, did the king tell you? In case you should inexplicably feel the urge to run away. Not that Alexander wants you any more. Did Henry tell you that too? The King of Scots has refused leave for you to travel north again. He has lost interest in you. But you knew that, didn't you? And if your behaviour gives me any cause for worry, I have the king's permission to lock you up.' He paused. 'And chastise you as I think fit. And no Scot, noble or baseborn, king or peasant, is going to stop me.'

VII

FOTHERINGHAY ❖ Easter 1245

Within four months she was pregnant and on Easter Day the following year she went into labour. Robert stood by the bed as pain after pain tore through her straining body. He was smiling.

'At least this time I know it's mine. My son.' He was completely sober. He watched with detached interest as Eleyne's women scuttled around her preparing the room. The carpenter had brought a crib up to the bedchamber that morning, beautifully carved and polished, furnished with small sheets and blankets, and the new swaddling bands hung by the fire to warm.

Alice Goodwife stood beside Eleyne, her hand firmly pressed to her mistress's distended stomach. 'He'll come soon now, my lady. I can feel your muscles all tightened and ready. Girl, fetch a cloth for my lady's face!' Alice did not stop her expert gropings as one of the servants wiped Eleyne's forehead. Eleyne groaned. Neither of her two previous births had prepared her for this pain. Both had been quick, the babies small. She moaned, throwing herself away from the midwife's probing fingers, hunching her knees towards her stomach. Then she sat up.

'I must walk about. I can't stand this any more. Help me up.' The sweat was pouring down her face.

'Best lie still, my lady.' Alice pushed her back on the pillows with surprising strength.

'I can't lie still! For pity's sake. An animal walks –'

'And you are no animal, my lady. Do you think our Blessed Virgin made such a fuss when she bore her sweet babe?' The woman leaned close, her eyes narrowed; her breath stank of onions. 'For the sake of the baby now, you be still.'

'No.' Eleyne pushed her away. 'I have to walk. I have to.' She kicked off the blankets and tried to swing her legs over the side of the bed. Her shift was soaked in blood.

'Lie still, Eleyne.' Robert's voice was harsh above the sound of her laboured breathing and the agitated tones of the women. 'Or I shall have you tied to the bed. I won't have my son harmed.'

Eleyne closed her eyes, aware that Alice's expression had not changed. 'Take no notice, my lady,' Alice said softly, 'but lie still, please.'

'So your son can be saved, but not your wife!' Eleyne cried, through clenched teeth.

'I'm sure there will be no need for choice.' Robert folded his arms and turned to Alice. 'How much longer?' He affected a yawn. Outside it was growing dark.

'As long as God wills,' Alice retorted. 'Women are born to travail. The babe will come when it's ready and not before.'

'I reckon it needs turning.' The old woman who had been tending the fire joined her by the bed. 'I've seen births like this before. The babe is feet first, you mark. He'll have to be turned.'

Eleyne bit her lip as another spasm tore through her body and she tasted salt blood on her tongue as she realised that she was too tired to argue. Her body was exhausted. She felt the pain carry and lift her as though it were a wave and leave her in soft darkness. Then the next contraction dragged her back to screaming wakefulness. 'For God's sake do something!' She clutched at Alice's hands. She threw her head back, fighting the pain. As she did so she caught sight of Robert, lounging against the wall, his arms folded. Several times he had left the room and gone away to eat and drink and rest, but he had always returned. 'Go away!' she screamed. 'Go away! Get out of here. Get out!'

'Not until I've seen my son born.' His voice was calm, but she did not hear him. She had thrown herself back against the pillows, grabbing at the twisted sheet which had been tied to the bedpost for her to pull. Alice put a cloth soaked in coriander in Eleyne's hand and encouraged her to put it to her face. 'Breathe it in, my lady, breathe in the fumes. They'll make it easier.'

'If the child's legs are across the way to freedom, it will never come and they will both die.' The old woman shook her head gloomily. 'I've turned babies before, my lady, you'd do best to let me see.' Elbowing Alice aside at last she pulled back the sheets and began to feel with surprising gentleness beneath Eleyne's bloodstained shift. 'No, 'tis a normal birth, Blessed Mother be praised. I can feel the head. It won't be long now.' She wiped her fingers fastidiously on the corner of the sheet and looked down at Eleyne as she lay in an exhausted doze. 'This child will live, my dear, and grow tall and healthy.' She put her hand on Eleyne's forehead. 'A few more pushes, my lady, and she will be born.'

'She?' Eleyne's eyes flickered open.

The woman gave a fruity chuckle. 'I'd lay money on it,' she said.

Twenty minutes later the baby was born. Robert stepped forward. 'My son!' he said exultantly.

'Your daughter, sir.' Alice held the naked child aloft, the pulsating cord still dangling from its belly.

Robert's face darkened. 'But I wanted a son!' He stepped back in disgust.

'We get what God sends us!' Alice handed the baby to the old woman.

Eleyne lying exhausted on the bed turned her head slowly towards him. 'It takes a man to father a son,' she whispered hoarsely.

'And you think I am not a man?' Robert's voice was dangerously low. He stepped forward threateningly. 'You contrived this. To spite me! You with your spells and your foresight. Well, you will be sorry, my lady, very sorry.' He looked as though he would hit her.

Alice stepped between him and the bed. 'My lady must sleep now, sir. You can see how tired she is . . .' She folded her arms in a gesture so adamant that Robert stopped, then turned on his heel.

Eleyne did not want the child. She turned her head away and closed her eyes and Alice beckoned forward the wetnurse who had been waiting.

The old woman who had stood watching as they cleaned Eleyne's torn and aching body and changed the stinking sheets sat down on the bed. 'I told you. She will live.'

'The others died.' Tears slid down Eleyne's cheeks. 'My two little boys. I watched them die in my arms.' She had wanted them; prayed for them; planned for them. And all for nothing.

'Look, my lady.' The old woman took the swaddled baby from the nurse. 'See, it's you she wants, bless her. See her tiny face. She'll be a beauty, this child of yours.'

'If she lives.' Eleyne's eyes were closed.

'She will live.' The woman's voice was so forceful that everyone in the room stopped what they were doing and stared.

Eleyne opened her eyes and the woman thrust the baby at her, folding Eleyne's limp arms around her. 'She is your child, my lady, yours,' she whispered. 'What does the father matter? She is of your blood, your body. It's your love she wants.'

Almost unwillingly, Eleyne found herself looking down at the swaddled bundle in her arms. The fuzz of hair on the baby's head was dark, the eyes, which looked directly and unblinkingly into hers, a deep midnight blue. Involuntarily, her arms tightened and, without knowing she had done it, she bent to nuzzle the small soft head.

Three days later as she slept, with the baby beside her in its carved cradle, Robert rode out of the castle and took the road south. He had waited only for the baptism. His daughter had been named Joanna.

VIII
ROXBURGH CASTLE

Marie de Couci waited until her husband's chancellor had left the room, followed by the clerks and servants of the chancellery. Alexander looked up at her and waited. He was weary after an afternoon of intense discussion; he wanted food and wine and relaxation. His wife's expression was smug, and he felt his heart sink. Why did she take such an unholy pleasure in bad news? No doubt it was bad news.

'So, my dear, you have something to tell me.'

Marie looked at the floor, her expression veiled. 'My lord, if I don't tell you, someone else will. You have to know.' The triumphant glance she threw him was so swift he all but missed it. 'Lady Chester has been brought to bed of a daughter.' She paused. 'By her husband.'

Alexander had long ago schooled his expression to give nothing away. She would never have the satisfaction of knowing how the news hurt him.

ABER ❖ February 1246

Isabella looked for a long time staring at the letter before her then slowly she stood up and walking to the fire she dropped it on to the flames. So, Eleyne's child continued to thrive. She had had reports over the last ten months from one of Eleyne's servants, since that first tentative note after the baby's birth. Each time she had cried, always secretly, always bitterly, for her own barren womb. And her tears this time had been more anguished than ever as Dafydd had drawn up the details of the succession with Ednyfed Fychan, who had been his father's most trusted adviser and now was Dafydd's. It was unthinkable that Henry of England should remain Dafydd's heir. The line must after all revert, now Gruffydd was dead, to Gruffydd's eldest son, Owain, released from the Tower the previous August; Owain who had three younger brothers behind him, all robust and healthy. What hurt Isabella so much was the way they all assumed now that there would be no direct heir; no son for Dafydd. She stamped her foot petulantly and sighed.

The death of Gruffydd had removed any need for restraint on Dafydd's part. At first, although he had expected it, Henry did not take the renewed rebellion seriously, but news had reached them now that he had resolved on a major campaign in Wales. Soon the war would resume in earnest. Isabella frowned at the snow which whirled thickly down. It was the first day of Lent.

Dafydd had eaten something that disagreed with him in the wild Shrove Tide feasting the night before and had retired to his chamber with a belly ache. A few hours later he had begun to vomit violently and this morning he had been worse. She sighed again; she resented anything which kept him from her bed. She needed him with a deep aching hunger which was more than physical – it had become an obsession. The more often they made love, the more chance that she would conceive. Her hand strayed to her throat. Three amulets hung there now, three amulets to ward off the evil eye and counteract Eleyne's curse. Because it was Eleyne's fault that she had no child.

She walked back to the fire and kicked out spitefully at the logs where the letter from Fotheringhay had disintegrated into ash. Perhaps it would happen tonight. The stars were propitious and Dafydd would be recovered by then. She would bathe in rose water in front of the fire and have her servants rub scented oils into her skin. She touched her breasts gently and closed her eyes. Two days before she had vowed her most beautiful necklace to the shrine at Holywell if she should conceive. Surely the Virgin would help her tonight.

But that night Dafydd was worse. He was contorted with pain and now he had developed a fever. Isabella was suddenly afraid. 'What is it?' She looked at the ring of learned doctors around the bed. 'What's wrong with him?'

Ednyfed was standing near her, his face set with worry. 'There's a hard swelling in the belly,' he said softly. 'The doctors fear there's some kind of obstruction.' He glanced at the huddle of physicians who were examining samples of Dafydd's urine, holding up their flasks to the candlelight.

'He's not going to die?' she cried, her voice sliding out of a whisper in her panic.

Ednyfed frowned at her sharply. 'Of course he's not going to die!'

'But you sent for the priest to give him the last rites?' She had only just noticed the man kneeling in the corner. She had begun to shake violently. 'Dafydd! Dafydd *bach*?' She threw herself towards the bed. 'What is it? What's wrong with you?'

He opened his eyes with an effort. 'Too much wine and good living, sweetheart, that's all. I'll soon be better.' He reached out for her hand. 'Don't worry, I'll be as right as rain tomorrow, you'll see. Then we'll celebrate, eh?' He managed the ghost of a grin.

She nodded, biting her lip, and she squeezed his fingers.

Soon after that he drifted into an uneasy sleep, but later he awoke, contorted in agony, clutching at her hand. This time he was delirious. He did not know her.

As the grey February daylight began to lighten the chamber he lay still at last and opened his eyes. He gave her the ghost of a smile. 'The pain has gone,' he said wonderingly. 'The Blessed Virgin be thanked, the pain has gone.'

'Thank God.' She had not moved from his side all night. She bent and kissed his forehead.

'Drink this, my lord.' One of the physicians stepped forward with a phial of medicine. Dafydd sipped it with a grimace then lay back on the pillows and closed his eyes.

Two hours later he was dead.

'No,' Isabella cried in disbelief. 'He was better. No, he's not dead, he's asleep.'

'Princess –' Ednyfed had tears running down his face.

'No.' She went on shaking her head. 'He's asleep.'

'Princess –'

'He's asleep I tell you!' She threw herself on the bed, and clutched at his hands. 'He'll wake up. He was better. He's not dead. He's not.' She pulled at him frantically and his head rolled sideways on the pillow. A little mucus trickled from the side of his mouth and his eyes opened. 'Dafydd! Dafydd! You see? He's alive! I told you he was alive.' Suddenly

428

she was sobbing, her whole body shaking with the strength of her weeping.

It was a long time before they could persuade her to leave the stiffening body and half carry, half drag her to a hastily prepared chamber on the far side of the *llys*. A messenger had already departed to find Owain Goch ap Gruffydd. And already the news was crossing the mountains from mouth to mouth and ear to ear towards King Henry's court.

X

FOTHERINGHAY ❖ 1 March 1246

Eleyne was playing with her little daughter when word came of her brother's death. She read the letter twice and sat gazing into space, the letter dangling from nerveless fingers. Joanna crawled towards her, reaching for the red wax seal on its ribbon.

Eleyne was numb; she had loved both her brothers and now she had lost them both. She had not seen Dafydd for a long time and she had often disagreed with him violently, but that did not mean she was any less devastated. Her eyes filled with tears and little Joanna, her small fists knotted into Eleyne's gown, stared up with solemn eyes at her mother's face. Eleyne stooped to pick the child up with a sad smile, and Joanna stabbed a chubby finger at Eleyne's cheek. Eleyne hugged her, knocking the letter to the floor and, burying her face in Joanna's curls, she began to sob.

Nesta wrote to Rhonwen, and Rhonwen came.

'So Owain Goch is prince now.' Rhonwen cuddled Joanna and tucked a sweetmeat into the child's mouth. 'Gruffydd is avenged.'

'Rhonwen.' Eleyne was reproachful.

'Well? You should be pleased too! I only hope young Llywelyn will be prepared to support his brother. He has no respect for Owain at all; he's much the stronger character! And you, *cariad*? What are you still doing here at Fotheringhay? Your husband has gone. I had no doubt that you would ride to Scotland as soon as you were recovered from the birth.'

Eleyne frowned. 'Alexander sent no messages –'

'Of course not. No doubt Queen Marie has told him you are lying every night in your husband's arms. So, you never intend to see him again?' Rhonwen carried Joanna over to the door.

'Of course I do . . .'

'Then what are you waiting for? Your husband's permission?' Her tone was acidic. She handed the child to a nurse and walked back to

Eleyne. 'You still have a child to bear for Scotland, *cariad*. I don't know how or why, but that is your destiny.' Her eyes burned with a sudden fanaticism.

'That's not true, Einion was wrong.'

'He was never wrong.' Rhonwen's face had become deeply lined over the last months and there was a permanent frown between her eyes. 'You have a darling child there, but she is not the child the gods have promised you.' She paused. 'You must not let her father touch you again.'

'No.' Eleyne was watching the nurse carry Joanna from the room.

'He would be better dead.' Rhonwen's voice was very soft.

There was a long pause. 'Yes.' Eleyne bit her lip.

Rhonwen gave a quick triumphant smile. 'I'm glad you agree.'

Eleyne swung round. 'I will not have him killed.'

'Why not?'

'I – am – his – wife.' The words were scarcely audible.

'No.' Rhonwen shook her head. 'You were forced to make vows that meant nothing, before a god who cares nothing!' She put her hands over Eleyne's wrists. 'And you hate him!'

'Yes, I hate him.' Eleyne's eyes flashed. She snatched her hands away. 'But I will not be responsible for his death.' She moved away from Rhonwen. 'I didn't go to Scotland because I won't crawl to Alexander. If he wants me he must send for me.' She straightened her shoulders.

Rhonwen smiled. 'I am sure he will, *cariad*,' she said meekly, 'I am sure he will.'

XI
DYSERTH ❖ March 1246

Philip de Bret, Constable of Dyserth Castle, bowed gravely to the cleric who stood before him. He glanced at Isabella. 'The Princess of Aberffraw has been a most welcome guest here, my lord abbot.'

The Abbot of Basingwerk bowed back. Both men looked as if they were tiptoeing on thin ice as they turned as one to Isabella. She stared back at them resentfully. 'So? Why did you want to see me, my lord abbot?'

'As you know, princess, your late husband was a patron of our abbey . . .'

'And endowed it handsomely.' Her voice was waspish. 'If you come for a donation, my lord abbot, you are out of luck. I have no money until my dower is arranged.'

'You misunderstand me, princess.' The abbot bowed again. 'I have not come to ask for your generosity.' He took a deep breath. 'I have come at the command of the king.'

'Oh?' She looked at him suspiciously.

'It appears that his grace has decided that for now –' he paused and licked his lips nervously – 'he would like you to go to the sisters at Godstow.'

'What exactly do you mean?' Isabella's hands had gone cold.

Henry had after all allowed Owain to succeed Dafydd, but only after he and his brother, Llywelyn, had acknowledged the King of England as their overlord.

The abbot glanced at de Bret for support. 'His grace commands that I escort you to Godstow. He feels that as a highborn widow –'

'He is not going to turn me into a nun!' Her voice rose sharply. 'I hope his grace does not intend to try to make me stay there.'

The abbot shrugged. 'I have my orders, madam. To deliver you to the Lady Flandrina, Abbess of Godstow. That is the king's command.'

'I won't go! I'll marry again.' She looked from one man to the other wildly. 'It's because I can't have children, that's it, isn't it? No man will want me if I'm barren. But I can have children! Ask anyone. I was cursed. But the curse can be lifted –'

'Princess.' The old abbot shook his head. 'Please don't distress yourself. I am sure the arrangement is only temporary.'

'Sure? How can you be sure?' Her hands were shaking. 'The king doesn't confide in you, does he? No, of course he doesn't. Suppose they lock me up and keep me there forever?'

'Why should they do such a thing?' Philip de Bret forced himself to speak calmly. He disliked excitable women in general and he was beginning to dislike this one in particular. Since her arrival at Dyserth the smooth running of the royal castle had been relegated to the least of his worries. Instead he had found himself summoned to a series of increasingly stormy interviews with the princess, who had been packed into his care by Henry and her two nephews the moment Dafydd's death had been announced.

'When Eleyne was widowed, the king didn't send her to a nunnery.' Isabella's voice had risen to a tight, nervous whine. 'Why should he send me there? And to Godstow. It's so far away. No, I won't go. I shall return to Aber until the matter of my dower is arranged.'

The abbot sighed. 'Princess, I'm sorry, but that is not possible. The King of England's command must be obeyed, and it is also the wish of the new Prince of Aberffraw.' He nodded to himself smugly. Those two boys had not been able to wait, so he had heard, to get rid of her!

'Not if I refuse.' She shook her finger under his nose. 'I'm sorry, my lord abbot. I hate to disappoint you but you must return without me.'

She took his hand and kneeling to give his ring a perfunctory kiss – some inches above the cold amethyst on an equally cold finger – she rose and swept from the room.

De Bret shrugged. 'I had hoped we could avoid using force.'

'And I.' The abbot stared sadly at the door which still reverberated from the force with which Isabella had flung it shut behind her. 'Poor woman. She is still young for such an incarceration.'

De Bret raised an eyebrow. 'I'm surprised to hear you of all people call going into a convent incarceration. A strong word, surely.'

The abbot frowned. 'What else is it, my friend, if the postulant is unwilling and must stay there for the rest of her life?'

XII

ROXBURGH CASTLE ❖ August 1246

The house was on the main street in Roxburgh, not far from the bakehouse where she and Alexander had spent such happy hours. The rich tradesman who owned it was not interested in the identity of the two merchants' wives who had agreed to rent the ground-floor rooms. They had heavy purses and were well dressed beneath their sober cloaks: that was all that mattered. They had two servants, a nurse for the baby and a great dog. He did not ask their business in Roxburgh.

He was not there when the elder woman took water from the silver Tweed and setting her bowl on the bank beneath the stars drew down the moonlight into the water with her muttered incantations, stirring glittering circles into the black depths of the pot before taking it indoors and making the younger woman drink. The spell was to hide her identity; to make her invisible to all but the king and in his eyes to make her irresistible.

XIII

The great hall of the castle was as always crowded and Alexander was in jovial mood after the midday meal. He had called for his horse and his hawk and was looking forward to an afternoon's sport after a morning closeted with his nobles. Marie had left the table early to go and fuss over the boy. Even that small respite improved his mood.

He rose from the table with a contented sigh and began to make his way slowly down the hall towards the door. He could already hear the scraping of the horses' hooves on the cobbles as they waited in the courtyard and the high piping call of the bird waiting on the fist of his falconer.

He wasn't sure why the woman caught his eye; her stillness in the midst of so much confusion? The angle of her head as she waited unobtrusively in the shadows near the door? Shadows made blacker by the wedge of brilliant sunshine which streamed into the high-roofed great hall attended by a myriad of dancing dust motes. He squinted across the sun and stopped dead. Immediately the crowd around him stopped too, but their chatter did not cease; the stamping of the hooves did not cease. And yet it was the woman's silence he heard: her silence and her power.

Sweet Christ! She had come back to him at last. At last she had tired of her husband and come back!

He looked about him swiftly. Whom could he trust? No one else had recognised her; no one else had even noticed her in the general mêlée which accompanied him everywhere.

He moved on without giving any sign that he had seen her, out on to the steps and down to his horse. Only then did he beckon one of the grooms and whisper into his ear. The groom found her, still standing in the shadows, though she was now alone. He peered at her inquisitively and shrugged; if the king wanted to play riddles with a heavily veiled townswoman who hadn't even the wit to put on her best gown when she came to court it was none of his business. What was his business was the reward he had been promised if he got the message right.

Her smile was like the sunrise after a night of rain. He glimpsed it only for a moment beneath her veil as he whispered the message and then he felt a coin pressed into his palm – a coin hot from her own hand. With a flurry of skirts she was gone and by dusk when the king returned the groom would be richer by far than he had ever dreamed.

XIV

The mist was lying across the grass, drifting amongst the trees, hiding the river. She rode slowly, the reins loose, her eyes on the hill in front of her. It stood silhouetted against the sky, conical in shape, not very high, the tumbled ruins of the old fort clear in the moonlight. She knew at once why he had chosen it. It belonged now to the old people; to the fairies. The locals would go nowhere near it. She shivered, feeling the skin on the back of her neck stir and tighten and as if sensing her thoughts, Tam Lin laid back his ears and side-stepped at the shadows.

His horse was already there, tethered beneath the trees. She tied Tam Lin beside it and stood for a moment looking towards the hill top, Donnet at her heels. The moon had drifted higher, farther away from the earth, its light no longer soft and diffused. Now it shed a cold uncaring beam on the soft, sheep-cropped grass. Gathering her skirts, she commanded Donnet to stay and began to climb.

By the time she reached the top, her heart was pounding and the back of her throat was dry and tight. She stopped and looked around, trying to catch her breath. It must have been a castle of the ancient Picts. The huge, rough-cut blocks of stone lay tossed into the grass at crazy angles, throwing black wedges of shadow on the moon-silvered ground. Far below she could see Tweeddale laid out before her, the low-lying river valley brimming with mist. She closed her eyes and made the sign of protection. They were still here, the old ones, watching.

Alexander was sitting on a block of masonry, wrapped in his thick cloak, his arms around his knees. A naked sword lay beside him, its blade glinting in the moonlight.

She went to him without a word and stood in front of him, looking at his face as she raised her veil. If he no longer wanted her, she would know.

He smiled. Opening his cloak he drew her into its folds and held her close. For a long time neither of them spoke.

'So. Finally you grew tired of your husband?' he said at last.

Her eyes widened. 'I don't live with my husband; I haven't seen him since Joanna was born.'

'Joanna.' His voice was thoughtful, then he went on. 'So, why did you wait until now to come?'

'I didn't know if you wanted me.'

'Wanted you!' he echoed. 'I wanted you so much I nearly went mad when they told me you had gone back to de Quincy.'

'Who told you?'

'King Henry.'

'And you believed him?'

He was silent for a moment. 'There must be honour among kings, Eleyne. You had ignored my gifts, my letters. I thought you wanted no more of me. After I heard about the bairn. I suppose I thought that after the two that died . . .' His voice trailed away.

She smiled sadly. 'I wanted *you*, my lord. Not letters, or gifts. I wanted you.'

Slowly he raised his hand and touched her face. 'Why did you come this time?' he asked softly.

'You wrote and said you couldn't live without me any more. I suspect that Rhonwen told you what to say, but it was what I needed to hear.'

He shook his head. 'I knew what to say, woman. The Lady Rhonwen merely told me to say it again. Sweet Christ! How could we have wasted so much time? Every day that has passed, I've missed you in my arms!' He pulled her closer. 'You are defying your king by coming here, Eleyne.'

She nestled closer to him. 'I would defy the world, if you wanted me to,' she said. 'And I still have a son to carry for Scotland. A son who will live and one day be the ancestor of a line of kings.' She put her finger against his lips. 'Don't frown. I know you and I can never marry. I am content to be your mistress. We'll leave destiny to see to the legitimacy of our children.'

As they kissed she pulled open the bodice of her gown. His fingers were calloused and cold from the moonlit rock, and she heard herself gasp as his arms slid around her naked body.

'I'm never going to let you go away again, Eleyne,' he murmured. 'I want you to be mine forever.'

CHAPTER EIGHTEEN

I

GODSTOW, OXFORDSHIRE ❖
Ash Wednesday, 13 February 1247

Isabella was staring out of the window of her cell towards the dark sky. It was ice-cold in the small room and in spite of the fur-lined cloak over her black habit, her hands and feet were blue. Soon she would go to the warming room and sit with the other sisters, huddled around the fire. They were only supposed to sit near it for short periods between work and prayer, but somehow the majority of them managed to congregate there as often as possible. She sniffed. She had not gone down the night stairs for matins, or lauds or prime. Only when her maid had brought her a hot drink and helped her change her linen would she appear grudgingly at terce. This was a rich convent; many of the ladies were aristocratic relicts like herself, dumped by the king out of sight, out of mind. Some of them would leave the convent; she meant to be one of them.

The moon was high, its face a strange blood-red, shedding a weird half-light over the snow-covered roofs of the convent buildings. She did not remember ever having seen it like that before and for some reason it frightened her. It had upset the animals too. She could hear the horses stirring in the stables behind the dorter and somewhere beyond the convent walls a dog was howling.

With a shiver, she picked up her candle and carried it to the coffer which served as bookrest, cupboard and table. On it lay a small book of hours and the precious piece of parchment she had bribed from Sister Maude in the scriptorium together with quills and ink. This would be her fifth letter – carried out of the convent by one of the lay sisters to be consigned to the doubtful mercies of anyone passing who looked trustworthy enough to take it at least part of its way towards its destination.

This one was to go to Eleyne. She knelt before the coffer and nibbled thoughtfully at the feathered end of the quill. *Dear Sweet Sister*. That was a good start. *For the sake of our long love for one another I must ask you one last favour.*

Get me out of here, that was the gist of it. She was desperate, a prisoner in all but name, destined never to see another man unless she counted the old priest who took their services and the bishop who came to scold mother abbess about the slackness of the house and its signs of wealth and comfort. Comfort! Isabella snorted to herself. This place was the nearest thing to hell she could imagine. Eleyne had to get her out; she had the entrée to King Henry's court. Surely she could help.

She bent again to the small circle of candlelight, scribbling laboriously, unused to handling a pen, watching in despair as the nib split and spat a fine shower of ink across the page.

The low rumble in the distance sounded at first like thunder. She looked up, puzzled, then she frowned. The floor she knelt on had seemed to move under her. She dropped the pen and clutched at the coffer. The pewter candlestick rocked violently and fell over. It rolled to the edge of the coffer and fell to the ground. The candle had gone out and she saw that a faint daylight showed at the window.

The sound of screams in the distance brought her to her feet. Scrabbling for the doorknob, she let herself out into the cold corridor as the whole world around her seemed to shake itself like a dog. Tiles cascaded from the roof of the cloister and in the distance there was a louder sound of falling masonry.

Then it was over. As suddenly as it had begun, the tremor died away and left total silence.

Isabella stood still, her heart thumping with fear, watching from the cloister as the other nuns streamed out of the chapel. Some were crying, some had been injured. She could see at least two with blood pouring from their heads; all were shocked. Without warning, as their voices were raised in the ethereal beauty of the plainsong of the morning office, the great rood screen had collapsed and huge chunks of masonry had fallen from the roof into the choir. The lovely rose window which had decorated the western wall had exploded into a million pieces. The abbess, her hands clasped, her face as white as her wimple, made her way from one trembling nun to the next, seeing how many were hurt. It was a miracle that no one had been killed.

As Isabella joined the others, stooping over the injured to see if she could help, the abbess stopped and stared at her. 'Where were you? Were you not in the chapel?' Isabella's fingers were covered in ink and she still clutched the broken quill in her right hand. There were spots of ink on her wimple and even on her face beneath the dust.

'I was in my cell, writing, mother abbess.' In her shock Isabella blurted out the truth. 'What is it? What happened?'

'I believe it was an earthquake.' The abbess pursed her lips. 'I have read of such things. They are a sign of God's extreme displeasure; of his wish to punish the wicked and the backsliders.' She wrung her

437

hands. 'Only yesterday I received another letter from the bishop warning me. He said we had fallen into sinful ways. He said we had strayed too far from the rule. He said we would be punished! He said God would not condone our ways. He said I must be stern and now we have been sent a sign.' She dropped to her knees amongst the broken tiles and the glass and, sobbing, began to pray. Crossing themselves, the other nuns followed suit as the blood moon sank in the west and a pale watery sun began to climb out of the mist behind the chapel.

That same day the nuns divested themselves of their comforts; they donned hair shirts, the servants were dismissed and the abbess announced that they would double the rigours of their Lenten fast. There would be no more fires, no extra blankets, no wine and no speaking. There would be no further contact with the lay community.

Isabella, as frightened as the rest, put her unfinished letter to Eleyne on the great bonfire in the garth which consumed so many of their comforts. The food and blankets were given to the poor and the nuns turned back in earnest to their prayers. They had no way of knowing that their fear and their terror at God's warning was being echoed up and down southern England and Wales; that the newly rebuilt tower of St David's Cathedral had fallen, that King Henry III was ordering prayers throughout the land and that the end of the world was being predicted.

II

ROXBURGH ❖ February 1247

Alexander laughed. 'So God has blasted London and rocked the English to their foundations! I trust Henry takes heed of the warning and spends the next year on his knees!' He drew little Joanna on to his lap. 'Have you had any news of your dower lands and property in the south? Has there been much damage?'

Eleyne shrugged. She was watching the king play with her daughter.

He glanced up. 'I think you must find out, Eleyne.' His expression was suddenly very sober.

She met his gaze steadily and saw the sadness there with a sinking heart. 'You are telling me that I must go?'

He nodded. 'Marie knows. I don't know how we have kept your presence here a secret so long, but she has found out. I don't want you exposed and humiliated before three nations.'

They had not seen each other more than once a week, sometimes, when he was away, less than that. When they had met, they had not

438

mentioned Marie, but her presence had always been there between them.

'I don't care about that!' she cried.

'I know you don't, my love. But I do,' he said gently. 'Let me deal with Marie in my own way. I have to go to the west. I still plan to buy the Western Isles from Norway and settle once and for all the problems caused by the lords and their battle fleets. I must attend to the problems of the far corners of my kingdom and while I'm away you must go. I will call you back very soon.'

Without his protection, her life would be worth nothing once he had left for the Western Isles. Marie had made that clear. It was not a risk he was prepared to take.

She would not plead. She rose from her place on the cushions by the fire and took her daughter from him. 'I can come back? You promise?' She closed her eyes, waiting for his answer, determined that he would not see her devastating unhappiness.

He smiled and the smile showed his pain more clearly than any tears could have done. 'I promise,' he said gently. He stood up and taking the little girl's hand used her to draw her mother closer to him. Burying his face in the child's stomach, he made the little girl giggle. He dropped a kiss into her fist, closed the chubby fingers over it and blew gently to seal the pledge, making her squeal with pleasure. Then he stepped away from her. 'I have a gift for you –'

'I don't want a gift!' The sharpness of Eleyne's tone revealed her hurt and her misery and she knew she sounded like a spoiled child.

'You do.' He grinned, suddenly cheerful. 'I had it made specially. Look.' He reached into the velvet scrip which hung from his belt and produced a packet. 'Open it.'

She put Joanna on the floor and took it from him. 'I don't want anything but your love,' she repeated.

'You have that. Always.' He put his hand over hers. 'But it is not always possible to have me, and this way you can have something of me with you. Our secret pledge. A link between us, however far apart we find ourselves.'

She raised her eyes to his and smiled. 'But I will see you again?' She needed his reassurance. Somewhere near them, out of sight, a shadow hovered over them. She felt it with a sudden shiver.

'You will see me again. You have my most solemn promise.'

She held his gaze then, reassured, she turned the small packet over in her hand and began to unwrap the covering. She could tell by its feel and weight that it was some kind of jewellery.

A fine gold chain tumbled out over her fingers. Attached to it was a jewelled and enamelled pendant. She gasped. 'It's beautiful.'

'Can you guess what it is?' He waited while she examined it.

'It's like an eagle, an eagle rising from the fire.'

'Not an eagle.' He smiled. 'A phoenix.' He raised a finger to her face and gently touched the scars on her temple. 'For my phoenix, who rose from the fire more beautiful than ever.'

She gazed down at the jewel. The golden bird had tiny rubies for its eyes and the flames from which it sprang were brilliantly enamelled gold with lapis and ruby flames. 'Did you know I was born in a fire?'

He raised an eyebrow. 'Nothing surprises me about my Eleyne. It's doubly right then. You are a child of the phoenix in every way. Wear it for me. It will bring us together, always. When you need me, hold it in your hand and think of me. I'll know and, if I can, I'll come.' He smiled, then his face became serious. She could see the anguish in his eyes. 'If we can't have each other in this life, Eleyne, then beyond death you will be mine, I swear it. This is a symbol of my undying love through all eternity.'

Again she felt the shadow hovering near, and with a prickle of something like fear at the overwhelming intensity of his love, she unfastened the chain and slipped it around her neck. 'I will come back to Scotland. One day,' she whispered. 'We will be together one day, my love. I know it.'

She still owed him a child; a son who would live and thrive.

He kissed her and the moment of tension had passed. 'I know you will,' he said.

III
LLANFAES ❖ April 1247

In the manor house Joanna ran wild, the sound of her high-pitched laughter everywhere. Donnet followed her, as anxious as a mother, constantly on watch, sitting in the corner of the room, his large brown eyes on the child, submitting to the hugs and squeezes, the chubby legs astride his grey silky flanks and looking up from time to time, pleading with Eleyne to rescue him from the onslaught. It was a welcome distraction for all of them when the two young rulers of Aberffraw, her nephews Owain Goch and Llywelyn, asked her to go with them to Woodstock.

At first she said she couldn't go. She could not run the risk of meeting Robert.

'Uncle Henry has particularly requested that you come with us,' Owain wheedled in the dusty bachelor fortress that was Aber now. 'Now that we have a treaty with John de Gray, we are going to sort things out with him properly and pay homage for Gwynedd.'

'So Henry has won.' Eleyne looked from one young man to the other.

Owain shrugged, but she saw a flash of rebellion in Llywelyn's eyes. 'It will give us time to consolidate, Aunt Eleyne,' he said grimly. 'Time is what we need now. Let Henry think everything is going his way. Later we will re-establish Gwynedd's greatness, have no fear.'

Eleyne eyed her nephew with amusement. She had a feeling that if the future were left to Llywelyn, Gwynedd would indeed one day be great again.

IV
WOODSTOCK ❖ April 1247

She was finally persuaded to go with them when a letter came from Henry himself commanding her to wait on him with her nephews. 'There are matters to discuss concerning the Honour of Huntingdon and the earldom of Chester and the confirmation of your dower.' Five years before, Henry had bought out the heiresses of the Chester lands. The right to the title was now his alone.

Almost the first person she saw in the great hall of the king's palace at Woodstock was Robert de Quincy. She froze, but he had seen her as the princes' party made their way indoors after the long days in the saddle.

Eleyne stopped. Frantically she looked round for an escape but the king was coming towards her.

'Lady Chester!' His voice was imperious. She dropped a deep curtsey. 'You and your husband will present yourselves in an audience with me tomorrow. Alone.'

Sweet Bride, was she never to be free of him? She wanted to run away. She wanted to scream.

'Face him, Aunt Eleyne.' Llywelyn was standing near her. 'Tell him you want to live separately from Robert. Tell him how much you hate him. He'll understand.' The young man's eyes were intense. 'He doesn't want you to be unhappy.' He reached out and took her hands. 'He wants to keep Alexander's friendship. He'll help you.'

'Are you sure?'

'I'm sure.' A handsome young man in his early twenties, he was confident of his own infallibility.

It was raining. She could hear it pouring down the gutter outside her window and splashing on the paving of the small courtyard beyond her room. On the far side of the walls it thundered on to the new red-green leaves of the unfurling oaks. Nesta and Joanna and her nurse, Meggie, were all asleep in the darkness of the room. Eleyne raised herself on to her elbow and peered around, holding her breath. Then

441

she heard it again; the latch was moving. Slowly the door creaked open. She knew it was Robert even before she saw him outlined against the light of the torch in the passage outside.

She grabbed her bedcovers and held them tightly to her breasts. Next to her Nesta groaned.

'What do you want?' Her voice sounded shockingly loud in the silence. Robert jumped and the two women sat up in fright. Joanna began to cry.

Robert lurched against the wall, looking blankly into the darkness. 'I want my wife.' His speech was slurred. Waving his arms, he stumbled into the room and grabbed at Nesta's arm. 'Get out. Take the brat with you.'

'Stay where you are!' Eleyne said urgently to Nesta. 'Go away, Robert. Now. You're drunk! Leave us alone or I'll call the guard.'

'Call away.' Robert hiccuped loudly. His eyes were growing used to the darkness. 'They can throw out these women.' He glared at the screaming child and lunged forward, catching Eleyne's shoulder in his hand and pulling away the sheets. He narrowed his eyes as the jewelled pendant on its chain between her breasts caught the light and reflected a thousand prisms across her white skin. 'Pretty bauble! Worth a fortune no doubt.' He grabbed it and wrenched it from her, snapping the chain.

Eleyne gave a scream. She tried to snatch it back but he had staggered out of reach. 'It'll buy me some wine,' he crowed. 'Oh dear! So upset! Who gave it to you? Or can I guess?'

'Give it to me.' Eleyne snatched her bed gown from the end of the bed and, flinging it on, she pushed her feet out on to the cold floor. Joanna's screams had risen hysterically in spite of Meggie's frantic rocking. Holding the phoenix high, dangling on the end of its chain so that it flashed in the flickering torchlight, Robert backed away from her. She caught him as he reached the door and with a vicious lunge he pushed her to the floor, laughing as he tucked the pendant into his scrip.

By the time she had scrambled to her feet, he had gone.

'Did he hurt you, my lady?' Nesta ran to help her.

Mutely, Eleyne shook her head. His blow had glanced off her shoulder. She flung herself at the door and looked out, but there was no sign of Robert. He had disappeared into the warren of buildings and passages which made up the huge sprawling palace.

Eleyne could not sleep even when Joanna had at last been soothed and tucked back into bed, and the breathing of the two women had grown even once more. She was seething with fury, and it was still dark when she made her way to the stables. She had left Donnet with Tam. Quietly she called the dog and, putting the temptation to ride behind her, she went to walk in the orchards beyond the park wall. By the time she was to see her uncle, she was calm.

It did not surprise her to see that Robert was at the king's side first. He eyed her smugly, sober, his hair and beard freshly barbered. His gown looked new.

Eleyne curtseyed to the king, her hand on Donnet's head.

Henry smiled. 'So, niece. I have some documents here for you to sign –'

'Do you value your alliance with Scotland, your grace?' Eleyne held her uncle's eye challengingly. Her voice was clear and steady as she interrupted him.

He frowned, astonished. 'We are not here to discuss Scotland –'

'I think we are. The King of Scots gave me a valuable jewel; it was to be my security and part of my dower. Last night, my husband . . .' she flicked Robert the barest glance – 'stole it.'

Henry frowned. 'I hardly think –'

'If I tell Alexander that you condoned that theft,' Eleyne went on, 'he will be angry and disappointed. He has always told me that you are a man of honour and I agreed with him. Yet this has happened under your roof.'

Henry sighed. 'Give it back to her, de Quincy.'

Robert shook his head. 'A whore's bauble? I sold it.'

Eleyne gasped. 'You can't have. You haven't had time . . .'

'Find it!' Henry's voice cut in angrily. 'I give you twelve hours to restore this jewel to your wife, Sir Robert, or you will be charged with the theft. Now leave me. Both of you. I have grown bored with your quarrels.' He had forgotten why he wanted to speak to them in the first place.

Eleyne left the king's room. She went straight to the stables and gave orders for Tam Lin to be saddled. Her anger and exhaustion after the sleepless night and the long ride the day before had made her restless. And she missed her pendant. She had grown used to the feel of it nestling between her breasts. It brought her close to Alexander.

Llywelyn's voice brought her back to herself as she watched the groom fitting Tam's bridle.

'Would you ride with me, Aunt Eleyne? Our talks with the king don't begin until tomorrow, so I thought I would go to Godstow to see Aunt Isabella. I owe her that much.' He looked sheepish.

'So your conscience troubles you. It was unkind to force her to leave Aber.'

'I didn't force her!' Stung, he met her eye. 'The king ordered her to the nunnery.'

'But you didn't argue, did you?' Eleyne asked gently. 'I'll come with you. Poor Isabella.' Even a visit to her would be better than staying under the same roof as her husband.

They found her thin and pale. The black habit of the Benedictines did not suit her. She looked from Llywelyn to Eleyne and back and then she laughed. 'So. To what good fortune do I owe this visit? Or are you here to take me home?'

Llywelyn looked down. 'It is for the king to say when you leave, Aunt Isabella. We came to see if you were well.'

'And to gloat?' Isabella walked restlessly across the parlour and back. 'Well, now you have seen, I am well. You may go back to King Henry and tell him so. Tell him I am deliriously happy! Tell him I thrive. Tell him I pray for him daily!' She kicked at the rush-strewn floor with a sandalled foot. 'And you, *sister*' – She faced Eleyne, her eyes narrowed. 'Are you pleased with your success? Oh it was so clever wasn't it? To ensure Gruffydd's sons succeeded Dafydd . . .' Suddenly she was crying.

'Isabella!' Anguished, Eleyne moved towards her. 'Oh my dear, please . . .'

'Don't touch me!' Isabella flinched and turned her back on them. 'Go away! Both of you. Leave me to God!'

V

WOODSTOCK

King Henry summoned Eleyne to his private office that evening. He was not alone. With him was his son. At eight years old, Edward was tall for his age, very thin, and as handsome as his father in his own way. Precocious, with a cruel, malicious tongue which did not endear him to his father's courtiers, Edward had his own household and apartments at Woodstock. Having escaped his new tutor, Peter of Wakering, he was sitting on a small stool, waiting impatiently to go riding. He glared at Eleyne with resentment as she came in and, feeling the child's eyes on her, she glanced at him as she curtseyed to the king. Edward returned the look with a scowl. He did not like people intruding on the precious time when he should have his father to himself.

Henry ignored him. As Eleyne waited silently for him to speak, he paced the floor from the small ornately leaded window to the door and back, then he moved across to the high desk.

'I have your jewel here.' He picked it up and weighed it in his hand.

Eleyne felt her heart leap, but she kept a cautious eye on Henry's face, trying to read his expression. Edward eyed the pendant speculatively.

'It's a beautiful trinket,' Henry said at last, making no effort to give it to her.

'Indeed, sire, I'm very fond of it.'

'You say the King of Scots gave it to you.' Henry looked up.

She swallowed, then nodded, uncertain which way the conversation was going. Edward listened to every word; he had become adept at picking up interesting snippets of information about the members of his father's court.

'I don't want to offend Alexander,' Henry went on thoughtfully. 'As you know I respect and honour him, and I am very fond of the Countess of Pembroke, his sister . . . but neither do I want to offend the King of France, who naturally supports the Queen of Scots.' He turned from her, the pendant still in his hand. 'I cannot openly condone your visits to Scotland,' he said slowly, 'and I cannot vouch for your husband's discretion. The man is a hothead and a drunkard.' Holding out his hand he dropped the phoenix into her palm. 'I wish you well, niece, but I think it best if I hear no more of these visits of yours, do you understand?' His piercing blue eyes met hers and held them. 'And in exchange for my lack of perspicacity I would appreciate your good offices in ensuring that your nephews toe the line in regard to the Welsh settlement. And before you ask, I want to hear no more about Isabelle de Braose either. I am pestered morning, noon and night about that woman. I wish to hear no more about her, and I wish to see no more of Sir Robert de Quincy.'

'Sir Robert has left the palace, papa,' Edward put in, 'I heard him tell Prince Llywelyn he was going.' He was looking with a strangely calculating expression at Eleyne.

The king swung round. He had forgotten his eldest son was there. 'Wait for me in the courtyard, boy,' he said curtly.

'Yes, papa.' Edward leaped to his feet and bowed meekly. He turned towards the door, then he stopped. 'Sir Robert was very angry,' he smiled maliciously. 'He said all sorts of bad things about Lady Eleyne.'

Eleyne closed her eyes. Whatever Robert had said, she didn't want to hear it. She clutched the precious phoenix tightly, as a talisman. When she opened her eyes she found Edward watching her closely.

'He said nobody could trust her,' Edward rushed on before his father could stop him. 'And he said she was a witch and a murderer.'

'That is enough, Edward,' Henry thundered. 'I told you to wait outside.'

'Yes, papa.' Edward lowered his eyes. He had surprisingly long lashes for a boy. They made him look almost demure. 'I just thought you'd like to know what he said.'

445

VI

FOTHERINGHAY

For three weeks Eleyne waited for Robert to appear. He did not come. Joanna settled back into her routine and, at Eleyne's summons, Rhonwen joined them from London.

'So, *cariad*.' Rhonwen had inspected the nursery and toured the castle, then she had nodded, content that all was running like clockwork. 'When are you going back to Scotland? Surely you are not going to wait for him to summon you now he is back from the west?' Together they began to plan.

It was the beginning of July when Eleyne and Hal Longshaft, who had returned to Fotheringhay as her steward, set off alone for the north, disguised in plain roughspun cloaks.

She enjoyed the ride, unencumbered by baggage or attendants. She enjoyed the empty roads, the disguise, the speed of their travel, and she enjoyed the challenge and excitement of getting a message undetected to Alexander. And above all, she enjoyed the thought of being with him again.

In the event he was at Berwick without the queen and they were able to meet easily in the house where she was lodging below the castle.

'No one will ever know I have been in Scotland.' She nuzzled against him, her hands busy inside his gown. 'I'm a shadow. No more than a wisp of dust motes in a sunbeam. When you blink you'll find I've gone.'

He laughed, pulling her on to his knee, his hands on her breasts. 'Then I must be careful not to blink too soon.' He lowered his head to her nipples, circling first one and then the other with his tongue until she cried out with pleasure.

They had only a short time together; he had to ride north almost at once and she could not go with him, but her visit had given them hope. 'I'll tell you if I can when I'm away from the queen, and you can come to me.' He kissed her greedily, trying to take as much of her as he could before they parted. 'That way we'll be together sometimes and I shall carry the dream of you with me.' He took the phoenix in his hand and pulled it gently, so that she had to move towards him, slipping obediently on to his knee, her breasts pressing urgently against his chest. 'You must never take this off. It links us. It joins my soul to yours.' His mouth sought hers and she felt his tongue urgent, probing, take her captive, demanding her surrender.

She rode to Scotland twice more that year, three times the next and once in the following spring. Each time Hal went with her. Each time, as far as she knew, her visits went undetected. Each time she wept when she discovered there was still no child. The months between were gentle times, occupied with Joanna and with her horses, when her body slept. Her beauty was at its ripest, but she covered herself with mantles and veils and played the chaste housewife with demure skill. Of her husband there was no sign at all.

VII
ROXBURGH ✤ April 1249

It was dark inside the small bedchamber, though the night was luminous. Eleyne stood at the window gazing at the huge pale moon. He would be here for only a few more days, then he was going once more to the Western Isles to try yet again to establish his authority amongst the warring barons.

This visit had not been a success. The king had been distracted in the short times he had been with her, and she wasn't sure if he were coming now. For only the second time he had secreted her in the castle itself to be near him, but her presence there meant they had to be more careful. She fingered the phoenix longingly. Her hair was loose, as the king liked it, heavy on her shoulders, and beneath the silky green velvet of her mantle she was naked. She had stroked perfumes and soft oils on to her skin and she could smell the fragrance of rose and jasmine as she moved.

She leaned from the window of the tower and looked out across the moonlit countryside. The burgh was out of sight here, the country a kaleidoscope of silver shadow, the heavy cold of the dew lying like a silk scarf across trees and grass. This corner tower in the outer wall was a deserted place, used as a storeroom. She could not hear the noise of the courtyards and the stables. The silence was broken only by the calls of a pair of owls hunting across the river, and in the distance she heard the howl of a wolf.

She was asleep, huddled in the darkness, when he came at last. He did not have a candle or a lantern as he let himself in silently and bolted the door. There was no fire. The room was icy. He stood in the moonlight staring down at her, then as she stirred and turned towards him sleepily he took her in his arms.

He was still with her when she awoke at dawn, his head on her shoulder, his hand on her breast, sleeping deeply as the first rays of sunlight showed across the eastern hills. She watched him, taking in greedily every detail of his sleeping face, trying to memorise every inch of him, every hair, every pore, every golden eyelash as he turned sleepily and reached for her again.

It was a long time later that she was able to speak. 'You'll miss mass, I can hear the bell in the distance.'

'I'll hear mass before we ride, later.'

'Must you go today?' She clung to him.

'You know I must, Eleyne.' He sat up and swung his legs over the edge of the bed. Then he put his hand to her lips. 'You know I hate goodbyes.' He reached to stroke a heavy breast, and at the last moment touched the pendant instead, gently, with his forefinger.

He dressed, but she made no move to put on her own clothes. When he was ready, he bent and dropped a quick kiss on the top of her head.

'God go with you, my love,' she whispered. Then he was gone.

VIII

FOTHERINGHAY

In her dream she looked down at Einion's grave. Wild daffodils danced in the wind beneath the lichen-covered stone. When she put her hand on it it was very cold.

'So where is Scotland's son?' she whispered out loud. 'Where? All your predictions were lies.' Her hands went sadly to the phoenix on the chain around her neck. Behind her from beyond the damp bitter-sweet woods and meadows, across the white-topped waves of the tide race, the south wind carried the fragrance of the mountain air. The vast silences of the lonely peaks, broken only by the cry of the eagle and the rush of waterfalls high on the rocky scree, reached out to her. He was there, near her. She saw Tam Lin's ears flatten against his head. She saw Donnet's hackles rise as a blackbird flew screaming from the thicket and she saw the whirl of dead leaves in the grassy ride.

Go back. The voice was inside her head. *Go back to Scotland, go back.*

The echoing silence of the woods was full of menace. The air as it touched her skin carried a hint of ice.

If you want to keep him go back – now.

High in the *cwms* of Eryri the snows still lingered. Wolves prowled the valleys looking for lambs. The echoing cry of a chough from the high cliffs reverberated through the crystal silence.

Go back, go back.

She stepped back, her hand going to the dog's head for reassurance as the leaves settled. Then, thoughtfully, she turned away.

How could she go back, when Alexander himself had sent her away?

Alexander lay on a pile of rugs, gazing up at the furled sails. His head throbbed and swam. The sky, brilliant blue behind the web of stays which held the mast, seemed to be moving, pulsing like a blood-filled heart.

He heard himself groan and felt at once the cool softness of a wet cloth on his forehead. He must force himself to his feet. He had to show himself to his men. Where were they? He groaned again, trying to lift his head, and then fell back. God's bones! but he felt ill. What was the matter with him? Was it something he had eaten or something to do with the accursed pain in his head? He had never been ill in his life before. It wasn't as though there had been any fighting. The visit had been peaceful; successful even. He closed his eyes, but the pain didn't go away.

'Sire.' He could hear the voice near him, urgently trying to attract his attention. 'Sire? Can you hear me?'

Of course he could hear. Couldn't the fool see that he could hear? He tried to open his eyes, but he was too tired to make the effort.

'Sire.' The voice came again, insistent, annoying, not letting him sleep.

'Sire, we are going to take you ashore to the island of Kerrera.'

The king turned his head restlessly. Don't bother. He thought he had said it out loud. But it was he who had given the orders earlier; he had told them to take him ashore. He had insisted, before this wretched illness had taken hold so badly, while he was still strong enough to speak. Kneeling at his side, the two senior captains of his fleet looked at one another grimly. One summoned the litter they had made from a sail.

For two days he lay ill on the island of Kerrera in Oban Bay. On the third his fever lessened and he opened his eyes.

'Eleyne?' He could see her clearly, sitting in the window, her hair glinting in the sunlight. He smiled. How cross she had been when he teased her about the silver streaks in the glossy chestnut. He was glad she had come back to Scotland. He always missed her so much when she went away; it was as though a limb were missing from his body.

'Eleyne?' He tried again, but she didn't seem to hear him. She was gazing out of the window towards the west. He could see the sunset behind her, the flaming sky throwing her into silhouette, as if her hair were on fire. Daughter of the phoenix, child of the fire. Why didn't she come to him? Why did she not press her lips to his? He wanted her. He needed her. He tried to stretch out his hand.

A priest knelt near him, his lips moving silently in prayer. His attendants and companions stood looking down at their king, their faces tense. The leech they had fetched from the mainland shook his head again. The king would die with the sun; he knew the signs. There was nothing he or anyone could do.

Alexander frowned a little as he tried to keep her in focus. The sunset was fading; she was less distinct now. She must look after his son; she must keep watch over the boy, for Scotland's sake. Why didn't she come to him? He wanted so much to touch her. Perhaps he should go to her.

He gathered the last of his strength with a supreme effort of will-power, concentrating every ounce of determination on keeping her in sight. He had to stay with her. Wherever she went, he would go with her into the darkness or into the light beyond.

As the sun set and the room sank into darkness the king sat up, astonished to find it was so easy. He rose and turned for a moment to look at the bed on which he had been lying and he frowned. His body still lay there, hunched against the fever. Around it he could see his friends staring down in disbelief.

'He's dead, my lords.' He heard the words of the leech as from a great distance but already he had moved away. Somewhere out there in the dark behind the setting sun he had to find Eleyne.

X

FOTHERINGHAY ❖ 8 July 1249

Eleyne woke suddenly, listening. As the sound of the watchman's horn died into reverberations in the silence, she heard the beating of her heart very loud in her ears. The bedchamber was in darkness and she was alone. Her household here was small; her ladies slept elsewhere in the keep: Rhonwen, in her own chamber, with her own servants, on the north side near the nursery; Nesta, next door.

She slipped from the bed, pulled on her shift and ran to the window. Moonlight glittered on the great loop of the River Nene. Beyond it fields and marshes and woods merged into a flat chessboard of silver and black. Somewhere towards the convent she could hear two owls calling as they hunted across the cut hay meadows and closer at hand the tiny calls of bats, pinpricks of sound in the night.

Still numb with sleep it was a moment before she realised that her throat was tight with fear, her whole body cold with dread. She leaned on the sill, looking out into the moonlight, and felt the chill of the night air touching her face. Her hands were shaking.

'Alexander.'

She whispered his name, but there was no answer in the dark. She opened the small coffer on the table where she kept her jewellery and took out the enamelled phoenix. The fine chain was broken. She had meant to summon a goldsmith from Northampton, but somehow it had slipped her mind. She held it for a moment in her hands, gazing at it in the darkness. Even without candles it seemed to gleam, the ruby eyes reflecting a starlight which had not penetrated the room. She felt the tears starting in her eyes. She kissed it sadly and put it back in the coffer. She shivered.

Alexander.

His name would not go away. There was something wrong. He needed her.

Snatching up a silk shawl she threw it around her shoulders over her shift. The castle was silent; they kept early hours unless they had guests. Her last visitor, Isabel Bruce, had left for Scotland three weeks before. Still barefoot she ran down the stairs, Donnet at her heels, and crossed the lower chamber. Some dozen people were asleep there, wrapped in their cloaks around the gently ticking embers of the great fire. None of them seemed to have heard the horn.

She made her way to the door and pulled it open – there was no sign of the watchman.

The stone steps down from the keep were ice-cold and wet with dew, but she scarcely felt them as she ran down and over the high slippery cobbles of the courtyard past the great hall towards the gate-house. The moat lay black and still in the shadow of the stone wall, a veil of white mist over the water. The drawbridge was up and there was no sign of life from the guardroom. As Eleyne ran in, the guards leaped to their feet.

'I heard the horn sound,' she cried. 'There is a messenger.'

The captain of the guard stepped forward sheepishly jerking his tunic into place. 'There was no alarm, my lady.' He looked sharply at his men. 'There has been no one on the road since dusk.'

'But I heard it!' She knew how she must look. The long white shift, bare feet, the silk shawl, her hair loose, without her veil.

'Not from here, lady.' His garments straightened to his satisfaction, the captain felt more confident.

'Then I dreamt it.' She sounded puzzled. Her shoulders slumped and her voice lost its sharpness. 'I'm sorry.' As they watched her go, the captain crossed himself fervently.

At dawn the dream, if dream it were, returned. She heard the horn, jumped from the bed in a panic and ran to the window. The weather was breaking. The dawn was hot and thundery and the sweet scent of the earth mingled with the cool green smell of the river.

The touch on her shoulder was featherlight. For a moment she ignored it, then she swung around. There was no one there. A draught

451

had stirred the wall hangings, that was all. Her jewellery box lay open on the table, she was certain she had closed it. She went to it and picked up the phoenix again, staring at it in the dim light of the dawn. She slipped the chain from its loop and dropped it back into the casket, then she threaded the pendant on to a black silk ribbon and hung it around her neck, feeling the hard bright enamel cold as death between her breasts.

It had been a long time since she had looked into the fire. Kneeling before the hearth, she pushed aside the turves and blew on the embers. She was trembling violently and the cold dread which filled her had nothing to do with dreams.

Alexander!

She leaned towards the flames. Her eyes were blurred. She could see nothing and suddenly she realised she was crying.

Alexander!

The door rattled on its hinges as the wall hangings billowed. Ash blew towards her across the hearth and a log cracked from end to end in a shower of sparks.

There were no pictures in the flames, only the sound of weeping.

XI

Robert de Quincy's horse was soaked with sweat and he was alone. Eleyne was sitting in the great hall with the entire household as he swaggered in. She knew at once that he was very drunk. It was the first time she had seen him in over two years.

She watched, taut with apprehension as he made his way towards the high table on the dais, where she sat with Rhonwen and some of the senior members of the household.

'You know, of course, what I am here to tell you.' He stood, hands on hips, one leg thrust forward, his elegant surcoat mud-spattered and torn, his tunic stained with sweat.

'Indeed not.' She tried to keep her voice neutral.

'What? No pyromancy to tell your fortune in the flames?' He was speaking deliberately loudly, ensuring silence in the hall.

Eleyne heard the priest next to her draw in his breath sharply and she clenched her fists. 'What is it you have to tell me?'

Robert laughed. 'So, you don't know! How strange. You're happy, yet in a few minutes you're going to be devastated.' He looked at her almost clinically, with total detachment. 'I'm about to break your heart!'

Eleyne could feel the fear building inside her. 'Do you intend to make a public spectacle of this announcement?' she asked coldly. 'If so, you should hurry before the horn sounds for supper.'

452

Turn away, keep your back to him, keep your back to the hall. Don't give him the pleasure of seeing it hurt, whatever it is.

But she knew. She had known for a whole week. And her heart was already breaking.

Robert was giggling now, quietly. He stepped towards the dais, missed his footing and decided to sit on the edge of the step instead. So he was facing down the great hall when at last he spoke, tears of laughter running down his face.

'He's dead, sweetheart. Your king is dead! I was with King Henry when the messengers brought the news from Scotland. We thought it only seemly to bring you the news at once . . .'

His voice had faded into a mist. It swirled and eddied around her, muffling her ears, enveloping her head, blinding her eyes. She took a step forward, and felt an arm around her. Rhonwen's. Her back was straight; she was not crying. With Rhonwen at her side, she stepped slowly off the dais past her giggling husband and walked the length of the hall to the door.

She went into the chapel and knelt on the ornate tiles before the altar, aware that Rhonwen had waited at the door. Beeswax candles glowed before a statue of the Virgin; she did not see them. She saw nothing. Her mind was a spinning emptiness; a whirl of nameless pain.

Robert came for her a long time later. He had eaten and drunk more, but now he was steadier on his feet. He strode into the chapel and found her still on her knees, her eyes closed, her face transparent with exhaustion and unhappiness.

He pulled her to her feet. 'Enough of prayer! Now perhaps you will pay some attention to your husband.'

Wearily she looked at him. 'I do not have a husband who merits my attention.'

'No?' His lips twisted into a sneer. 'Then perhaps this will encourage it.' The blow from his ringed hand tore open her cheek and the blood trickled like warm tears down her face.

'You hit me in the presence of Our Lady?' Eleyne backed towards the niche with its candlelit statue. Neither of them noticed that the door had banged shut. The air around them was full of anger.

'I shall hit you where I please!'

She could not fight him and no one in the household would stand against him as he dragged her across the inner courtyard up the steep steps into the gatehouse, past crowds of openly staring men and women and on up towards the bedchambers. She did not sleep in the lord's chamber, the room which had been John's, but that was where he took her now. The great bed stood without hangings in the darkness, the deep feather mattress musty and full of mice, the flagstone floor swept bare of strewing herbs.

She did not even try to fight him. She submitted as he dragged off her clothes and tied her hands; she knelt like a frozen statue as he swaggered towards her and commanded that she open her mouth and later as she lay back painfully on her bound hands on the bare mattress, and let him thrust again and again inside her, her mind shut off entirely from the degradation of her body and allowed her to drift away.

Her wrists were still bound when Rhonwen found her at daybreak. Robert had slept for a few hours, sprawled across her inert body, then he had woken and staggered off in search of more wine. He had not returned.

'Do you still forbid me to kill him?' Tight-lipped, Rhonwen slid the blade of her small knife into the thongs around Eleyne's wrists.

'What good would his death achieve now?' Eleyne's fingers were white and lifeless and she watched, strangely detached still, as Rhonwen began gently to rub them.

'It would free you of him for good.'

XII

A week later Eleyne received a letter from Malcolm of Fife. Robert was out riding when the messenger arrived for which she was thankful because the letter made her cry. It was courteous and restrained, and gave her the facts.

Alexander had been struck down by a sudden fever while his fleet was at anchor in Oban Bay. He struggled on, insisting on being rowed ashore to the island of Kerrera to complete their business there and there he had died. His body had been taken for interment to Melrose Abbey, as he had long ago specified in his will. His eight-year-old son had been crowned five days after he died, at Scone, elevated on the sacred stone by Malcolm himself, following the ancient tradition that the Earls of Fife alone had that right. But already, it appeared, there was quarrelling amongst the magnates. The king's closest henchman, Sir Alan Durward, and Lord Menteith were locked in conflict over who should have power during the young king's minority. At the end of his letter Malcolm gave her the crumb of comfort she so desperately needed. 'I am assured, my lady, that in his last delirium the king mentioned your name several times and begged that you pray for his soul's eternal rest.' As the tears flooded her eyes, she threw down the letter. It was not until a long time later that she read the closing sentence. 'Please be assured, my lady, of my lasting devotion and my service, which shall be yours as long as I draw breath.'

XIII

By the beginning of November she knew she was once again with child. Robert had stayed only a few days at Fotheringhay then, bored with tormenting her and afraid, though he would not admit it even to himself, of the cold, considered hatred which seemed to emanate from the very stones of the castle and from the air around him, he had finally obtained the king's permission to return to court. That same day she had made them take out the bed on which, though she did not yet know it, her child had been conceived and burn it in the outer court.

It seemed strange that life went on as usual once he had gone. She oversaw the stud farm and rode regularly about the manor. She ate and slept and sewed and talked and waited indifferently as her belly began to grow. It would be a girl. Robert would father no sons, of that she was certain.

Her dreams were at an end. Her love was dead; her heart a lead weight inside her. She had no place in history. Her sons would never be kings. Einion had been a charlatan, her own visions the demon-inspired ramblings of a fevered brain. She would not return to Scotland where her godson was now king, firmly tied to his mother's apron strings whilst Alan Durward governed as justiciar. Scotland was a place of dreams and memories; a place of broken destiny.

The ghostly woman who haunted the deserted rooms of the castle gave her little comfort. Their mutual unhappiness was part of the fabric of history. It entwined and encircled them and held them together in a web of eternity from which neither could break free.

XIV

FOTHERINGHAY

Hawisa was born on St George's Day 1250, and two weeks after her birth Robert returned. He stared for a long time at the mite in the heavy wooden cradle, then he looked up at Eleyne. 'Another girl?'

'That was God's will.'

'Was it? Or did you use charms and potions to ensure it?' His expression was flat and hard.

Eleyne shrugged. 'It did not matter to me what sex the child was. She is healthy and baptised.'

'So caring a mother!' He bent over the cradle and lifted out the swaddled bundle. 'At least it's obvious that she is mine.' The baby's hair was thick and dark, her eyes set close above the small nose. 'Where is Joanna?' When he had come to Fotheringhay the summer before, he had not once asked to see his daughter.

Eleyne tensed. 'Somewhere with her nurses,' she said guardedly.

'Don't you know?' His tone was half accusing, half mocking.

'Of course I know. She's safe with them.' Eleyne was suddenly afraid. She did not want him to see her beautiful daughter; did not want him to have any claim over the child at all.

'I hope so.' He put the baby down.

She dreaded his appearance at her bedside that night, but he did not come. She lay awake, afraid to close her eyes, but her night was undisturbed.

When Rhonwen came to her in the morning, her eyes were glittering with hatred. 'He has taken the little one.'

'Taken?' Though still half asleep, the word slammed into Eleyne's brain. She pushed herself upright in the bed and peered into the cradle.

'Not the baby, *cariad*, Joanna. He has taken Joanna.' Rhonwen's voice broke.

'Sweet Mother of God!' At Eleyne's desperate cry, Hawisa began to sob, but her mother ignored her. Flinging her cloak around her shoulders, she was halfway to the door before Rhonwen stopped her. 'It's no use; they're long gone. He took her in the night. Little Sarah Curthose tried to stop him and had her face beaten to pulp for her pains.'

'He'll have taken Joanna to London.' Eleyne's breasts ached as the baby cried. Scooping Hawisa into the crook of her arm, she opened the front of her shift and felt the usual sharp wince of pain as the small mouth clamped on to her nipple. 'We'll go after him. Now, as soon as the horses are made ready.' Her face was bleak. 'See to it for me, Rhonwen.'

Encumbered by servants and the baby, they did not reach London until noon the following day. Within two hours Eleyne, in her finest gown, was riding towards the Palace of Westminster. She could barely stay on her horse; tired to the point of collapse, her body still weak from giving birth, she nevertheless rode to the door and slid from Tam Lin's back. As a groom ran to take the horse's bridle, she staggered slightly.

The great hall was crowded, but she could see the king surrounded as usual by noblemen and servants. He appeared to be studying a huge book as Eleyne pushed her way towards the dais. He looked up as she approached and frowned. 'Niece, I did not give you leave to come to court.'

Eleyne managed a deep curtsey. 'My child was safely delivered, your grace, and I am churched, but my husband has returned to London. I need to see him urgently and hoped to find him near you.'

Henry smiled coldly. 'He has been here, but not, I think, today. If you and he are once more together, that pleases me.' He leaned forward and looked into her face. 'You are well, niece?'

'Well enough, sire, thank you.' She saw sympathy in his eyes. For what? The heartache and loneliness now that Alexander was dead? Henry had never condoned her love, never admitted he knew about it save in that one interview three years before.

She took a step forward, afraid that he was going to wave her away. 'Robert has taken our little girl, and I'm afraid for her.' She could not hold back the words. 'You must help me to find her. Please.' Her eyes filled with tears. 'She doesn't know him. He was drunk. He nearly killed her nurse . . .' Oblivious of the people around her she caught his hand and sank to her knees. 'Please help me. Please.'

Henry frowned down at her. 'You are talking about his daughter.'

'I am talking about a little girl who would not even recognise him.'

'A common enough occurrence.'

'What is not common, sire, is for a man to take away a child without so much as a nursemaid to take care of her.'

'But why should he do such a thing?' Henry looked puzzled. He had not tried to release his hand from her grip.

'Because he knew it would hurt me. He has always enjoyed hurting me.' She held his gaze until the king looked away uncomfortably.

'Very well. I will send men to find him for you,' he mumbled. 'I will send to you when we have found her.'

The king watched as she made her way back down the hall. She had been so beautiful once, his niece, so spirited. Now it was as if her vital flame had dimmed. He had long ago stopped reproaching himself for marrying her to de Quincy to teach that old fox, her father, a lesson, but now his conscience pricked him again. He snapped to his secretary, 'See that Robert de Quincy is found without delay and that his daughter is recovered and returned to her mother.'

But Robert de Quincy and Joanna were nowhere to be found.

XV

GODSTOW ❖ July 1250

Isabella was sitting in the sun in the garden sewing when the nun came to fetch her to the abbess's parlour. She was thin and pale and her eyes were dull with boredom. Her contrition and fear after the earthquake, like that of her companions, had lasted several months, but as the convent returned to normal and the end of the world did not come her piety faded.

She had begun to write letters again: to the king; to her de Braose relatives; to her nephews in Wales, long pathetic letters begging for her release. She hated the convent. Like the other rich ladies who lived there, for one reason or another out of society, she once again had servants to wait on her, her habits were of the richest silk, her food appetising and plentiful, with only the merest nod towards fasting, and she had the best wine with every meal. But she was still a prisoner. She could never leave the convent walls.

Abbess Flandrina had died two years before, to be succeeded by the tall, elegant Emma Bloet, a kind sincere woman who was deeply sympathetic to her unwilling charge, had Isabella but realised it. She entered the abbess's parlour with a scowl. No doubt the abbess was about to administer further penance for yet another of her small transgressions.

It was only as she raised her eyes after kneeling to kiss her superior's ring that she saw the tall young man in the livery of the King of England. Her heart turned over with excitement. At last the king had taken pity on her; he had seen the pointlessness of shutting her away. Dafydd was dead. She was not Welsh. At last he was going to free her.

She could feel herself expanding and glowing beneath the young man's eyes like a wilted flower which has been put into water. 'At last you have come to take me to court!' Even her voice had sparkle in it as she turned to the young man, but it was the abbess who answered for him.

'No, sister, he has not come to take you anywhere.' Her tone was a mixture of exasperation and sympathy. 'Sir John is here to make enquiries about the whereabouts of your sister-in-law Lady Chester's child.'

Isabella didn't understand. Her hope had been so high, the moment of excitement and relief so intense that the truth was incomprehensible.

'Lady Chester's child?' she echoed blankly.

'The child's father has abducted her and it is believed he will have sequestered her somewhere in the country,' Sir John volunteered awkwardly. He had seen the hunger in the eyes of the Princess of Aberffraw and he pitied her. She must have been pretty once, though now she was faded and her features were hard. 'The king thought of you immediately, as Lady Chester's sister-in-law.'

'I told Sir John that you have no visitors,' said the abbess, 'and there is no possibility of the little girl being hidden here.'

'No.' Isabella's voice was hard. 'There is no possibility of her being hidden here.'

Three times she had written to Eleyne and not once had she received an answer. That all her recent letters had been brought by her chosen messenger – a lay sister from the convent farm – straight to the abbess, read and burned, never occurred to her. Her messenger always took her money and promised to send the letters on their way. She believed her, and she went on writing. Eleyne, like everyone else, was probably rejoicing in her captivity and her unhappiness, or so she believed.

She looked from under her lashes at Sir John, self-preservation overriding her bitterness. 'I would help if I could. My sister, Eleyne, has always been very dear to me. Perhaps if you could take me to her . . .'

'You know that is impossible, my dear,' the abbess put in quietly. She had seen the melting look Isabella had thrown at the young knight. 'All you can do is pray for the child, as all the sisters will do with all their hearts. Please tell the king, Sir John, that we cannot help your quest. I'm sorry.'

She stood beside Isabella at the parlour window and watched as Sir John's squire led his master's horse to the door. Both young men mounted and rode away without a backward glance. Looking covertly at Isabella, the abbess sighed. On this occasion, she would turn a blind eye to the woman's tears.

XVI

GRACECHURCH STREET ❖ August 1250

Eleyne stooped over the tall pitcher and scooped some of the cool water into her palms. She splashed it over her face gratefully, aware that long nights of crying had reddened her eyes and engraved black circles beneath them. There was still no word of Joanna. A thick fetid heat had settled over London and there was plague in the city, but still she stayed. The court had long gone, as had most of the nobility. The great houses were closed.

She stooped again, ready to sink her hands up to the wrists in the cool river water when she stopped and frowned, staring into the shadowy depths of the jug. For a moment she thought she had seen a face in the water. Not her own reflection – her red-gold hair flattened by the head-dress she had discarded on the bed – but a smaller, darker head. A child's head. Not daring to believe her eyes, she tried to peer through the shadows, seeing the movement of the water as it lapped the rough glaze. She was there: Joanna, her arms outstretched, calling silently and behind her – Eleyne concentrated, terrified the vision would break – a castle. A castle surrounded by water.

She swung round so suddenly that she swept the pitcher off the coffer and it broke on the floor, soaking the dusty woodruff which covered the boards. The sound brought Rhonwen running. 'What is it, *cariad*? What have you done?'

'Joanna! She is in Scotland. He has taken her to Loch Leven!' Eleyne was feverish with excitement. 'What fools we were not to think of it! Order the horses quickly.'

'Thank all the gods that she's all right.' Rhonwen did not question how Eleyne knew or remind her of her vow never to set foot in Scotland again.

XVII
LOCH LEVEN

It was dusk when the four riders arrived at last on the shores of the loch and stared across the dark, still water towards the castle on its island. Eleyne had left Hawisa and her wetnurse in London with Luned and her three children and she and Rhonwen had ridden north at breakneck speed attended by two of her knights, Sir Thomas Bohun and Sir David Paris. There had been no time to think about the past.

'How will we get there, lady?' Sir Thomas leaned forward in his saddle and slapped his horse's sweating neck. 'Are there boats?'

'You should ask Lord Fife to help us,' Rhonwen put in quietly. 'He would do anything for you.' She shivered. This place held nothing but unhappy memories.

Dismounting, Sir Thomas led his exhausted horse to the water's edge and let it drink, watching the water dribble from its soft lips. 'Is Lord Fife close?' He stood, squinting at the island.

'There must be a boat. If we ride towards Kinross, we'll find something.' Now that she was so close Eleyne could not tolerate the thought of another delay. The castle's walls seemed very remote. There was no sign of life on the island as far as she could see and the water was deserted save for sleeping gulls.

Sir David had ridden a little way away from them, pushing his horse breasthigh into the reeds. 'There's a boat of sorts here,' he called softly. 'Pulled up out of the water.'

A flat-bottomed punt, the paddles still in it, was hidden carefully in the reeds. Eleyne caught her breath with excitement. 'We three will go. Rhonwen, you stay with the horses.' She squeezed the woman's hand, well aware of the horror she must feel at the thought of setting sail in the dark on the water which had so nearly drowned her. 'If we have not returned by dawn ride to Falkland Castle and find the Earl of Fife. Tell him everything and bring him to look for us.'

Rhonwen watched as the boat drew slowly away. It was hard to see, but the drip of water from the paddles as the two young men propelled it away from the shore sounded loud in the silence. She stood there for a long time. To David and Thomas it was all a great adventure, but she had seen the expression on Eleyne's face; the fear, the strain, the terrible weight of sorrow which coming back here had reawakened. One day soon – very soon – Sir Robert de Quincy was going to pay for his cruelty with his life.

The bushes were thick near the gateway to the castle and the track was overgrown. Peering cautiously out of the shadows Thomas cursed as the moon floated serenely free of the clouds and flooded the island with silver light. A slight mist had begun to drift across the water. It lapped the shore and floated hesitantly towards the walls.

'You have to demand entry,' Eleyne whispered. 'Hammer on the gates. You are friends of Lord Fife's. They will let you two in.'

'And you?' David looked at her doubtfully.

'See who is here. If Robert is here, you must find Joanna and bring her to me. If he is not, you can let me in.' She touched each gently on the shoulder. There was no doubt in her mind that Joanna was in the castle.

She held her breath as they moved stealthily back towards the landing stage. Once there, they stepped brazenly into the moonlight and walked arm-in-arm up the track to the castle gate. Thomas hammered on it with the hilt of his sword and they both began to shout.

For a long time she thought no one was there, then at last she saw a small figure appear on the battlements. He was carrying a horn lantern.

'Andrew,' she breathed.

Minutes later the pass door in the iron-bound gates swung open and the two men disappeared inside. She closed her eyes and whispered a prayer of gratitude – so far, so good.

They did not reappear. Leaning against the trunk of the tree, she watched as the moonlight travelled slowly across the grey stone walls. Robert must be there. If he wasn't, they would have come at once to fetch her. She felt a knife-thrust of fear in her stomach. She had not thought beyond this moment. Her child was here; her child had called to her across hundreds of miles and she had come, and she could do nothing. Her fingers went for comfort to the pendant beneath her gown. Pulling her cloak around her more closely she sank down on the damp grass, her back against the rough tree trunk, and drew up her knees with a shiver.

The eastern sky was a blaze of green when the door opened once again and three figures slipped out into the cold dawn. One of them was carrying a sleeping child wrapped in a blanket. Her eyes closing with fatigue and stiff with cold, Eleyne jerked awake and scrambled to her feet. Her heart was thudding with excitement. She ran towards them, but Thomas was waving her back under the trees, his finger to his lips.

'Don't wake her. She's all right.' He grinned at his companion, who was carrying the child. Behind them came a hooded figure. Eleyne stared at her and then smiled. 'Annie.'

461

'She had to come,' Thomas said curtly. 'Robert would have killed her for losing the little girl.'

'And I wanted to come,' Annie put in hastily. 'I wanted to serve you, my lady, if you will have me.' There was no pleading in her voice, only a cool certainty that Eleyne would indeed want her.

'So. Robert was there.'

Thomas nodded grimly. 'We drank him under the table. It didn't take much. He was pretty nearly unconscious when we got there. Andrew says he'll sleep all morning, but we can't be sure of that. We've got to get away fast.'

Handing Eleyne and then Annie into the boat, he and David passed Joanna carefully down into Eleyne's arms. The child was still three-quarters asleep. Warm and heavy, she snuggled into her mother's lap with a little smile.

As the boat slid silently through the mist, the sky turned slowly from green to gold. Somewhere nearby a moorhen called as they passed, the sound echoing across the still water. Eleyne tightened her grip on the little girl and kissed the small closed eyes.

They rode all morning, Annie on the crupper of David's saddle. They found a boat across the Forth almost at once and headed south again, aware that Robert could already be on the road behind them. Fully awake now, Joanna was talkative. Her papa had given her a new pony. He had given her clothes and toys and she was devastated at leaving them behind. While pleased to see her mother, she had obviously enjoyed her stay.

As they rode past Melrose, she knew she had to stop. However fast they needed to travel, however frightened she was, there was one last farewell she had to make.

Abbot Matthew greeted her alone in the new hall of the old abbey beneath the Eildon Hills. If he guessed who she was he gave no sign, listening to her quiet request with a gracious inclination of the head. 'It is of course our blessing that many pilgrims come to visit the grave of our late king,' he said. He stared thoughtfully at the heavily veiled, unknown woman who had asked for an audience with him and knelt to kiss his ring with such humility, sensing her tightly controlled grief.

He was a realist. He knew the king had had many lady friends in his time. The numbers of royal bastards married into the prominent families of Scotland bore witness to the fact, but this woman intrigued him. She was younger than the others, more vulnerable, and more dignified. He guessed who she was: the whole of Scotland knew that during his later years Alexander had eyes for only one woman. The old man gave an indulgent smile. He had decided that he personally would lead her into the great abbey church.

462

The king's tomb lay before the high altar, the carved alabaster of his effigy lit by four tall candles. Eleyne stopped before it and stared at the cold stiff features of the sculpted face, the hard formal ringlets of the beard, the helm surmounted by the crown. Her heart was beating very fast, and there was a lump in her throat. She couldn't breathe. The light, which filtered, cool and dim, through the coloured glass of the great east window, bathed the pale stone in shadows. The abbey was completely silent.

The abbot moved back and stood, his hood pulled forward over his head, his arms folded deep within his sleeves, his lips moving in prayer. It was as though she were alone. For several moments she stood, trying to control the pain which filled her chest, then she moved to kneel at the prayer stool at the foot of the tomb. Swallowing hard, she raised her eyes to the window. The stained glass was blurred. She could see nothing.

They were ten miles from Roxburgh when the horsemen caught up with them. They wore the royal livery.

Eleyne froze in the saddle. Her joy at having Joanna sitting before her, her chubby legs stuck straight out on either side of the pommel, her small gown rucked up to her thighs, vanished in another wave of misery which almost overwhelmed her. These were not Alexander's men; Alexander would never send for her again. These riders wore the livery of her godson. Fighting to contain her tears and knowing they could not outride their pursuers, she ordered her companions to rein in and waited, silently praying that Robert was still drunkenly asleep in Fife.

The leading rider saluted. 'Sir Thomas, Sir David, Lady Chester. Her grace the queen demands that you attend her at Roxburgh Castle.'

'The queen?' Eleyne echoed.

'How did you know we were in Scotland?' Thomas enquired sharply.

'You were seen yesterday on your way north, sir.' One of the riders had made himself spokesman. 'Her grace was not pleased that you did not have the courtesy to call on her, especially as Lady Chester had not asked permission to come to Scotland and had no safe conduct for the journey.'

Eleyne cursed herself under her breath for walking into Marie's trap. 'That was my fault, I was in a hurry.'

'Indeed, madam.' The man's smile was knowing. 'So her grace imagined.'

Eleyne felt her anger mounting. This oaf was going to delay them and Robert would catch up with them. 'I shall explain to the queen,' she said haughtily. 'I am sure she will understand and allow us on our way.'

'I'm sure she will.' He had fallen in beside her, and she had no doubt that he would remain at her side until they reached their destination.

XVIII
ROXBURGH CASTLE

Queen Marie was seated in state on the dais when Eleyne was ushered into the great hall, still holding Joanna by the hand, the two young men beside her and Rhonwen and Annie behind them.

'I am given to understand that you have been visiting your husband in Fife,' the queen began without preamble.

Eleyne tried to conceal her hatred of this woman, who had taken Alexander from her. 'You are well informed, ma'am,' she said drily.

'Of course. Whilst the king – my son – is so young, I make it my business to know everything that goes on in Scotland.' She leaned back in her ornate chair. 'And I hear you have also visited Melrose.' Her face darkened. 'Can you not leave him alone even now?' she hissed. She glared at Eleyne.

Her next question was silky with innocence. 'Is your husband not returning with you?'

'Not yet, your grace.' Eleyne's voice was icy. 'He is unwell.'

'Indeed.' The queen gave a pert, humourless laugh. 'Poor Sir Robert. Though it must be a great relief to him to have you all to himself at last.' Her voice was heavy with innuendo, the smile honeyed. Satisfied that she had scored a hit, she turned her attention to the child who was hiding in Eleyne's skirts. 'Is this your daughter?'

'This is my daughter, Joanna –' Too late she tried to hold the name back; the woman's eyes hardened at the name of Alexander's first wife. 'Named for my mother, Joan,' Eleyne said softly. She could feel Joanna's wary restlessness as the child sensed the tension in the atmosphere.

'You have no sons, I think.' The queen retaliated with a knife twist.

'No sons, your grace,' Eleyne repeated firmly. 'No sons who lived.'

'Quite.' Marie smiled again. 'I intend to keep you here, my lady, until your husband is well enough to ride south with you.' A look of triumph swept across her face as she saw Eleyne recoil. 'You will be a very welcome guest, I assure you.' She turned to Thomas. 'Your father is here, Sir Thomas. I am sure you will be pleased to see him. And Lord Fife has joined us with Sir Alan Durward. We shall be a very merry gathering this evening.'

Eleyne stepped forward. 'Do you really wish to keep us here, your grace?' she asked forcefully. 'The memories I bring back for you cannot be happy ones.'

The queen flinched as if Eleyne had hit her, and for a moment she didn't speak. 'Yes, my lady, I really wish you to stay here. I want to see you given back to your husband with my own eyes.'

XIX

Malcolm of Fife found Eleyne outside the great hall. His hair was greying now and there was an ugly scar across his cheek from a fall from his horse the year before, but his charm seemed undiminished.

'You have to help me get Joanna away.' Eleyne wasted no time in drawing him into a corner. 'I feel as though I'm a prisoner here for her amusement!'

Malcolm nodded. 'I am afraid that's exactly what you are. She knows Joanna was taken against your will. Robert bragged of it openly, as he bragged that he beat you. Our gracious queen makes no secret of her hatred of you. She will make you suffer as much as she possibly can. You stole too much from her.'

Eleyne looked away. 'It was she who stole from me.' Her voice was full of pain.

He frowned again. 'I can take you and the child to Falkland. It's a risk, but I'm prepared to do it for you.' He looked sheepish. 'I can protect you and I can deal with your husband.'

She hesitated. To go with Malcolm would be moving from one trap to another, yet what alternative was there? And it was she who had begged his help.

He grinned amiably. 'Surely, by the process of elimination, I am the least of all evils.'

She laughed out loud. 'Perhaps you are, my lord, but I have no wish to return north. I have made my home in England.'

'With Robert de Quincy?'

'As my own mistress. If he comes back, I shall go to my nephews in Wales. Robert will never find me if I hide myself in the mountains of Eryri. No one would find me there.'

'I would find you.' He was gazing at her with undisguised hunger in his eyes. 'You will be mine one day, Eleyne. Why fight it? Why not let me take you away from your boor of a husband? I could make you content and I could give you sons.'

She flinched, 'I want no sons.'

'Rubbish, every woman wants sons. The king has gone, Eleyne, forget him.'

'I'll never forget him!' She rounded on him. 'How could you even ask it?' Her composure was cracking. Why couldn't they leave her alone

465

with her memories? Why did they have to plague her like this? 'I'm sorry, my lord, but I can't come with you.'

He raised an eyebrow. 'Then I can't help you, you'll have to stay here.' He bowed. 'But one day you'll come, Eleyne, I promise you that. And one day soon.'

XX

Rhonwen, Joanna and Annie had been escorted to the nursery quarters which had once belonged to the young king when Eleyne found herself once more before the queen that evening. Marie was smiling as Eleyne walked swiftly, her head high, up the great hall towards her, bitterly aware of her shabbiness, of her lack of attendants, and of the wagging spiteful tongues. As she curtseyed before the throne – Alexander's throne – Eleyne saw the triumph in her rival's eyes.

'I have a surprise for you, Lady Chester,' Marie said sweetly. 'I sent someone to see how your husband was, and he was already on his way south after you. Wasn't it nice that we were able to tell him where you were? Sir Robert?' She turned and beckoned Robert from the shadows at the back of the dais.

Husband and wife stared at each other, oblivious of the silence that had fallen over the entire hall. He was dressed in a soiled tunic, his rich, embroidered mantle torn. His eyes were bloodshot and his face blurred by drink.

'So.' He managed to make the one word accusing, triumphant and threatening all at once. He was panting slightly.

'So.' Her echo was icy.

'Where is she?'

'Safe.'

A group of men pushed past them, coming in from the courtyard. Neither Eleyne nor Robert noticed.

'We'll go back to Loch Leven,' he said. 'Get her ready.'

'No.' Eleyne clenched her fists, well aware of the enjoyment on Marie's face. 'I think you will find that at last you have outstayed your welcome in Fife.'

'Indeed.' Robert suppressed a belch. 'Then we'll go elsewhere.'

A second group of people appeared in the doorway and Eleyne recognised with a sinking heart that one of them was Robert's brother, the Constable of Scotland. Roger de Quincy regarded Robert sternly. He stood as if deep in thought, then walked purposefully towards the group of people around the throne and dropped on one knee before the queen.

'I am sorry to see my brother here in such a state, your grace. I hoped it wasn't true when I was told that he had followed his wife and child to Roxburgh. I have instructions from King Henry that he and Lady Chester are to return south. If either of them disobeys the order, the child, Joanna de Quincy, will be made a royal ward.'

There was a stunned silence in the hall. The queen frowned. 'King Henry has no jurisdiction here.'

'Indeed not, madam, but my brother and his wife are King Henry's subjects.' Roger's voice was firm.

'They are my son's subjects too,' she said uncertainly.

'I think you must allow them to go, your grace.' Roger gave her the practised smile of a courtier. 'Scotland does not want to antagonise Henry over so minor a matter. I shall escort them south myself.'

It was obvious that the queen respected him; in his role as constable Roger de Quincy was one of her closest advisers. But she had not realised until today how much she hated this woman; to see her quail before her drunken oaf of a husband would have given her enormous satisfaction. But she did not dare anger Henry of England. 'Very well.' She made up her mind at last. 'Take them.'

XXI

For two days on the long slow ride Robert did not speak to her. He rode apart at the back of the group of horsemen, ignoring his brother, casting baleful looks at Rhonwen, who threw murderous glances back, and from time to time reaching into the bag which hung at his saddle bow for a stoppered jug of wine, which he hung from his forefinger and tipped to his mouth with his arm.

The third night they spent in the guesthouse of a lonely abbey on the Yorkshire moors, wrapped in their cloaks in the single small room beneath the vaulted stone roof. Outside the men of the escort slept with the horses.

Eleyne lay, her head cushioned on her saddlebags, looking up at the shadowy ceiling, listening to the sounds of the men around her. Robert snored loudly, a wineskin lying empty beside him. Beyond him his brother slept enveloped in his cloak. Joanna had cuddled up to Rhonwen who, so far, had kept well out of Robert's way. Eleyne stirred uncomfortably. The floor was hard and the dying fire left the room cold and damp in spite of the huddled sleepers.

Slowly she sat up. Cautiously, so as not to disturb any of the others, she felt in her saddlebag. There, at the bottom, wrapped in a silk kerchief, was the phoenix pendant. She had hidden it there, afraid that Robert would see it around her neck. She took it out and stared at it, watching the way even the dying fire reflected in the dark glitter of the eyes. She looked at it for a long time, then slipped the chain around her neck and tucked the jewel inside the bodice of her gown so that it nestled between her breasts. It always brought her closer to him.

Hugging her knees, she gazed out of the open door. The soaring roof of the abbey was black against the stars and she could smell the cool sweetness of the night above the staleness of the bodies around her. Quietly she rose and tiptoed to the door. The man on guard stirred and nodded in silent recognition. The grass was ice-cold, wet with dew as she walked through it away from the guesthouse towards the great looming shadow of the abbey grange. Behind her Joanna slept securely in the curve of Rhonwen's arm. She was safe now, but what would happen when they reached the king? What would he do, confronted with both de Quincys?

Roger had already told his brother sharply to sober up before they reached the king and Robert had smiled and nodded that he would do it. By the time they walked into Henry's presence his barber would have trimmed his beard and hair, he would be washed and scented with oils and pomades and wearing one of the new gowns he had no doubt ordered already to be waiting for him when he returned to London. He would look the picture of reliable and loyal manhood.

There was only one way to be rid of him now that she could see. She had to leave Fotheringhay, run back to Wales with the children and hide in the mountains. He would never find her there. She would lose everything: her income, her property, her status, but she would be free and never again would she have to suffer the endless nightmares thinking about what Robert was going to do to her, or what, in a drunken frenzy, he might do to his own daughters. She closed her eyes, breathing in the sweet night air.

In the doorway to the guesthouse Robert watched his wife as she moved steadily away from him into the darkness. His arms were folded and he was swaying slightly. Pushing himself away from the doorpost he walked around the side of the building and relieved himself against the wall, then he turned to follow her.

He made no effort to walk quietly but she didn't hear him as he trod unsteadily through the long grasses, feeling them cold and wet at the hem of his mantle. Deep in thought, she wandered more and more slowly, seeing, not the velvet Yorkshire sky, but the ice-covered peaks of Yr Wyddfa, where she would live with Owain's and Llywelyn's help in one of the mountain castles her father had built and where her daughters could grow up free and unafraid.

When she turned and saw him, only feet away from her, his hands on his hips and a disarmingly pleasant smile on his face, it was too late to run.

'At last.' He spoke slowly and distinctly. 'Some privacy. I don't like taking my wife before an audience.' He put his hand around her wrist. 'I find it inhibiting. It spoils the fun.'

468

She broke his grip. 'Don't touch me.'

'Why not? You are my wife. Before God and the law you belong to me.'

'No.' She backed away, keeping just out of reach. 'I belong to no one, no one at all.'

'Now that your Scots king has abandoned you.' He lunged and managed to catch her cloak. She pulled away, but she was off balance and he had sobered during the walk through the icy grass. This time he pulled her into his arms and sought her mouth with his own. 'We need to tie your hands to make you obedient, don't we?' he murmured as he sucked at her face, his lips wet and hot, his breath stinking of stale wine. 'Remind my beautiful wife who is her master. I have something. I have a rope especially for you, to keep you still. So we can enjoy ourselves.'

He held her with one hand and fumbled at his girdle as she kicked and struggled with grim fury. Her nails connected with his face, then he was pulling a loop of cord around her wrist, drawing it tight, forcing her arm behind her, groping for her other hand.

The swirl of ice-cold wind in the stillness of the night sent them both reeling. Robert staggered off balance, staring into the darkness; there was something there, something between him and Eleyne. A figure. He screamed and lashed out at it, but he missed. His fist passed straight through it; there was nothing there but the shadows from the starlight. He was stunned, then recovering himself he lunged after her, catching the rope which trailed from her wrist and giving it a vicious tug. It was the accursed drink which had fuddled his wits and made him imagine things.

'Robert!'

Roger de Quincy's voice was shockingly loud against the sound of his brother's laboured breathing. So was the smack of bone on flesh as his fist caught Robert full in the face. Robert crumpled and lay still.

Eleyne was too shocked to move, then she looked up and stared round. Roger de Quincy's arrival had rescued her. But before that, in the icy darkness. Her mind grappled with the implications of what she had seen. Who or what had attacked her husband out of the shadows? Whatever it was, it had saved her.

Her brother-in-law's gentle hand on her shoulder brought her back to reality.

'Thank you.' She smiled at him shakily as he unknotted the cord from her wrist.

Roger's mouth had set in a hard line. 'I'm sorry, I gave the king my word that in future Robert would behave as a knight should.'

Gathering her cloak round her Eleyne groped for the phoenix. She stared down at her husband's crumpled form. 'If only you could.' Her voice was husky with shock.

Roger smiled. His sister-in-law's beauty and dignity touched him every time he saw her, but on this occasion there was something there he had never seen before, something wild and untouchable as she gazed past him into the night. It reminded him of an untrained falcon.

'He will live as a knight, madam,' he assured her. 'Men all over Christendom are taking the cross in response to the King of France's call. King Henry has decided that your husband will be one of those who goes to the Holy Land.'

Her green eyes were huge in her pale face. 'The Holy Land?' she echoed.

He nodded. 'Your husband will not bother you or your family again for a very long time, my dear. He is to ride to Jerusalem.'

Behind them, on the lonely moors, the wind warmed a little and the air was suddenly clear.

BOOK FOUR

1253–1270

CHAPTER NINETEEN

I

SUCKLEY MANOR ✧ June 1253

The soft morning air was still sparkling with dew as Eleyne drew the colt gently to a walk and smiled across at her companion. 'He'll do. You can start training him tomorrow.'

'It'll be a pleasure to ride him, my lady.' Narrowing his eyes in the sunlight, Michael watched the two great wolfhounds gambolling at the colt's heels. The animal was used to the dogs; he had known them since he was foaled. She was never without her dogs; they followed her everywhere, as did her two little girls.

Sliding from his horse, he ducked under its head to help her dismount, but as always she beat him to it, slipping off as gracefully as a dancer, laughing at the crestfallen face of her marshal of horses.

Since her husband had sailed for France at the beginning of his trip to the Holy Land Eleyne had moved her base from Fotheringhay to this dower house in the Malvern Hills which her father had given to her on her marriage to John. Behind them the old manor house which she now called home sprawled in the early sunshine, its soft peach-coloured stone walls nestling between the orchards, parks and fields of the home farm. She ran the place like a kingdom. The manor farms, the stud, the outlying tenants all spoke of prosperity and peace.

Twice there had been letters from Robert, the last two years ago, then silence. Michael had reason to remember de Quincy well. In one of his drunken rages he had beaten the quiet stable boy who was now in charge of the Countess of Chester's brood mares.

'I'll go in, Michael.' She was smiling at him now, that beautiful, slow smile which melted a man's gut and made him wonder, just for a moment if she – but no, of course she wouldn't. She showed no interest in men. At thirty-five, she was always the virtuous wife; she loved her children and tended her estates and slept, as far as he knew, chastely alone. He knew the rumours, of course, who didn't? That his lady had a ghostly lover, a tall presence seen sometimes at her side in the twilight, but who would believe that?

He took the colt's rein and watched as she walked towards the manor house, her dogs at her heels. No other lady he had ever heard

473

of would ride without attendants and stride tall and free about her estates as did Lady Chester, but perhaps her dogs were escort enough. He eyed them wryly. Tall, grizzled Lyulf and Ancret, both three years old now, the pups of old Donnet who, rumour had it, had been given to her by the King of Scots. When she reached the house, the dogs would throw themselves down in the shade by the door, waiting for her orders. Only then would the ladies of the house get a chance to speak to their mistress. The ladies were ruled over by the Lady Rhonwen, who kept them in order as she did the two children who would otherwise, if their mother had her way, run barefoot and wild like the children of the serfs on the manor farm. He could see little Hawisa now, a sturdy small girl with a determined chin and the dark good looks of her father, rushing out of the house and hurling herself into her mother's arms. With a grin, Michael began to lead the horses towards the stables. He wouldn't see Lady Chester again today if Hawisa had her way.

'We're to have new gowns for the midsummer revels!' Hawisa gabbled with excitement as she swung from her mother's hand.

Eleyne looked down at her fondly. 'Tell me about them.' Half her mind was still in the stables where her finest stallion rested a badly gashed leg. The only son of Invictus who actually looked like his dead sire, he was an especial favourite. She brought her attention back firmly to the child and stooped to give her a hug.

'Mine is yellow, with little bows here and here and here,' the child's flying hands seemed to indicate every part of her small person, 'and Joanna's is red. And we've got ribbons to go around the necks of Ancret and Lyulf – one red and one yellow.'

Eleyne laughed in delight. 'They'll like that, they're very vain dogs.'

She lived in semi-retirement now. Only once had she gone back to Aber, for the funeral of her sister Gwladus. The death had saddened her, but she and Gwladus had never been close; the gap in their ages had been too great. She had spent several days with Margaret and Angharad in the *ty hir* and then sadly she had come home. Once or twice she had been tempted to court and much against her better judgement she had ridden to York two years before, to attend the marriage of her ten-year-old godson, Alexander, to her cousin Margaret, King Henry's youngest daughter. The visit was not a success. Miserable and lonely, snubbed by the Scottish queen and her ladies, and paid an unwelcome degree of attention by Malcolm of Fife, she had returned home and tried to forget them all.

She never thought about Scotland now. She had forbidden Rhonwen to talk about the past and she had no interest in the future. The present was sufficient. She had never been so content. The lonely place in her heart which had once been full of Alexander was walled off in a corner somewhere deep inside her. The children, the horses, the dogs: they were enough. For now. In daylight. And if sometimes at night in her dreams she allowed that wall to crumble and let herself imagine that Alexander still watched over her, that was a secret she shared with no one.

One thing hadn't changed: she still treasured her solitude. She would ride alone for miles with only her dogs for protection and she still insisted on sleeping alone, something at which her ladies had long ago stopped looking askance. They delighted in her eccentricities. She was their countess, the king's niece; a princess once, they sometimes remembered, and she bred the best horses in ten counties!

She closed the door with a sigh and stretched her arms above her head luxuriously. It had been a tiring day, but she had enjoyed it. The stallion's leg was healing cleanly and the preparations for the revels after today's fast were well in hand. She smiled. The girls were almost sick with excitement; their gowns were ready and she had ordered a chased bangle for each of them from a silversmith in Worcester as a surprise.

She walked to the window embrasure and leaned out. It was a glorious evening, the June air full of the magical scents of summer: newly scythed hay, roses and honeysuckle from the hedgerows and the elusive wild smell of the Malvern Hills which reminded her, a little, of Eryri.

She frowned. This was a moment to enjoy, a moment of perfect happiness, and yet for a fraction of a second she had felt a whisper of unease. She stared out into the luminous darkness, listening intently, but there was nothing there beyond the usual sounds of the night. With a shiver she turned away from the window. There was one thing she had to do before she called her ladies to unlace her gown and brush her hair. She stood before her writing desk and picked up the letter which lay there. It was from Isabella. This, of all her letters, had been entrusted to a party of pilgrims who had stopped at the convent guesthouse on their way to Canterbury, and they had sent it safely on its way.

'. . . If you beg the king for my release he will allow it. He has always loved you. Please, for the love of the Holy Virgin, help me. I am dying in this place . . .'

She sighed. Presumably the warm June night with its whispers of sweetness and promise filtered into the cold stone cells at Godstow too. It would take only a few moments to write to the king and to Isabella, promising her at least a little hope. She had been staring at that letter for much too long, knowing that she would have to offer Isabella a home, knowing Isabella would cause nothing but trouble here at Suckley. But it was her duty to help and she must put it off no longer.

The candle had almost burned down when the letters were finished and she rang at last for Nesta. 'Take these and have Sam ride tonight, first to Godstow and then to London.'

'Tonight?' Nesta stared. 'My lady, it must be midnight!'

'Tonight,' Eleyne repeated. She went back to the window to wait for Nesta's return. Leaning on the broad sill, she found she had tensed again, listening, her ears straining beyond the calls of the owls hunting the home park where the mares grazed with their foals. Something was out there. There was a strange indefinable feeling of menace in the air. It had been a long time since she had felt anything like this.

She wanted to leave the window, to bury her face in her pillow and pull the covers over her head and hide. She looked at the dogs; they were both asleep in their accustomed place by the hearth, where a dull glow showed the small summer fire, damped down to embers. They sensed nothing. She moved towards them, the hairs on her arms prickling with fear, and Lyulf raised his head and gazed at her. He felt her disquiet at once and rose to his feet, his hackles stirring, his eyes puzzled as he looked round the room for the source of his beloved mistress's fright.

When Nesta returned, she was still standing there, her hand on the dogs' heads. To Nesta, it looked as if she were listening to something very far away.

'My lady?'

Eleyne shook her head. 'It's nothing, I thought I heard something –'

She gestured the dogs back to the hearth and sat down so that Nesta could unfasten her hair. 'Where are the children?'

'Asleep, my lady. Where else would they be?' Nesta laughed.

'I didn't kiss them goodnight.' Why was it suddenly so important?

'You kissed them a thousand times between dawn and supper!' Nesta picked up the comb and began to unplait Eleyne's hair. 'And they'll be up again at dawn for Midsummer's Day – as you will. There's John's Mass fires on the hills. You can see them from the tower.' The fires were to keep away the evil spirits which roamed so freely abroad on this night of all nights of the year. Was that what she had sensed? Was there evil here tonight? Had Einion returned after so long to perpetuate his lies? Eleyne frowned. 'Send Rhonwen to me.' She pushed away Nesta's hand. 'Quickly, I must speak to her.'

She stood up and went across to her jewel casket, which stood on the clothes chest near her bed. Her hand hesitated over the lid, then she opened it. The phoenix lay on top of her other jewels, wrapped in a scrap of silk. She stared at it as it glowed in her hand. She was aware of him, when she held it; felt him near her. It was at night, when she took the pendant and put it under her pillow, that it was so easy to imagine that he was there in the darkness. And it was when the sensation grew too strong to bear that she took the pendant and put it in her jewel box. Only that way could she keep her sanity. The door opened and guiltily she put the pendant down on the table.

Rhonwen had been asleep. 'What is it, *cariad*?' She moved more slowly now; her joints were stiff and her bones ached even in the warmth of the summer.

'Listen!' Eleyne held up her hand. 'Can you hear anything?' Nesta had followed Rhonwen into the room and they both listened. The ashes shifted softly in the hearth and Ancret sighed. 'There is something wrong. Is it Einion?'

Rhonwen looked surprised. 'It's a long time since you spoke of him, I thought you no longer believed.'

'I don't believe in his prophecies! How could I?' Eleyne said bitterly. 'But he still haunts me.'

'No, *cariad*, whatever it is, it is not him, not here.' Rhonwen sat down on the edge of the bed. She had her suspicions. She had heard the rumours that Eleyne walked with ghosts, and she had smiled secretly to herself. The child had always walked with ghosts, but now there was one special ghost, who watched over her; if it was the man she thought it was, she blessed them both. The love of Eleyne and her king had been sanctified by the gods. With their blessing even death could not separate them.

'Nothing is wrong. Why don't you go to sleep? Those children of yours will have me awake at first light if I know them.' She smiled indulgently.

The dogs heard the footsteps in the hall before the women, but the loud knocking surprised them all. Hal Longshaft pushed into the room before Nesta had a chance to answer his knock; he was visibly distressed.

'My lady, there are armed men on the road.'

'Armed men?' So that was it. There was a human danger out there in the night. Robert! Robert had returned from the Holy Land. Robert, whom she had hoped never to see again. Her stomach began to churn with fear.

'Hugh Fletcher saw them, my lady. He was going to ride a bit of the way with Sam, but when they saw the men he turned back to warn us. I've called the men awake and the gates are under double guard. Hugh didn't know their leader. He said they wore dark cloaks over the devices on their surcoats, but he was certain it wasn't Sir Robert, my lady.'

So, he had read her mind. 'Issue arms to all the men,' she said quietly, 'and pray.' What good could her servants, her household do against armed men? There was no garrison here, no bodyguard. If this

477

was an attack from the armies of thieves and outlaws who lived in the wild border march, they could do nothing. She turned to Rhonwen as Hal hurried away. 'Why didn't I see the danger sooner –?'

'Your senses have grown lazy, *cariad*.' Rhonwen shook her head. 'They've had no need to develop here. Don't reproach yourself, you chose the other path. Those content with the present don't seek to see into the future. Besides, perhaps there is no danger.' Her voice was reassuring. 'They could be harmless travellers passing along the road.'

'Take the children, Rhonwen. Take them into the woods below the brook.' Eleyne caught her hand and pulled her to her feet. 'Quickly. I want them out of the house and as far away as possible. Take Annie with you. Everyone else must stay and fight if necessary.'

'But *cariad* –'

'Do as I say. Quickly. Please. To be safe. I'll send Hal to find you as soon as the danger is over. Take the dogs, they'll guard the children with their lives.' She ran towards the door, the dogs at her heels. 'Go. Now. Go with Rhonwen.' She pointed at Rhonwen and the two dogs obeyed her. Lyulf looked back once, and she saw the reproach in his eyes. With a quick look at Eleyne's face, Rhonwen hurried away.

Eleyne was standing on the steps outside the front door of the old house when the horsemen drew up outside the gates and shouted for entry.

'Who asks?' The gateward's voice sounded thin in the warm night air.

'Tell Lady Chester that Malcolm of Fife has come to call.' The voice sounded clearly across the cool green moat beyond the wall.

A wave of relief swept over Eleyne. She realised that her fists had been clenched so tightly that her nails had cut into the palms of her hands. Malcolm of Fife might not be welcome under most circumstances, but tonight, in the wake of her panic, he counted as a friend. 'Open the gates,' she called. 'Make our guests welcome,' and she stepped forward as the old oak gates creaked open and the armed men trooped across the bridge and into the courtyard.

Malcolm dismounted and bowed. 'Lady Chester! It has been too long.'

She smiled at him. 'You are welcome.'

'I hope so.' He followed her into the great hall of the manor house as she gave orders for the fire to be rekindled and lights to be placed in the sconces.

'You have ridden a long way, Sir Malcolm,' she commented as she sat in her chair and gestured him towards the other, 'if you have come all the way from Scotland.'

'I have come from Fife.'

'And you are on your way south? To Bristol perhaps to see the king?'

'No.' He sat down and leaned forward, his elbows on his knees, his eyes on her face. 'I came for you.'

She smiled guardedly, her apprehension returning. 'For me?'

'Your husband is dead, Eleyne. You are free to remarry.' He kept his voice low, aware of the curious glances in their direction from Eleyne's sleepy household.

'Dead?' The shock of his words cut through her fear like a knife. 'Robert is dead?'

'Didn't you guess? You haven't heard from him for two years.'

'Who told you? Who told you Robert was dead?'

'I have my informants.' He leaned back in his chair with a smile. 'The fate of Robert de Quincy was, after all, of special importance to me. The reports I received seem conclusive. He is dead and buried. He will not come back to pester you again. You are free.'

Her immediate sense of relief was short-lived as she considered what Malcolm had said. 'If I am, I intend to stay that way.' She was painfully aware of her helplessness. She had opened the gates. She had invited him in and now some three dozen fully armed men were inside her walls, men who, while accepting the wine her servants had offered, had not laid down their swords. Conscious of the sudden stillness in his expression, she forced herself to soften her voice. 'You do me great honour, my lord, but I will never marry again. And I have the assurance of my uncle, the King of England, on that.' She hadn't, but Malcolm would never know.

'I do not intend to ask the king your uncle, madam.' Malcolm's voice dropped slightly. 'I have waited too long. You are mine now.'

'Perhaps we could discuss this in the morning?' She was thinking frantically. Nearby she could see Michael standing, his hand on his sword. She frowned. She had never seen her horse marshal wear a sword before. 'You and your men must be tired and such important matters must be talked about with due ceremony.'

He laughed softly. 'There is nothing to talk about. We leave tonight.'

'No!' Her eyes were blazing. She stepped towards him, aware of the silence in the hall. 'Leave my house, now, before I call my guard!'

Cautiously Nesta crept closer to her. Her small embroidery shears were hidden in her hand.

'I thought this was your guard.' With a smile Malcolm looked around the shadowy hall.

They were all there: her maids, her ladies, Hal, Michael, most of the stable lads, even Kenrick, her cook, and his kitchen boys and the three pages who were serving her until they moved to a household where the head of house was a knight from whom they could learn the chivalric arts. She was sick with fear for them all. The only people absent were Sam and Rhonwen and Annie and the children. She breathed a little prayer that Rhonwen had taken them into the woods as she had asked, then she looked Malcolm full in the eyes. 'Please leave my house, sir. I am sorry, but your attentions are not welcome.' There was a sudden coldness in the air.

'I am sure you will learn to like me, Eleyne, and I am sorry I have to do this, but as you say, your uncle is the king, and it would be more politic if he didn't know what had become of you. We'll leave quietly, and disappear into the darkness forever. If you do as I say, no one will be hurt.'

'No.' She raised her voice. 'I'm not coming with you!'

'Then I am afraid I must use force. You have condemned these people to death, Eleyne of Chester, out of your own mouth.' He snapped his fingers and his men in the hall drew their swords, the rasp of steel ugly in the peaceful old house.

Michael did not hesitate. With a shout of anger, he raised his sword and ran towards her, but he had taken only half a dozen steps before he was cut down.

'*Michael!*' She heard herself scream as Malcolm lunged forward and caught her wrist, swinging her into his arms. Nesta, sweet faithful Nesta, raised her hand, the wickedly sharp shears glinting in her fist. A man-at-arms stepped towards her and Nesta doubled up with a soundless gurgle, his sword through her stomach. There was nothing Eleyne could do. Malcolm had pinioned her arms as he carried her through the uproar, striding towards the door, ignoring her frantic struggles. The shadowy hall was splashed with gore. Women lay in pools of blood on the floor amongst the men and in the far corner she saw a sheet of flame race across the hangings which backed the dais, as one of Malcolm's men snatched up a torch and touched it systematically to the tapestries.

The courtyard was cool and silent after the horror of the hall. Without a word, he carried her to his horse and threw her across the saddle, mounting behind her and kicking the animal into a gallop almost in the same movement. Two of his men were behind them. The last thing she saw before she blacked out was a glimpse of them through her streaming hair as the horse thundered through the gates and up the dust road in the moonlight.

II
GODSTOW

Isabella opened the letter with shaking hands. The seal of Chester was sharp and defiant beneath her fingers, the seal of a woman who was her own mistress and free. She grimaced with a glance at the almoner who sat near her, her beads twisted in her arthritic fingers. Did they think she wouldn't notice that the letter had been opened? That the seal had been lifted with a knife blade and then melted – probably with the same knife but hot this time from the fire – long enough to hold it closed?

Eleyne's letter was short. It was dated St John's Eve, two days before. 'Be patient, dear Isabella. I have written to the king on your behalf and I am sure he will allow you to journey to me on my undertaking to keep you here . . .'

Her undertaking! Isabella echoed the words furiously. Then she shrugged. What did it matter what undertakings Eleyne gave if it got her out of this damned convent? It was the mention of the king's name which had forced them at last to give her this letter. They were afraid to burn it, which they would have done if they had dared. Never mind. She had it now. She clenched her fist over the crackling parchment. Let Eleyne promise anything she wanted; once she was out of the convent it would take more than Eleyne of Chester to imprison her again.

III

The children; she had to get to the children.

The thought pounded in her head, round and round, in time to the beating hooves of the horse.

The children; Sweet Virgin, the children.

She tried to move, but her limbs were like lead and her head swam sickeningly when she tried to open her eyes. She realised it was now bright day: was it two days they had been on the road, or three? She had lost all track of time. She could feel the sun beating down on the hood of her cloak; she was so hot she could hardly breathe and the iron band around her ribs grew tighter every minute.

'Joanna, Hawisa –' Their names came out as a whisper, but someone heard. Abruptly the horse's pace slackened and the band around her waist loosened. It was a man's arm.

'Are you awake?' Malcolm peered at her, pulling the heavy cloak away from her face. 'We'll stop and rest as soon as we're across the border.'

'The border?' Her lips were so dry she could hardly speak.

He grinned. 'Aye, it'll not be long now.'

'Joanna, Hawisa.' She tried to push his arm away, but he didn't seem to notice. Kicking the horse back into a slow canter, he turned and shouted to his men to follow. Her mind was blank; she remembered nothing of the killing; only the terrible overwhelming fear for her two little girls. 'Joanna, Hawisa.' Her lips framed the words again, but no sound came.

They stopped in the wild empty hills as the sun was setting and bivouacked in the heather. Eleyne staggered away from the men and sinking down beside a peaty pool of brown water bathed her face, trying to clear her head. She was dizzy and her temples throbbed sickeningly. Malcolm followed her and stood, hands on hips, watching her. Her hands and face were dripping as she knelt on the coarse heather stems. 'What happened?' she asked. The past days were a blur of terror and confusion. She could remember nothing but shouting and fire. Her mind refused to work properly. 'Joanna, Hawisa!'

'Don't you bother about them.' His face was hard. 'Forget them.'

'How can you say that?' Her eyes blazed at him. 'There was a fire! My children! My two little girls! What have you done to them? Where are they? What's happened to them?'

'Nothing happened to them.' For a moment he dropped his gaze. 'I saw no children. The people scattered when we burned the place. No one was hurt.'

'You burned it?' For a moment she was too shocked to speak. Suckley, her beautiful, peaceful home. 'And the horses? You burned the stables too?'

He shook his head emphatically. 'You know me better than that. The stables were untouched.'

'You spared the horses.' She seemed able only to repeat everything he said. Her mind had blotted out most of what had happened.

Malcolm nodded. 'Those which can travel are being brought north. I know how much you cared for them.'

'So, you act like a reiver. You steal my horses and you burn my house.'

'I'm no horsethief, Eleyne.' He looked very grave. 'The horses are yours.'

'And I am yours?' It was barely a question.

'You are mine.'

'And if I choose not to be yours?'

'You will, given time.' He folded his arms. 'If you want food, you must come to the fire.'

'I'll not eat with you.' She rose unsteadily to her feet and faced him. 'I'll not eat with you and I'll not sleep with you, if that's what you're hoping.'

She moved a few paces away. All around them the heather bent stretched empty beneath the crimson sky. In the silence a curlew called.

'Eat or not as you choose, my lady,' he called after her. 'But sleep with me you will. Tonight and every night, for the rest of your life.'

'No!' She flung herself round. 'Never!'

He smiled 'If it's your good name you're worried about, we shall be wed as soon as we reach Falkland. Though I always got the impression that your reputation didn't worry you much.' He put his head on one side. 'I've waited a long time for you, Eleyne – an unconscionable long time. I don't intend to wait any longer. But for now, I can see you won't be satisfied until you've tried to run. Go on then, see how far you get. I'll come for you when I'm ready.'

She watched as he strode towards the fire where already venison was roasting on the makeshift spit. She could smell the cooking flesh and her stomach turned with revulsion even as it growled with hunger. She knew it was no use. There was nowhere to hide. The folded ground was a wilderness of heather and grass, dotted with stunted thorn and pine. All round her the wild Cheviot Hills formed a barrier of loneliness and desolation. She walked for several minutes, stumbling on the tussocky ground, watching the bog cotton as it bobbed in the falling dusk. Curlew called in the distance, their liquid trills emphasising the emptiness of the hills.

The men settled around their fire. She could hear their laughter and their shouts as they lounged on the soft ground. She stopped at last by an old pine tree and leaned against it, closing her eyes. She could not escape: wherever she went, whatever she did, Malcolm would find her; she suspected he would follow her now to the ends of the earth. It was as if he had been her destiny all along. She smiled grimly to herself. Was this what Einion had predicted? A life and a death, in Scotland.

It was a long time before Malcolm came for her. 'Are you ready for some food now?' he asked softly. 'It'll do no good to starve yourself.'

She pushed herself away from the tree. 'I won't marry you,' she said.

'We'll talk about that tomorrow.' He took her arm.

His men moved aside for her and she sat down on his folded cloak while they brought her a portion of roast hart from one of the animals Malcolm's men had hunted down on their ride that morning, laughing that though they stole the king's stag it was at least in season, and they gave her wine from a leather bottle. While she ate, one of the young men produced a bird-bone pipe and began to play a slow, wistful tune which echoed in the swiftly falling night. It was midsummer – there would be no darkness.

483

She made no attempt to struggle when at last Malcolm folded her into his cloak a little apart from his men, near the dying embers of the fire. As he pulled up her gown and entered her with almost gentle eagerness, it was another man's face she saw in the glowing peat over his shoulder — the face of the man who had been his king.

IV
WESTMINSTER ❖ 28 June 1253

King Henry looked at the letter for a long time before he looked up at Roger de Quincy. 'When did this happen?'

'St John's Eve. The place was completely destroyed, no one was left, no one. They seem to have been after the horses. The animals in that stud were worth a fortune.' Roger took a deep breath. He had seen it. He had ridden west at once when he received the report and arrived within a few hours. The burned house was still smouldering, the butchered men and women, even children, still unburied, as were the few horses they had left — killed in the stable yard.

'And my niece?' Henry's voice was muffled.

'She must have died too, sire. And her children with her. There was no sign of them. And many –' Roger paused and cleared his throat – 'many of the bodies were unrecognisable.'

'Sweet Christ's bones! Has any attempt been made to catch the murdering thieves?'

'Everything possible is being done, sire. There are so many outlaws in the forests up there. Who knows, maybe it was that rascal Robin Fitzooth, Robin Hood, some are calling him now, who – outlaw though he's become for this thieving ways – claims to be the Earl of Huntingdon. He rides somewhere in that area, I've heard, and he'd have reason to know of her wealth and be jealous of it.'

Henry picked up the parchment again. 'You will have to write to your brother and tell him of his wife's death, and his children.' He shook his head. 'It's time he came home.'

'Indeed, sire, I shall send for him at once. There was a report that he'd been killed, but I'm glad to say it proved unfounded. He has been at Acre for the last few months, and I'm sure he will be pleased to be allowed back.' Roger tightened his lips. 'Poor Eleyne, she didn't have a happy life.'

'Indeed not, with your brother.' Henry threw down the parchment and reached for the book of hours which lay as usual on his desk. 'I shall order masses to be said for her soul.' He sighed. 'And I shall begin to settle her affairs. Her dower lands are rich. They are very valuable.'

The priest was very drunk. He gabbled the words over them, blessed them perfunctorily and passed out on the floor. Malcolm laughed. 'So, my lady, how does it feel to be wife of the Earl of Fife and Thane of Falkland? Is it not good to be back in Scotland?' The ring he had put on her finger was a heavy cabochon ruby. It clung tightly, like a manacle, above her knuckle.

'This marriage is not valid,' she flashed at him. 'No one will ever recognise it.'

'Indeed they will.' He took her hand and threaded it through his arm. 'And I shall have the king's blessing on our union before the week is out.'

The castle had been prepared for her. The great hall and their bedchamber were decorated with garlands of flowers. He had ordered servants, and bales of fabric were waiting to make her gowns and mantles and cloaks. An ivory comb and mirror and three brooches of chased gold and enamel waited in a cedarwood coffer by her bed. Malcolm, his ambition fulfilled at last, was as pleased as a dog with two tails.

'I'll not stay with you.' Now that her exhaustion was easing and the first dull shock of what had happened had passed, her anger was growing. Though she still had no memory of what had happened that night; however hard she tried, she could fill in no details in her own mind amidst the fear and confusion and smoke. But how dare this man come and pluck her like a fruit from the bough just because he wanted her? This marriage was not even a political decision by a king; this was one man's greed and lust. 'I swear before God, I will not stay here with you.'

Behind them the chapel of Falkland Castle was ablaze with candles. The priest lay snoring in stentorian tones across his own threshold, his feet stuck out on the cobbles of the yard, his head within the sanctuary of his church.

Malcolm laughed. 'Don't make me lock you up, sweetheart. You would hate it, and so would I.' He squeezed her arm. 'Here you shall have horses, your own and more – as many as you want,' he promised recklessly, 'and freedom, anything your heart desires, and a man to satisfy you. Fight me and I shall have to make you my prisoner. You would have no horses, sweetheart, and only bread and water until you learned obedience.' He looked at her soberly. 'Henry would have married you to someone else in the end, you know that as well as I. Come on, admit it. I can make you happy. You'll soon forget your bairns. They'll be safe in England. We'll have more children. Sons, plenty of sons.' His arm encircled her waist. 'I *will* make you happy, sweetheart.'

She bit back a retort. Arguing with him was not going to get her anywhere. To escape, she would have to be subtle; subtle and very careful.

He slept with his arm across her breasts, the weight of his thigh across her legs, the heat of his body intolerable against her skin, but at least his lovemaking was straightforward, gentle in comparison to Robert. In a strange, half-shy way he wanted to give her pleasure, and his anxiety to please her warred strangely with his exultant triumph of ownership. She lay awake for a long time looking up into the shadows of the bedchamber after he had fallen asleep at last, her hair entwined in his fists, his prisoner as absolutely as if he had tied her, as Robert had so often done, to the bed.

Alexander!

In the silence she thought she had cried the name out loud. But no one came. The only sound was from the wind in the chimney of the room.

They had a visitor the following day. Marie de Couci was radiant in silks sewn with pearls as she was shown into the great hall, followed by a train of attendants.

'So, I was right, the beautiful Lady Chester is here. Is it true? Have you made her your wife?'

'Indeed I have. News travels fast, madam.'

The queen's smile broadened. Walking past Malcolm she sat down on the best chair in the hall and arranged her skirts carefully around her. 'Your wooing was a little rough, I hear,' she said lightly. She had addressed no word directly to Eleyne.

Malcolm moved towards her uneasily. 'Madam, I –'

'And did you really kill everyone in the house?' she went on relentlessly. 'Every single person? How you must have lusted after her, Malcolm, my friend!' She eyed Eleyne with cold appraisal. 'She obviously knows how to attract men.' She stretched out a foot and eyed the toe of her shoe. It was stitched with silver thread. 'They think she's dead, you know. Or did you plan that too?'

Malcolm said nothing, but Eleyne moved forward. At the queen's words, her heart had stopped beating. 'What do you mean, he killed everyone in the house?' Her voice was icy as she stepped on to the dais. Her eyes were so large they seemed like great hollow shadows in her skull. 'What do you mean?'

The queen shrank back in her chair. 'My dear, I am only repeating what I heard. You were there. You must know what happened.'

The two women looked at each other, then Eleyne turned to Malcolm. 'How many people did you kill?' she asked. Her voice sounded thin and high in her ears.

'I killed no one.'

'But your men did. My children. They killed my children –' Her voice rose sharply, the fear which had been lurking at the back of her mind suddenly unspeakably close and real.

'No.' He cut in sharply. 'I never saw your children.'

'Do you think I believe that?' Her voice was shaking now. 'Joanna, Hawisa. Rhonwen. What did you do to them?'

'I told you, I saw none of them.' He was growing irritated. 'I have no idea what happened to them and I couldn't care less. They belong to the past. Forget them. You are here now. With me.'

'You think I could stay with the man who murdered my babies?' The pictures were returning. Flashes of violent, blood-soaked terror. Nesta, gentle, faithful Nesta, a sword through her belly, her eyes huge with agonised pleading. Michael, his dark blue gown scarlet from the gaping hole in his chest as he collapsed at her feet.

'You will do as you are told!' Malcolm's patience snapped. 'And you will remember that her grace is our guest at Falkland.' He moved towards Eleyne threateningly.

'Murderer!' Eleyne screamed. 'Her grace's son will release me from this pretence of a marriage!' She had begun to tremble violently as she backed away from him, her memories spinning in her mind, a blackened, bloody nightmare.

The queen settled back to enjoy herself. 'I don't think so, my dear. Alexander was very pleased to hear of Malcolm's marriage, very pleased. He has already given it his blessing.'

Eleyne shook her head. 'He would never do that. And nor will the King of England, my uncle, when he hears what has happened.'

She was wrong.

VI

WESTMINSTER ❖ July

'What do you mean, she's alive?' Henry thundered at the Earl of Winchester. 'How can she still be alive?'

Roger de Quincy took another few paces around the table. 'She is alive and well. My steward has seen her with his own eyes. Word is in Scotland that she has run off with her lover! The whole thing was arranged. He came and burned the place to make it look as though she were dead and carried her off.' He struck his fists together in fury. 'She fooled me, the scheming Jezebel! She fooled us all. I believed her when she told us Robert mistreated her. We all believed her.' The expansive sweep of his hand included the king, who flinched slightly. 'She was just making sure that we got rid of Robert for her; God's bones, but I was an idiot!'

'And who is her latest lover, pray?' After an initial moment of disbelief, Henry was recovering from the shock of Lord Winchester's statement.

'Lord Fife. He has taken her back to Scotland. He is even pretending she is his wife.'

Henry raised an eyebrow. 'So, she still sees herself as a Scots whore, no matter who the man.' His anger had been slow in surfacing. 'So be it, I'll not raise another finger to help that woman, or save her reputation. I did enough when I sent Sir Robert to the Holy Land and played right into her hands. All right. She wants to be dead to her English friends and family, let her stay that way. As far as England is concerned, my niece died in that fire. Her lands and property are confiscated. They will be redistributed amongst the Chester heirs. See that the enquiries post mortem are set in train. Are her children alive then? For that at least we might be grateful.'

Roger shook his head grimly. 'My informers say they are not in Scotland. It looks as though they died. I cannot believe she meant that to happen, that she could be such an unnatural mother, but they were Robert's children . . .' His voice trailed away and he sighed. 'And Robert?' Roger asked at last. 'What do I tell my brother?'

The king sat down and beckoned his clerks. On the desk was Eleyne's letter about Isabella. In his sorrow over Eleyne's death he had been about to carry out her last wish and order that Isabella be released from her captivity at Godstow. He stared at the letter as if he had never seen it before, then tossed it to the nearest secretary. 'Destroy this,' he said curtly. 'I never wish to hear Isabella de Braose's name again.' He turned back to Roger. 'Tell your brother that his wife is dead,' he said succinctly. 'Otherwise he will probably kill her himself and imperil his immortal soul.'

VII

DUNFERMLINE CASTLE

Eleyne looked at the twelve-year-old king, so agonisingly like his father, and her throat tightened. 'You have to help me. You have to tell Lord Fife to let me go home.' Her voice was shaking and she was painfully aware of the queen and Lord Fife standing immediately behind her. They had all ridden to Dunfermline that same afternoon.

Alexander glanced at his mother and then at Alan Durward, who was at his side. 'Lord Fife is our trusted friend,' he said solemnly, his high voice clear against the murmur of voices in the vaulted audience chamber. 'Mama says I must not offend him.'

'And me? Am I not your friend?' She held out her hands to him and, startled, the boy stepped towards her and took them in his own.

'Yes, of course you are.'

'Then, please.' Clutching his hot fingers, she sank to her knees. 'Please help me.'

He was distressed. 'I don't want you to be unhappy –'

'Then don't interfere. Sir.' Malcolm added the last word as an after-thought. 'Leave my wife to me.'

Marie de Couci smiled reassuringly at her son. 'Lady Fife is still feeling strange in our country, but I am sure she will settle soon. And until she does, Malcolm must keep her at Falkland. We do not want her upsetting the king.'

On the ride back to Falkland Castle Eleyne was silent. Malcolm's men surrounded her and he rode close at her side, looking from time to time at her closed face.

'Do you like the horse you are riding?' he asked at last as they splashed through the shallow water of the River Leven. They had left the misty waters of the loch to their left, the castle barely visible on its island. Eleyne had not even glanced at it. Now before them the Lomond Hills rose, folded and dark against the sky. Eleyne nodded mutely. Even through her anger and misery she had taken unconscious note of the delicate white palfrey she rode. 'He is half-brother to your Tam Lin,' Malcolm went on, 'and he's yours.'

She stared down at the horse's neck. Her slim brown hands were steady on the soft leather reins; on her hand Malcolm's ring still clung to her finger. Why had she not thrown it away as she had thrown away Robert's ring sixteen years before?

'You cannot buy me, Malcolm,' she said quietly. 'No amount of horses will make me want to stay with you.'

He grinned at her amicably. 'Just so long as you do stay.'

That night she slipped from his bed as he lay flat on his back, snoring, exhausted by his passionate lovemaking. Gritting her teeth in impatience, she dressed in the darkness of the bedchamber and crept towards the door. The latch creaked as she opened it, but he did not stir. Outside the passage was empty and the narrow newel stair in darkness. Her shoes in her hand, she groped her way to the stair and crept down it, the only sound the slight rustle of her skirts on the stone steps. A smell of old woodsmoke drifted up, and the air grew cold as she crept down towards the lower chamber.

Half a dozen men were asleep there, wrapped in their cloaks in the dim light of a guttering tallow candle. She surveyed the round room.

The door on the far side was closed and a guard dozed beside it, slumped on his heels, his chin on his chest, his hand fallen from the sword which lay at his side. The only way out of the tower was past him.

'Do you plan a midnight ride, perhaps?' Malcolm's voice was light and friendly as he stood in the doorway behind her. There was a candle in his hand. Her eyes went to it automatically and she felt her throat tighten.

'I felt restless, I thought I would walk in the courtyard.' She held his eye in the dim, flickering light.

'Good, then we'll walk together.' He sighed. 'You shan't escape me, Eleyne. No one can leave the castle without my knowledge, and this tower is guarded at all times.' Beside the door on the far side of the chamber the guard was now standing to attention, the sword held menacingly across his chest. 'Don't make me lock you up, lass.'

The sleepers on the floor had stirred at the sound of his voice. One sat up, hugging his knees, and viewed with every sign of enjoyment his lord and his new lady engaged in combat.

The castle had seethed with gossip since Malcolm had brought Eleyne home, and now the answer to the question so many had asked for so long – why had the Earl of Fife remained so long unmarried – was answered at last. He had loved Eleyne, daughter of Llywelyn of Wales, since the day he had first set eyes on her eighteen years before and from that day he had meant to have her for his own. There wasn't a man, woman or child in Falkland Castle, if not the whole of Fife, who did not wish their earl well of her.

The onlookers waited to see what would happen. She hesitated as though wondering whether to go on and walk in the dark of the court-yard with her husband, but she moved past him, back to the stairs.

VIII

Four days later she escaped. She slipped past the guards at dawn, swathed in the dark cloak of one of her maids. The man on duty at the gate, which was open for the first wagons of flour being brought in from the mill, did not look at her face or question her. Two hours later he paid for his carelessness with his life.

She did not get far: Malcolm's dogs tracked her down when she was only two miles from the castle. Instinctively she had turned towards the dark shoulder of the Lomond, seeking safety in the mountain, but it was no use. She turned at bay, like a trapped animal, mad with grief and anger.

'I will not come back with you. You have to let me go! How can I live with the man who killed my children, who killed my friends!' It haunted her every moment, waking and sleeping, the picture of the

490

two little girls – so happy on St John's Eve, longing to wear their new gowns, plaiting ribbon collars for the two dogs – and superimposed was the memory of Nesta and of Michael, dear gentle Michael who had never hurt anyone in his life, spitted on a sword like an animal as he tried to come to her aid. She could feel the cold agony of the sword in her children's flesh, hear their screams echoing in her ears, see their little hands outstretched towards her, begging her to save them.

'I did not kill your children.' He faced her, leaning on his sword. She had lost her veil and her hair was down; her gown was grass-stained and torn and her face and hands were burned by the sun as she faced him, proud and furious as a wild cat. His facc softened. He could not restrain a smile. She was all he had dreamed of, this beautiful Welsh princess. And at last she was his.

She did not see his smile. 'Someone killed them! The queen said so –'

'The queen wanted to hurt you, Eleyne. She has never forgiven you for stealing her husband. My men did not kill your children. I gave specific orders to that effect. Little girls are no danger to me. Sons might have been different, but you had no sons. I left them to the de Quincys, where they belong. And you must forget them. Think instead of the sons you will bear me.

'No, never.'

He smiled tolerantly. 'You will. You will do exactly as I wish, my dear.'

IX

FOTHERINGHAY CASTLE ❖ July 1253

The castle slept in the early sunshine. The gates were still closed, but smoke rose from the bakehouse chimneys. Rhonwen stood at the bend in the track and peered at the walls. She was exhausted, but her anger and despair drove her on. Beside her Annie stood in the middle of the road with the two small children, all three bemused with sleep, their bare feet dusty, their clothes in rags. Beside them sat the two great dogs.

'Will mama be here?' Joanna's small hand slid into Rhonwen's.

Rhonwen tried to hide her grief. 'No, *cariad*, she won't be here.'

She had crept back and seen the smoking ruins, the butchered servants, the corpses burned beyond recognition. Clinging to the remnants of her sanity, she had searched for Eleyne's body. She had not found her, but she knew in her heart that her beloved child was dead. Their attackers, whoever they had been, had been too thorough, too sudden. No one could have escaped that conflagration. Heartbroken, she clawed through the still-hot ashes and in the burned-out ruins of the solar she had found the phoenix pendant on the charred table where Eleyne had dropped it on Midsummer's Eve. Somehow it had escaped the looters who had followed the fire. Rhonwen had rubbed it clean of the cloying soot and, tears pouring down her cheeks, she kissed it and tucked it into her purse. Then she had clambered out of the building, gone to the courtyard and picked her way amongst slaughtered horses. Some had gone, but Tam Lin was there, his leg broken, his head smashed in with a spike. Rhonwen stared at the flyblown remains of the beautiful horse, her stomach heaving with disgust. At last she had turned away.

X

Dervorguilla Balliol had arrived at Fotheringhay the day before, unaware that since it was no longer part of Eleyne's dower lands, the great castle and its property would soon revert to her as part of her inheritance from her uncle, John the Scot.

On her way from London to Scotland, this daughter of John's sister Margaret and the Lord of Galloway was taking the news of Eleyne's death to her husband, John Balliol. It had seemed fitting to stop overnight at Fotheringhay, where Eleyne had spent so much of her life.

When the arrivals were announced, she looked up in disbelief. 'Lady Rhonwen? And the children?' She almost ran down the hall. 'Eleyne? Where is Aunt Eleyne? Oh thank Sweet Blessed Christ you are all all right.' On her knees she hugged the two little girls to her.

Rhonwen's silence made her look up at last. 'Aunt Eleyne?' she repeated in a whisper.

Wordlessly, Rhonwen shook her head.

Dervorguilla crossed herself. She stood up slowly and sighed. 'Will you take them to London?'

'No, I'll leave them with you. Annie can look after them. I mean to find out who did it.' Rhonwen's face was bleak, her eyes devoid of expression. She put her hand on Lyulf's head. 'I'll find out his name and then I shall kill him.'

XI

LOCH LEVEN CASTLE ❖ August 1253

She found them all on the island – mugwort, ash, apple, wormwood and skullcap. They burned slowly at first, smoky, acrid, the flames dull and sluggish. But they would clear.

She looked across the narrow strip of dry white sand where she had built her little fire, towards the grey walls of the castle. They couldn't see her here and they wouldn't come looking for her, not until dusk. Behind her the waters of the loch were a clear, bright blue. Small ripples played on the sand and sparkling lights danced around the island, teasing her eyes.

She had tried to escape from him so often that at last Malcolm, with a sigh, had brought her to Loch Leven Castle. 'It's only for a short time while I'm with the king,' he said. 'I have to go to Stirling, but when I return I shall bring you back to Falkland. By then, perhaps you will have learned to appreciate me more.'

At first she was pleased; it was a relief to be free of him, to call her body her own again, to have time to think; to watch the moon rise above the Bishop's Hill and be able to plan her escape. She was allowed the run of the island and served with some state, but the men and women with her were all Malcolm's trusted servants. Andrew and Janet, she discovered, had long ago gone to live with their son in Cupar. There was no way to reach the mainland. Bribery, cajolery, pleading and fury all failed. Her jailers were polite, even obsequious to Lady Fife, but all were adamant.

As time passed she thought she would go mad with frustration. There were no horses, no dogs, no entertainers, no gossips, no music. There were no books and no writing materials; nothing to do but eat and sleep and sit with her embroidery and mourn her children. It had been a moment of inspiration to look again into the fire and summon the visions.

She leaned closer to the flames, piling on another handful of herbs. They were too green. She should have dried them, but that would have taken days or weeks and there wasn't time. She needed to see now. She needed to see why Alexander no longer came to her.

Her head began to spin, but it was not an unpleasant sensation. She sat back and arranged her skirts. As soon as the flames burned more brightly, the pictures would come.

She saw the horseman first. He reined in slightly, his animal prancing, its flanks steaming in the rain. She could see the wind, the thrashing banner, his hands wet on the reins.

Show me your face, please show me your face.

She bent yet closer. Who was he, this broad-shouldered man, and what was he to her? Why did she keep seeing him? But he had turned away, urging his horse forward, and he was riding on, out of her sight into the mists conjured from the flames.

Eleyne cursed softly.

Show me more, show me my future, mine!

Her head was heavy now and she felt a little sick, but there were other pictures there, shifting, changing. A man – Alexander! Her Alexander. With a whimper she reached out and she saw him smile. He stretched out his hand to her and their fingers almost touched. Then he was gone.

Her eyes were full of tears. The knowledge had been there all the time, had she been able to face the truth. Without the pendant she could not reach him and the phoenix, the precious link which held him to her, had gone, lost in the fire at Suckley.

But there were other pictures now. Children. She could see children. Several of them, playing on the beach beyond the flames. She rubbed her eyes. There were two little girls, playing by the water, intent on gathering stones and tossing them into the ripples. Joanna? Hawisa?

She half rose, a huge lump in her throat, holding out her arms. But they had gone. There was no one there, nothing but the empty sand. Tears ran down her cheeks again and she turned to look for the others. They were running away: five boys and two other girls, running, skipping towards the trees.

Come back!

She tried once more to rise to her feet but her legs were cramped and she stumbled. She could hear them laughing, the sound echoing amongst the trees. In a moment they would be out of sight. She sank back on the ground before the fire and stared at it again. But the flames were empty and dying.

'Have you seen any children on the island?' she asked that night.

'Children, my lady?' Her maid, Emmot, looked puzzled.

'Did they come from the mainland?'

'No boats came today, my lady, none at all.'

Eleyne did not mention them again. She had not seen their faces; she had not really heard their voices. Only as shouts, mingled with the breeze, teasing the leaves on the trees.

Two weeks later she knew that she was pregnant with Malcolm's child.

CHAPTER TWENTY

I

LOCH LEVEN CASTLE ❖ 1253

It became easier each time. After a while she didn't need the fire. As the muggy August days gave way to clear warm September she found she could see pictures in the water too. She watched the children playing in the depths of her earthenware bowl; she saw Tam Lin lying slaughtered on the ground and, through her tears, knew he had been killed quickly and mercifully because his leg was broken when he panicked in the fire. She saw the dogs gambolling in the sun and knew as she whispered their names that somehow they heard her. Sometimes she saw Joanna and Hawisa playing with them, but she could never know, never be sure, that they were alive.

Then Malcolm came. He rode from Dunfermline with gifts and wine. That night as he entered her chamber and dismissed her ladies he was eager for her, unfastening the neck of her shift and pushing it back from her shoulders with shaking hands. He saw the fullness of her breasts; slowly he raised his hands to them, cupping their heaviness in his palms.

'You're even more beautiful than I remembered,' he breathed.

She woke to find him gazing at her naked body, his hand on the curve of her belly as he sat beside her on the bed. 'You're carrying my son.' He sounded awed. When she nodded, he bent and kissed her stomach. 'So soon! I shall take you back to Falkland. I want you at my side.'

He treated her as though she were made of precious glass. She wasn't to lift a finger. He surrounded her with servants, plied her with new gowns and stayed with her every second that he could. When she asked for a Welsh harper he sent for one; when she asked for a garden to the south of the castle wall he had one dug and planted. When she asked him not to touch her any more, he backed off sheepishly and left her alone to her dreams.

II
September

Rhonwen put her hand again to the dagger she carried hidden in her gown and gave a grim smile. Ancret and Lyulf had come with her and it was almost as if they understood. She put her hand on Lyulf's head as Eleyne used to do and the dog looked up and growled a little in his throat.

She was sorry it was the Earl of Fife who had murdered Eleyne. When she had first heard the rumour that he was behind the raid which had destroyed their lives, it had been with shocked disbelief. He was the kind of man she could almost admire. She had waited silently, listening to the gossip which flew through the halls of Lady Lincoln's castles, and at last she was convinced. Eleyne was dead. The king had ordered masses for her soul and begun to dismantle her estates, but no one was going to pursue Malcolm. No one was going to punish him. Rhonwen made her preparations.

The children were safe. With their mother dead and their father still in the Holy Land, they had been made the king's wards and were for the time being to be reared by their cousin, the gentle Countess of Lincoln, whom Rhonwen liked and trusted. Besides, they would be safe with Annie.

Unobtrusively one night she had slipped away and set off on her grim journey north.

Before her, Falkland Castle lay in the shadow of the Lomond, the earl's standard, depicting a mounted knight with a drawn sword, hanging limply from the Great Tower. The gates stood open. She watched a loaded wain creak slowly under the gatehouse, the shadows of the spikes of the raised portcullis falling obliquely across its load as it disappeared inside. It all looked so normal; so peaceful. Yet within the day the earl would be dead and so probably would she. Touching the dagger again, she smiled and walked forward, leading her horse.

The man-at-arms on the gate must have recognised her from her previous visits to Falkland for he did not question her. He merely smiled and waved her in. 'Where is the earl?' Her voice was husky with exhaustion.

'He's away, but the countess is here, my lady. You'll find her in her rooms in the Great Tower.'

Rhonwen wanted no truck with Lord Fife's countess, whoever she might be. She had nerved herself to kill – today.

The man was waving her on and another huge cart was looming in the gateway behind her and suddenly Lyulf was growling in his throat. As she stepped back out of the way of the heavy iron-bound wheels, the hound leaped away from her across the courtyard. Ancret too tore herself from Rhonwen's restraining hand and followed him.

Rhonwen ran after them, her anger and astonishment at the dogs' desertion mixed with a small incredulous flicker of hope. She had never seen them run like that before; not for a long time seen them look so eager or so excited.

No one challenged her as she ran up the stairs into the lower chamber of the tower. The dogs had vanished, but she ran on across the room to the stair up to the higher floors. At the doorway to the earl's chamber she stopped, gasping for breath.

Eleyne was there, her arms around Lyulf's great neck, kissing the dog's head whilst Ancret tried to push between them, licking her hands. It was a long time before she looked up, tears pouring down her face, and saw Rhonwen in the doorway. She straightened and held out her arms. 'Rhonwen! Joanna? Hawisa? Where are they?'

The shock was so great that Rhonwen could not move, but the terror in Eleyne's face as she misinterpreted Rhonwen's silence catapulted her back to reality. 'They're safe, *cariad*, and well.' For a long time the two women hugged each other in silence, with Eleyne's ladies looking on in astonishment, then Emmot stepped forward. 'I don't know that my lord would want you to have visitors without his knowledge, my lady,' she ventured timidly.

Eleyne smiled. 'He would not object to Rhonwen.' She turned to the eager dogs, kissing their heads in turn. 'Oh, Rhonwen. I can't believe you are here! I thought you were dead!' She was crying through her laughter.

'As I thought you.' Rhonwen's voice was strangely flat. 'What happened to you? The whole world thinks you are dead. King Henry has had masses said for your soul and your lands have been redistributed. The girls have become the king's wards.' Her practised eyes ran over Eleyne's figure. 'Had you forgotten us?'

Eleyne gave a sob. 'Forgotten! How can you say that? I was brought here against my will, forced into marriage. Guarded day and night!'

'You're married already. How can they force you to marry again?' Rhonwen asked.

'Robert is dead!' Flinging away Rhonwen's questioning hand Eleyne paced across the floor.

'Dead, is it?' Rhonwen's voice followed her. 'Then no one in England knows it. They say he is on his way back from Acre.'

There was a long pause.

'Are you sure?' Eleyne's voice was no more than a whisper. Unconsciously her hand had gone to her belly where Malcolm's child lay, not yet quickened, beneath her ribs.

'When I took the children from the Lady Dervorguilla at Fothering-hay to Lady Lincoln, who has been made their guardian, she said they had sent letters to him to come back as soon as he could.'

'Sweet Jesus!' Eleyne stared at her appalled.

'My lady.' Ann Douglas, one of her new companions, had been listening in increasing distress and now she was wringing her hands. 'It's not true. What this woman tells you is a lie. You are married before God and the law!'

'Am I?' Eleyne was numb. Her joy at realising the children were safe had drained away as the full horror of the truth began to dawn on her. Malcolm's plan had worked. The whole world thought her dead. Her children had been given to another woman and the king had reclaimed her lands. A wave of fury hit her. She shook off Ann Douglas's restraining hand.

'At least now I know the truth! That's why no one looked for me; no one came to help me. I didn't believe him! I didn't believe people would think I was dead.' She paused. 'But you must be wrong about Robert. Malcolm would not have married me if he were still alive. He couldn't have. That would be the most terrible sin.'

He had told her the truth when he said the children were alive; he had told her the truth when he had said that Henry thought her dead. This too must be the truth; it had to be. If it wasn't, what did it make her and the child she carried?

'You find that you like Lord Fife after all, do you, *cariad*?' Rhonwen asked at last. She was staring into Eleyne's eyes. Did her ghostly lover still visit her, or was he too forgotten? She reached surreptitiously into her bundle and touched the phoenix which lay there. But she did not give it to Eleyne.

'Like him!' Eleyne turned on her furiously. 'He brought me here as a captive.'

'You don't look like a captive now though.' There had been no guards save at the castle gatehouse.

'No, because every person in this castle is my guard! She is my guard!' She flung her arm in Ann's direction. 'And she.' This time it was Emmot. 'Every time I escaped – and I did – I was brought back. All my letters were intercepted!' She paced the floor, solemnly followed by the two dogs who pressed close on either side of her. 'And now I carry his child! What am I to do? Where am I to go?' The words were a ringing challenge.

Rhonwen walked stiffly to a chair and sat down with a sigh. Perhaps after all she would still need her dagger. But the tension was pouring out of her and she felt limp and exhausted. 'There is always Aber,' she said wearily. 'Young Llywelyn loves you. He would welcome you, you know that.'

Eleyne paused in her pacing. 'Must I always run back to Aber?'

'No, my lady!' Ann caught her wrist. 'Please, we love you. Your home is here at Falkland now.'

Eleyne shrugged. Only one thing mattered now. 'Would Malcolm send for my daughters?'

Ann smiled. 'I think he would do anything if it would make you happy, my lady.'

III

November

Her letters to Margaret of Lincoln went unanswered; Malcolm's more circumspect requests to King Henry received the curt reply that, now that their mother was dead, the children had been given to their cousin's charge and were safe and well in her care. There was no acknowledgement of Malcolm's interest and no hint that Henry knew the identity of his new countess. There was no mention of the children's father.

'Be patient!' Malcolm was bored by the whole business. 'You'll have another bairn soon to occupy you.'

The phrase was repeated often before he left once more for Stirling.

'You have to go and fetch them.' Eleyne's patience, at best frail, had snapped. She caught Rhonwen's hand. 'You must go and bring them to Falkland. Malcolm will give you an escort. Steal them, kidnap them, anything. But please, please bring them. Go now, before winter sets in.'

The night before she left, Rhonwen put a small packet into Eleyne's hands. Eleyne looked down at it. For a long time she did not move. She could feel him: Alexander. He was there beside her in the room; there between her hands; in the shadows. She closed her eyes and brought the package to her lips. 'The phoenix?' she said wonderingly.

Rhonwen nodded grimly. 'I found it in the ruins of the fire.'

Eleyne unfolded the piece of soft leather and held the pendant in her palm. 'He always said I had nothing to fear from Malcolm,' she whispered. Her hand went to her shoulder almost as though another hand rested there – a strange, intimate gesture and Rhonwen, seeing it, suddenly smiled.

IV

Snow came at the beginning of January: drifts which blocked the roads and made riding impossible. The great fires were banked high and minstrels and harpists kept the household amused.

Eleyne slept late each morning, her body heavy and uncomfortable and constantly tired. The salt-meat diet of winter did not suit her, nor did the narrow indoor life. She wanted to ride; she wanted her children and, strangest of all in that crowded environment, with her husband beside her every night, his hand resting proprietorially on her belly, she was lonely; desperately and deeply lonely, for her lover had not returned. She had not dared to put the phoenix around her neck for fear that Malcolm would see it and recognise it. Instead she kept it hidden. But she kept it close – yet still he did not come.

One visitor came however, in the shadows and in the cold winter sunlight, a visitor who was never seen by others. The lady in black velvet was here too, only now her clothes were white and silver and she smiled, and Eleyne knew that at Falkland she was happy. 'Who are you?' She spoke the words out loud as the lady drifted across the snow-covered gardens, a wraith scarcely more visible than the snow itself.

Marie . . .

Perhaps she had imagined the name of the woman who shared her blood and whose destiny was bound with hers at Fotheringhay, at Falkland and in the bitter loneliness of Loch Leven, but her presence comforted Eleyne in the long desolate days.

Weeks passed and there was still no word from Rhonwen. At first Eleyne waited calmly, filling her days with her horses, cooped up in their stables, and organising the castle, for the first time assuming her full role as Malcolm's wife. He responded by turning over to her the financial running of his estates. Fife was not a rich earldom, or a large one. One of the seven ancient earldoms of Scotland, it was tiny compared with the lands she had overseen as Countess of Chester, but it had power and influence in Scotland and some pretensions to be pre-eminent because of the tradition which gave the Earls of Fife the ancient right of sanctuary beneath the sacred cross of the Clan Macduff and the right to place the crown on the king's head at his coronation.

She kept herself busy, but there was no privacy; nowhere she could go to stare into fire or water to see how Rhonwen fared; nowhere she could go to try to summon Alexander. Night after night she lay awake listening to Malcolm's quiet, regular snores, trying to ease her body on the deep mattress as the wind howled across the central flat lands of Fife and beat against the ice-coated walls of the castle. This night in particular was colder than any before. Her back ached; her legs ached. Her heart ached. She pulled herself up on the pillows wondering if she should get up yet again to visit the garderobe. But the room was bitter. The fire, banked for the night, gave off little heat and she was reluctant to crawl from beneath the warm bedcovers. She slipped her hand beneath the pillow where she had tucked the phoenix, wrapped in a

500

blue silk handkerchief. Easing herself once more on to her side, she closed her eyes, pressing the cold jewel against her lips.

The hand on her breast wakened her. The sheets were thrown back as though she had been dreaming, her breasts aroused. She frowned: Malcolm had up to now respected her wish not to be touched. Then she heard his snore from beside her. He was fast asleep. She lay still, confused, then she felt the touch on her breast again, as though lips caressed her in the velvety darkness. Were her eyes open or closed? She wasn't sure. Was she awake or asleep? Again the light touch, the whisper of fingers over her breasts and down her belly, the warmth of a mouth on hers. With a secret shiver of recognition, she eased herself down on the pillows and opened her arms. She could feel his warmth, his strength, his longing and at last she felt the brush of his lips on hers as her thighs parted to receive him. Malcolm was still asleep when some time later Eleyne gave a gasp of pleasure in fulfilment of her waking dream.

He came every night after that; she never saw him and she never tried to speak, but he brought her reassurance and pleasure in her lonely bed. Then one night Malcolm awoke. For a while he lay still, aware of his wife awake in the darkness beside him. He could feel her tenseness; feel her excitement. He frowned. She had made it clear that she didn't want him while her belly was so huge and uncomfortable, and yet he knew she was aroused. Cautiously he put out his hand and cupped it around a heavy breast.

Half-asleep, not knowing if it was a dream or reality, Eleyne turned to him. She wanted the hardness of a man inside her, his lips on her breasts, his skin on hers. Glancing at her face in the shadowy firelight he saw the hunger there and he smiled. She closed her eyes. It wasn't Alexander. She had realised it too late. It was her husband and yet at that moment she wanted him.

He was less gentle that night than he had ever been and she responded in kind, tearing at his shoulders with her nails, sinking her teeth into the sinews of his neck, gripping his hips with her thighs as though she would suck him dry of his seed. She took no pleasure from him though and somewhere in the darkness of the room she could feel Alexander's anger and despair. When at last he fell away from her, spent, she turned towards the wall and wrapping her arms around herself she felt the tears pouring down her face.

501

V

March 1254

When Rhonwen arrived back the children were not with her.

'They didn't want to come, *cariad*. They love their Cousin Margaret, and they thought you were dead. Yes, yes, I told them you weren't.' She raised her hand as Eleyne tried to interrupt. 'But that made it worse. Joanna got very angry; angry that you had left them. I tried to explain, again and again, but they are only little, and it has been a long time since they saw you. I know it's unfair, but Joanna blames you. She has been hurt too much. Hawisa is too little to know anything but that she loves her sister and she loves Margaret Lincoln and they both adore Annie, who looks after them and runs a nursery of ten children!' She smiled. 'They are happy and secure and well looked after there –'

'You are telling me to leave them there –'

'*Cariad* –'

'You are! You are telling me to leave them. To abandon them! You never cared for them because they were Robert's children.'

'That's not true, and you know it.' Rhonwen's temper flared. 'I love them and I love you. If you loved the devil himself, I would find him for you! But in this you have no choice.' Rhonwen took her hands. 'Listen to me. It's their father's wish that they stay.'

'What?' Eleyne stared at her, white-faced.

'He has written to them. I saw the letter. He is in the service of King Louis in Acre. He told the girls that you were dead, and that their Cousin Margaret would take care of them.'

'So. He *is* alive!' Eleyne sat down heavily; she put her hand to her side.

'He was three months ago.'

'Then my child will be born a bastard!' She stood up again. 'Three months, you said? Anything could happen in three months. The war in the Holy Land is cruel, they say.'

Rhonwen watched her closely. 'You are happy then with Lord Fife?'

'No.' Her reply was swift and unequivocal. 'Resigned, perhaps. It might have been different when Hawisa and Joanna came. He's good to me and he loves me. But I can never forgive what he did at Suckley. And he lied.' She shook her head, her voice heavy with despair. 'He lied about Robert's death.'

'No, he wouldn't have lied about that, not when he had to make vows before the priest.' If Alexander tolerated Malcolm, so would Rhonwen – for now. 'He must have believed that Robert was dead. He had been away three years without a word, after all.' Rhonwen smiled coaxingly. '*Cariad*, surely Malcolm of Fife is a thousand times a better man than Robert de Quincy. If Henry can declare you officially dead, then surely you can do the same for Sir Robert. He is dead for you. And Malcolm of Fife is now your chosen man.'

Eleyne did not deny it.

VI

As if to console her for the loss of the girls, the birth was an easy one and the baby, a boy, was a healthy, happy child. Malcolm was speechless with delight, embarrassed and astonished by the perfection of his son, touching the child's hands with one cautious finger as if to test if he were real. Eleyne saw the wonder on his face and found herself almost liking him.

'He's beautiful,' he said at last.

She smiled, exhausted but content. He was christened Colban. She had been terrified that he would want to call the baby after the king, but perhaps after all he had more tact.

As before, she recovered quickly from the birth, her muscles snapping back into place swiftly and firmly as she took once more to the saddle and the energetic life which Malcolm allowed her freely now he was confident that she no longer wanted to flee. And once more she wrote to Margaret of Lincoln.

VII

GODSTOW ❖ April 1254

Isabella stared at the abbess. 'I don't believe you. I had a letter from Lady Chester less than a year ago. She said I could go to her. She promised. She said she would speak to the king . . .'

'I'm sorry.' Emma Bloet had so hoped that Isabella would settle to her retirement with the grace and dignity which her rank and position demanded. This endless struggle was wearing for them both.

'Eleyne of Chester is dead, my dear. Nothing can change that.'

'No, she's my friend. She's my sister –'

The abbess sighed. 'We must pray for her soul.'

'And me? What will happen to me now?' Isabella clasped her hands together to stop them shaking.

'You will stay here, my daughter.' The abbess suddenly ran out of patience. 'In God's house. Until you die.'

VIII
FALKLAND CASTLE ❖ Winter 1256

'You're not Michael.'

Eleyne regarded the tall, wild-haired man who stood before her, his gown still damp from the rain which beat down outside.

'Michael the Wizard is no longer with us, my lady.' The man bowed gravely. 'I served him while he was in Scotland and at the court of the emperor and I learned his art. He told me you would call on him one day and that when you did I should come.'

Eleyne frowned. 'He offered to teach me once.' Rhonwen sat near the fire, stitching in the light of a branch of candles; otherwise they were alone in the shadowy solar. A rumble of thunder rolled around the Lomond Hills. 'I want you to look into the future for me,' she said slowly.

It was two years now since Colban's birth. She had had no further word from Margaret of Lincoln, in spite of her stream of frantic letters, unaware that King Henry and John de Lacy had forbidden her to reply. Neither had she become pregnant again. Malcolm had hidden his disappointment well, but he came home to her more and more often, sometimes riding from Dunfermline only to dine and to take her to bed before setting off to the court again at dawn. She lay beneath him submissively, wanting a child as much as he did, aware that her lack of passion disappointed him and cooled his ardour, but unable to respond. Never again did she react to him as she had that night when she was pregnant with Colban, when she had released all the passion and frustration her phantom lover had aroused. She was, she supposed, content with him. She would not fight him, but that was all. For passion she looked only into the shadows.

The dark eyes scrutinised her face carefully. Adam Scot had learned well from his master: he could read her soul. 'You have the power to see, Lady Fife, why do you not use it? Why do you resort to herbs and stars and water when you were born with the power of vision; when you were born with the ability to walk between the worlds?'

Her skin crawled with revulsion. The man's power was tangible, reaching out to her, probing her mind. She resisted the urge to fend him off. She had after all begged for his help.

'My powers are untrained, I cannot command them.'

'I will train you.' He smiled faintly.

The power frightened her, but it would give her the means to reach Joanna and Hawisa. Through it she could persuade them to ask Margaret to send them to her. And it would bring Alexander to her more often.

Feeling his eyes still on her face, she veiled her thoughts quickly.

504

She had no desire for this dirty, unkempt man to know her most precious secrets. He gave a supercilious smile, seeing the veil and knowing already the reason; but he retreated at once. Don't frighten her. Don't pry. Somehow this woman held the future of the kingdom in her hand.

'You are wondering about your children,' he said, softening his voice. What should he tell her?

'The truth,' she murmured, as if she read his mind in turn.

'The child you carry now will be a soldier.' He smiled in triumph as he saw her look of surprise. So she didn't even know herself about the new life in her belly. 'He will live to full manhood and he will die gloriously in battle in the service of his king.'

Her hands went to her stomach protectively. 'You are certain of this?'

'It is written, my lady.' He bowed.

'And what of Colban? And my daughters? Can you see my daughters?' Her voice sharpened.

He shook his head. The truth would cause her too much pain. 'The picture there is blurred. Let me teach you, my lady, then you may seek to see them yourself.'

She looked beyond Rhonwen to the fire. 'Sometimes I see in the flames, but they frighten me. They seem to draw me in.' That was where Alexander waited, in the heart of the flame. He and the other – the man on horseback. She shivered.

Adam studied her gravely, 'We must all look where the pictures come. I can help you conjure them more clearly.'

'And Einion Gweledydd? Can you bring him to me?' Eleyne fixed him with a cold look, aware that Rhonwen had risen to her feet at the name. The room was silent, and suddenly very cold.

Adam didn't move; he was staring beyond her, through the castle walls into the whirling darkness and the cold rain. Einion Gweledydd had tried to warn her of what was to come and he had failed. Somewhere out there, beyond the night, his soul flailed in the darkness, seeking forgiveness and peace.

Rhonwen's face was white. 'Can you reach him?' she echoed, her voice husky with fear.

Adam's eyes focused again. 'I will try.' He folded his arms inside the long sleeves of his gown, and addressed Eleyne. 'If it is truly your wish.'

Eleyne nodded faintly. 'I must know the truth. I must know why he lied to me.'

Beyond the walls there was a moment of turmoil in the darkness – a whirlwind – which vanished across the parkland and into the forest. Adam frowned. He could feel the protest, the denial, the yearning to put right a great wrong. It spun out of nothing in the rain, spattering on the shuttered windows, then it was gone.

IX
FALKLAND CASTLE ❖ January 1257

Malcolm stood with his back to the fire, feeling the warmth drying the rain out of his clothes. He tipped the goblet of wine down his throat and held it out for a refill, sighing. The manoeuvres for power at the boy king's court were becoming wearisome. A couple of days at Falkland and two nights in his wife's bed would restore him. He eased his shoulders with a grunt, feeling the knotted muscles protest and he grinned at his companions. 'We'll hunt well tomorrow if this accursed weather improves a bit.'

'Where is Lady Fife?' Alan Durward asked, holding out his goblet for more wine. 'The great hall is dull without her.'

Malcolm beckoned a servant and despatched him to Eleyne's solar, but it was Rhonwen who came. Tall and austere, she stood gazing thoughtfully at Malcolm and he shivered. He disliked the woman intensely, though he was always careful to hide his hostility.

'My lady has retired to bed,' she said finally. 'She was feeling unwell.'

'Unwell?'

Rhonwen gave a slight smile. It was not for her to divulge a pregnancy revealed by a seer.

She was about to speak again when the door at the end of the hall burst open and a rain-soaked figure appeared. Malcolm's eyes narrowed as he recognised John Keith, one of his most trusted messengers, a man he had despatched a month previously on yet another visit to Margaret of Lincoln, to try to persuade her to allow the children at least to visit their mother.

Keith pushed his way through the crowds huddled around the great fires in the hall, until he had reached Malcolm. Without ceremony, he pulled him to one side. 'I have to talk to you in private.'

'What is it, man?' Malcolm looked around angrily; they were out of earshot of his men. 'Speak up.'

'Robert de Quincy is in London.' John Keith lowered his voice.

Malcolm went white. Over the years the rumours had persisted that de Quincy was alive, but he had not let himself believe them. He dared not let himself believe them. Nothing could be permitted to jeopardise his marriage.

'Are you sure?'

'Aye, he's at Henry's court. And he has visited your wife's children.'

506

Malcolm cursed. 'By Our Lady! I can't believe it!' He banged his fists together in fury.

'Lord Fife.' Rhonwen's quiet voice at his elbow made him swing round, cursing again. Her eyes were almost colourless in the firelight and he felt a superstitious shiver run up his spine. She had heard, God damn it! She had heard!

She smiled coldly at him. 'My lady would not welcome Sir Robert's return,' she said. 'She should not be told.' Those clear, fathomless eyes met his and held them. 'Not until he is dead.'

Malcolm resisted the urge to cross himself. Sweet Christ, the woman actually frightened him! 'It seems our thoughts run on the same road, Lady Rhonwen.'

She nodded. 'It should be done without delay.'

So, she was on his side after all. He looked at John Keith. 'The man is presumably shriven by his visit to the Holy Land. He is prepared for death. Let it come to him – swiftly.'

John Keith bowed. His face was grim. 'I'll see to it, my lord.'

Malcolm nodded curtly. 'And see to it also that no one knows how or why it came.'

Keith grinned. 'Not even Sir Robert himself will know that, my lord,' he said.

507

CHAPTER TWENTY-ONE

I

February 1257

'I shall come with you.'

John Keith turned in surprise at the soft voice at his elbow as he prepared to mount his horse. It was the countess's nurse, the Lady Rhonwen.

'My lord's orders are that I should ride fast. I go on his business.'

'I know your business, Master Keith,' she replied. 'And I shall come with you.' Her smile made his blood run cold.

It took five days to reach London, changing horses frequently along the road. Once there, Rhonwen led the way to the house in Gracechurch Street. It belonged now to Dervorguilla Balliol, who had inherited it on Countess Clemence's death four years before, but Rhonwen was still welcome there. It was dark when they rode into the courtyard and the gates closed behind them.

He had planned an attack in the street – quick, easy and anonymous, as would be his escape, but Rhonwen shook her head. A knife in the ribs was too quick. Too easy. Too anonymous. She wanted him to know where his death came from and she had it all planned. A bolt of finest silk from Luned's stock was to be the bait.

As he woke up, Robert realised it was St Gilbert's Day: February the fourth, a dismal day, a day of ill omen. Not a day when he would normally have undertaken any enterprise more energetic than climbing out of bed and pouring himself a goblet of wine. Nevertheless, the bargains he had been promised by the whispering servant the day before were very hard to resist. How could it be unlucky to go abroad when such riches had been vaunted? Silk. The finest, and at a ludicrous price. He found his way to the empty shop at the back of Paul's and left his servant outside with the horses as instructed. When he recognised Rhonwen, the door behind him was already bolted.

She had spread the silk across the table. 'Do you like it?' She stood, arms folded, watching him. John Keith, by the door, had the dirk ready.

Robert glanced at the fabric. Soft and sensuous, a beautiful scarlet, it was the colour of blood. His mouth suddenly dry, he nodded. His own dagger was in the scrip at his belt beneath his cloak. He took a couple of steps back towards the door. 'I hear my wife has run off with yet another lover,' he blustered with a sneer. 'Didn't you go with her, Lady Rhonwen? Is she finally tired of your murdering, heathen ways?'

Rhonwen smiled. 'She knows nothing of my murdering ways, Sir Robert. Nothing. But you, on the other hand, are about to find out all about them.' She still hadn't moved.

He had seen the silent man by the door. He was slightly built, but wiry; strong, Robert calculated. He wished he hadn't drunk so much the night before. The bitch was dangerous as a viper, and probably as quick. He eased his hand towards his dagger, but John Keith was too quick for him. Before Robert realised what had happened, the Scotsman had his dirk at his throat. 'Keep still,' he growled, 'and do as she says.'

Rhonwen still hadn't moved. His neck drawn back, rigid with fear before the gleaming blade, Robert's eyes slid sideways to her face.

Again she smiled. She stepped towards the table. 'I'm glad you like the silk. It shall be your shroud.' From beneath the soft folds she produced a length of rope.

He paled. 'You daren't touch me –'

'No?' She coiled it over her arm, stroking the twisted hemp.

It took them only a few moments to tie his hands behind him and drag him to the upright beam in the middle of the dusty floor. He was struggling violently, but they managed it at last, hobbling his legs and pushing a rag into his mouth to stop him shouting for his servants.

Rhonwen stood back calmly and surveyed him. 'See how you like it, my lord, being tied and helpless. Does it give you pleasure when it is done to you?' She saw the fear in his eyes.

'What else did you do to her, my lord?' she went on quietly. 'Oh, she never told me. She never told anyone. She was too ashamed. But do you think I don't know? Did you think you would get away with it? You are going to be very sorry that the infidel hordes did not get their hands on you, my lord, because what I am going to do to you is a thousand times worse than anything they have thought of.'

Without looking at John Keith, she held out her hand; her meaning was clear. He put the dirk into it. He was beginning to feel a little sick himself. This wasn't what he had in mind. A knife in the ribs. A throat cut in a back alley. That was a man's work, but this . . .

Carefully keeping his face impassive he stepped back and folded his arms. He had the feeling she didn't need him any more.

By the time she had finished he had vomited in the corner, his ears ringing with Robert's stifled screams, muffled at last to a dying gurgle as she forced his severed genitals into his mouth.

The silence that followed was as appalling as the noise had been. John Keith stared at her, the bile still rising in his gorge. He had seen many men die; he had killed a few himself, but never had he seen anyone kill with such slow and calculated hatred.

She was covered in blood, but her face was impassive as she wiped clean the dirk and held it out to him. 'I shall change,' she said calmly, 'then we can ride north. Go down and fetch my saddlebag, and while you are there send his servants away. Tell them he is riding with us to Fotheringhay. By the time someone finds the body we shall be in Scotland. Well, go on, man. What are you waiting for?'

His hands were shaking. Sweet Christ but there had been true madness in her eyes! He nodded. What matter how it was done? Lord Fife had been obeyed.

'John.' Her voice was gentle now. 'He hurt my lady very badly.' It was all she offered by way of explanation.

II

FALKLAND CASTLE ❖ 9 February 1257

Eleyne looked up from the fodder accounts she was studying as Malcolm walked in, her mind still full of the price of oats and hay, beans and pease and horsebread. He stood for a moment with a strange expression on his face. She tried to read it. He was still a good-looking man, but more grizzled now and hardened. 'What is it, what has happened?'

He did not answer. His gaze slid from her face to her belly; in its fourth month now, the pregnancy had just begun to show.

'We have to ride to St Andrews.'

'Why?' She put down her pen, stretching cramped fingers.

'I have to see the archdeacon.'

'And do I need to come?'

'I think you do.'

She walked to his side. 'What has happened, Malcolm?' She had never seen him like this – tense, excited, his muscles taut, like a man about to ride into battle.

He smiled at her. 'Get ready, my love. We ride at once.'

'Is it the bishop? Has he returned from exile?' Bishop Gamelin, the government's choice for Bishop of St Andrews, had fled abroad two years before.

He shook his head. 'Our business is with the archdeacon.'

III

It was cold and stormy. The Castle of St Andrews, on its bleak promontory, rose dark in the early twilight. Below it, the sea crashed on the fingers of rock which stretched into it, crawling back in an uneasy lace of foam, then hurling itself again against the low hollow cliffs below the outer castle wall. Inside, the high stone created an oasis of quiet shelter out of the wind.

The archdeacon met them in the gatehouse. He bowed as Malcolm greeted him. 'All is ready, my lord.'

'Is it to be in the cathedral?'

'Aye, my lord, all is arranged.' He gave Eleyne a tight smile. 'Would you like to rest first, my lady, after your long ride?'

'Thank you, archdeacon, I shall rest later. First I want to know what is happening.' Eleyne turned to her husband. 'I think it is time you told me why we are here.' She surveyed his face, her eyes steady.

The archdeacon shuffled his feet uncomfortably. Malcolm frowned. 'We are to be married.'

'Married?' Eleyne was stunned, too astonished even to speak.

'It appears I was misinformed when I was told originally that your husband had died,' he went on gruffly. 'Now I have absolute proof of his death. This marriage is to seal the bond between us without any possibility of doubt.'

Eleyne was silent for a moment. 'When did he die?' she asked at last. There was no sadness, only a cold curiosity and relief.

'I believe he died in London,' Malcolm replied. Cautiously he glanced at her face.

She met his gaze. 'How did he die?'

'Of a fever I understand, but whatever the reason, he is dead now without a doubt. We have come here to be absolved of any sin in our bigamous union, to marry again, to confirm that all is legal beyond question and to confirm that Colban is my legitimate heir. We ride to Edinburgh tomorrow, where I shall have a private audience with the king. He has agreed to sign a document to confirm the church's blessing on the house of Fife and I shall have it sealed with the great seal as confirmation of Colban's legitimacy.'

'I see.' Eleyne's voice was bleak. 'So, for the last four years I have been your whore.'

'No, my lady, no.' The archdeacon stepped forward. 'You married in good faith in the belief you were a widow. This must be the substance of your confession. God and Our Blessed Lady will look kindly on your sin. You will be absolved.'

'By you?' She drew herself up and turned to Malcolm. 'You kidnapped me, you raped me and you forced me into marriage. But it is my sin we come here to absolve.' Her voice was heavy. 'And I suppose mine will be the penance as well.'

The two men glanced at each other. 'Lord Fife was not already married, my lady,' the archdeacon said uncomfortably.

'No.' Eleyne resisted the urge to put her hand protectively over the gentle swelling of her stomach.

'Your penance will not be arduous, my lady,' the archdeacon went on, 'Lord Fife has assured me of your innocence and the chaste nature of your love.' He looked at the ground.

'Let's get on with it!' Malcolm was growing restless. 'I want it done as soon as possible.' He turned to the door.

The storm was increasing. In the great cathedral the candles flickered and streamed, spattering wax across the floor tiles as they let themselves in by the passdoor set into the huge oak doors at the west end. The archdeacon led the way to a side chapel, the sound of his sandals lost in the echoes as the monks in the choir sang vespers.

Eleyne stood, the rain dripping off her cloak, gazing at the altar as more candles were lit. The chapel was dedicated to St Margaret. Seven years before Scotland's blessed queen had been elevated at last to full sainthood and chapels dedicated to her all over the country.

For Colban's sake, and for the sake of her unborn child, she would go through with this ceremony; she would confess to a sin which was none of her making; she would marry Malcolm to secure their legitimacy and she would if necessary go down on her knees before her godson and beg his connivance for Colban's sake.

As she knelt before the archdeacon and received his gabbled absolution and accepted with bowed head the penance he imposed, she felt no awe and no relief. The storm that crashed over their heads and threw the sea against the rocks showed the displeasure of the gods; no meek Virgin, no saintly queen, could absolve fate for depriving her of her king, the man she loved. Had Robert de Quincy died nine years before she could have been Alexander's queen.

IV

June 1257

Macduff, Eleyne's second son by the Earl of Fife, was born on a soft, balmy day full of the sweetness of flowers. She gazed at the child in her arms and smiled at this small scrap, destined, if Adam was to be believed, for a career as a soldier and a glorious death in battle in the fullness of his years. She pulled open the neck of her shift and put the small questing mouth to her breast, feeling at once the eager tug which brought the strange cramps to her womb. The wetnurse had been ready these last two weeks, with her own child at her heavy breast. She frowned; if the countess decided to feed the baby herself, she would not be paid and her other children would starve.

Adam would tell her no more about Macduff's future, and about Colban he had spoken little. As he cast the boy's horoscope, he saw no long life or happiness. He saw a line blighted and doomed; he saw storms and lightning and blood. Closing his books and setting aside his charts and tables, he concentrated instead on Eleyne. It was her future which fascinated him. As Einion had done before him, he saw the promise of a destiny far beyond the small kingdom of Fife.

He taught her all he knew. She was quick to understand the science of astrology; she was adept at divination; she already knew more than he of herbs and their powers. But there were areas where she would not go. One of them was the fire.

'But it's your natural element, my lady. It's where the pictures come,' he argued. 'I can show you how to see the future in water, or in the flights of birds, or in your dreams, but in the fire you will see your destiny written.' She was adamant however. She did not feel able to face the fire. She shielded her dreams from him deliberately. He could read nothing of them. Once or twice he had tried to probe, delicately trying to read her soul, but she had flinched as though he had touched raw flesh and he drew back.

She was still not sure whether they were dreams or whether Alexander came to her in reality. Sometimes he came as she lay in bed beside her sleeping husband, but more often it was when she slept alone, as the beam of moonlight crept across the floor and slid between the curtains of the bed, or the early dawn light, cold and grey as the sea, touched her face. It was then she felt his lips on hers, his hands on her breasts and, lying sleepy and acquiescent, she would feel her thighs part at his command.

V

DUNFERMLINE ❖ September 1257

King Alexander III had had enough of politics for that morning. The touchy, raw-tempered lords of his court were like so much kindling on a fire-swept moor: one spark and they would be at one another's throats again. But agreement was close between the opposing parties in the government at last, and Lord Menteith and Lord Mar, for one faction, stood on one side of him, with Durward on his other side, as the Earl of Fife led his wife up the hall.

Alex greeted Eleyne with alacrity. 'Aunt Eleyne, I want you to see my new horse.' He grinned at her conspiratorially. 'You know more about horses than any of my advisers.'

Eleyne laughed. 'I am flattered you should think so, sire.'

'Lady Fife.' Queen Margaret had put her hand on her husband's

513

arm as she leaned forward. A pretty, bubbly, good-natured girl, she was still a child whilst her husband was at last becoming a man, and horses bored her except as a means of transport. 'We shall all visit the stables presently, no doubt, but first you must meet my latest adoring squire.' Giggling, she put her hand out to the young man who had been sitting on the dais at her feet. 'Donald, this is Lady Fife.'

The Earl of Mar's son was tall, dark-haired like his father, and astonishingly handsome, Eleyne noticed with unconscious approval as with the shy grace of a young mountain stag he scrambled to his feet and bowed over her hand.

'If you capture his heart, Aunt Eleyne, he will write you a poem.' The king chuckled good-naturedly. 'He bombards my wife with them.'

With a glance at the glowering face of the Earl of Mar at the king's shoulder, Eleyne smiled at the young man. He was at least a year or two older than the king, and she could see he was the focus of much covert interest on the part of the queen's ladies.

'Then I shall have to set out to capture his heart,' she said at once. 'I love poems, and it is many years since anyone wrote one for me.'

Donald glanced at her shyly: 'My heart is pledged to the queen, my lady,' he said with quiet dignity, 'but if she permits it, I shall write you the most beautiful poem in the world.'

Eleyne's attention was caught. There was a strength in his voice and a calm confidence in his words which spoke of maturity far beyond his years.

Margaret giggled. 'Do it, Donald, I beg you. You have my permission to dedicate your next hundred poems to Lady Fife. I already have far too many.' She rose, bustling cheerfully, and did not notice the crestfallen look in the young man's eyes. 'Come on, let's go to the stables. I'm bored with so much talk.'

As they turned to follow King Alexander from the dais, Lord Mar stepped forward. He knew his son was the object of much admiration among the ladies of the court and he had encouraged his friendship with the young king and queen and watched it flourish with a benevolent eye, but as he saw Donald raise Eleyne's hand to his lips he scowled. He drew his son to one side as the party made its way towards the stables.

'Keep away from Eleyne of Fife, my boy,' he murmured. 'She causes nothing but trouble wherever she goes.'

'I only offered to write her a poem, father. I serve the queen, you know that.'

William of Mar looked heavenwards, and Lord Buchan, next to him, grinned sympathetically. The boy was obsessed with the notion of courtly love. Let be. A few months in the cold northern mountains with a sword in his hand and the icy highland rain pouring down his neck would soon cure that.

VI

Eleyne was sitting in the window of the chamber at Dunfermline, staring south across the silver Forth. While Malcolm was involved in yet another round of talks with Menteith, Mar and Durward, becoming more angry and frustrated daily, she was expected to sit with the queen and the other ladies, but this time she had pleaded a headache. She was missing her children. Colban at three and a half an adorable puppy of a child, and little Macduff, only three months old and now in the care of his wetnurse and of Rhonwen, had remained at Falkland. Besides, since Queen Marie and her new French husband had joined the court the atmosphere had chilled rapidly. The carefree giggling coterie had changed into a solemn, hostile group whose eyes seemed to watch her whenever she entered the queen's presence.

The castle was quiet, their chamber deserted. The servants were elsewhere and she had sent her own ladies down to the hall. For the first time in a long while she was completely alone.

She looked behind her into the silent room and felt a sudden catch in her throat. He was here: Alexander, her Alexander. She always felt closer to him at Dunfermline than anywhere else, but he had never come to her here. Not like this. She felt a breath on her cheek, the slightest brush against her breast and a whisper in the shadows. Obediently she rose and walked towards the bed, sleepily, languid with the autumn heat, already opening the front of her gown.

The quiet knock seemed part of her daydream, no more. She glanced lazily across the room and smiled.

The knock came a second time, louder. As suddenly as it had come, the presence in the room had gone. She was once more alone. Hastily adjusting her gown, she called to come in.

The door opened and Donald of Mar peered round it.

'My Lady Eleyne? They told me you weren't well. The queen said I should bring you my poem . . .' He blushed, still holding the ring of the door handle.

Eleyne's irritation vanished. With a smile, she beckoned him in. Alexander – her own tiny dead Alexander – would be this young man's age now if he had lived. 'As you see, I am quite alone and very bored. I should love to hear your poem, sir.' Her ghostly visitor was forgotten. She did not feel the anguish in the room, or sense the chill as she gestured Donald towards a stool. It did not occur to her to call for a chaperone.

He came into the chamber and closed the door with care. The roll

515

of parchment was tucked into his girdle, but although he brought it out he did not need to read it. He had his poem by heart.

Eleyne listened. His voice was deep and musical and the words had power and beauty. She listened, amused and touched, unaware that her near encounter with her phantom lover had left her eyes huge and lustrous and brought a colour and softness to her skin which reminded Donald of the innermost part of the delicate petal of sweet eglantine.

After he finished there was a long silence. The words had been in places stylised and clumsy, but running through them was a note of sensuousness which made her catch her breath. 'You are a true poet, Donald,' she said at last. 'Such men are greatly honoured in my country.'

He smiled gravely. 'As they are in Scotland, Lady Eleyne, though not if they are the eldest son of an earl.' The bitterness in his voice did not suit his handsome face and clear grey eyes.

'Your father does not like having a poet for a son?' she asked, surprised.

'It's not that. Squires are supposed to write poetry and play court to their lady. Only —'

'Only they should not be so good at it, perhaps,' she prompted.

He laughed, half embarrassed, half pleased. 'I don't enjoy the lists or the quintain. You'll think me a girl for that.' He went on shyly: 'You ride better than most men, my lady.'

'I've never ridden in a tournament though,' she teased. 'I don't think I should acquit myself well there. Please, recite another poem.'

'Really?' He tried to hide his eagerness.

'Really,' she insisted.

He came often after that. New poems in her honour followed hard upon one another's heels and then, shyly presented, gifts. A rose; a ribbon; a ring of gold and sea pearls.

Malcolm roared with laughter. 'The pup is besotted! Have a care, my dear, or the queen will be jealous. He has stopped writing for her, you know! In fact he barely looks at her now.'

Ridiculously, Eleyne felt herself blushing. Donald was no pup. Youthful though he might be, he was a man and she was half shocked, half intrigued by her reaction to him. His attraction was tangible and the more she saw of him, the harder she found it to resist him.

'The boy is a poet,' she said defensively. 'He would recite poems to anyone who listens and the queen is too busy.'

'And you are not.'

They looked at each other in silence: the usual gulf had opened between them. Malcolm looked away first. 'I am returning to Falkland when the court moves to Stirling,' he said abruptly. 'There is business which requires my attention. The king and queen have asked that you remain with them; no doubt they want you to write to Prince Llywelyn or speak to his ambassador, who I understand is on his way, so I shall leave you to your poet.' He laughed harshly. 'Be gentle with him, my dear. Remember, he is only a boy.'

He was still laughing as he vaulted on to his horse and rode away.

VII

In the great hall at Stirling Donald sought her out. As usual, there was a group around the young king, and the Earl of Mar was amongst them. Eleyne saw him look across at his son and then at her; his expression was thoughtful.

'Your husband has not come to Stirling?' Donald's voice was painfully eager; he did not like Malcolm's teasing.

Eleyne shook her head.

'And you are not going to follow him?' Suddenly the reason for the anxiety in the young man's eyes was apparent.

Impulsively Eleyne laid her hand on Donald's sleeve. 'No, I am staying here, I don't want to be parted from my poet.' She was aware suddenly that she spoke the truth; she was becoming dangerously fond of this young man. He represented so much that her soul craved: poetry; chivalry; charm. He was young, romantic. What woman could resist such a combination after years with Robert and then with Malcolm? 'I shall command that you attend me faithfully and wait on my every whim.' Her voice took on a note of mock sternness. 'When we go tomorrow with the king and queen for our banquet in the forest, I shall want you to be my squire.'

Donald's face cleared. He bowed low, with a little flourish of his hand. 'I am yours to command, lady.'

The picnic had been arranged as a distraction for the king and queen, a relief from the monotony of grey council meetings and the quarrels of the leading members of the court. A clearing had been chosen in the king's park and spread with cloths, and from dawn baskets of food and wine had been carried out for the feast. Cooking fires had been lit hours before. Musicians, tumblers, troubadours and minstrels were clustered beneath the trees waiting for the guests to appear in all their finery.

It was a hot, airless day. The trees still threw a heavy shade across the grass, though a carpet of crisp golden leaves lay across the parched sward, and the men and women who trooped out of the castle sought it eagerly, seating themselves around the food-laden cloths. The air was loud with talk and laughter and soon the cheerful notes of pipe and drum, harp and fiddle echoed beneath the trees.

Eleyne watched Donald, aware that several other wistful pairs of eyes were fixed on the handsome son of the Earl of Mar. She was amused as the young man piled food on to her manchet, choosing from each great trencher what he considered the most succulent portions. He was wearing a new gown of dark green fabric tied with a simple leather girdle and he had brushed his hair until it shone. His beard was scant, but carefully trimmed, and in the scrip at his belt she guessed there would be another gift. She knew that she should discourage him. She knew that she was playing with fire, but she could not stop herself.

Most of the ladies at the English court played at love. They encouraged their admirers to write them poetry; they accepted gifts. They flirted and sang and laughed with their adoring swains, and wore their favours at the tournaments. It meant nothing; husbands turned a blind eye; it was the accepted way.

Here in Scotland it was the same, surely, though the court was less light-hearted. The factions which had torn the government this way and that for the last ten years were reflected in a certain grimness which permeated the atmosphere. It was that which had upset the little queen and distressed her father King Henry when he heard of it, and which Lords Menteith and Mar and their advisers were trying to alleviate with parties like this one. Eleyne saw the royal pair seated on their chairs beneath an oak tree, from which was suspended the royal canopy of state. Queen Marie was with them, her husband a little apart. The little queen was too thin, her face pinched and white. Eleyne felt a shiver of unease as she looked at her.

Something touched her hand and she glanced down. Donald's long sensitive fingers lay over her own, then he moved his hand. 'Your food, my lady,' he said softly, 'it grows cold.'

'I'm sorry.'

'You were staring at the queen as though you saw a ghost,' Donald went on. He had seen the colour drain from her face.

Eleyne shook her head hastily. 'I was thinking of other things. Come, distract me. You must pay with a poem before I permit you to eat!'

She watched him as he recited, picking only lethargically at her food. The planes of his handsome face had not yet hardened into full manhood. Above the beard his cheeks still had the soft bloom of youth, unmarred by the acne which disfigured some of his contemporaries, and she found herself longing to touch the curve of his cheek.

His poem done, he threw himself down beside her on the rug and reached for his food. There was nothing pale or romantic about his appetite. He ate like a horse, addressing his meal with enthusiasm. Eleyne hid a smile and pushed her own helping towards him. It was a shame to waste the succulent pieces he had chosen with such care.

When the meal was done many settled themselves to sleep in the shade as the harper stroked his instrument into a lazy lullaby. Eleyne felt restless, and scrambling to her feet, she held out her hand to Donald. 'Shall we walk amongst the trees? It's cooler in the forest. I have no desire to sit and listen to a hundred people belch and then lie down to snore.'

She didn't wait to see if he had followed. The cool shade of the forest closed around her almost at once and within a few paces she was out of earshot of the music. The silence of the afternoon was suffocating; tangible. Every creature in the forest slept. Running her hand around the back of her neck, she lifted the weight of her hair in the snood and veil which covered her head, and turned to smile at Donald close behind her. She had left the phoenix tucked into the bottom of her coffer.

'I imagine you would rather be swimming naked in the burn than walking here with me.' She leaned against a tree trunk, aware of the damp perspiration below her breasts.

'No, I would rather be nowhere else on earth.' He stepped towards her. 'My lady. Eleyne –'

'No, Donald.' Aware of the expression on his face, she raised her hand. The intensity of passion in the young man's eyes frightened her.

What would you have done if your lover had beckoned you one night and kissed you in the shadows beneath the moon? What if he beguiled you away from everyone else on a ride and you found yourself alone with him . . .

From somewhere at the back of her memory came the echo of the conversation she had had with her mother all those years before when Joan had spoken to her about William de Braose. At last she understood her mother's terrible plight. Oh yes, at last she understood.

'Eleyne, please.' Donald's voice broke through her reverie. 'I love you so much. Surely you can grant me one small kiss?'

'No, Donald.' She ached to reach out to him. 'No,' she repeated, more softly this time. This was no longer a chivalric pretence of love. 'It would not be right; I'm old enough to be your mother.' Neither of them noticed that she had not mentioned her husband.

She pushed herself away from the tree and ducked past him, running a few steps down the grassy ride.

'You will never look old to me, my lady,' Donald called after her. 'On the day you are a hundred, you will be as beautiful as a new budded rose and I shall kiss your eyelids and your lips as velvet petals in the sunlight.'

Eleyne suppressed a smile. She had to stop this now or he was going to get hurt. 'Donald –' she said.

He shook his head sternly. 'Only one kiss, my lady, that's all I crave. You wouldn't deny me that, surely?'

She know that however much she enjoyed his company and his gifts and his poems and his compliments, however much fun it was to be courted and wooed and worshipped with such open admiration, however attractive she found him, she had to put a stop to it now. 'No, Donald, we should go back to the others.'

'Soon.' He was standing between her and the path which led back to the clearing. 'First I demand a forfeit for cutting short our walk.' His voice was light but his eyes were serious as he stepped towards her.

'Donald,' she said uncertainly.

'Ssssh!' He put his hands on her shoulders and drew her to him. 'Just one forfeit.'

His lips were cool and firm on hers. There was nothing boyish or diffident about him now. The hands which held her were those of a man. Shocked, she was overwhelmed by the wave of longing which swept through her, the temptation to abandon herself to his embrace. When she pushed him away, she was trembling. 'You shouldn't have done that, Donald. We must go back to the others.'

The forest had suddenly become very cold. The sun had vanished and a small spiteful whirlwind had whipped the dead leaves into spinning, dusty vortices. Uncomfortably Eleyne looked round. She could feel the anger in the air like a lightning charge, and she was afraid. 'Donald,' she said, 'we flirted, you wrote me beautiful poems and I am flattered. But it can never be more than that.' She tried to make her voice gentle, to cover the raw ache he had awakened in her. 'Be sensible. It's too dangerous. You must find someone to marry.' A girl your own age, she was about to say, but the words stuck in her throat. She turned from him and began to walk back towards the clearing, conscious that the atmosphere was lightening.

'Eleyne.' Donald had not moved. He didn't even raise his voice. 'One day you will change your mind.'

She didn't look back.

The following day, with the king's permission, she rode back to Falkland.

VIII

FALKLAND CASTLE ❖ October 1257

The moonlight falling through the narrow window poured across the bed. Eleyne stared at it sleepily, listening to the steady breathing of the man who slept beside her. Malcolm groaned as though he felt the moonlight with pain and he shrugged the shadowy covers over him. Eleyne lay still, waiting for him to settle again.

Alexander . . . she was calling the name in her head.

Alexander, where are you?

She stirred restlessly, her fingers reaching for the phoenix beneath her pillow, feeling the moonlight lapping over her, seductive, secret, touching her body with warmth and longing.

Alexander.

But the shadows were empty.

IX

November 1257

Robert Bruce, since his father's death Lord of Annandale, and since his mother's death two years before vastly richer for her share of the great Chester estates, arrived at Falkland a week later.

'Aunt Eleyne!' He kissed her fondly, his irrepressible humour and energy a tangible aura around him. 'How are you?' He noticed her pale, tired face. 'What have you been up to?'

'Getting married, having babies, getting old, nephew,' she replied tartly.

He raised an eyebrow. 'A new husband already? Have you grown tired of poor old Malcolm, then?'

She laughed in spite of herself. 'It was poor old Malcolm I married – again.' She sighed. The story had not become general gossip. Robert de Quincy's death had gone unremarked in Scotland. She had heard none of the rumours which had swept London after his vicious murder until they had been replaced by some other newer scandal. 'Enough, Rob, it's a long story. Tell me, how are you? How is your beautiful wife?'

Robert was married to Isabel, a daughter of the Earl of Clare and Gloucester and niece of the earl marshal. Fifteen months after their marriage in 1240, she had produced a son. Mother and child were, between them, Robert's pride and joy. 'She's well, and Robbie thrives, though I could wish he had a bit more energy and spirit. You must come and stay with us at Lochmaben, Aunt Eleyne. I know they would love to see you.' He paused. 'You haven't been there since mama died, have you? You must miss her.'

Eleyne smiled sadly, 'I was very fond of your mother.' She put her head on one side. 'Are you going to call me Aunt Eleyne when we're both seventy, Rob?'

'Undoubtedly, and you will call me nephew – and give me a penny on my birthday.' He sighed. 'And now to the reason for my visit. I have brought messages from the court for Malcolm. A great deal has happened since you both returned here and buried yourselves in the country.' He looked at her quizzically. 'The factions around the king are at one another's throats again. The Earls of Mar and Menteith have more or less captured him. Durward has fallen from power.'

'When?' Sternly Eleyne suppressed the longing which the name of

Mar was able to induce. She did not allow herself to think about Donald. 'Why haven't we heard about this?' She was shocked.

'It happened last month.'

'That won't please Malcolm.'

'No.' Robert narrowed his eyes. Anything that befell the king was of especial interest to him. Since the birth of his cousins, Hugh and John Balliol, Dervorguilla's sons, he was no longer heir presumptive to the throne. They were the grandsons of his mother's elder sister, but he still harboured a secret ambition; he had come too close to the throne to lose sight of it now, and whilst Alexander was still childless anything might happen.

Malcolm was, as predicted, angry at the news, but he had to accept the situation just as Durward himself had done. None of them had been with the king when Mar and Menteith had struck. Had they been there, perhaps things would have been different. He nursed his fury over the winter, but was somewhat mollified when Lord Menteith came to Falkland to see them, though not when he knew why.

'The King of England has ordered his northern barons to prepare to come north and fight us,' Menteith said curtly. 'He wants to interfere in the regency again, making his daughter's unhappiness his excuse. Not that she is unhappy,' he interrupted himself. 'My view is that there is no chance that he will do it – he has distractions enough in the south – but it is King Alexander's wish that we form an alliance with our neighbours in Wales. We are entering into negotiations with your nephew, Prince Llywelyn, my lady.' He turned to Eleyne as the true reason for his visit emerged. 'Although your husband does not support our government, we know that you are both loyal to King Alexander. Would you be prepared to write in our favour to the prince?' He eyed her cautiously: her face was tired, but he could see her beauty still; the beauty which had captivated a king. He had heard that she had been passionate in the Welsh cause once, and if he could enlist her help he would have a stronger hand.

Eleyne returned his gaze. The man was tall, lean, his face grim. There was no attempt to charm her into supporting him. She suspected he had been one of those who had dissuaded Alexander from marrying her, yet she knew his request made sense for Scotland and for Wales. She nodded. 'I shall write to him for you, Lord Menteith; such a union would have my complete blessing.'

Menteith bowed slightly. 'King Alexander will be grateful for your help, my lady. He . . .' He hesitated almost imperceptibly. 'Although he is only sixteen he is rapidly becoming his own man and it is his wish that the different factions in this country unite.'

X

ROXBURGH CASTLE ❖ December 1257

When Malcolm was summoned to the king's council at Roxburgh Eleyne went with him, leaving the boys with Rhonwen yet again.

Donald of Mar was at the castle with his father; he was attending the council meetings, attentive, serious, and waiting once more upon the queen. The young man had grown taller; his shoulders had broadened and the beard which before had been thin now framed his face, giving it strength. Eleyne studied him covertly, shocked and half amused to find that her heart was beating faster than normal. He did not appear to have seen her, but that evening, as she sat with some of the other ladies, embroidering as they listened to the songs of a French *trouvère*, a note was pressed into her hand.

The queen's garden at the hour of vespers. It was unsigned.

Donald had his back to her as he talked animatedly to Lord Buchan. She tucked the note inside her gown; there could be no question of doing as it asked.

XI

'You came.'

The whisper in the darkness came from behind her. At first she had thought the garden empty. The narrow gravelled paths were raked smooth in the moonlight and the shadow of the castle wall cut a harsh diagonal across the regular beds of herbs.

She turned slowly. 'I came.'

'I knew you would. Lord Fife doesn't know?'

'Of course not.' She held her breath: what was she doing here, trysting with him in a moonlit garden?

She had tried to put Donald out of her mind over the past months, but time and again the memory of his kiss had come back to her. She had burned his note – but she had come. Was it the excitement she could not resist? Or the thought of an illicit rendezvous? Or was it her longing for Donald himself, for his charm, his good looks, his consideration, his gentleness, and the memory of that kiss?

Donald had exhaled audibly. He took a step nearer and she saw he was holding a frosted white rosebud in his hand. 'For you.' He proffered it and she took it with a smile.

Donald looked down at the flower. He wanted to tell Eleyne that she was the most beautiful creature he had ever seen; she was so gracious, so lovely, so flawless in spite of the burn marks on her face and hands. He longed to kiss her, to feel her skin beneath his lips. She was so voluptuous compared with the maidens whom his parents

523

paraded before him; so cool and composed compared to the queen's ladies who giggled and simpered and ogled him behind their hands. Sweet Blessed Virgin, how he wanted her!

He frowned, torn. He must not, could not, think of her like that, she was a perfect wife, chaste, pure, the mother of two little boys, yet here she was in front of him in the moonlight, here in obedience to his summons. He clenched his fists and raised his eyes.

'This is madness.' She could feel him, that other presence, her king, her phantom lover, nearby. He was angry. The air crackled with cold impotent fury.

Donald smiled and nodded, holding out his hands to her. 'I want you,' he said helplessly.

She almost went to him. She reached out her hand, then lowered it. 'Donald –'

'I'm sorry.' He made a supreme effort to control himself. 'I had no right, forgive me.'

'There's nothing to forgive.' She smiled. 'What woman could be angry with you?'

Reaching up she kissed him, once, lightly on the cheek, then, turning, she fled.

XII

William of Mar was pacing up and down the room when Donald appeared. He swung to face his son. 'So there you are. Where have you been?'

Donald took a step back at the anger in his father's voice. 'With the horses, father.' His face coloured slightly.

'The horses or the whore?' William's voice dropped to a hiss. 'God's blood! If what I hear is true I shall flay you alive, boy!'

Donald straightened. 'I am no longer a boy, father.'

'Really? Did she tell you that?' William's voice slid into a sneer.

Donald looked his father in the eye. He respected William and had always gone rather in awe of him, but now his temper flared. 'I don't know what you have heard, father, or who you heard it from,' he said with enormous dignity. 'But I have formed no liaisons of which I should be ashamed and I have done nothing to dishonour myself or any lady at this court.' He had wanted to – Sweet Virgin how he had wanted to. But he had respected her wishes. He had not followed her; instead he had stood for what had seemed like hours alone in the icy garden, staring up at the moon.

William took a turn around the table, his hands beating sonorous time, fist on palm, as he tried to regain control of his temper. 'I understand your feelings, Donald, believe me. She is a beautiful woman.

She's almost led better men than you to their doom. You do know she was the old king's mistress?'

Donald scowled at him. 'That's a lie!'

'No, boy, it started before you were born. *Before you were born,*' he repeated. 'Sweet Jesu, Donald, the woman is twice your age! She carried Alexander's bastard. There was a time when he wanted to marry her, to make it his heir. Thank Christ good sense prevailed and he married Marie. Have you never wondered why Queen Marie hates Lady Fife so much? Have you never wondered why Lady Fife is the king's godmother?' He regarded his son with sympathy. 'She's an attractive woman, Donald, damned attractive. But not for you. Not for anyone. She's married, and Lord Fife would tolerate no one meddling with his wife. Up to now he has seen your attentions as a joke. He hasn't taken them seriously. But if he hears the rumours I have heard, he will find it a joke no longer.'

'But she loves me.' Donald's chin stuck out mutinously.

'I dare say she does, you're a handsome enough young man and I hear her fleshly appetites are insatiable! No doubt she has used her magical arts to ensnare you just as she did the king.' He sighed. 'But you have to leave her alone.'

'She has not ensnared me. I love her. I have loved her from the first moment I saw her. I have loved her all her life . . .'

'I don't care if you've loved her for all eternity!' William suddenly lost patience. 'You will not see her again. And you will go back to Kildrummy with me if I have to knock you senseless and tie you across your horse.' He glared at his son. 'And to make your decision easier, you may as well know that Lord Fife is taking his wife away from court. A word in his ear was all it took.'

'You told him?' Donald was white to the lips.

'Of course I didn't tell him. Do you think I want my son and heir gralloched like a slaughtered stag? He has been told that his presence is not required in the government and that it would be as well if he and his wife returned to Fife for the time being.'

XIII

Donald met Eleyne that night in the dark angle of the herb garden wall.

'What is it?' She put her hand to his cheek; his note had been so abrupt, so urgent she had been unable to ignore it.

'My father knows,' he blurted out. 'We must have been seen! He has ordered me back to Kildrummy.'

Eleyne's hand dropped to her side; perhaps it was as well. 'So,' she said listlessly. 'And are you going to obey him?'

He shook his head violently. 'How could I leave you? But he said . . . he said you and your husband were leaving.'

She gave a wry smile. 'We are. Malcolm has been excluded from the king's council. I thought it was because they did not trust him, but it seems that it is my fault.'

'If my father knows I love you, your husband will find out,' Donald said.

Eleyne stood leaning against the wall. The stone was icy. 'I don't care that much for what Malcolm thinks.' She snapped her fingers in the air. 'But he is a jealous man, Donald. He would kill you if he thought I returned your love.' The matter-of-factness in her voice made the hairs prickle on the back of his neck. 'Perhaps it would be better for you to go to Kildrummy and forget me.' And better for me. The words were unspoken. Before my foolishness leads us both into real danger.

'No.'

She faced him, scanning his face with serious eyes in the icy starlight: 'You would risk so much for me?'

'More, much more, my lady. Dragons, monsters of the deep!'

She laughed. 'Oh, Donald! And ghosts? Would you brave ghosts?' The question hovered in the silence.

'And more still! Manticoras; unicorns; the deadly cockatrice!' Without thinking he pulled her into his arms, his eyes sparkling. 'Oh, my darling!'

'Wait –' she tensed – 'someone is coming.' She pushed him away.

Donald listened, 'No, it's the wind.' He caught her hand and drew her to him again. 'There's a storm coming. You can hear the trees in the park outside the walls.'

Was it the wind? Or was it Alexander, watching from the shadows? Eleyne could feel a coldness on her skin, a sense of dread in the air. Then, as suddenly as it had come, it was gone.

She relaxed. 'Dragons fighting perhaps.'

'Or mating in the dark. The roar you hear is their cry of ecstasy.' He put his arms around her. 'Don't go with him tomorrow, please.'

This time she did not push him away. 'I have to,' she whispered, 'I have to, Donald, or we'll both be lost!' She touched his face gently. 'I have to see my children.'

'But you will come back to court?'

She caught her breath, frightened by the longing, so like a hunger, which overwhelmed her as he pulled her against him again. 'Of course I shall come back.'

'Soon.'

'Soon, I promise.' She glanced over her shoulder. 'I must go.'

Donald frowned. 'You won't –' He paused, unable to summon the words. 'You won't let Lord Fife touch you –' His voice trailed into silence.

Eleyne touched his lips with her forefinger. 'He is my husband, Donald,' she said gently, 'I cannot prevent him.'

As she made her way back alone towards the great keep of the castle, its doors and windows alight with candlelight, there were tears in her eyes. She had let it all go too far; she must not see him again. For a wonderful, glorious moment she had begun to see Donald of Mar as her lover, but for his sake, and for hers, that could never be.

XIV

FALKLAND CASTLE ✧ Christmas 1257

Rhonwen eyed Malcolm warily; this man had always earned her grudging respect in spite of the violence of his methods and Eleyne seemed content with him. She was prepared to listen to anything he had to say.

Malcolm smiled to himself as he read correctly what was going on in her mind. He had listened in silence to John Keith's account of the murder of Robert de Quincy and, like him, had felt a shudder of horror at the thought of a woman capable of such cold-blooded killing. Such a man he would have welcomed amongst his followers; about a woman, whose loyalty was to his wife and not to himself, he was far less sanguine. She had meekly resumed her duties in the nursery, without once, as far as he knew, arousing Eleyne's suspicion. Was there madness in those eyes, he wondered, behind that cold stare? Once again he shivered.

'You did well in London, Lady Rhonwen,' he said. 'My thanks.'

Rhonwen bowed.

'You would do much I think for my wife,' he went on thoughtfully.

'I would die for her.'

'Let us hope that will not be necessary,' Malcolm said grimly. He strolled across to the table. 'I heard disturbing rumours while she and I were at Dunfermline and I am at a loss as to how to deal with them,' he went on carefully. He took a letter from the table and held it up, his back still towards her. 'I wonder whether you can advise me.'

Rhonwen made no reply and after a moment he went on: 'It seems that she is being pursued by a young court gallant.' He turned, his face carefully expressionless. He had thought Donald's attentions a joke. His informant, anonymous, but seemingly knowledgeable, thought otherwise. 'The young man is the son of a colleague – a friend – whom I have no wish to upset. However, the boy's attentions are causing Eleyne much distress. Much distress,' he repeated with emphasis. 'That is one of the reasons I insisted that she return here with me, but I fear he may try to follow her here.'

'And pursue her under your roof?' Rhonwen raised an eyebrow.

He shrugged elaborately. 'He has a way with words, I understand.'

'A way my lady can't resist?' Rhonwen was incredulous.

'He saps her will to fight.' Malcolm's voice grew angry. 'When she is here, apart from him, she is in despair, begging to be saved from his bewitchment, then she falls back under his spell and asks me to do nothing; to spare him for his youth and foolishness.' He leaned towards her. 'She has pleaded with me to save her. I ride back to Stirling this afternoon to rejoin the court. You must come with me and remain behind when I return to Falkland.' He held her gaze. 'I think you will know what to do, Lady Rhonwen, now that you have experience in these matters. You do understand me?'

Rhonwen nodded.

'And you will not speak to my wife of your mission. It would only distress her unnecessarily.'

Rhonwen's eyes narrowed. 'I would not act without knowing what she wanted. I only do what I think is best for her. Ever.'

Malcolm took a deep breath. 'I have already told you what she wants, Lady Rhonwen. That is why she is begging for our help. She is enslaved by this young man. That is why I have asked you to assist me. Do you think I would have done so did I not want someone who understands my wife and who loves her unreservedly? I could send anyone to dispose of him. John Keith would do my bidding without a second thought as you know well. But I would rather it were you.'

Rhonwen was half flattered, half wary, but he swept on, not giving her time to think. 'He threatens your lady's happiness; he threatens her very life, Lady Rhonwen. Don't fail her.'

He met her eye and held it and she wondered if he knew. Was he aware of his wife's secret lover? Did he know that he shared her with a ghost? Was this what he was saying: that Alexander, too, wanted the boy's death?

'Help me, I beg you,' he repeated quietly. 'You would be above suspicion; you would have access to him and he will come to you, knowing you are her friend, hoping to enlist your aid.' He smiled coldly. 'You would have the perfect opportunity, Lady Rhonwen. It can be done quickly and quietly, without fuss, in a way which would cause the minimum distress.'

He knew better than to mention a bribe. If she did it, it would be for love of Eleyne. Her reward, if she were caught, would be his complete disavowal of her and total condemnation of her act – whatever it was.

STIRLING CASTLE ❖ January 1258

Rhonwen sought out Donald in the king's hall as the young man walked towards the door as supper finished.

'A word with you, my lord,' she murmured.

He stopped and stared at her, but his expression cleared as he recognised the Welsh woman who had from time to time accompanied Eleyne to court.

'You have a message for me?' he asked eagerly. They stood aside as a noisy group of court attendants pushed giggling past them.

'You expect a message?' Rhonwen surveyed him coldly.

He nodded. 'She said she would think of me every day, and she has asked the king to call her back to court as soon as possible so that we can be together.' His eyes were shining.

'You think this is what she wants?'

He nodded vigorously.

'And what of her husband and children?' Rhonwen lowered her voice. 'Does she no longer care for them?'

Donald was now the sulky boy again. 'She has never loved her husband, and as for the children, I thought you were supposed to be looking after them.'

'I am.' Her tone became silky. 'I look after everyone my lady loves.'

'Oh.' His face cleared into a radiant smile. 'I'm glad.'

He did not add that he was much relieved; her icy manner had begun to unnerve him.

XVI

In the chamber she shared with four other ladies, Rhonwen knelt before her coffer and lifted the lid. Taking the small phial from the pocket beneath her gown, she looked at it for a few moments, then tucked it carefully beneath her spare shift. Closing the coffer, she locked it. For the time being she would reserve judgement on Donald of Mar.

XVII

When she arrived back at Falkland Rhonwen found Eleyne sitting on the straw in the stables, watching Ancret nursing a litter of puppies.

'So what was so urgent at Stirling you had to ride there without asking my permission?'

'Lord Fife wanted me to carry a message to the Welsh ambassadors,' Rhonwen said. 'He needed someone who spoke the language and whom he could trust. He knew you didn't want to ride back so soon after you had come home.'

Eleyne nodded absent-mindedly. She reached for one of the pups and cradled it with gentle hands. 'I trust you gave them my good wishes to pass on to Llywelyn *bach*.'

To her sorrow, Eleyne's four nephews in Wales had given up all attempts at settling their jealousies amicably and Owain and Dafydd had tried to oust Llywelyn from power completely. He, showing the flair for leadership which had been apparent so early in his boyhood, had defeated them easily and they had both been taken captive. Owain was still in prison.

Eleyne had written to Llywelyn warning him that the brothers had to keep a united front before Henry if they hoped for any credibility at all, and he had written back a letter full of charm and wit, telling her in the nicest possible way to mind her own business, but that what he would really like was the support of the King of Scots. Eleyne had smiled indulgently; in her heart she knew he was right. He was the strongest of the brothers and she was very fond of him; besides, she would always back the alliance of Wales and Scotland. It seemed both countries wanted the same thing.

But for all that she missed her homeland, Gwynedd was a world away. And for now she was distracted. She could not put Donald out of her mind. What was it about him that she found so attractive? Time and again she tried to analyse her feelings: he wasn't just a handsome, attentive squire; he was more, far more. There was a depth to him, she decided, a maturity far beyond his years; a sensitivity and an inner strength which she found irresistible. He was so different from Malcolm; so different from Robert. He was everything a woman could want in a man. He did not compare with Alexander; she did not even attempt the comparison. Alexander had been her man; her king; her god. He had been everything to her. But Donald awakened in her a physical longing she could not deny, even though it shocked her that the thought of him could arouse her. She wanted him so badly, she could think of nothing else. She knew she must never see him again. If she did she would not be able to trust herself.

A passing groom looked at the two women, then, not yet used to his countess's ways, he stared askance as he recognised who it was who sat with the dogs in the straw.

'I hear there were many attractions at court,' Rhonwen said cautiously.

'There are always attractions near the king.'

'Young handsome attractions,' Rhonwen persisted, 'who write you beautiful poems.'

Eleyne felt herself colouring and frowned sternly. 'All the squires write poems. They cluster round the ladies and imagine themselves constantly in love just as they do at King Henry's court.'

'And refuse to take no for an answer, is it? And pestering the daylights out of you.'

Eleyne dropped the puppy and climbed to her feet, plainly annoyed.

'All right, if you must know the young man did pester me. I don't want to talk about it. I don't want to think about him, do you hear? I don't even want his name mentioned!' She walked swiftly back across the great courtyard.

Rhonwen stooped and gently picking up the distressed puppy laid it with its brothers and sisters on its mother's stomach. She frowned down at the dogs thoughtfully. For Eleyne to throw down that pup was so out of character as to betray her distress. But why was she so distressed? Did she really hate and fear the Master of Mar so much?

XVIII

'There will be no knighthood!' William of Mar confronted his son, his hand on his hips. 'That is where this woman has got you. You are not fit to be knighted! the king has refused to convey the accolade.'

He turned away from Donald, his face working furiously. 'That this should happen to us! I can't believe it. The disgrace! The humiliation! That you of all people, who claim to serve the cause of chivalry before all others –' He spluttered to a stop, speechless with fury. 'I was so sure you would be granted it, young though you are. The king had agreed! It was all arranged! And now the king says he is not prepared to knight you, ever. And if he will not, neither will anyone else! Of course the queen mother is behind this,' he went on after a moment. 'We all know how much she hates Eleyne of Fife. Alexander is too fond of you – and fond of Lady Fife – to think of this by himself.'

Exhausted by his anger, he slumped into the chair at the head of the table, and for the first time looked at his son. Donald was standing quite still, his face chalk-white, his fists clenched. To his horror, his father suspected that the young man was near to tears.

'No knighthood?' It was a whisper. 'Ever?'

'No knighthood,' William repeated with merciless emphasis, and leaning forward he smashed his fist on the table.

XIX

It would have to be the poison. Rhonwen considered the small phial on the table in front of her. Monkshood worked fast and with no possibility of error. Today, whilst Eleyne was preoccupied with the pups and with Colban, who was fretful with a heavy head cold. She could

531

ride to Stirling and be back before dawn; be back before they had even found the young man's body.

She told no one where she was going. John Keith called for a fast horse for her. He asked no questions and he watched her go with something like admiration in his eyes. If anyone asked, he would swear he had not seen her for three days.

She left the sweating horse in the stables and made her way into the castle, her hood pulled down over her face. Donald of Mar would guess who it was who had put the poison in his wine, but he would not tell anyone. Ever.

Swiftly she threaded her way across the great hall, where the servants were putting out the trestle tables for supper. She could see the vast ornate silver-gilt salt on the white linen cloth of the high table, the goblets, the baskets of bread. Two young men had hauled a huge log to the fire and levered it on to the dogs in the hearth. She would find a place at one of the lower tables. Later, much later, when the wine was flowing and the great hall was thick with the aroma of food and sweat and smoke from the fire, she could easily make her way to the high table, goblet in hand. On pretext of whispering a lover's message, she would give him the poisoned wine.

No one noticed the woman in the dark green woollen cloak who sat at one of the lower tables. She ate little and spoke not at all as the hall filled around her. Her eyes were fixed on the high table. She watched the young king and queen take their places with Marie de Couci and her husband and Lord Menteith, and next to him Alan Durward and his wife. She frowned. Margaret Durward was an openly acknowledged bastard daughter of King Alexander II, conceived long before he had met and loved Eleyne, but nevertheless of his blood. Her eye moved on down the table. There was no sign of the Earl and Countess of Mar and no sign of their son.

It was some time before she found someone who knew.

'The Mars have gone. Lord Mar would no longer sit at the same table as Alan Durward. Durward is claiming that the earldom of Mar is rightfully his and has sent a petition to the pope asking him to depose William and give him the earldom instead.'

'And Donald of Mar? The queen's squire? Where is he?' Rhonwen's question cut through the excited babble of gossip and scandal.

'He went with them. Lord Mar wanted his son at Kildrummy. They left yesterday . . .'

The story went on, but Rhonwen had turned away.

For the time being Donald of Mar was safe.

XX

'The earl and his son have ridden back to Kildrummy.'

Marie de Couci had summoned Eleyne back to Stirling. She was in her solar, but their interview was far from private. Several other ladies were present as were Sir Alan Durward and Robert Bruce.

'You cannot, I am sure, be unaware of the disgrace. To be unworthy of knighthood, for a squire seeking such an honour, is to be unworthy of life.'

Eleyne's mouth was dry. She saw Robert looking at her with sympathy and felt a quick stab of gratitude. He was her only ally in the room, probably in the whole castle.

'I expect you want to know why he was judged unworthy,' the queen mother went on relentlessly.

'No, your grace, I don't wish to know,' she replied, holding the woman's gaze.

Marie smiled. 'Oh, I think you should.'

Robert coughed. 'Your grace, I don't think any of us wishes to know. It would be unchivalrous to speculate on such a matter. Our sympathies go out to Lord Donald, let us leave it at that.'

Eleyne breathed a sigh of gratitude.

The queen mother's mouth had tightened angrily, but in the face of Robert's firm tone even she could not take the subject further. She inclined her head in acknowledgement of his quiet victory. Turning away from Eleyne she seated herself in the cushioned chair by the fire and put her feet on the footstool one of her ladies pushed into place.

XXI

The long spring and summer away from court brought Eleyne to her senses at last. Her life at Falkland was full and pleasant. The children were growing fast, she rode and hunted and went hawking and the demands Malcolm made upon her as his wife, though frequent, grew less and less arduous. And Alexander had returned.

It had taken a long time, but at last she had put aside all thoughts of Donald of Mar. Her sorrow and guilt over the fact that his liaison with her – however brief and tentative – had blighted his life were profound, but there was nothing she could do. It was better that they forget each other.

It was then that her thoughts had turned wistfully back to Alexander. For a long time she thought that he had gone for good. Distressed, she had risen night after night and tiptoed to the west-facing window to gaze at the slowly moving stars. Night after night she called him in her mind, the phoenix in her hand, her arms aching with emptiness, knowing her lover was jealous and angry still. Night after night she waited in vain.

She summoned Adam at last. 'You have ways of calling back the spirits of the dead?' She could not ask Rhonwen and she mistrusted the fire. She did not want to find Einion at her side instead of her lover.

'There are ways, my lady, but as you know there are better methods to seek the future. Easier, safer methods.'

'I do not wish to know the future.'

'May I ask what other reason there could be for consulting the spirits?'

'That is my business.' She met his gaze steadily. 'All I need to know from you is the method you recommend.'

'I can teach you that, lady.' He folded his arms. 'And also the spells you will need if you seek vengeance and retribution on those who have harmed you.'

'I do not intend to make spells, Master Adam.'

'No?' his smile was cynical.

'No.'

For a moment he watched her, then he turned away. 'Very well, I will tell you what you must do.'

The hardest part was getting out of the castle. Men had died before for letting the countess leave. But in the end she managed it, wearing the cloak of one of the nursemaids while Malcolm was with the king at Kinross. She guided her horse along the path which led up into the wooded lower slopes of the Lomond and within minutes was out of sight of the watchmen's fires. It was a hot airless night but as she dismounted and tethered her horse she found she was shivering. Old Lyulf was at her heels as she climbed from the track, following the natural contour of the hill in the starlight. No one would follow her here. It was well known that the hills were haunted, magic places. She glanced down at the dog and feeling her eyes on him he nuzzled her hand and whined.

She needed the fire after all, it seemed. She set it with the ease of long practice, piling dried twigs and leaves within the circle of stones, striking the flint and steel to the birchbark kindling and throwing on the herbs and berries from the pouch Adam had given her. Then she took the phoenix into her hands.

Lyulf growled uneasily deep in his throat, and Eleyne stopped, listening to the silence of the hills. A slight breeze touched her skin, and the night was full of the scent of wild thyme. Somewhere in the distance her horse whickered softly.

'Alexander? My lord?' The words were barely a whisper. The pendant was clutched between her fingers. 'Why are you still angry with me? He's gone, gone back to Mar.'

The wind moaned in the trees in the small glen behind her and she knew she was no longer alone.

'Alexander,' she whispered again. 'Where are you?'

She woke beside the cold ashes of the fire as dawn broke across the plain behind her. Her hair was unbound, otherwise there was no trace of her ghostly lover. It might all have been a dream.

XXII

EDINBURGH CASTLE ❖ December 1259

'Donald of Mar is here.'

Rhonwen confronted Eleyne in the small bedchamber the Fifes had been allocated in the great tower of the castle, where they were summoned by the king the following winter. Outside, the wind howled across the Nor Loch, battering against the wooden window shutters and rattling the heavy doors as though they were made of thin board.

Eleyne tensed. She had seen Lord Mar in the great hall with the king, but there had been no sign of Donald and, after an initial moment of wistful longing, she had put the young man firmly out of her head.

She turned away to hunt in her coffer for an enamelled necklace which would go with her gown the next day. Her heart was beating fast. Donald of Mar was here, in Edinburgh, beneath the same roof. She took a deep breath; she must not think about him, she must not even look at him in the great hall. Her fingers went automatically to the phoenix pendant at her throat. Hardly realising what she was doing, she slipped the chain over her head, put the pendant into the jewel casket and closed the lid.

In front of the fire Ancret and two of her pups, Raoulet and Sabina – old Lyulf had died in his sleep the previous spring – were stretched out on the carpet of warm heather. Already the beds for Rhonwen and Eleyne's two maids were pulled out and heaped with blankets. The curtains around the great bed had been pulled back and the feather mattress put in place. Malcolm was with the king and his lords in the great hall; he had shown no inclination to go to bed yet.

'I trust you are not going to allow him to pester you again,' Rhonwen said as she helped Eleyne off with her mantle and folded it over her arm.

'I have no reason to think he will pester me at all,' Eleyne returned sharply. 'I had no idea he was here. It's two years since I saw him.'

'Oh, he's here. And he was watching you. He was watching you all the time.'

'Then he is a fool.' Eleyne turned so that Rhonwen could unlace

535

her gown. She could not believe that he had been in the hall and she had not seen him.

'You'd tell me, *cariad*, if you wanted him chased away,' Rhonwen said softly.

'I'd tell you,' Eleyne answered in a whisper.

She was already in bed, the curtains closed, when the tap at the door brought Rhonwen to her feet in the firelight. The other two women, curled tightly in their truckle beds, were fast asleep.

Rhonwen opened the door cautiously. Donald of Mar stood in the passage outside, a flickering torch in his hand. 'I'm sorry. I thought —'

'You thought this was the Countess of Fife's room.' Rhonwen spoke in a harsh whisper. 'She doesn't want to see you. She wants nothing to do with you. Do you understand?' She was almost sorry for the young man, his expression in the unsteady light was so crestfallen. 'Now go. Go, before Lord Fife comes up and finds you here.'

'Lord Fife is busy with my father and Sir Alan Durward. They will be talking for hours . . .' Donald peered past Rhonwen towards the bed, and his face lit up. 'My lady!'

Hearing the muffled whispers at the door, Eleyne had pushed back the bed curtains. Her hair loose, her shoulders bare beneath the cloak she had pulled around her, she swung her legs over the edge of the bed and stood up. 'Donald.' Her voice was husky. Suddenly her heart was thudding under her ribs. 'What are you doing here?'

'Eleyne! My lady!' Pushing past Rhonwen he threw himself at Eleyne's feet and kissed her hand. 'Oh sweet lady, it's been so long. I've missed you so much.'

Eleyne looked across at the two sleeping women and then at Rhonwen. 'Watch the door!' she commanded in a low voice. She took Donald's hand and pulled him to his feet. 'Over here, in the window embrasure. We must talk.'

Rhonwen had extracted the small dagger she still wore at her belt beneath her cloak. 'I can call for help, my lady.'

'Don't be such a fool!' Eleyne cried impatiently. 'Can't you see I want this! If you love me, help us. Keep watch and don't say a word!'

Leaving Rhonwen staring, her mouth slightly open, she pulled Donald towards the window, where a heavy curtain divided the chilly embrasure from the room. In the ice cold beyond the curtain they stood staring at each other in the darkness. Tentatively Donald put out his hands, 'My sweet love.'

Her hands met his and he pulled her gently towards him. All her resolutions had vanished at the sight of his face. Malcolm was forgotten; her dreams of Alexander were forgotten; the last two years were forgotten. He had grown if anything more handsome. Nothing mattered but that she should feel his lips on hers. Desperately she shook her head. 'Donald, this is mad.'

'I can't help it. I need you so much. And you want me, don't deny it.' After a moment's hesitation his hands slid gently inside her cloak. She caught her breath but did not push him away. Almost reluctantly she raised her face and felt his lips on hers. This was not the airy kiss of a phantom lover. This was the real kiss of a passionate man. The shock of her own reaction shook her.

'We mustn't do this,' she breathed as she returned his kiss.

'I think we must,' he replied, his own doubts forgotten, as were his protestations that he wanted to worship her from afar. For the last two years he had dreamed of Eleyne of Fife and in his dreams she had been his absolutely. Throwing caution away his hands were suddenly more demanding, pushing back her cloak. 'You want this as much as I, don't pretend you don't.' She could hear his smile in the darkness.

'Donald –' Her whisper was almost a groan. Her knees were growing weak. He was right. She did want him. Desperately. She could not resist him as he dropped his cloak on the cramped stone floor between the window seats and pulled her down.

By the door Rhonwen stood, arms folded, staring at the heavy curtain, the knife still in her hand. So Malcolm of Fife had lied – her lady loved Donald of Mar and the husband and ghost lover were no longer needed. Sitting down, she held out her hands to the warmth of the hearth.

Eleyne lay still at last, her body sated with the young man who lay asleep, his thighs slack between hers, his head heavy on her breast. She felt no guilt, no shame. She was unutterably content, but she knew she had to wake him. The floor was agonisingly hard beneath the cloak and besides, Malcolm might return at any moment. But she could not bear to end it. She raised her hand to touch his tumbled curls.

Opening her eyes she was looking up towards the stone arch above their heads when something caught her eye: a darker shadow in the darkness. She narrowed her eyes, straining to see better; it was almost as if someone was sitting on the edge of the seat, watching.

The grief and anger, when they hit her, were like tangible weights, filling the embrasure, encompassing her and Donald like a miasma.

Alexander! Her lips framed the words, though no sound came. *I'm sorry, oh, my dear, I'm so sorry.*

XXIII

Malcolm regarded Rhonwen coldly. 'I expected you to deal with the situation.'

'What situation, my lord?' She met his gaze blankly.

'Donald of Mar.' He hissed the name softly. 'You know what I mean.'

'I believe Lord Mar's son is here as part of his father's entourage,' Rhonwen replied. 'If you feel he should not remain, perhaps you should speak to the grand chamberlain, his father, yourself.' With a small curtsey, she left Malcolm glaring furiously after her.

XXIV

GODSTOW ❖ January 1260

Emma Bloet, Abbess of Godstow, stared at the tall red-haired young man who confronted her. He and his two companions wore dark cloaks over their mail and she could see no identifying arms stitched to their surcoats, but his arrogance betrayed his breeding. She drew herself up.

'I am sorry. Nobody can see the Princess of Aberffraw.' Her tone implied clearly that she found his use of the title distasteful.

'Why not?' Eyeing her with a distrust and dislike which matched her own, Llywelyn was beginning to regret coming to Godstow. To rescue his uncle's widow from the clutches of King Henry and incarceration in a convent of old women had seemed a good idea at the time. It would tweak Henry's nose when the King of England, embroiled in his barons' demands for reform, could ill afford any more problems on his doorstep. And having Isabella de Braose back in Wales would serve his purpose well now, provided he kept her away from Aber. But his boyish romantic plan – light relief from his quarrel with Owain and his new-found pre-eminence as Prince of Wales, a title he had used only in the last year or two – seemed to have misfired.

He had planned to be in and out of England within three days, but this woman with her starched wimple and foot-long carved crucifix at her belt had kept him outside the convent wall like a supplicant for that long already. He was wishing heartily that he had brought some Welsh footsoldiers with him. They would have walked all over this grey forbidding place and liberated every pretty nun in the place. He hid the smile which threatened to replace the scowl on his face and with a sigh tried again.

'Holy mother, I beg you, allow me to see her. I was like a son to the princess. She would want to see me, I assure you.' He was sure Isabella would forgive the lie. The second part of his statement would undoubtedly be true.

For the first time the abbess's face softened. 'You didn't say you were close to her.'

'Very close.' He smiled winningly. He could hardly tell her how

538

close or the wretched woman might guess she had the Prince of Wales in her parlour!

The abbess seemed to be making up her mind. 'Under the circumstances, perhaps I can allow you to see her. Poor woman, she has had few enough visitors all these years. Perhaps your presence will ease her last hours.'

'Her last hours?' Llywelyn echoed. 'What do you mean?'

The abbess frowned. 'I'm sorry. I thought you knew. I thought that was why you had come. Sister Isabella is dying.'

XXV

Isabella lay in the end bed in the infirmary, nearest the fire. The others were occupied by two frail old nuns who no longer had the strength to walk, and a novice whose agonising sore throat and fever did not prevent her from pulling herself up in bed to watch the tall young stranger follow the infirmarian down the room.

He sat on Isabella's bed; dismissing his guide curtly, he took her hand. It was thin and brittle between his own.

'Aunt Isabella? You have to get better. I've come to take you back to Wales.' His whisper seemed loud in the silent room.

He thought she hadn't heard him, but after a minute or two she opened her eyes.

'Llywelyn *bach*?' Her voice was very weak.

He grinned. 'The same.'

'You'd take me back to Aber?'

He squeezed her hand gently. 'As soon as you are fit to travel.'

'I was fit enough to travel last year.' Her voice assumed some of its old tartness, 'And the year before that and the year before that. Why did you not come then? Why did you not answer my letters?'

'The time was not right.' He met her gaze steadily.

'The time was not right.' She repeated the words softly. 'And now the time is not right for me. It's too late, Llywelyn *bach*, I'll never go back to Aber now.'

'Of course you will . . .' His tone was bracing. 'We'll have you carried there in a litter.'

'No. If you did that, it would be my corpse you carried home.' She smiled and he saw the pain in her eyes. 'And it's not worth doing that. Liberating my poor bones would scarcely annoy Henry at all. That's what you had in mind, didn't you?' She smiled again. 'I thought so. We'd have made a pair, you and I, Llywelyn son of Gruffydd, if we'd had the chance to know each other. We're both realists.'

She eased herself up painfully against the pillows. Her bedlinen was soft and clean, he noted, whereas the old nun in the next bed had sheets so coarse he could see the rough weave from where he sat.

'I nearly got away, you know,' she went on, 'Eleyne agreed to take me.' She snorted. 'I pestered her with letters until I got to her conscience and she persuaded Henry. Then she died.'

'Aunt Eleyne isn't dead.'

Isabella ignored him. 'There was a fire. No one told me, no one bothered. They forgot.' Her voice was thin and bitter. 'Then the abbess heard. Eleyne was killed. The poppy syrup they give me for the pain makes me confused, but I remember that. Eleyne was killed at Suckley.'

There was compassion in Llywelyn's eyes as he leaned forward. 'No. Henry chose to believe she was dead, but it isn't true. She was taken to Scotland by Lord Fife.'

For a moment he wondered if she had heard what he said. Her eyes were closed, and it was several moments before she spoke again. 'She's alive?' she asked weakly. 'In Scotland?'

He nodded. 'She and Lord Fife were married.'

'I see.' She turned her head away from him. 'And do they have children?'

'They have two sons.'

'I see.' Her voice was muffled. 'Was she so much more beautiful than me, that men rushed to marry her and fight for her body and take care of her, while I was left to rot, childless and without love?'

Llywelyn cursed himself under his breath for telling her the truth. 'She could not help herself, Aunt Isabella; and she could not help you. I suspect had she had the choice she would have wished to remain her own mistress as you have done. After all, to the English courts she is dead. Her dower, her lands, her two daughters by de Quincy – all were taken from her. As far as the English records are concerned, she died in 1253.'

Isabella's eyes were wet with tears. 'And as far as the English records are concerned, I shall probably never die. The death of a nun in an English convent does not merit an entry in the records. My dower has gone to the church. There are no children of my womb to mourn. No one will read what happened to Isabella de Braose, the widow of Dafydd ap Llywelyn.'

'Of course they will.' Llywelyn took her hands again, his voice cheerful. 'When you die, full of years and with a dozen grandchildren, the world shall read about you in the chronicles. My bards will compose poems about you which each take a month to recite and your beauty will be sung to harps all over Wales.'

She smiled. 'You are like your Uncle Dafydd, you have charm when you want. Are you married yet?' He shook his head and she sighed. 'You must marry, have children, ensure there are heirs to follow you.' She patted his hand. 'Your grandfather would have been so proud of you. Now, go home, forget me. I'll be dead before you reach the Welsh border. Pay someone to say a requiem mass for me in Hay. I was so happy there when I was a child. Go.' She pushed him away feebly. 'Before the abbess guesses who you are.'

Reluctantly he stood up. 'Is there anything you want?'

She shook her head. 'Just tell the Countess of Fife that her curse worked better than she could ever have dreamed. My body has been eaten day by day by the crab she set growing in my womb with her evil eye and her vicious spells. As she cursed me, so I curse her. I pray that her famous fertility will be her downfall. I pray she will die in Scotland in as much agony as I die in, here in England, and I shall no doubt meet her again in hell!'

Her voice had risen and the other nuns stared at her in horror.

With a sob, the girl with the sore throat hauled herself out of bed and staggered to Isabella, pulling off the crucifix she wore around her neck. 'Sister, for pity's sake, for the love of the Blessed Virgin don't say such things! That is mortal sin!' She pressed Isabella's fingers around the cross. 'Please say you didn't mean it.'

'I meant it!' Isabella summoned the last of her strength to sit up and hurl the cross from her. 'I meant every word!'

CHAPTER TWENTY-TWO

I

FIFE ❖ Autumn 1262

The track was narrow and dangerous. Donald leaned low over his horse's neck, peering into the heavy rain. It would soon be dark. He shrugged himself deeper into his sodden cloak. His latest poems and a gift – a pretty ring engraved with the words 'love for eternity' – were tucked deep inside his scrip. He shook the rain from his eyes and kicked his horse on; he must be nearly there.

A gust of wind bent the trees and roared on through the woods, leaving him even wetter than before, and in the distance he heard the howl of a wolf. Then he saw it at last, the lonely tower standing above the trees on its crag. From here it seemed formidable, an impregnable defence against the foe, but it had been long abandoned, the walls crumbling in places, the oak door hanging off on its hinges, a lonely forgotten outpost of the earldom of Fife. It was the perfect trysting place, according to Eleyne, where they could meet in absolute safety.

He guided his horse up the tortuous path, hearing its hooves strike rock at every step and, half blinded by the rain, dismounted at last by an old stone outbuilding; it was freshly roofed with thatch, just as she had described it. The shepherds used it in the summer but tonight it was going to serve as a stable. Pulling his horse's rein over its ears, he led it inside. Her horse was already there. There was fodder enough for the two of them, and a spare rug to throw over his animal's steaming flanks. He unsaddled swiftly, his hands shaking with anticipation and, wedging the door shut, he left the animals alone. Trust Eleyne to think of their comfort first. He suspected he would find that she was quite prepared to lie on the cold stone. Well, he had thought of that. He was wearing his thickest cloak, lined with fur. At the thought of lying anywhere with Eleyne, he felt his body tense with excitement.

They managed to meet so seldom, he and this beautiful woman who was his mistress, that when they were together the poignancy and rightness of their love seemed almost unbearable. He had never mentioned the king's continued refusal to grant him knighthood – something he had buried deep within himself, unfaceable and unfaced – and neither had she. Their love was the most important thing in his life, and he had convinced himself that any sacrifice was worth making for it.

His saddlebags over his shoulder, he ran for the doorway. The lower chamber of the old tower was deserted, the floor a mess of rubble and weeds; a strong animal smell came from the darkness. He wrinkled his nose and peered round. The stair in the thickness of the wall was pitch dark.

'Eleyne!' he called softly. 'Nel? Are you there?'

There was no reply.

Cautiously he set his foot on the lowest step. 'Nel?' His hand in front of him in the blackness, he began to mount, his feet crunching on the loose stones and mortar. Stumbling heavily on the stairs, he reached the upper chamber at last. Smaller than the one below, it too was empty.

'Nel?' He heard the anxiety in his voice. 'Where are you?'

He almost ran across the dusty floor to the gaping darkness in the wall opposite, which revealed the entrance to another stair. Once more he peered up into the darkness. This spiral stair was narrow and extremely steep. He felt his way up carefully, one hand on the cold stone of the newel post, one feeling the steps before him. At the top he stopped, out of breath. The smallest chamber had lost part of its roof and the rain spattered on to the stone floor. It too was empty. He heard again the lonely howl of a wolf, the sound echoing in the wind.

'Nel!' He called sharply. There was real anxiety in his voice now and suddenly over the sound of the rain he heard a stifled giggle.

'Nel?' he repeated again, his heart leaping. So she was hiding. Dropping his saddlebags in the archway, he stepped out into the room and looked round. There was nowhere she could hide save the ruined archway which had once been the window. He tiptoed towards it. There she was, crouched against the loose rubble, only feet from the three-storey drop to the rocky ground. Seizing her wrist with a shout of triumph, he pulled her into his arms and covered her face with kisses.

'You foolish woman! you might have slipped!' He held her tightly, revelling in the feel of her warm flesh beneath the soft damp wool of her gown. He reached around to unfasten it, but she shook her head. Still laughing, she freed herself and pushed him away. 'Let's go down a floor. There's firewood in the hearth – a hundred old jackdaws' nests have fallen down the chimney – and there's quite a bit of old dry bracken and I've left food and a rug down there.' She was breathless too, as eager as he.

He laughed in delight. 'And I have wine and some bridies, and gifts for my dearest love.' He gestured towards his saddlebags.

It was his turn to make her wait while he kindled the fire and laid out two silver goblets, a skin of wine, the food and his cloak. Then he beckoned her with a grin. 'The fire will soon warm us, but I think you should take off those wet clothes.'

She laughed. 'I will, if you will.' She knelt on the rugs and stared, distracted, at the fire which crackled and spat angrily over the damp twigs. She thought she had seen something moving in the flames and felt a quiver of anguish in the air, but that was foolish. The phoenix was in a locked casket at Falkland. She never wore it now.

She had no way of knowing that Rhonwen, noticing that it had been put aside, had taken the pendant from its hiding place. It was a powerful talisman, she had guessed that much; it was special, it carried the king's love and it protected Eleyne. Without saying anything, she had sewed it into the hem of Eleyne's cloak. With the weight of the furs, Eleyne would never notice and she would carry the talisman's protection wherever she went.

Donald followed the direction of Eleyne's gaze as she sat looking into the fire. 'You don't think someone will see the smoke?' he asked anxiously.

'No one. We shall be quite safe.' The moment of unease, the feeling that something was wrong had gone as swiftly as it had come. 'It will be dark quite soon.'

'And no one will come after you?' He approached her almost reverently and began to unplait her hair.

'No one. Rhonwen will cover for me. We're quite safe.'

She smiled as he fumbled with the laces of her gown. Gently she took his hands in hers and kissed his cold, clumsy fingers, then she undressed herself swiftly. With a shiver half of cold, half of anticipation, she knelt before him naked, and began to undo the brooch which held his mantle closed.

'Oh, Nel.' He pulled her against him, unable to keep still another moment. 'Oh my love, how I've prayed this moment would come. It has been so long since last time. I thought I would go mad, thinking about you and waiting.' Winding his fingers into her hair, he pulled her against him and kissed her again and again.

The air of the tower was icy on their naked flesh, draughts spinning round the dark chamber, the wind screaming in through the two narrow window slits. Donald pulled the rug over them both and smiled. 'I'll have to find some more wood for the fire soon.' He leaned over and pushed her hair back from her face. 'Are you comfortable, my love?'

Below her the floor was cold and hard beneath his cloak. She felt its dampness and the chill striking up through her bones as his weight pressed her down. The heat of his body warmed her body, but her feet were freezing. It was impossible to be comfortable, but she didn't care.

Her body was alive and tingling with anticipation. She looked up into his eyes and smiled.

The crash of the falling stone brought Donald scrambling to his feet with an exclamation of shock. He stared around, trying to see into the darkness. 'What was that?'

'The wind, it must have been the wind.' Eleyne sat up. She pulled the discarded rug around her shoulders, shivering violently. She realised that the fire had died and no longer gave any light. 'Come back.' She held out her hand, but he was standing with his back to her, peering into the darkness.

'There's someone here,' he whispered.

Eleyne clenched her fists. 'Don't be silly, there can't be. No one comes here.'

'I'll check all the same.' His voice was grim. He pulled on his gown, and reached for the dirk which hung from his girdle. He unsheathed it silently; the blade gleamed in the light of a stray pale flame which licked across the cooling embers and was gone almost as soon as it had flared.

Outside, the wind moaned through the trees and the sound of the rain on the autumn leaves grew louder. He smiled reassuringly at her, then he put his finger to his lips. They were both straining their ears trying to hear the inner silence of the old tower beyond the storm.

The touch of the hand on her shoulder was so sudden that she screamed. Donald swung round, the dirk outstretched before him. 'What is it?'

'There *is* someone here, he touched me.' Eleyne clutched the rug, staggered to her feet and backed towards the wall. Her teeth were chattering with cold and fear. 'Don't leave me, don't go down. There's someone here, in this room.'

'There can't be.' Donald's voice was steadying, reassuringly firm. 'Wait, let me throw something on the fire.' He stooped, scrabbling among the rubbish on the floor for a handful of jackdaw sticks and old bracken. He tossed it on the embers, his dirk still in his hand, and turned back towards the room. As the kindling flared the empty echoing chamber was full of shadows. His own fell across the floor and up the stone wall. As he moved, it foreshortened grotesquely and thickened but, in the leaping reflections of the flames, they could see the room was empty.

'He's gone downstairs,' Donald breathed. 'Stay here.'

'Don't go –' Her anguished plea was barely audible. Her terror was increasing. 'Donald, can't you feel it? There's something here, in this room.'

The feeling of anger was palpable: a cold, calculated fury which was building with the storm outside. As the firelight settled into a steady glow, she saw that Donald too could feel it now. The dirk was still held out before him as he moved steadily backwards towards her.

'What is it?' he breathed. 'What's happening?' The dust was whirling round his feet and a shower of mortar fell from the vaulted roof above their heads.

'Alexander,' she breathed, staring around wildly. 'Alexander, no, please!'

'Who is it? Where is he?' Donald's jaw was set, his face grim. 'Sweet Jesus, Nel, I can't see him, where is he?' He swore as another stone fell from the ceiling. 'This place is falling apart. Come on, we must get out of here –'

'No!' Eleyne ran forward and clutched at his sleeve. 'No, that's what he wants. He wants us out in the storm, so he can separate us. Stay here. Leave us alone, please,' she cried to the shadows. 'I don't want you, don't you understand? I don't want you any more!' Her voice rose hysterically as she addressed the darkness.

'Nel! What is it? Who is it?' The hairs on Donald's neck were rising like the hackles on a dog. 'Sweet Jesus, Nel, what is it?'

'Give me your dagger!' Eleyne held out her hand. 'Quickly, give it to me!'

Without thinking, he reversed the dirk and handed it to her, hilt first. Behind him the fire was dying again. Eleyne raised the dirk before her, hilt upwards, in the age-old sign of protection and blessing.

'In the name of the holy cross I command you to leave us.' She raised her voice in a wild cry against the scream of the wind. 'Leave us now, I don't want you. I love Donald of Mar. You're dead, don't you understand? You're dead, and I'm alive! I need a living man. Don't torment yourself. Please go. Now!' Her eyes filled with tears and she was shaking so much she couldn't stand. She collapsed on her knees, the dirk still clutched in her fingers. Donald's face was white. He crossed himself, then he squatted down beside her and put his arms around her.

'Has he gone?' The room was still full of the sound of the wind and rain.

She raised her head, and after a moment she nodded. Wordlessly she clutched at Donald's arm, trembling violently. 'I'm sorry,' she whispered, 'I'm so sorry.'

He squeezed her shoulder. 'It's all right, it's all over.' He kissed her gently on the cheek, then he released her. 'I'll get us some wine.' His mouth was dry and his voice husky, and when he unstoppered the wineskin and tried to pour the wine he found his hands were shaking uncontrollably. He managed it at last and turned back to her. She had pulled on her gown and her cloak and was sitting silently, her arms clasped tightly around her knees.

546

He put the silver goblet into her hand and closed her fingers around the stem. 'Drink that.'

Obediently she sipped, feeling the rough red wine slipping down her throat. She sipped again, watching as Donald threw more rubbish on the fire, followed by the end of an old oak beam which had been lying in the corner of the chamber. The fire flared and settled into a steady glow.

'Can you tell me what that was all about?' His voice was carefully neutral.

'Alexander.' She licked her lips and took a deep nervous breath. 'He was someone who loved me very much.' She took another sip of wine.

Donald said nothing; his wine remained untouched in the goblet in his hand.

She saw the expression on his face with a sinking heart. 'He died,' she went on.

There was a long silence, then Donald raised his goblet to his lips and tipped the wine down his throat. 'Do I take it we are talking about the late king?' His voice was curiously flat.

She nodded.

'He must indeed have loved you.'

She smiled wistfully then she nodded again.

'And did you love him?' Tossing the goblet aside, he folded his arms. It was a curiously defensive gesture and her heart went out to him.

'Yes.' There was no way she could lie about her feelings for Alexander, however much it hurt Donald. 'But that was a long time ago. It's you I love now.' She looked up at him pleadingly. 'Oh, Donald, help me.'

He shook his head, bewildered. 'I thought Lord Fife was my rival. I can fight a flesh and blood man, but a ghost?' He crossed himself again.

'You can fight a ghost too,' she said softly, 'if your love is strong enough.'

'Can I?' He faced her. 'I can't bolt the doors against a ghost! I can't carry you off and hide you from a ghost! We came here to escape people; you promised no one could find us here, but he did! Your ghost found us and stood over us while we made love, as no doubt he has done before, though I've been too preoccupied to notice! How can I fight that?' His voice rose in anguish.

Eleyne bit her lip. 'I don't know, but you have to fight him. You have to.'

'Does he come like that when you are with Lord Fife?'

'No.'

'Why not?'

'Because I don't love Malcolm. He's not jealous of Malcolm.' She scrambled to her feet. 'Don't you see? It's because I love you so much that he has come to haunt us. He's jealous.' The tears poured down her cheeks. 'Donald, I don't know how to fight him, I don't know how to make him go away. I loved him. I went on loving him until I met you, but now –'

'Now?'

'Now I want a real man; I want a flesh and blood lover. I want someone who can hold me in his arms and crush the breath out of me!'

He smiled and put out his hands to draw her to him. Her body was as cold as ice. 'Then we must fight him together. Tell him to go away and find himself a lady phantom to keep him warm.' When he smiled his eyes crinkled at the edges.

She stood on tiptoe and kissed his mouth.

'Did you bring me a poem?' she asked. She was still trembling.

He nodded. Releasing her, he walked over to his mantle and found the scrip which he had worn at his girdle. 'And something else, a present for you.' He produced the small box which contained the ring. Opening it, he took it out and brought it to her.

'Close your eyes and give me your hand.' The ring fitted the third finger on her right hand. She stared at it in delight, holding her hand to the fire, trying to make out the inscription.

'What does it say?'

'Love for eternity.' Their eyes met and he saw her sadness. 'Perhaps not entirely a good choice, under the circumstances,' he said quietly.

She shook her head. 'The perfect choice,' she said.

II

The first thing Eleyne did when she returned to Falkland was go to the casket where she had hidden the phoenix. She threw back the lid and rummaged amongst her jewels. The pendant wasn't there.

Rhonwen had come into the room on silent feet, and she stood watching as Eleyne tipped the contents of the casket on to her bed. 'What are you looking for, *cariad*?' Eleyne had not even taken off her cloak.

'The phoenix, where is the phoenix?' Eleyne spread the jewels with a sweep of her hand. 'It isn't here.'

How had Alexander followed her to her meeting place with Donald? How had he been so strong?

'Why do you want it so urgently you cannot even take off your wet cloak first?' Rhonwen looked at the muddy hem of the cloak; there was no sign that it had been torn open.

'I need it.' Eleyne's hands were shaking.

'Then I'll find it for you.' Rhonwen's voice was soothing. 'Let me take the cloak and order some mulled wine while you wash your hands. See, the girl has brought hot water for you.' Unfastening the brooch on Eleyne's shoulder, she retrieved the cloak. It took only moments in the ladies' solar to unpick the stitching with her small shears. When she took the pendant back to Eleyne, it was wrapped in a wisp of blue silk. 'Here it is, *cariad*, you had put it in the coffer next door. I thought I had seen it there.'

Eleyne took the pendant with shaking hands. 'Please leave me, Rhonwen, I wish to be alone.'

The phoenix lay in her hand, glowing gently in the firelight. It brought him close; she could feel him now. No longer angry, he was a gentle, loving shade hovering at her shoulder. But he was not real.

'Oh, my dear,' she murmured. 'Can't you understand? I don't want you any more. Please let me go.'

Outside Rhonwen pressed her ear to the thick wood of the door but she could hear nothing. Something had happened when Eleyne had gone to meet her lover. Something that involved the phoenix. But what?

III

February 1263

It was four months before Donald and Eleyne were able to meet again. This time it was at Macduff's Castle, on the southern edge of the kingdom of Fife. Malcolm seldom went there now. Named for their Macduff ancestors, like her little son, it was primitive and bare, dating back to the years when the first Mormaers of Fife held sway.

This time Rhonwen was with her and two of her ladies with two knights to escort them. All hand-picked by Rhonwen for their loyalty and their ability to keep a secret, or rather to ignore the handsome squire who appeared out of the darkness on his showy bay horse and slipped up the spiral staircase to where their lady waited. This time there was no phoenix; the jewel lay wrapped in its silk in the jewel casket at Falkland. Rhonwen had checked where it was, and she had left it. She would be there to watch over Eleyne in person, there would be no need of a talisman.

They had mulled wine and hot food, brought to the door by Hylde, one of her new, trusted maids. The mound of dried heather and bracken which would serve as their bed was covered by sheets and rugs and

549

furs, and the fire was fed from a solid stack of logs. Eleyne had dressed in a silk gown; under it was a shift of the finest, almost transparent lawn. She wore Donald's ring on her finger and her skin was anointed with rose-scented salve.

At the sight of her he stopped in the doorway and smiled.

'You are the most beautiful woman in the world, did you know?'

She laughed. 'If at my age I am even a little beautiful in your eyes, then I am content.'

'I've brought you another gift.' He closed the door behind him and slid the bolt across. Then he came to her side and went down on one knee. 'See.'

She looked down at his closed fist. 'You are spoiling me.'

'Of course.'

'What is it?'

'Close your eyes and I'll put it on you.'

She did as he asked, feeling his hands on her shoulders and the cold slither of a fine chain around her neck.

'Now, look.'

She opened her eyes and squinted down at her breasts. Nestling between them, on the blue silk of her gown, was a pendant. It was shaped like a horse. Her moment of horror at the feel of the accustomed weight around her neck turned into a gasp of delight. 'Donald! It's lovely.'

'I had it specially made.' He looked gratified. 'Now, let me have some wine. I hear we have hot food waiting and I'm starved.' He sat down on the floor and inspected the tray of dishes which had been left near the hearth to keep warm. She smiled, her fingers stroking the jewel at her throat. He was, after all, a strong man, in his prime; he needed his food. What she hungered for was his body, but she could wait as long as she could feast her eyes on him while he ate.

It was some time later that he looked up and smiled. 'You've been watching me.'

'Of course.'

'And you've hardly touched anything yourself.'

'I have some wine.'

He laughed. 'I like this place better than that fearful haunted tower.' He refilled his goblet and leaned forward to fill hers. 'It was all our imagination, wasn't it? What happened then? It was just the storm and the shadows and the noise of the wind. We frightened ourselves.'

For a moment she was silent. Then she nodded slowly. 'Yes, we frightened ourselves.' She glanced over his shoulder towards the door and then at the window, shuttered against the night. It was raining tonight as well, and a southerly gale was hurling the waves against the rocks below the castle, but the fire was bright and the candles were lit and she had walked thrice in a circle around the room, sealing it against Alexander and as she had done it she had imagined that she felt sadness and his helpless rage.

She shivered slightly. 'Shall we go to bed?'

Donald nodded, but he made no move towards the pile of rugs. He too had looked towards the window, and he reached again for the wine.

'Shall I undress?' She rose and felt behind her for the laces of her gown.

At last she saw his eyes gleaming with desire. He raised his goblet in a toast. 'Undress there, in the firelight. I shall watch.'

'Watch then.' She eased the laces through the eyelets which held them, and slipped the gown forward over her shoulders to the ground. His eyes widened when he saw the filmy shift beneath it. The fine stuff clung to her breasts, revealing the dark shadow of her nipples below. He ran his tongue across his lips and put down the goblet.

'Come here.' His voice was husky.

She obeyed him. They were within the circle. No one could harm them here. She stood before him as he ran his hands gently over her body. Nothing mattered here; not Alexander; not Malcolm; not the difference in their ages. Nothing mattered but that he was with her and she was his. Her hunger for him was physical, like a pain. She went to the makeshift bed and lay down on it, beckoning him to her side. He threw himself down next to her and slowly, sensuously, he began to push up her shift, running his hand up her leg from her ankle towards her thigh.

Five minutes later he pulled away and sat up. He was sweating. 'Sweet Christ, I'm sorry! I just can't get it out of my mind that any minute I'll feel a hand on my shoulder!' He put his face in his hands. 'I know it was all my imagination! I know nothing happened, but I can't get it out of my head!' He got up, walked back to the fire and picked up his empty goblet. He reached for the wine. 'I'll be all right in a minute! Oh Christ, Nel, what must you think of me! you'll think I'm a girl . . .'

'Donald.' Eleyne held out her arms. 'Come back, you're quite safe. He won't come, I promise.'

'I know he won't come. He doesn't exist.' Donald threw back the wine and poured himself another cupful. 'It's just I can feel that ice-cold hand on my shoulder!' He shuddered.

Eleyne stared at him. 'He touched you before?'

'Yes . . . no, I don't know!'

She went to him and took the goblet out of his hand. 'He can't come near us, Donald. I've drawn a circle in the room, and he can't cross it. We are safe.'

'You've done what?' His face was as white as her shift.

She looked at him anxiously. 'I've drawn a circle.'

'So you do believe he's real?' He stepped away from her.

'I was afraid, I didn't know what to believe.'

But he wasn't listening. 'You do! You believe in him. You think he's real! You said you went on loving him after he was dead! Did you mean that? Is that what happened? Blessed Virgin! What did you let him do to you?'

'Donald, please.' Suddenly she was frightened. 'Forget him —'

'How can I forget him? If he were a real man I could fight him. I could take you away and hide you from him. I could see him, for Christ's sake! But this!'

Her hands had begun to shake. 'There is no danger. There's no one there. It's you I love.'

For a moment he continued to stare at her, then he reached again for the wine. 'Is it true you bore him a child?'

'Yes.' She did not dare tell him there had been two children, her two little boys.

Almost timidly she put her hand on his shoulder. He froze. 'Does he lie with you, this ghost? Like some foul incubus?'

'No!'

'Oh yes, he does. I can see it in your eyes.' His anger evaporated and there was nothing left but terrible hurt. 'Oh, Nel, how can I compete with a king? I don't know if he's real, or if he's just in your mind, or if he's just in my mind, but I can't compete with him. Every time I see you I shall imagine I see him at your shoulder. Every time I touch you I shall imagine he's touching you too.'

He stooped and picking up his mantle he began to shrug it on.

'What are you doing?' Her voice rose in panic. 'Donald, you can't leave me.'

'I'm sorry, my love, I can't stay.' He looked at her with terrible sadness in his eyes. 'You belong to King Alexander. Malcolm may not mind sharing you with him, but I can't. I'm sorry.'

She was too shocked and frightened to speak as he turned towards the door. When he was halfway across the room he stopped and hesitated. He groped in his scrip and pulled out a folded piece of parchment. Without turning round, he tossed it on to the table, then he walked out.

It was his poem.

IV
August 1263

Rhonwen sat in the large chamber which had served as nursery, play-room and, while they were young enough, before their tutors came, as schoolroom to the two young Fifes. On the table before her were a dozen small piles of embroidery silks, all carefully graded by quality and colour. Her eyes weren't as keen as they used to be. The long hours of needlework, the fine stitches, the poor light had all made her near-sighted. She peered at one of the tangled skeins and, sighing, put it down.

Behind her two young women were threading the loom. The pattern of the woollen warp was complicated and repetitive and involved much serious counting as they knotted the loom weights into place. The finished length of cloth would make a fine plaid: the broad warm multi-coloured strip of cloth the men and women of Fife wrapped around themselves against the vicious east wind which whipped across the forest from the bitter North Sea. If it turned out fine enough and warm enough, she would give it to Eleyne. She smiled fondly, then frowned.

She had known at once that the affair with Donald of Mar was over. Eleyne had hidden her devastation well. Outwardly her life con-tinued as before, the life of a country woman above all else, less con-cerned with the goings-on at court, where her husband spent most of his time, and more passionately involved with her horses and the new stud farm she was building. Her aching heart was invisible to all, Rhonwen suspected, except herself. She had pondered what to do about it, once or twice going to the casket where the phoenix lay and gazing thoughtfully at it. Her cautious enquiries revealed that Donald had disappeared back to Mar. Her mistress's pride would not tolerate a man brought back unwillingly. And did she want him back? Rhonwen watched and waited.

One morning as she sat with Eleyne, working on the tiny gold knots which were to decorate the neck of one of Macduff's tunics, Rhonwen found herself contemplating yet again the younger woman's preoccu-pied face. Eleyne's fingers were inky like a child's; she had been copying lists of horses into the great ledger she had begun, listing every foal bred at Falkland since her arrival, but she had written nothing for some minutes. The ink was drying on her quill as she stared into space, the expression on her face transparent. With a frisson of shock, Rhonwen found herself reading it with ease. Eleyne of Fife had a new lover! The glow on her skin, the excitement in her eyes, combined with the dreamy expression, could only mean one thing – a man.

The embroidery dropped unnoticed on Rhonwen's knee as all her senses sharpened. It wasn't possible! Not without her knowledge! And it certainly wasn't Donald of Mar. Her curiosity was aroused.

She watched for days, surreptitiously and with great caution. The obvious place for the meetings was the stables. In the old days she had often wondered if Eleyne hadn't found comfort with that pleasant young man who had been her master of horse at Suckley. He had died for her, that young man; there were perhaps many who would do the same.

The marshal of the horse in the Falkland stables was Thomas of Cupar, a man in his mid-sixties, who had been shiningly and aggressively bald for more than forty years. He was a brilliant, dedicated horseman, and undoubtedly he and Eleyne respected and liked each other enormously – but lovers? No. Rhonwen was sure not. Stealthily, she tracked Eleyne around the castle and found her the same with all the men she spoke to. She had a way with men, as she had had since she was a child. From the most senior of the household to the most junior of the pages, she spoke with gracious dignity, combined with an almost invisible flirtation of the eyes which told them that, though their countess appreciated them as men and found them attractive, they must not overstep the mark.

Her eyes alight with wry amusement, Eleyne refused to be drawn by Rhonwen's casual attempts to trick her into giving herself away. She still loved Rhonwen, the older woman was sure of that, but she confided in her less and less. There was a reservation there which hurt and saddened her and Rhonwen guessed why. She had been away too much; she had left Eleyne when Eleyne had needed her most, and when she had returned the habit of keeping her own counsels was established. That Eleyne had ever resented her prying and manipulation over their long years together never entered her head. Nor had she noticed that sometimes it was Eleyne who watched her, as though she too were trying to resolve a problem which would not go away.

Rhonwen sucked in her cheeks and doggedly pursued her quest. There was someone. She saw the signs again and again, but only when Eleyne was alone and thought herself unobserved; and she never saw her single out any particular man for so much as an extra smile.

So. It must be at night. He must somehow go to her at night right here in the castle under everyone's noses. It was so convenient, her strange habit of wanting to sleep by herself when her husband was away; so easy when her servants were used to leaving her alone; no fear of interruption, no possibility of discovery; no guards save at the main entrance to the Great Tower.

The man in question had therefore to secrete himself in the Tower, in the evening, after supper in the great hall and before the door was closed and bolted for the night. Rhonwen, her eyes everywhere, watched and waited her chance.

Eleyne's new young maid, Meg, was somewhat in awe of her mistress's old nurse: the hawklike nose, the glittering eyes, the imperious voice with its strange foreign intonation all frightened her, as did the woman's reputation amongst the lower servants as a witch, though the old woman had never been anything other than kind to her and she knew the children adored her. So when Rhonwen demanded that she let her wait behind the heavy curtains which screened off the window embrasure in Eleyne's chamber, she agreed without a word.

'Your lady and I have to talk alone late,' Rhonwen confided, 'and I don't want the other servants tattling about it or trying to guess what we have to say to each other. So don't give so much as a sign that I'm there, do you understand?' If Eleyne discovered her, she would claim she had had a message after all these years of silence from Lady Lincoln, and that her embarrassment at being inadvertently trapped in Eleyne's room had caused her to hide. It was a flimsy excuse, and unlikely, but it would have to do.

She took a warm wrap into her hiding place and a cushion for the cold stone seat and smiled reassuringly at Meg as the girl pulled the heavy curtain across. It was bitterly cold in the embrasure in spite of the window glass, and the wind, with the scent of woodsmoke, the cold woods and marshes and the far distant sea, sneaked through a dozen cracks in the ill-fitting leads.

It was late when Eleyne came at last to her chamber. She had been sitting in the great hall, listening to the music of their harper, Master Elias. The young man had been blind since birth, but the music his fingers stroked from the strings was like the voices of angels. He was, Eleyne was sure, the most accomplished harper she had ever heard, though as a patriotic Welsh woman she would never admit as much to her husband. Malcolm was at Dunfermline – or Roxburgh – or Edinburgh – she didn't know which and she didn't care. Undoubtedly he was with the king; as long as he was not at Falkland, she was content.

She sat back in her chair, listening, her eyes closed, a goblet of wine in her hand, until long after the usual time she went to bed, and it was a long time before she realised that Elias was playing for her alone. Most of the men and women in the great hall had crept away and those who remained had long ago fallen asleep, the tables and benches removed, their cloaks wrapped around them for the night. She stood up and walked over to where the man sat, gently strumming the strings as though reluctant to silence the instrument for the night. She often asked one or other of the musicians to play for her and her ladies in the bedchamber before she retired for the night. It was restful there.

She could close her eyes in the chair by the fire and let her thoughts roam as the women quietly prepared the room for the night.

'Will you come upstairs and play for me?'

'I will always play for you, my lady.'

She smiled. 'Tell your boy to bring your harp and come to my chamber.' He was a handsome man; not tall, and with a slight build, but his arms were muscular and his fingers agile with the telltale calluses of the harper. When he stood up, he was a head shorter than she. 'My music speaks to your soul, my lady?' He looked directly at her as though he saw her clearly.

She nodded and though he could not see the gesture he seemed content with her answer. He followed her, his stick in his hand, and behind him came his servant with the precious harp.

After the heat of the great hall the courtyard was very cold. She hurried across it, her head lowered against the wind, followed by two of her ladies, and behind them Elias and his servant. The staircase in the Great Tower was broad and steep, lighted by the burning torches which had been left in the sconces on each landing. The one outside her bedchamber spluttered and spat, spilling resin on the floor.

Meg was asleep in the chair by the fire when Eleyne walked in. The chamber was lit by a single candle. The girl jumped to her feet with a squeak of fright, glancing, in spite of herself, at the curtain across the embrasure. 'My lady! I'm sorry.'

'That's all right, child. I'm sorry I was so late. Go to bed. And Annabel and Hylde, you go too. Leave me with my music.' She sat down on a stool and indicated that the harper should take her chair. His servant set down the instrument with great care and guided his master to the seat. Then he withdrew to sit silently in the shadows as Elias gently tweaked the strings back into tune before he began to play.

V

Behind the curtain Rhonwen too had fallen asleep. She awoke with a start as the door opened and Eleyne came into the room. She almost cried out in fright, but somehow she stifled the sound, remembering at once where she was. She heard the murmur of voices from beyond the curtain, and then the sound of the closing door. She held her breath. Was Eleyne alone, or was someone there with her? For the first time she realised that she was in the only obvious hiding place in the room; if anyone had been going to hide, to wait for Eleyne to be alone, this is where they would have secreted themselves.

She shivered, half expecting to see the curtains twitch before her eyes and a figure slip between them. But nothing happened. She waited in the darkness, holding her breath, and then she heard the first tentative notes of the harp. She could hear no voices now, just the single notes, dropping into the silence as they were tuned, then the music. It was slow, gentle music; soothing, lilting, seductive. Rhonwen edged closer to the curtain and pulled it cautiously a fraction of an inch from the wall; she put her eye to the gap. The room was lit by a single candle and the soft glow from the fire. She saw Eleyne sitting peacefully on the stool, leaning on the table with her elbows. The candle flickered gently, throwing shadows across her face. The harper had his back half turned towards her, sitting near the fire, his fingers stroking the sounds from the strings. They appeared to be alone. There was no sign of Meg or of Annabel or Hylde. Rhonwen eased her position, aware of the cold seeping into her bones so that she was stiff and achy. The wind was moaning through a crack in the window behind her: a desolate, lonely sound. Was it the harper then, this lover who brought the glow to Eleyne's cheeks? Rhonwen moved, trying to get a better view of his face, though she knew it was Elias. No one else could play like that. She listened, thinking over this new idea, and then shook her head in the darkness. She doubted if Elias was the man.

She moved back from the curtain and sat down on the window seat. She was cold and stiff and she wanted to go to her bed, but she was trapped. She would have to stay there, in the window embrasure, until Eleyne had gone to sleep, and then hope that she could creep unnoticed from the room. She felt cheated and not a little angry.

The sound of voices awakened her a second time. The music had stopped, and Elias was speaking. She crept towards the curtain again and listened.

'The time has come for you to be alone, my lady,' he said softly. 'I shall play for you tomorrow.'

Eleyne sat up straight, and Rhonwen saw the sudden suspicion on her face. 'You know.' Her voice was sharp in the silence.

Elias smiled. 'I know, my lady. I need no eyes to see, so I see things which others miss.' He rose and his servant scrambled to his feet and hurried to his master's side. Rhonwen was startled. She hadn't even noticed the young man sitting against the wall by the door.

Eleyne waited courteously as Elias moved towards the door, guided by his servant, and only when they had descended the stairs towards the lower floors of the Great Tower did she walk over to the door and bolt it behind them, then she turned back to the fire and threw on several logs. It flared a little in its bed of ash. Eleyne nodded, as though satisfied that it would burn steadily for the rest of the night. She blew out the candle on the table and moved towards her bed. She was obviously not going to call her maids.

The room was almost dark. The warm firelight flickered up the walls and threw deep velvet shadows across the floor and Rhonwen realised that Eleyne was not, after all, alone. A man was standing near her, in the pool of deeper darkness near the bed. She caught her breath so painfully she was sure they would hear her gasp, but neither figure turned in her direction. Where had he been hiding? Had he been in the room when Rhonwen had come in? Unaware that the hairs on the back of her neck and on her arms were standing on end, Rhonwen pressed her eye closer to the curtain and watched as Eleyne moved towards him slowly, almost as though she were in a dream. Rhonwen saw the figure, scarcely more than a greater darkness against the darkness of the bed curtains, open his arms and enfold her.

A log slipped in the hearth and Rhonwen jumped as a shower of sparks shot up the broad chimney, but neither Eleyne nor her lover moved. They were totally preoccupied with each other. Rhonwen watched, fascinated, half ashamed at her own prurient interest but unable to look away as she saw Eleyne turn at last from his embrace. Still moving in a dreamlike trance, Eleyne began to undress. The man made no move to help her. He had stepped away, and Rhonwen found she had to stare very hard to be sure he was still there. His shape merged with the curtains of the bed as he waited in the moving shadows. Eleyne's gown fell to the floor, and Rhonwen saw the white glow of her arms as she raised her hands to unbraid her hair. She shook it free and then pulled her shift over her head, stretching languidly upwards as she did so, flaunting her body sensuously as she dropped the garment in a tangled heap at her feet. Only then did he step forward again and Rhonwen saw that he too was naked. Her scalp prickled warningly. She had not seen him undress; she had not seen him move.

Without warning, she was very afraid. Not once had she seen his face; she couldn't even guess who he was and, she realised, she was shaking like a leaf, half from cold and half from terror.

The room was growing darker as the fire burned low; she could barely see them now. They were still standing up, lost in one another's arms, as if almost reluctant to fall on the bed and consummate their passion. Rhonwen's throat had gone dry, and the room was so cold that her feet had gone numb. She looked longingly at the fire and, almost in response to her yearning for more heat, a log slipped from the sluggishly burning pile. A sheet of flame spurted up, throwing a swathe of clear amber light across the room. Rhonwen looked towards the bed and saw his face.

For a moment her terror was so great she could not breathe; she stepped back, forgetting her hands were clutching the curtain, and as they swung inwards she stumbled and fell, pulling them open. With a moan, she crumpled in a heap between the two window seats and brought her arms around her head.

Eleyne's voice was sharp with anger: 'What are you doing there? Get up!'

Rhonwen raised her head, searching in wild terror for the dead king. He had gone. Eleyne stood in front of her, alone. She had pulled on her bed gown, and her face was white with fury. Rhonwen saw the gleam of the phoenix between her breasts.

'How long have you been there?'

Rhonwen was shaking so violently she could not stand. 'I was asleep. I must have fallen asleep waiting for you –' Her mind groped for excuses even as it flitted around the reality of what she had seen. 'I'm sorry, *cariad*, I must have fallen off the seat. So silly.' She was kneeling at Eleyne's feet, and she realised that tears were pouring down her face. She raised her hands pathetically and Eleyne took them, her face softening.

'You've been asleep all the time?' She sounded relieved.

Rhonwen nodded violently, unable to meet Eleyne's eye. 'I was dreaming, I dreamt I heard music, then I woke and found myself on the floor. I'm sorry, I must have given you such a fright.' She was trying desperately to pull herself together; she had known that the king visited Eleyne, but to see him as real as another man, taking her in his arms . . . she was overcome with shock. He was still a man and he could still love Eleyne like a man. Grunting with the effort, Rhonwen stood and walked stiffly over to the fire.

'This room is very cold, *cariad*,' she said, her voice trembling.

'That's because it is the middle of the night,' Eleyne said gently. 'I'll come with you to your room and make sure you get to bed.' She bent and threw on another log. The fire was burning brightly now. Eleyne reached for the candle and thrust it into the flames. The light spread to the dark corners near the bed. There was no one there; nothing, not even a shadow.

CHAPTER TWENTY-THREE

I

T hree nights passed before Alexander returned. Watching Eleyne's face, following her, waiting for her at every opportunity, Rhonwen knew when he had come back. From the shadow of the wall she could see the dreamy contentment in Eleyne's eyes, feel the heavy sensuality of her body as she moved across the courtyard and towards the stables.

Her lips set in a tight, straight line, Rhonwen hurried up the winding stairs towards Eleyne's bedchamber. It was deserted, as she had known it would be. Sliding silently through the door, she closed it and slid the bolt. The fire had been banked up to smoulder quietly all day. The shutters were open and the heavy embrasure curtain drawn back. Rain was falling and a dull light filtered into the room. It strayed across the floor towards the bed, playing on the heavy bed hangings.

Rhonwen looked towards the bed where she had seen the tall shadowy figure and she made herself walk towards it. It had been neatly made by the bed maids, who every morning smoothed the sheets and covers with the long sticks which enabled them to reach to the very middle of the broad high bed, and it was covered with a heavy embroidered coverlet. There was no sign now of Eleyne's companion of the night.

'Are you there?' Rhonwen murmured aloud. She waited, half afraid, half relieved at the echoing emptiness and silence of the room. 'Where are you?' She listened again, peering around. 'I'm on your side. I know how much you loved her, I've always known. She can still bear your child.' She fell slowly to her knees. 'I'll help you, I'll do anything you wish. Einion Gweledydd was right, wasn't he? He was right all along. She belongs to you. She will bear your child. Your son will die without an heir and then you will need my Eleyne, my *cariad*. Then you will give her a child and I will take care of him. I take care of all my Eleyne's babes. If I'd been there before, your little ones would not have died.' The thin daylight lay in a flat wash across the floor. In the hearth the fire smoked. The bedchamber was empty.

'Listen to me!' she cried out again. 'Please. Listen.'

She scrambled to her feet and hurrying to the jewel casket on the table she threw back the lid. She rummaged through Eleyne's jewels, her arthritic fingers clumsy with cold, and at last she found the phoenix. She clutched it with an exclamation of triumph and turned back to the bed. 'You see, I have it! This is how she calls you, isn't it? This is how you reach her. Your talisman. She doesn't know I know. She thinks I'm a silly old woman, but I'm not.' Her eyes narrowed craftily. 'I see everything. And I wait. And I am your servant, most gracious prince.' She was out of breath. Was that a movement at last, near the wall, behind the heavy columnar folds of the bed curtains? 'I'll do whatever you wish.' Painfully she knelt, addressing the curtain. 'I'll get rid of the earl for you.' Her voice dropped confidentially. 'I know of poisons which no one will suspect; I've used them before, for her. She won't know but she'll be free. She'll be yours absolutely.' She looked down coquettishly at the enamelled phoenix. 'My pretty bird. You'll help us, won't you? You'll serve your king and his lady and bring them together.' She put her head on one side. 'But now I must put you away. We don't want anyone to know our secret, do we?' She climbed to her feet again. 'No one but you and me and the king and my sweet, sweet lady.'

Hylde pressed her eye closer to the keyhole of the door. She saw the woman clearly as she knelt near the bed, but she was too far away to be heard. Only once had she raised her voice. 'Listen to me,' she had cried, 'please listen!' She was pleading with someone. Hylde pressed closer to the door. Who was in there with her? She was deeply suspicious of Rhonwen. Meg had confided that the old woman had hidden in her lady's chamber three nights before and Hylde had immediately begun to watch her. The mad old witch was up to something.

She saw something glitter in Rhonwen's hand as she raised it before her. She was holding it the way people would hold a crucifix or something holy, to ward off evil. Was there a crucifix among her lady's jewels? She had never seen one, other than the carved cross she sometimes wore with her beads. Hylde crossed herself and wished she could see who Rhonwen was talking to. She found she was trembling and glanced behind her. The empty staircase wound out of sight, dimly lit from the doorway at the bottom. In the silence she heard the gentle moan of the wind.

When Rhonwen at last left the chamber, Hylde was hidden in the darkness of the stairs above her. She waited until Rhonwen's shuffling steps had died away into silence, then she tiptoed down. Only one person had left the room, so whoever had been talking to Rhonwen was still there.

Not giving herself time to think, she threw open the door and sailed in. 'What are you doing in my lady's room —' She stopped in her tracks and stared around. The room was empty, but there had been someone here with Rhonwen. The woman had not been alone, she was sure of

561

it. Methodically she began to search – the garderobe, the coffers, the window embrasure, the gap behind the bed, the heavy bed hangings; she even stepped into the hearth and peered up through the smoke into the chimney. There was no one: the room was empty.

The small hairs on her arms prickled with fear. She walked over to the jewel casket and pulled back the hasp – unlocked in spite of her warnings – then she threw back the lid and stared at the jumble of brooches and chains and earrings which lay there. At the bottom of the casket, wrapped in wisps of silk, lay two pendants. She had never seen the countess wear either, but she had unwrapped them once to show Hylde: a fabulous gleaming phoenix with jewelled eyes springing from a nest of flames and a beautiful prancing horse. Also wrapped in the bottom of the casket was a small engraved gold ring. As she had thought, there was no crucifix; no ring which contained a holy relic. She lowered the lid and pulled the hasp back across its loop. There was only one explanation left of what Rhonwen was doing: she was casting a spell.

Hylde took her suspicions to Eleyne that evening, as Eleyne was changing for supper. She chased the countess's other women away before confessing cheerfully to her eavesdropping, and informed her mistress that Rhonwen had hidden in her chamber three nights before as well. She waited for a reaction, and she was not disappointed. Anger and fear chased each other across Eleyne's features before she controlled her emotions and smiled at Hylde who was holding her mantle ready.

'You think she was casting a spell?'

Hylde shrugged. 'She was talking out loud, my lady, and holding something up before her like this.' She held her hand out in front of her nose. 'She sounded as if she were pleading with someone. I searched the room, but there was no one here.' She looked around, conscious that once more her arms were covered in gooseflesh.

Settling her mantle over her shoulders, Eleyne turned to her jewel casket. Hylde watched. If someone had been rummaging through them, would her lady notice? But Eleyne merely picked out a brooch to fasten her mantle and dropped the lid of the casket without a second glance.

'Don't say anything to anyone,' she said to Hylde. 'I'll talk to her. If she's casting spells to make me bear a child, at my age, I shall be very cross.' She smiled. 'I love my children dearly, but if Our Lady has seen fit to make me barren at last, then so be it. I shall not complain!'

And with that Hylde had to be content.

II

Eleyne summoned Rhonwen to her chamber that very evening when supper was finished. Dismissing her other ladies, she turned on the old woman as soon as they were alone.

'I hear you have been spying on me. Why?' Her eyes were hard. She was afraid. Rhonwen was the one person she could not deceive.

Rhonwen sat down slowly by the fire and looked at Eleyne. 'I know.'

'You know what?'

'I saw him.'

There was a long silence as Eleyne gazed steadily at her, trying to gauge what she meant. 'Who exactly did you see?' she asked.

'The king.' Rhonwen spoke in a whisper. 'Don't worry, *cariad*, your secret is safe with me. You have been chosen for great things, and I can help you.' She smiled confidently. 'I spoke to him, you see. I told him I would help you –'

'You spoke to him!' Eleyne was as white as a sheet. 'You saw him?'

Rhonwen nodded emphatically. 'You will bear his child, *cariad*. A child who will be a king – just as Einion Gweledydd foretold. He spoke the truth, all those years ago. You see? It has all come right in the end.'

'I will bear the king's child?' Eleyne stared at her incredulously. 'No, you don't understand, it's not like that. He's not real.' She twisted her fingers together unhappily. 'You should not have spied on me, Rhonwen. That was wrong, and you know it.'

Rhonwen shook her head. 'He was pleased. He needs my help to get rid of Lord Fife. We have to get rid of Lord Fife, *cariad*. He's in the way now –'

'No!' Eleyne squatted beside her and took her hands in her own. Rhonwen had begun to look like an old woman, but her eyes had the cold steadiness of the fanatic. Looking at them, Eleyne was afraid. 'Rhonwen, you must not harm Lord Fife. I am sure the king did not tell you to. You haven't done anything yet, have you?'

Rhonwen shook her head. 'With the earl away –'

'He is coming back soon. And I do not want him harmed, do you understand?' Eleyne clasped her hands tightly. She was frightened, not of Rhonwen knowing, but of what she might do; terrified even of acknowledging her fears of what Rhonwen was capable of doing. 'He did not take me from Alexander, that was Robert. Malcolm is the father of my children, and if, *if* I should ever bear another child, before the whole world Malcolm would be its father. What would happen if I had a child and I was a widow? Think, Rhonwen, think what would be said!'

'But the king –'

'Leave the king to me, my dear.' Eleyne dropped a light kiss on the older woman's head. 'Now, go to bed and leave me. I want to hear no more about this, do you understand?'

Rhonwen stood up slowly. 'If you need me –'

'If I need your help, I will call on you, I promise.'

Eleyne sat for a long time after Rhonwen had gone. Not once did she stare into the shadows. She shivered and sat closer to the fire. If Rhonwen had really seen him, he was growing stronger, and she was suddenly very afraid.

III

October 1263

The news Malcolm brought on his return put all other thoughts out of Eleyne's head.

'You can't do it!' She looked at her husband in horror. 'There can be no question of a marriage alliance with the Durwards!'

Malcolm scowled. 'It's all arranged!'

'Then you must unarrange it. My son will not marry a child of that ambitious, lying, cheating, jumped-up nobody!'

'I told you, Eleyne, it's done.' Malcolm's face darkened with anger. 'The match pleases me.'

'Well, it doesn't please me!' she retorted. 'Think, Malcolm, think who they are.'

'Little Anna is the grand-daughter of the late king,' Malcolm said with deceptive mildness. His eyes gleamed. 'That should please you.'

'Please me!' Eleyne wondered for a moment if he had forgotten or if he were being deliberately obtuse. 'That her mother was King Alexander's bastard?' She paused, afraid suddenly even to be saying his name out loud. 'And perhaps it should also please me that Durward has been pursuing the earldom of Mar through the Vatican courts in a pathetic attempt to cheat himself into the noble blood he does not possess – a claim he was quick to drop when his own legitimacy was questioned!' She was white with rage.

'You are strangely defensive about the earldom of Mar, my dear.' Malcolm took her wrist and pulled her towards him sharply. 'I had thought that business with Donald of Mar finished. Can it be that I was wrong? Why should you care a jot for the earldom of Mar and who holds it?'

'I don't care!' Eleyne rounded on him in fury. 'I don't care at all except that it proves the lengths to which Durward will go, to try to win himself position and influence in one of the ancient earldoms of this land. Don't you see? He failed to get himself the earldom of Mar. Now he wants Fife!'

564

'And his daughter shall have it,' Malcolm growled, 'with my blessing!'

IV

Later he sat staring glumly at the empty flagon of wine on the table. His belly ached and he felt sick and old. He looked around dazedly and gave a painful belch. His sons had gone out riding with their hawks after Eleyne had stormed out and he found himself feeling lonely. He sighed. Not so very long ago he would have worried that perhaps she still dangled after the Mar boy. Boy! He checked himself. Donald was in his twenties now. But Lady Rhonwen had put his mind at rest on that subject years ago. Donald of Mar's infatuation had waned as quickly as it had begun. There was nothing to fear there. Eleyne had been kind to the boy, no more, and yet, sometimes, he had wondered. He had caught sight of her face at an unguarded moment, seen the secret dreaminess in her eyes and, just occasionally, he thought she had the look of a woman who had a lover.

He had given orders that she be watched, but Donald of Mar was far away, and no other man had been seen in her company. She had remained a good and faithful wife. And beautiful. It was a pity there had been no more children, but he was very proud of his two sons.

It was Sir Alan Durward who had made the suggestion: a marriage between his spirited daughter, Anna, and Colban. Malcolm had known that Eleyne would hate the idea. She had never liked Sir Alan. But he intended the marriage to go through. He was still out of the immediate government, but his initial anger at being excluded had waned when he found others in the same boat: Eleyne's nephew, Robert Bruce, Lord of Annandale, for instance. And in the inner council or not, he had remained close to Durward and, more important still, close to the king, who had now been in full control of the country for four years or more. Little Queen Margaret too had grown up at last and was even now expecting her first child. That was good for Scotland; it would bring back some feeling of stability to the succession.

He eased his position in his chair and groaned again. The marriage should take place without delay, then he would once more be accepted into the king's closest circle. That was part of the deal, that and the girl's dowry, a fair exchange for the fact that Sir Alan's daughter would one day be the Countess of Fife. One day sooner rather than later, if this accursed pain did not go away.

V
FIFE

Eleyne kicked the grey palfrey into a gallop, feeling the cold wind whipping tears into her eyes, seeing the two great dogs, Raoulet and Sabina, lengthen their strides to catch up as she bent low on the horse's neck. Her anger was still white-hot, but there was nothing she could do; she had long ago learned that. If Malcolm had made up his mind, then Colban would marry Anna Durward and nothing she could say would alter the fact.

It was a long time since she had consulted Adam and she had never before visited him in the cave he called home, but her anger and frustration after her latest quarrel with Malcolm had driven her to seek him out for Colban's sake. Adam would know; she was sure he knew more about Colban than he had told her.

The track narrowed as it came close to the edge of the low cliffs. Below her she saw the gleam of the Firth of Forth through the trees. The water glittered in the icy wind, tossing white-topped wavelets on to the narrow curve of the beach. Her wild ride had brought her to a part of the coast near Macduff's Castle.

The low cliffs flattened out at the end of the bay, and the rocks ran in great black ribs out into the sea. Squinting into the brightness, she could see the Isle of May and beyond it the great mist-shrouded hump of the Bass Rock. She reined her horse in and looked out to sea. The rush of the wind and the sea filled her ears, and she strained to hear beyond them. She glanced around. There was no one there. Nothing but the wind dancing in the tossing birch and alder, and no one but the impatient horse and the two eager dogs. She walked the palfrey on, and it was barely a quarter of a mile before she saw the path. It led, zigzag, down the cliff face to the beach below. Sliding from the saddle, she tied the horse to a tree and calling the dogs to heel she began to walk down, sliding on the loose earth and sand, clutching at the coarse stems of grass to steady herself, her ears full of the rush and ebb of the sea.

The boy was at her side almost before she realised he was there, running towards her up the beach on bare feet. He bowed, gazing warily at the dogs, and stopped several yards from her.

'My master says you are welcome, my lady.' He grinned, a friendly cheeky grin from a dirty face, lit by two brilliant blue eyes. He gestured towards the rocks as though they formed an anteroom to a presence chamber. It was almost as if she were expected! Eleyne smiled at him, intrigued, liking his brazen, confident gaze.

'And who might your master be, young sir?' She had already

guessed, but she wanted to be sure. She put her hand on Raoulet's head as he growled warningly in his throat. The boy's eyes went to the dog's face and she saw him hesitate nervously. 'He won't hurt you,' she reassured him.

He took a cautious step closer. 'My master is the greatest wizard in all Scotland.' He did not take his eyes off Raoulet's teeth as the dog sat panting at Eleyne's side.

Relieved that she had found Adam so easily, she looked around. The cave where he spent the short summer months had, so she had been told, belonged to Michael and before him probably to a long line of seers and holy men.

The implications of the boy's welcome sank in. 'Your master was expecting me?'

'Oh yes.' The boy nodded vigorously. 'He said that today was the conjunction of two destinies.' He repeated the words carefully. 'He saw it in the stars many months ago and then again when he read the signs.' He straightened his shoulders, full of self-importance. 'It was me who fetched Lord Donald. I had to ride to Dunfermline on the mule and take a message to the king's hall.'

'Lord Donald?' Eleyne echoed. A knot of excitement tightened in her stomach.

She began to run up the beach in the direction from which the boy had appeared, the two dogs bounding beside her, barking. Her shoes filled with sand and she stumbled on her skirts as she flew panting towards the base of the low cliffs, where already she had spotted the entrance to the cave.

It was dark inside, and she stood still, blinded after the bright sunshine. As her eyes grew accustomed to the gloom, she saw a faint gleam coming from the wall ahead of her. The cave led back into the cliff and then took a right-angled bend towards the source of the warm glow of candlelight. She snapped her fingers at the two dogs, who immediately fell behind, crouching on the sand floor of the cave to wait. Then she tiptoed forward. Her heart was pounding in her throat as she reached the bend in the cave wall and peered around it. The walls of the cave were carved with strange symbols – signs of the old gods and with them early Christian crosses. This had long been a special, sacred place. The two figures bent over the driftwood table with its single candle were lost in thought, their concentration on something which she could not see. Adam's tall spare figure, so stooped at the shoulders, was turned away from her. It was the other man she was staring at. His face clearly lit by the flickering candle flame, Donald of Mar was tracing something on the table with his finger.

Her heart ached with longing. He had changed in the last six months. His shoulders had broadened even more, his face had grown

567

heavier and had more authority, but it had, she noticed sadly, lost something of its wistful dreaminess.

'Please come in, my lady.' Adam had not turned, but his voice echoed around the cave. 'We have been waiting for you.'

She edged forward obediently, half mesmerised, and stood in the candlelight, her eyes on Donald's face. She saw his eyes narrow, though he did not look surprised to see her there.

'How did you know I would come?' To her astonishment, her voice was quite steady.

'I saw.' Adam straightened at last. 'It was written. I took the liberty of lending fate a helping hand by arranging for Lord Donald to come here to wait for you. Time is short. Nothing can be left to chance.'

'It sounds as though you don't believe in chance at all,' she replied softly. She felt something strange happening to her insides, as though a great stone were melting inside her. Her misery and hurt, so carefully hidden and buried after that terrible night at Macduff's Castle, when Donald had walked out on her and ridden back to the great dark mountains of the north, were dissolving into a strange half-dreaming warmth.

Adam folded his arms austerely. 'One can hinder the gods as one can help them. One can never defy them. Sometimes one man's destiny is out of step with another's; one dies, and another must step in to fulfil his fate. All will follow the ordained path in the end.'

There was a short silence. Eleyne and Donald were gazing at each other, half dazzled by the candlelight.

'And my destiny is here?' Eleyne asked at last.

'Your destiny is in Mar,' Adam said slowly.

VI

It was two days later.

'Where is she?'

Malcolm was pacing the great hall at Falkland. 'For the love of the Blessed Virgin, she can't have disappeared off the face of the earth.'

'She has her dogs with her, my lord.' John Keith stood before the earl, his face creased with worry. 'She is not in any danger with those great creatures to protect her, and I'm sure she is safe. She's decided to take refuge somewhere from the storms, that's all. There are scores of places where she could have gone.'

Outside the thunder rolled again around the Lomonds and shook the window screens. In the forest to the north of the castle the leaves were being torn from the ancient oaks, streaming on the wind like gold coins to lie in soggy heaps, their glory eclipsed. Sir Alan Durward was standing by the fire, warming his hands. 'She's sulking. You said as much yourself. She'll come back when she finds out the wedding will take place whether she approves it or not.' Colban was sitting restlessly at the trestle table, forcing himself to concentrate on a game of backgammon with his brother; Macduff was beating him with ease.

Durward and Malcolm had just fixed the date of the wedding: it would be three weeks hence.

Malcolm frowned. There was something wrong; he could sense it. And it was more than just the fact that he and Eleyne had had a fight. Something had changed in the air and he watched as a lightning flash lit the high narrow windows of the great hall, followed by another crash of thunder.

She came back three days later, unrepentant, refusing to tell him where she had been. But there was a new lightness to her step and a glow on her skin which stirred his old desire. His wife was radiant.

VII

FALKLAND CASTLE ❖ October 1263

She was afraid. Not of Malcolm, he would discover nothing. But of Alexander – he knew, and he was angry. She erected a wall against him and surrounded herself with it, a mental screen behind which she did not think of him, dream of him or even remember him. He was a thing of the past. She had taken off the phoenix and wrapping it carefully in a dark silk scarf, she locked it in a small casket and tucked the casket into a chest in her solar. Then, deliberately, she put Alexander out of her mind.

Her whole present and future were centred on Donald and the need to be with him. But she could do nothing before the wedding. And when she did, she could not involve Rhonwen in her plans. Rhonwen belonged to Alexander.

VIII

The marriage of Colban and Anna Durward took place on a stormy day at the end of the month. The bride was a plump and cheerful fourteen-year-old; the bridegroom, excited, confident, boasting his prowess, was just twelve. Within months his wife had confirmed she was with child.

Donald was vastly amused. 'Why are you so shocked?' He was stroking Eleyne's shoulders as she sat on the floor, leaning against his knees before the fire at Macduff's Castle, where at last they had met again. The rugs heaped before the hearth were already tumbled with their lovemaking. The light of the flames played across their naked bodies, resting and relaxed. He saw her heavy breasts, the rounded flesh of her thighs and felt the excitement begin to build again. Her body was taut and hard; she had the figure still of a woman half her age, but it was her maturity, her ripeness which excited him. The bouncy charm of a young woman like Anna Durward left him completely unmoved.

'I suppose I'm shocked because Colban is still my child. It's such a short time since he was a baby.' She shrugged. 'I can't see him as a man.'

'He isn't a man,' Donald snorted. 'He's a precocious boy, but he will be a man soon enough. Give him some freedom, let him find his feet.' His hands began to roam across her body commandingly. 'Now forget him and forget Durward. I have. You pay attention to me, my lady.'

Much later she turned to him again, sleepy and spent. 'Why did you not come back before, if you still loved me?'

'I rode back to Kildrummy to try to forget you. I listened to my father. I decided I could never fight Alexander. I suppose I was afraid.' He spoke the name openly, seemingly without fear.

Eleyne turned from her position on the floor so that she could see his face. 'But you're not afraid now?'

'No. I never stopped thinking about you, however hard I tried. I used to see you sometimes at court. I used to watch you. Oh, I made sure you never saw me, but I saw you often. I used to dream about how I would fight Alexander for you; duel with him in the clouds; seek the entrance to hell and follow him there if I had to. Twice I consulted Adam when he came to court, and he hinted that I had a place in your future, but he could not tell me what. Not until now. Then he sent for me and told me that you were going to come to his cave and that the stars foretold our union.' He smiled. 'He was right. I want you, Nel and I'm not prepared to live without you. I know that now.' He wound his fingers into her hair. 'I'll face anything to keep you.' She saw the new confidence and strength in his face as he bent and kissed her on the lips. 'Does he still visit you?'

She did not have to be told who he meant. It was strange that neither of them had given a thought to Malcolm, her husband. She nodded and felt him grow tense. 'I was lonely,' she whispered, 'I couldn't fight him.'

'And you didn't want to.' He was looking deep into her eyes.

'No, I didn't want to, I couldn't. I was torn, but it was as if I were under his spell.'

'And if I'm there, will you still welcome him to your bed?'

She saw the muscles around his jaw tighten imperceptibly as he waited for her answer. Slowly she shook her head. 'You are what I want.'

Neither of them noticed the sudden chill in the room.

IX

Alexander had not returned since Donald had come back into her life. Once, twice, perhaps three times she had imagined she sensed him near her and she had willed him out of her mind, feeling him dwindle and fade, confident that her love for Donald could hold him at bay.

Her physical obsession with Donald of Mar kept her totally enthralled. Somehow they managed to meet often; the custodians of the outlying castles of Fife grew used to seeing their countess and her hitherto infrequent visits became a regular occurrence. She checked the accounts, toured the demesne and after a night or two moved on, riding one or other of her beautiful grey palfreys and followed always by her stately wolfhounds and a minimum of carefully chosen attendants.

If she was often joined by a tall, handsome squire, who attended her with austere silent attention, it was scarcely noticed. Only her own servants knew that at night the squire took their countess to bed and none of them, hand-picked by Hylde and sworn to secrecy on pain of unspeakable and lingering deaths, ever said a word.

She no longer confided in Rhonwen. Rhonwen's eagle eye had at once detected a difference in her mistress on her return to Falkland after that first meeting with Donald at Adam's cave. The old woman cornered her alone. 'What has happened, *cariad*?' Rhonwen fixed her with a coldly analytical stare. 'Where have you been?'

Eleyne returned her gaze unflinchingly. 'I don't think that's any of your business, Rhonwen,' she said, her resentment building. 'I've put you in charge of my nurseries to leave me free to administer the Fife lands. What I do is not your province.'

'But if you are unfaithful to the king, that *is* my province. I have promised to serve him.'

'We have all given our allegiance to the king.' Eleyne wilfully misunderstood her. But her stomach tightened with warning: she had seen that fanatical light in Rhonwen's eye too often before. It spelt danger; danger to Donald and danger to herself. 'Please don't meddle in affairs which do not concern you. You have built something up in your mind which does not exist, something which is not possible.' She raised her hand as Rhonwen opened her mouth to contradict her. 'No, I don't want to discuss it any more. Your province is the nursery and I do not want to find you creeping around my rooms again, do you understand?'

The two women's eyes locked, their friendship and love lost in mutual suspicion and resentment. Eleyne had not spoken to Rhonwen

571

for several days, and then it was to give her curt orders about the running of the nurseries. When she next left the castle, she made sure that Rhonwen did not know where she was going, and she gave Hylde stricter than ever instructions about the secrecy their visits required.

How Donald managed to evade his father and his ever-increasing duties, Eleyne never asked. Sufficient that he was there for her. The infrequency of their meetings, the danger, the inconveniences and sometimes the discomfort added to the excitement. Their lovemaking was passionate beyond anything she had ever dreamed. There was no room for Alexander.

There was no question of marrying Donald, they both knew that. She had toyed with the idea of asking the king to have her marriage to Malcolm annulled; it had after all been bigamous and there should be some way of using that to untie the knots which held her to an unloved husband. Once she had hinted as much to Donald, but he had frowned and looked embarrassed and she realised sadly that she was pushing him too hard. He could see her as a lover, but not as a wife; never as a wife. She had not mentioned the matter again, and nor had he.

X

June 1264

Rhonwen threw the pile of clothes back into the coffer, dropped the lid and turned to the next one. She had been hunting through Eleyne's belongings for several days and still she hadn't found it. The phoenix was missing. She had spotted immediately Eleyne had ceased to wear it, but it wasn't in the jewel casket, nor in the coffer near Eleyne's bed, or under her pillows.

'I'll find it, sire, I'll find it for you!' Rhonwen addressed the air somewhere near the bed curtains. 'She still loves you. She is still yours.' The rain rattled against the window, and a rumble of thunder echoed in the distance.

Eleyne was busy, happy, confident, but Rhonwen's instincts told her that something had changed. Her first thought was that Donald of Mar had returned, but there was no sign of him and Eleyne made no attempts that she could see to arrange any secret meetings. It never crossed her mind that Eleyne would confide in Hylde or Meg and not in her.

She turned back to rummaging through the coffers. If it wasn't here in the bedchamber, she would have to look further afield.

She found the phoenix at last, pulling the small package from the coffer in the solar with a triumphant smile. Why had Eleyne gone to so much trouble to hide it? Unwrapping it, she held it on the palm of her hand; the enamels glowed gently against the dark blue of the silk. It was almost as though she could feel the jewel humming with a life of its own.

She took it back into the bedchamber, and making sure she was alone she closed the door.

'I've found it!' Her whisper was husky with excitement. 'I've found it for you. Now you can reach her, you can come to her again.' She tucked it under the pile of pillows and bolsters and smoothed the coverlet down. She sent a quick darting look around the room, but there was no movement, no sign that anybody heard.

XI

Eleyne tossed uneasily on her bed. The storms had returned and the night was humid. She heard the heavy rain drumming on the roof of the chapel below her window.

She and Donald had planned to meet soon. She was to ride to the Abbey of Balmerino and nearby in one of the summer granges they would be able to spend a day together before returning to their public life. She sighed with longing at the thought of him.

The touch on her shoulder was sudden and very firm. Her eyes flew open and she stared into the darkness as a flash of lightning flickered at the window. She sat up slowly and felt her heart thudding with fear.

'Go away,' she whispered. 'Please.' Another flicker of lightning showed behind the glass, sending eldritch shadows lancing across the room. She pulled the sheet tightly around her. There was no fire: the night was too muggy. In the intervals between the flickers of summer lightning the room was dark as a tomb.

He came in the darkness, his lips commanding, the touch of his hands sure. She could not fight him, he knew her too well. Her body responded, obedient, slavelike, accepting him, opening to him, drugged with the heat of the night and the languor of her dreams. As she drifted into sleep, the perspiration cooling between her breasts, her hair damp on the pillow, there was a smile on her lips and Donald was forgotten.

XII

It was easy to remove the pendant before the maids made the bed in the morning. Whisking it out of sight, Rhonwen tucked it back in its hiding place in the solar. One look at Eleyne's face told her that her ruse had worked. It would be simple to hide it again the following night.

XIII

The huge tithe barn was swept and empty, waiting for the harvest. It was a strange place to meet. Eleyne gazed up at the slanting sunbeams as they pierced its high walls; there was no sign of Donald. She had slipped out of the abbey guesthouse and stood absorbed in the view across the Tay to the blue mountains beyond, then as dusk fell she had made her way into the fragrant darkness rich with the scent of decades of harvested riches.

The slanting sunbeams had long gone when Donald came at last, slipping through the door and leading in his horse before pushing it closed with his shoulder. She watched, her mouth dry with desire as he tied the animal and threw down some hay for it, then she slipped out of the shadows.

His mouth on hers was firm, his arms around her so strong she gasped for breath as he swept her off her feet and carried her into the darkest corner of the building before throwing down his cloak and pulling her to the ground.

They had no warning. The ice-cold wind tore through the barn, whirled the hay into the air and crashed the doors back against the wall. The horse whinnied its terror, backing so hard that its halter snapped. It turned and galloped out into the night.

Donald drew Eleyne to him, trying to pull his wildly flapping cloak around them for shelter, ducking his head against the whirlwind trapped inside the barn, which threatened to tear the great roof beams apart.

'Sweet Christ, Nel, what's happening!' There was a crash as a hay-fork, long forgotten in a corner, flew up into the air and slammed into the ground only inches from him. Donald threw his body on top of her, trying to protect her from the flying debris which filled the air, passion forgotten as the sky above Fife split and sizzled with lightning which forked, split again and buried itself in the soil.

Her face pressed into the earth floor of the barn, Eleyne was trembling like a leaf. 'No, please, leave us alone.' She didn't need the commanding touch of the invisible hand on her head to know that Alexander was there. 'Please, leave us alone.' She did not guess then or later that Rhonwen had sewn a small packet into the heavy train of her mantle which she would remove when Eleyne returned to Falkland.

Donald sat up. She could barely make out his face in the darkness, and she thought he was going to push her away. But his arms enfolded her as he climbed to his feet, helping her up. He glared around and narrowed his eyes against the flying dust.

'Don't think I won't fight you for her!' he yelled into the blackness.

'It's me she wants, *me*! Get back to the hell you came from and leave us in peace!'

Eleyne closed her eyes in terror, clinging to Donald, waiting for some new sign, but the wind had died as swiftly as it had come. The only sound now was the thunder of rain pouring on to the wet ground. The air was full of the sweet scent of the earth.

XIV

Adam's cave was deserted. There were all the signs of his presence – the neatly stowed bed roll, the books, the astrolabe, the bottles and boxes of herbs – but there was no sign of him or his boy. She glanced at the carvings on the walls, with their strange ancient power, then went back to the cave mouth and looked up and down the beach. It had not crossed her mind that he would not be there.

The weather had broken with the storm and a sweet south wind ruffled the waters of the Forth, carrying the heavy scent of the Pentland Hills.

'Good day, my lady.' Adam's voice at her elbow made her jump. He had appeared as silently as a shadow on the path behind her. He saw her pale face, the dark rings under her eyes, the tenseness of her hands as she clutched her cloak, and he frowned. 'Lord Donald is not with you,' he observed quietly.

'No.' She bit her lip, then she held out her hands to him. 'Please, you have to help me!'

Donald had gone. They had planned another meeting, but the shadow of Alexander had been between them as they parted.

'Of course. I am here to help, my lady. Please come in.' He gestured her towards one of the three-legged stools which stood on either side of the rough plank table. There was no sign of the boy who had been with him before.

She sat down, her green eyes fixed on his fathomless dark ones. 'It's the king,' she said.

Adam met her eye steadily. He did not need her to explain which king. 'When a man has loved a woman through all eternity, it's hard for him to let go,' he said with a wry smile. 'You must help him.'

'How? How can I help him?' she cried. 'I'm torn between them, torn between the living and the dead. I love them both, but –' She broke off abruptly.

'But you prefer the living to the dead.' Adam looked at his long brown fingers linked loosely before him on the table. 'And you know your future lies in Mar.'

She nodded.

He walked across to the cave mouth, his shadow long on the sandy floor behind him.

'Your destiny is linked to the royal blood line of Scotland,' he said at last, narrowing his eyes and gazing out across the silver glitter of the water. 'I saw it the first time I met you and Michael saw it before me. Across the centuries you tie the ancient blood of Alba and Albion to the future destiny of this land. Your descendants will one day rule half the world.'

He turned to face her. Silhouetted against the light she could not see his expression. His hair stood out in a wild tangle around his head, highlighted by the sun behind him. 'I have studied the stars and read your fortune a thousand times, Lady Fife, but I can tell you no details beyond that. Which of your children will carry your blood into the future I cannot see. I cannot see if the father is king or earl or commoner. I'm sorry.'

'But you know that my future lies in Mar? Where does my husband come into all this? And my son and his wife who is of bastard royal blood? Alexander's blood.' Eleyne stood up so suddenly that the stool fell over on to the sand.

Adam shook his head. The shadows hung heavily over the house of Fife, that much he had seen, but he had no intention of telling her. 'I can tell you no more,' he said. 'I'm sorry. You must reconcile your royal lover and your earthly one, your husband and your sons and daughters yourself. The gods will guide you to your future. I can't.'

XV

FALKLAND CASTLE ✢ August 1264

King Alexander III had agreed to knight Colban, young though he was, at the persuasion of Sir Alan Durward. At the feast which followed Eleyne sat at Malcolm's side and smiled at her eldest son with enormous pride. He had grown tall – taller now at last than his wife, with whom he was obviously delighted. He had matured too since the birth of Anna's baby. His tutors reported better of him; he had calmed down and no longer fought spitefully with his younger brother. Her eyes moved to Macduff, a serious nine-year-old whose gravity and gentleness belied the warlike future foretold for him.

Beyond her, at the centre of the table, sat young King Alexander, his queen beside him. He had grown very like his father now, and she felt a pang of acute sadness and longing as she looked at him.

She watched him wistfully, detached from the noise which crescendoed around her. The king was laughing; he had raised one of their precious silver goblets and was drinking a toast with Malcolm. The light of hundreds of candles caught and condensed on the bright metal, blinding her for a moment. She blinked, confused as the noise around her ebbed and died, to be replaced by the roar of the sea. She could see the wind catch the king's hair and pull it back from his face, feel the storm tearing at his cloak, see his horse plunge through the rain with a screaming whinny as it reared and began to fall. Confused, she tried to rise, to hold out her hand towards him. She cried out, seeing behind the king the shadow of his father's cloak, his father's hand, then the vision had gone, leaving her shaking like a leaf at the king's side.

'It's all right, my lady, I'm here.' The arms firmly around her shoulders were Rhonwen's. 'Nobody has noticed, *cariad*, nobody saw.' She pressed a goblet of wine into Eleyne's hand, 'Breathe deeply and calm yourself.'

Eleyne was trembling, the tears wet on her face. 'What happened?' She clutched at the wine and sipped it, feeling its warmth flow through her chilled body.

'The Sight was returned to you.' Rhonwen looked at her with compassion. 'The goddess has laid her hand on you again.'

'How can you know –'

'I know, I've seen it happen a hundred times.' Rhonwen bent closer. 'You were looking at the king. Was it his future you saw?'

Eleyne watched the young king as he laughed and joked with her husband. He caught her eye and raised his goblet in a toast then turned away again, the candlelight catching the gems of the coronet he wore.

Slowly Eleyne shook her head. 'I don't remember, I don't remember what I saw.'

The noise had increased. Above the shouts and laughter and roar of conversation she heard the thin music of the harp. Beef had been brought in, and venison, swimming in blood gravy, and the pages were carrying around the wine yet again. Smoke from the candles rose into the high rafters and was lost in the darkness. Beyond the king she saw Sir Alan Durward lean forward, laughing, as was his wife, the king's half-sister, the woman Durward had once tried to have declared Alexander's heir. If that woman should die, and the king and the king's baby son, Anna, her daughter-in-law, could come very close to the throne. Eleyne looked at her and then at Colban, and she put her hand to her aching head. Was this then the way it would go? Was it possible that one day her son's child would be the King of the Scots?

Rhonwen was whispering in her ear. 'My lady, people are looking.' She took Eleyne's hand and chafed it. 'You are too pale, drink some more wine.'

Malcolm had also turned, and looked at his wife sharply. His own face was ruddy from the heat and wine. His pain was better of late and he felt stronger than he had for a long time. 'Are you unwell?'

'Just a little overcome.' Eleyne touched his hand with something like affection. 'This is a great day for us, my husband.'

He grinned. 'Indeed it is.'

A messenger arrived as the final courses of the feast were being carried in. Eleyne, tired, waved them away, watching in detached amusement as heads on the tables below the dais began one by one to fall among the debris of bread and bones, and snores began to mingle with the shouts and laughter and the music. It was then she noticed the man weaving his way between the tables. It was a long time since she had seen the Countess of Lincoln's livery; many years since her niece had deigned to answer her desperate letters about her daughters' welfare. No day passed without her thinking of them; no night without her remembering them in her prayers, but she had long ago given up any real hope of seeing them again.

She watched as he made his way towards her, pushing between the crowded benches. Why after all this time should Margaret of Lincoln send her a message?

When he reached the dais the young man called, 'I seek the Lady Rhonwen.' His eyes met Eleyne's as though aware of her sharp pang of disappointment, then he looked away.

Rhonwen rose from her seat at the foot of the dais and touched his shoulder. Eleyne saw a letter change hands, saw the flash of a coin as Rhonwen directed the man to a place at one of the lower tables where he could eat. She saw the parchment in Rhonwen's hand as she opened it and read. When Rhonwen looked up Eleyne's eyes were on her face. Rhonwen made her way towards the high table.

The letter wasn't from the Countess of Lincoln. One of her ladies, whom Rhonwen had befriended, had taken it upon herself to inform the household of Fife that Eleyne's eldest daughter Joanna, now seventeen years old, had been married in the summer. Her husband was the recently widowed Sir Humphrey de Bohun, heir to the Earl Marshal of England; a man whose son was two years the girl's senior.

The following day Eleyne sent Joanna a wedding gift: a silver casket and a gem-studded chaplet with a letter.

Eight weeks later the gifts were returned. Inside the casket she found her letter cut in two.

Within a year Joanna would be a widow. This time Eleyne did not write.

Eleyne had given orders that her companions be ready to leave at first light. Whatever the destiny foretold for them by Adam, Eleyne and Donald had managed to meet seldom and then only briefly: a few quiet words here, a lightly touched hand there, a glance in the great hall of the king, no more; always the shadow of Alexander was between them.

Donald was constantly in the north, administering his father's earldom, distracted by disputes with his highland neighbours. It was increasingly difficult for him to get away, but as the stranglehold of ice, borne on the east wind, threatened to make Mar impassable he turned his horse south in obedience to her summons. Aching to be with him, Eleyne planned another meeting at Macduff's Castle.

Malcolm was irascible. 'Why go? For pity's sake, woman, it's madness! We don't need to check on anything in this weather, let alone that old place.'

His chest hurt, he was visibly irritated and tired. Their small grandson, normally kept out of his way by his doting nurses, was playing noisily near his feet and he'd had another quarrel with Macduff; his younger son's quietness was now revealing itself as a stubborn arrogance.

It was a long time since Malcolm had spent so much time under the same roof as his wife, and she too had begun to irritate him. The night before he had found himself impotent again. It was her fault — she was old; unattractive. What he needed was a younger woman. And a woman who was faithful. At first he hadn't believed the rumours, but quietly, over the months, he had watched and now he was sure. He didn't know when the affair had started, but by God she wasn't going to make a fool of him any more.

'I have to go.' She pulled on her gloves. 'You don't normally argue about the way I run your estates. Nor do you complain about the results. Your estates are worth nearly £500 each year under my management!'

'I know, I know, I just don't want you to go now.'

'I have to go now.' She was hungry for Donald, a physical yearning which she could not fight.

'I forbid it.' Malcolm stood up and put his hand to his chest, wincing.

'You forbid it?' She stared at him. 'You can't!'

'I can and I do, you are my wife, you will obey me.' His colour was rising. 'Take that brat away!' he said to Duncan's nurses. 'And you, boy,' he yelled at his younger son, 'go and tell them to put your mother's horses away.'

Macduff hesitated.

'Did you hear me?' Malcolm turned on him in a fury. 'I have forbidden your mother to go out. And do you know why? Do you want to know the real reason why?' He turned on her. 'Did you think I didn't know? Did you think I would never find out? All this care for my estates! All this meek, dutiful quartering of the lands of Fife! At every stop your lover is waiting for you with his poems and his kisses!'

He raised his hand as though to strike her, then he turned away. 'You are a whore, madam. You've been a whore all your life; first with the king – while you were still married to Lord Chester, for all I know – then . . .'

'Then with you,' Eleyne's voice cut in like a whiplash. 'You made me a whore, Malcolm, when you married me bigamously. And if Robert hadn't died when he did, I would have been a whore to this day, with your connivance.' She noticed with horror that Macduff was still standing in the room, his face white with shock. Her heart turned over with guilt.

'Go away, please. Your father and I have to talk.'

Macduff ran towards her. 'Please, mama, the whole castle is listening!' Already the boy was conscious of the need to keep silent before the household; the need to keep the rift between his parents hidden. He was nearly in tears. 'Don't quarrel!' Behind him in the body of the hall a dozen people had paused in their tasks to listen.

'Then the whole castle can find out the truth!' Malcolm roared furiously. 'Enough is enough!' He stopped, then staggered a step backwards. A strange look of puzzlement appeared on his face.

'Malcolm?' Eleyne put out her hand. He had clutched at his throat. 'Malcolm, what is it?' He stumbled to his knees and before their appalled eyes fell to the floor and lay still.

'Blessed Bride!' Eleyne was too shocked to move. Then: 'Quickly, Macduff, help your father!' She dropped down beside him, groping for his hand. For a moment Macduff didn't stir, then he turned to the hall. 'Fetch a physician someone,' he cried, his voice shrill with fear. 'And you – two of you – help me carry my father to his bed. Quickly!'

Rhonwen caught Eleyne's cloak as she followed her husband's prostrate body, borne on a trestle top towards the earl's bedchamber. Her eyes were wild. 'So. You lied. All this time you lied!' she spat. 'You have been seeing Donald of Mar; you betrayed your king!'

'I told you a long time ago it was none of your business!' Eleyne snapped.

'It *is* my business, I promised King Alexander –'

Eleyne grabbed Rhonwen's arm and pulled her aside. 'You promised a shadow, a phantom, a creation of your own mind!' she hissed, with a glance at the staring men and women around them. At her side Macduff listened in round-eyed terror, shocked at the outburst. 'He does not exist! He never existed! Donald is real. A real man! And Malcolm is a real man. My husband, who might be dying at this moment . . .'

'And if he is dying, you will be free at last! Free for the king! Free to be with him,' Rhonwen gloated.

Eleyne stared at her in horror, then stepped back sharply, wrenching her cloak from Rhonwen's grasp. 'Do you realise what you are saying? Do you? For me to join the king I'd have to be dead!'

Rhonwen paled, and lifted her eyes to Eleyne's without a word. The two women looked at each other long and hard then Eleyne swung round and ran after the men who were carrying her husband upstairs.

Malcolm was unconscious when Eleyne reached him. The friar at his bedside, a travelling physician who had stopped providentially at Falkland on his way to St Andrews, had his hand on Malcolm's forehead. 'It's a seizure, my lady. There was too much choler in his body.'

Eleyne looked down at her husband. 'Will he live?'

The friar shrugged. 'If he lives the day and the night he may recover, but the moon wanes and the tides are low. That does not augur well.'

She bit her lip. 'Poor Malcolm.' She put her hand on his with a sigh and looked at Macduff. 'Go and find your brother, he should be here. And Macduff –' she smiled at her son sadly, 'tell them to put away the horses. I won't be riding today after all.'

As night fell, candles were lighted in the chamber. Colban and Anna stood beside the bed, with Macduff at its foot. There was antagonism in Anna's gaze as she looked at Eleyne.

Eleyne was seated near her husband's head when he opened his eyes and forced himself to smile.

'So. Will you marry him when I am gone?'

Eleyne shook her head. 'You will get better.'

'No.' He closed his eyes and held out his hand towards her. After a moment's hesitation she took it. 'There is something I should tell you,' he said haltingly. 'Something on my conscience.'

'The priest is here.' In the corner of the room the castle's chaplain waited with the viaticum.

'No, no, I'll confess to him later.' He had difficulty speaking. 'No, there is something I have to confess to you if I am to die easy in my soul.'

'What is it?' It was strange that she felt so little. She had shared this man's bed for nearly fourteen years and learned to accept him; sometimes she even almost liked him, but most of the time he had meant nothing to her at all. She had never loved him; she respected him, and obeyed him. That was all.

'Robert de Quincy – your husband.' Malcolm tried to catch his breath and there was a long silence. When she didn't speak, he struggled on. 'I really thought he was dead when I came for you, then I heard he was still alive. I . . . I had him killed.'

'I see.' Her voice was flat.

'It was your nurse who did it,' he went on. 'She's a killer by instinct.' He gave a faint chuckle. 'A dangerous woman.'

She did not appear to have heard him; her eyes were on Colban's white face.

'Eleyne –' Malcolm went on faintly, 'you do forgive me? I did it for you.'

His fingers slipped from her clasp and she made no effort to take them again. She stood up and looked down at his face for a long moment, then she turned away.

'Eleyne.' He struggled to raise his head. 'Eleyne, please, come back.' His voice broke into sobs.

She stood before the door until one of the weeping servants opened it for her, then she walked down the spiral stairs. She did not look back.

Colban found her in the stables two hours later. The boy's eyes were red with weeping.

'Is it over?'

He nodded.

'And was he shriven by the priest?' Her voice was heavy with bitterness.

Again Colban nodded. 'Mama. Is it true? Am I a bastard?'

Eleyne frowned. Slowly she rose to her feet and put her arms around her son's narrow shoulders. 'No, you are not a bastard. I married your father in good faith . . . twice. And your legitimacy was confirmed by the church, the king and the chancellor of Scotland. You are the Earl of Fife now, Colban, and no one can deny it, though I suppose you will have to wait until you come of age for the king to confirm you in the title.' She gave a weary smile. 'God rest your father's soul. I hope he finds at God's feet the forgiveness he seeks.'

'Why did he marry you?' Colban shuffled his feet uncomfortably.

'Because he loved me.'

'And did you ever love him?' Colban's eyes were full of pain. For a moment she was tempted to lie, but she shook her head.

'No. I never loved him.'

'And did you ever love us?'

'Oh, Colban!' She gave a miserable little laugh. 'Of course I loved you! You made life worth living. You were everything to me. Everything.' She paused. 'When I lost little Joanna and Hawisa, I thought I would die of unhappiness. But then you came along, you and your brother. You mean everything to me, Colban, everything.'

'And Donald of Mar?' His voice had fallen to a whisper.

She sighed. So. Macduff had told him. 'We can't choose who we fall in love with, Colban, it just happens. One minute you're your own person, free and in charge of your own destiny, the next you are enslaved. But it never affected my love for you and Macduff and it never will.' She caught his hands. 'You must believe that. You are married. You know the love of a man and woman for each other is different from the love one feels for one's babies.' She smiled.

'I don't think I love Anna in the way you describe.' His voice was sad.

'You will. You will grow to love her.' Her voice did not betray her sudden misgivings. 'Poor Malcolm. There's such a lot to be done now. Come, let's go in.'

'Mama.' Colban had not moved.

'What is it?'

'Will you go to him?'

She did not pretend not to know what he meant. 'I don't know what will happen,' she said quietly, 'I don't know at all.'

XVII

She let the lid of the coffer drop. It wasn't there; the phoenix had gone. She turned back towards her bedchamber, then stopped. Rhonwen was standing in the doorway. 'Are you looking for something, *cariad*?'

'My embroidered girdle. It isn't in my clothes chest.'

'It's on the bracket where Meg left it. Your eyes must be going, if you couldn't see it.' Rhonwen stepped forward into the light. 'You're not going to wear that, surely, for my lord's funeral?'

The phoenix was already there, beneath the feather bed. Tonight, and every night from now on, Eleyne would have the king to console her.

CHAPTER TWENTY-FOUR

I

FALKLAND CASTLE

Donald arrived at Falkland two weeks after the funeral. Eleyne received him alone in the small solar in the Great Tower. He kissed her hand and looked up at her tired face. 'You know why I'm here.'

Her heart was beating very fast. She found she couldn't speak. She wanted him to touch her so badly, she thought she would throw herself at him. But he had been the one to make it clear that they had no future together, whatever Adam said. Besides, Alexander was there. He was everywhere in the castle, at her side, in her bed; he had been there when Donald had not, stronger all the time. And he was near her. Now.

Donald held out his arms and pulled her to him. His mouth on hers was demanding, as hungry as hers, but after a moment he pushed her away. 'I've come here to ask you to be my wife.'

'Donald.' It was a whisper.

She could feel the anguish in the shadows around her.

'You will, won't you?'

'I thought you would want to marry someone else; I thought you would want to marry someone younger –' Brutally she forced herself to say the word which had tormented her for so long.

'You don't want to –?' Anger and disappointment vied for predominance in his face.

'No, no! I want to, you know I want to, but –' She waved her hand to encompass the walls of the room and through them the rest of the world. 'It would never be allowed.'

'Why not?' He took her hand again and lifted it to his lips. 'I have already spoken to the king; our king; his son.' His voice was harsh.

'You have?' She looked at him in astonishment.

'I went straight to court when I heard of Malcolm's death. Only that would have kept me from you so long.' He smiled. 'The king likes me and he has always loved you. And the queen mother wasn't there to interfere.' His voice was suddenly bitter. 'He said he would do anything to make us happy.'

'And your father?'

'We won't tell my father until it's done. I'm of age. So are you. We are both free. Oh yes, we are. Your ghost won't follow us to Mar and we have the king's approval. What more do we need?' He pulled her once more into his arms.

Rhonwen was waiting for her in her bedchamber, holding something in her hand. Eleyne's eyes went to the open jewel casket on the table. 'I thought I told you not to come to my room!' she said sharply. 'I didn't summon you.'

Rhonwen smiled. 'No, someone else summoned me.' She lifted her hand slightly and Eleyne saw the gleam of gold as the jewelled pendant swung between her fingers. 'Someone else, who doesn't want you to receive Donald of Mar.'

Eleyne spun around. 'Hylde, Meg, leave us alone,' she ordered. They did not wait. They scuttled away, closing the door behind them.

Eleyne turned back to Rhonwen. 'Put that pendant down.'

'Why?' Rhonwen smiled again.

'Because I say so. Put it back in the casket.'

'It brings him to you, doesn't it?' Rhonwen held the jewel up to the light. Her eyes narrowed. 'Why don't we try it now? Why don't we call him and ask him what he thinks about Donald of Mar coming here to Falkland? Why don't we call him –'

'*No!*' Eleyne cried. 'I forbid it.'

'You forbid me to call him? But you said he was nothing but a dream. If he was only a dream, how can I call him?' Rhonwen moved swiftly behind the table, still holding the phoenix aloft. 'Come!' she cried out loud. 'Come, your grace, come to her now. If you don't, it will be too late. Donald of Mar will take her . . .'

'It's already too late,' Eleyne said softly. 'I have promised to marry Donald.'

Rhonwen stopped in mid-sentence and her mouth fell open. 'You have done what?'

'I have promised to marry Donald of Mar.' Eleyne leaned across the table and snatched the pendant from Rhonwen's slack fingers. For a moment she stood looking at it, then she threw it down into the casket and slammed the lid on top of it. 'Alexander is dead, Rhonwen! I am alive! We can be nothing to each other any more. I shall always treasure his memory. I shall always love him in my heart, but he is dead and gone. Donald is alive. I love *him*, I want to marry *him*. For the first time in my life I have the chance to live with someone I love and trust. Would you deny me that?' She took Rhonwen's cold fingers between her own. 'Please, give me your blessing.' Desperately she willed Rhonwen to understand.

There was a long silence. Slowly Rhonwen extricated her hands from Eleyne's. 'I can't,' she whispered.

'Why?'

'You belong to King Alexander. Einion Gweledydd foretold it –'

'Einion's prophecies were false.'

'No!'

'They were. Listen, you have seen Adam and you remember Michael, his master. They foretold the future for me too. They both said my future lay in Mar. If I am to found a royal dynasty, it is through Colban and Anna. She is King Alexander's grand-daughter –'

'Her mother was a bastard –' Rhonwen spat the words out furiously.

'Sir Alan Durward has great ambitions for his daughter, nevertheless. Please, Rhonwen, forget Einion Gweledydd. Think of me.'

'I am thinking of you, *cariad*.' Rhonwen folded her arms grimly into the sleeves of her mantle and drew herself up to her full height. 'You should have been a queen.'

'I shall be a countess again when Donald inherits from his father. That is sufficient glory for me.' Eleyne smiled pleadingly. 'Rhonwen. I cannot be the consort of a dead man.'

Rhonwen shook her head slowly. 'Call him. Explain it to him. See what the king thinks. Go on.' The old woman's eyes were blazing again. She swept towards the fire and fumbling in the scrip attached to her girdle she produced a handful of crushed herbs. 'You see, I carry them with me. I have them always in case he needs me – the magic herbs to summon the spirits.'

'No!' Eleyne cried. 'No, I forbid it!'

'You forbid your king, *cariad*? That is treason!' She raised her hand and flung the handful of dusty twigs on to the smouldering logs. They crackled and spat and gave off an acrid sulphurous smell which filled the room.

'You silly old fool!' Eleyne cried in despair. 'It won't work!'

But it was working. She could feel him approaching. The room was growing cold. She could feel his anger and his despair like a blanket across the air. She looked round frantically: 'Go away! Please, go away! I love Donald. I'm going to marry him. Please, go away!'

The candles on the table began to stream in trails of smoke as the window shutters rattled. Outside, a pall of sleet swept across the countryside, blotting out the sky.

Rhonwen dropped to her knees, her face lit by a triumphant smile. 'He's coming. He's coming for you. You belong to him, *cariad*. You won't escape him. Not now you are free!'

'Sweet Holy Mother!' Eleyne's veil was torn from her hair as the wind roared in the window and the shutter crashed to the floor. She spun round protecting her face with her arms as the candles blew out, showering hot wax across the table. In the hearth the fire flared up angrily, sucked up the high chimney as the wind whirled westwards across the hills.

II

She could not bring herself to throw the phoenix into the well. For a long time she stood, the jewel in her hand, contemplating the circle of black water so far below. The cold enamel, the rubies, the ice-blue sapphires would be no danger in the water and her link with Alexander would be gone forever. He was there at her side. She could feel him pleading. Her eyes filled with tears.

'Please, let me go, my love,' she whispered into the darkness of the well chamber. 'Don't begrudge me happiness with Donald. Let me go to him.'

She stretched out her hand. The chain hung glinting from her fingers over the water for a moment, then abruptly she withdrew it. She couldn't bring herself to drop it, but she would hide it where it would never be found and once she had left Falkland she would leave Alexander behind.

She wrapped the pendant in its piece of silk and, turning in a whirl of skirts, she ran back to the stair. On the second floor of the Great Tower she ran into the small private chapel next to the earl's bedroom. It was very dark and the air was heavy with incense. Only one small candle burned before the statue of Our Lady. She moved hesitantly towards the altar.

Wedging the small package behind the reredos she pushed it down as far as she could reach, then she stepped back and murmured a quick prayer. Crossing herself, she ran from the incense-rich gloom.

Rhonwen stepped quickly back out of sight. Later she would break the habit of a lifetime and enter the chapel. Later, when the king commanded it. Until then the phoenix was safe where it was.

III

Shrove Tuesday 1266

They married secretly. The King and Queen of Scots witnessed their wedding at Kinross whilst obligingly ensuring that the Earl and Countess of Mar were at Roxburgh, and Donald and Eleyne rode north towards Mar the same afternoon. Snow was falling and the tracks were treacherous but they were both too happy to notice. Wagonloads of Eleyne's possessions would follow them north as soon as the snows melted, together with some of her horses. The dogs were at her heels.

She had bidden a tearful farewell to Colban and Macduff and her little grandson, Duncan. 'I'll come back and see you all very soon,' and she hugged each in turn. Her farewell to Anna was a little more restrained. Her daughter-in-law had begun to treat her with a reserve that bordered on antipathy and Eleyne had the feeling the girl was glad to see her go. Eleyne had ordered Rhonwen to stay at Falkland to look after the nurseries. Both Malcolm's sons had been made royal wards on his death, but the king had promised that Eleyne would remain their guardian.

'Just give Donald and me a little time together,' she whispered to her eldest son. 'Just a little time, then I'll come back to you.'

IV
KILDRUMMY CASTLE, MAR ❖ Lent 1266

Kildrummy Castle lay huge and squat in the broad valley of the Don. Snow had swept the landscape of mountains and broad river valley, moorland and forest to a uniform whiteness and the towers and walls were frosted with crystals which glittered in the sunlight. Eleyne reined in with an exclamation of delight. 'It looks as though it's built from snow! A snow tower in a snowy land. It's lovely.'

Donald grinned at her. Swathed in white furs, riding a white horse, she looked like a snow princess.

He took Eleyne at once to their circular bedchamber. A huge fire had been lighted in the hearth and a dozen candles burned in the sconces as he unfastened her cloak and threw it down. Laughing, blowing on his frozen fingers to warm them, he undressed her and pulled her on to the bed. 'At last!' He kissed her eyes and nose and ears. 'You are mine at last. And no one, ever, can take you away from me!' His hands on her breasts were cold and she caught her breath and squealed like a girl as he flung himself on to her with a cry of triumph and pressed his mouth over hers.

For the next two weeks, to the vast amusement of the Kildrummy household, they were very seldom out of bed. The servants, giggling, brought them food and wine on huge trays and kept the fires and candles alight, vainly trying not to look at the drawn bed curtains or hear the stifled laughter from behind them.

V

19 March 1266

It was on St Joseph's Day – a beautiful day which presaged, according to the legend, a fertile year and a lucky life to any born on it – that the Earl and Countess of Mar arrived home.

A frantic knocking on the chamber door alerted the newlyweds. As Donald pushed Eleyne reluctantly from him, Hugh Leslie, the earl's steward, entered the room. A small earnest conscientious man in his fifties, his face was pale and he was gesturing frantically behind him.

William and Elizabeth stood in the doorway; both still wore their travelling cloaks. The snow crystals clung for a moment then melted in the heat of the fire.

Donald had barely had time to pull on his tunic and run his fingers through his hair before he faced his father defiantly. 'Could you not wait to greet us downstairs, father? Were you so eager you had to come to our bedroom?'

'Is it true?' William was apoplectic with rage. 'Is it true that you are married?' His pale eyes strayed to Eleyne, who knelt on the bed only half covered by a sheet, her hair tangled and wild down her back. The distaste in his face was plain to see.

'Yes, it's true.' Donald tried to keep the defensiveness out of his voice. 'Lady Fife has done me the great honour of becoming my wife, with the blessing of the king and queen.'

'Sweet Jesus!' Elizabeth of Mar's voice was harsh. 'Do you know what you have done?'

'Yes, mama.' Donald was keeping his tone even with great difficulty. 'I have married the most beautiful woman in the world.'

'Indeed.' Elizabeth's cold sarcasm was cutting. 'A woman who runs from bed to bed like a bitch in heat. A woman who was already married before I – your own mother! – was born! You have married yourself, you stupid boy, to a woman who is probably past the age of childbearing! Sweet Blessed Virgin, did you not think of that? Are you so besotted by her flesh that you did not think of your duty to the earldom?'

Donald had blushed scarlet. 'Mama, how dare you! Please leave this room, both of you.' He walked back to the bed and sitting down put his arm around Eleyne's shoulders. She was still kneeling on the sheets, white-faced and speechless with shock. He turned back to his parents. 'You will apologise to my wife, both of you, or we will leave this castle and never return.'

William said, 'It is for you, Donald, to think of apologies. You have destroyed this family. And by your careless selfishness, you have caused Lady Fife this embarrassment. You would do well to apologise to her and then to us.'

Turning on his heel he walked out, but his wife did not immediately follow. The sister of the Earl of Buchan, Elizabeth Comyn was a formidable woman. Her dark eyes were black pebbles in her aquiline face as she glared at Eleyne for several long seconds, then she too turned away. Her cloak trailed melted snow on to the dried heather floor covering as she walked from the room, followed by an acutely uncomfortable Hugh Leslie, who closed the door softly behind him.

'Get dressed.' Donald stood up. His hands were shaking with anger.

'What are you going to do?'

'We are leaving.'

She shook her head. 'If we do that, they will have won.'

He was astonished. 'You want to confront them again after that?'

'No, I never want to see them again, but I will. You and I will sit with them at the high table tonight and we will show them we are too happy and too strong to be beaten by their prejudice.' Dropping the sheet, she climbed off the bed.

Donald's eyes strayed down her body and she tensed as she saw his slight frown.

'It's not true, Donald,' she whispered. 'I'm not too old to bear your children.' She put her arms around his neck and pressed herself against him, swaying slightly. 'I'll bear you a dozen sons, my love,' she crooned.

He smiled, and kissed her.

'Half that number will do,' he whispered and he laughed. 'How you shock them, my poor darling. Why is it that they hate you so?'

'Your father has always hated me,' Eleyne said sadly. Pushing him away she pulled the sheet around her shoulders and walked over to the fire. 'And he always will. You must accept that.'

He scowled. 'I'll never accept it . . . and I shall tell him so.'

It was the first time Donald and Eleyne had appeared in William's newly built great hall since their arrival, but Eleyne did not look at the roof with its ornately carved beams, or at the two huge fireplaces built of stone. Her eyes were fixed on the high table. She had taken the greatest trouble with her hair and gown. Around her neck she wore the carved silver horse Donald had given her and on her fingers she wore his rings.

The Mars greeted them coldly as they took their places.

'You may as well know, father, that Eleyne and I intend to live at Falkland Castle,' Donald said as the first courses of food were carried in. 'I do not want my wife to live in a household where she is insulted.'

Elizabeth put down her knife. 'I'm afraid you are going to be disappointed, Donald. Sir Alan and Lady Durward have moved into Falkland for the time being, to be with their daughter and grandson. Sir Alan does not seem to approve of your marriage any more than we do.' She gave a harsh laugh. 'I believe he has declared that your wife will return only over his dead body.'

Donald gritted his teeth. 'I am sure that can be arranged . . .'

'Don't be a fool, boy.' William took a huge helping of pike stewed in fish liquor and then turned to eye the oysters on their bed of ginger and saffron. 'You can stay here, both of you. Out of harm's way. We'll be going back south within a few days if the roads stay open, and I'll leave you to manage the earldom.'

'William!' Elizabeth burst out. 'You can't allow this!'

'There's nothing to be done, Elizabeth.' William sighed and picked up his spoon. 'The marriage is legal and the king has given it his blessing. There is nothing to be done.'

'There is nothing to be done!' Donald echoed later in a gruff imitation of his father's tone. He burst into laughter. 'Of course there's nothing to be done and they know it.' He pulled Eleyne into his arms. 'Oh, my love, I'm so sorry they came and said such awful things, but we won't let them spoil it. Once they're gone, Kildrummy will be our own kingdom again.'

They were gone within two days and Eleyne breathed a sigh of relief. Slowly they toured the castle and Donald introduced her to the vast household. Some of them were suspicious, some amused, but most were friendly. She chose two girls, Agnes and Bethoc, to join Meg as her personal maidens and she and Donald moved into the earl's chamber, a large room with arched windows on the first floor of what was already being called the Snow Tower.

Slowly the spring grew warmer. There was no word from the south. The earl and countess were with the Scottish court; in Fife, in spite of Eleyne's anxious letters, Rhonwen remained obstinately silent. Still obsessed with Donald and their life together Eleyne kept her worries about the boys at bay just as she refused to face the other problem which haunted her.

She was not yet pregnant. Never in all the years of their illicit lovemaking had she become pregnant and she had borne no children for nine years. Elizabeth's cruel comments had cut her to the quick and she brooded on them constantly. Was it true? Was she too old to give Donald the heir he must have?

Secretly she cast her horoscope. It spoke of many children and in disgust she swept her charts aside. The stars mocked her. She looked, cautiously at first, then more anxiously, into the flames. There were no pictures there.

Also in secret she stood beside the bed, staring down at her naked figure. She had no way of knowing how she looked. Donald still took enormous delight in her body, but did he also notice the slight slackening of her skin, the little wrinkles at the corners of her eyes, the streaks of silver in her hair which had broadened over the years?

She took Meg into her confidence and between them in the stillroom they made up a soft balm scented with rose petals which she rubbed on her skin to keep it soft. Donald noticed the smell at once. He buried his face between her breasts and threatened never to leave her bed again.

VI

FALKLAND CASTLE ❖ July 1266

The king had given them time enough. Rhonwen felt him growing restless. Twice she thought she saw him, shadowy on the turnpike stair above her – reproachful, angry that she had done nothing to bring Eleyne back to him. Afraid, she began to form a plan.

She stood for a long time at the door of the chapel. It was dark. The castle was asleep, but one candle burned before the statue of Our Lady, replaced and trimmed before the priest had gone to his bed. Rhonwen could feel the prickle of fear on the back of her neck, and peered at the altar. It was somewhere at the back that Eleyne had hidden the pendant. She had to break the taboo; she had to enter this chapel of the priests, but what would happen to her if she laid a hand on the fabric of this holy place? Her fingers went automatically to the amulet at her throat.

With a muttered prayer to the goddess of her Welsh mountains, she took two tiptoed steps inside the door and held her breath. The small chapel smelt of cold incense; it was impregnated in the stones of the walls and in the air around her. Her heart beating very fast she crept towards the altar and, her back to the wall, her eyes fixed on the crucifix between the candles, she made her way towards the eastern wall.

Reaching the reredos at last, she felt behind it. Sweat dripped into her eyes. She was breathing audibly through her mouth. Blessed Bride, she couldn't feel it. There was nothing there. She pushed harder, trying to wedge her whole arm behind the carved oak panel.

The candle flame flickered. A few drops of pale wax spattered on the shelf before the statue and a trail of smoke spiralled into the air. The shadow in the corner of the chapel behind the faldstool was no more than smoke itself. Rhonwen's hands were shaking violently.

Driven by panic to one last effort, she pushed again, groping in the emptiness with desperate fingers, and suddenly she touched something soft. The sensation was so unexpected that she let out a whimper of fright. Then she remembered. Eleyne had always wrapped the pendant. Cautiously she hooked her fingers into the object again in the darkness and slowly, carefully, she managed to draw the wisp of silk towards her.

VII

KILDRUMMY

Sometimes they rode together, exploring the neighbourhood, and sometimes, when Donald was occupied with the affairs of the earldom, Eleyne rode alone, realising how much she had missed her solitary rides with only the dogs for company. Gradually she extended her range, beyond the crofts and the tofts around the township and up the broad river valley, following the meandering course of the River Don and into the mountains beyond, feeling immediately at home, although these mountains were unlike those of Eryri. These were rounded shoulders, humped massively from the great backbone of the Grampians beneath a vast north-eastern sky.

It was here, in a lonely glen where she had ridden with only the dogs for escort, that she met Morna. The woman was gathering flowers by the river as Eleyne stopped to let her horse drink. She straightened to look at Eleyne, her face solemn, her eyes direct, showing no shyness as the Master of Mar's wife slid from her saddle. The two women looked at each other with the strange empathy that brings immediate liking, though neither had spoken a word.

Eleyne smiled. 'Good day, mistress.' The woman, whom Eleyne judged to be only a little younger than herself, was heavily pregnant.

She nodded gravely in return. 'You'll be wanting a drink too, perhaps.' Her voice was low and musical. She glanced at the horse and Raoulet and Sabina, and Sabina's son, Piers, as the animals drank greedily from the cool brown water. There was no need to ask who her visitor was. Word of Lord Donald's wife, with her silks and velvets, riding her horse unescorted like a man, followed by the three great hounds, had spread for miles around.

'I can drink with them.' Eleyne dropped the horse's rein and pushed up the sleeves of her gown.

The other woman smiled. 'I have something you might prefer: there's blaeberry wine in my house if you would care to follow me, my lady.' She set off without looking back, the withy basket full of flowers on her arm.

Her house, set back from the shingle bank of the river, on the side of a small hill, was a small stone-built bothy, roofed with turves. She led the way inside and gestured Eleyne to sit on the rug-covered heap of heather which served as a bed. The place was spotless, swept with a heather besom which stood against the wall, furnished sparingly with a rough oak coffer, a girnel kist, a table and two stools and by the fire a polished bannock stone. The cup in which she offered the wine was a finely chased silver. Eleyne took it without comment. Such was the woman's dignity it did not occur to her that it was out of place in such a poor hut, and that it might be stolen. She sipped the wine and smiled. 'This is good.'

'Aye.' The woman nodded. 'It's the best you'll taste in Mar.' Her hand to her back, she sat down gracefully on the floor, her ragged checked skirts swirling in the dust of the dry earth floor.

'Is your husband a shepherd?' Eleyne looked around the hut.

'I've no husband, lady. I prefer my own company. The bairn –' The woman put her hand on her stomach with a possessive gesture of affection. 'Well, maybe she's a child of the fairies.' She gave a humorous scowl, and shook her head in mock despair. 'I'm Morna, my lady. I'm the spaewife, or so the cottars call me.'

'I see.' Eleyne smiled. 'Yes. I've heard about you. The people of the castle think very highly of your powers.'

She was much loved, this Morna of the glens. Eleyne had heard her name repeated often with tales of healing and magic and love spells. She leaned forward and set her cup down on the ground before her. 'Perhaps you could help me.'

'You want to know your fortune?' The woman sounded incredulous. 'Usually the lasses come out to me to know the name of the lad they'll marry. You already have your husband.'

'But will I give him a son?' Eleyne wasn't aware how desperate she sounded until the words were out.

The woman leaned forward and took Eleyne's hands in hers. She turned them palm up and looked at them. The only sound in the bothy was the high trickling song of the skylark, lost in the brilliance of the sky above the glen, and the small murmur of the river outside. Eleyne found she was holding her breath. Her hands grew hot in the woman's cool grasp. When at last Morna looked up, she was smiling. 'You will give your husband three sons.'

'Three!' Eleyne echoed in astonishment. She laughed, half in disbelief, half in delight. 'I had suspected I was past the age of childbearing. I still have my courses, but it's nine years since I conceived. If you are right, I shall be the happiest woman in the world.'

'I hope so, lady.'

'When? Can you see when it will happen?'

The other woman nodded. 'You already carry your first son.'

Eleyne stood up. She walked outside the small house and stood staring down towards the river numb with shock.

Morna followed her. 'Why do you ask me all this? You have the Sight yourself.'

Eleyne shook her head. 'I see other things: visions of the past and of the future, but never for myself. I've tried to learn, but I can never understand; never see clearly.'

'Perhaps you try too hard.' Morna folded her arms across her stomach. 'You have lived too long in the castles and courts of the south. If you want to see, the mountains of Mar will teach you. All you have to do is listen and watch with stillness in your heart.'

VIII

It was another six weeks before Eleyne was sure in her own mind. Only then did she tell Donald. Solemnly he undressed her and kneeling before her he kissed her stomach. Then he gave her a twisted rope of sea pearls.

'Don't tell your parents, Donald.' Suddenly she was afraid.

'Why?' He pulled her on to his knees, 'They'll be delighted.'

'Suppose something goes wrong?'

'It won't.' He touched her belly again, gently stroking it, 'Nothing could go wrong now.'

It was an idyllic time. The long summer drowsed over the hills. She and Donald made love as often as before, though he was more careful with her now, watching in wonder as her breasts and belly grew. Sometimes they rode together into the hills and he would undress her there, on his cloak, spread on the heather amongst the wild marjoram by the burns, surrounded by clouds of butterflies.

She would still ride out alone though not so far now. More often than not she went to visit Morna, taking gifts for the woman and her coming baby, and they would talk for a long time, companionably, sitting by the babbling river or, if the soft highland rain poured down, by Morna's fire. Morna's knowledge of the magic of the hills was vast; Eleyne found herself listening enthralled to her hostess's tales, and then almost without realising it she was talking too, about Einion and his prophecies, and about Alexander.

She still feared sometimes that he would return, suddenly while she and Donald were together. But it had not happened; he had not come to Kildrummy.

'Perhaps he could not follow me here,' she said softly. 'Perhaps he has forgotten me at last.'

Morna was watching her closely. 'If his love was as great and as deep as you say, he will never forget you,' she said slowly. 'He will love you through all eternity and through all ages.'

Eleyne was silent.

'Did you love him as much?' Morna asked.

Eleyne nodded. 'He was everything to me, but he turned his back on me. If he had really wanted, he could have had me as his wife, but he chose not to. He chose not to make our sons legitimate. He put Scotland's honour before mine.' She considered for a minute. 'Malcolm of Fife killed so that he could have me as his wife. Does that not make his love the greater?'

'Do you measure love in bloodshed and honour?' Morna's voice was sharp. 'Has Malcolm returned from the grave to make you his own again? Would Lord Donald?' She was stern. 'Has not the king crossed the greatest boundary there is, for you?'

'You sound as though you would make me choose between Donald and a dead man,' Eleyne replied, 'and there is no choice, not for me.'

'Perhaps it is not up to you – one day the gods will decide: ghost or mortal; king or man.'

Eleyne went white. 'There is no choice,' she repeated. 'Donald is my husband. You are frightening me.'

Morna was apologetic. 'I didn't mean to do that. Of course Donald is your husband and you belong to him. Perhaps the prophecy your Einion spoke of will yet be fulfilled. You have four children and another on the way. One of them may be a king or the father of kings.'

'Can't you see?' Eleyne sat forward.

'I have no powers like that. I see who is to fall in love with whom, in the hills; I look into a woman's wame and see how many bairns she is to carry. I don't see people's destiny; I don't see their deaths.' Morna touched Eleyne's hand. 'Forget your king; forget the past. Live now, for the present, for your child, and be happy.' She smiled fondly. 'Now, go back to your lord. He is waiting for you full of anxiety because you have ridden out alone and he dares not reprimand you.' She laughed.

Donald and Eleyne rode back to Kildrummy late on a hot August evening when they had been alone together in the hills. Donald had taken her on his horse before him and held her in his arms, Eleyne's palfrey following loose behind them. They rode back along the slow Don, made shallow by the hot summer, past the lonely monastery of Cabrach, its stone buildings dozing in the late summer's warmth, and turned in at last under the gatehouse and into the courtyard of the castle. It was crowded with horses and wagons and milling crowds of people.

Donald reined in his horse and looked around, his heart sinking. 'My mother!'

'Oh no.' Eleyne turned in his arms, appalled.

'It is. See, her standard, and the carts bear her coat-of-arms.' He slipped from the horse and lifted Eleyne down.

'You told her about the baby!' she said accusingly.

'I didn't, my love, but you can't expect people to keep it a secret forever.' He looked fondly at her thickening waistline. 'Come, let's find out what she wants.'

The Countess of Mar was in the great hall. She wore a cloak and gloves in spite of the heat of the evening, and stared in horror at the sight of her daughter-in-law's loosely knotted hair and tanned face and arms.

'So, it's true.' Her eyes travelled down to Eleyne's belly. 'You do carry my son's child. I can see it's just as well that I came.' She turned to Donald. 'I hear you have been using the earl's chamber. Please give orders for it to be cleared for me. You and your wife can sleep elsewhere. I suggest, madam,' she addressed Eleyne, 'that you dress yourself decently and cover your hair. I cannot imagine what my household think of you. I hear, Donald,' she swept on, 'that you have been neglecting the running of the estates, just as you have been neglecting the affairs of the kingdom. Now I am here, you can turn your attention back to both. I shall look after your wife.'

Eleyne could not believe Donald would allow his mother to speak to him like that, but he said nothing. Sheepishly he asked, 'You won't mind moving to another chamber, my love?'

'Of course not,' she said as coolly as she could. 'I shall give orders at once. Please, excuse me, Lady Mar. As you say, I need to change my gown.'

She bowed to Elizabeth and walked from the great hall. Donald did not follow her.

'No one forbids me to ride, Lady Mar,' Eleyne said coldly to her mother-in-law who had walked into the bedchamber the following morning and dismissed Eleyne's servants from the room.

'Then you should forbid yourself, madam.' Elizabeth sat on the chair near the hearth. 'If you value your child's life. Surely I need not point out to you that at your age it is scarcely suitable to be galloping around the country in your condition. You should rest.'

'I do not need to rest.' Eleyne reined in her temper with difficulty. 'I am accustomed to riding and I assure you it will not harm me. I rode in all my pregnancies until the week of my delivery.'

'And you lost two children, as I recall.' Lady Mar looked her in the eye.

Eleyne blanched. 'Neither died as a result of my riding I assure you.' She changed the subject. 'Do you intend to stay at Kildrummy long?'

'It is my home. I intend to live here, and to run the estates.' Elizabeth's eyes gleamed with triumph. 'You may have been accustomed to running the Fife lands, madam, and you may have learned to expect your own way, but here from now on things will be very different, I think you will find. You are not the mistress of these lands or this castle; I am. Here, you are nothing but the wife of the heir.'

CHAPTER TWENTY-FIVE

I

FALKLAND CASTLE ❖ Summer 1266

Colban sat at his father's desk looking blankly down at the empty area of oak in front of him. 'All you have to do is give the order, boy,' Sir Alan Durward had said. 'Do it now.' He had walked from the room, leaving Colban staring unhappily at the servant standing just inside the door. Colban cleared his throat and took a deep breath. 'Please. Fetch the Lady Rhonwen here,' he said. His voice slid and squeaked uncomfortably from tenor to falsetto and the servant, hiding a smile, bowed and turned away.

Still upright, still slim, her hair white beneath her coif, Rhonwen entered slowly. She was, she calculated, in her sixty-sixth summer, like the century.

Seeing Colban standing so formally behind the desk, she smiled to herself. He had done well in his efforts to step into his father's shoes. He missed Lord Fife and she knew he had been devastated by what he saw as his mother's defection, but he had not showed it. He had turned his attention to Anna and to his son and concentrated on learning how to run the Fife estates. If he resented the overbearing interference of his father-in-law, he gave no sign.

'You sent for me, my lord?'

He nodded and she saw him swallow nervously. 'Lady Rhonwen, I'm sorry, but Sir Alan and Lady Durward feel – that is, I feel – that it's time someone a little younger ran the nurseries here.' She could see the sweat breaking out on his upper lip. 'I shall of course give you a pension. And I shall always love you –' that bit was not part of the speech he had prepared and he blushed unhappily – 'but I think it's better if you go.'

Rhonwen was not surprised. One by one Eleyne's personal servants and companions had been demoted and sent to remote castles in the earldom. It had only been a matter of time.

As it happened the decision suited her plans very well. 'I'm glad you told me yourself, *cariad bach*. I shall be sad not to see to the growing up of little Duncan and I shall miss you and your brother, but, as you say, I am growing old.' She shook her head ruefully.

599

'What will you do, Rhonwen?' Suddenly he was a boy again. He ran round the desk and took her hand.

'Why, I shall go to your mother, of course. She'll look after me.'

'My mother.' Colban turned away, shoulders stiffening, his eyes unhappy. 'She has forgotten us; she never writes to us.'

'She hasn't forgotten you.' Rhonwen's voice was gentle. 'Have you ever wondered if perhaps her letters don't reach you?' Surely the boy could see that Durward would never willingly let Eleyne contact her sons. 'Remember how she loves Joanna and Hawisa, even though they determined to shut her out of their lives. Don't ever do that to her, Colban.' She reached out and touched his shoulder, feeling the unhappiness in the boy's rigidity. 'You'll be your own master soon, *cariad*, then you can visit her as often as you like and you'll see she still loves you.'

'But why did she go with Donald of Mar so quickly?' He looked bewildered. 'Why didn't she wait and say goodbye properly?'

Rhonwen knew the answer to that. She had fled because otherwise she would not have had the strength to fight Alexander. 'She went quickly because too many people wanted to stop her marrying. If she had waited they would have succeeded, and your mother thought that would make her unhappy.'

'And is she happy now?'

'I don't know.' Her fixed smile betrayed her true feelings. 'I hope so.'

II

KILDRUMMY CASTLE ❖ August 1266

Elizabeth of Mar summoned her son to her side whilst Eleyne was out visiting Morna. 'You are happy with your wife, Donald?' she asked doubtfully.

Donald stiffened. 'You know I am. Eleyne is the most wonderful thing that has ever happened to me.' He straightened his shoulders, unconsciously preparing for the attack he knew to be coming. His mother always made him feel like an unruly child and he hated her for it.

Elizabeth could read her son like a book. She concealed a smile as she seated herself on the chair nearest the fire. 'Perhaps your father and I were wrong to try to put you off marrying her. For all her age, she seems a healthy woman and she has brought a good terce to the marriage as her dower from Fife. Her ladies tell me she carries the child with ease.' She paused. 'Because of that you do not seem to have realised just how delicate a woman in her condition is.' She watched

600

him mockingly. 'I am sure she is anxious to please you in every way she knows, but for her sake you must leave her alone. I am surprised that you have not realised that yourself. You cannot continue to share her bed.'

'That is none of your business –'

'I think it is. Obviously she hasn't the strength or the wit to tell you this herself, so I have to do it for her. It is customary for a man to leave his wife alone in the later stages of pregnancy. Amuse yourself elsewhere. Bed that pretty red-haired wench who eyes you constantly in the hall. Your wife will understand. All she will ask is that you do it discreetly. She will be nothing but relieved that you have freed her from what must be a dreadful ordeal for her.' She paused. 'What you have been doing, Donald, is a mortal sin.' She hissed the word at him without warning and was gratified to see him flinch as though she had struck him.

Donald's face was white, then slowly it blushed to a deep crimson. 'I never thought.'

'Men never do.' She watched him with grim satisfaction. Once she had weaned him from his wife's bed, his infatuation would be doomed. It was too late to annul the marriage and the child might yet be a boy, but at least she would have the satisfaction of being proved right. Her son would realise what a terrible mistake he had made.

III

Morna's baby arrived at dawn on Lammas Day. She delivered the girl-child herself neatly and efficiently and alone, then wrapped her in the lacy shawl Eleyne had brought the week before. She called her Mairi and when Eleyne came – no longer alone: for the sake of peace and quiet at home she brought one of her ladies with her now – the baby was sleeping peacefully in a woven reed cradle. Eleyne bent over the child and smiled. Then her smile faltered. Just for a moment in the shadows of the cottage she thought she had seen flames licking around the cradle. She put out her hand as if to snatch the baby up, but the flames had gone. Morna had not seen what had happened. 'Blessed Virgin; Sweet Bride, protect you,' she murmured soundlessly. Perhaps it was her own birth she had seen, no more – an image which had floated up from the past. Though the August day was airless and muggy, she had begun to shiver.

Morna came up behind her and stared past her at the child. 'It'll be your turn soon,' she said softly. 'And yours will be a boy.'

September 1266

Eleyne sat on the edge of the high bed and watched as Agnes and Bethoc hung her gown on a bracket on the wall, put away her shoes and readied the room for the night. It was the tenth night that Donald had not appeared. Her back ached and she felt heavy and ill and bored, cut off from the world by her condition and the very remoteness of Mar, which before she had loved. She looked down at the bulk of her stomach and groaned.

She could no longer pretend to herself that Donald found her attractive. Now that her belly had grown, he had drawn away, no longer pulling off her clothes to kiss her stomach, no longer touching her at all, no longer sharing her bed. Overwhelmed by misery and loneliness, she turned away so that her ladies could not see her tears.

'Agnes,' she asked, 'will you fetch me a posset? It will help me to sleep.'

She had lost him. He had gone. Her bed was empty and cold. Agnes nodded sypathetically. 'I'll fetch it at once, my lady.'

Dismissing Meg and Bethoc, Eleyne leaned against the pillows. She was feeling strangely uneasy. Her head ached and her eyes were tired. She glanced towards the narrow lancet windows. West-facing they had seen the last of the stormy sun sink into a black pall of cloud.

Alexander.

It was many weeks since she had thought of him, but suddenly she found herself longing for his presence. She was lonely for him, lost without either of the men she loved.

When Agnes returned, she was not alone to Eleyne's astonishment; Rhonwen was with her.

Eleyne stared at the old woman for a full minute in complete silence, then she levered herself off the bed. She understood now why her thoughts had returned to Alexander and she felt a momentary wave of panic sweep over her.

'You're pasty-faced, *cariad*, and your eyes are puffy. What have you been doing to yourself?'

'You can see what I have been doing!' Eleyne moved awkwardly to a stool and sat down. 'Why have you come to Kildrummy? I did not send for you.' She did not want Rhonwen here. She did not want the fear and the suspicion and the dread.

Rhonwen sat down near her. She was exhausted after her long journey, accompanied by two servants and three armed men. Her worldly possessions had been loaded on two packmules. 'Sir Alan forced your son to send me away. He wants no friends of yours left at Falkland.'

'I see.' Eleyne looked at her thoughtfully. 'And are you my friend?'

Rhonwen looked despairing. 'How can you ask that? Of course I'm your friend. I love you, and I want what is best for you.'

'It didn't seem like that to me,' Eleyne retorted harshly.

Rhonwen shrugged. 'I did what I had to.'

'And do you still serve Alexander?'

Rhonwen looked away. 'He has not returned since you left.' The phoenix was in her saddlebag, carefully wrapped in lambswool and wedged inside a box of dried lavender heads.

'Good.' Eleyne was watching her carefully. 'If you stay here, I shall want your complete and undivided loyalty to be given to my husband. I do not want Alexander here.'

'Of course, *cariad*,' Rhonwen replied meekly. 'I shall serve you in whatever way you wish. He would not come anyway, while you carry another man's child.'

Dismissing Agnes, Eleyne poured two beakers of mulled wine and passed one to Rhonwen. 'We need not speak about it any more. Drink this, then tell me what has been happening at Falkland. How are my boys?'

When Rhonwen had finished speaking at last, Eleyne laid her head in her arms. 'Poor Colban, poor Macduff. I've written to them both a score of times. Do they really think I would have forgotten them?'

Rhonwen shook her head. 'They realise now Sir Alan would intercept anything you sent. You must send messages they are bound to get. Write to the young king, *cariad*. The Durwards can't stop him from giving them your love.'

Rhonwen found out at once where Donald had gone. The pretty wench from the castle dairies had long glossy red hair and skin like curds. It was Elizabeth of Mar's maiden, Maggie, who told Bethoc who told Rhonwen that Elizabeth had told Donald to leave his wife alone; had told him that pursuing her was a sin whilst she was with child and pushed the red-haired girl – who looked a little as Eleyne had when she was a child – in his direction. It took no one to tell Rhonwen that when he had lain with the slim girl, he would turn away in revulsion from Eleyne's swollen body.

Rhonwen was torn: part of her wanted to rejoice that Donald had proved a broken reed; part of her, convinced that Alexander would want nothing to do with Eleyne while she carried another man's child, wanted to comfort Eleyne's misery.

When she told Eleyne where he had gone for his comforts, Eleyne wept.

'I knew it, I suppose. I've seen them together,' she sobbed. 'He was looking at her the way he always looked at me. And can you blame him!' She pressed her hands to her sides. 'Look at me! I'm disgusting.'

'You're beautiful, *cariad*. And seeing that you know where your husband spends his nights, you should know as well that Lady Mar told him to leave you alone.'

'Lady Mar?' Eleyne looked up, the tears sparkling on her lashes.

'Who else?' Rhonwen had very quickly formed an unfavourable opinion of the Countess of Mar. 'He wouldn't have left you had she not told him it was a mortal sin to lie with his wife whilst she was with child.'

'Mortal sin?' Eleyne was aghast.

Rhonwen nodded. 'Be thankful he's not in your bed now, while you are so large and uncomfortable. He'll come back to you as soon as you are delivered. You'll see.'

V
October 1266

Gratney was born at midnight as the first great gale of the autumn swept up the strath, battering the walls of the castle, toppling the battlements on the south-western gatehouse, turning the burn which flowed down the Den, the ravine behind the castle, into a raging torrent.

He was a large baby, with his father's hair and eyes. The delivery was easy and quick and even Elizabeth was satisfied that her first grandson made a lusty heir.

Exhausted, Eleyne lay back on the bed. She had been bathed and lay in fresh lavender-scented linen, her hair brushed loose on her shoulders. Only then did she let them bring Donald to her. He sat on the bed and took her hand. 'My beautiful, clever love.' He leaned forward and kissed her on the mouth.

Beside them the baby lay asleep in its carved oak cradle.

VI

Donald was standing alone on the battlements of the Snow Tower staring at the distant hills. Behind him the castle drowsed in the winter sunshine. The great fortress, built largely by his father at the instigation of King Alexander II over forty years before, was still in the process of being finished; the tower in the south-west angle of the wall near him was at this moment covered in scaffolding, though there were no workmen to be seen.

He had come from the bedchamber where he had been sitting with Eleyne and the baby, watching them as they drifted together into a warm, milky sleep. He leaned on the cold stonework, his chin in his cupped hand. His son was the most beautiful child he had ever seen:

tiny, delicate, his violet eyes fringed with long dark lashes which, when he slept, lay on a skin as white as alabaster. It was unheard of to write a poem about a child, unless it was the Blessed Saviour himself, but already the words of adoration were pounding through his head.

It was a moment before he realised that there was someone behind him. Annoyed at the intrusion he was tempted to do nothing in the hope that whoever it was would take the hint and go away; then some sixth sense made him swing round.

There was no one there.

Puzzled, he stared across the stone slabs which roofed the tower. The door into the stairwell stood open as he had left it. Inside, it was in deep shadow. He strode across the roof and, stooping, peered in. The staircase disappeared down into the darkness. There was no sound of retreating footsteps from the deeper recesses of the tower.

Ducking back into the sunlight he looked around again uneasily, the skirt of his heavy gown blowing against the stonework near him.

Across the steep sides of the ravine behind the castle he saw the trees on the hillside opposite, behind the quarry where the stone for building came from, stirring gently as the wind strengthened, moaning amongst the boughs of the tall Scots pine, rustling the last crisped leaves of oak and birch to the ground. If he listened hard, he could hear the sound of the burn tumbling over the rocks far below into the boggy ground of the Den.

He shivered violently. Sweet Christ, he could feel the cold sweat of fear between his shoulder blades! He stared round again, then he dived for the staircase.

'Nel!'

Two at a time he hurtled down the narrow, winding staircase, floor after floor until he reached the bedchamber, gasping for breath.

'Nel! Are you all right?' Without realising it, he had his hand on his dagger.

She was startled into wakefulness. Pulling herself up on the pillows, her eyes were wide with fear.

'What is it? What's wrong?' She clutched little Gratney tightly in her arms.

He looked down at her and sheepishly pushed the dagger into its gilded leather sheath. His relief that she was all right was palpable, the flood of adrenalin in his body draining away, leaving him weak and exhausted.

'I'm sorry, my darling. I shouldn't have woken you –'

'What was it?' She reached out her hand to him. She was afraid now as suddenly, staring at his face, she knew what had happened.

'Alexander is here?' Soundlessly her lips framed the question, while her eyes held his.

605

He shrugged. 'I saw nothing. I can't believe he would follow us. How could he? It was my imagination.'

'No, you're right. He's here.' Her arms tightened around the baby. Rhonwen had brought him somehow and now that she no longer carried Donald's child in her womb he was searching for her.

She could taste the strange metallic sharpness of fear in her throat. Slowly she knelt up on the bed, peering around the dimly lit chamber. Only a ray or two of pale winter sunshine pierced the double lancets of the window.

'Please go away,' she called softly. 'Please, my lord; my love. Give me time with Donald and with his son. Please, if you love me, go away.'

Donald held his breath. He realised his hands were shaking and he clasped them together over the hilt of his dagger.

'Please, don't take me now.' Eleyne's voice was pleading and there were tears in her eyes. 'Please, not yet.'

'Sweet Christ!' Donald whispered. 'What do you mean, not yet?' He threw himself towards the bed, enveloping Eleyne and the baby in his arms, and buried his face in her neck. 'What do you mean?' he repeated in anguish.

Eleyne was trembling. 'I . . . I don't know.' She swallowed. 'I suppose that one day I'll grow old. I'll grow old long before you, Donald . . .'

'Don't talk like that!' His eyes blazed with anger. 'I forbid you to talk like that! It's obscene! He's not getting you, not ever, do you hear me? I've already told you –' he was shaking his head like a wounded animal – 'I've already told you that I will fight him in hell itself if I have to. You are not going to him, Nel, not ever. You are mine. Do you hear me? You are mine!'

He realised suddenly that she was crying and, trapped between them, Gratney let out a thin wail, his little face screwed up with misery. Eleyne kissed him gently then she looked up at Donald and smiled through her tears.

'We'll fight him together,' she said softly. 'Somehow we'll fight him. It will be all right, I promise.'

VII

Rhonwen's eyes were unfathomably hard. 'I don't know what you mean, *cariad*. Why should the king come here? There's nothing for him here, surely.' She looked at the cradle by the bed. 'Unless Lord Donald has grown bored with you, of course.'

'He hasn't grown bored,' Eleyne retorted. 'He'll come back to my bed as soon as I am churched.'

'I am glad to hear it. Just as long as you are happy with him. It's when you're unhappy the other will come to claim you.'

'He'll have to kill me first, Rhonwen,' Eleyne said slowly. 'Don't you realise that?'

'No.' Rhonwen shook her head. 'You've to bear his child.'

'No!' Eleyne grabbed her by the shoulders and shook her. 'No, I'll never bear his child. Can't you get that into your head? Never!'

She was angry to find she was trembling like a leaf. Stooping over the cradle, she scooped Gratney into her arms and hugged him. The women of the castle were afraid of Rhonwen, she knew; there were whispers that the old woman with her cold eyes and her fanatical concern for Eleyne was mad. Eleyne had heard them and sometimes she felt the doubt creeping back. 'I want no more babies, Rhonwen, no more at all. But if I must have them, they will be my husband's.'

Rhonwen smiled. 'Of course, *cariad*,' she said. She glanced at the bed. There, safely hidden beneath the pillows and bolsters, the phoenix lay where she had left it. As long as it was there, Eleyne belonged to her king.

VIII

The first time Donald returned to his wife's bed he was shy and tentative, like a stranger. He had watched her trace the circle of protection around their bed, seen her command Alexander to leave them alone. It seemed too easy; too simple a way to hold their fear at bay, but she believed the king had gone and she was hungry for Donald.

Laughing, she had to guide his hands to her hard flat belly, her soft breasts, but from that moment she had to guide him no longer. Their lovemaking, after so long an abstinence, was almost better than before.

IX

JEDBURGH ✧ February 1267

Donald took her south to the king's court when the snows turned to rain and the frozen ground began to thaw. He wanted to get her away from Kildrummy, away from his mother, away from the ghost which haunted them. The lively atmosphere of the court would distract her, and surely the dead king would not come near his son.

As he had hoped, the castle was crowded, noisy and full of good humour. The great hall rang with music and laughter. Troubadours and minstrels, acrobats and animal trainers vied with one another to amuse the king and queen in the frenzied run up to the austerities of

Lent. It was a shock to discover that one of the reasons for the excitement was the visit of Prince Edward, the queen's brother. He had arrived from Haddington, where he was recruiting troops to fight the rebels in England. At twenty-eight, Edward was a fine figure of a man; tall, handsome in a reserved manner, he had been married since he was fifteen years old. His first two daughters had died in infancy but now he had a son, John, just a year old, named for their grandfather. The antipathy Eleyne felt for her English cousin was, she knew, more than returned. They regarded one another with dislike, suspicion and resentment, something which had grown and developed over the years on the rare occasions when they had met. She wasn't quite sure why, even from a child, he had marked her out for his spite. It didn't occur to her that he sensed in her a rebellious spirit which he would never be able to tame and that as such he regarded her as a personal threat.

His presence cast a blight over the visit. Eleyne avoided the king and queen and their guest as much as she could; but she could not escape Edward's attention entirely.

The lower tables had been removed and the guests had settled down to listen to the music of one of Prince Edward's minstrels, or sleep away their heavy meal, when Edward addressed her directly for the first time.

'So, our fair cousin is now wife to the heir to the Earl of Mar. I understand from my brother-in-law that there are five more earldoms in Scotland for you to collect.' He inclined his head towards those within earshot, waiting for their laughter. When it came, dutifully, it was muted.

Eleyne tensed, but Donald's hand was firm on her arm. He turned to Prince Edward. 'My wife is so fair she merits a thousand earldoms, your highness,' he said quietly.

A spot of colour appeared on Edward's cheeks, then he gave a slight bow. 'Your gallantry shames me, Lord Donald,' he said. He smiled coldly, then he turned away.

Donald and Eleyne looked at one another as the minstrel tuned his lute. Both had felt a shadow hover over the hall before the music soared towards the high rafters. Eleyne shivered. The happiness of the visit was spoiled.

X

By the time they returned to Kildrummy she knew she was pregnant again.

Instinctively certain that her condition kept her safe from Alexander, she tried to hide it from Donald for as long as possible. When at last she told him, he was overjoyed, but in spite of his reassurances and her pleas he left her even sooner this time. The red-haired girl in the dairy was married to the castle baker and hugely pregnant herself, and he had sworn he would not look, ever, at another woman, but even so he found it necessary to ride south to join his father at Dunfermline and she was left alone.

Rhonwen confronted her at once. 'So, *cariad*, he has left you again. Do you still swear that he loves you?'

Eleyne was sitting in the window embrasure, and did not turn round. 'I wouldn't blame him if he found me ugly. But it is his mother. He cannot argue with her. The church says it's a sin to touch me while I am great with child.' She wrapped her arms around herself miserably.

Rhonwen snorted. 'The church says,' she echoed mockingly. 'Your bitter, twisted church.' She bent close to Eleyne. 'Lord Donald is not for you, *cariad*. Have you not seen that yet? Have you not seen who it is who truly loves you?'

Eleyne turned to look at her, almost afraid of what she would see. Her face was drawn as she met Rhonwen's eyes. 'No one loves me while I am pregnant,' she said wearily. 'Alexander has no use for me while I carry another man's child.'

'I can bring him to you,' Rhonwen whispered. 'Look.' She produced her hand from behind her back. In it something sparkled, and as the enamelled jewel swung on its chain free of Rhonwen's fingers, Eleyne caught her breath.

'I hid that —'

'And he showed me where.' Rhonwen dangled it in front of Eleyne's eyes. 'He guided me to it, he commanded me to bring it to you. It binds you to him. You cannot throw it away. You cannot hide it. It will always find you.'

Eleyne reached out but Rhonwen took a quick step backwards. 'I'm going to take care of it, *cariad*. We cannot have it lost again, can we?'

Eleyne's eyes blazed with anger. 'You are meddling in matters which don't concern you, Rhonwen. Give that to me!'

Rhonwen shook her head. Turning, she skipped out of reach with surprising agility, slipping the phoenix through the slit in her skirt and into the pocket she wore at the waist of her shift. 'The king told me to guard it well,' she said triumphantly.

'He won't come.' Eleyne did not try to chase her. Aware of her dignity, she sat down and turned back to the window. 'He will never come while I am carrying Donald's child.'

Day after day Eleyne found herself seated next to Elizabeth at the high table. They ate in a silence occasionally broken by the gallant chatter of Hugh Leslie, Father Gillespie the castle chaplain, and Sir Duncan Comyn, Elizabeth's cousin and head of her personal household.

Elizabeth had grown very thin over the last twelve months. She kept more often to her rooms and sometimes failed to appear at meals at all, but when she did her tight-lipped dislike of Eleyne showed no respite.

Twice Elizabeth's brother, the Earl of Buchan, had come to Mar and on both occasions he brought his wife. With Elizabeth de Quincy at Lady Mar's side, Eleyne felt outnumbered.

'They sit side by side and glare at me,' she told Morna, taking little Mairi on her knee. 'I don't know which one of them hates me most.'

'Poor lady.' Morna laughed. 'You threaten them. You are young – oh yes you are, compared with them – you are beautiful and above all you are fertile, whilst their wombs have shrivelled and died.' Morna sat down on the grassy bank next to her. 'And neither of them can forget that you are loved by a king.'

'So, the story reaches even the glens of Mar.' She shivered.

'I need no gossips to know what happens to the people I love.' Morna sounded reproachful. 'I hear the news on the wind; I hear it in the rain and see it written in the clouds.'

'And the fire,' Eleyne said softly. 'Do you ever see it in the fire?' She touched Mairi's face with her fingertip.

For a moment Morna said nothing, studying Eleyne. 'No,' she said at last, 'I don't see things in the fire.'

There was a long silence. 'I hear things from the gossips as well, of course,' Morna went on in a more energetic tone. 'For instance they told me that your nephew Llywelyn has now been recognised as Prince of all Wales by Henry of England.'

Eleyne smiled. 'It's strange how the shadows from Yr Wyddfa stretch as far as the mountains of Scotland.' She shivered. 'I pray all goes well with him.'

'But you see trouble for him in the future?' Morna asked tentatively.

'Perhaps. I don't know what I see, except that destiny sits heavily on our family.' Eleyne sighed. When the news had come only the week before of her sister Angharad's death, she had wept bitterly. But it was so long since she had seen any of her sisters. Margaret, who had written to her to tell her the news, had herself been widowed for the second

610

time only three years before and had been too ill to go to Angharad's funeral.

Morna was watching her. 'Destiny sits heavy on you, my friend, certainly.' She smiled. 'To be loved by two men at once is never easy. It's even harder if you love them both in return.'

Eleyne looked up at her. 'You know that Alexander has followed me to Mar?'

Morna shrugged. 'As I said, I hear it in the wind and rain. One day you will have to make a choice.'

'But not yet.' It was a plea. Eleyne wrapped her arms around herself with a shiver. 'He doesn't come near me when I'm pregnant. It's as though he never existed, as though he were just a dream. I find it hard to believe in him at all when he's not there.'

'Perhaps he is a dream.'

'Perhaps I don't exist for him. Perhaps I'm the dream.' Eleyne put Mairi down and climbed restlessly to her feet. 'Oh, Morna, why did Donald go away again? Do I cease to exist for him too when I'm with child?'

'Perhaps.' Morna pulled her daughter to her and dropped a kiss on the toddler's head. 'But you still exist for yourself and that's the only true reality,' she said enigmatically. 'You are too much ruled by your passions, my dear.'

'I can't help it.' Eleyne shook her head. 'I love him so much.'

It was Donald she meant.

Elizabeth of Mar followed her on her next visit to Morna, her chestnut palfrey flanked by four mounted knights.

'So, this is where you come. I thought perhaps there was a man.' She snapped her fingers at one of her escorts. He dismounted and helped her down.

Little Mairi had fallen asleep in Eleyne's arms. Carefully she laid the child on the ground without waking her and stood up, controlling her anger with difficulty. 'How kind of you to be worried. As you see, I am not with a man, I am visiting a friend.'

'A friend?' The Countess of Mar looked down at Morna, who was sitting on the grass by the river, and raised a haughty eyebrow.

Morna smiled at her, unruffled. 'I could be a friend to you too, Lady Mar, if you would let me.' Her low voice halted Elizabeth in her tracks. 'I can see the pain inside you and I could help you, if you would let me.'

Elizabeth stared at her. Her face was white, her thin, lined face drawn with the effort of the long ride. 'Why? Are you some kind of leech?' For a moment there was something like longing in her eyes, then it was gone.

'No, but I know something of healing,' Morna replied, 'and I know of a holy well, the waters of which would help you and bless you with long life.'

'Indeed.' Elizabeth hesitated for only a fraction of a second, then she turned back to her horse. 'Then I suggest you use your knowledge in the clachan, where no doubt it would be of some use. Eleyne, accompany me, please.'

'I shall follow soon.' Eleyne kept her voice even. 'I had planned to return in time for the midday meal.' She made no move towards her horse, which waited with those of the two men who had escorted her. They were sitting playing a lazy game of knucklebones at the far end of the glen, well out of earshot of Morna's cottage. After a moment's hesitation Elizabeth beckoned the knight forward to help her mount, and rode off without looking back.

XII

'Why did you follow me?' Eleyne went straight to Elizabeth's chamber when she returned to the castle.

Her ladies, sitting around the broad table with their embroidery and their spindles, looked up in astonishment.

'Your husband suspects you of being unfaithful,' Elizabeth said.

'No, that would never cross Donald's mind. Not unless you suggested it to him, as you suggested to him that he leave my bed.' Eleyne held Elizabeth's gaze without wavering, and was gratified to see the countess look away first.

'I suggested he leave your bed, madam, to relieve you of a presence which must have become intolerable,' Elizabeth said stiffly. 'As for the other, it is as well I told him of your rides. No faithful wife goes completely alone, day after day, into the hills.'

'It is something I have always done,' Eleyne replied, 'and something I shall continue to do. When Donald is here, he often rides with me.'

'Indeed.' Elizabeth raised an eyebrow. 'How annoying for you. So, unwittingly I have done you a favour, it seems, in reminding my son of his duties at his father's side. You can once more ride alone. Though I must say, I'm astonished that you persist in riding in your condition. Tell me –' She changed the subject unexpectedly. 'Have your lonely rides taken you to this sacred well? Do you know where it is?'

'I know,' Eleyne said quietly. Guided by Morna, she had ridden there and splashed the crystal water over her face and breasts, leaving an offering to the gods in the hope that the magic waters would keep her young. Only days later she had conceived this second child.

612

XIII

When Eleyne arrived at Morna's cottage a few days later, she found her friend seated by the cool brown water of the river. The birch trees had scattered golden leaves in the whirling pools of the backwater eddies, and Morna was watching as Mairi tried to catch the flying leaves on the bank.

'Your mother-in-law was here again this morning,' Morna said as Eleyne sat down beside her. 'She arrived with such an escort I felt sure she had come to arrest me.'

'And why did she come?'

'To ask my help. Her heart pains her a great deal and she doesn't dare ask the castle physicians in case they tell her she is mortally sick.'

'And what did you tell her?' Eleyne raised an eyebrow.

'I told her, as I told her before, that I was no physician. If she doesn't want the doctor at the castle, she could send for the infirmarian at Cabrach. I sent her home with water from the sacred spring, and I told her to rest.' She smiled. 'And I told her you were a faithful and obedient wife.'

'Thank you.' Eleyne groaned as she sat down. 'What else could I be, like this? Look at me! I've never been so huge.'

'It won't be long,' Morna said comfortingly. 'Then you'll be slim again. And I will tell you what to do to prevent another baby coming.'

Eleyne stared at her. 'You can?'

The other woman nodded. 'When the time is right I will show you. But you must say nothing to anyone, especially your husband. Such things are considered a sin against God.'

XIV

September 1267

Eleyne was resting on her bed; her back ached and she was tired. The child in her womb did not kick so much now, held too tightly in its dark prison. She was larger than she had been with any of her other children. A few weeks before, while there was still room, it had kicked and flailed endlessly until Eleyne had wondered if she were going to give birth to a litter of pups, just as Sabina had done a few months before. She sighed, trying to ease her position on the bed. The command to go at once to Elizabeth's chamber did not please her at all.

Lady Mar was lying on her bed, her face very pale. It had been a hot day and the stone of the castle held the heat as one of the first of the heavy dews of autumn started to fall.

'You said you knew where the sacred well is?' Elizabeth began without preamble.

Eleyne nodded. A century or so before a hermit had built himself a stone hut beside it and now it sheltered pilgrims who came to bathe in its healing waters or make offerings to the saint who guarded it.

'I want to go there.' Elizabeth's hand was pressed against her chest.

Eleyne stared at her in astonishment. 'But it's a long way. It's up in the hills and hard to reach. Morna will give you more water from the spring –'

'That's no use!' Elizabeth lay back on the pillow, pressing her lips together tightly as a wave of pain hit her. 'Morna is away from her bothy. I hear she is sometimes away for days or weeks on end. I can't wait until she gets back. I want to go to the well myself.'

'You can't possibly!' Eleyne was shocked out of her attempt to comfort the woman. 'It's a long steep ride; even for someone who is fit it's difficult. Water can be fetched . . .'

'I want to go there. I have to go there,' Elizabeth repeated stubbornly, willing herself into a sitting position. 'I shall order a litter first thing tomorrow and you will guide me there.'

'I can't. It would be madness,' Eleyne cried. She was sorry for the anguish and fear she saw in the other woman's eyes; the fear of illness and death. 'It would be foolish for you to try to ride that far when you are unwell.'

'It will kill me if I don't go.' Elizabeth shook her head. 'I have to go, don't you see? I've been thinking about it for weeks. I remember hearing of the spring when I was a child in Buchan. My grandfather, Fergus, was full of old tales of the hills. He said if you bathed in its holy waters you would live forever. I had forgotten about it until that spaewife told me the story again. I have to get there, it's my only chance.'

Eleyne shook her head and put her hand to her stomach. 'I'm sorry, I can't ride that far, even if you can. My time is close . . .'

'I see!' Elizabeth's voice was mocking. 'You protest that you must ride all day to please yourself, but to save my life you're not prepared to ride at all –'

'That's not true!'

'Then come with me.' Elizabeth stood up. She staggered slightly, then straightened. 'I will order you a litter too. We have two I believe.'

'No.' Eleyne was looking at her in disbelief. 'Please. Neither of us is in a fit state to go.'

'I have to.' Elizabeth's face tightened in a grimace of pain. 'You are my daughter-in-law, it's your duty to obey me in this.' She snapped her fingers at one of her ladies. 'Go and order the litters and an escort of armed men. Tell them to be ready tomorrow after mass.' She turned again to Eleyne. 'Of course we have to take into account the fact that you are no longer as young as you were,' she said spitefully. 'But you have always insisted your age made no difference to your activities. Is that it? Are you afraid?'

Eleyne clenched her fists. 'Of course not.'

'Then you will come with me.'

XV

They had an escort of ten men. Elizabeth had forbidden any of her ladies to accompany them. Eleyne looked up at the sky as her groom brought her horse, and she shook her head. However much she hated the litter, she knew she could not ride.

The clouds were high and wild, though on the ground the air was still. Wind would come later, and with it rain. She could smell the cold and salt from the distant sea. She pulled her cloak more closely around her as one of her attendants came to help her awkwardly on to the cushions and she felt the baby move resentfully.

They travelled very slowly, leaving the track almost immediately and heading across the rough, slowly rising ground. Eleyne's litter was at the front of the riders, Ancret and Lyulf close beside her, a deeply disapproving Sir Duncan Comyn riding at her side. He had insisted on accompanying them and had hand-picked their escort.

Eleyne's back ached and she was very tired. Every now and then she called a halt, peering around to orientate herself to the unaccustomed view from the litter.

At one of the halts Duncan turned in his saddle. 'Do you think we should check to see if she is all right?'

Wearily Eleyne nodded, glad of the rest. She waited, slumped uncomfortably on the cushions, whilst he rode back. Above the rising wind she heard Elizabeth's harsh voice demanding to know why the devil they had stopped, and even more clearly, as he rode back towards her, she heard Sir Duncan's muttered imprecation that his cousin was a selfish vicious old harridan and deserved to roast in hell. She smiled. It was reassuring to know that she was not without allies on this journey.

They found the spring in the end and she climbed wearily out of the litter, gratefully allowing Sir Duncan to help her into the stone chapel and settle her on the long low ledge which had served the hermit all those years before both as seat and bed. He called his men to build a fire in the ring of blackened stones which had obviously formed the hearth over the centuries. Only then did he leave her to help Elizabeth from her litter.

The spring bubbled gently from beneath an overhang of rock, filling a shallow pool rimmed by smooth stones which had been used since time immemorial as a resting-place for people's offerings. Coloured bits of rag, stones and coins lay in the glistening spray, protected by small curling ferns, brilliant green in the late afternoon sun.

'Now, I want you to leave my daughter-in-law and me here. Take all your men. I want no one left here with us.' Elizabeth's grating voice was still strong as Sir Duncan helped her from the litter. 'You may return tomorrow at noon.'

'My lady, we can't leave you!' Sir Duncan was horrified.

'Why not? No one will harm us here. We have my daughter-in-law's great dogs to protect us. Build up the fire and leave enough wood to keep us warm and unpack the food and bring me all the rugs and towels from the litter. Then go. I have no intention of bathing with a dozen men ogling through the bracken.'

Sir Duncan appealed to Eleyne. 'My lady —?'

'Do as I say!' Elizabeth cut in sharply. 'I have to be alone and I have to bathe in the moonlight. It's part of the cure. She can stay and seek her own blessing from the water, but no one else. No one at all.' She staggered slightly, her hand to her breast. 'Go now.'

Eleyne closed her eyes in despair, wishing fervently that she hadn't come. The wild look in her mother-in-law's eyes frightened her. 'Surely, if Sir Duncan and his men wait out of sight,' she said, 'that will be good enough. Then they can take us back.'

'No!' Elizabeth cried in a frenzy. 'They have to go. I have to wait for the moon. It's my only chance. My only chance,' she repeated through gritted teeth.

'You had better do as she says,' Eleyne said softly to Sir Duncan. She glanced at Elizabeth. 'The Blessed Virgin and St Bride will protect us.' And so will the old gods who watch here, she added to herself silently. Whose power is still strong in these hills; whose watch over the sacred springs has never lessened.

With one final anxious glance at Eleyne, Sir Duncan did as he was bid. The rugs and towels were piled in the chapel, the fire built up and a neat stack of firewood fetched from the copse at the foot of the rocks; dried rowan and pine and birch and even sharp, prickly thorn were heaped in the corner, then the escort left and they were alone.

Eleyne and Elizabeth watched as the horsemen rode down the hillside, then Elizabeth turned to her. 'We'll eat while we wait for the moon to rise,' she said.

The two women sat before the fire in the deserted chapel as the dusk, coming in from the east, threw purple shadows across the glens. The light was dying fast. Through the open door, Eleyne looked up at the sky. It had turned to an opalescent aquamarine, remote and cold, streaked with carmine cloud. Between the mountains the shadows grew black and soft, folded in secrecy. From somewhere far away there was the howl of a wolf. Eleyne saw her dogs' ears flatten. The hackles on their necks had risen, but neither animal moved from its watch by the door.

'You're afraid.' Elizabeth's mocking voice was loud in the silence.

Eleyne clenched her fists. 'I'm afraid for you. Supposing you were taken ill –'

'I won't be taken ill. I've come here to be cured and as soon as the moon has risen, I shall bathe in the pool.' Elizabeth shivered suddenly. 'Throw some more wood on the fire and put the towels to warm.' She made no effort to move as Eleyne heaved herself awkwardly to her feet and did as she was bid. Her back was aching so much, she could barely move as she threw some branches on to the fire. For a moment she hesitated, staring down into the flames, seeing them beckon, then she forced herself to look away. Wearily she reached for the towels and spread them across the stone ledge.

'It's nearly dark.' Elizabeth sat forward. 'The moon will be up soon.'

'I'll go and see.' Eleyne went slowly out into the wind. It was cold outside. The red was nearly gone from the west. Cloud, shredded and black, streamed across the darkening sky. In the east she could see the glow of the rising moon behind the hills. In a few moments its silver rim would float clear of the clouds. The water behind her was black as velvet, bubbling quietly from the deep centre of the mountain.

'Is it time?' Elizabeth's husky voice behind her made her jump.

'The moon is nearly up.' Eleyne turned. She caught her breath in surprise. Elizabeth had removed her gown. Dressed only in a white shift beneath her cloak she was like an apparition in the darkness as the silver moonlight slowly spread across the mountainside.

Kicking off her shoes, Elizabeth began to walk, slowly and with laboured breath, towards the smooth flat rocks. Eleyne followed her, taking her arm as the woman stumbled. 'You can't mean to bathe completely. It's ice cold!' she protested.

'Hold my cloak. It'll serve to warm me when I come out.' Elizabeth groped with the fastening at her throat.

'Splash yourself. That will be enough.' Eleyne tried to hold her back. 'Here, let me get some water for you –'

'Leave me!' Elizabeth's voice rose sharply. She pushed Eleyne away and took the last few steps to the edge of the pool.

Moonlight flooded the dark water as the heavy strips of cloud scudded west, and Elizabeth paused, catching her breath as the pool turned silver. Cautiously she stepped into the shallow rock basin. The icy water clung to her shift, soaking her ankles then, as she took another step, her knees. She could hear her heart beating; her head was full of the sound. The moonlight filled her eyes. Slowly she raised her arms towards the sky.

On the bank Eleyne watched, a dog on each side of her. She saw

Elizabeth move cautiously to the centre of the pool and she saw her raise her hands towards the moon. She smiled ruefully. So this woman too, descendant as she was of the ancient Celtic line of the Earls of Buchan, remembered earlier gods. Eleyne shivered, huddled in her cloak as the wind freshened across the mountainside, wincing as the child in her belly moved sharply, as if sensing her unease. Preoccupied with her thoughts of the impatient life within her, it was a moment before she saw that Elizabeth had fallen to her knees in the pool. She took a step nearer, peering into the moonlit dazzle from the water.

'Help me!'

She barely heard Elizabeth's call over the trickle of the spring. Dropping the woman's cloak she ran to the edge of the pool. Elizabeth had slumped forward in the water, her arms flailing, her face contorted with pain.

Sabina got there first, bounding into the water with a fearful splash, dragging at the woman's gown. Eleyne reached her seconds later, scarcely feeling the cold on her legs as she caught Elizabeth's arm. The woman's head was lolling out of control. Gritting her teeth, Eleyne felt Elizabeth's weight sagging against her as she began to drag her bodily from the water, half helped, half hindered by the dogs.

A pain knifed through her back and she gasped, nearly dropping Elizabeth back into the water. She took a deep breath and, with a groan, put her hands beneath Elizabeth's arms, pulling her step by step towards the edge of the pool. Though thin, Elizabeth was a tall woman and with her shift soaked with water she was enormously heavy. Eleyne heard herself sobbing as she gave another heave. She was shaking uncontrollably, the pain in her back arcing through her belly.

At last she pulled Elizabeth halfway up the bank. She sank to the ground next to her, struggling for breath before she reached for the woman's cloak and tucked it around her gently. 'Are you all right? Can you hear me?' she gasped. She took one of the cold limp hands and began to chafe it. 'Can you hear me?' Her voice broke into a sob of pain.

She stared up towards the moon, taking deep breaths, trying to calm her heartbeat. Her whole body had contorted suddenly with agony.

'Blessed Bride, help me.'

She was alone on the empty mountainside with a sick woman – and her baby was coming.

Elizabeth, scarcely conscious, looked up at her. 'What is it?' she murmured. Through her own agony she had at last realised Eleyne's distress.

'My baby. It's going to be born.'

'You shouldn't have helped me.' Elizabeth grimaced. 'I'm sorry.' She closed her eyes, her breathing harsh and irregular. 'Leave me. Get into the warm,' she muttered. 'Go on.' She reached feebly towards Eleyne with a clawed hand. 'God bless you' – She paused. 'Daughter.'

Eleyne stared down at her. 'Don't die!' She gritted her teeth as another wave of pain hit her. 'You can't die, you've bathed in the pool. You have immortality.' She clutched at Elizabeth's hand. 'Please, don't die!' It was a frightened plea.

Elizabeth's head rolled sideways and her eyes opened slightly, but the life in them had gone. After the harshness of her breathing, the silence was even more terrifying. Eleyne dropped her hand and stared around in a panic. The mountainside was deserted. The night was silent. Only the silver moon watched the stricken woman as she knelt beside her mother-in-law's body, and the only sound now was the gentle bubbling of the spring.

She found she was shaking uncontrollably again and, after a moment's hesitation, she pulled the cloak from Elizabeth's body and wrapped it round her own. She dragged herself to her feet and staggered towards the chapel, the dogs pressing themselves against her anxiously as she sobbed out loud as each new pain took her. In the doorway she looked back at the dead woman sprawled on the soft bed of fern and moss by the side of the spring and for a moment she envied her peace.

Painfully she built up the fire and spread blankets on the stone bed before she collapsed on to it, clenching her teeth against each new onset of pain.

The dogs seemed to know what was happening. Raoulet remained on guard by the door, staring out into the night, whilst Sabina lay down beside Eleyne. It was the bitch's tongue on her face which revived her as she drifted in and out of consciousness, her shaggy coat to which Eleyne clung as spasm after spasm of agony knifed through her body.

It was just before dawn.

In a short lull between contractions, Eleyne pulled herself up slightly on the bed. The fire was dying; she had to put on more logs. Somehow she managed to do it, and to finish her preparations for the birth. She had torn strips from her shift to wrap the baby and had plenty of rugs to keep it and herself warm. She unpicked threads from her hem to tie the cord. Morna had borne her child alone; it was better that way, she had said. No fuss, no gossiping cronies taking the opportunity to poke around her house. At this moment Eleyne would have welcomed anyone poking around her house. At the end of the chapel, almost beyond the angle of her vision, the flat slab which acted as an altar carried a small carved Celtic cross, crude in its design. There were no statues in this deserted place. And no prospect of any pilgrims arriving to help her in her hour of need. She had to keep calm. Her baby's life, and probably her own, depended on it. She must think back to her previous births and cope on her own.

The first rays of sunlight were falling pale and cold across the floor when at last the child slipped free of her body and lay whimpering feebly. It was a boy. Eleyne did what was necessary. Gathering the last reserves of her strength, she tied the cord and nipped it with her teeth, then she dried the baby carefully in one of the towels, wrapped the tiny scrap in the piece of her shift and then a rug against the cold beyond the fire, and put the baby to her breast. Sabina whimpered in her throat and Eleyne smiled across at the dog. Moments later the contractions started again. She lay back, cuddling the baby to her. Once the afterbirth was passed, she would be free of pain. But the pain did not go: it grew worse and she became frightened. She looked down at the baby, which had fallen asleep in her arms, and laid it beside her. When were they coming back? Noon, Elizabeth had said and it was only just morning.

Beside her Sabina nuzzled the swaddled baby. 'Guard him, Sabina, guard him well,' Eleyne murmured. 'Take care of him for me.'

As the pain built again, she began to drift away. Her spent body tensed and fought the waves of agony and she slipped in and out of unconsciousness, to be awakened by renewed spasms of her contorted muscles as a second child was born. Somehow she found the strength again to tie off the cord and wrap the baby in the rug which lay near her, then she fell back exhausted.

Sabina sat up. Head to one side she looked down at the second baby lying at Eleyne's side, where it had slipped from the crook of her arm. The baby whimpered miserably and gently the bitch nuzzled it. Not swaddled like its brother, it waved its arms, dislodging the loosely wrapped rug, and as the small body began to grow chill it let out a feeble cry.

Sabina nudged it, agitated, then she began to lick it, her rough tongue covering every inch of the small human, working as efficiently as when she dealt with her own puppies. Satisfied at last that the baby was warm and dry, she stood up, shook herself and looked enquiringly at Eleyne. When there was no response from her mistress, she looked down again at the two babies. The smallest was crying weakly and the sound worried her. Leaping up beside the babies on to the stone bed, she curled her great shaggy body around them, nosed them gently and settled down to sleep.

Next to her Eleyne drifted further and further into blackness.

CHAPTER TWENTY-SIX

I

'They told you to return at noon?' Rhonwen confronted Sir Duncan in the great hall. 'And you left them alone?' She stared at the man in complete disbelief.

'Lady Mar ordered it,' he said crossly. 'She said they had to be alone.'

Rhonwen put her hand to her head. 'For the love of pity, they have been out there all night! A sick woman and a woman only weeks from giving birth!'

Outside the trees bent before the wind, their branches streaming, leaves whirling in vortices on the ground beneath. Above the castle, great patches of purple shadow raced across the hillsides.

Rhonwen took Agnes and Bethoc with her as she rode stiffly on her roan palfrey beside Sir Duncan. He guided them unerringly up the track, threading his way across the mountain until they came in view of the spring and drew up abreast at the edge of the holy place.

'Blessed Virgin!' Sir Duncan stared, appalled, at the body sprawled on the edge of the pool, one foot still trailing in the water. The ravens and kites had already begun work on her face. There was blood on the rocks and on her shift – the black slow blood of death. There was no sign of Eleyne.

At first Raoulet would not let them pass, but Rhonwen coaxed him out of the doorway so that she and Bethoc could get in.

'Holy Mother!' Bethoc's eyes got used to the dark in the windowless cell first. Eleyne lay half wrapped in a blood-soaked cloak, her face white, her eyes closed. Beside her the second great wolfhound had curled up with the two babies cuddled up in her fur. They were clean and warm and both very much alive.

Rhonwen and Bethoc were speechless, then at last Rhonwen spoke. 'Twins! And one is Alexander's child,' she breathed. 'Sweet lady, it's a miracle!' Her voice rose in triumph. 'Donald of Mar's son had to make room for his sovereign's child!'

Bethoc stared at her in bewilderment. She crossed herself, her face white. Then she tiptoed across the floor. 'Is my lady alive?' she asked in a whisper.

Rhonwen took Eleyne's hand and chafed it gently. 'She's breathing, but only just. It's a miracle this place stayed warm.' She looked across at the dying fire and shuddered. 'But there are great powers at work here; great powers to guard over the birth of a king's son.' She stooped and reverently picked up the baby which had been wrapped in the torn shift. 'This is he. The first-born. Lord Donald's child was not important to my lady. She did not even bother to wrap it.'

Bethoc gave a superstitious shiver, then she scowled. Deftly she caught up the second baby and wrapped it warmly in her own cloak. 'Whoever fathered these children, it is for us to take care of them, and of their mother,' she scolded sharply.

Rhonwen nodded. She could not contain her sense of triumph. At last, Alexander had his son!

II

'I swear before God they are both your sons!' Eleyne was terrified at the fury in Donald's face.

'How can they be! Everyone knows that twins are born only to women who have lain with two men. My mother warned me, and I didn't believe her!' He slammed his fist on the palm of his hand. 'God's bones! I should have listened to her!'

'Donald, please!' Eleyne was still too weak to get out of bed. It was three days since Elizabeth's funeral in the parish church in Kildrummy village; seven days since the twins had been baptised in the castle chapel by Father Gillespie. On Rhonwen's instructions they had been named Duncan and Alexander. Neither Donald nor Eleyne was present at the christening. Nor was Rhonwen.

'I swear I have not lain with another man. I swear it! I have been faithful to you.' Tears trickled down her cheeks and she clutched at his hand. 'I swear it, Donald.'

He moved to look down at the two cradles. 'Then it was Alexander,' he said quietly. 'Rhonwen is right. One of them is Alexander's son.'

'No!' Sobbing, Eleyne reached out towards him. 'How could it be? He was no more than a figment of the imagination! I haven't seen him or thought about him or dreamed about him since we came to Kildrummy. I swear it!'

Donald turned away. 'That's not true and we both know it,' he said softly. 'And the fact remains, you have given birth to twins and you called one of them Alexander.'

'I didn't call him Alexander, that was Rhonwen. Rhonwen!' She pulled herself up on her pillows and pushed her hair out of her eyes. 'Donald, you must believe me. I will swear on anything you hold holy. On the relics of the Blessed St Margaret. On the children's heads! Look at the boys, see how like each other they are. And they are both like you. How could they have had different fathers?'

Donald looked down at the babies. They were indeed alike and he had to admit they were like Gratney too. His eldest son had no qualms at all about his little brothers. He adored them and spent long hours with his nurse gazing at them in awed silence.

Donald turned back to the bed. 'You would swear on holy relics?' he asked uncertainly.

'I would swear on anything you like.'

He still looked doubtful. 'Mother was so sure.'

'Your mother was mistaken.' Eleyne's voice, though still weak, took on a firmness which he recognised. He smiled in spite of himself.

'I think perhaps she was.' He sighed. 'As she was mistaken about her illness. The physicians have told me she brought her death upon herself. The shock of the cold water on top of the exertion of the journey stopped her heart. There was nothing wrong with it until then.' He looked questioningly at the two cribs. 'But you have given birth to twins. How did it happen?'

Eleyne gave a tight unhappy laugh. 'How do you think, husband mine? We made love too much, that's how. I'm surprised it didn't happen when Gratney was born as well!' She raised an eyebrow at him provocatively and was relieved to see an answering light in his eye.

III

'I want the phoenix!' Eleyne fixed Rhonwen with a furious stare. 'How dare you hide it from me!'

'The king told me to hide it,' Rhonwen repeated stubbornly. 'He wants it near you, so that he can reach you.'

'I could have this castle torn apart,' Eleyne said slowly. 'And I'll do it. Rhonwen,' she appealed, 'I thought you loved me.'

'I do love you, *cariad*, I love you more than life itself. That's why I serve the man who is your destiny.'

'Donald is my destiny –'

'No, *cariad*.' Rhonwen raised her voice. 'He is an obsession – a passing passion. He is nothing. Einion Gweledydd knew. That is what he tried to tell you . . .'

'No –'

'Oh, yes, *cariad*, he knew. Donald of Mar is no one. So much thistle-down, tossed on the wind.' She snapped her fingers in the air. 'And now you have the king's son, Alexander, a child of royal blood –'

'No!' Eleyne raised her voice at last. 'I forbid you ever to say such a thing again, ever. Sandy and Duncan are both Donald's sons. Donald's, do you hear? Now give me the phoenix.'

Rhonwen shook her head.

Exasperated Eleyne took a deep breath, her anger mounting. 'Rhonwen, I have loved you for a very long time. I have stood by you and helped you when you have caused me nothing but heartache and trouble. You have not done me any favours by claiming all over the castle that Sandy is a dead man's son. My husband doubts my faithfulness and half the household think I am a whore or a witch or both. Now, give me the phoenix.'

'I haven't got it any more.' Rhonwen stared at her defiantly. 'It's gone.'

'You think I'd believe that?' Eleyne's voice was hard. She folded her arms wearily.

'Believe it or not, *cariad*,' Rhonwen said slowly, 'it's the truth.'

She curtseyed with only the smallest hint of mockery as Donald walked into the room and then she fled.

Eleyne stared after her in helpless fury.

'You look tired.' Donald's voice was gentle but there was still a certain constraint between them.

'I am tired.' Eleyne wanted to go to him, to touch his face, to feel his arms around her, but she sensed his distance from her. 'Rhonwen continues to make trouble.'

'Why don't you send that mad old baggage packing? Back to London? Didn't you say Mistress Luned had offered her a home?'

'It would break her heart.' Eleyne sat down at the table. She put her face in her hands. 'She won't give me the phoenix.'

'So.' His voice was bleak.

'We can fight him, my love.' She looked up at Donald pleadingly. 'Just as we have always fought him. Please.' She held out her arms.

'Has he come back to you?' Donald did not move.

She shook her head.

He shivered. 'Yet I feel him. He watches over you all the time.'

'No.' She went to him and put her arms around his neck. 'I am yours, Donald. Gratney, Duncan and Sandy are your sons. I have sworn it and I will swear it again.'

She reached up to the neck of her gown and pulled it open at the back, slipping the dark green velvet from her shoulders. She saw his eyes go at once to her heavy blue-veined breasts. He had begun to breathe deeply. 'Lock the door,' she whispered. She let her gown and then her shift fall slowly to her knees. He hesitated, then walking like a man in a dream, he did as she bid, and she opened her arms.

At dead of night in the cold moonlight she had traced a circle of protection around the castle walls: phoenix or no phoenix, Alexander was outside it, in the darkness. He could not come near her or her sons.

FALKLAND CASTLE ❖ 1268

The visit was not a success. Bethoc, Agnes and Rhonwen had remained behind to look after her three sons at Kildrummy, but Eleyne missed the children desperately. Colban and Macduff were reserved, though polite; Anna was hostile; Eleyne's grandson, Duncan, did not remember her at all. On her last evening at Falkland, Eleyne followed Colban to his father's countinghouse, set in the thickness of the grey wall which overlooked the Lomond Hills.

'Are you and Anna still content?' She put her hands on his shoulders and held him at arm's length, forcing him to meet her eye.

'We rub along well enough, mama.'

'And your brother, is he happy?' After greeting her happily enough, Macduff had disappeared. He had not been present at supper the night before.

Colban shrugged. 'I think so. Don't worry, mama, we're grown men. In two years I come of age. You worry about your new family.'

She held his eye a little longer, overwhelmed with love for her proud, independent boy, then she looked away. 'I love all my children equally, Colban, but there is always a special place in a mother's heart for her eldest son.' She smiled. 'I'm very proud of you.'

He looked embarrassed, then at last he put his arms around her and gave her a quick, tight hug.

From Falkland they rode to Dunfermline, where they spent some time in private with the king. When they left, Eleyne had letters for her nephew, for they were to ride on south to Wales.

She was torn: she badly wanted to go back to her boys, but the chance to go south again to Wales, the chance to show Yr Wyddfa to Donald was a temptation hard to resist. And the king's orders were clear. As his father had before him, he wanted her to be his go-between, his royal messenger, riding south on the pretext of visiting her family to discuss a Welsh–Scottish Celtic alliance with her nephew.

V

ABER ❖ June 1268

By Midsummer's Day, Eleyne was once more home at Aber.

'Well, has it changed?' Llywelyn, resplendent in the *talaith*, the gold coronet of the Welsh princes, stepped down off the dais in his great hall and hugged her.

She gazed around and shook her head. 'Yr Wyddfa is still there,

and the strait and beyond it the island. I can still smell the mountains;
I can still hear Afon Aber in the valley.' She looked at Rhonwen, who
had cried as once again they crossed the border into Wales. Ostensibly
it had been a last-minute act of kindness to send for Rhonwen before
they set out, so that she could visit her native Gwynedd again, but
Eleyne had two other reasons: she did not want the old woman left in
charge of the nurseries at Kildrummy; especially she did not want her
near Sandy. Also, she wondered secretly whether she could prevail
upon her nephew or one of her remaining sisters, Gwenllian or Margaret, to keep Rhonwen in Wales.

Llywelyn grimaced. 'You loved it here as a child, I remember.
Whereas I spent most of my childhood as a prisoner!' He sighed.

'Tell me about Isabella.' He had only said that she had died.

He shrugged. 'There's nothing to tell. She had a wasting disease.'

'And you were with her when she died?'

He nodded.

'Did she speak of me at all?'

'No,' he said abruptly.

She watched him thoughtfully as he walked away from her, aware
of a slight shiver down her back. She did not question him on the
subject again.

VI

'Donald.' She shook his shoulder gently. 'Donald, are you awake?' They
had made love long and passionately the night before and now he slept
heavily, one arm hanging over the edge of the bed. Smiling fondly, she
crept from beneath the bedcovers. The servants on the truckle beds
were all asleep; it was barely light.

Pulling on her shift and then her gown and cloak, she tiptoed to
the door. Nodding at the dogs to follow her, she let herself out on to
the dark stairs. Meg opened a sleepy eye and watched her, debating
whether to get up, but Eleyne was already outside. No doubt her lady
was going riding. Had she wanted a companion she would have woken
someone, not tiptoed from the room like a lover off to a secret meeting.

It was a long time since Eleyne had slipped from the prince's hall,
through the gate, past the night guard and out down the hill past the
forge and the church and the mill and out through the village. With a
rueful smile as she thought of all the years which had passed, she
walked along the river, the dogs gambolling at her side. She was not
tempted to go to the horses after spending the last three weeks in the
saddle. All she wanted was to walk quietly along the river, watching
the cold colourless early morning suffuse with light. And she wanted
to think; think about the past and the people who had gone. Her

father, her mother, Dafydd, Gruffydd, both buried with their father at Aberconwy, even Isabella.

She wandered out of sight of the village, following the valley. The air was cold beneath the trees, rich with the scent of rotting wood. The path, though well trodden, was deserted.

Behind her, Rhonwen paused, keeping well out of sight. She shivered in the cold dawn, and looked up through the trees at the slopes of the hillside which were still covered in mist. Almost, she decided to turn back.

Eleyne walked on, slowly and dreamily, smiling as she saw the blue flash of a kingfisher beneath the trees. She stopped, peering at the place it had vanished, and for the first time she realised how cold it was in the shady ravine. She pulled her cloak round her more tightly, and looked behind her. The mist had advanced through the trees, drifting closer, lapping around the gossamer-hung bushes, curling among the old rotting vegetation which hung over the path. Both dogs had disappeared, eagerly exploring the scents of the morning. The birds were silent, the mist drifting closer, and with it came the cold, suffocating aura of menace.

She hesitated, then firmly she walked on a few steps and stopped again. She pulled her cloak tighter still, glancing up at the hillside. The earlier patches of thin sunlight on the high western flanks of the mountain had gone – all she could see was the mist.

Suddenly she couldn't breathe. The mist was all around her, touching her face, soaking her clothes. Someone was near her, but she could see nothing. The silence beat against her eardrums.

'Who is there?' She spun round, holding out her hands in front of her. 'Who is it?'

But already she knew. She could feel him trying to speak, feel the frustration beating round her head, feel the cold air vibrating against her mouth, her eyes, her ears.

'Einion?' She turned round and round on the path, her feet slipping on the mud. 'Please leave me alone.'

A wind had arisen from nowhere. The air was alive, and near her the trees began to bend and creak, their branches thrashing the water, whipping it into spray, shredding the mist.

She had lost the path now. She could feel brambles catching at her skirts; nettles whipped across her face, and a briar wound itself around her arm, tearing her gown and leaving a long bleeding scratch. With a scream she lost her footing and fell on her knees among the flat pebbles on a shingly strip of beach where the low summer river had left the margin dry. The wind was still tearing at her head; she felt the hood of her cloak fall, felt her hair pulled free, tangling. Desperately she

627

closed her eyes and crouching down she wrapped her arms around her head.

It was then that she saw him: tall, his white hair blowing in the wind, his eyes a piercing fury in his head. 'My prophecy was true!' The words exploded in her mind. 'It was true! The child. The child. Your daughter. Your child . . .' The words were fading. 'Your child . . .'

'No!' Eleyne screamed. 'Leave me alone!' She flailed out desperately. 'Go away.' Frantically she tried to regain her feet, sobbing. 'I don't believe you, I don't want to know. Go away, leave me alone.' Her feet kept slipping on the pebbles as, blindly, she tried to find the steep bank. Her hand closed over a tree root and she tried to pull herself up. She was panting, unable to catch her breath. Clawing at the soft earth, she found a foothold, then another, and, hampered by her skirts, she pulled herself up on to the path once more. The mist was thinner there. Stray rays of sunlight filtered through the trees and she could see a figure running towards her.

'Cariad!' Rhonwen's breath was rasping in her throat, her hand pressed to her side. Behind her were the two dogs. 'I heard you scream! Dew! I couldn't go any faster. What is it? What's happened?' She stared in horror at Eleyne's torn stained clothes and her tearful face. 'What is it? Did you fall?' Rhonwen looked down the bank at the shingle. Wisps of mist still floated over the river between the trees. Somewhere nearby a dove had begun to croon, high in a treetop where the sunlight was suddenly strong.

Eleyne seized her arm. Her teeth were chattering. 'Einion!' she gasped.

'Einion?' White-faced, Rhonwen peered around. All she had seen was the silent white mist drifting down the hillside until it enveloped Eleyne and she had vanished from sight. 'What did he say?' She put her arms around Eleyne and held her tightly.

'I don't know. I didn't understand. He said the prophecy was true. He talked about a child.' She was crying.

Rhonwen could feel her whole body shaking. 'You must look in the fire, cariad, you will see the future there. Yours and little Alexander's. You never look in the fire now. You avoid it. I've seen you. You keep away from it, even when the east wind blows at Kildrummy.' She tried to smile. 'Almost as though you were afraid of it.'

Eleyne shook her head. 'I don't want to see the future. I don't want to know what happens next.' She bent and put her arms around Sabina's neck.

'Oh but you do, cariad. All your life, destiny has marked you for her own. Whatever is to happen to you, you are special. You must have courage, you must look.'

Eleyne shook her head again. Sunshine shone obliquely over the shoulder of the hill and caught the water, setting diamonds amongst the shadows. 'I used to think Alexander was my destiny,' she whispered. 'That I would marry him and be a queen . . . When he died, I wanted to die too. I couldn't bear to live without him.' She was talking to herself.

'And you didn't have to,' Rhonwen said softly.

'Then Donald came,' Eleyne ignored the interruption, 'and the shadows receded and I no longer thought about destiny. Our love was too strong to question. No other man could have been my destiny, only Donald.'

Rhonwen shook her head. 'No. Lord Donald stole you from the king.'

'No one stole me, Rhonwen.' Eleyne was feeling calmer now. The sun's beams had strengthened, and she could feel the heat of one striking through the soft leather of her shoe on the path.

'Oh, but he did,' Rhonwen insisted. 'Alexander was your destiny and somehow, something went wrong. Your life and his did not run parallel; destiny was out of line. And now the gods are trying to put things right. Lord Einion is their messenger. How can you still be happy with Lord Donald, when you think of the grief he has caused you?'

'That's over.' Eleyne was still trembling. With her hand on Sabina's head, she turned slowly back towards the village. 'Now his mother has gone, it will be different. We are happy again. He won't leave me any more.'

'I hope you are right.' Rhonwen walked ahead slowly. 'Because if ever he makes you unhappy again, I swear I shall kill him and give you back to your king.'

Eleyne stood still, staring at Rhonwen's retreating back. She was cold with horror at the flat note of certainty in Rhonwen's voice and, as if she heard them for the first time, Malcolm Fife's words rang in her head. *It was your nurse that did it. She's a killer by instinct.*

'Rhonwen!' Her voice was sharp.

Twenty yards ahead of her along the track, Rhonwen stopped and turned.

'Did you kill Robert de Quincy?'

Rhonwen smiled. 'Oh yes, *cariad*, I killed him. For you.'

VII

The August sun was unremittingly hot. The mountains baked; the earth dried and cracked. Grass and crops shrivelled and the trees began to shed their leaves as though it were autumn. In the lush orchards of Aber the trees carried small hard apples, red before their time on branches

629

crackling with dryness. The air was heavy, laden with dust and carried the acrid scent of a hundred scrub fires.

Donald and Eleyne lay together in their bedchamber after lunch. They were both naked. They had made love then slept. The whole world slept. The servants who usually shared their room had made their way to the hillside behind the castle where the trees and the bracken shaded them and a slight breeze blew from the strait.

Eleyne awakened suddenly and lay looking at the tester above the bed. She had been dreaming about Colban, and tried to recall the dream, but it had gone. Leaning on her elbow, she gazed down at Donald. At twenty-eight he was, if anything, more handsome than he had been at eighteen. His face had matured as his body had hardened and the small laugh lines at the corners of his eyes gave promise that he would grow more attractive still. Smiling secretly to herself, she kissed him lightly on the mouth and felt her body respond with instant excitement as, still half-asleep, he reached up and pulled her down.

The letter for him came that evening. He read it sitting at the high table beside the Prince of Wales, and at his exclamation of horror and anger Llywelyn turned to him.

'Bad news from Scotland, my friend?'

Eleyne leaned forward. 'What is it, Donald? what has happened?'

'Father!' Donald slammed the letter down on the table amongst the trenchers. 'He has remarried.'

'Your father is still an active man,' Llywelyn said. 'Surely you wouldn't deny him the comfort of a wife.'

'Who is it, Donald?' Eleyne put in. 'Who has he married?'

'Muriel, Malise of Strathearn's daughter.'

Eleyne forced a smile. 'I'm glad. She'll be good to him.'

Muriel of Strathearn was several years younger than she was.

'You shouldn't be glad!' Donald rounded on her. 'He'll have more children. He may even try to threaten the succession to the earldom.'

'You really think he hates me that much?' Eleyne was taken aback, then she shook her head. 'No. He adores Gratney and the twins. He would never do anything to oust them.' She reached across the table and touched his hand. 'It'll be all right, Donald, I promise.'

VIII

KILDRUMMY CASTLE ❖ September 1268

It was a joy to be home. However much she thought she would miss Wales, to be back with her three boys in the cool mountains of the north filled her with enormous pleasure. The fact that Rhonwen had refused to stay in Wales did not. She had tried persuasion; she had even tried to forbid her return, but Rhonwen, tight-lipped and cold, had been adamant, and Eleyne, unable to forget the woman's years of devotion, had at last given in. She had dismissed Rhonwen's claim to have killed Robert; no woman could have done such a thing. Almost wilfully her brain had blanked out the death of Cenydd: that had been an accident, a dreadful accident, no more.

Only days after her return north, she knew she was pregnant again. She went at once to see Morna.

'You told me those things would work!'

She had assiduously done what Morna had told her: the spells, the charms, the salves which would prevent another baby.

'And they do.' Morna was watching little Mairi playing by the burn.

'But they haven't. I did everything you said. I can't have this child. I will lose Donald. Morna, I'm too old to bear any more children. You must help me.'

Morna stared at her. 'You are asking me to help you lose it?'

'You've done it for cottar women, you told me.'

'But I won't do it for you. I'm sorry, but I can't.' Morna frowned. 'This baby is special. The gods would not have allowed you to carry her otherwise. Don't even think about trying to rid yourself of her. You would never forgive yourself if you did.'

'I would never forgive myself if I lost Donald,' Eleyne went on. 'Don't you see? Each time I've been pregnant, he's gone away. He can't stand the sight of me. Do you think he'll go on coming back? At my age? I am old, Morna, old! I have grey hairs and wrinkles on my face and neck. My breasts are sagging and my stomach is no longer flat. Another child and I'll look like his grandmother!'

Morna was amused. 'Let me tell you what I see: a beautiful woman with red-gold hair with some streaks of silver, and a slim, firm body. But she is more than just a body. She has charm and humour and intelligence and a knowledge of men and how to please them. And that's worth far more than the insipid body of a girl.' She smiled. 'Very few wives please their husbands as you please Lord Donald.' She paused and glanced up. 'I will make you a spell to keep your baby and your man.'

IX

A week later Donald was walking beside her in the herb garden which she had planted on the gently sloping ground outside the south wall beyond the great ditch.

'Muriel is pregnant,' he said without preamble. His father's wife had taken over Elizabeth's rooms in the Snow Tower. She was quiet and pleasant and seemed inclined to allow Eleyne to run the castle.

'I know.' Eleyne avoided his eye.

'She's a pretty creature.' Donald bent to pick a sprig of mint and twirled it between his fingers. 'Having a child seems to agree with her.'

Eleyne gritted her teeth.

He laughed out loud. 'I do know, my darling; I've learned to spot the signs. You too grow more beautiful every day.' He put a possessive hand on her stomach and patted it.

Eleyne caught his hand. 'You won't go away this time, will you? Promise me.' She despised herself for saying it, but she couldn't stop herself. 'If you need to go to court, take me with you. I can't bear to be away from you.'

He put his arm around her. 'I shan't leave you. I find you infinitely desirable, knowing you carry another of my sons.' He kissed her gently.

'And if it's a girl?' She heard an echo in her head of Einion's voice and of Morna's.

He grinned. 'If it's a girl, I shall be even more pleased. I would like a daughter, especially one who looks just like her mother.'

X
St Valentine's Eve 1269

A blizzard raged across the Grampian Mountains; thick snow blanketed everything; the skies behind the blinding whiteness were bruised and louring; the castle, in spite of the huge banked fires, was cold and draughty.

Eleyne and Muriel sat with their ladies around the fire in the great hall, embroidering by the light of a hundred candles whilst Donald and his father played chess at the table. In the body of the hall, where most of the household still sat, the trestle tables had been put away and a minstrel was playing a succession of old ballads with choruses in which everyone could join.

Eleyne looked at Donald surreptitiously. His move made, he was gazing down into the body of the hall whilst his father studied the board. She followed his gaze and her heart missed a beat. Catriona, the baker's wife, her red hair bundled beneath a green snood, was sitting near the minstrel. As Eleyne watched, she looked up at Donald and the two exchanged knowing smiles.

Eleyne closed her eyes. The night before Donald had failed to come to her bed. So. It had begun again and this time she could not blame his mother. Without realising it, she put down the piece of fine linen on which she was embroidering a border of flowers and her hand went to the gently swelling mound of her stomach.

Bethoc glanced at Agnes and both grimaced, sensing their mistress's unhappiness. Rhonwen, concentrating short-sightedly on her embroidery in the flickering light, appeared to notice nothing.

Eleyne stayed in the great hall until the candles had burned too low to see. She dreaded going to bed; she knew he would not come.

Not until the last flames began to gutter did she rise. Folding her work and putting it into a rush basket, she smiled wanly at Agnes who dozed near her, her head propped on her arms. In the body of the hall men and women were asleep, on benches or wrapped on the floor in their heavy cloaks. Donald and William had long ago disappeared. As had Catriona. Eleyne had not looked for her in the hall – she knew she would not be there.

Head erect, shoulders back, she walked slowly across the great hall, followed by Agnes who carried her basket, and out into the ice-cold darkness of the stone stair which led up to the Snow Tower.

The whole castle was alive with the scream of the wind as the whirling snow filled the air, drifting into every nook and cranny and every space; creeping beneath the doors, seeping through the ill-fitting glass of the windows and through the shutters. Agnes followed her, carrying a candle which she had collected in the ground-floor storeroom of the tower. The flame streamed, scattering hot wax across her wrist, and she flinched. At the doorway to her chamber Eleyne turned and held out her hand for it. 'Thank you, Agnes, I won't need you again tonight.'

'But my lady –' Agnes protested, the deep moving shadows on her face accenting her prominent nose and eyes, 'let me help you undress.'

'No.' Eleyne spoke sharply. 'I can manage. Goodnight, Agnes.' Taking the candle from her, she groped for the door handle and pushed open the heavy door. The room was completely dark. She closed the door and leaned against it. In the leaping shadows thrown by the single flame she could just see the great bed. The covers were smoothly drawn. It was empty.

Until that moment she had refused to let herself cry, but now the tears began to slide down her face. She stood there long after the candle in her hand had flickered, flared and died. Then she groped her way in total darkness to the bed and threw herself down on it.

She was awakened by a light shining in her eyes. Rhonwen was standing over her. 'You're cold, *cariad*,' she said. 'I called the boy to make up the fire. Come, let me help you into bed properly.'

'No, I'm all right.' Eleyne blinked, dazzled by Rhonwen's fresh candles. 'Please, let me sleep.'

'When I've tucked you in. Look at you!' Clucking and cajoling, Rhonwen pulled off Eleyne's shoes, then dragged at the bedcovers, piling them over her. 'I won't have you crying, *cariad*, not ever again.'

Rhonwen's face was grim. 'Now, you go to sleep and I'll look after everything.'

Eleyne buried her face in the pillows, welcoming the darkness as Rhonwen picked up the candles and carried them away, pulling the door shut behind her, taking the light.

Still enveloped in misery, she dozed for a while, then all of a sudden she was wide awake. Rhonwen's words had echoed back into her mind with appalling clarity.

'Donald!' She sat bolt upright. 'Sweet Blessed Virgin! Donald!' Groping in the darkness she found a candlestick beside her bed, then ran to the fireplace, guided by the glow of the newly banked peats. Thrusting in the candle, she waited impatiently for the wick to catch, then she ran to the door.

Where was he? Where would he and his mistress go? Sobbing, she ran down the stairs, realising for the first time that she was barefoot.

Kildrummy was a huge castle. Five towers linked by stone passages, the great gatehouse, the chapel, the kitchens, the bakehouse, the smithy, the stables and storerooms and the great hall itself, all within the high wall. He could have taken her anywhere.

The doorward stared at her sleepily as she ran, candle streaming, across the store chamber towards him. Behind her the great square wellhead hid the black, still water. 'Lady Rhonwen. Have you seen her?' she shouted. 'Quickly, man, she was here not long ago. Did she go outside again?'

'No, my lady. No one has gone out.' The man stared at her in bewilderment.

'Open the door, let me see.'

Ignoring his protests, she waited impatiently as he pulled back the bolts and dragged the door open. A whirling wall of whiteness greeted them. She could see nothing. Her candle blew out instantly, as did his lantern, and they were left in the darkness. 'No one could slip out past me, my lady,' he called, his voice lost against the roar of the wind.

'All right, shut it.' She watched him put his shoulder to the door and heave it shut, bracing his back against it to catch the massive latch, and she waited, her heart beating with fear, as he groped for kindling and held it in the fire to relight his lantern and then her candle. 'No one would go out on a night like this, lady,' he repeated.

'All right, thank you.' She turned. They were still in the tower then, or in one of the curtain towers linked by narrow wall passages to the great hall.

'Blessed Lady, help me! Let me be in time.' She turned left and headed towards the stairs again and the passage which linked the Snow

Tower with its neighbour. Used for visiting guests, the huge south-western tower, newly finished, was empty at this time of year – the servants and household preferring to huddle together by the fires in the great hall. The passages were deserted; the rush lamps which usually lit them had gone out; the corners were full of leaping shadows cast by her own candle.

'*Rhonwen!*' she screamed. She heard her voice echo dully against the stone and die below the shriek of the wind. '*Donald!*' Frantically, she peered into an empty storeroom opening off the passage. It was deserted. Opposite it, another store was full, packed with great earthenware jars of mustard and honey, barrels of dried fish and salt beef, loaves of sugar, locked spice chests and sacks of grain. She held her candle high, trying to see into the depths of the room, then she hurried on, throwing open door after door, her feet icy on the cold grey flags. The lower floors of the tower were deserted. She brushed the tears from her eyes and hurried on. A sharp pain knifed through her side and she stopped to catch her breath. It was a stitch, that was all. There was nothing wrong with the baby. In despair, she stood at the foot of the spiral staircase and stared up into the darkness.

'Donald!' Her voice was thin. It would never carry. Perhaps she was already too late. Slowly she began to climb, feeling the dryness of panic catching at the back of her throat, and the constriction of her chest as her breath came in shorter and shorter gasps.

'*Donald!*' She paused and stared upwards, seeing the shadow of her candle flame slanting across the underside of the steps above her as the stair wound upwards.

'Donald!' He would never hear her. Wherever he was, he had no doubt shut the door and was by now fully distracted by his red-haired love. Her only hope was that he had bolted himself in somewhere where Rhonwen could not reach him.

The echo of a door slamming above her in the empty tower brought a sob to throat. Frantically she began to climb again, tripping on her gown and nearly dropping her candle.

XI

Rhonwen held her candle high. Her soft leather shoes were silent on the stone flags, the whisper of her skirts lost in the howl of the wind. She crept on up the stairs. She had already searched the warden's tower and the half-built carcass of stone at the south-eastern corner of the walls. They weren't there, nor were they in the warm bakehouse or in the kitchens. Only the south-western tower remained. She gripped the candlestick more tightly, feeling the warm wax dripping on to her

635

fingers as she stumbled upwards. Pushed into her girdle was a newly sharpened knife.

She looked upwards. The door of the chamber on the top floor was closed. The candlelight veered wildly across the heavy oak. Pausing to catch her breath, she waited until the flame of her candle had steadied then she put her hand to the handle. The iron ring was ice-cold and heavy. With a silent curse she stooped and put down the candle, then she grasped the ring with both hands and began to turn it. The door was stiff. Holding her breath, she pushed. It creaked as it began to swing open, but the noise was lost in the roar of the wind from the unglazed lancets. Her candle went out.

She inched into the dark echoing chamber, silently taking the knife from her girdle, and stood looking at the scene before her.

Donald and his paramour were lying in each other's arms on a pile of empty flour sacks. In the small circle of lamplight, Catriona's pale body was indecently white against the flaming red of her hair, her eyes huge and terrified as she stared up at the old woman who stood over them with a naked dirk in her hand.

Behind her, the door banged in the draught.

XII

Her heart beating in her throat, Eleyne climbed the last flight of stairs. Her legs were trembling, and strange sharp pains were pulling at her chest. Desperately she sheltered the flame of her candle with her free hand, tripping on her skirts, her eyes blinded with tears.

'Donald!'

Her breathless cry was lost in the night.

XIII

'So.' Rhonwen looked down at Donald with scorn. 'You are no better than I thought, no better than any other man, for all my lady thought you were some sort of god!' She tightened her grip on the dirk. 'And no doubt you will bleed like any other man.'

Donald, his gown around his waist, looked up at her helplessly. His mantle and his belt, with his own dirk, lay in a heap on the dusty floor outside the circle of light and out of reach. He was pinned by the slack weight of the frightened woman who lay half across his body.

'Rhonwen!' His voice was a husky whisper. 'You don't understand!' He tried to push the woman off, but paralysed with fright she could not move.

'Please, Rhonwen, wait.' His eyes went towards his own weapon and then back to her, drawn irresistibly to the gleaming blade in her hand.

'I've waited long enough,' Rhonwen said softly. 'In fact, I've waited too long for this moment. You've caused my lady nothing but heartache and misery. You are worthless. Trash. Even Robert de Quincy was a knight.' She smiled as she saw his eyes darken and her fingers tightened imperceptibly on the hilt of her knife as she raised it above her head.

The door crashed open.

'Rhonwen! No!' Eleyne's scream brought Rhonwen up short, but she was distracted only for a moment. 'It has to be, *cariad*, I have to do this.' She raised her arm until the blade caught the soft lamplight. 'He betrayed you. He is not fit to live. I shall give you back to your king.'

As she lunged downwards at Donald, Eleyne threw herself across the floor, grabbing for the hand that held the knife. The door banged again. Only the small flame in the lamp on the floor beside the lovers lit the scene. 'No you can't! You can't kill him! I forbid it!' She was sobbing as her fingers locked around Rhonwen's wrist. How could she have been so stupid as to let Rhonwen return to Kildrummy? Why hadn't she seen the extent of the woman's madness? Why had she fooled herself for so long? 'Drop it! For Sweet Jesus' sake, drop it!'

'I have to, *cariad*.' Even as she struggled, Rhonwen's voice remained totally calm. 'I have to give you back to your king. I have to.' She was panting slightly as Donald, at last disentangling himself, rose to his knees, his gown falling into place to cover his nakedness. Breaking free of Eleyne's clutches, Rhonwen lunged at him with an animal growl and plunged her knife into his shoulder.

Eleyne grabbed for her hand. 'No!' she screamed as blood poured down Donald's arm. 'For pity's sake, no!'

The two women swayed back and forth, slipping on the scattered sacks. Rhonwen's eyes were blank. Her lips were fixed in a snarl as she threw herself at Donald once more.

She was surprisingly strong for a woman of her years and Eleyne, already bulky, had not yet recovered her breath from her desperate climb up the stairs, but at last the strength seemed to go out of Rhonwen's arm. Forcing the dirk as hard as she could away from Donald, Eleyne felt the woman's arm give way.

There was a moment's total silence as Rhonwen stepped back, a look of astonishment on her face. Her mouth opened. 'You've killed me, *cariad*,' she murmured. 'Silly child. I was doing it for you –' She crumpled to her knees. A trickle of blood had appeared at the corner of her mouth. The dagger was embedded in her chest she fell backwards on to the piled sacks and lay still. Eleyne staggered and leaned against the wall gasping for breath, tears pouring down her face as Catriona grabbed her shift and fled from the room.

'Is she dead?' Eleyne whispered at last, her voice all but lost in the howl of the wind.

'Yes.' Donald bit his lip. 'She's dead.' He stooped and, pulling out the dirk, he flung it on the ground.

He went to his wife and tried to put his arms around her, but she pushed him away. 'Don't touch me!'

'Eleyne!' His hands dropped to his sides. 'I know you're upset, but –'

'But what?' Her eyes were blazing. 'I just found you making love to another woman and –'

'That didn't mean anything.'

'Of course it meant something! Why else would you have done it?' She was almost hysterical. 'I nearly lost my baby trying to follow Rhonwen to save you and now – and now –' her eyes flooded with tears – 'and now she is dead and I killed her.'

'You saved my life, my darling.'

'I killed her!' Rhonwen lay sprawled on her back, her eyes wide open, gazing sightlessly upwards at the shadowy vaulted ceiling. 'I killed her . . .' She held out her hands in front of her, staring at them in revulsion.

'And how many people has she killed in her life, Nel?' Donald asked gently. He did not try to touch her again. 'You told me that she admitted having killed Robert de Quincy. You told me you suspected there were other people she had poisoned: John of Chester, Alexander's queen – even Malcolm himself perhaps! Sweet Christ, Eleyne! She nearly succeeded in killing me!' He clamped his hand to his shoulder, where his gown was slowly turning red, and brought it away, his fingers sticky with blood. 'Do you realise that woman might have been responsible for the deaths of all your husbands! Christ only knows why you kept her near you!'

For a moment they both stood staring down at Rhonwen's body. Eleyne was shaking her head. 'But she loved *me*!' she whispered. 'And I killed her!'

'She was a dangerous, mad woman, Eleyne.' Wearily Donald stooped and picking up a sack he threw it over Rhonwen's face and shoulders. 'Come away now.'

'Someone will have to be with her.'

'I'll deal with it.' He picked up the lantern. 'How did you know where to come?'

'I searched the whole tower.'

'And you knew what she was going to do?'

Eleyne nodded. 'It was something she said in Wales. That if you made me cry she would kill you.'

'And I made you cry.' Donald's face was full of anguish.

'It was tonight that I realised you had gone to that woman again and I knew this time you wouldn't come back.' She gave a helpless, angry shrug. 'We both knew this would happen one day; that I would grow old.'

She knelt beside Rhonwen and gently pulled back the sack.

'Old!' Donald shook his head. 'How could you be old? You are carrying my child!'

'And it makes me unattractive to you.' She shrugged, not looking at him. 'I understand.'

She touched Rhonwen's face with a gentle hand and closed the staring eyes. Then, summoning all her dignity, she stood up and turned towards the door. The shock was beginning to hit her afresh, and she could feel herself trembling. 'I think I'll go to bed.'

'Eleyne.' His voice stopped her. 'I love you. That whore meant nothing. Nothing at all, I swear it.'

She smiled faintly. 'Goodnight,' she said.

He did not follow her. When she looked back from the door at the head of the stairway, he was standing looking down at Rhonwen's body.

CHAPTER TWENTY-SEVEN

I

KILDRUMMY CASTLE ❖ 1269

Eleyne's daughter, Isabella, was born at the end of May. To commemorate the occasion, Donald gave his wife a gold filigree chain. To his new daughter, for a christening present, he gave a silver casket.

Neither of them ever mentioned the events of Valentine's Eve. Rhonwen was buried without the benefit of the Christian requiem, which she would have abhorred, in an unmarked grave in the woods far to the north of the castle. When at last the snows thawed, her embalmed body was lowered into the ground by four men from the village. It was left to Morna, at Eleyne's request, to plant flowers on the spot and whisper prayers to the old gods for the comfort of her soul. Catriona and her husband were sent to Aberdeen with enough money to set themselves up as baxters to the burgesses there.

A few days after Rhonwen died, Bethoc brought a small wooden coffer to Eleyne's chamber and put it on the table. 'I've given all her clothes away as you asked, my lady,' she said gently, 'but there are more personal things. I thought . . .' She hesitated, looking at Eleyne's pale strained face, 'I thought you might want them.'

She did not touch the coffer for a long time, then at last she moved across to it and laid her hand on the wood. It was heavily carved in the Welsh fashion. She remembered it from when she was a small child, following Rhonwen everywhere, from Aber to Llanfaes, from Caernarfon to Degannwy to Hay and later to Chester and Fotheringhay and London. Fighting her tears, she turned the key in the lock and pushed back the lid. There were pitifully few possessions – an ivory comb, a few enamelled buckles and a silver brooch, some beads and a silk kerchief. Eleyne's hands strayed to the kerchief, then she took it out and unwrapped it.

The phoenix lay in her palm. She stared at it with a pang of longing. It was so beautiful, catching the thin morning sunlight which slanted through the lancet windows. Carrying it, she went to the window seat and sat down. Until her child was born there was nothing to fear. But then . . . Thoughtfully she weighed it in her hand. It was the link and she must get rid of it.

Donald did not return to Eleyne's bed until Isabella was nearly three months old, but as far as she knew he did not seek comfort elsewhere. When he came back, they were both changed by what had happened: calmer, more reticent and sad. It was a complete surprise when he brought up the subject of Alexander again.

'Rhonwen believed he had come back, didn't she?' he said as they rode side by side through the woods towards Glenbuchat Tower.

Eleyne's hands tightened involuntarily on her palfrey's reins and the horse threw up its head in resentment. 'She believed in him, yes,' she said quietly.

He examined her: her seat on a horse was still neat and beautiful, her head erect as she looked straight ahead between the horse's ears. She was a princess, he reminded himself; perhaps she should have been a queen.

She went on without looking at him, her words painfully slow as she confronted her memories. 'She thought she saw him once and she believed he was waiting for me and that only you stood in his way.'

'We believe that too, don't we?' Donald put in. He didn't give her a chance to reply. 'How did she propose to give you back to him once I was dead?'

Eleyne was staring ahead towards the mountains. 'I think in the end she would have killed me too.'

She thought for a minute. 'It's his love that brings him back, Donald. He doesn't mean to frighten me and he would certainly not want to hurt me.' It was hard for her to speak calmly about something she kept buried so deep. 'I think perhaps it was my belief that first allowed his spirit to return. When I was married to Robert and then to Malcolm, I had to believe he was still there to keep my sanity and because I longed for him so much I allowed him to come to me.'

'Through the pendant.' Donald had reined in beside her.

She nodded. 'It was as though he had planned it that way when he gave it to me all those years ago. I think he knew we would never be together in this life. He uses it as a link; a bridge of some kind. But I don't think he needs it any more.' He was still there, she was sure of it, even though the phoenix was no longer at Kildrummy. She glanced across at him, pain and something like fear in her eyes. 'I think he's growing stronger all the time. It's love gone mad. Out of control. Even without the phoenix.' She bit her lip. 'He's no longer a king, so he sees no reason for us to be apart. He doesn't have to think about Scotland or what men like your father think. All he cares about is me.' It was a relief to have voiced her fears at last.

641

Donald reached across and touched her hands. 'But you can control him. He can't cross your magic circle.'

'No.' It was a whisper. 'He can't cross it. He can't come back without the phoenix. Not yet.'

'And Rhonwen has gone.'

'He didn't need Rhonwen, Donald. He doesn't need anyone. He doesn't even see anyone else. Except you.'

Donald could feel the hairs standing up on the back of his neck.

'It was when I met you. I tried to turn my back on him and he knew. He knew that I loved you.' She looked at him for the first time. 'No ghost could compete with the love I felt for you.'

He blushed and she smiled. She loved the way he still coloured at her compliments, like a boy.

'And do you still feel that way about me?' he asked after they had ridden on some way.

'I think I must . . .'

'Even after I betrayed you?'

'Even then.'

He stared at her. She was still the most beautiful woman he had ever seen. 'I think you bewitched me the first time I met you, and I think you have kept me bewitched ever since.'

She laughed. 'I sincerely hope so.'

'I'm a very lucky man. Poor Alexander.'

The laughter died in her eyes. 'We're making him so unhappy. I've tried to tell him I hate to hurt him but he makes me afraid.'

His eyes sought hers. 'Where is the phoenix now?'

'Gone for good, where no one will find it.'

'I see.' He urged his horse on thoughtfully. 'But you don't think that will keep him at bay?'

Her eyes went back to the mountains in the distance. 'I don't know any more,' she murmured. Then she went on, so quietly he didn't hear her words, 'I can only pray, because if he gets much stronger I shan't be able to control him.'

II

KILDRUMMY CASTLE ❖ January 1270

She adored the children unreservedly. Gratney at three was a chubby, mischievous child, into everything, already a determined rider, hanging on to the mane of the tiny fat pony she had found for him at the horse fair in Aberdeen. His twin brothers seemed equally extrovert and equally determined to succeed, tumbling over one another like the puppies they played with, and the three children were noisy favourites throughout the castle.

Secretly Donald watched the twins as they played, searching for signs of differences between them, searching in spite of himself for the clues or mannerisms which would identify one of the children as the son of another man, a man who had been dead for twenty years, but it was impossible. As they chuckled and wrestled and climbed over him on his visits to the nursery, he found himself responding with equal delight and love to all the smothering eager little bodies which hung around his neck. As did his wife. Never once did he catch Eleyne making any difference in her treatment of the children. Kisses for Duncan matched kisses for Alexander and so did slaps. There was no sign that she considered any of her sons to be of different blood.

When she found she was pregnant again in her fifty-second year, Eleyne cried. She was bouncing with health. She felt no sickness or aches or pains. Her hair was glossier and thicker than ever and Donald had been, if anything, more attentive than at any time in the last four years. This time she told him at once. He stared at her. Then he laughed. Then he kissed her. 'My lovely fruitful wife!'

'You will stay with me, Donald?' She could not keep the fear out of her voice.

'I promise.' He kissed her again.

III

KILDRUMMY ❖ March 1270

She had no premonition of disaster, no seeing in the flames. When Donald came to her in the stillroom, he found her with an apron over her gown poring over an old book of recipes.

'Nel –' Curtly he dismissed the servants and, with one look at his face, they all obeyed immediately.

'What is it?' Guiltily she slid a box of dried orris over the parchment page. The recipe was one for ensuring the fidelity of one's husband.

Donald hesitated. How could he tell her? His mouth was dry. He didn't know what to say. He should have brought the letter to her, shown her that.

She was suddenly full of misgivings. 'What is it? What has happened?'

'It's Colban.'

'Colban? What's wrong with Colban?'

'He's dead, Eleyne.'

'Dead?' Her face drained of colour. 'That's not possible.'

643

'His horse fell. I'm sorry.' He was doing it all wrong, but he didn't know how else to break the news.

She stood, stunned, the pestle she had been using still in her hand.

'No.' Her whisper was pitiful. 'I would have known. It can't be true. It can't.'

'I'm so sorry, my darling.' He put out his arms and blindly she went to him.

'I must go to him.'

He frowned. 'Do you think that's wise?'

'Of course it's wise!' she flashed. 'I have to go to him! I have to be there. Don't you see?' Her voice was broken. 'I have to see him.'

IV

FALKLAND CASTLE

'I'm sorry, my lady.' John Keith looked unhappy and embarrassed. 'Lady Fife will not receive you.'

'What do you mean?' Exhausted after the precipitous ride from Mar, Eleyne had ridden to the door of the great hall at Falkland with all the confidence of long ownership. It had not crossed her mind that she would be denied entry.

'I think there is some mistake, Sir John,' Donald said sharply. 'My wife has come to be with Lady Fife and her son at this terrible time.'

'I know.' Keith shrugged miserably. 'She has told me not to let you in.'

'Where is my son's body?' Eleyne's voice was very tight.

'In the chapel, my lady.'

'I take it Lady Fife does not object to my going there.' She did not wait for an answer. Riding to the chapel door – the scene of her first marriage to Malcolm, the place where both her eldest sons had been baptised – she slid from her horse and went into the cool darkness.

His body lay on a bier before the altar, his sword clasped between his hands. Candles burned at his head and his feet. Eleyne walked slowly to his side and stood staring down at him, ignoring the monks who prayed near him. Colban looked younger than when she had last seen him the year before. His face was serene, boyish, happy. He was seventeen years old.

Closing her eyes, she felt a wave of dizziness sweep over her. She did not cry – she hadn't cried since the news had come. Leaning over, she kissed him gently on the forehead and then went to kneel on the faldstool at his feet.

Behind her Sir Alan Durward had come into the chapel. He stood beside Donald for a moment without speaking, gazing at Eleyne.

'I'm sorry that Anna was so cruel,' he said quietly at last to Donald. The two men eyed each other with hostility, the long court case between Sir Alan and Donald's father over the earldom of Mar as always in both their minds when they met. Simultaneously they made the decision to ignore it for Eleyne's sake. 'Anna is beside herself with grief. Of course you are both welcome here. It's unthinkable that you should not be at the funeral.'

His sympathy was not endorsed by his wife or daughter. Neither Margaret nor Anna would speak to Eleyne and, to her fathomless grief, they refused to let her see her grandson, Duncan.

'I'm sorry, mama,' Macduff was red-eyed and pale, 'Anna doesn't want you to go near him.' He didn't know how to say that his sister-in-law thought his mother possessed the evil eye.

'Why?' Eleyne was bewildered and hurt.

He shrugged. 'Give her time. She'll get over it.' He grinned wanly. 'I had a little chat with Duncan, uncle to nephew, you know, and he sends you his love.'

'Does he realise what has happened?' Eleyne asked Macduff. He was like his brother in many ways, though she had to admit a sturdier and more reliable version. Her heart went out to him as she watched him fighting his tears.

'He knows his father is dead. He knows he is the new earl, or will be one day.' Macduff grinned ruefully. 'It's a shame a brother no longer seems to have a claim to inherit. This fashion for primogeniture is a disaster for the Earls of Fife. I'd have made a good earl.'

Eleyne gave a wistful smile. 'Yes, you would.' She put her arm around the boy and hugged him.

'You told me once I'd be a great soldier, that you had seen it in the stars. Did you see this for Colban? Did you know he was going to die?' he asked, biting his lip.

Eleyne shook her head. 'It wasn't me. It was Adam, the wizard, who saw your futures. He never told me what he saw for Colban, so perhaps I should have guessed.' Her eyes filled with tears. 'Why did it happen?'

He shook his head. 'Why does anything happen? Bad luck. A bird went up under his horse's feet. He wasn't paying attention. He was never as good a rider as me –' He stopped guiltily at the sound of his own boasting – it had come so automatically – and she smiled reassuringly.

'It's true, you always were the better horseman, even when you were both small.'

He grimaced. 'The earldom has been in a minority for four years already. Do you realise they will have to wait now until Duncan is twenty-one before there is someone in Fife who can administer the earldom personally? In the meantime, no doubt, the king will take the revenues again.' The king was already taking the revenues on the few lands left directly to Macduff by his father.

Eleyne nodded thoughtfully. 'When you are twenty-one, I will speak to the king for you. I'm sure he will make you one of the earldom's guardians and give you some of its revenue so that you can set up your own household.' She smiled fondly. 'Fife will need you, my darling,' she said gently. 'For the sake of your father's people you must be patient.'

V

May 1270

When Donald left Kildrummy again, twelve weeks after they had returned home, to join his father in the king's council, Eleyne smiled and kissed him and wished him well. If it were the will of the gods, he would come home. He did, three days after Marjorie's birth in August, with gifts for her and all the children and an invitation from the king.

'He commands your presence at court, my darling,' he said as they sat at table in the great hall with Muriel. His father's wife had become Eleyne's friend. Childless after a first, sad miscarriage, the Countess of Mar, though younger than Eleyne, had assumed with ease the role of the grandmother and confidante to the children. 'He says you have been away too long. As soon as you are fully recovered from the birth we will ride south.'

Donald adored his two daughters. They both had their mother's hair and eyes; they both laughed a lot and played with the toys he brought for them. As he surveyed his overflowing nursery, he sometimes found it hard to believe all these children could be his. Five children in four years. Three sons, two daughters and a wife who, to his infatuated eyes, seemed younger than ever.

VI

Now she did resort to magic and to the tricks that Morna taught her; to go alone into the hills and whisper to the gods; to stand naked under the moon and let its cold benign light stroke her skin and iron away the signs of age. There would be no more children. The knowledge had come to her as suddenly and as surely as she knew now that Donald would return each time he went away; knowing it, she was more certain, more alluring, when they were together. But it was less often. She accepted that now too.

As if to make up for the lessening at last of passion, the Sight returned. On the hills she had visions. She felt the tides of magic which ebbed and flowed with the moon and she grew less afraid. She foresaw that the young man Agnes loved would tumble from the back of a wagon and break his leg. She knew when Sir Duncan Comyn would fall ill with fever and she knew he would recover. Three times she had the vision of the horseman in the storm. But still she could not see his face. And unknowingly, as she opened her heart to worlds beyond the whirling darkness, she allowed Alexander back into her life. With her collusion, even though it was unwitting, he had no need of the phoenix. He was growing stronger.

The night of the first full moon in September he returned. Eleyne was watching Isabella as she took her first unsteady steps from one nursemaid to another in the warm afternoon sunshine. All the children were there. The three boys playing boisterously with a ball, little Marjorie asleep in a plaited straw basket and Isabella. For some reason it was to this one child above all the others – not to Sandy – that her heart reached out, and with it a fear she couldn't name. It was then that she felt it: the faintest breath against her cheek, a touch on her arm so light it could have been her imagination. For a moment she didn't understand.

Eleyne . . .

She heard her name so clearly she looked around, puzzled. There was no one there, save the children and their nurses. No one who would dare to call her Eleyne.

Eleyne . . .

It was fainter this time, just an echo in her mind, but suddenly she understood. She stepped backwards, her heart beating fast, staring around her. She had given the phoenix to the gods at the sacred spring, thrown far out into the pool where Elizabeth of Mar had died. How could he be here? How could he? What had she done to allow him near her?

'My lady, look!'

'Mama! Look at Isabella!'

'Mama! She's walking by herself!' The chorus of cries claimed her, pulled her back to the present and he was gone.

That night she clung to Donald as though she would never let him go, worshipping his body, touching him with greedy fingers, kissing him, pulling him inside her with a hunger that delighted him. When they lay apart at last, spent and exhausted, she peered into the shadowy corners of the room with something like fear. 'Don't come again, please,' she murmured into the emptiness. 'Don't take me from him.' With her heart closed and without the phoenix, surely he could not come near her?

647

'You have to help me,' she said to Morna. 'There's no one else I can talk to. It's as though he's trying to win me back, as though he's pulling me. Tearing me in half. I got rid of the phoenix, but still he comes.'

She put her head in her hands. 'I think I'm going mad. He's there all the time even when Donald is with me. I can feel him, sense him – he won't leave me alone. Why suddenly, after all these years? Why has he come back?'

Morna shrugged. 'Something has happened to give him hope.' She sighed. 'You have learned to walk in the world of the moonlight. He senses you near him there and his love is so strong that it builds the bridge between you. Perhaps you should do as Lord Donald wishes and go to the king. You said before that you thought he would not follow you near his son.'

VIII

SCONE PALACE ❖ September 1270

The king greeted Eleyne and Donald warmly and at once drew them inside. 'Lord Donald, your father has reminded me that you, the most chivalrous and knightly of men, have never been given the accolade of knighthood. It is my intention to confer it upon you here at Michaelmas.' He took Donald's hand and clapped him on the shoulder, then he glanced at Eleyne with an embarrassed little shrug. 'I'm glad we can put it right at last and that you can be presented with your spurs by your king.'

Eleyne's heart was bursting with pride. In all their years together, they had never discussed the terrible day when the king had denied his knighthood. Eleyne had never mentioned it: her guilt was too profound. If he thought about it, he kept it to himself. He had never reproached her, never given any sign that he thought about it at all. But now the incredulous joy on his face reminded her of how much he had been prepared to give up for her. Silently she touched his arm; he smiled and that smile told her what she wanted to know. His love for her still came first. He would give up a thousand knighthoods for her if she commanded it. She gave him a little push and stood back as Donald knelt before his king and kissed his hand.

The day after the ceremony of knighthood Eleyne walked in the great park at Scone. Bethoc was with her, half-heartedly twirling a spindle as she followed her mistress. 'You look happy, my lady,' she smiled. 'You must have been so proud of Sir Donald.'

Eleyne stopped. 'I am.'

She had much to be happy about: Donald. Their children. Macduff. Little Duncan.

There was a special place in her heart for Joanna and Hawisa, apart, toughened to keep the pain at bay, and another there for Colban and her two dead babies by the king and for Rhonwen, but she did not let herself dwell on them. Her mourning for them was done in the dark and in her prayers. And there was Alexander. Her love for Alexander – a thing apart, a piece of her future after she too had died. She frowned. What had made her think such a thing? Alexander was nothing to her now, nothing. There was no place for him near her or near his son. But even as she thought it she knew that was not true. She had been wrong to think he would not come near his son. He was here. He was everywhere. This was still his kingdom and next to her he loved Alexander more than anyone on earth.

The sun was reflecting on the distant curve of the river, sending zigzags of silver across the rippled water. Bethoc's voice came to her in waves, advancing, retreating, muffled as the silver broadened and merged into a carpet which darkened and flattened under the weight of the rain.

The horse was a grey, a stallion, its eyes wild, its neck arched, its scarlet bridle studded and decorated with gold. The rider sat forward eagerly, his hands wet on the slippery reins as he urged the animal forward through the storm. He was excited, exhilarated by the crash of thunder around him, alone with the darkness and the elements.

'Slow down,' Eleyne could hear herself calling, 'slow down, be careful, please.' Behind her Alexander – her Alexander – was watching with her. She could feel him, feel his fear.

He was going faster now, the animal's great muscles bunching and flexing as it covered the ground. A flash of lightning sliced through the sky and the horse shied, nearly unseating him. She heard him curse above the roar of the wind; another flash of lightning and the horse reared with a piercing scream. In that moment he turned his head and for a fleeting second she saw his face at last.

'My lady.' Bethoc was shaking her arm, her face white. 'My lady? What's the matter? what is it?' The woman looked terrified.

Eleyne looked at her blankly.

'My lady, what is it?' Bethoc repeated, shaking Eleyne's arm. 'Shall I call someone? What's wrong?'

'The king,' Eleyne whispered, 'I have to see the king.' She turned as though Bethoc wasn't there and began to run up the park back towards the palace. 'I have to see him, now, alone.'

She was gasping when she reached the king's hall, and pressed her hand to her side as the pain of a stitch knifed through her, barely aware of how she must look to the staring attendants. Her gown was dusty and her face pale. Her head-dress had fallen back and her braids hung loose around her shoulders. 'Please. I have to see him, now –'

Her raised voice must have reached the king for he looked up from the table where he was studying some documents with two of his advisers. 'Aunt Eleyne . . . ?'

'Please, I have to talk to you. Alone.' Trying to steady her breath and talk calmly, Eleyne hastened towards him.

'Of course.' After one puzzled glance at her anguished face, Alexander gestured those around him away. 'Sit down. Here, let me pour you some wine.'

Eleyne collapsed on to the stool he pulled forward and took the wine with a shaking hand. 'Forgive me, sire. I had to see you.'

'So, I am here.' He sat down opposite her and smiled. 'Tell me what's wrong.' He leaned forward, his elbows on his knees, his rich blue gown, stitched with silver, hitched up to show his cross-gartered hose. He was like his father, very like – his colouring, the strong face, the eyes which could within seconds turn from anger to compassion. He had shown himself a strong and effective monarch, and under his rule Scotland was prospering. He had two sons now and a daughter. He was absolutely in control of himself and of his country's destiny, so why was she filled with such a certainty of disaster?

She tore her eyes from his face and looked down. 'Ever since I was a child I have had the gift of the Sight. One of the visions I have had again and again was of a man riding his horse in a storm. The horse is scared by the lightning and throws his rider.'

There was total silence in the big room. The king did not move. His eyes were on hers.

'This morning I had that vision again, and for the first time I saw the rider's face.' Alexander had shown it to her. 'It was you, sire.'

At last he spoke. 'You think you have foreseen the manner of my death?' His voice was calm.

'I've never seen what happened after the rider falls, but my feeling is one of such fear and dread . . .' She opened her hands in a gesture of hopelessness.

He smiled. 'Perhaps I should take it as a warning never to ride again in a storm.' Standing up, he took her hands and raised her to her feet. 'Thank you for telling me.'

'What are you going to do?'

'What can I do? If the manner of my death is already written in the stars I cannot avoid it. Except, as I say,' he grinned, 'by keeping in out of the storm.'

'Please God the warning can save you.'

He nodded fervently. 'Amen to that! I receive many warnings – from sages, from soothsayers, from spaewives, as I ride around the

kingdom. Most of the time they are wrong, the Lord be thanked. Sometimes they are right.' He followed her to the edge of the dais, and
rubbed his hands over his face. 'You know, Michael Scot of Balwearie
once prophesied my horse would be the cause of my death. And
Thomas of Ercildoune himself has said I would be killed by a storm.
They would seem to have had the same premonition as you. So,' he
put his hand on her arm, 'just one more thing, before you go. What
colour was the horse?' There was laughter in his eyes now.

'Grey.'

'Then the answer is simple. Never again shall I ride a grey.'

IX

Alexander – her Alexander – came to her again that evening as she sat
at the table in her bedchamber writing a letter to Macduff. Bethoc was
near her, hemming a gown, her eyes narrowed as she held the garment
up to the last light from the window. Eleyne felt her pen slow and
falter as she became aware that someone was standing behind her.
When she looked around there was no one there and she turned back
to the letter but she did not pick up the pen. Alexander was at her
shoulder; she could feel him watching her, feel him wanting her to
turn to him and smile.

Trembling, she got to her feet and walked to the window, only
dimly hearing Bethoc's exclamation of irritation, hastily cut short, as
her mistress blocked the light. Bethoc looked up and for a brief instant
she thought she saw a tall shadow hovering at Eleyne's side. Her mouth
dropped open and she crossed herself, dropping her sewing on to the
table where light from the lancet window fell across the old polished
oak. 'My lady,' she whispered. Her mouth had gone dry.

Eleyne didn't appear to have heard her, then she turned. 'I'm
sorry?' The window was empty now, the shadow gone. Whatever it
was had disappeared as soon as Bethoc spoke.

'That's all right, my lady, it's just that I thought I saw
something . . .' Her words faded uncertainly.

Eleyne looked at her sharply. 'What do you mean?'

'I thought I saw someone standing in the window near you.'

'Who?'

'I don't know. It was only for a moment, then he was gone.'

Eleyne shook her head. 'That's nonsense. It was a trick of the light.
Come, let me help you with your stitching, then we must go down to
join the men in the hall for supper.'

She sat down, gathering her skirts neatly around her, and picked
up Bethoc's work basket, searching for needle and threads and thimble,

but twice Bethoc saw her glance back at the window where she had been standing. The expression on her face was troubled.

That night as Donald drew the curtains around their bed she clung to him with fear rather than passion. 'Nel, what is it, my darling?' He held her close, stroking her hair. Her skin was cold as ice.

'Hold me.' There was nothing flirtatious in the way she nestled into his arms. She reminded him more of a frightened child.

'What's wrong? What is it?' he whispered. Something in her fear was communicating itself to him. 'For pity's sake, tell me.' He tightened his arms protectively.

'He's here,' she whispered back. 'He wants me. And he's grown so strong!'

'Sweet Jesus!' He did not need to ask who she meant.

'Hold me, Donald. Don't let him take me.'

'No one will take you anywhere.' Sitting up, he pushed back the bed curtain and groped for the tinder. The sudden pale glow of the candle flame sent shadows leaping round the bedchamber, over the truckle beds along the far wall with the three sleeping women and up the hangings on one of the walls. The room was completely still.

'There's no one here, Eleyne. Look, the dogs are asleep. They wouldn't let anyone near you, you know that. It's your imagination, Nel. He wouldn't come here.'

She gave a doubtful smile. 'I'm sorry. It must have been a dream.'

The candle flame spluttered in an unseen draught and a spatter of wax spilled across the coffer where it was standing.

Eleyne stared into the shadows. It was no dream. He was there. She could feel him, feel the anguish, feel the longing. His raw pain made her flinch. It was like a scream deep inside her.

Donald felt it too. 'Why now? Why has he come back now?'

'It was my fault. It was because I let him back in.' Her voice was all but inaudible.

'How?' He sounded incredulous.

'I didn't mean to. It was after Marjorie was born, as if he knew I could no longer bear you any children.' Her voice broke into a sob. 'I was afraid I would grow ugly in your eyes, and I prayed to be beautiful again. I opened myself to the forces of magic, and he came back. Don't let him near me, please! Hold me!' She threw herself back into his arms, pressing her face against his chest.

'He can't hurt you, Eleyne,' he murmured, stroking her hair. 'If he loved you so much, he won't want to hurt you.'

'No?' She looked up at him. 'No,' she repeated thoughtfully, 'he doesn't want to hurt me. He knows he can't share me, not any more. So he wants to take me away from you.'

The truth had come to her in a flash. 'Today I told the king the manner of his death.' She swallowed hard. 'I foresaw it long ago, but I didn't understand. I never recognised him before. Then today I saw his face. I saw his face because Alexander showed it to me.' She pressed herself against Donald's chest. 'Now that he knows, now that I have warned him – there is no need for me to live. My purpose has been fulfilled and Alexander knows his son has been warned. Don't you see, Donald? He wants me dead!'

'Nonsense.' Donald looked over the top of her head into the darkness. 'He'd have to fight me for you.' The hair on his forearms was standing on end. He could feel an eerie coldness around them as he strained his eyes into the shadows. 'Tell him, tell him I'm not letting you go. Tell him to go away.'

'I have, I've begged him.' Her voice rose hysterically and Bethoc stirred and sat up.

'My lady?' she queried sleepily.

'Go back to sleep,' Donald commanded.

Gently pushing Eleyne from him he stood up and reached for the dagger which lay on the coffer beside him. Unsheathing it, he raised it before him, hilt uppermost, the thought of his all-night vigil in the royal chapel on the night before his knighthood still fresh in his mind. 'In the name of Our Lord Jesus Christ and of Our Blessed Lady, I command you to leave my wife alone. Go back to wherever you came from. Leave her in peace. Tell him.' He pressed the dirk into Eleyne's hand. 'Tell him this is what you want.'

'Please, Alexander, please go.' Eleyne raised the dirk in front of her, holding it in both hands. 'I loved you. I still love you, but I'm not ready to come to you, not yet. I want to stay with Donald and with my children as long as they need me. Please leave me. I'll watch over your son, I'll show him the danger, I'll keep him safe from the storm.'

In her bed Bethoc realised she had stopped breathing. Clutching her blankets under her chin, she watched the bed curtains, her heart thundering with fright. She could see the shadow again, quite clearly, standing over Eleyne.

Eleyne looked up as though she too could see it. 'Please,' she whispered brokenly, 'if you love me, go.'

He was fading now. Bethoc lost the shape amongst the shadows.

Eleyne felt him drawing away, his sadness tangible. 'Bless you, my love,' she whispered. 'God keep you. One day I'll come to you, I promise. One day, when they don't need me any more.'

'No!' Donald cried, anguished. 'Never!'

Eleyne laid down the dirk on the bed and put her arms around Donald's neck. 'Oh, my love, don't grudge him that. If I die before you, then you will marry again. Of course you will. Then I shall be with him.'

'Has he gone?' Donald stared over her head.

'Yes, he's gone.' She smiled faintly.

'And he won't come back?'

'No.' There were only empty shadows where the darker shadow had been. 'No. Now he knows that one day I shall be his, I don't think he'll come back. Not until I die.'

BOOK FIVE

1281–1302

CHAPTER TWENTY-EIGHT

I

It had rained for several weeks; torrential, cold, swelling the rivers and burns, lying in the great sodden mosses of the moors, cascading from the mountains in falls and leaps of white water. When the sun appeared at last it was balm upon the land.

The old man went regularly to the sacred well. He would hang a torn strip of cloth from a branch of thorn or leave a broken piece of bannock and once, in despair, he tossed a penny, a whole day's pay, into the spring before he dipped a jug of the pure, ice-cold water to take back to the high shielings where his wife lay ill with fever in their makeshift bothy.

The rain had deepened the pool. The trickle which usually bubbled gently from the rock had become a torrent. He could see where the shingle had been washed out of the pool by the force of the floodwater. It lay on the bank amongst the thin scattering of bog orchids and purple-black cornel like the sea strand. Something caught his eye, gleaming amongst the stones. He bent and picked it up. Trailing with soft, feathery moss, the phoenix lay in his palm and it seemed to him that it vibrated like a captive dragonfly. For a long time he looked at it, debating whether he should throw it back into the pool. Someone had left it as an offering, and it would be the worst of luck to take it. On the other hand, he could see the jewel was worth a king's ransom.

II

KILDRUMMY CASTLE ❖ July 1281

On the hills behind Kildrummy Castle the heather was beginning to turn to purple beneath the summer sun. Eleyne sat in her favourite room in the Snow Tower watching Marjorie and Isabella sew whilst she told them the stories of old Wales. Agnes brought in a pouch of letters which had just arrived from the south.

She had grown to dread the arrival of these letters. Too often, as the years passed, they contained bad news. The first had come four years before. A letter, out of the blue, from Alice Goodsire, Luned's eldest daughter.

It was very quick. Mama did not suffer at all. A seizure, the doctor said. She had a happy life and she remembered you always in her prayers.

Luned had left a doting husband, five children and sixteen grand-children to mourn her.

Her death shook Eleyne terribly. Her foster sister, her maid and her oldest friend, Luned had been her closest companion for so many years it did not seem possible that she could be dead, that she would never see her again . . .

Then five months ago the next blow had come, word of her sister Gwenllian's death, followed only three months later by news that her beloved Margaret had succumbed to a congestion of the lungs and died at last, giving orders that her heart be buried in her beloved husband Walter's coffin at Aconbury in the rolling hills of the border march.

So, they were all gone now. Luned, Gruffydd and Senena, Dafydd and Isabella, Gwladus, Angharad, Gwenllian and Margaret. She was the only one left of the brood of Llywelyn ap Iorwerth and Joan the daughter of John of England.

She frowned, lost in thought, the pouch dangling from her finger-tips. Henry of England had also died, nine years ago now; her Uncle Henry, the man who had declared her dead. In his eyes, in the eyes of England she had been dead for nearly thirty years! She had felt little sorrow when he had gone, he who had treated her as a pawn, to be handed without a second thought to a man like Robert de Quincy. She shivered. Even after all these years the thought of Robert could still make her skin crawl. The power of a king was frightening – a power of life and death; a power to treat his subjects like so many possessions. The great charter her grandfather had been forced to sign had changed little in the long run. And now another king ruled England: her cousin Edward. Unofficially he recognised her existence; he knew she was there and the thought filled her with unease. For a long time she had known that Edward regarded her as an enemy.

She gazed thoughtfully at the bag of letters.

Donald and his father were at Roxburgh with the Scots court. The letters were undoubtedly from them, full of last-minute instructions to do a thousand things on the estates which she had probably done two weeks ago. Her face cleared; smiling fondly, she picked up one sealed with Donald's seal.

The letter did indeed contain news. As Donald's father was still unwell Donald had been called to act as a witness to the marriage agreement between little Princess Margaret, King Alexander's youngest child, and Eric, King of Norway. The earl was, he said, travelling back to Kildrummy in easy stages. William, who had always been such a robust and energetic man, had been growing old visibly over the past few months, his decline speeded by Muriel's sudden death of congestion of the lungs. Eleyne put the letter down. Next to it on the pile was a letter in a hand she didn't recognise. It bore the seal of de Bohun; her heart began to thump uncomfortably.

'Mama! the story!' Isabella prompted. At twelve she was tall and slim as a sapling but showing at last the signs of great beauty to come. 'Please.'

'In a minute, my love.' Eleyne turned the letter over and over in her hands, then finally she broke the seal. When she looked up at last, there were tears in her eyes.

'Mama! Mama, what is it?' Isabella dropped her work and ran to put her thin arms around her mother's neck.

Eleyne smiled, barely able to speak for emotion. 'It's from your sister.'

'My sister?' Isabella looked uncertainly at Marjorie – at eleven, still a chubby tomboy.

'No, not your little sister, your big sister.' Eleyne drew her daughter down on to the seat near her. 'Long before you were born, I lived in England and I had two little girls, much like you and Marjorie. But when I came to live in Scotland with Macduff's father, I had to leave them behind.'

'You wouldn't leave me behind, would you?' Marjorie, sitting plumply on a stool of her own, sounded only half confident as she too put down her sewing ready for the new story.

'No, darling, I wouldn't leave you behind.' Eleyne smiled, hiding the terrible sadness those memories still brought back.

'What is she called. Our sister?' Isabella asked, eyeing the letter clutched in her mother's hands.

'She is called Joanna, and her sister is Hawisa.'

'What does she say?' Marjorie interrupted. 'Is she coming to see us?'

'She wants to see us, but she hasn't been very well,' Eleyne said slowly.

Forgive me my churlish behaviour in the past. I could not forgive you for leaving us and it is only lately, as I find myself increasingly a pawn of King Edward's marriage plans for me, that I realise how helpless we women are when men have decided our fate. Only my recurrent illness stopped his father remarrying me to someone else after Humphrey's death. Now I fear my illness will remove me from this world and from the marriage game sooner rather than later. I should so like to see you before I die. Please, mother, if you can forgive me, can we meet?

She did not say how ill she was, nor did she mention her sister.

'When will she come?' Marjorie asked eagerly. Scrambling to her feet, she came and leaned against her mother's knees and picking up the letter, she began to spell out some of the words. 'How old is she? Her writing is difficult to read. Or did she use a clerk?' The girl smiled. Her own writing had been condemned as execrable by the boys' tutor who had remained at Kildrummy after his charges had gone so that twice a week he could give the girls a lesson in reading and writing.

'She is grown up, my darling. I don't know when she'll come or if she'll be able to travel so far,' Eleyne said. 'It may be that I shall ride south to see her.'

'Then we won't meet her!' Isabella scowled. 'I know! You can take us to see Cousin Llywelyn in Wales. We'll meet her there and we can see Aber. Can we?'

It was a tempting idea. 'We'll see. I'll speak to your father. I would like to go to Aber again.' She sighed wistfully and stood up and stretched. Aber and Joanna. That would be perfect.

III

The heatwave which followed the rain broke in a massive storm. Lightning flashed across the mountains, turning heather and rock to blinding silver as the thunder reverberated over the moors and echoed around the corries.

Eleyne surveyed the women in her solar. They were restless, made uneasy by the thunder. At the table Isabella and Marjorie were squabbling quietly over a game of pick-a-sticks.

Eleyne went to stand in the window embrasure, flinching as a flash seemed to angle directly through the eighteen-foot-thick walls.

Donald and his father had still not returned to Mar. There had been no further word from them, and she was unsettled. Something was wrong. She closed her eyes; her head was throbbing dully and, in spite of the heat of the chamber, there was a strange coldness across her shoulders.

Eleyne . . .

She caught her breath. The whisper had been in her head, inside her brain.

Her eyes flew open and she looked across the room. In spite of the heat, they had had to light candles to sew by. She could see the perspiration on the faces of the women, the dampness of the clinging wimples, dark stains spreading on thin silk. The rankness of their bodies was beginning to fill the room, overpowering the floral scents they used and the sweetness of the beeswax candles.

Eleyne spun around. A dozen faces turned towards her, then turned back to their work.

Eleyne . . .

There it was again. Clearer this time, stronger.

She couldn't breathe. 'Blessed Virgin. Holy Mother of God.' Soundlessly her lips framed the words. Another lightning flash illuminated the room and she saw Isabella flinch, her hand across her eyes. The child looked near to tears.

'It's all right.' Her voice sounded distant and disembodied above the muted gabble of conversation. 'It will pass over soon. Bethoc, where is your lute? Play for us. It will take our minds off the storm.'

She went back to the table, feeling the drag of her skirts intolerably hot and heavy against her legs, and she put her hand on Isabella's for a moment as it hovered over the pile of cut rushes they were using for their game.

'Mama!' Marjorie's protest was anguished. 'Now you've spoiled it –'

'I'm sorry, darling, I didn't mean to.' Eleyne smiled at her youngest daughter contritely.

He was there near her; unbelievably, he was there. The women, seated in groups around the candles or at the heavy oak trestle, had sensed nothing. The deep window embrasure was empty and yet she could feel him. For the first time in years she could feel him.

'Why? Why have you come back?' She mouthed the words silently over her daughters' bent heads but she knew the answer.

She hadn't called him, it was the phoenix.

Someone had found the phoenix.

IV

Eleyne put the idea of a visit to Wales to Donald as soon as he came home with his father two weeks later. It was the only way to escape, to be sure that Alexander would not follow.

'That would give you real pleasure? To go back to Wales?'

'You know it would.'

She was trying to hide her anxiety, her terror that Alexander had come back for her at last. She had to get away from Scotland and in Wales surely he couldn't reach her.

'I want to see Llywelyn again. And Aber. I'm getting old, Donald. Soon I won't be able to contemplate the idea of such a long journey.'

He laughed. 'You old? Never!'

At sixty-three she was as upright and slim as ever and as full of energy. She could still outride him, still sit up all night with a foaling mare, not trusting his horse masters, and be as alert at breakfast as the children. And she was still as desirable as ever. There were times – when she returned from her long lonely rides in the hills with only her two dogs, Lucy and Saer, the latest in the long line of Donnet's

descendants to guard her — when he wondered what magic she practised in secret beneath the moon. There was a glow to her skin and a
gleam in her eye, a strange glamour over her, which bewitched him as
strongly as when he had first met her.

He frowned. Out of nowhere the fear had returned, the suspicion,
the secret dread, that on those lonely trips she met with Alexander's
ghost.

V
August 1281

William summoned Eleyne to his bedside soon after he and Donald
returned. His face had thinned to the point of gauntness and his voice
had weakened, but he had lost none of his acerbity when addressing
his daughter-in-law.

'I bring greetings from the king. He thanks you for your messages
of condolence.' Alexander's second son, David, had died in June.

He groaned as he eased the pain in his joints. 'You've heard no
doubt that I was too ill to attend the finalising of the marriage settlement between young Margaret and the King of Norway. Donald was
there, though. He'll be a valuable adviser to the king when I'm gone,
if you let him.' He frowned through his bushy eyebrows. 'You're a
powerful woman, Eleyne, and you still have my son exactly where you
want him. Don't stand in his way.'

Eleyne eyed him coolly. 'I have never stood in his way.'

'Oh yes you have. You keep him dangling here at Kildrummy when
he should be with the king; you keep him on a leash like one of your
damn dogs. And it's not good for him. Let him go, woman.' He shot
his neck forward and glared at her. 'I'll be dead soon and he'll be the
earl. You've given him three sons and all credit to you for that.' He
paused thoughtfully, visibly wondering how she had done it. 'You stay
here and look after the earldom. You're a good administrator. And let
Donald go to court.' He coughed feebly. 'Are you afraid he'll find himself another woman now you're old?' The glance he gave her out of
the corner of his eye was pure malice.

She smiled. 'No, I'm not afraid of that.' She wasn't, not any more.

'Nor should you be.' Grudgingly he smiled. 'You've the looks of a
woman half your age still, though, Blessed Margaret, I don't know how
you do it. One last point.' His cough grew harsher. 'I'm sending men
from Mar as part of the army, keeping the peace in Wales. Wait —!' He
raised his hand as she opened her mouth to speak. 'This is my duty,
according to the agreements made between England and Scotland, and
I abide by it, as Donald will be expected to do. You will not try to

662

interfere. The politics of Wales are no longer your concern even if the king permits you to visit Llywelyn as you've asked. If there are Scotsmen helping Edward of England keep the peace, it is because your nephew was unable to do so himself. He lost the best part of Wales through his own weakness. Now, with Edward building castles all around him, he'll be forced to abide by English rules, and there's nothing you can do about it!'

Eleyne grimaced. He was right, but it hurt to think of foreign soldiers on Welsh soil.

So much had happened in Wales since she had been there last. Ever since Edward's accession to the English throne, the working relationship which had existed between his father and Llywelyn had deteriorated, until in the face of Llywelyn's persistent refusal to submit to his new English overlord, Edward had invaded Wales, accompanied by Llywelyn's ever-rebellious and still jealous younger brother, Dafydd.

The combination of king and brother had inflicted a resounding defeat on Llywelyn, reducing the prince's territory to the northern part of Gwynedd and forcing him to release his and Dafydd's elder brother, Owain, whom Llywelyn, in his anxiety to keep him away from the centre of power, had kept so long a prisoner.

Edward had compromised in the interests of peace. He did not take away Llywelyn's title of Prince of Wales and he had allowed him at long last to marry Eleanor, the daughter of Simon de Montfort, to whom he had been betrothed for so long, in a wonderful ceremony in Worcester Cathedral. That had been the last time Eleyne had seen her nephew. She and Donald had ridden south to attend the wedding, and she had been overjoyed to think that at last Wales would find some kind of peace.

The peace, however, had been an uneasy one.

Lord Mar shook his head grimly. 'There was a time when I thought Wales and Scotland would unite to keep English ambition in check. It's sad for Wales that that did not happen, for Edward is a very different man from his father.' He fell silent, staring grumpily at his gnarled hands.

Eleyne took a deep breath. She was too old a hand at sparring with William to rise to most of the challenges he had flung at her. 'Are you confident that Edward will not challenge Scottish supremacy one day?' she asked mildly. She had never trusted Edward, from that day when as a boy he had stared at her with such hostile eyes at Woodstock. And she had sensed something in him – a cold-bloodedness – which set him apart even from his father.

'He and Alexander get on well, they always have. There is no reason why Edward should threaten us. We are an independent kingdom with a strong king and an effective government.' He frowned. 'Though I could wish Prince David had not died. The king's eldest son, Lord Alexander, is not a strong boy either. He is a fragile defence to have between the king and destiny, especially since the queen died and the king has not remarried.'

His words sparked off some strange warning bell inside Eleyne's head. 'But the king has chosen a wife,' she said.

William nodded. 'It's not yet announced, but he has talked to the Count of Flanders about his daughter. There has been too much delay.' He shook his head slowly. 'He's a strong, robust man; he needs a woman now, and a dozen new sons as soon as possible. In case.'

Eleyne frowned: her vision of Alexander on his horse had never returned. It was as if by telling him about it she had pre-empted fate. Certainly it was well known now that he would never ride a grey.

She stood up and dropped a dutiful kiss on her father-in-law's head. 'I must leave you now. You are tired.'

He scowled. 'Yes, Goddamnit, I'm tired.'

Two weeks later William of Mar was dead.

VI

GWYNEDD ❖ 1281

The new Earl of Mar and Thane of Cabrach travelled to Wales with his wife in November. Their intention was to spend Christmas with Prince Llywelyn at Aber and meet at long last with Joanna.

On the way they stopped at King Edward's great new castle of Rhuddlan, with its canal diversion of the River Clwyd. Solemnly they allowed themselves to be given a tour of the new building by King Edward's castle builder, Master James of St George, admiring not only the provision for stables and granaries and workshops in the outer ward but also the king's and queen's halls with their painted timber walls and, already, the start of the queen's garden and her little fish pond.

In their lavishly appointed guest chamber Donald turned to one of his coffers and brought out his writing materials. Within minutes he was deeply engrossed in a sketch of the lay-out of the castle.

Eleyne stood behind him, watching. 'Are you going to show it to Llywelyn?'

He glanced up. 'I doubt if there's any secret about the strength of this place, my love. And it bodes ill for Llywelyn. No, I'm taking these drawings back with me to show to my stonemasons. We could gain some useful ideas for strengthening Kildrummy, with the king's approval.' He reached up and pulled her down to kiss her. 'Are the children settled?'

She nodded. 'They're all tired and excited.'

He gave her a fond, sideways glance. 'So are you?'

'Not as tired as all that, Donald!' She raised an eyebrow sharply. 'As you will see, later!' She left him to his sketching and wandered across to the window which overlooked the broad waters of the diverted River Clwyd. The east wind was beginning to scream through the half-built sections of the inner towers and darkness was setting in.

They had spent the previous night at Chester, a strange echo from earlier times. Tomorrow they would spend the night at the guesthouse of Conwy Abbey, so she could pray at the tombs of her father and her two brothers. Then at last they would be at Aber.

The low cloud racing in on the wind had cut out all views from the castle now. The inner ward was dank and murky as it grew dark. A boy had come in to light the candles and throw logs on the fire. All ought to be well, but she could not throw off a feeling of unease.

At Aber Llywelyn and Eleanor greeted them with enthusiasm and made them all at home. But at once Llywelyn had disappointing news. 'Lady de Bohun has written to say she is not well enough to travel, Aunt Eleyne. I'm so sorry.' He handed her Joanna's letter.

Eleyne gazed unseeing at the parchment in her hands. 'I knew she wouldn't come.' Her voice was flat.

Eleanor frowned at her husband; he needn't have told her so soon. He could have allowed her the pleasure of coming home first. She smiled at Eleyne. 'It just means you must come again, next summer perhaps. When the weather is better and she has had a chance to recover.'

'And when we will have a new member of the family to show you.' Llywelyn put his arm around his wife's waist fondly. 'June or thereabouts would be about right, I'd say.'

Eleyne put Joanna's letter away. 'So, you are to have a daughter, I'm so pleased.' She spoke without thinking as she kissed Eleanor's cheek.

'A son, Aunt Eleyne,' Llywelyn said sharply, 'we are expecting a son.'

She looked at him. His handsome face had aged since she had last seen him, and the shadows of exhaustion surrounded his eyes. She shivered slightly as a cold draught whistled through the great hall, gone as soon as it had come.

'Of course,' she said. 'A son.'

ABER

Einion was not there. Almost defiantly she stood by the river in memory of Rhonwen and threw a late frost-hardened rosebud into the whirling waters as an offering to the past. Her children watched in silence. Gratney was tall and handsome, very like his father, as were the twins; at fourteen, he was a squire now, in the household of his cousin, her nephew and friend of so many years, Robert Bruce of Annandale. The twins were pages with the Earl of Buchan at Slains. All three had been summoned home for the pilgrimage to their mother's birthplace, and were enjoying for the first time the fact of her royal birth.

She showed them Yr Wyddfa; she showed them the strait and Llanfaes and the views of the great cloud-covered mass of Eryri, the high *cwms* already deep with snow, but it was Sandy alone who rode with her to the site of Einion's grave. So like his brother in looks, he was a gentler, dreamier version. Dismounting, he held his mother's horse as she stood looking down at the lichen-covered stone.

'These woods are strange,' he said with a shiver.

'In what way?' Squinting at him against the frosty sunlight, she studied his face. Handsome, square-jawed, his nose liberally sprinkled with freckles, his sandy hair as usual awry beneath his cap, he was gazing into the distance, his grey eyes unfocused.

'There are ghosts, spirits.' He shrugged, dismissing the thought, and began to fondle the horse's muzzle. 'Duncan doesn't notice, so I don't talk about it much.' His voice was carefully casual.

'You mean you've seen them before?' Eleyne asked softly. She had a vivid memory of her own cautious questioning of Isabella de Braose when they were children, her withdrawal when Isabella's scorn told her other people didn't see the things she did.

Sandy nodded.

'At Kildrummy too?'

He nodded again. 'And at Slains. And on the mountains.' He hesitated. 'You see them, don't you?'

'Yes,' she said quietly, 'I see them.'

'There's one in particular,' he went on in a rush, the words tumbling over each other in his eagerness to speak to her on her own at last, now that he had dared to broach the subject. 'I sometimes think he follows me about.'

Eleyne forced herself to smile. She felt suddenly sick with fear. 'Perhaps it is your guardian angel,' she whispered. She put her hands on the boy's shoulders. 'What does he look like? Have you ever really seen him?'

Sandy met her gaze steadily. A slight blush had coloured his cheeks and was spreading to the back of his neck. 'He's shadowy, tall, with dark, watching eyes. I've never seen him clearly.' He broke away from her, his embarrassment overcoming his longing to confide. 'It's silly. He's not really there . . . I just feel him.'

Eleyne could hardly breathe. 'And he watches over you?'

Sandy nodded.

Alexander.

'Well.' Eleyne took a deep breath. 'Whoever it is, he must love you very much.' She kissed him on the forehead. 'Having the Sight is hard to live with, Sandy. It's a burden. The people who don't see into the other worlds are very lucky.' She paused. 'Does Duncan ever see anything?'

He shook his head violently. 'It's the only thing that comes between us. We're so close otherwise. It's as though we're part of each other. I know when he's hurt, I know when he's sad, even when Lord Buchan has taken one of us to court and left the other at Slains . . . he makes us take turns. But Dunc never sees. Not like me.'

'Then the gods have chosen you for some reason,' Eleyne said quietly. 'You have their blessing and their protection.'

'And Dunc hasn't?' Sandy was uncertain whether to be pleased for himself or upset for his twin.

'Duncan has other blessings.' Eleyne smiled reassuringly and with that he had to be content.

She turned away, unable to school her face any longer. She was shaking like a leaf. Was the spirit who watched over her elder twin Alexander of Scotland? Had he after all fathered one of her sons?

That night, alone in the bedchamber in the tower room at the end of the *ty hir*, while Donald lingered in the great hall with Llywelyn, she went to the north-facing window and tore open the shutters, staring out across the black sea towards Llanfaes and the beaches which stretched in the direction of Penmon.

'Where are you?' she cried out loud into the darkness. 'Where are you? Why don't you come to me and tell me the truth?'

There was no reply. Alexander had not followed her to Wales.

VIII

KILDRUMMY CASTLE ❖ February 1282

Isabella was the most pleased to be back. She had enjoyed their month-long stay in Gwynedd and she had grown very fond of her splendid glamorous cousin who was the Prince of Wales, but she missed her home. She had spent all her twelve years in Mar and had grown used to the mountains and the broad straths of north-east Scotland. The violent crags and the ice-hung gullies and *cwms* of Yr Wyddfa were to her sinister in their wild beauty and, back in Eryri, her mother's remote feyness seemed more threatening.

Isabella had a special hiding place which even Meg and the nursery maids did not know about: a small storeroom in the tower, right under the roof, and there she would sit for hours, dreaming or reading her mother's precious book of the Mabinogi, or playing with one or other of the dozens of castle kittens. Best of all, Marjorie and her brothers had never found her there. Twice her younger sister had plodded up to the storeroom, calling her, but on both occasions she had missed the little door, carefully hidden behind some empty wooden chests, which led into the small room beyond, her own private sanctuary, and she had heard the plaintive calls getting fainter again as Marjorie went away.

Only a few hours after reaching the castle she made her way up to her hidy-hole clutching a new treasure, a new book of stories, laboriously copied for her by one of Llywelyn's scribes. It too told of kings and princes; of fairies and magic, and of wonderful princesses with whom she passionately identified.

Wrapping herself in her cloak, she huddled closer to her candle for warmth. Outside the narrow slit window snow flurries whirled up the valley. Soon it would be time for supper but in the meantime she had already forgotten the long ride and the black cliffs and icy crags of Gwynedd. She was lost in her dreams.

It was a severe shock when her mother came into the room, silent as a shadow, and sat down next to her on the dusty floor. 'So, this is where you hide away.' Eleyne smiled. 'Do you mind me knowing?'

'Not as long as you don't tell Marjorie.'

Eleyne laughed. Isabella loved the way her mother's eyes crinkled at the corners when she laughed. It made her look young and carefree. 'I won't tell her, I promise.' Eleyne was studying her daughter's face. 'You didn't like Wales, did you?'

Isabella knew better than to pretend. 'It was frightening. And sad.'

Eleyne sighed. 'I wish you could have seen it in the summer, when the snow on the mountains has gone and the *cwms* are full of flowers.' She smiled. 'So. You come up here to read.'

Isabella nodded shyly.

'I've always loved to be alone. But all my special places have been outside – or in the stables. Are you going to come down now? It's so cold up here. And the horn will call us to supper soon.'

'Mama.' Closing the book, Isabella tucked it carefully into a small coffer by the wall. 'Can I ask you something?'

'Of course.' Eleyne wrapped her arms around her legs and sat, chin on knees.

'Who am I going to marry?'

'Who knows?'

'Haven't you and papa arranged my marriage?'

Eleyne shook her head. 'We've talked about it, of course, and we've thought of various possibilities. But there's nothing arranged. There's plenty of time to think about it yet.'

'Did you ever dream about who you would marry?' Isabella edged closer, her eyes huge in the candlelight.

Eleyne nodded. 'I did, but you see, it was different for me. I was married when I was a young child, so I always knew who my husband was.'

'And was he very handsome?' Isabella sat forward on her knees.

'He was very handsome and very kind.'

'And he was Joanna's father?'

Slowly Eleyne shook her head, 'No, John and I had no children. Joanna's father was my second husband.'

Isabella was silent for a moment. 'And was he handsome too?' she asked.

'I suppose so.'

'And then came Macduff's father.'

Eleyne smiled. 'And then yours.'

'Will I have four husbands?'

'I don't think so. I think you'll have just one. Someone you'll love very much.'

'Is that written in the stars?' Isabella loved Eleyne's almanacs and star charts. She and Marjorie had both spent hours poring over them, seeing the pictures in the heavens.

'Yes, it's written in the stars.'

'And will I have lots of children?'

Eleyne leaned forward and took Isabella's hands in hers. 'That's enough questions, sweetheart. I don't know how many children you'll have, or when, or who you will marry. Come on, let's leave the future to take care of itself and go down to supper.'

IX

MAR ❖ April 1282

Morna looked down at the woman lying on the straw pallet on the floor at Mossat. She was pale and shivering, the sweat pouring from her body. She shook her head. 'The fever hasn't broken. She's worse.'

The woman's husband had brought her down from the high shielings in the autumn, carrying her on his back. Her fever had returned a dozen times since then and he had had to let the other men go to the lambing without him.

'Last summer I went to the well. I thought the water would cure her,' he admitted unhappily. He was twisting his cap in his hands in agitation as he looked down at his wife.

Morna frowned. 'That wouldn't help for this. What we need to do is break the fever once and for all,' she said practically. She turned to her bag of remedies. The woman needed medicine now as well as spells.

She knelt, propping the woman's head on her arm as she fed her the hot green tea. The man felt in his pouch and produced a scrap of sacking. 'I took something from the spring,' he said shamefaced. 'I shouldna have done it. I knew it would bring ill luck.'

Morna was shocked. 'You stole from the guardians of the spring?'

He nodded. 'Will you take it back for me? Please. Will you make it all right? She won't get better until it's done.'

Morna helped the sick woman drink the last of the decoction, then she laid her gently on the ground and covered her with sheepskin rugs. 'I'll take it back, but I can't promise the spirits will withdraw their anger,' she said sternly. 'You've done a terrible thing, Eddie, stealing from the gods.' She held out her hand and taking the sacking she slipped it into her herb bag without looking at it. 'Keep Jinnie warm. Give her some more of this tea at dusk and again at dawn. I'll come and see her in the morning.' She crouched down and laid her hand for a moment on the burning forehead, then she slipped from the house out into the village street.

It wasn't until Mairi was asleep that night and Morna was sitting exhausted as her fire died, trying to summon the strength to go to her own bed, that she remembered the package and reaching for her bag of dried herbs took it out. She unwrapped the fraying piece of sacking in the firelight and sat looking down at what it contained.

He had packed the phoenix in dried moss. Tiny curls of it clung to the creature's beak and claws. In the flickering light its eyes were red and malicious, glaring up at her. She, like the old man, could feel its energy.

For a long time she looked at it, then with gentle reverence she wrapped it up again. The fire was dead and the embers cold before she went to sleep.

X

April 1282

Robert Bruce, Lord of Annandale, was always a welcome visitor at Kildrummy. With him was his son, another Robert, a grown man and father himself now, who had taken the title of Earl of Carrick from his wife, Marjorie.

'So, how was Wales?' Robert of Annandale raised a goblet of wine and toasted Eleyne and Donald cheerfully.

'Beautiful, as always,' Eleyne replied. 'But you haven't come all this way to ask us about Wales, Robert.' The two men had not so far divulged the reason for their visit. 'I trust you haven't come to complain about your squire.' Gratney had gone back to the Bruces at Lochmaben two months before.

'On the contrary, he's a charming young man. He does you both great credit, doesn't he, father?' Robert of Carrick said. 'You should be very proud of your children.'

'We are.' Donald stretched out and took his wife's hand. 'As you should be of yours.'

Carrick laughed. He already had a clutch of sons and daughters, and his wife, Marjorie, was pregnant again. 'I am. My eldest son is so like his grandfather! They get on too well by far.' He looked fondly at his father. 'Though Robert is only seven, he is a bright, ambitious boy. And Christian is like mama in looks. She'll make someone a good wife one day.' He glanced at Eleyne sideways.

Eleyne smiled. 'Subtlety was never your strong point, Robbie.'

Carrick threw back his head and laughed. 'No, I'll leave that to my father and my son. Subtlety and the Lochaber Axe, that's about their mark. An unbeatable combination! But seriously, keep us in mind when you think of a match for Gratney. That's one of the things we came to say. I think we could negotiate something which would please us all.'

Eleyne could not keep the happiness out of her eyes. 'That would be wonderful,' she said softly, 'absolutely wonderful.'

'And now that we've settled that,' Robert of Annandale remarked, 'on to the subject of the king's remarriage. Does anyone yet know whom he has in mind?'

'I do.' Eleyne answered, though Robert had been looking at her husband. 'It is to be Yolande de Dreux, the daughter of the Count of Flanders.' She laughed at the thunderstruck faces of the three men.

'Who told you?' Robert asked.

'The king, who else? He has made his mind up who to marry, but it's when that he cannot decide. It's not easy for him so soon after one son's death to acknowledge that his eldest son is far from strong and may not live. But he will do what he must.'

Without realising it, her eyes had moved to the fire. The flames were intensifying, curdling over the peats, licking and sparking along the pine logs filling the chamber with their bitter scent.

There were pictures there, part of the flames: she saw the horseman, the storm clouds massing round him, but in a flash he had gone and there was nothing but the orange glow, like the living centre of the sun, searing her eyeballs.

The hands on her shoulders jerked her back to reality. 'Eleyne,' asked Donald, 'are you all right?'

'Of course.'

'What did you see?' Robert of Carrick whispered, awestruck.

She shook her head. 'Nothing.'

XI

Morna took Eleyne's hand and led her to the window embrasure, drawing the curtain across the alcove to give them privacy. Behind them in the solar a wall painter was meticulously working on the last corner of the room, sketching in the outlines of two figures with sinopia before he began to colour the dry plaster. Near him, his apprentice stencilled a pattern of rosettes on the green wall. The room already glowed with colour.

'I must know what you want me to do. If you wish, I will return it to the sacred spring.' Eddie's wife was improving. Obviously the gods had forgiven the man's intrusion. 'Or I can keep it at my house.' Morna paused. 'Or I can bring it here.'

Eleyne sat down. Her heart was beating very fast. 'I knew it had been found,' she said. She took a deep shaky breath.

'Has he come back?' Morna studied her face sympathetically.

Eleyne nodded. 'Nothing frightening, not yet, but he's here.' She kneaded her hands together nervously in her lap. 'He's growing impatient.' She stood up, every movement betraying her fear. 'What shall I do, Morna?'

Morna was doubtful. 'His power is growing. However much you beg him not to come he can reach you now the pendant is out of the water, even though it's not here in the castle.'

'I draw a circle round our bed,' Eleyne said sadly, 'and he has never crossed the line. And I draw a circle here in my solar and another around the castle walls.'

Morna raised an eyebrow. 'You believe that will keep him away?'

'A powerful wizard told me how to do it. But one day,' Eleyne clutched at Morna's hands, 'one day he'll come when I'm outside the circle. And then he'll take me from Donald.'

'Has anyone else seen him?' Morna murmured.

'Yes,' Eleyne said, 'Sandy.'

XII

Eleyne held the phoenix in her cupped hands. She felt its power; felt the colours vibrating beneath her fingers. She opened them and gazed down at the jewel. Flecks of moss still clung beneath the creature's claws.

Gently, she packed it into an intricately carved ivory box and wedged it with lambswool. She fitted the lid with care and made her way towards the chapel. She climbed the stairs which led up over the undercroft to the first floor and went into the shadowy body of the building.

Father Gillespie was kneeling before the altar. Crossing himself, he rose to his feet and turned as he heard her footsteps. He had lit the candles on the altar and before the statue of the Virgin.

'Are you ready, father?' Eleyne was tense with nerves.

'I am.' His face was deeply lined, his eyes narrowed and watery from years of peering at the crabbed writing in his missals and books of hours. Surreptitiously he looked at her face – his countess looked pale and strained. He knew a little of her torment from her confessions; he also suspected that she paid more than lip service to another, older god, but he did not pursue the matter. There were many gods in the mountains, and he was a tolerant man. He knew she liked him and respected him and he liked and respected her. She would have his compassion and she would have his prayers. The Blessed Christ and the Blessed Virgin would succour her in her hour of need. And was not the old king the great-great-grandson of the blessed St Margaret herself? 'You have the object, my lady?' He was staring at the box in her hand.

She nodded. 'You will bless it, father, so that no one can . . . so no one can use it any more.'

'I shall weave a prayer around it, my lady, and beg Our Sweet Lord and his mother and all the saints to guard it. I can do no more.'

She gave him a tight smile. 'Thank you, father.'

There was a strange coldness in the chapel. She shivered. She could see where he meant to put it: he had raised some of the new, painted tiles on the step before the altar, and beneath them a board had been removed. A cavity yawned black between the floor joists.

The candle flames were flickering wildly. She saw him look at them anxiously and again she felt the cold.

'Put the box on the altar, my lady.' His voice was strained.

Her mouth dry, Eleyne stepped forward. He was here, in the chapel. She could feel him, feel the protest and the anger in the air around her. Out of the corner of her eye she saw Father Gillespie cross himself twice in quick succession.

Eleyne . . .

'*Ave Maria, gratia plena, intercede pro nobis . . .*' The words John of Chester had repeated so often at her side filled her head. 'Pray for me now and in the hour of my need . . .'

Eleyne . . .

She laid the box before the crucifix and crossed herself, then she knelt at her usual prayer desk and closed her eyes.

Eleyne . . .

Father Gillespie had begun his prayers. As he became more confident, his voice strengthened.

Eleyne . . .

The call was growing weaker.

'*Requiem aeternam dona ei, Domine . . .*' The priest's voice filled the high vault of the chapel. '*Requiescat in pace . . . in pace . . . in pace . . .*'

The call died away, and Eleyne felt tears burning on her cold cheeks.

Father Gillespie picked up the box and knelt on the step. He lowered the box into the darkness, then he fitted back the floorboard and replaced the tiles. He climbed to his feet and, strenuously rubbing the dirt from his hands on his chasuble, he smiled. 'It is done, my lady.'

'Thank you.' She rose from her knees. 'And you will tell no one, ever.'

'My lips are sealed. I will have one of the masons come in and cement down the tiles. He will not know why they came loose.'

The candles burned steadily now in the silence. She and the priest were completely alone in the chapel.

All she had to do now was to leave another offering of gold at the holy spring where Elizabeth had died. Then she would be left in peace.

XIII

May 1282

We are surrounded on all sides. By sea, Edward attacks Anglesey. He is trying to establish a blockade around Eryri. But he won't succeed. Llywelyn knows his people and his mountains too well, and he has even ordered the digging of a secret tunnel from the palace to the valley so we can flee in safety if Edward traps us here. Would that I could help him more, but my time is near, and he has to leave valuable men here at Aber to guard me and our son when he is born. Pray for us, dear Eleyne, and if you have the King of Scots' ear, beg him to send us help. If Wales falls to this tyrant ambition, who knows but that Scotland might be next . . .

Eleyne put down Eleanor's letter, smuggled out of Aber, and her eyes filled with tears. Her nephew Dafydd, Llywelyn's younger brother, disenchanted at last with his treacherous adherence to King Edward, had launched the revolt against the English tyranny in Wales only weeks after Eleyne and Donald had left Aber. Within days the revolt had spread and all Wales was again in arms with Llywelyn at her head.

Gwynedd was far from Mar, but she did not need Llywelyn's brief heartbroken note a week later to know that Eleanor was already dead, and that the longed-for heir to the Prince of Wales was a daughter. She had seen the woman's agony in the candle flame and heard Wales's sorrow in the wind on the moors.

XIV
ROXBURGH CASTLE

She and Donald were at court a week later, and Eleyne lost no time in seeking a private audience with the king.

'You have to do something; you must send my nephew help! Don't you see how dangerous, how disastrous, it would be if Edward were to conquer Wales?'

Alexander shook his head thoughtfully. 'I am deeply sorry for Llywelyn and I hope he manages to save the situation, but the matter is terribly delicate, Aunt Eleyne. So many of my vassals are also vassals of Edward of England. You know yourself how many Scots have English estates and vice versa. I should be asking them to choose between their allegiances for a matter which does not concern Scotland.'

'It will,' Eleyne flashed. 'If Wales falls, where do you think Edward will look next for conquest?'

'Not to Scotland, I assure you.' Alexander folded his arms. 'Edward and I have an understanding. We respect each other. Scotland's sovereignty is safe.'

'Is it?' She met his eye. 'You should not trust Edward Plantagenet. I know my cousin of old; ever since he was a boy he has been ambitious, devious, and vicious. Don't put him to the test.'

'I won't.' Alexander scowled. 'Because, unlike you, I get on well with him and have no reason to cross him. And I am not going to make reason by taking arms with Wales, much as I might like to for sentiment's sake.'

'You made an alliance before, against Henry —'

'An informal alliance which is no longer valid. No, I'm sorry.'

Eleyne looked at him in despair. 'I have seen pictures of war and disaster in the fire,' she said quietly. 'Your father would have listened to me.'

'Then my father would have been listening to his heart, not his head,' Alexander replied sharply. 'Now, if you please, Aunt Eleyne, I have matters to attend to.'

Alexander, why don't you show yourself to him . . . why don't you tell him of the danger . . . for Scotland's sake?

She sighed. 'Then listen at least to one other thing I have to say. When your advisers beg you to fix a date for your marriage, listen to them,' she pleaded. 'I know how much you miss Margaret, and I know how much you love Alexander and what a credit he is to you, but you must have other sons.'

His face darkened. 'You are presuming too much, Aunt Eleyne.'

'No, I'm taking a privilege allowed to old ladies!' She raised an eyebrow imperiously and he laughed out loud.

'Old? You? Never!' He sighed. 'I'm not a fool. I know I have to remarry. I even understand that if I die without a strong heir to succeed me that might give Edward an excuse to interfere in Scotland's business.' His voice was rueful. 'I do not take unnecessary risks, I promise you. After all, I have banned grey horses from my stables and I never ride in storms.'

'I'm glad.' Taking his hand, she dropped a deep curtsey and raised his fingers to her lips. 'Take care, my sovereign lord. I see black clouds everywhere, and it makes me afraid.'

XV
11 December 1282

Isabella had woven ribbon collars for the dogs. Seeing them brought a lump to Eleyne's throat as she thought of the Midsummer's Eve celebrations all those years ago. There had been no further word from Joanna since her letter at Christmas the year before. Eleyne moved closer to the fire, shivering violently.

'What is it, mama? Aren't you well?' Isabella was knotting the plaited silk around the wolfhounds' great, shaggy necks.

'I don't know.' Eleyne closed her eyes. A wave of terrible cold had swept over her. She turned to the fire, overwhelmed by the strange despair which had swept away her happiness. 'It's as though a light has gone out. Someone is dead —'

Isabella crossed herself nervously. 'Who?' she whispered. 'Not papa?' Her voice slid up into a frightened squeak; her father was once more with the king.

'No, not papa.'

'Why don't you know?' Isabella was used to her mother's second sight. Though Sandy was the only one who showed signs of having inherited it, all her children accepted it as being part of the normal way of things, a short cut sometimes to the truth.

Eleyne shrugged in despair. 'I don't know. I can't always see what

I want to; the flames don't answer my questions.' She leaned closer to the fire. 'I can't see anything; I can't hear anything but the howling of the wind in the hills.'

Isabella stared at her. 'There's no wind, mama, not here.' She slid her arms unhappily around Saer's neck and the dog turned and licked the girl's face.

'No.' It was a whisper. 'No, it's a Welsh wind.'

XVI

Llywelyn ap Gruffydd, separated from his men as he directed an attack on Builth in central Wales, was killed by a lance wielded by a member of the Shropshire levy, a man called Stephen Frankton. He did not even realise whom he had killed.

By the time confirmation of the news reached Scotland, Llywelyn's head was being paraded before Edward's troops on Anglesey and his tiny orphaned daughter and heir, Gwenllian, was Edward's prisoner. The child was to spend the rest of her life in a nunnery.

CHAPTER TWENTY-NINE

I

ROXBURGH CASTLE ❖ 1284

'**D**o I have to close my eyes and raise my arms above my head and go into a trance to convince you, sire?' Eleyne, wrapped in a scarlet fur-lined cloak against the cold, addressed the king wearily.

She's getting old after all, he thought to himself. *She is still a beautiful woman, but the tiredness which shows in her eyes is new, as is the despair.*

Behind them Master Elias, the king's harper, played gently in the shadows, his sightless eyes fixed blankly on the wall. It had been Eleyne's suggestion after Malcolm's death that he leave Falkland and enter royal service, and his fame at court had spread far and wide. Apart from the harper they were alone.

The king stood up and took her hands in his. 'No, you don't have to do that. I know you foresee a dire future for Scotland and for me. And I know that now both my sons are dead, I can put it off no longer. I must take steps to meet it.' His third child, too, had died in far-off Norway, leaving as the king's only heir her small daughter, Margaret. 'When all the arrangements have been made the chancellor will go to France to fetch Yolande.'

'She is a wife of whom England approves?' Eleyne raised an eyebrow.

'She is.'

'So you have bought us more peace.'

Wales had fallen to the English. Owain and Rhodri were dead and Dafydd was dead, beheaded by Edward of England, his sons captured. Gwynedd was a proud, independent principality no more.

'I hope so.' He turned away. 'I have done what everyone wants, so why do I hear disapproval in your voice?'

'Do you?' She shrugged. 'I see danger from England ahead. It's no more than an instinct, but I know Edward.'

'I thought it was more than an instinct; I thought it was foresight.'

She shrugged. 'What use is foresight if I can see only faintly and not understand?'

'You are able to warn people of what the stars intend and they can step away from fate,' he answered.

'But I saw nothing for Llywelyn. Could I not have foreseen his death and warned him?'

'As you did mine? Perhaps he was too far away. Perhaps his was a fate which could not be avoided.' The king put his arm around her shoulders kindly. 'Go and celebrate Lord Fife's good fortune in winning himself a beautiful wife, and stop worrying about me.'

When Duncan of Fife, twenty-one at last, inherited his father's earldom, he had triumphantly announced his impending marriage to Joanna de Clare, daughter of the Earl of Gloucester and a niece of Robert of Annandale's wife. Eleyne was very proud of him.

'Are you coming to his wedding?'

He nodded. 'Fife is one of the great earldoms of Scotland. How could I miss such a ceremony?'

'You didn't come to my wedding to his grandfather as I recall,' she replied tartly, her voice heavy with irony.

He gave a sheepish shrug. 'I was very young.'

'Indeed you were, and under your mother's thumb.' She gathered her cloak around her. 'May the gods bless you, Alexander of Scotland. I shall wait in turn for an invitation to *your* wedding!'

II

FIFE

Joanna de Clare was fair-haired and pretty, with large blue eyes, the daughter of one of England's greatest earls and a close kinswoman of King Edward. Duncan was inordinately proud of her.

The wedding ceremony was held in St Andrews Cathedral, covered in wooden scaffolding still after the great storm which had brought down the whole west front a few years before. This was not a hasty ceremony in a side chapel lit by midnight candles but a full nuptial mass before the high altar in the presence of the king and all the greatest nobles in the land.

Among the guests were the Lord of Annandale and his wife, the bride's aunt, and the Earl and Countess of Carrick and their eldest son and daughters, and it was here that Gratney met his bride-to-be, Christian Bruce, for the first time since they had been told of the plan for their betrothal.

'I know she's only eight years old,' Eleyne said gently. 'Remember, it will be a long time before you marry and if you don't like each other when you're grown up we can always change our minds.'

He scowled. 'She's just a baby!'

'So she is, but in six years she will be of marriageable age.'

'If we are betrothed, I can't change my mind,' he went on, determined to be awkward.

'You can if you want it badly enough. But we won't arrange a betrothal unless you are happy with the idea.' Patiently, she gave him a little push. 'Go on, greet her. She knows about the idea and she has always liked you.'

Smiling at Marjorie, Countess of Carrick, she stepped forward and the two women exchanged kisses. Behind her formidable mother Christian was tall for her age and slim with huge dark eyes and long ash-blonde hair held by a chaplet of gilded flowers. She was an extraordinarily pretty child.

Seeing Gratney, her brother Robert, youngest of the Robert Bruces, dug her in the ribs with his elbow. She blushed violently and Gratney found himself smiling. He liked all the Bruce children. Perhaps, after all, she wouldn't make such a bad wife – one day.

III

1285

Isabella was the first to hear of Duncan's and Joanna's baby. The messenger was telling everyone as he dismounted in the outer courtyard. 'It's a girl! The Earl and Countess of Fife have a daughter! The Fifes have a daughter!'

'My first great-grandchild.' Eleyne clasped her hands. 'I must go to see her.'

'May I come, mama?' Isabella at sixteen had turned into a beautiful young woman. She had inherited only a little of her mother's colouring. Her hair was red-gold, but her eyes were grey and her skin almost transparent in its fairness. They had still not arranged a marriage for her. Donald had talked to several families, but no one was good enough for his Isabella.

Eleyne frowned. 'No, darling, not this time.'

'Why not?' Isabella's eyes were so full of disappointment her mother felt a pang of guilt. There was no reason why she should not go. No logical reason for her refusal and yet in the back of her mind a warning bell was ringing. Isabella of Mar and Isobel of Fife. Somehow their destinies were linked, and the link was not a happy one.

IV

Anna, the Dowager Countess of Fife, was waiting for Eleyne in her bower at Falkland. 'I do not want you to see my grandchild.' Her eyes glittered. 'You bring nothing but grief when you come here.' It was a scene that had been played before.

Eleyne studied her. 'After all this time can you not let the quarrel rest? It was your father and my husband's father who had the fight. And even they in the end could let it go. Can't you forget it?'

Anna scowled. 'It's not that stupid court case. It's the bad luck you bring with you –'

'I bring no bad luck –'

'No?' Anna's voice slid up the scale. 'My husband died when he was scarcely a man. My son died before he came into his earldom and now Duncan has a daughter –'

'You blame me for that?' Eleyne said uneasily. 'When I have not even seen the child?'

'There is no need for you to see her. Bad blood will out.' Anna was swaying her head from side to side. Still only thirty-six years old, she had all the mannerisms of an old woman. 'It's your fault, all of it.'

'Rubbish,' Eleyne said crisply, getting to her feet. 'I've never heard such nonsense. You,' she turned on one of the staring ladies in attendance on the dowager in the crowded, stuffy room, 'take me to the countess and her baby.'

Joanna was cradling the baby in her arms, propped up in the huge bed which had once belonged to Eleyne and Malcolm. Now it was painted and gilded and hung with bright, fresh curtains. She looked up eagerly as Eleyne came in and smiled. 'Grandmama! Come and see my Isobel.' She held out the baby.

Eleyne stopped beside the bed and gazed down at the baby. It was tiny: a delicate, faery child with dark hair and deep violet eyes. As Eleyne looked at her, she looked unwinkingly back at her great-grandmother. Then she smiled.

Sweet Blessed Bride! The air around the child was full of whirling shadows! 'No.' It was only a murmur, but Joanna heard it. She paled. 'What is it?' she asked, 'what can you see?'

Eleyne didn't hear her. She hugged the baby to her, burying her face in the woollen shawl. 'No,' she begged softly again. She looked at Joanna and there were tears on her cheeks. 'She's lovely,' and she tried to smile.

'And you see her doom.' Joanna was as white as a sheet. 'Is she going to die?'

Eleyne shook her head. 'No. She will live to be a woman and to fulfil her destiny.' A destiny which involved Isabella of Mar. She stared over the baby's head at the fire as though seeking the answer there, then, hearing Joanna's weeping, she looked at her grandson's wife. 'I'm sorry, my dear, I've frightened you.' She touched the baby's face with her finger and smiled as the little face turned instinctively towards the gentle pressure. 'Take no notice of the ramblings of an old woman. I saw shadows and they made me afraid. This child has the mark of the gods on her; she will one day serve her nation and her king and she will be glorious.' She cradled the baby closer, pulling aside the swaddling bands so she could see the child more clearly. 'And she is beautiful.'

'And she is not a boy.' Joanna had recovered from her moment of panic, but her voice was flat. 'Duncan is very disappointed.'

'Then Duncan is a fool!' Eleyne's voice was sharp. 'No man could be what this child will be.' She gave a sudden half-apologetic laugh. 'I must be going mad, I talk in certainties yet I don't know what I'm talking about!' Gently she handed the baby back to Joanna. 'That has been my curse.' She stepped back. 'My dear, I'll leave you to rest. We'll talk again later. Don't let anything I say upset you. Isobel will grow up to be a beautiful, happy, healthy young woman and,' she put her head on one side, 'your next child will be a son.'

V

'I hear you've been terrifying Joanna out of her mind with your spooks and your fortune-telling, grandmama.' Duncan of Fife cornered her in the great hall as they made their way towards the table for supper. 'I wish you wouldn't do it.'

He turned to rinse his hands in the bowl of scented water held for him by a page and dried his hands energetically on the proffered towel.

Eleyne looked him in the eye. 'I'm sorry if she's upset. I can't always control the visions when they come . . .'

'Did you speak the truth when you said we would have a son?' His grey eyes were hard, she noticed.

'I believe so.'

He smiled, satisfied. 'That's all that matters. The destiny of a girl is not important as long as she marries well.'

Eleyne looked at him steadily. 'Quite so,' she said drily.

VI
KILDRUMMY CASTLE

'Morna, would you consider letting Mairi go to Falkland? She can learn how to be a nurserymaid and later she can be Isobel's nurse and companion. It would be a position full of prestige and honour.' Eleyne had picked up Morna's spindle, and began idly to twirl the wool between her fingers. They had often discussed the girl's future. Morna was ambitious for her.

'You fear for the child?' Morna asked.

'Yes,' Eleyne admitted.

'Will Mairi be strong enough to help her?'

'She is your daughter, she has your strength. I can think of no one better.' Eleyne sighed. 'I don't know what is to come. I saw storms; I saw much unhappiness and I saw the hand of destiny over the child's cradle. But why? How? I don't know. And I will probably never know. That's why I want to send someone young and strong to be with her. My grandson has agreed; if you do, we could send Mairi to Falkland almost at once. She will earn good money, and learn the ways of the castle. She could have a very good future there and she can tell Isobel the stories of the hills; show her a little of the magic that is ours.'

Morna nodded slowly. 'She can certainly do that. And it will be with my blessing.'

VII

'Well? Was there something special about her?'

Isabella cornered her mother in the herb garden as Eleyne tended her plants, clipping and snipping with a pair of embroidery shears.

She straightened her back with a groan. 'Special about who?'

'Isobel of Fife.' Isabella folded her arms defensively.

Oh yes, there was something special. But the words remained unsaid. Eleyne threw down her shears and put her arm around Isabella's shoulder. 'She was just a very pretty baby,' she said gently. 'I don't know why I didn't want you to come to see her. It was one of my funny feelings.' She smiled. 'I expect you and she will be great friends one day.'

She stopped with a shiver. A cold wind had arisen, scattering the clippings of hyssop and thyme and lavender in her basket. Her eyes were fixed on the girl's face.

'Mama? What is it?' Isabella paled. 'What's wrong?'

'I don't know. For a moment I thought I saw someone . . . I saw a crown . . .' Suddenly Eleyne was crying.

Isabella threw her arms around her. 'Mama, don't, please. What is it?'

'Nothing.' It was gone so fast. 'I'm sorry, my darling, I think I'm going in. I feel so chilled.' She stooped to pick up the shears and her basket. 'Don't worry, next time I go to Fife, you shall come.'

Isabella was playing with Lucy's pups when her father found her. 'Those dogs are already too rough for you, my darling,' he said, 'they'll bite you.'

'No they won't.' Isabella laughed. 'They love me.' The wind ruffled her hair. Her face saddened. 'Papa, you said you'd tell me who you'd chosen for my husband.' Pushing away the wrestling puppies she stood up. There were grass smears on her skirt.

'Your mother and I haven't decided yet.'

'But papa, I'm sixteen –'

'And already you're left on the shelf?' Donald laughed. 'Poor Bella, don't rush. Your mother and I want the very best for you – a veritable prince amongst men.' He sighed. 'Your mother's very protective of you, sweetheart. She has three marriages behind her and two of them were not happy. Neither of us wants that to happen to you. We couldn't bear you to be unhappy.' He shook his head. 'Be patient a little longer. We'll find the right man soon, I promise.'

VIII

November 1285

Rain, cold and heavy and driven horizontally by the wind, soaked through the cloaks of the riders and chilled them to the bone as they rode towards the royal castle of Jedburgh. There, the Lady Yolande, daughter of the Count of Dreux, awaited her king, accompanied by the Chancellor of Scotland Master Thomas Charteris, Patrick Graham, William Soules and William Sinclair, the four emissaries of the King of Scots, who had ridden to France to escort her through the length of England with the King of England's blessing.

Donald and Eleyne were riding with the king, having spent the last few nights in Roxburgh waiting to hear that the lady who would be Scotland's new queen had arrived. In the broad valley the trees leaned away from the gale, their leaves brown and torn, trampled into the mud.

Alexander refused to be downhearted. He had ordered minstrels, feasts, finery, paid for by the crown for his entourage, his bride and himself, and he was smiling broadly at Eleyne who rode beside him. His black stallion danced sideways, shaking its bridle, irritated by the wind. 'So, shall you and I gallop, my lady, and leave the sluggards behind? There's no thunder and my horse is as sable as the night. I should be safe!' His words were caught by the wind and almost indistinguishable to Eleyne as she urged her chestnut palfrey forward beside him along the muddy track. Behind them the king's banners drummed and cracked like snapping twigs in the wind, straining the staffs to which they were fastened, and the colourful caparisons flogged wetly around the horses' legs.

Donald shook his head at her sternly and she resisted the urge to stick out her tongue at him like a naughty child. She knew he disapproved of her riding fast. He thought it undignified and dangerous for a woman in her sixties to rush about the country with her hair tumbling around her ears. She caught a mocking gleam in the king's eye. It was enough of a challenge. She gathered her reins more tightly and urged the palfrey on.

She and Alexander reached the town gates only a short way ahead of the escort, who had gamely whipped their horses into a gallop in hot pursuit of their king. In the castle courtyard he jumped from his horse and came to Eleyne's side. 'A king has to gallop to see his bride, does he not?' His eyes were full of laughter.

'Indeed he does.' She smiled down at him, still out of breath. 'No, go on, my lord, don't wait to help me. There is only one lady you must give your hand to today.'

She had seen the heavy doors opening in the wall of the keep at the top of the stairs. A group of people appeared in the archway. 'Go to her, my lord.' She remained in her saddle, watching as the king turned and ran two at a time up the stairs.

'Are you pleased with yourself now?' Donald's voice at her elbow was light and teasing. She realised suddenly how mud-splashed they all were, and found she was laughing. Donald shook his head in despair and vaulting from his horse came to help her down.

At the top of the stairs, the king was gazing at his bride. Tall and slim, fair-skinned, with large grey eyes and a wide, humorous mouth, Yolande de Dreux curtseyed to her future husband, taking in his muddy finery, the glow of the wind-swept cheeks and the fiery hair. By the time he took her hand and kissed it she had decided she would find it easy to fall in love with her Scottish king.

'Nel? I said, shall I help you?' Donald was standing with his hand on the bridle of Eleyne's horse, and he saw his wife's face. She was staring at the king and his bride with a strangely troubled expression.

'What is it? Don't you like her?' Donald had found the bride attractive enough.

'She's very beautiful.' Eleyne sounded abstracted. A strange chill had settled over her.

'And the wedding tomorrow will be a grand affair,' Donald said cheerfully. He put his hands over her cold wet fists as they rested, still clutching her gilded reins, on the horse's wet mane. 'Come on, let's find our quarters and get you dry.' He squeezed her hands gently. 'Nel?'

'There's something wrong.'

Inside the castle courtyard all was bustle and noise as fifty horses milled about and their riders dismounted and began to sort themselves out. But outside the walls, beyond the small teeming burgh with its lovely abbey, the hills and moors were dreich beneath the rain and the wind howled mournfully like an animal prowling before the coming darkness. Donald resisted the urge to make the sign against the evil eye and took the reins firmly from her chilled fingers. 'Rubbish, you're cold and wet and chilled. When you've had a mug of mulled wine and got your feet by the hearth you'll feel better.'

However, even in the warm curtained bed in the brightly painted roof chamber which they had been allocated and with her husband's arms around her, Eleyne could not shake off her feeling of dread. It lingered all next day until the wedding and the feast which followed it.

IX

Eleyne was sitting at the king's left hand. She eyed him surreptitiously. After the years of procrastination over this wedding, he appeared at last to have put every reservation aside and thrown himself totally into the joy of his new marriage. Yolande sat close to him, her face glowing with happiness, her hand straying often at the same time as his to the dish they shared so that their fingers touched in the sensuous warmth and scent of sauces and gravies and sweet creams and junkets.

Below the dais, in the crowded heat of the hall, the noise of talk and laughter had risen to a deafening pitch which drowned the playing of the minstrels in the space between the tables. Course after course of food continued to arrive, and with it a positive river of rich Gascon wine.

In one of the rare moments when he took his eyes off his wife, Alexander turned to Eleyne and was astounded. How had he ever imagined that Eleyne of Mar looked old? She was radiant. Her trained velvet gown was an exquisite deep green trimmed with gold, her girdle heavy with gilt, her mantle of russet silk trimmed with fox fur, but it was her eyes which caught his attention. They were as green as emeralds in the golden candlelight, large and lustrous. And full of laughter.

Outside, the thunder rumbled gently around the hills. He laughed and touched her arm. 'Thank you.'

He mouthed the words above the noise and she smiled. He wasn't sure what he was thanking her for – for helping sway him finally into remarriage, perhaps; perhaps for caring; for having loved the father he could barely remember but who came to him sometimes in his dreams.

He frowned, aware suddenly that there was someone standing behind them, between his great chair and Eleyne's smaller one. He saw her look over her shoulder and her face paled, all the animation dying before his eyes.

He swung around, angry at the interruption, and caught his breath. There was no one there. Yet he felt it, felt it as clearly as she obviously had. Someone had been there, his shadow cutting off the light from the huge candelabra which burned on the dais behind them.

Eleyne closed her eyes, aware of the sudden cold in the heat of the great hall.

'No.' She didn't realise that she had spoken out loud. 'No, please.'

She felt Donald's arm around her shoulders. 'What is it, Nel?'

Her knife had fallen on the table. Gravy from the roast peacock had soaked into the linen cloth. Her hand went unconsciously to her throat, to the silver pendant she wore there, Donald's pendant. The phoenix lay within a circle of power, imprisoned beneath the floor in the chapel of Kildrummy, sealed under the tiles with rough lime mortar.

It was Alexander. She had known that at once. But he had not come to Jedburgh to see her: he had come to be with his son.

The candles flickered and she was aware suddenly that a strange hush was falling over the great hall as table by table the hundreds of guests fell silent. Beside her the king had half turned in his seat and was staring into the wildly flickering candlelight, his normally ruddy complexion grey.

'Holy Mother of God!' She heard his whispered gasp. 'Who are you?'

She could see something now, a shadow, tall and indistinct, hovering over the king, feel the anguish around them.

Below the high table every face had turned to stare. The new queen was as white as a sheet as she too saw the tossing shadows.

Beware.

Eleyne heard the words in the howling wind.

Beware, my son, beware.

Alexander swallowed, and Eleyne realised that his hand had gone automatically to the ornamental jewelled dirk he wore at his girdle. She saw his knuckles white around the cruciform hilt.

In the quiet one could have heard a pin drop, then from the shadowy body of the hall a woman screamed. The sound tore through the silence, echoing up into the carved roof beams as she pointed towards the high table. It was a signal for total panic. Screams and the crash of overturning tables and benches almost drowned the words.

Too late.

He was fading.

Too late, my son.

The wind in the chimneys reached a crescendo and showers of sparks and ashes blew back into the hall from the two hearths.

Only a scant handful of people actually saw the ghost at the wedding feast of King Alexander III and Yolande of Dreux, but within days the story had spread around Scotland and beyond the border, south. Only three of them – Alexander himself, and Eleyne and Donald – knew who he was, but two whole nations knew that such a spectre was an omen of doom.

X

'It's all right. Please, my dear, calm yourself.' Eleyne cradled the hysterical queen's head in her arms. 'There's nothing to be afraid of, nothing.' She turned the queen's face gently towards her. 'He came to give you his blessing. He came to be with his son.'

Yolande lifted a tear-streaked face. 'But everyone is saying the ghost spoke of death . . .'

'No.' Eleyne shook her head. 'No, I heard him. He made no mention of death. He came to bless you both.' She forced herself to smile. 'Forget him, your grace, be happy with your husband.'

While you still have him. The words hung in the silence between them until Eleyne shrugged them away.

She quickly became very fond of Yolande. The new queen made a confidante of her in the loneliness of her new country, explaining how apprehensive she had been, especially in the care of her solemn, humourless escort of Scotsmen. Her French companions, there for the wedding only, had nearly all departed, leaving only a handful of ladies with her. 'But Alexander, he is different,' she said in her heavy accent. 'He laughs and he makes me laugh and he is kind.'

Eleyne smiled. 'I'm glad. My godson is a good man.'

'Soon I shall give him a son. And then another and then another!'

Eleyne laughed. 'That will please him, my dear, but at the moment he seems perfectly delighted with you.'

Yolande looked away, embarrassed. 'I know how to make him happy.'

'I can see that.' Patting the young woman's shoulder, Eleyne hid a smile.

'And you, you will stay my friend?' Yolande became anxious. 'Alexander says you live in the far north.'

'I do indeed. But I spend my life in the saddle,' Eleyne said, touched at the loneliness the remark betrayed, for all the queen's outward happiness. 'I shall come and see you often, have no fear.'

XI

KILDRUMMY CASTLE ❖ December 1285

Isabella had brought cushions and a thick tapestry to her eyrie in the Snow Tower while her parents were at the king's wedding. One servant had been allowed into the secret and now there was a fire up there, beside which Isabella read her books by candlelight.

'You've turned it into a real bower.' Eleyne admired it, pulling her cloak around her. In spite of the merrily blazing little fire, the vaulted chamber was dark and cold, the roughly plastered walls unpainted. Outside, heavy sleet lashed the castle walls and turned the heather on the hills to a black sodden mass.

'Tell me about the wedding.' Isabella sat cross-legged on the tapestry which she had spread on the floor. 'What did the queen wear?'

Eleyne described the queen's gown, her mantle, the jewellery she had worn and the golden chaplet in her hair, which had hung loose, brushed until it lay like polished ebony over the scarlet samite of her wedding gown.

'It must be wonderful to marry a king.' Isabella put her elbows on her knees, cupping her chin wistfully in her linked fingers.

She dreamed often of the man she would marry. He would be tall and handsome – a prince – like her heroic cousin Llywelyn – a poet like her father; gentle and kind and above all loving. Her father had promised her as much but no one who had yet sought her hand, and there had been many, was good enough for his beautiful Bella.

Eleyne looked away from her daughter's face. 'Isabella, while we were at Jedburgh, your father and Robert of Carrick had a long talk.'

'About Gratney and Christian? Have you fixed a date for their betrothal?'

Eleyne nodded, and held out her hand. 'They were also discussing young Robert's future marriage.'

'Oh?' Isabella was studying her mother's face.

'He is an exceptional young man: charming, intelligent, full of courage . . .'

'Why are you telling me this?'

'We have always liked the Bruces. I have known Robert's grandfather for fifty years and his mother and I were once very close –'

'So?'

There was a long silence.

'I always thought you liked Christian's brothers,' Eleyne said at last.

'Mama!' Her daughter jumped to her feet. 'You don't mean it! You can't mean it! Robert is a boy! He is years younger than me.'

'Not so much younger,' Eleyne coaxed. 'Only five years. Your father is twenty years younger than me.'

'That is different!'

'How is it different?'

'Because it is.' Isabella's voice rose passionately. 'Mama! It will be so long. When he's ready for a wife, I shall be . . . *old!*' Her voice rose to a wail. 'You promised! You promised that I should love my husband! You promised, mama!'

Eleyne flinched at the accusation. 'You will grow to love Robert Bruce,' she said softly. 'I do promise. He will make you a good husband; and he will one day be an earl.'

It must be wonderful to marry a king. Isabella's wistful words rose between them for a moment. Eleyne repeated, 'You will love him, my darling, I do promise it.'

That night in the bedchamber Eleyne sat beside the fire brushing out her hair slowly, watching the reflection of the flames throw glints into the curls. There was more white now, but it still crackled with energy as she pulled the comb through. 'I hope we have done right.'

Donald was poring over some documents by the light of the great candelabra near the shuttered windows. Behind him they could hear the sleet rattling against the glass.

He did not look up. 'She will get used to the idea. He's a fine boy. He'll grow up soon enough.'

'It is a big gap, though.' Eleyne put down her comb.

'*You* say that?' Donald grinned mischievously and she nodded vehemently.

'Yes, I say that. You were a man when I met you. Isabella has to wait for him to grow. And she will have to wait while her blood is yearning for a lover.'

Walking across, Donald put his arm around her shoulder and dropped a kiss on her head. 'If she were destined for the convent, she would have to wait forever,' he said gently. 'It will do her no harm at all. Take her with you when you ride to Fife and take her with you when you go to court; present her to the queen. Give the girl some fun, some distractions, and the time will soon pass. I'll bet that boy could father a child in a year or two given half a chance!' He laughed. 'Who knows? Maybe the marriage will come sooner than she thinks.'

XII

FALKLAND CASTLE ❖ March 1286

Mairi at seventeen was a tall, shy girl with huge eyes. To Eleyne's surprise Joanna seemed happy to hand her daughter over to the girl's care at once.

'She looks strong and competent – that's all that matters. The nurses here are old.' The Countess of Fife wrinkled her nose. 'And they obey my mother-in-law rather than me!' She paused, a puzzled look on her beautiful face. 'Why should you want to give the child a nurse from Mar?'

Eleyne touched the baby's cheek with her fingertip. 'I think one day she'll have need of a friend.'

'And a nursemaid will be her friend?' Joanna sounded scandalised.

'My nurse was my friend.' Eleyne paused. 'If anything she loved me too much,' she added almost inaudibly. The thought of Rhonwen still hurt; still haunted her dreams. 'Mairi will not make that mistake but she will be there when Isobel needs her.' She frowned. 'I only hope she will be strong enough when the time comes.'

The girl's calm acceptance of her fate had worried her slightly. There had been no tears at the thought of leaving her mother; no obvious fear at the thought of the long journey to Fife and the strange household she would be joining, so different from Morna's small lonely cottage. Mairi had taken the journey well; she was shy, and she spoke only Gaelic, though she understood some French and English, but she had picked up the baby with affection and nodded contentedly when she was shown the nursery quarters and introduced to the other nurse-maids. By some strange instinct they seemed to know that they were to be superseded by this quiet northern girl, yet they seemed to regard her without resentment.

Eleyne was watching Mairi bustling competently around the nursery when Isabella came into the room. On the eve of their departure she had had qualms about taking Isabella to Fife. It had been there again, the warning at the back of her mind, the fear that something was wrong. But what could be wrong? What possible danger could a baby be to a girl of seventeen?

Her daughter, tall and pretty, her long hair the colour of ripe corn, held back by a chaplet of woven silk, stood in the doorway. 'Mama! you're here, I've been looking for you.' She moved forward, a slight graceful figure, and looked down into the cradle. Without realising it, Eleyne was holding her breath. The baby looked back at Isabella steadily from dark, smoky eyes and the girl smiled uncertainly. 'What a pretty little thing.' She put her hand down towards the baby, then withdrew it without touching her. 'Are you coming, mama?'

'Of course.' Eleyne was watching little Isobel. The solemn small face was still watching her daughter as if fascinated by the girl. Eleyne turned to Mairi. 'My dear, you'll be happy here. And Isobel is your responsibility, you understand that?'

Mairi nodded gravely. 'I'll take care of her for you, my lady, I promise.'

XIII
17 March 1286

From Falkland they rode to Kinghorn where Queen Yolande was staying. She greeted Eleyne warmly, kissed her on both cheeks and smiled at Isabella, before ushering them into her bower. In the doorway Eleyne stopped: this was the room Alexander had used as his own – her Alexander. The hearth was heaped high with crackling driftwood and the small room was hot and stuffy. The windows had been glassed in now and were heavily shuttered.

Seating herself on a cushion Yolande held out her hand to Isabella. 'So, this is your daughter, Lady Mar. Is she going to come and serve me as one of my maidens?'

'Would you like that, my dear?' Eleyne asked Isabella. She had not planned it, but the queen was offering her a great honour; one which could not be refused and one which would help to pass the time until a boy became a man.

She held her breath, seeing the shyness in her daughter's eyes turning to terror as the implications of the queen's warm-hearted invitation hit her. Isabella shook her head. 'I don't know, mama . . .'

'I think she would be honoured, your grace,' Eleyne replied gently. 'My daughter will serve the queen with all her heart.'

Yolande smiled. 'She will soon become accustomed to the idea. Tell me, child, are you betrothed?' She leaned forward, still holding Isabella's hand.

Isabella was speechless and again Eleyne answered for her. 'She is, your grace, to Robert Bruce, the eldest son of the Earl of Carrick.'

'Ah,' the queen nodded, 'I have met the Lady Marjorie, his mother. A formidable lady!' She laughed good-naturedly. 'Now, let us call some of my other maidens. They can take Isabella away while I talk with her mother.'

Eleyne ignored Isabella's pleading look as two young women came in answer to the queen's call and bore her off. As the door closed behind the chattering girls, a strange silence fell on the room. Eleyne turned from the queen towards the fire, feeling a cold draught playing on her spine. The fire had died; the embers glowed weakly where only moments before a cheerful blaze had crackled up the chimney.

The queen exclaimed crossly, 'Call the boy to bring more wood!' She shivered ostentatiously. 'The fires at Kinghorn gobble fuel like greedy monsters. This is a godforsaken country when it comes to the weather!'

The spell was broken. Whatever had hung above the room had gone. Eleyne found she could breathe more easily suddenly and she laughed. 'Our winters can be bad, your grace, but spring always comes – in the end.'

'Good.' Yolande folded her arms and leaned forward conspiratorially. 'May I tell you a secret?' Her eyes sparkled. 'No one knows it yet, not even the king, but I have to tell someone.' She patted the bench beside her and when Eleyne sat down took her hand in excitement. 'I think I am with child.'

'That's wonderful, your grace!' Eleyne smiled, but there was something wrong; her skin prickled a warning. The room had grown colder again. Standing up, she went to the door and called the page in attendance outside. 'We need wood for the fire quickly. The queen's bower is freezing.'

Turning, she looked at the queen. The room was shimmering with cold; the patterns on the wall hangings stood out in extraordinary detail; she could see every board in the painted shutters, dark though they were in the candlelight. She could hear the wind moaning over the Forth as it funnelled in from the North Sea. A haze of spume hit the small panes of leaded glass, running down on to the sills and streaming down the walls. She could not see it, but her ears, suddenly preternaturally sensitive, picked up the sound and interpreted it correctly.

Yolande was watching her. 'What is it?' she breathed. 'What is wrong?'

Eleyne did not hear her. The air was full of danger. It crackled with the coldness of ice in the atmosphere of the stuffy little room. She heard the storm building until it was in the room with them. The howl of the wind; the crash of the waves and suddenly a knife blade of lightning, zigzagging through the air around the queen. Eleyne gasped and stepped forward, expecting to see Yolande drop, but the queen was still sitting exactly where she had been, her face a mask of astonishment.

'Lady Mar? Eleyne, my dear? What is it?'

Eleyne was shaking from head to foot. 'Didn't you see it?'

'See what?' At last the queen stood up. 'What's the matter? Shall I call a physician? Or one of your ladies?' She put her hand on Eleyne's arm, seeing her as an old woman, her face lined, her shoulders stooped.

'The storm. The lightning touched you –' Eleyne was confused.

Yolande smiled. She shook her head. 'There is no storm. Listen.' She gestured towards the shuttered windows.

Eleyne could hear the gentle moan of the wind, no more. Walking wearily over to the fireplace, she stared down at the hot embers. 'Forgive me, I must be more tired than I thought.'

'I'll call for some wine,' the queen said reassuringly, 'then you must rest. Your daughter can attend you. Tomorrow if you're well enough we shall travel together to Edinburgh, to Alexander.'

'To Alexander?' Eleyne was disorientated. 'Alexander is dead.'

The queen went white. 'What do you mean? Alexander is in Edinburgh with his council!'

'No, no, I'm sorry.' Eleyne shook her head. 'I was muddled. I was thinking of his father . . .'

Yolande's face had closed, and she turned away frowning. The woman was indeed growing old. 'I think you should rest, my lady. Tomorrow we shall ride.'

'No!' Eleyne's voice was suddenly sharp. 'No, you mustn't ride to Edinburgh.' The air was spinning around the queen's head, crackling with warning. 'Please, you mustn't. If you ride, something terrible will happen. Wait, you must wait here. Let Alexander come to you. You can tell him about the child you carry then. Tell him to come here.'

Yolande had swung to face her again. 'Go and rest, my lady,' she repeated. Her eyes were full of pity, mixed with not a little apprehension. 'We can talk about it all in the morning. Here is the boy with the logs. Leave me now. Call your daughter and rest.'

Eleyne smiled sadly. 'I'm sorry. I've frightened you. I didn't mean to. It is just that I see things sometimes . . .'

'You mean you are *clairvoyante*!'

'Yes.'

'And you saw danger for my baby?' The queen put her hand to her stomach protectively.

'I saw no baby, madame. But I did see danger. I saw danger all around you.'

'Then I shall not ride. You were quite right to tell me.' Yolande went back to her seat and sat down firmly. 'I shall send a messenger to Alexander to come to me. Tomorrow. As soon as he can.' She was suddenly coquettish. 'I don't think he will find this a hardship.'

Isabella was sharing her mother's bed. In the darkness she snuggled against Eleyne's back, exhausted and pleased now with her new role as one of the queen's maidens and it was not long before Eleyne heard the girl's breathing grow steady as she fell asleep.

Eleyne lay looking into the glowing fire, listening as the wind grew stronger. Like the queen's bower, their bedchamber looked out across the Forth. Behind the ill-fitting shutters and the glass, so loosely set in its leads that it rattled, she heard the waves beating on to the shore. Her mind was churning with images: Mairi, so far from home and, at the whim of Joanna de Clare, in charge of the nursery at Falkland at the age of seventeen. Shadows hung over that girl's head, and over little Isobel's. And Isabella. Shadows hung over the whole land.

She eased herself away from Isabella so as not to wake her, and crept out of bed. She pulled her cloak around her shoulders and went over to the fire. Reaching for the poker, she pushed aside the turves which covered it and threw on a couple of pieces of wood. Then she sat on a stool facing it, huddling for warmth in the folds of her thick cloak. Behind her Isabella flung out an arm in her sleep and gave a little murmur.

Staring into the flames, trying to see pictures which would not come, Eleyne was aware that there was someone with her. The room was dark save where the light of the fire sent flickering shadows leaping up the walls and across the floor. She smiled sadly and reached out her hand, but there was no one to take it. Only a whisper too soft to hear above the sigh of the ash beneath the logs.

Alexander! The name floated soundlessly in the air around her.

'Alexander. My love!'

Her eyes widened. How could he be here? The phoenix was hidden.

The shadows were uneasy. The air tense and unhappy. Outside the window the sound of a gull's laughing cry, shredded on the night wind, tumbled into the room and was gone, borne away on the storm.

Alexander! The name again, in her head, a cry of despair.

She was afraid. 'What is it?' She spoke out loud and heard Isabella groan. The shadows were growing blacker. She shivered and looked down at the fire. The flames had died, the logs lay sullenly black and suddenly the room was full of the noise of the storm. Staggering to her feet, Eleyne groped her way to the narrow window. The shutter had blown open and the fragile glass was rattling in its frame. As she reached it, two opaque panes blew in and broke at her feet on the floor of the window embrasure.

'Mama! What is it?' Isabella sat up in fright. 'What's happened?'

'Nothing, my darling. Stay in bed.' Eleyne groped for the flailing shutter. 'The storm has blown in the window, that's all. I can fix the shutter.' She felt a sharp pain as she stood on a piece of broken glass. Rain was spattering on the floor and ice-cold on to her face and arms as she struggled with the heavy shutter. At last she pushed it back across the window and wedged the bar home in its slot. The room grew still and dark once more.

A light flared as Isabella pushed a taper into the fire and lit a candle. 'Are you all right?' Her voice was high and frightened.

'I've cut my foot.' Eleyne could feel the blood running down her instep.

'The storm has got so bad!' Isabella ran to her and knelt at her mother's feet. 'I'll fetch some ointment from your coffer and bind it up for you. Poor mama, you should have called a servant to fix the shutter.' She bustled away, the candle in her hand throwing a crazy whirl of shadows on the walls.

695

Eleyne hobbled to the bed and hoisted herself on to the high mattress with a groan. The frightened hammering in her chest slowed. Whatever, whoever, had been in the room, had gone.

The next day the storm had blown itself out. The sun sparkled on the blue waters of the Forth and they could see clearly across the firth.

After breakfast the queen sent for Eleyne. 'Are you rested, my lady?' she asked warily and Eleyne noted with weary amusement that she had made the sign against the evil eye.

'Thank you, yes.' Eleyne refrained from mentioning the sleepless night or her swollen painful foot.

'I've taken your advice,' Yolande went on, 'and sent a messenger to Edinburgh begging the king to come to me as soon as his meetings are over.' She smiled. 'I'm sure he won't stay away from me a moment longer than he need.'

'I'm sure he won't.' Eleyne's head was as heavy as lead. There were dark circles beneath her eyes. Lethargically she took her place beside the queen and reached for the embroidery which the queen's ladies had laid ready for the day. Isabella had vanished, already whispering secrets to a new-found friend.

'You still look tired.' Yolande noticed the paleness of her companion's face.

Eleyne gave a wry smile. 'I do feel tired. I fear I'm getting old.'

But it was not tiredness or age weighing her down; it was a feeling of oppression and despair which seemed to fill her soul.

XIV

18 March 1286

In Edinburgh Castle Alexander walked to the door of the great keep and stared out at the storm. As the day went on, the weather had grown worse again. The blue sky vanished; black cloud raced in from the east, and with it snow. The weather was set for the night, probably for weeks. Cursing, he turned back into the hall, then stopped. He had had enough of meetings, enough of discussion, enough of argument, on a day which the gossips and old wives whispered was to be a day of doom. What he wanted was to ride with the wind and rain and ice on his face until he was exhausted, a drink and bed with his highly desirable wife.

He thought again of the note she had sent him that morning and the unspecified delights it promised. He had hoped that the meetings would be finished by midday and that he would be with her by dark.

So be it: he would ride now and be with her by midnight. Surprise her; come cold of face and hot of body to her bed.

Without a word to the assembled nobles and courtiers, who stood drinking around the great fire waiting for the horn to call them to the evening meal, he ran down the staircase and into the slanting rain.

His great black horse whickered as he glanced into its stall and he rubbed its nose fondly. 'Saddle him up, James, and find four men to ride with me to Kinghorn,' he ordered the groom.

'Kinghorn, my lord?' The man glanced out at the rain. 'You'll not be crossing the water in this weather?'

'Why not? I'll find a sturdy boatman to take me over.' Alexander slapped him on the back. 'Hurry, man, before my friends see I've gone and insist on coming too.'

Suddenly the expedition had turned to an adventure, and he wanted no one urging caution. He wanted to gallop, to forget the discussions, the voices of sober restraint and shout his warcry into the storm.

The ride to Dalmeny was wild. He galloped ahead of the four men who rode with him and when they arrived he had already called the ferryman from his bed, smacking the great bell at the water's edge with the flat of his sword, hearing the wild note ring out across the white-topped waves to be lost in the scream of the wind.

'You'll not take the horses tonight, my lord,' James shouted, pitching the full power of his lungs against the storm. 'Not in an open boat. Best leave them here and pick up new mounts on the other side.'

'It's too bad, my lord!' the boatman said, his beard streaming in the wind. 'I'll not take my boat out tonight.'

'Yes, tonight!' Alexander shouted back, exhilarated. He threw his horse's rein to James. 'You stay. Take them back to the castle. And you, my friend –' he spoke to the ferryman – 'a bag of silver pennies to you when I set foot on the other side. You're not afraid, surely!' He laughed out loud as he saw the greedy light in the man's eyes.

The ferryman wagged his head in mock resignation. 'No doubt I could not die in better company,' he acknowledged grumpily as they all looked out across the water.

The wind had backed to the south and the sturdy ferry set out into the waves, bucking violently, sending cascades of spray over the bows. In the stern the boatman stood at the steering oar, his eyes narrowed, watching the sail which strained in a great arc before the mast.

The journey was fast. They were all soaked to the skin by the time they reached the shore at Inverkeithing and Alexander's mood was if anything more exhilarated than before.

Leaping ashore he turned to the ferryman, 'A bag of silver for the crossing and another for your men, my friend. You did your king great

697

service tonight. Summon the bailie and have him find us horses, then you can go.'

The bailie tried to persuade the king to go no further, but Alexander would not listen and reluctantly the man found horses for his king and his three companions, plus two local men to guide them.

By the light of the torches which spluttered under the rain the king surveyed the horses. Three of them were greys, the finest a rig with an arched neck and proudly carried tail, its harness gilded and studded with gleaming metal. For a moment Alexander hesitated, then he swung himself into the high saddle. It was not far to Kinghorn and in his present mood he wanted no delay. With a shout, he turned the horse's head towards the track and set it at a gallop into the darkness, his companions in hot pursuit.

He could smell the sharp resin of the pines as the track turned inland, following the contours of the land. Amongst the trees the strange twilight of the darkness grew absolute, and he was forced to slow the horse, realising for the first time that it had a mouth of iron and a will to match. It had caught his mood of wild excitement and was thundering up the track parallel with the edge of the low cliff. Far out to sea the first flicker of lightning cut across the sky and above the roar of the wind in the pine boughs he heard a grumble of thunder. He reined the horse in to a rearing halt and looked back the way he had come. There was no sign of the others. Cursing, he narrowed his eyes in the wind-borne sleet, aware of the shifting moaning mass of the firth to his right, hidden between the pine trees with their whipping branches.

When the lightning came, it cut through the darkness like a steel blade, slamming into one of the old Scots pines and igniting it like a burning torch. The horse let out a piercing scream of fear and plunged off the track into the narrow belt of trees which fringed the top of the cliff. Desperately Alexander dragged at the reins trying to turn its head but its hooves were slipping, scrabbling in the soft slippery mud at the edge of the cliff. He tried to throw himself from the saddle but they were already falling, man and horse together, into the blackness of the night.

XV

19 March 1286

'NO!'

Eleyne sat up in the bed, the scream ringing in her ears.

'Mama, what is it?' Terrified, Isabella sat up, but her mother had already scrambled from the bed, swinging her heavy cloak around her.

698

Eleyne ran towards the door and pulled it open. Barefoot, she flew down the stairs and through the silent building, trying to drag open the heavy outer door with her hands.

'My lady?' The sleepy doorward stepped forward and unbolted it for her, swinging it open to let in the rush of the storm.

She ran outside, staring up at the sky, feeling the icy sleet on her face and throat, knowing the wind had seized her cloak and torn it open.

'No! No!' She was sobbing violently as Isabella caught up with her in the courtyard.

'Mama, what is it? Was it a dream?' Isabella tried to put her arms around her, pulling the cloak across her mother's nakedness.

'A dream! A nightmare!' Eleyne screamed. 'Oh sweet Blessed Virgin, why? I warned him! I told him! Thomas told him and Michael of Balwearie! He knew!' Suddenly she froze. 'I told the queen to send for him. I told her to tell him to come to Kinghorn. It was me! It was my fault!' Tears streamed down her face.

'What was you, mama? What has happened?'

Behind Isabella figures had appeared in the doorway. The doorward had raised a lighted torch high and the flames streamed past his head.

'What has happened?' Eleyne turned to her daughter in despair. 'You don't know! No one knows! The king is dead! That is what has happened! If my destiny was to save him and to save Scotland I have failed!' She tore at her hair in despair. 'I saw, I saw what was to come and I failed to stop it. I told the queen to send for him. And I killed him!'

XVI

The room was lit by a single lamp, its faint light steady on the table. Eleyne lay gazing up at the ceiling above her head. She was shivering violently, and her teeth were chattering.

Isabella had brought her back to bed, put the sleeping draught to her lips and held her hands until she dozed. The household was in turmoil. The queen had collapsed in hysterics and been escorted to her own bed, sobbing wildly, whilst every able-bodied man in the place had ridden out into the storm to search.

To search for what? A wild-eyed half-naked old woman had run out into the courtyard in the middle of the night, screaming that the king was dead, that the king had fallen from his horse! And that she was to blame. More than one person that night looked at Eleyne of Mar and crossed their fingers against the evil eye.

Her head felt heavy and her eyes were red and sore with weeping, but she was unable to sleep again. If she moved her head slightly, she could see Isabella sitting by the fire. Wrapped in a blue velvet cloak, the child was dozing in her chair.

She heard a log move and fall from the firedogs on to the hearth. The fire flared briefly, sending reflected lights dancing over the walls of the room. Here near the bed the walls were stencilled with green and silver patterns, a repetitive, gentle decoration designed to soothe and calm the weary as they climbed into the high bed.

Her eyes closed. She was still shaking, still so very, very cold. Turning on her side, she humped herself into the foetal position, clutching her cloak around her ice-cold body beneath the bedcovers.

Eleyne . . . Eleyne . . .

Her eyes flew open. The room was full of voices.

The child . . . the girl . . . Isabella . . .

'Einion!' Her lips were stiff. After so many years the name was unfamiliar.

Eleyne . . . Eleyne . . .

'Alexander!' She was crying now, the tears scalding her frozen skin. Her head was spinning and she was still trembling violently. Was that a figure in the corner of the room, or was she asleep, her mind a black hell of nightmares?

She tried to sit up, but she couldn't move. 'Isabella!' She tried to call, but no sound came. Was it a tall figure by the wall, the white hair and beard incandescent round his head, or had the fire, blown back by the wind, belched smoke into the room?

'Einion Gweledydd,' she whispered again. She was terribly afraid. 'I tried to warn him, I tried . . .'

But he had gone.

'Alexander, please, I tried to warn him . . .'

The lamp was guttering. The gentle light played for a moment over Isabella's face, then it went out, leaving only the firelight to flicker in the shadows of the room.

They found King Alexander's body at first light, on the beach below the cliffs. His neck was broken. The dead horse lay several yards away from him. They brought him first to Kinghorn. Then he was taken to Dunfermline where he was to lie near the shrine of St Margaret.

Eleyne was too ill to view the body. By morning, when they brought the king to his wife's bed, she was delirious with fever. If she knew that her nephew lay beneath the same roof, she gave no sign. The country, stunned by the news, hummed to the rumours that the Countess of Mar had foretold the king's death. Isabella sent for Mairi to come from Falkland and between them they nursed her from the brink of insanity.

It was several weeks before she was well enough to return to Kildrummy, leaving Mairi once more with her charge, and sending Isabella to be with the queen. There in the lonely northern hills she rode and paced and ran in the wind and rain, railing against the uncaring gods who had allowed the death of the king. All her life she had seen what was to happen, but it could not be prevented. Alexander's death, like every other death, had been written in the stars. Nothing had been allowed to change the course of destiny.

CHAPTER THIRTY

I

May 1286

'So. That is that!' Donald flung himself into the elegantly carved X-chair before the hearth in the solar of the Snow Tower. 'The parliament at Scone has elected a group of guardians to rule Scotland until she has a king again, and I am not amongst them. No doubt the fact that my wife made a public spectacle of her foolishness helped them make their decision.'

'Donald.' Eleyne could not hide the pain in her voice. 'Please. Don't you think there's enough on my conscience without adding this to it?' She took a deep breath, trying to steady herself against the storm of emotions which welled up within her. 'Where is the queen now?'

'She is at Stirling Castle. And Isabella is with her. God help Scotland! What a choice of rulers we have! The king's grandchild, a slip of a girl in Norway under the thumb of a foreign king, or an unborn babe. Who would have thought such a disaster could strike this kingdom?' He paced the floor. 'Duncan of Fife is to be one of the guardians, you'll be pleased to hear, in spite of his youth.' He scowled. 'And Alexander of Buchan and James Stewart, with a brace of bishops to keep us all holy.'

'And Robert of Carrick or his father?' Eleyne asked, trying to concentrate on the implications of what Donald was saying. She had grown very thin and there were dark shadows beneath her eyes.

Donald shook his head. 'Bruce and Balliol are eyeing each other like gamecocks ready for the fight. They both remember their royal descent, remote though it is. Your nephew, old Robert Bruce of Annandale, is strutting round reminding everyone that he was once named heir to the throne in the old king's day.' He studied Eleyne's face, but it remained shuttered with strain and exhaustion as the memory of the late King Alexander and their own private terror hovered in the air between them.

'How could I forget that?' she sighed. 'It was when John died. Poor John, he was so sure he would one day be a king.'

Donald nodded. 'Well, the lords of the realm decided in their wisdom that neither a Bruce nor a Balliol should be amongst the guardians. If the queen loses this baby – if there is a baby –' he added cynically, 'and if anything happens to Margaret of Norway who is the present acknowledged heir and to whom we have all now taken an oath of fealty, one of those two men will no doubt one day be our king.'

Eleyne caught her breath. 'And our daughter is betrothed to the Bruce heir,' she whispered. *It must be wonderful to marry a king.* Isabella's voice echoed in her head.

Donald smiled grimly. 'Don't start seeing crowns on Isabella's head yet, my love. There are four lives at least between young Robert Bruce and the throne of Scotland, his father and grandfather being two of them, and probably an ocean of blood if John Balliol has anything to say in the matter.' He stood up. 'Where is Gratney?'

'He and the twins took their hawks out this morning. I doubt if they'll be back before dark.'

Donald walked across to Eleyne and dropped a kiss on the top of her head. 'Forgive me, my darling, it's not your fault I'm not named a guardian. They know we are close to the Bruces and so have already, in a sense, declared our hand. Young Duncan was only chosen because they revere the earldom of Fife's old traditions and acknowledge that the Earl of Fife, above all men, has the right to crown the next king.' He paused. 'Or queen, God help us. I suspect it is that, rather than Duncan's talent as an administrator, which has caused his elevation to these dizzy heights.' He grimaced sourly. 'Has he told you his latest plan for his little daughter?'

'No. She's only a baby, Donald, he can't have made plans yet.'

'You were married as a baby, my love.' He folded his arms. 'Lord Buchan has approached him, it seems. He would like the Fife alliance and he proposes little Isobel for his eldest son. Duncan agreed with alacrity.'

Eleyne closed her eyes and shook her head. 'John of Buchan is already a grown man. Surely he won't wait for her.' She stared down at the hearth where the wolfhound, Sarra, lay asleep, head on paws, and she pushed the sudden feeling of apprehension aside. Never again would she listen to the voices inside her head, or heed the Sight when it came. Fate could not be side-stepped. What the gods ordained, they carried through ruthlessly and without mercy. There was nothing any puny man or woman could do to save themselves from the destiny which awaited them. Knowing about it beforehand just made it harder to bear.

She walked across to the window and looked out. On the ridge behind the castle, against the brilliant spring sky, she saw the silhouettes of a herd of hinds as they made their way east. In a moment they were out of sight on the far slopes of Garlat Hill.

Turning, she saw her husband looking at her, and she shrugged. 'So be it. If it's what Duncan wants. One day the child will be Countess of Buchan. I can only hope she is strong enough for whatever lies ahead.'

II

With Isabella still in attendance on Queen Yolande, her hideaway was empty and Eleyne found her way there more and more often. She was growing tired. Gratney and Donald quarrelled endlessly, mainly over the intentions of the King of England. To Donald he was a danger, ever present on their border. Gratney, on the other hand, admired Edward enormously, proud of his close kinship with the King of England; they were after all first cousins once removed. His two brothers, Alexander and Duncan, supported their father and Marjorie, outspoken beyond her years, joined in the family quarrels with alacrity, her hair flaming, her thin face screwed up with passion, supporting her eldest brother whom she adored unreservedly. Sometimes Eleyne felt the castle would never be free of the passionate, ringing voices of the young Mars, or of the slamming doors as one or another of them stormed out of the latest quarrel.

In the autumn Isabella came home, with tales of Queen Yolande's tearful admission that she was not – and never had been – pregnant; that there would be no direct male heir to the ancient line of Scotland and that now without a doubt little Margaret of Norway, King Alexander II's great-grand-daughter, was their queen.

'Yolande is to go to France, to remarry, no doubt,' Isabella said sadly. 'So she has sent all her Scottish maidens home. Look, she gave me a gift.' She held out her hand and showed them the ring which sparkled on her third finger. Made from twisted gold wire, it was set with a crystal which caught the firelight as it moved.

'Poor lady.' Eleyne sighed.

Isabella looked pityingly at her mother. 'She found it hard to forgive you at first, mama, but she did in the end. She said you had no way of knowing what would happen . . .' Her voice trailed away. 'But you did know, didn't you?'

'Yes, I knew.'

'Why didn't you do something, mama?' It was a whisper.

'Because I didn't know *when* it would happen.' Eleyne clutched her hands together, her knuckles white. 'He knew! He knew he should not ride in a storm. He knew he must never ride a grey, but he did both. He went ahead and did both, anyway! Because we cannot change what is to be.' She turned to her daughter. 'Scotland's destiny was in my hands, but I could change nothing, *nothing*! I was not strong enough. Perhaps once I could have done it. If I had studied with Einion or with

704

Michael or Adam, perhaps I could have altered the course of history. I don't know.'

'Who was Einion?' Isabella asked.

Eleyne considered for a moment. 'A wise man, a descendant of the ancient Druids. But even he made mistakes. He saw my children as kings . . .' She paused.

Isabella grimaced. 'My Robert's grandfather will claim to be king if anything happens to little Queen Margaret.'

She went to look out of the high narrow window. The sky was a clear washed blue, cold and harsh above the mountains. 'That means Robert might one day be king. Then your Druid's prophecy will come true, if I am his wife.'

Eleyne gave a small smile. So Isabella too had seen a crown in her dreams. 'Did you see more of your betrothed when you were at Stirling?'

Isabella tossed her head. 'He is always at Turnberry or Lochmaben. But he came with his grandfather to see James the Stewart and Duncan last week.'

'And do you like him better now?' Eleyne asked the question lightly.

Isabella considered for a moment. 'I suppose he's quite handsome,' she said at last, reluctantly. 'And he's as tall as I am. And at least now he is a squire.'

Eleyne smiled. 'Well,' she said. 'It seems he's improving.'

III

John of Strathbogie, Earl of Atholl, twenty-two years old, with dark wavy hair and handsome regular features, shook hands solemnly with Donald and smiled.

'I'll take care of her,' he said firmly. 'And I'll make her happy.'

'You make sure you do,' Donald said gruffly. Then he grinned. 'She's a handful, mind. It's all that red hair. And she's like her mother. Determined!'

Atholl laughed. 'So am I, my friend, I assure you. I'll cope.'

He and Donald had just signed the marriage contract drawn up by their respective advisers. Two months hence, on John the Baptist's Day, the twenty-fourth of June, Midsummer, Lord Atholl would marry Marjorie, youngest daughter of the Earl of Mar.

'I don't believe it!' Isabella raged at her sister. 'That's not fair. You'll be married before me. And he's older than you. Much older than Robert, and he's an earl. I'm the eldest! He should have married me!'

'It was me he wanted!' Marjorie performed a little twirl of excitement and resisted the urge to stick her tongue out at her sister. 'Anyway, you wouldn't break off your betrothal to Robert. I thought you liked him.'

'I do like him, but he's a boy still.' Isabella sat down abruptly. Her face crumpled. 'You'll be a countess.'

'So will you, one day.'

'But not for years and years and years!'

Marjorie frowned. Suddenly her triumph didn't look so fine after all. 'He'd have chosen you if you'd been free,' she said coaxingly. 'I'm sure he would. I wasn't his first choice, after all. He's been married before and his wife died.' She bit her lip. 'She was only eighteen. She died in childbirth.' Both girls were silent for a moment, then Marjorie shrugged. 'I'm sure that won't happen to me. I'll give him lots of sons,' she said. She did not sound altogether convinced.

Only weeks after Marjorie's betrothal came another. Duncan the twin was to marry Christiana, the only child and heir of Alan Macruarie of the great lordship of Garmoran in the Western Isles.

'So, the brood are taking wing at last.' Fondly Donald put his arm around Eleyne's shoulders.

'It's wonderful to see them so happy.' All three sons had been knighted by the king, Gratney on his twenty-first birthday, and the twins on theirs a year later.

'Sandy hasn't said much about his twin's marriage,' she commented.

'He's a strange young man, that one. He's determined not to marry himself, you know.' Donald shook his head, and there was a moment of tension between them. It was always there, the uncertainty, even after all these years. Donald fought it constantly, and if anything showed Sandy greater favour than the others, ashamed of his doubts. Sandy reciprocated with a special shy affection for his father, without ever realising the cause of his father's extra warmth.

Eleyne took Sandy to walk with her in the herb garden and made him hold her basket while she cut lavender and marjoram and new shooting fennel.

'Your father tells me you're not upset that Duncan is going to be married,' she said gently. 'Is that true?'

Sandy smiled. He took the shears from her hands and began to cut for her, expertly choosing the right shoots. 'Of course I'm not upset. I shall miss him when he goes off to the Hebrides, of course I shall. It's a long way. But he and I don't have to be together to be close, you know that.'

Eleyne smiled. 'I know. And he'll come back and see us often, I'm sure. Sandy, about your marriage . . .'

'No, mama.' Sandy put the shears and basket on the grass and took her hands. 'It's right for Gratney to marry. He's the heir. And it's right for Duncan as the youngest to marry an heiress, so his son will be a great lord one day too. But not me.' He held her gaze with his strangely fathomless eyes. 'There's no place for my children in history.'

Eleyne felt pinpricks of cold tiptoeing up and down her spine. 'How do you know that?' she asked. Her mouth had gone dry.

'Let's just say I know.' He raised her hands and kissed her fingers lightly. 'And now, little mama, I suggest we go in. The wind is cold and I can feel you shivering.'

Later, alone in the chapel, she stood looking at the Holy Rood and then down at the floor beneath the tall lancet windows. The tiles were covered now by a richly woven carpet. Beneath the carpet, incarcerated in wood and cement and clay, inside its ivory box bound with a web of prayer, the phoenix lay wrapped in lambswool and silk. Around it, when Father Gillespie was elsewhere, she had woven a circle of power to hold it prisoner until it was time for her to join her king.

She was puzzled as she stood in the cool shadows of the chapel. Did Alexander visit his son within the great walls of Kildrummy? Was the hand of destiny resting on Sandy's head? He had been so certain, so sure that it was not to be. It was almost as though he knew his future already and that it was bleak. She walked to the prayer desk near the chancel steps and knelt, then she buried her face in her hands and wept.

IV

KILDRUMMY ❖ September 1289

It was early autumn when Eleyne had her first serious illness, lying in bed tossing feverishly day after day without the strength to rise.

Morna came, fetched from her bothy by Sandy when Eleyne refused to see a physician.

Her bones ached; her body felt tired; she had no desire to leave the room in spite of the call of the brilliant smoky day outside, and she scowled at Morna who had brought her a new infusion of herbs. Donald was away in Perth, Sandy had ridden to visit the Countess of Buchan at Ellon, and Marjorie had gone to her handsome earl, leaving Gratney in charge of the castle and Isabella to fuss endlessly over her mother. It was the fussing which eventually forced Eleyne from her bed.

'Help me to my chair. If that child sponges my forehead once more, I shall scream.' She leaned on Morna's arm and walked the few steps to the chair by the hearth. 'Bless her, I love her dearly, but she'll fuss me into my grave. Give me my medicine. I have to be better by the time Donald returns.'

Kneeling at her side, Morna handed her the goblet. Eleyne sipped it with a grimace. 'Go on, say it: I'm the worst patient you have ever treated.'

'You're not used to being ill. You've never learned patience.'

'And I never intend to!' Eleyne leaned back in the chair with a groan. 'Do you know how old I am? I'm seventy-one, Morna! I've outlived my time.'

'Rubbish.' Morna handed the goblet to a waiting servant and settled herself comfortably on a stool near Eleyne's feet. 'Your first proper illness in years –' the illness at Kinghorn had been an illness of the mind '– and you are talking mournfully of death. What would your husband say? Or the children? You'll be up and in the saddle within days, my friend, I'd stake my reputation on it.' She laughed her deep melodious laugh. 'And I intend to take the credit for it. Did you see the way that old monk from Cabrach looked at me when I said I'd given you enough physic and he was to keep his leeches in his scrip.' She leaned forward. 'I had a letter from Mairi. The folk in Fife think her illiterate, you know, because she's quiet and keeps her counsel, but she writes as well as a scribe. I taught her myself, as you well know. She says she's proud of your little great-grand-daughter. She says the child reminds her of you. She rides already and the little madam has a mind of her own.'

Eleyne smiled. 'I'll take that as a compliment. I'm glad Mairi is there to take care of Isobel. Something in that household worries me.'

'Have you heard from Lord and Lady Fife?' Morna asked.

'Not for months. I was planning to visit Falkland before the weather got bad, but now . . .' Eleyne looked forlorn.

'So you didn't know that Lady Fife is expecting another child.'

'No.' Eleyne straightened. 'That's good news. Is Duncan pleased?'

'Mairi did not say. She only said that he was away. They have moved from Falkland for the last months of the summer. Then after Lady Fife's confinement they will travel south.'

'Then I must try and get better in time to ride down to see them,' Eleyne said.

V

It was three weeks more before she was strong enough to order the horses to take her and her companions to Fife. Her sons had left the week before at their father's command to join him at Stirling. Only Isabella remained to take care of her mother – Isabella, still unmarried as she waited for her fifteen-year-old suitor to become a man.

708

'I shall leave you to ensure the last of the stores are brought in, and the marts hung for the winter,' Eleyne directed briskly the night before she left. 'Check that we have sugar, ginger, mace, citron, figs, raisins . . .' She ticked them off on her fingers. 'Salt beef, hams, sturgeon, lampreys. The stewards have my lists. You must make sure they check the merchants don't cheat us. You will be in sole charge of Kildrummy.' She kissed her daughter's cheek fondly.

'And you will come back soon, mama,' Isabella put her hand over her mother's, 'and not tire yourself too much.'

Eleyne laughed. 'I'm as fit as I ever was, child. Don't you worry, I can cope with anything.'

VI

FIFE

The ride to Macduff's Castle was not unduly tiring, but as they turned towards the coast and saw the walls of the castle rise before them against the evening sky Eleyne felt such a wave of weariness sweep over her that it nearly bore her from her saddle. She reined in her horse and looked at the castle, built long ago by one of Malcolm's ancestors. Behind it, in the green evening sky, a skein of duck flew westwards towards the last yellow flash of daylight. In the fields nearby, the small black cattle grazed unconcerned.

'Something is wrong.' She saw smoke rising from the chimney in the corner of the keep and another column from the kitchens inside the outer wall. Nothing seemed amiss there – the smoke was clear, spiced with apple wood. She raised her hand to shade her eyes, looking for the earl's barred standard on the tower. No flag flew. The gates were closed although it was not yet dusk.

Urging her horse into a canter, she was first at the castle gatehouse, and she waited impatiently, her eyes on the postern, as one of her men-at-arms hammered on it with the hilt of his sword.

It was Master Elias, the blind harper, retired now from court and once more in his beloved Fife, who greeted her in the great hall. 'My lady, I knew you would come.' The old man had risen to his feet. He groped his way towards her and held out his hands. Taking them, Eleyne felt a suffocating sense of fear. 'What has happened? Where is Lady Fife?'

Elias lowered his head. 'It's the beginning of the end, my lady. Lord Fife is dead, murdered by his own kinfolk.' His hands tightened over hers as he heard her sharp intake of breath. 'His body was taken to Coupar Angus. Lady Fife and the household rode there this morning.'

709

'My husband . . . my son . . . and now my grandson,' Eleyne whispered. 'Sweet Blessed Margaret! The house of Fife is cursed.' She put her hands over her face. 'Where is Macduff?'

'Your son, Macduff, has ridden to Coupar Angus too. He will await you there.' The blind eyes seemed all-seeing. 'Lady Fife carries a son in her womb, my lady, another child to inherit the earldom, but it's the little lass who will fulfil Fife's destiny.' He smiled sadly. 'Give her your blessing this night, for that destiny is already in train.'

Eleyne took his hands again and pressed them gently. Then she turned away, blinking back her tears.

She called for lighted torches. The stables were empty, so they had no choice but to remount their weary horses and turn back north into the coming darkness.

VII

COUPAR ANGUS

The abbey was dark save for the four great candles around the bier. The monks who watched over the body of their patron as it lay beneath the silk banner, embroidered with the rampant lion of Fife, scarcely looked up from beneath their cowls at the old woman who walked in, upright in spite of her tiredness, and stood at the Earl of Fife's feet. For a long time she remained without moving, then at last she walked closer, lifting the corner of the flag to gaze for the last time on her grandson's face. If she was appalled at his wounds, she gave no sign. She bent to kiss his forehead, as cold already as the marble that would be his tomb.

At the requiem mass the following day, she stood side by side with her son, the dead earl's uncle, listening to the voices of the monks as they rose in unison towards the vaulted roof of the church. *Requiem aeternam.* How many times had she heard those words? She looked at Macduff. At thirty-two, he was a handsome, stocky man, much respected by his followers, married at last to a quiet, attractive, adoring wife and with two sons of his own. Sensing her eyes on him, he turned to her and took her arm. The Countess of Fife was not there. In the guesthouse of the abbey she lay enveloped in the agony of a premature labour brought on by the shock of her husband's death and the precipitate ride to be at his interment. And now she was near her time. Eleyne raised her eyes to the statue of the Blessed Virgin above the side altar near her and prayed silently for Joanna's deliverance. For the baby she had no fears. Like Master Elias, she knew that he would live.

*

710

She found Mairi much later with little Isobel in the monks' orchards. The child was white-faced, her small features pinched with fear and exhaustion.

'So, little one.' She took Isobel on her knee and looked at Mairi. 'Are you happy to have a little brother?'

Isobel shook her head dumbly.

'Why not?'

'He's already more important than me.' Isobel buried her face in her great-grandmother's gown. 'Even Mairi went away to be with him.'

'Is this true?' Eleyne asked the girl; Mairi nodded her head unhappily.

'They made me attend the countess, my lady. No one knew what to do.'

'I see.' Eleyne pursed her lips and turned back to the child. 'Surely you don't begrudge your mama the help she needed when she was ill?'

'She was having a new earl.' Isobel screwed up her small fists. 'And I hate him!' She glanced up to see what effect the words would have on her great-grandmother. 'I shall never, ever have a baby. Not if it hurts so much it makes you scream, like mama did.' Her voice trembled and Eleyne tightened her arms around the child. 'Having babies kills you.' Isobel went on in a whisper. 'One of mama's ladies told me. It might kill mama!' She burst into tears. 'I don't want to have a baby, ever!'

'Hush, my love.' Mairi sank to her knees and pulled the child into her lap. 'Your mama is safe and well. I told you last night. And you won't have to have babies if you don't want to.' Her eyes met Eleyne's challengingly over the child's dark curls. 'I'll show you what to do to stop them coming, then you'll never need to cry like your mama.'

Joanna looked wan and exhausted when Eleyne sat on her bed in the vaulted guesthouse and took the tiny red-faced swaddled baby in her arms.

'I've called him Duncan for his father,' Joanna said, her voice croaky and faint.

'I'm glad.'

'And I'm sending Isobel to Buchan. It's all decided, Elizabeth de Quincy will have the job of bringing her up.' Joanna lay back on the heaped pillows, her face pallid and damp with perspiration. 'No, don't argue, grandmama, please.' She had seen the shocked surprise on Eleyne's face. 'I can't cope with the child; it would be better for her to be brought up by her future husband's family.' Eleyne saw tears sliding slowly down her cheeks. 'It's what Duncan wanted, and it's best for everyone. Then I can go home. To England.' She turned her head away. Eleyne stood up. She gazed down for a moment at the small puckered face of the baby in her arms and sighed, then she handed him to one of Joanna's maids. At least she could insist that Mairi go with Isobel to Slains. Beyond that she could do no more.

VIII
LOCHMABEN CASTLE ❖ 1290

Gratney married his fifteen-year-old bride, Christian Bruce, at the end of September the following year. Christian, known as Kirsty to her adoring family, was attended by Isabella and Marjorie of Atholl, by her own two sisters, Mary and Isobel, and by Duncan's wife, Christiana Macruarie. She brought as her dower the lordship of the Garioch, a huge area of land which abutted the eastern side of the earldom of Mar.

The day after the wedding the first of the rumours reached them. Old Robert Bruce of Annandale stormed into the great hall at Lochmaben waving a letter above his head. Seventy-two now, like Eleyne, and like her as active as ever, his eyes glittered above a red-veined nose.

'So. It has happened. I knew it! I knew it! Little Queen Margaret is dead!'

There was silence as shocked eyes turned to him.

Donald stood up, looking at his son-in-law, John of Atholl. Only moments before they had been discussing the little queen's imminent arrival in Scotland. 'Where did that news come from? If it's true it's a sad day for this country. How did she die?'

Robert Bruce shrugged. 'I don't know. But if it's true . . .' His eyes gleamed with excitement, 'I am heir to the throne. That makes me Scotland's king!'

He glared around the great hall. 'Oh, I know I'll have to fight for the crown. And fight I will, make no mistake. John Balliol is not going to take the crown with his claims. It's mine! I was confirmed as his heir by King Alexander II, and I am the most senior of the descendants of David of Huntingdon, we all know that.'

'There are more claimants than John Balliol, papa,' Robert of Carrick put in mildly. In his view John Balliol, the grandson of the elder sister of John of Chester, had more claim than his father, who though one generation closer to John was the son of the younger sister. 'There are at least two others; probably more. For Scotland's sake we should pray your informant is mistaken and that Margaret is still alive. At least her succession has been confirmed by everyone and the preparations are under way for her coronation.'

Robert smiled. He winked at his grandson, who was waiting nearby, wide-eyed with excitement. 'So be it. We shall go to Scone as arranged. We shall all go.' His gesture took in the Earls of Mar and Atholl. 'And we shall take a goodly contingent of men, to show our support for the little queen. And if by any sad chance this news is true and she has died, we'll have the advantage when it comes to establishing our claim.' He laughed softly. 'We'll have a great advantage: several hundred fully armed men.'

IX

SCONE ❖ October 1290

Eleyne, tired after the long days of feasting for the wedding and the precipitate journey, was lying down in their bedchamber when Donald brought her the confirmation that the little queen was truly dead. There were no details of her illness, but it appeared that she had succumbed to some childish ailment. She, like her mother and her two uncles, had never been strong.

'So.' She sighed, putting her arm across her eyes to try to suppress the throbbing headache which assaulted her temples. 'What happens now?'

'You tell me.' Donald sat down beside her and took her hands. 'It is you who sees Scotland's future.'

Eleyne turned her head away sharply. 'I see blood and fire.'

Donald's face was lined with worry. 'I fear you may be right,' he said drily. 'I gather that the guardians of the realm are resolved to ask King Edward for his advice. They are not prepared to give the throne to either a Bruce or a Balliol or any of the other claimants, at present. They don't seem to be able to make up their minds what to do.'

Eleyne sat up. 'And so it starts. Do they really think Edward will give impartial advice? Do they think he will stand by to see a strong king set up on his northern border?' She put her head in her hands. 'Persuade them, Donald, persuade them to see how foolish they are being. They are handing Scotland to Edward on a platter.'

There were many who agreed with her, but it seemed that Bishop Fraser, one of the guardians, had already written to Edward. It proved too late to hold back his letter and by May the following year King Edward I of England had claimed overlordship over Scotland and demanded fealty from her nobility before announcing whom he had chosen as the country's next king. His decision fell on John Balliol, in his view, the view of the lawyers and of a substantial majority of Scots the senior claimant to the throne as grandson of John of Chester's eldest sister. On St Andrew's Day 1292, King John Balliol was crowned at Scone, the crown put on his head not by Duncan, Earl of Fife, who was but a baby, but by Sir John de St John in the young earl's name. It remained to be seen what kind of a king he would make.

X
KILDRUMMY CASTLE ❖ 1292

Isabella was sitting in her bower, reading. The November wind was finding its way into the lonely chamber under the roof; she could hear it whistling and screaming up the stairs. It was a dismal sound. She shrugged herself deeper into her cloak, knowing she should be downstairs helping her mother supervise the accounts. Guiltily she turned the page of her vellum-bound book and read on. Only a few more minutes, then she would blow out her candle, put the book into her book chest and creep downstairs.

The door opening behind her brought her out of her reverie a long time later. The candle was nearly gone and her legs were an agony of pins and needles. She looked up, expecting to see her mother's face.

Young Robert Bruce was standing in the doorway. He grinned at her. 'I did knock but you didn't hear.'

'Robert!' Isabella stared at her betrothed in confusion. The book slipped from her fingers and, squatting down, he picked it up and gave it back to her. 'I hope you don't mind my coming up here. Your mother told me where you were. She thought you'd not mind too much . . .' He faltered to a stop and shrugged, his eyes full of laughter.

'Of course I don't mind.' Isabella tried to hide how flustered she was. 'It's just I wasn't expecting anyone.'

'Grandfather and I came to see your father and Kirsty,' Robert said.

She loved the way his eyes narrowed when he smiled, his strong face softening momentarily. And it was a strong face; there was no longer any sign of the unformed features of the adolescent, or of the slightly gauche shyness he had displayed last time they had met. As he sat near her on the dusty floor his tunic and surcoat fell gracefully round his knees as he crossed his long legs clad in soft leather boots; he was totally composed.

'What are you reading?'

She glanced down at the book lying in her lap on the azure velvet of her gown. 'It's the story of Branwen, the daughter of Llyr.' It was her favourite.

There was an awkward silence. 'I was sorry to hear that your mama had died,' Isabella said at last.

She looked up in time to see the intense sadness in his eyes.

'I shall miss her very much,' he said. 'It's strange. It's as though I'd lost a best friend. I got on far better with her – ' He left the sentence unfinished, the words 'than with my father' unsaid, hanging in the air between them.

'And you're the Earl of Carrick now,' Isabella went on. 'Does your papa mind very much?'

Robert's father had been Earl of Carrick only in right of his wife. Now that she had died the title was no longer his. It had passed to her eldest son, leaving her husband, only heir himself to the lordship of Annandale, without a title.

'I don't think he minds much,' Robert replied, 'and he can go on using it if he wants to. I don't mind. But my father is totally without ambition.' He tried to keep the scorn out of his voice. He was fond of his father, but the two found each other mutually incomprehensible. It was with his ambitious, fiery, romantic grandfather, Robert Bruce of Annandale, that Robert identified. Completely.

He wrapped his arms around his knees and rested his chin on them, watching her. 'Aunt Eleyne said I should bring you down to join her and my sister in her solar before you freeze to death,' he said.

She smiled. 'I'll come now.' Scrambling to her feet, she put her precious book into the coffer by the wall and, turning back to him, she let out a little squeak of surprise. He had risen swiftly and silently to his feet and was standing immediately behind her.

They looked into each other's eyes, all shyness forgotten as he raised his hands to her shoulders and drew her to him. His kiss was firm and sure and she was taken by surprise by her own reaction to it. Her legs began to grow weak as she found herself sliding her arms around his neck, drawing his face down for a second lingering kiss.

It was a long time before they drew apart and she looked away, unable to meet his eyes. She was trembling all over.

'I came up here to ask you something,' Robert said softly. He reached for her hand. 'I wanted to know if you thought I was old enough yet to get married.'

She caught the irrepressible amusement in his eyes.

'I've tried so hard to grow up quickly,' he went on, teasing. He pulled her towards him again and looked down at her. Her head was level with his shoulders. 'What do you think?' His voice had dropped to a husky whisper.

Her breath was catching in her throat; her hand was shaking in his; all she wanted in the world was for him to take her once more into his arms.

She frowned, hesitating, seeming to give the matter serious thought, and was grateful to see a moment of uncertainty in his eyes. Trying very hard to hide her eagerness, she reached out her other hand and took his.

'I think you're old enough, my lord,' she said.

715

XI

KILDRUMMY CASTLE ❖ 1293

'Macduff of Fife has been arrested by King John Balliol and thrown into prison!' John Keith, still one of the most trusted administrators of the beleaguered earldom of Fife, stood in front of Eleyne, his face white with anger. 'Is there no end to the iniquities this man is prepared to authorise!'

'Macduff?' Eleyne's embroidery shears fell unnoticed from her fingers. 'Arrested?'

'Yes, my lady. He has been pursuing the restoration of his lands — the lands your late husband, his father, left him in Creich and Rires. With the earldom for so long in minority he has been deprived of what was rightfully his. And now Balliol denies him his claim and throws him into a cell for his pains!'

Eleyne's lips tightened. 'John Balliol oversteps the mark all too often. He is a weak man, playing the strong.' She stood up. 'This is not to be borne. Macduff must be released. Where is he being held?'

Keith shrugged. 'At first at Kinross. Then he was taken before the king at Stirling. My lady, you should seek help from the Bruces and their friends.'

'And stir the cauldron?' Eleyne said softly. 'Is that what you would like?'

'I, and many others. Balliol is not the king for Scotland.'

'He is the chosen king.'

'Chosen by God or by man?' Keith paused. 'What will Lord Mar do, my lady?'

Eleyne looked up, searching his face. 'That will remain to be seen, my friend, when I have told him about Macduff.'

XII

TURNBERRY CASTLE

Turnberry Castle stood on a promontory, the sea protecting it on three sides. It was an ancient stronghold, the seat of the Earls of Carrick. Standing on the high walls which surrounded the castle, Eleyne looked out to sea, stunned by the overwhelming homesickness which had hit her. This was her sea; the sea which washed the shores of Gwynedd; the sea which had echoed in her ears as a child. She could smell the cold, salt freshness above the warmth of the land, the sea spice vying with the sweetness of thyme and roses and whin, the hint of vast distances lost in the haze, a backdrop to the warmth and greenness of the land.

She stood mesmerised, oblivious of the people around her on the wall walk. Below, the sea lapped the rocks exposed by the low tide, hardly moving, licking at the drifting wood, clear as a mountain stream.

When she turned back, they had brought a chair up to the battlements for old Robert Bruce of Annandale.

She frowned. She had caught herself thinking of him as an old man; his followers obviously thought of him as an old man. No one had volunteered to bring her a chair. Yet they were of an age, she and this robust, cantankerous patriarch of the house of Bruce. She put the thought behind her briskly. 'So, what are we going to do? What about Macduff?'

The Lord of Annandale leaned back in his chair and stretched his legs in front of him with a groan. 'Calm down, lass. Let your old nephew speak! Macduff is free. Balliol has already ordered his release.'

'Are you sure? When?'

Eleyne and Donald had set off for John Balliol's court soon after hearing of Macduff's arrest. Then they had changed their minds, and ridden west instead towards the stronghold of opposition to their elected king.

'He let him go almost at once.' Robert grinned. He had lost two of his front teeth the previous year and his smile had a piratical wickedness which Donald found fascinating. Even knowing how foolish it was, he felt a shiver run up his spine at the sight of the old man smiling. There was a joyful malevolence there. Robert's next words confirmed his fears.

'Macduff is to appeal against Balliol,' he said quietly. 'If the appeal doesn't come out his way, he has threatened to go over his head to King Edward. Balliol is being shown up for his true worth. The man is an ineffectual fool who can't handle the smallest problem, never mind a kingdom.'

'And you could,' Donald said quietly.

'Of course I could, I was born to it!' Robert stood up and paced across to lean against one of the wall merlons, his whole body betraying his energy and frustration. He turned abruptly as his son ducked out of the stairwell and on to the roof leads.

The former Lord Carrick greeted Eleyne and Donald warmly. 'So, what's the old man plotting now?' he asked, putting his arm around his father's shoulders. 'Not more plans for the royal line of Bruce?'

'Yes, more plans.' Robert turned to his son with a flash of impatience. 'And as usual you're not here to discuss them. It will be your throne, boy! You're the one who will inherit it. I'm too old, Goddamn it! Balliol is a broken reed and the other claimants are so much dust in the wind!' He smacked his hands together in frustration. 'And I'm stuck with a son who would rather sit about watching the sheep eat grass than buckle on his armour and win himself a kingdom!'

He turned to Eleyne and Donald. 'I've negotiated a match for his daughter,' he gestured towards his son, 'that will bring them all up by the ears! Young Isabel, Robert and Kirsty's sister, is going to marry the King of Norway! What do you think of that?' He was bursting with pride. 'King Eric obviously sees the Bruces as a royal family and I shall have a king for a son-in-law.'

Donald raised an eyebrow. 'Edward of England won't like that!'

'No, he won't.' The old man chuckled and put his head on one side. 'My grandson, Rob, is a man now. Shall we fix a date for his wedding too? Your lass, Isabella, must have given up hoping her husband will ever be out of clouts!' He threw back his head and laughed.

Eleyne shook her head at him reprovingly. 'I think you'll find the young people have already decided they are ready,' she said fondly. 'The date is all that's missing.'

Robert Bruce the younger looked at his father and then at the Mars and cleared his throat self-consciously. 'There's something I'd like to say. Rob is the Earl of Carrick now. He's nineteen years old. As you say, he's a man. And, as you say, I'm not.' He looked at the ground and they saw the contortion of his throat muscles as he swallowed.

'No, no, I didn't say that!' his father put in testily. 'You're over-reacting, boy. I didn't mean anything – '

'Yes, you did, father, and you're right.' The younger man straightened his shoulders and looked Robert of Annandale in the eye. 'I would rather be a farmer than a soldier, and I have no stomach for fighting for a throne. It's best we all recognise the fact. Make Rob your heir, and I will stand back from any claims you make.'

There was silence for a moment. Robert the elder cleared his throat. 'That is a courageous decision, my son. But I'm not sure it's possible.'

His son shrugged. 'Why not? I've always supported you. And I'll support Rob as loyally.' He smiled. 'And I think you'll find the people of Scotland would rather follow Rob than me.'

Donald took his hand and shook it solemnly. 'That's a brave thing to say, my friend, and I for one will support Rob as his grandfather's heir.'

Eleyne reached up and kissed her great-nephew on the cheek. 'Does Rob know what you feel?'

'He will soon enough. It was something I didn't need to consult him over. That boy has the makings of a king, I don't. It's as simple as that.'

XIII

Isabella of Mar and young Robert Bruce, Earl of Carrick, were married in the Great Chapel at Kildrummy eight weeks before Christmas. He was nineteen, his bride was twenty-three. She wore a gown of cloth of silver with a mantle of blue, trimmed with white fox fur. Robert, in scarlet and green, was taller than any of the bride's brothers. He had grown into a man fit indeed, in Isabella's eyes, to be her prince. She looked up at him as they knelt side by side at the altar during the nuptial mass. Sensing her look, he smiled and held out his hand.

Isabella hesitated. For a moment she was too overwhelmed to move, then slowly she held out her own to meet his.

Behind them Eleyne saw the gesture and her eyes filled with tears. Donald put his arm around her shoulders and brought his mouth to her ear. 'They will be happy,' he said. 'They will be very happy.'

CHAPTER THIRTY-ONE

I

February 1296

S andy found his mother in the chapel. He stood in the doorway watching her as – unaware that he was there – she knelt at the prayer desk facing the altar. Her eyes were open and her hands gripped the front of the desk so that they were white at the knuckles. He could not see her face, which was just as well: its expression was of deepest desolation.

'Mama.'

She didn't hear him.

'Mama!' He raised his voice slightly.

She started and tensed her shoulders, then she turned her face to him. She was pale and her eyes were red-rimmed.

'Sandy. I didn't hear you.' At seventy-eight her voice was as strong and clear as ever. 'Has your father ridden back with you?'

Sandy nodded, and helped her to her feet. 'We were present at the ratification of the treaty. Scotland and France are now allies against Edward of England.' He stood looking at her sadly, as though trying to read her face. 'We have as good as declared war on England, mama. And Edward has already ordered his host to assemble at Newcastle. I'm afraid we are going to have to fight.'

Eleyne groped for his hand. 'You and your brothers?' Her mouth had gone dry.

'And papa. He must lead the men of Mar. All the lords of Scotland will be mustering their armies.'

'But he's too old to fight!' Eleyne was horrified. 'Your father can't possibly go!'

'He's scarcely older than King Edward, mama,' Sandy said ruefully, 'and he is as fit as I am. He wouldn't want to be left behind, you know that as well as I do.'

He took her hands in his and squeezed them, horrified at how ice-cold they were. 'We've brought someone else home with us.' He tried to cheer her up. 'Rob and Isabella were at Scone. He wants her to be here with you over the next months until the baby is born.

720

Lochmaben and Turnberry wouldn't be safe if there's an invasion, so she has come home with us.'

Eleyne's face lit up. 'So, he's seen sense! He's joining the loyal Scots –'

'No!' Sandy shook his head. 'It seems my brother-in-law would rather fight for the English than support Balliol.' He did not try to hide his disgust. 'He swears he is biding his time, but I think it's pretty odd. In fact it's damn near treason, to my mind!' Sandy, who so seldom raised his voice, was trembling with anger.

Eleyne felt a terrible lump in her throat: her second son was normally so quiet, so pacific. She closed her eyes, seeing him armed, sword in hand, his eyes narrowed, his jaws tensed, every muscle straining –

'Mama? Are you all right?' His hand under her elbow was gentle. There was no sword. There never had been a sword except in training. All those long hours at the quintain, or with his instructors or fighting mock duels with his brothers. He was no soldier. No more was his father. Eleyne's eyes went automatically to the floor of the chapel. Alexander, her Alexander, had been a soldier, but not Donald. Not her poet husband. She doubted if he had ever raised a weapon in anger in his life.

'Come and see Isabella, mama.' Sandy put his arm around her thin shoulders.

For a moment she didn't respond. Then she nodded. In the shadows, below the triple lancet windows, just for a moment, she had thought she saw the figure of a man. Then it was gone.

II

Isabella was five months pregnant and radiant. She sat down next to Sandy at the high table and they shared a plate. At the far end sat Duncan, newly arrived from the west where he had left Christiana with their baby son, Ruairi. Next to him sat Kirsty, then Gratney, then her mother and father, sitting close together, both slightly strained. Every now and again, she noticed, her mother's hand strayed to touch Donald's. The atmosphere at the table was very subdued.

'She's never had to send him off to war before,' Sandy said quietly, following the direction of Isabella's gaze. 'In all the years they've been married, papa has never been called to arms.'

Isabella smiled sadly. 'They seem to be as much in love as ever. Yet mother is nearly eighty!'

'It's her magic powers!' Sandy was only half joking. He gave a deep sigh. 'And you and I will both be dead long before her –' He spoke without thinking, and stopped, appalled, as he saw his sister's face. She had gone as white as a sheet, her hand flying automatically to her

721

stomach where the outline of her child was scarcely visible yet.

'I don't mean literally,' he said quickly, 'I meant it's as though she's immortal. There's something special about her, something that keeps her young.' He paused. What he had said, trying hastily, desperately, to cover up his terrible blunder, was in a sense true.

He reached for some coffined lamprey made just the way he liked it, with the finest white bread and wine and served with a ginger and wine syrup, and taking a piece of the pastry on the tip of his knife he held it to Isabella's lips, trying to distract her.

'You're sure you haven't seen my death?' she whispered. To his horror he saw that her hand was shaking.

'No, no. Oh, Bella! I never meant that! Blessed Lady, I never meant you to think that.' Sandy dropped the knife and leaned across to put his hand gently on his sister's stomach. Then he laughed, genuinely amused. 'The little Bruce is kicking!' he said in delight.

She smiled. 'Indeed he is.'

It was special, this child of Isabella's. Sandy didn't need the stars to tell him that; nor did he need them to tell him that he would never see it.

III

The war progressed too fast; the Scots were overconfident. Their first attacks across the border were not pressed home, and Edward was able to concentrate his forces at Berwick and take the town so quickly the townspeople barely had time to fight. The castle garrison surrendered and the citizens were slaughtered. Appalled, the Scots army hurried eastwards towards Dunbar and there on the twenty-seventh of April they met the English under Earl Warenne and were totally defeated. Amongst those captured were Donald of Mar and his son, Alexander.

IV

KILDRUMMY CASTLE ❖ May 1296

'Well, what is your news?' Eleyne looked down at the panting, gasping man who knelt at her feet. Her face was white.

'The battle was lost, my lady.' The man took a gulp of air. 'Lost. All lost. The English king walked all over our host.'

'Donald?' Her mouth had gone dry, and the word came out as less than a whisper. She was clenching her fists tightly.

The man had not heard. He was still kneeling before her, his head bent, and there were tears coursing down his grimy, weathered face.

Eleyne felt a moment of compassion as he knelt there. 'My husband,' she repeated desperately. 'Where is Lord Mar?'

'Captured, my lady. And Sir Alexander with him.' The man knuckled his eyes fiercely and took a deep breath. 'And most of the lords of Scotland.'

'Captured,' she echoed, numb with shock. 'By Edward? What is to happen to them? Where are they? Where is Lord Gratney?'

He shrugged. 'All was confusion at Dunbar. The English king is in complete control, and opposition to him has collapsed. Many of the prisoners are being sent south to England. I think it likely that Lord Mar is amongst them. The king is sending south all the leaders of what he called the rebellion.'

'And our king?' Eleyne's voice was heavy. 'What of our King John? Was he captured too?' She was fighting off the despair which threatened to overwhelm her.

'He was not taken. I don't know where he is.'

'You don't know?' Eleyne cried. 'What kind of king is this who allows his kingdom to fall about his ears and his people don't know where he is?' She took a deep breath. 'I must go to Donald, I must find him. Is King Edward still at Dunbar? I must leave at once – today.' She turned and almost ran to the door. As she reached it Gratney appeared. He had been but minutes behind his father's messenger when he drew his mud-stained slavering horse to a halt in the courtyard.

'It's all right, mama, papa is unhurt. He is safe and with Sandy in honourable custody. Would you expect any less of King Edward?'

Eleyne stared at her eldest son. 'You weren't fighting for Edward!' Her voice was husky with shock.

Gratney shook his head. 'Of course not. I am loyal to Scotland, mama. But like the Bruces it does not suit me to fight for Balliol. I'm not prepared to answer his summons as meekly as father is. But I would not fight my own people, either. Never!' He gave her a sheepish grin. 'So I was a bit late for the battle. I fought on neither side. I knew papa and the twins would provide enough Mar blood between them. No, no!' He raised his hand as she went white. 'None of them has shed any of it. I heard Duncan is safe, though I haven't seen him. I'm fairly sure he escaped.'

He frowned. 'I'm not a coward, mama, I'll fight when the time comes. But this was not the time. Please don't think badly of me, I did what I thought was right. Listen, I shall ride south again at once to negotiate their release. I admire Edward and he trusts me. He will let them go. He does not mean to harm Scotland. He does what's best for our land.'

'Is it best to invade us and fight a war?'

'No. He invaded because of Balliol's alliance with the French. In his eyes that was treachery.' Gratney stepped forward and put his arm around her shoulders. 'It will all turn out all right, mama.' He smiled reassuringly. 'Will you look after Kirsty for me if I leave her here while I ride south?'

She was troubled. 'You think you can free your father and Sandy?'

'I'm sure I can.'

She walked away from the door at last, to stand in front of the smouldering fire. 'I couldn't live if anything happened to Donald, Gratney. He has been my whole life for so many years.' Tiny blue flames licked across the logs; the deep red heart of the burning wood glowed and pulsed before her eyes. 'I always assumed I would die first. It's just not possible that anything could happen to him. We've had so many years of peace in Scotland. I can't believe it has come to war. And yet it had to happen. When Alexander died . . . it had to happen.'

Gratney regarded her fondly. Upright, strong, indomitable, his mother looked twenty years younger than her age. He had never heard her say anything before which came so close to despair and defeat.

'I shall bring him home, mama, I promise.' He put his hands on her shoulders, turning her to face him. 'I know you can't live without him.' He took her hands in his. 'The love affair that rocked Scotland. I know the story. And it will have a happy ending, I promise.'

V

KILDRUMMY ❖ July 1296

'There is nothing you can do.' Kirsty's arms were around Eleyne and she hugged her. Beside her stood her sister, Mary, also a refugee from the south, come to be with Isabella at the birth. 'You said yourself that you dislike Edward and he dislikes you. I find it hard to believe, but if it's true you are the last person to plead for your husband's release. Leave it to Gratney. He gets on well with Edward. Besides, Isabella needs you here.'

In the upper bedchamber of the Snow Tower Isabella was asleep, worn out by the heat and the bulk of the child not yet born.

'I hope Robert arrives soon,' his younger sister, Mary, whispered to Kirsty. 'He'll be distraught if anything awful happens.'

'Nothing awful is going to happen!' Kirsty snapped. Their nerves were on edge. The huge castle, populated mainly by women, seemed claustrophobic, an island beneath the beating sun as the afternoon wore on. It was several days since the messengers had ridden south to find the young Earl of Carrick and tell him his wife's labour had started. Since then the pains had stopped and started several times. Isabella was no nearer giving birth, but she was growing weaker. Timidly Kirsty touched Eleyne's arm. 'You said she would have a son,' she said quietly. 'You're sure?'

'She will have a son,' Eleyne repeated. 'The heir to Scotland. The destiny Einion foresaw. At last.'

Kirsty glanced at Mary and grimaced fondly. She had grown used to her mother-in-law's incomprehensible asides and ignored them. In Eleyne's more straightforward predictions she had the utmost confidence. 'Poor Isabella.' She looked towards the white disc of the sun. 'I hope the child is born soon.'

It was three days before Isabella's labour pains began again in earnest and still Robert had not appeared.

Sitting with her daughter, holding her hand in the stifling bedchamber, Eleyne looked up as one of Isabella's ladies came in. 'Is there no sign of him?' She winced as Isabella's hand tightened over hers.

'None, my lady.' The woman wrung out a fresh cloth in the cold-water pitcher and gently wiped Isabella's face.

'Mama!' Isabella threw her head from side to side on the hot pillow. 'Where is he?'

'He'll come soon, my darling.' Eleyne took the cloth from the woman's hands and gestured her away. 'Don't worry. Just concentrate on saving your strength.'

'You know he's in love with someone else.' Isabella closed her eyes and gritted her teeth as another wave of pain took her.

Eleyne stared at her in shocked disbelief. For a moment the air in the room seemed to shimmer over the bed, then all was normal again. 'I'm sure that's not true,' she said gently.

'It is. Perhaps he's with her. She's young and beautiful. I heard one of the grooms talking. He would have married her if he could; if he hadn't been betrothed to me for so long.'

'I don't believe it!' Eleyne sponged her daughter's face again. 'Robert worships you. You have only to see the way he looks at you.'

'He looks at me with guilt.' Isabella could feel the tears coming as the pain built once more.

'No, no, I won't believe it.' Eleyne laid her hand on the linen sheet which covered the contorted muscles of her daughter's belly. She felt every pain as if it were in her own body. 'He loves you, and if it's humanly possible he will come.'

'Can't you see? Can't you see in the fire?' Isabella's voice rose unsteadily. 'Look, mama. Please. See where he is.'

Nearby the two midwives, sitting side by side telling their beads, looked at each other and one crossed herself.

In the hearth the fire burned in spite of the heat of the day. One of the maids sprinkled dried rose petals and coriander on it every so often, using a small wooden scoop, and the room was full of aromatic, spicy scent. Reluctantly Eleyne walked across to it, feeling the heat on her face. Beneath her veil, the perspiration started out on the back of her neck. On the bed Isabella groaned again.

Eleyne pursed her lips and stared into the depth of the flames, feeling the heat against her eyes, willing the picture to come – the picture that would tell her beyond all doubt that Isabella would be safe and that the child would be a son, but there was nothing there. Nothing but the red heart of the burning wood. And then she saw it: a shadow in the heat, no more. She leaned forward – a standard. Surely it was a standard. A flag flying in the wind, a flag of red and gold – the standard of the king.

'My lady –'

Only the hand on her elbow had saved her from toppling into the fire. Shaken, she saw the maid standing beside her, holding her arm, watching her with frightened eyes. 'I thought you were going to fall, my lady.' The woman dropped her hand apologetically.

'Thank you.' Eleyne collected herself with difficulty. 'I was dizzy for a moment with the heat. How is she?' She turned back to the high bed.

'She's coming on nicely.' One of the midwives smiled. 'I reckon it will be here with the dawn.'

It was Robert who arrived with the dawn, throwing himself, exhausted, from his horse, taking the stairs to the bedchamber two at a time. He was allowed only a moment to touch his wife's hand and kiss her forehead before he was ushered from the room. Childbirth was women's work. There was no room here for a man, save perhaps a priest. The midwives scanned Isabella with practised eyes. She was strong, but tired already and old for a first child. The baby was positioned wrong; it should have been here long since. Shaking their heads, they bent over the bed again.

The sight of her husband and the touch of his hand had done more for Isabella than all the charms and potions with which the two women had been plying her for the last two days. She reached for Eleyne's hand. 'He came.'

Eleyne nodded. 'He came.'

The child was born four hours later. It was a girl.

'No.' Eleyne shook her head as the small scrap of humanity was held out to her, wrapped in a bloodstained sheet. 'No. It is not possible. He was to be a boy.'

'Well, if he's a boy, he's got some precious baubles missing, my lady.' One of the midwives took the baby, chuckling, and began to wash and wrap her. 'This bairn will be no prince.' Everyone in the castle knew of Eleyne's prediction.

'No.' Eleyne shook her head disbelievingly. She walked towards the bed and took Isabella's hand, but her daughter had drifted already into an exhausted sleep.

'You must tell Lord Carrick, my lady.' The woman smiled spitefully. 'He too expected a son.'

VI

Robert was asleep, his head on the table beside an overturned goblet. For a moment she stood looking down at him, not wanting to wake him, aware of the whispers in the body of the hall, full of compassion for the young man's disappointment.

As if sensing her standing over him, he raised his head and with the instincts of a soldier was instantly awake. She took a deep breath.

'You have a daughter.'

If there was dismay in his face, it was veiled as soon as it appeared. 'Isabella? Is she all right?'

Eleyne nodded with a rush of warmth for her son-in-law. He cared for Isabella. Of course he cared. Isabella was wrong. 'She'll be all right; she's exhausted now. Go up and see her later.' They both understood there was no need to rush upstairs to view the baby – a daughter could wait.

'I'm sorry.' She lowered her head, defeated. 'I got it wrong. I was so sure this child was to be the progenitor of kings.'

Robert grinned. 'I'm the one who intends to be the progenitor of kings.' He lurched wearily to his feet. 'Don't blame yourself. I'm content to wait for destiny. There will be other children.'

'I hope so,' she said sadly.

He frowned. 'There's something wrong –'

'No! No.' The wave of terrible unhappiness had gone as soon as it had come. 'No, I'm very tired, that's all. Forgive me, Robert, if I go and rest. I'm too old to stay up all night.' She smiled at him. 'Isabella is all right. And so is the baby. What shall you call her?'

'Marjorie. After my mother.'

'God bless you, my dear.' She put her hand up to his cheek for a moment, then turned to climb wearily to her bedchamber.

VII

The next evening Robert and Eleyne dined alone at the high table. Father Gillespie had been called away, the officers of the household were visiting the manors of the Garioch, Eleyne's ladies were down the far end of the table and Mary and Kirsty were both with Isabella. For the first time it was possible to talk in private.

'Do you have news of what is happening in the south?' She had been wanting all day to talk of the war and Donald.

Robert nodded as he raised his wine to his lips. 'Gratney is with King Edward and has put in a plea for Donald's release. All the high-ranking captives are being sent south. To Chester or to the Tower.' He saw her flinch at the words. 'Don't be afraid, he'll be all right. They're being treated well. My concern is what Edward means to do with Scotland now that our noble King John has abdicated like a craven fool.' His voice was full of contempt for the man who after his defeat had been captured and forced to surrender his crown.

'You, like me, suspect the worst of our interfering neighbour.' Eleyne leaned forward, her elbows on the table. 'When are you going to act, Robert? The country is waiting for your lead.'

The year before, on Maundy Thursday, 31 March, her old friend and nephew Robert Bruce of Annandale had died, defiant and cantankerous to the last. His loss had been a terrible blow to Eleyne, as it had to all the supporters of the Bruces.

Robert demurred. 'What can I do? My father has no stomach for battle, and he is still the heir to our claims to the throne, not I. However much grandfather wanted it, he couldn't replace papa in the succession, and I'm afraid I'll have to play a waiting game. I will not support John Balliol or the Comyns while I wait, which means in a world that is black and white that I must be seen to support Edward. For now.' He grinned at her. 'You and I know better.'

'Be careful.' She smiled, responding as always to the young man's charm. 'You're playing a dangerous game.'

'I know.' He reached for the wine and refilled her goblet. 'My grandfather would have loved this, and I am like him. I play for high stakes, but I play to win. It may take time, but I intend to take the prize.'

'I believe you.' She hesitated, then she turned to face him again. 'Tell me, Robert, while we confide in each other over our cups. Are you unfaithful to my daughter?' Having sprung the question, she studied his profile, aware of the sudden tenseness.

There was a silence which lasted just too long. 'I love my wife. And I am faithful to her as is my duty as a husband and a knight.'

'And if you were not a husband and a knight? What then?'

'Then nothing. The other lady is also married.'

'I see.' Eleyne poked idly at the food on the manchet of bread before her with her small bone-handled knife. She swallowed her anger and disappointment in him. 'Thank you for being open with me. Have you lost your heart to this other lady?'

'No.' He put down his goblet, shaking his head. 'No, I know it's madness. She is trouble. Trouble for everyone near her. It's when I'm near her . . .' The sentence remained unfinished.

'And she reciprocates your feelings, does she? This troublesome lady?' Eleyne persisted sternly.

He nodded.

'But you would never betray Isabella.' It was a command rather than a question.

He shook his head. 'I love Isabella. I would never do anything to hurt her, never.' Suddenly he frowned. 'It wasn't Isabella who told you this?'

'However much you think you've kept your feelings hidden, your servants have noticed. Did you expect them to keep your secret?' Her voice was harsh.

Robert closed his eyes wearily. 'I suppose I did expect them to keep it a secret as there was nothing to tell.' He sounded disillusioned. 'I'm sorry. I would not have had that happen for the world. The last thing I wanted was to upset Isabella. You must believe me. Did she tell you who the lady is?'

'No, I don't know who she is, and I don't want to. And I don't think Isabella knows,' Eleyne said more gently. 'If she suspects she did not tell me.'

He looked relieved. 'I shall make it up to her . . . and I shall see that the lady and I are not alone together again.'

Eleyne raised an austere eyebrow. 'Please do,' she said.

VIII

He left Kildrummy a week later. Neither she nor Robert had referred to their conversation again, but Eleyne detected from his demonstrative affection for his wife that she had pricked his conscience. She kissed him farewell fondly; and watched as he kissed Isabella, then little Marjorie, who was already showing signs of having inherited her paternal grandmother's flaming hair and her temper.

Kirsty watched her brother leave, then turned to her mother-in-law and took her hands.

'What is it, mama? What's wrong?'

'Why should anything be wrong, child?'

'I don't know, I just feel it.' Kirsty shrugged. 'Something to do with Robert.'

Eleyne looked dejected. 'I let him down. I told him he would have a son. All my predictions – everything – pointed to this child being the ancestor of kings . . .' Her voice died away. 'My powers have never been strong. Now I believe they have left me altogether.' She tightened her mouth angrily. 'I see nothing, Kirsty. I cannot see your father or

Sandy, however hard I try. I can see nothing for Scotland but blood.' She shuddered. 'I'm too old. I've lived too long.'

'That's not true, mama.' Gently Kirsty took her hand. 'I want you to do something for me. I want you to ride with me to the Garioch. I have a plan, which I want to discuss with you.'

'I should stay with Isabella –'

'There's no need. She'll spare you for a couple of days.' Kirsty looked at her shrewdly. 'You need a ride as much as I do. It's stifling here, and we are all brooding too much. A canter on the hills and a ride around Bennachie and up to Drumdurno will do us both good.'

IX

The horses stood panting, their heads hanging low as the two women gazed around. The low hills stretched into the distance behind them, a wilderness of heath and moor and bog, with small areas of woodland and scattered birch. In front the great fang of Bennachie rose up against a sky as clear and blue as amethyst. Kirsty had reined in at an ancient circle of stones near the track. Sliding from her horse, she came to Eleyne's side as the groom helped her down and she led her into the centre of the stone ring.

'This is a very special place,' she said quietly, glancing up. The sky was empty.

'It belongs to the old gods.' Eleyne smiled. The air was strangely still; there were no birds; no sound broke the intense silence. Even the grooms, waiting a few hundred yards away, made no sound in the heat of the afternoon. 'Why have you brought me here?'

'I wanted you to approve. I've decided to build a chapel here, dedicated to Our Lady. I have so many prayers; so many petitions . . .' She stopped, half embarrassed. 'I vowed a chapel to her if she would hear me and one day, when I am old, I shall be buried here.' She walked to one of the great recumbent stones and touched it reverently. 'Do you think I've done right?'

Eleyne didn't answer. She was staring into the distance. The air was full of the scent of grass and flowers, the resinous odour of pine and juniper, the clear cold overtones from the mountain a hint only beneath the heat. Around Kirsty the heat reflecting from the stone on which she had laid her hand made the air quiver. She looked insubstantial, almost ghostly, a wraith from the past; a ghost from the future. Eleyne shivered, then she nodded. 'Yes,' she said quietly, 'I approve.'

The weather grew even hotter; the haze on the hills as they turned for home was heavy with brooding thunderheads. The horses were lethargic and they were walking slowly when the party was met by

730

James Leslie, one of Gratney's squires, galloping as fast as he could, his horse lathered, gobbets of foam flying from the animal's bit.

'My lady, thank God!' The man reined to a rearing halt. 'The king is on his way to Kildrummy! Lord Gratney has arrived there, and he sent me to fetch you.' He wiped the sweat from his eyes with his forearm.

'I thought the king had been taken prisoner.'

'Not King John, my lady.' The man was almost gibbering with anxiety. 'King Edward of England.'

'Edward?' An icy shiver tiptoed up Eleyne's spine, for all the heat of the day.

James nodded, still gulping for breath. 'He's making a progress around Scotland, visiting the greatest castles, taking oaths of fealty from everyone.'

Eleyne stiffened. 'Taking oaths for Scottish lands?'

James nodded. 'Last night he was at Elgin. He's coming by way of Inverharroch and will go to the monks at Cabrach. My lady, he expects you at Kildrummy to greet him.'

Eleyne scowled. 'Where is Lord Mar? Is he with the king?'

'He has been sent south, with the other prisoners, my lady.'

Her eyes narrowed. 'Then there are things I wish to say to my cousin of England.' She kicked her horse on. 'And as soon as possible. If he chooses to wait on me at Kildrummy, so much the better.'

She rode the last few miles in grim silence, only half aware of the apprehension of the men and women who rode with her.

At Kildrummy there was as yet no sign of the King of England or his outriders. Eleyne handed her horse to a groom and made her way towards her bedchamber. There would be time for a cool wash in scented water, fresh clothes and an interview with her eldest son before she had to nerve herself to meet Edward.

X

12 August 1296

It was twilight before he arrived and already clear that he intended to spend at least one night at Kildrummy, with the attendant colossal expense to the Mars of feeding hundreds of extra men and horses. Calmly Eleyne and Kirsty gave orders for the preparations to be made, and they were in the great hall, seated on the dais, when Edward at last appeared. Eleyne rose, giving only the slightest curtsey in greeting, the stiffness of old age exaggerated as she moved.

Edward, at fifty-seven, was a tall, energetic, wiry man with sharp all-seeing eyes and a grim set to his mouth. Wearing full armour

731

beneath his embroidered surcoat, with a golden circlet on his head, he radiated power as he walked towards the dais. 'Lady Mar,' he acknowledged with brisk formality, 'I have come to demand your allegiance and the keys of Kildrummy.'

'Indeed.' Eleyne met her cousin's eye haughtily. 'The keys are my husband's to give or withhold as he sees fit.'

'Your husband has taken the oath of fealty, madam.' Edward's eyes had hardened. 'An oath which every man and woman and child in Scotland will take before I have finished.'

'If he has taken the oath, why has he not come home?' Eleyne asked with deceptive mildness.

'Because I am not yet entirely convinced of his wholehearted loyalty. Because every man who stood against me at Dunbar will have to convince me of his loyalty before I release him.'

Eleyne turned and walked deliberately away from him. She stopped, her back still turned. 'I shall take no oath until my husband is returned to me,' she said. 'I have promised to obey him and he has given me no orders to swear allegiance to an enemy of this country.'

'An enemy, madam?' Edward's voice was icy. 'I am overlord of all Scotland, a country at present without a king and without any government save mine. I have removed to England all the emblems of government: the Scottish regalia – all that wasn't hidden – the crown jewels, the plate, the relics, the Black Rood of St Margaret and –' he paused and glared around the hall triumphantly – 'after I burned the palace and the abbey of Scone I took your precious Stone of Destiny.' He acknowledged the gasp of horror with a half-smile. 'It's on its way to the abbey at Westminster at this very moment and there it will stay – forever. I am the government of this country now and my son will be the next monarch crowned on your coronation stone. Face me, madam, when I am addressing you!' His voice was a whiplash.

Eleyne turned, hiding her horror as best she could, not wanting to give him the satisfaction of seeing how shaken she was by his sacrilege. Giving him a long disdainful look, she was aware that the great hall was crowded with the men and women of the household and beyond them, in grim, serried ranks, Edward's men-at-arms. The eyes of all were on her as she spoke.

'You will not destroy Scotland's independence by stealing the things she holds most sacred,' she said confidently. Her face was drawn and tight with anger. 'Nor will you win the allegiance of her people that way. As for me, I owe you no allegiance, Edward of England. Your father declared me dead! He took my land, my inheritance, my name, even my children! I owe you nothing!'

'Of course.' Edward smiled. 'You are not just a rebellious Scot! How could I have forgotten the escapades of your youth? And how could I

732

have forgotten how thickly the blood of Welsh rebels runs in your veins? Perhaps I should arrest you, madam, and send you to join your nephew Owain in Bristol Castle, or to the Tower with the pathetic Scots king who seems to have your enthusiastic allegiance. If I had considered allowing your husband to return north, now I know I am right to keep him in London, safely away from his rebellious wife. You have one last chance.' He shot his head forward and glared at her coldly. 'You take the oath or you spend the rest of your days in my dungeons at the Tower with him.' He folded his arms. 'Let us waste no more time. Decide.' He held her eyes steadily.

It was Eleyne who looked away. The threat of Edward's dungeon was too real and too terrible to contemplate. And what use would she be to Donald or the children or to Scotland if she were a prisoner? Cursing her own weakness, she forced herself to kneel on the hard dais before him and put her hands between his. She repeated the oath through clenched teeth and saw the triumph in his eyes at the humiliation of her public defeat. She could barely hold back her tears.

She went to the chapel. Kneeling in the near darkness, she looked at the statue of Our Lady. She was tired, so tired. Her back straight, her hands gripping the edge of the prayer desk, she tried to pray. The image of the Virgin was indistinct, blurred by her tears, the flame of the candle at her feet shimmering, beckoning, a tiny speck of fire in the cool darkness of the great chapel.

She wasn't aware of standing up or of moving towards the altar. The only sound was of the light shushing of her skirts on the paving slabs as she was drawn towards it. The heavy carpet was shadowy in the candlelight, the embroidered Virgin and Child unmoving, their eyes fixed emptily on infinite distances. She stooped, her hand going involuntarily to the heavy fabric as she began to pull it aside. It was as though someone else was directing her actions; someone else guiding her hand. She was not thinking as her stiff, gnarled fingers touched the tiles. She did not realise that she was pulling at them, scrabbling with her nails, working one of them back and forth until the ill-mixed mortar crumbled and cracked and the tile came free of the floor, loosening its neighbours. She was not aware that she had lifted the loose board, groped beneath it, taken out the dusty box, and tucked it into the bosom of her gown. Replacing the board and tiles she allowed the heavy carpet to fall back into place. Even when she knelt again at the faldstool, she was unaware of what she had done.

For the two days King Edward spent at Kildrummy, Eleyne kept to her solar, and he did not insist that she appear again. Access to one of the richest and best-stocked castles in the north of Scotland was sufficient for Edward; he saw to the replenishing of his packhorses and the feeding of his men at Mar's expense. Only when he was satisfied that all were rested and replete did he give the order to move on. Before he left, he commanded Eleyne to attend him once more in the great hall.

She kept him waiting long enough to put on her best gown and call for a jewelled chaplet for her hair. When she walked at last into the hall, tall and stately, attended by four of her ladies, it was as a princess of the royal blood, and it was as a princess that she curtseyed gracefully before him, her aches and pains forgotten.

He acknowledged her arrival with a curt nod.

'I am about to take my leave, Lady Mar. A word before I go.' She heard the silence echoing in the rafters of the hall as every man, woman and child held their breath. 'Kildrummy will be held for me by your son, Lord Gratney. I shall direct my master builder to strengthen your defences. Scotland's castles, like those in Wales, will provide me with the bases I need to keep the country obedient. And its people.' He paused. 'Don't, ever, defy me again, madam. If you do, you will pay dearly for it. Do I make myself understood?'

She forced herself to smile. 'Indeed you do, cousin.' The mockery in the ultimate word brought a spot of colour to his cheeks but without another word he turned and strode towards the great double doors to the courtyard. No one else moved until at a sharp command from one of Edward's knights the men-at-arms stood to attention, rapping their lances on the stone floor and, turning, marched out.

Eleyne felt herself sway slightly, then a hand was on her arm and another and another. Kirsty and Mary and her ladies surrounded her. The household was closing ranks once more. In a few minutes the king and his men would be clear of the gatehouse and on the long road south.

Eleyne straightened. Somehow she found the strength to stand upright and smile. 'Thank you all,' she said in ringing tones which carried to the farthest corners of the hall. 'Let us try to forget this interlude. Let us all return to our duties, securing Kildrummy, strengthened or not, for Earl Donald and holding it safe for his return. And let us all remember,' she looked proudly around her, 'that whatever oaths your earl and countess may have been forced to take by our self-appointed overlord, we are all by birth or by marriage,' she paused with a smile, 'Scots!'

XI

Her bedchamber was cooler now it was fully dark. Wearing only a light linen bed gown, her hair brushed loose down her back, Eleyne sent her ladies away at last. She walked into the garderobe. On a rail there hung her winter furs together with some of Donald's; his fur-trimmed mantles, his heaviest woollen gowns. Unhooking one, she gathered it into her arms and buried her face in its folds, smelling faintly the scent of her husband.

She crossed to the window and sat stiffly on the cushioned window seat in the cool depth of the embrasure. Far away to the south, was Donald too staring out of a window thinking wistfully of his home? The tears began to trickle down her cheeks, unchecked in the darkness. It was the first time she had broken down since his capture, the first time she had acknowledged even to herself how desperately she missed him, and how hard it was for her to carry on alone.

For a moment she didn't notice the gentle touch on her cheek – featherlight, hesitant, no more than a whisper against her skin. Still hugging Donald's robe, she turned her head towards the window. Not a breath of wind stirred the trees in the back den below the castle wall or opposite the ravine, above the quarry. The pale sky was sewn with a myriad stars and even as she watched a shooting star, trailing its tail of luminous green, hurled itself across the heavens in the throes of its fiery death. The second touch was firmer, brushing aside the tears which trickled down on either side of her nose, tracing the network of fine lines wrought by the weather and time on her face.

She felt the stomach-churning beginning of terror, and her arms tightened around Donald's gown.

'No,' she whispered. 'You can't come for me now. I'm not ready, not yet.' Her back was pressed against the stone wall behind the seat, she levered herself to her feet, her eyes wide, peering into the blackness of the room as she clutched Donald's mantle to her chest.

Still wrapped in its dusty lambswool, the phoenix lay in its box in a coffer near the bed. She had no memory of having put it there.

She backed away from the window, her eyes straining in the darkness. 'Go away. Please,' she breathed. 'Go away.'

She was working her way steadily towards the table where the candelabra stood. Nearby a small rush lamp burned, its light so weak it illuminated no more than a tiny circle on the table around it. Her heart was beating loudly in her ears as inch by inch she edged across the room.

Still clutching Donald's mantle like a talisman with her left hand, she stretched out her right towards the table and felt her fingers brush another hand. Somehow she bit back the scream which rose in her throat. 'No, please. Go away.' She stood still, trembling. 'Please. Let me light the candles –'

She stepped forward into the darkness and came up hard against the edge of the table with a gasp. Dropping the gown, she groped blindly for the candles and felt her hand close over the rush light holder.

Her fingers were trembling so much she could not bring the feeble flame to the candle wicks. A sob escaped her as again and again the shaking flame flickered. For a moment one of the candles caught and in the flare of light she glanced behind her. The room was empty; she could see no one. Then as quickly as it flared the candle died. She was weeping openly now as she felt a hand close over her wrist. Donald's robe slid to the floor and she felt herself pulled gently away from the table. The rush light fell from her fingers and extinguished itself on the floor. She was lost in the pitch darkness.

She could feel his breath on her cheek, his hands on her wrists. She tried to pull away, but she was held fast and then his arms were around her and she could feel his lips upon hers.

There was no sound as she was drawn towards the bed. She did not struggle. She found herself obeying. If it were time for her to die and go to him, so be it. His hands were on her body now, his mouth on hers, and she pulled aside her gown herself to bare her flat withered breasts to his lips.

'Alexander.' She breathed his name out loud. 'My love.' She could not fight him; Donald was a part of the past. She felt her thighs falling open, her body for so long dry and old, moist again with longing acquiescence. The cry of joy and release she gave at last was the cry of a young woman in the arms of her lover. The woman who curled warmly into the bed beneath the covers as he drew away was young again and content as she drifted into a heavy, exhausted sleep.

XII

She awoke to find the room full of the faint light of early dawn. She lay quite still, half dreaming, a slight smile on her lips. Then she remembered, and sat up, her body heavy with guilt. A candle had been knocked unlit from the candelabra, the rush light lay on the floor, its little pottery holder smashed, and in the corner, crumpled in a pile, lay Donald's robe. She climbed out of the bed and with a shiver she walked across and picked it up.

'Alexander?' The room was empty. There was nothing to show what had happened save the warm tingling of her body. She went to the window. The countryside beyond the walls was colourless, as yet untouched by the sun. Mist curled between the battlements and wreathed the trees. She walked back to the bed and, groaning, hauled herself into it, Donald's robe in her arms. When Bethoc came to wake her, she was fast asleep.

XIII

Robert had brought gifts for his wife and daughter, and a small ivory casket, bound with silver, for Eleyne. His face was grey with fatigue and worry.

'Poor Scotland.' He sat on his wife's bed, holding Isabella's hand. 'That it should come to this, that he should take the Stone of Scone! It's an outrage no one will forgive. But at least, now he has gone, the country will have time to consolidate. We have to find a new leader to tide us over.' Unspoken was the implication that one day there would be a permanent leader, and that that leader would be him. He knew he was criticised; he knew his loyalty was being questioned as he hung back from supporting Balliol. Only a few, a very few people – his wife and mother-in-law amongst them – knew that he had to play for time.

He frowned as Isabella clutched at his hand. 'Does your leg still hurt, my love?' He had been astonished and worried to find her still in bed so many weeks after the birth.

She nodded, biting her lip. Her strength had still not returned enough for her to get up and now there was a strange pain deep in her leg. 'It doesn't matter. It's only a cramp.' She pulled herself up on the pillows. 'Don't worry about me, I want to hear about your plans. How will the next King of Scots be crowned without the coronation stone?' Her eyes were fixed adoringly on his face, her fingers wound in his. She knew that in the dreams of both of them he would be that king.

She had been as disappointed that the baby was not a boy as he was, but they had promised themselves that next time it would be all right, that next time Eleyne's prediction would come true. They talked together late into the night, making plans, dreaming of the future, choosing names for their next six children. At last he kissed her goodnight, pulled the covers over her and tucked her in before turning to go down to the great hall.

He was asleep when they came for him at dawn. The pain in her leg had moved inexorably upwards through her body to her chest. By the time he arrived, she was coughing and gasping, unable to catch her breath.

'Isabella?' Robert cried out as he saw her. 'Isabella? My darling, what is it? Where's Lady Mar? Fetch her quickly.'

Father Gillespie, sitting by the bed, kissed his cross and tucked it away in his robes. He shook his head sadly. 'She's going, my lord. I'm sorry. It's God's will.'

'What do you mean?' Robert was white with shock. 'She's not going to die? No! It can't be God's will! We had such plans.' Bending over Isabella, he took her hands in his. They were cold as ice. She lay white and drained, a wraith on the pale linen sheets, her hair spread out around her on the pillows dampened by the water with which they had been sponging her face.

'Sweetheart.' He put his lips to hers, trying to will her eyes open. 'Please, don't leave me. Isabella!' His voice rose in panic.

'It's no good, my lord.' The remaining midwife stepped forward. 'She's gone.' The other had packed her bags an hour before when it became obvious that their charge was dying. Given the duty of fetching Robert to his wife's bedside while Isabella was still capable of recognising him, she had instead fled into the dawn.

Robert would not believe it. 'She was all right. She was laughing. She was to be my queen . . .' His voice broke and he buried his face in the bedclothes, trying to coax warmth back into her body with his own.

Behind him Kirsty and Eleyne had arrived at last. They stood huddled together in disbelief, both with tears pouring down their cheeks. Eleyne was numb. Isabella could not be dead; her daughter had been so vital, so alive, so precious. The shock was so total, so complete, she could not understand what had happened. There had been no sign, no premonition, no warning. Yet again the gods were punishing her for her presumption in thinking she could foretell the future. Her daughter's son would not beget a line of kings; her fate and that of those around her were as random and as arbitrary as the throw of a dice.

She sank to her knees as her tears dried, leaving the sharp bitter taste of defeat and the overwhelming taste of disappointment. Her own, but above all Isabella's. The marriage, so long awaited, so long anticipated and at last so happy, had lasted barely three years.

It was a long time before she moved. Rising stiffly, she went to the bed. Bending, she kissed her daughter once on the forehead, then she turned away.

In the crib in the corner little Marjorie slept on, blissfully unaware that her mother was dead.

Eleyne went to the stables.

Hal Osborne, the blacksmith, was shoeing some dray-horses. Lamed by a kick from one of Eleyne's brood mares, the farrier, an Englishman who had come to Kildrummy two years before with Gratney's followers, was unable to fight and was one of the few men who had remained at Kildrummy throughout the war. He acknowledged her with a curt nod as he hauled a heavy hoof into the lap of his leather apron. She watched him for a few moments, her wolfhound Senga at her side, then she sought the sweet-smelling dim light of the stables. Her favourite mare, Starlight, was pulling greedily at a bag of hay. She acknowledged her mistress with a whicker of welcome and a shake of the head, then went back to her food. Eleyne put her arms around the horse's neck and wept.

CHAPTER THIRTY-TWO

I

TOWER OF LONDON ❖ June 1297

Donald of Mar was standing at a window in the White Tower, staring down into the cages of the king's menagerie below. He shuddered. He hated the sight of those poor thin caged beasts – the leopards, the mangy lion and the bears. They reminded him too sharply of himself. He turned wearily and went back to his seat at the table. He had grown painfully thin during his year of captivity and his body was racked with pains. The king had sent a physician to tend his cough, but the medicines seemed to have done little good. He sighed. If only he were at home. Eleyne would know how to cure the pain in his damn chest.

He bitterly resented his captivity and every precious second it kept him away from home and from his wife. He resented the fact that when she had needed him most, when his beloved, beautiful Isabella had died, he had not been there. He resented the fact that he had not had the chance to say goodbye to his favourite daughter, that he would never see her again. He resented that his new little grand-daughter was growing up without him there to see her, and he resented above all else that time was passing. Each day he and Eleyne were apart meant that less time was left to them. His frustration was enormous. He reached for the flask of wine on the table, then pushed it aside impatiently. That wasn't the way. It was too easy to find oblivion there; besides it was at the bottom of the wine goblet that his worst fears lurked: that while he was a prisoner Alexander had returned; that even now he might have claimed Eleyne for his own.

Sandy was a welcome distraction from his dark thoughts. His son too had lost weight. His handsome face was drawn and his skin had a transparency which had he but known was reflected in his own.

'How are you, papa?' During the day the Scots captives wandered freely about their floor of the White Tower. The royal apartments had now been removed to the Wakefield Tower, built by Edward's father, which left more room in the vast old keep. Only at night were they consigned to their cells and locked in.

'Not good.' Donald scowled.

740

'Then I have news to cheer you up. A letter has been smuggled in
– look.' He brandished a small piece of parchment. 'The revolt against
Edward in Scotland has spread. It's being led by Andrew Moray and
Sir William Wallace. Robert has ceased prevaricating and, claiming he
cannot fight for a Balliol, has joined us at long last. Macduff has brought
out the men of Fife!' He slapped his father on the shoulder. 'The tide
of luck is turning.' He paused, glancing quickly at his father's pale face.
'While you were ill, the Scots amongst the prisoners here have been
negotiating with Edward,' he said, dropping his voice. 'There's a way
out because he's worried and he's offering us a deal.'

Donald looked at his son, not daring to allow himself to hope.
'What sort of deal?' He turned away, trying to suppress his cough,
aware of his son frowning.

When he had recovered, Sandy went on. 'He's talking of allowing
us home if we agree to help suppress the revolt –'

'Never!' Donald interrupted.

'Wait.' Sandy put his finger to his lips. 'The Scots lords are being
asked to attempt – only attempt –' he grinned – 'to put down the
revolt. So, if we fail, too bad. He also wants us to pledge to serve in the
war against France. There's a new campaign in Flanders, it seems.' He
lowered his voice even further. 'Edward is under pressure, and he's
unsure of the future. He needs our co-operation. He needs our men.'

Donald said thoughtfully, 'It would be a way to get out of here.'

Sandy nodded.

'Soon.'

'So I hear.' Sandy reached forward and drew the mug of medication
across the table. 'You'd better drink this and get your strength back,
papa. It could be you'll need it sooner than you ever hoped.'

II

'No.' Donald was staring at the king. 'I will not return to Scotland
without my son.'

'Then you will not return to Scotland.' Edward sat in his carved
chair in the great chamber. 'I need Sir Alexander here – as insurance.'
Edward's smile was tight-lipped. 'Just to make sure you abide by the
conditions of your release.'

'I have given you my word. That is enough!' Donald glared at his
wife's cousin with open dislike.

'I'm afraid it isn't.' The king's tone was silky. 'I shall require assurance from all the lords of Scotland before I release them. Once you
have fulfilled your part of the bargain, your son will be returned to
you.'

Sandy's face paled when Donald told him, but he forced himself to smile. 'It doesn't matter, papa. What is important is that you go as soon as possible. For mama's sake as well as yours.' He hugged his father and turned away quickly, so that Donald did not see the disappointment and despair in his eyes. 'It won't be for long. We'll all be released in the end, you'll see.'

Not to smell again the cold fragrant air of the mountains; not to ride across the moors; not to hawk and hunt and laugh with his twin. He could feel himself weeping deep inside himself as he embraced his father and said his final farewells. Then he turned away. The sense of impending doom which swept over him was like a black cloud from which there would be no escape.

III

KILDRUMMY CASTLE

Eleyne waited on tenterhooks; the castle was *en fête*, a banquet planned for the earl's arrival. But there was no sign of him. She was in her solar looking out across the hills when Duncan came to find her. He and Gratney were both at Kildrummy with her.

'I think I should ride south to meet him, mama,' Duncan said. 'He could have been delayed for any number of reasons.' He shivered. For all its warmth and the band of sunshine thrown across the floor from the window, the room was cold and brooding. It was as though something lurked there, unseen. His mother must have noticed too. He saw her glance behind her as she came to kiss him. 'I'll hurry him up, never fear.' He hugged her affectionately. 'We can't have him philandering in the borders while we plan a feast for him here!'

Dismissing her attendants, Eleyne went later to sit on the grass bench in her garden. Wanting to be alone, she frowned and hesitated as she realised that someone else was already there until she saw that it was Kirsty. She sat down next to her daughter-in-law. For a long time neither of them spoke. Their silence was companionable. Around them the flowers were full of bees and butterflies and the warmth of the sunshine was soporific.

It was Kirsty who spoke first. 'Have you noticed something strange in the air?' she asked. Her tone was diffident. 'Something almost frightening, as though someone or something is watching us all.' She snapped off a piece of lavender and rubbed it nervously between her fingers. In the clear sunlight of the garden where no shadows lurked, it seemed a foolish question.

Eleyne closed her eyes. For a moment Kirsty thought she wasn't going to answer. She watched a bee bumble amongst the flowering heads of the marjoram on the bank behind them.

When her mother-in-law spoke at last, she was appalled by the pain in Eleyne's voice. 'There is someone here, and he doesn't want Donald to come back.'

'Who?' It was a scandalised whisper.

'You would never believe me if I told you.'

'Why?' Kirsty scanned Eleyne's face. The woman was incredible; in her late seventies, she was still as active as someone half her age. The hair beneath her veil was, Kirsty knew, still predominantly the rich auburn of her youth, streaked with bands of silver. Her eyes were as sharp as ever, her mind agile and acute. Only her body now betrayed a certain stiffness which Eleyne went to great pains to deny. She looked at Eleyne's face. The high cheekbones, the fair skin, so finely networked with the thousand lines of old age, were still beautiful and still proud. And suddenly Kirsty didn't want to know the answer to her question. It was too ridiculous, the sudden conviction that her mother-in-law, a woman of nearly eighty, had a lover.

His presence was everywhere – in the solar, in the bedchamber, in the stables and the stores, in the great hall and even in the chapel with its triple lancet window, where she would go sometimes to sit alone in the cool parti-coloured light. And Kirsty was not the only person to have sensed it; on more than one occasion she had seen people shiver and look over their shoulders as the brooding cloud which seemed to hang over Kildrummy deepened.

Eleyne was torn; half of her wanted to hide from him, to send him away, to exorcise him from her life so she could welcome Donald back with uncomplicated and unreserved love; the other half, the treacherous side of her, wanted to give in, to stop fighting him, to welcome to her bed a lover who saw her still as a young woman and who coaxed from her body the responses of a young woman.

'Have you heard from Robert?' It was Eleyne who changed the subject.

Kirsty shook her head sadly. 'Not lately. He's still devastated. He won't even talk about Isabella. He spends all his time with his friends, plotting and scheming. I suppose that is something: that he commits himself more and more to Scotland's cause.' She smiled the indulgent smile of an elder sister. 'He adores Marjorie, though, so he'll always come back to us, to visit her. He spoils her terribly.' Robert had left Marjorie at Kildrummy to be brought up by his sister.

There was a long silence. When she looked at Eleyne there was a defensive expression on her face. 'You never ask why Gratney and I have no children yet.'

Eleyne sighed wearily. 'I have learned to mistrust my visions of the future, but I am certain all will be well for you. There is no hurry. When God wills it, you will have a baby.'

God.

Did she no longer believe then in the gods of her native hills?

Kirsty was frowning. 'I hope so, but at the same time I'm afraid. Poor Isabella. It was so terrible for her . . .' Her voice trailed away.

Eleyne took her hand. 'Isabella didn't die in childbirth, Kirsty. Whatever unkind fate killed her, it could not have been that. There is nothing to be afraid of, child. Look at me. I have borne eleven children and survived to an irascible old age.' Apart from her two babies – Alexander's babies, taken from her by the jealous gods – all her children had lived to grow up. Was she greedy to wish for more? Her children had lived to grow up, but she had seen too many deaths, too soon. Her eldest son, Colban, and his son and grandson. And Isabella. Her eyes filled with tears as she thought again about her beautiful daughter and she turned her head away sharply so that Kirsty could not see.

IV

SLAINS CASTLE, BUCHAN

Morna regarded her daughter in horror. The girl had spoken very softly, her voice lost in the crash of the sea on the cliffs around the lonely castle on its wild shore, but what she had said was devastating.

Isobel of Fife, married now to her childhood betrothed, the Earl of Buchan, was rebellious, unhappy, untamable. The fact that there was no child of this disastrous, incompatible marriage was no accident, it seemed. 'Years ago, mama, I promised Iseabail there would be no baby.' The soft Gaelic name was a musical whisper on her lips. 'I have taught her everything I know, everything you taught me –' The girl smiled her shy, wide-eyed smile. 'My lady has vowed never to bear Lord Buchan a child. Never.' She looked behind her into the shadowy corners of the room. 'And she will stay barren or die.'

Morna closed her eyes in horror. 'Why have you never told me this before?' It was her first visit to her daughter in all the years Mairi had been with Isobel.

'Iseabail made me swear not to. She is terribly afraid.' Mairi stepped closer to her mother. 'There are other things, terrible things, things I cannot tell you.'

But Morna, when she had seen the beautiful face of the Countess of Buchan bruised from her husband's fist, had already guessed that she had heard only part of the story. She could read it in Isobel's eyes: the young Countess of Buchan had a lover. And if her husband found out, he would kill her.

744

V

KILDRUMMY CASTLE ❖ July

The parched earth sucked up the rain greedily, filling the air with its rich warm scent, and in her bedchamber Eleyne sat at the window watching it grow dark.

'Shall I light the candles, my lady?' Bethoc was moving with her slow stooped gait around the room, tidying away Eleyne's clothes. In her seventies herself now, Bethoc refused resolutely to retire, and Eleyne was glad of her companionship. So many of her old friends and servants had gone, it was good to have someone who remembered the past.

Morna was with her, seated at the table. There was no sewing, no spinning in her hands. For once she sat unmoving, her fingers idle. Morna too was growing older. In her late sixties now, her hair was snow-white beneath her veil.

'I don't want lights yet. They will bring in the moths. I'll call one of the pages when we're ready.' She smiled indulgently as the old woman shuffled out of the room and closed the door behind her. With her creaking joints, her swollen legs and her endless quiet grumbling, Bethoc was the only person at Kildrummy who made Eleyne feel she was still comparatively young.

'I'm sorry to bring you such news, but you had to know.' Morna had waited until Bethoc had gone, then as Eleyne sat opposite her friend at the table she had begun to talk. She shook her head sadly as Eleyne sharply drew in her breath. 'Lady Isobel has no one to turn to but Mairi and now you.'

Eleyne, sitting with her elbows on the table, put her face in her hands. 'Blessed Lady! How could I not have known how unhappy she was? I must ride and see her.'

'She will be with the earl at Stirling by now. They were leaving as I set off home. But I haven't told you everything yet. There were things Mairi would not tell even me, so I'm guessing.' Morna hesitated. 'I think Lady Buchan has a lover.'

Eleyne looked up quickly. 'And does her husband suspect this too?'

Morna shrugged. 'Mairi is too loyal to her mistress to discuss such things, even with me. She is protective, like a mother hen.' She smiled indulgently. 'You made a good decision when you sent her to take care of your great-grand-daughter.'

Eleyne nodded. 'I love the child. And for her father's sake and her grandfather's I wanted to watch over her. Her mother never cared. I can't forgive that woman for leaving for England the way she did, abandoning one child while she took the other with her.' It was the cause of some resentment in Scotland that the young earl was being brought up as an Englishman.

'Lady Buchan is a brave lass; spirited, beautiful.' Morna smiled. She had fallen completely under the spell of Isobel's charm. 'Mairi will take care of her as far as she can, but if Lord Buchan finds out . . .' The two women were silent as they contemplated the earl's fury if he should discover that his wife was unfaithful. 'I think it would be a good thing if you could speak to her. Let her know she's not alone. Tell her to be careful.'

Silence fell on the room again. Suddenly Morna wondered if Eleyne were listening. Her attention had been withdrawn; she seemed to be hearing something far away. Her eyes were fixed blankly on the far wall of the room. Morna studied her expression, puzzled. It wasn't the first time she had seen that look on Eleyne's face, that strange luminous quality which shone from her eyes.

Into the silence of the room came the distant sound of a horn, but Eleyne did not seem to hear it. She was half smiling, a thousand miles away.

Outside the rain fell in a heavy curtain; the sound of it filled the air and in the empty hearth a succession of stray raindrops hit the flags.

Morna pulled her shawl around her, then she gave a little cry of fright as a cold wind swept through the open window. A rolled parchment on the far end of the table fell to the floor. It was suddenly very dark.

Eleyne felt her heart pounding uncomfortably in her chest.

Go away. The words were unspoken, but it seemed to her that she had screamed them out loud.

'Please, go away.' This time the whisper was audible and Morna's eyes became enormous.

'Who are you talking to?'

But even as she spoke she knew.

The tall, broad-shouldered figure standing immediately behind Eleyne was so indistinct he was scarcely more than a shadow, but she could see him clearly enough to make out the flaming hair and the beard, and the intense expression as he looked down at the woman seated in front of him.

From the gatehouse came the sound of the watchman's horn again, strangely muted by the rain. Neither woman heard it. Morna held her breath. The spirit, if that is what he was, seemed oblivious of her presence. His eyes were fixed on Eleyne as though trying to will her to turn round and face him.

Eleyne had not moved; she seemed frozen to the spot and her fists were clenched.

Morna reached out towards the flint and steel which lay on the empty table at the foot of the candlestick. As her hand inched towards them, her eyes were fixed on the figure behind Eleyne. He had leaned forward slightly now and put his hands on her shoulders, a touch so light she showed no sign of feeling it.

The flint was in her hand. Slowly Morna raised her fists and brought it down on the steel with a snap. The spark flew into the box of tinder and in a second a spiral of blue smoke was rising and a small clear flame showed itself in her cupped hands.

She glanced up.

The figure had gone.

Standing up, she put the flame to the candles, watching Eleyne's face illuminated by the steadily growing circle of light.

'He must love you very much,' she said quietly.

Eleyne seemed to accept that Morna had seen him. 'I am a lucky woman. To have had two men love me is a great honour, I suppose.'

'Even though they are now rivals for you?' Morna walked around the table and put her hand on Eleyne's shoulder where the shadow hand had been. 'To choose a dead man would be to deny life,' she said softly.

'I know.' Stiffly Eleyne rose and walked to a coffer on the far side of the room. She brought out a small casket and found what she wanted. 'I don't know how this got here.' She put the flashing jewel on the table. 'I had hidden it in the chapel.'

Morna looked at it without touching it. 'The phoenix.'

Eleyne picked it up by the chain and held it so that it swung in the candlelight. The bird's ruby eyes and fiery feathers gleamed and rippled. 'I have tried again and again to be rid of it, but always it returns. But if Donald is to come home it must go.' For a long moment she stared at it, then she turned to Morna. 'Come with me.'

The sentry on guard at the postern gate stared after the two women as they walked out into the wet night. Within seconds they were lost to sight. The steps which led down into the back den were steep and rough beneath their feet. In the total darkness, Eleyne felt her ankle turn and she gave a gasp of pain, but she forced herself to go on.

'It's only a few steps further. Here, where the burn goes over the waterfall, before it gets all marshy.' She strained her eyes and gave a false laugh, strangely loud in the silence. 'I must get them to cut back the scrub here. If ever we should be attacked, our enemies could come up the burn here and get too close to the walls.'

Morna, who could see in the dark as well as a cat, was following her, sure-footed. 'Kildrummy will never be attacked. The very idea! Here, in the heartland of Mar?'

'I had to entertain an enemy here, in the heartland of Mar, Morna,'

Eleyne reminded her sharply. 'If Edward can come in peace, he can come in war.'

'You think he will return?' Morna could feel the hairs on the nape of her neck stirring.

'Who knows?' Eleyne's voice was non-committal. 'But if he ever did, I would be ready for him.'

'Where are we going?' Morna stopped to catch her breath.

'Not much further. Here, look, see how the burn tumbles over the rocks?' Eleyne had stopped on the edge of the water. Below, it disappeared into the darkness, falling into the bottom fo the shallow marshy gorge. At its foot the water was deep.

Eleyne stood for a moment looking down. She could see nothing. The sound of the water filled her ears. For a long time she did not move, forgetting completely her companion, who stood out of sight in the darkness near her. Then slowly she raised her hand. In it the jewelled pendant gleamed as though it had a light of its own.

Release me. Leave me for Donald.

The words were not spoken out loud, but they rang inside her head as she raised her arm and threw the phoenix as hard as she could out over the small waterfall. She smiled grimly to herself. 'So. Water extinguishes the fire at last. My gift to the gods once more. I hope now they are satisfied.'

Around her the night was empty.

For a moment both women stood staring into the darkness, then with a shrug Eleyne turned back towards the castle.

They were soaked through by the time they had scrambled back up the track and regained the arched door in the wall. The guard opened it to Eleyne's knock and they slipped through beneath the small portcullis, into the dark inner courtyard.

Several horses stood, riderless, near the entrance to the great hall which was open, spilling light on to the wet cobbles. Eleyne walked towards it, refusing to allow the slow-burning excitement inside her to surface. It might not be him. She had been disappointed so often in the last few days. But the phoenix had gone and with it the malign force which had kept Donald away. Her shoes squelched uncomfortably as she moved quickly towards the steps and began to climb them.

'My lady, thank the Blessed Virgin.' A face appeared in the doorway. 'She's here!' The figure shouted over his shoulder. 'The countess is here.'

'What has happened? Who is it?' Furious at her breathlessness, Eleyne forced herself almost to run up the steps, willing her stiff bones to move faster.

The far end of the great chamber was lit with a dozen candles and someone had stoked up the fire in one of the hearths despite the thundery warmth of the night.

She barely recognised him. It was fifteen months since she had seen him, and in that time he had changed out of all recognition. Her robust, handsome husband had become a living skeleton. He was seated, exhausted, near the fire as she came in, still wrapped in his wet riding cloak. His face was grey, his cheeks hollow, his eyes sunk deep in their sockets. Beside him stood Duncan. There was no sign of Sandy.

'Mother of Christ! What has Edward done to you?' Eleyne could not move, her dismay was so intense.

Donald smiled. With an effort he rose to his feet and, throwing off the cloak, he held out his arms to her.

'Nel, my love, don't look like that. They have done nothing. I was treated with great courtesy. I've not been well, that's all. Edward's own physicians attended me and now I'm better. Some good Scots beef and some of your magic strengthening potions and I shall be a new man.'

He folded her into his arms and they stood close for a few moments. Eleyne could feel the brittle thinness of his body as she clung to him, and the cold dryness of his wasted flesh. Desperately, she tried to warm it with some of her own vitality, willing her strength into him.

'Have you called for food and wine?' she scolded as she extricated herself from his arms. 'And dry clothes? Look how chilled you are.' *No, she could hear herself crying inside. No. Don't let him be taken from me. That's not fair. It is I who am old. It is I who should die first.*

She took his hands and kissed them; then she kissed his forehead again. Only then did she look around for Sandy.

'Where is he?' Her mouth was suddenly dry with fear.

'Still in the Tower.' Donald shook his head. He had been afraid to tell her, dreading this moment. He looked at Duncan and saw the twin's distress, swiftly veiled as his youngest son put his arm round his mother's shoulders.

'Why?' Eleyne's voice was husky.

'Surety for my good behaviour.' Donald was very bitter. 'Edward is a clever unscrupulous man. He gives with one hand and takes with the other. He keeps a guarantee that I will serve him even as he releases me.' He broke off in a fit of coughing. 'And of course it will work. I shall have to obey him.'

'Papa, enough talking for now.' Duncan took his father's hand gently. 'Come and rest. We'll talk later and think then what to do.' *Did his mother too feel the raw bleeding wound inside which was Sandy's pain?* Seeing her face, he knew that she did.

Somehow Donald found the strength to reach their private rooms in the Snow Tower, to eat a little of the fragrant chicken broth the cook had warmed for him and to drink a goblet of good red wine, but the effort exhausted him. It took Eleyne and one of his men to undress him and almost carry him to the great bed. Only then could Eleyne dismiss the servants and be alone with her husband.

'I've sent for Gratney and Kirsty. They have been waiting for you here, but they rode to the Garioch today. They'll spend the night at Inverurie and be back tomorrow,' she said as she sat on the bed. 'Oh Donald, we've missed you so much.' Almost shyly she touched his hand.

He smiled. How often had he dreamed of this moment. How could he have remembered Eleyne as an old woman? Drowsy with the wine and his exhaustion, he could feel his eyes closing. He must tell her how much he loved her. Now, before he fell asleep – but already his hand had fallen limply at his side and he had drifted into a fitful doze.

When Donald awoke, Eleyne was lying beside him staring up at the tester above their heads.

'Did you sleep well, my dear?' She hadn't meant to share his bed; it was so long since she had done that. She had just meant to lie beside him for a few minutes, to feel the comfort of his presence.

He moved slightly, feeling for her hand. 'It's so good to be home.'

'And you weren't ill treated?'

'As I told you, King Edward sent me his own physicians when I fell ill, and special gifts of food and wine. I'm on the mend, Nel. I'll soon be my old self.'

'Of course you will.' She raised his hand to her lips and kissed it. 'Oh, my love, I'm so pleased you're home.' She did not mention Sandy and neither did he.

Gratney and Christian arrived back later that morning. Donald and his eldest son hugged each other for a long, silent moment, then Gratney punched his father gently on the arm. 'So, what news of King Edward?' The moment of emotion was over.

'He has sent us a master mason and a team of builders to strengthen our fortifications.' Donald smiled grimly. 'Do you remember Master James of St George at Rhuddlan?' He glanced at his wife. 'He is to supervise the building of a new gatehouse for us, it seems, and see to the strengthening of our walls.' He coughed weakly. 'The king leaves for Flanders within the month. I have undertaken to go with him.'

Gratney looked at his mother and caught the flash of tight-lipped disapproval. He hid a smile. 'Mama will forbid it if she can.'

Donald chuckled. 'I know she will – and fight me tooth and nail for supporting her greatest enemy. But we have no choice.' There was a tense silence, then he went on, 'But in this case my lack of health may be on her side. At the moment I can barely sit a horse, I'm so accursed weak!'

As though to substantiate his words, he sat down heavily on a stool.

750

His face was grey with fatigue though he had walked only from the bedchamber to the solar.

Eleyne bit her lip, trying not to show her dismay. 'Some wine for your father, Gratney, to put some colour into his cheeks,' she ordered cheerfully. 'Not that I'm sure I want to put flesh on him to serve Edward Plantagenet.'

Her tone was sufficiently tart to bring a fond smile to her husband's lips. 'That's my Nel.' He took the wine from his son and drank it in one draught. Two spots of livid colour appeared on his cheekbones. 'You know, I think I'll go and rest for a little.' He staggered to his feet with a tremendous effort.

Gratney stepped forward. 'Let me help you, papa.'

Eleyne thought he would refuse, but Donald gave a curt nod and took his son's arm. By the time they reached the door Gratney was almost carrying him.

VI

SLAINS CASTLE

Kirsty smiled at the Dowager Countess of Buchan and accepted the cup of wine her hostess offered. 'My mother-in-law was hoping to visit you herself,' she said, 'but as you know my father-in-law has just been released from the Tower. He is unwell and she didn't want to leave him.'

Elizabeth de Quincy bowed slightly and raised an austere eyebrow. 'Your mother-in-law does not make a habit of visiting me, Lady Christian. Besides, at her age I would have thought her past riding.' She folded her arms inside her mantle. 'If the reason for your visit is to see Isobel, I suggest you say so. That young woman needs a sound beating in my opinion. However, perhaps you can talk some sense into her. If you don't, she will end up killing herself.'

Kirsty's gasp of horror drew no more than a glare from the countess who, with an imperious click of her fingers, summoned a maid to take Kirsty to Isobel's solar.

Isobel had just returned from a ride. Her gown was muddy and crumpled and her face streaked with dust. She looked exhausted.

Mairi showed Kirsty to the window embrasure overlooking the sea, and guided Isobel to sit opposite her; then she pulled a screen across the alcove and left them together. The air was full of the wild ringing cries of gulls.

'Your great-grandmother is very worried about you,' Kirsty began softly. 'Mairi's mother told her how unhappy you are.' To her horror

751

she saw Isobel's eyes flood with tears. 'My dear, is there anything I can do?'

Isobel pressed her lips together, shaking her head. It was several moments before she was sufficiently composed to speak. 'Tell grandmama I'm all right.'

'But you're not.' In spite of herself, Kirsty found her eyes straying to Isobel's stomach. The girl was so thin the pregnancy showed even at this early stage.

'I'm all right,' Isobel repeated desperately.

'And your baby?'

'There is no baby!' Isobel jumped to her feet, pulled her mantle around herself defensively, and stood staring out of the unglazed window at the sea.

'I see.' Kirsty bit her lip, not sure how to proceed. 'Isobel —'

Isobel swung round. 'You're Robert's sister, aren't you? How is he?' There was a hungry gleam in her eye which Kirsty found almost frightening.

'He's well,' she said guardedly.

'And his wife's dead,' Isobel said quietly. 'And his daughter is being brought up by you.'

Kirsty nodded, but Isobel had turned back to the window. Outside the sea was darkly heaving slate, relieved now and then by towering white horses which rode the swells and crested against the shore. 'He must have a son,' Isobel went on. 'He must have a son. He will be king, you know.' She swung round.

Kirsty smiled. 'I believe so.'

'And he must marry again.'

'I suppose he must,' Kirsty said thoughtfully, 'but not yet, not while he is still grieving for Isabella.'

'He's not grieving for her, not really.' Isobel's voice was muffled.

'I think he is,' Kirsty said. She was beginning to understand the reason for this desperate tirade. As Robert's eldest sister she had met too many girls who thought themselves in love with her glamorous brother not to know the signs. She sighed. 'Eleyne told me to tell you she will come to see you when Donald is better. She said you must be courageous and patient and that she loves you and is praying for you.'

Isobel turned suddenly. 'Have you ever had a baby?' It was as though she had not heard a word Kirsty had said.

Kirsty shook her head.

'You don't want one?'

The question appeared to be artless, but Kirsty sensed there was more behind it than appeared. 'Yes, I want one very much,' she said wistfully. 'But God has not yet seen fit to send us one.'

'I see.' There was disillusion in Isobel's voice.

'You'll love it very much when you have one,' Kirsty said cautiously.

'I'm not going to have one.'

The tension in the thin shoulders, the angle of her head, the white, tightly clenched fists all proclaimed a denial of the fact.

Sadly Kirsty stood up. She held out her hands and took Isobel's tense fists in hers. 'Is Mairi looking after you?'

Isobel nodded. 'Ask great grandmama to come,' she whispered.

'As soon as Donald is better, she'll come, I promise.' But Kirsty knew she couldn't burden Eleyne with this further worry. Not now. Not yet.

VII

KILDRUMMY CASTLE

'Mother. He's dying.' Gratney sat opposite Eleyne, holding her hands tightly in his. Two weeks had passed and Donald was worse. 'Anyone can see it. You have to prepare yourself.'

'No.' She shook her head stubbornly. 'He says he's getting stronger. He wrote to King Edward today –'

'And he couldn't hold the pen. His clerk had to take down the letter. He's wasting away before our eyes.'

Kirsty and Duncan were standing together watching them. Duncan put his arm around Eleyne's shoulder. 'He's right, mama. You must accept it. For papa's sake. There must be things you want to say to each other . . .' He shrugged, suddenly embarrassed. 'You loved each other so much.'

'You talk as if he were already dead.' Eleyne stood up stiffly. Her heart was breaking, deep inside, but her brain refused to acknowledge what was happening. 'I thought I would die first,' she cried in anguish, 'and I'm having to watch his pain –'

She went back to Donald's bedside and sat down. Outside, the short summer night was luminous with stars. The mountains were hunched shadows, heavy with the rich scents of blaeberry and thyme and the sharp tang of pine. Somewhere out in the darkness a vixen screamed to her cubs.

'Nel?' Donald had opened his eyes with difficulty. His eyelids were heavy, his breathing laboured.

She leaned across and kissed his forehead. 'I'm here, my love.'

'I need something, one of your potions.' He found it hard to speak now. 'Please.'

She turned towards the table where a shaded candle burned and reached towards the draught she had made him, but he shook his head. 'No use. Something stronger. Please, Nel.'

'Something stronger?' Eleyne looked at him silently.

He nodded. 'The pain is worse every minute. I'm dying, Nel. We both know it. Please, help me.' He coughed a little and she saw the flecks of blood on his chin. She wiped his face gently. His breathing was rattling in his chest and every breath was an effort. His hands clawed at the sheets. 'I love you, Nel. You've made me so happy.' He tried to smile.

Eleyne forced herself to blink back the tears. She leaned forward and kissed him again. 'I'll call Bethoc to sit with you, my darling,' she whispered. 'I won't be long. I promise.'

VIII

26 July 1297

The stillroom was dark. Closing the door behind her, Eleyne stood for a moment without moving, holding her candle high. The pale light flickered along the shelves of jars and pots and clusters of dried herbs. The spicy scent of the room enveloped her, bringing with it a sense of peace and calm. She put the candle on the workbench and moved towards the shelves.

Something to deaden the pain; something to help him sleep. That was what she wanted. That was all she wanted. The juice of the white poppy and the hemlock. Her hand hovered across the containers of dried herbs and the bottles of syrup. With shaking hands, she seized the pestle and mortar and reached down the first of her tightly stoppered jars.

When she returned to their bedchamber, Donald was lying back against the pillows racked with coughing. He could no longer leave the bed; no longer raise himself on the pillows. She stood in the doorway, her candle guttering, aware of the watching eyes in the room. Servants busied themselves while Bethoc dozed in the chair near the fire. By the bed Gratney had jerked awake as she opened the door. He gave her a wan smile; near him Duncan was dozing as he sat on one of the coffers.

Her eyes returned to her husband's face. In the candlelight she could see the sheen of sweat on the grey skin, see the agony in his eyes which belied his attempt at a smile.

'Nel.' His whisper was so faint she did not hear it. She approached the bed and setting down her candle and the flask of thick syrup she had brought with her she leaned over and kissed him. 'Donald?' His skin beneath her lips was ice-cold and clammy. He looked up at her. For a moment she thought he didn't recognise her. Then he gave her a faint smile. His fingers tightened over hers in a spasm of pain and she

754

heard the breath rattle in his lungs. He coughed again and a fleck of bloody sputum appeared on his lip.

'Gratney, would you and Duncan and Bethoc and the servants leave us alone for a little?' Eleyne asked, smiling reassuringly at her son. He held her gaze, then slowly he stood up. He bent and kissed his father's forehead.

'Goodnight, papa.'

'Goodnight, my son.' Donald's eyes focused with difficulty on Gratney's face. 'God bless you.'

Duncan followed. He too kissed his father, and Eleyne saw the tears streaming down his face.

She stood for a long time after the door had closed. She was staring at the candlelight.

'Nel.' Donald's hand closed over hers. 'The sleeping draught?'

'I have it here.' She turned and forced herself to smile down at him.

'You've made it strong enough to take away my pain?' His eyes were clearer than they had been for many days.

'It's the strongest draught I've ever made.'

'Good.' His hand fell back on the sheet and the room was silent save for his laboured breathing.

'I could have wished for a more glorious death,' he said after a long silence. He managed a wry smile. 'One worthy of a romance perhaps.' Another spasm of coughing shook his frame. 'I've been so happy with you, Nel,' he said when at last he could speak again.

She blinked back her tears. 'And I with you, my darling.' She took his hands in hers and kissed each in turn. His skin had the dryness of dead leaves.

'Perhaps I shall return like Alexander.' He gave a faint chuckle. 'I'll have something to say to him if we meet at the gates of purgatory.' He winced as a new wave of pain tore him momentarily beyond lucidity.

Eleyne could not hold back her tears, and they coursed down her cheeks. Gently she released herself from his grasp and reaching for the flask she poured some syrup into the empty wine goblet which stood on the chest beside the bed.

'Drink, my darling,' she whispered. 'It will take away the pain.'

'Help me.' He had no strength to sit up. Carefully she raised his head and put the cold silver to his lips.

The metal clouded slightly under his breath and she could see the movement of his muscles as he swallowed, almost see the liquid as it slid down his throat. The effort was nearly too much for him. She put the goblet down and dabbed his lips with a napkin. His fists clenched over hers as a new spasm of pain took him. 'Will it take long?' He was fighting for breath.

She shook her head. 'Not long, my darling.' She stroked his face. 'Close your eyes.'

'I want to see you,' he smiled faintly, 'and the candle is dying.' His words were becoming slurred. 'It's getting dark. Come closer –'

She touched his forehead with her lips. 'Sleep well, my darling,' she whispered. 'No more pain.'

The flame by the bed had died and grown cold before she moved. His hands in hers were icy and stiff, the harshness of his breathing stilled at last.

There were no tears left. She sat on, still holding his hands as the chamber slowly grew light. She did not hear as Gratney pushed open the door and tiptoed across the shadowy floor. He stood for a long time without saying anything, his face heavy with grief. Then at last he put his hands on his mother's shoulders.

'Come and rest, mama. You can do no more for him now.'

She looked up at him, so cold and stiff she could barely move. 'I couldn't bear to see him in such pain –'

'I know.'

'It was what he wanted . . .'

'I know, mama.' Carefully he raised her to her feet. Bethoc had tiptoed into the room. She stood looking down at the earl's body and crossed herself slowly, then she came to Eleyne's side.

'Come and sleep, my lady. We'll do all that has to be done now,' she said.

Behind her Duncan had appeared in the shadowy room. Eleyne looked from one to the other of her sons with tear-filled eyes. But she could not speak.

IX

She dreamed that Donald was young again. She touched the springy curls of his hair, the softness of his skin. She touched his hand and he pushed a role of parchment into her fingers. He smiled. 'A poem,' he whispered. 'Just for you.'

She had begun to unfold it when a hand reached over her shoulder and snatched the parchment from her. She tried to cry out in protest but no sound came. There were hands on her arms, turning her away from Donald, and she could not fight them; she did not want to fight them.

Alexander looked at her and smiled. He reached up to touch her cheek with the back of his forefinger. 'Mine,' he whispered. 'You are mine now.'

'No.' She shook her head, but she could not resist him. Unprotesting, she walked with him away from Donald. Donald stood staring after her, his hands outstretched, but he was fading. A mist seemed to be forming around him. She turned once to look at him one last time. He raised a hand in farewell, then he was gone.

X

It was midday when she awoke. Morna was sitting on the window seat looking out across the valley.

For a moment Eleyne stared at her, disorientated, then slowly she pulled herself up against the pillows.

'He has gone,' Morna said. She came to the bed and studied Eleyne's face, troubled. 'I saw him,' she went on gently. 'Lord Mar stood beside your bed to bid you farewell. You will meet again in another life, but not as lovers.' She sat down and put her hands over Eleyne's. 'The other was here too, and it's to his destiny that yours is linked and always has been through the ages.'

'So, I am to die soon too.' Eleyne no longer found the idea frightening. 'And then I shall be with him.'

Morna closed her eyes. She was shaking her head. 'I don't know what is to happen. Death is only passing through a door. People should not fear it the way they do.' She smiled. 'But you know that as well as I do.'

XI

The countryside was locked in silence. Snow blanketed the mountains; ice slowed the rivers. Only the tiny specks of birds, desperately hunting for food, and deer, forced through hunger into the towns and villages, moved in the grey freezing landscape. The howl of the wolves echoed with the howl of the wind.

Eleyne shunned the great hall. Her chamber in the Snow Tower was warm and bright with candles and she and her ladies spent much of their time there. Morna had moved into the castle – her own bothy was buried feet deep in snowdrifts. Kirsty was there too with little Marjorie. And big Marjorie was there with her John and their three children – David, John and Isabel – and Duncan's wife, Christiana Macruarie with their son, Ruairi. The close-knit family had drawn around Eleyne for comfort.

The victory of William Wallace and Andrew Moray over an army of English knights at Stirling Bridge barely three weeks after Donald had died had been a triumph for Scotland, marred by Moray's death from his wounds. The patriots were at last in control. Those who had vacillated over their allegiance over the months and years, swinging first this way, then the other – like Robert and Gratney and John,

Earl of Buchan – had opted wholeheartedly for the Scots, under the leadership now of Wallace alone. Only the onset of winter had brought a halt to the hostilities and to Wallace's exuberant raids on northern England, and English and Scots alike retreated to recoup their losses and plan their strategy for the following spring.

One person was missing from the family gathering. Sandy was still in the Tower. Eleyne's desperate letters informing Edward of Donald's death and begging for her son's release had produced one curt refusal. Then silence.

The first messenger to fight his way up the strath on snowshoes was not from the south. He brought a letter from Macduff. 'I returned to Slains with the Comyns as the weather turned. There has been unusually deep snow here on the coast. Isobel has lost the baby she was expecting. Come as soon as you can travel, mama. She needs you.' The letter was dated three weeks earlier.

XII

SLAINS CASTLE ❖ February 1298

Isobel was with her husband's niece, Alice Comyn, and Elizabeth de Quincy when Eleyne arrived exhausted after the long cold journey from Mar. Most of the men, including Isobel's husband, had gone, impatiently riding away from Slains as soon as the snows began to melt.

Eleyne was appalled at the sight of her great-grand-daughter. Isobel's beauty was ravaged by pain and grief, her eyes huge in the pinched paleness of her face. She looked so vulnerable, so wild, trapped in the cold, dark room with Alice Comyn and her mother-in-law that Eleyne's heart went out to the child.

'I would like to talk to Isobel alone,' she said firmly. She held out her hand and Isobel came to her. She recognised the angle of the girl's head, the straightness of her shoulders. She had felt like this herself a thousand times in the past – defiant, desolate, despairing. Isobel of Buchan was far, far more like her than any of her own children had been.

She did not speak until they were seated in the window embrasure, both very conscious of the Countess of Buchan's thoughtful gaze.

'I'm so sorry, my darling,' Eleyne said. 'You're so thin, Isobel. You look as though one breath of wind could break you in two.'

Isobel looked down at her hands and Eleyne noticed the nails were bitten to the quick. 'I'm well enough, grandmama.'

'Are you?' Eleyne's voice dropped to a whisper. 'Does Mairi take care of you?'

Isobel nodded numbly. Then, 'Grandmama!' and she threw herself into Eleyne's arms.

'My darling.' Eleyne cradled her close for a long time, aware of Alice and Mairi retiring discreetly to the far side of the solar. Elizabeth stayed where she was. Beyond the shuttered windows Eleyne could hear the sound of the sea, crashing icily on the rocks in the narrow bay.

'How did it happen?' Eleyne held the girl at arm's length, feeling the narrow bones almost brittle beneath her thinness.

Isobel shook her head mutely. 'We were snowed up at one of the castles along the coast. John was so angry with me.' Her eyes flooded with tears. 'He thought I did it on purpose,' she burst out. 'That is the stupid part! I had tried everything to get rid of it, but nothing worked. Then he came in and he pushed me and I fell against the corner of the coffer –' She put her face in her hands as the tears coursed down her cheeks. 'Are you terribly shocked?' The words were almost inaudible through her fingers.

Eleyne shifted uneasily on the cushioned seat. The cold wind and the tiring ride in the uncomfortable litter had set her bones aching so much she found it painful to sit still. She pulled Isobel to her and the girl subsided on the dried heather at her feet, her arms on Eleyne's knees.

'No, I'm not shocked, I'm just distressed that you should be so unhappy.' Eleyne looked into Isobel's eyes. 'I know what it is like to be married to a man you hate.'

'You do?' Isobel looked up almost eagerly. 'How did you bear it?'

Eleyne did not answer for a while. She frowned, trying to remember. 'For a long time I was in love with someone else,' she said at last. 'The thought of him helped a little.'

She was taken aback by the blaze of excitement in Isobel's eyes. 'King Alexander! I remember! I know the story! It's the same with me! Oh, great-grandmama, there's someone I love too! Someone handsome and brave – and young!' Her eyes flooded with tears again. 'But I can't go to him, I'm a prisoner here.' Her voice rose passionately.

'Hush, child.' The others were talking together at the table and did not appear to have heard. Only Mairi was looking in their direction, her expression wary and thoughtful.

'I'm sure your husband would let you come to Kildrummy,' Eleyne said gently. She was horrified by how cold Isobel's hands were. 'I will tell him I've invited you to keep me company for a while. The men of this country will be kept busy fighting for Scotland's freedom – I suspect for a very long time. Edward is not going to give in easily, I know him. He will not forgive the defeat at Stirling Bridge. He will come back from Flanders bent on revenge.'

Isobel subsided on to her heels. The fire in her eyes had died. Then she looked up again. 'Who do you believe should be King of Scots, grandmama?'

Eleyne sat back. 'I must confess I favour the Bruces' claim. Both John Balliol and Robert are descended from the royal house of Canmore through my first husband's sisters, but Isabel Bruce, my friend, was John's mother's younger sister. Dervorguilla, John Balliol's mother, as daughter of the elder sister, inherited Fotheringhay forty years ago when I forfeited my dower lands, and I believe the lawyers were probably right that Balliol has the senior claim.' She raised her hand to fend off the storm of protest she could see building in Isobel's eyes. 'But I also believe that Robert is a leader of men. John Balliol, with the best will in the world, is not.'

She paused thoughtfully. Isobel had blushed scarlet. Seeing her great-grandmother had noticed, the girl buried her face in her arms on Eleyne's knee. Eleyne put her hand on Isobel's head. 'So, that's it,' she said. 'Oh, Isobel, my dear.'

Wordlessly Isobel shook her head without looking up.

'Does he know?' But even as she said the words Eleyne remembered her conversation with Robert the night after Marjorie was born. *She is trouble. Trouble for everyone near her. It's when I'm near her . . .*

Eleyne swallowed the wave of grief that it should be this child, this beloved great-grand-daughter, who had caused her own daughter so much unhappiness in the last weeks of her life.

As though sensing what her great-grandmother was thinking, Isobel looked up. 'I know he was married to Isabella, but I loved him first!' she cried in anguish. 'I have loved him since I was four years old! By rights he is mine!'

'My dear, you have a husband, Robert can never be yours.' Eleyne kept her voice steady. 'You should not even think about him.'

'You had a husband when you were King Alexander's mistress!' Isobel cried rebelliously. 'You just admitted it. And the whole country knew about your affair!'

'I suppose Lady Buchan told you that,' Eleyne said drily. Elizabeth de Quincy was the daughter of Roger, the Constable of Scotland, and thus her dead husband Robert's niece.

'So, you should understand how I feel.' Isobel's voice was passionate. 'I thought you would understand.' She sounded cheated.

'I do understand.' Eleyne cupped the girl's stormy face between her hands. 'Believe me, I understand. I also understand that John of Buchan is a very different man from Robert de Quincy! Be careful, my darling. Be very, very careful.'

There was a thoughtful silence, then Isobel looked up again. 'Grand-mama, don't you see?' Her eyes again blazed with excitement. 'It is I who am going to fulfil your destiny! My father told mama a long time ago – he didn't know I was listening – that it was foretold that one of your children would be a queen. It's me! It has to be me. John will die and I will marry Robert! Don't you see?' She knelt up, her forearms on Eleyne's knees. 'I am to fulfil the prophecy of your Welsh bard! All we have to do now is help Robert become king!'

'Isobel –'

'I know it's true, great-grandmama! I know it, I feel it here.' She hugged her chest dramatically. 'Please, you must understand, you're the only one who can.'

Eleyne sighed. And so that foolish story went on, from generation to generation.

'Great-grandmama?' Isobel was looking up at her, pleading.

Eleyne smiled. 'I shall certainly do all I can to help Robert become king one day,' she said. 'John Balliol is not the man to rule this country.'

XIII

March 1298

Duncan rode the horse on a loose rein, deep in thought. The snows were melting fast, the air was full of the clean wet cold smell of the newly released waters which cascaded down the hills.

They had killed a wild boar and he had left his men to load the carcass on to the garron and bring it home. There would be fresh meat at the high table when his mother returned to Kildrummy.

Christiana was waiting for him there with Ruairi. He should be content. Why then did he feel so strange? He reined in, his hand pressed to his chest. He could feel his heart thumping as though he had been involved in some violent wrestling match. His breath was constricted, labouring. Sweat had broken out on his brow; something was wrong.

Sandy is in trouble . . . The conviction came to him suddenly. It was like that: if either of them were ill or hurt, the other would know immediately, however great the distance between them. And this time the distance was very great. Sandy was still Edward's prisoner.

Duncan turned in his saddle, looking down the strath towards the south, as though he could see through the hills and forests and the high stone walls which separated his brother from himself. His eyes were, shamefully, full of unmanly tears.

XIII

KILDRUMMY

Eleyne was scrambling over the rocks in the marshy bed of the burn at the foot of the small waterfall. Her fingers were bleeding, her gown soaked and cold, dragging around her legs. She was crying.

'Mama? Mama, please don't.' Duncan had found her there, and he leaped down the steep sides of the den, putting his arms around her. His own eyes were red with weeping. 'What are you doing? Come back before you freeze to death.'

'I'm looking for something I lost.' Shaking with cold, she clung to him. 'Something Sandy's father gave me long ago.'

Sandy's father. As she said the words she began to sob. Sandy's father. Not your father. Duncan frowned as his arms tightened around her thin shoulders. 'We'll find it,' he said gently, 'whatever it is, we'll find it, but you must come in now. It won't help anyone if you get a congestion in the lungs.' Carefully he helped her up the steep slope, half carrying her, conscious for the first time of how light she had become. He broke off an ashplant for her to lean on, and guided her feet on to the precipitous path. Below them the sun reflected on the water in the deep ravine, glittering like a thousand precious gems.

The letter from London had merely stated that Alexander of Mar had died of a sudden fever. His body had been interred in the precincts of the rebuilt church of St Peter ad Vincula within the great curtain wall of the Tower. The king had asked for his condolences to be conveyed to the Mars. That was all: a few lines of black, crabbed, clerical script on a regulation sheet of parchment from the king's chancery.

'What is it, mama? What did you lose down there?' His arm around her shoulders, Duncan drew his mother down to sit on a tree stump to rest. Her breath was coming in painful gasps and her face was alarmingly white.

'My phoenix.' She smiled wanly. 'A pendant. It was so beautiful, so precious . . .'

'How did it get in the back den?'

'I threw it there.' She straightened her shoulders. 'One day I'll tell you the story, Duncan. One day I'll tell all of you. But not yet.' She sighed. 'There's no point in looking for it; if it wishes to return, it will. It always has in the past.' She gave a faint smile. 'Give me your hand. Let's go back indoors.' She rose stiffly, leaning on the ashplant. She stared at it for a moment, then she gave a light, astonished laugh. 'And have someone cut me a proper walking stick. I give in, I need one at last.' Her voice was still young and vibrant, even in her unhappiness. She reached up to kiss him. 'Don't grieve too much for your brother,

Duncan. He's still there, and he still loves us. We'll all be together again one day.'

She walked ahead of him up the path. In spite of the bright, cold sunlight, the shadows were gathering over Scotland. She shivered. There would be more deaths before the year was out; she had seen them in the flames.

XIV
FALKIRK ❖ 22 July 1298

Macduff eased himself deeper into his saddle. His mail felt heavy on his shoulders; his sword dragged at the baldric across his shoulder. It was hot and muggy, the sun hidden behind a bronzed pall of cloud. It was the Feast of St Mary Magdalene and the whole army had heard mass at first light.

Macduff frowned. The vast English host was massed beyond the hill, in the direction of Linlithgow. He had been forward in the white mist of the pre-dawn two days before to peer through the trees towards the Burgh Muir where Edward had bivouacked, and he had felt his stomach clench with fear at the sight of the army camp there with its seemingly invincible cavalry – a cavalry feared throughout Europe for its massive strength. Even the Scots commander, Wallace, was afraid of that cavalry; it had proved itself again and again. He frowned. Well, they were as ready as they would ever be. The English might be superior in weight and numbers, but this time the Scots were ready.

Edward had returned from Flanders in March. Making it clear that the subjection of Scotland was now his top priority, he had made York his headquarters rather than London, and had summoned the host so that by the first of July he was ready for the advance into Scotland. The time for retribution was at hand.

Wallace had formed up his spearmen on the south-eastern side of the hill. They were grouped into tightly packed divisions, each massed behind a barrier of sharpened stakes and flanked by archers, with the Scots cavalry behind them in a solid mass. Macduff was proud of the men of Fife, with his own two sons at their head immediately behind him. They were smart and well trained and eager for battle. Somewhere beyond them, up the line, were the men of Buchan and Mar. Robert Bruce, Earl of Carrick, was there too, swallowing his pride to fight in the name of Balliol in this crucial confrontation. But not all the Scots nobles were there. It would be to their eternal shame that they were not behind Wallace today, keeping aloof because they did not wish to follow a mere knight, however well proven he was as a soldier in the field.

Macduff edged his warhorse forward a few steps, feeling its excitement as it plunged against the bit. Below them, beyond the spearmen and the archers, a broad shallow loch separated the two armies; he could see the first oblique rays of sunlight shining on the helmets and spears of the enemy and reflecting on the green water, every reed throwing a long black shadow horizontally before it. If only their spearmen could stand firm when the attack came, as it would come – soon. The men below were tensing, the English army closing formation. His mouth had gone dry. His gauntleted fist opened and closed on the hilt of his sword.

Wallace had addressed the army earlier: 'Remember. Go for their horses,' he had shouted to the assembled forces. 'Without their horses, they are nothing.' Then he had raised his arms, grinning at the spearmen, the men of Scotland who had come to fight for Scotland's liberty. 'I've brought you to the ring, my friends,' he yelled with all the power in his lungs, as he gestured at the tight formation of the schiltrons, so like the formation of the popular dance. 'Now, hop circles round them if you can!' and the men had answered with a great roar of acclaim.

'They're coming, father.' The voice on his right, tight with excitement, brought him back to the present with a jerk. He could see the two outer wings of the English cavalry wheeling towards them; dust rose in clouds and he heard the thunder of thousands of hooves.

'Sweet Blessed Christ!' He heard the awestruck, terrified cry somewhere to his left. 'Oh, Sweet Jesus, we can't fight that!'

'Fight! Fight! Follow Macduff!' Macduff hefted his shield more securely on to his arm and drawing his sword from his scabbard he raised it above his head with a flourish, then he drove his vicious, rowelled spurs into his horse's sides. It leaped forward and charged straight down the hill. The men of Fife followed without hesitation, but beyond them men were faltering. The knight who had called out reined in his horse, fighting it as it tried to plunge after the others, then he swung it away towards the north. 'It's no good,' he yelled. 'It will be a massacre! Save yourselves!'

Macduff did not see the greater part of the Scots cavalry turn and flee. The bloodlust was on him, the glow of red already in his eyes. The weight of his sword carried it lethally back and forth on either side. He felt it hit bone and heard a scream of agony, but he did not know if it was horse or man. The air was thick with dust; behind his helmet he could see little now. Sweat coursed down his face and into his eyes. He was no longer thinking, no longer aware of his surroundings beyond the great swinging arc of his sword blade. Once he heard his eldest son, Jamie, shout, 'A Macduff! A Macduff!' and he grinned wildly, echoing the cry as he hacked on through the surrounding enemy.

He never saw the man who felled him. He felt a sudden massive blow against his ribs beneath his sword arm, and tipped sideways in the saddle. He tried to brace his left leg into the stirrup to save himself, but he could feel nothing. His whole body had gone numb. He saw his sword fall from his fingers, but a black haze had already filled his visor. He had a moment to wonder why he felt so cold. Then he was falling. He was dead before he hit the ground.

XV

KILDRUMMY CASTLE

The news of the Scots defeat at Falkirk and of her son's death was brought to Eleyne by the Earl of Buchan.

'Macduff died a hero, as did his sons. His name will go down in history,' he said formally. He hated having to do this, but he had been there, close to the ranks of the men of Fife who had proved themselves so brave. It was right that he should tell her.

To his surprise she did not seem as distraught as he had expected. It was as though she had known what he was going to tell her. Wearily Eleyne sat down and gestured at the chair opposite her. 'So. It comes at last.' She looked up with a deep sigh. 'And what of Scotland now?'

'Wallace must go of course. He led Scotland on sufferance – a lowborn soldier who has lost all credibility.' He gave a grudging shrug. 'Though one must give him his due. He was there when his country needed him, but now others must take over the leadership. My guess is that it will be Robert Bruce of Carrick and my cousin John of Badenoch.'

Eleyne scanned Buchan's face thoughtfully as he mentioned Robert's name, but his tone had remained neutral. 'Where is King Edward now?' She shivered.

'He stayed a while at Stirling and there were rumours that he was wounded, but if so he has made a quick recovery, for I hear he has marched west after the Bruce. Our men are scattered. We are in disarray, God help us, but we will regroup. Scotland is more united now than she has been for a long time. Edward Longshanks knows how to make enemies here, and those enemies will stand together against him.'

She smiled wanly. 'I'm glad to hear it.' The pain, the grieving would come later. Macduff had been a soldier, destined to die in battle. But in defeat? Surely it was not meant to be in defeat? And with his sons?

Fiercely she pulled herself together and concentrated on her great-grand-daughter's husband. 'Tell me, how is Isobel?' He hadn't mentioned his wife since his arrival.

His face darkened. 'A trial, as always. My beloved wife accused me of cowardice for leaving the battlefield alive!'

'The girl has an indomitable spirit; it makes her wayward –'

'She is no longer a wayward girl!' he snapped. 'She is my wife, a grown woman. She should be a mother. She must learn to grow up and learn her place. Things will go very badly for her if she does not learn to respect me as her husband. If you have any influence with her, Lady Eleyne, you should tell her so.'

Eleyne did not say anything for several seconds. 'I will do so, of course I will, but you must make allowances and you must help her a little. She is still very young and she is very courageous. She will be a valuable friend to you, if only you will let her.'

XVI
1301

She stared into the fire, her eyes long used to the strange leaping shapes, the licking flames, the crack and hiss of logs and twigs which turned without warning to pictures and as swiftly back to smoke. The room behind her was silent; she often sat there, alone by her own choice, lost in her memories. So many people gone. So much love. So much hate. And still it went on. Still there was no release to join Donald and Sandy and Macduff and all the others she had loved so much. She sighed. Alexander no longer visited her. He had not come even in her dreams, since the night Donald had died. Probably he had only ever been a dream. The phoenix was lost. Wales was lost. Scotland was lost. If her destiny had been to play any part in a nation's history it had slipped past her with the years and been lost as well.

Gratney closed the door silently and looked fondly at his mother. She seemed to be dozing and he sighed. He had brought her yet more news to hurt her and he wondered whether he should keep it from her if it would save her more pain. He sat down quietly in the chair facing hers across the hearth.

Her eyes opened. 'More news, I see? Tell me, Gratney.'

He reached forward and took her hand between his own. 'King Edward has made his son Prince of Wales, mama,' he said gently.

She closed her eyes. 'So. Poor Wales.'

He sat watching her for a few moments. Her face was very pale and thin, her skin networked into a thousand fine wrinkles, framed by the snow-white wimple and veil she wore. She was still a beautiful woman. The passing years seemed to affect her little. The high cheekbones, the broad forehead, the firm mouth, all had remained. He found himself grinning wryly. He was pretty sure she still had every one of her teeth;

766

he himself had had a tooth drawn only a few days before and his jaw still ached from the pain of it.

Only her hands gave away her age. When other women pampered their hands with rose water and buttermilk and kept themselves out of the sun, his mother had worked in the stables like a peasant and it showed. Her hands were rough and coarsened, disfigured by freckles and by old ugly scars. She still insisted on going down to see her horses almost every day, in spite of the pain it gave her to walk. She no longer rode; she might never ride again, though he knew she would rather die than admit it.

He realised suddenly that she was looking at him. 'As you know, in my opinion Edward of England is an evil man,' she said slowly, 'but he is clever. You have to give him that. He never puts a foot wrong!' She was suddenly blazing with fury. 'The Welsh will be pleased he has given them a prince. He has let them think no doubt that he is doing them a favour and poor Wales, without a strong man to pull all her princelings together, will wag her tail like a petted dog and run to heel.' She dropped a hand over the edge of her chair and immediately Grizel, yet another generation of the descendants of old Donnet, was there to nuzzle her fingers. 'I've lived too long, Gratney. I don't want any more of it. I don't want to live to see young Edward Plantagenet pronounced King of Scots as well!'

'That will never happen, mama.' Gratney straightened with a groan and stood up shivering, his back to the fire. 'Scotland is larger and stronger than Wales and far more united.'

'Is it?' She grimaced. 'When Bruce and Comyn are at each other's throats year after year, and one man after another is made guardian of the kingdom, and Edward returns again and again to southern Scotland to torment us. No, it will be Scotland's turn next.' She scowled as she eased herself back on the cushions of her chair. 'I don't want to see it happen. It's time for me to die, Gratney. I want to be rid of this treacherous old body of mine!'

Gratney frowned. It was unlike her to sound so defeated. 'Mama, don't say such things. A few days of warm weather and you'll be down supervising the foaling and bossing the grooms about as usual! Hal Osborne doesn't know what to do without you there to bully him.'

'I'd like to think so. I want to keep an eye on those stables. You should get after them, Gratney.'

'I know.' He shrugged, his eyes alight with humour, and she felt her heart turn over suddenly, he looked so like his father. But the humour was gone in an instant. 'Robert is reputed to have repledged his allegiance to Edward, mama. I didn't know if you had heard.' He shook his head. 'Doesn't he see how it must look to others when he changes sides all the time? Doesn't he realise what it does to his credibility? I know he works to a plan, I know he believes that one day the throne will be his, but in the meantime the lords all see him vacillate and change with every wind. And now he is to marry again.'

'Marry?' She straightened in her chair, her thoughts going immediately to Isobel of Buchan and her impossible dream. 'Are you sure?'

He nodded. 'It appears it is to be Elizabeth, the daughter of the Earl of Ulster.'

Richard de Burgh of Ulster was a staunch supporter of the King of England. 'So. He would even marry to please Edward!' Groping for her walking stick, she pushed herself out of her chair, unable to sit still in her agitation. 'I had such high hopes of Robert. The whole country had such hopes for him. I know he always has good reasons for why he changes sides, but I can't believe he would do this!' She poked at the fire irritably with the end of her stick. 'I suppose he will want to take Marjorie away from Kirsty, and that will break your wife's heart.' There was a moment's silence. There was still no heir to the earldom of Mar after eleven years of marriage.

'Don't think too badly of him, mama.' Gratney put his arm around her. 'I think he may still surprise us all. He's playing a very complicated game, but he has not lost sight of his goal for one second. And that goal is an independent kingdom with Robert Bruce as its king.'

'You still believe that?' Eleyne asked wistfully.

'I believe it. He is to come, I understand, to the meeting of the leaders of the realm at Scone. No doubt he will justify his actions there, yet again.'

Eleyne scowled. 'I wish I could come with you.' She said it half hopefully and Gratney laughed.

'No, mama, you stay here at Kildrummy and help Kirsty take care of Mar for me. I'll tell you everything that happens at Scone, I promise. And before you ask, you can be sure I will tell Robert what you think of him!'

XVII

Spring 1302

Morna sat on the bank of the burn and, setting down her spindle, eased her back for a moment. Every winter now she moved into the castle; each spring, as the land warmed and the days lengthened, she packed her belongings into a bundle and set off on foot for the township and beyond it her bothy in the shadow of the hill. There she found the villagers had swept it for her and cut fresh heather sprigs for her bed and laid a fire in the hearth. Now that she was back, there would be milk each day and sometimes an egg or two in a twisted dock leaf or a plaited rush basket – little gifts from the men and women who found their way to her door when their troubles came upon them.

Leaning back, she stared up at the sky, listening to the quavering mournful cry of a whaup high on the hillside behind her. She shivered. It was the sound of sadness; the sound of loneliness; the cry of a soul in pain.

She shook herself like a dog; she had spent too long with the Countess of Mar. Eleyne had been uncharacteristically gloomy over the past few weeks and uncharacteristically pessimistic. The castle had been full of builders: masons and labourers under the direction of Master James of St George, strengthening the walls, building up the south-west tower, enlarging the gatehouse. It meant the thought of war was always with them, even when the spring fair was held in the grassy fields before the castle and the men and women of Kildrummy and Strathdon were *en fête*.

Morna stood up and gathered her spindle and the soft oily wool. She was tucking it into her basket when she heard the thud of hooves from the direction of the village. Whoever was coming was riding at full gallop, making no allowances for the rough ground. With a sudden sense of foreboding she glanced skywards again as the curlew flew over her house towards the east: the curlew – the whaup – the bird that carried the souls of the new dead to the next world.

Her heart thundering unsteadily in her chest she waited, her basket in her hand, while the riders drew nearer. She could see them now, two of them. A man on a lathered bay horse and a second on a mule. She recognised the mule; it belonged to Ewan, the miller. Reaching her, the two men flung themselves from their mounts. 'Mistress, you must come to the castle. We have to fetch help,' Ewan gasped.

'What's happened?' Morna was staring at the stranger, noting almost absent-mindedly the shock of fair sweat-darkened hair, the brilliant blue eyes, the torn mantle, as she prepared herself for what was to come.

He tried to catch his breath. 'It's terrible, mistress,' he gasped at last. 'Lord Buchan has accused his wife of heresy and child murder and your daughter Mairi with her. The church has condemned Mairi to burn!'

Morna stared at him, frozen, her eyes enormous, riveted to his face.

Ewan stepped forward and put a burly supporting arm around her shoulders. He smelled of flour and sweat, and she leaned on him instinctively, trying to draw strength from his. 'I'll put you on to the beast,' he said gently, 'and run beside you. Lady Mar will know what to do.'

He lifted her on to the mule and she found herself being led at a trot towards the castle.

She was still numb with shock when the two men helped her into Eleyne's solar in the Snow Tower. She stood, dazed, as they gabbled their story, not noticing Eleyne's white face or the speed with which, forgetting her age and stiffness, the countess flew to the door and shouted for her squire.

Within half an hour they were mounted and riding east. They were a party of fourteen: six men-at-arms, two knights and two squires, and two ladies escorted the two elderly women. Only the sight of Eleyne being lifted on to a grey palfrey shook Morna out of her frozen silence. 'You can't ride all that way!'

'Try and stop me!' Eleyne replied through gritted teeth. It had happened at last. The explosion of hatred and jealousy and fear she had half expected for so many years. Poor Isobel! Sweet Bride, let them be in time to save her. She gathered up her reins and kicked the horse into a canter, refusing to acknowledge the pain which exploded through her frail frame as the horse's hooves hit the hard ground. They rode without rest for more than twenty miles, then, exhausted, they stopped to eat and change horses as darkness fell. Neither woman could eat; both drank some ale, then they remounted and kicked their new mounts forward towards Ellon by the light of flaring torches.

The great Buchan castle stood in the elbow of the River Ythan, the beech trees around it swaying lightly in the breeze. From the road, in the pale dawn light, they could see the river, broad and fast-flowing between sandy dunes.

In the meadow below the castle walls there was a great blackened circle in the grass.

For several moments they stood staring down at it.

'We're too late,' Morna whispered at last. Her hands were white on the leather rein of her horse, her face almost transparent with exhaustion. 'Blessed Bride, we're too late!'

Wordlessly, Eleyne kicked her horse on. They crossed the river and rode up towards the castle gatehouse, intensely aware of the raked, blackened circle by the water. Above them rooks circled in the beech trees, cawing in the silence which reigned over the castle. There were none of the usual noises: no horses, no cheerful clanging from the blacksmith, no shouts of children from the courtyard, and yet, above the central keep, the Buchan standard with the golden wheatsheaf rippled cheerfully beneath the high mackerel cloud.

'The Countess of Buchan will receive you in her solar, my lady.' The servant who came forward as they rode into the courtyard bowed gravely. Eleyne breathed a silent prayer of gratitude. So, Isobel at least was safe.

Almost too tired to stand, but spurred on by their terror, she and Morna followed the man up the long staircase to the second floor of the keep. There they found not Isobel but the dowager, Elizabeth de Quincy. She raised an eyebrow austerely at the sight of Eleyne.

'Please sit down, you look exhausted.'

'I am exhausted.' Eleyne remained standing, her back ramrod straight. 'Where is Isobel? And where is her nurse, Mairi?' She heard Morna give a small whimper beside her, like an animal in pain, but Eleyne held Elizabeth's gaze.

'The woman Mairi was condemned as a heretic,' Elizabeth said coldly, 'and she died a heretic's death yesterday morning.' She broke off as Morna let out a piteous wail and collapsed on the ground.

Eleyne fixed Elizabeth with an icy glare. 'This —' she flung out her arm — 'is Mairi's mother.'

'I'm sorry,' Elizabeth said without a trace of remorse. 'You should not have brought her here.'

'We came to see justice done,' Eleyne said softly. 'To find out the truth. To save her life. Was there no appeal? Was there no time to reconsider? Was there no talk of clemency?'

'None.' Elizabeth walked slowly to a chair and sat down. 'The woman was guilty.' Her head shot forward aggressively. 'She helped my son's wife prevent conception — a mortal sin — she helped her to kill the child she carried and she worshipped the devil!' Her mouth closed with a snap.

Morna looked up, her eyes huge and black, the tears pouring down her cheeks. 'That's a lie,' she cried. 'A terrible lie!'

'Mairi would never do such a thing,' Eleyne whispered in horror. 'And you know it. How could you have allowed it to happen? Where is your son? And where is Isobel? What have you done with Isobel?'

Elizabeth smiled. 'Oh, Isobel is safe. She is going to learn how to be a good wife at last. My youngest son, William, who is as you know provost of St Mary's at St Andrews, has taken charge of her punishment and her penance, while her husband is helping to run the country. When she has learned her lesson, no doubt she will return to us. Until then, she must remain where she can do no more harm to others or to herself.'

'And where is that?' Eleyne demanded.

Elizabeth gave a supercilious smile. 'Somewhere suitable,' she said in a tone which implied she would brook no further questions. 'Now, may I suggest you take that woman away. It will only be distressing for her to remain here. We'll find fresh horses for you immediately.'

Morna was rocking silently back and forth on her knees, her arms clasped across her chest, her mouth working in a frenzy of grief.

Eleyne looked at Elizabeth once, despising her for her inhumanity, then she stooped and tried to raise Morna to her feet. 'Come, there's nothing we can do here.'

Morna rose and walked obediently to the door, then she snatched her arm from Eleyne's grasp and turned back.

'Where are her ashes?' she cried. 'What have you done with my daughter's ashes?'

'They were thrown into the river. By now I should imagine they are in the sea.'

Morna gasped. She took a step towards Elizabeth. 'May God curse you and your sons forever!' She pulled off her veil and threw it on to the floor, then she pulled the pins from her hair and let the yellow-grey locks fall around her shoulders. She spat on the heather floor covering. 'May your house be barren; may all its children die before they draw breath! I curse you, Elizabeth of Buchan, and I curse the sons you bore in your poisoned womb!'

BOOK SIX

1304–1306

CHAPTER THIRTY-FOUR

I

KILDRUMMY CASTLE ❖ Spring 1304

The night Morna hanged herself Eleyne dreamed again of the fire. She could hear the roar of the flames, smell the smoke; her eyes streamed and she awoke choking and gasping.

Bethoc, still half-asleep, dragged herself out of her bed and went to her. 'My lady, what is it? What's the matter?'

'The fire!' Eleyne pointed at the hearth, still dazed with sleep.

Bethoc turned. The room was lit only by a rush lamp. A small fire smouldered in the hearth. As they watched, the wind blew back down the chimney and a puff of bitter smoke strayed into the room.

'It's getting stormy, my lady. The wind must have woken you.'

The west wind roared in the chimneys and they heard the trees in the Den thrashing their new leaves. 'I'll call for turves to damp the fire down.' She pulled the bedcovers over Eleyne and tucked them in firmly, but Eleyne pushed them back with shaking hands. 'Something's wrong, I know it.' The dream had been so real, so vivid. She had dreamed it a dozen times in the two years since Mairi died, but each time she had remembered nothing but the fire.

Wrapping her nightgown around her, she lowered her feet to the floor with a groan at the stiffness in her joints and, reaching for her stick, walked slowly to the hearth. 'Build it,' she commanded suddenly. 'Build it into a good blaze.'

Bethoc summoned the sleepy page who went to call the log boy and within ten minutes a blaze had been achieved.

Eleyne sat looking at it, her thin body wrapped in the scarlet silk and velvet gown, her feet pushed into velvet slippers, her hair in a heavy plait, hanging over one shoulder. In the flickering firelight her face looked young again. Watching her surreptitiously, Bethoc sucked in her cheeks and shook her head. The expression on her lady's face was strange. She had raised her head as though listening to something far away and then she had smiled. Bethoc shivered violently and crossed herself before she turned away.

The picture in the flames was clear. She saw the man walking through the crowds and she heard the roar of their acclaim; she saw the scarlet lion of Scotland thundering triumphantly in the wind beside the silver saltire of St Andrew on its azure ground, and then she saw the woman, tall and slim, a flame herself in a scarlet gown, and in her hands a crown . . .

'Mama!'

She started violently as Gratney put his hand on her shoulder. 'My dear! I didn't hear you come in.' For a moment she was disorientated, far away, not wanting to lose the vision. But it had gone. With a sigh she looked up at her son, scrutinising his face in the firelight, wondering why he had come to her chamber in the middle of the night. 'What is it? What's happened?'

'I'm sorry. There's no easy way to tell you this. It's Morna.'

Her eyes held his steadily. 'She's dead.' So, she had chosen the moment to walk through the door and end her loneliness.

He nodded.

'How?'

'She hanged herself.' He looked away, unable to bear the agony in her eyes.

'It's my fault.'

'No, mama, how could it have been your fault?'

'I sent Mairi to Isobel.'

'You weren't to know what would happen.'

'Wasn't I?' She stood up. Her stick slipped to the floor, but she ignored it. 'Blessed Virgin! Am I to have no rest from blame? How many deaths must haunt me?'

'Mama –'

'Please leave me, Gratney.' Her narrow shoulders were tense with pain.

He hesitated. Then he nodded slowly.

For a long time after he had gone she sat unmoving, her face in her hands, then at last she looked up.

'Where are you? Why don't you take me?' she cried out loud. '*Alexander?*'

The great solar remained silent. She rubbed her face, trying to deny the tears which channelled down her cheeks, but they would not stop.

'Goddamn you, Alexander, why don't you show yourself, now I need you? Why don't you speak to me? Why don't you come any more?' She stared around the room. 'You showed yourself to her. Why not to me?' She clenched her fists. 'Isn't it my turn to die? You wanted me enough before. Am I too old now, even for you?' She pushed herself to her feet, leaning on the chairback for support. 'Or don't you exist at all? Were you just the imaginings of a lonely, frustrated woman? That's it, isn't it? You were nothing but a dream! You don't exist! You're dead! Like Morna. Like Mairi! Like Donald –' Her voice wavered and she

776

began to sob out loud. 'You never existed. You died on Kerrera. You died!'

Outside the door a page was waiting, his ear pressed to the door. He leaped to his feet guiltily as Kirsty appeared at the top of the stairs behind him.

'Lady Mar! I'm sorry, I thought perhaps the Lady Eleyne was ill. She was shouting –'

Kirsty waved him aside. Pulling open the heavy door, she went in and to his intense disappointment closed it behind her.

'Mama?'

Her mother-in-law was staring down at the fire, tears coursing down her cheeks. She didn't seem to hear.

'Mama, are you all right?' The room seemed very cold. Kirsty went to put her hand, almost timidly, on Eleyne's arm. 'I'm so sorry about Morna.'

Eleyne sighed. She groped for her handkerchief and shook her head. 'I'm being foolish, Kirsty. For a moment I felt I couldn't take any more.' She blew her nose firmly and managed a watery smile. 'But of course, one does. I'm sorry, my dear, it's old age. It gets harder to hide the pain. I must pull myself together and arrange –' Her voice broke for a moment and she had to fight to continue. 'I have to arrange for something to be done with her body.'

'There is no need. It was Ewan the miller who found her. He cut her down and the villagers have taken care of her. They loved her too, mama. She did so much for them.'

'She wanted to be buried on the brae below the sacred spring – we discussed it once.'

It had been the October before when Edward of England had appeared once more at Kildrummy, checking on the building works, letting it be known once more that he was Scotland's overlord. Eleyne, forewarned, and vowing that never again would she bow the knee to Edward, had slipped down the glen to Morna and stayed there alone in the bothy by the gently flowing river until her cousin had gone. The two women had talked then, long into the summer nights.

'She wanted no Christian burial. They won't know what to do –'

'They know what she wanted, mama. They're burying her exactly where she wished, and I have already ordered flowers for her grave.' The two women were silent, each lost in her own thoughts. Then at last Kirsty looked up. 'I only hope I can be as brave as you when it's needed,' she said. 'May I tell you a secret to cheer you up? Even Gratney doesn't know yet.' She took Eleyne's hand and led her carefully to her chair. When she was seated, Kirsty knelt at her feet. 'Mama, I'm going to have a baby. I thought I wouldn't be able to bear it when Robert took Marjorie away to live with him and his new wife, I was so lonely, but after all these years of hoping and praying, after all the offerings I have made at my chapel, it has happened.'

Eleyne gazed at her incredulously, then she smiled. 'So. An heir for the earldom at last. Oh, Kirsty, I'm so pleased, my dear.'

'If it's a boy, I shall call him Donald and if it's a girl I shall call her Eleyne.' Kirsty smiled, pleased to see the unhappiness leave her mother-in-law's face.

'And your husband gets no say in the matter?' Eleyne asked, half scolding.

'None at all!' Kirsty laughed. 'Mama, things will get better, I know they will. You mustn't despair. Poor Morna never recovered after Mairi died. You must allow her her choice to be with her daughter. That's what you believe, don't you? You don't believe either of them has gone to hell.'

'Not if there is any justice in the firmament. If the hell the church speaks of exists, it must be reserved for the truly evil.' Eleyne stared down at the fire again, lost in thought. 'Morna said it was like going through a door,' she said quietly. 'That's what she's done. She has stepped through a door.'

'I have more good news, mama,' Kirsty went on. 'Robert and Nigel are coming to Kildrummy.' She fell silent, thinking about her two eldest brothers. 'While father was still alive, Robert felt he couldn't act. He was hamstrung because papa did not want the throne. But when papa died in April Robert made one or two decisions about the future.'

'Did he indeed,' Eleyne said ironically, 'and about time.'

'I know he seems to be at King Edward's beck and call again.' Kirsty's voice took on a defensive tone. 'But he couldn't afford to show his hand too soon, and there are still obstacles. John Balliol and Sir William Wallace, for instance . . .'

'And his new wife, the daughter of one of Edward's supporters.' Eleyne could not keep the tartness out of her voice. 'I shall have a few things to say to your brother when he arrives, not least about the high-handed way he took Marjorie away from you when he married that woman!'

If Kirsty's intentions had been to distract Eleyne from her sadness with the news of Robert's imminent arrival, it worked and when he reached Kildrummy with his brother Nigel, she was waiting for him.

'So. Just what game are you playing now, Robert?' she asked tartly. They were alone in her solar on her instructions.

He grinned. 'A waiting game.'

'And just how long do you intend to wait?'

'As long as it takes.'

'And meanwhile you fight for Edward?' She was tight with indignation.

778

'In the meantime, I stir the pot.' He smiled. 'Now, are you too angry with me to do me a favour?'

She narrowed her eyes suspiciously. 'So, your visit is not a social one?'

'Of course it's social.' He grinned again. 'I came to see my sister – the beautiful and *enceinte* Countess of Mar. I came to see my most favourite mother-in-law,' he paused, 'and I should like to see her great-grand-daughter.'

'You know that's impossible!' Eleyne's hand whitened on the handle of her walking stick. 'Lord Buchan took Isobel to France with him when her so-called penance was done after Mairi died. You know very well he is one of the Scots envoys at the French king's court.'

'And I know it was your idea that he take Isobel; and I know it was you who persuaded him to release her. I know how much you love her.' Robert took Eleyne's hand. 'And now he too has made a temporary and expedient peace with King Edward and they are back at Slains.' He walked towards the window and then swung back towards her rest- lessly. 'I need to know what the King of France's views are on our situation in Scotland.'

'And you want Isobel to tell you?' Eleyne raised an eyebrow sharply. She held Robert's gaze challengingly. 'Do you remember once you told me that Isobel was trouble, Robert,' she said softly. 'Is that still true?'

He looked down uncomfortably. 'So, you know. I'm glad.' He paused. 'I wrote to her while she was in France. She has information I need and I can hardly ask Buchan himself. May I send one of my most trusted men to fetch her? No one would question an invitation to Kildrummy to visit you. She would be in no danger.'

'And I would be condoning anything that happened between you,' Eleyne said thoughtfully.

'Nothing will happen, I promise.' He smiled. 'Or nothing that you need know about!'

II

Robert's henchman, Gilbert of Annandale, brought Isobel of Buchan to Kildrummy three days later.

Isobel stood in the doorway of her great-grandmother's solar and the two looked at each other for several seconds. Isobel was very thin, but she looked far better than when Eleyne had previously seen her and her face, lightly tanned from the sea voyage from France and the ride through the mountains to Mar, glowed with happiness. She was undeniably very beautiful. Eleyne sighed. How could she blame Robert – or indeed any man – for loving such a woman? She held out her arms. Together they sat in the window embrasure, where they could be sure of privacy.

'It's been so long, child! Come, tell me about France,' Eleyne said, 'and then, if you wish, tell me about the rest.'

Isobel talked for a long time. At first she spoke in short stilted sentences about her time in France at the court of King Philippe. Then she spoke of the endless weeks at Dundarg Castle in the far north of Buchan, where her husband had sent her to repent of her long list of sins. Finally she spoke of Mairi and at last the tears came. 'It was because of me she died. He wanted to punish me.'

'To punish you for losing your baby?' Eleyne prompted. She put her hands on Isobel's veil as the girl sat at her feet, her head in Eleyne's lap.

Isobel shook her head wordlessly, choked with sobs, then at last she looked up, her eyes bright with tears. 'That was the excuse they used, that she helped me get rid of the baby.' Her voice was harsh. 'Even though it was *his* fault it happened. He hit me and I fell . . . No, he did it because I was seen.' Two tears hung on her eyelashes, then dropped and ran down her face. 'I was seen with Robert.' Her whisper was so faint Eleyne had to bend her head to hear at all.

'Seen?' Eleyne queried.

'At Scone. We met in the monk's garden among the ruins of the burned abbey and – someone saw us . . . making love.' Isobel's broken murmur was almost inaudible.

'My poor child –'

'I love him so much,' Isobel whispered. 'I would die for him.'

'We may all have to die for him one day, when he is our king,' Eleyne said slowly. 'But, Isobel, child, not for that . . . not because he has made you betray your marriage vows.'

'Yes. For that.' Eleyne saw the passion she remembered from their last meeting blazing in the girl's eyes again. She sighed, then in spite of herself she smiled. She kissed Isobel's forehead. 'Take care, my darling, won't you,' she said.

Isobel bit her lip, then she scrambled to her feet. 'You must be tired, great-grandmama. Shall I leave you a while to rest?' The girl was so eager to see him, it was cruel to keep her here.

'I think that would be nice, my child. I shall see you in the great hall later.' Eleyne tried to quell the feeling of unease that filled her, but there was no putting it off. Isobel's fate, like that of all of them, was already written in the flames. 'There is someone else here, I believe, who would like to talk to you about France.' She looked grave and raised her gnarled fingers to Isobel's cheek. 'Take care, my darling. Remember your husband.' As Isobel bent to kiss her, she saw the colour flooding into the girl's face.

She walked slowly to the fireside as soon as Isobel had gone and stood looking down into the flames. In spite of the heat of the long summer outside, she kept the fire burning constantly now. She frowned, screwing up her eyes, but there were no pictures there. Nothing but empty heat.

III

August 1305

Duncan looked from his brother to his mother and back with a despairing shrug. 'I pray no one else falls into King Edward's hands. The man doesn't know the meaning of mercy.' He had just read out a letter they had received from London.

It gave the news that Eleyne's great-nephew Owain, Dafydd's son, still a prisoner after so many years in Bristol Castle, had been dragged from his cell in one of the towers and thrown into a cage. There the king had determined to keep him, like an animal, for the rest of his days.

'A cage? Sweet Lady! Why?' Eleyne closed her eyes, picturing the bars, the horror, the despair of the poor, lonely young man.

'My guess is he wants to frighten anyone who might think of opposing him. He is a vindictive, vicious man,' Duncan replied. 'There's another letter, mama, and I'm afraid it's worse.'

Sir William Wallace had been captured at last. He had been taken to London in chains, dragged through the streets and hanged. His body had been quartered. His head had been put on London Bridge and his four quarters were being set up at Newcastle, Berwick, Stirling and Perth, as a salutary example to the Scots.

Eleyne was aware that everyone in the room was silently making the sign of the cross. 'Poor Sir William,' she said softly. 'May God rest his soul.'

She glanced at Gratney sitting at the table, a goblet of mulled wine in his hand. He was shivering and feverish, having caught a bad cold while visiting Kirsty's chapel of the Garioch the week before. 'So, do you still admire Edward? Would you tell your sons to follow him?' Little Donald had been born three months earlier and flourished noisily to his grandmother's delight, and Kirsty, as though to prove her new-found fertility, was already pregnant again.

Gratney shook his head. 'Mama, I've told you, Edward is a good king. He's strong, he's a brilliant tactician. That doesn't mean I condone what he has done.' His voice was hoarse and he reached for the flagon near him for more wine.

'There is yet more news, mama,' Duncan interrupted. 'Lord Buchan and Isobel were in London when Wallace was tried and executed. Lord

Buchan is to be one of the Scots lords supposed to represent us in the new English parliament. I understand his wife did not care for London, and has retired to their manor at Whitwick in Leicestershire for the summer.'

Eleyne nodded, satisfied. Isobel would be out of harm's way in England. She wondered if the girl had seen her brother while she was in London. Duncan of Fife still lived in England; still served the English king. She shook her head sadly. How could her sons and grandsons be so blind? Why did they not understand the danger? She stood up. 'I shall go and rest and pray for Sir William's soul.' She put her hand on Gratney's shoulder. 'Take care of that cough, my son, or I shall have to dose you with one of my concoctions.' She bent and kissed the top of his head.

Gratney reached for her hand affectionately. 'Not that, please, mama!' He smiled. 'A fate worse than death, one of your nasty medicines!'

The cough grew worse. Four days later it had descended to his lungs, and three days after that, in spite of his mother's medicines and the distraught family's anguished prayers, Gratney, Earl of Mar, died. He was thirty-eight years old. His son and heir was a baby, his daughter not yet born.

IV

December 1305

Little Eleyne of Mar made her appearance four months later at Kildrummy as a blizzard raged around the cold stone walls. In spite of her tiny size, the baby snuggled against a succession of warmed wrapped stones, thrived and proved as lusty a crier as her brother had been.

Kirsty looked wearily at her brother when he came to visit her a week after the birth. Robert, still high in King Edward's trust, had been made little Donald's guardian, and was now constable of his ward's great castle at Kildrummy, in charge of overseeing the continuation of its building works. He sat down on Kirsty's bed and peered at the baby in the crook of her arm. 'Gratney would have adored her,' he said gently.

She nodded.

'There is someone downstairs who would like to come up to see you and pay his respects.'

Kirsty bit her lip. 'Christopher?'

'Who else? He's so laden with gifts for the new mother, he will need a dozen servants to help carry them up to you.' Robert hesitated.

'He has asked me for your hand, Kirsty. It would be my dearest wish for you to marry him, but it's up to you. I would never force you. I know how much you loved Gratney.' His voice tailed away into silence as he watched his sister's face.

One of Robert's closest friends and supporters, Sir Christopher Seton had declared his love for Kirsty three months after Gratney had died, and in her frozen misery she had sent him away. He had persisted, however, gently and with dogged good humour and slowly she had begun to respond to his charm. She lay back on her pillow, looking down at the baby in her arms. 'It's too soon, Robert. Give me time.'

'Of course.' He smiled. 'Can he come up, or shall I send him out into the snow?'

'Of course he can come up.' She looked up at her brother fondly. 'I should welcome a little distraction.'

V

February 1306

Eleyne had remained strong when Gratney died; she had arranged the funeral in Kirsty's chapel of the Blessed Virgin of the Garioch; she had sustained Kirsty through her tears and through little Eleyne's birth and through her remarriage two months after that. But as a second freeze had locked the land she had fallen ill and at last she had taken to her bed. There was no fight left in her. Pale and thin as a wraith, she ate nothing, holding on to life by a tenuous thread. Even the pure spring song of a robin on a tree beyond the wall, once one of her favourite sounds, did not reach her.

She was asleep when Kirsty tiptoed to the bed, holding little Donald by the hand. 'Mama, are you awake?' She lifted Donald on to the bed and sat down. She had ordered Eleyne's ladies from the room. 'Mama, are you awake?' Her voice was shaking with excitement. 'Christopher and I have just arrived and we have incredible news!'

Donald crawled gleefully across the covers and pulled the sheets from his grandmother's face. 'Boo!' he said hopefully. He adored the old lady, and pestered her unceasingly whenever he could get near her.

Eleyne smiled wanly. She pulled herself up on her pillows. 'How could I not be awake when you plonk that monster on top of my frail bones?' she said sharply. 'Move him, Kirsty, before he breaks my ribs.'

Kirsty swept her son on to her knee, ignoring his wails of protest. 'Listen! It has begun! Robert has declared himself king!' Her face was pinched with excitement.

Eleyne leaned forward, suddenly wide awake. 'When? Why now? What has happened?'

Kirsty jiggled Donald up and down on her knee. 'He quarrelled with John Comyn of Badenoch and they fought. Comyn was killed! Christopher says the fight was in a kirk but I don't believe that, Robert would never do such a terrible thing; but the upshot was that Robert has declared himself at last. Men are flocking to his standard from all over Scotland!' Her eyes sparkled. 'He has taken Dumfries and Ayr and his followers have taken Rothesay. The Bishop of Glasgow is with him, and Bishop Lamberton. He has demanded that Edward recognise him as king.' She gave a half-frightened giggle. 'And he is to be crowned at Scone!'

For a moment Eleyne stared at her without a word, then, purposefully, she swung her legs over the edge of the bed. Her cheeks were bright with colour.

'At last! At last!' she cried exultantly. 'I must get up. What a fool I've been to lie in bed like this. There are things to be done. A coronation to attend! And then –' She paused soberly. 'And then, make no mistake, Kirsty, my dear, there will be a war to fight. I suspect we've seen nothing yet to compare with what will come when Edward Plantagenet hears about this.'

She walked stiffly towards the window. Impatiently she called a page to open the shutter. Suddenly she was stifled with the heat of the room. She wanted to be outside; she wanted to ride. She stepped towards the window and stared up at the sky. She could see nothing but the reflection of the candles in the glass, then, as her eyes grew used to the darkness beyond, she gasped. A shimmer of pale colour blazed on the horizon. 'Kirsty, the sky –'

'I know, mama. We saw them as we rode in. You must come outside and see them properly. It is the *cailleachan*, the storm hags. They've sent the Merry Dancers to bid Scotland rejoice in her new king!'

VI
SCONE ❖ Lady Day, March 1306

Scone was crowded by the time the contingent from Mar arrived, their numbers increased by John of Atholl with Marjorie, and Duncan and Christiana with their respective children. Eleyne's litter was lowered at last outside the rambling, half-ruined palace and she was shown the spot where their tents were being erected. Tents and pavilions crowded the meadows around the abbey; the air was full of smoke from hundreds of fires and braziers fanned by the cold March wind and the noise of thousands of people shouting and laughing and dancing in a wild excitement.

Kirsty and Christopher, John and Marjorie, Eleyne, and little

Donald – the king's nephew and a senior peer of the realm for all his small size – were all given places of honour in the abbey and watched with tears in their eyes as the Bishop of St Andrews, flanked by the Bishops of Glasgow and Moray and the Abbots of Scone and Inchaffray, lifted a golden coronet high and placed it on Robert's head and the rafters rang to the cheers of Robert's willing subjects as he faced them as their crowned king.

'He should be seated on the sacred stone, and Lord Fife should be putting that crown on his head,' John Atholl murmured to Eleyne as they stood in the closely packed crowd. 'And it should be the true crown.'

Earls of Fife had from time immemorial crowned Scotland's sovereign on the ancient coronation stone. It did not augur well for Robert's reign that tradition had been flouted not once but twice in this ceremony. But what could they do? Duncan of Fife was to all intents and purposes an Englishman now, in the household of Edward of Caernarfon, and the stone itself had been carted to England and, rumour had it, Edward had built it into a chair in Westminster Abbey: the chair on which one day his son would be crowned King of England. With it had gone the crown and nearly all the Scots regalia.

'Say nothing,' she whispered. 'It's so long since we crowned a proper king in this country, perhaps there are few who will remember.'

But their memories were to be jogged the following evening at the second of the feasts to follow the crowning ceremony.

The great hall in the palace was packed, the trestle tables groaning under mountains of hastily assembled food and wine, and lit by a thousand candles from the precious stocks of the loyal abbeys of Scotland. The noise, following the grace, was deafening.

Eleyne was seated near the new king at the high table. Between her and Kirsty, little Donald dozed on a pile of cushions. Laughing, Robert had insisted, 'He's one of the senior earls of my kingdom and he's my ward. How can he miss my coronation feast!' And he had kissed his nephew roundly. Beyond him and his tight-lipped, disapproving queen, Elizabeth, sat his daughter Marjorie, herself only ten, but so proud and excited she was far beyond sleep.

Kirsty looked at Eleyne across Donald's head and grimaced. 'Our new queen seems none too pleased at the situation. I take it, coming from a family who is so completely in King Edward's shadow, that she does not support her husband wholeheartedly.' She shot a malevolent glance at her sister-in-law.

'It would seem not.' Eleyne sighed. 'I wish she could find it in her at least to smile –'

She broke off as a hush fell over the noisy scene and she turned to stare, as everyone else was doing, towards the far end of the hall, beyond the leaping torchlight. The lone figure of a woman had appeared in the doorway and begun to walk towards them. She was dressed in a wet, muddy cloak, the hood thrown back to reveal wildly tangled dark hair.

'Isobel?' Eleyne's lips formed the word incredulously, but no sound came.

Total silence fell on the great hall as the Countess of Buchan drew near the dais, her eyes on Robert's face. As she approached him, he stood up, his crown glinting in the light of the candles. She stopped so close to her great-grandmother that Eleyne could see the dark rings beneath the girl's eyes, the peaty mud stains on her fair skin. She looked so exhausted she seemed about to collapse, but it was with enormous composure and even triumph that she sank on her knees in front of Robert.

'Your grace, I bring you the allegiance of the House of Duff,' she cried in ringing tones. 'I bring my brother's greeting and his blessing and I claim the right, in his stead, to set you on the throne of Scotland.' She raised her hands towards his in a gesture of submission and fealty and Robert took them.

He smiled. 'Your allegiance I accept and gladly, Lady Buchan, but I am already crowned.'

There was a buzz of excited conversation behind them in the hall. Kirsty glanced at Eleyne and raised an eyebrow.

Beyond Robert old Bishop Lamberton had scrambled to his feet, his eyes alight with excitement as he looked at Isobel. 'The Countess of Buchan brings you the seal of tradition. The ancient right of the Earls of Fife to enthrone the king is not to be denied!'

Robert looked around at him. 'Would you have me crowned twice, my lord bishop?'

John of Atholl jumped to his feet, and thumped Robert on the shoulder with a shout of delight. 'Why not! By God, that would be a splendid start to your reign, Robert! Of course she must enthrone you!'

'But where?' Lord Menteith sat back in his chair. 'The Earls of Fife have always enthroned our kings upon the Stone of Destiny, and that has gone with so much else to England.'

Eleyne saw Isobel tense. She was trembling with excitement now.

'I have the power of the stone in my hands,' she said, her voice so quiet it was almost a whisper. 'I went to St Edward's shrine at Westminster, and I laid my hands upon it, where it lies in the chair Edward of England has had carved to hold it prisoner, and I prayed for its power so that I could pass it on to you, my king. And the stone gave me its blessing. I felt its power!'

Eleyne's eyes were on Isobel's hands as they lay between Robert's, and she saw with amusement that Robert let go of them suddenly, almost as though they had burned him.

Beyond the king Bishop Lamberton glanced at his colleague, Bishop Wishart. 'This is part of the sacred inheritance of Scotland.'

Wishart nodded. 'We should ask the countess to perform the ceremony without delay. Tomorrow. It will be Palm Sunday.' The old man's face was solemn. 'Thus may our king, Robert, enter his kingdom twice, and in the footsteps of Our Lord.'

There was an awed silence. Eleyne felt her eyes fill with tears. The emotion amongst Robert's followers was raw and explosive in the hall below them. Only a few, sitting near the king and queen at the high table, heard the queen's quiet words as she addressed her husband. With a small snort of derision she gave Isobel a withering glance. 'These are the games of children! Do you seriously expect this woman to crown you again? Surely one such farce is enough!'

There was a gasp of horror from Eleyne's neighbours.

Isobel looked at the floor, her face white, her fists clenched in the folds of her muddy cloak. 'I am here to serve my king if he desires it,' she said softly. To Eleyne it seemed as though her love must be obvious to every person in the hall.

'And he does desire it!' Robert reached for her hand once more with a small bow. 'Tomorrow, my lady, you shall enthrone me in the ancient manner upon the sacred hill outside the abbey before the people of Scotland.' He smiled, then his face sobered. 'Tell me, my lady, does the Earl of Buchan know what you are doing?'

Eleyne saw Isobel bite her lip suddenly. 'I have no doubt that by now he knows, sire.' She glanced up at Robert under her eyelashes. 'I hope this time you won't tell me to go back to him.' It was as if the two of them were alone in the great hall, oblivious of anyone else; Eleyne strained her ears to hear his quiet reply: 'Not this time, my lady. This time I shall keep you with me.'

The new queen scowled furiously. She pushed back her heavy chair and stood up. 'My lord, it is time for us to retire,' she said sharply.

'It is too soon, madam. Please sit down,' Robert replied. 'All of you, sit down and make a place for Lady Buchan. It seems our celebrations are only half over after all.'

Eleyne slept badly. The tent was noisy; their neighbours had no intention of cutting short the celebrations just because the feast was over, and the whole field was full of music and laughter throughout the night, the sound carried on the wind, augmented by the wildly flapping tents and banners.

She had crept away from the feast early, too tired to remain longer, taking Donald with her and handing him over to his nurses. Isobel too was tired; she could see her exhaustion as she sat next to Robert, but she was buoyed up by her excitement. Not once had she taken her eyes off Robert; not once had she acknowledged by so much as a smile that her great-grandmother was there at the table with her. She had seen no one but her king. Eleyne buried her hurt sternly. This was Isobel's moment of glory, her destiny. The scene she had foretold in her dream. Her own time was past: the moment for which she had lived so long had come, but she was not to be at the centre of the stage.

She tossed uncomfortably on the camp bed and willed herself unsuccessfully to sleep.

By the king's orders in deference to her eighty-eight years, they provided her with a chair the next day, close to the sacred place of enthronement on the Moot Hill outside the abbey. It was a brilliant clear day, bitterly cold, and she huddled, shivering, in her furs as the ceremony got under way.

A new stone had been found for the occasion, hewn from the heart of the mountains to be blessed by the bishops and sprinkled with holy water and anointed with oil. In England the king himself was anointed at his coronation, but in Scotland's more ancient ceremony the crowning and enthronement were the important acts.

Finishing their part, the bishops stood back and Isobel stepped forward. She was richly dressed in borrowed velvets and furs, and on her dark hair there was a diadem of Scottish silver, provided by the Bishop of Glasgow who had kept what survived of the Scottish regalia hidden from the invading armies, producing it proudly for Robert's coronation. Nearby the king waited quietly, resplendent in his own hastily assembled robes and finery.

Isobel knelt down on the grass before the stone and put her hands upon it reverently. Around her the watching crowds fell silent. For several moments she did not move, her concentration entirely on the cold grey granite, then at last she stood up and turning towards Robert she took his hand as behind them the Abbot of Scone devoutly spread a cloth of gold upon the stone.

When Robert was seated, she took the crown from the waiting bishop and held it for a long moment high in the air. Then at last she lowered it and placed it on Robert's head and the crowd, massed around the flat-topped man-made hill which was Scotland's most sacred site, roared their approval and their assent.

Near Eleyne, the queen was standing with John of Atholl and Marjorie watching the ceremony, tight-lipped. 'This is asinine,' she whispered to Lord Atholl in a tone which was perfectly audible to Eleyne and probably to a great many people around her. 'We shall be king and queen for the summer if we are lucky! Robert cannot defeat Edward of England. No one can!'

Lord Atholl hid his irritation with difficulty. 'The king will reign for longer than a summer, madam. Be sure of that!' he retorted sharply. Noticing Eleyne's quizzical expression, he gave her a grim smile. 'Much longer,' he repeated fervently, 'with God's good grace.'

VII

There was no time for a parliament after the coronation. Robert planned to march back to the south-west immediately and with him went all his supporters. All save Eleyne. She saw him alone the night before he left and knelt to kiss his hand.

'I'm too old to follow the drum, Robert,' she said with a grimace. 'Would that I could, but I'll be with you in spirit, my dear. God speed. Isobel is going with you, I suppose?' She looked him in the eye.

He nodded. 'She can never go back to her husband now. She stole his horses and half his men, God bless her, and left him to run bleating to Edward. I think there's little doubt that he would kill her if he got his hands on her again.'

'Then take care of her, Robert. She has more courage in her little finger than many men have in their whole bodies. Don't hurt her. Don't fling her love back in her face.'

He shook his head. 'I would never do that.' He smacked his hands together in frustration. 'If only I could have married her! Think what a queen she would have made! But we never had the chance. I'll take care of her. I'll take care of all of you, with God's help.'

She sighed. Would she once have made a queen of whom a king could be proud? Like Isobel, she had somehow missed her place in history. Her thoughts went back to her beloved daughter, Isabella, who had dreamed of marrying a prince, who had been so sure that one day she would be the wife of a king. For her, too, time had been out of joint and it was Eleyne's grand-daughter, Marjorie, Isabella's child, who was the princess – little red-haired Marjorie, with her temper and her passion. Perhaps it was she who would inherit the prophecy and one day be a queen. She sighed again. Was Alexander here, somewhere in the shadows? Had he come to watch the crowning of his distant cousin? If he had, he had given her no sign.

She turned back to Robert. 'I shall relieve you of one small charge. I'm taking Donald back to Kildrummy with me. Kirsty wants to stay with you and Christopher, but I think the Earl of Mar is too young for war.' She paused. 'If ever an old woman can help you, Robert, remember me. And remember Kildrummy, which will always be a refuge for you and yours should you need it. I flatter myself it could withstand any siege, strengthened as it has been at Edward's expense,' she smiled grimly, 'and I shall see that it is stocked and ready.' She took his hand

and raised it to her lips. 'God speed, Robert. God save you, my king.'

VIII

KILDRUMMY CASTLE ❖ April 1306

There was a visitor waiting for Eleyne when she arrived home. The sky was a dazzling blue, streaming with soft white cloud as her litter took her at last across the drawbridge over the ditch, and through the massive new gatehouse into the familiar courtyard. Behind her, a second litter carried Donald's nurse and the child himself, fast asleep in her arms after all the excitement of the last few days.

Stiff and weary Eleyne climbed out and smiled at the wildly leaping young wolfhound who greeted her. Grizel's only pup, Eleyne had named him Donnet after his ancestor, knowing in her heart that this would be the last dog she would ever own. She greeted the remaining senior members of her household who had stayed behind and turned at last towards the entrance to the Snow Tower. Overhead a buzzard circled, its yelping cry echoing over the countryside beyond the walls. She shivered, and pulling her heavy cloak around her she began stiffly to climb the staircase, followed by her ladies.

At the door to her solar she was met by one of the women who had remained behind, Gillot, who, finger to her lips, motioned her to one side.

'You have a visitor, my lady,' she whispered. She gestured over her shoulder. 'She's been here a week, but she won't tell us her name.'

Eleyne reached up to the brooch which fastened her cloak and fumbled at it with stiff fingers. 'I'll speak to her, then I think I must lie down. I am so tired I can hardly move.' She handed her cloak to Gillot and turned towards the fireplace where several ladies sat talking and sewing by the light of a dozen candles.

She had already identified the stranger, a tall woman in her late fifties or early sixties seated straightbacked in Eleyne's own chair by the fire. She wore a plain gown of rich dark blue velvet and a mantle held by a silver brooch shaped like a boar.

As Eleyne walked into the room, Donnet at her heels, the woman rose. She was staring at the dog. 'Lyulf,' she murmured.

Eleyne stopped dead, her knuckles white on the handle of her stick, aware of the inquisitive eyes of her ladies on her.

The woman took a hesitant step forward. 'Mother?' she said.

Eleyne could not speak. For several seconds she did nothing, then, her heart thudding with excitement and fear, she held out her free hand. 'Joanna?' It was a whisper.

The woman nodded. She did not take Eleyne's hand. Instead she glanced, half embarrassed, around the room.

'I've chosen a stupid time to travel. It appears Scotland is once again in revolt –'

'Scotland has just crowned her rightful king,' Eleyne corrected gently. She turned to Gillot. 'Please, fetch me some mulled wine, then I would ask you all to leave us.'

They did not speak until they were alone. Then Joanna took a seat opposite her mother. 'Of course, it can't be Lyulf.'

Eleyne shook her head. 'One of his descendants. The last one I shall have; I'm too old for dogs.' She sipped her wine, glad of the warmth of the goblet between her fingers.

For a moment neither of them said anything. Eleyne gazed into the opaque depths of the wine between her hands. 'Where is Hawisa?' she asked at last.

'She died many years ago of a scarlet fever.'

Eleyne closed her eyes. 'I didn't want to leave you,' she said at last in a broken whisper.

'I know that now.'

'Why did you come after all this time?' Eleyne could still feel her heart thudding unsteadily between her ribs.

Joanna was embarrassed. 'I hadn't realised you were still alive. I think for me you had been dead for many years –' She realised how cruel that sounded as she said it, but there was no taking it back. Her eyes on her mother's face, she went on: 'Then, one day, I heard you mentioned at court. It was when your son died. The Earl of Mar. They were talking about the dowager, and the king mentioned your Welsh blood –'

'Should I be flattered that the king persists in remembering it?'

For the first time Joanna smiled. 'I doubt it. He did not intend it as a compliment. I reminded him that I was your daughter and he looked down his long nose at me –' she paused to imitate her sovereign's haughty expression, making Eleyne smile, 'and he said: "you had better hope that I forget that fact, Lady de Bohun, lest I suspect you of being a rebel too!"' She hesitated. 'I am not often at court, in case you are wondering why the matter did not come up sooner.'

'You had better hope that he does forget it, and immediately,' Eleyne said crisply. 'He does not care for the family of King Robert either and I am now part of that family. The king's daughter and heir is my grandchild and your niece.'

Joanna grinned ruefully. 'So I understand. I have had plenty of time while I was waiting for you to work out to whom I am related in Scotland, and I have decided to retire from public life as soon as I return to England.'

791

'How soon must you go back?' Eleyne looked at her wistfully. 'I don't suppose you would consider staying?'

Joanna shook her head. 'Coming here was something I had to do, for both our sakes. But having done it I must go home. My life is there, and my loyalty.' She returned Eleyne's look and her face was sad. 'We are of different worlds; different nations. We have nothing to join us together save a tenuous thread of blood.' She stood up and putting her goblet down she came to stand by Eleyne's chair. 'My marriage lasted so short a time. Humphrey died of his wounds after the battle of Evesham. Did you know,' she asked, 'that Humphrey's first wife was a sister of Isabella de Braose? He said she used to talk about you.' She was rueful. 'After Humphrey's death, the king decided that I was no more use to him in the marriage market. I had little dower, and my child was dead.' She smiled sadly. 'Most of my life I have given to the Lincolns who looked after me when –' She stopped abruptly. 'Cousin Margaret was good to me. Hawisa and I were happy there. And we had Rhonwen for a while to provide the link with our old lives. What happened to Rhonwen?'

'She died.' Eleyne did not elaborate further and after a moment Joanna shrugged. She went back to her chair and held out her hand to Donnet who went and sat beside her, leaning against her knees. 'I missed these dogs so much,' she said after a minute. 'But I never kept a wolfhound of my own. It reminded me too much . . .' Her voice tailed away and she fell silent again.

'I am sorry.' Eleyne shook her head, feeling the weight of her sorrow as almost intolerable. 'So very, very sorry.'

Joanna looked up again. 'Do we . . . I mean, do I have any sisters?'

Eleyne nodded. 'Marjorie. She is married to Lord Atholl. My eldest daughter, Isabella, died.'

'I'm your eldest daughter, mother,' Joanna said softly.

'Oh, my dear.' For a moment Eleyne was aghast, then she held out her hands. 'Oh, Joanna.'

Joanna came to her, then almost shyly she took her hands and, bending, kissed the knotted old fingers. 'I'm glad I came,' she whispered. 'For a long time I didn't want to. I didn't want to see you again, ever. Once, when I was going to come to you at Aber I changed my mind. I couldn't face it. I hated you for leaving us, and I hated you because Hawisa died without knowing you. She couldn't even remember you. Cousin Margaret was the only mother she ever knew. And Annie. And Rhonwen. She loved Rhonwen.' She noticed again the way her mother's face hardened at the mention of Rhonwen's name and she sighed. There was so much she would never know, now, about this enigmatic old woman.

As if sensing that somewhere, somehow a line had been drawn,

792

Eleyne slowly withdrew her hands and reached for her stick. Unsteadily she pushed herself to her feet and walked towards the table in the centre of the room. 'My dear, I'm so pleased you came,' she said, 'but you are right. It would be better if you did not stay here.' She stood where she was, looking at the soft dark shine on the old oak table, her narrow shoulders squared defensively as if she expected Joanna to protest. 'Scotland is at war. Kildrummy supports her present constable, who is now Scotland's king. If you are a subject of King Edward, you cannot remain here without being compromised.' She looked Joanna squarely in the eye. 'The countryside is already overrun by soldiers. It may already be unsafe for you to travel, but if you stay here –'

'I don't want to stay, mother.' Joanna's voice was firm and unemotional. 'There's no place for me here. Whatever your allegiance, whatever country you belong to now, my father was an Englishman.'

'Indeed he was,' Eleyne replied at last, drily.

'And as you say, there are soldiers everywhere further south. I shall go as soon as I can – tomorrow.'

'So. We shall have only one night together.' Eleyne bit her lip. 'I wish I could have known you; I wish I had seen you both grow up.' She smiled sadly. 'We won't see each other again,' Joanna was looking down at her hands, trying to resist the sudden stupid bitter tears which had flooded into her eyes, 'but I shall treasure this meeting in my heart. Perhaps in another lifetime we'll be permitted to know each other better.'

'Another lifetime?' Joanna looked shocked. She laughed uncomfortably. 'In heaven, you mean?'

Eleyne shook her head. 'Who knows what I mean? I just feel there will be a time, a place where we'll see the people we've loved. There has to be. It can't all just end.'

'Mother –'

'No, my dear, don't say any more. Please call one of the pages to take Donnet into the courtyard while I change. My gown is soiled from travelling and we must go down to the great hall for dinner. I want to show you off –' She managed a smile.

It was Joanna who took Donnet down to the courtyard, anxious to have a few moments to herself to compose her thoughts. She stood looking up at the luminous night sky with its myriads of stars, breathing the cool freshness after the smoky heat of the solar.

From the battlements she heard the measured tread of one of the few remaining men-at-arms as he patrolled the curtain wall. She could smell the mountains; the rich, acid tang of peat and heather and thyme carried by the wind; the acrid scent of smoke from the dozens of smoke-holes and chimneys in the huge castle and, beneath it, the ever present sick odour of effluence from the ditches and open drains which carried away the castle's waste.

Donnet whined and looked up at her face. She patted his head. 'If you knew how I loved Ancret and Lyulf,' she whispered, 'I missed them so much when Rhonwen took them away . . .'

IX

'I want you to take him.' Eleyne had put the leash into Joanna's hands. 'He will protect you on your ride home. He's a young dog, barely more than a puppy, for all he's so huge, and I'm too old for him. I always have to ask others to give him exercise and he seems to have become very attached to you already.'

'Mother!' Joanna protested, 'you can't mean it. You wouldn't part with one of your dogs!'

Eleyne nodded. 'I'll have no more dogs, Joanna,' she said sadly. 'Once I would sooner have parted with an arm or a leg than one of my beauties.' She put her hands on either side of Donnet's head and kissed his nose. 'But no more. I shall be dead before he is even fullgrown – oh yes,' she hurried on as Joanna tried to protest, 'I'm quite realistic about it. It would put my mind at rest to know he has gone with someone who will love him as much as I do. It is the most precious gift I have to give you, my darling. Please take him, with my blessings and my love.'

She walked to the drawbridge after Joanna had gone and gazed for a long time after the riders as they wound their way down the strath and into the distance, the rangy grey form of the dog, as large as a small pony already, loping beside Joanna's dun mare in front of her small escort – a maid and two squires.

When she turned back into the outer bailey her face was wet with tears.

X

The garrison left at Kildrummy was small and many of the men were elderly. Most of the men of Mar were with their king. Only those unfit for active service or too young or too old remained to hold the castles and work the farms and crofts of the mountains. Eleyne called her steward, Alan Gordon, and her remaining knights together that very afternoon, trying in her own determined fashion to forget the lonely figure of her daughter disappearing into the distance at the beginning of her long dangerous ride south.

It was the start of several frenzied days of activity. The castle was to be made ready for a possible siege.

Gordon frowned. 'My lady, the fighting is all to the south. The English king will never besiege Kildrummy. Our King Robert will never let him get this far, God bless him.'

'The English king was here in person not three years ago,' Eleyne retorted. 'And five years before that, when I had to give him the keys on my knees. Never, never will I do that again. If all does not go well with King Robert, this will be one of the castles where he can find support and refuge – and look at us!' She waved her hand energetically towards the high walls. 'The underbrush comes so close to the ditch, ten armies could hide there and we wouldn't know it.'

She was tireless in her supervision of her household over the next days, not admitting even to herself how much she missed the presence of her dog beside her as she watched the undergrowth hacked and scythed back, checking herself the lists of provisions in the storerooms, sending out for more from markets as far away as Huntly and Aberdeen. Stocks were low. It had been a cold winter and it was a late spring. The small fields around the village were hazed green with new-planted oats and barley, but it would be a long time until the harvest.

Bethoc watched her lady's feverish activity with alarm and delight. Only five months earlier Lady Eleyne had seemed within weeks of death; now she was everywhere, her stiffness and weakness all but forgotten. The tapping of her walking stick became a familiar sound in the courtyards and corridors of the castle. Once again she was often in the stables, watching her mares as they fed, or leaning thoughtfully against the wall in the smithy as Hal Osborne paused from forging weapons to fit new shoes, missing nothing as he laid the red-hot irons on his anvil, hammering them to shape before plunging them into the tank of water and clamping them to the horses' hooves in clouds of steam.

She was standing outside the postern, scanning the men who were cutting back the undergrowth in the Den when one of the men perched on the rocks above the burn gave a shout. She saw him jump down out of sight into the rocks, then he reappeared and began to scramble up towards her.

Even before she saw it in his hand she knew what he had found. She tensed, her fingers tightening on the handle of her walking stick.

'My lady.' It was John of Mossat, a small man with bright brown eyes and a head of unruly dark hair, the reason for his absence from the war immediately apparent as she saw his twisted withered right arm. He polished something against the grubby hodden of his belted tunic and held it out to her.

The phoenix.

'Someone must have dropped it, my lady,' he said, puzzled that she did not put out her hand to take it. 'It's gey pretty.'

Even the encrustation of mud and moss could not dull the gemstone flames. She stared at it for a long time before she remembered the man standing before her. She looked up and he was astonished to see tears in her eyes.

'Thank you,' she said.

He shrugged and turned away, disappointed at her reaction. He had already forgotten it when two days later Alan Gordon appeared himself at the door of his bothy and pressed a small bagful of silver coins, a fortune beyond his wildest dreams, into his hand as a reward.

XI

'So you have come back to me.' In the silence of her bedchamber, Eleyne poured some water from a ewer into an earthenware bowl. By the light of a single branch of candles, she dropped the jewel into the water and agitated it gently, watching the dirt float to the surface.

When it was clean, she dried it carefully on a scrap of silk, then she held it up to the light.

'Where are you?' she whispered. Her hands, holding the phoenix, had begun to tremble.

The room was very quiet. On the floor above, Bethoc and the ladies were sitting quietly around their own fire, gossiping as they sewed or spun. Like the men of the castle they viewed their countess's frenetic preparations for a siege with long-suffering scepticism, putting her caution down to old age, but half afraid deep down that maybe she had had a premonition . . .

Alexander? Eleyne's fingers tightened on the phoenix. 'Where are you?'

The room was completely silent; the fire burned low. *Please don't forsake me now. I need you.* She stared down at the jewelled bird in her hands. *Scotland needs you.* But there was no reply. The room was cold and empty and there was no gentle touch on her shoulder to reassure her that she was not alone.

With a small sigh she rummaged in her jewel casket for a chain, her stiff swollen fingers picking over treasures which brought back so many memories. She found one at last, and threading the pendant on to it, put it around her neck, slipping it beneath the soft fabric of gown and shift. The enamelled jewels were cold beneath her breasts, and she caught her breath as she shut the casket lid and turned towards the fire. She would never take the phoenix off again.

*

796

She was asleep when he came at last, a shadow in the darkness, cast upon the wall by the dying candles. For a long time he stood, looking down at the sleeping face, then at last he smiled. His touch upon her hair was no more than the gentle shiver of a passing draught.

XII

The lack of news was the worst part of the next few weeks. The castle waited through the long spring without word from the south. From time to time rumours reached them of the activities of King Edward's armies, under the direction of Aymer de Valence, Earl of Pembroke. He had arrived in Scotland under the dragon banner – the fearful symbol of total destruction which would give no quarter. Neither women nor children would be spared if they supported the rebel king. Eleyne heard the news white-faced and went to look down into the castle courtyard. She had done all she could to prepare. Little Donald and her name-sake, Ellie, were safe at Kildrummy. Now they could do nothing but wait.

XIII

June

The last thing she expected was to find King Robert on her doorstep. He slipped into the castle in the strange half-light of the early June night, accompanied by a few dozen men and several women. 'I want you to keep my daughter here, mother-in-law.'

He raised Eleyne to her feet as, wrapped in a bed gown, her hair loose down her back, she knelt before him in the great hall. 'I'm terrified what would happen to her if she were captured. And my queen. And Kirsty and Mary, and Isobel. I'm going to leave Nigel and Robert Boyd here to help you hold the castle.' He glanced over his shoulder at the Countess of Buchan who stood near him and Eleyne saw them exchange smiles. 'Things are not going well for us.' He scowled with weariness. 'We'll stay a day or two, to rest my men, then we'll be on our way. We have to confront Pembroke and drive him out of Scotland. Unless we can do that, we're lost. I'll feel safer if I know the ladies are here out of harm's way.'

He was as good as his word. For three days the men ate and slept and repaired their weapons, then in the dawn of the fourth, they slipped away as quietly as they had come.

Sir Nigel Bruce came to the Snow Tower to tell Eleyne that they had gone. A tall young man, with his brother's good looks and hazel eyes, he smiled when he saw her dismay at his news. 'He thought it better to leave quietly. He didn't want any scenes. Elizabeth has not made it easy for him, and she is not making it easy for Isobel either. I suppose you can't blame her. She knows of course that they are lovers.' He looked at the old woman to gauge her reaction, and noted with approval her lack of shock or surprise. 'They've tried to hide it, they've been very careful, but it's hard. Travelling, camping . . . We have tried to allow them time together when they can find it, and Elizabeth of course has resented it bitterly.' He shrugged. 'But she is no support to Robert. He needs someone who is behind him totally, and Isobel gives him that. She's as passionate in her support of the cause as she is in her love for him.'

Eleyne pulled her bed gown around her thin shoulders. 'Then I'm glad they've had some time together. Tell Isobel to come to me here later. I should like to talk to her. And make sure our queen,' she grimaced at the words, 'has all the comforts that Kildrummy can offer her. It will perhaps mollify her a little. I shall pray for Robert. And for Scotland.'

Sir Nigel scowled. 'So shall we all, Lady Eleyne, so shall we all.'

Eleyne was dressed and poring over one of the account ledgers when Isobel found her way to her great-grandmother's solar. She hesitated, as though unsure of her welcome, then as Eleyne looked up and dropping her pen rubbed her cramped fingers, she ran to Eleyne and hugged her. 'Are you very angry with me?'

'Angry?' Eleyne asked her in astonishment.

'For crowning him. For making an exhibition of myself. For loving him?' Isobel sank to the floor in front of the old lady and clasped her hands tightly.

Eleyne smiled. 'How could I be angry? I'm very, very proud of you, my darling. It took enormous courage to put the crown on Robert's head before the whole world.'

'Robert told me you were there.'

'Yes. I was there.'

'And I never saw you. I'm sorry.'

'You had other things on your mind.' Eleyne took the young woman's hands in her own, and held them, palm up, on her knee. 'You had the magic of the stone in your fingers that day. With the blessing of the ancient gods of Scotland, and that of our Blessed Lord, Robert will succeed.'

There was a sudden tension in the room.

'You really believe in the ancient gods?'

'Oh yes, they still have power. I have always believed in them. I was brought up to see them in the Welsh mountains. My first husband tried to make me believe they were wicked and sinful; he taught me the beauty of the church's teachings. But they're still there, the old gods. And when we call upon them, they answer.'

798

'And they support Robert?'

Eleyne nodded slowly. 'I believe so.'

'I'm going to go after him.' Isobel's voice dropped suddenly to a whisper. 'They don't want me here. Elizabeth hates me. Nigel says Robert has mustered a further band of men from the mountains here and as soon as they are ready to follow him, I am going with them.'

Eleyne shook her head. 'Isobel, he doesn't want you with him, my dear. You add to his worries . . .'

'He needs me, great-grandmama.' Isobel stuck out her chin stubbornly. 'Please, don't try to stop me. I shan't tell the others, I shall just slip away when the time is right. I shan't get in his way. I'm not stupid. I know he doesn't need any distractions, but I shall be there if he needs me. He is going to find Lord Pembroke and defeat him. This will be the most important battle of his life, grandmama.'

Eleyne nodded again. 'I shan't prevent you going, Isobel. I'd have done the same in your place. Perhaps . . .' She paused. 'Perhaps if I had gone with Alexander to the Western Isles he would not have died. Who knows?' She gazed across the table, lost in a dream.

Isobel glanced up at her, still holding her grandmother's cold hands, then she followed the old woman's gaze and stared. A man was standing by the wall watching them: a tall, handsome man in his early fifties, his rich blue mantle caught on his shoulder by a gold brooch. His hair, red-gold and streaked with grey, was encircled by a golden coronet. She gasped. It was the same gold crown with which she had crowned Robert King of Scots. Her face white, Isobel scrambled to her feet. She was shaking.

Eleyne blinked several times, then she turned back to the young woman. One look at Isobel's face told her what she wanted to know. Alexander had been in the room. 'You saw him?' she whispered.

Isobel was staring at the place the man had been standing. For a moment he had remained, his eyes on hers, then he had faded from sight.

'Who was it?' Isobel gasped. She crossed herself quickly with a shaking hand.

So this child too could see him clearly. What else had she inherited, this great-grand-daughter of hers? Could she see the future too? Eleyne shivered. 'He is someone who blesses our cause, my dear. The man who once recognised Robert's grandfather as his heir.'

'King Alexander?' Isobel whispered. 'Oh, grandmama! He was wearing the crown – the crown I put on Robert's head.'

Eleyne sighed. Sweet Jesus, why could *she* not see him? Why would he not show himself to her? Was her belief not strong enough? All she had seen was a shadow; a patch of darkness against the wall.

'He wore that often. The Bishop of Glasgow kept it hidden when the wars started, to preserve it from Edward.' She pulled herself to her feet with a groan and groped for her stick. 'Isobel, my dear, I know I don't have to tell you to keep silent about what you have seen. There are people who have seen him – Kirsty is one of them – but he's my secret.' She forced herself to smile. 'I don't want panic to break out in the castle.'

'Even though he's here to give us hope?'

'Even though he supports us and will help us.' Leaning heavily on her stick, Eleyne went to Isobel and hugged her. 'Leave me now. Let me rest. We'll talk again later.' She moved painfully towards her chair. Then she stopped. 'Promise me one thing, my darling. Don't leave without saying goodbye.'

'I promise.'

Eleyne held back her tears until the door had closed, then she fell back in her chair, letting them roll freely down her cheeks. *Why won't you show yourself to me?* she murmured. *Oh Alexander, why?*

XIV

12 June 1306

It was ten days before the last group of men were mustered from the mountains and braes of Mar, and assembled in the courtyard at Kildrummy. The night before they were due to march south, towards Perth, Isobel came to say goodbye to Eleyne. 'We're leaving as soon as the first light touches the strath. Before the castle is awake. May I take your blessing to Robert?'

'Of course.' Eleyne touched the young woman's face.

'And . . . his . . . King Alexander's?'

'If you think it right. Robert should know that the shades of his ancestors are watching over him.'

'And you will pray for us. To your old gods.'

'To the one god and all the gods.' Eleyne smiled. 'Bless you, Isobel. Bring Robert some happiness. I shall take care of his family here, and we'll be waiting for him when his battles are won.'

XV

Robert did not let her remain with him, but it was many days before Isobel returned to Kildrummy. And when she did it was with news of a disaster. At the sight of the anxious faces awaiting her in the great hall, she dissolved into tears and they heard the story of Robert's defeat.

'He sent me away the night before the battle. Two of James Stewart's men were to escort me back here, but I made them turn back

800

to him. I couldn't leave him, I couldn't.' She began to cry again.

'What happened?' Eleyne asked at last in the silence of the great hall. She raised a thin beringed hand to her own shoulder, caressing it slightly, almost as though it covered someone else's hand.

As Isobel seemed unable to speak, one of the two men who had ridden back with her took up the story. 'They were defeated, my lady. Near Methven. Terribly defeated. The king's army was massacred. The survivors are scattered.'

'And my husband?' Elizabeth whispered.

'And Christopher?' Kirsty added, her face white.

The man shrugged. 'As far as we know the king wasn't injured. We met men from the battlefield, who said it was his own men who dragged him away in the end to save his life. I don't know about Sir Christopher, my lady. Most of the men we saw were from Lord Pembroke's army. They are everywhere, burning villages and farms, slaughtering the people they find.' He passed a weary hand across his face.

For a long time there was no more news. Nigel sent out scouts daily as the castle remained on full alert, the small garrison constantly at the ready for the sign of Lord Pembroke's army. But no one came and there was no news.

The days grew hotter as a blue, cloudless sky settled over Scotland, and Kildrummy was shrouded by a heat haze. The first sign that they had not been forgotten by the world came in the shape of a messenger wearing the Pembroke colours. One man alone, the scouts confirmed; there was no army behind him. He brought a letter for Elizabeth from her father, the Earl of Ulster. It informed her that as her husband's cause was lost she should return to England at once. If she did so, he would intercede with Edward for her. Reading the letter through twice, Elizabeth passed it to Nigel. 'My father says I should go to him, but my place is with Robert,' she said. 'Robert is my husband.' She eyed Isobel coldly. 'In spite of what you all think of me, I shall stand by him.'

Nigel looked up at her and she saw the admiration in his eyes. She gave a tight smile. 'I may not believe in what he has done. But I could not turn my back on him now,' she added.

The women spent most of their days in the solar in the Snow Tower. The tension was enormous. There was no more news as the sky turned from blue to copper in the heat. Isobel and Elizabeth avoided one another as best they could whilst Kirsty spent her time with her children and Marjorie in the nurseries. Finally another messenger found his way to Mar. Exhausted and badly injured, he had been sent by Neil Campbell, Mary Bruce's betrothed. He was well, as was Robert, but Sir Christopher Seton, Kirsty's husband, had been captured on the battlefield. No one knew what had happened to him.

Alone with the nurses and her children, Kirsty wept. Before the

801

other women she tried to keep a brave face, but in the nurseries her mask slipped. She had little hope that she would see Christopher again. How could fate deprive her so soon of two husbands, two men whom she had loved? She had barely got to know Christopher in the short time they had been married; she had borne him no children. But she loved him dearly.

Eleyne understood. She comforted the young woman, knowing her need to keep her grief secret, and knowing in her heart that Kirsty was right. She would never see her husband again.

XVI

July

One of her ladies shook Eleyne awake. The rainswept night was unusually dark. Eleyne sat up, confused. 'A messenger has arrived from King Robert, my lady,' the woman said. 'He is waiting in the hall. The other ladies and Sir Nigel are being called.'

Eleyne pushed her legs wearily from under the sheets, groping for her velvet slippers. Her heart was thumping with fear. Pulling on her bed gown, she allowed the woman to comb her hair quickly and knot it back with a piece of ribbon, then she grabbed her stick and began to make her painful way downstairs. The others were already in the great hall. The messenger was Gilbert of Annandale and with him were two companions. One had a blood-soaked bandage around his arm.

'The king and his men are hiding in the hills of Drumalban.' Gilbert looked round the hushed gathering, pitying the women with their tired anxious faces. He knew how frustrating it was to wait without news. Then for the news to be bad . . . 'He has decided that it would be best if you all joined him there.' He looked first to Nigel and then at Eleyne. 'The Earl of Pembroke is set on capturing the royal family and no quarter is to be given. I don't have to tell you the danger. The king feels he can give you more protection in the mountains to the west, where he has men and much support. We should set out at once.'

Eleyne saw Nigel's face light up with excitement. 'At last! I have been a nursemaid too long!' he burst out. Then he glanced embarrassed at Elizabeth and then at Eleyne. 'Forgive me, I didn't mean . . . it's just that I want to be with Robert! I want to see some fighting!'

Gilbert gave a grim smile. 'You'll see fighting soon enough, Sir Nigel, have no fear,' he said. 'More than you want, no doubt.'

XVII

It did not take long for the women to pack their belongings. They were all as eager as the king's brother to end their self-imposed imprisonment and ride as fast as possible to be with Robert. Only Eleyne did not prepare.

She cornered Kirsty in the nurseries. 'Leave the children here with me, my dear. Donald's place is at Kildrummy and they will be safe here. Poor little Marjorie must go to her father, but small children and old ladies would only add to Robert's worries.' She smiled wryly. 'It's a terrible thing to say, but once you've all gone Kildrummy will no longer be in danger.'

Kirsty started to protest, then she looked down at the sleeping children and nodded. 'You're right. They'll be safe with you.' She hugged Eleyne and then she turned away, not trusting herself even to kiss them goodbye.

Nigel demurred when he heard Eleyne had resolved to stay. 'I'm not sure you're right, Lady Eleyne. I am sure the children will be safe but for some reason King Edward harbours grudges towards you. I think Robert would want you with us.'

Eleyne patted him on the arm. 'Bless you, my boy. It's nice to think that I'm important. But I'm too old to ride with you. I'll be all right. No one is interested in an old woman. You go, and God go with you.'

When they had ridden out of sight, she gave the order for the gates to be closed. Then she walked into the chapel. Only the small lamp burning in the sanctuary, and the faintest light from the sky at the east window, lit the blackness. She went to the altar and stood gazing up at the crucifix which hung there, its soft silver carving gleaming.

It was a long time before she realised that she was no longer alone. *You can watch over them*, she pleaded silently. *You can go with them. Please help them.*

He was standing near her. She could feel his presence and his pain. Did he understand her agony and her frustration, the despair of being locked inside the frail body of an old woman when her spirit wanted to ride the wind, to fight, to be beside the king when at last he came into his own?

She opened her eyes. There was no one there. Just the empty chapel, lighter now as the dawn began to colour the east window, its tall narrow lancets inset with stained glass. She was leaning with both hands on the handle of her stick. There were no prayers in her heart. Nothing. She could not marshal her thoughts. She wanted to rest her head on his shoulder, feel his arms around her, comforting and supporting her. She wanted someone to look after her and take away the misery and the fear which overwhelmed her. But already he had gone and she was again alone.

CHAPTER THIRTY-THREE

I

July 1306

T he dream had returned. The ground was slimy with blood; horses were screaming; men were dying beneath their hooves. In the mist she could see little save the gleam of swords and axes as they cut through bone and fell to the wet mud. Somewhere in the thick of the battle she saw the scarlet lion flag fall to the ground, where it was trampled until it disappeared from sight. Then came the flames: the roar of fire, the howl of the storm which would wake her. Each time Bethoc or one of the others soothed her, making her chamomile tea and sitting with her until she slept again. Each time left her weaker.

Gritting her teeth, she forced herself to walk the castle walls, staring down the strath into the heat haze, seeing the summer lightning flash around the hills. Several times she ordered a fire lit in spite of the heat and she sat gazing into the embers trying to see. But no pictures came to order. Nothing came save an increasing feeling of impending doom.

The scouts saw the straggling group of riders as soon as they appeared on the track from the west. Long before they could identify them Eleyne had ordered the great gates open. She was waiting for them in the courtyard when they arrived.

The party was larger this time. Nigel Bruce was accompanied by John Atholl and several men as well as the queen, the king's sisters, little Marjorie and Isobel. All were exhausted and bedraggled, their clothes torn and filthy. Half their horses were lame.

Eleyne watched as the riders dismounted, then she moved to Isobel's side and kissed the girl tenderly. 'Thank God you are safe. I had such terrible dreams. Where is Robert?'

Isobel shrugged, tears streaming down her face. It was Nigel who told Eleyne of the second terrible defeat of Robert's hastily reconstituted army in the mountains beyond Strathfillan and of the king's decision that he could not after all keep his loved ones safe. 'He is hoping to lead the enemy away into the far west. He wants you to give us your hospitality again and to keep the ladies here after all.' He grimaced wearily. 'Either he will join us, or he will go to Ireland. He thinks it might be best if we go on from here and try and reach Norway, but I'm damned if I'll leave Scotland now.'

'Poor Nigel – a nursemaid for the second time.' Eleyne pressed his arm sympathetically. 'Stay here, you'll be safe at Kildrummy.'

The travellers recovered slowly and they settled once more into the steady routine of castle life. Each in their own way was under enormous strain, but they all tried to hide it. Only Isobel, growing daily thinner, the dark circles under her eyes becoming more and more marked, found it impossible to hide her grief, but even she spoke seldom of Robert, trying to follow the queen's example and put on a brave face as time passed and there was still no news.

The long dreary days were filled with chores, with spinning and embroidery, playing with the children and then at last with the harvest.

The harvest was good. The granaries were filled to overflowing and rather than use the outlying granges Eleyne ordered the superfluous grain to be stored within the castle itself, in the towers, against the walls and even in the great hall. There was now only the smallest garrison at Kildrummy, but the old men and the boys all helped the women of the township bring in the corn and side by side with them worked the king's family. Even Eleyne herself went into the fields, sitting in the shade of the hedgerows, a man's broad-brimmed hat over her veil to protect her from the sun, watching the younger people work amongst the splashed scarlet of late poppies.

There was no more news from Drumalban. The king had vanished into the haze.

II

September 1306

It was afternoon and Eleyne was playing chess with the queen when John Atholl burst into the solar. 'I'm afraid our idyll is at an end,' he said grimly. His face was white and strained. 'The English army has been sighted heading into Mar.'

Elizabeth and Eleyne looked at him in horror. For a moment none of them spoke. Then the silence was broken by a sharp crack as the ivory piece in Elizabeth's hand snapped between her tightly clasped fingers. It was her queen. The eyes of every person in the room were on the splintered pieces as she dropped them on the table.

A meeting was called at once in the great hall.

'How far away are they?' Nigel asked.

'Perhaps a day's ride. Their outriders are moving fast. Too fast.' John Atholl's face was bleak. 'And they march here under the banner of the Prince of Wales.' He glanced up as he heard Eleyne catch her breath. 'We cannot stay here. We must go on. We have to save the women at all cost. We must take them north and try to reach Norway. We'll be safe there with Nigel's sister, the Queen of Norway.'

They were all in a state of shock. Kildrummy's size and power had lulled them into a feeling of security. Its position in the north had made it seem unlikely that the English armies would attack them. They had felt safe there.

John Atholl looked at the queen. 'We can't abandon Kildrummy; we have to hold it for Robert. But we must get you ladies away to safety in case the worst happens.' He looked back at Nigel who had seated himself gloomily on one of the piled sacks of barley. 'How can we do it?'

Nigel stood up. 'What do you say, shall we toss for it, John? One of us will go with the ladies, and one of us will stay and hold the castle for Robert.'

Nigel lost the toss. It was he who must stay. He gave Eleyne a gallant bow, trying hard to hide his disappointment. 'It's my job to hold the castle for its earl and I shall stay. But this time you should go.'

Eleyne shook her head. 'My mind has not changed, Nigel. I intend to stay here. I am too old to excite Edward any more. It's the king's immediate family he wants. I shall stay here and take care of the children. Kildrummy will hold out for months if necessary. Edward of Caernarfon –' she pronounced it the Welsh way, her tongue accentuating the word which had once been so familiar – 'will grow bored with besieging us long before we run out of food. And our well runs deep and pure. We will hold out until doomsday.'

They were ready to leave as soon as darkness fell. Eleyne made her way out into the courtyard, lit by a dozen spluttering torches. It was crowded with people as the townsfolk and crofters made their way in to the safety of the castle's great walls, driving their animals with them, knowing full well that when they eventually came out again, their homes and fields would have been burned.

Lord Atholl's small band – two of his best men, their wounds healed, and the women – was ready, wrapped in black cloaks which would give them some cover in the dark, and leading Eleyne's last horses, those which remained after the men had gone to join Robert's standard. Nearby the blacksmith, Hal Osborne, stood scowling. He had demanded to go with them, but Nigel had refused. 'With your damaged leg you'll slow them down, man. You're more use to us here,' he commanded brusquely. 'We need weapons and we need some strong men to man the walls.'

When the last man was inside the great gates, they heard the grating of the portcullis as it came down and the squeak of wood on metal as the drawbridge was raised and the gates were closed for the last time.

The only way into or out of the castle now was by the postern gate which led directly into the back den.

There was a hush in the courtyard, broken only by the stamping of the horses and the hiss of the resin-burning torches. Eleyne looked round, trying to hide the sudden fear which had made her heart thump unsteadily beneath her ribs, the desperate urge to change her mind, to go with them, to escape from this great castle which had been her home for so long, but was now a trap. Her hand went to the pendant at her breast. Forcing herself to smile, she stepped forward. One by one she kissed the women who were leaving, giving Kirsty and Isobel special long hugs which left all of them near tears. Then she took John Atholl's hand. 'Take care of them, John, they are all very precious people.' She dropped her voice so that Kirsty could not hear. 'I thank God daily that your Marjorie is safe and far away with the children. At least that's one thing you needn't worry about.'

Bending, he kissed her. 'You'll be safe too. My bet is that they will besiege you for a few weeks then grow bored when they realise the castle is impregnable. The Prince of Wales is not one to sit around doing nothing all day. He'll crave glory, especially if his father starts to chase him for results. Be patient, mama-in-law, and keep your courage up.'

'I shall, John. Don't give us a thought. You concentrate on saving yourselves. Now go; before the clouds clear and the moon gives you away.'

She followed them to the postern and stood back as one by one the party led their horses through it and down the zigzag path into the deep ravine. As soon as the last man was through, the door was pushed shut and the bars dropped into place; behind it the small postern portcullis was lowered for the last time. Kildrummy was sealed.

III

Eleyne had retired to her solar after they had gone. She looked at the empty hearth, tempted to order a page to call for logs. Then she remembered: firewood and peats too must be conserved. If the siege lasted more than a few weeks – if it ran on for months – they would be glad of heat when the nights grew really cold. Huddled in a fur to keep her old bones warm against the chill of the September dark, she stood at the window which looked down across the broad strath. The candlelight turned the thick glass opaque with shadows; she could see nothing beyond the window and after a while she turned away.

The lookouts on the walls could see little either. The attack when it came took the whole castle by surprise. The shouts, the rain of arrows, the thundering upon the gates and the first hurled missiles from hastily erected siege engines bouncing harmlessly from the great walls, began almost exactly at midnight and went on for several hours. No one within the castle was hurt. From the walls the archers shot back at the enemy and hurled the first of their stockpiled rocks. Some fired flaming arrows to start a few harmless scrub fires in the dry grass and several found their mark, judging from the screams below. By dawn the enemy had pulled back to a safe distance.

All the next day they watched the besieging army moving into place around the castle, erecting tents and pavilions, dragging more and more siege engines into place and digging defensive ramparts behind which their archers could stand. Eleyne went up on to the battlements after mass and stood beside Nigel looking down through the arrow loops at the activity below. 'I can't believe it,' she murmured. 'Not here. Not Kildrummy. This place has always been so safe.'

'And it will remain safe.' Nigel put his arm around her shoulder.

'Do you think the others got away?' Eleyne peered towards the distant peak of Tap o'Noth and the hills to the north.

'Of course they did. John Atholl would never let anything happen to them. You know that as well as I do. Besides,' Nigel shrugged, 'being totally realistic, we both know that, if they had been captured, young Edward there would not be able to resist letting us know. John's head would be on a pole outside his tent by now.' He shuddered. They both stared down at the largest pavilion which marked the prince's base. Above it, on the huge banner, the three Plantagenet leopards ramped merrily across their scarlet field in the wind. It was twice the size of that of the Earl of Pembroke with its bars and birds, which flew beside it.

Once the siege was under way and the inhabitants of the castle had become used to the sinister presence beyond their walls, the days settled down to a routine once more. Food was carefully rationed, and the storerooms locked, though so much food filled the castle that much of it was openly available to those who wanted it. But there was good discipline amongst the people. Conscientiously they regulated themselves and obeyed the rules which Eleyne and Nigel had drawn up.

After the first onslaught, it was several days before the siege weapons were in use and a sense of almost peaceful anticipation filled the men and women in the castle. It did not last long. As the huge ballistas and trebuchets swung into action, hurling massive missiles at and across the walls, they had their first casualties. Two men from the Garioch died as they crossed the open courtyard. Roofs within the curtain walls collapsed; chunks of masonry flew from the massive walls and the walls of the chapel and the great hall both sustained hits which cracked the stone. After that people became more cautious.

A week later Prince Edward sent the first of many messengers to the castle gate under a white flag of truce to negotiate with Nigel and, they soon discovered, to try to establish if the Queen and Princess of Scotland were still at Kildrummy.

The castle flew two banners. The royal lion of Scotland and the cross-crosslets of Mar. On his first visit the messenger, Sir John Appleby, found out nothing save that they were well stocked with grain, and that Sir Nigel Bruce and the dowager Countess of Mar at least were there behind the granite walls and that they were confident and defiant.

On his second visit, three weeks later, he had another mission besides his message for Sir Nigel. As he walked across the courtyard beneath his white flag, his eyes were everywhere, scanning the faces of the men and women who stared at him from the shelter of the outbuildings. They were looking to see if the rumour that Englishmen had tails was true. He was looking for signs of a different kind: rebellion, frustration, avarice – the bag of jingling coins openly bouncing at his belt might possibly speak to one of the people who were watching him now.

Carefully trained by King Edward's negotiators, the messenger looked to left and right, scrutinising the faces around him, and as he left the castle, ostensibly disappointed by his defiant reception, he smiled. He reckoned he had spotted his man.

IV

September

The dream came again. Not the battle, but the fire. Eleyne woke sobbing, to find Bethoc shaking her. 'My lady, please, what is it?' The woman was frightened.

Eleyne felt her pillows damp with her tears. The dream had gone. Elusive as a shadow, it had been there at the edge of her consciousness, then it had vanished into blackness. She stared across the room, lit only by the one tallow candle, and frowned. 'The fire is out.'

'It hasn't been lit for weeks, my lady,' Bethoc said gently. 'Only the cooking fires are lit and those only during the day.'

'Of course, I had forgotten.' Eleyne closed her eyes. 'Is it nearly dawn?'

'Near enough, my lady.' Bethoc glanced towards the window. The glow outside came from the great fires which burned all night in the camp around their walls, openly defying the cold darkness of the castle in the first rawness of autumn.

Bethoc tucked the covers around Eleyne once more and crawled back into her own bed, shivering. In minutes she was asleep.

Eleyne lay looking up at the grey shadows on the ceiling as imperceptibly it grew lighter. Without realising it, her hand had gone to the phoenix lying over her thin, bony chest. The enamel was warm, vibrant between her fingers; his hands, when they touched her shoulder, were gentle and persuasive, soothing her pounding heart, stroking away her fear, making her forget her aged, treacherous body. Beneath the warm covers of her bed, she began to smile.

V

Edward of Caernarfon was sitting in his pavilion when Sir John Appleby returned to the camp. At twenty-two, Edward was tall, cool, uninvolved, like his father in many ways, and yet different – a paler, weaker version. Always there was that soft centre, that lack of resolution, which meant he would never be the king his father was. It showed even now amongst his men. He sat back on his stool and looked at Sir John's face. One glance told him what he wanted to know, and he threw down his quill. 'You found someone?' He stretched his legs in front of him with a groan. He was bored with the siege; he wanted quick results. And glory.

Sir John nodded. He bowed formally, then took the stool Prince Edward indicated and drew it forward. Above their heads, the sun threw dappled shadows on to the canvas of the pavilion. He could smell the crushed grass beneath the floor coverings. Outside, the brazier burned merrily; a page was feeding twigs into the flames. 'Yes, sire, I think I've found my man. Strong, but disabled. Frustrated; angry and resentful. I saw his eye follow me, and I saw it linger a long time on the gates as they opened for me. My bet is that he noticed my purse and he'd sell his own grandmother for it.'

Edward smiled. 'Good.' He picked up his pen again and tapped it on the folding table where he was sitting. 'This siege begins to bore me. The sooner it's over, the sooner I'll be pleased. Did you see the Bruce's family?'

'I spoke to Sir Nigel. They're there all right.'

'But did you see them?' Edward's eyes narrowed.

'No one but Sir Nigel and the Countess of Mar. The old girl looked daggers at me.' He shivered. 'I wouldn't like to be the one to put chains on her. Quite a nest of vipers we have holed up here, my lord. Once you have them the Bruce will be hamstrung. Wife, mistress, child! What a gift for the king, your father!'

'What a gift indeed.' Edward stood up and strode to the tent's doorway. He stood gazing at the curtain wall of the castle, so high and thick his siege engines could make no impression on them. Kildrummy would never fall to them. He smiled cynically. Those walls and that gatehouse had been reconstructed under his father's orders at the direction of Master James of St George. They were impregnable! He gave an ironic little laugh. Then his face sobered. Only treachery would bring Kildrummy to its knees.

VI

Sir Nigel spent a great deal of time now in the solar in the Snow Tower. He had grown fond of Eleyne and they talked and played chess and backgammon to while away the long hours when he was not patrolling the walls and supervising weapons practice amongst his few men. It was hard to keep morale high; harder to keep them from the boredom which would miss the scaling ladder in the dark. Women as well as men were being trained to use any weapons which came to hand and to take their turn on the walls.

'What will happen, Nigel?' Eleyne had put down her sewing. Her eyes tired easily now. She rubbed them and blinked. Even on the sunniest days, and with the window glass removed to give light – and so that the lead could be melted down to make shot for their catapults – she found it harder to place the intricate stitches.

He shrugged. 'Prince Edward looks set for a long siege.'

'Through the winter?'

'I suspect so. He can only guess how much food we have here, but he knows we can last a long, long time. No doubt we'll have more proposals for terms of surrender soon.'

Eleyne shuddered. 'Sir John made it clear there would be little quarter given.' He had promised the women their lives, no more. And he had promised to return for their reply. 'I suspect that quarter would be withdrawn when he found there was no one here he wanted but you and me.' She smiled grimly. 'I would be a grave disappointment to my dear cousin, who's hoping for far more exotic pickings.'

Nigel was silent for a while, then he sat down opposite her. He leaned forward and picked up her embroidery. She had stitched a bird into the linen. An eagle? An osprey? It looked as though it were sitting in a nest of fire. 'You, of all of us, have the most royal blood, you know,' he said with a laugh.

'And Edward cannot wait to shed it.' Eleyne took the sewing from him and tucked it neatly into her sewing basket. She sighed. 'How strange. I was once so sure that my royal blood would bring me to a throne and now it looks as though it will bring me to my death.'

That night she dreamed again. This time the dream was triumphant. She saw Robert crowned; she saw Elizabeth and Isobel at his side and Marjorie tall and radiant, and at her side another child – a son; a prince for Scotland. She lay awake a long time thinking about it the next morning as, slowly, the chamber grew light. Had she dreamed truly or was the dream just the form of her longings? She could still see in her mind the faces of the men and women who had walked through the bright halls, and the boy – Elizabeth's son – the son who would take away her grand-daughter's right to the crown, and the chance of her own blood succeeding, ever, to the throne of Scotland.

It was several minutes before she felt a hand on her shoulder gently caressing her beneath the silk coverlet. She smiled and relaxed back on to the pillows, looking up at the hangings above her head as a stray beam of sunlight reflected into the narrow east window. *'Can you see what will happen, my dear?'* she whispered out loud. *'Will Robert win? Will he come to our rescue?'* Slowly she sat up. That was it! That was what the dream meant. Robert was on his way. He was coming to rescue them. He had regrouped his men.

For the first time in weeks she felt a small ray of hope and it acted as a tonic to her stiff bones. Climbing from her bed, she picked up the bell and rang it for Bethoc, then she walked to the window, without the aid of her stick, and looked down the strath. A fresh wind was blowing and she could see the royal banner above Edward's tent rippling merrily on its tall staff. There was little activity in the camp of their enemy. She could see the cooking fires, newly built, with smoking cauldrons of something hot suspended over them. Her stomach growled with hunger. She shook her head. They had enough to eat, and she of all the men and women in the castle needed least to sustain her old bones.

Bethoc entered the room and stood looking at her mistress's back, silhouetted in the window. In the bright red-gold rays of the rising sun, her hair, hanging down over her shoulders in a wild tangle, looked deep auburn again; her figure straight and girlish, the slim active figure of a young woman, up early to run down the long winding staircase and jump on her horse to ride in the bright cold dawn.

The face Eleyne turned to her faithful waiting woman was radiant. 'I dreamed we were going to win, Bethoc. I dreamed King Robert is on his way to save us.'

'Oh, my lady!' Bethoc had complete faith in Eleyne's predictions. 'Oh my lady, thank the Blessed Virgin! And the queen and her ladies got away? I knew they had! But it's not easy, not knowing for sure.'

'They got away. They are safe. All of them. And the queen will have a son.'

Neither of them doubted for a moment that her dream was true.

By the time those in the castle who were not needed to defend the walls were assembled in the great hall for their breakfast of oat cakes and ale, the entire garrison knew of the countess's dream. The effect on morale was astounding. Faces which had been weary and depressed were full of smiles. There was a spring in the step of the men on the walls and their taunts, hurled at the besiegers below, had a new defiance which was not lost on the men in Edward's camp.

At midday the prince sent for Sir John. 'I want you back in that castle. Find out what has made them so confident suddenly. And bring me the name of the man who will get us in there.'

Sir John was ready within the hour with his standard bearer and the white flag of truce. And he was ready with his message. As the small passdoor in the great gates opened, he ushered his standard bearer in ahead of him and followed, stooping stiffly in his mail. In the court-yard he paused. The countess's aged steward was there once more to greet him. There were a dozen or so men and women busy about their activities and on the walls the usual quota of armed men, looking outward, uninterested in the enemy's envoy. Sir John missed nothing: the corn was piled high still − enough for several months if properly rationed; there were no signs of distress. He could see the heaps of stones and lead balls for the catapults. The castle was ordered and calm.

Sir Nigel met him once more in the great hall. This time he was alone. There was no sign of the Countess of Mar.

Sir John bowed stiffly. 'Have you given thought to my offer? If the castle surrenders, we will spare the lives of the ladies and children.' He had seen a small child playing near the smithy in the courtyard.

'And the men of the garrison?' Nigel looked him in the eye.

Sir John looked uncomfortable. 'That is for the king to decide.'

'Not a reassuring thought.' Nigel grinned at him amiably. 'And one which thankfully I do not have to contemplate. The end of the siege is indeed at hand. Our information is that a large army is on its way with our relief in view.'

Sir John gaped at him. 'A large army? Whose army, sir?' He laughed, an unexpected bark of humour which rang around the hall.

'My brother's army,' Nigel said quietly. 'And with my brother are the ladies who give him so much support, his queen, his daughter, the Countess of Buchan.'

'But they are here . . .'

'No.' The quiet certainty with which Nigel spoke brought Sir John's blustered denial to an abrupt halt. There was a moment's silence.

Sir John narrowed his eyes. 'If that is true, sir, God help you and Lady Mar when the king finds out. Your lives won't be worth that!' He snapped his fingers under Nigel's nose. 'For pity's sake, give in, man. Your life may be forfeit, but won't you think about that old woman? Are you prepared to see her dragged to London in chains? Do you think King Edward would spare her anything?'

Following the sudden change of direction of Nigel's eyes, he swung round and found himself facing Eleyne who had entered the hall as he spoke. She bowed to him coldly. 'I am grateful for your concern for my welfare, Sir John, but I am confident it's not necessary. I have no intention of allowing Edward the satisfaction of having me as his prisoner. Kildrummy will soon be free. And if the man who dares to call himself Prince of Wales wants to save his skin, I suggest he raises this siege and returns to England as soon as he possibly can.'

Sir John scowled. 'And just what makes you think this great army is on its way to help you?' His voice was full of sarcasm. 'You've had a message from them, I suppose?'

'Yes.' Eleyne smiled serenely. 'We've had a message.'

'That's not possible. No one could get in or out of this place. It's sealed as tight as a drum of butter.' Sir John fingered the empty scabbard which hung at his sword belt. His weapon, according to the conventions of the flag of truce, had been left behind in his tent.

Neither Nigel nor Eleyne spoke, but both looked too sure, too pleased with themselves. For the first time he had a real qualm of doubt. 'Very well, I can see you're not going to listen to reason. On your own heads be it.' He bowed curtly, first to Eleyne then to Nigel, and turned on his heel.

He walked slowly through the hall, his eyes darting here and there in the crowd of staring men and women: villagers, crofters, servants, a few of the castle garrison, resting between spells of duty. Perhaps he had miscalculated. His man was not there. But then he saw him, lounging near the door, his leather apron stained. He was chewing a stem of straw.

Sir John stopped and deliberately caught the man's eye. Then he turned, addressing the whole hall. 'The man who burns this place to the ground and delivers Kildrummy Castle to the King of England will win the safety of his wife and children and a bag of gold so large he cannot carry it away!' His ringing tones carried the length of the great hall.

From the dais Nigel roared back: 'There isn't a man in this castle who would take up your offer, Sir John. Don't waste your breath, my friend. Go back to your camp and keep your gold!' A subdued murmur of support came from the hall around them.

Sir John bowed silent acknowledgement of Nigel's words and turned on his heel.

'Did he really think any of our people would betray us?' Eleyne was tight-lipped with anger as she gripped the handle of her walking stick. 'Foolish man.'

'He's desperate. Edward of Caernarfon won't like the news that his mission has failed, or the titbit about the imminent arrival of Robert's army.' Nigel stopped. 'I suppose . . . No, no, of course there's no doubt. He is on his way.'

She smiled at him serenely. 'There is no doubt, Nigel. Trust me.'

VII

Hal Osborne was standing at the entrance to his smithy. The fire was
out, the bellows silent. His small sons were playing in the dust on the
floor. The eldest, Ned, was old enough to work those bellows for short
periods, heating his father's roaring furnace to white heat. If the castle
fell, the men would die. Ned might die. He was old enough for a man's
work; he was old enough to use a catapult; perhaps he was old enough
for a man's death.

He looked sourly across the courtyard, where Sir Nigel Bruce was
talking to one of the men-at-arms near the bakehouse. But for Bruce
he would have gone with the queen, and if it wasn't for the countess's
ill-tempered horse, his leg would be whole. Christ and all his devils
curse them both to hell! He could have gone. It was her fault he was
here, her fault that if the castle fell, he would die. What loyalty did he
owe her? He folded his arms, his eyes going back to the two boys as
they scuffled in the dust. None. What chance was there of the siege
being lifted? None.

And think of the gold.

VIII

Eleyne was already undressed, wrapped in her bed gown, when Nigel
was ushered into her bedchamber by Bethoc, who poured them each
a goblet of spiced wine and then left them alone. He sat down opposite
her and cradled the hot goblet between his hands. 'Can you summon
your visions at will?' he began without preamble.

Eleyne stared down at the empty hearth. 'Sometimes.' She gave an
involuntary shiver.

'Could you do it now?'

She didn't answer for a long time. 'Perhaps. I need fire.'

'Fire?' He looked at the single candle burning on the table near
them.

'Fire. I see the pictures in the flames; in the embers. There are
things I can sprinkle on the flames which help; dried herbs. What do
you want to know?'

'I need to know how long.' He stood up in a sudden lithe movement, nervy as a cat, and began to pace the floor. 'I have a bad feeling
here.' He thumped his chest. 'Something is wrong.'

'With the castle?'

'I don't know, I'm just worried. Supposing they don't come! Supposing your dream was just that – a dream?' He rubbed his cheek with

the flat of his hand. 'Supposing Kirsty and the others didn't make it. Supposing Robert decided to leave Scotland and go to Ireland for a while. Supposing we are alone!'

'You can suppose any number of things, my dear,' Eleyne said gently. 'We all have our nightmares as well as our dreams.' She took a sip from her drink. 'Did you check the night guard?'

He nodded. 'They'll change when the chapel bell rings.' He resumed his pacing. 'If I were to have a small fire made up here – we can say it's because of your age and aching bones –' He gave her a mischievous look, gone as soon as it had come to be replaced by a look of infinite weariness. 'Would you consider looking into it for me?'

'Of course I will. But I can promise nothing. I'll go down to the stillroom and find the right herbs.' She was groping for her stick when she sat back in her chair, her head cocked to one side, listening.

'What is it?' He was watching her tensely.

'I thought I heard something. A horn . . .'

He was at the window in two strides, leaning out, staring down the glen. The silence in the room was intense. Then he turned back to her, disappointment clear on his face. 'I can see nothing.'

'He will come,' Eleyne said firmly.

IX

In the silence of the stillroom she peered around, her candle held high. The room was so full of memories; so many deaths: Donald, Gratney, William, Elizabeth, Muriel; so many illnesses cured: childhood snuffles and croups, broken bones, earaches and headaches and wounds. So many visions, conjured from the flames with the aid of mugwort and apple and ash and rosemary and lavender and thyme. The air was heavy with the fragrance of dried herbs, the beams hanging with this year's crop. Taking a small linen bag from the hook beneath the high workbench, she went deftly from jar to jar collecting what she needed. Then she blew out the candle.

As she did every evening, she stopped in the nursery to say good-night to her grandchildren. They were asleep together, bathed and in clean nightgowns, two small dark heads on the pillow. She stood looking down at them, smiling, then stiffly she bent to kiss each one in turn. 'Sweet Bride keep you safe.' Her knuckles were white on the handle of her stick, and suddenly her eyes were full of tears.

The castle was silent. On the walls the watch patrolled up and down, their eyes ever straining for a sign of siege ladders or engines being pushed closer under cover of darkness. In the smithy Hal Osborne leaned against the wall, chewing a stalk of barley between his teeth. His leg ached unbearably. Beyond him, in the back of the small heather-thatched building which was his home and place of work, his wife and two children slept on their straw pallets. She was a local girl, from a farm beyond the village. One day it would be his and then it would be his sons'. His chest tightened with love as he listened to the small snoring sounds his younger son made as he slept, his throat clogged by mucus. If the castle was taken that child would die, both his children would die, and his wife too, after she had been raped a dozen times.

Unless.

Silently he stood up. The English envoy had made the position clear. There was money and safety waiting for the man who gave Kildrummy Castle to the English.

On silent feet he walked across the courtyard, feeling the cold cut of the wind from the hills. The place was deserted. He made his way across to the bakehouse, where the ovens were already heating to bake the morning's bread. Only one woman was there, sleepily feeding firewood to the blaze. Behind her the long trays of barley loaves lay on a table, proving beneath their linen cloths. Her face lightened when she saw Hal. 'It's early, my friend. If you've come for breakfast you're too soon.' Her arms were still floury; but there were smears of soot across her apron.

He eyed her for a moment, wondering what would happen to her. She was a cheerful motherly soul; at least four children played round her skirts when she was away from her duties in the kitchen. He remembered her. She wasn't part of the castle household. She was the baker's wife from Mossat. He could see the signs of the siege on her face – the drawn lines around her mouth, the black circles beneath her eyes, the thinness of her arms. Her husband had taken his bow and his sword and gone at the very beginning with the first muster of men.

For a moment he hesitated.

'Out of my way.' She bustled around him busily. 'I've no one to help this morning. If you've nothing to do but stand around like a gowk, you can help me put the bread in the ovens. The castle will be awake at first light.'

He shook his head slowly. 'I've duties to perform, mistress. I need a light for my lantern.' He produced the horn lantern which used to hang above the door of the smithy in the hours of darkness.

She tossed her head. 'Take it then, and get out of my way.' Already she had turned away to her loaves.

He took a spill and thrust it into the fire. The tallow candle in the lantern lit easily, burning with a feeble flickering flame which stank immediately of rancid meat as, carefully, he shut the transparent horn door. He grinned at her uncomfortably. He wanted to say something, something to prepare her, but there was nothing he could say. He

817

turned away and vanished into the pre-dawn dark. Within seconds she had forgotten that he had been there.

The great hall, the mekill hall, the people of Kildrummy called it, was virtually empty when he pushed the door ajar and slipped into the smoky darkness. A few figures slept on straw pallets around the hearth, but there was no fire there. The smoke in the air was an echo from long-dead fires trapped in the cold air below the high vaulted roof.

The lantern light was too faint to light much more than a foot or two around him. Silently he crept towards the largest pile of sacks. There was barley, oats, a little wheat for the countess's table and stacked straw sheaves, bound into bales and piled into heaps which reached higher than a man. He glanced round. No one was awake. No one had seen him.

Slipping behind one of the piles he opened the door of the lantern. Pulling a handful of straw from one of the sheaves, he thrust it inside and held it above the candle. In seconds it had caught. It burned with a fierce crackle in the silence, but still no one had awakened. With fear catching at his throat, he swiftly drew the burning straw across the base of the nearest pile of sheaves, seeing the sparks catching in a bright trail. Hurrying now, he turned to another pile then another and another, hearing the crackle behind him growing louder. A murmur came from the far side of the hall and he heard a sudden shout. Hurling his lantern high into the pile of stacked sacks, he turned and dived for the door. Coughing, his eyes streaming from the acrid smoke, he ran silently down the side of the hall and dived through the darkness to his smithy. Running inside he stooped and shook his wife awake. 'Bring the children! Hurry! We're getting out of here.'

'What is it? What's happened?' Sleepily she sat up, then in the open doorway she saw the first glow of fire. 'What is it, Hal? What's happened?'

'The castle is being attacked,' he said grimly, 'but you and I will be safe. Come quickly. Follow me.' He snatched up the sleepy boy and ran for the doorway.

The first tocsin began to ring as he stepped out into the courtyard and he could hear angry, frightened shouts from the watch. Someone ran across in front of him, a bucket in each hand from the deep well in the base of the Snow Tower – he could see the water slopping uselessly on to the dry cobbles.

He ran swiftly towards the gatehouse, his son clutched in his arms. Behind him he could smell the smoke now, and hear the crackle of the fire as the vast stockpile of grain and fodder in the hall caught. The noise was growing louder – turning into a dull roar.

Beside him a man appeared: the watch from the gatehouse tower. He was running towards the hall, shouting. He passed so close, Hal could have reached out and touched him, then he was gone, plunging into the smoke which billowed from the double doors of the great hall, leaving his post unmanned.

Hal smiled grimly. Putting the child down, he felt his way along the wall to the narrow stairway which led up into the winding chamber. There the windlass stood which raised the portcullis. Normally it took several men to work it, but his desperation gave him the strength of several men. Spitting on his calloused palms, he braced himself against the bar and began to push, his muscles straining and bulging. For a long moment nothing happened, then there was a groan from the pulley which led to the heavy counterweights in the ceiling. Sweat poured off him. He shut his eyes and pushed harder, hearing from below the lost wail of the little boy, waiting in the dark, and the terrified voice of his wife comforting him as they hid in the shadows. The sound gave him strength. Another superhuman shove and the windlass began to turn. Outside, beneath the gatehouse, slowly the portcullis began to rise. When it was only halfway up he knocked in the oak wedge and, his muscles screaming with agony, threw himself back down the stairs. Ducking under the ominously hanging spikes of the portcullis he reached the iron-studded gates and felt along them until he touched the passdoor with its triple bars. It was pitch-black in the shadow of the gatehouse. Gritting his teeth he heaved at the first bar. It was jammed. He pulled harder and at last it slid from its slots and fell to the ground. The second was easier, and the third. Grasping the heavy ring handle, he turned it and pulled the door open. Beyond it, the black barrier of the raised drawbridge barred the way.

He could hear Ned crying, the boy's thin wail a lonely frightened sound beneath the echoing arch of the gateway. Ignoring the cry grimly, Hal threw himself at the wheel which controlled the drawbridge. It was wedged by a pin; he needed something to strike it free. Desperately he groped around. But there was nothing there.

Behind him there was a deafening crash. Part of the roof of the great hall had fallen in. The flames which shot up into the sky roared like demons in the night. For a fraction of a second he stopped and turned to stare, awed by what he had done. Then his eye was caught by the glint of steel in the light of the flames, and he saw the rack of axes on the wall near the watchman's door. Seizing one, he swung it in his powerful arms and struck out the pin in one swift stroke. With a rumble and creak, the drawbridge began to fall on its counterweights as the first ladders were thrown up against the undefended walls by the enemy outside.

X

Standing in front of his tent, Prince Edward watched with folded arms, his eyes squinting in the darkness as the flames poured upwards, clearly visible above the curtain walls. It was only minutes since the fire had been noticed, but already the highly trained teams of men had run forward to take advantage of the distraction and run the siege towers forward. Beside them ladders were thrown up and already they swarmed with men. There was no opposition. He could already see Englishmen on the battlements when the drawbridge began to fall.

He turned to Sir John who stood beside him, barely suppressing his excitement. 'So. Your bait was taken.' Both men watched as a figure appeared at the far end of the bridge – a man, with a child in his arms.

Edward smiled. 'Your man, I suspect, Sir John, come to claim his reward!'

XI

Eleyne had spent an hour staring into the fire which burned in her hearth. The acrid scent of the herbs still hung in the air. The visions had come. She had seen Robert wearing his crown; she had seen him with his son. She had seen little Marjorie as a grown woman with a child of her own in her arms and she had wept for joy. Then the pictures had changed. She had seen blood; she had heard the clash of steel. She had seen iron bars in the embers, and behind them a succession of faces, hands reaching out in supplication, and she had felt herself grow cold as death. She wept again.

Bethoc had tiptoed into the room. Silently the woman had wrapped a shawl around her mistress's shoulders as she sat staring into the glowing peats. Eleyne did not notice. There were faces now from the past: her father; her mother; Einion, his hair flying in the raw winds of Gwynedd, his eyes wild as he raised his arms towards her; John of Chester was there, and Robert de Quincy and Malcolm. And her children. The children who had died. Hawisa, a young woman now, her two royal babes, Colban and his son with him, and Macduff, and the twins, and Isabella. Tears pouring down her face, Eleyne held out her hands towards the embers. Donald was there. Donald smiling at her, young again, handsome. And he was pointing. Pointing away towards another time, another place.

She sat forward, the shawl falling unnoticed from her shoulders. 'Donald,' she whispered, 'wait for me. You were right. We will meet again. We will . . .'

Around her the shadows swirled. The fumes of the herbs filled the room and Bethoc, waiting patiently in the corner, felt herself grow dizzy. Choking, she began to cough.

The pounding feet on the stairs outside brought Bethoc to her feet before the bell began to peal in the darkness of the courtyard. As the door burst open, Eleyne looked up dazed. Lost in her world of dreams, she did not recognise Nigel as he caught her arm.

'Quickly! For Christ's sake. Our only hope is to get to the Warden's Tower. We are betrayed! Help her, Bethoc!' He was dragging Eleyne to her feet.

'Betrayed?' Eleyne's eyes were still full of visions. The room swam around her and she staggered against the young man's arm.

'Betrayed,' he repeated grimly. 'Our only chance is to hold the tower. Hurry!'

'But Robert is coming. He will win. He will be king . . .'

'I'm sure he will, but we have to wait for him in the Warden's Tower.' Almost lifting her, Nigel hurried her down the long winding staircase of the Snow Tower and out of the open door at its base.

In the swirling smoke they stopped, staring at the mass of flame which had once been the great hall of Kildrummy Castle.

'Sweet Virgin!' Eleyne was horror-stricken. Sparks from the hall had carried to the chapel roof, which was already ablaze, as were several of the outbuildings which nestled against the inside of the curtain wall. The heat seared across the ward, smoke hanging above the shimmering, static air.

A figure appeared before them, sword in hand. His surcoat carried the leopards of England. With a shout of anger, Nigel drew his sword, thrusting Eleyne behind him. She staggered and nearly fell as the two men met head on. Behind them was another man-at-arms and then another. She was trying to see through the smoke as she backed away from the whirling sword blades when a tall figure materialised beside her and she recognised Sir John Appleby.

Lowering his sword, he bowed to her. 'There is no hope. I have a thousand men inside the castle, and I am here to accept your surrender, Lady Mar.'

She drew herself up, her head miraculously clear suddenly. 'There will be no surrender, Sir John. I hold Kildrummy for my king and for my grandson, the earl.' Her voice carried proudly across the sound of fighting.

'I am sorry, my lady, but you hold nothing.' He looked round and, following his gaze, she saw Nigel backing grimly away from her. His sword had gone, and there were at least three men around him, their sword points at his throat. Beyond him more and more men, wearing the Prince of Wales's colours, filled the courtyard. The small garrison was overwhelmed as she watched. Behind her there was another crash. The roof of the smithy fell in and showers of sparks shot up into the smoky air. 'Surrender, my lady. Tell your men to stop fighting,' Sir John called out.

'Never!'

She backed towards the chapel. They were dragging Nigel away, and she saw they had bound his hands behind his back. Behind him, she saw old Sir Alan throw down his sword. A figure ran through the smoke and she saw a child in his arms. She heard the high-pitched scream and her heart turned over.

'Little Donald –' she cried. 'Oh Sweet Blessed Lady, Donald! Where is my grandson?' She whirled to face Sir John.

'The Earl of Mar is my prisoner, madam.' The cool voice of her cousin Edward was suddenly at her elbow. 'As you are. My father will be so pleased to have you in chains at last.' He laughed out loud, then he held out his arm, in mock gallantry. 'Please, come this way. The chapel is alight now. There's nothing left here for you.'

The heat from the burning straw was intense.

Eleyne shook her head. She stared around. She was alone. Bethoc had disappeared – dragged screaming from the castle by two men-at-arms; little Ellie and her nurse had gone, following Donald across the drawbridge to the prince's camp where the prisoners were being corralled, surrounded by a strong guard. There was no one left to defend her.

Eleyne turned to him. 'Who betrayed us?' she cried, through dried, blistered lips. 'Who?'

'Your blacksmith, cousin. He was seduced by the thought of English gold!' Edward smiled. 'And he has been given his reward. I dislike traitors.' he added almost as an afterthought. 'He betrayed you – he would have betrayed me as easily.'

'So. You've killed him?' Eleyne found herself looking into his face with almost dispassionate curiosity.

'Oh yes, we've killed him, and his spawn with him.' Edward smiled. 'We planned something rather special for him. The gold he wanted so much. I had it smelted in my forge while he watched. Apt for a blacksmith, don't you think? Then it was poured down his throat.'

Eleyne shuddered. 'And what fate do you reserve for me, cousin? Something equally dramatic?'

He laughed. 'Still looking for the centre place on the stage, Lady Mar? That's just as well, because that's where you will be. I understand my father has planned to immure you in a cage at his Tower in London. So the populace can stare at you to their hearts' content. A daughter of Llewelyn; a husband-killer; a rebel witch; the mother-in-law of the so-called King of Scots!' He folded his arms. 'Your chains await you, Cousin Eleyne.'

His face was illuminated by the flaring flames as they ran across the gaping chapel door. The roof creaked ominously and a shower of sparks flew into the air. Edward flinched. He brushed a piece of burning ash from his surcoat.

Eleyne drew herself up. Her fear and disgust had gone, to be replaced by white-hot anger. She looked him in the eye. 'You'd cage me like an animal? As you've done, so they tell me, to my nephew, Owain? Never! Tell my cousin your father that I decline his invitation, that I am not going to England. I am not going anywhere with you.'

The chapel door was hanging open, only a few paces away up the steps. Inside, the centre of the chapel was dark. Again, the roof creaked and a beam fell before the altar in a blaze of flame. It illuminated the whole interior of the building, and before the altar on the chancel step, silhouetted against the triple window, she saw the figure of a man. He smiled and beckoned, and her heart leaped.

Alexander! Her hand went to the pendant around her neck.

Edward, following her gaze, saw the man: tall, red-haired, a gold coronet on his head, the royal lion of Scotland emblazoned on his surcoat. He opened his arms and called Eleyne's name.

Edward shrank back, his skin crawling with superstitious terror as the man stepped forward, the flames licking around him. Eleyne could not move – her joy was too intense. She could see him! She could see him clearly, waiting for her. She glanced at Edward, and seeing his expression she laughed out loud and at last she saw her chance. Turning, she ran up the steps towards the chapel door. Before Edward had the time to react, she had vanished through the flaming doorway.

For a brief second, through the smoke, he saw her reach her king and he saw them in each other's arms. Then, in a blaze as intense as any furnace, the chapel roof fell in and she was gone.

AFTERWORD

The story of Isobel of Buchan and what happened following the siege of Kildrummy Castle is told in *Kingdom of Shadows*.

Donald, Earl of Mar, was taken as a prisoner to England, where he was held in Bristol Castle, although the records assure us that he was not fettered because he was so young. Later he was brought up at the English court, where he served King Edward II loyally, not returning to Scotland to be restored to his earldom until 1327. In 1332 he was made Regent of Scotland, in the minority of his eight-year-old cousin, King David II.

Donald's sister, Elyne (the spelling of the name used for Eleyne's grand-daughter), married Sir John Menteith. Their mother Christian Bruce survived her imprisonment and married for the third time, Andrew Murray of Bothwell. She died about 1357 and was buried in her chapel of the Blessed Virgin of the Garioch.

Although King Robert and Queen Elizabeth had a son, who inherited his father's kingdom in 1329 as King David II, he died without issue, and it was Eleyne's great-grandson, the son of Marjorie Bruce and Walter the Steward of Scotland, who next inherited the throne as King Robert II, the first of the Stewart line, in fulfilment of Einion's prophecy.

AUTHOR'S NOTE

The story of Eleyne of Mar is the result of a pilgrimage deep into the remote archives of my family, and is a part of a legend with which I grew up. This legend told of romance and excitement in Scotland in the time of Robert the Bruce and Isobel of Buchan, which I first wrote about in *Kingdom of Shadows*. It was while researching the historical sections of that novel that I realised how closely Eleyne (or Helen or Ellen), the great-grandmother of Isobel and the mother of Isabella, Robert's first wife, was bound up with their story and I began to wonder what kind of a woman she was. It was the start of a quest which turned out to be convoluted and full of irreconcilable puzzles and which led in the end to the writing of this novel.

Like any good detective I began my research into Helen's life with the part I already knew, or thought I knew, when she was the Countess of Mar. Thirteenth-century Scotland is fairly well documented. There are chronicles, there are records, there is the wonderful narrative poem 'The Bruce', written by John Barbour, the Archdeacon of Aberdeen, only seventy or so years after the siege of Kildrummy. I felt it would be easy to find out about 'Helen' and her world.

There she was, in the Peerage: 'Donald, Earl of Mar m. Helen, widow of Malcolm, Earl of Fife (who d. 1266), and da. of Llywelyn, Prince of North Wales. She was living in Feb. 1294/5.' The entry under Fife confirms her name. It was those words 'daughter of Llywelyn' which intrigued me. How had this daughter of a Welsh prince ended up the great-grandmother of a Scots king?

I was to discover, however, that there are very few mentions of her extant in original records. One of the few is to be found in the Pipe Roll of King Edward I where we have, in an account by Walter de Cambo of the Issues of Lands and Tenements belonging to Duncan, Earl of Fife: '*Et Elenae, comitissae de Mar, pro parte dotis suae xl s. per idem tempus*', an entry which is repeated a few months later, and lists the 'pension' which followed Ellen/Helen into her last marriage. This entry was brief, but appeared to establish her existence beyond any doubt. It was a start. But how had this daughter of Wales reached Scotland in the first place?

I turned to Welsh history. There were two Llywelyns who might be called 'Prince of North Wales', although the term was not strictly used for either of them. Llywelyn ap Iorwerth, or Llywelyn the Great, was Prince of Aberffraw and Lord of Snowdon. He was the ruler of Gwynedd and so could be said to have been Prince of North Wales. Then there was his grandson, Llywelyn ap Gruffydd, who in the latter part of his rule was to call himself Prince of Wales. The former appeared to be the most likely candidate for Helen's father and there indeed in all the textbooks and family trees was the information that Llywelyn ap Iorwerth and his wife, Joan, had a daughter called Ellen or Helen. Her brother and two of her sisters were married to de Braoses, a fact which I registered with a shock of recognition as I had become so familiar with that family while researching *Lady of Hay*. Ellen/Helen herself was married to John the Scot, Earl of Huntingdon and Chester. This seemed at once to establish a Scots connection, albeit a somewhat tenuous one. I read on.

Ellen/Helen married John in 1222. But my Scots Ellen/Helen married the Earl of Mar sometime after 1266 and went on to bear him five children. If she was the same person the dates did not fit unless she married John of Huntingdon as a baby. There is a great deal of information available about this wedding between the daughter of Prince Llywelyn and the heir to the great and powerful earldom of Chester. We know where and when, we know some of the gifts, we know who the witnesses were. But nowhere does it say the bride was a baby or even a child or that the wedding was by proxy. By now doubting that this could after all be my Ellen/Helen I read on about the Countess of Huntingdon, looking for clues. There were for instance no children by this marriage. That would fit if most of it was spent growing up. If she was a small child in 1222, at her husband's death in 1237 she would have been in her teens. Of course there could be many reasons for her childlessness, such as his ill health – he was a comparatively young man when he died. (It was later that I was to find the intriguing information that at the time she was suspected of having procured his death by poison.)

The records chart Ellen/Helen's removal to Chester Castle, where she was to be kept in honourable and fitting state until Henry decided what to do with her, and her swift remarriage to Robert de Quincy. We read from the Dunstable annalist the remark about Llywelyn's indignation at the haste of the wedding and at his new son-in-law's low rank. We learn of her two daughters and can determine their ages. We know about Joanna's marriage, we lose track of Hawisa while still a minor shortly after her father's death. We know that Robert de Quincy took the Cross (but not if he actually went to the Holy Land) and we know when he died.

I assumed that at this point, if Ellen/Helen was my Ellen/Helen, she would now have remarried for the third time, on this occasion to

Malcolm, Earl of Fife. There would have been plenty of time then for her to have had two sons by him before he died in 1266.

But no.

Following the records further, I found that in 1253 the story of the Countess of Huntingdon and Chester abruptly ended when her dower lands were redistributed amongst her heirs. The obvious inference was that she was dead and I must admit I was very disappointed. I had become fascinated with my Welsh Ellen/Helen and now I was left, so it seemed, with two Ellen/Helens and an unbridgeable gap between them.

Where to go from there?

Families in medieval times commonly and confusingly had siblings with the same Christian name. Did Llywelyn ap Iorwerth have two daughters called Ellen? Back came an unequivocal answer from North Wales, no, although at this point some information emerged about an interesting variation on Welsh Ellen's birth. Two sources, one collected in the sixteenth or seventeenth century, state that she was not Joan's daughter, as all the modern history books said, but the eldest daughter of Tangwystl, Llywelyn's mistress or first wife. (Margaret and Gwladus were also, according to this source, daughters of Tangwystl.) This record does agree however that she married John the Scot. Intriguing, but the authorities who claim the three girls as Joan's daughters seem to outnumber those who uphold that they were Tangwystl's.

At this point I took a step back to take a more oblique look at Welsh history. There were at least a dozen Llywelyns, lesser princelings and lords, extant at the relevant period. Could my Scots Ellen/Helen be the daughter of one of them, and had he become transmogrified over the centuries into 'the' Llywelyn by her descendants?

I put this idea on hold whilst considering the other major contender for the title of Llywelyn, Prince of North Wales, Llywelyn ap Gruffydd. I had at first discounted him because, as far as the majority of history books and records are concerned, he had only one child, the unfortunate Gwenllian who died without issue. But . . .

In a collection of traditional Welsh pedigrees in the College of Arms in London, consulted for me by Peter Gwynn-Jones, the Lancaster Herald, there are at least two which contain a record of Llywelyn's marriage to Eleanor, daughter of Simon de Montfort, and go on to speak of their only child, Catherine Lackland, who married first Philip ap Ifor and second MALCOLM, EARL OF FIFE!

Catherine?

This was a shock. And it couldn't be right! Llywelyn married Eleanor in 1278, twelve years after Malcolm died! Perhaps Catherine was a bastard daughter of Llywelyn ap Gruffydd, conceived in his youth? (That might explain her name of Lackland.) Works based on pedigrees in the National Library of Wales do not mention her at all, speaking only of Gwenllian.

I was by now feeling very confused. Obviously there had been a marriage between some member of the house of Gwynedd and Malcolm, Earl of Fife. At the Scots end, the lady's name was believed to have been Ellen/Helen; at the Welsh end, the only actual mention of Malcolm of Fife is linked with a putative daughter of Llywelyn ap Gruffydd, called Catherine.

It seemed to be a good time to return to the Scots records and once again to consult the experts, confronting them with Catherine. There is quite a lot of information in existence about the Mar family at that date. We know Donald was knighted rather late in life (but not why). We know who his children were and whom they married. Obviously their close relationship with the Bruces is well documented. We know Alexander was kept in the Tower (the cost of the Scots nobles and their retinues 'staying' in the Tower after the Battle of Dunbar was noted in Edward I's account book as being £407 6s. ½d) and we know he is not heard of again. But sadly it proved impossible to learn any more than I already knew about Donald's wife, namely that she was Malcolm's widow, that her name was Ellen or Helen and that she was a daughter of a Llywelyn.

It was frustrating, the more so when I learned that many of the charters of the noble families of Scotland had been taken by Oliver Cromwell and had been lost in a storm in the Forth on their way to England. Amongst these, gone forever, were perhaps the very documents which might have mentioned Ellen of Fife, her origins and her marriage to Donald of Mar.

I should have been dismayed, but by this time the strange alchemy had begun by which a fictional character is born. Based on legend or fact, one person or two, Eleyne, my Eleyne (or Ellen or Helen), was beginning to stir. And yes, she was the daughter of Llywelyn ap Iorwerth and Joan. And yes, she had four husbands, in a life which spanned nearly a century, and yes, she had nine children, at least. And, yes, in 1253 her dower lands had been redistributed. But seizing on the fact that nowhere did it actually say that she had died at that point, an alternative reason for this drastic action began to present itself and a novel was born.

I kept reminding myself that I am neither genealogist, nor historian, nor biographer. I am a novelist. My Eleyne, though based loosely on fact, was fiction. Probably I would never know the truth about her, so all I could do was listen to the story which she was beginning to whisper in my ear.

Her love affair with Alexander was her idea – it formed no part of my original synopsis. But time and again I found the facts, where they could be checked, fitted exactly the story she was dictating so insistently in my head. Alexander II did indeed have many lady friends – why not Eleyne? He had several bastard children, why could she too not carry his babies? Her heroic role, her triumphs and her failures, all came from her. And as for ghosts and predictions, Michael the Scot and Thomas of Ercildoune are part of Scots history, as are their predictions of Alexander III's doom. Even the ghost at his wedding is recorded in the chronicles – a story retold with lip-licking gusto by Hector Boece:

> At that mariage tak tent I sall tell
> So greit ane wounder on ane nycht befell . . .
> Into the figure that tyme of ane man,
> But flesche or blude, haiffand nocht ellis than,
> Bot like ane bogill all of ratland banis . . .
> And as tha stude to farlie on that thing,
> So laithlie wes thair in the candill licht
> Richt suddanlie it vaneist out of sicht.

Also from Eleyne came the prompt that her marriage to Robert was unhappy – nothing in the records says as much. All we have to go on is the difference in their rank, her father's disapproval of the marriage and umpteen references to the endless litigation in which they were engaged – they were forever fighting their neighbours over boundaries and rents which conveys an impression that at least one of them was quarrelsome (and by now I was too partisan to believe it could have been Ellen/Helen).

There is always, in handling a historical theme, a conflict between the promptings of fiction and the actualities of fact. Reconciling them without compromising historical accuracy too much is part of the joy and the nightmare of writing a novel like this. I hope I have succeeded in making an enjoyable and credible story, but please, no examination theses based on Eleyne's life!

As portrayed here I now think Eleyne probably did not exist. She is a composite; a family legend of the type which converts dingy oil paintings into Rembrandts and Victorian paste beads into aquamarines. But, if the two Ellen/Helens were indeed the same person she must have been a woman cast in the mould of Eleanor of Aquitaine – tough, fertile, healthy and long-lived! She would have been a formidable lady. Whoever she was she is an ancestor of whom I'm extremely proud.

The spelling of Elyne is taken from the form of the name adopted by my great-aunt when she copied the pedigrees from her grandfather's version. It survived in the Erskine family, the descendants of Eleyne's grand-daughter, as Elyne, which is, I suspect, a Victorian etymological amalgam or mis-spelling and as such admirably suits my enigmatic and evasive heroine.